EVERYMAN'S LIBRARY

EVERYMAN,
I WILL GO WITH THEE,
AND BE THY GUIDE,
IN THY MOST NEED
TO GO BY THY SIDE

VICTOR HUGO

Les Misérables

Translated by Charles E. Wilbour

with an Introduction by
Peter Washington

———

E V E R Y M A N ' S   L I B R A R Y

Alfred A. Knopf New York Toronto

239

THIS IS A BORZOI BOOK

PUBLISHED BY ALFRED A. KNOPF, INC.

First included in Everyman's Library, 1909
Introduction, Bibliography and Chronology Copyright © 1997 by
David Campbell Publishers Ltd.
Typography by Peter B. Willberg

ISBN 0-375-40317-5

Book Design by Barbara de Wilde and Carol Devine Carson

Typeset by AccComputing, Castle Cary, Somerset

Printed and bound in Germany
by Graphischer Grossbetrieb Pössneck GmbH

LES MISÉRABLES

INTRODUCTION

Victor Hugo might be regarded as the Mr Toad of French literature: vain, arrogant, pompous, selfish, cold and stingy; a windbag, a humbug and a fraud, absurdly puffed up with the immensity of his own greatness. But unlike Mr Toad, he was also an astute and energetic promoter of his own image as a Great Man. The process began early. Writing in Hugo's lifetime, Virginie Ancelot recalls the reception the young poet received in literary drawing-rooms when he arrived to read his latest ode.

... There was a few moments' silence; then someone rose and approached him with visible emotion, took his hand and raised their eyes to heaven.
The multitude listened.
A single word was heard, to the great surprise of the uninitiated. And this word, which echoed in every corner of the salon, was:
'Cathedral!'
Then the orator returned to his place; another rose and cried out:
'Ogive!'
A third looked round him and ventured:
'Egyptian Pyramid!'
The assembly applauded, and then it was lost in profound reflection.

To the Anglo-Saxon mind – and, it should be said, to many Frenchmen – this is Parisian literary life at its worst: the posturing, the pretension, the self-regard, masquerading under the name of art. Yet Hugo is the man who wrote a handful of the most exquisite lyrics – 'Victor Hugo, hélas!' said Gide when someone asked him to name the finest French poet – and at least one novel judged to be supreme. In his person, he sums up all that is most monstrous in writerly vanity; in his best work he transcended his failings. How did he do it? How did a monster come to write the masterpiece that is *Les Misérables*?

*

LES MISÉRABLES

In an early essay on Scott, Hugo prophesies that

After the picturesque but prosaic novel of Walter Scott, there will still be another novel to create ... It is the novel which is at once drama and epic, picturesque and poetic, real and ideal, true and great, the novel which will enshrine Walter Scott in Homer.

These words were written in 1823, just after the publication of his own first novel, *Han d'Islande*, and there is no doubt that Hugo had himself in mind as the man who could 'enshrine Walter Scott in Homer'. Anyone who can still get through this book may take a rather different view. Set in seventeenth-century Norway and dripping with gore on every page, *Han d'Islande* is nearer to the Gothic horror tradition than to Scott. For the man who really succeeded in reconciling the genres of epic and historic fiction we have to look further afield, to Hugo's own admirer, Tolstoy. Yet it was Tolstoy who vindicated the French novelist's early ambition by judging *Les Misérables* one of the world's great novels, if not the greatest, and acknowledged its effect on his own work.

Les Misérables was completed in 1862, shortly before the Russian novelist began *War and Peace*. The two novels are set in the same period. It cannot be said that Hugo had much to teach his junior about structure or characterization; like all his attempts at epic, in prose and verse, *Les Misérables* rambles, there are huge digressions and absurdities of plot, the characters are often thin, the action melodramatic. But in spacious, vigorous story-telling, in the use of an historical framework, in the relating of human events to a larger philosophical and spiritual context, in the deployment of fiction as a social and political weapon, in the exaltation of 'the people' as a supreme authority, in the treatment of suffering as a dominant theme – in all these matters Hugo exerted a profound influence on Tolstoy. Without his example, *War and Peace* might have been a very different novel.

Perhaps the most extraordinary point of contact between them concerns Napoleon. One might expect the emperor to intrigue European writers in the early nineteenth century, as he intrigues Byron, Balzac and Stendhal, among others, but by the 1860s almost half a century had passed since Waterloo, yet Hugo and Tolstoy are still trying to unravel the mystery of one whose shadow falls across the entire century.

For Tolstoy, Napoleon is pre-eminently a human being – an extraordinary man, certainly, the instrument of destiny, but still a man. For Hugo he is more like a superman, a mysterious brooding presence with almost divine powers. The point is made by an ironic comparison between Napoleon and Wellington. Hugo's argument seems to be that Napoleon *ought* to have won Waterloo by sheer force of genius – indeed, that he *did* win it, when judged according to the rules of natural justice – but that Wellington achieved a victory on points by taking more care to spy out the lay of the battlefield and to estimate the balance of forces. Calculation is everything to the mundane Englishman, imagination nothing. When lightning flashes round the emperor's head, the duke looks like a very ordinary man. While Napoleon surveys the heavens, Wellington consults his watch.

Clearly, the image of general as genius was vital to Hugo's own project of himself as a literary Napoleon, but there is more to it than that. Commentators have often lamented the digression on Waterloo which is quite unnecessary to the plot and, coming early in the book, throws it decisively out of its narrative stride. But Hugo, though careless of structural refinement, does have a more serious purpose here – a purpose from which Tolstoy must have learnt much, and not only in his description of Borodino. For Hugo, who in turn learnt so much from Scott, grasped the fact that by imprinting the significance of a decisive historical moment on the minds of his readers he could hugely enlarge the scope of his novel. Precisely because *Les Misérables* is about little people, the history of a great man is one means of linking their petty lives with the Infinite. (The link is made touchingly explicit in the chapter called 'In which Little Gavroche Takes Advantage of Napoleon the Great'.) Even events as great as Waterloo, we are told, can hinge on details: the location of a ditch, the arrival of a platoon. Conversely, the most trivial life may exemplify a great truth – and in that sense, all lives are equally significant, for every existence embodies these truths.

At the same time, Hugo's treatment of Waterloo makes it

clear that realities and appearances diverge as much in everyday life as they do in historical interpretation – and that the two divergences are linked. What a post-Waterloo Frenchman thinks of Napoleon helps to shape what he thinks of himself. Sometimes we try to envision history in our own image; sometimes we use it to understand ourselves; at all times we are formed by it without our knowledge. One function of fiction is to help us achieve that knowledge. *Les Misérables* is, among other things, an attempt to explain the people of the mid-nineteenth century to themselves. Jean Valjean finds himself in a certain situation because he is a poor Frenchman at a particular time. This is one version of Fate – the sociological and political explanation of things. But Valjean is like Waterloo: his life also has a deeper purpose, a hidden meaning. Hugo has a number of names for this meaning – Fate, Destiny, God, the Infinite. But whatever he calls it, we observe a complex dialogue throughout the book between the surface causes of Valjean's predicament – poverty and ignorance – and their deeper meaning, to which he penetrates through suffering.

*

Hugo was a mythologizer of genius. Like most writers, he drew on his own life for his mythology; unlike most, he made himself a central figure in the drama. 'Victor Hugo' was not only to be the author of poems, plays and novels; from an early age it is clear that he meant to be a public figure playing a significant role in French history – a personage, a presence, a name. As V.S. Pritchett observed, the narrator of *Les Misérables* sometimes seems to mistake himself for God.

One might even say that the process began before he was born. The son of a rising star in Napoleon's Spanish army, he was thrust into the very midst of a struggle over French national identity which continues to this day. In later life he himself was torn between vaunting his relationship to the emperor and hinting at aristocratic descent. Typically, the first claim was exaggerated and the second a lie. Hugo was only a step away from peasant origins, his paternal grandfather having been a carpenter in Besançon where the novelist himself was born. But he saw himself as a natural aristocrat, a lord of the imagination – and imagination is a notoriously accommodating medium when it comes to reconciling fact and fantasy. Louis Philippe's eventual grant of a peerage made the reconciliation complete, while at the same time underlining the fact that Hugo was neither Napoleonic nor Bourbon but a typical product of the bourgeois age. The irony seems to have been lost on the new baron.

General Hugo and his wife lived separate lives. Occasionally threatening each other with divorce, they were just grand enough to ensure that the imperial court stepped in to prevent such a discreditable scandal among Napoleon's new elite. Despite visits to his father in Spain, where the general was serving with Napoleon's brother Joseph, recently installed on the Spanish throne, Victor and his two brothers lived with their mother. She indulged their literary ambitions, as French mothers are apt to do – one thinks of Mmes Balzac, Flaubert and Proust, among others. This is possibly a sign of the esteem in which the French hold literature, or at least authorial status. Hugo's early hero was the royalist writer Chateaubriand; Madame Hugo was a royalist, perhaps to spite her husband, and Victor himself a sympathizer. Chateaubriand encouraged the boy from afar, calling him 'l'enfant sublime', until he met and disliked him – not an uncommon response to Hugo. He was hugely prolific and enormously ambitious, announcing that there was no point in being a writer unless one could be the best: 'Chateaubriand ou rien!'

In 1823 Hugo's first novel appeared, and in 1827 his first play. At 500 pages of text, *Cromwell* is far too long to perform and hardly bears re-reading. With occasional flashes of eloquence, it has all the faults for which Hugo was soon to become notorious: windy rhetoric, over-complicated imagery and an hilariously cavalier way with the facts. In a later play about Mary Tudor he manages to confuse the heroine with Mary, Queen of Scots, a very different sort of lady. In Hugo's defence, it should be said that he had a genuine contempt for pedantry. What interested him were ideas, great conflicts, historical visions, not petty details. But *Cromwell* also brings out his chauvinism: the hero is significant for the parallels with Napoleon. Although he drew on their history for several major works, Hugo despised the British. He is more careful with French history, either because he regards the French as the historic bearers of a destiny to lead and civilize the world, or because he was born in Besançon.

His dislike of Britain might have complicated the preface to *Cromwell* – the only part of this drama still alive – where Hugo champions Shakespeare against the classicizing tradition of French drama, but the problem is neatly side-stepped when it becomes clear that Hugo has never read the earlier dramatist. Nor had he done so with any care by the time he wrote *William Shakespeare* almost forty years later. In fact, Hugo is not interested in Shakespeare, except as a vehicle for his own ideas about the relationships between nature and art, theatre and life, reality and language. Like Berlioz and Delacroix, he uses the Shakespearean name as shorthand for the Romantic creed he was expounding – though, as many contemporaries pointed out, he wasn't really a Romantic at all. But Hugo needed a platform to stand on, a movement to lead, and Romanticism was the radical aesthetic watchword of the hour. It would do as well as anything else. In the preface to *Cromwell* he seized the leadership of literary France and remained a dominant figure in cultural politics until his death fifty-eight years later.

*

The following decades were hugely productive. Besides many volumes of verse and a number of novels – among them *Notre-Dame de Paris*, now best known for parodies of Charles Laughton's starring role as the hunchback Quasimodo in the film of the book – Hugo found success in the theatre with a series of colourful historical dramas: *Lucrèce Borgia, Marion Delorme, Marie Tudor, Le Roi s'amuse, Ruy Blas, Les Burgraves* and, most famous of all, *Hernani*, which achieved instant fame by provoking uproar at its first performance in 1830, thus sealing the author's reputation as a rebel and a romantic. These plays, rarely performed today, remind us of three important things about Hugo, all relevant to *Les Misérables*: his immersion in public life, his dramatic instinct and his belief in popular literature.

The relationship between literature and politics in France is a perpetual puzzle to Anglophone observers, who assume that a writer's activities are restricted to entertaining and instructing his public. But in France, writers have a third role which is more important than either: they *intervene*. Given the chronic inability of the French to develop a working relationship with their governing elite since the upheavals of 1789, and the existence in Paris of a distinct intellectual class which pre-dates the Revolution, it is natural that French writers play a part in articulating political ideas to and for the nation. Often they go further, involving themselves directly in politics in the certainty that their professional status gives them a special right to be heard. The theatre and the publishing house are political platforms, plays and novels are political events.

Occasionally, individuals deliberately abjure this role. Flaubert is a case in point. Others, like Genet, use it to shock. But from Voltaire to Barthes, major literary figures have taken their political importance for granted, and none more so than Hugo, whether by participating in politics directly, either as deputy and peer, and in revolutionary action; or by pronouncing on political matters from his vantage point as a famous author. One might go further and say that, for Hugo, as for Diderot or Sartre, literature is by its nature political, the author inevitably a politician, even (in Hugo's case) a statesman. This does not mean identification with a single party. On the contrary, French writers are inclined to exploit their detachment from the formal political process by insisting on the freedom to intervene as and when they like. So Hugo's views evolved from royalism through Bonapartism and republicanism to the highly personal and quasi-mystical form of socialism we can see in *Les Misérables*. But at every stage he made his opinions noisily public, considering it not only his privilege but his duty to do so.

Two points of reference survive all his changes of mind: his belief in Man and his belief (or attempt to believe) in a divine force which might as well be called God. These were the twin poles about which his thought revolved. Morally and politically, Hugo was a humanitarian in the Voltairean tradition. He attacked poverty, cruelty and ignorance, he opposed capital punishment and he believed in the perfectibility of Man, hence his ultimate subscription to a form of socialism in which pity and compassion for suffering play more important roles than theoretical definitions of equality and fraternity.

His theology is harder to pin down. As in politics he evolved from royalism to socialism, so in religion Hugo began in orthodoxy, passed through liberalism and doubt, and ended in a faith of his own making which rejected the traditional Christian scheme while making use of its symbolism. Like Tolstoy, he came to see life in Manichean terms as a war between darkness and light. As so often in the nineteenth century, Hugo's very personal religion and his radical politics eventually coalesced into an overarching and not always very coherent vision of Humanity's apotheosis. When this vision is expressed directly, as it is in many of the later attempts at verse epic, it lapses more often than not into vacuous apostrophes to Infinity, Eternity and Immortality. It comes into its own when providing a background to realistic action, and this is its function in *Les Misérables* where it supplies the sense of purpose, meaning and larger significance.

This sense is articulated by means of that favourite nineteenth-century plot mechanism, the coincidence, so beloved of Dickens and Balzac and so crucial to nineteenth-century opera. Hugo's work was enormously popular with composers. In the eighty years following its publication in 1831, no fewer than seventeen composers made operas out of *Notre-Dame de Paris* and several tried their hands at the far more daunting *Les Misérables*. Verdi had an early success with *Hernani*, and out of *Le Roi s'amuse* made the libretto for one of his greatest triumphs, *Rigoletto*. More generally, Hugo's writings about dramaturgy had a profound influence on the practice of librettists, and many of Verdi's early and middle-period operas bear their mark.

Much of this influence must be put down to the fact that Hugo's work was perceived as simultaneously theatrical yet realistic, and nowhere more so than in his use of coincidence.

INTRODUCTION

As the later works of Wagner and Verdi were to show, opera can combine dramatic force and simplicity with emotional and psychological subtlety to a degree fiction finds it hard to match. At his best, Hugo too achieves this combination. In European literature up to the late eighteenth century, coincidence is a synonym for the workings of Divine Grace in the world. By Hugo's time, few writers subscribed to this view, though we can still find it in novels by George Eliot where the language and symbolism of Christianity survive the metaphysical reality. For most nineteenth-century novelists and librettists, coincidence is simply a lazy way of jazzing up the plot or moving things forward, but in Hugo it seems to take on a genuine dramatic and philosophical value. Like Dickens at his best, he uses coincidence to articulate a sense of order and inevitability amidst the terrifying flux of modern life. Even as we recognize how unlikely it is that Valjean would encounter Javert in the street, or that Marius and the Thénardiers would settle in the same house, we accept the *dramatic* truth of events which are superficially unrealistic. This is the essence of great opera, the deployment of preposterous artifice to express unavoidable reality.

One might well apply the same formula to the best popular literature of Hugo's time, and he is certainly far closer in spirit and manner to popular contemporaries like Sue and Dumas than he is to more 'literary' writers such as Flaubert and Stendhal. Sue, in particular, combines sensational fiction with an interest in social reform and other humanitarian causes in a manner very reminiscent of *Les Misérables*. In his early writings, Hugo had worked hard for the appreciation of the literary elite while simultaneously courting popular success. And although he had staged a revolt against the tyranny of French verse forms, he also accepted the major literary conventions. But by 1862, though still eager for mass sales, he was interested in rather different notions of popularity and propriety. His royalism had long given way to socialism and he well understood the value of fiction in spreading this gospel to the widest possible audience. He had also moved away from an earlier preoccupation with the lives of the great – which we see reflected in the historical dramas – towards a concern with the poor, the deprived and the ordinary. There is certainly nothing very ordinary about Jean Valjean's life, or about the plot of *Les Misérables*, but both are really less important than the complete world – or underworld – Hugo presents in his novel. This is the world English readers will recognize from Dickens and Mayhew, the world of the forgotten and the destitute, the people of the streets and the slums. If *Les Misérables* is a popular novel, its popularity is a matter of more than sales: it has to do with notions of literary democracy and cultural equality which were beginning to find expression on both sides of the Atlantic at this time. As the cliché has it, the Age of the Common Man was dawning, and in Hugo's novel we see it at sunrise.

*

By the 1860s, all the elements for *Les Misérables* were in place: the mastery of popular fiction, the operatic manner, the engagement with social reform, the personal philosophy, the understanding of how to make a political gesture. These were combined with the novelist's unfailing belief in his own powers, an inexhaustible energy and a determination always to be the best. When the book appeared they were supported by a formidable propaganda campaign. In 1848 Hugo had founded a daily paper, *L'Evénement*, which taught him how to manipulate the popular press to good account. Even his family were involved in making publicity. On the novel's publication in Paris, Henri Blaze de Bury wrote to his wife that

The book is now the talk of the town. And you should see the advertisements for it. All the papers in Europe have been infested by them for the past month. Madame Hugo and her sons are here; they spend their time drawing up advertisements and interviewing journalists.

Their time was not wasted. Despite critical reservations, *Les Misérables* was a huge popular success, and deservedly so.

Hugo's engagement with journalism had taught him two other lessons, about style and subject. His style in *Les Misérables* combines the delicacy of a poet, the vividness of a dramatist and the popular touch of the reporter. Whatever its failings in structure and characterization, there is no doubt that much of the novel is written in a dazzling manner. Hugo's native pomposity, his tendency to oracular pronouncements of little meaning, and his fondness for over-elaborate visual imagery, are tamed not only by the sheer emotional power of the story but by a style which is by turns epigrammatic, tender and energetic. It is equally suited to powerful narratives, such as the account of Valjean's escape through the sewers of Paris with the wounded body of Marius on his back; to portraits, such as the devastating account of Louis Philippe; and to operatic set-pieces, such as Valjean's exit from the convent in a coffin, when Hugo permits himself a comic exchange between the abbess and the gardener which is worthy of Scott.

But Hugo – like Dickens – had also learnt from journalism how to write effective non-fiction. His most interesting work in the genre is *Le Dernier Jour d'un condamné* of 1829 (a piece of 'faction'), which offers a graphic account of the social and psychological effects of capital punishment, on both the condemned man and his judges. Hugo had been fascinated by execution ever since childhood experiences in Spain, and he studied inmates in the Bicêtre prison near Paris for this work. It was the beginning of a life-long fascination with prison and concealment, and a vigorous involvement in debate about the causes of crime and the efficacy of punishment. In *Les Misérables* he offers a long and complex meditation on the relationship between guilt, innocence, repentance and forgiveness which is at the heart of the book, extending even to its imagery. The novel is filled with allusions to imprisonment, to light hidden in darkness and overcoming it. Confinement and concealment are shown to be both dangerous and infectious. Himself used to being kept under close supervision, Valjean tries to confine Cosette in the cell of his love. Again like Dickens, Hugo shows that imprisonment is not merely a punishment, but a state of mind which may itself produce crime.

Underlying this imagery is a belief in the supreme importance of enlightenment, which links Hugo directly to the liberal philosophers of the eighteenth century. Involved with this belief is an equally eighteenth-century view that truth will prevail, a view which Hugo develops into the moral imperative that the truth must be told, though the heavens fall. Goethe once said that only the fruitful is true. Hugo might have responded that only the truth is fruitful. Central to *Les Misérables* is Valjean's struggle with himself to be honest. This is first and most powerfully presented when Valjean has long been settled and prosperous under a new name as Monsieur Madeleine, only to find that another man, mistaken for him, is in danger of being returned to the galleys in his place. Valjean realizes that he can simply sit back and let the man suffer. After all, the fellow is probably guilty of something else for which he has not yet been punished. Besides, if Monsieur Madeleine reveals that he is really Valjean and gives himself up to justice, the business he has created will collapse and hundreds will suffer hardship. What is the fate of one man, compared with theirs? Valjean endures a terrible night, wrestling with his conscience, but in the end he knows that he must submit, whatever the consequences. He knows that to perpetrate an injustice on another man is to collude in the system which has devastated his own life. He surrenders to the court. He is arrested, his business fails and his workmen lose their livelihood. But injustice has been avoided and truth prevails.

On the subject of justice, critics have made a good deal of the fact that *Les Misérables* is a pioneering detective novel. This commentary is surely wide of the mark. Hugo has no interest whatever in the forensic aspects of detection which intrigued Poe, Collins and Conan Doyle. The processes and methods by which the police conduct their business are almost entirely absent from his novel, which is obvious if we compare his sketchy treatment of police procedure with the passion he brings to describing convict life. He is far closer to Dickens and Dostoevsky who present policemen as the embodiment of blind justice, unable to distinguish between crime and human frailty. Valjean is given little depth of character, despite the care Hugo takes to exhibit the workings of his conscience; but Javert, who pursues Valjean throughout most of the novel, has even less. Even more than pursuer and pursued in *Martin Chuzzlewit* and *Dombey and Son*, Valjean and Javert are meant to be seen as mythical prototypes; complementary figures who require one another for their lives to have meaning. The defining detail of detective fiction is quite absent from Hugo's novel. To that extent we might want to see Javert as the externalization of Valjean's unassuageable guilt, a guilt which – like his punishment – is out of all proportion to any crime he may ever have committed.

This disproportion allows us to view Valjean, should we so wish, either as a Christ figure, carrying the sins of a whole society on his shoulders, or as an existential hero, a precursor of Camus' Outsider. It would be a mistake to take either interpretation too far: *Les Misérables* remains a realistic novel about poverty, injustice and inequality in nineteenth-century France. However, Hugo's constant appeal from the limited lives of his characters to a sphere of broader philosophical debate allows such interpretations to enrich the narrative. Indeed, it may be wise, given the thinness of characterization and the simplicity of the story, to focus precisely on such an approach, as Hugo himself seems to do. There is no point in searching this book for the psychological depth of character we find in George Eliot, Flaubert or Dostoevsky, any more than we would when reading Dickens. Hugo is offering a different kind of fiction. So when readers complain that his female characters are mere stereotypes, they are quite right but they miss the point. Fantine and Cosette are meant to be stereotypes. So are all the other fictional characters. Oddly enough, the only figures in the book who are *not* are those taken from life: the bishop of Digne, Louis Philippe, Napoleon, all so brilliantly drawn. This is not a failing on Hugo's part, but it does require readers accustomed to nineteenth-century fiction's emphasis on character to read in a different way. Here, the richness belongs to the historical and philosophical context of the novel, to the poetic descriptions of Paris, in all its glory and horror; and to the extraordinarily wide panorama of French life in the lower reaches of society.

Hugo was passionately applauded and bitterly criticized in his time for concentrating his attention on the poor: the beggars, prostitutes and convicts, the starving children, failing tradesmen and petty thieves who populate this novel in such large numbers. Many readers still took the Aristotelian view that such sordid characters were below the dignity of great literature. Narrower minds simply didn't want to know about them. Some shared the opinion, expressed by certain characters in the book, that the poor were always poor for very good reasons. Hugo's political supporters, on the other hand, hailed his revelation of the cess-pit which lay beneath the grandeur of Paris, as a necessary step, as they saw it, on the road to reform. Others delighted in the sheer realism of his descriptions, pointing especially to the brilliant pages on street urchins and the magnificent rendering of the 1832 *émeute*. It is in such moments that the novel really comes to life for this reader, when Hugo reveals his intimate and loving knowledge of street life. In the best realistic tradition, he forbears to moralize or to lecture, simply presenting the urban underworld as it is.

And this ability to present the extremes of experience 'as they are' is, in the end, Hugo's great gift, when he has done with his lofty theorizing about the terrors of the Infinite and the abominations of French Justice. We can only suppose that its new life as a musical – and what an appropriate fate for that most operatic novelist – will help to bring *Les Misérables* to the attention of a new generation of readers, reminding them, perhaps, that the abuses Hugo catalogues are still alive elsewhere, awaiting their own chroniclers in the brave new world of the twenty-first century.

Peter Washington

Everyman's Library publish the classic translation of *Les Misérables* by Hugo's friend CHARLES E. WILBOUR, which appeared in the same year as the novel was published in France. PETER WASHINGTON, who introduces this edition, is the General Editor of Everyman's Library and the author of *Literary Theory and the End of English* and *Madame Blavatsky's Baboon*.

SELECT BIBLIOGRAPHY

There is a readable short biography by Joanna Richardson (Weidenfeld and Nicolson, 1976) but one of the best general books in English is still the version of André Maurois' critical biography *Victor Hugo*, translated by Gerard Hopkins and published by Jonathan Cape in 1956. Like the Richardson, this volume also offers an extensive bibliography of French works about Hugo. However, both are superseded by Graham Robb's *Victor Hugo*, Picador, 1997, which appears as we go to press.

The novelist's highly-coloured version of his own life is provided in *Victor Hugo raconté par un témoin de sa vie*, published in 1863. Nominally written by his wife, it is largely his own work and interesting more for that reason than for its accuracy as an historical record.

Despite a vast body of commentary in French, English and American critics have shown little interest. Hugo's verse is hard to translate and he does not fit easily into schematic histories of the French novel, which may be why he appears only fleetingly in many accounts of nineteenth-century French literature, where he is treated primarily as a poet who happened to write fiction.

Les Misérables is given more substantial treatment in H. J. Hunt's *The Epic in Nineteenth-Century France*, Basil Blackwell, 1941, and there is an interesting essay by Eugène Schulkind in *French Literature and its Background*, vol. IV, edited by J. Cruickshank, Oxford University Press, 1969. There is no sustained treatment of Hugo in Harry Levin's classic study of French realism, *The Gate of Horn*, Oxford University Press, 1963, but he is frequently mentioned.

Finally, readers in search of more recent commentary will find some in *Paris and the Nineteenth Century*, Basil Blackwell, 1992, by Christopher Prendergast. Though marred by jargon, this is a fascinating study of how Hugo and his contemporaries saw the city they loved so much.

CHRONOLOGY

DATE	AUTHOR'S LIFE	LITERARY CONTEXT
1797		Goethe: *Hermann und Dorothea*.
1798		Coleridge & Wordsworth: *Lyrical Ballads*.
1799		Schiller: *Wallenstein*.
1802	Victor Hugo born in Besançon, 26 February.	Mme de Staël: *Delphine*. Chateaubriand: *Génie du Christianisme*.
1804		Schiller: *William Tell*.
1805		Chateaubriand: *René*.
1808		Goethe: *Faust* (I).
1810		Mme de Staël: *De l'Allemagne*.
1811	Taken to Spain where his father is a brigadier-general in the army of Joseph Bonaparte, now king of Spain.	
1812	Returns from Spain with his mother and brother Eugène. They settle in Paris.	Byron: *Childe Harold* (I & II).
1813	General Hugo returns to France after fall of King Joseph.	Byron: *The Corsair, The Giaour*.
1814	General Hugo and his wife separate unofficially.	Scott: *Waverley*. Hoffmann: *Tales* (to 1815).
1815	Eugène and Victor sent to boarding school (until 1818).	Scott: *Guy Mannering*. Wordsworth: *Poems*.
1816	Hugo starts writing poetry: 'I want to be Chateaubriand or nothing'.	Constant: *Adolphe*. Coleridge: 'Christabel', 'Kubla Khan'.
1818	General Hugo and his wife separate officially. Victor and his brothers live with their mother.	Mary Shelley: *Frankenstein*.
1819	The Hugo brothers found a periodical, *Le Conservateur littéraire*, in emulation of Chateaubriand's *Le Conservateur*. Victor falls in love with Adèle Foucher.	Maistre: *Du Pape*. Scott: *Ivanhoe*. Byron: *Don Juan* (to 1824). Shelley: *The Mask of Anarchy*.

HISTORICAL EVENTS

French invasion of Austria; Peace of Campo Formio.

Napoleon's Egyptian expedition. Nelson defeats French in the battle of the Nile.

Second coalition against France. Coup d'état of 18 *brumaire*. Napoleon becomes First Consul.

Peace of Amiens between France and Britain; war resumes the following year. Concordat between France and Roman Catholic Church. Napoleon made Consul for life.

Napoleon becomes emperor.

Third Coalition against France. Nelson defeats Franco-Spanish fleet at battle of Trafalgar. French occupation of Vienna and victory at Austerlitz.

Joseph Bonaparte king of Spain. Peninsular War begins.

Napoleon divorces Josephine and marries Archduchess Marie-Louise of Austria.

Napoleon invades Russia. Battle of Borodino. Retreat from Moscow. Wellington takes Madrid.

Napoleon defeated by Allied forces at battle of Leipzig. Wellington crosses the Pyrenees.

Allies invade France. Fall of Paris. Abdication of Napoleon and exile to Elba. Restoration of Louis XVIII. Congress of Vienna (to 1815).

Napoleon's Hundred Days and defeat at Waterloo. Second Bourbon Restoration. White Terror in Midi. Election of *Chambre introuvable*. Fall of government of Talleyrand and Fouché. First Richelieu ministry.

Dissolution of *Chambre introuvable*.

Congress of Aix-la-Chapelle: end of occupation of France. Richelieu replaced by Decazes.

Géricault's *The Raft of the Medusa*. Peterloo Massacre and Six Acts in England. Metternich's repressive Carlsbad Decrees (German Federation).

LES MISÉRABLES

CHRONOLOGY

HISTORICAL EVENTS

Assassination of duc de Berry, heir presumptive to French throne. Recall of Richelieu. Revolutions in Spain and Naples.

Death of Napoleon on St Helena. Fall of second Richelieu ministry. Ultras take over government. Greek War of Independence begins. Laibach Conference: Austria authorized to suppress Neapolitan revolution.

Villèle President of the Council. Congress of Verona. Delacroix's *Dante's Bark*.

French expedition into Spain.

Elections return an Ultra Chamber. Dismissal of Chateaubriand as Foreign Minister. Death of Louis XVIII; accession of Charles X. Delacroix's *The Massacre of Scio*.
Law against sacrilege. Indemnity to *émigrés* voted.

Niepce photographs from nature.

Combined French, British and Russian fleets defeat Turks in the battle of Navarino. Fall of Villèle. Delacroix's *Death of Sardanapalus*.

Government of Martignac. Delacroix's *Faust* lithographs.

DATE	AUTHOR'S LIFE	LITERARY CONTEXT
1829	*Les Orientales* reveals influence of Byron. *Le Dernier Jour d'un condamné* is a shockingly realistic study of the effects of capital punishment.	Balzac: *Les Chouans*. Dumas: *Henri III et sa Cour*. Mérimée: *La Chronique du règne de Charles IX*, 'Matteo Falcone'.
1830	On 25 February the first performance of *Hernani* causes uproar at the Théâtre-Français. Birth of Hugo's fourth and last child, Adèle.	Stendhal: *Le Rouge et le noir*. Gautier: *Premières poésies*. Comte: *Cours de philosophie positive* (6 vols to 1842).
1831	Hugo publishes an historical novel, *Notre-Dame de Paris*, and his poems *Les Feuilles d'automne*. Also has *Marion Delorme* performed.	Balzac: *Le Peau de chagrin*. Dumas: *Antony*.
1832	*Le Roi s'amuse* performed. Hugo moves into the Place Royale where he holds court in a literary salon.	Sand: *Indiana*. Sainte-Beuve: *Critiques et portraits littéraires* (to 1839).
1833	*Lucrèce Borgia* and *Marie Tudor* performed. Hugo meets and falls in love with one of the actresses, Juliette Drouet, formerly the mistress of Princess Mathilde's husband (among others).	Balzac: *Eugénie Grandet, Le Médecin de campagne*. Sand: *Lélia*. Heine: *De la France*. Michelet: *L'Histoire de France* (17 vols to 1867).
1834	*Claude Gueux*.	Sand: *Jacques*. Lammenais: *Paroles d'un croyant*.
1835	*Les Chants du crépuscule*.	Tocqueville: *De la démocratie en Amérique* (vol. I: vol. II, 1840). Vigny: *Servitude et grandeur militaires, Chatterton*. Balzac: *Le Père Goriot*. Gautier: *Mademoiselle de Maupin*. Musset: *Les Nuits* (to 1837).
1836		Lamartine: *Jocelyn*. Dumas: *Kean*.
1837	*Les Voix intérieures*. Hugo is nominated to the Legion of Honour.	Balzac: *Illusions perdues* (to 1843). Sand: *Mauprat*. Nodier: *Inès de la Sierras*.
1838	*Ruy Blas* performed.	Gautier: *La Comédie de la mort*. Dickens: *Oliver Twist*.

CHRONOLOGY

HISTORICAL EVENTS

Polignac forms government.

Conquest of Algiers. The Four Ordinances: Charles X dissolves newly elected Chamber, restricts the franchise and suppresses freedom of the press. July revolution. Abdication of Charles X; duc d'Orléans accepts lieutenant-generalcy of France, afterwards becoming 'King of the French' as Louis Philippe. New constitutional Charter. Risings in Belgium, Poland, Germany and central Italy. Berlioz's *Symphonie fantastique*. Delacroix's *Liberty leading the People*.

Anti-clerical riots in Paris. Casimir-Périer ministry. French expel Dutch from Belgium. Insurrection of Lyons silk-workers. Exhibition by painters of the Barbizon School. Cholera epidemic (to 1832). Russia crushes revolution in Poland.

Duchesse de Berry attempts to rouse Vendée (April). Death of Casimir-Périer (May). Attempted insurrection by Republicans in Paris (June). Death of the duc de Reichstadt, Napoleon's son (July). New ministry includes Broglie, Thiers and Guizot, with Marshal Soult as nominal head (October). Guizot's education law.

Revolt in Lyons. Unrest in Paris suppressed (rue Transnonain massacre). Berlioz' symphony *Harold en Italie*.

Fieschi's assassination attempt on Louis Philippe.

Attempted uprising by Louis Napoleon at Strasbourg. Molé forms government. Death of Charles X in exile.
Paris–Saint-Germain railway opened. Capture of Constantine (Algeria). Accession of Queen Victoria.

Death of Talleyrand.

DATE	AUTHOR'S LIFE	LITERARY CONTEXT
1839		Stendhal: *La Chartreuse de Parme.* Lamartine: *Recueillements poétiques.* Blanc: *Organisation du travail.* Louis Napoleon: *Les Idées napoléoniennes.* Poe: *Tales of the Grotesque and Arabesque.*
1840	*Les Rayons et les Ombres.*	Sainte-Beuve: *Port-Royal* (6 books to 1859). Mérimée: 'Colomba'. Proudhon: *Qu'est-ce que la propriété?*
1841	Elected to the Académie Française.	Musset: *Le Souvenir.* Lammenais: *Le Livre du peuple.* Dickens: *The Old Curiosity Shop.*
1842		Sue: *Les Mystères de Paris.* Sand: *Consuelo.*
1843	Hugo's daughter Léopoldine and her husband drown in a boating accident. *Les Burgraves.*	Dickens: *Martin Chuzzlewit* (to 1844).
1844		Dumas: *Le Comte de Monte Cristo, Les Trois Mousquetaires.* Sue: *Le Juif errant* (to 1845).
1845	Louis Philippe creates Hugo a peer of France.	Mérimée: 'Carmen'.
1846	In *Lettres sur le Rhin* Hugo claims that an alliance between France and Germany would check the imperialism of Britain and Russia.	Balzac: *La Cousine Bette.* Sand: *La Mare au diable.* Dickens: *Dombey and Son* (to 1848).
1847		Balzac: *Le Cousin Pons.* Michelet: *Histoire de la révolution française* (7 vols to 1853). Thackeray: *Vanity Fair.* C. Brontë: *Jane Eyre.* E. Brontë: *Wuthering Heights.*
1848	Hugo stands twice for election to the Assembly after the revolution but is defeated. Founds *L'Evénement*, a daily paper.	Sand: *La petite Fadette.* Thackeray: *Pendennis* (to 1850). Marx & Engels: *Communist Manifesto.* Mill: *Principles of Political Economy.*

CHRONOLOGY

Revolt of Abd-el-Kader. Fall of Molé. Berlioz's *Roméo et Juliette* symphony.

Inauguration of Bastille Column. Napoleon's ashes returned to Paris. Attempt of Louis Napoleon at Boulogne. Government of Thiers (March–October). Mehemet Ali crisis. Guizot forms ministry.

Franco-British entente cordiale.

Duc d'Orléans killed in accident. Guizot's railway law. Railway mania in France (to 1846).

Verdi's *Ernani* (based on Hugo's novel).

Bad harvests and potato blight affect most of western Europe 1845–6.

Escape of Louis Napoleon from Ham, where he had been imprisoned since 1840. Marriage of Louis Philippe's son, the duc de Montpensier, with the sister of Queen Isabella of Spain.

Economic crisis in France. Capture of Abd-el-Kader. Teste trial: prosecution of former minister for corruption discredits government. Opposition launch campaign of banquets (July–December) at which government is denounced.

France: February Revolution in Paris. Resignation of Guizot. Abdication of Louis Philippe. Provisional government proclaims universal suffrage. Slavery abolished. Demonstrations by National Guard (*bonnets à poil*); counter-demonstrations by Paris workers pacified by Minister of Interior, Ledru-Rollin (March). Election of Constituent Assembly (April). Unsuccessful left-wing 'push' (May). June Days: six days of street fighting in Paris as workers' rising put down by Cavaignac. Constitution of Second Republic (November). Election of Louis Napoleon as President. Government of Odilon Barrot (December).

DATE	AUTHOR'S LIFE	LITERARY CONTEXT
1848 cont.		
1849	Hugo is elected to the Assembly. Broadly supports Louis Napoleon.	Sue: *Les Mystères du peuple* (to 1856). Dickens: *David Copperfield* (to 1850).
1850	Gives a speech at Balzac's funeral.	Turgenev: *A Month in the Country*.
1851	Goes into voluntary exile after Louis Napoleon declares himself dictator. Settles in Jersey. Writes *Napoléon le petit*, an indictment of the new dictator.	Sainte-Beuve: *Causeries du lundi* (15 vols to 1862). Melville: *Moby-Dick*. Mayhew: *London Labour and the London Poor*.
1852	Formally expelled from France.	Dumas *fils*: *La Dame aux camélias*. Thackeray: *The History of Henry Esmond*.
1853	*Les Châtiments*.	
1854		Nerval: *Les Chimères*.
1855	Expelled from Jersey for attacking Queen Victoria's visit to Louis Napoleon (now Napoleon III). Settles in Guernsey.	Dumas *fils*: *Le Demi-monde*.
1856	Publishes *Les Contemplations*. Moves into Hauteville House in St Peter Port, Guernsey.	Tocqueville: *L'Ancien Régime*. Turgenev: *Rudin*.
1857		Flaubert: *Madame Bovary*. Baudelaire: *Les Fleurs du mal*. Dickens: *Little Dorrit*.
1858		Mazzini: *The Duties of Man*.
1859	*La Légende des siècles*. Napoleon III offers a general amnesty. Hugo refuses it but is henceforward a voluntary exile.	Darwin: *The Origin of Species*. Dickens: *A Tale of Two Cities*. Eliot: *Adam Bede*.
1860	Agitates in favour of Garibaldi and Italian independence.	Eliot: *The Mill on the Floss*. Collins: *The Woman in White*. Turgenev: *On the Eve*.
1861		Dickens: *Great Expectations*. Eliot: *Silas Marner*.

CHRONOLOGY

HISTORICAL EVENTS

Europe: Year of Revolutions notably in Vienna, Prague, Berlin, Venice, Milan, Parma, Rome and Naples. Chartists' demonstration in London. Election of Legislative Assembly (May). Attempted uprising in Paris fails (June). French restore Pius IX; fall of Roman republic (July). Dismissal of Barrot ministry (October). Austrians regain control of Venice. Kossuth declares a Hungarian republic.

Loi Falloux: clerical control of education extended. Left-wing victories in by-elections. Law restricting franchise. Hungarian republic defeated by Austria and Russia.

Legislative Assembly rejects constitutional reform. Louis Napoleon's coup d'état (2 December). Plebiscite. Re-establishment of absolutism in Austria and Prussia. Great Exhibition in London. Verdi's *Rigoletto* (based on Hugo's *Le Roi s'amuse*).

New constitution. Plebiscite on Empire. Proclamation of Empire (1 December). Foundation of Crédit Foncier and Crédit Mobilier.

Marriage of Napoleon III and Eugénie. France occupies New Caledonia. Hausmann made Prefect of the Seine (to 1870): embarks on reconstruction of Paris.

France enters Crimean War.

Exposition Universelle in Paris. Fall of Sebastopol.

Peace of Paris ends Crimean War.

Orsini bomb plot. Napoleon III and Cavour meet at Plombières. Vision at Lourdes. Offenbach's *Orphée en enfers*.

Construction of Suez Canal begun. War of Italian Unification; battles of Magenta and Solferino; armistice of Villafranca. Gounod's *Faust*.

France acquires Nice and Savoy. Free trade treaty with Britain. Anglo-French occupation of Peking. Expedition to Syria. First constitutional changes: Senate and Legislative Assembly permitted annual debates on the speech from the throne. First Italian parliament meets in Turin. Garibaldi and 'Redshirts' take Palermo and Naples.

French intervention in Mexico. Work on Garnier's Paris Opéra (completed 1875). Victor Emmanuel king of Italy. American Civil War begins. First bicycles manufactured, in France.

DATE	AUTHOR'S LIFE	LITERARY CONTEXT
1862	The first volume of *Les Misérables* appears in April, throughout Europe and America. The rest follows in May and June. It is a huge popular success.	Flaubert: *Salammbô*. Turgenev: *Fathers and Children*.
1863	Hugo's daughter Adèle, aged 33, runs away from home, following to Canada the man she is besotted with. After her discovery that he is already married, her mental health begins to deteriorate.	Renan: *Vie de Jésus*. Sainte-Beuve: *Nouveaux lundis* (13 vols to 1870).
1864	*William Shakespeare* a critical flop.	Tolstoy: *War and Peace* (to 1869). Dickens: *Our Mutual Friend* (to 1865).
1865	*Les Chansons des rues et des bois.*	
1866	*Les Travailleurs de la mer.*	Dostoevsky: *Crime and Punishment*.
1867		Marx: *Das Kapital* (I). Zola: *Thérèse Raquin*. Goncourt: *Manette Salomon*.
1868	Death of Madame Hugo.	Baudelaire: *Petits poèmes en prose*. Collins: *The Moonstone*.
1869	*L'Homme qui rit.*	Flaubert: *L'Education sentimentale*. Daudet: *Lettres de mon moulin*. Verlaine: *Les Fêtes galantes*.
1870	In July Hugo plants an acorn in his garden, dedicating the future tree to the 'United States of Europe'. In September, after the fall of Napoleon III, Hugo returns to France.	
1871	Elected deputy for Paris in the new Assembly but resigns after a few weeks. His son Charles dies, aged 44. As civil war breaks out between the new government and the Communards, Hugo sides with the rebels.	Zola: *La Fortune des Rougon*. Eliot: *Middlemarch* (to 1872). Dostoevsky: *The Possessed*.
1872	Stands again for the Assembly and is defeated. Hugo's daughter Adèle is finally brought back to France, declared mad and committed to an asylum – where she dies in 1915. Publishes *L'Année terrible*.	Zola: *La Curée*. Daudet: *Tartarin de Tarascon*. Nietzsche: *The Birth of Tragedy*.

CHRONOLOGY

HISTORICAL EVENTS

France annexes Cochin-China. Bismarck becomes Prussian prime minister. First performance of Berlioz's *Béatrice et Bénédict*.

Legislative elections. Fall of Persigny. Rouher becomes Minister of State. Salon des Refusés: founding of French Impressionist school. Revolt of Poland.

Schleswig-Holstein War. Maximilian proclaimed emperor in Mexico. Papal Syllabus of Errors (condemning liberalism). Offenbach's *La belle Hélène*.

Duruy's educational reforms.
Austro-Prussian War. Austrians defeated at Sadowa. French troops evacuate Mexico.
Letter of Napoleon III announcing constitutional changes. Proposals for re-armament. Crisis of Crédit Mobilier. Exposition Universelle in Paris.
Execution of Maximilian. Garibaldi repelled by French and papal troops at Mentana. Gounod's *Roméo et Juliette*.
French press laws relaxed.

Government of Ollivier. Suez Canal opens. Death of Berlioz.

Liberal reforms to constitution (April) supported by plebiscite (May). Franco-Prussian War begins (July). Fall of Ollivier (August). Surrender of Napoleon III at Sedan; republic declared; Government of National Defence set up; siege of Paris begins (September). Italian forces enter Rome; Papal States vote for union with Italy.

Bombardment and surrender of Paris (January). Election of Assembly; government of Thiers (February). Paris Commune (March–May). Treaty of Frankfurt (May). William I of Prussia becomes emperor of a united Germany.

LES MISÉRABLES

DATE	AUTHOR'S LIFE	LITERARY CONTEXT
1873	Hugo's final surviving child, François-Victor, dies of TB.	Verne: *Around the World in 80 Days.* Rimbaud: *Une Saison en enfer.* Tolstoy: *Anna Karenina* (to 1877). Dostoevsky: *The Idiot.*
1874	Hugo's last novel, *Quatre-vingt-treize.*	Verlaine: *Romances sans paroles.* Flaubert: *La Tentation de Saint-Antoine.* Trollope: *The Way We Live Now* (to 1875).
1877	*La Légende des siècles*, second series. *L'Art d'être grand-père.*	Zola: *L'Assommoir.*
1883	Death of Juliette Drouet. *La Légende des siècles*, third series.	Maupassant: *Une Vie.* Villiers de l'Isle-Adam: *Contes cruels.*
1885	Death of Victor Hugo, 22 May. He is given a state funeral in Paris and buried in the Pantheon.	Zola: *Germinal.* Maupassant: *Bel-Ami.*

CHRONOLOGY

LES MISÉRABLES

PREFACE

So long as there shall exist, by reason of law and custom, a social condemnation, which, in the face of civilisation, artificially creates hells on earth, and complicates a destiny that is divine, with human fatality; so long as the three problems of the age—the degradation of man by poverty, the ruin of woman by starvation, and the dwarfing of childhood by physical and spiritual night—are not solved; so long as, in certain regions, social asphyxia shall be possible; in other words, and from a yet more extended point of view, so long as ignorance and misery remain on earth, books like this cannot be useless.

HAUTEVILLE HOUSE, 1862.

CONTENTS

FANTINE

COSETTE

MARIUS

SAINT DENIS

JEAN VALJEAN

FANTINE

FANTINE
BOOK FIRST – AN UPRIGHT MAN

I

M. MYRIEL

In 1815, M. Charles François-Bienvenu Myriel was Bishop of D——. He was a man of seventy-five, and had occupied the bishopric of D—— since 1806. Although it in no manner concerns, even in the remotest degree, what we have to relate, it may not be useless, were it only for the sake of exactness in all things, to notice here the reports and gossip which had arisen on his account from the time of his arrival in the diocese.

Be it true or false, what is said about men often has as much influence upon their lives, and especially upon their destinies, as what they do.

M. Myriel was the son of a counsellor of the Parlement of Aix; of the rank given to the legal profession. His father, intending him to inherit his place, had contracted a marriage for him at the early age of eighteen or twenty, according to a widespread custom among parliamentary families. Charles Myriel, notwithstanding this marriage, had, it was said, been an object of much attention. His person was admirably moulded; although of slight figure, he was elegant and graceful; all the earlier part of his life had been devoted to the world and to its pleasures. The revolution came, events crowded upon each other; the parliamentary families, decimated, hunted, and pursued, were soon dispersed. M. Charles Myriel, on the first outbreak of the revolution, emigrated to Italy. His wife died there of a lung complaint with which she had been long threatened. They had no children. What followed in the fate of M. Myriel? The decay of the old French society, the fall of his own family, the tragic sights of '93, still more fearful, perhaps, to the exiles who beheld them from afar, magnified by fright—did these arouse in him ideas of renunciation and of solitude? Was he, in the midst of one of the reveries or emotions which then consumed his life, suddenly attacked by one of those mysterious and terrible blows which sometimes overwhelm, by smiting to the heart, the man whom public disasters could not shake, by aiming at life or fortune? No one could have answered; all that was known was that when he returned from Italy he was a priest.

9

In 1804, M. Myriel was curé of B—— (Brignolles). He was then an old man, and lived in the deepest seclusion.

Near the time of the coronation, a trifling matter of business belonging to his curacy—what it was, is not now known precisely—took him to Paris.

Among other personages of authority he went to Cardinal Fesch on behalf of his parishioners.

One day, when the emperor had come to visit his uncle, the worthy curé, who was waiting in the ante-room, happened to be on the way of his Majesty. Napoleon noticing that the old man looked at him with a certain curiousness, turned around and said brusquely:

"Who is this goodman who looks at me?"

"Sire," said M. Myriel, "you behold a good man, and I a great man. Each of us may profit by it."

That evening the emperor asked the cardinal the name of the curé and some time afterwards M. Myriel was overwhelmed with surprise on learning that he had been appointed Bishop of D——.

Beyond this, no one knew how much truth there was in the stories which passed current concerning the first portion of M. Myriel's life. But few families had known the Myriels before the revolution.

M. Myriel had to submit to the fate of every new-comer in a small town, where there are many tongues to talk, and but few heads to think. He had to submit, although he was bishop, and because he was bishop. But after all, the gossip with which his name was connected was only gossip: noise, talk, words, less than words—*palabres*, as they say in the forcible language of the South.

Be that as it may, after nine years of episcopacy, and of residence in D——, all these stories, topics of talk, which engross at first petty towns and petty people, were entirely forgotten. Nobody would have dared to speak of or even to remember them.

When M. Myriel came to D—— he was accompanied by an old lady, Mademoiselle Baptistine, who was his sister, ten years younger than himself.

Their only domestic was a woman of about the same age as Mademoiselle Baptistine, who was called Madame Magloire, and who after having been the servant of M. le curé, now took the double title of femme de chambre of Mademoiselle and housekeeper of Monseigneur.

Mademoiselle Baptistine was a tall, pale, thin, sweet person. She fully realised the idea which is expressed by the word "respectable;" for it seems as if it were necessary that a woman should be a mother to be venerable. She had never been pretty; her whole life, which had been but a succession of pious works, had produced upon her a kind of transparent whiteness, and in growing old she had acquired what may be called the beauty of goodness. What had been thinness in her youth had become in maturity transparency, and this etherialness permitted gleams of the angel within. She was more a spirit than a virgin mortal. Her form was shadow-like, hardly enough body to convey the thought of sex—a little earth containing a spark—large eyes, always cast down; a pretext for a soul to remain on earth.

Madame Magloire was a little, white, fat, jolly, bustling old woman, always out of breath, caused first by her activity, and then by the asthma.

M. Myriel, upon his arrival, was installed in his episcopal palace with the honours ordained by the imperial decrees, which class the bishop next in rank to the field-marshal. The mayor and the president made him the first visit, and he, on his part, paid like honour to the general and the prefect.

The installation being completed, the town was curious to see its bishop at work.

II
M. MYRIEL BECOMES MONSEIGNEUR BIENVENU

THE bishop's palace at D—— was contiguous to the hospital: the palace was a spacious and beautiful edifice, built of stone near the beginning of the last century by Monseigneur Henri Pujet, a doctor of theology of the Faculty of Paris, abbé of Simore, who was bishop of D—— in 1712. The palace was in truth a lordly dwelling: there was an air of grandeur about everything, the apartments of the bishop, the saloons, the chambers, the court of honour, which was very large, with arched walks after the antique Florentine style; and a garden planted with magnificent trees.

In the dining hall was a long, superb gallery, which was level with the ground, opening upon the garden; Monseigneur Henri

Pujet had given a grand banquet on the 29th of July, 1714,
to Monseigneur Charles Brûlart de Genlis, archbishop, Prince
d'Embrun, Antoine de Mesgrigny, capuchin, bishop of Grasse,
Philippe de Vendôme, grand-prior de France, the Abbé de Saint
Honoré de Lérins, François de Berton de Grillon, lord bishop
of Vence, Cesar de Sabran de Forcalquier, lord bishop of
Glandève, and Jean Soanen, priest of the oratory, preacher in
ordinary to the king, lord bishop of Senez; the portraits of these
seven reverend personages decorated the hall and this memorable date, July 29th, 1714, appeared in letters of gold on a white
marble tablet.

The hospital was a low, narrow, one story building with a
small garden.

Three days after the bishop's advent he visited the hospital;
when the visit was ended, he invited the director to oblige him
by coming to the palace.

"Monsieur," he said to the director of the hospital, "how
many patients have you?"

"Twenty-six, monseigneur."

"That is as I counted them," said the bishop.

"The beds," continued the director, "are very much
crowded."

"I noticed it."

"The wards are but small chambers, and are not easily
ventilated."

"It seems so to me."

"And then, when the sun does shine, the garden is very small
for the convalescents."

"That was what I was thinking."

"Of epidemics we have had typhus fever this year; two years
ago we had military fever, sometimes one hundred patients, and
we did not know what to do."

"That occurred to me."

"What can we do, monseigneur?" said the director; "we
must be resigned."

This conversation took place in the dining gallery on the
ground floor.

The bishop was silent a few moments: then he turned
suddenly towards the director.

"Monsieur," he said, "how many beds do you think this hall
alone would contain?"

"The dining hall of monseigneur!" exclaimed the director, stupefied.

The bishop ran his eyes over the hall, seemingly taking measure and making calculations.

"It will hold twenty beds," said he to himself; then raising his voice, he said:

"Listen, Monsieur Director, to what I have to say. There is evidently a mistake here. There are twenty-six of you in five or six small rooms: there are only three of us, and space for sixty. There is a mistake, I tell you. You have my house and I have yours. Restore mine to me; you are at home."

Next day the twenty-six poor invalids were installed in the bishop's palace, and the bishop was in the hospital.

M. Myriel had no property, his family having been impoverished by the revolution. His sister had a life estate of five hundred francs which in the vicarage sufficed for her personal needs. M. Myriel received from the government as bishop a salary of fifteen thousand francs. The day on which he took up his residence in the hospital building, he resolved to appropriate this sum once for all to the following uses. We copy the schedule then written by him.

Schedule for the Regulation of my Household Expenses

"For the little seminary, fifteen hundred livres.

Mission congregation, one hundred livres.

For the Lazaristes of Montdidier, one hundred livres.

Congregation of the Saint-Esprit, one hundred and fifty livres.

Seminary of foreign missions in Paris, two hundred livres.

Religious establishments in the Holy Land, one hundred livres.

Maternal charitable societies, three hundred livres.

For that of Arles, fifty livres.

For the amelioration of prisons, four hundred livres.

For the relief and deliverance of prisoners, five hundred livres.

For the liberation of fathers of families imprisoned for debt, one thousand livres.

Additions to the salaries of poor schoolmasters of the diocese, two thousand livres.

Public storehouse of Hautes-Alpes, one hundred livres.

Association of the ladies of D—— of Manosque and Sisteron for the gratuitous instruction of poor girls, fifteen hundred livres.

For the poor, six thousand livres.

My personal expenses, one thousand livres.

Total, fifteen thousand livres."

M. Myriel made no alteration in this plan during the time he held the see of D——; he called it, as will be seen, the regulation of his *household expenses*.

Mademoiselle Baptistine accepted this arrangement with entire submission; M. Myriel was to her at once her brother and her bishop, her companion by ties of blood and her superior by ecclesiastical authority. She loved and venerated him unaffectedly; when he spoke, she listened; when he acted, she gave him her co-operation. Madame Magloire, however, their servant, grumbled a little. The bishop, as will be seen, had reserved but a thousand francs; this, added to the income of Mademoiselle Baptistine, gave them a yearly independence of fifteen hundred francs, upon which the three old people subsisted.

Thanks, however, to the rigid economy of Madame Magloire, and the excellent management of Mademoiselle Baptistine, whenever a curate came to D——, the bishop found means to extend to him his hospitality.

About three months after the installation, the bishop said one day, "With all this I am very much cramped." "I think so too," said Madame Magloire: "Monseigneur has not even asked for the sum due him by the department for his carriage expenses in town, and in his circuits in the diocese. It was formerly the custom with all bishops."

"Yes!" said the bishop; "you are right, Madame Magloire."

He made his application.

Some time afterwards the conseil-général took his claim into consideration and voted him an annual stipend of three thousand francs under this head: "Allowance to the bishop for carriage expenses, and travelling expenses for pastoral visits."

The bourgeoisie of the town were much excited on the subject and in regard to it a senator of the empire, formerly a member of the Council of Five Hundred, an advocate of the

Eighteenth Brumaire now provided with a rich senatorial seat near D——, wrote to M. Bigot de Préameneu, Minister of Public Worship, a fault-finding confidential epistle, from which we make the following extract:—

"Carriage expenses! What can he want of it in a town of less than 4000 inhabitants? Expenses of pastoral visits! And what good do they do, in the first place; and then, how is it possible to travel by post in this mountain region? There are no roads; he can go only on horseback. Even the bridge over the Durance at Château-Arnoux is scarcely passable for oxcarts. These priests are always so; avaricious and miserly. This one played the good apostle at the outset: now he acts like the rest; he must have a carriage and post-chaise. He must have luxury like the old bishops. Bah! this whole priesthood! Monsieur le Comte, things will never be better till the emperor delivers us from these macaroni priests. Down with the pope! (Matters were getting embroiled with Rome.) As for me, I am for Cæsar alone," etc., etc., etc.

This application, on the other hand, pleased Madame Magloire exceedingly. "Good," said she to Mademoiselle Baptistine; "Monseigneur began with others, but he has found at last that he must end by taking care of himself. He has arranged all his charities, and so now here are three thousand francs for us."

The same evening the bishop wrote and gave to his sister a note couched in these terms:

Carriage and Travelling Expenses

"For beef broth for the hospital, fifteen hundred livres.

For the Aix Maternal Charity Association, two hundred and fifty livres.

For the Draguignan Maternal Charity Association, two hundred and fifty livres.

For Foundlings, five hundred livres.

For Orphans, five hundred livres.

Total, three thousand livres."

Such was the budget of M. Myriel.

In regard to the official perquisites, marriage licences, dispensations, private baptisms, and preaching, consecrations of churches or chapels, marriages, etc., the bishop gathered them from the wealthy with as much exactness as he dispensed them to the poor.

In a short time donations of money began to come in; those who had and those who had not, knocked at the bishop's door; some came to receive alms and others to bestow them, and in less than a year he had become the treasurer of all the benevolent, and the dispenser to all the needy. Large sums passed through his hands; nevertheless he changed in no wise his mode of life, nor added the least luxury to his simple fare.

On the contrary, as there is always more misery among the lower classes than there is humanity in the higher, everything was given away, so to speak, before it was received, like water on thirsty soil; it was well that money came to him, for he never kept any; and besides he robbed himself. It being the custom that all bishops should put their baptismal names at the head of their orders and pastoral letters, the poor people of the district had chosen by a sort of affectionate instinct, from among the names of the bishop, that which was expressive to them, and they always called him Monseigneur Bienvenu. We shall follow their example and shall call him thus; besides, this pleased him. "I like this name," said he; "Bienvenu counterbalances Monseigneur."

We do not claim that the portrait which we present here is a true one; we say only that it resembles him.

III
GOOD BISHOP – HARD BISHOPRIC

THE bishop, after converting his carriage into alms, none the less regularly made his round of visits, and in the diocese of D—— this was a wearisome task. There was very little plain, a good deal of mountain; and hardly any roads, as a matter of course; thirty-two curacies, forty-one vicarages, and two hundred and eighty-five sub-curacies. To visit all these is a great labour, but the bishop went through with it. He travelled on foot in his own neighbourhood, in a cart when he was in the plains, and in a *cacolet*, a basket strapped on the back of a mule, when in the mountains. The two women usually accompanied him, but when the journey was too difficult for them he went alone.

One day he arrived at Senez, formerly the seat of a bishopric, mounted on an ass. His purse was very empty at the time, and would not permit any better conveyance. The mayor of the city came to receive him at the gate of the episcopal residence, and saw him dismount from his ass with astonishment and mortification. Several of the citizens stood near by, laughing. "Monsieur Mayor," said the bishop, "and Messieurs citizens, I see what astonishes you; you think that it shows a good deal of pride for a poor priest to use the same conveyance which was used by Jesus Christ. I have done it from necessity, I assure you, and not from vanity."

In his visits he was indulgent and gentle, and preached less than he talked. He never used far-fetched reasons or examples. To the inhabitants of one region he would cite the example of a neighbouring region. In the cantons where the necessitous were treated with severity he would say, "Look at the people of Briançon. They have given to the poor, and to widows and orphans, the right to mow their meadows three days before any one else. When their houses are in ruins they rebuild them without cost. And so it is a country blessed of God. For a whole century they have not had a single murderer."

In villages where the people were greedy for gain at harvest time he would say, "Look at Embrun. If a father of a family, at harvest time, has his sons in the army, and his daughters at service in the city, and he is sick, the priest recommends him in his sermons, and on Sunday, after mass, the whole population of the village, men, women, and children, go into the poor man's field and harvest his crop, and put the straw and the grain into his granary." To families divided by questions of property and inheritance, he would say, "See the mountaineers of Devolny, a country so wild that the nightingale is not heard there once in fifty years. Well now, when the father dies, in a family, the boys go away to seek their fortunes, and leave the property to the girls, so that they may get husbands." In those cantons where there was a taste for the law, and where the farmers were ruining themselves with stamped paper, he would say, "Look at those good peasants of the valley of Queyras. There are three thousand souls there. Why, it is like a little republic! Neither judge nor constable is known there. The mayor does everything. He apportions the impost, taxes each one according to his judgment, decides their quarrels without charge, distributes their patrimony without fees, gives judgment without expense; and he is obeyed, because he is a just man among simple-hearted men." In the villages which he found without a schoolmaster, he would again hold up the valley of Queyras. "Do you know how they do?" he would say. "As a little district of twelve or fifteen houses cannot always support a teacher, they have schoolmasters that are paid by the whole valley, who go around from village to village, passing a week in this place, and ten days in that, and give instruction. These masters attend the fairs, where I have seen them. They are known by quills which they wear in their hatband. Those who teach only how to read have one quill; those who teach reading and arithmetic have two; and those who teach reading, arithmetic, and Latin, have three; the latter are esteemed great scholars. But what a shame to be ignorant! Do like the people of Queyras."

In such fashion would he talk, gravely and paternally, in default of examples he would invent parables, going straight to his object, with few phrases and many images, which was the very eloquence of Jesus Christ, convincing and persuasive.

IV
WORKS ANSWERING WORDS

His conversation was affable and pleasant. He adapted himself to the capacity of the two old women who lived with him, but when he laughed, it was the laugh of a school-boy.

Madame Magloire usually called him *Your Greatness*. One day he rose from his arm-chair, and went to his library for a book. It was upon one of the upper shelves, and as the bishop was rather short, he could not reach it. "Madame Magloire," said he, "bring me a chair. My greatness does not extend to this shelf."

One of his distant relatives, the Countess of Lô, rarely let an occasion escape of enumerating in his presence what she called "the expectations" of her three sons. She had several relatives, very old and near their death, of whom her sons were the legal heirs. The youngest of the three was to receive from a great-aunt a hundred thousand livres in the funds; the second was to take the title of duke from his uncle; the eldest would succeed to the peerage of his grandfather. The bishop commonly listened in silence to these innocent and pardonable maternal displays. Once, however, he appeared more dreamy than was his custom, while Madame de Lô rehearsed the detail of all these successions and all these "expectations." Stopping suddenly, with some impatience, she exclaimed, "My goodness, cousin, what are you thinking about?" "I am thinking," said the bishop, "of a strange thing which is, I believe, in St. Augustine: 'Place your expectations on him to whom there is no succession!' "

On another occasion, when he received a letter announcing the decease of a gentleman of the country, in which were detailed, at great length, not only the dignities of the departed, but the feudal and titular honours of all his relatives, he exclaimed: "What a broad back has death! What a wondrous load of titles will he cheerfully carry, and what hardihood must men have who will thus use the tomb to feed their vanity!"

At times he made use of gentle raillery, which was almost always charged with serious ideas. Once, during Lent, a young vicar came to D——, and preached in the cathedral. The subject of his sermon was charity, and he treated it very eloquently. He called upon the rich to give alms to the poor, if they would escape the tortures of hell, which he pictured in the most fearful colours, and enter that paradise which he painted as so desirable and inviting. There was a retired merchant of wealth in the audience, a little given to usury, M. Géborand, who had accumulated an estate of two millions in the manufacture of coarse cloths and serges. Never, in the whole course of his life, had M. Géborand given alms to the unfortunate; but from the date of this sermon it was noticed that he gave regularly, every Sunday, a penny to the old beggar women at the door of the cathedral. There were six of them to share it. The bishop chanced to see him one day, as he was performing this act of charity, and said to his sister, with a smile, "See Monsieur Géborand, buying a penny-worth of paradise."

When soliciting aid for any charity, he was not silenced by a refusal; he was at no loss for words that would set the hearers thinking. One day, he was receiving alms for the poor in a parlour in the city, where the Marquis of Champtercier, who was old, rich, and miserly, was present. The marquis managed to be, at the same time, an ultra-royalist and an ultra-Voltairian, a species of which he was not the only representative. The bishop coming to him in turn, touched his arm and said, "Monsieur le Marquis, you must give me something." The marquis turned and answered drily, "Monseigneur, I have my own poor." "Give them to me," said the bishop.

One day he preached this sermon in the cathedral:——

"My very dear brethren, my good friends, there are in France thirteen hundred and twenty thousand peasants' cottages that have but three openings; eighteen hundred and seventeen thousand that have two, the door and one window; and finally, three hundred and forty-six thousand cabins, with only one opening—the door. And this is in consequence of what is called the excise upon doors and windows. In these poor families, among the aged women and the little children, dwelling in these huts, how abundant is fever and disease? Alas! God gives light to men; the law sells it. I do not blame the law, but I bless God. In Isère, in Var, and in the Upper and the Lower Alps, the peasants have not even wheelbarrows, they carry the manure on their backs; they have no candles, but burn pine knots, and bits of rope soaked in pitch. And the same is the case all through the upper part of Dauphiné. They make bread once in six months, and bake it with the refuse of the fields. In the winter it becomes so hard that they cut it up with an axe, and soak it for twenty-four hours, before they can eat it. My brethren, be compassionate; behold how much suffering there is around you."

Born a Provençal, he had easily made himself familiar with all the patois of the south. He would say, "*Eh, bé! moussu, sès sagé?*" as in Lower Languedoc; "*Onté anaras passa?*" as in the Lower Alps; "*Puerte un bouen montou embe un bouen froumage grase,*" as in Upper Dauphiné. This pleased the people greatly, and contributed not a little to giving him ready access to their hearts. He was the same in a cottage and on the mountains as in his own house. He could say the grandest things in the most common language; and as he spoke all dialects, his words entered the souls of all.

Moreover, his manners with the rich were the same as with the poor.

He condemned nothing hastily, or without taking account of circumstances. He would say, "Let us see the way in which the fault came to pass."

Being, as he smilingly described himself, an *ex-sinner*, he had none of the inaccessibility of a rigorist, and boldly professed, even under the frowning eyes of the ferociously virtuous, a doctrine which may be stated nearly as follows:—

"Man has a body which is at once his burden and his temptation. He drags it along, and yields to it.

"He ought to watch over it, to keep it in bounds; to repress it, and only to obey it at the last extremity. It may be wrong to obey even then, but if so, the fault is venial. It is a fall, but a fall upon the knees, which may end in prayer.

"To be a saint is the exception; to be upright is the rule. Err, falter, sin, but be upright.

"To commit the least possible sin is the law for man. To live without sin is the dream of an angel. Everything terrestrial is subject to sin. Sin is a gravitation."

When he heard many exclaiming, and expressing great indignation against anything, "Oh! oh!" he would say, smiling. "It would seem that this is a great crime, of which they are all guilty. How frightened hypocrisy hastens to defend itself, and to get under cover."

He was indulgent towards women, and towards the poor, upon whom the weight of society falls most heavily; and said: "The faults of women, children, and servants, of the feeble, the indigent and the ignorant, are the faults of their husbands, fathers, and masters, of the strong, the rich, and the wise." At other times, he said, "Teach the ignorant as much as you can; society is culpable in not providing instruction for all and it must answer for the night which it produces. If the soul is left in darkness, sins will be committed. The guilty one is not he who commits the sin, but he who causes the darkness."

As we see, he had a strange and peculiar way of judging things. I suspect that he acquired it from the Gospel.

In company one day he heard an account of a criminal case that was about to be tried. A miserable man, through love for a woman and for the child she had borne him, had been making false coin, his means being exhausted. At that time counterfeiting was still punished with death. The woman was arrested for passing the first piece that he had made. She was held a prisoner, but there was no proof against her lover. She alone could testify against him, and convict him by her confession. She denied his guilt. They insisted, but she was obstinate in her denial. In this state of the case, the *procureur du roi* devised a shrewd plan. He represented to her that her lover was unfaithful, and by means of fragments of letters skilfully put together, succeeded in persuading the unfortunate woman that she had a rival, and that this man had deceived her. At once exasperated by jealousy, she denounced her lover, confessed all, and proved his guilt. He was to be tried in a few days, at Aix, with his accomplice, and his conviction was certain. The story was told, and everybody was in ecstasy at the adroitness of the officer. In bringing jealousy into play he had brought truth to light by means of anger, and justice had sprung from revenge. The bishop listened to all this in silence. When it was finished he asked:

"Where are this man and woman to be tried?"

"At the Assizes."

"And where is the *procureur du roi* to be tried?"

A tragic event occurred at D——. A man had been condemned to death for murder. The unfortunate prisoner was a poorly educated, but not entirely ignorant man, who had been a juggler at fairs, and a public letter-writer. The people were greatly interested in the trial. The evening before the day fixed for the execution of the condemned, the almoner of the prison fell ill. A priest was needed to attend the prisoner in his last moments. The curé was sent for, but he refused to go, saying, "That does not concern me. I have nothing to do with such drudgery, or with that mountebank; besides, I am sick myself; and moreover it is not my place." When this reply was reported to the bishop, he said, "The curé is right. It is not his place, it is mine."

He went, on the instant, to the prison, went down into the dungeon of the "mountebank," called him by his name, took him by the hand, and talked with him. He passed the whole day with him forgetful of food and sleep, praying to God for the soul of the condemned, and exhorting the condemned to join with him. He spoke to him the best truths, which are the simplest. He was father, brother, friend; bishop for blessing only. He taught him everything by encouraging and consoling him. This man would have died in despair. Death, for him, was like an abyss. Standing shivering upon the dreadful brink, he recoiled with horror. He was not ignorant enough to be indifferent. The terrible shock of his condemnation had in some sort broken here and there that wall which separates us from the mystery of things beyond, and which we call life. Through these fatal breaches, he was constantly looking beyond this world, and he could see nothing but darkness; the bishop showed him the light.

On the morrow when they came for the poor man, the bishop was with him. He followed him, and showed himself to

the eyes of the crowd in his violet camail, with his bishop's cross
about his neck, side by side with the miserable being, who was
bound with cords.

He mounted the cart with him, he ascended the scaffold
with him. The sufferer, so gloomy and so horror-stricken in the
evening, was now radiant with hope. He felt that his soul was
reconciled, and he trusted in God. The bishop embraced him,
and at the moment when the axe was about to fall, he said to
him, "whom man kills, him God restoreth to life, whom his
brethren put away, he findeth the Father. Pray, believe, enter
into life! The Father is there." When he descended from the
scaffold, something in his look made the people fall back. It
would be hard to say which was the most wonderful, his paleness
or his serenity. As he entered the humble dwelling which he
smilingly called his *palace*, he said to his sister, "I have been
officiating pontifically."

As the most sublime things are often least comprehended,
there were those in the city who said, in commenting upon the
bishop's conduct that it was affectation, but such ideas were
confined to the upper classes. The people, who do not look for
unworthy motives in holy works, admired and were softened.

As to the bishop, the sight of the guillotine was a shock to
him, from which it was long before he recovered.

The scaffold, indeed, when it is prepared and set up, has the
effect of a hallucination. We may be indifferent to the death
penalty, and may not declare ourselves, yes or no, so long as we
have not seen a guillotine with our own eyes. But when we see
one, the shock is violent, and we are compelled to decide and
take part, for or against. Some admire it, like Le Maistre; others
execrate it, like Beccaria. The guillotine is the concretion of the
law; it is called the Avenger; it is not neutral and does not permit
you to remain neutral. He who sees it quakes with the most
mysterious of tremblings. All social questions set up their points
of interrogation about this axe. The scaffold is vision. The scaffold is not a mere frame, the scaffold is not a machine, the
scaffold is not an inert piece of mechanism made of wood, of
iron, and of ropes. It seems a sort of being which had some
sombre origin of which we can have no idea; one would say
that this frame sees, that this machine understands, that this
mechanism comprehends; that this wood, this iron, and these
ropes, have a will. In the fearful reverie into which its presence

casts the soul, the awful apparition of the scaffold confounds itself with its horrid work. The scaffold becomes the accomplice of the executioner; it devours, it eats flesh, and it drinks blood. The scaffold is a sort of monster created by the judge and the workman, a spectre which seems to live with a kind of unspeakable life, drawn from all the death which it has wrought.

Thus the impression was horrible and deep, on the morrow of the execution, and for many days, the bishop appeared to be overwhelmed. The almost violent calmness of the fatal moment had disappeared; the phantom of social justice took possession of him. He, who ordinarily looked back upon all his actions with a satisfaction so radiant, now seemed to be a subject of self-reproach. By times he would talk to himself, and in an undertone mutter dismal monologues. One evening his sister overheard and preserved the following: "I did not believe that it could be so monstrous. It is wrong to be so absorbed in the divine law as not to perceive the human law. Death belongs to God alone. By what right do men touch that unknown thing?"

With the lapse of time these impressions faded away, and were probably effaced. Nevertheless it was remarked that the bishop ever after avoided passing by the place of execution.

M. Myriel could be called at all hours to the bedside of the sick and the dying. He well knew that there was his highest duty and his greatest work. Widowed or orphan families had no need to send for him; he came of himself. He would sit silent for long hours by the side of a man who had lost the wife whom he loved, or of a mother who had lost her child. As he knew the time for silence, he knew also the time for speech. Oh, admirable consoler! he did not seek to drown grief in oblivion, but to exalt and to dignify it by hope. He would say, "Be careful of the way in which you think of the dead. Think not of what might have been. Look steadfastly and you shall see the living glory of your well-beloved dead in the depths of heaven." He believed that faith is healthful. He sought to counsel and to calm the despairing man by pointing out to him the man of resignation, and to transform the grief which looks down into the grave by showing it the grief which looks up to the stars.

V

HOW MONSEIGNEUR BIENVENU
MADE HIS CASSOCK LAST SO LONG

THE private life of M. Myriel was full of the same thoughts as his public life. To one who could have seen it on the spot, the voluntary poverty in which the Bishop of D—— lived, would have been a serious as well as a pleasant sight.

Like all old men, and like most thinkers, he slept but little, but that little was sound. In the morning he devoted an hour to meditation, and then said mass, either at the cathedral, or in his own house. After mass he took his breakfast of rye bread and milk, and then went to work.

A bishop is a very busy man, he must receive the report of the clerk of the diocese, ordinarily a prebendary, every day; and nearly every day his grand vicars. He has congregations to superintend, licences to grant, all ecclesiastical bookselling to examine, parish and diocesan catechisms, prayer-books, etc., charges to write, preachings to authorise, curés and mayors to make peace between, a clerical correspondence, an administrative correspondence, on the one hand the government, on the other the Holy See, a thousand matters of business.

What time these various affairs and his devotions and his breviary left him, he gave first to the needy, the sick, and the afflicted; what time the afflicted, the sick, and the needy left him, he gave to labour. Sometimes he used a spade in his garden, and sometimes he read and wrote. He had but one name for these two kinds of labour; he called them gardening. "The spirit is a garden," said he.

Towards noon, when the weather was good, he would go out and walk in the fields, or in the city, often visiting the cottages and cabins. He would be seen plodding along, wrapt in his thoughts, his eyes bent down, resting upon his long cane, wearing his violet doublet, wadded so as to be very warm, violet stockings and heavy shoes, and his flat hat, from the three corners of which hung the three golden grains of spikenard.

His coming made a fête. One would have said that he dispersed warmth and light as he passed along. Old people and children would come to their doors for the bishop as they would for the sun. He blessed, and was blessed in return. Whoever was in need of anything was shown the way to his house.

Now and then he would stop and talk to the little boys and girls—and give a smile to their mothers. When he had money his visits were to the poor; when he had none, he visited the rich.

As he made his cassock last a very long time, in order that it might not be perceived, he never went out into the city without his violet doublet. In summer this was rather irksome.

On his return he dined. His dinner was like his breakfast.

At half-past eight in the evening he took supper with his sister, Madame Magloire standing behind them and waiting on the table. Nothing could be more frugal than this meal. If, however, the bishop had one of his curés to supper, Madame Magloire improved the occasion to serve her master with some excellent fish from the lakes, or some fine game from the mountain. Every curé was a pretext for a fine meal, the bishop did not interfere. With these exceptions there was rarely seen upon his table more than boiled vegetables, or bread warmed with oil. And so it came to be a saying in the city, "When the bishop does not entertain a curé, he entertains a Trappist."

After supper he would chat for half an hour with Mademoiselle Baptistine and Madame Magloire, and then go to his own room and write sometimes upon loose sheets, sometimes on the margin of one of his folios. He was a well-read and even a learned man. He has left five or six very curious manuscripts behind him; among them is a dissertation upon this passage in Genesis: *In the beginning the spirit of God moved upon the face of the waters.* He contrasts this with three other versions; the Arabic, which has: *the winds of God blew*; Flavius Josephus, who says: *a wind from on high fell upon all the earth*; and finally the Chaldean paraphrase of Onkelos, which reads: *a wind coming from God blew upon the face of the waters.* In another dissertation, he examines the theological works of Hugo, Bishop of Ptolemais, a distant relative of the writer of this book, and proves that sundry little tracts, published in the last century under the pseudonym of Barleycourt, should be attributed to that prelate.

Sometimes in the midst of his reading, no matter what book he might have in his hands, he would suddenly fall into deep meditation, and when it was over, would write a few lines on whatever page was open before him. These lines often have no connection with the book in which they are written. We have under our own eyes a note written by him upon the margin of a quarto volume entitled: "*Correspondance du Lord Germain avec les généraux Clinton, Cornwallis, et les amiraux de la Station de l'Amérique. A Versailles, chez Poinçot, Libraire, et à Paris, chez Pissot, Quai des Augustins.*"

And this is the note:

"Oh Thou who art!

"Ecclesiastes names thee the Almighty; Maccabees names thee Creator; the Epistle to the Ephesians names thee Liberty; Baruch names thee Immensity; the Psalms name thee Wisdom and Truth; John names thee Light; the book of Kings names thee Lord; Exodus calls thee Providence; Leviticus, Holiness; Esdras, Justice; Creation calls thee God; man names thee Father; but Solomon names thee Compassion, and that is the most beautiful of all thy names."

Towards nine o'clock in the evening the two women were accustomed to retire to their chambers in the second story, leaving him until morning alone upon the lower floor.

Here it is necessary that we should give an exact idea of the dwelling of the Bishop of D——.

VI

HOW HE PROTECTED HIS HOUSE

THE house which he occupied consisted, as we have said, of a ground floor and a second story; three rooms on the ground floor, three on the second story, and an attic above. Behind the house was a garden of about a quarter of an acre. The two women occupied the upper floor; the bishop lived below. The first room, which opened upon the street, was his dining-room, the second was his bedroom, and the third his oratory. You could not leave the oratory without passing through the bed-room, and to leave the bedroom you must pass through the dining-room. At one end of the oratory there was an alcove closed in, with a bed for occasions of hospitality. The bishop kept this bed for the country curés when business or the wants of their parish brought them to D——.

The pharmacy of the hospital, a little building adjoining the house and extending into the garden, had been transformed into a kitchen and cellar.

There was also a stable in the garden, which was formerly the hospital kitchen, where the bishop now kept a couple of cows, and invariably, every morning, he sent half the milk they gave to the sick at the hospital. "I pay my tithes," said he.

His room was quite large, and was difficult to warm in bad weather. As wood is very dear at D——, he conceived the idea of having a room partitioned off from the cow-stable with a tight plank ceiling. In the coldest weather he passed his evenings there, and called it his *winter parlour*.

In this winter parlour, as in the dining-room, the only furniture was a square white wooden table, and four straw chairs. The dining-room, however, was furnished with an old sideboard stained red. A similar sideboard, suitably draped with white linen and imitation lace, served for the altar which decorated the oratory.

His rich penitents and the pious women of D—— had often contributed the money for a beautiful new altar for monseigneur's oratory; he had always taken the money and given it to the poor. "The most beautiful of altars," said he, "is the soul of an unhappy man who is comforted and thanks God."

In his oratory he had two prie-dieu straw chairs, and an armchair, also of straw, in the bedroom. When he happened to have seven or eight visitors at once, the prefect, or the general, or the major of the regiment in the garrison, or some of the pupils of the little seminary, he was obliged to go to the stable for the chairs that were in the winter parlour, to the oratory for the prie-dieu, and to the bedroom for the arm-chair; in this way he could get together as many as eleven seats for his visitors. At each new visit a room was stripped.

It happened sometimes that there were twelve; then the bishop concealed the embarrassment of the situation by standing before the fire if it were winter, or by walking in the garden if it were summer.

There was another chair in the stranger's alcove, but it had lost half its straw, and had but three legs, so that it could be used only when standing against the wall. Mademoiselle Baptistine had also, in her room, a very large wooden easy-chair, that had once been gilded and covered with flowered silk, but as it had to be taken into her room through the window, the stairway being too narrow, it could not be counted among the movable furniture.

It had been the ambition of Mademoiselle Baptistine to be able to buy a parlour lounge, with cushions of Utrecht velvet, roses on a yellow ground, while the mahogany should be in the form of swans' necks. But this would have cost at least five hundred francs, and as she had been able to save only forty-two francs and ten sous for the purpose in five years, she had finally given it up. But who ever does attain to his ideal?

Nothing could be plainer in its arrangements than the bishop's bed-chamber. A window, which was also a door, opening upon the garden; facing this, the bed, an iron hospital-bed, with green serge curtains; in the shadow of the bed, behind a screen, the toilet utensils, still betraying the elegant habits of the man of the world; two doors, one near the chimney, leading into the oratory, the other near the book-case, opening into the dining-room. The book-case, a large closet with glass doors, filled with books; the fire-place, cased with wood painted to imitate marble, usually without fire; in the fire-place, a pair of andirons ornamented with two vases of flowers, once plated with silver, which was a kind of episcopal luxury; above the fire-place, a copper crucifix, from which the silver was worn off, fixed upon a piece of thread-bare black velvet in a wooden frame from which the gilt was almost gone; near the window, a large table with an inkstand, covered with confused papers and heavy volumes. In front of the table was the straw arm-chair, and before the bed, a prie-dieu from the oratory.

Two portraits in oval frames hung on the wall on either side of the bed. Small gilt inscriptions upon the background of the canvas indicated that the portraits represented one, the Abbé de Chaliot, bishop of Saint Claude, the other, the Abbé Tourteau, vicar-general of Agde, abbé of Grandchamps, order of Citeaux, diocese of Chartres. The bishop found these portraits when he succeeded to the hospital patients in this chamber, and left them untouched. They were priests, and probably donors to the hospital—two reasons why he should respect them. All that he knew of these two personages was that they had been named by the king, the one to his bishopric, the other to his living, on the same day, the 27th of April, 1785. Madame Magloire having taken down the pictures to wipe off the dust, the bishop had found this circumstance written in a faded ink upon a little square piece of paper, yellow with time, stuck with four wafers on the back of the portrait of the Abbé of Grandchamps.

He had at his window an antique curtain of coarse woollen stuff which finally became so old that, to save the expense of a new one, Madame Magloire was obliged to put a large patch in the very middle of it. This patch was in the form of a cross. The bishop often called attention to it. "How fortunate that is," he would say.

Every room in the house, on the ground floor as well as in the upper story, without exception, was whitewashed, as is the custom in barracks and in hospitals.

However, in later years, as we shall see by-and-by, Madame Magloire found, under the wall paper, some paintings which decorated the apartment of Mademoiselle Baptistine. Before it was a hospital, the house had been a sort of gathering-place for the citizens, at which time these decorations were introduced. The floors of the chambers were paved with red brick, which were scoured every week, and before the beds straw matting was spread. In all respects the house was kept by the two women exquisitely neat from top to bottom. This was the only luxury that the bishop would permit. He would say, "*That takes nothing from the poor.*"

We must confess that he still retained of what he had formerly, six silver dishes and a silver soup ladle, which Madame Magloire contemplated every day with new joy as they shone on the coarse, white, linen table-cloth. And as we are drawing the portrait of the Bishop of D—— just as he was, we must add that he had said, more than once, "It would be difficult for me to give up eating from silver."

With this silver ware should be counted two large, massive silver candlesticks which he inherited from a great-aunt. These candlesticks held two wax-candles, and their place was upon the bishop's mantel. When he had any one to dinner, Madame Magloire lighted the two candles and placed the two candlesticks upon the table.

There was in the bishop's chamber, at the head of his bed, a small cupboard in which Madame Magloire placed the six silver dishes and the great ladle every evening. But the key was never taken out of it.

The garden, which was somewhat marred by the unsightly structures of which we have spoken, was laid out with four walks, crossing at the drain-well in the centre. There was another walk round the garden, along the white wall which enclosed it. These walks left four square plats which were bordered with box. In three of them Madame Magloire cultivated vegetables; in the fourth the bishop had planted flowers, and here and there were a few fruit trees. Madame Magloire once said to him with a kind of gentle reproach: "Monseigneur, you are always anxious to make everything useful, but yet here is a plat that is of no use. It would be much better to have salads there than bouquets." "Madame Magloire," replied the bishop, "you are mistaken. The beautiful is as useful as the useful." He added after a moment's silence, "perhaps more so."

This plat, consisting of three or four beds, occupied the bishop nearly as much as his books. He usually passed an hour or two there trimming, weeding, and making holes here and there in the ground, and planting seeds. He was as much averse to insects as a gardener would have wished. He made no pretensions to botany, and knew nothing of groups or classification; he did not care in the least to decide between Tournefort and the natural method; he took no part either for the utricles against the cotyledons, or for Jussieu against Linnæus. He did not study plants, he loved flowers. He had much respect for the learned, but still more for the ignorant; and, while he fulfilled his duty in both these respects, he watered his beds every summer evening with a tin watering-pot painted green.

Not a door in the house had a lock. The door of the dining-room which, we have mentioned, opened into the cathedral grounds, was formerly loaded with bars and bolts like the door of a prison. The bishop had had all this iron-work taken off, and the door, by night as well as by day, was closed only with a latch. The passer-by, whatever might be the hour, could open it with a simple push. At first the two women had been very much troubled at the door being never locked; but Monseigneur de D—— said to them: "Have bolts on your own doors, if you like." They shared his confidence at last, or at least acted as if they shared it. Madame Magloire alone had occasional attacks of fear. As to the bishop, the reason for this is explained, or at least pointed at in these three lines written by him on the margin of a Bible: "This is the shade of meaning, the door of a physician should never be closed; the door of a priest should always be open."

In another book, entitled *Philosophie de la Science Medicale*, he wrote this further note: "Am I not a physician as well as they? I also have my patients; first I have theirs, whom they call the sick; and then I have my own, whom I call the unfortunate."

Yet again he had written: "Ask not the name of him who asks you for a bed. It is especially he whose name is a burden to him, who has need of an asylum."

It occurred to a worthy curé, I am not sure whether it was the curé of Couloubroux or the curé of Pomprierry, to ask him one day probably at the instigation of Madame Magloire, if monseigneur were quite sure that there was not a degree of imprudence in leaving his door, day and night, at the mercy of whoever might wish to enter, and if he did not fear that some evil would befall a house so poorly defended. The bishop touched him gently on the shoulder, and said: "*Nisi Dominus custodierit domum, in vanum vigilant qui custodiunt eam.*"*

And then he changed the subject.

He very often said: "There is a bravery for the priest as well as a bravery for the colonel of dragoons." "Only," added he, "ours should be quiet."

VII
CRAVATTE

THIS is the proper place for an incident which we must not omit, for it is one of those which most clearly shows what manner of man the Bishop of D—— was.

After the destruction of the band of Gaspard Bès, which had infested the gorges of Ollivolles, one of his lieutenants, Cravatte, took refuge in the mountains. He concealed himself for some time with his bandits, the remnant of the troop of Gaspard Bès, in the county of Nice, then made his way to Piedmont, and suddenly reappeared in France in the neighbourhood of Barcelonnette. He was first seen at Jauziers, then at Tuiles. He concealed himself in the caverns of the Joug de l'Aigle, from which he made descents upon the hamlets and villages by the ravines of Ubaye and Ubayette.

He even pushed as far as Embrun, and one night broke into the cathedral and stripped the sacristy. His robberies desolated the country. The gendarmes were put upon his trail, but in vain. He always escaped; sometimes by forcible resistance. He was a bold wretch. In the midst of all this terror, the bishop arrived. He was making his visit to Chastelar. The mayor came to see

---

* Unless God protects a house, they who guard it, watch in vain.

him and urged him to turn back. Cravatte held the mountains as far as Arche and beyond; it would be dangerous even with an escort. It would expose three or four poor gendarmes to useless danger.

"And so," said the bishop, "I intend to go without an escort."

"Do not think of such a thing," exclaimed the mayor.

"I think so much of it, that I absolutely refuse the gendarmes, and I am going to start in an hour."

"To start?"

"To start."

"Alone?"

"Alone."

"Monseigneur, you will not do it."

"There is on the mountain," replied the bishop, "a humble little commune, that I have not seen for three years; and they are good friends of mine, kind and honest peasants. They own one goat out of thirty that they pasture. They make pretty woollen thread of various colours, and they play their mountain airs upon small six-holed flutes. They need some one occasionally to tell them of the goodness of God. What would they say of a bishop who was afraid? What would they say if I should not go there?"

"But, monseigneur, the brigands?"

"True," said the bishop, "I am thinking of that. You are right. I may meet them. They too must need some one to tell them of the goodness of God."

"Monseigneur, but it is a band! a pack of wolves!"

"Monsieur Mayor, perhaps Jesus has made me the keeper of that very flock. Who knows the ways of providence?"

"Monseigneur, they will rob you."

"I have nothing."

"They will kill you."

"A simple old priest who passes along muttering his prayer? No, no; what good would it do them?"

"Oh, my good sir, suppose you should meet them!"

"I should ask them for alms for my poor."

"Monseigneur, do not go. In the name of heaven! you are exposing your life."

"Monsieur Mayor," said the bishop, "that is just it. I am not in the world to care for my life, but for souls."

He would not be dissuaded. He set out, accompanied only

by a child, who offered to go as his guide. His obstinacy was the talk of the country, and all dreaded the result.

He would not take along his sister, or Madame Magloire. He crossed the mountain on a mule, met no one, and arrived safe and sound among his "good friends" the shepherds. He remained there a fortnight, preaching, administering the holy rites, teaching and exhorting. When he was about to leave, he resolved to chant a Te Deum with pontifical ceremonies. He talked with the curé about it. But what could be done? there was no episcopal furniture. They could only place at his disposal a paltry village sacristy with a few old robes of worn-out damask, trimmed with imitation-galloon.

"No matter," said the bishop. "Monsieur le curé, at the sermon announce our Te Deum. That will take care of itself."

All the neighbouring churches were ransacked, but the assembled magnificence of these humble parishes could not have suitably clothed a single cathedral singer.

While they were in this embarrassment, a large chest was brought to the parsonage, and left for the bishop by two unknown horsemen, who immediately rode away. The chest was opened; it contained a cope of cloth of gold, a mitre ornamented with diamonds, an archbishop's cross, a magnificent crosier, all the pontifical raiment stolen a month before from the treasures of Our Lady of Embrun. In the chest was a paper on which were written these words: "Cravatte to Monseigneur Bienvenu."

"I said that it would take care of itself," said the bishop. Then he added with a smile: "To him who is contented with a curé's surplice, God sends an archbishop's cope."

"Monseigneur," murmured the curé, with a shake of the head and a smile, "God—or the devil."

The bishop looked steadily upon the curé, and replied with authority: "God!"

When he returned to Chastelar, all along the road, the people came with curiosity to see him. At the parsonage in Chastelar he found Mademoiselle Baptistine and Madame Magloire waiting for him, and he said to his sister, "Well, was I not right? the poor priest went among those poor mountaineers with empty hands; he comes back with hands filled. I went forth placing my trust in God alone; I bring back the treasures of a cathedral."

In the evening before going to bed he said further: "Have no fear of robbers or murderers. Such dangers are without, and are but petty. We should fear ourselves. Prejudices are the real robbers; vices the real murderers. The great dangers are within us. What matters it what threatens our heads or our purses? Let us think only of what threatens our souls."

Then turning to his sister: "My sister, a priest should never take any precaution against a neighbour. What his neighbour does, God permits. Let us confine ourselves to prayer to God when we think that danger hangs over us. Let us beseech him, not for ourselves, but that our brother may not fall into crime on our account."

To sum up, events were rare in his life. We relate those we know of, but usually he passed his life in always doing the same things at the same hours. A month of his year was like an hour of his day.

As to what became of the "treasures" of the Cathedral of Embrun, it would embarrass us to be questioned on that point. There were among them very fine things, and very tempting, and very good to steal for the benefit of the unfortunate. Stolen they had already been by others. Half the work was done; it only remained to change the course of the theft, and to make it turn to the side of the poor. We can say nothing more on the subject. Except that, there was found among the bishop's papers a rather obscure note, which is possibly connected with this affair, that reads as follows: "*The question is, whether this ought to be returned to the cathedral or to the hospital.*"

VIII
AFTER DINNER PHILOSOPHY

THE senator heretofore referred to was an intelligent man, who had made his way in life with a directness of purpose which paid no attention to all those stumbling-blocks which constitute obstacles in men's path, known as conscience, sworn faith, justice, and duty; he had advanced straight to his object without once swerving in the line of his advancement and his interest. He had been formerly a *procureur*, mollified by success, and was not a bad man at all, doing all the little kindnesses that he could to his sons, sons-in-law, and relatives generally, and even to his friends; having prudently taken the pleasant side of life, and availed himself of all the benefits which were thrown in his way. Everything else appeared to him very stupid. He was sprightly, and just enough of a scholar to think himself a disciple of Epicurus, while possibly he was only a product of Pigault-Lebrun. He laughed readily and with gusto at infinite and eternal things, and at the "crotchets of the good bishop." He laughed at them sometimes, with a patronising air, before M. Myriel himself, who listened.

At some semi-official ceremony, Count * * * (this senator) and M. Myriel remained to dinner with the prefect. At dessert, the senator, a little elevated, though always dignified, exclaimed: "Parbleu, Monsieur Bishop; let us talk. It is difficult for a senator and a bishop to look each other in the eye without winking. We are two augurs. I have a confession to make to you; I have my philosophy."

"And you are right," answered the bishop. "As one makes his philosophy, so he rests. You are on a purple bed, Monsieur Senator."

The senator, encouraged by this, proceeded:——

"Let us be good fellows."

"Good devils, even," said the bishop.

"I assure you," resumed the senator, "that the Marquis d'Argens, Pyrrho, Hobbes, and M. Naigeon are not rascals. I have all my philosophers in my library, gilt-edged."

"Like yourself, Monsieur le Comte," interrupted the bishop.

The senator went on:——

"I hate Diderot; he is an idealogist, a demagogue, and a revolutionist, at heart believing in God, and more bigoted than Voltaire. Voltaire mocked at Needham, and he was wrong; for Needham's eels prove that God is useless. A drop of vinegar in a spoonful of flour supplied the *fiat lux*. Suppose the drop greater and the spoonful larger, and you have the world. Man is the eel. Then what is the use of an eternal Father? Monsieur Bishop, the Jehovah hypothesis tires me. It is good for nothing except to produce people with scraggy bodies and empty heads. Down with this great All, who torments me! Hail, Zero! who leaves me quiet. Between us, to open my heart, and confess to my pastor, as I ought, I will confess that I have common sense. My head is not turned with your Jesus, who preaches in every corn-field renunciation and self-sacrifice. It is the advice of a miser to beggars. Renunciation, for what? Self-sacrifice, to what? I do not see that one wolf immolates himself for the benefit of another wolf. Let us dwell, then, with nature. We are at the summit and let us have a higher philosophy. What is the use of being in a higher position if we can't see further than another man's nose? Let us live gaily; for life is all we have. That man has another life, elsewhere, above, below, anywhere—I don't believe a single word of it. Ah! I am recommended to self-sacrifice and renunciation, that I should take care what I do; that I must break my head over questions of good and evil, justice and injustice; over the *fas* and the *nefas*. Why? Because I shall have to render an account for my acts. When? After death. What a fine dream! After I am dead it will take fine fingers to pinch me. I should like to see a shade grasp a handful of ashes. Let us who are initiated, and have raised the skirt of Isis, speak the truth; there is neither good nor evil; there is only vegetation. Let us seek for the real; let us dig into everything. Let us go to the bottom. We should scent out the truth, dig in the earth for it, and seize upon it. Then it gives you exquisite joy; then you grow strong and laugh. I am firmly convinced, Monsieur Bishop, that the immortality of man is a will-o'-the-wisp. Oh! charming promise. Trust it if you will! Adam's letter of recommendation! We have souls, and are to become angels, with blue wings to our shoulders. Tell me, now, isn't it Tertullian who says that the blessed will go from one star to another? Well, we shall be the grasshoppers of the skies. And then we shall see God. Tut tut tut. All these heavens are silly. God is a monstrous myth. I shouldn't say that in the *Moniteur*, of course, but I whisper it among my friends. *Inter pocula*. To sacrifice earth to paradise is to leave the substance for the shadow. I am not so stupid as to be the dupe of the Infinite. I am nothing; I call myself Count Nothing, senator. Did I exist before my birth? No. Shall I, after my death? No. What am I? A little dust, aggregated by an organism. What have I to do on this earth! I have the choice to suffer or to enjoy. Where will suffering lead me? To nothing. But I shall have suffered. Where will enjoyment lead me? To nothing. But I shall have enjoyed. My choice is made. I must eat or be eaten, and I choose to eat. It is better to be the tooth than the grass. Such is my philosophy. After which, as I tell you, there is the grave-digger—the pantheon for us—but all fall into the great gulf—the end; *finis*; total liquidation. This is the vanishing point. Death is dead, believe me. I laugh at the idea that there is any one there that has anything to say to me. It is an invention of nurses: Bugaboo for children; Jehovah for men. No, our morrow is night. Beyond the tomb are only equal nothings.

You have been Sardanapalus, or you have been Vincent de Paul—that amounts to the same nothing. That is the truth of it. Let us live, then, above all things; use your personality while you have it. In fact, I tell you, Monsieur Bishop, I have my philosophy, and I have my philosophers. I do not allow myself to be entangled with nonsense. But it is necessary there should be something for those who are below us, the bare-foots, knife-grinders, and other wretches. Legends and chimeras are given them to swallow, about the soul, immortality, paradise, and the stars. They munch that; they spread it on their dry bread. He who has nothing besides, has the good God—that is the least good he can have. I make no objection to it, but I keep Monsieur Naigeon for myself. The good God is good for the people."

The bishop clapped his hands.

"That is the idea," he exclaimed. "This materialism is an excellent thing, and truly marvellous; reject it who will. Ah! when one has it, he is a dupe no more; he does not stupidly allow himself to be exiled like Cato, or stoned like Stephen, or burnt alive like Joan of Arc. Those who have succeeded in procuring this admirable materialism have the happiness of feeling that they are irresponsible, and of thinking that they can devour everything in quietness—places, sinecures, honours, power rightly or wrongly acquired, lucrative recantations, useful treasons, savoury capitulations of conscience, and that they will enter their graves with their digestion completed. How agreeable it is! I do not say that for you, Monsieur Senator. Nevertheless, I cannot but felicitate you. You great lords have, you say, a philosophy of your own, for your special benefit—exquisite, refined, accessible to the rich alone; good with all sauces, admirably seasoning the pleasures of life. This philosophy is found at great depths, and brought up by special search. But you are good princes, and you are quite willing that the belief in the good God should be the philosophy of the people, much as goose with onions is the turkey with truffles of the poor."

IX

THE BROTHER PORTRAYED BY THE SISTER

To afford an idea of the household of the Bishop of D——, and the manner in which these two good women subordinated their actions, thoughts, even their womanly instincts, so liable to disturbance, to the habits and projects of the bishop, so that he had not even to speak, in order to express them; we cannot do better than to copy here a letter from Mademoiselle Baptistine to Madame la Viscontesse de Boischevron, the friend of her childhood. This letter is in our possession:—

D——, *Dec. 16th, 18*——.

MY DEAR MADAME: Not a day passes that we do not speak of you; that is customary enough with us; but we have now another reason. Would you believe that in washing and dusting the ceilings and walls, Madame Magloire has made some discoveries? At present, our two chambers, which were hung with old paper, whitewashed, would not disparage a château in the style of your own. Madame Magloire has torn off all the paper: it had something underneath. My parlour, where there is no furniture and which we use to dry clothes in, is fifteen feet high, eighteen feet square, and has a ceiling, once painted and gilded, with beams like those of your house. This was covered with canvas during the time it was used as a hospital; and then we have wainscoating of the time of our grandmothers. But it is my own room which you ought to see. Madame Magloire has discovered beneath at least ten thicknesses of paper some pictures, which, though not good, are quite endurable. Telemachus received on horseback, by Minerva, is one; and then again, he is in the gardens—I forget their name; another is where the Roman ladies resorted for a single night. I could say much more; I have Romans, men and women [*here a word is illegible*], and all their retinue. Madame Magloire has cleaned it all, and this summer she is going to repair some little damages, and varnish it, and my room will be a veritable museum. She also found in a corner of the storehouse two pier tables of antique style; they asked two crowns of six livres to regild them, but it is far better to give that to the poor; besides that they are very ugly, and I much prefer a round mahogany table.

"I am always happy: my brother is so good: he gives all he has to the poor and sick. We are full of cares: the weather is very severe in the winter, and one must do something for those who lack. We at least are warmed and lighted, and you know those are great comforts.

"My brother has his peculiarities; when he talks he says that a bishop ought to be thus. Just think of it that the door is never closed. Come in who will, he is at once my brother's guest; he fears nothing, not even in the night; he says that is his form of bravery.

"He wishes me not to fear for him, nor that Madame Magloire should; he exposes himself to every danger, and prefers that we should not even seem to be aware of it; one must know how to understand him.

"He goes out in the rain, walks through the water, travels in winter, he has no fear of darkness, or dangerous roads, or of those he may meet.

"Last year he went all alone into a district infested with robbers. He would not take us. He was gone a fortnight, and when he came back, though we had thought him dead, nothing had happened to him, and he was quite well. He said: 'See, how they have robbed me!' And he opened a trunk in which he had the jewels of the Embrun Cathedral which the robbers had given him.

"Upon that occasion, on the return, I could not keep from scolding him a little, taking care only to speak while the carriage made a noise, so that no one could hear us.

"At first I used to say to myself, he stops for no danger, he is incorrigible. But now I have become used to it. I make signs to Madame Magloire that she shall not oppose him, and he runs what risks he chooses. I call away Madame Magloire, I go to my room, pray for him, and fall asleep. I am calm, for I know very well that if any harm happened to him, it would be my death: I should go away to the good Father with my brother and my bishop. Madame Magloire has had more difficulty in getting used to what she calls his imprudence. Now the thing is settled: we pray together; we are afraid together, and we go to sleep. Should Satan even come into the house, no one would interfere. After all, what is there to fear in this house? There is always One with us who is the strongest: Satan may visit our house, but the good God inhabits it.

"That is enough for me. My brother has no need now even to speak a word. I understand him without his speaking, and we commend ourselves to Providence.

"It must be so with a man whose soul is so noble.

"I asked my brother for the information which you requested respecting the Faux family. You know how well he knows about it, and how much he remembers, for he was always a very good royalist, and this is really a very old Norman family, of the district of Caen. There are five centuries of a Raoul de Faux, Jean de Faux, and Thomas de Faux, who were of the gentry, one of whom was a lord of Rochefort. The last was Guy Etienne Alexandre, who was a cavalry colonel, and held some rank in the light horse of Brittany. His daughter Marie Louise married Adrien Charles de Gramont, son of Duke Louis de Gramont, a peer of France, colonel of the Gardes Françaises, and lieutenant-general of the army. It is written Faux, Fauq, and Faouq.

"Will you not, my dear madame, ask for us the prayers of your holy relative, Monsieur le Cardinal? As to your precious Sylvanie, she has done well not to waste the short time that she is with you in writing to me. She is well, you say; studies according to your wishes and loves me still. That is all I could desire. Her remembrance through you, reached me, and I was glad to receive it. My health is tolerably good; still I grow thinner every day.

"Farewell: my paper is filled and I must stop. With a thousand good wishes,

"BAPTISTINE

"P.S.—Your little nephew is charming; do you remember that he will soon be five years old? He saw a horse pass yesterday on which they had put knee-caps, and he cried out: 'What is that he has got on his knees?' The child is so pretty. His little brother drags an old broom about the room for a carriage, and says, hi!"

As this letter shows, these two women knew how to conform to the bishop's mode of life, with that woman's tact which understands a man better than he can comprehend himself. Beneath the gentle and frank manner of the Bishop of D——, which never changed, he sometimes performed great, daring, even grand acts, without seeming to be aware of it himself. They trembled, but did not interfere. Sometimes Madame Magloire would venture a remonstrance beforehand: never at the time, or afterwards; no one ever disturbed him by word or token in an action once begun. At certain times when he had no need to say it, when, perhaps, he was hardly conscious of it, so complete was his artlessness, they vaguely felt that he was acting as bishop, and at such periods they were only two shadows in the house. They waited on him passively, and if to obey was to disappear, they disappeared. With charming and instinctive delicacy they knew that obtrusive attentions would annoy him; so even when they thought him in danger, they understood, I will not say his thought, but his nature rather, to the degree of ceasing to watch over him. They entrusted him to God's keeping.

Besides, Baptistine said, as we have seen, that his death would be hers. Madame Magloire did not say so, but she knew it.

X

THE BISHOP IN THE PRESENCE
OF AN UNKNOWN LIGHT

A LITTLE while before the date of the letter quoted in the preceding pages, the bishop performed an act, which the whole town thought far more perilous than his excursion across the mountains infested by the bandits.

In the country near D——, there was a man who lived alone. This man, to state the startling fact without preface, had been a member of the National Convention. His name was G——.

The little circle of D—— spoke of the conventionist with a certain sort of horror. A conventionist, think of it; that was in the time when folks thee-and-thoued one another, and said "citizen." This man came very near being a monster; he had not exactly voted for the execution of the king, but almost; he was half a regicide, and had been a terrible creature altogether. How was it, then, on the return of the legitimate princes, that they had not arraigned this man before the provost court? He would not have been beheaded, perhaps, but even if clemency were necessary he might have been banished for life; in fact, an example, etc. etc. Besides, he was an atheist, as all those people are. Babblings of geese against a vulture!

But was this G—— a vulture? Yes, if one should judge him by the savageness of his solitude. As he had not voted for the king's execution, he was not included in the sentence of exile, and could remain in France.

He lived about an hour's walk from the town, far from any hamlet or road, in a secluded ravine of a very wild valley. It was said he had a sort of resting-place there, a hole, a den. He had no neighbours or even passers-by. Since he had lived there the path which led to the place had become overgrown, and people spoke of it as of the house of a hangman.

From time to time, however, the bishop reflectingly gazed

upon the horizon at the spot where a clump of trees indicated the ravine of the aged conventionist, and he would say: "There lives a soul which is alone." And in the depths of his thought he would add "I owe him a visit."

But this idea, we must confess, though it appeared natural at first, yet, after a few moments' reflection, seemed strange, impracticable, and almost repulsive. For at heart he shared the general impression and the conventionist inspired him, he knew not how, with that sentiment which is the fringe of hatred, and which the word "aversion" so well expresses.

However, the shepherd should not recoil from the diseased sheep. Ah! but what a sheep!

The good bishop was perplexed: sometimes he walked in that direction, but he returned.

At last, one day the news was circulated in the town that the young herdsboy who served the conventionist G—— in his retreat, had come for a doctor; that the old wretch was dying, that he was motionless, and could not live through the night. "Thank God!" added many.

The bishop took his cane, put on his overcoat, because his cassock was badly worn, as we have said, and besides the night wind was evidently rising, and set out.

The sun was setting; it had nearly touched the horizon when the bishop reached the accursed spot. He felt a certain quickening of the pulse as he drew near the den. He jumped over a ditch, cleared a hedge, made his way through a brush fence, found himself in a dilapidated garden, and after a bold advance across the open ground, suddenly, behind some high brushwood, he discovered the retreat.

It was a low, poverty-stricken hut, small and clean, with a little vine nailed up in front.

Before the door in an old chair on rollers, there sat a man with white hair, looking with smiling gaze upon the setting sun.

The young herdsboy stood near him, handing him a bowl of milk.

While the bishop was looking, the old man raised his voice.

"Thank you," he said, "I shall need nothing more;" and his smile changed from the sun to rest upon the boy.

The bishop stepped forward. At the sound of his footsteps the old man turned his head, and his face expressed as much surprise as one can feel after a long life.

"This is the first time since I have lived here," said he, "that I have had a visitor. Who are you, monsieur?"

"My name is Bienvenu-Myriel," the bishop replied.

"Bienvenu-Myriel? I have heard that name before. Are you he whom the people call Monseigneur Bienvenu?"

"I am."

The old man continued half-smiling. "Then you are my bishop?"

"Possibly."

"Come in, monsieur."

The conventionist extended his hand to the bishop, but he did not take it. He only said:

"I am glad to find that I have been misinformed. You do not appear to me very ill."

"Monsieur," replied the old man, "I shall soon be better."

He paused and said:

"I shall be dead in three hours."

Then he continued:

"I am something of a physician; I know the steps by which death approaches; yesterday my feet only were cold; to-day the cold has crept to my knees, now it has reached the waist; when it touches the heart all will be over. The sunset is lovely, is it not? I had myself wheeled out to get a final look at nature. You can speak to me; that will not tire me. You do well to come to see a man who is dying. It is good that these moments should have witnesses. Every one has his fancy; I should like to live until the dawn, but I know I have scarcely life for three hours. It will be night, but what matters it: to finish is a very simple thing. One does not need morning for that. Be it so: I shall die in the starlight."

The old man turned towards the herdsboy:

"Little one, go to bed: thou didst watch the other night: thou art weary."

The child went into the hut.

The old man followed him with his eyes and added, as if speaking to himself: "While he is sleeping, I shall lie: the two slumbers keep fit company."

The bishop was not as much affected as he might have been: it was not his idea of godly death; we must tell all for the little inconsistencies of great souls should be mentioned; he who had laughed so heartily at "His Highness," was still slightly shocked at not being called monseigneur, and was almost tempted to answer "citizen." He felt a desire to use the brusque familiarity common enough with doctors and priests, but which was not customary with him.

This conventionist after all, this representative of the people, had been a power on the earth; and perhaps for the first time in his life the bishop felt himself in a humour to be severe. The conventionist, however, treated him with a modest consideration and cordiality, in which perhaps might have been discerned that humility which is befitting to one so nearly dust unto dust.

The bishop, on his part, although he generally kept himself free from curiosity, which to his idea was almost offensive, could not avoid examining the conventionist with an attention for which, as it had not its source in sympathy, his conscience would have condemned him as to any other man; but a conventionist he looked upon as an outlaw, even to the law of charity.

G——, with his self-possessed manner, erect figure, and vibrating voice, was one of those noble octogenarians who are the marvel of the physiologist. The revolution produced many of these men equal to the epoch: one felt that here was a tested man. Though so near death, he preserved all the appearance of health. His bright glances, his firm accent, and the muscular movements of his shoulders seemed almost sufficient to disconcert death. Azrael, the Mahometan angel of the sepulchre, would have turned back, thinking he had mistaken the door. G—— appeared to be dying because he wished to die. There was freedom in his agony; his legs only were paralysed; his feet were cold and dead, but his head lived in full power of life and light. At this solemn moment G—— seemed like the king in the oriental tale, flesh above and marble below. The bishop seated himself upon a stone near by. The beginning of their conversation was *ex abrupto*:

"I congratulate you," he said, in a tone of reprimand. "At least you did not vote for the execution of the king."

The conventionist did not seem to notice the bitter emphasis placed upon the words "at least." The smiles vanished from his face and he replied:

"Do not congratulate me too much, monsieur; I did vote for the destruction of the tyrant."

And the tone of austerity confronted the tone of severity.

"What do you mean?" asked the bishop.

"I mean that man has a tyrant, Ignorance. I voted for the abolition of that tyrant. That tyrant has begotten royalty, which is authority springing from the False, while science is authority springing from the True. Man should be governed by science."

"And conscience," added the bishop.

"The same thing: conscience is innate knowledge that we have."

Monsieur Bienvenu listened with some amazement to this language, novel as it was to him.

The conventionist went on:

"As to Louis XVI.: I said no. I do not believe that I have the right to kill a man, but I feel it a duty to exterminate evil. I voted for the downfall of the tyrant; that is to say, for the abolition of prostitution for woman, of slavery for man, of night for the child. In voting for the republic I voted for that: I voted for fraternity, for harmony, for light. I assisted in casting down prejudices and errors: their downfall brings light! We caused the old world to fall; the old world, a vase of misery, reversed, becomes an urn of joy to the human race."

"Joy alloyed," said the bishop.

"You might say joy troubled, and, at present, after this fatal return of the blast which we call 1814, joy disappeared. Alas! the work was imperfect I admit; we demolished the ancient order of things physically, but not entirely in the idea. To destroy abuses is not enough; habits must be changed. The windmill has gone, but the Wind is there yet."

"You have demolished. To demolish may be useful, but I distrust a demolition effected in anger!"

"Justice has its anger, Monsieur Bishop, and the wrath of justice is an element of progress. Whatever may be said matters not, the French revolution is the greatest step in advance taken by mankind since the advent of Christ; incomplete it may be, but it is sublime. It loosened all the secret bonds of society, it softened all hearts, it calmed, appeased, enlightened; it made the waves of civilisation to flow over the earth; it was good. The French revolution is the consecration of humanity."

The bishop could not help murmuring: "Yes, '93!"

The conventionist raised himself in his chair with a solemnity well nigh mournful, and as well as a dying person could exclaim, he exclaimed:

"Ah! you are there! '93! I was expecting that. A cloud had

been forming for fifteen hundred years; at the end of fifteen centuries it burst. You condemn the thunderbolt."

Without perhaps acknowledging it to himself, the bishop felt that he had been touched; however, he made the best of it, and replied:

"The judge speaks in the name of justice, the priest in the name of pity, which is only a more exalted justice. A thunderbolt should not be mistaken."

And he added, looking fixedly at the conventionist: "Louis XVII.?"

The conventionist stretched out his hand and seized the bishop's arm.

"Louis XVII. Let us see! For whom do you weep?—for the innocent child? It is well; I weep with you. For the royal child? I ask time to reflect. To my view the brother of Cartouche, an innocent child, hung by a rope under his arms in the Place de Grève till he died, for the sole crime of being the brother of Cartouche, is no less sad sight than the grandson of Louis XV.; an innocent child, murdered in the tower of the Temple for the sole crime of being the grandson of Louis XV."

"Monsieur," said the bishop, "I dislike this coupling of names."

"Cartouche or Louis XV.; for which are you concerned?"

There was a moment of silence; the bishop regretted almost that he had come, and yet he felt strangely and inexplicably moved.

The conventionist resumed: "Oh, Monsieur Priest! you do not love the harshness of the truth, but Christ loved it. He took a scourge and purged the temple; his flashing whip was a rude speaker of truths; when he said, 'Sinite parvulos,' he made no distinctions among the little ones. He was not pained at coupling the dauphin of Barabbas with the dauphin of Herod. Monsieur, innocence is its own crown! Innocence has only to act to be noble! She is as august in rags as in the fleur de lys."

"That is true," said the bishop, in a low tone.

"I repeat," continued the old man; "you have mentioned Louis XVII. Let us weep together for all the innocent, for all the martyrs, for all the children, for the low as well as for the high. I am one of them, but then, as I have told you, we must go further back than '93, and our tears must begin before Louis

XVII. I will weep for the children of kings with you, if you will weep with me for the little ones of the people."

"I weep for all," said the bishop.

"Equally," exclaimed G——, "and if the balance inclines, let it be on the side of the people; they have suffered longer."

There was silence again, broken at last by the old man. He raised himself upon one elbow, took a pinch of his cheek between his thumb and his bent forefinger, as one does mechanically in questioning and forming an opinion, and addressed the bishop with a look full of all the energies of agony. It was almost an anathema.

"Yes, Monsieur, it is for a long time that the people have been suffering, and then, sir, that is not all; why do you come to question me and to speak to me of Louis XVII.? I do not know you. Since I have been in this region I have lived within these walls alone, never passing beyond them, seeing none but this child who helps me. Your name, has, it is true, reached me confusedly, and I must say not very indistinctly, but that matters not. Adroit men have so many ways of imposing upon this good simple people. For instance I did not hear the sound of your carriage. You left it doubtless behind the thicket, down there at the branching of the road. You have told me that you were the bishop, but that tells me nothing about your moral personality. Now, then, I repeat my question—Who are you? You are a bishop, a prince of the church, one of those men who are covered with gold, with insignia, and with wealth, who have fat livings—the see of D——, fifteen thousand francs regular, ten thousand francs contingent, total twenty-five thousand francs—who have kitchens, who have retinues, who give good dinners, who eat moor-hens on Friday, who strut about in your gaudy coach, like peacocks, with lackeys before and lackeys behind, and who have palaces, and who roll in your carriages in the name of Jesus Christ who went bare-footed. You are a prelate; rents, palaces, horses, valets, a good table, all the sensualities of life, you have these like all the rest, and you enjoy them like all the rest; very well, but that says too much or not enough; that does not enlighten me as to your intrinsic worth, that which is peculiar to yourself, you who come probably with the claim of bringing me wisdom. To whom am I speaking? Who are you?"

The bishop bowed his head and replied, "*Vermis sum.*"

"A worm of the earth in a carriage!" grumbled the old man.

It was the turn of the conventionist to be haughty, and of the bishop to be humble.

The bishop replied with mildness:

"Monsieur, be it so. But explain to me how my carriage, which is there a few steps behind the trees, how my good table and the moor-fowl that I eat on Friday, how my twenty-five thousand livres of income, how my palace and my lackeys prove that pity is not a virtue, that kindness is not a duty, and that '93 was not inexorable?"

The old man passed his hand across his forehead as if to dispel a cloud.

"Before answering you," said he, "I beg your pardon. I have done wrong, monsieur; you are in my house, you are my guest. I owe you courtesy. You are discussing my ideas; it is fitting that I confine myself to combating your reasoning. Your riches and your enjoyments are advantages that I have over you in the debate, but it is not in good taste to avail myself of them. I promise you to use them no more."

"I thank you," said the bishop.

G—— went on:

"Let us get back to the explanation that you asked of me. Where were we? What were you saying to me? that '93 was inexorable?"

"Inexorable, yes," said the bishop. "What do you think of Marat clapping his hands at the guillotine?"

"What do you think of Bossuet chanting the Te Deum over the dragonnades?"

The answer was severe, but it reached its aim with the keenness of a dagger. The bishop was staggered, no reply presented itself; but it shocked him to hear Bossuet spoken of in that manner. The best men have their fetishes, and sometimes they feel almost crushed at the little respect that logic shows them.

The conventionist began to gasp; the agonising asthma, which mingles with the latest breath, made his voice broken; nevertheless, his soul yet appeared perfectly lucid in his eyes. He continued:

"Let us have a few more words here and there—I would like it. Outside of the revolution which, taken as a whole, is an immense human affirmation, '93, alas! is a reply. You think

it inexorable, but the whole monarchy, monsieur? Carrier is a
bandit; but what name do you give to Montrevel? Fouquier-
Tainville is a wretch; but what is your opinion of Lamoignon
Bâville? Maillard is frightful, but Saulx Tavannes, if you please?
Le père Duchêne is ferocious, but what epithet will you furnish
me for le père Letellier? Jourdan-Coupe-Tête is a monster, but
less than the Marquis of Louvois. Monsieur, monsieur, I lament
Marie Antoinette, archduchess and queen, but I lament also
that poor Huguenot woman who, in 1685, under Louis le
Grand, monsieur, while nursing her child, was stripped to the
waist and tied to a post, while her child was held before her;
her breast swelled with milk, and her heart with anguish; the
little one, weak and famished, seeing the breast, cried with
agony; and the executioner said to the woman, to the nursing
mother, 'Recant!' giving her the choice between the death of
her child and the death of her conscience. What say you to
this Tantalus torture adapted to a mother? Monsieur, forget
not this; the French revolution had its reasons. Its wrath will
be pardoned by the future; its result is a better world. From its
most terrible blows comes a caress for the human race. I must
be brief. I must stop. I have too good a cause; and I am dying."

And, ceasing to look at the bishop, the old man completed
his idea in these few tranquil words:

"Yes, the brutalities of progress are called revolutions. When
they are over, this is recognised: that the human race has been
harshly treated, but that it has advanced."

The conventionist thought that he had borne down successively one after the other all the interior intrenchments of the
bishop. There was one left, however, and from this, the last
resource of Monseigneur Bienvenu's resistance, came forth
these words, in which nearly all the rudeness of the exordium
reappeared.

"Progress ought to believe in God. The good cannot have
an impious servitor. An atheist is an evil leader of the human
race."

The old representative of the people did not answer. He
was trembling. He looked up into the sky, and a tear gathered
slowly in his eye. When the lid was full, the tear rolled down
his livid cheek, and he said, almost stammering, low, and
talking to himself, his eye lost in the depths:

"O thou! O ideal! thou alone dost exist!"

The bishop felt a kind of inexpressible emotion.

After brief silence, the old man raised his finger towards heaven, and said:

"The infinite exists. It is there. If the infinite had no *me*, the *me* would be its limit; it would not be the infinite; in other words it would not be. But it is. Then it has a me. This *me* of the infinite is God."

The dying man pronounced these last words in a loud voice, and with a shudder of ecstasy, as if he saw some one. When he ceased, his eyes closed. The effort had exhausted him. It was evident that he had lived through in one minute the few hours that remained to him. What he had said had brought him near to him who is in death. The last moment was at hand.

The bishop perceived it, time was pressing. He had come as a priest; from extreme coldness he had passed by degrees to extreme emotion; he looked upon those closed eyes, he took that old, wrinkled and icy hand, and drew closer to the dying man.

"This hour is the hour of God. Do you not think it would be a source of regret, if we should have met in vain?"

The conventionist re-opened his eyes. Calmness was imprinted upon his face, where there had been a cloud.

"Monsieur Bishop," said he with a deliberation which perhaps came still more from the dignity of his soul than from the ebb of his strength, "I have passed my life in meditation, study, and contemplation. I was sixty years old when my country called me, and ordered me to take part in her affairs. I obeyed. There were abuses, I fought them; there were tyrannies, I destroyed them; there were rights and principles, I proclaimed and confessed them. The soil was invaded, I defended it; France was threatened, I offered her my breast. I was not rich; I am poor. I was one of the masters of the state, the vaults of the bank were piled with specie, so that we had to strengthen the walls or they would have fallen under the weight of gold and of silver; I dined in the Rue de l'Arbre-Sec at twenty-two sous for the meal. I succoured the oppressed, I solaced the suffering. True, I tore the drapery from the altar; but it was to staunch the wounds of the country. I have always supported the forward march of the human race towards the light, and I have sometimes resisted a progress which was without pity. I have, on occasion, protected my own adversaries, your friends. There is at Peteghem in Flanders, at the very place where the Merovingian kings had their summer palace, a monastery of Urbanists, the Abbey of Sainte Claire in Beaulieu, which I saved in 1793, I have done my duty according to my strength, and the good that I could. After which I was hunted, hounded, pursued, persecuted, slandered, railed at, spit upon, cursed, proscribed. For many years now, with my white hairs, I have perceived that many people believed they had a right to despise me; to the poor, ignorant crowd I have the face of the damned, and I accept, hating no man myself, the isolation of hatred. Now I am eighty-six years old; I am about to die. What have you come to ask of me?"

"Your benediction," said the bishop. And he fell upon his knees.

When the bishop raised his head, the face of the old man had become august. He had expired.

The bishop went home deeply absorbed in thought. He spent the whole night in prayer. The next day, some persons, emboldened by curiosity, tried to talk with him of the conventionist G——; he merely pointed to Heaven.

From that moment he redoubled his tenderness and brotherly love for the weak and the suffering.

Every allusion to "that old scoundrel G——," threw him into a strange reverie. No one could say that the passage of that soul before his own, and the reflex of that grand conscience upon his own had not had its effect upon his approach to perfection.

This "pastoral visit" was of course an occasion for criticism by the little local coteries of the place.

"Was the bed-side of such a man as that the place for a bishop? Of course he could expect no conversion there. All these revolutionists are backsliders. Then why go there? What had he been there to see? He must have been very curious to see a soul carried away by the devil."

One day a dowager, of that impertinent variety who think themselves witty, addressed this sally to him. "Monseigneur, people ask when your Grandeur will have the red bonnet." "Oh! ho! that is a high colour," replied the bishop. "Luckily those who despise it in a bonnet, venerate it in a hat."

XI
A QUALIFICATION

WE should be very much deceived if we supposed from this that Monseigneur Bienvenu was "a philosopher bishop," or "a patriot curé." His meeting, which we might almost call his communion with the conventionist G——, left him in a state of astonishment which rendered him still more charitable; that was all.

Although Monseigneur Bienvenu was anything but a politician, we ought here perhaps to point out very briefly his position in relation to the events of the day, if we may suppose that Monseigneur Bienvenu ever thought of having a position.

For this we must go back a few years.

Some time after the elevation of M. Myriel to the episcopacy, the emperor made him a baron of the empire, at the same time with several other bishops. The arrest of the pope took place, as we know, on the night of the 5th of July, 1809; on that occasion, M. Myriel was called by Napoleon to the synod of the bishops of France and Italy, convoked at Paris. This synod was held at Notre Dame, and commenced its sessions on the 15th of June, 1811, under the presidency of Cardinal Fesch. M. Myriel was one of the ninety-five bishops who were present. But he attended only one sitting, and three or four private conferences. Bishop of a mountain diocese, living so near to nature, in rusticity and privation, he seemed to bring among these eminent personages ideas that changed the temperature of the synod. He returned very soon to D——. When asked about this sudden return, he answered: "*I annoyed them. The free air went in with me. I had the effect of an open door.*"

Another time, he said: "*What would you have? Those prelates are princes. I am only a poor peasant bishop.*"

The fact is, that he was disliked. Among other strange things, he had dropped the remark one evening when he happened to be at the house of one of his colleagues of the highest rank: "What fine clocks! fine carpets! fine liveries! This must be very uncomfortable. Oh! how unwilling I should be to have all these superfluities crying for ever in my ears: 'There are people who hunger! there are people who are cold! there are poor! there are poor!'"

We must say, by the way, that the hatred of luxury is not an intelligent hatred. It implies a hatred of the arts. Nevertheless, among churchmen, beyond their rites and ceremonies, luxury is a crime. It seems to disclose habits which are not truly charitable. A wealthy priest is a contradiction. He ought to keep himself near the poor. But, who can be in contact continually, by night as well as day, with all distresses, all misfortunes, all privations, without taking upon himself a little of that holy poverty, like the dust of a journey? Can you imagine a man near a fire, who does not feel warm? Can you imagine a labourer working constantly at a furnace, who has not a hair burned, nor a nail blackened, nor a drop of sweat, nor a speck of ashes on his face? The first proof of charity in a priest, and especially a bishop, is poverty.

That is doubtless the view which the Bishop of D—— took of it.

It must not be thought, however, that he took part in the delicate matters which would be called "the ideas of the age." He had little to do with the theological quarrels of the moment, and kept his peace on questions where the church and the state were compromised; but if he had been pressed, he would have been found rather Ultramontane than Gallican. As we are drawing a portrait, and can make no concealment, we are compelled to add that he was very cool towards Napoleon in the decline of his power. After 1813, he acquiesced in, or applauded all the hostile manifestations. He refused to see him as he passed on his return from the island of Elba, and declined to order in his diocese public prayers for the emperor during the Hundred Days.

Besides his sister, Mademoiselle Baptistine, he had two brothers; one, a general, the other, a prefect. He wrote occasionally to both. He felt a coolness towards the first, because, being in a command in Provence, at the time of the landing at Cannes, the general placed himself at the head of twelve hundred men, and pursued the emperor as if he wished to let him escape. His correspondence was more affectionate with the other brother, the ex-prefect, a brave and worthy man, who lived in retirement at Paris in the Rue Cassette.

Even Monseigneur Bienvenu then had his hour of party spirit, his hour of bitterness, his clouds. The shadow of the passions of the moment passed over this great and gentle spirit in its occupation with eternal things. Certainly, such a man deserved to escape political opinions. Let no one misunderstand our idea; we do not confound what are called "political opinions" with that grand aspiration after progress, with that sublime patriotic, democratic, and human faith, which, in our days, should be the very foundation of all generous intelligence. Without entering into questions which have only an indirect bearing upon the subject of this book, we simply say: it would have been well if Monseigneur Bienvenu had not been a royalist, and if his eyes had never been turned for a single instant from that serene contemplation where, steadily shining, above the fictions and the hatreds of this world, above the stormy ebb and flow of human affairs, are seen those three pure luminaries, Truth, Justice and Charity.

Although we hold that it was not for a political function that God created Monseigneur Bienvenu, we could have understood and admired a protest in the name of right and liberty, a fierce opposition, a perilous and just resistance to Napoleon when he was all-powerful. But what is pleasing to us towards those who are rising, is less pleasing towards those who are falling. We do not admire the combat when there is no danger, and in any case, the combatants of the first hour have alone the right to be the exterminators in the last. He who has not been a determined accuser during prosperity, ought to hold his peace in the presence of adversity. He only who denounces the success at one time has a right to proclaim the justice of the downfall. As for ourselves, when providence intervened and struck the blow, we took no part; 1812 began to disarm us. In 1813, the cowardly breach of silence on the part of that taciturn corps Legislatif, emboldened by catastrophe, was worthy only of indignation, and it was base to applaud it; in 1814, from those traitorous marshals, from that senate passing from one baseness to another, insulting where they had deified, from that idolatry recoiling and spitting upon its idol, it was a duty to turn away in disgust; in 1815, when the air was filled with the final disasters, when France felt the thrill of their sinister approach, when Waterloo could already be dimly perceived opening before Napoleon, the sorrowful acclamations of the army and of the people to the condemned of destiny, were no subjects for laughter; and making every reservation as to the despot, a heart like that of the Bishop of D—— ought not perhaps to have refused to see what was august and touching, on the brink of the abyss, in the last embrace of a great nation and a great man.

To conclude: he was always and in everything just, true, equitable, intelligent, humble, and worthy, beneficent, and benevolent, which is another beneficence. He was a priest, a sage, and a man. We must say even that in those political opinions which we have been criticising, and which we are disposed to judge almost severely, he was tolerant and yielding, perhaps more than we, who now speak. The doorkeeper of the City Hall had been placed there by the emperor. He was an old subaltern officer of the old Guard, a legionary of Austerlitz, and as staunch a Bonapartist as the eagle. This poor fellow sometimes thoughtlessly allowed words to escape him which the law at that time defined as *seditious matters*. Since the profile of the emperor had disappeared from the Legion of Honour, he had never worn his badge, as he said, that he might not be compelled to bear his cross. In his devotion he had himself removed the imperial effigy from the cross that Napoleon had given him; it left a hole, and he would put nothing in its place. "*Better die,*" said he, "*than wear the three toads over my heart.*" He was always railing loudly at Louis XVIII. "*Old gouty-foot with his English spatterdashes!*" he would say, "*let him go to Prussia with his goat's-beard,*" happy to unite in the same imprecation the two things that he most detested, Prussia and England. He said so much that he lost his place. There he wàs without bread, and in the street with his wife and children. The bishop sent for him, scolded him a little, and made him doorkeeper in the cathedral.

In nine years, by dint of holy works and gentle manners, Monseigneur Bienvenu had filled the city of D—— with a kind of tender and filial veneration. Even his conduct towards Napoleon had been accepted and pardoned in silence by the people; a good, weak flock, who adored their emperor, but who loved their bishop.

XII
SOLITUDE OF MONSEIGNEUR BIENVENU

THERE is almost always a squad of young abbés about a bishop as there is a flock of young officers about a general. They are what the charming St. Francis de Sales somewhere calls "white-billed priests." Every profession has its aspirants who make up the cortège of those who are at the summit. No power is without its worshippers, no fortune without its court. The seekers of the future revolve about the splendid present. Every capital, like every general, has its staff. Every bishop of influence has his patrol of undergraduates, cherubs who go the rounds and keep order in the episcopal palace, and who mount guard over monseigneur's smile. To please a bishop is a foot in the stirrup for a sub-deacon. One must make his own way; the apostolate never disdains the canonicate.

And as there are elsewhere rich coronets so there are in the church rich mitres. There are bishops who stand well at court, rich, well endowed, adroit, accepted of the world, knowing how to pray, doubtless, but knowing also how to ask favours; making themselves without scruple the viaduct of advancement for a whole diocese; bonds of union between the sacristy and diplomacy; rather abbés than priests, prelates rather than bishops. Lucky are they who can get near them. Men of influence as they are, they rain about them, upon their families and favourites, and upon all of these young men who please them, fat parishes, livings, archdeaconates, almonries, and cathedral functions—steps towards episcopal dignities. In advancing themselves they advance their satellites; it is a whole solar system in motion. The rays of their glory empurple their suite. Their prosperity scatters its crumbs to those who are behind the scenes, in the shape of nice little promotions. The larger the diocese of the patron, the larger the curacy for the favourite. And then there is Rome. A bishop who can become an archbishop, an archbishop who can become a cardinal, leads you to the conclave; you enter into the rota, you have the pallium, you are auditor, you are chamberlain, you are monseigneur, and from grandeur to eminence there is only a step, and between eminence and holiness there is nothing but the whiff of a ballot. Every cowl may dream of the tiara. The priest is, in our days, the only man who can regularly become a king; and what a king! The supreme king. So, what a nursery of aspirations is a seminary. How many blushing chorus boys, how many young abbés, have the ambitious dairymaid's pail of milk on their heads! Who knows how easily ambition disguises itself under the name of a calling, possibly in good faith, and deceiving itself, saint that it is!

Monseigneur Bienvenu, a humble, poor, private person, was

not counted among the rich mitres. This was plain from the entire absence of young priests about him. We have seen that at Paris "he did not take." No glorious future dreamed of alighting upon this solitary old man. No young ambition was foolish enough to ripen in his shadow. His canons and his grand-vicars were good old men, rather common like himself, and like him immured in that diocese from which there was no road to promotion, and they resembled their bishop, with this difference, that they were finished, and he was perfected. The impossibility of getting on under Monseigneur Bienvenu was so plain, that as soon as they were out of the seminary, the young men ordained by him procured recommendations to the Archbishop of Aix or of Auch, and went immediately to present them. For, we repeat, men like advancement. A saint who is addicted to abnegation is a dangerous neighbour; he is very likely to communicate to you by contagion an incurable poverty, an anchylosis of the articulations necessary to advancement and, in fact, more renunciation than you would like; and men flee from this contagious virtue. Hence the isolation of Monseigneur Bienvenu. We live in a sad society. Succeed; that is the advice which falls drop by drop, from the overhanging corruption.

We may say, by the way, that success is a hideous thing. Its counterfeit of merit deceives men. To the mass, success has almost the same appearance as supremacy. Success, that pretender to talent, has a dupe,—history. Juvenal and Tacitus only reject it. In our days, a philosophy which is almost an official has entered into its service, wears its livery, and waits in its antechamber. Success; that is the theory. Prosperity supposes capacity. Win in the lottery, and you are an able man. The victor is venerated. To be born with a caul is everything. Have but luck, and you will have the rest; be fortunate, and you will be thought great. Beyond the five or six great exceptions, which are the wonder of their age, contemporary admiration is nothing but shortsightedness. Gilt is gold. To be a chance comer is no drawback, provided you have improved your chances. The common herd is an old Narcissus, who adores himself, and who applauds the common. That mighty genius, by which one becomes a Moses, an Æschylus, a Dante, a Michael Angelo, or a Napoleon, the multitude assigns at once and by acclamation to whoever succeeds in his object, whatever it may be. Let a notary rise to be a deputy; let a sham Corneille write *Tiridate*;

let a eunuch come into the possession of a harem; let a military
Prudhomme accidentally win the decisive battle of an epoch,
let an apothecary invent pasteboard soles for army shoes, and lay
up, by selling this pasteboard instead of leather for the army of
the Sambre-et-Meuse, four hundred thousand livres in the
funds; let a pack-pedlar espouse usury and bring her to bed of
seven or eight millions, of which he is the father and she the
mother; let a preacher become a bishop by talking through his
nose; let the steward of a good house become so rich on leaving
service that he is made Minister of Finance;—men call that
Genius, just as they call the face of Mousqueton, Beauty, and
the bearing of Claude, Majesty. They confound the radiance of
the stars of heaven with the radiations which a duck's foot leaves
in the mud.

XIII
WHAT HE BELIEVED

WE need not examine the bishop of D—— from an orthodox
point of view. Before such a soul, we feel only in the humour
of respect. The conscience of an upright man should be taken
for granted. Moreover, given certain natures, and we admit the
possible development of all the beauties of human virtues in a
faith different from our own.

What he thought of this dogmà or that mystery, are secrets
of the interior faith known only in the tomb where souls enter
stripped of all externals. But we are sure that religious difficulties
never resulted with him in hypocrisy. No corruption is possible
with the diamond. He believed as much as he could. *Credo in
Patrem*, he often exclaimed; and, besides, he derived from his
good deeds that measure of satisfaction which meets the
demands of conscience, and which says in a low voice, "thou
art with God."

We think it our duty to notice that, outside of and, so to say,
beyond his faith, the bishop had an excess of love. It is on that
account, *quia multum amavit*, that he was deemed vulnerable
by "serious men," "sober persons," and "reasonable people;"
favourite phrases in our sad world, where egotism receives its
key-note from pedantry. What was this excess of love? It was a
serene benevolence, overflowing men, as we have already indicated, and, on occasion, extending to inanimate things. He lived

without disdain. He was indulgent to God's creation. Every man, even the best, has some inconsiderate severity which he holds in reserve for animals. The Bishop of D—— had none of this severity peculiar to most priests. He did not go as far as the Brahmin, but he appeared to have pondered over these words of Ecclesiastes: "who knows whither goeth the spirit of the beast?" Ugliness of aspect, monstrosities of instinct, did not trouble or irritate him. He was moved and afflicted by it. He seemed to be thoughtfully seeking, beyond the apparent life, for its cause, its explanation, or its excuse. He seemed at times to ask changes of God. He examined without passion, and with the eye of a linguist decyphering a palimpsest, the portion of chaos which there is yet in nature. These reveries sometimes drew from him strange words. One morning, he was in his garden, and thought himself alone; but his sister was walking behind him; all at once he stopped and looked at something on the ground: it was a large, black, hairy, horrible spider. His sister heard him say:

"Poor thing! it is not his fault."

Why not relate this almost divine childlikeness of goodness? Puerilities, perhaps, but these sublime puerilities were those of St. Francis of Assisi and of Marcus Aurelius. One day he received a sprain rather than crush an ant.

So lived this upright man. Sometimes he went to sleep in his garden, and then there was nothing more venerable.

Monseigneur Bienvenu had been formerly, according to the accounts of his youth and even of his early manhood, a passionate, perhaps a violent, man. His universal tenderness was less an instinct of nature than the result of a strong conviction filtered through life into his heart, slowly dropping in upon him, thought by thought; for a character, as well as a rock, may be worn into by drops of water. Such marks are ineffaceable; such formations are indestructible.

In 1815, we think we have already said, he attained his seventy-sixth year, but he did not appear to be more than sixty. He was not tall; he was somewhat fleshy, and frequently took long walks that he might not become more so, he had a firm step, and was but little bowed; a circumstance from which we do not claim to draw any conclusion.—Gregory XVI., at eighty years, was erect and smiling, which did not prevent him from being a bad bishop. Monseigneur Bienvenu had what people call "a fine head," but so benevolent that you forgot that it was fine.

When he talked with that infantile gaiety that was one of his graces, and of which we have already spoken, all felt at ease in his presence, and from his whole person joy seemed to radiate. His ruddy and fresh complexion, and his white teeth, all of which were well preserved, and which he showed when he laughed, gave him that open and easy air which makes us say of a man: he is a good fellow; and of an old man: he is a good man. This was, we remember, the effect he produced on Napoleon. At the first view, and to one who saw him for the first time, he was nothing more than a good man. But if one spent a few hours with him, and saw him in a thoughtful mood, little by little the good man became transfigured, and became ineffably imposing; his large and serious forehead, rendered noble by his white hair, became noble also by meditation; majesty was developed from this goodness, yet the radiance of goodness remained; and one felt something of the emotion that he would experience in seeing a smiling angel slowly spread his wings without ceasing to smile. Respect, unutterable respect, penetrated you by degrees, and made its way to your heart; and you felt that you had before you one of those strong, tried, and indulgent souls, where the thought is so great that it cannot be other than gentle.

As we have seen, prayer, celebration of the religious offices, alms, consoling the afflicted, the cultivation of a little piece of ground, fraternity, frugality, self-sacrifice, confidence, study, and work, filled up each day of his life. Filled up is exactly the word; and in fact, the bishop's day was full to the brim with good thoughts, good words, and good actions. Nevertheless it was not complete if cold or rainy weather prevented his passing an hour or two in the evening, when the two women had retired, in his garden before going to sleep. It seemed as if it were a sort of rite with him, to prepare himself for sleep by meditating in presence of the great spectacle of the starry firmament. Sometimes at a late hour of the night, if the two women were awake, they would hear him slowly promenading the walks. He was there alone with himself, collected, tranquil, adoring, comparing the serenity of his heart with the serenity of the skies, moved in the darkness by the visible splendours of the constellations, and the invisible splendour of God, opening his soul to the thoughts which fall from the Unknown. In such

moments, offering up his heart at the hour when the flowers of
night inhale their perfume, lighted like a lamp in the centre of
the starry night, expanding his soul in ecstasy in the midst of the
universal radiance of creation, he could not himself perhaps
have told what was passing in his own mind; he felt something
depart from him, and something descend upon him; mysterious
interchanges of the depths of the soul with the depths of the
universe.

He contemplated the grandeur, and the presence of God; the
eternity of the future, strange mystery; the eternity of the past,
mystery yet more strange; all the infinities deep-hidden in every
direction about him; and, without essaying to comprehend the
incomprehensible, he saw it. He did not study God; he was
dazzled by the thought He reflected upon these magnificent
unions of atoms, which give visible forms to Nature, revealing
forces in establishing them, creating individualities in unity, proportions in extension, the innumerable in the infinite, and
through light producing beauty. These unions are forming and
dissolving continually; thence life and death.

He would sit upon a wooden bench leaning against a broken
trellis and look at the stars through the irregular outlines of his
fruit trees. This quarter of an acre of ground, so poorly cultivated, so cumbered with shed and ruins, was dear to him, and
satisfied him.

What was more needed by this old man who divided the
leisure hours of his life, where he had so little leisure, between
gardening in the day time, and contemplation at night? Was not
this narrow inclosure, with the sky for a background, enough to
enable him to adore God in his most beautiful as well as in his
most sublime works? Indeed, is not that all, and what more can
be desired? A little garden to walk, and immensity to reflect
upon. At his feet something to cultivate and gather; above his
head something to study and meditate upon; a few flowers on
the earth, and all the stars in the sky.

XIV
WHAT HE THOUGHT

A FINAL word.

As these details may, particularly in the times in which we
live, and to use an expression now in fashion,—give the Bishop

of D—— a certain "pantheistic" physiognomy, and give rise to the belief, whether to his blame or to his praise, that he had one of those personal philosophies peculiar to our age, which sometimes spring up in solitary minds, and gather materials and grow until they replace religion, we insist upon it that no one who knew Monseigneur Bienvenu would have felt justified in any such idea. What enlightened this man was the heart. His wisdom was formed from the light that came thence.

He had no systems; but many deeds. Abstruse speculations are full of headaches; nothing indicates that he would risk his mind in mysticisms. The apostle may be bold, but the bishop should be timid. He would probably have scrupled to sound too deeply certain problems, reserved in some sort for great and terrible minds. There is a sacred horror in the approaches to mysticism; sombre openings are yawning there, but something tells you, as you near the brink—enter not. Woe to him who does!

There are geniuses who, in the fathomless depths of abstraction and pure speculation—situated, so to say, above all dogmas, present their ideas to God. Their prayer audaciously offers a discussion. Their worship is questioning. This is direct religion, full of anxiety and of responsibility for him who would scale its walls. •

Human thought has no limit. At its risk and peril, it analyses and dissects its own fascination. We could almost say that, by a sort of splendid reaction, it fascinates nature; the mysterious world which surrounds us returns what it receives; it is probable that the contemplators are contemplated. However that may be, there are men on the earth—if they are nothing more—who distinctly perceive the heights of the absolute in the horizon of their contemplation, and who have the terrible vision of the infinite mountain. Monseigneur Bienvenu was not one of those men; Monseigneur Bienvenu was not a genius. He would have dreaded those sublimities from which some very great men even, like Swedenborg and Pascal, have glided into insanity. Certainly, these tremendous reveries have their moral use, and by these arduous routes there is an approach to ideal perfection. But for his part, he took the straight road, which is short—the Gospel.

He did not attempt to make his robe assume the folds of Elijah's mantle; he cast no ray of the future upon the dark scroll of events; he sought not to condense into a flame the glimmer of things; he had nothing of the prophet and nothing of the magician. His humble soul loved; that was all.

That he raised his prayer to a superhuman aspiration, is probable; but one can no more pray too much than love too much; and, if it was a heresy to pray beyond the written form, St. Theresa and St. Jerome were heretics.

He inclined towards the distressed and the repentant. The universe appeared to him like a vast disease; he perceived fever everywhere, he auscultated suffering everywhere, and, without essaying to solve the enigma, he endeavoured to staunch the wound. The formidable spectacle of created things developed a tenderness in him he was always busy in finding for himself, and inspiring others with the best way of sympathising and solacing; the whole world was to this good and rare priest a permanent subject of sadness seeking to be consoled.

There are men who labour for the extraction of gold; he worked for the extraction of pity. The misery of the universe was his mine. Grief everywhere was only an occasion for good always. *Love one another*; he declared that to be complete; he desired nothing more, and it was his whole doctrine. One day, this man, who counted himself "a philosopher," this senator before mentioned, said to the bishop: "See now, what the world shows; each fighting against all others; the strongest man is the best man. Your *love one another* is a stupidity." "*Well*," replied Monseigneur Bienvenu, without discussion, "*if it be a stupidity, the soul ought to shut itself up in it, like the pearl in the oyster.*" And he shut himself up in it, he lived in it, he was satisfied absolutely with it, laying aside the mysterious questions which attract and which dishearten, the unfathomable depths of abstraction, the precipices of metaphysics—all those profundities, to the apostle converging upon God, to the atheist upon annihilation; destiny, good and evil, the war of being against being, the conscience of man, the thought-like dreams of the animal, the transformation of death, the recapitulation of existences contained in the tomb, the incomprehensible engrafting of successive affections upon the enduring *me*, the essence, the substance, the Nothing and the Something, the soul, nature, liberty, necessity; difficult problems, sinister depths, towards which are drawn the gigantic archangels of the human race; fearful abyss, that Lucretius, Manou, St. Paul, and Dante contemplate with that flaming eye which seems, looking steadfastly into the infinite, to enkindle the very stars.

Monsieur Bienvenu was simply a man who accepted these mysterious questions without examining them, without agitating them, and without troubling his own mind with them; and who had in his soul a deep respect for the mystery which enveloped them.

BOOK SECOND – THE FALL

I

THE NIGHT OF A DAY'S TRAMP

An hour before sunset, on the evening of a day in the beginning of October, 1815, a man travelling afoot entered the little town of D——. The few persons who at this time were at their windows or their doors, regarded this traveller with a sort of distrust. It would have been hard to find a passer-by more wretched in appearance. He was a man of middle height, stout and hardy, in the strength of maturity; he might have been forty-six or seven. A slouched leather cap half hid his face, bronzed by the sun and wind, and dripping with sweat. His shaggy breast was seen through the coarse yellow shirt which at the neck was fastened by a small silver anchor; he wore a cravat twisted like a rope; coarse blue trousers, worn and shabby, white on one knee, and with holes in the other; an old ragged grey blouse, patched on one side with a piece of green cloth sewed with twine: upon his back was a well-filled knapsack, strongly buckled and quite new. In his hand he carried an enormous knotted stick: his stockingless feet were in hobnailed shoes; his hair was cropped and his beard long.

The sweat, the heat, his long walk, and the dust, added an indescribable meanness to his tattered appearance.

His hair was shorn, but bristly, for it had begun to grow a little and seemingly had not been cut for some time. Nobody knew him, he was evidently a traveller. Whence had he come? From the south—perhaps from the sea; for he was making his entrance into D—— by the same road by which, seven months before, the Emperor Napoleon went from Cannes to Paris. This man must have walked all day long; for he appeared very weary. Some women of the old city which is at the lower part of the town, had seen him stop under the trees of the boulevard Gassendi, and drink at the fountain which is at the end of the promenade. He must have been very thirsty, for some children who followed him, saw him stop not two hundred steps further on and drink again at the fountain in the market-place.

When he reached the corner of the Rue Poichevert he

turned to the left and went towards the mayor's office. He went in, and a quarter of an hour afterwards he came out.

The man raised his cap humbly and saluted a gendarme who was seated near the door, upon the stone bench which General Drouot mounted on the fourth of March, to read to the terrified inhabitants of D—— the proclamation of the *Golfe Juan*.

Without returning his salutation, the gendarme looked at him attentively, watched him for some distance, and then went into the city hall.

There was then in D——, a good inn called *La Croix de Colbas*; its host was named Jacquin Labarre, a man held in some consideration in the town on account of his relationship with another Labarre, who kept an inn at Grenoble called *Trois Dauphins*, and who had served in the Guides. At the time of the landing of the emperor there had been much noise in the country about this inn of the *Trois Dauphins*. It was said that General Bertrand, disguised as a wagoner, had made frequent journeys thither in the month of January, and that he had distributed crosses of honour to the soldiers, and handfuls of Napoleons to the country-folks. The truth is, that the emperor when he entered Grenoble, refused to take up his quarters at the prefecture, saying to the monsieur, after thanking him, *"I am going to the house of a brave man with whom I am acquainted,"* and he went to the *Trois Dauphins*. This glory of Labarre of the *Trois Dauphins* was reflected twenty-five miles to Labarre of the *Croix de Colbas*. It was a common saying in the town: *"He is the cousin of the Grenoble man!"*

The traveller turned his steps towards this inn, which was the best in the place, and went at once into the kitchen, which opened out of the street. All the ranges were fuming, and a great fire was burning briskly in the chimney-place. Mine host, who was at the same time head cook, was going from the fire-place to the saucepans, very busy superintending an excellent dinner for some wagoners who were laughing and talking noisily in the next room. Whoever has travelled knows that nobody lives better than wagoners. A fat marmot, flanked by white partridges and goose, was turning on a long spit before the fire; upon the ranges were cooking two large carps from Lake Lauzet, and a trout from Lake Alloz.

The host, hearing the door open, and a new-comer enter, said, without raising his eyes from his ranges——

"What will monsieur have?"

"Something to eat and lodging."

"Nothing more easy," said mine host, but on turning his head and taking an observation of the traveller, he added, "for pay."

The man drew from his pocket a large leather purse, and answered,

"I have money."

"Then," said mine host, "I am at your service."

The man put his purse back into his pocket, took off his knapsack and put it down hard by the door, and holding his stick in his hand, sat down on a low stool by the fire. D—— being in the mountains, the evenings of October are cold there.

However, as the host passed backwards and forwards, he kept a careful eye on the traveller.

"Is dinner almost ready?" said the man.

"Directly," said mine host.

While the new-comer was warming himself with his back turned, the worthy innkeeper, Jacquin Labarre, took a pencil from his pocket, and then tore off the corner of an old paper which he pulled from a little table near the window. On the margin he wrote a line or two, folded it, and handed the scrap of paper to a child, who appeared to serve him as lackey and scullion at the same time. The innkeeper whispered a word to the boy and he ran off in the direction of the mayor's office.

The traveller saw nothing of this.

He asked a second time: "Is dinner ready?"

"Yes; in a few moments," said the host.

The boy came back with the paper. The host unfolded it hurriedly, as one who is expecting an answer. He seemed to read with attention, then throwing his head on one side, thought for a moment. Then he took a step towards the traveller, who seemed drowned in troublous thought.

"Monsieur," said he, "I cannot receive you."

The traveller half rose from his seat.

"Why? Are you afraid I shall not pay you, or do you want me to pay in advance? I have money, I tell you."

"It is not that."

"What then?"

"You have money——"

"Yes," said the man.

"And I," said the host; "I have no room."

"Well, put me in the stable," quietly replied the man.

"I cannot."

"Why?"

"Because the horses take all the room."

"Well," responded the man, "a corner in the garret; a truss of straw: we will see about that after dinner."

"I cannot give you any dinner."

This declaration, made in a measured but firm tone, appeared serious to the traveller. He got up.

"Ah, bah! but I am dying with hunger. I have walked since sunrise; I have travelled twelve leagues. I will pay, and I want something to eat."

"I have nothing," said the host.

The man burst into a laugh, and turned towards the fireplace and the ranges.

"Nothing! and all that?"

"All that is engaged."

"By whom?"

"By those persons, the wagoners."

"How many are there of them?"

"Twelve."

"There is enough there for twenty."

"They have engaged and paid for it all in advance."

The man sat down again and said, without raising his voice: "I am at an inn. I am hungry, and I shall stay."

The host bent down his ear, and said in a voice which made him tremble:

"Go away!"

At these words the traveller, who was bent over, poking some embers in the fire with the iron-shod end of his stick, turned suddenly around, and opened his mouth, as if to reply, when the host looking steadily at him, added in the same low tone: "Stop, no more of that. Shall I tell you your name? your name is Jean Valjean, now shall I tell you *who* you are? When I saw you enter, I suspected something. I sent to the mayor's office, and here is the reply. Can you read?" So saying, he held towards him the open paper, which had just come from the mayor. The man cast a look upon it; the innkeeper, after a short silence, said: "It is my custom to be polite to all: Go!"

The man bowed his head, picked up his knapsack, and went out.

He took the principal street; he walked at random, slinking near the houses like a sad and humiliated man: he did not once turn around. If he had turned, he would have seen the innkeeper of the *Croix de Colbas*, standing in his doorway with all his guests, and the passers-by gathered about him, speaking excitedly, and pointing him out; and from the looks of fear and distrust which were exchanged, he would have guessed that before long his arrival would be the talk of the whole town.

He saw nothing of all this: people overwhelmed with trouble do not look behind; they know only too well that misfortune follows them.

He walked along in this way some time, going by chance down streets unknown to him, and forgetting fatigue, as is the case in sorrow. Suddenly he felt a pang of hunger; night was at hand, and he looked around to see if he could not discover a lodging.

The good inn was closed against him: he sought some humble tavern, some poor cellar.

Just then a light shone at the end of the street; he saw a pine branch, hanging by an iron bracket, against the white sky of the twilight. He went thither.

It was a tavern in the Rue Chaffaut.

The traveller stopped a moment and looked in at the little window upon the low hall of the tavern, lighted by a small lamp upon a table, and a great fire in the chimney-place. Some men were drinking and the host was warming himself, an iron-pot hung over the fire seething in the blaze.

Two doors lead into this tavern, which is also a sort of eating-house—one from the street, the other from a small court full of rubbish.

The traveller did not dare to enter by the street door; he slipped into the court, stopped again, then timidly raised the latch, and pushed open the door.

"Who is it?" said the host.

"One who wants supper and a bed."

"All right: here you can sup and sleep."

He went in, all the men who were drinking turned towards him; the lamp shining on one side of his face, the firelight on the other, they examined him for some time as he was taking off his knapsack.

The host said to him: "There is the fire; the supper is cooking in the pot; come and warm yourself, comrade."

He seated himself near the fire-place and stretched his feet out towards the fire, half dead with fatigue: an inviting odour came from the pot. All that could be seen of his face under his slouched cap assumed a vague appearance of comfort, which tempered the sorrowful aspect given him by long-continued suffering.

His profile was strong, energetic, and sad; a physiognomy strangely marked: at first it appeared humble, but it soon became severe. His eye shone beneath his eyebrows like a fire beneath a thicket.

However, one of the men at the table was a fisherman who had put up his horse at the stable of Labarre's inn before entering the tavern of the Rue de Chaffaut. It so happened that he had met, that same morning, this suspicious-looking stranger travelling between Bras d'Asse and—I forget the place, I think it is Escoublon. Now, on meeting him, the man, who seemed already very much fatigued, had asked him to take him on behind, to which the fisherman responded only by doubling his pace. The fisherman, half an hour before, had been one of the throng about Jacquin Labarre, and had himself related his unpleasant meeting with him to the people of the *Croix de Colbas*. He beckoned to the tavern-keeper to come to him, which he did. They exchanged a few words in a low voice; the traveller had again relapsed into thought.

The tavern-keeper returned to the fire, and laying his hand roughly on his shoulder, said harshly:

"You are going to clear out from here!"

The stranger turned round and said mildly,

"Ah! Do you know?"

"Yes."

"They sent me away from the other inn."

"And we turn you out of this."

"Where would you have me go?"

"Somewhere else."

The man took up his stick and knapsack, and went off. As he went out, some children who had followed him from the *Croix de Colbas*, and seemed to be waiting for him, threw stones at him. He turned angrily and threatened them with his stick, and they scattered like a flock of birds.

He passed the prison: an iron chain hung from the door attached to a bell. He rang.

The grating opened.

"Monsieur Turnkey," said he, taking off his cap respectfully, "will you open and let me stay here to-night?"

A voice answered:

"A prison is not a tavern: get yourself arrested and we will open."

The grating closed.

He went into a small street where there are many gardens; some of them are enclosed only by hedges, which enliven the street. Among them he saw a pretty little one-story house, where there was a light in the window. He looked in as he had done at the tavern. It was a large whitewashed room, with a bed draped with calico and a cradle in the corner, some wooden chairs, and a double-barrelled gun hung against the wall. A table was set in the centre of the room; a brass lamp lighted the coarse white table-cloth; a tin mug full of wine shone like silver, and the brown soup-dish was smoking. At this table sat a man about forty years old, with a joyous, open countenance who was trotting a little child upon his knee. Near by him a young woman was suckling another child; the father was laughing, the child was laughing, and the mother was smiling.

The traveller remained a moment contemplating this sweet and touching scene. What were his thoughts? He only could have told: probably he thought that this happy home would be hospitable, and that where he beheld so much happiness, he might perhaps find a little pity.

He rapped faintly on the window.

No one heard him.

He rapped a second time.

He heard the woman say, "Husband, I think I hear some one rap."

"No," replied the husband.

He rapped a third time. The husband got up, took the lamp, and opened the door.

He was a tall man, half peasant, half mechanic. He wore a large leather apron that reached to his left shoulder and formed a pocket containing a hammer, a red handkerchief, a powder-horn, and all sorts of things which the girdle held up. He turned his head; his shirt, wide and open, showed his bull-like throat, white and naked; he had thick brows, enormous black whiskers, and prominent eyes; the lower part of the face was covered, and had withal that air of being at home which is quite indescribable.

"Monsieur," said the traveller, "I beg your pardon; for pay can you give me a plate of soup and a corner of the shed in your garden to sleep in? Tell me; can you, for pay?"

"Who are you?" demanded the master of the house.

The man replied: "I have come from Puy-Moisson; I have walked all day; I have come twelve leagues. Can you, if I pay?"

"I wouldn't refuse to lodge any proper person who would pay," said the peasant; "but why do you not go to the inn?"

"There is no room."

"Bah! That is not possible. It is neither a fair nor a market-day. Have you been to Labarre's house?"

"Yes."

"Well?"

The traveller replied hesitatingly: "I don't know; he didn't take me."

"Have you been to that place in the Rue Chaffaut?"

The embarrassment of the stranger increased; he stammered: "They didn't take me either."

The peasant's face assumed an expression of distrust: he looked over the new-comer from head to foot, and suddenly exclaimed, with a sort of shudder: "Are you the man!"

He looked again at the stranger, stepped back, put the lamp on the table, and took down his gun.

His wife, on hearing the words, "*are you the man*," started up, and clasping her two children, precipitately took refuge behind her husband; she looked at the stranger with affright, her neck bare, her eyes dilated, murmuring in a low tone: "*Tso maraude!*"*

All this happened in less time than it takes to read it; after examining the man for a moment, as one would a viper, the man advanced to the door and said:

"Get out!"

"For pity's sake, a glass of water," said the man.

* Patois of the French Alps, "Chat de maraude."

"A gun shot," said the peasant, and then he closed the door violently, and the man heard two heavy bolts drawn. A moment afterwards the window-shutters were shut, and noisily barred.

Night came on apace; the cold Alpine winds were blowing; by the light of the expiring day the stranger perceived in one of the gardens which fronted the street a kind of hut which seemed to be made of turf; he boldly cleared a wooden fence and found himself in the garden. He neared the hut; its door was a narrow, low entrance; it resembled, in its construction, the shanties which the road-labourers put up for their temporary accommodation. He, doubtless, thought that it was, in fact, the lodging of a road-labourer. He was suffering both from cold and hunger. He had resigned himself to the latter; but there at least was a shelter from the cold. These huts are not usually occupied at night. He got down and crawled into the hut. It was warm there and he found a good bed of straw. He rested a moment upon his bed motionless from fatigue; then, as his knapsack on his back troubled him, and it would make a good pillow, he began to unbuckle the straps. Just then he heard a ferocious growling and looking up saw the head of an enormous bull-dog at the opening of the hut.

It was a dog-kennel!

He was himself vigorous and formidable; seizing his stick, he made a shield of his knapsack, and got out of the hut as best he could, but not without enlarging the rents of his already tattered garments.

He made his way also out of the garden, but backwards; being obliged, out of respect to the dog, to have recourse to that kind of manoeuvre with his stick, which adepts in this sort of fencing call *la rose couverte*.

When he had, not without difficulty, got over the fence, he again found himself alone in the street without lodging, roof, or shelter, driven even from the straw-bed of that wretched dog-kennel. He threw himself rather than seated himself on a stone, and it appears that some one who was passing heard him exclaim, "I am not even a dog!"

Then he arose, and began to tramp again, taking his way out of the town, hoping to find some tree or haystack beneath which he could shelter himself. He walked on for some time, his head bowed down. When he thought he was far away from all human habitation he raised his eyes, and looked about him inquiringly. He was in a field: before him was a low hillock covered with stubble, which after the harvest looks like a shaved head. The sky was very dark; it was not simply the darkness of night, but there were very low clouds, which seemed to rest upon the hills, and covered the whole heavens. A little of the twilight, however, lingered in the zenith; and as the moon was about to rise these clouds formed in mid-heaven a vault of whitish light, from which a glimmer fell upon the earth.

The earth was then lighter than the sky, which produces a peculiarly sinister effect, and the hill, poor and mean in contour, loomed out dim and pale upon the gloomy horizon: the whole prospect was hideous, mean, lugubrious, and insignificant. There was nothing in the field nor upon the hill, but one ugly tree, a few steps from the traveller, which seemed to be twisting and contorting itself.

This man was evidently far from possessing those delicate perceptions of intelligence and feeling which produce a sensitiveness to the mysterious aspects of nature; still, there was in the sky, in this hillock, plain, and tree, something so profoundly desolate, that after a moment of motionless contemplation, he turned back hastily to the road. There are moments when nature appears hostile.

He retraced his steps; the gates of D—— were closed. D——, which sustained sieges in the religious wars, was still surrounded, in 1815, by old walls flanked by square towers, since demolished. He passed through a breach and entered the town.

It was about eight o'clock in the evening: as he did not know the streets, he walked at hazard.

So he came to the prefecture, then to the seminary; on passing by the Cathedral square, he shook his fist at the church.

At the corner of this square stands a printing-office; there were first printed the proclamations of the emperor, and the Imperial Guard to the army, brought from the island of Elba, and dictated by Napoleon himself.

Exhausted with fatigue, and hoping for nothing better, he lay down on a stone bench in front of this printing-office.

Just then an old woman came out of the church. She saw the man lying there in the dark and said:

"What are you doing there, my friend?"

He replied harshly, and with anger in his tone:

"You see, my good woman, I am going to sleep."

The good woman, who really merited the name, was Madame la Marquise de R——.

"Upon the bench?" said she.

"For nineteen years I have had a wooden mattress," said the man; "tonight I have a stone one."

"You have been a soldier?"

"Yes, my good woman, a soldier."

"Why don't you go to the inn?"

"Because I have no money."

"Alas!" said Madame de R——, "I have only four sous in my purse."

"Give them then." The man took the four sous, and Madame de R—— continued:

"You cannot find lodging for so little in an inn. But have you tried? You cannot pass the night so. You must be cold and hungry. They should give you lodging for charity."

"I have knocked at every door."

"Well, what then?"

"Everybody has driven me away."

The good woman touched the man's arm and pointed out to him on the other side of the square, a little low house beside the bishop's palace.

"You have knocked at every door?" she asked.

"Yes."

"Have you knocked at that one there?"

"No."

"Knock there."

II
PRUDENCE COMMENDED TO WISDOM

THAT evening, after his walk in the town, the Bishop of D—— remained quite late in his room. He was busy with his great work on Duty, which unfortunately is left incomplete. He carefully dissected all that the Fathers and Doctors have said on this serious topic. His book was divided into two parts: First, the duties of all: Secondly, the duties of each, according to his position in life. The duties of all are the principal duties; there are four of them, as set forth by St. Matthew: duty towards God (Matt. vi.); duty towards ourselves (Matt. v. 29, 30); duty towards our neighbour (Matt. vii. 12); and duty towards animals

(Matt. vi. 20, 25). As to other duties the bishop found them defined and prescribed elsewhere; those of sovereigns and subjects in the Epistle to the Romans; those of magistrates, wives, mothers, and young men, by St. Peter; those of husbands, fathers, children, and servants, in the Epistle to the Ephesians; those of the faithful in the Epistle to the Hebrews; and those of virgins in the Epistle to the Corinthians. He collated with much labour these injunctions into a harmonious whole, which he wished to offer to souls.

At eight o'clock he was still at work, writing with some inconvenience on little slips of paper, with a large book open on his knees, when Madame Magloire, as usual, came in to take the silver from the panel near the bed. A moment after, the bishop, knowing that the table was laid, and that his sister was perhaps waiting, closed his book and went into the dining-room.

This dining-room was an oblong apartment, with a fire-place, and with a door upon the street, as we have said, and a window opening into the garden.

Madame Magloire had just finished placing the plates.

While she was arranging the table, she was talking with Mademoiselle Baptistine.

The lamp was on the table, which was near the fire-place, where a good fire was burning.

One can readily fancy these two women, both past their sixtieth year: Madame Magloire, small, fat, and quick in her movements; Mademoiselle Baptistine, sweet, thin, fragile, a little taller than her brother, wore a silk puce colour dress, in the style of 1806, which she had bought at that time in Paris, and which still lasted her. To borrow a common mode of expression, which has the merit of saying in a single word what a page would hardly express, Madame Magloire had the air of a peasant, and Mademoiselle Baptistine that of a lady. Madame Magloire wore a white funnel-shaped cap: a gold *jeannette* at her neck, the only bit of feminine jewellery in the house, a snowy fichu just peering out above a black frieze dress, with wide short sleeves, a green and red checked calico apron tied at the waist with a green ribbon, with a stomacher of the same pinned up in front; on her feet, she wore coarse shoes and yellow stockings like the women of Marseilles. Mademoiselle Baptistine's dress was cut after the fashion of 1806, short waist, narrow skirt, sleeves with epaulettes, and with flaps and buttons. Her grey

hair was hid under a frizzed front called *à l'enfant*. Madame
Magloire had an intelligent, clever, and lively air; the two corners of her mouth unequally raised, and the upper lip projecting
beyond the under one, gave something morose and imperious
to her expression. So long as monseigneur was silent, she talked
to him without reserve, and with a mingled respect and freedom; but from the time that he opened his mouth as we have
seen, she implicitly obeyed like mademoiselle. Mademoiselle
Baptistine, however, did not speak. She confined herself to
obeying, and endeavouring to please. Even when she was
young, she was not pretty; she had large and very prominent
blue eyes, and a long pinched nose, but her whole face and
person, as we said in the outset, breathed an ineffable goodness.
She had been fore-ordained to meekness, but faith, charity,
hope, these three virtues which gently warm the heart, had
gradually sublimated this meekness into sanctity. Nature had
made her a lamb; religion had made her an angel. Poor, sainted
woman! gentle, but lost souvenir.

Mademoiselle Baptistine has so often related what occurred
at the bishop's house that evening, that many persons are still
living who can recall the minutest details.

Just as the bishop entered, Madame Magloire was speaking
with some warmth. She was talking to *Mademoiselle* upon a
familiar subject, and one to which the bishop was quite accustomed. It was a discussion on the means of fastening the front
door.

It seems that while Madame Magloire was out making provision for supper, she had heard the news in sundry places. There
was talk that an ill-favoured runaway, a suspicious vagabond,
had arrived and was lurking somewhere in the town, and that
some unpleasant adventures might befall those who should
come home late that night; besides, that the police was very
bad, as the prefect and the mayor did not like one another, and
were hoping to injure each other by untoward events; that it
was the part of wise people to be their own police, and to
protect their own persons; and that every one ought to be careful to shut up, bolt, and bar his house properly, and *secure his door
thoroughly*.

Madame Magloire dwelt upon these last words; but the
bishop having come from a cold room, seated himself before the
fire and began to warm himself, and then, he was thinking of

something else. He did not hear a word of what was let fall by Madame Magloire, and she repeated it. Then Mademoiselle Baptistine, endeavouring to satisfy Madame Magloire without displeasing her brother, ventured to say timidly:

"Brother, do you hear what Madame Magloire says?"

"I heard something of it indistinctly," said the bishop. Then turning his chair half round, putting his hands on his knees, and raising towards the old servant his cordial and good-humoured face which the firelight shone upon, he said: "Well, well! what is the matter? Are we in any great danger?"

Then Madame Magloire began her story again, unconsciously exaggerating it a little. It appeared that a bare-footed gipsy man, a sort of dangerous beggar, was in the town. He had gone for lodging to Jacquin Labarre, who had refused to receive him; he had been seen to enter the town by the boulevard Gassendi, and to roam through the street at dusk. A man with a knapsack and a rope, and a terrible-looking face.

"Indeed!" said the bishop.

This readiness to question her encouraged Madame Magloire; it seemed to indicate that the bishop was really well-nigh alarmed. She continued triumphantly: "Yes, monseigneur; it is true. There will something happen to-night in the town: everybody says so. The police is so badly organised (a convenient repetition). To live in this mountainous country, and not even to have street lamps! If one goes out, it is dark as a pocket. And I say, monseigneur, and mademoiselle says also——"

"Me?" interrupted the sister; "I say nothing. Whatever my brother does is well done."

Madame Magloire went on as if she had not heard this protestation:

"We say that this house is not safe at all; and if monseigneur will permit me, I will go and tell Paulin Musebois, the locksmith, to come and put the old bolts in the door again; they are there, and it will take but a minute. I say we must have bolts, were it only for to-night; for I say that a door which opens by a latch on the outside to the first comer, nothing could be more horrible: and then monseigneur has the habit of always saying 'Come in,' even at midnight. But, my goodness! there is no need even to ask leave——"

At this moment there was a violent knock on the door.

"Come in!" said the bishop.

III
THE HEROISM OF PASSIVE OBEDIENCE

THE door opened.

It opened quickly, quite wide, as if pushed by some one boldly and with energy.

A man entered.

That man, we know already; it was the traveller we have seen wandering about in search of a lodging.

He came in, took one step, and paused, leaving the door open behind him. He had his knapsack on his back, his stick in his hand, and a rough, hard, tired, and fierce look in his eyes, as seen by the firelight. He was hideous. It was an apparition of ill omen.

Madame Magloire had not even the strength to scream. She stood trembling with her mouth open.

Mademoiselle Baptistine turned, saw the man enter, and started up half alarmed; then, slowly turning back again towards the fire, she looked at her brother, and her face resumed its usual calmness and serenity.

The bishop looked upon the man with a tranquil eye.

As he was opening his mouth to speak, doubtless to ask the stranger what he wanted, the man, leaning with both hands on his club, glanced from one to another in turn, and without waiting for the bishop to speak, said in a loud voice:

"See here! My name is Jean Valjean. I am a convict; I have been nineteen years in the galleys. Four days ago I was set free, and started for Pontarlier, which is my destination; during those four days I have walked from Toulon. To-day I have walked twelve leagues. When I reached this place this evening I went to an inn, and they sent me away on account of my yellow passport, which I had shown at the mayor's office, as was necessary. I went to another inn, they said: 'Get out!' It was the same with one as with another; nobody would have me. I went to the prison, and the turnkey would not let me in. I crept into a dog-kennel, the dog bit me, and drove me away as if he had been a man; you would have said that he knew who I was. I went into the fields to sleep beneath the stars: there were no stars; I thought it would rain, and there was no good God to stop the drops, so I came back to the town to get the shelter of some doorway. There in the square I lay down upon a stone, a good woman showed me your house, and said: 'Knock there!' I have knocked. What is this place? Are you an inn? I have money; my savings, one hundred and nine francs and fifteen sous which I have earned in the galleys by my work for nineteen years. I will pay. What do I care? I have money. I am very tired—twelve leagues on foot, and I am so hungry. Can I stay?"

"Madame Magloire," said the bishop, "put on another plate."

The man took three steps, and came near the lamp which stood on the table. "Stop," he exclaimed; as if he had not been understood, "not that, did you understand me? I am a galley-slave—a convict—I am just from the galleys." He drew from his pocket a large sheet of yellow paper, which he unfolded. "There is my passport, yellow as you see. That is enough to have me kicked out wherever I go. Will you read it? I know how to read, I do. I learned in the galleys. There is a school there for those who care for it. See, here is what they have put in the passport: 'Jean Valjean, a liberated convict, native of ——,' you don't care for that, 'has been nineteen years in the galleys; five years for burglary; fourteen years for having attempted four times to escape. This man is very dangerous.' There you have it! Everybody has thrust me out; will you receive me? Is this an inn? Can you give me something to eat, and a place to sleep? Have you a stable?"

"Madame Magloire," said the bishop, "put some sheets on the bed in the alcove."

We have already described the kind of obedience yielded by these two women.

Madame Magloire went out to fulfil her orders.

The bishop turned to the man:

"Monsieur, sit down and warm yourself: we are going to take supper presently, and your bed will be made ready while you sup."

At last the man quite understood; his face, the expression of which till then had been gloomy and hard, now expressed stupefaction, doubt, and joy, and became absolutely wonderful. He began to stutter like a madman.

"True? What! You will keep me? you won't drive me away? a convict! You call me *Monsieur* and don't say 'Get out, dog!' as everybody else does. I thought that you would send me away, so I told first off who I am. Oh! the fine woman who sent me here! I shall have a supper! a bed like other people with mattress and sheets—a bed! It is nineteen years that I have not slept on a bed. You are really willing that I should stay? You are good people! Besides I have money: I will pay well. I beg your pardon, Monsieur Innkeeper, what is your name? I will pay all you say. You are a fine man. You are an innkeeper, an't you?"

"I am a priest who lives here," said the bishop.

"A priest," said the man. "Oh, noble priest! Then you do not ask any money? You are the curé, an't you? the curé of this big church? Yes, that's it. How stupid I am, I didn't notice your cap."

While speaking, he had deposited his knapsack and stick in the corner, replaced his passport in his pocket, and sat down. Mademoiselle Baptistine looked at him pleasantly. He continued:

"You are humane, Monsieur Curé; you don't despise me. A good priest is a good thing. Then you don't want me to pay you?"

"No," said the bishop, "keep your money. How much have you? You said a hundred and nine francs, I think."

"And fifteen sous," added the man.

"One hundred and nine francs and fifteen sous. And how long did it take you to earn that?"

"Nineteen years."

"Nineteen years!"

The bishop sighed deeply.

The man continued: "I have all my money yet. In four days I have spent only twenty-five sous which I earned by unloading wagons at Grasse. As you are an abbé, I must tell you, we have an almoner in the galleys. And then one day I saw a bishop; monseigneur they called him. It was the Bishop of Majore from Marseilles. He is the curé who is over the curés. You see—beg pardon, how I bungle saying it, but for me, it is so far off! you know what we are. He said mass in the centre of the place on an altar; he had a pointed gold thing on his head, that shone in the sun; it was noon. We were drawn up in line on three sides, with cannons and matches lighted before us. We could not see him well. He spoke to us, but he was not near enough, we did not understand him. That is what a bishop is."

While he was talking, the bishop shut the door, which he had left wide open.

Madame Magloire brought in a plate and set it on the table.

"Madame Magloire," said the bishop, "put this plate as near the fire as you can." Then turning towards his guest, he added: "The night wind is raw in the Alps; you must be cold, monsieur."

Every time he said this word monsieur, with his gently solemn, and heartily hospitable voice, the man's countenance lighted up. *Monsieur* to a convict, is a glass of water to a man dying of thirst at sea. Ignominy thirsts for respect.

"The lamp," said the bishop, "gives a very poor light."

Madame Magloire understood him, and going to his bed-chamber, took from the mantel the two silver candlesticks, lighted the candles, and placed them on the table.

"Monsieur Curé," said the man, "you are good; you don't despise me. You take me into your house; you light your candles for me, and I hav'n't hid from you where I come from, and how miserable I am."

The bishop, who was sitting near him, touched his hand gently and said: "You need not tell me who you are. This is not my house; it is the house of Christ. It does not ask any comer whether he has a name, but whether he has an affliction. You are suffering; you are hungry and thirsty; be welcome. And do not thank me; do not tell me that I take you into my house. This is the home of no man, except him who needs an asylum. I tell you, who are a traveller, that you are more at home here than I; whatever is here is yours. What need have I to know your name? Besides, before you told me, I knew it."

The man opened his eyes in astonishment:

"Really? You knew my name?"

"Yes," answered the bishop, "your name is my brother."

"Stop, stop, Monsieur Curé," exclaimed the man. "I was famished when I came in, but you are so kind that now I don't know what I am; that is all gone."

The bishop looked at him again and said:

"You have seen much suffering?"

"Oh, the red blouse, the ball and chain, the plank to sleep on, the heat, the cold, the galley's crew, the lash, the double chain for nothing, the dungeon for a word,—even when sick in bed, the chain. The dogs, the dogs are happier! nineteen years! and I am forty-six, and now a yellow passport. That is all."

"Yes," answered the bishop, "you have left a place of

suffering. But listen, there will be more joy in heaven over the tears of a repentant sinner, than over the white robes of a hundred good men. If you are leaving that sorrowful place with hate and anger against men, you are worthy of compassion; if you leave it with goodwill, gentleness, and peace, you are better than any of us."

Meantime Madame Magloire had served up supper; it consisted of soup made of water, oil, bread, and salt, a little pork, a scrap of mutton, a few figs, a green cheese, and a large loaf of rye bread. She had, without asking, added to the usual dinner of the bishop a bottle of fine old Mauves wine.

The bishop's countenance was lighted up with this expression of pleasure, peculiar to hospitable natures. "To supper!" he said briskly, as was his habit when he had a guest. He seated the man at his right. Mademoiselle Baptistine, perfectly quiet and natural, took her place at his left.

The bishop said the blessing, and then served the soup himself, according to his usual custom. The man fell to, eating greedily.

Suddenly the bishop said: "It seems to me something is lacking on the table."

The fact was, that Madame Magloire had set out only the three plates which were necessary. Now it was the custom of the house when the bishop had any one to supper, to set all six of the silver plates on the table, an innocent display. This graceful appearance of luxury was a sort of childlikeness which was full of charm in this gentle but austere household, which elevated poverty to dignity.

Madame Magloire understood the remark; without a word she went out, and a moment afterwards the three plates for which the bishop had asked were shining on the cloth, symmetrically arranged before each of the three guests.

IV

SOME ACCOUNT OF THE DIARIES OF PONTARLIER

Now, in order to give an idea of what passed at this table, we cannot do better than to transcribe here a passage in a letter from Mademoiselle Baptistine to Madame de Boischevron, in which the conversation between the convict and the bishop is related with charming minuteness.

"This man paid no attention to any one. He ate with the voracity of a starving man. After supper, however, he said:

"'Monsieur Curé, all this is too good for me, but I must say that the wagoners, who wouldn't have me eat with them, live better than you.'

"Between us, the remark shocked me a little. My brother answered:

"'They are more fatigued than I am.'

"'No,' responded this man; 'they have more money. You are poor, I can see. Perhaps you are not a curé even. Are you only a curé? Ah! if God is just, you well deserve to be a curé.'

"'God is more than just,' said my brother.

"A moment after he added:

"'Monsieur Jean Valjean, you are going to Pontarlier?'

"'A compulsory journey.'

"I am pretty sure that is the expression the man used. Then he continued:

"'I must be on the road to-morrow morning at daybreak. It is a hard journey. If the nights are cold, the days are warm.'

"'You are going,' said my brother, 'to a fine country. During the revolution, when my family was ruined, I took refuge first in Franche-Comté, and supported myself there for some time by the labour of my hands. There I found plenty of work, and had only to make my choice. There are paper-mills, tanneries, distilleries, oil-factories, large clock-making establishments, steel manufactories, copper foundries, at least twenty iron foundries, four of which, at Lods, Châtillon, Audincourt, and Beure, are very large.'

"I think I am not mistaken, and that these are the names that my brother mentioned. Then he broke off and addressed me:

"'Dear sister, have we not relatives in that part of the country?'

"I answered:

"'We had; among others Monsieur Lucenet, who was captain of the gates at Pontarlier under the old régime.'

"'Yes,' replied my brother, 'but in '93, no one had relatives; every one depended upon his hands. I laboured. They have, in the region of Pontarlier, where you are going, Monsieur Valjean, a business which is quite patriarchal and very charming, sister. It is their dairies, which they call *fruitières*.'

"Then my brother, while helping this man at table, explained

to him in detail what these *fruitières* were;—that they were
divided into two kinds: the *great barns*, belonging to the rich,
and where there are forty or fifty cows, which produce from
seven to eight thousand cheeses during the summer; and the
associated *fruitières*, which belong to the poor; these comprise
the peasants inhabiting the mountains, who put their cows into
a common herd, and divide the proceeds. They hire a cheese-
maker, whom they call a *grurin*; the *grurin* receives the milk
of the associates three times a day, and notes the quantities in
duplicate. Towards the end of April—the dairy work commences, and about the middle of June the cheese-makers drive
their cows into the mountains.

"The man became animated even while he was eating. My
brother gave him some good Mauves wine, which he does not
drink himself, because he says it is too dear. My brother gave
him all these details with that easy gaiety which you know is
peculiar to him, intermingling his words with compliments for
me. He dwelt much upon the good condition of a *grurin*, as if
he wished that this man should understand, without advising
him directly, and abruptly, that it would be an asylum for him.
One thing struck me. This man was what I have told you. Well!
my brother, during the supper, and during the entire evening,
with the exception of a few words about Jesus, when he entered,
did not say a word which could recall to this man who he himself was, nor indicate to him who my brother was. It was apparently a fine occasion to get in a little sermon, and to set up the
bishop above the convict in order to make an impression upon
his mind. It would, perhaps, have appeared to some to be a duty,
having this unhappy man in hand, to feed the mind at the same
time with the body, and to administer reproof, seasoned with
morality and advice, or at least a little pity accompanied by an
exhortation to conduct himself better in future. My brother
asked him neither his country nor his history; for his crime lay
in his history, and my brother seemed to avoid everything which
could recall it to him. At one time, as my brother was speaking
of the mountaineers of Pontarlier, who have *a pleasant labour
near heaven, and who*, he added, *are happy, because they are innocent*,
he stopped short, fearing there might have been in this word
which had escaped him something which could wound the feelings of this man. Upon reflection, I think I understand what was
passing in my brother's mind. He thought, doubtless, that this

man, who called himself Jean Valjean, had his wretchedness too constantly before his mind; that it was best not to distress him by referring to it, and to make him think, if it were only for a moment, that he was a common person like any one else, by treating him thus in the ordinary way. Is not this really understanding charity? Is there not, dear madame, something truly evangelical in this delicacy, which abstains from sermonising, moralising, and making allusions, and is it not the wisest sympathy, when a man has a suffering point, not to touch upon it at all? It seems to me that this was my brother's inmost thought. At any rate, all I can say is, if he had all these ideas, he did not show them even to me: he was, from beginning to end, the same as on other evenings, and he took supper with this Jean Valjean with the same air and manner that he would have supped with Monsieur Gédéon, the provost, or with the curé of the parish.

"Towards the end, as we were at dessert, some one pushed the door open. It was Mother Gerbaud with her child in her arms. My brother kissed the child, and borrowed fifteen sous that I had with me to give to Mother Gerbaud. The man, during this time, paid but little attention to what passed. He did not speak, and appeared to be very tired. The poor old lady left, and my brother said grace, after which he turned towards this man and said: 'You must be in great need of sleep.' Madame Magloire quickly removed the cloth. I understood that we ought to retire in order that this traveller might sleep, and we both went to our rooms. However, a few moments afterwards, I sent Madame Magloire to put on the bed of this man a roebuck skin from the Black Forest, which is in my chamber. The nights are quite cold, and this skin retains the warmth. It is a pity that it is quite old, and all the hair is gone. My brother bought it when he was in Germany, at Totlingen, near the sources of the Danube, as also the little ivory-handled knife, which I use at table.

"Madame Magloire came back immediately, we said our prayers in the parlour which we use as a drying-room, and then we retired to our chambers without saying a word."

V
TRANQUILLITY

AFTER having said good-night to his sister, Monseigneur Bienvenu took one of the silver candlesticks from the table, handed the other to his guest, and said to him:

"Monsieur, I will show you to your room."

The man followed him.

As may have been understood from what has been said before, the house was so arranged that one could reach the alcove in the oratory only by passing through the bishop's sleeping chamber. Just as they were passing through this room Madame Magloire was putting up the silver in the cupboard at the head of the bed. It was the last thing she did every night before going to bed.

The bishop left his guest in the alcove, before a clean white bed. The man set down the candlestick upon a small table.

"Come," said the bishop, "a good night's rest to you: to-morrow morning, before you go, you shall have a cup of warm milk from our cows."

"Thank you, Monsieur l'Abbé," said the man.

Scarcely had he pronounced these words of peace, when suddenly he made a singular motion which would have chilled the two good women of the house with horror, had they witnessed it. Even now it is hard for us to understand what impulse he obeyed at that moment. Did he intend to give a warning or to throw out a menace? or was he simply obeying a sort of instinctive impulse, obscure even to himself? He turned abruptly towards the old man, crossed his arms, and casting a wild look upon his host, exclaimed in a harsh voice:

"Ah, now, indeed! you lodge me in your house, as near you as that!"

He checked himself, and added, with a laugh, in which there was something horrible:

"Have you reflected upon it? Who tells you that I am not a murderer?"

The bishop responded: "God will take care of that."

Then with gravity, moving his lips like one praying or talking to himself, he raised two fingers of his right hand and blessed the man, who, however, did not bow; and without turning his head or looking behind him, went into his chamber.

When the alcove was occupied, a heavy serge curtain was drawn in the oratory, concealing the altar. Before this curtain the bishop knelt as he passed out, and offered a short prayer.

A moment afterwards he was walking in the garden, surrendering mind and soul to a dreamy contemplation of these grand and mysterious works of God, which night makes visible to the eye.

As to the man, he was so completely exhausted that he did not even avail himself of the clean white sheets; he blew out the candle with his nostril, after the manner of convicts, and fell on the bed, dressed as he was, into a sound sleep.

Midnight struck as the bishop came back to his chamber.

A few moments afterwards all in the little house slept.

VI
JEAN VALJEAN

TOWARDS the middle of the night, Jean Valjean awoke.

Jean Valjean was born of a poor peasant family of Brie. In his childhood he had not been taught to read: when he was grown up, he chose the occupation of a pruner at Faverolles. His mother's name was Jeanne Mathieu, his father's Jean Valjean or Vlajean, probably a nickname, a contraction of *Voilà Jean*.

Jean Valjean was of a thoughtful disposition, but not sad, which is characteristic of affectionate natures. Upon the whole, however, there was something torpid and insignificant, in the appearance at least, of Jean Valjean. He had lost his parents when very young. His mother died of malpractice in a milkfever: his father, a pruner before him, was killed by a fall from a tree. Jean Valjean now had but one relative left, his sister, a widow with seven children, girls and boys. This sister had brought up Jean Valjean, and, as long as her husband lived, she had taken care of her younger brother. Her husband died, leaving the eldest of these children eight, the youngest one year old. Jean Valjean had just reached his twenty-fifth year: he took the father's place, and, in his turn, supported the sister who reared him. This he did naturally, as a duty, and even with a sort of moroseness on his part. His youth was spent in rough and ill-recompensed labour: he never was known to have a sweetheart; he had not time to be in love.

At night he came in weary and ate his soup without saying a

word. While he was eating, his sister, *Mère Jeanne*, frequently took from his porringer the best of his meal, a bit of meat, a slice of pork, the heart of the cabbage, to give to one of her children. He went on eating, his head bent down nearly into the soup, his long hair falling over his dish, hiding his eyes; he did not seem to notice anything that was done. At Faverolles, not far from the house of the Valjeans, there was on the other side of the road a farmer's wife named Marie Claude; the Valjean children, who were always famished, sometimes went in their mother's name to borrow a pint of milk, which they would drink behind a hedge, or in some corner of the lane, snatching away the pitcher so greedily one from another, that the little girls would spill it upon their aprons and their necks; if their mother had known of this exploit she would have punished the delinquents severely. Jean Valjean, rough and grumbler as he was, paid Marie Claude; their mother never knew it, and so the children escaped.

He earned in the pruning season eighteen sous a day: after that he hired out as a reaper, workman, teamster, or labourer. He did whatever he could find to do. His sister worked also, but what could she do with seven little children? It was a sad group, which misery was grasping and closing upon, little by little. There was a very severe winter; Jean had no work, the family had no bread; literally, no bread, and seven children.

One Sunday night, Maubert Isabeau, the baker on the Place de l'Eglise, in Faverolles, was just going to bed when he heard a violent blow against the barred window of his shop. He got down in time to see an arm thrust through the aperture made by the blow of a fist on the glass. The arm seized a loaf of bread and took it out. Isabeau rushed out; the thief used his legs valiantly; Isabeau pursued him and caught him. The thief had thrown away the bread, but his arm was still bleeding. It was Jean Valjean.

All that happened in 1795. Jean Valjean was brought before the tribunals of the time for "burglary at night, in an inhabited house." He had a gun which he used as well as any marksman in the world and was something of a poacher, which hurt him, there being a natural prejudice against poachers. The poacher, like the smuggler, approaches very nearly to the brigand. We must say, however, by the way, that there is yet a deep gulf between this race of men and the hideous assassin of the city.

The poacher dwells in the forest, and the smuggler in the mountains or upon the sea; cities produce ferocious men, because they produce corrupt men; the mountains, the forest, and the sea, render men savage; they develop the fierce, but yet do not destroy the human.

Jean Valjean was found guilty: the terms of the code were explicit; in our civilisation there are fearful hours; such are those when the criminal law pronounces shipwreck upon a man. What a mournful moment is that in which society withdraws itself and gives up a thinking being for ever. Jean Valjean was sentenced to five years in the galleys.

On the 22nd of April, 1796, there was announced in Paris the victory of Montenotte, achieved by the commanding-general of the army of Italy, whom the message of the Directory, to the Five Hundred, of the 2nd Floréal, year IV., called Buonaparte; that same day a great chain was riveted at the Bicêtre. Jean Valjean was a part of this chain. An old turnkey of the prison, now nearly ninety, well remembers this miserable man, who was ironed at the end of the fourth plinth in the north angle of the court. Sitting on the ground like the rest, he seemed to comprehend nothing of his position, except its horror: probably there was also mingled with the vague ideas of a poor ignorant man a notion that there was something excessive in the penalty. While they were with heavy hammer-strokes behind his head riveting the bolt of his iron collar, he was weeping. The tears choked his words, and he only succeeded in saying from time to time: "I was a *pruner at Faverolles.*" Then sobbing as he was, he raised his right hand and lowered it seven times, as if he was touching seven heads of unequal height, and at this gesture one could guess that whatever he had done, had been to feed and clothe seven little children.

He was taken to Toulon, at which place he arrived after a journey of twenty-seven days, on a cart, the chain still about his neck. At Toulon he was dressed in a red blouse, all his past life was effaced, even to his name. He was no longer Jean Valjean: he was Number 24,601. What became of the sister? What became of the seven children? Who troubled himself about that? What becomes of the handful of leaves of the young tree when it is sawn at the trunk?

It is the old story. These poor little lives, these creatures of God, henceforth without support, or guide, or asylum; they passed away wherever chance led, who knows even? Each took a different path, it may be, and sank little by little into the chilling dark which engulfs solitary destinies; that sullen gloom where are lost so many ill-fated souls in the sombre advance of the human race. They left that region; the church of what had been their village forgot them; the stile of what had been their field forgot them; after a few years in the galleys, even Jean Valjean forgot them. In that heart, in which there had been a wound, there was a scar; that was all. During the time he was at Toulon, he heard but once of his sister; that was, I think, at the end of the fourth year of his confinement. I do not know how the news reached him: some one who had known him at home had seen his sister. She was in Paris, living in a poor street near Saint Sulpice, the Rue du Geindre. She had with her but one child, the youngest, a little boy. Where were the other six? She did not know herself, perhaps. Every morning she went to a bindery, No. 3 Rue du Sabot, where she was employed as a folder and book-stitcher. She had to be there by six in the morning, long before the dawn in the winter. In the same building with the bindery, there was a school, where she sent her little boy, seven years old. As the school did not open until seven, and she must be at her work at six, her boy had to wait in the yard an hour, until the school opened—an hour of cold and darkness in the winter. They would not let the child wait in the bindery, because he was troublesome, they said. The workmen, as they passed in the morning, saw the poor little fellow sometimes sitting on the pavement nodding with weariness, and often sleeping in the dark, crouched and bent over his basket. When it rained, an old woman, the portress, took pity on him; she let him come into her lodge, the furniture of which was only a pallet bed, a spinning-wheel, and two wooden chairs; and the little one slept there in a corner, hugging the cat to keep himself warm. At seven o'clock the school opened and he went in. That is what was told Jean Valjean. It was as if a window had suddenly been opened looking upon the destiny of those he had loved, and then all was closed again, and he heard nothing more for ever. Nothing more came to him; he had not seen them, never will he see them again! and through the remainder of this sad history we shall not meet them again.

Near the end of this fourth year, his chance of liberty came to Jean Valjean. His comrades helped him as they always do in that dreary place, and he escaped. He wandered two days in freedom through the fields; if it is freedom to be hunted, to turn your head each moment, to tremble at the least noise, to be afraid of everything, of the smoke of a chimney, the passing of a man, the baying of a dog, the gallop of a horse, the striking of a clock, of the day because you see, and of the night because you do not; of the road, of the path, the bush, of sleep. During the evening of the second day he was retaken; he had neither eaten nor slept for thirty-six hours. The maritime tribunal extended his sentence three years for this attempt, which made eight. In the sixth year his turn of escape came again; he tried it, but failed again. He did not answer at roll-call, and the alarm cannon was fired. At night the people of the vicinity discovered him hidden beneath the keel of a vessel on the stocks; he resisted the galley guard which seized him. Escape and resistance. This the provisions of the special code punished by an addition of five years, two with the double chain, thirteen years. The tenth year his turn came round again; he made another attempt with no better success. Three years for this new attempt. Sixteen years. And finally, I think it was in the thirteenth year, he made yet another, and was retaken after an absence of only four hours. Three years for these four hours. Nineteen years. In October, 1815, he was set at large: he had entered in 1796 for having broken a pane of glass, and taken a loaf of bread.

This is a place for a short parenthesis. This is the second time, in his studies on the penal question and on the sentences of the law, that the author of this book has met with the theft of a loaf of bread as the starting-point of the ruin of a destiny. Claude Gueux stole a loaf of bread, Jean Valjean stole a loaf of bread; English statistics show that in London starvation is the immediate cause of four thefts out of five.

Jean Valjean entered the galleys sobbing and shuddering: he went out hardened; he entered in despair: he went out sullen. What had been the life of this soul?

VII
THE DEPTHS OF DESPAIR

LET us endeavour to tell.

It is an imperative necessity that society should look into these things: they are its own work.

He was, as we have said, ignorant, but he was not imbecile. The natural light was enkindled in him. Misfortune, which has also its illumination, added to the few rays that he had in his mind. Under the whip, under the chain, in the cell, in fatigue, under the burning sun of the galleys, upon the convict's bed of plank, he turned to his own conscience, and he reflected.

He constituted himself a tribunal.

He began by arraigning himself.

He recognised that he was not an innocent man, unjustly punished. He acknowledged that he had committed an extreme and a blamable action; that the loaf perhaps would not have been refused him, had he asked for it; that at all events it would have been better to wait, either for pity, or for work; that it is not altogether an unanswerable reply to say: "could I wait when I was hungry?" that, in the first place, it is very rare that any one dies of actual hunger; and that, fortunately or unfortunately, man is so made that he can suffer long and much, morally and physically, without dying; that he should, therefore, have had patience; that that would have been better even for those poor little ones; that it was an act of folly in him, poor, worthless man, to seize society in all its strength, forcibly by the collar, and imagine that he could escape from misery by theft; that that was, at all events, a bad door for getting out of misery by which one entered into infamy; in short, that he had done wrong.

Then he asked himself:

If he were the only one who had done wrong in the course of his fatal history? If, in the first place, it were not a grievous thing that he, a workman, should have been in want of work; that he, an industrious man, should have lacked bread. If, moreover, the fault having been committed and avowed, the punishment had not been savage and excessive. If there were not a greater abuse, on the part of the law, in the penalty, than there had been, on the part of the guilty, in the crime. If there were not an excess of weight in one of the scales of the balance—on the side of the expiation. If the discharge of the penalty were not the effacement of the crime; and if the result were not to reverse the situation, to replace the wrong of the delinquent by the wrong of the repression, to make a victim of the guilty, and a creditor of the debtor, and actually to put the right on the side of him who had violated it. If that penalty, taken in connection with its successive extensions for his attempts to escape, had not at last come to be a sort of outrage of the stronger on the weaker, a crime of society towards the individual, a crime which was committed afresh every day, a crime which had endured for nineteen years.

He questioned himself if human society could have the right alike to crush its members, in the one case by its unreasonable carelessness, and in the other by its pitiless care; and to keep a poor man for ever between a lack and an excess, a lack of work, an excess of punishment.

If it were not outrageous that society should treat with such rigid precision those of its members who were most poorly endowed in the distribution of wealth that chance had made, and who were, therefore, most worthy of indulgence.

These questions asked and decided, he condemned society and sentenced it.

He sentenced it to his hatred.

He made it responsible for the doom which he had undergone, and promised himself that he, perhaps, would not hesitate some day to call it to an account. He declared to himself that there was no equity between the injury that he had committed and the injury that had been committed on him; he concluded, in short, that his punishment was not, really, an injustice, but that beyond all doubt it was an iniquity.

Anger may be foolish and absurd, and one may be irritated when in the wrong; but a man never feels outraged unless in some respect he is at bottom right. Jean Valjean felt outraged.

And then, human society had done him nothing but injury; never had he seen anything of her, but this wrathful face which she calls justice, and which she shows to those whom she strikes down. No man had ever touched him but to bruise him. All his contact with men had been by blows. Never, since his infancy, since his mother, since his sister, never had he been greeted with a friendly word or a kind regard. Through suffering on suffering he came little by little to the conviction, that life was a war, and that in that war he was the vanquished. He had no weapon but his hate. He resolved to sharpen it in the galleys and to take it with him when he went out.

There was at Toulon a school for the prisoners conducted by some not very skilful friars, where the most essential branches were taught to such of these poor men as were willing. He was one of the willing ones. He went to school at forty and learned to read, write, and cipher. He felt that to increase his knowledge was to strengthen his hatred. Under certain circumstances, instruction and enlightenment may serve as rallying-points for evil.

It is sad to tell; but after having tried society, which had caused his misfortunes, he tried Providence which created society, and condemned it also.

Thus, during those nineteen years of torture and slavery, did this soul rise and fall at the same time. Light entered on the one side, and darkness on the other.

Jean Valjean was not, we have seen, of an evil nature. His heart was still right when he arrived at the galleys. While there he condemned society, and felt that he became wicked; he condemned Providence, and felt that he became impious.

It is difficult not to reflect for a moment here.

Can human nature be so entirely transformed from top to bottom? Can man, created good by God, be made wicked by man? Can the soul be changed to keep pace with its destiny, and become evil when its destiny is evil? Can the heart become distorted and contract deformities and infirmities that are incurable, under the pressure of disproportionate woe, like the vertebral column under a too heavy brain? Is there not in every human soul, was there not in the particular soul of Jean Valjean, a primitive spark, a divine element, incorruptible in this world, immortal in the next, which can be developed by good, kindled, lit up, and made resplendently radiant, and which evil can never entirely extinguish?

Grave and obscure questions, to the last of which every physiologist would probably, without hesitation, have answered *no*, had he seen at Toulon, during the hours of rest, which to Jean Valjean were hours of thought, this gloomy galley-slave, seated, with folded arms, upon the bar of some windlass, the end of his chain stuck into his pocket that it might not drag, serious, silent, and thoughtful, a pariah of the law which views man with wrath, condemned by civilisation which views heaven with severity.

Certainly, we will not conceal it, such a physiologist would have seen in Jean Valjean an irremediable misery; he would perhaps have lamented the disease occasioned by the law; but he would not even have attempted a cure; he would have turned from the sight of the caverns which he would have beheld in that soul; and, like Dante at the gate of Hell, he would have wiped out from that existence the word which the finger of God has nevertheless written upon the brow of every man—*Hope*!

Was that state of mind which we have attempted to analyse as perfectly clear to Jean Valjean as we have tried to render it to our readers? Did Jean Valjean distinctly see, after their formation, and had he distinctly seen, while they were forming, all the elements of which his moral misery was made up? Had this rude and unlettered man taken accurate account of the succession of ideas by which he had, step by step, risen and fallen, till he had reached that mournful plane which for so many years already had marked the internal horizon of his mind? Had he a clear consciousness of all that was passing within him, and of all that was moving him? This we dare not affirm; we do not, in fact, believe it. Jean Valjean was too ignorant, even after so much ill fortune, for nice discrimination in these matters. At times he did not even know exactly what were his feelings. Jean Valjean was in the dark; he suffered in the dark; he hated in the dark; we might say that he hated in his own sight. He lived constantly in the darkness, groping blindly and as in a dream. Only, at intervals, there broke over him suddenly, from within or from without, a shock of anger, an overflow of suffering, a quick pallid flash which lit up his whole soul, and showed all around him, before and behind, in the glare of a hideous light, the fearful precipices and the sombre perspectives of his fate.

The flash passed away; the night fell, and where was he? He no longer knew.

The peculiarity of punishment of this kind, in which what is pitiless, that is to say, what is brutalising, predominates, is to transform little by little, by a slow stupefaction, a man into an animal, sometimes into a wild beast. Jean Valjean's repeated and obstinate attempts to escape are enough to prove that such is the strange effect of the law upon a human soul. Jean Valjean had renewed these attempts, so wholly useless and foolish, as often as an opportunity offered, without one moment's thought of the result, or of experience already undergone. He escaped wildly, like a wolf on seeing his cage-door open. Instinct said to him: "Away!" Reason said to him: "Stay!" But before a temptation so mighty, reason fled; instinct alone remained. The beast alone was in play. When he was retaken, the new severities that were inflicted upon him only made him still more fierce.

We must not omit one circumstance, which is, that in physical strength he far surpassed all the other inmates of the prison. At hard work, at twisting a cable, or turning a windlass, Jean Valjean was equal to four men. He would sometimes lift and hold enormous weights on his back, and would occasionally act the part of what is called a *jack*, or what was called in old French an *orgeuil*, whence came the name, we may say by the way, of the Rue Montorgeuil near the Halles of Paris. His comrades had nicknamed him Jean the Jack. At one time, while the balcony of the City Hall of Toulon was undergoing repairs, one of Puget's admirable caryatides, which support the balcony, slipped from its place, and was about to fall, when Jean Valjean, who happened to be there, held it up on his shoulder till the workmen came.

His suppleness surpassed his strength. Certain convicts, always planning escape, have developed a veritable science of strength and skill combined,—the science of the muscles. A mysterious system of statics is practised throughout daily by prisoners, who are eternally envying the birds and flies. To scale a wall, and to find a foothold where you could hardly see a projection, was play for Jean Valjean. Given an angle in a wall, with the tension of his back and his knees, with elbows and hands braced against the rough face of the stone, he would ascend, as if by magic, to a third story. Sometimes he climbed up in this manner to the roof of the galleys.

He talked but little, and never laughed. Some extreme emotion was required to draw from him, once or twice a year, that lugubrious sound of the convict, which is like the echo of a demon's laugh. To those who saw him, he seemed to be absorbed in continually looking upon something terrible.

He was absorbed, in fact.

Through the diseased perceptions of an incomplete nature and a smothered intelligence, he vaguely felt that a monstrous weight was over him. In that pallid and sullen shadow in which he crawled, whenever he turned his head and endeavoured to raise his eyes, he saw, with mingled rage and terror, forming, massing, and mounting up out of view above him with horrid escarpments, a kind of frightful accumulation of things, of laws, of prejudices, of men, and of acts, the outlines of which escaped him, the weight of which appalled him, and which was no other than that prodigious pyramid that we call civilisation. Here and there in that shapeless and crawling mass, sometimes near at hand, sometimes afar off, and upon inaccessible heights, he distinguished some group, some detail vividly clear, here the jailer with his staff, here the gendarme with his sword, yonder the mitred archbishop; and on high, in a sort of blaze of glory, the emperor crowned and resplendent. It seemed to him that these distant splendours, far from dissipating his night, made it blacker and more deathly. All this, laws, prejudices, acts, men, things, went and came above him, according to the complicated and mysterious movement that God impresses upon civilisation, marching over him and crushing him with an indescribably tranquil cruelty and inexorable indifference. Souls sunk to the bottom of possible misfortune, and unfortunate men lost in the lowest depths, where they are no longer seen, the rejected of the law, feel upon their heads the whole weight of that human society, so formidable to him who is without it, so terrible to him who is beneath it.

In such a situation Jean Valjean mused, and what could be the nature of his reflections?

If a millet seed under a millstone had thoughts, doubtless it would think what Jean Valjean thought.

All these things, realities full of spectres, phantasmagoria full of realities, had at last produced within him a condition which was almost inexpressible.

Sometimes in the midst of his work in the galleys he would stop and begin to think. His reason, more mature, and, at the same time, perturbed more than formerly, would revolt. All that had happened to him would appear absurd; all that surrounded him would appear impossible. He would say to himself: "it is a dream." He would look at the jailer standing a few steps from him; the jailer would seem to be a phantom; all at once this phantom would give him a blow with a stick.

For him the external world had scarcely an existence. It would be almost true to say that for Jean Valjean there was no sun, no beautiful summer days, no radiant sky, no fresh April dawn. Some dim window light was all that shone in his soul.

To sum up, in conclusion, what can be summed up and reduced to positive results, of all that we have been showing, we will make sure only of this, that in the course of nineteen years, Jean Valjean, the inoffensive pruner of Faverolles, the terrible galley-slave of Toulon, had become capable, thanks to the training he had received in the galleys, of two species of crime; first, a sudden, unpremeditated action, full of rashness, all instinct, a sort of reprisal for the wrong he had suffered; secondly, a serious, premeditated act, discussed by his conscience, and pondered over with the false ideas which such a fate will give. His premeditations passed through the three successive phases to which natures of a certain stamp are limited—reason, will, and obstinacy. He had as motives, habitual indignation, bitterness of soul, a deep sense of injuries suffered, a reaction even against the good, the innocent, and the upright, if any such there are. The beginning as well as the end of all his thoughts was hatred of human law; that hatred which, if it be not checked in its growth by some providential event, becomes, in a certain time, hatred of society, then hatred of the human race, and then hatred of creation, and reveals itself by a vague and incessant desire to injure some living being, it matters not who. So, the passport was right which described Jean Valjean as *a very dangerous man*.

From year to year this soul had withered more and more, slowly but fatally. With this withered heart, he had a dry eye. When he left the galleys, he had not shed a tear for nineteen years.

VIII
THE WATERS AND THE SHADOW

A MAN overboard!

What matters it! the ship does not stop. The wind is blowing, that dark ship must keep on her destined course. She passes away.

The man disappears, then reappears, he plunges and rises again to the surface, he calls, he stretches out his hands, they hear him not; the ship, staggering under the gale, is straining every rope, the sailors and passengers see the drowning man no longer; his miserable head is but a point in the vastness of the billows.

He hurls cries of despair into the depths. What a spectre is that disappearing sail! He looks upon it, he looks upon it with frenzy. It moves away; it grows dim; it diminishes. He was there but just now, he was one of the crew, he went and came upon the deck with the rest, he had his share of the air and of the sunlight, he was a living man. Now, what has become of him? He slipped, he fell; and it is finished.

He is in the monstrous deep. He has nothing under his feet but the yielding, fleeing element. The waves, torn and scattered by the wind, close round him hideously; the rolling of the abyss bears him along; shreds of water are flying about his head; a populace of waves spit upon him; confused openings half swallow him; when he sinks he catches glimpses of yawning precipices full of darkness; fearful unknown vegetations seize upon him, bind his feet, and draw him to themselves; he feels that he is becoming the great deep, he makes part of the foam; the billows toss him from one to the other; he tastes the bitterness; the greedy ocean is eager to devour him; the monster plays with his agony. It seems as if all this were liquid hate.

He tries to defend himself, he tries to sustain himself; he struggles; he swims. He—that poor strength that fails so soon—he combats the unfailing.

But yet he struggles.

Where now is the ship? Far away yonder. Hardly visible in the pallid gloom of the horizon.

The wind blows in gusts; the billows overwhelm him. He raises his eyes, but sees only the livid clouds. He, in his dying agony, makes part of this immense insanity of the sea. He is tortured to his death by its immeasurable madness. He hears sounds, which are strange to man, sounds which seem to come not from earth, but from some frightful realm beyond.

There are birds in the clouds, even as there are angels above human distresses, but what can they do for him? They fly, sing, float, while he is gasping.

He feels that he is buried at once by those two infinities, the ocean and the sky; the one is a tomb, the other a pall.

Night descends, he has been swimming for hours, his strength is almost exhausted; that ship, that far off thing, where there were men, is gone; he is alone in the terrible gloom of the abyss; he sinks, he strains, he struggles, he feels beneath him the shadowy monsters of the unseen; he shouts.

Men are no more. Where is God?

He shouts. Help! Help! He shouts incessantly.

Nothing in the horizon. Nothing in the sky.

He implores the blue vault, the waves, the rocks; all are deaf. He supplicates the tempest; the imperturbable tempest obeys only the infinite.

Around him are darkness, storm, solitude, wild and

unconscious tumult, the ceaseless tumbling of the fierce waters; within him, horror and exhaustion. Beneath him the engulfing abyss. No resting place. He thinks of the shadowy adventures of his lifeless body in the limitless gloom. The biting cold paralyses him. His hands clutch spasmodically, and grasp at nothing. Winds, clouds, whirlwinds, blasts, stars, all useless! What shall he do? He yields to despair; worn out, he seeks death; he no longer resists; he gives himself up; he abandons the contest, and he is rolled away into the dismal depths of the abyss for ever.

O implacable march of human society! Destruction of men and of souls marking its path! Ocean, where fall all that the law lets fall! Ominous disappearance of aid! O moral death!

The sea is the inexorable night into which the penal law casts its victims. The sea is the measureless misery.

The soul drifting in that sea may become a corpse. Who shall restore it to life?

IX

NEW GRIEFS

WHEN the time for leaving the galleys came, and when there were sounded in the ear of Jean Valjean the strange words: *You are free!* the moment seemed improbable and unreal, a ray of living light, a ray of the true light of living men, suddenly penetrated his soul. But this ray quickly faded away. Jean Valjean had been dazzled with the idea of liberty. He had believed in a new life. He soon saw what sort of liberty that is which has a yellow passport.

And along with that there were many bitter experiences. He had calculated that his savings, during his stay at the galleys, would amount to a hundred and seventy-one francs. It is proper to say that he had forgotten to take into account the compulsory rest on Sundays and holydays, which, in nineteen years, required deduction of about twenty-four francs. However that might be, his savings had been reduced, by various local charges, to the sum of a hundred and nine francs and fifteen sous, which was counted out to him on his departure.

He understood nothing of this, and thought himself wronged, or to speak plainly, robbed.

The day after his liberation, he saw before the door of an orange flower distillery at Grasse, some men who were unloading bags. He offered his services. They were in need of help and accepted them. He set at work. He was intelligent, robust, and handy; he did his best; the foreman appeared to be satisfied. While he was at work, a gendarme passed, noticed him, and asked for his papers. He was compelled to show the yellow passport. That done, Jean Valjean resumed his work. A little while before, he had asked one of the labourers how much they were paid per day for this work and the reply was: thirty sous. At night, as he was obliged to leave the town next morning, he went to the foreman of the distillery, and asked for his pay. The foreman did not say a word, but handed him fifteen sous. He remonstrated. The man replied: "*That is good enough for you.*" He insisted. The foreman looked him in the eyes and said: "*Look out for the lock-up!*"

There again he thought himself robbed.

Society, the state, in reducing his savings, had robbed him by wholesale. Now it was the turn of the individual, who was robbing him by retail.

Liberation is not deliverance. A convict may leave the galleys behind, but not his condemnation.

This was what befell him at Grasse. We have seen how he was received at D——.

X
THE MAN AWAKES

As the cathedral clock struck two, Jean Valjean awoke.

What awakened him was, too good a bed. For nearly twenty years he had not slept in a bed, and, although he had not undressed, the sensation was too novel not to disturb his sleep.

He had slept something more than four hours. His fatigue had passed away. He was not accustomed to give many hours to repose.

He opened his eyes, and looked for a moment into the obscurity about him, then he closed them to go to sleep again.

When many diverse sensations have disturbed the day, when the mind is preoccupied, we can fall asleep once, but not a second time. Sleep comes at first much more readily than it comes again. Such was the case with Jean Valjean. He could not get to sleep again, and so he began to think.

He was in one of those moods in which the ideas we have

in our minds are perturbed. There was a kind of vague ebb and flow in his brain. His oldest and his latest memories floated about pell mell, and crossed each other confusedly, losing their own shapes, swelling beyond measure, then disappearing all at once, as if in a muddy and troubled stream. Many thoughts came to him, but there was one which continually presented itself, and which drove away all others. What that thought was, we shall tell directly. He had noticed the six silver plates and the large ladle that Madame Magloire had put on the table.

Those six silver plates took possession of him. There they were, within a few steps. At the very moment that he passed through the middle room to reach the one he was now in, the old servant was placing them in a little cupboard at the head of the bed. He had marked that cupboard well: on the right, coming from the dining-room. They were solid; and old silver. With the big ladle, they would bring at least two hundred francs, double what he had got for nineteen years' labour. True; he would have got more if the "*government*" had not "*robbed*" him.

His mind wavered a whole hour, and a long one, in fluctuation and in struggle. The clock struck three. He opened his eyes, rose up hastily in bed, reached out his arm and felt his haversack, which he had put into the corner of the alcove, then he thrust out his legs and placed his feet on the ground, and found himself, he knew not how, seated on his bed.

He remained for some time lost in thought in that attitude, which would have had a rather ominous look, had any one seen him there in the dusk—he only awake in the slumbering house. All at once he stooped down, took off his shoes, and put them softly upon the mat in front of the bed, then he resumed his thinking posture, and was still again.

In that hideous meditation, the ideas which we have been pointing out, troubled his brain without ceasing, entered, departed, returned, and became a sort of weight upon him; and then he thought, too, he knew not why, and with that mechanical obstinacy that belongs to reverie, of a convict named Brevet, whom he had known in the galleys, and whose trousers were only held up by a single knit cotton suspender. The checked pattern of that suspender came continually before his mind.

He continued in this situation, and would perhaps have remained there until daybreak, if the clock had not struck the quarter or the half-hour. The clock seemed to say to him: "Come along!"

He rose to his feet, hesitated for a moment longer and listened; all was still in the house; he walked straight and cautiously towards the window, which he could discern. The night was not very dark; there was a full moon, across which large clouds were driving before the wind. This produced alternations of light and shade, out-of-doors eclipses and illuminations, and in-doors a kind of glimmer. This glimmer, enough to enable him to find his way, changing with the passing clouds, resembled that sort of livid light, which falls through the window of a dungeon before which men are passing and repassing. On reaching the window, Jean Valjean examined it. It had no bars, opened into the garden, and was fastened, according to the fashion of the country, with a little wedge only. He opened it; but as the cold, keen air rushed into the room, he closed it again immediately. He looked into the garden with that absorbed look which studies rather than sees. The garden was enclosed with a white wall quite low, and readily scaled. Beyond, against the sky, he distinguished the tops of trees at equal distances apart, which showed that this wall separated the garden from an avenue or a lane planted with trees.

When he had taken this observation, he turned like a man whose mind is made up, went to his alcove, took his haversack, opened it, fumbled in it, took out something which he laid upon the bed, put his shoes into one of his pockets, tied up his bundle, swung it upon his shoulders, put on his cap, and pulled the vizor down over his eyes, felt for his stick, and went and put it in the corner of the window, then returned to the bed, and resolutely took up the object which he had laid on it. It looked like a short iron bar, pointed at one end like a spear.

It would have been hard to distinguish in the darkness for what use this piece of iron had been made. Could it be a lever? Could it be a club?

In the day-time, it would have been seen to be nothing but a miner's drill. At that time, the convicts were sometimes employed in quarrying stone on the high hills that surround Toulon, and they often had miners' tools in their possession. Miners' drills are of solid iron, terminating at the lower end in a point, by means of which they are sunk into the rock.

He took the drill in his right hand, and holding his breath, with stealthy steps, he moved towards the door of the next room, which was the bishop's, as we know, On reaching the door, he found it unlatched. The bishop had not closed it.

XI
WHAT HE DOES

JEAN VALJEAN listened. Not a sound.

He pushed the door.

He pushed it lightly with the end of his finger, with the stealthy and timorous carefulness of a cat. The door yielded to the pressure with a silent, imperceptible movement, which made the opening a little wider.

He waited a moment, and then pushed the door again more boldly.

It yielded gradually and silently. The opening was now wide enough for him to pass through; but there was a small table near the door which with it formed a troublesome angle, and which barred the entrance.

Jean Valjean saw the obstacle. At all hazards the opening must be made still wider.

He so determined, and pushed the door a third time, harder than before. This time a rusty hinge suddenly sent out into the darkness a harsh and prolonged creak.

Jean Valjean shivered. The noise of this hinge sounded in his ears as clear and terrible as the trumpet of the Judgment Day.

In the fantastic exaggeration of the first moment, he almost imagined that this hinge had become animate, and suddenly endowed with a terrible life; and that it was barking like a dog to warn everybody, and rouse the sleepers.

He stopped, shuddering and distracted, and dropped from his tiptoes to his feet. He felt the pulses of his temples beat like trip-hammers, and it appeared to him that his breath came from his chest with the roar of wind from a cavern. It seemed impossible that the horrible sound of this incensed hinge had not shaken the whole house with the shock of an earthquake: the door pushed by him had taken the alarm, and had called out; the old man would arise, the two old women would scream; help would come; in a quarter of an hour the town would be alive with it, and the gendarmes in pursuit. For a moment he thought he was lost.

He stood still, petrified like the pillar of salt, not daring to stir. Some minutes passed. The door was wide open; he ventured a look into the room. Nothing had moved. He listened. Nothing was stirring in the house. The noise of the rusty hinge had wakened nobody.

This first danger was over, but still he felt within him a frightful tumult. Nevertheless he did not flinch. Not even when he thought he was lost had he flinched. His only thought was to make an end of it quickly. He took one step and was in the room.

A deep calm filled the chamber. Here and there indistinct, confused forms could be distinguished; which by day, were papers scattered over a table, open folios, books piled on a stool, an arm-chair with clothes on it, a *prie-dieu*, but now were only dark corners and whitish spots. Jean Valjean advanced, carefully avoiding the furniture. At the further end of the room he could hear the equal and quiet breathing of the sleeping bishop.

Suddenly he stopped: he was near the bed, he had reached it sooner than he thought.

Nature sometimes joins her effects and her appearances to our acts with a sort of serious and intelligent appropriateness, as if she would compel us to reflect. For nearly a half hour a great cloud had darkened the sky. At the moment when Jean Valjean paused before the bed the cloud broke as if purposely, and a ray of moonlight crossing the high window, suddenly lighted up the bishop's pale face. He slept tranquilly. He was almost entirely dressed, though in bed, on account of the cold nights of the lower Alps, with a dark woollen garment which covered his arms to the wrists. His head had fallen on the pillow in the unstudied attitude of slumber; over the side of the bed hung his hand, ornamented with the pastoral ring, and which had done so many good deeds, so many pious acts. His entire countenance was lit up with a vague expression of content, hope, and happiness. It was more than a smile and almost a radiance. On his forehead rested the indescribable reflection of an unseen light. The souls of the upright in sleep have vision of a mysterious heaven.

A reflection from this heaven shone upon the bishop.

But it was also a luminous transparency, for this heaven was within him; this heaven was his conscience.

At the instant when the moonbeam overlay, so to speak, this

inward radiance, the sleeping bishop appeared as if in a halo. But it was very mild, and veiled in an ineffable twilight. The moon in the sky, nature drowsing, the garden without a pulse, the quiet house, the hour, the moment, the silence, added something strangely solemn and unutterable to the venerable repose of this man, and enveloped his white locks and his closed eyes with a serene and majestic glory, this face where all was hope and confidence—this old man's head and infant's slumber.

There was something of divinity almost in this man, thus unconsciously august.

Jean Valjean was in the shadow with the iron drill in his hand erect, motionless, terrified, at this radiant figure. He had never seen anything comparable to it. This confidence filled him with fear. The moral world has no greater spectacle than this; a troubled and restless conscience on the verge of committing an evil deed, contemplating the sleep of a good man.

This sleep in this solitude, with a neighbour such as he, contained a touch of the sublime, which he felt vaguely but powerfully.

None could have told what was within him, not even himself. To attempt to realise it, the utmost violence must be imagined in the presence of the most extreme mildness. In his face nothing could be distinguished with certainty. It was a sort of haggard astonishment. He saw it; that was all. But what were his thoughts; it would have been impossible to guess. It was clear that he was moved and agitated. But of what nature was this emotion?

He did not remove his eyes from the old man. The only thing which was plain from his attitude and his countenance was a strange indecision. You would have said he was hesitating between two realms, that of the doomed and that of the saved. He appeared ready either to cleave this skull, or to kiss this hand.

In a few moments he raised his left hand slowly to his forehead and took off his hat; then, letting his hand fall with the same slowness, Jean Valjean resumed his contemplations, his cap in his left hand, his club in his right, and his hair bristling on his fierce-looking head.

Under this frightful gaze the bishop still slept in profoundest peace.

The crucifix above the mantelpiece was dimly visible in the

moonlight, apparently extending its arms towards both, with a benediction for one and a pardon for the other.

Suddenly Jean Valjean put on his cap, then passed quickly, without looking at the bishop, along the bed, straight to the cupboard which he perceived near its head; he raised the drill to force the lock; the key was in it; he opened it; the first thing he saw was the basket of silver, he took it, crossed the room with hasty stride, careless of noise, reached the door, entered the oratory, took his stick, stepped out, put the silver in his knapsack, threw away the basket, ran across the garden, leaped over the wall like a tiger, and fled.

XII
THE BISHOP AT WORK

THE next day at sunrise, Monseigneur Bienvenu was walking in the garden. Madame Magloire ran towards him quite beside herself.

"Monseigneur, monseigneur," cried she, "does your greatness know where the silver basket is?"

"Yes," said the bishop.

"God be praised!" said she, "I did not know what had become of it."

The bishop had just found the basket on a flower-bed. He gave it to Madame Magloire and said: "There it is."

"Yes," said she, "but there is nothing in it. The silver?"

"Ah!" said the bishop, "it is the silver then that troubles you. I do not know where that is."

"Good heavens! it is stolen. That man who came last night stole it."

And in the twinkling of an eye, with all the agility of which her age was capable, Madame Magloire ran to the oratory, went into the alcove, and came back to the bishop. The bishop was bending with some sadness over a cochlearia des Guillons, which the basket had broken in falling. He looked up at Madame Magloire's cry:

"Monseigneur, the man has gone! the silver is stolen!"

While she was uttering this exclamation her eyes fell on an angle of the garden where she saw traces of an escalade. A capstone of the wall had been thrown down.

"See, there is where he got out; he jumped into Cochefilet lane. The abominable fellow! he has stolen our silver!"

The bishop was silent for a moment, then raising his serious eyes, he said mildly to Madame Magloire:

"Now first, did this silver belong to us?"

Madame Magloire did not answer; after a moment the bishop continued:

"Madame Magloire, I have for a long time wrongfully withheld this silver; it belonged to the poor. Who was this man? A poor man evidently."

"Alas! alas!" returned Madame Magloire. "It is not on my account or mademoiselle's; it is all the same to us. But it is on yours, monseigneur. What is monsieur going to eat from now?"

The bishop looked at her with amazement:

"How so! have we no tin plates?"

Madame Magloire shrugged her shoulders.

"Tin smells."

"Well, then, iron plates."

Madame Magloire made an expressive gesture.

"Iron tastes."

"Well," said the bishop, "then, wooden plates."

In a few minutes he was breakfasting at the same table at which Jean Valjean sat the night before. While breakfasting, Monseigneur Bienvenu pleasantly remarked to his sister who said nothing, and Madame Magloire who was grumbling to herself, that there was really no need even of a wooden spoon or fork to dip a piece of bread into a cup of milk.

"Was there ever such an idea?" said Madame Magloire to herself, as she went backwards and forwards: "to take in a man like that, and to give him a bed beside him; and yet what a blessing it was that he did nothing but steal! Oh, my stars! it makes the chills run over me when I think of it!"

Just as the brother and sister were rising from the table, there was a knock at the door.

"Come in," said the bishop.

The door opened. A strange, fierce group appeared on the threshold. Three men were holding a fourth by the collar. The three men were gendarmes; the fourth Jean Valjean.

A brigadier of gendarmes, who appeared to head the group, was near the door. He advanced towards the bishop, giving a military salute.

"Monseigneur," said he—

At this word Jean Valjean, who was sullen and seemed entirely cast down, raised his head with a stupefied air—

"Monseigneur!" he murmured, "then it is not the curé!"

"Silence!" said a gendarme, "it is monseigneur, the bishop."

In the meantime Monsieur Bienvenu had approached as quickly as his great age permitted:

"Ah, there you are!" said he, looking towards Jean Valjean. "I am glad to see you. But! I gave you the candlesticks also, which are silver like the rest, and would bring two hundred francs. Why did you not take them along with your plates?"

Jean Valjean opened his eyes and looked at the bishop with an expression which no human tongue could describe.

"Monseigneur," said the brigadier, "then what this man said was true? We met him. He was going like a man who was running away, and we arrested him in order to see. He had this silver."

"And he told you," interrupted the bishop, with a smile, "that it had been given him by a good old priest with whom he had passed the night. I see it all. And you brought him back here? It is all a mistake."

"If that is so," said the brigadier, "we can let him go."

"Certainly," replied the bishop.

The gendarmes released Jean Valjean, who shrank back—

"Is it true that they let me go?" he said in a voice almost inarticulate, as if he were speaking in his sleep.

"Yes! you can go. Do you not understand?" said a gendarme.

"My friend," said the bishop, "before you go away, here are your candlesticks; take them."

He went to the mantelpiece, took the two candlesticks, and brought them to Jean Valjean. The two women beheld the action without a word, or gesture, or look, that might disturb the bishop.

Jean Valjean was trembling in every limb. He took the two candlesticks mechanically, and with a wild appearance.

"Now," said the bishop, "go in peace. By the way, my friend, when you come again, you need not come through the garden. You can always come in and go out by the front door. It is closed only with a latch, day or night."

Then turning to the gendarmes, he said:

"Messieurs, you can retire." The gendarmes withdrew.

Jean Valjean felt like a man who is just about to faint.

The bishop approached him, and said, in a low voice:

"Forget not, never forget that you have promised me to use this silver to become an honest man."

Jean Valjean, who had no recollection of this promise, stood confounded. The bishop had laid much stress upon these words as he uttered them. He continued, solemnly:

"Jean Valjean, my brother: you belong no longer to evil, but to good. It is your soul that I am buying for you. I withdraw it from dark thoughts and from the spirit of perdition, and I give it to God!"

XIII
PETIT GERVAIS

JEAN VALJEAN went out of the city as if he were escaping. He made all haste to get into the open country, taking the first lanes and by-paths that offered, without noticing that he was every moment retracing his steps. He wandered thus all the morning. He had eaten nothing, but he felt no hunger. He was the prey of a multitude of new sensations. He felt somewhat angry, he knew not against whom. He could not have told whether he were touched or humiliated. There came over him, at times, a strange relenting which he struggled with, and to which he opposed the hardening of his past twenty years. This condition wearied him. He saw, with disquietude, shaken within him that species of frightful calm which the injustice of his fate had given him. He asked himself what should replace it. At times he would really have liked better to be in prison with the gendarmes, and that things had not happened thus; that would have given him less agitation. Although the season was well advanced, there were yet here and there a few late flowers in the hedges, the odour of which, as it met him in his walk, recalled the memories of his childhood. These memories were almost insupportable, it was so long since they had occurred to him.

Unspeakable thoughts thus gathered in his mind the whole day.

As the sun was sinking towards the horizon, lengthening the shadow on the ground of the smallest pebble, Jean Valjean was seated behind a thicket in a large reddish plain, an absolute desert. There was no horizon but the Alps. Not even the steeple of a village church. Jean Valjean might have been three leagues from D——. A by-path which crossed the plain passed a few steps from the thicket.

In the midst of this meditation, which would have heightened not a little the frightful effect of his rags to any one who might have met him, he heard a joyous sound.

He turned his head, and saw coming along the path a little Savoyard, a dozen years old, singing, with his hurdygurdy at his side, and his marmot box on his back.

One of those pleasant and gay youngsters who go from place to place, with their knees sticking through their trousers.

Always singing, the boy stopped from time to time, and played at tossing up some pieces of money that he had in his hand, probably his whole fortune. Among them there was one forty-sous piece.

The boy stopped by the side of the thicket without seeing Jean Valjean, and tossed up his handful of sous; until this time he had skilfully caught the whole of them upon the back of his hand.

This time the forty-sous piece escaped him, and rolled towards the thicket, near Jean Valjean.

Jean Valjean put his foot upon it.

The boy, however, had followed the piece with his eye, and had seen where it went.

He was not frightened, and walked straight to the man.

It was an entirely solitary place. Far as the eye could reach there was no one on the plain or in the path. Nothing could be heard, but the faint cries of a flock of birds of passage, that were flying across the sky at an immense height. The child turned his back to the sun, which made his hair like threads of gold, and flushed the savage face of Jean Valjean with a lurid glow.

"Monsieur," said the little Savoyard, with that childish confidence which is made up of ignorance and innocence, "my piece?"

"What is your name?" said Jean Valjean.

"Petit Gervais, monsieur."

"Get out," said Jean Valjean.

"Monsieur," continued the boy, "give me my piece."

Jean Valjean dropped his head and did not answer.

The child began again:

"My piece, monsieur!"

Jean Valjean's eye remained fixed on the ground.

"My piece!" exclaimed the boy, "my white piece! my silver!"

Jean Valjean did not appear to understand. The boy took him by the collar of his blouse and shook him. And at the same time he made an effort to move the big, iron-soled shoe which was placed upon his treasure.

"I want my piece! my forty-sous piece!"

The child began to cry. Jean Valjean raised his head. He still kept his seat. His look was troubled. He looked upon the boy with an air of wonder, then reached out his hand towards his stick, and exclaimed in a terrible voice: "Who is there?"

"Me, monsieur," answered the boy. "Petit Gervais! me! me! give me my forty sous, if you please! Take away your foot, monsieur, if you please!" Then becoming angry, small as he was, and almost threatening:

"Come, now, will you take away your foot? Why don't you take away your foot?"

"Ah! you here yet!" said Jean Valjean, and rising hastily to his feet, without releasing the piece of money, he added: "You'd better take care of yourself!"

The boy looked at him in terror, then began to tremble from head to foot, and after a few seconds of stupor, took to flight and ran with all his might without daring to turn his head or to utter a cry.

At a little distance, however, he stopped for want of breath, and Jean Valjean in his reverie heard him sobbing.

In a few minutes the boy was gone.

The sun had gone down.

The shadows were deepening around Jean Valjean. He had not eaten during the day; probably he had some fever.

He had remained standing, and had not changed his attitude since the child fled. His breathing was at long and unequal intervals. His eyes were fixed on a spot ten or twelve steps before him, and seemed to be studying with profound attention the form of an old piece of blue crockery that was lying in the grass. All at once he shivered; he began to feel the cold night air.

He pulled his cap down over his forehead, sought mechanically to fold and button his blouse around him, stepped forward and stooped to pick up his stick.

At that instant he perceived the forty-sous piece which his foot had half buried in the ground, and which glistened among the pebbles. It was like an electric shock. "What is that?" said he, between his teeth. He drew back a step or two, then stopped without the power to withdraw his gaze from this point which his foot had covered the instant before, as if the thing that glistened there in the obscurity had been an open eye fixed upon him.

After a few minutes, he sprang convulsively towards the piece of money, seized it, and, rising, looked away over the plain, straining his eyes towards all points of the horizon, standing and trembling like a frightened deer which is seeking a place of refuge.

He saw nothing. Night was falling, the plain was cold and bare, thick purple mists were rising in the glimmering twilight.

He said: "Oh!" and began to walk rapidly in the direction in which the child had gone. After some thirty steps, he stopped, looked about, and saw nothing.

Then he called with all his might "Petit Gervais! Petit Gervais!"

And then he listened.

There was no answer.

The country was desolate and gloomy. On all sides was space. There was nothing about him but a shadow in which his gaze was lost, and a silence in which his voice was lost.

A biting norther was blowing, which gave a kind of dismal life to everything about him. The bushes shook their little thin arms with an incredible fury. One would have said that they were threatening and pursuing somebody.

He began to walk again, then quickened his pace to a run, and from time to time stopped and called out in that solitude, in a most desolate and terrible voice:

"Petit Gervais! Petit Gervais!"

Surely, if the child had heard him, he would have been frightened, and would have hid himself. But doubtless the boy was already far away.

He met a priest on horseback. He went up to him and said:

"Monsieur curé, have you seen a child go by?"

"No," said the priest.

"Petit Gervais was his name?"

"I have seen nobody."

He took two five-franc pieces from his bag, and gave them to the priest.

"Monsieur curé, this is for your poor. Monsieur curé, he is a little fellow, about ten years old, with a marmot, I think, and a hurdygurdy. He went this way. One of these Savoyards, you know?"

"I have not seen him."

"Petit Gervais? is his village near here? can you tell me?"

"If it be as you say, my friend, the little fellow is a foreigner. They roam about this country. Nobody knows them."

Jean Valjean hastily took out two more five-franc pieces, and gave them to the priest.

"For your poor," said he.

Then he added wildly:

"Monsieur abbé, have me arrested. I am a robber."

The priest put spurs to his horse, and fled in great fear.

Jean Valjean began to run again in the direction which he had first taken.

He went on in this wise for a considerable distance, looking around, calling and shouting, but met nobody else. Two or three times he left the path to look at what seemed to be somebody lying down or crouching; it was only low bushes or rocks. Finally, at a place where three paths met, he stopped. The moon had risen. He strained his eyes in the distance, and called out once more "Petit Gervais! Petit Gervais! Petit Gervais!" His cries died away into the mist, without even awakening an echo. Again he murmured: "Petit Gervais!" but with a feeble, and almost inarticulate voice. That was his last effort; his knees suddenly bent under him, as if an invisible power overwhelmed him at a blow, with the weight of his bad conscience; he fell exhausted upon a great stone, his hands clenched in his hair, and his face on his knees, and exclaimed: "What a wretch I am!"

Then his heart swelled, and he burst into tears. It was the first time he had wept for nineteen years.

When Jean Valjean left the bishop's house, as we have seen, his mood was one that he had never known before. He could understand nothing of what was passing within him. He set himself stubbornly in opposition to the angelic deeds and the gentle words of the old man, "you have promised me to become an honest man. I am purchasing your soul, I withdraw it from the spirit of perversity and I give it to God Almighty." This came back to him incessantly. To this celestial tenderness, he opposed pride, which is the fortress of evil in man. He felt dimly that the pardon of this priest was the hardest assault, and the most formidable attack which he had yet sustained; that his hardness of heart would be complete, if it resisted this kindness; that if he yielded, he must renounce that hatred with which the acts of other men had for so many years filled his soul, and in which he found satisfaction; that, this time, he must conquer or be conquered, and that the struggle, a gigantic and decisive struggle, had begun between his own wickedness, and the goodness of this man.

In view of all these things, he moved like a drunken man. While thus walking on with haggard look, had he a distinct perception of what might be to him the result of his adventure at D——? Did he hear those mysterious murmurs which warn or entreat the spirit at certain moments of life? Did a voice whisper in his ear that he had just passed through the decisive hour of his destiny, that there was no longer a middle course for him, that if, thereafter, he should not be the best of men, he would be the worst, that he must now, so to speak, mount higher than the bishop, or fall lower than the galley slave; that, if he would become good, he must become an angel; that, if he would remain wicked, he must become a monster?

Here we must again ask those questions, which we have already proposed elsewhere: was some confused shadow of all this formed in his mind? Certainly, misfortune, we have said, draws out the intelligence; it is doubtful, however, if Jean Valjean was in a condition to discern all that we here point out. If these ideas occurred to him, he but caught a glimpse, he did not see; and the only effect was to throw him into an inexpressible and distressing confusion. Being just out of that misshapen and gloomy thing which is called the galleys, the bishop had hurt his soul, as a too vivid light would have hurt his eyes on coming out of the dark. The future life, the possible life that was offered to him thenceforth, all pure and radiant, filled him with trembling and anxiety. He no longer knew really where he was. Like an owl who should see the sun suddenly rise, the convict had been dazzled and blinded by virtue.

One thing was certain, nor did he himself doubt it, that he was no longer the same man, that all was changed in him, that it was no longer in his power to prevent the bishop from having talked to him and having touched him.

In this frame of mind, he had met Petit Gervais, and stolen his forty sous. Why? He could not have explained it, surely; was it the final effect, the final effort of the evil thoughts he had brought from the galleys, a remnant of impulse, a result of what is called in physics *acquired force*? It was that, and it was also perhaps even less than that. We will say plainly, it was not he who had stolen, it was not the man, it was the beast which, from habit and instinct, had stupidly set its foot upon that money, while the intellect was struggling in the midst of so many new and unknown influences. When the intellect awoke and saw this act of the brute, Jean Valjean recoiled in anguish and uttered a cry of horror.

It was a strange phenomenon, possible only in the condition in which he then was, but the fact is, that in stealing this money from that child, he had done a thing of which he was no longer capable.

However that may be, this last misdeed had a decisive effect upon him; it rushed across the chaos of his intellect and dissipated it, set the light on one side and the dark clouds on the other, and acted upon his soul, in the condition it was in, as certain chemical reagents act upon a turbid mixture by precipitating one element and producing a clear solution of the other.

At first, even before self-examination and reflection, distractedly, like one who seeks to escape, he endeavoured to find the boy to give him back his money; then, when he found that that was useless and impossible, he stopped in despair. At the very moment when he exclaimed: "What a wretch I am!" he saw himself as he was, and was already so far separated from himself that it seemed to him that he was only a phantom, and that he had there before him, in flesh and bone with his stick in his hand, his blouse on his back, his knapsack filled with stolen articles on his shoulders, with his stern and gloomy face, and his thoughts full of abominable projects, the hideous galley slave, Jean Valjean.

Excess of misfortune, we have remarked, had made him, in some sort, a visionary. This then was like a vision. He veritably saw this Jean Valjean, this ominous face, before him. He was on the point of asking himself who that man was, and he was horror-stricken by it.

His brain was in one of those violent, and yet frightfully calm, conditions where reverie is so profound that it swallows up reality. We no longer see the objects that are before us, but we see, as if outside of ourselves, the forms that we have in our minds.

He beheld himself then, so to speak, face to face, and at the same time, across that hallucination, he saw, at a mysterious distance, a sort of light which he took at first to be a torch. Examining more attentively this light which dawned upon his conscience, he recognised that it had a human form, and that this torch was the bishop.

His conscience weighed in turn these two men thus placed before it, the bishop and Jean Valjean. Anything less than the first would have failed to soften the second. By one of those singular effects which are peculiar to this kind of ecstasy, as his reverie continued, the bishop grew grander and more resplendent in his eyes, Jean Valjean shrank and faded away. At one moment he was but a shadow. Suddenly he disappeared. The bishop alone remained.

He filled the whole soul of this wretched man with a magnificent radiance.

Jean Valjean wept long. He shed hot tears, he wept bitterly, with more weakness than a woman, with more terror than a child.

While he wept, the light grew brighter and brighter in his mind—an extraordinary light, a light at once transporting and terrible. His past life, his first offence, his long expiation, his brutal exterior, his hardened interior, his release made glad by so many schemes of vengeance, what had happened to him at the bishop's, his last action, this theft of forty sous from a child, a crime meaner and the more monstrous that it came after the bishop's pardon, all this returned and appeared to him, clearly, but in a light that he had never seen before. He beheld his life, and it seemed to him horrible; his soul, and it seemed to him frightful. There was, however, a softened light upon that life and upon that soul. It seemed to him that he was looking upon Satan by the light of Paradise.

How long did he weep thus? What did he do after weeping? Where did he go? Nobody ever knew. It is known simply that, on that very night, the stage-driver who drove at that time on the Grenoble route, and arrived at D—— about three o'clock in the morning, saw, as he passed through the bishop's street, a man in the attitude of prayer, kneel upon the pavement in the shadow, before the door of Monseigneur Bienvenu.

I
THE YEAR 1817

THE year 1817 was that which Louis XVIII., with a certain royal assumption not devoid of stateliness, styled the twenty-second year of his reign. It was the year when M. Bruguière de Sorsum was famous. All the hairdressers' shops, hoping for the return of powder and birds of Paradise, were bedizened with azure and fleurs-de-lis. It was the honest time when Count Lynch sat every Sunday as churchwarden on the official bench at Saint Germain des Prés, in the dress of a peer of France, with his red ribbon and long nose, and that majesty of profile peculiar to a man who has done a brilliant deed. The brilliant deed committed by M. Lynch was that, being mayor of Bordeaux on the 12th of March, 1814, he had surrendered the city a little too soon to the Duke of Angoulême. Hence his peerage. In 1817 it was the fashion to swallow up little boys from four to six years old in great morocco caps with ears, strongly resembling the chimney-pots of the Esquimaux. The French army was dressed in white after the Austrian style; regiments were called legions, and wore, instead of numbers, the names of the departments. Napoleon was at St Helena, and as England would not give him green cloth, had had his old coats turned. In 1817, Pellegrini sang; Mademoiselle Bigottini danced; Potier reigned; Odry was not yet in existence. Madame Saqui succeeded to Forioso. There were Prussians still in France. M. Delalot was a personage. Legitimacy had just asserted itself by cutting off the fist and then the head of Pleignier, Carbonneau, and Tolleron. Prince Talleyrand, the grand chamberlain, and Abbé Louis, the designated minister of the finances, looked each other in the face, laughing like two augurs; both had celebrated the mass of the Federation in the Champ-de-Mars on the 14th of July, 1790; Talleyrand had said it as bishop, Louis had served him as deacon. In 1817, in the cross-walks of this same Champ-de-Mars, were seen huge wooden cylinders painted blue, with traces of eagles and bees, that had lost their gilding, lying in the rain, and rotting in the grass. There were the columns which, two years before, had supported the estrade of the emperor in the Champ-de-Mai. They were blackened here and there from the bivouac-fires of

the Austrians in barracks near the Gros-Caillou. Two or three
of these columns had disappeared in the fires of these bivouacs,
and had warmed the huge hands of the kaiserlics. The Champ-
de-Mai was remarkable from the fact of having been held in the
month of June, and on the Champ-de-Mars. In the year 1817
two things were popular—Voltaire-Touquet and Chartist snuff-
boxes. The latest Parisian sensation was the crime of Dautun,
who had thrown his brother's head into the fountain of the
Marché-aux-Fleurs. People were beginning to find fault with
the minister of the navy for having no news of that fated frigate,
La Méduse, which was to cover Chaumareix with shame, and
Géricault with glory. Colonel Selves went to Egypt, there to
become Soliman-Pacha. The palace of the Thermes, Rue de La
Harpe, was turned into a cooper's shop. On the platform of the
octagonal tower of the hotel de Cluny, the little board shed was
still to be seen, which had served as observatory to Messier, the
astronomer of the navy under Louis XVI. The Duchess of Duras
read to three or four friends, in her boudoir, furnished in sky-
blue satin, the manuscript of *Ourika*. The N's were erased from
the Louvre. The bridge of Austerlitz abdicated its name, and
became the bridge of the Jardin-du-Roi, an enigma which disguised at once the bridge of Austerlitz and the Jardin-des-
Plantes. Louis XVIII., absently annotating Horace with his
finger-nail while thinking about heroes that had become
emperors, and shoemakers that had become dauphins, had two
cares, Napoleon and Mathurin Bruneau. The French Academy
gave as a prize theme, *The happiness which Study procures*. M.
Bellart was eloquent, officially. In his shadow was seen taking
root the future Attorney-General, de Broë, promised to the
sarcasms of Paul Louis Courier. There was a counterfeit
Chateaubriand called Marchangy, as there was to be later a
counterfeit Marchangy called d'Arlincourt. *Claire d'Albe* and
Malek Adel were masterpieces; Madame Cottin was declared
the first writer of the age. The Institute struck from its list the
academician, Napoleon Bonaparte. A royal ordinance established a naval school at Angoulême, for the Duke of Angoulême
being Grand Admiral, it was evident that the town of Angoulême had by right all the qualities of a seaport, without which
the monarchical principle would have been assailed. The question whether the pictures, representing acrobats, which spiced
the placards of Franconi and drew together the blackguards of

the streets, should be tolerated, was agitated in the cabinet councils. M. Paër, the author of *l'Agnese*, an honest man with square jaws and a wart on his cheek, directed the small, select concerts of the Marchioness de Sassenaye, Rue de la Ville-l'Evêque. All the young girls sang *l'Ermite de Saint Avelle*, words by Edmond Géraud. The *Nain juane* was transformed into the *Miroir*. The Café Lemblin stood out for the emperor in opposition to the Café Valois, which was in favour of the Bourbons. A marriage had just been made with a Sicilian princess for the Duke of Berry, who was already in reality regarded with suspicion by Louvel. Madame de Staël had been dead a year. Mademoiselle Mars was hissed by the body-guards. The great journals were all small. The form was limited, but the liberty was large. *Le Constitutionnel* was constitutional; *La Minerve* called Chateaubriand, *Chateaubriant*. This excited great laughter among the citizens at the expense of the great writer.

In purchased journals, prostituted journalists insulted the outlaws of 1815; David no longer had talent, Arnault no longer had ability, Carnot no longer had probity, Soult had never gained a victory; it is true that Napoleon no longer had genius. Everybody knows that letters sent through the post to an exile rarely reach their destination, the police making it a religious duty to intercept them. This fact is by no means a new one; Descartes complained of it in his banishment. Now, David having shown some feeling in a Belgian journal at not receiving the letters addressed to him, this seemed ludicrous to the royalist papers, who seized the occasion to ridicule the exile. To say, *regicides*, instead of *voters*, *enemies* instead of *allies*, *Napoleon* instead of *Buonaparte*, separated two men more than an abyss. All people of common sense agreed that the era of revolutions had been for ever closed by King Louis XVIII., surnamed "The immortal author of the Charter." At the terreplain of the Pont Neuf, the word *Redivivus* was sculptured on the pedestal which awaited the statue of Henri IV. M. Piet at Rue Thérèse, No. 4, was sketching the plan of his cabal to consolidate the monarchy. The leaders of the Right said, in grave dilemmas, "We must write to Bacol." Messrs. Canuel O'Mahony and Chappedelaine made a beginning, not altogether without the approbation of Monsieur, of what was afterwards to become the "conspiracy of the Bord de l'Eau." L'Epingle Noire plotted on its side; Delaverderie held interviews with Trogoff; M. Decazes, a mind

in some degree liberal, prevailed. Chateaubriand, standing every
morning at his window in the Rue Saint Dominique, No. 27,
in stocking pantaloons and slippers, his grey hair covered with a
Madras handkerchief, a mirror before his eyes, and a complete
case of dental instruments open before him, cleaned his teeth
which were excellent, while dictating *La Monarchie selon la
Charte* to M. Pilorge, his secretary. The critics in authority preferred Lafon to Talma. M. de Féletz signed himself A., M.
Hoffman signed himself Z. Charles Nodier was writing *Thérèse
Aubert*. Divorce was abolished. The lyceums called themselves
colleges. The students, decorated on the collar with a golden
fleur-de-lis, pommelled each other over the King of Rome.
The secret police of the palace denounced to her royal highness,
Madame, the portrait of the Duke of Orleans, which was everywhere to be seen, and which looked better in the uniform of
colonel-general of hussars than the Duke of Berry in the uniform of colonel-general of dragoons—a serious matter. The city
of Paris regilded the dome of the Invalides at its expense. Grave
citizens asked each other what M. de Trinquelague would do in
such or such a case; M. Clausel de Montals differed on sundry
points from M. Clausel de Coussergues; M. de Salaberry was
not satisfied. Comedy-writer Picard, of the Academy to which
comedy-writer Molière could not belong, had *Les deux Phili-
berts* played at the Odeon, on the pediment of which, the
removal of the letters still permitted the inscription to be read
distinctly: THEATRE DE L'IMPÉRATRICE. People took sides for or
against Cugnet de Montarlot. Fabvier was factious; Bavoux was
revolutionary. The bookseller Pelicier published an edition of
Voltaire under the title, *Works of Voltaire*, of the French Academy. "That will attract buyers," said the naive publisher. The
general opinion was that M. Charles Loyson would be the
genius of the age; envy was beginning to nibble at him, a sign
of glory, and the line was made on him——

"Même quand Loyson vole, on sent qu'il a despattes."

Cardinal Fesch refusing to resign, Monsieur de Pins, Archbishop of Amasie, administered the diocese of Lyons. The quarrel of the Vallée des Dappes commenced between France and
Switzerland by a memorial from Captain, afterwards General
Dufour. Saint-Simon, unknown, was building up his sublime
dream. There was a celebrated Fourier in the Academy of

Sciences whom posterity has forgotten, and an obscure Fourier in some unknown garret whom the future will remember. Lord Byron was beginning to dawn; a note to a poem of Millevoye introduced him to France as a *certain Lord Baron*. David d'Angers was endeavouring to knead marble. The Abbé Caron spoke with praise, in a small party of Seminarists in the cul-de-sac of the Feuillantines, of an unknown priest, Félicité Robert by name, who was afterwards Lamennais. A thing which smoked and clacked on the Seine, making the noise of a swimming dog, went and came beneath the windows of the Tuileries, from the Pont Royal to the Pont Louis XV.; it was a piece of mechanism of no great value, a sort of toy, the day-dream of a visionary, a Utopia—a steamboat. The Parisians looked upon the useless thing with indifference. Monsieur Vaublanc, wholesale reformer of the Institute by royal ordinance and distinguished author of several academicians, after having made them, could not make himself one. The Faubourg Saint-Germain and the Pavillon Marsan desired Monsieur Delaveau for prefect of police, on account of his piety. Dupuytren and Récamier quarrelled in the amphitheatre of the Ecole de Médicine, and shook their fists in each other's faces, over the divinity of Christ. Cuvier, with one eye on the book of Genesis and the other on nature, was endeavouring to please the bigoted reaction by reconciling fossils with texts and making the mastodons support Moses. Monsieur François de Neufchâteau, the praiseworthy cultivator of the memory of Parmentier, was making earnest efforts to have *pomme de terre* pronounced *parmentière*, without success. Abbé Grégoire, ex-bishop, ex-member of the National Convention, and ex-senator, had passed to the condition of the "infamous Grégoire," in royalist polemics. The expression which we have just employed, "passed to the condition," was denounced as a neologism by Monsieur Royer-Collard. The new stone could still be distinguished by its whiteness under the third arch of the bridge of Jena, which, two years before, had been used to stop up the entrance of the mine bored by Blücher to blow up the bridge. Justice summoned to her bar a man who had said aloud, on seeing Count d'Artois entering Notre-Dame, "Sapristi! I regret the time when I saw Bonaparte and Talma entering the Bal-Savage, arm in arm." Seditious language. Six months' imprisonment.

Traitors showed themselves stripped even of hypocrisy; men

who had gone over to the enemy on the eve of a battle made no concealment of their bribes, and shamelessly walked abroad in daylight in the cynicism of wealth and dignities; deserters of Ligny and Quatre-Bras, in the brazenness of their purchased shame, exposed the nakedness of their devotion to monarchy, forgetting the commonest requirements of public decency.

Such was the confused mass of events that floated pell-mell on the surface of the year 1817, and is now forgotten. History neglects almost all these peculiarities, nor can it do otherwise; it is under the dominion of infinity. Nevertheless, these details, which are wrongly called little—there are neither little facts in humanity nor little leaves in vegetation—are useful. The physiognomy of the years makes up the face of the century.

In this year, 1817, four young Parisians played "a good farce."

II
DOUBLE QUATUOR

THESE Parisians were, one from Toulouse, another from Limoges, the third from Cahors, and the fourth from Montauban; but they were students, and to say student is to say Parisian; to study in Paris is to be born in Paris.

These young men were remarkable for nothing; everybody has seen such persons, the four first comers will serve as samples; neither good nor bad, neither learned nor ignorant, neither talented nor stupid; handsome in that charming April of life which we call twenty. They were four Oscars; for at this time, Arthurs were not yet in existence. *Burn the perfumes of Arabia in his honour*, exclaims the romance. *Oscar approaches! Oscar, I am about to see him!* Ossian was in fashion, elegance was Scandinavian and Caledonian; the pure English did not prevail till later, and the first of the Arthurs, Wellington, had but just won the victory of Waterloo.

The first of these Oscars was called Félix Tholomyès, of Toulouse; the second, Listolier, of Cahors; the third, Fameuil, of Limoges; and the last, Blacheville, of Montauban. Of course each had his mistress. Blacheville loved Favourite, so called, because she had been in England; Listolier adored Dahlia, who had taken the name of a flower as her *nom de guerre*, Fameuil idolised Zéphine, the diminutive of Josephine, and Tholomyès had Fantine, called *the Blonde*, on account of her beautiful hair, the colour of the sun. Favourite, Dahlia, Zéphine, and Fantine were four enchanting girls, perfumed and sparkling, something of workwomen still, since they had not wholly given up the needle, agitated by love-affairs, yet preserving on their countenances a remnant of the serenity of labour, and in their souls that flower of purity, which in woman survives the first fall. One of the four was called the child, because she was the youngest; and another was called the old one—the Old One was twenty-three. To conceal nothing, the three first were more experienced, more careless, and better versed in the ways of the world than Fantine, the Blonde, who was still in her first illusion.

Dahlia, Zéphine, and Favourite especially, could not say as much. There had been already more than one episode in their scarcely commenced romance, and the lover called Adolphe in the first chapter, was found as Alphonse in the second, and Gustave in the third. Poverty and coquetry are fatal counsellors; the one grumbles, the other flatters, and the beautiful daughters of the people have both whispering in their ear, each on its side. Their ill-guarded souls listen. Thence their fall, and the stones that are cast at them. They are overwhelmed with the splendour of all that is immaculate and inaccessible. Alas! was the Jungfrau ever hungry?

Favourite, having been in England, was the admiration of Zéphine and Dahlia. She had had at a very early age a home of her own. Her father was a brutal, boasting old professor of mathematics, never married, and a rake, despite his years. When young, he one day saw the dress of a chambermaid catch in the fender, and fell in love through the accident. Favourite was the result. Occasionally she met her father, who touched his hat to her. One morning, an old woman with a fanatical air entered her rooms, and asked, "you do not know me, mademoiselle?"— "No."—" "I am your mother."—The old woman directly opened the buffet, ate and drank her fill, sent for a bed that she had, and made herself at home. This mother was a devotee and a grumbler; she never spoke to Favourite, remained for hours without uttering a word, breakfasted, dined and supped for four, and went down to the porter's lodge to see visitors and talk ill of her daughter.

What had attracted Dahlia to Listolier, to others perhaps, to indolence, was her beautiful, rosy finger-nails. How could such nails work! She who will remain virtuous must have no compassion for her hands. As to Zéphine, she had conquered Fameuil by her rebellious yet caressing little way of saying "yes, sir."

The young men were comrades, the young girls were friends. Such loves are always accompanied by such friendships.

Wisdom and philosophy are two things; a proof of which is that, with all necessary reservations for these little, irregular households, Favourite, Zéphine, and Dahlia, were philosophic, and Fantine was wise.

"Wise!" you will say, and Tholomyès? Solomon would answer that love is a part of wisdom. We content ourselves with saying that the love of Fantine was a first, an only, a faithful love.

She was the only one of the four who had been petted by but one.

Fantine was one of those beings which are brought forth from the heart of the people. Sprung from the most unfathomable depths of social darkness, she bore on her brow the mark of the anonymous and unknown. She was born at M——— on M———. Who were her parents? None could tell, she had never known either father or mother. She was called Fantine—why so? because she had never been known by any other name. At the time of her birth, the Directory was still in existence. She could have no family name, for she had no family; she could have no baptismal name, for then there was no church. She was named after the pleasure of the first passer-by who found her, a mere infant, straying barefoot in the streets. She received a name as she received the water from the clouds on her head when it rained. She was called little Fantine. Nobody knew anything more of her. Such was the manner in which this human being had come into life. At the age of ten, Fantine left the city and went to service among the farmers of the suburbs. At fifteen, she came to Paris, to "seek her fortune." Fantine was beautiful and remained pure as long as she could. She was a pretty blonde with fine teeth. She had gold and pearls for her dowry; but the gold was on her head and the pearls in her mouth.

She worked to live; then, also to live, for the heart too has its hunger, she loved.

She loved Tholomyès.

To him, it was an amour; to her a passion. The streets of the Latin Quarter, which swarm with students and grisettes, saw the beginning of this dream. Fantine, in those labyrinths of the hill of the Pantheon, where so many ties are knotted and unloosed, long fled from Tholomyès, but in such a way as always to meet him again. There is a way of avoiding a person which resembles a search. In short, the eclogue took place.

Blacheville, Listolier, and Fameuil formed a sort of group of which Tholomyès was the head. He was the wit of the company.

Tholomyès was an old student of the old style; he was rich, having an income of four thousand francs—a splendid scandal on the Montagne Sainte-Geneviève. He was a good liver, thirty years old and ill preserved. He was wrinkled, his teeth were broken, and he was beginning to show signs of baldness, of which he said, gaily: "*The head at thirty, the knees at forty.*" His digestion was not good, and he had a weeping eye. But in proportion as his youth died out, his gaiety increased; he replaced his teeth by jests, his hair by joy, his health by irony, and his weeping eye was always laughing. He was dilapidated, but covered with flowers. His youth, decamping long before its time, was beating a retreat in good order, bursting with laughter, and displaying no loss of fire. He had had a piece refused at the Vaudeville; he made verses now and then on any subject; moreover, he doubted everything with an air of superiority—a great power in the eyes of the weak. So, being bald and ironical, he was the chief. Can the word *iron* be the root from which irony is derived?

One day, Tholomyès took the other three aside, and said to them with an oracular gesture:

"For nearly a year, Fantine, Dahlia, Zéphine, and Favourite have been asking us to give them a surprise; we have solemnly promised them one. They are constantly reminding us of it, me especially. Just as the old women at Naples cry to Saint January, '*Faccia gialluta, fa o miracolo*, yellow face, do your miracle,' our pretty ones are always saying: 'Tholomyès, when are you going to be delivered of your surprise?' At the same time our parents are writing for us. Two birds with one stone. It seems to me the time has come. Let us talk it over."

Upon this, Tholomyès lowered his voice, and mysteriously articulated something so ludicrous that a prolonged and enthusiastic giggling arose from the four throats at once, and Blacheville exclaimed: "What an idea!"

An ale-house, filled with smoke, was before them; they entered and the rest of their conference was lost in its shade.

The result of this mystery was a brilliant pleasure party, which took place on the following Sunday, the four young men inviting the four young girls.

III
FOUR TO FOUR

IT is difficult to picture to one's self, at this day, a country party of students and grisettes as it was forty-five years ago. Paris has no longer the same environs; the aspect of what we might call circum-Parisian life has completely changed in half a century; in place of the rude, one-horse chaise, we have now the railroad car; in place of the pinnace, we have now the steamboat; we say Fécamp to-day, as we then said Saint Cloud. The Paris of 1862 is a city which has France for its suburbs.

The four couples scrupulously accomplished all the country follies then possible. It was in the beginning of the holidays, and a warm, clear summer's day. The night before, Favourite, the only one who knew how to write, had written to Tholomyès in the name of the four: "It is lucky to go out early." For this reason, they rose at five in the morning. Then they went to Saint Cloud by the coach, looked at the dry cascade and exclaimed: "How beautiful it must be when there is any water!" breakfasted at the *Tête Noire*, which Castaing had not yet passed, amused themselves with a game of rings at the quincunx of the great basin, ascended to Diogenes' lantern, played roulette with macaroons on the Sèvres bridge, gathered bouquets at Puteaux, bought reed pipes at Neuilly, ate apple puffs everywhere, and were perfectly happy.

The young girls rattled and chattered like uncaged warblers. They were delirious with joy. Now and then they would playfully box the ears of the young men. Intoxication of the morning of life! Adorable years! The wing of the dragon-fly trembles! Oh, ye, whoever you may be, have you memories of the past? Have you walked in the brushwood, thrusting aside the branches for the charming head behind you? Have you glided laughingly down some slope wet with rain, with the woman of your love, who held you back by the hand, exclaiming: "Oh, my new boots! what a condition they are in!"

Let us hasten to say that that joyous annoyance, a shower, was wanting to this good-natured company, although Favourite had said on setting out, with a magisterial and maternal air: "The snails are crawling in the paths. A sign of rain, children."

All four were ravishingly beautiful. A good old classic poet, then in renown, a good man who had an Eléanore, the Chevalier de Labouïsse, who was walking that day under the chestnut trees of Saint Cloud, saw them pass about ten o'clock in the morning, and exclaimed, thinking of the Graces: "There is one too many!" Favourite, the friend of Blacheville, the Old One of twenty-three, ran forward under the broad green branches, leaped across ditches, madly sprang over bushes, and took the lead in the gaiety with the verve of a young faun. Zéphine and Dahlia, whom chance had endowed with a kind of beauty that was heightened and perfected by contrast, kept together through the instinct of coquetry still more than through friendship, and, leaning on each other, affected English attitudes; the first *keepsakes* had just appeared, melancholy was in vogue for women, as Byronism was afterwards for men, and the locks of the tender sex were beginning to fall dishevelled. Zéphine and Dahlia wore their hair in rolls. Listolier and Fameuil, engaged in a discussion on their professors, explained to Fantine the difference between M. Delvincourt and M. Blondeau.

Blacheville seemed to have been created expressly to carry Favourite's dead-leaf-coloured shawl upon his arm on Sunday.

Tholomyès followed, ruling, presiding over the group. He was excessively gay, but one felt the governing power in him. There was dictatorship in his joviality; his principal adornment was a pair of nankeen pantaloons, cut in the elephant-leg fashion, with under-stockings of copper-coloured braid; he had a huge ratten, worth two hundred francs, in his hand, and as he denied himself nothing, a strange thing called a cigar in his mouth. Nothing being sacred to him, he was smoking.

"This Tholomyès is astonishing," said the others, with veneration. "What pantaloons! what energy!"

As to Fantine, she was joy itself. Her splendid teeth had evidently been endowed by God with one function—that of laughing. She carried in her hand rather than on her head her little hat of sewed straw, with long, white strings. Her thick blonde tresses, inclined to wave, and easily escaping from their confinement, obliging her to fasten them continually, seemed designed for the flight of Galatea under the willows. Her rosy lips babbled with enchantment. The corners of her mouth, turned up voluptuously like the antique masks of Erigone, seemed to encourage audacity; but her long, shadowy eyelashes were cast discreetly down towards the lower part of her face as if to check its festive tendencies. Her whole toilette was indescribably harmonious and enchanting. She wore a dress of mauve barège, little reddish-brown buskins, the strings of which were crossed over her fine, white, open-worked stockings, and that species of spencer, invented at Marseilles, the name of which, *canezou*, a corruption of the words *quinze août* in the Canebière dialect, signifies fine weather, warmth, and noon. The three others, less timid as we have said, wore low-necked dresses, which in summer, beneath bonnets covered with flowers, are full of grace and allurement; but by the side of this daring toilette, the canezou of the blonde Fantine, with its transparencies, indiscretions, and concealments, at once hiding and disclosing, seemed a provoking godsend of decency; and the famous court of love, presided over by the Viscountess de Cette, with the sea-green eyes, would probably have given the prize for coquetry to this canezou, which had entered the lists for that of modesty. The simplest is sometimes the wisest. So things go.

A brilliant face, delicate profile, eyes of a deep blue, heavy eyelashes, small, arching feet, the wrists and ankles neatly encased, the white skin showing here and there the azure arborescence of the veins; a cheek small and fresh, a neck robust as that of Egean Juno; the nape firm and supple, shoulders modelled as if by Coustou, with a voluptuous dimple in the centre, just visible through the muslin: a gaiety tempered with reverie, sculptured and exquisite—such was Fantine, and you divined beneath this dress and these ribbons a statue, and in this statue a soul.

Fantine was beautiful, without being too conscious of it. Those rare dreamers, the mysterious priests of the beautiful, who silently compare all things with perfection, would have had a dim vision in this little workwoman, through the transparency of Parisian grace, of the ancient sacred Euphony. This daughter of obscurity had race. She possessed both types of beauty—style and rhythm. Style is the force of the ideal, rhythm is its movement.

We have said that Fantine was joy; Fantine also was modesty.

For an observer who had studied her attentively would have found through all this intoxication of age, of season, and of love, an unconquerable expression of reserve and modesty. She was somewhat restrained. This chaste restraint is the shade which separates Psyche from Venus. Fantine had the long, white, slender fingers of the vestals that stir the ashes of the sacred fire with a golden rod. Although she would have refused nothing to Tholomyès, as might be seen but too well, her face, in repose, was in the highest degree maidenly; a kind of serious and almost austere dignity suddenly possessed it at times, and nothing could be more strange or disquieting than to see gaiety vanish there so quickly, and reflection instantly succeed to delight. This sudden seriousness, sometimes strangely marked, resembled the disdain of a goddess. Her forehead, nose, and chin presented that equilibrium of line, quite distinct from the equilibrium of proportion, which produces harmony of features; in the characteristic interval which separates the base of the nose from the upper lip, she had that almost imperceptible but charming fold, the mysterious sign of chastity, which enamoured Barbarossa with a Diana, found in the excavations of Iconium.

Love is a fault; be it so. Fantine was innocence floating upon the surface of this fault.

IV

THOLOMYÈS IS SO MERRY THAT HE SINGS
A SPANISH SONG

THAT day was sunshine from one end to the other. All nature seemed to be out on a holiday. The parterres of Saint Cloud were balmy with perfumes; the breeze from the Seine gently waved the leaves; the boughs were gesticulating in the wind; the bees were pillaging the jessamine, a whole crew of butterflies had settled in the milfoil, clover, and wild oats. The august park of the King of France was invaded by a swarm of vagabonds, the birds.

The four joyous couples shone resplendently in concert with the sunshine, the flowers, the fields, and the trees.

And in this paradisaical community, speaking, singing, running, dancing, chasing butterflies, gathering bindweed, wetting their open-worked stocking in the high grass, fresh, wild, but not wicked, stealing kisses from each other indiscriminately now and then, all except Fantine, who was shut up in her vague, dreary, severe resistance, and who was in love. "You always have the air of being out of sorts," said Favourite to her.

These are true pleasures. These passages in the lives of happy couples are a profound appeal to life and nature, and call forth endearment and light from everything. There was once upon a time a fairy, who created meadows and trees expressly for lovers. Hence comes that eternal school among the groves for lovers, which is always opening, and which will last so long as there are thickets and pupils. Hence comes the popularity of spring among thinkers. The patrician and the knife-grinder, the duke and peer, and the peasant, the men of the court, and the men of the town, as was said in olden times, all are subjects of this fairy. They laugh, they seek each other, the air seems filled with a new brightness; what a transfiguration is it to love! Notary clerks are gods. And the little shrieks, the pursuits among the grass, the waists encircled by stealth, that jargon which is melody, that adoration which breaks forth in a syllable, those cherries snatched from one pair of lips by another—all kindle up, and become transformed into celestial glories. Beautiful girls lavish their charms with sweet prodigality. We fancy that it will never end. Philosophers, poets, painters behold these ecstasies and know not what to make of them. So dazzling are they. The departure for Cythera! exclaims Watteau; Lancret, the painter of the commonalty, contemplates his bourgeois soaring in the sky; Diderot stretches out his arms to all these loves, and d'Urfé associates them with the Druids.

After breakfast, the four couples went to see, in what was then called the king's square, a plant newly arrived from the Indies, the name of which escapes us at present, and which at this time was attracting all Paris to Saint Cloud: it was a strange and beautiful shrub with a long stalk, the innumerable branches of which, fine as threads, tangled, and leafless, were covered with millions of little, white blossoms, which gave it the appearance of flowing hair, powdered with flowers. There was always a crowd admiring it.

When they had viewed the shrub, Tholomyès exclaimed, "I propose donkeys," and making a bargain with a donkey-driver, they returned through Vanvres and Issy. At Issy, they had an adventure. The park, Bien-National, owned at this time by the commissary Bourguin, was by sheer good luck open. They passed through the grating, visited the mannikin anchorite in his grotto, and tried the little, mysterious effects of the famous cabinet of mirrors—a wanton trap, worthy of a satyr become a millionaire, or Turcaret metamorphosed into Priapus. They swung stoutly in the great swing, attached to the two chestnut trees, celebrated by the Abbé de Bernis. While swinging the girls, one after the other, and making folds of flying crinoline that Greuze would have found worth his study, the Toulousian Tholomyès, who was something of a Spaniard—Toulouse is cousin to Tolosa—sang in a melancholy key, the old *gallega* song, probably inspired by some beautiful damsel swinging in the air between two trees.

> *Soy de Badaioz.*
> *Amor me llama.*
> *Toda mi alma*
> *Es en mi ojos*
> *Porque enseñas*
> *A tus piernas.*

Fantine alone refused to swing.

"I do not like this sort of air," murmured Favourite, rather sharply.

They left the donkeys for a new pleasure, crossed the Seine in a boat, and walked from Passy to the Barrière de l'Etoile. They had been on their feet, it will be remembered, since five in the morning, but *bah! there is no weariness on Sunday*, said Favourite; on Sunday fatigue has a holiday. Towards three o'clock, the four couples, wild with happiness, were running down to the Russian mountains, a singular edifice which then occupied the heights of Beaujon, and the serpentine line of which might have been perceived above the trees of the Champs-Elysées.

From time to time Favourite exclaimed:

"But the surprise? I want the surprise."

"Be patient," answered Tholomyès.

V

AT BOMBARDA'S

THE Russian mountains exhausted, they thought of dinner, and the happy eight, a little weary at last, stranded on Bombarda's, a branch establishment, set up in the Champs-Elysées by the celebrated restaurateur, Bombarda, whose sign was then seen on the Rue de Rivoli, near the Delorme arcade.

A large but plain apartment, with an alcove containing a bed at the bottom (the place was so full on Sunday that it was necessary to take up with this lodging room); two windows from which they could see, through the elms, the quai and the river; a magnificent August sunbeam glancing over the windows; two tables; one loaded with a triumphant mountain of bouquets, interspersed with hats and bonnets, while at the other, the four couples were gathered round a joyous pile of plates, napkins, glasses, and bottles; jugs of beer and flasks of wine; little order on the table, and some disorder under it.

Says Molière:

> Ils faisaient sous la table,
> Un bruit, un trique-trac de pieds épouvantable.*

Here was where the pastoral, commenced at five o'clock in the morning, was to be found at half-past four in the afternoon. The sun was declining, and their appetite with it.

The Champs-Elysées, full of sunshine and people, was nothing but glare and dust, the two elements of glory. The horses of Marly, those neighing marbles, were curveting in a golden cloud. Carriages were coming and going. A magnificent squadron of body-guards with the trumpet at their head, were coming down the avenue of Neuilly; the white flag, faintly tinged with red by the setting sun, was floating over the dome of the Tuileries. The Place de la Concorde, then become Place Louis XV. again, was overflowing with pleased promenaders. Many wore the silver fleur-de-lis suspended from the watered white ribbon which, in 1817, had not wholly disappeared from the buttonholes. Here and there in the midst of groups of applauding spectators, circles of little girls gave to the winds a Bourbon doggerel rhyme, intended to overwhelm the Hundred Days, and the chorus of which ran:

> Rendez-nous notre père de Gand,
> Rendez-nous notre père.†

Crowds of the inhabitants of the faubourgs in their Sunday

---

* And under the table they beat
  A fearful tattoo with their feet.
† Give us back our *Père de Gand*.
  Give us back our sire.

clothes, sometimes even decked with fleurs-de-lis like the citizens, were scattered over the great square and the square Marigny, playing games and going around on wooden horses; others were drinking; a few, printer apprentices, had on paper caps; their laughter resounded through the air. Everything was radiant. It was a time of undoubted peace and profound royal security; it was the time when a private and special report of Prefect of Police Anglès to the king on the faubourgs of Paris, ended with these lines: "Everything considered, sire, there is nothing to fear from these people. They are as careless and indolent as cats. The lower people of the provinces are restless, those of Paris are not so. They are all small men, sire, and it would take two of them one upon the other, to make one of your grenadiers. There is nothing at all to fear on the side of the populace of the capital. It is remarkable that this part of the population has also decreased in stature during the last fifty years, and the people of the faubourgs of Paris are smaller than before the Revolution. They are not dangerous. In short, they are good canaille."

That a cat may become changed into a lion, prefects of police do not believe possible; nevertheless, it may be, and this is the miracle of the people of Paris. Besides, the cat, so despised by the Count Anglès, had the esteem of the republics of antiquity; it was the incarnation of liberty in their sight, and, as if to serve as a pendant to the wingless Minerva of the Piræus, there was, in the public square at Corinth, the bronze colossus of a cat. The simple police of the Restoration looked too hopefully on the people of Paris. They are by no means such good canaille as is believed. The Parisian is among Frenchmen what the Athenian was among Greeks. Nobody sleeps better than he, nobody is more frankly frivolous and idle than he, nobody seems to forget things more easily than he; but do not trust him, notwithstanding; he is apt at all sorts of nonchalance, but when there is glory to be gained, he is wonderful in every species of fury. Give him a pike, and he will play the tenth of August; give him a musket, and you shall have an Austerlitz. He is the support of Napoleon, and the resource of Danton. Is France in question? he enlists; is liberty in question? he tears up the pavement. Beware! his hair rising with rage is epic; his blouse drapes itself into a chlamys about him. Take care! At the first corner, Grenétat will make a Caudine Forks. When the tocsin sounds, this dweller in the faubourgs will grow; this little man will arise, his look will be terrible, his breath will become a tempest, and a blast will go forth from his poor, frail breast that might shake the wrinkles out of the Alps. Thanks to the men of the Paris faubourgs, the Revolution infused into armies, conquers Europe. He sings, it is his joy. Proportion his song to his nature, and you shall see! So long as he had the Carmagnole merely for his chorus, he overthrew only Louis XVI.; let him sing the Marseillaise, and he will deliver the world.

Writing this note in the margin of the Anglès report, we will return to our four couples. The dinner, as we have said, was over.

VI

A CHAPTER OF SELF-ADMIRATION

TABLE talk and lovers' talk equally elude the grasp; lovers' talk is clouds, table talk is smoke.

Fameuil and Dahlia hummed airs; Tholomyès drank, Zéphine laughed, Fantine smiled. Listolier blew a wooden trumpet that he had bought at Saint Cloud. Favourite looked tenderly at Blacheville and said:

"Blacheville, I adore you."

This brought forth a question from Blacheville:

"What would you do, Favourite, if I should leave you?"

"Me!" cried Favourite. "Oh! do not say that, even in sport! If you should leave me, I would run after you, I would scratch you, I would pull your hair, I would throw water on you, I would have you arrested."

Blacheville smiled with the effeminate foppery of a man whose self-love is tickled. Favourite continued:

"Yes! I would cry watch! No! I would scream, for example: rascal!"

Blacheville, in ecstasy, leaned back in his chair, and closed both eyes with a satisfied air.

Dahlia, still eating, whispered to Favourite in the hubbub:

"Are you really so fond of your Blacheville, then?"

"I detest him," answered Favourite, in the same time, taking up her fork. "He is stingy; I am in love with the little fellow over the way from where I live. He is a nice young man; do you know him? Anybody can see that he was born to be an actor! I love actors. As soon as he comes into the house, his mother cries out: 'Oh, dear! my peace is all gone. There, he is going to hallo! You will split my head;' just because he goes into the garret among the rats, into the dark corners, as high as he can go, and sings and declaims—and how do I know that they can hear him below! He gets twenty sous a day already by writing for a pettifogger. He is the son of an old chorister of Saint-Jacques du Haut-Pis! Oh, he is a nice young man! He is so fond of me that he said one day, when he saw me making dough for pancakes: 'Mamselle, make your gloves into fritters and I will eat them.' Nobody but artists can say things like these; I am on the high road to go crazy about this little fellow. It is all the same, I tell Blacheville that I adore him. How I lie! Oh, how I lie!"

Favourite paused, then continued:

"Dahlia, you see I am melancholy. It has done nothing but rain all summer; the wind makes me nervous and freckles me. Blacheville is very mean; there are hardly any green peas in the market yet, people care for nothing but eating; I have the spleen, as the English say; butter is so dear! and then, just think of it—it is horrible! We are dining in a room with a bed in it. I am disgusted with life."

VII
THE WISDOM OF THOLOMYÈS

MEANTIME, while some were singing, the rest were all noisily talking at the same time. There was a perfect uproar. Tholomyès interfered.

"Do not talk at random, nor too fast!" exclaimed he; "we must take time for reflection, if we would be brilliant. Too much improvisation leaves the mind stupidly void. Running beer gathers no foam. Gentlemen, no haste. Mingle dignity with festivity, eat with deliberation, feast slowly. Take your time. See the spring; if it hastens forward, it is ruined; that is, frozen. Excess of zeal kills peach and apricot trees. Excess of zeal kills the grace and joy of good dinners. No zeal, gentlemen! Grimod de la Reynière is of Talleyrand's opinion."

"Tholomyès, let us alone," said Blacheville.

"Down with the tyrant!" cried Fameuil.

"Bombarda, Bombance, and Bamboche!" exclaimed Listolier.

"Sunday still exists," resumed Listolier.

"We are sober," added Fameuil.

"Tholomyès," said Blacheville, "behold my calmness (*mon calme*)."

"You are its marquis," replied Tholomyès.

This indifferent play on words had the effect of a stone thrown into a pool. The Marquis de Montcalm was a celebrated royalist of the time. All the frogs were silent.

"My friends!" exclaimed Tholomyès, in the tone of a man resuming his sway. "Collect yourselves. This pun, though it falls from heaven, should not be welcomed with too much wonder. Everything that falls in this wise is not necessarily worthy of enthusiasm and respect. The pun is the dropping of the soaring spirit. The jest falls, it matters not where. And the spirit, after freeing itself from the folly, plunges into the clouds. A white spot settling upon a rock does not prevent the condor from hovering above. Far be it from me to insult the pun! I honour it in proportion to its merits—no more. The most august, most sublime, and most charming in humanity and perhaps out of humanity, have made plays on words. Jesus Christ made a pun on St. Peter, Moses on Isaac, Æschylus on Polynices, Cleopatra on Octavius. And mark, that this pun of Cleopatra preceded the battle of Actium, and that, without it, no one would have remembered the city of Toryne, a Greek name signifying dipper. This conceded, I return to my exhortation. My brethren, I repeat, no zeal, no noise, no excess, even in witticisms, mirth, gaiety and plays on words. Listen to me; have the prudence of Amphiaraüs, and the boldness of Cæsar. There must be a limit, even to rebuses; *Est modus in rebus*. There must be a limit even to dinners. You like apple-puffs, ladies; do not abuse them. There must be, even in puffs, good sense and art. Gluttony punishes the glutton. Gula punishes Gulax. Indigestion is charged by God with enforcing morality on the stomach. And remember this: each of our passions, even love, has a stomach that must not be overloaded. We must in everything write the word *finis* in time; we must restrain ourselves, when it becomes urgent; we must draw the bolt on the appetite, play a fantasia on the violin, then break the strings with our own hand.

"The wise man is he who knows when and how to stop. Have some confidence in me. Because I have studied law a little, as my examinations prove, because I know the difference between the *question mue* and the *question pendante*, because I have written a Latin thesis on the method of torture in Rome at the time when Munatius Demens was quæstor of the Parricide; because I am about to become doctor, as it seems, it does not follow necessarily that I am a fool. I recommend to you moderation in all your desires. As sure as my name is Félix Tholomyès, I speak wisely. Happy is he, who when the hour comes, takes a heroic resolve, and abdicates like Sylla or Origenes."

Favourite listened with profound attention. "Félix!" said she, "what a pretty word. I like this name. It is Latin. It means prosperous."

Tholomyès continued:

"*Quirites*, gentlemen, *caballeros*, *mes amis*, would you feel no passion, dispense with the nuptial couch and set love at defiance? Nothing is easier. Here is a recipe: lemonade, over exercise, hard labour; tire yourselves out, draw logs, do not sleep, keep watch; gorge yourselves with nitrous drinks and ptisans of water-lilies; drink emulsions of poppies and agnus-castus; enliven this with a rigid diet, starve yourselves, and add cold baths, girdles of herbs, the application of a leaden plate, lotions of solution of lead and fomentations with vinegar and water."

"I prefer a woman," said Listolier.

"Woman!" resumed Tholomyès, "distrust the sex. Unhappy is he who surrenders himself to the changing heart of woman! Woman is perfidious and tortuous. She detests the serpent through rivalry of trade. The serpent is the shop across the way."

"Tholomyès," cried Blacheville, "you are drunk."

"The deuce I am!" said Tholomyès.

"Then be gay," resumed Blacheville.

"I agree," replied Tholomyès.

Then, filling his glass, he arose.

"Honour to wine! *Nunc te, Bacche, canam*. Pardon, ladies, that is Spanish. And here is the proof, *señoras*; like wine-measure, like people. The arroba of Castile contains sixteen litres, the cantaro of Alicante twelve, the almuda of the Canaries twenty-five, the cuartin of the Baleares twenty-six, and the boot of Czar Peter thirty. Long live the czar, who was great, and long live his boot, which was still greater! Ladies, a friendly counsel! deceive your neighbours, if it seems good to you. The characteristic of love is to rove. Love was not made to cower and crouch like an English housemaid whose knees are callused with scrubbing. Gentle love was made but to rove gaily! It has been said to err is human; I say, to err is loving. Ladies, I idolise you all. O Zéphine, or Josephine, with face more than wrinkled, you would be charming if you were not cross. Yours is like a beautiful face, upon which some one has sat down by mistake. As to Favourite, oh, nymphs and muses, one day, as Blacheville was crossing the Rue Guerin-Boisseau, he saw a beautiful girl with white, well-gartered stockings, who was showing them. The prologue pleased him, and Blacheville loved. She whom he loved was Favourite. Oh, Favourite! Thou hast Ionian lips. There was a Greek painter, Euphorion, who was surnamed painter of lips. This Greek alone would have been worthy to paint thy mouth. Listen! before thee, there was no creature worthy the name. Thou wert made to receive the apple like Venus, or to eat it like Eve. Beauty begins with thee. I have spoken of Eve; she was of thy creation. Thou deservest the patent for the invention of beautiful women. Oh, Favourite, I cease to thou you, for I pass from poetry to prose. You spoke just now of my name. It moved me; but, whatever we do, let us not trust to names, they may be deceitful. I am called Félix, I am not happy. Words are deceivers. Do not blindly accept the indications which they give. It would be a mistake to write to Liège for corks or to Pau for gloves. Miss Dahlia, in your place, I should call myself Rose. The flower should have fragrance, and woman should have wit. I say nothing of Fantine, she is visionary, dreamy, pensive, sensitive; she is a phantom with the form of a nymph, and the modesty of a nun, who has strayed into the life of a grisette, but who takes refuge in illusions, and who sings, and prays, and gazes at the sky without knowing clearly what she sees nor what she does, and who, with eyes fixed on heaven, wanders in a garden among more birds than exist there. Oh, Fantine, know this: I, Tholomyès, am an illusion—but she does not even hear me—the fair daughter of chimeras! Nevertheless, everything on her is freshness, gentleness, youth, soft, matinal clearness. Oh, Fantine, worthy to be called Marguerite or Pearl, you are a jewel of the purest water. Ladies, a second counsel, do not marry; marriage is a graft; it may take well or ill. Shun the risk. But what do I say? I am wasting my words. Women are incurable on the subject of weddings, and all that we wise men can say will not hinder vestmakers and gaiter-binders from dreaming about husbands loaded with diamonds. Well, be it so; but, beauties, remember this: you eat too much sugar. You have but one fault, oh, women! it is that of nibbling sugar. Oh, consuming sex, the pretty, little white teeth adore sugar. Now, listen attentively! Sugar is a salt. Every salt is desiccating. Sugar is the most desiccating of all salts. It sucks up the liquids from the blood through the veins; thence comes the coagulation, then the solidification of the blood; thence tubercles in the lungs; thence death. And this is why diabetes borders on consumption. Crunch no sugar, therefore, and you shall live! I turn towards the men: gentlemen, make conquests. Rob each other without remorse of your beloved. Chassez and cross over. There are no friends in love. Wherever there is a pretty woman, hostility is open. No quarter; war to the knife. A pretty woman is a *casus belli*; a pretty woman is a *flagrans delictum*. All the invasions of history have been determined by petticoats. Woman is the right of man. Romulus carried off the Sabine women; William carried off the Saxon women; Cæsar carried off the Roman women. The man who is not loved hovers like a vulture over the sweethearts of others; and for my part, to all unfortunate widowers, I issue the sublime proclamation of Bonaparte to the army of Italy, "Soldiers, you lack for everything. The enemy has everything."

Tholomyès checked himself.

"Take breath, Tholomyès," said Blacheville.

At the same time, Blacheville, aided by Listolier and Fameuil, with an air of lamentation hummed one of those workshop songs made up of the first words that came, rhyming richly and not at all, void of sense as the movement of the trees and the sound of the winds, and which are borne from the smoke of the pipes, and dissipate and take flight with it. This is the couplet by which the group replied to the harangue of Tholomyès:

> Les pères dindons donnèrent
> De l'argent à un agent
> Pour que mons Clermont-Tonnerre
> Fût fait pape à la Saint-Jean;
> Mais Clermont ne put pas être
> Fait pape, n'étant pas prêtre;
> Alors leur agent rageant
> Leur rapporta leur argent.

This was not likely to calm the inspiration of Tholomyès; he emptied his glass, filled it, and again began:

"Down with wisdom! forget all that I have said: Let us be neither prudes, nor prudent, nor prud'hommes! I drink to jollity; let us be jolly. Let us finish our course of study by folly and prating. Indigestion and the Digest. Let Justinian be the male, and festivity the female. There is joy in the abysses. Behold, oh, creation! The world is a huge diamond! I am happy. The birds are marvellous. What a festival everywhere! The nightingale is an Elleviou gratis. Summer, I salute thee. Oh, Luxembourg! Oh, Georgics of the Rue Madame, and the Allée de l'Observatoire! Oh, entranced dreamers! the pampas of America would delight me, if I had not the arcades of the Odeon. My soul goes out towards virgin forests and savannahs. Everything is beautiful; the flies hum in the sunbeams. The humming-birds whizz in the sunshine. Kiss me, Fantine!"

And, by mistake, he kissed Favourite.

VIII
DEATH OF A HORSE

"THE dinners are better at Edon's than at Bombarda's," exclaimed Zéphine.

"I like Bombarda better than Edon," said Blacheville. "There is more luxury. It is more Asiatic. See the lower hall. There are mirrors (glaces) on the walls."

"I prefer ices (glaces) on my plate," said Favourite.

Blacheville persisted.

"Look at the knives. The handles are silver at Bombarda's, and bone at Edon's. Now silver is more precious than bone."

"Except when it is on the chin," observed Tholomyès.

He looked out at this moment at the dome of the Invalides, which was visible from Bombarda's windows.

There was a pause.

"Tholomyès," cried Fameuil, "Listolier and I have just had a discussion."

"A discussion is good," replied Tholomyès, "a quarrel is better."

"We were discussing philosophy."

"I have no objection."

"Which do you prefer, Descartes or Spinoza?"

"Désaugiers," said Tholomyès.

This decision rendered, he drank, and resumed:

"I consent to live. All is not over on earth, since we can yet reason falsely. I render thanks for this to the immortal gods. We lie, but we laugh. We affirm, but we doubt. The unexpected shoots forth from a syllogism. It is fine. There are men still on earth who know how to open and shut pleasantly the surprise boxes of paradox. Know, ladies, that this wine you are drinking so calmly, is Madeira from the vineyard of Coural das Frerras, which is three hundred and seventeen fathoms above the level of the sea. Attention while you drink! three hundred and seventeen fathoms! and M. Bombarda, this magnificent restaurateur, gives you these three hundred and seventeen fathoms for four francs, fifty centimes."

Fameuil interrupted again.

"Tholomyès, your opinions are law. Who is your favourite author?"

"Ber—"

"Quin?"

"No. Choux."

And Tholomyès continued.

"Honour to Bombarda! he would equal Munophis of Elephanta if he could procure me an almée and Thygelion of Chæronea if he could bring me a hetaïra! for, oh, ladies, there were Bombardas in Greece and Egypt; this Apuleius teaches us. Alas! always the same thing and nothing new. Nothing more unpublished in the creation of the Creator! *Nil sub sole novum*, says Solomon; *amor omnibus idem*, says Virgil; and Carabine mounts with Carabin in the galliot at Saint Cloud, as Aspasia embarked with Pericles on the fleet of Samos. A last word. Do you know who this Aspasia was, ladies? Although she lived in a time when women had not yet a soul, she was a soul; a soul of a rose and purple shade, more glowing than fire, fresher than the dawn. Aspasia was a being who touched the two extremes of woman, the prostitute goddess. She was Socrates, plus Manon Lescaut. Aspasia was created in case Prometheus might need a wanton."

Tholomyès, now that he was started would have been stopped with difficulty, had not a horse fallen down at this moment on the quai. The shock stopped short both the cart and the orator. It was an old, meagre mare, worthy of the knacker, harnessed to a very heavy cart. On reaching Bombarda's, the beast, worn and exhausted, had refused to go further. This incident attracted a crowd. Scarcely had the carman, swearing and indignant, had time to utter with fitting energy the decisive word, "*mâtin!*" backed by a terrible stroke of the whip, when the hack fell, to rise no more. At the hubbub of the passers-by, the merry auditors of Tholomyès turned their heads, and Tholomyès profited by it to close his address by this melancholy strophe:

> Elle était de ce monde où coucous et carrosses
> Ont le même destin;
> Et, rosse, elle a vécu ce que vivent les rosses,
> L'espace d'un matin!

"Poor horse!" sighed Fantine.

Dahlia exclaimed:

"Here is Fantine pitying horses! was there ever anything so absurd?"

At this moment, Favourite, crossing her arms and turning round her head, looked fixedly at Tholomyès and said:

"Come! the surprise?"

"Precisely. The moment has come," replied Tholomyès. "Gentlemen, the hour has come for surprising these ladies. Ladies, wait for us a moment."

"It begins with a kiss," said Blacheville.

"On the forehead," added Tholomyès.

Each one gravely placed a kiss on the forehead of his mistress; after which they directed their steps towards the door, all four in file, laying their fingers on their lips.

Favourite clapped her hands as they went out.

"It is amusing already," said she.

"Do not be too long," murmured Fantine. "We are waiting for you."

IX
JOYOUS END OF JOY

THE girls, left alone, leaned their elbows on the window sills in couples, and chattered together, bending their heads and speaking from one window to the other.

They saw the young men go out of Bombarda's, arm in arm; they turned round, made signals to them laughingly, then disappeared in the dusty Sunday crowd which takes possession of the Champs-Elysées once a week.

"Do not be long!" cried Fantine.

"What are they going to bring us?" said Zéphine.

"Surely something pretty," said Dahlia.

"I hope it will be gold," resumed Favourite.

They were soon distracted by the stir on the water's edge, which they distinguished through the branches of the tall trees, and which diverted them greatly. It was the hour for the departure of the mails and diligences. Almost all the stagecoaches to the south and west passed at that time by the Champs-Elysées. The greater part followed the quai and went out through the Barrière Passy. Every minute some huge vehicle, painted yellow and black, heavily loaded, noisily harnessed, distorted with mails, awnings, and valises, full of heads that were constantly disappearing, grinding the curbstones, turning the pavements into flints, rushed through the crowd, throwing out sparks like a forge, with dust for smoke, and an air of fury. This hubbub delighted the young girls. Favourite exclaimed:

"What an uproar; one would say that heaps of chains were taking flight."

It so happened that one of these vehicles which could be distinguished with difficulty through the obscurity of the elms, stopped for a moment, then set out again on a gallop. This surprised Fantine.

"It is strange," said she. "I thought the diligences never stopped."

Favourite shrugged her shoulders:

"This Fantine is surprising; I look at her with curiosity. She wonders at the most simple things. Suppose that I am a traveller, and say to the diligence; 'I am going on; you can take me up on the quai in passing.' The diligence passes, sees me, stops and takes me up. This happens every day. You know nothing of life, my dear."

Some time passed in this manner. Suddenly Favourite started as if from sleep.

"Well!" said she, "and the surprise?"

"Yes," returned Dahlia, "the famous surprise."

"They are very long!" said Fantine.

As Fantine finished the sigh, the boy who had waited at dinner entered. He had in his hand something that looked like a letter.

"What is that?" asked Favourite.

"It is a paper that the gentlemen left for these ladies," he replied.

"Why did you not bring it at once?"

"Because the gentlemen ordered me not to give it to the ladies before an hour," returned the boy.

Favourite snatched the paper from his hands. It was really a letter.

"Stop!" said she. "There is no address; but see what is written on it:

"THIS IS THE SURPRISE."

She hastily unsealed the letter, opened it, and read (she knew how to read):

"Oh, our lovers!

"Know that we have parents. Parents—you scarcely know the meaning of the word, they are what are called fathers and mothers in the civil code, simple but honest. Now these parents bemoan us, these old men claim us, these good men and women call us prodigal sons, desire our return and offer to kill for us the fatted calf. We obey them, being virtuous. At the moment when you read this, five mettlesome horses will be bearing us back to our papas and mammas. We are pitching our camps, as Bossuet says. We are going, we are gone. We fly in the arms of Laffitte, and on the wings of Caillard. The Toulouse diligence snatches us from the abyss, and you are this abyss, our beautiful darlings! We are returning to society, to duty and order, on a full trot, at the rate of three leagues an hour. It is necessary to the country that we become, like everybody else, prefects, fathers of families, rural guards, and councillors of state. Venerate us. We sacrifice ourselves. Mourn for us rapidly, and replace us speedily. If this letter rends you, rend it in turn. Adieu.

"For nearly two years we have made you happy. Bear us no ill will for it."

Signed: BLACHEVILLE,
FAMEUIL,
LISTOLIER,
FÉLIX THOLOMYÈS.

"P.S. The dinner is paid for."

The four girls gazed at each other.

Favourite was the first to break silence.

"Well!" said she, "it is a good farce all the same."

"It is very droll," said Zéphine.

"It must have been Blacheville that had the idea," resumed Favourite. "This makes me in love with him. Soon loved, soon gone. That is the story."

"No," said Dahlia, "it is an idea of Tholomyès. This is clear."

"In that case," returned Favourite, "down with Blacheville, and long live Tholomyès!"

"Long live Tholomyès!" cried Dahlia and Zéphine.

And they burst into laughter.

Fantine laughed like the rest.

An hour afterwards, when she had re-entered her chamber, she wept. It was her first love, as we have said; she had given herself to this Tholomyès as to a husband, and the poor girl had a child.

BOOK FOURTH –
TO ENTRUST IS SOMETIMES TO ABANDON

I
ONE MOTHER MEETS ANOTHER

THERE was, during the first quarter of the present century, at Montfermeil, near Paris, a sort of chop-house; it is not there now. It was kept by a man and his wife, named Thénardier, and was situated in the Lane Boulanger. Above the door, nailed flat against the wall, was a board, upon which something was painted that looked like a man carrying on his back another man wearing the heavy epaulettes of a general, gilt and with large silver stars; red blotches typified blood; the remainder of the picture was smoke, and probably represented a battle. Beneath was this inscription: TO THE SERGEANT OF WATERLOO.

Nothing is commoner than a cart or wagon before the door of an inn; nevertheless the vehicle, or more properly speaking, the fragment of a vehicle which obstructed the street in front of the Sergeant of Waterloo one evening in the spring of 1815, certainly would have attracted by its bulk the attention of any painter who might have been passing.

It was the fore-carriage of one of those drays for carrying heavy articles, used in wooded countries for transporting joists and trunks of trees: it consisted of a massive iron axle-tree with a pivot to which a heavy pole was attached, and which was supported by two enormous wheels. As a whole, it was squat, crushing, and misshapen: it might have been fancied a gigantic gun-carriage.

The roads had covered the wheels, felloes, limbs, axle, and the pole with a coating of hideous yellow-hued mud, similar in tint to that with which cathedrals are sometimes decorated. The wood had disappeared beneath mud; and the iron beneath rust.

Under the axle-tree hung festooned a huge chain fit for a Goliath of the galleys.

This chain recalled, not the beams which it was used to carry, but the mastodons and mammoths which it might have harnessed; it reminded one of the galleys, but of cyclopean and superhuman galleys, and seemed as if unriveted from some monster. With it Homer could have bound Polyphemus, or Shakspeare Caliban.

Why was this vehicle in this place in the street, one may ask? First to obstruct the lane, and then to complete its work of rust. There is in the old social order a host of institutions which we find like this across our path in the full light of day, and which present no other reasons for being there.

The middle of the chain was hanging quite near the ground under the axle; and upon the bend, as on a swinging rope, two little girls were seated that evening in exquisite grouping, the smaller, eighteen months old, in the lap of the larger, who was two years and a half old.

A handkerchief carefully knotted kept them from falling. A mother, looking upon this frightful chain, had said: "Ah! there is a plaything for my children!"

The radiant children, picturesquely and tastefully decked, might be fancied two roses twining the rusty iron, with their triumphantly sparkling eyes, and their blooming, laughing faces. One was a rosy blonde, the other a brunette; their artless faces were two ravishing surprises; the perfume that was shed upon the air by a flowering shrub near by seemed their own out-breathings; the smaller one was showing her pretty little body with the chaste indecency of babyhood. Above and around these delicate heads moulded in happiness and bathed in light, the gigantic carriage, black with rust and almost frightful with its entangled curves and abrupt angles, arched like the mouth of a cavern.

The mother, a woman whose appearance was rather forbidding, but touching at this moment, was seated on the sill of the inn, swinging the two children by a long string, while she brooded them with her eyes for fear of accident with that animal but heavenly expression peculiar to maternity. At each vibration the hideous links uttered a creaking noise like an angry cry; the little ones were in ecstasies, the setting sun mingled in the joy, and nothing could be more charming than this caprice of chance which made of a Titan's chain a swing for cherubim.

While rocking the babes the mother sang with a voice out of tune a then popular song:

"Il le faut, disait un guerrier."

Her song and watching her children prevented her hearing and seeing what was passing in the street.

Some one, however, had approached her as she was beginning the first couplet of the song, and suddenly she heard a voice say quite near her ear:

"You have two pretty children there, madame."

"A la belle et tendre Imogine,"

answered the mother, continuing her song; then she turned her head.

A woman was before her at a little distance; she also had a child, which she bore in her arms.

She was carrying in addition a large carpet-bag, which seemed heavy.

This woman's child was one of the divinest beings that can be imagined: a little girl of two or three years. She might have entered the lists with the other little ones for coquetry of attire, she wore a head-dress of fine linen; ribbons at her shoulders and Valenciennes lace on her cap. The folds of her skirt were raised enough to show her plump fine white leg; she was charmingly rosy and healthful. The pretty little creature gave one a desire to bite her cherry cheeks. We can say nothing of her eyes except that they must have been very large, and were fringed with superb lashes. She was asleep.

She was sleeping in the absolutely confiding slumber peculiar to her age. Mothers' arms are made of tenderness, and sweet sleep blesses the child who lies therein.

As to the mother, she seemed poor and sad; she had the appearance of a working woman who is seeking to return to the life of a peasant. She was young,—and pretty? It was possible, but in that garb beauty could not be displayed. Her hair, one blonde mesh of which had fallen, seemed very thick, but it was severely fastened up beneath an ugly, close, narrow nun's head-dress, tied under the chin. Laughing shows fine teeth when one has them, but she did not laugh. Her eyes seemed not to have been tearless for a long time. She was pale, and looked very weary, and somewhat sick. She gazed upon her child, sleeping in her arms, with that peculiar look which only a mother possesses who nurses her own child. Her form was clumsily masked by a large blue handkerchief folded across her bosom. Her hands were tanned and spotted with freckles, the forefinger hardened and pricked with the needle; she wore a coarse brown delaine mantle, a calico dress, and large heavy shoes. It was Fantine.

Yes, Fantine. Hard to recognise, yet on looking attentively, you saw that she still retained her beauty. A sad line, such as is formed by irony, had marked her right cheek. As to her toilette—that airy toilette of muslin and ribbons which seemed as if made of gaiety, folly, and music, full of baubles and perfumed with lilacs—that had vanished like the beautiful sparkling hoarfrost, which we take for diamonds in the sun; they melt, and leave the branch dreary and black.

Ten months had slipped away since "the good farce."

What had passed during these ten months? We can guess.

After recklessness, trouble. Fantine had lost sight of Favourite, Zéphine, and Dahlia; the tie, broken on the part of the men, was unloosed on the part of the women; they would have been astonished if any one had said a fortnight afterwards they were friends; they had no longer cause to be so. Fantine was left alone. The father of her child gone—Alas! such partings are irrevocable—she found herself absolutely isolated, with the habit of labour lost, and the taste for pleasure acquired. Led by her liaison with Tholomyès to disdain the small business that she knew how to do, she had neglected her opportunities, they were all gone. No resource. Fantine could scarcely read, and did not know how to write. She had only been taught in childhood how to sign her name. She had a letter written by a public letter-writer to Tholomyès, then a second, then a third. Tholomyès had replied to none of them. One day, Fantine heard some old women saying as they saw her child: "Do people ever take such children to heart? They only shrug their shoulders at such children!" Then she thought of Tholomyès, who shrugged his shoulders at his child, and who did not take this innocent child to heart, and her heart became dark in the place that was his. What should she do? She had no one to ask. She had committed a fault; but, in the depths of her nature, we know dwelt modesty and virtue. She had a vague feeling that she was on the eve of falling into distress, of slipping into the street. She must have courage, she had it, and bore up bravely. The idea occurred to her of returning to her native village M—— sur M——; there perhaps some one would know her, and give her work. Yes, but she must hide her fault. And she had a confused glimpse of the possible necessity of a separation still more painful than the first.

Her heart ached, but she took her resolution. It will be seen that Fantine possessed the stern courage of life. She had already valiantly renounced her finery, was draped in calico, and had put all her silks, her gew-gaws, her ribbons, and laces on her daughter—the only vanity that remained, and that a holy one. She sold all she had, which gave her two hundred francs; when her little debts were paid, she had but about eighty left. At twenty-two years of age, on a fine spring morning, she left Paris, carrying her child on her back. He who had seen the two passing, must have pitied them. The woman had nothing in the world but this child, and this child had nothing in the world but this woman. Fantine had nursed her child; that had weakened her chest somewhat, and she coughed slightly.

We shall have no further need to speak of M. Félix Tholomyès. We will only say here, that twenty years later, under King Louis Philippe, he was a fat provincial attorney, rich and influential, a wise elector and rigid juryman; always, however, a man of pleasure.

Towards noon, after having, for the sake of rest, travelled from time to time at a cost of three or four cents a league, in what they called then the Petites Voitures of the environs of Paris, Fantine reached Montfermeil, and stood in Boulanger Lane.

As she was passing by the Thénardier chop-house, the two little children, sitting in delight on their monstrous swing, had a sort of dazzling effect upon her, and she paused before this joyous vision.

There are charms. These two little girls were one for this mother.

She beheld them with emotion. The presence of angels is a herald of paradise. She thought she saw above this inn the mysterious "HERE" of Providence. These children were evidently happy; she gazed upon them, she admired them, so much affected that at the moment when the mother was taking breath between the verses of her song, she could not help saying what we have been reading.

"You have two pretty children there, madame."

The most ferocious animals are disarmed by caresses to their young.

The mother raised her head and thanked her and made the stranger sit down on the stone step, she herself being on the doorsill: the two women began to talk together.

"My name is Madame Thénardier," said the mother of the two girls: "we keep this inn."

Then going on with her song, she sang between her teeth:

"Il le faut, je suis chevalier
Et je pars pour la Palestine."

This Madame Thénardier was a red-haired, brawny, angular woman, of the soldier's wife type in all its horror, and, singularly enough, she had a lolling air which she had gained from novel-reading. She was a masculine lackadaisicalness. Old romances impressed on the imaginations of mistresses of chop-houses have such effects. She was still young, scarcely thirty years old. If this woman, who was seated stooping, had been upright, perhaps her towering form and her broad shoulders, those of a movable colossus, fit for a market-woman, would have dismayed the traveller, disturbed her confidence, and prevented what we have to relate. A person seated instead of standing; fate hangs on such a thread as that.

The traveller told her story, a little modified.

She said she was a working woman, and her husband was dead. Not being able to procure work in Paris she was going in search of it elsewhere; in her own province; that she had left Paris that morning on foot, that carrying her child she had become tired, and meeting the Villemomble stage had got in; that from Villemomble she had come on foot to Montfermeil; that the child had walked a little but not much, she was so young, that she was compelled to carry her, and the jewel had fallen asleep.

And at these words she gave her daughter a passionate kiss which wakened her. The child opened its large blue eyes, like its mother's, and saw—what? Nothing, everything, with that serious and sometimes severe air of little children, which is one of the mysteries of their shining innocence before our shadowy virtues. One would say that they felt themselves to be angels, and knew us to be human. Then the child began to laugh, and, although the mother restrained her, slipped to the ground, with the indomitable energy of a little one that wants to run about. All at once she perceived the two others in their swing, stopped short, and put out her tongue in token of admiration.

Mother Thénardier untied the children and took them from the swing saying:

"Play together, all three of you."

At that age acquaintance is easy, and in a moment the little Thénardiers were playing with the new-comer, making holes in the ground to their intense delight.

This new-comer was very sprightly: the goodness of the mother is written in the gaiety of the child; she had taken a splinter of wood, which she used as a spade, and was stoutly digging a hole fit for a fly. The gravedigger's work is charming when done by a child.

The two women continued to chat.

"What do your call your brat?"

"Cosette."

For Cosette read Euphrasie. The name of the little one was Euphrasie. But the mother had made Cosette out of it, by that sweet and charming instinct of mothers and of the people, who change Jósefa into Pepita, and Françoise into Sillette. That is a kind of derivation which deranges and disconcerts all the science of etymologists. We knew a grandmother who succeeded in making from Théodore, Gnon.

"How old is she?"

"She is going on three years."

"The age of my oldest."

The three girls were grouped in an attitude of deep anxiety and bliss; a great event had occurred; a large worm had come out of the ground; they were afraid of it, and yet in ecstasies over it.

Their bright foreheads touched each other: three heads in one halo of glory.

"Children," exclaimed the Thénardier mother; "how soon they know one another. See them! one would swear they were three sisters."

These words were the spark which the other mother was probably awaiting. She seized the hand of Madame Thénardier and said:

"Will you keep my child for me?"

Madame Thénardier made a motion of surprise, which was neither consent nor refusal.

Cosette's mother continued:

"You see I cannot take my child into the country. Work forbids it. With a child I could not find a place there; they are so absurd in that district. It is God who has led me before your inn. The sight of your little ones, so pretty, and clean, and happy, has overwhelmed me. I said: there is a good mother; they will be like three sisters, and then it will not be long before I come back. Will you keep my child for me?"

"I must think over it," said Thénardier.

"I will give six francs a month."

Here a man's voice was heard from within:

"Not less than seven francs, and six months paid in advance."

"Six times seven are forty-two," said Thénardier.

"I will give it," said the mother.

"And fifteen francs extra for the first expenses," added the man.

"That's fifty-seven francs," said Madame Thénardier, and in the midst of her reckoning she sang indistinctly:

> "Il le faut, disait un guerrier."

"I will give it," said the mother; "I have eighty francs. That will leave me enough to go into the country if I walk. I will earn some money there, and as soon as I have I will come for my little love."

The man's voice returned:

"Has the child a wardrobe?"

"That is my husband," said Thénardier.

"Certainly she has, the poor darling. I knew it was your husband. And a fine wardrobe it is too, an extravagant wardrobe, everything in dozens, and silk dresses like a lady. They are there in my carpet-bag."

"You must leave that here," put in the man's voice.

"Of course I shall give it to you," said the mother; "it would be strange if I should leave my child naked."

The face of the master appeared.

"It is all right," said he.

The bargain was concluded. The mother passed the night at the inn, gave her money and left her child, fastened again her carpet-bag, diminished by her child's wardrobe, and very light now, and set off next morning, expecting soon to return. These partings are arranged tranquilly, but they are full of despair.

A neighbour of the Thénardiers met this mother on her way, and came in, saying:

"I have just met a woman in the street, who was crying as if her heart would break."

When Cosette's mother had gone, the man said to his wife:

"That will do me for my note of 110 francs which falls due tomorrow; I was fifty francs short. Do you know I should have had a sheriff and a protest? You have proved a good mousetrap with your little ones."

"Without knowing it," said the woman.

II

FIRST SKETCH OF TWO EQUIVOCAL FACES

THE captured mouse was a very puny one, but the cat exulted even over a lean mouse.

What were the Thénardiers?

We will say but a word just here; by-and-by the sketch shall be completed.

They belonged to that bastard class formed of low people who have risen, and intelligent people who have fallen, which lies between the classes called middle and lower, and which unites some of the faults of the latter with nearly all the vices of the former, without possessing the generous impulses of the workman, or the respectability of the bourgeois.

They were of those dwarfish natures, which, if perchance heated by some sullen fire, easily become monstrous. The woman was at heart a brute; the man a blackguard: both in the highest degree capable of that hideous species of progress which can be made towards evil. There are souls which, crablike, crawl continually towards darkness, going back in life rather than advancing in it; using what experience they have to increase their deformity; growing worse without ceasing, and becoming steeped more and more thoroughly in an intensifying wickedness. Such souls were this man and this woman.

The man especially would have been a puzzle to a physiognomist. We have only to look at some men to distrust them, for we feel the darkness of their souls in two ways. They are restless as to what is behind them, and threatening as to what is before them. They are full of mystery. We can no more answer for what they have done, than for what they will do. The shadow in their looks denounces them. If we hear them utter a word, or see them make a gesture, we catch glimpses of guilty secrets in their past, and dark mysteries in their future.

This Thénardier, if we may believe him, had been a soldier,

a sergeant he said; he probably had made the campaign of 1815, and had even borne himself bravely according to all that appeared. We shall see hereafter in what his bravery consisted. The sign of his inn was an allusion to one of his feats of arms. He had painted it himself, for he knew how to do a little of everything—badly.

It was the time when the antique classical romance, which, after having been *Clelié*, sank to *Lodoïska*, always noble, but becoming more and more vulgar, falling from Mdlle. de Scuderi to Madame Bournon-Malarme, and from Madame de Lafayette to Madame Barthélemy-Hadot, was firing the loving souls of the portresses of Paris, and making some ravages even in the suburbs. Madame Thénardier was just intelligent enough to read that sort of book. She fed on them. She drowned what little brain she had in them and that had given her, while she was yet young, and even in later life, a kind of pensive attitude towards her husband, a knave of some calibre; a ruffian, educated almost to the extent of grammar; at once coarse and fine, but so far as sentimentalism was concerned, reading Pigault Lebrun, and in "all which related to the sex," as he said in his jargon, a correct dolt without adulteration. His wife was twelve or fifteen years younger than he. At a later period, when the hair of the romantic weepers began to grow grey, when Mégère parted company with Pamela, Madame Thénardier was only a gross bad woman who had relished stupid novels. Now, people do not read stupidities with impunity. The result was, that her eldest child was named Eponine, and the youngest, who had just escaped being called Gulnare, owed to some happy diversion made by a novel of Ducray Duminil, the mitigation of Azelma.

However, let us say by the way, all things are not ridiculous and superficial in this singular epoch to which we allude, and which might be termed the anarchy of baptismal names. Besides this romantic element which we have noticed, there is the social symptom. To-day it is not unfrequent to see herdsboys named Arthur, Alfred, and Alphonse, and viscounts—if there be any remaining—named Thomas, Peter, or James. This change, which places the "elegant" name on the plebeian and the country appellation on the aristocrat, is only an eddy in the tide of equality. The irresistible penetration of a new inspiration is there as well as in everything else: beneath this apparent discordance there is a reality grand and deep—the French Revolution.

III
THE LARK

To be wicked does not insure prosperity—for the inn did not succeed well.

Thanks to Fantine's fifty-seven francs, Thénardier had been able to avoid a protest and to honour his signature. The next month they were still in need of money, and the woman carried Cosette's wardrobe to Paris and pawned it for sixty francs. When this sum was spent, the Thénardiers began to look upon the little girl as a child which they sheltered for charity, and treated her as such. Her clothes being gone, they dressed her in the cast-off garments of the little Thénardiers, that is in rags. They fed her on the orts and ends, a little better than the dog, and a little worse than the cat. The dog and cat were her messmates. Cosette ate with them under the table in a wooden dish like theirs.

Her mother, as we shall see hereafter, who had found a place at M—— sur M——, wrote, or rather had some one write for her every month, inquiring news of her child. The Thénardiers replied invariably:

"Cosette is doing wonderfully well."

The six months passed away: the mother sent seven francs for the seventh month, and continued to send this sum regularly month after month. The year was not ended before Thénardier said: "A pretty price that is. What does she expect us to do for her seven francs?" And he wrote demanding twelve francs. The mother, whom he persuaded that her child was happy and doing well, assented, and forwarded the twelve francs.

There are certain natures which cannot have love on one side without hatred on the other. This Thénardier mother passionately loved her own little ones: this made her detest the young stranger. It is sad to think that a mother's love can have such a dark side. Little as was the place Cosette occupied in the house, it seemed to her that this little was taken from her children, and that the little one lessened the air hers breathed. This woman, like many women of her kind, had a certain amount of caresses, and blows, and hard words to dispense each day. If she had not had Cosette, it is certain that her daughters, idolised as they were, would have received all, but the little stranger did them the service to attract the blows to herself; her children had only the caresses. Cosette could not stir that she did not draw down upon herself a hailstorm of undeserved and severe chastisements. A weak, soft little one who knew nothing of this world, or of God, continually ill-treated, scolded, punished, beaten, she saw beside her two other young things like herself, who lived in a halo of glory!

The woman was unkind to Cosette, Eponine and Azelma were unkind also. Children at that age are only copies of the mother; the size is reduced, that is all.

A year passed and then another.

People used to say in the village:

"What good people these Thénardiers are! They are not rich, and yet they bring up a poor child, that has been left with them."

They thought Cosette was forgotten by her mother.

Meantime Thénardier, having learned in some obscure way that the child was probably illegitimate, and that its mother could not acknowledge it, demanded fifteen francs a month, saying "that the 'creature' was growing and eating," and threatening to send her away. "She won't humbug me," he exclaimed. "I will confound her with the brat in the midst of her concealment. I must have more money." The mother paid the fifteen francs.

From year to year the child grew, and her misery also.

So long as Cosette was very small, she was the scapegoat of the two other children; as soon as she began to grow a little, that is to say, before she was five years old, she became the servant of the house.

Five years old, it will be said, that is improbable. Alas! it is true, social suffering begins at all ages. Have we not seen lately the trial of Dumollard, an orphan become a bandit, who, from the age of five, say the homicidal documents, being alone in the world, "worked for his living and stole!"

Cosette was made to run errands, sweep the rooms, the yard, the street, wash the dishes, and even carry burdens. The Thénardiers felt doubly authorised to treat her thus, as the mother, who still remained at M—— sur M——, began to be remiss in her payments. Some months remained due.

Had this mother returned to Montfermeil, at the end of these three years, she would not have known her child. Cosette, so fresh and pretty when she came to that house, was now thin and wan. She had a peculiar restless air. Sly! said the Thénardiers.

Injustice had made her sullen, and misery had made her ugly. Her fine eyes only remained to her, and they were painful to look at, for, large as they were, they seemed to increase the sadness.

It was a harrowing sight to see in the winter time the poor child, not yet six years old, shivering under the tatters of what was once a calico dress, sweeping the street before daylight with an enormous broom in her little red hands and tears in her large eyes.

In the place she was called the Lark. People like figurative names and were pleased thus to name this little being, not larger than a bird, trembling, frightened, and shivering, awake every morning first of all in the house and the village, always in the street or in the fields before dawn.

Only the poor Lark never sang.

BOOK FIFTH – THE DESCENT

I

HISTORY OF AN IMPROVEMENT IN JET-WORK

WHAT had become of this mother, in the meanwhile, who, according to the people of Montfermeil, seemed to have abandoned her child? where was she? what was she doing?

After leaving her little Cosette with the Thénardiers, she went on her way and arrived at M—— sur M—— .

This, it will be remembered, was in 1818.

Fantine had left the province some twelve years before, and M—— sur M—— greatly changed in appearance. While Fantine had been slowly sinking deeper and deeper into misery, her native village had been prosperous.

Within about two years there had been accomplished there one of those industrial changes which are the great events of small communities.

This circumstance is important and we think it well to relate it, we might even say to italicise it.

From time immemorial the special occupation of the inhabitants of M—— sur M—— had been the imitation of English jets and German black glass trinkets. The business had always been dull in consequence of the high price of the raw material, which reacted upon the manufacture. At the time of Fantine's return to M—— sur M—— an entire transformation had been effected in the production of these "black goods." Towards the end of the year 1815, an unknown man had established himself in the city, and had conceived the idea of substituting gum-lac for resin in the manufacture; and for bracelets, in particular, he made the clasps by simply bending the ends of the metal together instead of soldering them.

This very slight change had worked a revolution.

This very slight change had in fact reduced the price of the raw material enormously, and this had rendered it possible, first, to raise the wages of the labourer—a benefit to the country— secondly, to improve the quality of the goods—an advantage for the consumer—and thirdly, to sell them at a lower price even while making three times the profit—a gain for the manufacturer.

Thus we have three results from one idea.

In less than three years the inventor of this process had become rich, which was well, and had made all around him rich, which was better. He was a stranger in the Department. Nothing was known of his birth, and but little of his early history.

The story went that he came to the city with very little money, a few hundred francs at most.

From this slender capital, under the inspiration of an ingenious idea, made fruitful by order and care, he had drawn a fortune for himself, and a fortune for the whole region.

On his arrival at M—— sur M—— he had the dress, the manners, and the language of a labourer only.

It seems that the very day on which he thus obscurely entered the little city of M—— sur M——, just at dusk on a December evening, with his bundle on his back, and a thorn stick in his hand, a great fire had broken out in the town-house. This man rushed into the fire and saved, at the peril of his life, two children, who proved to be those of the captain of the gendarmerie, and in the hurry and gratitude of the moment no one thought to ask him for his passport. He was known from that time by the name of Father Madeleine.

II
MADELEINE

HE was a man of about fifty, who always appeared to be preoccupied in mind, and who was good-natured; this was all that could be said about him.

Thanks to the rapid progress of this manufacture, to which he had given such wonderful life, M—— sur M—— had become a considerable centre of business. Immense purchases were made there every year for the Spanish markets, where there is a large demand for jet work, and M—— sur M——, in this branch of trade, almost competed with London and Berlin. The profits of Father Madeleine were so great that by the end of the second year he was able to build a large factory, in which there were two immense workshops, one for men and the other for women: whoever was needy could go there and be sure of finding work and wages. Father Madeleine required the men to be willing, the women to be of good morals, and all to be honest. He divided the workshops, and separated the sexes in order that the girls and the women might not lose their modesty. On this point he was inflexible, although it was the only one in which he was in any degree rigid. He was confirmed in this severity by the opportunities for corruption that abounded in M—— sur M——, it being a garrisoned city. Finally his coming had been a beneficence, and his presence was a providence. Before the arrival of Father Madeleine, the whole region was languishing; now it was all alive with the healthy strength of labour. An active circulation kindled everything and penetrated everywhere. Idleness and misery were unknown. There was no pocket so obscure that it did not contain some money and no dwelling so poor that it was not the abode of some joy.

Father Madeleine employed everybody; he had only one condition, "Be an honest man!" "Be an honest woman!"

As we have said, in the midst of this activity, of which he was the cause and the pivot, Father Madeleine had made his fortune, but, very strangely for a mere man of business, that did not appear to be his principal care. It seemed that he thought much for others and little for himself. In 1820, it was known that he had six hundred and thirty thousand francs standing to his credit in the banking-house of Laffitte; but before setting aside this six hundred and thirty thousand francs for himself, he had expended more than a million for the city and for the poor.

The hospital was poorly endowed, and he made provision for ten additional beds. M—— sur M—— is divided into the upper city and the lower city. The lower city, where he lived, had only one school-house, a miserable hovel which was fast going to ruin; he built two, one for girls, and the other for boys, and paid the two teachers, from his own pocket, double the amount of their meagre salary from the government; and one day, he said to a neighbour who expressed surprise at this: "The two highest functionaries of the state are the nurse and the schoolmaster." He built, at his own expense, a house of refuge, an institution then almost unknown in France, and provided a fund for old and infirm labourers. About his factory, as a centre, a new quarter of the city had rapidly grown up, containing many indigent families, and he established a pharmacy that was free to all.

At first, when he began to attract the public attention, the good people would say: "This is a fellow who wishes to get rich." When they saw him enrich the country before he enriched himself, the same good people said: "This man is ambitious." This seemed the more probable, since he was religious and observed the forms of the church, to a certain extent, a thing much approved in those days. He went regularly to hear mass every Sunday. The local deputy, who scented rivalry everywhere, was not slow to borrow trouble on account of Madeleine's religion. This deputy, who had been a member of the Corps Legislatif of the Empire, partook of the religious ideas of a Father of the Oratory, known by the name of Fouché, Duke of Otranto, whose creature and friend he had been. In private he jested a little about God. But when he saw the rich manufacturer, Madeleine, go to low mass at seven o'clock, he foresaw a possible candidate in opposition to himself, and he resolved to outdo him. He took a Jesuit confessor, and went both to high mass and to vespers. Ambition at that time was, as the word itself imports, of the nature of a steeplechase. The poor, as well as God, gained by the terror of the honourable deputy, for he also established two beds at the hospital, which made twelve.

At length, in 1819, it was reported in the city one morning, that upon the recommendation of the prefect, and in consideration of the services he had rendered to the country, Father Madeleine had been appointed by the king, Mayor of M—— sur M——. Those who had pronounced the new-comer "an ambitious man," eagerly seized this opportunity, which all men desire, to exclaim:

"There! what did I tell you?"

M—— sur M—— was filled with the rumour, and the report proved to be well founded, for, a few days afterwards, the nomination appeared in the *Moniteur*. The next day Father Madeleine declined.

In the same year, 1819, the results of the new process invented by Madeleine had a place in the Industrial Exhibition, and upon the report of the jury, the king named the inventor a Chevalier of the Legion of Honour. Here was a new rumour for the little city. "Well! it was the Cross of the Legion of Honour that he wanted." Father Madeleine declined the Cross.

Decidedly this man was an enigma, and the good people gave up the field, saying, "After all, he is a sort of an adventurer."

As we have seen, the country owed a great deal to this man, and the poor owed him everything; he was so useful that all were compelled to honour him, and so kind that none could help loving him; his workmen in particular adored him, and he received their adoration with a sort of melancholy gravity. After he became rich, those who constituted "society" bowed to him as they met, and, in the city he began to be called Monsieur Madeleine;—but his workmen and the children continued to call him *Father Madeleine*, and at that name his face always wore a smile. As his wealth increased, invitations rained in on him. "Society" claimed him. The little exclusive parlours of M—— sur M——, which were carefully guarded, and in earlier days, of course, had been closed to the artisan, opened wide their doors to the millionaire. A thousand advances were made to him, but he refused them all.

And again the gossips were at no loss. "He is an ignorant man, and of poor education. No one knows where he came from. He does not know how to conduct himself in good society, and it is by no means certain that he knows how to read."

When they saw him making money, they said, "He is a merchant." When they saw the way in which he scattered his money they said, "He is ambitious." When they saw him refuse to accept honours, they said, "He is an adventurer." When they saw him repel the advances of the fashionable, they said, "He is a brute."

In 1820, five years after his arrival at M—— sur M——, the services that he had rendered to the region were so brilliant, and the wish of the whole population was so unanimous, that the king again appointed him mayor of the city. He refused again; but the prefect resisted his determination, the principal citizens came and urged him to accept, and the people in the streets begged him to do so; all insisted so strongly that at last he yielded. It was remarked that what appeared most of all to bring him to this determination, was the almost angry exclamation of an old woman belonging to the poorer class, who cried out to him from her door-stone, with some temper:

"A good mayor is a good thing. Are you afraid of the good you can do?"

This was the third step in his ascent. Father Madeleine had become Monsieur Madeleine, and Monsieur Madeleine now became Monsieur the Mayor.

III
MONEYS DEPOSITED WITH LAFFITTE

NEVERTHELESS he remained as simple as at first. He had grey hair, a serious eye, the brown complexion of a labourer, and the thoughtful countenance of a philosopher. He usually wore a hat with a wide brim, and a long coat of coarse cloth, buttoned to the chin. He fulfilled his duties as mayor, but beyond that his life was isolated. He talked with very few persons. He shrank from compliments, and with a touch of the hat walked on rapidly; he smiled to avoid talking, and gave to avoid smiling. The women said of him: "What a good bear!" His pleasure was to walk in the fields.

He always took his meals alone with a book open before him in which he read. His library was small but well selected. He loved books; books are cold but sure friends. As his growing fortune gave him more leisure, it seemed that he profited by it to cultivate his mind. Since he had been at M—— sur M——, it was remarked from year to year that his language became more polished, choicer, and more gentle.

In his walks he liked to carry a gun, though he seldom used it. When he did so, however, his aim was frightfully certain. He never killed an inoffensive animal, and never fired at any of the small birds.

Although he was no longer young, it was reported that he was of prodigious strength. He would offer a helping hand to any one who needed it, help up a fallen horse, push at a stalled wheel, or seize by the horns a bull that had broken loose. He always had his pockets full of money when he went out, and empty when he returned. When he passed through a village the ragged little youngsters would run after him with joy, and surround him like a swarm of flies.

It was surmised that he must have lived formerly in the country, for he had all sorts of useful secrets which he taught the peasants. He showed them how to destroy the grain-moth by sprinkling the granary and washing the cracks of the floor with a solution of common salt, and how to drive away the weevil by hanging up all about the ceiling and walls, in the pastures, and in the houses, the flowers of the orviot. He had recipes for clearing a field of rust, of vetches, of moles, of doggrass, and all the parasitic herbs which live upon the grain. He defended a rabbit warren against rats, with nothing but the odour of a little Barbary pig that he placed there.

One day he saw some country people very busy pulling up nettles; he looked at the heap of plants, uprooted, and already wilted, and said: "This is dead; but it would be well if we knew how to put it to some use. When the nettle is young, the leaves make excellent greens; when it grows old it has filaments and fibres like hemp and flax. Cloth made from the nettle is worth as much as that made from hemp. Chopped up, the nettle is good for poultry; pounded, it is good for horned cattle. The seed of the nettle mixed with the fodder of animals gives a lustre to their skin; the root, mixed with salt, produces a beautiful yellow dye. It makes, however, excellent hay, as it can be cut twice in a season. And what does the nettle need? very little soil, no care, no culture; except that the seeds fall as fast as they ripen, and it is difficult to gather them; that is all. If we would take a little pains, the nettle would be useful; we neglect it, and it becomes harmful. Then we kill it. How much men are like the nettle!" After a short silence, he added: "My friends, remember this, that there are no bad herbs, and no bad men, there are only bad cultivators."

The children loved him yet more, because he knew how to make charming little playthings out of straw and cocoanuts.

When he saw the door of a church shrouded with black, he entered: he sought out a funeral as others seek out a christening. The bereavement and the misfortune of others attracted him, because of his great gentleness; he mingled with friends who were in mourning, with families dressing in black, with the priests who were sighing around a corpse. He seemed glad to take as a text for his thoughts these funeral psalms, full of the vision of another world. With his eyes raised to heaven, he listened with a sort of aspiration towards all the mysteries of the infinite, to these sad voices, which sing upon the brink of the dark abyss of death.

He did a multitude of good deeds as secretly as bad ones are usually done. He would steal into houses in the evening, and furtively mount the stairs. A poor devil, on returning to his garret, would find that his door had been opened, sometimes even forced, during his absence. The poor man would cry out: "Some thief has been here!" When he got in, the first thing that he would see would be a piece of gold lying on the table. "The thief" who had been there was Father Madeleine.

He was affable and sad. The people used to say: "There is a rich man who does not show pride. There is a fortunate man who does not appear contented."

Some pretended that he was a mysterious personage, and declared that no one ever went into his room, which was a true anchorite's cell furnished with hour-glasses, and enlivened with death's heads and cross-bones. So much was said of this kind that some of the more mischievous of the elegant young ladies of M—— sur M—— called on him one day and said: "Monsieur Mayor, will you show us your room? We have heard that it is a grotto." He smiled, and introduced them on the spot to this "grotto." They were well punished for their curiosity. It was a room very well fitted up with mahogany furniture, ugly as all furniture of that kind is, and the walls covered with shilling paper. They could see nothing but two candlesticks of antique form that stood on the mantel, and appeared to be silver, "for they were marked," a remark full of the spirit of these little towns.

But none the less did it continue to be said that nobody ever went into that chamber, and that it was a hermit's cave, a place of dreams, a hole, a tomb.

It was also whispered that he had "immense" sums deposited with Laffitte, with the special condition that they were always at his immediate command, in such a way, it was added, that Monsieur Madeleine might arrive in the morning at Laffitte's, sign a receipt and carry away his two or three millions in ten minutes. In reality these "two or three millions" dwindled down, as we have said, to six hundred and thirty or forty thousand francs.

IV

MONSIEUR MADELEINE IN MOURNING

NEAR the beginning of the year 1821, the journals announced the decease of Monsieur Myriel, Bishop of D——, "surnamed *Monseigneur Bienvenu*," who died in the odour of sanctity at the age of eighty-two years.

The Bishop of D——, to add an incident which the journals omitted, had been blind for several years before he died, and was content therewith, his sister being with him.

Let us say by the way, to be blind and to be loved, is in fact, in this earth where nothing is complete, one of the most strangely exquisite forms of happiness. To have continually at your side a woman, a girl, a sister, a charming being, who is there because you have need of her, and because she cannot do without you, to know you are indispensable to her who is necessary to you, to be able at all times to measure her affection by the amount of her company that she gives you, and to say to yourself: she consecrates to me all her time, because I possess her whole heart; to see the thought instead of the face; to be sure of the fidelity of one being in the eclipse of the world; to imagine the rustling of her dress the rustling of wings; to hear her moving to and fro, going out, coming in, talking, singing, and to think that you are the centre of those steps, of those words, of that song; to manifest at every minute your personal attraction; to feel yourself powerful by so much the more as you are the more infirm; to become in darkness, and by reason of darkness, the star around which this angel gravitates; few happy lots can equal that. The supreme happiness of life is the conviction that we are loved; loved for ourselves—say rather, loved in spite of ourselves, this conviction the blind have. In their calamity, to be served, is to be caressed. Are they deprived of anything? No. Light is not lost where love enters. And what a love! a love wholly founded in purity. There is no blindness where there is certainty. The soul gropes in search of a soul, and finds it. And that soul, so found and proven, is a woman. A hand sustains you, it is hers; lips lightly touch your forehead, they are her lips; you hear one breathing near you, it is she. To have her wholly, from her devotion to her pity, never to be left, to have that sweet weakness which is your aid, to lean upon that unbending reed, to touch Providence with your hands and be able to grasp it in your arms; God made palpable, what transport! The heart, that dark but celestial flower, bursts into a mysterious bloom. You would not give that shade for all light! The angel-soul is there, for ever there; if she goes away, it is only to return; she fades away in dream and reappears in reality. You feel an approaching warmth, she is there. You overflow with serenity, gaiety, and ecstasy; you are radiant in your darkness. And the thousand little cares! The nothings which are enormous in this void. The most unspeakable accents of the womanly voice employed to soothe you, and making up to you the vanished universe! You are caressed through the soul. You see nothing, but you feel yourself adored. It is a paradise of darkness.

From this paradise Monseigneur Bienvenu passed to the other.

The announcement of his death was reproduced in the local paper of M—— sur M——. Monsieur Madeleine appeared next morning dressed in black with crape on his hat.

This mourning was noticed and talked about all over the town. It appeared to throw some light upon the origin of Monsieur Madeleine. The conclusion was that he was in some way related to the venerable bishop. "*He wears black for the Bishop of D——*," was the talk of the drawing-rooms; it elevated Monsieur Madeleine very much, and gave him suddenly, and in a trice, marked consideration in the noble world of M—— sur M——. The microscopic Faubourg Saint Germain of the little place thought of raising the quarantine for Monsieur Madeleine, the probable relative of a bishop. Monsieur Madeleine perceived the advancement that he had obtained, by the greater reverence of the old ladies, and the more frequent smiles of the young ladies. One evening, one of the dowagers of that little great world, curious by right of age, ventured to ask him: "The mayor is doubtless a relative of the late Bishop of D——?"

He said: "No, madame."

"But," the dowager persisted, "you wear mourning for him?"

He answered: "In my youth I was a servant in his family."

It was also remarked that whenever there passed through the city a young Savoyard who was tramping about the country in search of chimneys to sweep, the mayor would send for him, ask his name and give him money. The little Savoyards told each other, and many of them passed that way.

V

VAGUE FLASHES IN THE HORIZON

LITTLE by little in the lapse of time all opposition had ceased. At first there had been, as always happens with those who rise by their own efforts, slanders and calumnies against Monsieur Madeleine, soon this was reduced to satire, then it was only wit, then it vanished entirely; respect became complete, unanimous, cordial, and there came a moment, about 1821, when the words

Monsieur the Mayor were pronounced at M—— sur M——
with almost the same accent as the words Monseigneur the
Bishop at D—— in 1815. People came from thirty miles around
to consult Monsieur Madeleine. He settled differences, he prevented lawsuits, he reconciled enemies. Everybody, of his own
will, chose him for judge. He seemed to have the book of the
natural law by heart. A contagion of veneration had, in the
course of six or seven years, step by step, spread over the whole
country.

One man alone, in the city and its neighbourhood, held himself entirely clear from this contagion, and, whatever Father
Madeleine did, he remained indifferent, as if a sort of instinct,
unchangeable and imperturbable, kept him awake and on the
watch. It would seem, indeed, that there is in certain men the
veritable instinct of a beast, pure and complete like all instinct,
which creates antipathies and sympathies, which separates one
nature from another for ever; which never hesitates, never is
perturbed, never keeps silent, and never admits itself to be in
the wrong; clear in its obscurity, infallible, imperious, refractory
under all the counsels of intelligence, and all the solvents of
reason, and which, whatever may be their destinies, secretly
warns the dog-man of the presence of the cat-man, and the fox-
man of the presence of the lion-man.

Often, when Monsieur Madeleine passed along the street,
calm, affectionate, followed by the benedictions of all, it happened that a tall man, wearing a flat hat and an iron-grey coat,
and armed with a stout cane, would turn around abruptly
behind him, and follow him with his eyes until he disappeared,
crossing his arms, slowly shaking his head, and pushing his upper
with his under lip up to his nose, a sort of significant grimace
which might be rendered by: "But what is that man? I am sure
I have seen him somewhere. At all events, I at least am not his
dupe."

This personage, grave with an almost threatening gravity, was
one of those who, even in a hurried interview, command the
attention of the observer.

His name was Javert, and he was one of the police.

He exercised at M—— sur M—— the unpleasant, but useful,
function of inspector. He was not there at the date of Madeleine's arrival. Javert owed his position to the protection of
Monsieur Chabouillet, the secretary of the Minister of State,

Count Anglès, then prefect of police at Paris. When Javert arrived at M—— sur M—— the fortune of the great manufacturer had been made already, and Father Madeleine had become Monsieur Madeleine.

Certain police officers have a peculiar physiognomy in which can be traced an air of meanness mingled with an air of authority. Javert had this physiognomy, without meanness.

It is our conviction that if souls were visible to the eye we should distinctly see this strange fact that each individual of the human species corresponds to some one of the species of the animal creation; and we should clearly recognise the truth, hardly perceived by thinkers, that, from the oyster to the eagle, from the swine to the tiger, all animals are in man, and that each of them is in a man; sometimes even, several of them at a time.

Animals are nothing but the forms of our virtues and vices wandering before our eyes, the visible phantoms of our souls. God shows them to us to make us reflect. Only, as animals are but shadows, God has not made them capable of education in the complete sense of the word. Why should he? On the contrary, our souls being realities and having their peculiar end, God has given them intelligence, that is to say, the possibility of education. Social education, well attended to, can always draw out of a soul, whatever it may be, the usefulness that it contains.

Be this said, nevertheless, from the restricted point of view of the apparent earthly life, and without prejudice to the deep question of the anterior or ulterior personality of the beings that are not man. The visible *me* in no way authorises the thinker to deny the latent *me*. With this reservation, let us pass on.

Now, if we admit for a moment that there is in every man some one of the species of the animal creation, it will be easy for us to describe the guardian of the peace, Javert.

The peasants of the Asturias believe that in every litter of wolves there is one dog, which is killed by the mother, lest on growing up it should devour the other little ones.

Give a human face to this dog son of a wolf, and you will have Javert.

Javert was born in a prison. His mother was a fortune-teller whose husband was in the galleys. He grew up to think himself without the pale of society, and despaired of ever entering it. He noticed that society closes its doors, without pity, on two classes of men, those who attack it and those who guard it; he could choose between these two classes only; at the same time he felt that he had an indescribable basis of rectitude, order, and honesty, associated with an irrepressible hatred for that gypsy race to which he belonged. He entered the police. He succeeded. At forty he was an inspector.

In his youth he had been stationed in the galleys at the South.

Before going further, let us understand what we mean by the words human face, which we have just now applied to Javert.

The human face of Javert consisted of a snub nose, with two deep nostrils, which were bordered by large bushy whiskers that covered both his cheeks. One felt ill at ease the first time he saw those two forests and those two caverns. When Javert laughed, which was rarely and terribly, his thin lips parted, and showed, not only his teeth, but his gums; and around his nose there was a wrinkle as broad and wild as the muzzle of a fallow deer. Javert, when serious, was a bull-dog; when he laughed, he was a tiger. For the rest, a small head, large jaws, hair hiding the forehead and falling over the eyebrows, between the eyes a permanent central frown, a gloomy look, a mouth pinched and frightful, and an air of fierce command.

This man was a compound of two sentiments, very simple and very good in themselves, but he almost made them evil by his exaggeration of them, respect for authority and hatred of rebellion; and in his eyes, theft, murder, all crimes, were only forms of rebellion. In his strong and implicit faith he included all who held any function in the state, from the prime minister to the constable. He had nothing but disdain, aversion, and disgust for all who had once overstepped the bounds of the law. He was absolute, and admitted no exceptions. On the one hand he said: "A public officer cannot be deceived; a magistrate never does wrong!" And on the other he said: "They are irremediably lost; no good can come out of them." He shared fully the opinion of those extremists who attribute to human laws an indescribable power of making, or, if you will, of determining, demons, and who place a Styx at the bottom of society. He was stoical, serious, austere: a dreamer of stern dreams, humble and haughty, like all fanatics. His stare was cold and as piercing as a gimlet. His whole life was contained in these two words: waking and watching. He marked out a straight path through the most tortuous thing in the world; his conscience was bound up in his utility, his religion in his duties, and he was a spy as others are priests. Woe to him who should fall into his hands! He would have arrested his father if escaping from the galleys, and denounced his mother for violating her ticket of leave. And he would have done it with that sort of interior satisfaction that springs from virtue. His life was a life of privations, isolation, self-denial, and chastity: never any amusement. It was implacable duty, absorbed in the police as the Spartans were absorbed in Sparta, a pitiless detective, a fierce honesty, a marble-hearted informer, Brutus united with Vidocq.

The whole person of Javert expressed the spy and the informer. The mystic school of Joseph de Maistre, which at that time enlivened what were called the ultra journals with high-sounding cosmogonies, would have said that Javert was a symbol. You could not see his forehead which disappeared under his hat, you could not see his eyes which were lost under his brows, you could not see his chin which was buried in his cravat, you could not see his hands which were drawn up into his sleeves, you could not see his cane which he carried under his coat. But when the time came, you would see spring all at once out of this shadow, as from an ambush, a steep and narrow forehead, an ominous look, a threatening chin, enormous hands, and a monstrous club.

In his leisure moments, which were rare, although he hated books he read; wherefore he was not entirely illiterate. This was perceived also from a certain emphasis in his speech.

He was free from vice, we have said. When he was satisfied with himself, he allowed himself a pinch of snuff. That proved that he was human.

It will be easily understood that Javert was the terror of all that class which the annual statistics of the Minister of Justice include under the heading: *People without a fixed abode*. To speak the name of Javert would put all such to flight; the face of Javert petrified them.

Such was this formidable man.

Javert was like an eye always fixed on Monsieur Madeleine; an eye full of suspicion and conjecture. Monsieur Madeleine finally noticed it, but seemed to consider it of no consequence. He asked no question of Javert, he neither sought him nor shunned him, he endured this unpleasant and annoying stare without appearing to pay any attention to it. He treated Javert as he did everybody else, at ease and with kindness.

From some words that Javert had dropped, it was guessed that he had secretly hunted up, with that curiosity which belongs to his race, and which is more a matter of instinct than of will, all the traces of his previous life which Father Madeleine had left elsewhere. He appeared to know, and he said sometimes in a covert way, that somebody had gathered certain information in a certain region about a certain missing family. Once he happened to say, speaking to himself: "I think I have got him!" Then for three days he remained moody without speaking a word. It appeared that the clue which he thought he had was broken.

But, and this is the necessary corrective to what the meaning of certain words may have presented in too absolute a sense, there can be nothing really infallible in a human creature, and the very peculiarity of instinct is that it can be disturbed, followed up, and routed. Were this not so it would be superior to intelligence, and the beast would be in possession of a purer light than man.

Javert was evidently somewhat disconcerted by the completely natural air and the tranquillity of Monsieur Madeleine.

One day, however, his strange manner appeared to make an impression upon Monsieur Madeleine. The occasion was this:

VI
FATHER FAUCHELEVENT

MONSIEUR Madeleine was walking one morning along one of the unpaved alleys of M—— sur M——; he heard a shouting and saw a crowd at a little distance. He went to the spot. An old man, named Father Fauchelevent, had fallen under his cart, his horse being thrown down.

This Fauchelevent was one of the few who were still enemies of Monsieur Madeleine at this time. When Madeleine arrived in the place, the business of Fauchelevent, who was a notary of long-standing, and very well-read for a rustic, was beginning to decline. Fauchelevent had seen this mere artisan grow rich, while he himself, a professional man, had been going to ruin. This had filled him with jealousy, and he had done what he could on all occasions to injure Madeleine. Then came bankruptcy, and the old man, having nothing but a horse and cart, as he was without family, and without children, was compelled to earn his living as a carman.

The horse had his thighs broken, and could not stir. The old man was caught between the wheels. Unluckily he had fallen so that the whole weight rested upon his breast. The cart was heavily loaded. Father Fauchelevent was uttering doleful groans. They had tried to pull him out, but in vain. An unlucky effort, inexpert help, a false push, might crush him. It was impossible to extricate him otherwise than by raising the wagon from beneath. Javert, who came up at the moment of the accident, had sent for a jack.

Monsieur Madeleine came. The crowd fell back with respect.

"Help," cried old Fauchelevent. "Who is a good fellow to save an old man?"

Monsieur Madeleine turned towards the bystanders:

"Has anybody a jack?"

"They have gone for one," replied a peasant.

"How soon will it be here?"

"We sent to the nearest place, to Flachot Place, where there is a blacksmith; but it will take a good quarter of an hour at least."

"A quarter of an hour!" exclaimed Madeleine.

It had rained the night before, the road was soft, the cart was sinking deeper every moment, and pressing more and more on the breast of the old carman. It was evident that in less than five minutes his ribs would be crushed.

"We cannot wait a quarter of an hour," said Madeleine to the peasants who were looking on.

"We must!"

"But it will be too late! Don't you see that the wagon is sinking all the while?"

"It can't be helped."

"Listen," resumed Madeleine, "there is room enough still under the wagon for a man to crawl in, and lift it with his back. In half a minute we will have the poor man out. Is there nobody here who has strength and courage? Five louis d'ors for him!"

Nobody stirred in the crowd.

"Ten louis," said Madeleine.

The bystanders dropped their eyes. One of them muttered: "He'd have to be devilish stout. And then he would risk getting crushed."

"Come," said Madeleine, "twenty louis."

The same silence.

"It is not willingness which they lack," said a voice.

Monsieur Madeleine turned and saw Javert. He had not noticed him when he came.

Javert continued:

"It is strength. He must be a terrible man who can raise a wagon like that on his back."

Then, looking fixedly at Monsieur Madeleine, he went on emphasising every word that he uttered:

"Monsieur Madeleine, I have known but one man capable of doing what you call for."

Madeleine shuddered.

Javert added, with an air of indifference, but without taking his eyes from Madeleine:

"He was a convict."

"Ah!" said Madeleine.

"In the galleys at Toulon."

Madeleine became pale.

Meanwhile the cart was slowly settling down. Father Fauchelevent roared and screamed:

"I am dying! my ribs are breaking! a jack! anything! oh!"

Madeleine looked around him:

"Is there nobody, then, who wants to earn twenty louis and save this poor old man's life?"

None of the bystanders moved. Javert resumed:

"I have known but one man who could take the place of a jack; that was that convict."

"Oh! how it crushes me!" cried the old man.

Madeleine raised his head, met the falcon eye of Javert still fixed upon him, looked at the immovable peasants, and smiled sadly. Then, without saying a word, he fell on his knees, and even before the crowd had time to utter a cry, he was under the cart.

There was an awful moment of suspense and of silence.

Madeleine, lying almost flat under the fearful weight, was twice seen to try in vain to bring his elbows and knees nearer together. They cried out to him: "Father Madeleine! come out from there!" Old Fauchelevent himself said: "Monsieur Madeleine! go away! I must die, you see that; leave me! you will be crushed too." Madeleine made no answer.

The bystanders held their breath. The wheels were still sinking and it had now become almost impossible for Madeleine to extricate himself.

All at once the enormous mass started, the cart rose slowly, the wheels came half out of the ruts. A smothered voice was heard crying: "Quick! help!" It was Madeleine, who had just made a final effort.

They all rushed to the work. The devotion of one man had given strength and courage to all. The cart was lifted by twenty arms. Old Fauchelevent was safe.

Madeleine arose. He was very pale, though dripping with sweat. His clothes were torn and covered with mud. All wept. The old man kissed his knees and called him the good God. He himself wore on his face an indescribable expression of joyous and celestial suffering, and he looked with tranquil eye upon Javert, who was still watching him.

VII
FAUCHELEVENT BECOMES A GARDENER AT PARIS

FAUCHELEVENT had broken his knee-pan in his fall. Father Madeleine had him carried to an infirmary that he had established for his workmen in the same building with his factory, which was attended by two sisters of charity. The next morning the old man found a thousand franc bill upon the stand by the side of the bed, with this note in the handwriting of Father Madeleine: I have purchased your horse and cart. The cart was broken and the horse was dead. Fauchelevent got well, but he had a stiff knee. Monsieur Madeleine, through the recommendations of the sisters and the curé, got the old man a place as gardener at a convent in the Quartier Saint Antoine at Paris.

Some time afterwards Monsieur Madeleine was appointed mayor. The first time that Javert saw Monsieur Madeleine clothed with the scarf which gave him full authority over the city, he felt the same sort of shudder which a bull-dog would feel who should scent a wolf in his master's clothes. From that time he avoided him as much as he could. When the necessities of the service imperiously demanded it, and he could not do otherwise than come in contact with the mayor, he spoke to him with profound respect.

The prosperity which Father Madeleine had created at

M—— sur M——, in addition to the visible signs that we have
pointed out, had another symptom which, although not visible,
was not the less significant. This never fails. When the population is suffering, when there is lack of work, when trade falls
off, the tax-payer, constrained by poverty, resists taxation,
exhausts and overruns the delays allowed by law, and the government is forced to incur large expenditures in the costs of levy
and collection. When work is abundant, when the country is
rich and happy, the tax is easily paid and costs the state but little
to collect. It may be said that poverty and public wealth have an
infallible thermometer in the cost of the collection of the taxes.
In seven years, the cost of the collection of the taxes had been
reduced three-quarters in the district of M—— sur M——, so
that that district was frequently referred to especially by Monsieur de Villelè, then Minister of Finance.

Such was the situation of the country when Fantine
returned. No one remembered her. Luckily the door of M.
Madeleine's factory was like the face of a friend. She presented
herself there, and was admitted into the workshop for women.
The business was entirely new to Fantine; she could not be very
expert in it, and consequently did not receive much for her
day's work; but that little was enough, the problem was solved;
she was earning her living.

VIII

MADAME VICTURNIEN SPENDS
THIRTY FRANCS ON MORALITY

WHEN Fantine realised how she was living, she had a moment
of joy. To live honestly by her own labour; what a heavenly
boon! The taste for labour returned to her, in truth. She bought
a mirror, delighted herself with the sight of her youth, her fine
hair and her fine teeth, forgot many things, thought of nothing
save Cosette and the possibilities of the future, and was almost
happy. She hired a small room and furnished it on the credit of
her future labour; a remnant of her habits of disorder.

Not being able to say that she was married, she took good
care, as we have already intimated, not to speak of her little girl.

At first, as we have seen, she paid the Thénardiers punctually.
As she only knew how to sign her name she was obliged to
write through a public letter-writer.

She wrote often; that was noticed. They began to whisper in the women's workshop that Fantine "wrote letters," and that "she had airs." For prying into any human affairs, none is equal to those whom it does not concern. "Why does this gentleman never come till dusk?" "Why does Mr. So-and-so never hang his key on the nail on Thursday?" "Why does he always take the by-streets?" "Why does madame always leave her carriage before getting to the house?" "Why does she send to buy a quire of writing-paper when she has her portfolio full of it?" etc. etc. There are persons who, to solve these enigmas, which are more-over perfectly immaterial to them, spend more money, waste more time, and give themselves more trouble than would suffice for ten good deeds; and that gratuitously, and for the pleasure of it, without being paid for their curiosity in any other way than by curiosity. They will follow this man or that woman whole days, stand guard for hours at the corners of the street, under the entrance of a passage-way, at night in the cold and in the rain, bribe messengers, get hack-drivers and lackeys drunk, fee a chambermaid, or buy a porter. For what? for nothing. Pure crav-ing to see, to know, and to find out. Pure itching for scandal. And often these secrets made known, these mysteries published, these enigmas brought into the light of day, lead to catastrophes, to duels, to failures, to the ruin of families, and make lives wretched, to the great joy of those who have "discovered all" without any interest, and from pure instinct. A sad thing.

Some people are malicious from the mere necessity of talk-ing. Their conversation, tattling in the drawing-room, gossip in the ante-chamber, is like those fire-places that use up wood rapidly; they need a great deal of fuel; the fuel is their neighbour.

So Fantine was watched.

Beyond this, more than one was jealous of her fair hair and of her white teeth.

It was reported that in the shop, with all the rest about her, she often turned aside to wipe away a tear. Those were moments when she thought of her child; perhaps also of the man whom she had loved.

It is a mournful task to break the sombre attachments of the past.

It was ascertained that she wrote, at least twice a month, and always to the same address, and that she prepaid the postage. They succeeded in learning the address: *Monsieur, Monsieur*

Thénardier, inn-keeper Montfermeil. The public letter-writer, a simple old fellow, who could not fill his stomach with red-wine without emptying his pocket of his secrets, was made to reveal this at a drinking-house. In short, it became known that Fantine had a child. "She must be that sort of a woman." And there was one old gossip who went to Montfermeil, talked with the Thénardiers, and said on her return: "For my thirty-five francs, I have found out all about it. I have seen the child!"

The busybody who did this was a beldame, called Madame Victurnien, keeper and guardian of everybody's virtue. Madame Victurnien was fifty-six years old, and wore a mask of old age over her mask of ugliness. Her voice trembled, and she was capricious. It seemed strange, but this woman had been young. In her youth, in '93, she married a monk who had escaped from the cloister in a red cap, and passed from the Bernardines to the Jacobins. She was dry, rough, sour, sharp, crabbed, almost venomous; never forgetting her monk, whose widow she was, and who had ruled and curbed her harshly. She was a nettle bruised by a frock. At the restoration she became a bigot, and so energetically, that the priests had pardoned her monk episode. She had a little property, which she had bequeathed to a religious community with great flourish. She was in very good standing at the bishop's palace in Arras. This Madame Victurnien then went to Montfermeil, and returned saying "I have seen the child."

All this took time; Fantine had been more than a year at the factory, when one morning the overseer of the workshop handed her, on behalf of the mayor, fifty francs, saying that she was no longer wanted in the shop, and enjoining her, on behalf of the mayor, to leave the city.

This was the very same month in which the Thénardiers, after having asked twelve francs instead of six, had demanded fifteen francs instead of twelve.

Fantine was thunderstruck. She could not leave the city; she was in debt for her lodging and her furniture. Fifty francs were not enough to clear off that debt. She faltered out some suppliant words. The overseer gave her to understand that she must leave the shop instantly. Fantine was moreover only a moderate worker. Overwhelmed with shame even more than with despair, she left the shop, and returned to her room. Her fault then was now known to all!

She felt no strength to say a word. She was advised to see the mayor; she dared not. The mayor gave her fifty francs, because he was kind, and sent her away, because he was just. She bowed to that decree.

IX
SUCCESS OF MADAME VICTURNIEN

THE monk's widow was then good for something.

Monsieur Madeleine had known nothing of all this. These are combinations of events of which life is full. It was Monsieur Madeleine's habit scarcely ever to enter the women's workshop.

He had placed at the head of this shop an old spinster whom the curé had recommended to him, and he had entire confidence in this overseer, a very respectable person, firm, just, upright, full of that charity which consists in giving, but not having to the same extent that charity which consists in understanding and pardoning. Monsieur Madeleine left everything to her. The best men are often compelled to delegate their authority. It was in the exercise of this full power, and with the conviction that she was doing right, that the overseer had framed the indictment, tried, condemned, and executed Fantine.

As to the fifty francs, she had given them from a fund that Monsieur Madeleine had entrusted her with for alms-giving and aid to work-women, and of which she rendered no account.

Fantine offered herself as a servant in the neighbourhood; she went from one house to another. Nobody wanted her. She could not leave the city. The second-hand dealer to whom she was in debt for her furniture, and such furniture! had said to her: "If you go away, I will have you arrested as a thief." The landlord, whom she owed for rent, had said to her: "You are young and pretty, you can pay." She divided the fifty francs between the landlord and the dealer, returned to the latter three-quarters of his goods, kept only what was necessary, and found herself without work, without position, having nothing but her bed, and owing still about a hundred francs.

She began to make coarse shirts for the soldiers of the garrison, and earned twelve sous a day. Her daughter cost her ten. It was at this time that she began to get behindhand with the Thénardiers.

However, an old woman, who lit her candle for her when

she came home at night, taught her the art of living in misery. Behind living on a little, lies the art of living on nothing. They are two rooms; the first is obscure, the second is utterly dark.

Fantine learned how to do entirely without fire in winter, how to give up a bird that eats a farthing's worth of millet every other day, how to make a coverlid of her petticoat, and a petticoat of her coverlid, how to save her candle in taking her meals by the light of an opposite window. Few know how much certain feeble beings who have grown old in privation and honesty, can extract from a sou. This finally becomes a talent. Fantine acquired this sublime talent and took heart a little.

During these times, she said to a neighbour: "Bah! I say to myself: by sleeping but five hours and working all the rest at my sewing, I shall always succeed in nearly earning bread. And then, when one is sad, one eats less. Well! what with sufferings, troubles, a little bread on the one hand, anxiety on the other, all that will keep me alive."

In this distress, to have had her little daughter would have been a strange happiness. She thought of having her come. But what? to make her share her privation? and then, she owed the Thénardiers. How could she pay them? and the journey; how pay for that?

The old woman, who had given her what might be called lessons in indigent life, was a pious woman, Marguerite by name, a devotee of genuine devotion, poor, and charitable to the poor, and also to the rich, knowing how to write just enough to sign *Margeritte*, and believing in God, which is science.

There are many of these virtues in low places; some day they will be on high. This life has a morrow.

At first, Fantine was so much ashamed that she did not dare to go out.

When she was in the street, she imagined that people turned behind her and pointed at her; everybody looked at her and no one greeted her; the sharp and cold disdain of the passers-by penetrated her, body and soul, like a north wind.

In small cities an unfortunate woman seems to be laid bare to the sarcasm and the curiosity of all. In Paris, at least, nobody knows you, and that obscurity is a covering. Oh! how she longed to go to Paris! impossible.

She must indeed become accustomed to disrespect as she had to poverty. Little by little she learned her part. After two or three months she shook off her shame and went out as if there were nothing in the way. "It is all one to me," said she.

She went and came, holding her head up and wearing a bitter smile, and felt that she was becoming shameless.

Madame Victurnien sometimes saw her pass her window, noticed the distress of "that creature," thanks to her "put back to her place," and congratulated herself. The malicious have a dark happiness.

Excessive work fatigued Fantine, and the slight dry cough that she had increased. She sometimes said to her neighbour, Marguerite, "just feel how hot my hands are."

In the morning, however, when with an old broken comb she combed her fine hair which flowed down in silky waves, she enjoyed a moment of happiness.

X
RESULTS OF THE SUCCESS

SHE had been discharged towards the end of winter; summer passed away, but winter returned. Short days, less work. In winter there is no heat, no light, no noon, evening touches morning, there is fog, and mist, the window is frosted, and you cannot see clearly. The sky is but the mouth of a cave. The whole day is the cave. The sun has the appearance of a pauper. Frightful season! Winter changes into stone the water of heaven and the heart of man. Her creditors harassed her.

Fantine earned too little. Her debts had increased. The Thénardiers being poorly paid, were constantly writing letters to her, the contents of which disheartened her, while the postage was ruining her. One day they wrote to her that her little Cosette was entirely destitute of clothing for the cold weather, that she needed a woollen skirt, and that her mother must send at least ten francs for that. She received the letter and crushed it in her hand for a whole day. In the evening she went into a barber's shop at the corner of the street, and pulled out her comb. Her beautiful fair hair fell below her waist.

"What beautiful hair!" exclaimed the barber.

"How much will you give me for it?" said she.

"Ten francs."

"Cut it off."

She bought a knit skirt and sent it to the Thénardiers.

This skirt made the Thénardiers furious. It was the money that they wanted. They gave the skirt to Eponine. The poor lark still shivered.

Fantine thought: "My child is no longer cold, I have clothed her with my hair." She put on a little round cap which concealed her shorn head, and with that she was still pretty.

A gloomy work was going on in Fantine's heart.

When she saw that she could no longer dress her hair, she began to look with hatred on all around her. She had long shared in the universal veneration for Father Madeleine; nevertheless by dint of repeating to herself that it was he who had turned her away, and that he was the cause of her misfortunes, she came to hate him also, and especially. When she passed the factory at the hours in which the labourers were at the door, she forced herself to laugh and sing.

An old working-woman who saw her once singing and laughing in this way, said: "There is a girl who will come to a bad end."

She took a lover, the first comer, a man whom she did not love, through bravado, and with rage in her heart. He was a wretch, a kind of mendicant musician, a lazy ragamuffin, who beat her, and who left her, as she had taken him, with disgust.

She worshipped her child.

The lower she sank, the more all became gloomy around her, the more the sweet little angel shone out in the bottom of her heart. She would say: "When I am rich, I shall have my Cosette with me," and she laughed. The cough did not leave her, and she had night sweats.

One day she received from the Thénardiers a letter in these words: "Cosette is sick of an epidemic disease. A miliary fever they call it. The drugs necessary are dear. It is ruining us, and we can no longer pay for them. Unless you send us forty francs within a week the little one will die."

She burst out laughing, and said to her old neighbour:

"Oh! they are nice! forty francs! think of that! that is two Napoleons! Where do they think I can get them? Are they fools, these boors?"

She went, however, to the staircase, near a dormer window, and read the letter again.

Then she went down stairs and out of doors, running and jumping, still laughing.

Somebody who met her said to her: "What is the matter with you, that you are so gay?"

She answered: "A stupid joke that some country people have just written me. They ask for forty francs; the boors!"

As she passed through the square, she saw many people gathered about an odd-looking carriage on the top of which stood a man in red clothes, declaiming. He was a juggler and a travelling dentist, and was offering to the public complete sets of teeth, opiates, powders, and elixirs.

Fantine joined the crowd and began to laugh with the rest at this harangue, in which were mingled slang for the rabble and jargon for the better sort. The puller of teeth saw this beautiful girl laughing, and suddenly called out: "You have pretty teeth, you girl who are laughing there. If you will sell me your two incisors, I will give you a gold Napoleon for each of them."

"What is that? What are my incisors?" asked Fantine.

"The incisors," resumed the professor of dentistry, "are the front teeth, the two upper ones."

"How horrible!" cried Fantine.

"Two Napoleons!" grumbled a toothless old hag who stood by. "How lucky she is!"

Fantine fled away and stopped her ears not to hear the shrill voice of the man who called after her: "Consider, my beauty! two Napoleons! how much good they will do you! If you have the courage for it, come this evening to the inn of the *Tillac d'Argent*; you will find me there."

Fantine returned home; she was raving, and told the story to her good neighbour Marguerite: "Do you understand that? isn't he an abominable man? Why do they let such people go about the country? Pull out my two front teeth! why, I should be horrible! The hair is bad enough, but the teeth! Oh! what a monster of a man! I would rather throw myself from the fifth story, head first, to the pavement! He told me that he would be this evening at the *Tillac d'Argent*."

"And what was it he offered you?" asked Marguerite.

"Two Napoleons."

"That is forty francs."

"Yes," said Fantine, "that makes forty francs."

She became thoughtful and went about her work. In a quarter of an hour she left her sewing and went to the stairs to read again the Thénardiers' letter.

On her return she said to Marguerite, who was at work near her:

"What does this mean, a miliary fever? Do you know?"

"Yes," answered the old woman, "it is a disease."

"Then it needs a good many drugs?"

"Yes; terrible drugs."

"How does it come upon you?"

"It is a disease that comes in a moment."

"Does it attack children?"

"Children especially."

"Do people die of it?"

"Very often," said Marguerite.

Fantine withdrew and went once more to read over the letter on the stairs.

In the evening she went out, and took the direction of the Rue de Paris where the inns are.

The next morning, when Marguerite went into Fantine's chamber before daybreak, for they always worked together, and so made one candle do for the two, she found Fantine seated upon her couch, pale and icy. She had not been in bed. Her cap had fallen upon her knees. The candle had burned all night, and was almost consumed.

Marguerite stopped upon the threshold, petrified by this wild disorder, and exclaimed: "Good Lord! the candle is all burned out. Something has happened."

Then she looked at Fantine, who sadly turned her shorn head.

Fantine had grown ten years older since evening.

"Bless us!" said Marguerite, "what is the matter with you, Fantine?"

"Nothing," said Fantine. "Quite the contrary. My child will not die with that frightful sickness for lack of aid. I am satisfied."

So saying, she showed the old woman two Napoleons that glistened on the table.

"Oh! good God!" said Marguerite. "Why there is a fortune! where did you get these louis d'or?"

"I got them," answered Fantine.

At the same time she smiled. The candle lit up her face. It was a sickening smile, for the corners of her mouth were stained with blood, and a dark cavity revealed itself there.

The two teeth were gone.

She sent the forty francs to Montfermeil.

And this was a ruse of the Thénardiers to get money. Cosette was not sick.

Fantine threw her looking-glass out of the window. Long before she had left her little room on the second story for an attic room with no other fastening than a latch; one of those garret rooms the ceiling of which makes an angle with the floor and hits your head at every moment. The poor cannot go to the end of their chamber or to the end of their destiny, but by bending continually more and more. She no longer had a bed, she retained a rag that she called her coverlid, a mattress on the floor, and a worn-out straw chair. Her little rose-bush was dried up in the corner, forgotten. In the other corner was a butter-pot for water, which froze in the winter, and the different levels at which the water had stood remained marked a long time by circles of ice. She had lost her modesty, she was losing her coquetry. The last sign. She would go out with a dirty cap. Either from want of time or from indifference she no longer washed her linen. As fast as the heels of her stockings wore out she drew them down into her shoes. This was shown by certain perpendicular wrinkles. She mended her old, worn-out corsets with bits of calico which were torn by the slightest motion. Her creditors quarrelled with her and gave her no rest. She met them in the street; she met them again on her stairs. She passed whole nights in weeping and thinking. She had a strange brilliancy in her eyes, and a constant pain in her shoulder near the top of her left shoulder-blade. She coughed a great deal. She hated Father Madeleine thoroughly, and never complained. She sewed seventeen hours a day; but a prison contractor, who was working prisoners at a loss, suddenly cut down the price, and this reduced the day's wages of free labourers to nine sous. Seventeen hours of work, and nine sous a day! Her creditors were more pitiless than ever. The second-hand dealer, who had taken back nearly all his furniture, was constantly saying to her: "When will you pay me, wench?"

Good God! what did they want her to do? She felt herself hunted down, and something of the wild beast began to develop within her. About the same time Thénardier wrote to her that really he had waited with too much generosity, and that he must have a hundred francs immediately, or else little Cosette, just convalescing after her severe sickness, would be turned out of doors into the cold and upon the highway, and that she would become what she could, and would perish if she must. "A hundred francs," thought Fantine. "But where is there a place where one can earn a hundred sous a day?"

"Come!" said she, "I will sell what is left."

The unfortunate creature became a woman of the town.

XI
CHRISTUS NOS LIBERAVIT

WHAT is this history of Fantine? It is society buying a slave.

From whom? From misery.

From hunger, from cold, from loneliness, from abandonment, from privation. Melancholy barter. A soul for a bit of bread. Misery makes the offer, society accepts.

The holy law of Jesus Christ governs our civilisation, but it does not yet permeate it; it is said that slavery has disappeared from European civilisation. This is a mistake. It still exists: but it weighs now only upon woman, and it is called prostitution.

It weighs upon woman, that is to say, upon grace, upon feebleness, upon beauty, upon maternity. This is not one of the least of man's shames.

At the stage of this mournful drama at which we have now arrived, Fantine has nothing left of what she had formerly been. She has become marble in becoming corrupted. Whoever touches her feels a chill. She goes her ways, she endures you and she knows you not, she wears a dishonoured and severe face. Life and social order have spoken their last word to her. All that can happen to her has happened. She has endured all, borne all, experienced all, suffered all, lost all, wept for all. She is resigned, with that resignation that resembles indifference as death resembles sleep. She shuns nothing now. She fears nothing now. Every cloud falls upon her, and all the ocean sweeps over her! What matters it to her! the sponge is already drenched.

She believed so at least, but it is a mistake to imagine that man can exhaust his destiny, or can reach the bottom of anything whatever.

Alas! what are all these destinies thus driven pell-mell? whither go they? why are they so?

He who knows that, sees all the shadow.

He is alone. His name is God.

XII
THE IDLENESS OF MONSIEUR BAMATABOIS

THERE is in all small cities, and there was at M—— sur M——
in particular, a set of young men who nibble their fifteen hundred livres of income in the country with the same air with
which their fellows devour two hundred thousand francs a year
at Paris. They are beings of the great neuter species, geldings,
parasites, nobodies, who have a little land, a little folly, and a
little wit, who would be clowns in a drawing-room, and think
themselves gentlemen in a barroom, who talk about "my fields,
my woods, my peasants," hiss the actresses at the theatre to
prove that they are persons of taste, quarrel with the officers of
the garrison to show that they are gallant, hunt, smoke, gape,
drink, take snuff, play billiards, stare at passengers getting out of
the coach, live at the café, dine at the inn, have a dog who eats
the bones under the table, and a mistress who sets the dishes
upon it, hold fast to a sou, overdo the fashions, admire tragedy,
despise women, wear out their old boots, copy London as
reflected from Paris, and Paris as reflected from Pont-à-Mous-
son, grow stupid as they grow old, do no work, do no good,
and not much harm.

Monsieur Félix Tholomyès, had he remained in his province
and never seen Paris, would have been such a man.

If they were richer, we should say: they are dandies; if they
were poorer, we should say: they are vagabonds. They are simply
idlers. Among these idlers there are some that are bores, some
that are bored, some dreamers, and some jokers.

In those days, a dandy was made up of a large collar, a large
cravat, a watch loaded with chains, three waistcoats worn one
over the other, of different colours, the red and blue within, a
short olive-coloured coat with a fish-tail skirt, a double row of
silver buttons alternating with one another and running up to
the shoulder, and pantaloons of a lighter olive, ornamented at
the two seams with an indefinite, but always odd, number of
ribs, varying from one to eleven, a limit which was never
exceeded. Add to this, Blucher boots with little iron caps on the
heel, a high-crowned and narrow-brimmed hat, hair bushed
out, an enormous cane, and conversation spiced with the puns
of Potier. Above all, spurs and moustaches. In those days, moustaches meant civilians, and spurs meant pedestrians.

The provincial dandy wore longer spurs and fiercer moustaches.

It was the time of the war of the South American Republics against the King of Spain, of Bolivar against Morillo. Hats with narrow brims were Royalist, and were called Morillos; the liberals wore hats with wide brims which were called Bolivars.

Eight or ten months after what has been related in the preceding pages, in the early part of January, 1823, one evening when it had been snowing, one of these dandies, one of these idlers, a "well-intentioned" man, for he wore a morillo, very warmly wrapped in one of those large cloaks which completed the fashionable costume in cold weather, was amusing himself with tormenting a creature who was walking back and forth before the window of the officers' café, in a ball-dress, with her neck and shoulders bare, and flowers upon her head. The dandy was smoking, for that was decidedly the fashion.

Every time that the woman passed before him, he threw out at her, with a puff of smoke from his cigar, some remark which he thought was witty and pleasant as: "How ugly you are!" "Are you trying to hide?" "You have lost your teeth!" etc., etc. This gentleman's name was Monsieur Bamatabois. The woman, a rueful, bedizened spectre, who was walking backwards and forwards upon the snow, did not answer him, did not even look at him, but continued her walk in silence and with a dismal regularity that brought her under his sarcasm every five minutes, like the condemned soldier who at stated periods returns under the rods. This failure to secure attention doubtless piqued the loafer, who, taking advantage of the moment when she turned, came up behind her with a stealthy step and stifling his laughter stooped down, seized a handful of snow from the side walk, and threw it hastily into her back between her naked shoulders. The girl roared with rage, turned, bounded like a panther, and rushed upon the man, burying her nails in his face, and using the most frightful words that ever fell from the off-scouring of a guard-house. These insults were thrown out in a voice roughened by brandy, from a hideous mouth which lacked the two front teeth. It was Fantine.

At the noise which this made, the officers came out of the café, a crowd gathered, and a large circle was formed, laughing, jeering and applauding, around this centre of attraction composed of two beings who could hardly be recognised as a man and a woman, the man defending himself, his hat knocked off, the woman kicking and striking, her head bare, shrieking, toothless, and without hair, livid with wrath, and horrible.

Suddenly a tall man advanced quickly from the crowd, seized the woman by her muddy satin waist, and said: "Follow me!"

The woman raised her head; her furious voice died out at once. Her eyes were glassy, from livid she had become pale, and she shuddered with a shudder of terror. She recognised Javert.

The dandy profited by this to steal away.

XIII
SOLUTION OF SOME QUESTIONS OF MUNICIPAL POLICE

JAVERT dismissed the bystanders, broke up the circle and walked off rapidly towards the Bureau of Police, which is at the end of the square, dragging the poor creature after him. She made no resistance, but followed mechanically. Neither spoke a word. The flock of spectators, in a paroxysm of joy, followed with their jokes. The deepest misery, an opportunity for obscenity.

When they reached the Bureau of Police, which was a low hall warmed by a stove, and guarded by a sentinel, with a grated window looking on the street, Javert opened the door, entered with Fantine, and closed the door behind him, to the great disappointment of the curious crowd who stood upon tiptoe and stretched their necks before the dirty window of the guard-house, in their endeavours to see. Curiosity is a kind of glutton. To see is to devour.

On entering Fantine crouched down in a corner motionless and silent, like a frightened dog.

The sergeant of the guard placed a lighted candle on the table. Javert sat down, drew from his pocket a sheet of stamped paper, and began to write.

These women are placed by our laws completely under the discretion of the police. They do what they will with them, punish them as they please, and confiscate at will those two sad things which they call their industry and their liberty. Javert was impassible; his grave face betrayed no emotion. He was, however, engaged in serious and earnest consideration. It was one of those moments in which he exercised without restraint, but with all the scruples of a strict conscience, his formidable discretionary power. At this moment he felt that his policeman's stool was a bench of justice. He was conducting a trial. He was trying and condemning. He called all the ideas of which his mind was capable around the grand thing that he was doing. The more he examined the conduct of this girl, the more he revolted at it. It was clear that he had seen a crime committed. He had seen, there in the street, society represented by a property holder and an elector, insulted and attacked by a creature who was an outlaw and an outcast. A prostitute had assaulted a citizen. He, Javert, had seen that himself. He wrote in silence.

When he had finished, he signed his name, folded the paper, and handed it to the sergeant of the guard, saying: "Take three men, and carry this girl to jail." Then turning to Fantine: "You are in for six months."

The hapless woman shuddered.

"Six months! six months in prison!" cried she. "Six months to earn seven sous a day! but what will become of Cosette! my daughter! my daughter! Why, I still owe more than a hundred francs to the Thénardiers, Monsieur Inspector, do you know that?"

She dragged herself along on the floor, dirtied by the muddy boots of all these men, without rising, clasping her hands, and moving rapidly on her knees.

"Monsieur Javert," said she, "I beg your pity. I assure you that I was not in the wrong. If you had seen the beginning, you would have seen. I swear to you by the good God that I was not in the wrong. That gentleman, whom I do not know, threw snow in my back. Have they the right to throw snow into our backs when we are going along quietly like that without doing any harm to anybody? That made me wild. I am not very well, you see! and then he had already been saying things to me for some time. 'You are homely!' 'You have no teeth!' I know too well that I have lost my teeth. I did not do anything; I thought: 'He is a gentleman who is amusing himself.' I was not immodest with him, I did not speak to him. It was then that he threw the snow at me. Monsieur Javert, my good Monsieur Inspector! was there no one there who saw it and can tell you that this is true! I perhaps did wrong to get angry. You know, at the first moment, we cannot master ourselves. We are excitable. And then, to have something so cold thrown into your back when you are not expecting it. I did wrong to spoil the gentleman's hat. Why has he gone away? I would ask his pardon. Oh! I would beg his pardon. Have pity on me now this once, Monsieur Javert. Stop, you don't know how it is, in the prisons they only earn seven sous; that is not the fault of the government, but they earn seven sous, and just think that I have a hundred francs to pay, or else they will turn away my little one. O my God! I cannot have her with me. What I do is so vile! O my Cosette, O my little angel of the good blessed Virgin, what will she become, poor famished child! I tell you the Thénardiers are inn-keepers, boors, they have no consideration. They must have money. Do not put me in prison! Do you see, she is a little one that they will put out on the highway, to do what she can, in the very heart of winter; you must feel pity for such a thing, good Monsieur Javert. If she were older, she could earn her living, but she cannot at such an age. I am not a bad woman at heart. It is not laziness and appetite that have brought me to this; I have drunk brandy, but it was from misery. I do not like it, but it stupefies. When I was happier, one would only have had to look into my wardrobe to see that I was not a disorderly woman. I had linen, much linen. Have pity on me, Monsieur Javert."

She talked thus, bent double, shaken with sobs, blinded by tears, her neck bare, clenching her hands, coughing with a dry and short cough, stammering very feebly with an agonised voice. Great grief is a divine and terrible radiance which transfigures the wretched. At that moment Fantine had again become beautiful. At certain instants she stopped and tenderly kissed the policeman's coat. She would have softened a heart of granite; but you cannot soften a heart of wood.

"Come," said Javert, "I have heard you. Haven't you got through? March off at once! you have your six months! the Eternal Father in person could do nothing for you."

At those solemn words, *The Eternal Father in person could do nothing for you*, she understood that her sentence was fixed. She sank down murmuring:

"Mercy!"

Javert turned his back.

The soldiers seized her by the arms.

A few minutes before a man had entered without being noticed. He had closed the door, and stood with his back against it, and heard the despairing supplication of Fantine.

When the soldiers put their hands upon the wretched being, who would not rise, he stepped forward out of the shadow and said:

"One moment, if you please!"

Javert raised his eyes and recognised Monsieur Madeleine. He took off his hat, and bowing with a sort of angry awkwardness:

"Pardon, Monsieur Mayor—"

This word, Monsieur Mayor, had a strange effect upon Fantine. She sprang to her feet at once like a spectre rising from the ground, pushed back the soldiers with her arms, walked straight to Monsieur Madeleine before they could stop her, and gazing at him fixedly, with a wild look, she exclaimed:

"Ah! it is you then who are Monsieur Mayor!"

Then she burst out laughing and spit in his face.

Monsieur Madeleine wiped his face and said:

"Inspector Javert, set this woman at liberty."

Javert felt as though he were on the point of losing his senses. He experienced, at that moment, blow on blow, and almost simultaneously, the most violent emotions that he had known in his life. To see a woman of the town spit in the face of a mayor was a thing so monstrous that in his most daring suppositions he would have thought it sacrilege to believe it possible. On the other hand, deep down in his thought, he dimly brought into hideous association what this woman was and what this mayor might be, and then he perceived with horror something indescribably simple in this prodigious assault. But when he saw this mayor, this magistrate, wipe his face quietly and say: *set this woman at liberty*, he was stupefied with amazement; thought and speech alike failed him; the sum of possible astonishment had been overpassed. He remained speechless.

The mayor's words were not less strange a blow to Fantine. She raised her bare arm and clung to the damper of the stove as if she were staggered. Meanwhile she looked all around and began to talk in a low voice, as if speaking to herself:

"At liberty! they let me go! I am not to go to prison for six months! Who was it said that? It is not possible that anybody said that. I misunderstood. That cannot be this monster of a mayor! Was it you, my good Monsieur Javert, who told them to set me at liberty? Oh! look now! I will tell you and you will let me go. This monster of a mayor, this old whelp of a mayor, he is the cause of all this. Think of it, Monsieur Javert, he turned me away! on account of a parcel of beggars who told stories in the workshop. Was not that horrible! To turn away a poor girl who does her work honestly. Since that I could not earn enough, and all the wretchedness has come. To begin with, there is a change that you gentlemen of the police ought to make—that is, to stop prison contractors from wronging poor people. I will tell you how it is; listen. You earn twelve sous at shirt making, that falls to nine sous, not enough to live. Then we must do what we can. For me, I had my little Cosette, and I had to be a bad woman. You see now that it is this beggar of a mayor who has done all this, and then, I did stamp on the hat of this gentleman in front of the officers' café. But he, he had spoiled my whole dress with the snow. We women, we have only one silk dress, for evening. See you, I have never meant to do wrong, in truth, Monsieur Javert, and I see everywhere much worse women than I am who are much more fortunate. Oh, Monsieur Javert, it is you who said that they must let me go, is it not? Go and inquire, speak to my landlord; I pay my rent, and he will surely tell you that I am honest. Oh dear, I beg your pardon, I have touched—I did not know it—the damper of the stove, and it smokes."

Monsieur Madeleine listened with profound attention. While she was talking, he had fumbled in his waistcoat, had taken out his purse and opened it. It was empty. He had put it back into his pocket. He said to Fantine:

"How much did you say that you owed?"

Fantine, who had only looked at Javert, turned towards him:

"Who said anything to you?"

Then addressing herself to the soldiers:

"Say now, did you see how I spit in his face? Oh! you old scoundrel of a mayor, you come here to frighten me, but I am not afraid of you. I am afraid of Monsieur Javert. I am afraid of my good Monsieur Javert!"

As she said this she turned again towards the inspector:

"Now, you see, Monsieur Inspector, you must be just. I know that you are just, Monsieur Inspector; in fact, it is very simple, a man who jocosely throws a little snow into a woman's back, that makes them laugh, the officers, they must divert themselves with something, and we poor things are only for their amusement. And then, you, you come, you are obliged to keep order, you arrest the woman who has done wrong, but on reflection, as you are good, you tell them to set me at liberty, that is for my little one, because six months in prison, that would prevent my supporting my child. Only never come back again, wretch! Oh! I will never come back again, Monsieur Javert! They may do anything they like with me now, I will not stir. Only, to-day, you see, I cried out because that hurt me. I did not in the least expect that snow from that gentleman, and then, I have told you, I am not very well, I cough, I have something in my chest like a ball which burns me, and the doctor tells me: 'be careful.' Stop, feel, give me your hand, don't be afraid, here it is.''

She wept no more; her voice was caressing; she placed Javert's great coarse hand upon her white and delicate chest, and looked at him smiling.

Suddenly she hastily adjusted the disorder of her garments, smoothed down the folds of her dress, which, in dragging herself about, had been raised almost as high as her knees, and walked towards the door, saying in an undertone to the soldiers, with a friendly nod of the head:

"Boys, Monsieur the Inspector said that you must release me; I am going.''

She put her hand upon the latch. One more step and she would be in the street.

Javert until that moment had remained standing, motionless, his eyes fixed on the ground, looking, in the midst of the scene, like a statue which was waiting to be placed in position.

The sound of the latch roused him. He raised his head with an expression of sovereign authority, an expression always the more frightful in proportion as power is vested in beings of lower grade; ferocious in the wild beast, atrocious in the undeveloped man.

"Sergeant," exclaimed he, "don't you see that this vagabond is going off? Who told you to let her go?''

"I," said Madeleine.

At the words of Javert, Fantine had trembled and dropped the latch, as a thief who is caught, drops what he has stolen. When Madeleine spoke, she turned, and from that moment, without saying a word, without even daring to breathe freely, she looked by turns from Madeleine to Javert and from Javert to Madeleine, as the one or the other was speaking.

It was clear that Javert must have been, as they say, "thrown off his balance," or he would not have allowed himself to address the sergeant as he did, after the direction of the mayor to set Fantine at liberty. Had he forgotten the presence of the mayor? Had he finally decided within himself that it was impossible for "an authority" to give such an order, and that very certainly the mayor must have said one thing when he meant another? Or, in view of the enormities which he had witnessed for the last two hours, did he say to himself that it was necessary to revert to extreme measures, that it was necessary for the little to make itself great, for the detective to transform himself into a magistrate, for the policeman to become a judge, and that in this fearful extremity, order, law, morality, government, society as a whole, were personified in him, Javert?

However this might be, when Monsieur Madeleine pronounced that "I" which we have just heard, the inspector of police, Javert, turned towards the mayor, pale, cold, with blue lips, a desperate look, his whole body agitated with an imperceptible tremor, and, an unheard-of thing, said to him, with a downcast look, but a firm voice:

"Monsieur Mayor, that cannot be done."

"Why?" said Monsieur Madeleine.

"This wretched woman has insulted a citizen."

"Inspector Javert," replied Monsieur Madeleine, in a conciliating and calm tone, "listen. You are an honest man, and I have no objection to explaining myself to you. The truth is this. I was passing through the square when you arrested this woman; there was a crowd still there; I learned the circumstances; I know all about it; it is the citizen who was in the wrong, and who, by a faithful police, would have been arrested."

Javert went on:

"This wretch has just insulted Monsieur the Mayor."

"That concerns me," said Monsieur Madeleine. "The insult to me rests with myself, perhaps. I can do what I please about it."

"I beg Monsieur the Mayor's pardon. The insult rests not with him, it rests with justice."

"Inspector Javert," replied Monsieur Madeleine, "the highest justice is conscience. I have heard this woman. I know what I am doing."

"And for my part, Monsieur Mayor, I do not know what I am seeing."

"Then content yourself with obeying."

"I obey my duty. My duty requires that this woman spend six months in prison."

Monsieur Madeleine answered mildly:

"Listen to this. She shall not a day."

At these decisive words, Javert had the boldness to look the mayor in the eye, and said, but still in a tone of profound respect:

"I am very sorry to resist Monsieur the Mayor; it is the first time in my life, but he will deign to permit me to observe that I am within the limits of my own authority. I will speak, since the mayor desires it, on the matter of the citizen. I was there. This girl fell upon Monsieur Bamatabois, who is an elector and the owner of that fine house with a balcony, that stands at the corner of the esplanade, three stories high, and all of hewn stone. Indeed, there are some things in this world which must be considered. However that may be, Monsieur Mayor, this matter belongs to the police of the street; that concerns me, and I detain the woman Fantine."

At this Monsieur Madeleine folded his arms and said in a severe tone which nobody in the city had ever yet heard:

"The matter of which you speak belongs to the municipal police. By the terms of articles nine, eleven, fifteen, and sixty-six of the code of criminal law, I am the judge of it. I order that this woman be set at liberty."

Javert endeavoured to make a last attempt.

"But, Monsieur Mayor——"

"I refer you to article eighty-one of the law of December 13th, 1799, upon illegal imprisonment."

"Monsieur Mayor, permit——"

"Not another word."

"However——"

"Retire," said Monsieur Madeleine.

Javert received the blow, standing in front, and with open breast like a Russian soldier. He bowed to the ground before the mayor, and went out.

Fantine stood by the door and looked at him with stupor as he passed before her.

Meanwhile she also was the subject of a strange revolution. She had seen herself somehow disputed about by two opposing powers. She had seen struggling before her very eyes two men who held in their hands her liberty, her life, her soul, her child;

one of these men was drawing her to the side of darkness, the other was leading her towards the light. In this contest, seen with distortion through the magnifying power of fright, these two men had appeared to her like two giants; one spoke as her demon, the other as her good angel. The angel had vanquished the demon, and the thought of it made her shudder from head to foot; this angel, this deliverer was precisely the man whom she abhorred, this mayor whom she had so long considered as the author of all her woes, this Madeleine! and at the very moment when she had insulted him in a hideous fashion, he had saved her! Had she then been deceived? Ought she then to change her whole heart? She did not know, she trembled. She listened with dismay, she looked around with alarm, and at each word that Monsieur Madeleine uttered, she felt the fearful darkness of her hatred melt within and flow away, while there was born in her heart an indescribable and unspeakable warmth of joy, of confidence, and of love.

When Javert was gone, Monsieur Madeleine turned towards her, and said to her, speaking slowly and with difficulty, like a man who is struggling that he may not weep:

"I have heard you. I knew nothing of what you have said. I believe that it is true. I did not even know that you had left my workshop. Why did you not apply to me? But now: I will pay your debts, I will have your child come to you, or you shall go to her. You shall live here, at Paris, or where you will. I take charge of your child and you. You shall do no more work, if you do not wish to. I will give you all the money that you need. You shall again become honest in again becoming happy. More than that, listen. I declare to you from this moment, if all is as you say, and I do not doubt it, that you have never ceased to be virtuous and holy before God. Oh, poor woman!"

This was more than poor Fantine could bear. To have Cosette! to leave this infamous life! to live free, rich, happy, honest, with Cosette! to see suddenly spring up in the midst of her misery all these realities of paradise! She looked as if she were stupefied at the man who was speaking to her, and could only pour out two or three sobs: "Oh! oh! oh!" Her limbs gave way, she threw herself on her knees before Monsieur Madeleine, and, before he could prevent it, he felt that she had seized his hand and carried it to her lips.

Then she fainted.

BOOK SIXTH – JAVERT

I
THE BEGINNING OF THE REST

MONSIEUR MADELEINE had Fantine taken to the infirmary, which was in his own house. He confided her to the sisters, who put her to bed. A violent fever came on, and she passed a part of the night in delirious ravings. Finally, she fell asleep.

Towards noon the following day, Fantine awoke. She heard a breathing near her bed, drew aside the curtain, and saw Monsieur Madeleine standing gazing at something above his head. His look was full of compassionate and supplicating agony. She followed its direction, and saw that it was fixed upon a crucifix nailed against the wall.

From that moment Monsieur Madeleine was transfigured in the eyes of Fantine; he seemed to her clothed upon with light. He was absorbed in a kind of prayer. She gazed at him for a long while without daring to interrupt him; at last she said timidly:

"What are you doing?"

Monsieur Madeleine had been in that place for an hour waiting for Fantine to awake. He took her hand, felt her pulse, and said:

"How do you feel?"

"Very well. I have slept," she said. "I think I am getting better—this will be nothing."

Then he said, answering the question she had first asked him, as if she had just asked it:

"I was praying to the martyr who is on high."

And in his thought he added: "For the martyr who is here below."

Monsieur Madeleine had passed the night and morning in informing himself about Fantine. He knew all now, he had learned, even in all its poignant details, the history of Fantine.

He went on:

"You have suffered greatly, poor mother. Oh! do not lament, you have now the portion of the elect. It is in this way that mortals become angels. It is not their fault; they do not know how to set about it otherwise. This hell from which you have come out is the first step towards Heaven. We must begin by that."

He sighed deeply; but she smiled with this sublime smile from which two teeth were gone.

That same night, Javert wrote a letter. Next morning he carried this letter himself to the post-office of M—— sur M——. It was directed to Paris and bore this address: "To Monsieur Chabouillet, Secretary of Monsieur the Prefect of Police."

As the affair of the Bureau of Police had been noised about, the postmistress and some others who saw the letter before it was sent and who recognised Javert's handwriting in the address, thought he was sending in his resignation. Monsieur Madeleine wrote immediately to the Thénardiers. Fantine owed them a hundred and twenty francs. He sent them three hundred francs, telling them to pay themselves out of it, and bring the child at once to M—— sur M——, where her mother, who was sick, wanted her.

This astonished Thénardier.

"The Devil!" he said to his wife, "we won't let go of the child. It may be that this lark will become a milch cow. I guess some silly fellow has been smitten by the mother."

He replied by a bill of five hundred and some odd francs carefully drawn up. In this bill figured two incontestable items for upwards of three hundred francs, one of a physician and the other of an apothecary who had attended and supplied Eponine and Azelma during two long illnesses. Cosette, as we have said, had not been ill. This was only a slight substitution of names. Thénardier wrote at the bottom of the bill: "*Received on account three hundred francs.*"

Monsieur Madeleine immediately sent three hundred francs more, and wrote: "Make haste to bring Cosette."

"Christy!" said Thénardier, "we won't let go of the girl."

Meanwhile Fantine had not recovered. She still remained in the infirmary.

It was not without some repugnance, at first, that the sisters received and cared for "this girl." He who has seen the bas-reliefs at Rheims will recall the distension of the lower lip of the wise virgins beholding the foolish virgins. This ancient contempt of vestals for less fortunate women is one of the deepest instincts of womanly dignity; the sisters had experienced it with the intensification of Religion. But in a few days Fantine had disarmed them. The motherly tenderness within her, with her soft and touching words, moved them. One day the sisters heard her say in her delirium: "I have been a sinner, but when I shall have my child with me, that will mean that God has pardoned me. While I was bad I would not have had my Cosette with me; I could not have borne her sad and surprised looks. It was for her I sinned, and that is why God forgives me. I shall feel this benediction when Cosette comes. I shall gaze upon her; the sight of her innocence will do me good. She knows nothing of it all. She is an angel, you see, my sisters. At her age the wings have not yet fallen."

Monsieur Madeleine came to see her twice a day, and at each visit she asked him:

"Shall I see my Cosette soon?"

He answered:

"Perhaps to-morrow. I expect her every moment."

And the mother's pale face would brighten.

"Ah!" she would say, "how happy I shall be."

We have just said she did not recover: on the contrary, her condition seemed to become worse from week to week. That handful of snow applied to the naked skin between her shoulder-blades had caused a sudden check of perspiration, in consequence of which the disease, which had been forming for some years, at last attacked her violently. They were just at that time beginning in the diagnosis and treatment of lung diseases to follow the fine theory of Laënnec. The doctor sounded her lungs and shook his head.

Monsieur Madeleine said to him:

"Well?"

"Has she not a child she is anxious to see?" said the doctor.

"Yes."

"Well then, make haste to bring her."

Monsieur Madeleine gave a shudder.

Fantine asked him: "What did the doctor say?"

Monsieur Madeleine tried to smile.

"He told us to bring your child at once. That will restore your health."

"Oh!" she cried, "he is right. But what is the matter with these Thénardiers that they keep my Cosette from me? Oh! She is coming! Here at last I see happiness near me."

The Thénardiers, however, did not "let go of the child;" they gave a hundred bad reasons. Cosette was too delicate to travel in the winter time, and then there were a number of little petty debts, of which they were collecting the bills, etc., etc.

"I will send somebody for Cosette," said Monsieur Madeleine, "if necessary, I will go myself."

He wrote at Fantine's dictation this letter, which she signed. "Monsieur Thénardier:

"You will deliver Cosette to the bearer.

"He will settle all small debts.

"I have the honour to salute you with consideration.

"FANTINE."

In the meanwhile a serious matter intervened. In vain we chisel, as best we can, the mysterious block of which our life is made; the black vein of destiny reappears continually.

II

HOW JEAN CAN BECOME CHAMP

ONE morning Monsieur Madeleine was in his office arranging for some pressing business of the mayoralty, in case he should decide to go to Montfermeil himself, when he was informed that Javert, the inspector of police, wished to speak with him. On hearing this name spoken, Monsieur Madeleine could not repress a disagreeable impression. Since the affair of the Bureau of Police, Javert had more than ever avoided him, and Monsieur Madeleine had not seen him at all.

"Let him come in," said he.

Javert entered.

Monsieur Madeleine remained seated near the fire, looking over a bundle of papers upon which he was making notes, and which contained the returns of the police patrol. He did not disturb himself at all for Javert: he could not but think of poor Fantine, and it was fitting that he should receive him very coldly.

Javert respectfully saluted the mayor, who had his back towards him. The mayor did not look up, but continued to make notes on the papers.

Javert advanced a few steps, and paused without breaking silence.

A physiognomist, had he been familiar with Javert's face, had he made a study for years of this savage in the service of civilisation, this odd mixture of the Roman, Spartan, monk and corporal, this spy, incapable of a lie, this virgin detective—a physiognomist, had he known his secret and inveterate aversion for Monsieur Madeleine, his contest with the mayor on the subject of Fantine, and had he seen Javert at that moment, would have said: "What has happened to him?"

It was evident to any one who had known this conscientious, straightforward, clear, sincere, upright, austere, fierce man, that Javert had suffered some great interior commotion. There was nothing in his mind that was not depicted on his face. He was, like all violent people, subject to sudden changes. Never had his face been stranger or more startling. On entering, he had bowed before Monsieur Madeleine with a look in which was neither rancour, anger, nor defiance; he paused some steps behind the mayor's chair, and was now standing in a soldierly attitude with the natural, cold rudeness of a man who was never kind, but has always been patient; he waited without speaking a word or making a motion, in genuine humility and tranquil resignation, until it should please Monsieur the Mayor to turn towards him, calm, serious, hat in hand, and eyes cast down with an expression between that of a soldier before his officer and a prisoner before his judge. All the feeling as well as all the remembrances which we should have expected him to have, disappeared. Nothing was left upon this face, simple and impenetrable as granite, except a gloomy sadness. His whole person expressed abasement and firmness, an indescribably courageous dejection.

At last the mayor laid down his pen and turned partly round:

"Well, what is it? What is the matter Javert?"

Javert remained silent a moment as if collecting himself; then raised his voice with a sad solemnity which did not, however, exclude simplicity: "There has been a criminal act committed, Monsieur Mayor."

"What act?"

"An inferior agent of the government has been wanting in respect to a magistrate, in the gravest manner. I come, as is my duty, to bring the fact to your knowledge."

"Who is this agent?" asked Monsieur Madeleine.

"I," said Javert.

"You?"

"I."

"And who is the magistrate who has to complain of this agent?"

"You, Monsieur Mayor."

FANTINE 207

Monsieur Madeleine straightened himself in his chair. Javert continued, with serious looks and eyes still cast down.

"Monsieur Mayor, I come to ask you to be so kind as to make charges and procure my dismissal."

Monsieur Madeleine, amazed, opened his mouth. Javert interrupted him:

"You will say that I might tender my resignation, but that is not enough. To resign is honourable; I have done wrong. I ought to be punished. I must be dismissed."

And after a pause he added:

"Monsieur Mayor, you were severe to me the other day, unjustly. Be justly so to-day."

"Ah, indeed! why? What is all this nonsense? What does it all mean? What is the criminal act committed by you against me? What have you done to me? How have you wronged me? You accuse yourself: do you wish to be relieved?"

"Dismissed," said Javert.

"Dismissed it is then. It is very strange. I do not understand you."

"You will understand, Monsieur Mayor," Javert sighed deeply, and continued sadly and coldly:

"Monsieur Mayor, six weeks ago, after that scene about that girl, I was enraged and I denounced you."

"Denounced me?"

"To the Prefecture of Police at Paris."

Monsieur Madeleine, who did not laugh much oftener than Javert, began to laugh:

"As a mayor having encroached upon the police?"

"As a former convict."

The mayor became livid.

Javert, who had not raised his eyes, continued:

"I believed it. For a long while I had had suspicions. A resemblance, information you obtained at Faverolles, your immense strength; the affair of old Fauchelevent; your skill as a marksman; your leg which drags a little—and in fact I don't know what other stupidities; but at last I took you for a man named Jean Valjean."

"Named what? How did you call that name?"

"Jean Valjean. He was a convict I saw twenty years ago, when I was adjutant of the galley guard at Toulon. After leaving the galleys this Valjean, it appears, robbed a bishop's palace, then he committed another robbery with weapons in his hands, in a highway, on a little Savoyard. For eight years his whereabouts have been unknown, and search has been made for him. I fancied—in short, I have done this thing. Anger determined me, and I denounced you to the prefect."

M. Madeleine, who had taken up the file of papers again, a few moments before, said with a tone of perfect indifference: "And what answer did you get?"

"That I was crazy."

"Well!"

"Well; they were right."

"It is fortunate that you think so!"

"It must be so, for the real Jean Valjean has been found."

The paper that M. Madeleine held fell from his hand; he raised his head, looked steadily at Javert, and said in an inexpressible tone:

"Ah!"

Javert continued:

"I will tell you how it is, Monsieur Mayor. There was, it appears, in the country, near Ailly-le-Haut Clocher, a simple sort of fellow who was called Father Champmathieu. He was very poor. Nobody paid any attention to him. Such folks live, one hardly knows how. Finally, this last fall, Father Champmathieu was arrested for stealing cider apples from——, but that is of no consequence. There was a theft, a wall scaled, branches of trees broken. Our Champmathieu was arrested; he had even then a branch of an apple-tree in his hand. The rogue was caged. So far, it was nothing more than a penitentiary matter. But here comes in the hand of Providence. The jail being in a bad condition, the police justice thought it best to take him to Arras, where the prison of the department is. In this prison at Arras there was a former convict named Brevet, who is there for some trifle, and who, for his good conduct, has been made turnkey. No sooner was Champmathieu set down, than Brevet cried out: 'Ha, ha! I know that man. He is a *fagot*.' *

" 'Look up here, my good man. You are Jean Valjean.' 'Jean Valjean, who is Jean Valjean?' Champmathieu plays off the astonished. 'Don't play ignorance,' said Brevet. 'You are Jean Valjean; you were in the galleys at Toulon. It is twenty years

---

* Former convict.

ago. We were there together.' Champmathieu denied it all. Faith! you understand; they fathomed it. The case was worked up and this was what they found. This Champmathieu thirty years ago was a pruner in divers places, particularly in Faverolles. There we lose trace of him. A long time afterwards we find him at Auvergne; then at Paris, where he is said to have been a wheelwright and to have had a daughter—a washerwoman, but that is not proven, and finally in this part of the country. Now before going to the galleys for burglary, what was Jean Valjean? A pruner. Where? At Faverolles. Another fact. This Valjean's baptismal name was Jean; his mother's family name, Mathieu. Nothing could be more natural, on leaving the galleys, than to take his mother's name to disguise himself, then he would be called Jean Mathieu. He goes to Auvergne, the pronunciation of that region would make *Chan* of *Jean*—they would call him Chan Mathieu. Our man adopts it, and now you have him transformed into Champmathieu. You follow me, do you not? Search has been made at Faverolles; the family of Jean Valjean are no longer there. Nobody knows where they are. You know in such classes these disappearances of families often occur. You search, but can find nothing. Such people, when they are not mud, are dust. And then as the commencement of this story dates back thirty years, there is nobody now at Faverolles who knew Jean Valjean. But search has been made at Toulon. Besides Brevet there are only two convicts who have seen Jean Valjean. They are convicts for life; their names are Cochepaille and Chenildieu. These men were brought from the galleys and confronted with the pretended Champmathieu. They did not hesitate. To them as well as to Brevet it was Jean Valjean. Same age; fifty-four years old; same height; same appearance, in fact the same man; it is he. At this time it was that I sent my denunciation to the Prefecture at Paris. They replied that I was out of my mind, and that Jean Valjean was at Arras in the hands of justice. You may imagine how that astonished me; I who believed that I had here the same Jean Valjean. I wrote to the justice; he sent for me and brought Champmathieu before me."

"Well," interrupted Monsieur Madeleine.

Javert replied, with an incorruptible and sad face:

"Monsieur Mayor, truth is truth. I am sorry for it, but that man is Jean Valjean. I recognised him also."

Monsieur Madeleine said in a very low voice:

"Are you sure?"

Javert began to laugh with the suppressed laugh which indicates profound conviction.

"H'm, sure!"

He remained a moment in thought, mechanically taking up pinches of the powdered wood used to dry ink, from the box on the table, and then added:

"And now that I see the real Jean Valjean, I do not understand how I ever could have believed anything else. I beg your pardon, Monsieur Mayor."

In uttering these serious and supplicating words to him, who six weeks before had humiliated him before the entire guard, and had said "Retire!" Javert, this haughty man, was unconsciously full of simplicity and dignity. Monsieur Madeleine answered his request, by this abrupt question:

"And what did the man say?"

"Oh, bless me! Monsieur Mayor, the affair is a bad one. If it is Jean Valjean, it is a second offence. To climb a wall, break a branch, and take apples, for a child is only a trespass; for a man it is a misdemeanour; for a convict it is a crime. Scaling a wall and theft includes everything. It is not a case for a police court, but for the assizes. It is not a few days' imprisonment, but the galleys for life. And then there is the affair of the little Savoyard, who I hope will be found. The devil! There is something to struggle against, is there not? There would be for anybody but Jean Valjean. But Jean Valjean is a sly fellow. And that is just where I recognise him. Anybody else would know that he was in a hot place, and would rave and cry out, as the tea-kettle sings on the fire; he would say that he was not Jean Valjean, et cetera. But this man pretends not to understand, he says: 'I am Champmathieu: I have no more to say.' He puts on an appearance of astonishment; he plays the brute. Oh, the rascal is cunning! But it is all the same, there is the evidence. Four persons have recognised him, and the old villain will be condemned. It has been taken to the assizes at Arras. I am going to testify. I have been summoned."

Monsieur Madeleine had turned again to his desk, and was quietly looking over his papers, reading and writing alternately, like a man pressed with business. He turned again towards Javert:

"That will do, Javert. Indeed all these details interest me very little. We are wasting time, and we have urgent business, Javert; go at once to the house of the good woman Buseaupied, who sells herbs at the corner of Rue Saint Saulve, tell her to make her complaint against the carman Pierre Chesnelong. He is a brutal fellow, he almost crushed this woman and her child. He must be punished. Then you will go to Monsieur Charcellay, Rue Montre-de-Champigny. He complains that the gutter of the next house when it rains throws water upon his house, and is undermining the foundation. Then you will inquire into the offences that have been reported to me, at the widow Doris's, Rue Guibourg, and Madame Renée le Bossé's, Rue du Garraud Blanc, and make out reports. But I am giving you too much to do. Did you not tell me you were going to Arras in eight or ten days on this matter?"

"Sooner than that, Monsieur Mayor."

"What day then?"

"I think I told monsieur that the case would be tried to-morrow, and that I should leave by the diligence to-night."

Monsieur Madeleine made an imperceptible motion.

"And how long will the matter last?"

"One day at longest. Sentence will be pronounced at latest to-morrow evening. But I shall not wait for the sentence, which is certain; as soon as my testimony is given I shall return here."

"Very well," said Monsieur Madeleine.

And he dismissed him with a wave of his hand.

Javert did not go.

"Your pardon, monsieur," said he.

"What more is there?" asked Monsieur Madeleine.

"Monsieur Mayor, there is one thing more to which I desire to call your attention."

"What is it?"

"It is that I ought to be dismissed."

Monsieur Madeleine arose.

"Javert, you are a man of honour and I esteem you. You exaggerate your fault. Besides, this is an offence which concerns me. You are worthy of promotion rather than disgrace. I desire you to keep your place."

Javert looked at Monsieur Madeleine with his calm eyes, in whose depths it seemed that one beheld his conscience, un-enlightened, but stern and pure, and said in a tranquil voice:

"Monsieur Mayor, I cannot agree to that."

"I repeat," said Monsieur Madeleine, "that this matter concerns me."

But Javert, with his one idea, continued:

"As to exaggerating, I do not exaggerate. This is the way I reason. I have unjustly suspected you. That is nothing. It is our province to suspect, although it may be an abuse of our right to suspect our superiors. But without proofs and in a fit of anger, with revenge as my aim, I denounced you as a convict—you, a respectable man, a mayor, and a magistrate. This is a serious matter, very serious. I have committed an offence against authority in your person, I, who am the agent of authority. If one of my subordinates had done what I have, I would have pronounced him unworthy of the service, and sent him away. Well, listen a moment, Monsieur Mayor; I have often been severe in my life towards others. It was just. I did right. Now if I were not severe towards myself, all I have justly done would become injustice. Should I spare myself more than others? No. What! if I should be prompt only to punish others and not myself, I should be a wretch indeed! They who say: 'That black-guard, Javert,' would be right. Monsieur Mayor, I do not wish you to treat me with kindness. Your kindness, when it was for others, enraged me; I do not wish it for myself. That kindness which consists in defending a woman of the town against a citizen, a police agent against the mayor, the inferior against the superior, that is what I call ill-judged kindness. Such kindness disorganises society. Good God, it is easy to be kind, the difficulty is to be just. Had you been what I thought, I should not have been kind to you; not I. You would have seen, Monsieur Mayor. I ought to treat myself as I would treat anybody else. When I put down malefactors, when I rigorously brought up offenders, I often said to myself: 'You, if you ever trip; if ever I catch you doing wrong, look out!' I have tripped, I have caught myself doing wrong. So much the worse! I must be sent away, broken, dismissed, that is right. I have hands: I can till the ground. It is all the same to me. Monsieur Mayor, the good of the service demands an example. I simply ask the dismissal of Inspector Javert."

All this was said in a tone of proud humility, a desperate and resolute tone, which gave an indescribably whimsical grandeur to this oddly honest man.

"We will see," said Monsieur Madeleine.

And he held out his hand to him.

Javert started back, and said fiercely:

"Pardon, Monsieur Mayor, that should not be. A mayor does not give his hand to a spy."

He added between his teeth:

"Spy, yes; from the moment I abused the power of my position, I have been nothing better than a spy!"

Then he bowed profoundly, and went towards the door.

There he turned around: his eyes yet downcast.

"Monsieur Mayor, I will continue in the service until I am relieved."

He went out. Monsieur Madeleine sat musing, listening to his firm and resolute step as it died away along the corridor.

BOOK SEVENTH –
THE CHAMPMATHIEU AFFAIR

I
SISTER SIMPLICE

THE events which follow were never all known at M—— sur M——. But the few which did leak out have left such memories in that city, that it would be a serious omission in this book if we did not relate them in their minutest details.

Among these details, the reader will meet with two or three improbable circumstances, which we preserve from respect for the truth.

In the afternoon following the visit of Javert, M. Madeleine went to see Fantine as usual.

Before going to Fantine's room, he sent for Sister Simplice.

The two nuns who attended the infirmary, Lazarists as all these Sisters of Charity are, were called Sister Perpétue and Sister Simplice.

Sister Perpétue was an ordinary village-girl, summarily become a Sister of Charity, who entered the service of God as she would have entered service anywhere. She was a nun as others are cooks. This type is not very rare. The monastic orders gladly accept this heavy peasant clay, easily shaped into a Capuchine or an Ursuline. Such rustics are useful for the coarser duties of devotion. There is no shock in the transition from a cow-boy to a Carmelite; the one becomes the other without much labour; the common basis of ignorance of a village and a cloister is a ready-made preparation, and puts the rustic at once upon an even footing with the monk. Enlarge the smock a little and you have a frock. Sister Perpétue was a stout nun, from Marines, near Pontoise, given to patois, psalm-singing and muttering, sugaring a nostrum according to the bigotry or hypocrisy of the patient, treating invalids harshly, rough with the dying, almost throwing them into the face of God, belabouring the death agony with angry prayers, bold, honest, and florid.

Sister Simplice was white with a waxen clearness. In comparison with Sister Perpétue she was a sacramental taper by the side of a tallow candle. St. Vincent de Paul has divinely drawn the figure of a Sister of Charity in these admirable words in which he unites so much liberty with so much servitude. "Her only

convent shall be the house of sickness; her only cell, a hired
lodging; her chapel the parish church; her cloister the streets of
the city, or the wards of the hospital; her only wall obedience;
her grate the fear of God; her veil modesty.'' This ideal was
made alive in Sister Simplice. No one could have told Sister
Simplice's age; she had never been young, and seemed as if
she never should be old. She was a person—we dare not say a
woman—gentle, austere, companionable, cold, and who had
never told a lie. She was so gentle that she appeared fragile; but
on the contrary she was more enduring than granite. She
touched the unfortunate with charming fingers, delicate and
pure. There was, so to say, silence in her speech; she said just
what was necessary, and she had a tone of voice which would
at the same time have edified a confessional, and enchanted a
drawing-room. This delicacy accommodated itself to the serge
dress, finding in its harsh touch a continual reminder of Heaven
and of God. Let us dwell upon one circumstance. Never to
have lied, never to have spoken, for any purpose whatever, even
carelessly, a single word which was not the truth, the sacred
truth, was the distinctive trait of Sister Simplice; it was the mark
of her virtue. She was almost celebrated in the congregation for
this imperturbable veracity. The Abbé Sicard speaks of Sister
Simplice in a letter to the deaf mute, Massieu. Sincere and pure
as we may be, we all have the mark of some little lie upon our
truthfulness. She had none. A little lie, an innocent lie, can such
a thing exist? To lie is the absolute of evil. To lie a little is not
possible; he who lies, lies a whole lie; lying is the very face of
the demon. Satan has two names; he is called Satan, and he is
called the Liar. Such were her thoughts. And as she thought, she
practised. From this resulted that whiteness of which we have
spoken, a whiteness that covered with its radiance even her lips
and her eyes. Her smile was white, her look was white. There
was not a spider's web, not a speck of dust upon the glass of that
conscience. When she took the vows of St. Vincent de Paul, she
had taken the name of Simplice by especial choice. Simplice of
Sicily, it is well known, is that saint who preferred to have both
her breasts torn out rather than answer, having been born at
Syracuse, that she was born at Segesta, a lie which would have
saved her. This patron saint was fitting for this soul.

Sister Simplice, on entering the order, had two faults of
which she corrected herself gradually; she had had a taste for

delicacies, and loved to receive letters. Now she read nothing but a prayer-book in large type and in Latin. She did not understand Latin, but she understood the book.

The pious woman had conceived an affection for Fantine, perceiving in her probably some latent virtue, and had devoted herself almost exclusively to her care.

Monsieur Madeleine took Sister Simplice aside and recommended Fantine to her with a singular emphasis, which the sister remembered at a later day.

On leaving the sister, he approached Fantine.

Fantine awaited each day the appearance of Monsieur Madeleine as one awaits a ray of warmth and of joy. She would say to the sisters: "I live only when the mayor is here."

That day she had more fever. As soon as she saw Monsieur Madeleine, she asked him:

"Cosette?"

He answered with a smile:

"Very soon."

Monsieur Madeleine, while with Fantine, seemed the same as usual. Only he stayed an hour instead of half an hour, to the great satisfaction of Fantine. He made a thousand charges to everybody that the sick woman might want for nothing. It was noticed that at one moment his countenance became very sombre. But this was explained when it was known that the doctor had, bending close to his ear, said to him: "She is sinking fast."

Then he returned to the mayor's office, and the office boy saw him examine attentively a road-map of France which hung in his room. He made a few figures in pencil upon a piece of paper.

II

SHREWDNESS OF MASTER SCAUFFLAIRE

FROM the mayor's office he went to the outskirts of the city, to a Fleming's, Master Scaufflaer, Frenchified into Scaufflaire, who kept horses to let and "chaises if desired."

In order to go to Scaufflaire's, the nearest way was by a rarely frequented street, on which was the parsonage of the parish in which Monsieur Madeleine lived. The curé was, it was said, a worthy and respectable man, and a good counsellor. At the moment when Monsieur Madeleine arrived in front of the parsonage, there was but one person passing in the street, and he remarked this: the mayor, after passing by the curé's house, stopped, stood still a moment, then turned back and retraced his steps as far as the door of the parsonage, which was a large door with an iron knocker. He seized the knocker quickly and raised it; then he stopped anew, stood a short time as if in thought, and after a few seconds, instead of letting the knocker fall smartly, he replaced it gently, and resumed his walk with a sort of haste that he had not shown before.

Monsieur Madeleine found Master Scaufflaire at home busy repairing a harness.

"Master Scaufflaire," he asked, "have you a good horse?"

"Monsieur Mayor," said the Fleming, "all my horses are good. What do you understand by a good horse?"

"I understand a horse that can go twenty leagues in a day."

"The devil!" said the Fleming, "twenty leagues!"

"Yes."

"Before a chaise?"

"Yes."

"And how long will he rest after the journey?"

"He must be able to start again the next day in case of need."

"To do the same thing again?"

"Yes."

"The devil! and it is twenty leagues?"

Monsieur Madeleine drew from his pocket the paper on which he had pencilled the figures. He showed them to the Fleming. They were the figures, 5, 6, $8\frac{1}{2}$.

"You see," said he. "Total, nineteen and a half, that is to say, twenty leagues."

"Monsieur Mayor," resumed the Fleming, "I have just what you want. My little white horse, you must have seen him sometimes passing; he is a little beast from Bas-Boulonnais. He is full of fire. They tried at first to make a saddle horse of him. Bah! he kicked, he threw everybody off. They thought he was vicious, they didn't know what to do. I bought him. I put him before a chaise; Monsieur, that is what he wanted; he is as gentle as a girl, he goes like the wind. But, for example, it won't do to get on his back. It's not his idea to be a saddle horse. Everybody has his peculiar ambition. To draw, but not to carry: we must believe that he has said that to himself."

"And he will make the trip?"

"Your twenty leagues, all the way at a full eight hours. But there are some conditions."

"Name them."

"First, you must let him breathe an hour when you are half-way; he will eat and somebody must be by to prevent the tavern boy from stealing his oats, for I have noticed that at taverns oats are oftener drunk by the stable boys than eaten by the horses."

"Somebody shall be there."

"Secondly—is the chaise for Monsieur the Mayor?"

"Yes."

"Monsieur the Mayor knows how to drive?"

"Yes."

"Well, Monsieur the Mayor will travel alone and without baggage, so as not to overload the horse."

"Agreed."

"But Monsieur the Mayor, having no one with him, will be obliged to take the trouble of seeing to the oats himself."

"So said."

"I must have thirty francs a day, the days he rests included. Not a penny less, and the fodder of the beast at the expense of Monsieur the Mayor."

Monsieur Madeleine took three Napoleons from his purse and laid them on the table.

"There is two days, in advance."

"Fourthly, for such a trip, a chaise would be too heavy; that would tire the horse. Monsieur the Mayor must consent to travel in a little tilbury that I have."

"I consent to that."

"It is light, but it is open."

"It is all the same to me."

"Has Monsieur the Mayor reflected that it is winter?"

Monsieur Madeleine did not answer; the Fleming went on:

"That it is very cold?"

Monsieur Madeleine kept silence.

Master Scaufflaire continued:

"That it may rain?"

Monsieur Madeleine raised his head and said:

"The horse and the tilbury will be before my door to-morrow at half-past four in the morning."

"That is understood, Monsieur Mayor," answered

Scaufflaire, then scratching a stain on the top of the table with his thumb-nail, he resumed with that careless air that Flemings so well know how to associate with their shrewdness:

"Why, I have just thought of it! Monsieur the Mayor has not told me where he is going. Where is Monsieur the Mayor going?"

He had thought of nothing else since the beginning of the conversation, but without knowing why, he had not dared to ask the question.

"Has your horse good forelegs?" said Monsieur Madeleine.

"Yes, Monsieur Mayor. You will hold him up a little going downhill. Is there much downhill between here and where you are going?"

"Don't forget to be at my door precisely at half-past four in the morning," answered Monsieur Madeleine, and he went out.

The Fleming was left "dumb-founded," as he said himself some time afterwards.

The mayor had been gone two or three minutes, when the door again opened; it was the mayor.

He had the same impassive and absent-minded air as ever.

"Monsieur Scaufflaire," said he, "at what sum do you value the horse and the tilbury that you furnish me, the one carrying the other?"

"The one drawing the other, Monsieur Mayor," said the Fleming with a loud laugh.

"As you like. How much?"

"Does Monsieur the Mayor wish to buy them?"

"No, but at all events I wish to guarantee them to you. On my return you can give me back the amount. At how much do you value horse and chaise?"

"Five hundred francs, Monsieur Mayor!"

"Here it is."

Monsieur Madeleine placed a banknote on the table, then went out, and this time did not return.

Master Scaufflaire regretted terribly that he had not said a thousand francs. In fact, the horse and tilbury, in the lump, were worth a hundred crowns.

The Fleming called his wife, and related the affair to her. Where the deuce could the mayor be going? They talked it over. "He is going to Paris," said the wife. "I don't believe it," said the husband. Monsieur Madeleine had forgotten the paper on which he had marked the figures, and left it on the mantel. The Fleming seized it and studied it. Five, six, eight and a half? this must mean the relays of the post. He turned to his wife: "I have found it out." "How?" "It is five leagues from here to Hesdin, six from Hesdin to Saint Pol, eight and a half from Saint Pol to Arras. He is going to Arras."

Meanwhile Monsieur Madeleine had reached home. To return from Master Scaufflaire's he had taken a longer road, as if the door of the parsonage were a temptation to him and he wished to avoid it. He went up to his room, and shut himself in, which was nothing remarkable, for he usually went to bed early. However, the janitress of the factory, who was at the same time Monsieur Madeleine's only servant, observed that his light was out at half-past eight, and she mentioned it to the cashier who came in, adding:

"Is Monsieur the Mayor sick? I thought that his manner was a little singular."

The cashier occupied a room situated exactly beneath Monsieur Madeleine's. He paid no attention to the portress's words, went to bed, and went to sleep. Towards midnight he suddenly awoke; he had heard, in his sleep, a noise overhead. He listened. It was a step that went and came, as if some one were walking in the room above. He listened more attentively, and recognised Monsieur Madeleine's step. That appeared strange to him; ordinarily no noise was made in Monsieur Madeleine's room before his hour of rising. A moment afterwards, the cashier heard something that sounded like the opening and shutting of a wardrobe, then a piece of furniture was moved, there was another silence, and the step began again. The cashier rose up in bed, threw off his drowsiness, looked out, and through his window-panes, saw upon an opposite wall the ruddy reflection of a lighted window. From the direction of the rays, it could only be the window of Monsieur Madeleine's chamber. The reflection trembled as if it came rather from a bright fire than from a light. The shadow of the sash could not be seen, which indicated that the window was wide open. Cold as it was, this open window was surprising. The cashier fell asleep again. An hour or two afterwards he awoke again. The same step, slow and regular, was coming and going constantly over his head.

The reflection continued visible upon the wall, but it was

now pale and steady like the light of a lamp or candle. The window was still open.

Let us see what was passing in Monsieur Madeleine's room.

III
A TEMPEST IN A BRAIN

THE reader has doubtless divined that Monsieur Madeleine is none other than Jean Valjean.

We have already looked into the depths of that conscience; the time has come to look into them again. We do so not without emotion, nor without trembling. There exists nothing more terrific than this kind of contemplation. The mind's eye can nowhere find anything more dazzling nor more dark than in man; it can fix itself upon nothing which is more awful, more complex, more mysterious or more infinite. There is one spectacle grander than the sea, that is the sky; there is one spectacle grander than the sky, that is the interior of the soul.

To write the poem of the human conscience, were it only of a single man, were it only of the most infamous of men, would be to swallow up all epics in a superior and final epic. The conscience is the chaos of chimeras, of lusts and of temptations, the furnace of dreams, the cave of the ideas which are our shame, it is the pandemonium of sophisms, the battle-field of the passions. At certain hours, penetrate within the livid face of a human being who reflects, and look at what lies behind; look into that soul, look into that obscurity. There, beneath the external silence, there are combats of giants as in Homer, mêlées of dragons and hydras, and clouds of phantoms as in Milton, ghostly labyrinths as in Dante. What a gloom enwraps that infinite which each man bears within himself, and by which he measures in despair the desires of his will, and the actions of his life!

Alighieri arrived one day at an ill-omened door before which he hesitated. Here is one also before us, on the threshold of which we hesitate. Let us enter notwithstanding.

We have but little to add to what the reader already knows, concerning what had happened to Jean Valjean, since his adventure with Petit Gervais. From that moment, we have seen, he was another man. What the bishop had desired to do with him, that he had executed. It was more than a transformation—it was a transfiguration.

He succeeded in escaping from sight, sold the bishop's silver, keeping only the candlesticks as souvenirs, glided quietly from city to city across France, came to M—— sur M——, conceived the idea that we have described, accomplished what we have related, gained the point of making himself unassailable and inaccessible, and thence forward, established at M—— sur M——, happy to feel his conscience saddened by his past, and the last half of his existence giving the lie to the first, he lived peaceable, reassured, and hopeful, having but two thoughts: to conceal his name, and to sanctify his life; to escape from men and to return to God.

These two thoughts were associated so closely in his mind, that they formed but a single one; they were both equally absorbing and imperious, and ruled his slightest actions. Ordinarily they were in harmony in the regulation of the conduct of his life, they turned him towards the dark side of life; they made him benevolent and simple-hearted; they counselled him to the same things. Sometimes however, there was a conflict between them. In such cases, it will be remembered, the man, whom all the country around M—— sur M—— called Monsieur Madeleine, did not waver in sacrificing the first to the second, his security to his virtue. Thus, in despite of all reserve and of all prudence, he had kept the bishop's candlesticks, worn mourning for him, called and questioned all the little Savoyards who passed by, gathered information concerning the families at Faverolles, and saved the life of old Fauchelevent, in spite of the disquieting insinuations of Javert. It would seem, we have already remarked, that he thought, following the example of all who have been wise, holy, and just, that his highest duty was not towards himself.

But of all these occasions, it must be said, none had ever been anything like that which was now presented.

Never had the two ideas that governed the unfortunate man whose sufferings we are relating, engaged in so serious a struggle. He comprehended this confusedly, but thoroughly, from the first words that Javert pronounced on entering his office. At the moment when that name which he had so deeply buried was so strangely uttered, he was seized with stupor, and as if intoxicated by the sinister grotesqueness of his destiny, and through that stupor he felt the shudder which precedes great shocks; he bent like an oak at the approach of a storm, like a soldier at the approach of an assault. He felt clouds full of thunderings and lightnings gathering upon his head. Even while listening to Javert, his first thought was to go, to run, to denounce himself, to drag this Champmathieu out of prison, and to put himself in his place; it was painful and sharp as an incision into the living flesh, but passed away, and he said to himself: "Let us see! Let us see!" He repressed this first generous impulse and recoiled before such heroism.

Doubtless it would have been fine if, after the holy words of the bishop, after so many years of repentance and self-denial, in the midst of a penitence admirably commenced, even in the presence of so terrible a conjecture, he had not faltered an instant, and had continued to march on with even pace towards that yawning pit at the bottom of which was heaven; this would have been fine, but this was not the case. We must render an account of what took place in that soul, and we can relate only what was there. What first gained control was the instinct of self-preservation; he collected his ideas hastily, stifled his emotions, took into consideration the presence of Javert, the great danger, postponed any decision with the firmness of terror, banished from his mind all consideration of the course he should pursue, and resumed his calmness as a gladiator retakes his buckler.

For the rest of the day he was in this state, a tempest within, a perfect calm without; he took only what might be called precautionary measures. All was still confused and jostling in his brain, the agitation there was such that he did not see distinctly the form of any idea; and he could have told nothing of himself, unless it were that he had just received a terrible blow. He went according to his habit to the sick bed of Fantine, and prolonged his visit, by an instinct of kindness, saying to himself that he ought to do so, and recommend her earnestly to the sisters, in case it should happen that he would have to be absent. He felt vaguely that it would perhaps be necessary for him to go to Arras; and without having in the least decided upon this journey, he said to himself that, entirely free from suspicion as he was, there would be no difficulty in being a witness of what might pass, and he engaged Scaufflaire's tilbury, in order to be prepared for any emergency.

He dined with a good appetite.

Returning to his room he collected his thoughts.

He examined the situation and found it an unheard-of one; so unheard-of that in the midst of his reverie, by some strange impulse of almost inexplicable anxiety, he rose from his chair, and bolted his door. He feared lest something might yet enter. He barricaded himself against all possibilities.

A moment afterwards he blew out his light. It annoyed him. It seemed to him that somebody could see him.

Who? Somebody?

Alas! what he wanted to keep out of doors had entered; what he wanted to render blind was looking upon him. His conscience.

His conscience, that is to say, God.

At the first moment, however, he deluded himself; he had a feeling of safety and solitude; the bolt drawn, he believed himself invisible. Then he took possession of himself; he placed his elbows on the table, rested his head on his hand, and set himself to meditating in the darkness.

"Where am I? Am I not in a dream? What have I heard? Is it really true that I saw this Javert, and that he talked to me so? Who can this Champmathieu be? He resembles me then? Is it possible? When I think that yesterday I was so calm, and so far from suspecting anything! What was I doing yesterday at this time? What is there in this matter? How will it turn out? What is to be done?"

Such was the torment he was in. His brain had lost the power of retaining its ideas; they passed away like waves, and he grasped his forehead with both hands to stop them.

Out of this tumult, which overwhelmed his will and his reason, and from which he sought to draw a certainty and a resolution, nothing came clearly forth but anguish.

His brain was burning. He went to the window and threw it wide open. Not a star was in the sky. He returned and sat down by the table.

The first hour thus rolled away.

Little by little, however, vague outlines began to take form and to fix themselves in his meditation; he could perceive, with the precision of reality, not the whole of the situation, but a few details.

He began by recognising that, however extraordinary and critical the situation was, he was completely master of it.

His stupor only became the deeper.

Independently of the severe and religious aim that his actions had in view, all that he had done up to this day was only a hole that he was digging in which to bury his name. What he had always most dreaded, in his hours of self-communion, in his sleepless nights, was the thought of ever hearing that name pronounced; he felt that would be for him the end of all; that the day on which that name should reappear would see vanish from around him his new life, and, who knows, even perhaps his new soul from within him. He shuddered at the bare thought that it was possible. Surely, if any one had told him at such moments that an hour would come when that name would resound in his ear, when that hideous word, Jean Valjean, would start forth suddenly from the night and stand before him; when this fearful glare, destined to dissipate the mystery in which he had wrapped himself, would flash suddenly upon his head, and that this name would not menace him, and that this glare would only make his obscurity the deeper, that this rending of the veil would increase the mystery, that this earthquake would consolidate his edifice, that this prodigious event would have no other result, if it seemed good to him, to himself alone, than to render his existence at once more brilliant and more impenetrable, and that, from his encounter with the phantom of Jean Valjean, the good and worthy citizen, Monsieur Madeleine, would come forth more honoured, more peaceful and more respected than ever—if any one had said this to him, he would have shaken his head and looked upon the words as nonsense. Well! precisely that had happened; all this grouping of the impossible was now a fact, and God had permitted these absurdities to become real things!

His musings continued to grow clearer. He was getting a wider and wider view of his position.

It seemed to him that he had just awaked from some wondrous slumber, and that he found himself gliding over a precipice in the middle of the night, standing, shivering, recoiling in vain, upon the very edge of an abyss. He perceived distinctly in the gloom an unknown man, a stranger, whom fate had mistaken for him, and was pushing into the gulf in his place. It was necessary, in order that the gulf should be closed, that some one should fall in, he or the other.

He had only to let it alone.

The light became complete, and he recognised this: That his place at the galleys was empty, that do what he could it was always awaiting him, that the robbing of Petit Gervais sent him back there, that this empty place would await him and attract him until he should be there, that this was inevitable and fatal. And then he said to himself: That at this very moment he had a substitute, that it appeared that a man named Champmathieu had that unhappy lot, and that as for himself, present in future at the galleys in the person of this Champmathieu, present in society under the name of Monsieur Madeleine, he had nothing more to fear, provided he did not prevent men from sealing upon the head of this Champmathieu that stone of infamy which, like the stone of the sepulchre, falls once never to rise again.

All this was so violent and so strange that he suddenly felt that kind of indescribable movement that no man experiences more than two or three times in his life, a sort of convulsion of the conscience that stirs up all that is dubious in the heart, which is composed of irony, of joy, and of despair, and which might be called a burst of interior laughter.

He hastily relighted his candle.

"Well, what!" said he, "what am I afraid of? why do I ponder over these things? I am now safe? all is finished. There was but a single half-open door through which my past could make an irruption into my life; that door is now walled up! for ever! This Javert who has troubled me so long, that fearful instinct which seemed to have divined the truth, that had divined it, in fact! and which followed me everywhere, that terrible blood-hound always in pursuit of me, he is thrown off the track, engrossed elsewhere, absolutely baffled. He is satisfied henceforth, he will leave me in quiet, he holds his Jean Valjean fast! Who knows! it is even probable that he will want to leave the city! And all this is accomplished without my aid! And I have nothing to do with it! Ah, yes, but, what is there unfortunate in all this! People who should see me, upon my honour, would think that a catastrophe had befallen me! After all, if there is any harm done to anybody, it is in nowise my fault. Providence has done it all. This is what He wishes apparently. Have I the right to disarrange what He arranges? What is it that I ask for now? Why do I interfere? It does not concern me. How! I am not satisfied! But what would I have then? The aim to which I have aspired for so many years, my nightly dream, the object of my prayers to heaven, security, I have gained it. It is God's will. I must do nothing contrary to the will of God. And why is it God's will? That I may carry on what I have begun, that I may do good, that I may be one day a grand and encouraging example, that it may be said that there was finally some little happiness resulting from this suffering which I have undergone and this virtue to which I have returned! Really I do not understand why I was so much afraid to go to this honest curé and tell him the whole story as a confessor, and ask his advice; this is evidently what he would have said to me. It is decided, let the matter alone! let us not interfere with God."

Thus he spoke in the depths of his conscience, hanging over what might be called his own abyss. He rose from his chair, and began to walk the room. "Come," said he, "let us think of it no more. The resolution is formed!" But he felt no joy.

Quite the contrary.

One can no more prevent the mind from returning to an idea than the sea from returning to a shore. In the case of the sailor, this is called the tide; in the case of the guilty, it is called remorse. God upheaves the soul as well as the ocean.

After the lapse of a few moments, he could do no otherwise, he resumed this sombre dialogue, in which it was himself who spoke and himself who listened, saying what he wished to keep silent, listening to what he did not wish to hear, yielding to that mysterious power which said to him: "think!" as it said two thousand years ago to another condemned: "march!"

Before going further, and in order to be fully understood, it is necessary that we should make with some emphasis a single observation.

It is certain that we talk with ourselves; there is not a thinking being who has not experienced that. We may say even that the word is never a more magnificent mystery than when it goes, in the interior of a man, from his thought to his conscience, and returns from his conscience to his thought. It is in this sense only that the words must be understood, so often employed in this chapter, *he said*, *he exclaimed*; we say to ourselves, we speak to ourselves, we exclaim within ourselves, the external silence not being broken. There is a great tumult within; everything within us speaks, except the tongue. The realities of the soul, because they are not visible and palpable, are not the less realities.

He asked himself then where he was. He questioned himself upon this "resolution formed." He confessed to himself that all that he had been arranging in his mind was monstrous, that "to let the matter alone, not to interfere with God," was simply horrible, to let this mistake of destiny and of men be accomplished, not to prevent it, to lend himself to it by his silence, to do nothing, finally, was to do all! it was the last degree of hypocritical meanness! it was a base, cowardly, lying, abject, hideous crime!

For the first time within eight years, the unhappy man had just tasted the bitter flavour of a wicked thought and a wicked action.

He spit it out with disgust.

He continued to question himself. He sternly asked himself what he had understood by this: "My object is attained." He declared that his life, in truth, did have an object. But what object? to conceal his name? to deceive the police? was it for so petty a thing that he had done all that he had done? had he no other object, which was the great one, which was the true one? To save, not his body, but his soul. To become honest and good again. To be an upright man! was it not that, above all, that alone, which he had always wished, and which the bishop had enjoined upon him! To close the door on his past? But he was not closing it, great God! he was reopening it by committing an infamous act! for he became a robber again, and the most odious of robbers! he robbed another of his existence, his life, his peace, his place in the world, he became an assassin! he murdered, he murdered in a moral sense a wretched man, he inflicted upon him that frightful life in death, that living burial, which is called the galleys! on the contrary, to deliver himself up, to save this man stricken by so ghastly a mistake, to reassume his name, to become again from duty the convict Jean Valjean; that was really to achieve his resurrection, and to close for ever the hell from whence he had emerged! to fall back into it in appearance, was to emerge in reality! he must do that! all he had done was nothing, if he did not do that! all his life was useless, all his suffering was lost. He had only to ask the question: "What is the use?" He felt that the bishop was there, that the bishop was present all the more that he was dead, that the bishop was looking fixedly at him, that henceforth Mayor Madeleine with all his virtues would be abominable to him, and the galley slave, Jean Valjean, would be admirable and pure in his sight. That men saw his mask, but the bishop saw his face. That men saw his life, but the bishop saw his conscience. He must then go to Arras, deliver the wrong Jean Valjean, denounce the right one. Alas! that was the greatest of sacrifices, the most poignant of victories, the final step to be taken, but he must do it. Mournful destiny! he could only enter into sanctity in the eyes of God, by returning into infamy in the eyes of men!

"Well," said he, "let us take this course! let us do our duty! Let us save this man!"

He pronounced these words in a loud voice, without perceiving that he was speaking aloud.

He took his books, verified them, and put them in order. He threw into the fire a package of notes which he held against needy small traders. He wrote a letter, which he sealed, and upon the envelope of which might have been read, if there had been any one in the room at the time: *Monsieur Laffitte, banker, Rue d'Artois, Paris.*

He drew from a secretary a pocket-book containing some banknotes and the passport that he had used that same year in going to the elections.

Had any one seen him while he was doing these various acts with such serious meditation, he would not have suspected what was passing within him. Still at intervals his lips quivered; at other times he raised his head and fixed his eye on some point of the wall, as if he saw just there something that he wished to clear up or to interrogate.

The letter to Monsieur Laffitte finished, he put it in his pocket as well as the pocket-book, and began to walk again.

The current of his thought had not changed. He still saw his duty clearly written in luminous letters which flared out before his eyes, and moved with his gaze: "*Go! avow thy name! denounce thyself!*"

He saw also, and as if they were laid bare before him with sensible forms, the two ideas which had been hitherto the double rule of his life, to conceal his name, and to sanctify his soul. For the first time, they appeared to him absolutely distinct, and he saw the difference which separated them. He recognised that one of these ideas was necessarily good, while the other might become evil; that the former was devotion, and that the latter was selfishness; that the one said: "*the neighbour,*" and that the other said: "*me*;" that the one came from the light, and the other from the night.

They were fighting with each other. He saw them fighting. While he was looking, they had expanded before his mind's eye; they were now colossal; and it seemed to him that he saw struggling within him, in that infinite of which we spoke just now, in the midst of darkness and gloom, a goddess and a giantess.

He was full of dismay, but it seemed to him that the good thought was gaining the victory.

He felt that he had reached the second decisive movement of his conscience, and his destiny; that the bishop had marked the first phase of his new life, and that this Champmathieu marked the second. After a great crisis, a great trial.

Meanwhile the fever, quieted for an instant, returned upon him little by little. A thousand thoughts flashed across him, but they fortified him in his resolution.

One moment he had said: that perhaps he took the affair too much to heart, that after all this Champmathieu was not worthy of interest, that in fact he had committed theft.

He answered: If this man has in fact stolen a few apples, that is a month in prison. There is a wide distance between that and the galleys. And who knows even? has he committed theft? is it proven? the name of Jean Valjean overwhelms him and seems to dispense with proofs. Are not prosecuting officers in the habit of acting thus? They think him a robber, because they know him to be a convict.

At another moment the idea occurred to him that, if he should denounce himself, perhaps the heroism of his action, and his honest life for the past seven years, and what he had done for the country, would be considered, and he would be pardoned.

But this supposition quickly vanished, and he smiled bitterly at the thought, that the robbery of the forty sous from Petit Gervais made him a second offender, that that matter would certainly reappear, and by the precise terms of the law he would be condemned to hard labour for life.

He turned away from all illusion, disengaged himself more and more from the earth, and sought consolation and strength elsewhere. He said to himself that he must do his duty; that perhaps even he should not be more unhappy after having done his duty than after having evaded it; that if he let matters alone, if he remained at M—— sur M——, his reputation, his good name, his good works, the deference, the veneration he commanded, his charity, his riches, his popularity, his virtue, would be tainted with a crime, and what pleasure would there be in all these holy things tied to that hideous thing? while, if he carried out the sacrifice, in the galleys, with his chain, with his iron collar, with his green cap, with his perpetual labour, with his pitiless shame, there would be associated a celestial idea.

Finally, he said to himself that it was a necessity, that his destiny was so fixed, that it was not for him to derange the arrangements of God, that at all events he must choose, either virtue without, and abomination within, or sanctity within, and infamy without.

In revolving so many gloomy ideas, his courage did not fail, but his brain was fatigued. He began in spite of himself to think of other things, of indifferent things.

His blood rushed violently to his temples. He walked back and forth constantly. Midnight was struck first from the parish church, then from the city hall. He counted the twelve strokes of the two clocks, and he compared the sound of the two bells. It reminded him that, a few days before, he had seen at a junkshop an old bell for sale, upon which was this name: *Antoine Albin de Romainville.*

He was cold. He kindled a fire. He did not think to close the window.

Meanwhile he had fallen into his stupor again. It required not a little effort to recall his mind to what he was thinking of before the clock struck. He succeeded at last.

"Ah! yes," said he, "I had formed the resolution to denounce myself."

And then all at once he thought of Fantine.

"Stop!" said he, "this poor woman!"

Here was a new crisis.

Fantine, abruptly appearing in his reverie, was like a ray of unexpected light. It seemed to him that everything around him was changing its aspect; he exclaimed:

"Ah! yes, indeed! so far I have only thought of myself. I have only looked to my own convenience! It is whether I shall keep silent or denounce myself, conceal my body or save my soul, be a despicable and respected magistrate, or an infamous and venerable galley slave: it is myself, always myself, only myself. But, good God! all this is egotism. Different forms of egotism, but still egotism! Suppose I should think a little of others? The highest duty is to think of others. Let us see, let us examine! I gone, I taken away, I forgotten; what will become of all this? I denounce myself? I am arrested, this Champmathieu is released, I am sent back to the galleys, very well, and what then? what takes place here? Ah! here, there is a country, city, factories, a business, labourers, men, women, old grandfathers, children, poor people! I have created all this, I keep it all alive; wherever a chimney is smoking, I have put the brands in the fire and the meat in the pot; I have produced ease, circulation, credit; before me there was nothing; I have aroused, vivified, animated, quickened, stimulated, enriched, all the country; without me, the soul is gone. I take myself away; it all dies. And this woman who has suffered so much, who is so worthy in her fall, all whose misfortunes I have unconsciously caused! And that child which I was going for, which I have promised to the mother! Do I not also owe something to this woman, in reparation for the wrong that I have done her? If I should disappear, what happens? The mother dies. The child becomes what she may. This is what comes to pass if I denounce myself, and if I do not denounce myself? Let us see, if I do not denounce myself?"

After putting this question, he stopped; for a moment he hesitated and trembled; but that moment was brief, and he answered with calmness:

"Well, this man goes to the galleys, it is true, but, what of that? He has stolen! It is useless for me to say he has not stolen, he has stolen! As for me, I remain here, I go on. In ten years I shall have made ten millions; I scatter it over the country, I keep nothing for myself, what is it to me? What I am doing is not for myself. The prosperity of all goes on increasing, industry is quickened and excited, manufactories and workshops are multiplied, families, a hundred families, a thousand families, are happy; the country becomes populous; villages spring up where there were only farms, farms spring up where there was nothing; poverty disappears, and with poverty disappear debauchery, prostitution, theft, murder, all vices, all crimes! And this poor mother brings up her child! and the whole country is rich and honest! Ah, yes! How foolish, how absurd I was! What was I speaking of in denouncing myself? This demands reflection, surely, and nothing must be precipitate. What! because it would have pleased me to do the grand and the generous! That is melodramatic after all! Because I only thought of myself, of myself alone, what! to save, from a punishment perhaps a little too severe, but in reality just, nobody knows who, a thief, a scoundrel at any rate. Must an entire country be let go to ruin! must a poor hapless woman perish in the hospital! must a poor little girl perish on the street! like dogs! Ah! that would be abominable! And the mother not even see her child again! and the child hardly have known her mother! And all for this old whelp of an apple-thief who, beyond all doubt, deserves the galleys for something else, if not for this. Fine scruples these, which save an old vagabond who has, after all, only a few years to live, and who will hardly be more unhappy in the galleys than in his hovel, and which sacrifice a whole population, mothers, wives, children! This poor little Cosette who has no one but me in the world, and who is doubtless at this moment all blue with cold in the hut of these Thénardiers! They too are miserable rascals! And I should fail in my duty towards all these poor beings! And I should go away and denounce myself! And I should commit this silly blunder! Take it at the very worst. Suppose there were a misdeed for me in this, and that my conscience should someday reproach me; the acceptance for the good of others of these reproaches which weigh only upon me, of this misdeed which affects only my own soul, why, that is devotion, that is virtue."

He arose and resumed his walk. This time it seemed to him that he was satisfied.

Diamonds are found only in the dark places of the earth; truths are found only in the depths of thought. It seemed to him that after having descended into these depths, after having groped long in the blackest of this darkness, he had at last found one of these diamonds, one of these truths, and that he held it in his hand; and it blinded him to look at it.

"Yes," thought he, "that is it! I am in the true road. I have the solution. I must end by holding fast to something. My choice is made. Let the matter alone! No more vacillation, no more shrinking. This is in the interest of all, not in my own. I am Madeleine, I remain Madeleine. Woe to him who is Jean Valjean! He and I are no longer the same. I do not recognise that man, I no longer know what he is; if it is found that anybody is

Jean Valjean at this hour, let him take care of himself. That does not concern me. That is a fatal name which is floating about in the darkness, if it stops and settles upon any man, so much the worse for that man."

He looked at himself in the little mirror that hung over his mantelpiece and said:

"Yes! To come to a resolution has solaced me! I am quite another man now!"

He took a few steps more, then he stopped short.

"Come!" said he, "I must not hesitate before any of the consequences of the resolution I have formed. There are yet some threads which knit me to this Jean Valjean. They must be broken! There are, in this very room, objects which would accuse me, mute things which would be witnesses; it is done, all these must disappear."

He felt in his pocket, drew out his purse, opened it, and took out a little key.

He put this key into a lock the hole of which was hardly visible, lost as it was in the darkest shading of the figures on the paper which covered the wall. A secret door opened; a kind of false press built between the corner of the wall and the casing of the chimney. There was nothing in this closet but a few refuse trifles; a blue smock-frock, an old pair of trousers, an old haversack, and a great thorn stick, iron-bound at both ends. Those who had seen Jean Valjean at the time he passed through D——, in October, 1815, would have recognised easily all the fragments of this miserable outfit.

He had kept them, as he had kept the silver candlesticks, to remind him at all times of what he had been. But he concealed what came from the galleys, and left the candlesticks that came from the bishop in sight.

He cast a furtive look towards the door, as if he were afraid it would open in spite of the bolt that held it; then with a quick and hasty movement and at a single armful, without even a glance at these things which he had kept so religiously and with so much danger during so many years, he took the whole, rags, stick, haversack, and threw them all into the fire.

He shut up the false press, and, increasing his precautions, henceforth useless, since it was empty, concealed the door behind a heavy piece of furniture which he pushed against it.

In a few seconds, the room and the wall opposite were lit up

with a great, red flickering glare. It was all burning; the thorn
stick cracked and threw out sparks into the middle of the room.

The haversack, as it was consumed with the horrid rags
which it contained, left something uncovered which glistened
in the ashes. By bending towards it, one could have easily
recognised a piece of silver. It was doubtless the forty sous piece
stolen from the little Savoyard.

But he did not look at the fire; he continued his walk to and
fro, always at the same pace.

Suddenly his eyes fell upon the two silver candlesticks on the
mantel, which were glistening dimly in the reflection.

"Stop!" thought he, "all Jean Valjean is contained in them
too. They also must be destroyed."

He took the two candlesticks.

There was fire enough to melt them quickly into an unrecognisable ingot.

He bent over the fire and warmed himself a moment. It felt
really comfortable to him. "The pleasant warmth!" said he.

He stirred the embers with one of the candlesticks.

A minute more, and they would have been in the fire.

At that moment, it seemed to him that he heard a voice
crying within him: "Jean Valjean!" "Jean Valjean!"

His hair stood on end; he was like a man who hears some
terrible thing.

"Yes! that is it, finish!" said the voice, "complete what you
are doing! destroy these candlesticks! annihilate this memorial!
forget the bishop! forget all! ruin this Champmathieu, yes! very
well. Applaud yourself! So it is arranged, it is determined, it is
done. Behold a man, a greybeard who knows not what he is
accused of, who has done nothing, it may be, an innocent man,
whose misfortune is caused by your name, upon whom your
name weighs like a crime, who will be taken instead of you; will
be condemned, will end his days in abjection and in horror!
very well. Be an honoured man yourself. Remain, Monsieur
Mayor, remain honourable and honoured, enrich the city, feed
the poor, bring up the orphans, live happy, virtuous, and
admired, and all this time while you are here in joy and in the
light, there shall be a man wearing your red blouse, bearing your
name in ignominy, and dragging your chain in the galleys! Yes!
this is a fine arrangement! Oh, wretch!"

The sweat rolled off his forehead. He looked upon the

candlesticks with haggard eyes. Meanwhile the voice which spoke within him had not ended. It continued:

"Jean Valjean! there shall be about you many voices which will make great noise, which will speak very loud, and which will bless you; and one only which nobody shall hear, and which will curse you in the darkness. Well, listen, wretch! all these blessings shall fall before they reach Heaven; only the curse shall mount into the presence of God!"

This voice, at first quite feeble, and which was raised from the most obscure depths of his conscience, had become by degrees loud and formidable, and he heard it now at his ear. It seemed to him that it had emerged from himself, and that it was speaking now from without. He thought he heard the last words so distinctly that he looked about the room with a kind of terror.

"Is there anybody here?" asked he, aloud and in a startled voice.

Then he continued with a laugh, which was like the laugh of an idiot:

"What a fool I am! there cannot be anybody here."

There was One; but He who was there was not of such as the human eye can see.

He put the candlesticks on the mantel.

Then he resumed this monotonous and dismal walk, which disturbed the man asleep beneath him in his dreams, and wakened him out of his sleep.

This walk soothed him and excited him at the same time. It sometimes seems that on the greatest occasions we put ourselves in motion in order to ask advice from whatever we may meet by change of place. After a few moments he no longer knew where he was.

He now recoiled with equal terror from each of the resolutions which he had formed in turn. Each of the two ideas which counselled him, appeared to him as fatal as the other. What a fatality! What a chance that this Champmathieu should be mistaken for him! To be hurled down headlong by the very means which Providence seemed at first to have employed to give him full security.

There was a moment during which he contemplated the future. Denounce himself, great God! Give himself up! He saw with infinite despair all that he must leave, all that he must resume. He must then bid farewell to this existence, so good, so pure, so radiant; to this respect of all, to honour, to liberty! No more would he go out to walk in the fields, never again would he hear the birds singing in the month of May, never more give alms to the little children! No longer would he feel the sweetness of looks of gratitude and of love! He would leave this house that he had built, this little room! Everything appeared charming to him now. He would read no more in these books, he would write no more on this little white wood table! His old portress, the only servant he had, would no longer bring him his coffee in the morning. Great God! instead of that, the galley-crew, the iron collar, the red blouse, the chain at his foot, fatigue, the dungeon, the plank-bed, all these horrors, which he knew so well! At his age, after having been what he was! If he were still young! but so old, to be insulted by the first comer, to be tumbled about by the prison guard, to be struck by the jailer's stick! To have his bare feet in iron-bound shoes! To submit morning and evening his leg to the hammer of the roundsman who tests the fetters! To endure the curiosity of strangers who would be told: *This one is the famous Jean Valjean, who was mayor of M—— sur M——!* At night, dripping with sweat, overwhelmed with weariness, the green cap over his eyes, to mount two by two, under the sergeant's whip, the step-ladder of the floating prison. Oh, what wretchedness! Can destiny then be malignant like an intelligent being, and become monstrous like the human heart?

And do what he might, he always fell back upon this sharp dilemma which was at the bottom of his thought. To remain in paradise and there become a demon! To re-enter into hell and there become an angel!

What shall be done, great God! what shall be done?

The torment from which he had emerged with so much difficulty, broke loose anew within him. His ideas again began to become confused. They took that indescribable, stupefied, and mechanical shape, which is peculiar to despair. The name of Romainville returned constantly to his mind, with two lines of a song he had formerly heard. He thought that Romainville is a little wood near Paris, where young lovers go to gather lilacs in the month of April.

He staggered without as well as within. He walked like a little child that is just allowed to go alone.

Now and then, struggling against his fatigue, he made an

effort again to arouse his intellect. He endeavoured to state, finally and conclusively, the problem over which he had in some sort fallen exhausted. Must he denounce himself? Must he be silent? He could see nothing distinctly. The vague forms of all the reasonings thrown out by his mind trembled, and were dissipated one after another in smoke, but this much he felt, that by whichever resolve he might abide, necessarily, and without possibility of escape, something of himself would surely die; that he was entering into a sepulchre on the right hand, as well as on the left; that he was suffering a death-agony, the death-agony of his happiness, or the death-agony of his virtue.

Alas! all his irresolutions were again upon him. He was no further advanced than when he began.

So struggled beneath its anguish this unhappy soul. Eighteen hundred years before this unfortunate man, the mysterious being, in whom are aggregated all the sanctities and all the sufferings of humanity, He also, while the olive trees were shivering in the fierce breath of the Infinite, had long put away from his hand the fearful chalice that appeared before him, dripping with shadow and running over with darkness, in the star-filled depths.

IV
FORMS ASSUMED BY SUFFERING DURING SLEEP

THE clock struck three. For five hours he had been walking thus, almost without interruption, when he dropped into his chair.

He fell asleep and dreamed.

This dream, like most dreams, had no further relation to the condition of affairs than its mournful and poignant character, but it made an impression upon him. This nightmare struck him so forcibly that he afterwards wrote it down. It is one of the papers in his own handwriting, which he has left behind him. We think it our duty to copy it here literally.

Whatever this dream may be, the story of that night would be incomplete if we should omit it. It is the gloomy adventure of a sick soul.

It is as follows: upon the envelope we find this line written: "*The dream that I had that night.*"

"I was in a field. A great sad field where there was no grass. It did not seem that it was day, nor that it was night.

"I was walking with my brother, the brother of my childhood; this brother of whom I must say that I never think, and whom I scarcely remember.

"We were talking, and we met others walking. We were speaking of a neighbour we had formerly, who, since she had lived in the street, always worked with her window open. Even while we talked, we felt cold on account of that open window.

"There were no trees in the field.

"We saw a man passing near us. He was entirely naked, ashen-coloured, mounted upon a horse which was of the colour of earth. The man had no hair; we saw his skull and the veins in his skull. In his hand he held a stick which was limber like a twig of grape vine, and heavy as iron. This horseman passed by and said nothing.

"My brother said to me: 'Let us take the deserted road.'

"There was a deserted road where we saw not a bush, nor even a sprig of moss. All was of the colour of earth, even the sky. A few steps further, and no one answered me when I spoke. I perceived that my brother was no longer with me.

"I entered a village which I saw. I thought that it must be Romainville (why Romainville?).*

"The first street by which I entered was deserted. I passed into a second street. At the corner of the two streets was a man standing against the wall. I said to this man: 'What place is this? Where am I?' The man made no answer. I saw the door of a house open. I went in.

"The first room was deserted. I entered the second. Behind the door of this room was a man standing against the wall. I asked this man: 'Whose house is this? Where am I?' The man made no answer. The house had a garden.

"I went out of the house and into the garden. The garden was deserted. Behind the first tree I found a man standing. I said to this man: 'What is this garden? Where am I?' The man made no answer.

"I wandered about the village, and I perceived that it was a city. All the streets were deserted, all the doors were open. No living being was passing along the streets, or stirring in the

* This parenthesis is in the hand of Jean Valjean.

rooms, or walking in the gardens. But behind every angle of a wall, behind every door, behind everything, there was a man standing who kept silence. But only one could ever be seen at a time. These men looked at me as I passed by.

"I went out of the city and began to walk in the fields.

"After a little while, I turned and I saw a great multitude coming after me. I recognised all the men that I had seen in the city. Their heads were strange. They did not seem to hasten, and still they walked faster than I. They made no sound in walking. In an instant this multitude came up and surrounded me. The faces of these men were the colour of earth.

"Then the first one whom I had seen and questioned on entering the city, said to me: 'Where are you going? Do you not know that you have been dead for a long time?'

"I opened my mouth to answer, and I perceived that no one was near me."

He awoke. He was chilly. A wind as cold as the morning wind made the sashes of the still open window swing on their hinges. The fire had gone out. The candle was low in the socket. The night was yet dark.

He arose and went to the window. There were still no stars in the sky.

From his window he could look into the court-yard and into the street. A harsh, rattling noise that suddenly resounded from the ground made him look down.

He saw below him two red stars, whose rays danced back and forth grotesquely in the shadow.

His mind was still half buried in the mist of his reverie: "Yes!" thought he, "there are none in the sky. They are on the earth now."

This confusion, however, faded away; a second noise like the first awakened him completely; he looked, and he saw that these two stars were the lamps of a carriage. By the light which they emitted, he could distinguish the form of a carriage. It was a tilbury drawn by a small white horse. The noise which he had heard was the sound of the horse's hoofs upon the pavement.

"What carriage is that?" said he to himself. "Who is it that comes so early?"

At that moment there was a low rap at the door of his room.

He shuddered from head to foot and cried in a terrible voice: "Who is there?"

Some one answered:

"I, Monsieur Mayor."

He recognised the voice of the old woman, his portress.

"Well," said he, "what is it?"

"Monsieur Mayor, it is just five o'clock."

"What is that to me?"

"Monsieur Mayor, it is the chaise."

"What chaise?"

"The tilbury."

"What tilbury?"

"Did not Monsieur the Mayor order a tilbury?"

"No," said he.

"The driver says that he has come for Monsieur the Mayor."

"What driver?"

"Monsieur Scaufflaire's driver."

"Monsieur Scaufflaire?"

That name startled him as if a flash had passed before his face.

"Oh yes!" he said, "Monsieur Scaufflaire!"

Could the old woman have seen him at that moment she would have been frightened.

There was a long silence. He examined the flame of the candle with a stupid air, and took some of the melted wax from around the wick and rolled it in his fingers. The old woman was waiting. She ventured, however, to speak again:

"Monsieur Mayor, what shall I say?"

"Say that it is right, and I am coming down."

V
CLOGS IN THE WHEELS

THE postal service from Arras to M——— sur M——— was still performed at this time by the little mail wagons of the date of the empire. These mail wagons were two-wheeled cabriolets lined with buckskin, hung upon jointed springs, and having but two seats, one for the driver, the other for the traveller. The wheels were armed with those long threatening hubs which keep other vehicles at a distance, and which are still seen upon the roads of Germany. The letters were carried in a huge oblong box placed behind the cabriolet and making a part of it. This box was painted black and the cabriolet yellow.

These vehicles, which nothing now resembles, were

indescribably misshapen and clumsy, and when they were seen
from a distance crawling along some road in the horizon, they
were like those insects called, I think, termites, which with a
slender body draw a great train behind. They went, however,
very fast. The mail that left Arras every night at one o'clock,
after the passing of the courier from Paris, arrived at M—— sur
M—— a little before five in the morning.

That night the mail that came down to M—— sur M——
by the road from Hesdin, at the turn of a street just as it was
entering the city, ran against a little tilbury drawn by a white
horse, which was going in the opposite direction, and in which
there was only one person, a man wrapped in a cloak. The
wheel of the tilbury received a very severe blow. The courier
cried out to the man to stop, but the traveller did not listen and
kept on his way at a rapid trot.

"There is a man in a devilish hurry!" said the courier.

The man who was in such a hurry was he whom we have
seen struggling in such pitiable convulsions.

Where was he going? He could not have told. Why was he
in haste? He did not know. He went forward at haphazard.
Whither? To Arras, doubtless; but perhaps he was going elsewhere also. At moments he felt this, and he shuddered. He
plunged into that darkness as into a yawning gulf. Something
pushed him, something drew him on. What was passing within
him, no one could describe, all will understand. What man has
not entered, at least once in his life, into this dark cavern of the
unknown?

But he had resolved upon nothing, decided nothing, determined nothing, done nothing. None of the acts of his conscience had been final. He was more than ever as at the first
moment.

Why was he going to Arras?

He repeated what he had already said to himself when he
engaged the cabriolet of Scaufflaire, that, whatever might be the
result, there could be no objection to seeing with his own eyes,
and judging of the circumstances for himself, that it was even
prudent, that he ought to know what took place; that he could
decide nothing without having observed and scrutinised; that in
the distance every little thing seems a mountain; that after all,
when he should have seen this Champmathieu, some wretch
probably, his conscience would be very much reconciled to

letting him go to the galleys in his place; that it was true that Javert would be there, and Brevet Chenildieu, Cochepaille, old convicts who had known him; but surely they would not recognise him; bah! what an idea! that Javert was a hundred miles off the track; that all conjectures and all suppositions were fixed upon this Champmathieu, and that nothing is so stubborn as suppositions and conjectures; that there was, therefore, no danger.

That it was no doubt a dark hour, but that he should get through it; that after all he held his destiny, evil as it might be, in his own hand; that he was master of it. He clung to that thought.

In reality, to tell the truth, he would have preferred not to go to Arras.

Still he was on the way.

Although absorbed in thought, he whipped up his horse, which trotted away at that regular and sure full trot that gets over two leagues and a half an hour.

In proportion as the tilbury went forward, he felt something within him which shrank back.

At daybreak he was in the open country, the city of M——— sur M——— was a long way behind. He saw the horizon growing lighter; he beheld, without seeing them, all the frozen figures of a winter dawn pass before his eyes. Morning has its spectres as well as evening. He did not see them, but, without his consciousness, and by a kind of penetration which was almost physical, those black outlines of trees and hills added to the tumultuous state of his soul an indescribable gloom and apprehension.

Every time he passed one of the isolated houses that stood here and there by the side of the road, he said to himself: "But yet, there are people there who are sleeping!"

The trotting of the horse, the rattling of the harness, the wheels upon the pavement, made a gentle, monotonous sound. These things are charming when one is joyful, and mournful when one is sad.

It was broad day when he arrived at Hesdin. He stopped before an inn to let his horse breathe and to have some oats given him.

This horse was, as Scaufflaire had said, of that small breed of the Boulonnais which has too much head, too much belly, and not enough neck, but which has an open chest, a large rump, fine and slender legs, and a firm foot, a homely race, but strong and sound. The excellent animal had made five leagues in two hours, and had not turned a hair.

He did not get out of the tilbury. The stable-boy who brought the oats stooped down suddenly and examined the left wheel.

"Have you gone far so?" said the man.

He answered, almost without breaking up his train of thought:

"Why?"

"Have you come far?" said the boy.

"Five leagues from here."

"Ah!"

"Why do you say: ah?"

The boy stooped down again, was silent a moment, with his eye fixed on the wheel, then he rose up saying:

"To think that this wheel has just come five leagues, that is possible, but it is very sure that it won't go a quarter of a league now."

He sprang down from the tilbury.

"What do you say, my friend?"

"I say that it is a miracle that you have come five leagues without tumbling, you and your horse, into some ditch on the way. Look for yourself."

The wheel in fact was badly damaged. The collision with the mail wagon had broken two spokes and loosened the hub so that the nut no longer held.

"My friend," said he to the stable-boy, "is there a wheelwright here?"

"Certainly, monsieur."

"Do me the favour to go for him."

"There he is, close by. Hallo, Master Bourgaillard!"

Master Bourgaillard the wheelwright was on his own doorstep. He came and examined the wheel, and made such a grimace as a surgeon makes at the sight of a broken leg.

"Can you mend that wheel on the spot?"

"Yes, monsieur."

"When can I start again?"

"To-morrow."

"To-morrow!"

"It is a good day's work. Is monsieur in a great hurry?"

"A very great hurry. I must leave in an hour at the latest."

"Impossible, monsieur."

"I will pay whatever you like."

"Impossible."

"Well! in two hours."

"Impossible to-day. There are two spokes and a hub to be repaired. Monsieur cannot start again before to-morrow."

"My business cannot wait till to-morrow. Instead of mending this wheel, cannot it be replaced?"

"How so?"

"You are a wheelwright?"

"Certainly, monsieur."

"Have not you a wheel to sell me? I could start away at once."

"A wheel to exchange?"

"Yes."

"I have not a wheel made for your cabriolet. Two wheels make a pair. Two wheels don't go together haphazard."

"In that case, sell me a pair of wheels."

"Monsieur, every wheel doesn't go on to every axle."

"But try."

"It's of no use, monsieur. I have nothing but cart wheels to sell. We are a small place here."

"Have you a cabriolet to let?"

The wheelwright, at the first glance, had seen that the tilbury was a hired vehicle. He shrugged his shoulders.

"You take good care of the cabriolets that you hire! I should have one a good while before I would let it to you."

"Well, sell it to me."

"I have not one."

"What! not even a carriole? I am not hard to suit, as you see."

"We are a little place. True, I have under the old shed there," added the wheelwright, "an old chaise that belongs to a citizen of the place, who has given it to me to keep, and who uses it every 29th of February. I would let it to you, of course it is nothing to me. The citizen must not see it go by, and then, it is clumsy; it would take two horses."

"I will take two post-horses."

"Where is monsieur going?"

"To Arras."

"And monsieur would like to get there to-day?"

"I would."

"By taking post-horses?"

"Why not?"

"Will monsieur be satisfied to arrive by four o'clock to-morrow morning?"

"No, indeed."

"I mean, you see, that there is something to be said, in taking post-horses. Monsieur has his passport?"

"Yes."

"Well, by taking post-horses, monsieur will not reach Arras before to-morrow. We are a cross-road. The relays are poorly served, the horses are in the fields. The ploughing season has just commenced; heavy teams are needed, and the horses are taken from everywhere, from the post as well as elsewhere. Monsieur will have to wait at least three or four hours at each relay, and then they go at a walk. There are a good many hills to climb."

"Well, I will go on horseback. Unhitch the cabriolet. Somebody in the place can surely sell me a saddle."

"Certainly, but will this horse go under the saddle?"

"It is true, I had forgotten it, he will not."

"Then——"

"But I can surely find in the village a horse to let?"

"A horse to go to Arras at one trip?"

"Yes."

"It would take a better horse than there is in our parts. You would have to buy him too, for nobody knows you. But neither to sell nor to let, neither for five hundred francs nor for a thousand will you find such a one."

"What shall I do?"

"The best thing to do, like a sensible man, is that I mend the wheel and you continue your journey to-morrow."

"To-morrow will be too late."

"Confound it!"

"Is there no mail that goes to Arras? When does it pass?"

"To-night. Both mails make the trip in the night, the up mail as well as the down."

"How! must you take a whole day to mend this wheel?"

"A whole day, and a long one!"

"If you set two workmen at it?"

"If I should set ten."

"If you should tie the spokes with cords?"

"The spokes I could, but not the hub. And then the tyre is also in bad condition, too."

"Is there no livery stable in the city?"

"No."

"Is there another wheelwright?"

The stable-boy and the wheelwright answered at the same time, with a shake of the head—

"No."

He felt an immense joy.

It was evident that Providence was in the matter. It was Providence that had broken the wheel of the tilbury and stopped him on his way. He had not yielded to this sort of first summons; he had made all possible efforts to continue his journey; he had faithfully and scrupulously exhausted every means, he had shrunk neither before the season, nor from fatigue, nor from expense; he had nothing for which to reproach himself. If he went no further, it no longer concerned him. It was now not his fault; it was, not the act of his conscience, but the act of Providence.

He breathed. He breathed freely and with a full chest for the first time since Javert's visit. It seemed to him that the iron hand which had gripped his heart for twenty hours was relaxed.

It appeared to him that now God was for him, was manifestly for him.

He said to himself that he had done all that he could, and that now he had only to retrace his steps, tranquilly.

If his conversation with the wheelwright had taken place in a room of the inn, it would have had no witnesses, nobody would have heard it, the matter would have rested there, and it is probable that we should not have had to relate any of the events which follow, but that conversation occurred in the street. Every colloquy in the street inevitably gathers a circle. There are always people who ask nothing better than to be spectators. While he was questioning the wheelwright, some of the passers-by had stopped around them. After listening for a few minutes, a young boy whom no one had noticed, had separated from the group and ran away.

At the instant the traveller, after the internal deliberation which we have just indicated, was making up his mind to go back, this boy returned. He was accompanied by an old woman.

"Monsieur," said the woman, "my boy tells me that you are anxious to hire a cabriolet."

This simple speech, uttered by an old woman who was brought there by a boy, made the sweat pour down his back. He thought he saw the hand he was but now freed from reappear in the shadow behind him, all ready to seize him again.

He answered:

"Yes, good woman, I am looking for a cabriolet to hire."

And he hastened to add:

"But there is none in the place."

"Yes, there is," said the dame.

"Where is it then?" broke in the wheelwright.

"At my house," replied the dame.

He shuddered. The fatal hand had closed upon him again.

The old woman had, in fact, under a shed, a sort of willow carriole. The blacksmith and the boy at the inn, angry that the traveller should escape them, intervened.

It was a frightful go-cart, it had no springs, it was true the seat was hung inside with leather straps, it would not keep out the rain, the wheels were rusty and rotten, it couldn't go much further than the tilbury, a real jumper! This gentleman would do very wrong to set out in it, etc., etc."

This was all true, but this go-cart, this jumper, this thing, whatever it might be, went upon two wheels and could go to Arras.

He paid what was asked, left the tilbury to be mended at the blacksmith's against his return, had the white horse harnessed to the carriole, got in, and resumed the route he had followed since morning.

The moment the carriole started, he acknowledged that he had felt an instant before a certain joy at the thought that he should not go where he was going. He examined that joy with a sort of anger, and thought it absurd. Why should he feel joy at going back? After all, he was making a journey of his own accord, nobody forced him to it.

And certainly, nothing could happen which he did not choose to have happen.

As he was leaving Hesdin, he heard a voice crying out: "Stop! stop!" He stopped the carriole with a hasty movement, in which there was still something strangely feverish and convulsive which resembled hope.

It was the dame's little boy.

"Monsieur," said he, "it was I who got the carriole for you."

"Well!"

"You have not given me anything."

He, who gave to all, and so freely, felt this claim was exorbitant and almost odious.

"Oh! is it you, you beggar?" said he, "you shall have nothing!"

He whipped up the horse and started away at a quick trot.

He had lost a good deal of time at Hesdin, he wished to make it up. The little horse was plucky, and pulled enough for two; but it was February, it had rained, the roads were bad. And then, it was no longer the tilbury. The carriole ran hard, and was very heavy. And besides there were many steep hills.

He was almost four hours going from Hesdin to Saint Pol. Four hours for five leagues.

At Saint Pol he drove to the nearest inn, and had the horse taken to the stable. As he had promised Scaufflaire, he stood near the manger while the horse was eating. He was thinking of things sad and confused.

The innkeeper's wife came into the stable.

"Does not monsieur wish breakfast?"

"Why, it is true," said he, "I have a good appetite."

He followed the woman, who had a fresh and pleasant face. She led him into a low hall, where there were some tables covered with oilcloth.

"Be quick," said he, "I must start again. I am in a hurry."

A big Flemish servant girl waited on him in all haste. He looked at the girl with a feeling of comfort.

"This is what ailed me," thought he. "I had not breakfasted."

His breakfast was served. He seized the bread, bit a piece, then slowly put it back on the table, and did not touch anything more.

A teamster was eating at another table. He said to this man:

"Why is their bread so bitter?"

The teamster was a German, and did not understand him.

He returned to the stable to his horse.

An hour later he had left Saint Pol, and was driving towards Tinques, which is but five leagues from Arras.

What was he doing during the trip? What was he thinking about? As in the morning, he saw the trees pass by, the thatched roofs, the cultivated fields, and the dissolving views of the country which change at every turn of the road. Such scenes are sometimes sufficient for the soul, and almost do away with thought. To see a thousand objects for the first and for the last time, what can be deeper and more melancholy? To travel is to be born and to die at every instant. It may be that in the most shadowy portion of his mind, he was drawing a comparison between these changing horizons and human existence. All the facts of life are perpetually in flight before us. Darkness and light alternate with each other. After a flash, an eclipse; we look, we hasten, we stretch out our hands to seize what is passing; every event is a turn of the road; and all at once we are old. We feel a slight shock, all is black, we distinguish a dark door, this gloomy horse of life which was carrying us stops, and we see a veiled and unknown form that turns him out into the darkness.

Twilight was falling just as the children coming out of school beheld our traveller entering Tinques. It is true that the days were still short. He did not stop at Tinques. As he was driving out of the village, a countryman who was repairing the road raised his head and said:

"Your horse is very tired."

The poor beast, in fact, was not going faster than a walk.

"Are you going to Arras?" added the countryman.

"Yes."

"If you go at this rate, you won't get there very early."

He stopped his horse and asked the countryman:

"How far is it from here to Arras?"

"Near seven long leagues."

"How is that? the post route only counts five and a quarter."

"Ah!" replied the workman, "then you don't know that the road is being repaired. You will find it cut off a quarter of an hour from here. There's no means of going further."

"Indeed!"

"You will take the left, the road that leads to Carency, and cross the river; when you are at Camblin, you will turn to the right; that is the road from Mont Saint-Eloy to Arras."

"But it is night, I shall lose my way."

"You are not of these parts?"

"No."

"Besides, they are all cross-roads."

"Stop, monsieur," the countryman continued, "do you want I should give you some advice? Your horse is tired; go back to Tinques. There is a good house there. Sleep there. You can go on to Arras to-morrow."

"I must be there to-night—this evening!"

"That is another thing. Then go back all the same to that inn, and take an extra horse. The boy that will go with the horse will guide you through the cross-roads."

He followed the countryman's advice, retraced his steps, and a half hour afterwards he again passed the same place, but at a full trot, with a good extra horse. A stable-boy, who called himself a postillion, was sitting upon the shaft of the carriole.

He felt, however, that he was losing time. It was now quite dark.

They were driving through a cross-path. The road became frightful. The carriole tumbled from one rut to the other. He said to the postillion:

"Keep up a trot, and double drink-money."

In one of the jolts the whiffle-tree broke.

"Monsieur," said the postillion, "the whiffle-tree is broken; I do not know how to harness my horse now, this road is very bad at night, if you will come back and stop at Tinques, we can be at Arras early to-morrow morning."

He answered: "Have you a piece of string and a knife?"

"Yes, monsieur."

He cut off the limb of a tree and made a whiffle-tree of it.

This was another loss of twenty minutes; but they started off at a gallop.

The plain was dark. A low fog, thick and black, was creeping over the hill-tops and floating away like smoke. There were glimmering flashes from the clouds. A strong wind, which came from the sea, made a sound all around the horizon like the moving of furniture. Everything that he caught a glimpse of had an attitude of terror. How all things shudder under the terrible breath of night.

The cold penetrated him. He had not eaten since the evening before. He recalled vaguely to mind his other night adventure in the great plain near D——, eight years before; and it seemed yesterday to him.

Some distant bell struck the hour. He asked the boy:

"What o'clock is that?"

"Seven o'clock, monsieur; we shall be in Arras at eight. We have only three leagues."

At this moment he thought for the first time, and it seemed strange that it had not occurred to him sooner, that perhaps all the trouble he was taking might be useless; that he did not even know the hour of the trial; that he should at least have informed himself of that; that it was foolish to be going on at this rate, without knowing whether it would be of any use. Then he figured out some calculations in his mind, that ordinarily the sessions of the courts of assize began at nine o'clock in the morning; that this case would not occupy much time; this apple-stealing would be very short; that there would be nothing but a question of identity; four or five witnesses and some little to be said by the lawyers; that he would get there after it was all over!

The postillion whipped up the horses. They had crossed the river, and left Mont Saint-Eloy behind them.

The night grew darker and darker.

VI
SISTER SIMPLICE PUT TO THE PROOF

MEANWHILE, at that very moment, Fantine was in ecstasies.

She had passed a very bad night. Cough frightful, fever redoubled; she had bad dreams. In the morning, when the doctor came, she was delirious. He appeared to be alarmed, and asked to be informed as soon as Monsieur Madeleine came.

All the morning she was low-spirited, spoke little and was making folds in the sheets, murmuring in a low voice over some calculations which appeared to be calculations of distances. Her eyes were hollow and fixed. The light seemed almost gone out, but then, at moments, they would be lighted up and sparkle like stars. It seems as though at the approach of a certain dark hour, the light of heaven infills those who are leaving the light of earth.

Whenever Sister Simplice asked her how she was, she answered invariably: "Well. I would like to see Monsieur Madeleine."

A few months earlier, when Fantine had lost the last of her modesty, her last shame and her last happiness, she was the shadow of herself; now she was the spectre of herself. Physical suffering had completed the work of moral suffering. This creature of twenty-five years had a wrinkled forehead, flabby cheeks, pinched nostrils, shrivelled gums, a leaden complexion, a bony neck, protruding collar-bones, skinny limbs, an earthy skin, and her fair hair was mixed with grey. Alas! how sickness extemporises old age.

At noon the doctor came again, left a few prescriptions, inquired if the mayor had been at the infirmary, and shook his head.

Monsieur Madeleine usually came at three o'clock to see the sick woman. As exactitude was kindness, he was exact.

About half-past two, Fantine began to be agitated. In the space of twenty minutes, she asked the nun more than ten times: "My sister, what time is it?"

The clock struck three. At the third stroke, Fantine rose up in bed—ordinarily she could hardly turn herself—she joined her two shrunken and yellow hands in a sort of convulsive clasp, and the nun heard from her one of those deep sighs which seem to uplift great weight. Then Fantine turned and looked towards the door.

Nobody came in; the door did not open.

She sat so for a quarter of an hour, her eyes fixed upon the door, motionless, and as if holding her breath. The sister dared not speak. The church clock struck the quarter. Fantine fell back upon her pillow.

She said nothing, and again began to make folds in the sheet.

A half-hour passed, then an hour, but no one came; every time the clock struck, Fantine rose and looked towards the door, then she fell back.

Her thought could be clearly seeen, but she pronounced no name, she did not complain, she found no fault. She only coughed mournfully. One would have said that something dark was settling down upon her. She was livid, and her lips were blue. She smiled at times.

The clock struck five. Then the sister heard her speak very low and gently: "But since I am going away to-morrow, he does wrong not to come to-day!"

Sister Simplice herself was surprised at Monsieur Madeleine's delay.

Meanwhile, Fantine was looking at the canopy of her bed.

She seemed to be seeking to recall something to her mind. All at once she began to sing in a voice as feeble as a whisper. The nun listened. This is what Fantine sang:

> Nous achèterons de bien belles choses
> En nous promenant le long des faubourgs.
> Les bleuets sont bleus, les roses sont roses,
> Les bleuets sont bleus, j'aime mes amours.
>
> La vierge Marie auprès de mon poêle
> Est venue hier en manteau brodé;
> Et m'a dit:—Voici, caché sous mon voile,
> Le petit qu'un jour tu m'as demandé.
> Courez à la ville, ayez de la toile,
> Achetez du fil, achetez un dé.
>   Nous achèterons de bien belles choses
>   En nous promenant le long des faubourgs.
>
> Bonne sainte Vierge, auprès de mon poêle
> J'ai mis un berceau de rubans orné;
> Dieu me donnerait sa plus belle étoile,
> J'aime mieux l'enfant que tu m'as donné.
> Madame, que faire avec cette toile?
> Faites en trousseau pour mon nouveau-né.
>   Les bleuets sont bleus, les roses sont roses,
>   Les bleuets sont bleus, j'aime mes amours.
>
> Lavez cette toile.—Où?—Dans la rivière.
> Faites-en, sans rien gâter ni salir,
> Une belle jupe avec sa brassière
> Que je veux broder et de fleurs emplir.
>   L'enfant n'est plus là, madame, qu'en faire?
>   Faites-en un drap pour m'ensevelir.
>
> Nous achèterons de bien belles choses
> En nous promenant le long des faubourgs.
> Les bleuets sont bleus, les roses sont roses,
> Les bleuets sont bleus, j'aime mes amours.*

This was an old nursery song with which she once used to sing her little Cosette to sleep, and which had not occurred to her mind for the five years since she had had her child with her.

She sang it in a voice so sad, and to an air so sweet, that it could not but draw tears even from a nun. The sister, accustomed to austerity as she was, felt a drop upon her cheek.

The clock struck six. Fantine did not appear to hear. She seemed no longer to pay attention to anything around her.

Sister Simplice sent a girl to inquire of the portress of the factory if the mayor had come in, and if he would not very soon come to the infirmary. The girl returned in a few minutes.

Fantine was still motionless, and appeared to be absorbed in her own thoughts.

The servant related in a whisper to Sister Simplice that the mayor had gone away that morning before six o'clock in a little

---

* We will buy very pretty things
A walking through the faubourgs.
Violets are blue, roses are red,
Violets are blue, I love my loves.

The Virgin Mary to my bed
Came yesterday in broidered cloak
And told me: "Here hidden in my veil
Is the babe that once you asked of me."
"Run to the town, get linen,
Buy thread, buy a thimble."
    We will buy very pretty things,
    A walking through the faubourgs.

Good holy Virgin, by my bed
I have put a cradle draped with ribbons;
Were God to give me his fairest star
I should love the babe thou hast given me more.
"Madame, what shall be done with this linen?"
"Make a trousseau for my new-born."
    Violets are blue, roses are red,
    Violets are blue, I love my loves.

Wash this linen. "Where?" In the river.
Make of it, without spoiling or soiling,
A pretty skirt, a very long skirt,
Which I will broider and fill with flowers.
"The child is gone, madame, what more?"
"Make of it a shroud to bury me."

We will buy very pretty things
A walking in the faubourgs.
Violets are blue, roses are red,
Violets are blue, I love my loves.

tilbury drawn by a white horse, cold as the weather was; that he went alone, without even a driver, that no one knew the road he had taken, that some said he had been seen to turn off by the road to Arras, that others were sure they had met him on the road to Paris. That when he went away he seemed, as usual, very kind, and that he simply said to the portress that he need not be expected that night.

While the two women were whispering, with their backs turned towards Fantine's bed, the sister questioning, the servant conjecturing, Fantine, with that feverish vivacity of certain organic diseases, which unites the free movement of health with the frightful exhaustion of death, had risen to her knees on the bed, her shrivelled hands resting on the bolster, and with her head passing through the opening of the curtains, she listened. All at once she exclaimed:

"You are talking there of Monsieur Madeleine! why do you talk so low? what has he done? why does he not come?"

Her voice was so harsh and rough that the two women thought they heard the voice of a man; they turned towards her affrighted.

"Why don't you answer?" cried Fantine.

The servant stammered out:

"The portress told me that he could not come to-day."

"My child," said the sister, "be calm, lie down again."

Fantine, without changing her attitude, resumed with a loud voice, and in a tone at once piercing and imperious:

"He cannot come. Why not? You know the reason. You were whispering it there between you. I want to know."

The servant whispered quickly in the nun's ear: "Answer that he is busy with the City Council."

Sister Simplice reddened slightly; it was a lie that the servant had proposed to her. On the other hand, it did seem to her that to tell the truth to the sick woman would doubtless be a terrible blow, and that it was dangerous in the state in which Fantine was. This blush did not last long. The sister turned her calm, sad eye upon Fantine, and said:

"The mayor has gone away."

Fantine sprang up and sat upon her feet. Her eyes sparkled. A marvellous joy spread over that mournful face.

"Gone away!" she exclaimed. "He has gone for Cosette!"

Then she stretched her hands towards heaven, and her whole

countenance became ineffable. Her lips moved; she was praying in a whisper.

When her prayer was ended: "My sister," said she, "I am quite willing to lie down again, I will do whatever you wish; I was naughty just now, pardon me for having talked so loud; it is very bad to talk loud; I know it, my good sister, but see how happy I am. God is kind, Monsieur Madeleine is good; just think of it, that he has gone to Montfermeil for my little Cosette."

She lay down again, helped the nun to arrange the pillow, and kissed a little silver cross which she wore at her neck, and which Sister Simplice had given her.

"My child," said the sister, "try to rest now, and do not talk any more."

Fantine took the sister's hand between hers; they were moist; the sister was pained to feel it.

"He started this morning for Paris. Indeed he need not even go through Paris. Montfermeil is a little to the left in coming. You remember what he said yesterday, when I spoke to him about Cosette: *Very soon, very soon!* This is a surprise he has for me. You know he had me sign a letter to take her away from the Thénardiers. They will have nothing to say, will they? They will give up Cosette. Because they have their pay. The authorities would not let them keep a child when they are paid. My sister, do not make signs to me that I must not talk. I am very happy, I am doing very well. I have no pain at all, I am going to see Cosette again, I am hungry even. For almost five years I have not seen her. You do not, you cannot imagine what a hold children have upon you! And then she will be so handsome, you will see! If you knew, she has such pretty little rosy fingers! First, she will have very beautiful hands. At a year old she had ridiculous hands,—so! She must be large now. She is seven years old. She is a little lady. I call her Cosette, but her name is Euphrasie. Now, this morning I was looking at the dust on the mantel, and I had an idea that I should see Cosette again very soon! Oh, dear! how wrong it is to be years without seeing one's children! We ought to remember that life is not eternal! Oh! how good it is in the mayor to go—true, it is very cold! He had his cloak, at least! He will be here to-morrow, will he not? That will make to-morrow a fête. To-morrow morning, my sister, you will remind me to put on my little lace cap. Montfermeil is a country place. I made the trip on foot once. It was a long way for me. But the diligences go very fast. He will be here to-morrow with Cosette! How far is it from here to Montfermeil?"

The sister, who had no idea of the distance, answered: "Oh! I feel sure that he will be here to-morrow."

"To-morrow! to-morrow!" said Fantine, "I shall see Cosette to-morrow! See, good Sister of God, I am well now. I am wild; I would dance, if anybody wanted me to."

One who had seen her a quarter of an hour before could not have understood this. Now she was all rosy; she talked in a lively, natural tone; her whole face was only a smile. At times she laughed while whispering to herself. A mother's joy is almost like a child's.

"Well," resumed the nun, "now you are happy, obey me—do not talk any more."

Fantine laid her head upon the pillow, and said in a low voice:

"Yes, lie down again; be prudent now that you are going to have your child. Sister Simplice is right. All here are right."

And then, without moving, or turning her head, she began to look all about with her eyes wide open and a joyous air, and she said nothing more.

The sister closed the curtains, hoping that she would sleep.

Between seven and eight o'clock the doctor came. Hearing no sound, he supposed that Fantine was asleep, went in softly, and approached the bed on tiptoe. He drew the curtains aside, and by the glimmer of the twilight he saw Fantine's large calm eyes looking at him.

She said to him: "Monsieur, you will let her lie by my side in a little bed, won't you?"

The doctor thought she was delirious. She added:

"Look, there is just room."

The doctor took Sister Simplice aside, who explained the matter to him, that Monsieur Madeleine was absent for a day or two, and that, not being certain, they had not thought it best to undeceive the sick woman, who believed the mayor had gone to Montfermeil; that it was possible, after all, that she had guessed aright. The doctor approved of this.

He returned to Fantine's bed again, and she continued:

"Then you see, in the morning, when she wakes, I can say good morning to the poor kitten; and at night, when I am awake, I can hear her sleep. Her little breathing is so sweet it will do me good."

"Give me your hand," said the doctor.

She reached out her hand, and exclaimed with a laugh:

"Oh, stop! Indeed, it is true you don't know! but I am cured. Cosette is coming to-morrow."

The doctor was surprised. She was better. Her languor was less. Her pulse was stronger. A sort of new life was all at once reanimating this poor exhausted being.

"Doctor," she continued, "has the sister told you that Monsieur the Mayor has gone for the little thing?"

The doctor recommended silence, and that she should avoid all painful emotion. He prescribed an infusion of pure quinine, and, in case the fever should return in the night, a soothing potion. As he was going away he said to the sister: "She is better. If by good fortune the mayor should really come back to-morrow with the child, who knows? there are such astonishing crises; we have seen great joy instantly cure diseases; I am well aware that this is an organic disease, and far advanced, but this is all such a mystery! We shall save her perhaps!"

VII
THE TRAVELLER ARRIVES AND
PROVIDES FOR HIS RETURN

IT was nearly eight o'clock in the evening when the carriole which we left on the road drove into the yard of the Hotel de la Poste at Arras. The man whom we have followed thus far, got out, answered the hospitalities of the inn's people with an absent-minded air, sent back the extra horse, and took the little white one to the stable himself, then he opened the door of a billiard-room on the first floor, took a seat, and leaned his elbows on the table. He had spent fourteen hours in this trip, which he expected to make in six. He did himself the justice to feel that it was not his fault, but at bottom he was not sorry for it.

The landlady entered.

"Will monsieur have a bed? will monsieur have supper?"

He shook his head.

"The stable-boy says that monsieur's horse is very tired!"

Here he broke silence.

"Is not the horse able to start again to-morrow morning?"

"Oh; monsieur! he needs at least two days' rest."

He asked:

"Is not the Bureau of the Post here?"

"Yes, sir."

The hostess led him to the Bureau; he showed his passport and inquired if there were an opportunity to return that very night to M—— sur M—— by the mail coach; only one seat was vacant, that by the side of the driver; he retained it and paid for it. "Monsieur," said the booking clerk, "don't fail to be here ready to start at precisely one o'clock in the morning."

This done, he left the hotel and began to walk in the city.

He was not acquainted with Arras, the streets were dark, and he went haphazard. Nevertheless he seemed to refrain obstinately from asking his way. He crossed the little river Crinchon, and found himself in a labyrinth of narrow streets, where he was soon lost. A citizen came along with a lantern. After some hesitation, he determined to speak to this man, but not until he had looked before and behind, as if he were afraid that somebody might overhear the question he was about to ask.

"Monsieur," said he, "the court house, if you please?"

"You are not a resident of the city, monsieur," answered the citizen, who was an old man, "well, follow me, I am going right by the court house, that is to say, the city hall. For they are repairing the court house just now, and the courts are holding the sessions at the city hall, temporarily."

"Is it there," asked he, "that the assizes are held?"

"Certainly, monsieur; you see, what is the city hall to-day was the bishop's palace before the revolution. Monsieur de Conzié, who was bishop in 'eighty-two, had a large hall built. The court is held in that hall."

As they walked along, the citizen said to him:

"If monsieur wishes to see a trial, he is rather late. Ordinarily the sessions close at six o'clock."

However, when they reached the great square, the citizen showed him four long lighted windows on the front of a vast dark building.

"Faith, monsieur, you are in time, you are fortunate. Do you see those four windows? that is the court of assizes. There is a light there. Then they have not finished. The case must have been prolonged and they are having an evening session. Are you interested in this case? Is it a criminal trial? Are you a witness?"

He answered:

"I have no business; I only wish to speak to a lawyer."

"That's another thing," said the citizen. "Stop, monsieur, here is the door. The doorkeeper is up there. You have only to go up the grand stairway."

He followed the citizen's instructions, and in a few minutes found himself in a hall where there were many people, and scattered groups of lawyers in their robes whispering here and there.

It is always a chilling sight to see these gatherings of men clothed in black, talking among themselves in a low voice on the threshold of the chamber of justice.

It is rare that charity and pity can be found in their words. What are oftenest heard are sentences pronounced in advance. All these groups seem to the observer, who passes musingly by, like so many gloomy hives where buzzing spirits are building in common all sorts of dark structures.

This hall, which, though spacious, was lighted by a single lamp, was an ancient hall of the Episcopal palace, and served as a waiting-room. A double folding door, which was now closed, separated it from the large room in which the court of assizes was in session.

The obscurity was such that he felt no fear in addressing the first lawyer whom he met.

"Monsieur," said he, "how are they getting along?"

"It is finished," said the lawyer.

"Finished!"

The word was repeated in such a tone that the lawyer turned around.

"Pardon me, monsieur, you are a relative, perhaps?"

"No. I know no one here. And was there a sentence?"

"Of course. It was hardly possible for it to be otherwise."

"To hard labour?"

"For life."

He continued in a voice so weak that it could hardly be heard:

"The identity was established, then?"

"What identity?" responded the lawyer. "There was no identity to be established. It was a simple affair. This woman had killed her child, the infanticide was proven, the jury were not satisfied that there was any premeditation; she was sentenced for life."

"It is a woman, then?" said he.

"Certainly. The Limousin girl. What else are you speaking of?"

"Nothing, but if it is finished, why is the hall still lighted up?"

"That is for the other case, which commenced nearly two hours ago."

"What other case?"

"Oh! that is a clear one also. It is a sort of a thief, a second offender, a galley slave; a case of robbery. I forget his name. He looks like a bandit. Were it for nothing but having such a face, I would send him to the galleys."

"Monsieur," asked he, "is there any means of getting into the hall?"

"I think not, really. There is a great crowd. However, they are taking a recess. Some people have come out, and when the session is resumed, you can try."

"How do you get in?"

"Through that large door."

The lawyer left him. In a few moments, he had undergone, almost at the same time, almost together, all possible emotions. The words of this indifferent man had alternately pierced his heart like icicles and like flames of fire. When he learned that it was not concluded, he drew breath; but he could not have told whether what he felt was satisfaction or pain.

He approached several groups and listened to their talk. The calendar of the term being very heavy, the judge had set down two short, simple cases for that day. They had begun with the infanticide, and now were on the convict, the second offender, the "old stager." This man had stolen some apples, but that did not appear to be very well proven; what was proven, was that he had been in the galleys at Toulon. This was what ruined his case. The examination of the man had been finished, and the testimony of the witnesses had been taken; but there yet remained the argument of the counsel, and the summing up of his prosecuting attorney; it would hardly be finished before midnight. The man would probably be condemned; the prosecuting attorney was very good, and never *failed* with his prisoners; he was a fellow of talent, who wrote poetry.

An officer stood near the door which opened into the court-room. He asked this officer:

"Monsieur, will the door be opened soon?"

"It will not be opened," said the officer.

"How! it will not be opened when the session is resumed? is there not a recess?"

"The session has just been resumed," answered the officer, "but the door will not be opened again."

"Why not?"

"Because the hall is full."

"What! there are no more seats?"

"Not a single one. The door is closed. No one can enter."

The officer added, after a silence: "There are indeed two or three places still behind Monsieur the Judge, but Monsieur the Judge admits none but public functionaries to them."

So saying, the officer turned his back.

He retired with his head bowed down, crossed the ante-chamber, and walked slowly down the staircase, seeming to hesitate at every step. It is probable that he was holding counsel with himself. The violent combat that had been going on within him since the previous evening was not finished; and, every moment, he fell upon some new turn. When he reached the turn of the stairway, he leaned against the railing and folded his arms. Suddenly he opened his coat, drew out his pocket-book, took out a pencil, tore out a sheet, and wrote rapidly upon that sheet, by the glimmering light, this line: *Monsieur Madeleine, Mayor of M—— sur M——*, then he went up the stairs again rapidly, passed through the crowd, walked straight to the officer, handed him the paper, and said to him with authority: "Carry that to Monsieur the Judge."

The officer took the paper, cast his eye upon it, and obeyed.

VIII
ADMISSION BY FAVOUR

WITHOUT himself suspecting it, the Mayor of M—— sur M—— had a certain celebrity. For seven years the reputation of his virtue had been extending throughout Bas-Boulonnais; it had finally crossed the boundaries of the little county, and had spread into the two or three neighbouring departments. Besides the considerable service that he had rendered to the chief town by reviving the manufacture of jet-work, there was not one of the hundred and forty-one communes of the district of M——

sur M—— which was not indebted to him for some benefit. He had even in case of need aided and quickened the business of the other districts. Thus he had, in time of need, sustained with his credit and with his own funds the tulle factory at Boulogne, the flax-spinning factory at Frévent, and the linen factory at Boubers-sur-Canche. Everywhere the name of Monsieur Madeleine was spoken with veneration. Arras and Douai envied the lucky little city of M—— sur M—— its mayor.

The Judge of the Royal Court of Douai, who was holding this term of the assizes at Arras, was familiar, as well as everybody else, with this name so profoundly and so universally honoured. When the officer quietly opening the door which led from the counsel chamber to the court-room, bent behind the judge's chair and handed him the paper, on which was written the line we have just read, adding: "*This gentleman desires to witness the trial,*" the judge made a hasty movement of deference, seized a pen, wrote a few words at the bottom of the paper and handed it back to the officer, saying to him: "Let him enter."

The unhappy man, whose history we are relating, had remained near the door of the hall, in the same place and the same attitude as when the officer left him. He heard, through his thoughts, some one saying to him: "Will monsieur do me the honour to follow me?" It was the same officer who had turned his back upon him the minute before, and who now bowed to the earth before him. The officer at the same time handed him the paper. He unfolded it, and, as he happened to be near the lamp, he could read:

"The Judge of the Court of Assizes presents his respects to Monsieur Madeleine."

He crushed the paper in his hands, as if those few words had left some strange and bitter taste behind.

He followed the officer.

In a few minutes he found himself alone in a kind of panelled cabinet, of a severe appearance, lighted by two wax candles placed upon a table covered with green cloth. The last words of the officer who had left him still rang in his ear: "Monsieur, you are now in the counsel chamber; you have but to turn the brass knob of that door and you will find yourself in the court-room, behind the judge's chair." These words were associated in his thoughts with a vague remembrance of the narrow corridors and dark stairways through which he had just passed.

The officer had left him alone. The decisive moment had arrived. He endeavoured to collect his thoughts, but did not succeed. At those hours especially when we have sorest need of grasping the sharp realities of life do the threads of thought snap off in the brain. He was in the very place where the judges deliberate and decide. He beheld with a stupid tranquillity that silent and formidable room where so many existences had been terminated, where his own name would be heard so soon, and which his destiny was crossing at this moment. He looked at the walls, then he looked at himself, astonished that this could be this chamber, and that this could be he.

He had eaten nothing for more than twenty-four hours; he was bruised by the jolting of the carriole, but he did not feel it; it seemed to him that he felt nothing.

He examined a black frame which hung on the wall, and which contained under glass an old autograph letter of Jean Nicolas Pache, Mayor of Paris, and Minister, dated, doubtless, by mistake, June 9th, year II., in which Pache sent to the Commune the list of the ministers and deputies held in arrest within their limits. A spectator, had he seen and watched him then, would have imagined, doubtless, that this letter appeared very remarkable to him, for he did not take his eyes off from it, and he read it two or three times. He was reading without paying any attention, and without knowing what he was doing. He was thinking of Fantine and Cosette.

Even while musing, he turned unconsciously, and his eyes encountered the brass knob of the door which separated him from the hall of the assizes. He had almost forgotten that door. His countenance, at first calm, now fell. His eyes were fixed on that brass knob, then became set and wild and little by little filled with dismay. Drops of sweat started out from his head, and rolled down over his temples.

At one moment he made, with a kind of authority united to rebellion, that indescribable gesture which means and which so well says: *Well! who is here to compel me?* Then he turned quickly, saw before him the door by which he had entered, went to it, opened it, and went out. He was no longer in that room; he was outside, in a corridor, a long, narrow corridor, cut up with steps and side-doors, making all sorts of angles, lighted here and there by lamps hung on the wall similar to nurse-lamps for the sick; it was the corridor by which he had come. He drew breath and listened; no sound behind him, no sound before him; he ran as if he were pursued.

When he had doubled several of the turns of this passage, he listened again. There was still the same silence and the same shadow about him. He was out of breath, he tottered, he leaned against the wall. The stone was cold; the sweat was icy upon his forehead; he roused himself with a shudder.

Then and there, alone, standing in that obscurity, trembling with cold and, perhaps, with something else, he reflected.

He had reflected all night, he had reflected all day; he now heard but one voice within him, which said: "Alas!"

A quarter of an hour thus rolled away. Finally, he bowed his head, sighed with anguish, let his arms fall, and retraced his steps. He walked slowly and as if overwhelmed. It seemed as if he had been caught in his flight and brought back.

He entered the counsel chamber again. The first thing that he saw was the handle of the door. That handle, round and of polished brass, shone out before him like an ominous star. He looked at it as a lamb might look at the eye of a tiger.

His eyes could not move from it.

From time to time, he took another step towards the door.

Had he listened, he would have heard, as a kind of confused murmur, the noise of the neighbouring hall; but he did not listen and he did not hear.

Suddenly, without himself knowing how, he found himself near the door, he seized the knob convulsively; the door opened.

He was in the court-room.

IX
A PLACE FOR ARRIVING AT CONVICTIONS

HE took a step, closed the door behind him, mechanically, and remained standing, noting what he saw.

It was a large hall, dimly lighted, and noisy and silent by turns, where all the machinery of a criminal trial was exhibited, with its petty, yet solemn gravity, before the multitude.

At one end of the hall, that at which he found himself, heedless judges, in threadbare robes, were biting their finger-nails, or closing their eyelids; at the other end was a ragged rabble; there were lawyers in all sorts of attitudes; soldiers with honest and hard faces; old, stained wainscoting, a dirty ceiling, tables covered with serge, which was more nearly yellow than green; doors blackened by finger-marks; tavern lamps, giving more smoke than light, on nails in the panelling; candles, in brass candlesticks, on the tables; everywhere obscurity, unsightliness, and gloom; and from all this there arose an austere and august impression; for men felt therein the presence of that great human thing which is called law, and that great divine thing which is called justice.

No man in this multitude paid any attention to him. All eyes converged on a single point, a wooden bench placed against a little door, along the wall at the left hand of the judge. Upon this bench, which was lighted by several candles, was a man between two gendarmes.

This was the man.

He did not look for him, he saw him. His eyes went towards him naturally, as if they had known in advance where he was.

He thought he saw himself, older, doubtless, not precisely the same in features, but alike in attitude and appearance, with that bristling hair, with those wild and restless eyeballs, with that blouse—just as he was on the day he entered D——, full of hatred, and concealing in his soul that hideous hoard of frightful thoughts which he had spent nineteen years in gathering upon the floor of the galleys.

He said to himself, with a shudder: "Great God! shall I again come to this?"

This being appeared at least sixty years old. There was something indescribably rough, stupid, and terrified in his appearance.

At the sound of the door, people had stood aside to make room. The judge had turned his head, and supposing the person who entered to be the mayor of M—— sur M——, greeted him with a bow. The prosecuting attorney, who had seen Madeleine at M—— sur M——, whither he had been called more than once by the duties of his office, recognised him and bowed likewise. He scarcely perceived them. He gazed about him, a prey to a sort of hallucination.

Judges, clerk, gendarmes, a throng of heads, cruelly curious —he had seen all these once before, twenty-seven years ago. He had fallen again upon these fearful things; they were before him, they moved, they had being; it was no longer an effort of his memory, a mirage of his fancy, but real gendarmes and real judges, a real throng, and real men of flesh and bone. It was done; he saw reappearing and living again around him, with all the frightfulness of reality, the monstrous visions of the past.

All this was yawning before him.

Stricken with horror, he closed his eyes, and exclaimed from the depths of his soul: "Never!"

And by a tragic sport of destiny, which was agitating all his ideas and rendering him almost insane, it was another self before him. This man on trial was called by all around him, Jean Valjean!

He had before his eyes an unheard-of vision, a sort of representation of the most horrible moment of his life, played by his shadow.

All, everything was there—the same paraphernalia, the same hour of the night—almost the same faces, judge and assistant judges, soldiers and spectators. But above the head of the judge was a crucifix, a thing which did not appear in court-rooms at the time of his sentence. When he was tried, God was not there.

A chair was behind him; he sank into it, terrified at the idea that he might be observed. When seated, he took advantage of a pile of papers on the judges' desk to hide his face from the whole room. He could now see without being seen. He entered fully into the spirit of the reality; by degrees he recovered his composure, and arrived at that degree of calmness at which it is possible to listen.

Monsieur Bamatabois was one of the jurors.

He looked for Javert, but did not see him. The witnesses' seat was hidden from him by the clerk's table. And then, as we have just said, the hall was very dimly lighted.

At the moment of his entrance, the counsel for the prisoner was finishing his plea. The attention of all was excited to the highest degree; the trial had been in progress for three hours. During these three hours, the spectators had seen a man, an unknown, wretched being, thoroughly stupid or thoroughly artful, gradually bending beneath the weight of a terrible probability. This man, as is already known, was a vagrant who had been found in a field, carrying off a branch, laden with ripe apples, which had been broken from a tree in a neighbouring close called the Pierron inclosure. Who was this man? An examination had been held, witnesses had been heard, they had been unanimous, light had been elicited from every portion of the trial. The prosecution said: "We have here not merely a fruit thief, a marauder; we have here, in our hands, a bandit, an outlaw who has broken his ban, an old convict, a most dangerous wretch, a malefactor, called Jean Valjean, of whom justice has been long in pursuit, and who, eight years ago, on leaving the galleys at Toulon, committed a highway robbery, with force and arms, upon the person of a youth of Savoy, Petit Gervais by name, a crime which is specified in Article 383 of the Penal Code, and for which we reserve the right of further prosecution when his identity shall be judicially established. He has now committed a new theft. It is a case of second offence. Convict him for the new crime; he will be tried hereafter for the previous one." Before this accusation, before the unanimity of the witnesses, the principal emotion evinced by the accused was astonishment. He made gestures and signs which signified denial, or he gazed at the ceiling. He spoke with difficulty, and answered with embarrassment, but from head to foot his whole person denied the charge. He seemed like an idiot in the presence of all these intellects ranged in battle around him, and like a stranger in the midst of this society by whom he had been seized. Nevertheless, a most threatening future awaited him; probabilities increased every moment; and every spectator was looking with more anxiety than himself for the calamitous sentence which seemed to be hanging over his head with ever increasing surety. One contingency even gave a glimpse of the possibility, beyond the galleys, of a capital penalty should his identity be established, and the Petit Gervais affair result in his conviction. Who was this man? What was the nature of his apathy? Was it imbecility or artifice? Did he know too much or nothing at all? These were questions upon which the spectators took sides, and which seemed to affect the jury. There was something fearful and something mysterious in the trial; the drama was not merely gloomy, but it was obscure.

The counsel for the defence had made a very good plea in that provincial language which long constituted the eloquence of the bar and which was formerly employed by all lawyers, at Paris as well as at Romorantin or Montbrison, but which, having now become classic is used by few except the official orators of the bar, to whom it is suited by its solemn rotundity and majestic periods; a language in which husband and wife are called *spouses*, Paris, *the centre of arts and civilisation*, the king, *the monarch*, a bishop, *a holy pontiff*, the prosecuting attorney, *the eloquent interpreter of the vengeance of the law*, arguments, *the accents which we have just heard*, the time of Louis XIV., *the illustrious age*, a theatre, *the temple of Melpomene*, the reigning family, *the august blood of our kings*, a concert, *a musical solemnity*, the general in command, *the illustrious warrior who*, etc., students of theology, *those tender Levites*, mistakes imputed to newspapers, *the imposture which distils its venom into the columns of these organs*, etc., etc. The counsel for the defence had begun by expatiating on the theft of the apples,—a thing ill suited to a lofty style; but Benign Bossuet himself was once compelled to make allusion to a hen in the midst of a funeral oration, and acquitted himself with dignity. The counsel established that the theft of the apples was not in fact proved. His client, whom in his character of counsel he persisted in calling Champmathieu, had not been seen to scale the wall or break off the branch. He had been arrested in possession of this branch (which the counsel preferred to call *bough*); but he said that he had found it on the ground. Where was the proof to the contrary? Undoubtedly this branch had been broken and carried off after the scaling of the wall, then thrown away by the alarmed marauder; undoubtedly, there had been a thief.—But what evidence was there that this thief was Champmathieu? One single thing. That he was formerly a convict. The counsel would not deny that this fact unfortunately appeared to be fully proved; the defendant had resided at Faverolles; the defendant had been a pruner, the name of Champmathieu might well have had its origin in that of Jean Mathieu; all this was true, and finally, four witnesses had positively and without hesitation identified Champmathieu as the galley slave, Jean Valjean; to these circumstances and this testimony the counsel could oppose nothing but the denial of his client, an interested denial; but even supposing him to be the convict Jean Valjean, did this prove that he had stolen the apples? that was a presumption at most, not a proof. The accused, it was true, and the counsel "in good faith" must admit it, had adopted "a mistaken system of defence." He had persisted in denying everything, both the theft and the fact that he had been a convict. An avowal on the latter point would have been better certainly, and would have secured to him the indulgence of the judges; the counsel had advised him to this course, but the defendant had obstinately refused, expecting probably to escape punishment entirely, by admitting nothing. It was a mistake, but must not the poverty of his intellect be taken into consideration? The man was evidently imbecile. Long suffering in the galleys, long suffering out of the galleys, had brutalised him, etc., etc.; if he made a bad defence, was this a reason for convicting him? As to the Petit Gervais affair, the counsel had nothing to say, it was not in the case. He concluded by entreating the jury and court, if the identity of Jean Valjean appeared evident to them, to apply to him the police penalties prescribed for the breaking of ban, and not the fearful punishment decreed to the convict found guilty of a second offence.

The prosecuting attorney replied to the counsel for the defence. He was violent and flowery, like most prosecuting attorneys.

He complimented the counsel for his "frankness," of which he shrewdly took advantage. He attacked the accused through all the concessions which his counsel had made. The counsel seemed to admit that the accused was Jean Valjean. He accepted the admission. This man then was Jean Valjean. This fact was conceded to the prosecution, and could be no longer contested. Here, by an adroit autonomasia, going back to the sources and causes of crime, the prosecuting attorney thundered against the immorality of the romantic school—then in its dawn, under the name of the *Satanic school*, conferred upon it by the critics of the *Quotidienne* and the *Oriflamme*; and he attributed, not without plausibility, to the influence of this perverse literature, the crime of Champmathieu, or rather of Jean Valjean. These considerations exhausted, he passed to Jean Valjean himself. Who was Jean Valjean? Description of Jean Valjean: a monster vomited, etc. The model of all such descriptions may be found in the story of Théramène, which as tragedy is useless, but which does great service in judicial eloquence every day. The auditory and the jury "shuddered." This description finished, the prosecuting attorney resumed with an oratorical burst, designed to excite the enthusiasm of the *Journal de la Préfecture* to the highest pitch next morning. "And it is such a man," etc. etc. A vagabond, a mendicant, without means of existence, etc., etc. Accustomed through his existence to criminal acts and profiting little by his past life in the galleys, as is proved by the crime committed upon Petit Gervais, etc., etc. It is such a man who, found on the highway in the very act of theft, a few paces from a wall that had been scaled, still holding in his hand the subject of his crime, denies the act in which he is caught, denies the theft, denies the escalade, denies everything, denies even his name, denies even his identity! Besides a hundred other proofs, to which we will not return, he is identified by four witnesses—Javert—the incorruptible inspector of police. Javert—and three of his former companions in disgrace, the convicts Brevet, Chenildieu, and Cochepaille. What has he to oppose to this overwhelming unanimity? His denial. What depravity! You will do justice, gentlemen of the jury, etc., etc. While the prosecuting attorney was speaking the accused listened open-mouthed, with a sort of astonishment, not unmingled with admiration. He was evidently surprised that a man could speak so well. From time to time, at the most "forcible" parts of the argument, at those moments when eloquence, unable to contain itself, overflows in a stream of withering epithets, and surrounds the prisoner like a tempest, he slowly moved his head from right to left, and from left to right—a sort of sad, mute protest, with which he contented himself from the beginning of the argument. Two or three times the spectators nearest him heard him say in a low tone: "This all comes from not asking for Monsieur Baloup!" The prosecuting attorney pointed out to the jury this air of stupidity, which was evidently put on, and which denoted, not imbecility, but address, artifice, and the habit of deceiving justice, and which showed in its full light the "deep-rooted perversity" of the man. He concluded by reserving entirely the Petit Gervais affair, and demanding a sentence to the full extent of the law.

This was, for this offence, as will be remembered, hard labour for life.

The counsel for the prisoner rose, commenced by complimenting "Monsieur, the prosecuting attorney, on his admirable argument," then replied as best he could, but in a weaker tone; the ground was evidently giving way under him.

X

THE SYSTEM OF DENEGATIONS

THE time had come for closing the case. The judge commanded the accused to rise, and put the usual question: "Have you anything to add to your defence?"

The man, standing, and twirling in his hands a hideous cap which he had, seemed not to hear.

The judge repeated the question.

This time the man heard, and appeared to comprehend. He started like one awaking from sleep, cast his eyes around him, looked at the spectators, the gendarmes, his counsel, the jurors, and the court, placed his huge fists on the bar before him, looked around again, and suddenly fixing his eyes upon the prosecuting attorney, began to speak. It was like an eruption. It seemed from the manner in which the words escaped his lips, incoherent, impetuous, jostling each other pell-mell, as if they were all eager to find vent at the same time. He said:

"I have this to say: That I have been a wheelwright at Paris; that it was at M. Baloup's too. It is a hard life to be a wheel-wright, you always work out-doors, in yards, under sheds when you have good bosses, never in shops, because you must have room, you see. In the winter, it is so cold that you thresh your arms to warm them; but the bosses won't allow that; they say it is a waste of time. It is tough work to handle iron when there is ice on the pavements. It wears a man out quick. You get old when you are young at this trade. A man is used up by forty. I was fifty-three; I was sick a good deal. And then the workmen are so bad! When a poor fellow isn't young, they always call you old bird, and old beast! I earned only thirty sous a day, they paid me as little as they could—the bosses took advantage of my age. Then I had my daughter, who was a washerwoman at the river. She earned a little for herself; between us two, we got on; she had hard work too. All day long up to the waist in a tub, in rain, in snow with wind that cuts your face when it freezes, it is all the same, the washing must be done; there are folks who haven't much linen and are waiting for it; if you don't wash you lose your customers. The planks are not well matched, and the water falls on you everywhere. You get your clothes wet through and through; that strikes in. She washed too in the laundry of the Enfants-Rouges, where the water comes in through pipes. There you are not in the tub. You wash before you under the pipe, and rinse behind you in the trough. This is under cover, and you are not so cold. But there is a hot lye that is terrible and ruins your eyes. She would come home at seven o'clock at night, and go to bed right away, she was so tired. Her husband used to beat her. She is dead. We wasn't very happy. She was a good girl; she never went to balls, and was very quiet. I remember one Shrove Tuesday she went to bed at eight o'clock. Look here, I am telling the truth. You have only to ask if 'tisn't so. Ask! how stupid I am! Paris is a gulf. Who is there that knows Father Champmathieu? But there is M. Baloup. Go and see M. Baloup. I don't know what more you want of me."

The man ceased speaking, but did not sit down. He had uttered these sentences in a loud, rapid, hoarse, harsh, and guttural tone, with a sort of angry and savage simplicity. Once, he stopped to bow to somebody in the crowd. The sort of affirmations which he seemed to fling out haphazard, came from him like hiccoughs, and he added to each the gesture of a man chopping wood. When he had finished, the auditory burst into laughter. He looked at them, and seeing them laughing and not knowing why, began to laugh himself.

That was an ill omen.

The judge, considerate and kindly man, raised his voice:

He reminded "gentlemen of the jury" that M. Baloup, the former master wheelwright by whom the prisoner said he had been employed, had been summoned, but had not appeared. He had become bankrupt, and could not be found. Then, turning to the accused, he adjured him to listen to what he was about to say, and added: "You are in a position which demands reflection. The gravest presumptions are weighing against you, and may lead to fatal results. Prisoner, on your own behalf, I question you a second time, explain yourself clearly on these two points. First, did you or did you not climb the wall of the Pierron close, break off the branch and steal the apples, that is to say, commit the crime of theft, with the addition of breaking into an inclosure? Secondly, are you or are you not the discharged convict, Jean Valjean?"

The prisoner shook his head with a knowing look, like a man who understands perfectly, and knows what he is going to say. He opened his mouth, turned towards the presiding judge, and said:

"In the first place——"

Then he looked at his cap, looked up at the ceiling, and was silent.

"Prisoner," resumed the prosecuting attorney, in an austere tone, "give attention. You have replied to nothing that has been asked you. Your agitation condemns you. It is evident that your name is not Champmathieu, but that you are the convict, Jean Valjean, disguised under the name at first, of Jean Mathieu, which was that of his mother; that you have lived in Auvergne; that you were born at Faverolles, where you were a pruner. It is evident that you have stolen ripe apples from the Pierron close, with the addition of breaking into the inclosure. The gentlemen of the jury will consider this."

The accused had at last resumed his seat; he rose abruptly when the prosecuting attorney had ended, and exclaimed:

"You are a very bad man, you, I mean. This is what I wanted to say. I couldn't think of it first off. I never stole anything. I am a man who don't get something to eat every day. I was coming from Ailly, walking alone after a shower, which had made the ground all yellow with mud, so that the ponds were running over, and you only saw little sprigs of grass sticking out of the sand along the road, and I found a broken branch on the ground with apples on it; and I picked it up not knowing what trouble it would give me. It is three months that I have been in prison, being knocked about. More'n that, I can't tell. You talk against me and tell me 'answer!' The gendarme, who is a good fellow, nudges my elbow, and whispers, 'answer now.' I can't explain myself, I never studied; I am a poor man. You are all wrong not to see that I didn't steal. I picked up off the ground things that was there. You talk about Jean Valjean, Jean Mathieu—I don't know any such people. They must be villagers. I have worked for Monsieur Baloup, Boulevard de l'Hopital. My name is Champmathieu. You must be very sharp to tell me where I was born. I don't know myself. Everybody can't have houses to be born in; that would be too handy. I think my father and mother were strollers, but I don't know. When I was a child they called me Little One; now, they call me Old Man. They're my Christian names. Take them as you like. I have been in Auvergne, I have been at Faverolles. Bless me! can't a man have been in Auvergne and Faverolles without having been at the galleys? I tell you I never stole, and that I am Father Champmathieu. I have been at Monsieur Baloup's; I lived in his house. I am tired of your everlasting nonsense. What is everybody after me for like a mad dog?"

The prosecuting attorney was still standing; he addressed the judge:

"Sir, in the presence of the confused but very adroit

denegations of the accused, who endeavours to pass for an idiot, but who will not succeed in it—we will prevent him—we request that it may please you and the court to call again within the bar the convicts, Brevet, Cochepaille, and Chenildieu, and the police-inspector Javert, and to submit them to a final interrogation, concerning the identity of the accused with the convict Jean Valjean."

"I must remind the prosecuting attorney," said the presiding judge, "that police-inspector Javert, recalled by his duties to the chief town of a neighbouring district, left the hall, and the city also as soon as his testimony was taken. We granted him this permission, with the consent of the prosecuting attorney and the counsel of the accused."

"True," replied the prosecuting attorney; "in the absence of Monsieur Javert, I think it a duty to recall to the gentlemen of the jury what he said here a few hours ago. Javert is an estimable man, who does honour to inferior but important functions, by his rigorous and strict probity. These are the terms in which he testified: 'I do not need even moral presumptions and material proofs to contradict the denials of the accused. I recognise him perfectly. This man's name is not Champmathieu; he is a convict, Jean Valjean, very hard, and much feared. He was liberated at the expiration of his term, but with extreme regret. He served out nineteen years at hard labour for burglary; five or six times he attempted to escape. Besides the Petit Gervais and Pierron robberies, I suspect him also of a robbery committed on his highness, the late Bishop of D——. I often saw him when I was adjutant of the galley guard at Toulon. I repeat it; I recognise him perfectly.'"

This declaration, in terms so precise, appeared to produce a strong impression upon the public and jury. The prosecuting attorney concluded by insisting that, in the absence of Javert, the three witnesses, Brevet, Chenildieu, and Cochepaille, should be heard anew and solemnly interrogated.

The judge gave an order to an officer, and a moment afterwards the door of the witness-room opened, and the officer, accompanied by a gendarme ready to lend assistance, led in the convict Brevet. The audience was in breathless suspense, and all hearts palpitated as if they contained but a single soul.

The old convict Brevet was clad in the black and grey jacket of the central prisons. Brevet was about sixty years old; he had the face of a man of business, and the air of a rogue. They sometimes go together. He had become something like a turn-key in the prison—to which he had been brought by new mis-deeds. He was one of those men of whom their superiors are wont to say, "He tries to make himself useful." The chaplain bore good testimony to his religious habits. It must not be for-gotten that this happened under the Restoration.

"Brevet," said the judge, "you have suffered infamous pun-ishment, and cannot take an oath."

Brevet cast down his eyes.

"Nevertheless," continued the judge, "even in the man whom the law has degraded there may remain, if divine justice permit, a sentiment of honour and equity. To that sentiment I appeal in this decisive hour. If it still exist in you, as I hope, reflect before you answer me; consider on the one hand this man, whom a word from you may destroy; on the other hand, justice, which a word from you may enlighten. The moment is a solemn one, and there is still time to retract if you think yourself mistaken. Prisoner, rise. Brevet, look well upon the prisoner; collect your remembrances, and say, on your soul and con-science, whether you still recognise this man as your former comrade in the galleys, Jean Valjean."

Brevet looked at the prisoner, then turned again to the court.

"Yes, your honour, I was the first to recognise him, and still do so. This man is Jean Valjean, who came to Toulon in 1796, and left in 1815. I left a year after. He looks like a brute now, but he must have grown stupid with age; at the galleys he was sullen. I recognise him now, positively."

"Sit down," said the judge. "Prisoner, remain standing."

Chenildieu was brought in, a convict for life, as was shown by his red cloak and green cap. He was undergoing his punish-ment in the galleys of Toulon, whence he had been brought for this occasion. He was a little man, about fifty years old, active, wrinkled, lean, yellow, brazen, restless with a sort of sickly feebleness in his limbs and whole person, and immense force in his eye. His companions in the galleys had nicknamed him Je-nie-Dieu.

The judge addressed nearly the same words to him as to Brevet. When he reminded him that his infamy had deprived him of the right to take an oath, Chenildieu raised his head and looked the spectators in the face. The judge requested him to collect his thoughts, and asked him as he had Brevet, whether he still recognised the prisoner.

Chenildieu burst out laughing.

"Gad! do I recognise him! we were five years on the same chain. You're sulky with me, are you, old boy?"

"Sit down," said the judge.

The officer brought in Cochepaille; this other convict for life, brought from the galleys and dressed in red like Chenildieu, was a peasant from Lourdes, and a semi-bear of the Pyrenees. He had tended flocks in the mountains, and from shepherd had glided into brigandage. Cochepaille was not less uncouth than the accused, and appeared still more stupid. He was one of those unfortunate men whom nature turns out as wild beasts, and society finishes up into galley slaves.

The judge attempted to move him by a few serious and pathetic words, and asked him, as he had the others, whether he still recognised without hesitation or difficulty the man standing before him.

"It is Jean Valjean," said Cochepaille. "The same they called Jean-the-Jack, he was so strong."

Each of the affirmations of these three men, evidently sincere and in good faith, had excited in the audience a murmur of evil augury for the accused—a murmur which increased in force and continuance, every time a new declaration was added to the preceding one. The prisoner himself listened to them with that astonished countenance which, according to the prosecution, was his principal means of defence. At the first, the gendarmes by his side heard him mutter between his teeth: "Ah, well! there is one of them!" After the second, he said in a louder tone, with an air almost of satisfaction, "Good!" At the third, he exclaimed, "Famous!"

The judge addressed him:

"Prisoner, you have listened. What have you to say?"

He replied:

"I say—famous!"

A buzz ran through the crowd and almost invaded the jury. It was evident that the man was lost.

"Officers," said the judge, "enforce order. I am about to sum up the case."

At this moment there was a movement near the judge. A voice was heard exclaiming:

"Brevet, Chenildieu, Cochepaille, look this way!"

So lamentable and terrible was this voice that those who heard it felt their blood run cold. All eyes turned towards the spot whence it came. A man, who had been sitting among the privileged spectators behind the court, had risen, pushed open the low door which separated the tribunal from the bar, and was standing in the centre of the hall. The judge, the prosecuting attorney, Monsieur Bamatabois, twenty persons recognised him, and exclaimed at once:

"Monsieur Madeleine!"

XI
CHAMPMATHIEU MORE AND MORE ASTONISHED

IT was he, indeed. The clerk's lamp lighted up his face. He held his hat in hand; there was no disorder in his dress; his overcoat was carefully buttoned. He was very pale, and trembled slightly. His hair, already grey when he came to Arras, was now perfectly white.

It had become so during the hour that he had been there. All eyes were strained towards him.

The sensation was indescribable. There was a moment of hesitation in the auditory. The voice had been so thrilling, the man standing there appeared so calm, that at first nobody could comprehend it. They asked who had cried out. They could not believe that this tranquil man had uttered that fearful cry.

This indecision lasted but few seconds. Before even the judge and prosecuting attorney could say a word, before the gendarmes and officers could make a sign, the man, whom all up to this moment had called Monsieur Madeleine, had advanced towards the witnesses, Cochepaille, Brevet, and Chenildieu.

"Do you not recognise me?" said he.

All three stood confounded, and indicated by a shake of the head that they did not know him. Cochepaille, intimidated, gave the military salute. Monsieur Madeleine turned towards the jurors and court, and said in a mild voice:

"Gentlemen of the jury, release the accused. Your honour, order my arrest. He is not the man whom you seek; it is I. I am Jean Valjean."

Not a breath stirred. To the first commotion of astonishment had succeeded a sepulchral silence. That species of religious awe was felt in the hall which thrills the multitude at the accomplishment of a grand action.

Nevertheless, the face of the judge was marked with sympathy and sadness; he exchanged glances with the prosecuting attorney and a few whispered words with the assistant judges. He turned to the spectators and asked in a tone which was understood by all:

"Is there a physician here?"

The prosecuting attorney continued:

"Gentlemen of the jury, the strange and unexpected incident which disturbs the audience, inspires us, as well as yourselves, with a feeling we have no need to express. You all know, at least by reputation, the honourable Monsieur Madeleine, Mayor of M—— sur M——. If there be a physician in the audience, we unite with his honour the judge in entreating him to be kind enough to lend his assistance to Monsieur Madeleine and conduct him to his residence."

Monsieur Madeleine did not permit the prosecuting attorney to finish, but interrupted him with a tone full of gentleness and authority. These are the words he uttered; we give them literally, as they were written down immediately after the trial, by one of the witnesses of the scene—as they still ring in the ears of those who heard them, now nearly forty years ago.

"I thank you, Monsieur Prosecuting Attorney, but I am not mad. You shall see. You were on the point of committing a great mistake; release that man. I am accomplishing a duty; I am the unhappy convict. I am the only one who sees clearly here, and I tell you the truth. What I do at this moment, God beholds from on high, and that is sufficient. You can take me, since I am here. Nevertheless, I have done my best. I have disguised myself under another name, I have become rich, I have become a mayor, I have desired to enter again among honest men. It seems that this cannot be. In short, there are many things which I cannot tell. I shall not relate to you the story of my life: some day you will know it. I did rob Monseigneur the Bishop—that is true; I did rob Petit Gervais—that is true. They were right in telling you that Jean Valjean was a wicked wretch. But all the blame may not belong to him. Listen, your honours; a man so abased as I, has no remonstrance to make with Providence, nor advice to give to society; but, mark you, the infamy from which I have sought to rise is pernicious to men. The galleys make the galley slave. Receive this in kindness, if you will. Before the galleys, I was a poor peasant, unintelligent, a species of idiot; the galleys changed me. I was stupid, I became wicked; I was a log, I became a firebrand. Later, I was saved by indulgence and kindness, as I had been lost by severity. But, pardon, you cannot comprehend what I say. You will find in my house, among the ashes of the fire-place, the forty-sous piece of which, seven years ago, I robbed Petit Gervais. I have nothing more to add. Take me. Great God! the prosecuting attorney shakes his head. You say 'Monsieur Madeleine has gone mad;' you do not believe me. This is hard to be borne. Do not condemn that man, at least. What! these men do not know me! Would that Javert were here. He would recognise me!"

Nothing could express the kindly yet terrible melancholy of the tone which accompanied these words.

He turned to the three convicts:

"Well! I recognise you, Brevet, do you remember——"

He paused, hesitated a moment, and said:

"Do you remember those checkered, knit suspenders that you had in the galleys?"

Brevet started as if struck with surprise, and gazed wildly at him from head to foot. He continued:

"Chenildieu, surnamed by yourself Je-nie-Dieu, the whole of your left shoulder has been burned deeply, from laying it one day on a chafing dish full of embers, to efface the three letters T. F. P., which yet are still to be seen there. Answer me, is this true?"

"It is true!" said Chenildieu.

He turned to Cochepaille:

"Cochepaille, you have on your left arm, near where you have been bled, a date put in blue letters with burnt powder. It is the date of the landing of the emperor at Cannes, *March 1st*, 1815. Lift up your sleeve."

Cochepaille lifted up his sleeve; all eyes around him were turned to his naked arm. A gendarme brought a lamp, the date was there.

The unhappy man turned towards the audience and the court with a smile, the thought of which still rends the hearts of those who witnessed it. It was the smile of triumph; it was also the smile of despair.

"You see clearly," said he, "that I am Jean Valjean."

There were no longer either judges, or accusers, or gendarmes in the hall; there were only fixed eyes and beating hearts. Nobody remembered longer the part which he had to play; the prosecuting attorney forgot that he was there to prosecute, the judge that he was there to preside, the counsel for the defence that he was there to defend. Strange to say no question was put, no authority intervened. It is the peculiarity of sublime spectacles that they take possession of every soul, and make of every witness a spectator. Nobody, perhaps, was positively conscious of what he experienced; and, undoubtedly, nobody said to himself that he there beheld the effulgence of a great light, yet all felt dazzled at heart.

It was evident that Jean Valjean was before their eyes. That fact shone forth. The appearance of this man had been enough fully to clear up the case, so obscure a moment before. Without need of any further explanation, the multitude, as by a sort of electric revelation, comprehended instantly, and at a single glance, this simple and magnificent story of a man giving himself up that another might not be condemned in his place. The details, the hesitation, the slight reluctance possible were lost in this immense, luminous fact.

It was an impression which quickly passed over, but for the moment it was irresistible.

"I will not disturb the proceeding further," continued Jean Valjean. "I am going, since I am not arrested. I have many things to do. Monsieur the prosecuting attorney knows where I am going, and will have me arrested when he chooses."

He walked towards the outer door. Not a voice was raised, not an arm stretched out to prevent him. All stood aside. There was at this moment an indescribable divinity within him which makes the multitudes fall back and make way before a man. He passed through the throng with slow steps. It was never known who opened the door, but it is certain that the door was open when he came to it. On reaching it he turned and said:

"Monsieur the Prosecuting Attorney, I remain at your disposal."

He then addressed himself to the auditory.

"You all, all who are here, think me worthy of pity, do you not? Great God! when I think of what I have been on the point of doing, I think myself worthy of envy. Still, would that all this had not happened!"

He went out, and the door closed as it had opened, for those who do deeds sovereignly great are always sure of being served by somebody in the multitude.

Less than an hour afterwards, the verdict of the jury discharged from all accusation the said Champmathieu; and Champmathieu, set at liberty forthwith, went his way stupefied, thinking all men mad, and understanding nothing of this vision.

BOOK EIGHTH – COUNTER-STROKE

I

IN WHAT MIRROR M. MADELEINE
LOOKS AT HIS HAIR

DAY began to dawn. Fantine had had a feverish and sleepless night, yet full of happy visions; she fell asleep at daybreak. Sister Simplice, who had watched with her, took advantage of this slumber to go and prepare a new potion of quinine. The good sister had been for a few moments in the laboratory of the infirmary, bending over her vials and drugs, looking at them very closely on account of the mist which the dawn casts over all objects, when suddenly she turned her head, and uttered a faint cry. M. Madeleine stood before her. He had just come in silently.

"You, Monsieur the Mayor!" she exclaimed.

"How is the poor woman?" he answered in a low voice.

"Better just now. But we have been very anxious indeed."

She explained what had happened, that Fantine had been very ill the night before, but was now better, because she believed that the mayor had gone to Montfermeil for her child. The sister dared not question the mayor, but she saw clearly from his manner that he had not come from that place.

"That is well," said he. "You did right not to deceive her."

"Yes," returned the sister, "but now, Monsieur the Mayor, when she sees you without her child, what shall we tell her?"

He reflected for a moment, then said:

"God will inspire us."

"But, we cannot tell her a lie," murmured the sister, in a smothered tone.

The broad daylight streamed into the room, and lighted up the face of M. Madeleine.

The sister happened to raise her eyes.

"O God, monsieur," she exclaimed. "What has befallen you? Your hair is all white!"

"White!" said he.

Sister Simplice had no mirror; she rummaged in a case of instruments and found a little glass which the physician of the infirmary used to discover whether the breath had left the body of a patient. M. Madeleine took the glass, looked at his hair in it, and said, "Indeed!"

He spoke the word with indifference, as if thinking of something else.

The sister felt chilled by an unknown something, of which she caught a glimpse in all this.

He asked: "Can I see her?"

"Will not Monsieur the Mayor bring back her child?" asked the sister, scarcely daring to venture a question.

"Certainly, but two or three days are necessary."

"If she does not see Monsieur the Mayor here," continued the sister timidly, "she will not know that he has returned; it will be easy for her to have patience, and when the child comes, she will think naturally that Monsieur the Mayor has just arrived with her. Then we will not have to tell her a falsehood."

Monsieur Madeleine seemed to reflect for a few moments, then said with his calm gravity:

"No, my sister, I must see her. Perhaps I have not much time."

The nun did not seem to notice this "perhaps," which gave an obscure and singular significance to the words of Monsieur the Mayor. She answered, lowering her eyes and voice respectfully:

"In that case, she is asleep, but monsieur can go in."

He made a few remarks about a door that shut with difficulty, the noise of which might awaken the sick woman; then entered the chamber of Fantine, approached her bed, and opened the curtains. She was sleeping. Her breath came from her chest with that tragic sound which is peculiar to these diseases, and which rends the heart of unhappy mothers, watching the slumbers of their fated children. But this laboured respiration scarcely disturbed an ineffable serenity, which overshadowed her countenance, and transfigured her in her sleep. Her pallor had become whiteness, and her cheeks were glowing. Her long, fair eyelashes, the only beauty left to her of her maidenhood and youth, quivered as they lay closed upon her cheek. Her whole person trembled as if with the fluttering of wings which were felt, but could not be seen, and which seemed about to unfold and bear her away. To see her thus, no one could have believed that her life was despaired of. She looked more as if about to soar away than to die.

The stem, when the hand is stretched out to pluck the flower, quivers, and seems at once to shrink back, and present itself. The human body has something of this trepidation at the moment when the mysterious fingers of death are about to gather the soul.

Monsieur Madeleine remained for some time motionless near the bed, looking by turns at the patient and the crucifix, as he had done two months before, on the day when he came for the first time to see her in this asylum. They were still there, both in the same attitude, she sleeping, he praying; only now, after these two months had rolled away, her hair was grey and his was white.

The sister had not entered with him. He stood by the bed, with his finger on his lips, as if there were some one in the room to silence. She opened her eyes, saw him, and said tranquilly, with a smile:

"And Cosette?"

II
FANTINE HAPPY

SHE did not start with surprise or joy; she was joy itself. The simple question: "And Cosette?" was asked with such deep faith, with so much certainty, with so complete an absence of disquiet or doubt that he could find no word in reply. She continued:

"I knew that you were there; I was asleep, but I saw you. I have seen you for a long time; I have followed you with my eyes the whole night. You were in a halo of glory, and all manner of celestial forms were hovering around you!"

He raised his eyes towards the crucifix.

"But tell me, where is Cosette?" she resumed. "Why not put her on my bed that I might see her the instant I woke?"

He answered something mechanically, which he could never afterwards recall.

Happily, the physician had come and had been apprised of this. He came to the aid of M. Madeleine.

"My child," said he, "be calm, your daughter is here."

The eyes of Fantine beamed with joy, and lighted up her whole countenance. She clasped her hands with an expression full of the most violent and most gentle entreaty:

"Oh!" she exclaimed, "bring her to me!"

Touching illusion of the mother; Cosette was still to her a little child to be carried in the arms.

"Not yet," continued the physician, "not at this moment. You have some fever still. The sight of your child will agitate you, and make you worse. We must cure you first."

She interrupted him impetuously.

"But I am cured! I tell you I am cured! Is this physician a fool? I will see my child!"

"You see how you are carried away!" said the physician. "So long as you are in this state, I cannot let you have your child. It is not enough to see her, you must live for her. When you are reasonable, I will bring her to you myself."

The poor mother bowed her head.

"Sir, I ask your pardon. I sincerely ask your pardon. Once I would not have spoken as I have now, but so many misfortunes have befallen me that sometimes I do not know what I am saying. I understand, you fear excitement; I will wait as long as you wish, but I am sure that it will not harm me to see my daughter. I see her now, I have not taken my eyes from her since last night. Let them bring her to me now, and I will just speak to her very gently. That is all. Is it not very natural that I should wish to see my child, when they have been to Montfermeil on purpose to bring her to me? I am not angry. I know that I am going to be very happy. All night, I saw figures in white, smiling on me. As soon as the doctor pleases, he can bring Cosette. My fever is gone, for I am cured; I feel that there is scarcely anything the matter with me; but I will act as if I were ill, and do not stir so as to please the ladies here. When they see that I am calm, they will say: 'You must give her the child.'"

M. Madeleine was sitting in a chair by the side of the bed. She turned towards him, and made visible efforts to appear calm and "very good," as she said, in that weakness of disease which resembles childhood, so that, seeing her so peaceful, there should be no objection to bringing her Cosette. Nevertheless, although restraining herself, she could not help addressing a thousand questions to M. Madeleine.

"Did you have a pleasant journey, Monsieur the Mayor? Oh! how good you have been to go for her! Tell me only how she is. Did she bear the journey well? Ah! she will not know me. In all this time, she has forgotten me, poor kitten! Children have no memory. They are like birds. To-day they see one thing, and to-morrow another, and remember nothing. Tell me only, were her clothes clean? Did those Thénardiers keep her neat? How did they feed her? Oh, if you knew how I have suffered in asking myself all these things in the time of my wretchedness! Now, it is past. I am happy. Oh! how I want to see her! Monsieur the Mayor, did you think her pretty? Is not my daughter beautiful? You must have been very cold in the diligence? Could they not bring her here for one little moment? they might take her away immediately. Say! you are master here, are you willing?"

He took her hand. "Cosette is beautiful," said he. "Cosette is well; you shall see her soon, but be quiet. You talk too fast; and then you throw your arms out of bed, which makes you cough."

In fact, coughing fits interrupted Fantine at almost every word.

She did not murmur; she feared that by too eager entreaties she had weakened the confidence which she wished to inspire, and began to talk about indifferent subjects.

"Montfermeil is a pretty place, is it not? In summer people go there on pleasure parties. Do the Thénardiers do a good business? Not many great people pass through that country. Their inn is a kind of chop-house."

Monsieur Madeleine still held her hand and looked at her with anxiety. It was evident that he had come to tell her things before which his mind now hesitated. The physician had made his visit and retired. Sister Simplice alone remained with them.

But in the midst of the silence, Fantine cried out:——

"I hear her! Oh, darling! I hear her!"

There was a child playing in the court—the child of the portress or some workwoman. It was one of those chances which are always met with, and which seem to make part of the mysterious representation of tragic events. The child, which was a little girl, was running up and down to keep herself warm, singing and laughing in a loud voice. Alas! with what are not the plays of children mingled! Fantine had heard this little girl singing.

"Oh!" said she, "it is my Cosette! I know her voice!"

The child departed as she had come, and the voice died away. Fantine listened for some time. A shadow came over her face, and Monsieur Madeleine heard her whisper, "How wicked it is of that doctor not to let me see my child! That man has a bad face!"

But yet her happy train of thought returned. With her head on the pillow she continued to talk to herself. "How happy we shall be! We will have a little garden in the first place; Monsieur Madeleine has promised it to me. My child will play in the garden. She must know her letters now. I will teach her to spell. She will chase the butterflies in the grass, and I will watch her. Then there will be her first communion. Ah! when will her first communion be?"

She began to count on her fingers.

"One, two, three, four. She is seven years old. In five years. She will have a white veil and open-worked stockings, and will look like a little lady. Oh, my good sister, you do not know how foolish I am; here I am thinking of my child's first communion!"

And she began to laugh.

He had let go the hand of Fantine. He listened to the words as one listens to the wind that blows, his eyes on the ground, and his mind plunged into unfathomable reflections. Suddenly she ceased speaking, and raised her head mechanically. Fantine had become appalling.

She did not speak; she did not breathe; she half-raised herself in the bed, the covering fell from her emaciated shoulders; her countenance, radiant a moment before, became livid, and her eyes, dilated with terror, seemed to fasten on something before her at the other end of the room.

"Good God!" exclaimed he. "What is the matter, Fantine?"

She did not answer; she did not take her eyes from the object which she seemed to see, but touched his arm with one hand, and with the other made a sign to him to look behind him.

He turned, and saw Javert.

III
JAVERT SATISFIED

LET us see what had happened.

The half hour after midnight was striking when M. Madeleine left the hall of the Arras Assizes. He had returned to his inn just in time to take the mail-coach, in which it will be remembered he had retained his seat. A little before six in the morning he had reached M—— sur M——, where his first care had been to post his letter to M. Laffitte, then go to the infirmary and visit Fantine.

Meanwhile he had scarcely left the hall of the Court of Assizes when the prosecuting attorney, recovering from his first shock, addressed the court, deploring the insanity of the honourable Mayor of M—— sur M——, declaring that his convictions were in no wise modified by this singular incident, which would be explained hereafter, and demanding the conviction of this Champmathieu, who was evidently the real Jean Valjean. The persistence of the prosecuting attorney was visibly in contradiction to the sentiment of all—the public, the court, and the jury. The counsel for the defence had little difficulty in answering this harangue, and establishing that, in consequence of the revelations of M. Madeleine—that is, of the real Jean Valjean—the aspect of the case was changed, entirely changed, from top to bottom, and that the jury now had before them an innocent man. The counsel drew from this a few passionate appeals, unfortunately not very new, in regard to judicial errors, etc., etc.; the judge, in his summing up, sided with the defence; and the jury, after a few moments' consultation, acquitted Champmathieu.

But yet the prosecuting attorney must have a Jean Valjean, and having lost Champmathieu he took Madeleine.

Immediately upon the discharge of Champmathieu the prosecuting attorney closeted himself with the judge. The subject of their conference was, "Of the necessity of the arrest of the person of Monsieur the Mayor of M—— sur M——." This sentence, in which there is a great deal of *of*, is the prosecuting attorney's, written by his own hand, on the minutes of his report to the attorney-general.

The first sensation being over, the judge made few objections. Justice must take its course. Then to confess the truth, although the judge was a kind man, and really intelligent, he was at the same time a strong, almost zealous royalist, and had been shocked when the mayor of M—— sur M——, in speaking of the debarkation at Cannes, said the *Emperor* instead of *Buonaparte*.

The order of arrest was therefore granted. The prosecuting attorney sent it to M—— sur M—— by a courier, at full speed, to police-inspector Javert.

It will be remembered that Javert had returned to M—— sur M—— immediately after giving his testimony.

Javert was just rising when the courier brought him the warrant and order of arrest.

The courier was himself a policeman, and an intelligent man; who, in three words, acquainted Javert with what had happened at Arras.

The order of arrest, signed by the prosecuting attorney, was couched in these terms:—

"Inspector Javert will seize the body of Sieur Madeleine, Mayor of M—— sur M——, who has this day been identified in court as the discharged convict Jean Valjean."

One who did not know Javert, on seeing him as he entered the hall of the infirmary, could have divined nothing of what was going on, and would have thought his manner the most natural imaginable. He was cool, calm, grave; his grey hair lay perfectly smooth over his temples, and he had ascended the stairway with his customary deliberation. But one who knew him thoroughly and examined him with attention, would have shuddered. The buckle of his leather cravat, instead of being on the back of his neck, was under his left ear. This denoted an unheard-of agitation.

Javert was a complete character without a wrinkle in his duty or his uniform, methodical with villains, rigid with the buttons of his coat.

For him to misplace the buckle of his cravat, he must have received one of those shocks which may well be the earthquakes of the soul.

He came unostentatiously, had taken a corporal and four soldiers from a station-house near-by, had left the soldiers in the court, had been shown to Fantine's chamber by the portress, without suspicion, accustomed as she was to see armed men asking for the mayor.

On reaching the room of Fantine, Javert turned the key, pushed open the door with the gentleness of a sick-nurse, or a police spy, and entered.

Properly speaking, he did not enter. He remained standing in the half-opened door, his hat on his head, and his left hand in his overcoat, which was buttoned to the chin. In the bend of his elbow might be seen the leaden head of his enormous cane, which disappeared behind him.

He remained thus for nearly a minute, unperceived. Suddenly, Fantine raised her eyes, saw him, and caused Monsieur Madeleine to turn round.

At the moment when the glance of Madeleine encountered that of Javert, Javert, without stirring, without moving, without approaching, became terrible. No human feeling can ever be so appalling as joy.

It was the face of a demon who had again found his victim.

The certainty that he had caught Jean Valjean at last brought forth upon his countenance all that was in his soul. The disturbed depths rose to the surface. The humiliation of having lost the scent for a little while, of having been mistaken for a few moments concerning Champmathieu, was lost in the pride of having divined so well at first, and having so long retained a true instinct. The satisfaction of Javert shone forth in his commanding attitude. The deformity of triumph spread over his narrow forehead. It was the fullest development of horror that a gratified face can show.

Javert was at this moment in heaven. Without clearly defining his own feelings, yet notwithstanding with a confused intuition of his necessity and his success, he, Javert, personified justice, light, and truth, in their celestial function as destroyers of evil. He was surrounded and supported by infinite depths of authority, reason, precedent, legal conscience, the vengeance of the law, all the stars in the firmament; he protected order, he hurled forth the thunder of the law, he avenged society, he lent aid to the absolute; he stood erect in a halo of glory; there was in his victory a reminder of defiance and of combat; standing haughty, resplendent, he displayed in full glory the superhuman beastliness of a ferocious archangel; the fearful shadow of the deed which he was accomplishing, made visible in his clenched fist, the uncertain flashes of the social sword; happy and indignant, he had set his heel on crime, vice, rebellion, perdition, and hell, he was radiant, exterminating, smiling; there was an incontestable grandeur in this monstrous St. Michael.

Javert, though hideous, was not ignoble.

Probity, sincerity, candour, conviction, the idea of duty, are things which, mistaken, may become hideous, but which, even though hideous, remain great; their majesty, peculiar to the human conscience, continues in all their horror; they are virtues with a single vice—error. The pitiless, sincere joy of a fanatic in an act of atrocity preserves an indescribably mournful radiance which inspires us with veneration. Without suspecting it, Javert, in his fear-inspiring happiness, was pitiable, like every ignorant man who wins a triumph. Nothing could be more painful and terrible than this face, which revealed what we may call all the evil of good.

IV

AUTHORITY RESUMES ITS SWAY

FANTINE had not seen Javert since the day the mayor had wrested her from him. Her sick brain accounted for nothing, only she was sure that he had come for her. She could not endure this hideous face, she felt as if she were dying, she hid her face with both hands, and shrieked in anguish:

"Monsieur Madeleine, save me!"

Jean Valjean, we shall call him by no other name henceforth, had risen. He said to Fantine in his gentlest and calmest tone:

"Be composed; it is not for you that he comes."

He then turned to Javert and said:

"I know what you want."

Javert answered:

"Hurry along."

There was in the manner in which these two words were uttered, an inexpressible something which reminded you of a wild beast and of a madman. Javert did not say "Hurry along!" he said: "Hurr-'long!" No orthography can express the tone in which this was pronounced; it ceased to be human speech; it was a howl.

He did not go through the usual ceremony; he made no words; he showed no warrant. To him Jean Valjean was a sort of mysterious and intangible antagonist, a shadowy wrestler with whom he had been struggling for five years, without being able to throw him. This arrest was not a beginning, but an end. He only said: "Hurry along!"

While speaking thus, he did not stir a step, but cast upon Jean Valjean a look like a noose, with which he was accustomed to draw the wretched to him by force.

It was the same look which Fantine had felt penetrate to the very marrow of her bones, two months before.

At the exclamation of Javert, Fantine had opened her eyes again. But the mayor was there, what could she fear?

Javert advanced to the middle of the chamber, exclaiming:

"Hey, there; are you coming?"

The unhappy woman looked around her. There was no one but the nun and the mayor. To whom could this contemptuous familiarity be addressed? To herself alone. She shuddered.

Then she saw a mysterious thing, so mysterious that its like had never appeared to her in the darkest delirium of fever.

She saw the spy Javert seize Monsieur the Mayor by the collar; she saw Monsieur the Mayor bow his head. The world seemed vanishing before her sight.

Javert, in fact, had taken Jean Valjean by the collar.

Javert burst into a horrid laugh, displaying all his teeth.

"There is no Monsieur the Mayor here any longer!" said he.

Jean Valjean did not attempt to disturb the hand which grasped the collar of his coat. He said:

"Javert——"

Javert interrupted him: "Call me Monsieur the Inspector!"

"Monsieur," continued Jean Valjean, "I would like to speak a word with you in private."

"Aloud, speak aloud," said Javert, "people speak aloud to me."

Jean Valjean went on, lowering his voice.

"It is a request that I have to make of you——"

"I tell you to speak aloud."

"But this should not be heard by any one but yourself."

"What is that to me? I will not listen."

Jean Valjean turned to him and said rapidly and in a very low tone:

"Give me three days! Three days to go for the child of this unhappy woman! I will pay whatever is necessary. You shall accompany me if you like."

"Are you laughing at me!" cried Javert. "Hey! I did not think you so stupid! You ask for three days to get away, and tell me that you are going for this girl's child! Ha, ha, that's good! That is good!"

Fantine shivered.

"My child!" she exclaimed, "going for my child! Then she is

not here! Sister, tell me, where is Cosette? I want my child! Monsieur Madeleine, Monsieur the Mayor!"

Javert stamped his foot.

"There is the other now! Hold your tongue, hussy! Miserable country, where galley slaves are magistrates and women of the town are nursed like countesses! Ha, but all this will be changed; it was time!"

He gazed steadily at Fantine, and added, grasping anew the cravat, shirt, and coat collar of Jean Valjean:

"I tell you that there is no Monsieur Madeleine, and that there is no Monsieur the Mayor. There is a robber, there is a brigand, there is a convict called Jean Valjean, and I have got him! That is what there is!"

Fantine started upright, supporting herself by her rigid arms and hands; she looked at Jean Valjean, then at Javert, and then at the nun; she opened her mouth as if to speak; a rattle came from her throat, her teeth struck together, she stretched out her arms in anguish, convulsively opening her hands, and groping about her like one who is drowning; then sank suddenly back upon the pillow.

Her head struck the head of the bed and fell forward on her breast, the mouth gaping, the eyes open and glazed.

She was dead.

Jean Valjean put his hand on that of Javert which held him, and opened it as he would have opened the hand of a child; then he said:

"You have killed this woman."

"Have done with this!" cried Javert, furious. "I am not here to listen to sermons; save all that; the guard is below; come right along, or the handcuffs!"

There stood in a corner of the room an old iron bedstead in a dilapidated condition, which the sisters used as a camp-bed when they watched. Jean Valjean went to the bed, wrenched out the rickety head bar—a thing easy for muscles like his—in the twinkling of an eye, and with the bar in his clenched fist, looked at Javert. Javert recoiled towards the door.

Jean Valjean, his iron bar in hand, walked slowly towards the bed of Fantine. On reaching it, he turned and said to Javert in a voice that could scarcely be heard:

"I advise you not to disturb me now."

Nothing is more certain than that Javert trembled.

He had an idea of calling the guard, but Jean Valjean might profit by his absence to escape. He remained, therefore, grasped the bottom of his cane, and leaned against the framework of the door without taking his eyes from Jean Valjean.

Jean Valjean rested his elbow upon the post, and his head upon his hand, and gazed at Fantine, stretched motionless before him. He remained thus, mute and absorbed, evidently lost to everything of this life. His countenance and attitude bespoke nothing but inexpressible pity.

After a few moments' reverie, he bent down to Fantine, and addressed her in a whisper.

What did he say? What could this condemned man say to this dead woman? What were these words? They were heard by none on earth. Did the dead woman hear them? There are touching illusions which perhaps are sublime realities. One thing is beyond doubt; Sister Simplice, the only witness of what passed, has often related that, at the moment when Jean Valjean whispered in the ear of Fantine, she distinctly saw an ineffable smile beam on those pale lips and in those dim eyes, full of the wonder of the tomb.

Jean Valjean took Fantine's head in his hands and arranged it on the pillow, as a mother would have done for her child, then fastened the string of her night-dress, and replaced her hair beneath her cap. This done, he closed her eyes.

The face of Fantine, at this instant, seemed strangely illumined.

Death is the entrance into the great light.

Fantine's hand hung over the side of the bed. Jean Valjean knelt before this hand, raised it gently, and kissed it.

Then he rose, and, turning to Javert, said:

"Now, I am at your disposal."

V
A FITTING TOMB

JAVERT put Jean Valjean in the city prison.

The arrest of Monsieur Madeleine produced a sensation, or rather an extraordinary commotion, at M—— sur M——. We are sorry not to be able to disguise the fact that, on this single sentence, *he was a galley slave,* almost everybody abandoned him. In less than two hours, all the good he had done was forgotten, and he was "nothing but a galley slave." It is just to say that the details of the scene at Arras were not yet known. All day long, conversations like this were heard in every part of the town: "Don't you know, he was a discharged convict!" "He! Who?" "The mayor." "Bah! Monsieur Madeleine." "Yes." "Indeed!" "His name was not Madeleine; he has a horrid name, Béjean, Bojean, Bonjean!" "Oh! bless me!" "He has been arrested." "Arrested!" "In prison, in the city prison to await his removal." "His removal! where will he be taken?" "To the Court of Assizes for a highway robbery that he once committed." "Well! I always did suspect him. The man was too good, too perfect, too sweet. He refused fees, and gave sous to every little blackguard he met. I always thought that there must be something bad at the bottom of all this."

"The drawing-rooms," above all, were entirely of this opinion.

An old lady, a subscriber to the *Drapeau Blanc*, made this remark, the depth of which it is almost impossible to fathom:

"I am not sorry for it. That will teach the Bonapartists!"

In this manner the phantom which had been called Monsieur Madeleine was dissipated at M—— sur M——. Three or four persons alone in the whole city remained faithful to his memory. The old portress who had been his servant was among the number.

On the evening of this same day, the worthy old woman was sitting in her lodge, still quite bewildered and sunk in sad reflections. The factory had been closed all day, the carriage doors were bolted, the street was deserted. There was no one in the house but the two nuns, Sister Perpétue and Sister Simplice, who were watching the corpse of Fantine.

Towards the time when Monsieur Madeleine had been accustomed to return, the honest portress rose mechanically, took the key of his room from a drawer, with the taper-stand that he used at night to light himself up the stairs, then hung the key on a nail from which he had been in the habit of taking it, and placed the taper-stand by its side, as if she were expecting him. She then seated herself again in her chair, and resumed her reflections. The poor old woman had done all this without being conscious of it.

More than two hours had elapsed when she started from her reverie and exclaimed, "Why, bless me! I have hung his key on the nail!"

Just then, the window of her box opened, a hand passed through the opening, took the key and stand, and lighted the taper at the candle which was burning.

The portress raised her eyes; she was transfixed with astonishment; a cry rose to her lips, but she could not give it utterance.

She knew the hand, the arm, the coat-sleeve.

It was M. Madeleine.

She was speechless for some seconds, thunderstruck, as she said herself, afterwards, in giving her account of the affair.

"My God! Monsieur Mayor!" she exclaimed, "I thought you were—"

She stopped; the end of her sentence would not have been respectful to the beginning. To her, Jean Valjean was still Monsieur the Mayor.

He completed her thought.

"In prison," said he. "I was there, I broke a bar from a window, let myself fall from the top of a roof, and here I am. I am going to my room; go for Sister Simplice. She is doubtless beside this poor woman."

The old servant hastily obeyed.

He gave her no caution, very sure she would guard him better than he would guard himself.

It has never been known how he had succeeded in gaining entrance into the court-yard without opening the carriage-door. He had, and always carried about him, a pass-key which opened a little side door, but he must have been searched, and this taken from him. This point is not yet cleared up.

He ascended the staircase which led to his room. On reaching the top, he left his taper-stand on the upper stair, opened his door with little noise, felt his way to the window and closed the shutter, then came back, took his taper, and went into the chamber.

The precaution was not useless; it will be remembered that his window could be seen from the street.

He cast a glance about him, over his table, his chair, his bed, which had not been slept in for three days. There remained no trace of the disorder of the night before the last. The portress had "put the room to rights." Only, she had picked up from the ashes and laid in order on the table, the ends of the loaded club, and the forty-sous piece, blackened by the fire.

He took a sheet of paper and wrote: *These are the ends of my loaded club and the forty-sous piece stolen from Petit Gervais, of which I spoke at the Court of Assizes*; then placed the two bits of iron and the piece of silver on the sheet in such a way that it would be the first thing perceived on entering the room. He took from a wardrobe an old shirt which he tore into several pieces and in which he packed the two silver candlesticks. In all this there was neither haste nor agitation. And even while packing the bishop's candlesticks, he was eating a piece of black bread. It was probably prison-bread, which he had brought away in escaping.

This has been established by crumbs of bread found on the floor of the room, when the court afterwards ordered a search.

Two gentle taps were heard at the door.

"Come in," said he.

It was Sister Simplice.

She was pale, her eyes were red, and the candle which she held trembled in her hand. The shocks of destiny have this peculiarity; however subdued or disciplined our feelings may be, they draw out the human nature from the depths of our souls, and compel us to exhibit it to others. In the agitation of this day the nun had again become a woman. She had wept, and she was trembling.

Jean Valjean had written a few lines on a piece of paper, which he handed to the nun, saying: "Sister, you will give this to the curé."

The paper was not folded. She cast her eyes on it.

"You may read it," said he.

She read: "I beg Monsieur the Curé to take charge of all that I leave here. He will please defray therefrom the expenses of my trial, and of the burial of the woman who died this morning. The remainder is for the poor."

The sister attempted to speak, but could scarcely stammer out a few inarticulate sounds. She succeeded, however, in saying:

"Does not Monsieur the Mayor wish to see this poor unfortunate again for the last time?"

"No," said he, "I am pursued; I should only be arrested in her chamber; it would disturb her."

He had scarcely finished when there was a loud noise on the staircase. They heard a tumult of steps ascending, and the old portress exclaiming in her loudest and most piercing tones:

"My good sir, I swear to you in the name of God, that

nobody has come in here the whole day, and the whole evening; that I have not even once left my door!"

A man replied: "But yet, there is a light in this room."

They recognised the voice of Javert.

The chamber was so arranged that the door in opening covered the corner of the wall to the right. Jean Valjean blew out the taper, and placed himself in this corner.

Sister Simplice fell on her knees near the table.

The door opened.

Javert entered.

The whispering of several men, and the protestations of the portress were heard in the hall.

The nun did not raise her eyes. She was praying.

The candle was on the mantel, and gave but a dim light.

Javert perceived the sister, and stopped abashed.

It will be remembered that the very foundation of Javert, his element, the medium in which he breathed, was veneration for all authority. He was perfectly homogeneous, and admitted of no objection, or abridgment. To him, be it understood, ecclesiastical authority was the highest of all; he was devout, superficial, and correct, upon this point as upon all others. In his eyes, a priest was a spirit who was never mistaken, a nun was a being who never sinned. They were souls walled in from this world, with a single door which never opened but for the exit of truth.

On perceiving the sister, his first impulse was to retire.

But there was also another duty which held him, and which urged him imperiously in the opposite direction. His second impulse was to remain, and to venture at least one question.

This was the Sister Simplice, who had never lied in her life. Javert knew this, and venerated her especially on account of it.

"Sister," said he, "are you alone in this room?"

There was a fearful instant during which the poor portress felt her limbs falter beneath her. The sister raised her eyes, and replied:

"Yes."

Then continued Javert—"Excuse me if I persist, it is my duty—you have not seen this evening a person, a man—he has escaped and we are in search of him—Jean Valjean—you have not seen him?"

The sister answered—"No."

She lied. Two lies in succession, one upon another, without hesitation, quickly, as if she were an adept in it.

"Your pardon!" said Javert, and he withdrew, bowing reverently.

Oh, holy maiden! for many years thou hast been no more in this world; thou hast joined the sisters, the virgins, and thy brethren, the angels, in glory; may this falsehood be remembered to thee in Paradise.

The affirmation of the sister was to Javert something so decisive that he did not even notice the singularity of this taper, just blown out, and smoking on the table.

An hour afterwards, a man was walking rapidly in the darkness beneath the trees from M—— sur M—— in the direction of Paris. This man was Jean Valjean. It has been established, by the testimony of two or three wagoners who met him, that he carried a bundle, and was dressed in a blouse. Where did he get this blouse? It was never known. Nevertheless, an old artisan had died in the infirmary of the factory a few days before, leaving nothing but his blouse. This might have been the one.

A last word in regard to Fantine.

We have all one mother—the earth. Fantine was restored to this mother.

The curé thought best, and did well perhaps, to reserve out of what Jean Valjean had left, the largest amount possible for the poor. After all, who were in question?—a convict and a woman of the town. This was why he simplified the burial of Fantine, and reduced it to that bare necessity called the Potter's field.

And so Fantine was buried in the common grave of the cemetery, which is for everybody and for all, and in which the poor are lost. Happily, God knows where to find the soul. Fantine was laid away in the darkness with bodies which had no name; she suffered the promiscuity of dust. She was thrown into the public pit. Her tomb was like her bed.

COSETTE

COSETTE
BOOK FIRST – WATERLOO

I
WHAT YOU MEET IN COMING FROM NIVELLES

ON a beautiful morning in May, last year (1861), a traveller, he who tells this story, was journeying from Nivelles towards La Hulpe. He travelled a-foot. He was following, between two rows of trees, a broad road, undulating over hills, which, one after another, upheave it and let it fall again, like enormous waves. He had passed Lillois and Bois-Seigneur-Isaac. He saw to the west the slated steeple of Braine l'Alleud, which has the form of an inverted vase. He had just passed a wood upon a hill, and at the corner of a cross-road, beside a sort of worm-eaten sign-post, bearing the inscription—*Old Toll-Gate, No. 4*—a tavern with this sign:—*The Four Winds. Echlaleau, Private Café.*

Half a mile from this tavern, he reached the bottom of a little valley, where a stream flowed beneath an arch in the embankment of the road. The cluster of trees, thin-sown but very green, which fills the vale on one side of the road, on the other spreads out into meadows, and sweeps away in graceful disorder towards Braine l'Alleud.

At this point there was at the right, and immediately on the road, an inn, with a four-wheeled cart before the door, a great bundle of hop-poles, a plough, a pile of dry brush near a quick-set hedge, some lime which was smoking in a square hole in the ground, and a ladder lying along an old shed with mangers for straw. A young girl was pulling weeds in a field, where a large green poster, probably of a travelling show at some annual fair, fluttered in the wind. At the corner of the inn, beside a pond, in which a flotilla of ducks was navigating, a difficult foot-path lost itself in the shrubbery. The traveller took this path.

At the end of a hundred paces, passing a wall of the fifteenth century, surmounted by a sharp gable of crossed bricks, he found himself opposite a great arched stone doorway, with recti-linear impost, in the solemn style of Louis XIV., and plain med-allions on the sides. Over the entrance was a severe façade, and a wall perpendicular to the façade almost touched the doorway, flanking it at an abrupt right angle. On the meadow before the door lay three harrows, through which were blooming, as best they could, all the flowers of May. The doorway was closed. It was shut by two decrepit folding-doors, decorated with an old rusty knocker.

The sunshine was enchanting; the branches of the trees had that gentle tremulousness of the month of May which seems to come from the birds' nests rather than the wind. A spruce little bird, probably in love, was singing desperately in a tall tree.

The traveller paused and examined in the stone at the left of the door, near the ground, a large circular excavation like the hollow of a sphere. Just then the folding-doors opened, and a peasant woman came out.

She saw the traveller, and perceived what he was examining.

"It was a French ball which did that," said she.

And she added—

"What you see there, higher up, in the door, near a nail, is the hole made by a Biscay musket. The musket has not gone through the wood."

"What is the name of this place?" asked the traveller.

"Hougomont," the woman answered.

The traveller raised his head. He took a few steps and looked over the hedges. He saw in the horizon, through the trees, a sort of hillock, and on this hillock something which, in the distance, resembled a lion.

He was on the battle-field of Waterloo.

II
HOUGOMONT

HOUGOMONT—this was the fatal spot, the beginning of the resistance, the first check encountered at Waterloo by this great butcher of Europe, called Napoleon; the first knot under the axe.

It was a château; it is now nothing more than a farm. Hougomont, to the antiquary, is *Hugomons*. This manor was built by Hugo, sire de Somerel, the same who endowed the sixth chaplainship of the abbey of Villiers.

The traveller pushed open the door, elbowed an old carriage under the porch, and entered the court.

The first thing that he noticed in this yard was a door of the sixteenth century, which seemed like an arch, everything having fallen down around it. The monumental aspect is often produced by ruin. Near the arch opens another door in the wall, with keystones of the time of Henry IV., which discloses the trees of an orchard. Beside this door were a dung-hill, mattocks and shovels, some carts, an old well with its flag-stone and iron pulley, a skipping colt, a strutting turkey, a chapel surmounted by a little steeple, a pear-tree in bloom, trained in espalier on the wall of the chapel; this was the court, the conquest of which was the aspiration of Napoleon. This bit of earth, could he have taken it, would perhaps have given him the world. The hens are scattering the dust with their beaks. You hear a growling: it is a great dog, who shows his teeth, and takes the place of the English.

The English fought admirably there. The four companies of guards under Cooke held their ground for seven hours, against the fury of an assaulting army.

Hougomont seen on the map, on a geometrical plan, comprising buildings and inclosure, presents a sort of irregular rectangle, one corner of which is cut off. At this corner is the southern entrance, guarded by this wall, which commands it at the shortest musket range. Hougomont has two entrances: the southern, that of the château, and the northern, that of the farm. Napoleon sent against Hougomont his brother Jerome. The divisions of Guilleminot, Foy, and Bachelu were hurled against it; nearly the whole corps of Reille was there employed and there defeated, and the bullets of Kellermann were exhausted against this heroic wall-front. It was too much for the brigade of Bauduin to force Hougomont on the north, and the brigade of Soye could only batter it on the south—it could not take it.

The buildings of the farm are on the southern side of the court. A small portion of the northern door, broken by the French, hangs dangling from the wall. It is composed of four planks, nailed to two cross-pieces, and in it may be seen the scars of the attack.

The northern door, forced by the French, and to which a piece has been added to replace the panel suspended from the wall, stands half open at the foot of the court-yard; it is cut squarely in a wall of stone below, and brick above, and closes the court on the north. It is a simple cart-door, such as are found on all small farms, composed of two large folding-doors, made of rustic planks; beyond this are the meadows. This entrance was furiously contested. For a long time there could be seen upon the door all sorts of prints of bloody hands. It was there that Bauduin was killed.

The storm of the combat is still in this court: the horror is visible there; the overturn of the conflict is there petrified, it lives; it dies; it was but yesterday. The walls are still in death agonies; the stones fall, the breaches cry out; the holes are wounds; the trees bend and shudder, as if making an effort to escape.

This court, in 1815, was in better condition than it is to-day. Structures which have since been pulled down formed redans, angles, and squares.

The English were barricaded there; the French effected an entrance, but could not maintain their position. At the side of the chapel, one wing of the château, the only remnant which exists of the manor of Hougomont, stands crumbling, one might almost say disembowelled. The château served as donjon; the chapel served as block-house. There was work of extermination. The French, shot down from all sides, from behind the walls, from the roofs of the barns, from the bottom of the cellars, through every window, through every air-hole, through every chink in the stones, brought faggots and fired the walls and the men: the storm of balls was answered by a tempest of flame.

A glimpse may be had in the ruined wing, through the iron-barred windows, of the dismantled chambers of a main building; the English guards lay in ambush in these chambers; the spiral staircase, broken from foundation to roof, appears like the interior of a broken shell. The staircase has two landings; the English, besieged in the staircase, and crowded upon the upper steps, had cut away the lower ones. These are large slabs of blue stone, now heaped together among the nettles. A dozen steps still cling to the wall: on the first is cut the image of a trident. These inaccessible steps are firm in their sockets; all the rest resembles a toothless jawbone. Two old trees are there; one is dead, the other is wounded at the root, and does not leaf out until April. Since 1850 it has begun to grow across the staircase.

There was a massacre in the chapel. The interior, again restored to quiet, is strange. No mass has been said there since the carnage. The altar remains, however—a clumsy wooden altar, backed by a wall of rough stone. Four whitewashed walls, a door opposite the altar, two little arched windows, over the door a large wooden crucifix, above the crucifix a square open-ing in which is stuffed a bundle of straw; in a corner on the ground, an old glazed sash all broken, such is this chapel. Near the altar hangs a wooden statue of St. Anne of the fifteenth century; the head of the infant Jesus has been carried away by a musket-shot. The French, masters for a moment of the chapel, then dislodged, fired it. The flames filled this ruin; it was a furnace; the door was burned, the floor was burned, but the wooden Christ was not burned. The fire ate its way to his feet, the blackened stumps of which only are visible; then it stopped. A miracle, say the country people. The infant Jesus, decapitated, was not so fortunate as the Christ.

The walls are covered with inscriptions. Near the feet of the Christ we read this name: *Henquinez*. Then these others: *Conde de Rio Maior Marques y Marquesa de Almagre (Habana)*. There are French names with exclamation points, signs of anger. The wall was whitewashed in 1849. The nations were insulting each other on it.

At the door of this chapel a body was picked up holding an axe in its hand. This body was that of second-lieutenant Legros.

On coming out of the chapel, a well is seen at the left. There are two in this yard. You ask: why is there no bucket and no pulley to this one? Because no water is drawn from it now. Why is no more water drawn from it? Because it is full of skeletons.

The last man who drew water from that well was Guillaume Van Kylsom. He was a peasant, who lived in Hougomont, and was gardener there. On the 18th of June, 1815, his family fled and hid in the woods.

The forest about the Abbey of Villiers concealed for several days and several nights all that scattered and distressed popula-tion. Even now certain vestiges may be distinguished, such as old trunks of scorched trees, which mark the place of these poor trembling bivouacs in the depths of the thickets.

Guillaume Van Kylsom remained at Hougomont "to take care of the château," and hid in the cellar. The English disco-vered him there. He was torn from his hiding place, and, with blows of the flat of their swords, the soldiers compelled this frightened man to wait upon them. They were thirsty; this Guillaume brought them drink. It was from this well that he drew the water. Many drank their last quaff. This well, where drank so many of the dead, must die itself also.

After the action, there was haste to bury the corpses. Death has its own way of embittering victory, and it causes glory to be followed by pestilence. Typhus is the successor of triumph. This well was deep, it was made a sepulchre. Three hundred dead were thrown into it. Perhaps with too much haste. Were they all dead? Tradition says no. It appears that on the night after the burial, feeble voices were heard calling out from the well.

This well is isolated in the middle of the court-yard. Three walls, half brick and half stone, folded back like the leaves of a screen, and imitating a square turret, surround it on three sides. The fourth side is open. On that side the water was drawn. The back wall has a sort of shapeless bull's-eye, perhaps a hole made by a shell. This turret had a roof, of which only the beams remain. The iron that sustains the wall on the right is in the shape of a cross. You bend over the well, the eye is lost in a deep brick cylinder, which is filled with an accumulation of shadows. All around it, the bottom of the walls is covered by nettles.

This well has not in front the large blue flagging stone, which serves as a curb for all the wells of Belgium. The blue stone is replaced by a cross-bar on which rest five or six misshapen wooden stumps, knotty and hardened, that resemble huge bones. There is no longer either bucket, or chain, or pulley; but the stone basin is still there which served for the waste water. The rain water gathers there, and from time to time a bird from the neighbouring forest comes to drink and flies away.

One house among these ruins, the farm-house, is still inhabited. The door of this house opens upon the court-yard. By the side of a pretty Gothic key-hole plate there is upon the door a handful of iron in trefoil, slanting forward. At the moment that the Hanoverian lieutenant Wilda was seizing this to take refuge in the farm-house, a French sapper struck off his hand with the blow of an axe.

The family which occupies the house calls the former gardener Van Kylsom, long since dead, its grandfather. A grey-haired woman said to us: "I was there. I was three years old. My sister, larger, was afraid, and cried. They carried us away into the woods; I was in my mother's arms. They laid their ears to the ground to listen. For my part, I mimicked the cannon, and I went *boom, boom.*"

One of the yard doors, on the left, we have said, opens into the orchard.

The orchard is terrible.

It is in three parts, one might almost say in three acts. The first part is a garden, the second is the orchard, the third is a wood. These three parts have a common inclosure; on the side of the entrance the buildings of the château and the farm, on the left a hedge, on the right a wall, at the back a wall. The wall on the right is of brick, the wall on the back is of stone. The garden is entered first. It is sloping, planted with currant bushes, covered with wild vegetation, and terminated by a terrace of cut stone, with balusters with a double swell. It is a seignorial garden, in this first French style, which preceded the modern; now ruins and briers. The pilasters are surmounted by globes which look like stone cannon balls. We count forty-three balusters still in their places; the others are lying in the grass, nearly all show some scratches of musketry. A broken baluster remains upright like a broken leg.

It is in this garden, which is lower than the orchard, that six of the first Light Voltigeurs, having penetrated thither, and being unable to escape, caught and trapped like bears in a pit, engaged in a battle with two Hanoverian companies, one of which was armed with carbines. The Hanoverians were ranged along these balusters and fired from above. These voltigeurs, answering from below, six against two hundred, intrepid, with the currant bushes only for a shelter, took a quarter of an hour to die.

You rise a few steps, and from the garden pass into the orchard proper. There, in these few square yards, fifteen hundred men fell in less than a hour. The wall seems ready to recommence the combat. The thirty-eight loopholes, pierced by the English at irregular heights, are there yet. In front of the sixteenth, lie two English tombs of granite. There are no loopholes except in the south-wall, the principal attack came from that side. This wall is concealed on the outside by a large quickset hedge; the French came up, thinking there was nothing in their way but the hedge, crossed it, and found the wall, an obstacle and an ambush, the English Guards behind, the thirty-eight loopholes pouring forth their fire at once, a storm of grape and of balls; and Soye's brigade broke there. Waterloo commenced thus.

The orchard, however, was taken. They had no scaling ladders, but the French climbed the wall with their hands. They fought hand to hand under the trees. All this grass was soaked with blood. A battalion from Nassau, seven hundred men, was annihilated there. On the outside, the wall against which the two batteries of Kellermann were directed, is gnawed by grape.

This orchard is as responsive as any other to the month of May. It has its golden blossoms and its daisies; the grass is high; farm horses are grazing; lines on which clothes are drying cross the intervals between the trees, making travellers bend their heads; you walk over that sward, and your foot sinks in the path of the mole. In the midst of the grass you notice an uprooted trunk, lying on the ground, but still growing green. Major Blackmann leaned back against it to die. Under a large tree near by fell the German general, Duplat, of a French family which fled on the revocation of the edict of Nantes. Close beside it leans a diseased old apple tree swathed in a bandage of straw and loam. Nearly all the apple trees are falling from old age. There is not one which does not show its cannon ball or its musket shot. Skeletons of dead trees abound in this orchard. Crows fly in the branches; beyond it is a wood full of violets.

Bauduin killed, Foy wounded, fire, slaughter, carnage, a brook made of English blood, of German blood, and of French blood, mingled in fury; a well filled with corpses, the regiment of Nassau and the regiment of Brunswick destroyed, Duplat killed, Blackmann killed, the English Guards crippled, twenty French battalions, out of the forty of Reille's corps, decimated, three thousand men, in this one ruin of Hougomont, sabred, slashed, slaughtered, shot, burned; and all this in order that to-day a peasant may say to a traveller: *Monsieur, give me three francs; if you like, I will explain to you the affair of Waterloo.*

III
THE 18TH OF JUNE, 1815

LET us go back, for such is the story-teller's privilege, and place ourselves in the year 1815, a little before the date of the commencement of the action narrated in the first part of this book.

Had it not rained on the night of the 17th of June, 1815, the future of Europe would have been changed. A few drops of water more or less prostrated Napoleon. That Waterloo should be the end of Austerlitz, Providence needed only a little rain, and an unseasonable cloud crossing the sky sufficed for the over-throw of a world.

The battle of Waterloo—and this gave Blücher time to come up—could not be commenced before half-past eleven. Why? Because the ground was soft. It was necessary to wait for it to acquire some little firmness that the artillery could manoeuvre.

Napoleon was an artillery officer, and he never forgot it. The foundation of this prodigious captain was the man who, in his report to the Directory upon Aboukir, said: *Such of our balls killed six men*. All his plans of battle were made for projectiles. To converge the artillery upon a given point was his key of victory. He treated the strategy of the hostile general as a citadel, and battered it to a breach. He overwhelmed the weak point with grape; he joined and resolved battles with cannon. There was marksmanship in his genius. To destroy squares, to pulverise regiments, to break lines, to crush and disperse masses, all this was for him, to strike, strike, strike incessantly, and he entrusted this duty to the cannon ball. A formidable method, which, joined to genius, made this sombre athlete of the pugilism of war invincible for fifteen years.

On the 18th of June, 1815, he counted on his artillery the more because he had the advantage in numbers. Wellington had only a hundred and fifty-nine guns; Napoleon had two hundred and forty.

Had the ground been dry, and the artillery able to move, the action would have been commenced at six o'clock in the morning. The battle would have been won and finished at two o'clock, three hours before the Prussians turned the scale of fortune.

How much fault is there on the part of Napoleon in the loss of this battle? Is the shipwreck to be imputed to the pilot?

Was the evident physical decline of Napoleon accompanied at this time by a corresponding mental decline? had his twenty years of war worn out the sword as well as the sheath, the soul as well as the body? was the veteran injuriously felt in the captain? in a word, was that genius, as many considerable historians have thought, under an eclipse? had he put on a frenzy to disguise his enfeeblement from himself? did he begin to waver, and be bewildered by a random blast? was he becoming, a grave fault in a general, careless of danger? in that class of material great men who may be called the giants of action, is there an age when their genius becomes short-sighted? Old age has no hold on the geniuses of the ideal; for the Dantes and the Michael

Angelos, to grow old is to grow great; for the Hannibals and the Bonapartes is it to grow less? had Napoleon lost his clear sense of victory? could he no longer recognise the shoal, no longer divine the snare, no longer discern the crumbling edge of the abyss? had he lost the instinct of disaster? was he, who formerly knew all the paths of triumph, and who, from the height of his flashing car, pointed them out with sovereign finger, now under such dark hallucination as to drive his tumultuous train of legions over the precipices? was he seized, at forty-six years, with a supreme madness? was this titanic driver of Destiny now only a monstrous break-neck?

We think not.

His plan of battle was, all confess, a masterpiece. To march straight to the centre of the allied line, pierce the enemy, cut them in two, push the British half upon Hal and the Prussian half upon Tongres, make of Wellington and Blücher two fragments, carry Mont Saint Jean, seize Brussels, throw the German into the Rhine, and the Englishman into the sea. All this, for Napoleon, was in this battle. What would follow, anybody can see.

We do not, of course, profess to give here the history of Waterloo; one of the scenes that gave rise to the drama which we are describing hangs upon that battle; but the history of the battle is not our subject; that history moreover is told, and told in a masterly way, from one point of view by Napoleon, from the other point of view by Charras. As for us, we leave the two historians to their contest; we are only a witness at a distance, a passer in the plain, a seeker bending over this ground kneaded with human flesh, taking perhaps appearances for realities; we have no right to cope in the name of science with a mass of facts in which there is doubtless some mirage; we have neither the military experience nor the strategic ability which authorises a system; in our opinion, a chain of accidents overruled both captains at Waterloo; and when destiny is called in this mysterious accused, we judge like the people, that artless judge.

IV

A

THOSE who would get a clear idea of the battle of Waterloo have only to lay down upon the ground in their mind a capital

A. The left stroke of the A is the road from Nivelles, the right stroke is the road from Genappe, the cross of the A is the sunken road from Ohain to Braine l'Alleud. The top of the A is Mont Saint Jean, Wellington is there; the left-hand lower point is Hougomont, Reille is there with Jerome Bonaparte; the right-hand lower point is La Belle Alliance, Napoleon is there. A little below the point where the cross of the A meets and cuts the right stroke, is La Haie Sainte. At the middle of this cross is the precise point where the final battle-word was spoken. There the lion is placed, the involuntary symbol of the supreme heroism of the Imperial Guard.

The triangle contained at the top of the A, between the two strokes and the cross, is the plateau of Mont Saint Jean. The struggle for this plateau was the whole of the battle.

The wings of the two armies extended to the right and left of the two roads from Genappe and from Nivelles; D'Erlon being opposite Picton, Reille opposite Hill.

Behind the point of the A, behind the plateau of Mont Saint Jean, is the forest of Soignes.

As to the plain itself, we must imagine a vast undulating country; each wave commanding the next, and these undulations rising towards Mont Saint Jean, are there bounded by the forest.

Two hostile armies upon a field of battle are two wrestlers. Their arms are locked; each seeks to throw the other. They grasp at every aid; a thicket is a point of support; a corner of a wall is a brace for the shoulder; for lack of a few sheds to lean upon a regiment loses its footing; a depression in the plain, a movement of the soil, a convenient cross path, a wood, a ravine, may catch the heel of this colossus which is called an army, and prevent him from falling. He who leaves the field is beaten. Hence, for the responsible chief, the necessity of examining the smallest tuft of trees and appreciating the slightest details of contour.

Both generals had carefully studied the plain of Mont Saint Jean, now called the plain of Waterloo. Already in the preceding year, Wellington, with the sagacity of prescience, had examined it as a possible site for a great battle. On this ground and for this contest Wellington had the favourable side, Napoleon the unfavourable. The English army was above, the French army below.

To sketch here the appearance of Napoleon, on horseback, glass in hand, upon the heights of Rossomme, at dawn on the 18th of June, 1815, would be almost superfluous. Before we point him out, everybody has seen him. This calm profile under the little chapeau of the school of Brienne, this green uniform, the white facings concealing the stars on his breast, the overcoat concealing the epaulettes, the bit of red sash under the waist-coat, the leather breeches, the white horse with his housings of purple velvet with crowned N.'s and eagles on the corners, the Hessian boots over silk stockings, the silver spurs, the Marengo sword, this whole form of the last Cæsar lives in all imaginations, applauded by half the world, reprobated by the rest.

That form has long been fully illuminated; it did have a certain traditional obscurity through which most heroes pass, and which always veils the truth for a longer or shorter time; but now the history is luminous and complete.

This light of history is pitiless; it has this strange and divine quality that, all luminous as it is, and precisely because it is luminous, it often casts a shadow just where we saw a radiance; of the same man it makes two different phantoms, and the one attacks and punishes the other, and the darkness of the despot struggles with the splendour of the captain. Hence results a truer measure in the final judgment of the nations. Babylon violated lessens Alexander; Rome enslaved lessens Cæsar; massacred Jerusalem lessens Titus. Tyranny follows the tyrant. It is woe to a man to leave behind him a shadow which has his form.

V

THE QUID OBSCURUM OF BATTLES

EVERYBODY knows the first phase of this battle; the difficult opening, uncertain, hesitating, threatening for both armies, but for the English still more than for the French.

It had rained all night; the ground was softened by the shower; water lay here and there in the hollows of the plains as in basins; at some points the wheels sank into the axles; the horses' girths dripped with liquid mud; had not the wheat and rye spread down by that multitude of advancing carts filled the ruts and made a bed under the wheels, all movement, particularly in the valleys on the side of Papelotte, would have been impossible.

The affair opened late; Napoleon, as we have explained, had a habit of holding all his artillery in hand like a pistol, aiming now at one point, anon at another point of the battle, and he desired to wait until the field-batteries could wheel and gallop freely; for this the sun must come out and dry the ground. But the sun did not come out. He had not now the field of Austerlitz. When the first gun was fired, the English General Colville looked at his watch and noted that it was thirty-five minutes past eleven.

The battle commenced with fury, more fury perhaps than the emperor would have wished, by the left wing of the French at Hougomont. At the same time Napoleon attacked the centre by hurling the brigade of Quiot upon La Haie Sainte, and Ney pushed the right wing of the French against the left wing of the English which rested upon Papelotte.

The attack upon Hougomont was partly a feint; to draw Wellington that way, to make him incline to the left; this was the plan. This plan would have succeeded, had not the four companies of the English Guards, and the brave Belgians of Perponcher's division, resolutely held the position, enabling Wellington, instead of massing his forces upon that point, to limit himself to reinforcing them only by four additional companies of guards, and a Brunswick battalion.

The attack of the French right wing upon Papelotte was intended to overwhelm the English left, cut the Brussels road, bar the passage of the Prussians, should they come, to carry Mont Saint Jean, drive back Wellington upon Hougomont, from thence upon Braine l'Alleud, from thence upon Hal; nothing is clearer. With the exception of a few incidents, this attack succeeded. Papelotte was taken; La Haie Sainte was carried.

Note a circumstance. There were in the English infantry, particularly in Kempt's brigade, many new recruits. These young soldiers, before our formidable infantry, were heroic; their inexperience bore itself boldly in the affair; they did especially good service as skirmishers; the soldier as a skirmisher, to some extent left to himself, becomes, so to speak, his own general; these recruits exhibited something of French invention and French fury. This raw infantry showed enthusiasm. That displeased Wellington.

After the capture of La Haie Sainte, the battle wavered.

There is in this day from noon to four o'clock, an obscure

interval; the middle of this battle is almost indistinct, and partakes of the thickness of the conflict. Twilight was gathering. You could perceive vast fluctuations in this mist, a giddy mirage, implements of war now almost unknown, the flaming colbacks, the waving sabretaches, the crossed shoulder-belts, the grenade cartridge boxes, the dolmans of the hussars, the red boots with a thousand creases, the heavy shakos festooned with fringe, the almost black infantry of Brunswick united with the scarlet infantry of England, the English soldiers with great white circular pads on their sleeves for epaulettes, the Hanoverian light horse, with their oblong leather cap with copper bands and flowing plumes of red horse-hair, the Scotch with bare knees and plaids, the large white gaiters of our grenadiers; tableaux, not strategic lines, the need of Salvator Rosa, not of Gribeauval.

A certain amount of tempest always mingles with a battle, *Quid obscurum, quid divinum.* Each historian traces the particular lineament which pleases him in this hurly-burly. Whatever may be the combinations of the generals, the shock of armed masses has incalculable recoils in action, the two plans of the two leaders enter into each other, and are disarranged by each other. Such a point of the battle-field swallows up more combatants than such another, as the more or less spongy soil drinks up water thrown upon it faster or slower. You are obliged to pour out more soldiers there than you thought. An unforeseen expenditure. The line of battle waves and twists like a thread; streams of blood flow regardless of logic; the fronts of the armies undulate; regiments entering or retiring make capes and gulfs; all these shoals are continually swaying back and forth before each other; where infantry was, artillery comes; where artillery was, cavalry rushes up, battalions are smoke. There was something there; look for it; it is gone; the vistas are displaced; the sombre folds advance and recoil; a kind of sepulchral wind pushes forwards, crowds back, swells and disperses these tragic multitudes. What is a hand to hand fight? an oscillation. A rigid mathematical plan tells the story of a minute, and not a day. To paint a battle needs those mighty painters who have chaos in their touch. Rembrandt is better than Vandermeulen. Vandermeulen, exact at noon, lies at three o'clock. Geometry deceives; the hurricane alone is true. This is what gives Folard the right to contradict Polybius. We must add that there is always a certain moment when the battle degenerates into a combat, particu-

larises itself, scatters into innumerable details, which, to borrow
the expression of Napoleon himself, "belong rather to the biography of the regiments than to the history of the army." The
historian, in this case, evidently has the right of abridgment. He
can only seize upon the principal outlines of the struggle, and it
is given to no narrator, however conscientious he may be, to
fix absolutely the form of this horrible cloud which is called a
battle.

This, which is true of all great armed encounters, is particularly applicable to Waterloo.

However, in the afternoon, at a certain moment, the battle
assumed precision.

VI

FOUR O'CLOCK IN THE AFTERNOON

TOWARDS four o'clock the situation of the English army was
serious. The Prince of Orange commanded the centre, Hill the
right wing, Picton the left wing. The Prince of Orange, desperate and intrepid, cried to the Hollando-Belgians: *Nassau! Brunswick! never retreat!* Hill, exhausted, had fallen back upon
Wellington. Picton was dead. At the very moment that the
English had taken from the French the colours of the 105th of
the line, the French had killed General Picton by a ball through
the head. For Wellington the battle had two points of support,
Hougomont and La Haie Sainte; Hougomont still held out, but
was burning; La Haie Sainte had been taken. Of the German
battalion which defended it, forty-two men only survived; all
the officers, except five, were dead or prisoners. Three thousand
combatants were massacred in that grange. A sergeant of the
English Guards, the best boxer in England, reputed invulnerable
by his comrades, had been killed by a little French drummer.
Baring had been dislodged, Alten put to the sword. Several
colours had been lost, one belonging to Alten's division, and
one to the Luneburg battalion, borne by a prince of the family
of Deux-Ponts. The Scotch Grays were no more; Ponsonby's
heavy dragoons had been cut to pieces. That valiant cavalry had
given way before the lancers of Bro and the cuirassiers of Travers; of their twelve hundred horses there remained six hundred;
of three lieutenant-colonels, two lay on the ground, Hamilton
wounded, Mather killed. Ponsonby had fallen, pierced with

seven thrusts of a lance. Gordon was dead, Marsh was dead. Two divisions, the fifth and the sixth, were destroyed.

Hougomont yielding, La Haie Sainte taken, there was but one knot left, the centre. That still held; Wellington reinforced it. He called thither Hill who was at Merbe Braine, and Chassé who was at Braine l'Alleud.

The centre of the English army, slightly concave, very dense and very compact, held a strong position. It occupied the plateau of Mont Saint Jean, with the village behind it and in front the declivity, which at that time was steep. At the rear it rested on this strong stone-house, then an outlying property of Nivelles, which marks the intersection of the roads, a sixteenth-century pile so solid that the balls ricocheted against it without injuring it. All about the plateau, the English had cut away the hedges here and there, made embrasures in the hawthorns, thrust the mouth of a cannon between two branches, made loopholes in the thickets. Their artillery was in ambush under the shrubbery. This punic labour, undoubtedly fair in war, which allows snares, was so well done that Haxo, sent by the emperor at nine o'clock in the morning to reconnoitre the enemy's batteries, saw nothing of it, and returned to tell Napoleon that there was no obstacle, except the two barricades across the Nivelles and Genappe roads. It was the season when grain is at its height; upon the verge of the plateau, a battalion of Kempt's brigade, the 95th, armed with carbines, was lying in the tall wheat.

Thus supported and protected, the centre of the Anglo-Dutch army was well situated.

The danger of this position was the forest of Soignes, then contiguous to the battle-field and separated by the ponds of Groenendael and Boitsfort. An army could not retreat there without being routed; regiments would have been dissolved immediately, and the artillery would have been lost in the swamps. A retreat, according to the opinion of many military men—contested by others, it is true—would have been an utter rout.

Wellington reinforced this centre by one of Chassé's brigades, taken from the right wing, and one of Wincke's from the left in addition to Clinton's division. To his English, to Halkett's regiments, to Mitchell's brigade, to Maitland's guards, he gave as supports the infantry of Brunswick, the Nassau contingent, Kielmansegge's Hanoverians, and Ompteda's Germans. *The right wing*, as Charras says, was bent back behind the centre. An enormous battery was faced with sand-bags at the place where now stands what is called "the Waterloo Museum." Wellington had besides, in a little depression of the ground, Somerset's Horse Guards, fourteen hundred. This was the other half of that English cavalry, so justly celebrated. Ponsonby destroyed, Somerset was left.

The battery, which, finished, would have been almost a redoubt, was disposed behind a very low garden wall, hastily covered with sand-bags and a broad, sloping bank of earth. This work was not finished; they had not time to stockade it.

Wellington, anxious, but impassible, was on horseback, and remained there the whole day in the same attitude, a little in front of the old mill of Mont Saint Jean, which is still standing, under an elm which an Englishman, an enthusiastic vandal, has since bought for two hundred francs, cut down and carried away. Wellington was frigidly heroic. The balls rained down. His aide-de-camp, Gordon, had just fallen at his side. Lord Hill, showing him a bursting shell, said: *My Lord, what are your instructions, and what orders do you leave us, if you allow yourself to be killed?—To follow my example,* answered Wellington. To Clinton, he said laconically: *Hold this spot to the last man.* The day was clearly going badly. Wellington cried to his old companions of Talavera, Vittoria, and Salamanca: *Boys! We must not be beat: what would they say of us in England!*

About four o'clock, the English line staggered backwards. All at once only the artillery and the sharp-shooters were seen on the crest of the plateau, the rest disappeared; the regiments, driven by the shells and bullets of the French, fell back into the valley now crossed by the cow-path of the farm of Mont Saint Jean; a retrograde movement took place, the battle front of the English was slipping away, Wellington gave ground. Beginning retreat! cried Napoleon.

VII
NAPOLEON IN GOOD HUMOUR

THE emperor, although sick and hurt in his saddle by a local affliction, had never been in so good humour as on that day. Since morning, his impenetrable countenance had worn a smile. On the 18th of June, 1815, that profound soul masked in marble, shone obscurely forth. The dark-browed man of Austerlitz was gay at Waterloo. The greatest, when foredoomed, present these contradictions. Our joys are shaded. The perfect smile belongs to God alone.

Ridet Cæsar, Pompeius flebit, said the legionaries of the Fulminatrix Legion. Pompey at this time was not to weep, but it is certain that Cæsar laughed.

From the previous evening, and in the night, at one o'clock, exploring on horseback, in the tempest and the rain, with Bertrand, the hills near Rossomme, and gratified to see the long line of the English fires illuminating all the horizon from Frischemont to Braine l'Alleud, it had seemed to him that destiny, for which he had made an appointment, for a certain day upon the field of Waterloo, was punctual; he stopped his horse, and remained some time motionless, watching the lightning and listening to the thunder; and this fatalist was heard to utter in the darkness these mysterious words: "We are in accord." Napoleon was deceived. They were no longer in accord.

He had not taken a moment's sleep; every instant of that night had brought him a new joy. He passed along the whole line of the advanced guards, stopping here and there to speak to the pickets. At half-past two, near the wood of Hougomont, he heard the tread of a column in march; he thought for a moment that Wellington was falling back. He said: *It is the English rear guard starting to get away. I shall take the six thousand Englishmen who have just arrived at Ostend prisoners.* He chatted freely; he had recovered that animation of the disembarkation of the first of March, when he showed to the Grand Marshal the enthusiastic peasant of Gulf Juan crying: *Well, Bertrand, there is a reinforcement already!* On the night of the 17th of June, he made fun of Wellington: *This little Englishman must have his lesson*, said Napoleon. The rain redoubled; it thundered while the emperor was speaking.

At half-past three in the morning one illusion was gone; officers sent out on a reconnaissance announced to him that the enemy was making no movement. Nothing was stirring, not a bivouac fire was extinguished. The English army was asleep. Deep silence was upon the earth; there was no noise save in the sky. At four o'clock, a peasant was brought to him by the scouts; this peasant had acted as guide to a brigade of English cavalry, probably Vivian's brigade on its way to take position at the village of Ohain, at the extreme left. At five o'clock, two Belgian deserters reported to him that they had just left their regiment, and that the English army was expecting a battle. *So much the better!* exclaimed Napoleon, *I would much rather cut them to pieces than repulse them.*

In the morning, he alighted in the mud, upon the high bank at the corner of the road from Planchenoit, had a kitchen table and a peasant's chair brought from the farm of Rossomme, sat down, with a bunch of straw for a carpet, and spread out upon the table the plan of the battle-field, saying to Soult: "*Pretty chequer-board!*"

In consequence of the night's rain, the convoys of provisions mired in the softened roads, had not arrived at dawn; the soldiers had not slept, and were wet and fasting; but for all this Napoleon cried out joyfully to Ney: *We have ninety chances in a hundred.* At eight o'clock the emperor's breakfast was brought. He had invited several generals. While breakfasting, it was related, that on the night but one before, Wellington was at a ball in Brussels, given by the Duchess of Somerset; and Soult, rude soldier that he was, with his archbishop's face, said: *The ball is to-day.* The emperor jested with Ney, who said: *Wellington will not be so simple as to wait for your majesty.* This was his manner usually. *He was fond of joking,* says Fleury de Chaboulon. *His character at bottom was a playful humour,* says Gourgaud. *He abounded in pleasantries, oftener grotesque than witty,* says Benjamin Constant. These gaieties of a giant are worthy of remembrance. He called his grenadiers "the growlers;" he would pinch their ears and would pull their moustaches. *The emperor did nothing but play tricks on us*; so one of them said. During the mysterious voyage from the island of Elba to France, on the 27th of February, in the open sea, the French brig-of-war *Zephyr* having met the brig *Inconstant,* on which Napoleon was concealed, and having asked the *Inconstant* for news of Napoleon, the emperor, who still had on his hat the white and amaranth cockade, sprinkled with bees, adopted by him in the island of Elba, took the speaking-trumpet, with a laugh, and answered himself: *the emperor is getting on finely.* He who laughs in this way is on familiar terms with events; Napoleon had several of these bursts of laughter during his Waterloo breakfast. After breakfast, for a quarter of an hour, he collected his thoughts; then two generals were seated on the bundle of straw, pen in hand, and paper on knee, and the emperor dictated the order of battle.

At nine o'clock, at the instant when the French army, drawn up and set in motion in five columns, was deployed, the divisions upon two lines, the artillery between the brigades, music at the head, playing marches, with the rolling of drums and the sounding of trumpets—mighty, vast, joyous,—a sea of casques, sabres, and bayonets in the horizon, the emperor, excited, cried out, and repeated: "Magnificent! magnificent!"

Between nine o'clock and half-past ten, the whole army, which seems incredible, had taken position, and was ranged in six lines, forming, to repeat the expression of the emperor, "the figure of six V's." A few moments after the formation of the line of battle, in the midst of this profound silence, like that at the commencement of a storm, which precedes the fight, seeing as they filed by the three batteries of twelve pounders, detached by his orders from the three corps of D'Erlon, Reille, and Lobau, to commence the action by attacking Mont Saint Jean at the intersection of the roads from Nivelles and Genappe, the emperor struck Haxo on the shoulder, saying: *There are twenty-four pretty girls, General.*

Sure of the event, he encouraged with a smile, as they passed before him, the company of sappers of the first corps, which he had designated to erect barricades in Mont Saint Jean, as soon as the village was carried. All this serenity was disturbed by but a word of haughty pity; on seeing, massed at his left, at a place where there is to-day a great tomb, those wonderful Scotch Grays, with their superb horses, he said: "*It is a pity.*"

Then he mounted his horse, rode forward from Rossomme, and chose for his point of view a narrow grassy ridge, at the right of the road from Genappe to Brussels, which was his second station during the battle. The third station, that of seven o'clock between La Belle Alliance and La Haie Sainte, is terrible; it is a considerable hill which can still be seen, and behind which the guard was massed in a depression of the plain. About this hill the balls ricocheted over the paved road up to Napoleon. As at Brienne, he had over his head the whistling of balls and bullets. There have been gathered, almost upon the spot pressed by his horse's feet, crushed bullets, old sabre blades, and shapeless projectiles, eaten with rust. *Scabra rubigine.* Some years ago, a sixty-pound shell was dug up there, still loaded, the fuse having broken off even with the bomb. It was at this last station that the emperor said to his guide Lacoste, a hostile peasant, frightened, tied to a hussar's saddle, turning around at every volley of grape, and trying to hide behind Napoleon: *Dolt, this is shameful. You will get yourself shot in the back.* He who writes these lines has himself found in the loose slope of that hill, by turning up the earth, the remains of a bomb, disintegrated by the rust of forty-six years, and some old bits of iron which broke like alder twigs in his fingers.

The undulations of the diversely inclined plains, which were the theatre of the encounter of Napoleon and Wellington, are, as everybody knows, no longer what they were on the 18th of June, 1815. In taking from that fatal field wherewith to make its monument its real form was destroyed: history, disconcerted, no longer recognises herself upon it. To glorify it, it has been disfigured. Wellington two years afterwards, on seeing Waterloo, exclaimed: *They have changed my battle-field.* Where to-day is the great pyramid of earth surmounted by the lion, there was a ridge which sank away towards the Nivelles road in a practicable slope, but which, above the Genappe road, was almost an escarpment. The elevation of this escarpment may be measured to-day by the height of the two great burial mounds which embank the road from Genappe to Brussels; the English tomb at the left, the German tomb at the right. There is no French tomb. For France that whole plain is a sepulchre. Thanks to thousands and thousands of loads of earth used in the mound of a hundred and fifty feet high and a half a mile in circuit, the plateau of Mont Saint Jean is accessible by a gentle slope; on the day of the battle, especially on the side of La Haie Sainte, the declivity was steep and abrupt. The descent was there so precipitous that the English artillery did not see the farm below them at the bottom of the valley, the centre of the combat. On the 18th of June, 1815, the rain had gullied out this steep descent still more; the mud made the ascent still more difficult; it was not merely laborious, but men actually stuck in the mire. Along the crest of the plateau ran a sort of ditch, which could not possibly have been suspected by a distant observer.

What was this ditch? we will tell. Braine l'Alleud is a village of Belgium, Ohain is another. These villages, both hidden by the curving of the ground, are connected by a road about four miles long which crosses an undulating plain, often burying itself in the hills like a furrow, so that at certain points it is a ravine. In 1815, as now, this road cut the crest of the plateau of Mont Saint Jean between the two roads from Genappe and Nivelles; only, to-day it is on a level with the plain; whereas then it was sunk between high banks. Its two slopes were taken away for the monumental mound. That road was and is still a trench for the greater part of its length; a trench in some parts a dozen feet deep, the slopes of which are so steep as to slide down here and there, especially in winter, after showers. Accidents happen there. The road was so narrow at the entrance of Braine l'Alleud that a traveller was once crushed by a wagon, as is attested by a stone cross standing near the cemetery, which gives the name of the dead, *Monsieur Bernard Debrye, merchant of Brussels*, and the date of the accident, February, 1637.* It was so deep at the plateau of Mont Saint Jean, that a peasant, Matthew Nicaise, had been crushed there in 1783 by the falling of the bank, as another stone cross attested; the top of this has disappeared in the changes, but its overturned pedestal is still visible upon the sloping bank at the left of the road between La Haie Sainte and the farm of Mont Saint Jean.

On the day of the battle, this sunken road, of which nothing gave warning, along the crest of Mont Saint Jean, a ditch at the summit of the escarpment, a trench concealed by the ground, was invisible, that is to say terrible.

VIII

THE EMPEROR PUTS A QUESTION TO THE GUIDE LACOSTE

On the morning of Waterloo then, Napoleon was satisfied.

He was right; the plan of battle which he had conceived, as we have shown, was indeed admirable.

After the battle was once commenced, its very diverse

---

* The inscription is as follows:

> DOM CY A ETE ECRASE
> PAR MALHEUR
> SOUS UN CHARIOT
> MONSIEUR BERNARD
> DE BRYE MARCHAND
> A BRUXELLE LE (illegible)
> FEVRIER 1637

fortune, the resistance of Hougomont, the tenacity of La Haie Sainte, Bauduin killed, Foy put *hors de combat*, the unexpected wall against which Soye's brigade was broken, the fatal blunder of Guilleminot in having neither grenades nor powder, the miring of the batteries, the fifteen pieces without escort cut off by Uxbridge in a deep cut of a road, the slight effect of the bombs that fell within the English lines, burying themselves in the soil softened by the rain and only succeeding in making volcanoes of mud, so that the explosion was changed into a splash, the uselessness of Piré's demonstration upon Braine l'Alleud, all this cavalry, fifteen squadrons, almost destroyed, the English right wing hardly disturbed, the left wing hardly moved, the strange mistake of Ney in massing, instead of drawing out, the four divisions of the first corps, the depth of twenty-seven ranks and the front of two hundred men offered up in this manner to grape, the frightful gaps made by the balls in these masses, the lack of connection between the attacking columns, the slanting battery suddenly unmasked upon their flank, Bourgeois, Donzelot, and Durutte entangled, Quiot repulsed, Lieutenant Vieux, that Hercules sprung from the Polytechnic School, wounded at the moment when he was beating down with the blows of an axe the door of La Haie Sainte under the plunging fire of the English barricade barring the turn of the road from Genappe to Brussels, Marcognet's division, caught between infantry and cavalry, shot down at arm's length in the wheat field by Best and Pack, sabred by Ponsonby, his battery of seven pieces spiked, the Prince of Saxe Weimar holding and keeping Frischemont and Smohain in spite of Count D'Erlon, the colours of the 105th taken, the colours of the 43rd taken, this Prussian Black Hussar, brought in by the scouts of the flying column of three hundred chasseurs scouring the country between Wavre and Planchenoit, the disquieting things that this prisoner had said, Grouchy's delay, the fifteen hundred men killed in less than an hour in the orchard of Hougomont, the eighteen hundred men fallen in still less time around La Haie Sainte—all these stormy events, passing like battle clouds before Napoleon, had hardly disturbed his countenance, and had not darkened its imperial expression of certainty. Napoleon was accustomed to look upon war fixedly; he never made figure by figure the tedious addition of details; the figures mattered little to him, provided they gave this total: Victory; though beginnings went wrong he was not alarmed at it, he who believed himself master and possessor of the end; he knew how to wait, believing himself beyond contingency, and he treated destiny as an equal treats an equal. He appeared to say to Fate: thou would'st not dare.

Half light and half shadow, Napoleon felt himself protected in the right, and tolerated in the wrong. He had, or believed that he had, a connivance, one might almost say complicity, with events, equivalent to the ancient invulnerability.

However, when one has Beresina, Leipsic, and Fontainebleau behind him, it seems as if he might distrust Waterloo. A mysterious frown is becoming visible in the depths of the sky.

At the moment when Wellington drew back, Napoleon started up. He saw the plateau of Mont Saint Jean suddenly laid bare, and the front of the English army disappear. It rallied, but kept concealed. The emperor half rose in his stirrups. The flash of victory passed into his eyes.

Wellington hurled back on the forest of Soignes and destroyed; that was the final overthrow of England by France, it was Cressy, Poitiers, Malplaquet, and Ramillies avenged. The man of Marengo was wiping out Agincourt.

The emperor then, contemplating this terrible turn of fortune, swept his glass for the last time over every point of the battle-field. His guard standing behind with grounded arms, looked up to him with a sort of religion. He was reflecting; he was examining the slopes, noting the ascents, scrutinising the tuft of trees, the square rye field, the footpath; he seemed to count every bush. He looked for some time at the English barricades on the two roads, two large abattis of trees, that on the Genappe road above La Haie Sainte, armed with two cannon, which alone, of all the English artillery, bore upon the bottom of the field of battle, and that of the Nivelles road where glistened the Dutch bayonets of Chassé's brigade. He noticed near that barricade the old chapel of Saint Nicholas painted white, which is at the corner of the cross-road toward Braine l'Alleud. He bent over and spoke in an under tone to the guide Lacoste. The guide made a negative sign of the head, probably treacherous.

The emperor rose up and reflected. Wellington had fallen back. It remained only to complete this repulse by a crushing charge.

Napoleon, turning abruptly, sent off a courier at full speed to Paris to announce that the battle was won.

Napoleon was one of those geniuses who rule the thunder. He had found his thunderbolt.

He ordered Milhaud's cuirassiers to carry the plateau of Mont Saint Jean.

IX
THE UNLOOKED FOR

THEY were three thousand five hundred. They formed a line of half a mile. They were gigantic men on colossal horses. There were twenty-six squadrons, and they had behind them, as a support, the division of Lefebvre Desnouettes, the hundred and six gendarmes d'élite, the Chasseurs of the Guard, eleven hundred and ninety-seven men, and the Lancers of the Guard, eight hundred and eighty lances. They wore casques without plumes, and cuirasses of wrought iron, with horse pistols in their holsters, and long sabre-swords. In the morning, they had been the admiration of the whole army, when at nine o'clock, with trumpets sounding, and all the bands playing, *Veillons au salut de l'empire*, they came, in heavy column, one of their batteries on their flank, the other at their centre, and deployed in two ranks between the Genappe road and Frischemont, and took their position of battle in this powerful second line, so wisely made up by Napoleon, which, having at its extreme left the cuirassiers of Kellermann, and at its extreme right the cuirassiers of Milhaud, had, so to speak, two wings of iron.

Aide-de-camp Bernard brought them the emperor's order. Ney drew his sword and placed himself at their head. The enormous squadrons began to move.

Then was seen a fearful sight.

All this cavalry, with sabres drawn, banners waving and trumpets sounding, formed in column by division, descended with an even movement and as one man—with the precision of a bronze battering-ram opening a breach—the hill of La Belle Alliance, sank into that formidable depth where so many men had already fallen, disappeared in the smoke, then, rising from this valley of shadow, reappeared on the other side, still compact and serried, mounting at full trot, through a cloud of grape emptying itself upon them, the frightful acclivity of mud of the plateau of Mont Saint Jean. They rose, serious, menacing, imperturbable; in the intervals of the musketry and artillery could be heard the sound of this colossal tramp. Being in two divisions, they formed two columns; Wathier's division had the right, Delord's the left. From a distance they would be taken for two immense serpents of steel stretching themselves towards the crest of the plateau. That ran through the battle like a prodigy.

Nothing like it had been seen since the taking of the grand redoubt at La Moscowa by the heavy cavalry; Murat was not there, but Ney was there. It seemed as if this mass had become a monster and had but a single mind. Each squadron undulated and swelled like the ring of a polyp. They could be seen through the thick smoke, as it was broken here and there. It was one pell-mell of casques, cries, sabres; a furious bounding of horses among the cannon, and the flourish of trumpets, a terrible and disciplined tumult; over all, the cuirasses, like the scales of a hydra.

These recitals appear to belong to another age. Something like this vision appeared, doubtless, in the old Orphic epics which tell of centaurs, antique hippanthropes, those titans with human faces and chests like horses, whose gallop scaled Olympus, horrible, invulnerable, sublime; at once gods and beasts.

An odd numerical coincidence, twenty-six battalions were to receive these twenty-six squadrons. Behind the crest of the plateau under cover of the masked battery, the English infantry, formed in thirteen squares, two battalions to the square, and upon two lines—seven on the first, and six on the second—with musket to the shoulder, and eye upon their sights, waiting calm, silent, and immovable. They could not see the cuirassiers, and the cuirassiers could not see them. They listened to the rising of this tide of men. They heard the increasing sound of three thousand horses, the alternate and measured striking of their hoofs at full trot, the rattling of the cuirasses, the clicking of the sabres, and a sort of fierce roar of the coming host. There was a moment of fearful silence, then, suddenly, a long line of raised arms brandishing sabres appeared above the crest, with casques, trumpets, and standards, and three thousand faces with grey moustaches, crying, Vive l'empereur! All this cavalry debouched on the plateau, and it was like the beginning of an earthquake.

All at once, tragic to relate, at the left of the English, and on our right, the head of the column of cuirassiers reared with a frightful clamour. Arrived at the culminating point of the crest, unmanageable, full of fury, and bent upon the extermination of the squares and cannons, the cuirassiers saw between themselves and the English a ditch, a grave. It was the sunken road of Ohain.

It was a frightful moment. There was the ravine, unlooked for, yawning at the very feet of the horses, two fathoms deep between its double slope. The second rank pushed in the first, the third pushed in the second; the horses reared, threw themselves over, fell upon their backs, and struggled with their feet in the air, piling up and overturning their riders; no power to retreat; the whole column was nothing but a projectile. The force acquired to crush the English crushed the French. The inexorable ravine could not yield until it was filled; riders and horses rolled in together pell-mell, grinding each other, making common flesh in this dreadful gulf, and when this grave was full of living men, the rest marched over them and passed on. Almost a third of Dubois' brigade sank into this abyss.

Here the loss of the battle began.

A local tradition, which evidently exaggerates, says that two thousand horses and fifteen hundred men were buried in the sunken road of Ohain. This undoubtedly comprises all the other bodies thrown into this ravine on the morrow after the battle.

Napoleon, before ordering this charge of Milhaud's cuirassiers, had examined the ground, but could not see this hollow road, which did not make even a wrinkle on the surface of the plateau. Warned, however, and put on his guard by the little white chapel which marks its junction with the Nivelles road, he had, probably on the contingency of an obstacle, put a question to the guide Lacoste. The guide had answered no. It may almost be said that from this shake of a peasant's head came the catastrophe of Napoleon.

Still other fatalities must arise.

Was it possible that Napoleon should win this battle? We answer no. Why? Because of Wellington? Because of Blücher? No. Because of God.

For Bonaparte to be conqueror at Waterloo was not in the law of the nineteenth century. Another series of facts were preparing in which Napoleon had no place. The ill-will of events had long been announced.

It was time that this vast man should fall.

The excessive weight of this man in human destiny disturbed the equilibrium. This individual counted, of himself alone, more than the universe besides. These plethoras of all human vitality concentrated in a single head, the world mounting to the brain of one man, would be fatal to civilisation if they should endure. The moment had come for incorruptible supreme equity to look to it. Probably the principles and elements upon which regular gravitations in the moral order as well as in the material depend, began to murmur. Reeking blood, over-crowded cemeteries, weeping mothers—these are formidable pleaders. When the earth is suffering from a surcharge, there are mysterious moanings from the deeps which the heavens hear.

Napoleon had been impeached before the Infinite, and his fall was decreed.

He vexed God.

Waterloo is not a battle; it is the change of front of the universe.

X

THE PLATEAU OF MONT SAINT JEAN

At the same time with the ravine, the artillery was unmasked.

Sixty cannon and the thirteen squares thundered and flashed into the cuirassiers. The brave General Delord gave the military salute to the English battery.

All the English flying artillery took position in the squares at a gallop. The cuirassiers had not even time to breathe. The disaster of the sunken road had decimated, but not discouraged them. They were men who, diminished in number, grew greater in heart.

Wathier's column alone had suffered from the disaster; Delord's, which Ney had sent obliquely to the left, as if he had a presentiment of the snare, arrived entire.

The cuirassiers hurled themselves upon the English squares.

At full gallop, with free rein, their sabres in their teeth, and their pistols in their hands, the attack began.

There are moments in battle when the soul hardens a man even to changing the soldier into a statue, and all this flesh becomes granite. The English battalions, desperately assailed, did not yield an inch.

Then it was frightful.

All sides of the English squares were attacked at once. A whirlwind of frenzy enveloped them. This frigid infantry remained impassible. The first rank, with knee on the ground, received the cuirassiers on their bayonets, the second shot them down; behind the second rank, the cannoneers loaded their guns, the front of the square opened, made way for an eruption of grape, and closed again. The cuirassiers answered by rushing upon them with crushing force. Their great horses reared, trampled upon the ranks, leaped over the bayonets and fell, gigantic, in the midst of these four living walls. The balls made gaps in the ranks of the cuirassiers, the cuirassiers made breaches in the squares. Files of men disappeared, ground down beneath the horses' feet. Bayonets were buried in the bellies of these centaurs. Hence a monstrosity of wounds never perhaps seen elsewhere. The squares, consumed by this furious cavalry, closed up without wavering. Inexhaustible in grape, they kept up an explosion in the midst of their assailants. It was a monstrous sight. These squares were battalions no longer, they were craters; these cuirassiers were cavalry no longer, they were a tempest. Each square was a volcano attacked by a thunder-cloud; the lava fought with the lightning.

The square on the extreme right, the most exposed of all, being in the open field, was almost annihilated at the first shock. It was formed of the 75th regiment of Highlanders. The piper in the centre, while the work of extermination was going on, profoundly oblivious of all about him, casting down his melancholy eye full of the shadows of forest and lakes, seated upon a drum, his bagpipe under his arm, was playing his mountain airs. These Scotchmen died thinking of Ben Lothian, as the Greeks died remembering Argos. The sabre of a cuirassier, striking down the pibroch and the arm which bore it, caused the strain to cease by killing the player.

The cuirassiers, relatively few in number, lessened by the catastrophe of the ravine, had to contend with almost the whole of the English army, but they multiplied themselves, each man became equal to ten. Nevertheless some Hanoverian battalions fell back. Wellington saw it and remembered his cavalry. Had Napoleon, at that very moment, remembered his infantry, he would have won the battle. This forgetfulness was his great fatal blunder.

Suddenly the assailing cuirassiers perceived that they were assailed. The English cavalry was upon their back. Before them the squares, behind them Somerset; Somerset, with the fourteen hundred dragoon guards. Somerset had on his right Dornberg with his German light-horse, and on his left Trip, with the Belgian carbineers. The cuirassiers, attacked front, flank, and rear, by infantry and cavalry, were compelled to face in all directions. What was that to them? They were a whirlwind. Their valour became unspeakable.

Besides, they had behind them the ever thundering artillery. All that was necessary in order to wound such men in the back. One of their cuirasses, with a hole in the left shoulder-plate made by a musket ball, is in the collection of the Waterloo Museum.

With such Frenchmen only such Englishmen could cope.

It was no longer a conflict, it was a darkness, a fury, a giddy vortex of souls and courage, a hurricane of sword-flashes. In an instant the fourteen hundred horse guards were but eight hundred; Fuller, their lieutenant, fell dead. Ney rushed up with the lancers and chasseurs of Lefebvre-Desnouettes. The plateau of Mont Saint Jean was taken, retaken, taken again. The cuirassiers left the cavalry to return to the infantry, or more correctly, all this terrible multitude wrestled with each other without letting go their hold. The squares still held. There were twelve assaults. Ney had four horses killed under him. Half of the cuirassiers lay on the plateau. This struggle lasted two hours.

The English army was terribly shaken. There is no doubt, if they had not been crippled in their first shock by the disaster of the sunken road, the cuirassiers would have overwhelmed the centre and decided the victory. This wonderful cavalry astounded Clinton, who had seen Talavera and Badajos. Wellington, though three-fourths conquered, was struck with heroic admiration. He said in a low voice: "splendid!"

The cuirassiers annihilated seven squares out of thirteen, took or spiked sixty pieces of cannon, and took from the English regiments six colours, which three cuirassiers and three chasseurs of the guard carried to the emperor before the farm of La Belle Alliance.

The situation of Wellington was growing worse. This strange battle was like a duel between two wounded infuriates who, while yet fighting and resisting, lose all their blood. Which of the two shall fall first?

The struggle of the plateau continued.

How far did the cuirassiers penetrate? None can tell. One thing is certain: the day after the battle, a cuirassier and his horse were found dead under the frame of the hay-scales at Mont Saint Jean, at the point where the four roads from Nivelles, Genappe, La Hulpe, and Brussels meet. This horseman had pierced the English lines. One of the men who took away the body still lives at Mont Saint Jean. His name is Dehaze; he was then eighteen years old.

Wellington felt that he was giving way. The crisis was upon him.

The cuirassiers had not succeeded, in this sense, that the centre was not broken. All holding the plateau, nobody held it, and in fact it remained for the most part with the English. Wellington held the village and the crowning plain; Ney held only the crest and the slope. On both sides they seemed rooted in this funeral soil.

But the enfeeblement of the English appeared irremediable. The hæmorrhage of this army was horrible. Kempt, on the left wing, called for reinforcements. "*Impossible*," answered Wellington; "*we must die on the spot we now occupy.*" Almost at the same moment—singular coincidence which depicts the exhaustion of both armies—Ney sent to Napoleon for infantry, and Napoleon exclaimed: "*Infantry! where does he expect me to take them! Does he expect me to make them?*"

However, the English army was farthest gone. The furious onslaughts of these great squadrons with iron cuirasses and steel breastplates had ground up the infantry. A few men about a flag marked the place of a regiment; battalions were now commanded by captains or lieutenants. Alten's division, already so cut up at La Haie Sainte, was almost destroyed; the intrepid Belgians of Van Kluze's brigade strewed the rye field along the Nivelles road; there were hardly any left of those Dutch grenadiers who, in 1811, joined to our ranks in Spain, fought against Wellington, and who, in 1815, rallied on the English side, fought against Napoleon. The loss in officers was heavy. Lord Uxbridge, who buried his leg next day, had a knee fractured. If, on the side of the French, in this struggle of the cuirassiers, Delord, l'Heritier, Colbert, Dnop, Travers, and Blancard were *hors de combat*, on the side of the English Alten was wounded, Barne was wounded, Delancey was killed, Van Meeren was killed, Ompteda was killed, the entire staff of Wellington was decimated, and England had the worst share in this balance of blood. The second regiment of foot guards had lost five lieutenant-colonels, four captains, and three ensigns; the first battalion of the thirtieth infantry had lost twenty-four officers and one hundred and twelve soldiers; the seventy-ninth High-landers had twenty-four officers wounded, eighteen officers killed, and four hundred and fifty soldiers slain. Cumberland's Hanoverian hussars, an entire regiment, having at its head Col-onel Hacke, who was afterwards court-martialled and broken, had drawn rein before the fight, and were in flight in the Forest of Soignes, spreading the panic as far as Brussels. Carts, ammu-nition-wagons, baggage-wagons, ambulances full of wounded, seeing the French gain ground and approach the forest, fled precipitately; the Dutch, sabred by the French cavalry, cried murder! From Vert-Coucou to Groenendael, for a distance of nearly six miles in the direction towards Brussels, the roads, according to the testimony of witnesses still alive, were choked with fugitives. This panic was such that it reached the Prince of Condé at Malines, and Louis XVIII. at Ghent. With the excep-tion of the small reserve drawn up in echelon behind the hos-pital established at the farm of Mont Saint Jean, and the brigades of Vivian and Vandeleur on the flank of the left wing, Welling-ton's cavalry was exhausted. A number of batteries lay dis-mounted. These facts are confessed by Siborne; and Pringle, exaggerating the disaster, says even that the Anglo-Dutch army was reduced to thirty-four thousand men. The Iron Duke remained calm, but his lips were pale. The Austrian Commis-sary, Vincent, the Spanish Commissary, Olava, present at the battle in the English staff, thought the duke was beyond hope. At five o'clock Wellington drew out his watch, and was heard to murmur these sombre words: *Blücher, or night!*

It was about this time that a distant line of bayonets glistened on the heights beyond Frischemont.

Here is the turning-point in this colossal drama.

XI

SAD GUIDE FOR NAPOLEON; GOOD GUIDE FOR BULOW

WE understand the bitter mistake of Napoleon; Grouchy hoped for, Blücher arriving; death instead of life.

Destiny has such turnings. Awaiting the world's throne, Saint Helena became visible.

If the little cow-boy, who acted as guide to Bulow, Blücher's lieutenant, had advised him to debouch from the forest above Frischemont rather than below Planchenoit, the shaping of the nineteenth century would perhaps have been different. Napoleon would have won the battle of Waterloo. By any other road than below Planchenoit, the Prussian army would have brought up at a ravine impassable for artillery, and Bulow would not have arrived.

Now, an hour of delay, as the Prussian general Muffling declares, and Blücher would not have found Wellington in position; "the battle was lost."

It was time, we have seen, that Bulow should arrive. He had bivouacked at Dion le Mont, and started on at dawn. But the roads were impracticable, and his division stuck in the mire. The cannon sank to the hubs in the ruts. Furthermore, he had to cross the Dyle on the narrow bridge of Wavre; the street leading to the bridge had been fired by the French; the caissons and artillery wagons, being unable to pass between two rows of burning houses, had to wait till the fire was extinguished. It was noon before Bulow could reach Chapelle Saint Lambert.

Had the action commenced two hours earlier, it would have been finished at four o'clock, and Blücher would have fallen upon a field already won by Napoleon. Such are these immense chances, proportioned to an infinity, which we cannot grasp.

As early as mid-day, the emperor, first of all, with his field glass, perceived in the extreme horizon something which fixed his attention. He said: "I see yonder a cloud which appears to me to be troops." Then he asked the Duke of Dalmatia: "Soult, what do you see towards Chapelle Saint Lambert?" The marshal, turning his glass that way, answered: "Four or five thousand men, sire. Grouchy, of course." Meanwhile it remained motionless in the haze. The glasses of the whole staff studied "the cloud" pointed out by the emperor. Some said: "They are columns halting." The most said: "It is trees." The fact is, that the cloud did not stir. The emperor detached Domon's division of light cavalry to reconnoitre this obscure point.

Bulow, in fact, had not moved. His vanguard was very weak, and could do nothing. He had to wait for the bulk of his *corps d'armée*, and he was ordered to concentrate his force before entering into line; but at five o'clock, seeing Wellington's peril, Blücher ordered Bulow to attack, and uttered these remarkable words: "We must give the English army a breathing spell."

Soon after the divisions of Losthin, Hiller, Hacke, and Ryssel deployed in front of Lobau's corps, the cavalry of Prince William of Prussia debouched from the wood of Paris, Planchenoit was in flames, and the Prussian balls began to rain down even in the ranks of the guard in reserve behind Napoleon.

XII
THE GUARD

THE rest is known; the irruption of a third army, the battle thrown out of joint, eighty-six pieces of artillery suddenly thundering forth, Pirch the First coming up with Bulow, Ziethen's cavalry led by Blücher in person, the French crowded back, Marcognet swept from the plateau of Ohain, Durutte dislodged from Papelotte, Donzelot and Quiot recoiling, Lobau taken en echarpe, a new battle falling at night-fall upon our dismantled regiments, the whole English line assuming the offensive and pushed forward, the gigantic gap made in the French army, the English grape and the Prussian grape lending mutual aid, extermination, disaster in front, disaster in flank, the guard entering into line amid this terrible crumbling.

Feeling that they were going to their death, they cried out: *Vive l'Empereur!* There is nothing more touching in history than this death agony bursting forth in acclamations.

The sky had been overcast all day. All at once, at this very moment—it was eight o'clock at night—the clouds in the horizon broke, and through the elms on the Nivelles road streamed the sinister red light of the setting sun. The rising sun shone upon Austerlitz.

Each battalion of the guard, for this final effort, was commanded by a general. Friant, Michel, Roguet, Harlet, Mallet, Poret de Morvan, were there. When the tall caps of the grenadiers of the guard with their large eagle plates appeared, symmetrical, drawn up in line, calm, in the smoke of that conflict, the enemy felt respect for France; they thought they saw twenty victories entering upon the field of battle, with wings extended, and those who were conquerors, thinking themselves conquered, recoiled; but Wellington cried: "*Up, guards, and at them!*"

The red regiment of English guards, lying behind the hedges, rose up, a shower of grape riddled the tri-coloured flag fluttering about our eagles, all hurled themselves forward, and the final carnage began. The Imperial Guard felt the army slipping away around them in the gloom, and the vast overthrow of the rout; they heard the *sauve qui peut!* which had replaced the *vive l'Empereur!* and, with flight behind them, they held on their course, battered more and more and dying faster and faster at every step. There were no weak souls or cowards there. The privates of that band were as heroic as their generals. Not a man flinched from the suicide.

Ney, desperate, great in all the grandeur of accepted death, bared himself to every blow in this tempest. He had his horse killed under him. Reeking with sweat, fire in his eyes, froth upon his lips, his uniform unbuttoned, one of his epaulettes half cut away by the sabre stroke of a horse-guard, his badge of the grand eagle pierced by a ball, bloody, covered with mud, magnificent, a broken sword in his hand, he said: "*Come and see how a marshal of France dies upon the field of battle!*" But in vain, he did not die. He was haggard and exasperated. He flung this question at Drouet D'Erlon. "*What! are you not going to die?*" He cried out in the midst of all this artillery which was mowing down a handful of men: "*Is there nothing, then, for me? Oh! I would that all these English balls were buried in my body!*" Unhappy man! thou wast reserved for French bullets!

XIII
THE CATASTROPHE

THE route behind the guard was dismal.

The army fell back rapidly from all sides at once, from Hougomont, from La Haie Sainte, from Papelotte, from Planchenoit. The cry: *Treachery!* was followed by the cry: *Sauve qui peut!* A disbanding army is a thaw. The whole bends, cracks, snaps, floats, rolls, falls, crashes, hurries, plunges. Mysterious disintegration. Ney borrows a horse, leaps upon him, and without hat, cravat, or sword, plants himself in the Brussels road, arresting at once the English and the French. He endeavours to hold the army, he calls them back, he reproaches them, he grapples with the rout. He is swept away. The soldiers flee from him, crying: *Vive Marshal Ney!* Durutte's two regiments come and go, frightened, and tossed between the sabres of the Uhlans and the fire of the brigades of Kempt, Best, Pack, and Rylandt; rout is the worst of all conflicts; friends slay each other in their flight; squadrons and battalions are crushed and dispersed against each other, enormous foam of the battle. Lobau at one extremity, like Reille, at the other, is rolled away in the flood. In vain does Napoleon make walls with the remains of the guard; in vain does he expend his reserve squadron in a last effort. Quiot gives way before Vivian, Kellermann before Vandeleur, Lobau before Bulow, Moraud before Pirch, Domon and Lubervic before Prince William of Prussia. Guyot, who had led the emperor's squadrons to the charge, falls under the feet of the English horse. Napoleon gallops along the fugitives, harangues them, urges, threatens, entreats. The mouths, which in the morning were crying *vive l'Empereur!*, are now agape; he is hardly recognised. The Prussian cavalry, just come up, spring forward, fling themselves upon the enemy, sabre, cut, hack, kill, exterminate. Teams rush off, the guns are left to the care of themselves; the soldiers of the train unhitch the caissons and take the horses to escape; wagons upset, with their four wheels in the air, block up the road, and are accessories of massacre. They crush and they crowd; they trample upon the living and the dead. Arms are broken. A multitude fills roads, paths, bridges, plains, hills, valleys, woods, choked up by this flight of forty thousand men. Cries, despair, knapsacks and muskets cast into the rye, passage forced at the point of the sword; no more comrades, no more officers, no more generals; inexpressible dismay. Ziethen sabring France at his ease. Lions become kids. Such was this flight.

At Genappe there was an effort to turn back, to form a line, to make a stand. Lobau rallied three hundred men. The entrance to the village was barricaded, but at the first volley of Prussian grape, all took to flight again, and Lobau was captured. The marks of that volley of grape are still to be seen upon the old gable of a brick ruin at the right of the road, a short distance before entering Genappe. The Prussians rushed into Genappe, furious, doubtless, at having conquered so little. The pursuit was monstrous. Blücher gave orders to kill all. Roguet had set this sad example by threatening with death every French grenadier who should bring him a Prussian prisoner. Blücher surpassed Roguet. The general of the Young Guard, Duhesme, caught at the door of a tavern in Genappe, gave up his sword to a Hussar of Death, who took the sword and killed the prisoner. The victory was completed by the assassination of the vanquished. Let us punish, since we are history: old Blücher disgraced himself. This ferocity filled the disaster to the brim. The desperate rout passed through Genappe, passed through Quatre Bras, passed through Sombreffe, passed through Frasnes, passed through Thuin, passed through Charleroi, and stopped only at the frontier. Alas! who now was flying in such wise? The Grand Army.

This madness, this terror, this falling to ruins of the highest bravery which ever astonished history, can that be without cause? No. The shadow of an enormous right hand rests on Waterloo. It is the day of Destiny. A power above man controlled that day. Hence, the loss of mind in dismay; hence, all these great souls yielding up their swords. Those who had conquered Europe fell to the ground, having nothing more to say or to do, feeling a terrible presence in the darkness. *Hoc erat in fatis.* That day, the perspective of the human race changed. Waterloo is the hinge of the nineteenth century. This disappearance of the great man was necessary for the advent of the great century. One, to whom there is no reply, took it in charge. The panic of heroes is explained. In the battle of Waterloo, there is more than a cloud, there is a meteor. God passed over it.

In the gathering night, on a field near Genappe, Bernard and Bertrand seized by a flap of his coat and stopped a haggard, thoughtful, gloomy man, who, dragged thus far by the current of the rout, had dismounted, passed the bridle of his horse under his arm, and, with bewildered eye, was returning alone towards Waterloo. It was Napoleon endeavouring to advance again, mighty somnambulist of a vanished dream.

XIV
THE LAST SQUARE

A FEW squares of the guard, immovable in the flow of the rout as rocks in running water, held out until night. Night approaching, and death also, they waited this double shadow, and yielded unfaltering, to its embrace. Each regiment, isolated from the others, and having no further communication with the army, which was broken in all directions, was dying alone. They had taken position, for this last struggle, some upon the heights of Rossomme, others in the plain of Mont Saint Jean. There, abandoned, conquered, terrible, these sombre squares suffered formidable martyrdom. Ulm, Wagram, Jena, Friedland, were dying in them.

At dusk, towards nine o'clock in the evening, at the foot of the plateau of Mont Saint Jean, there remained but one. In this fatal valley, at the bottom of that slope which had been climbed by the cuirassiers, inundated now by the English masses, under the converging fire of the victorious artillery of the enemy, under a frightful storm of projectiles, this square fought on. It was commanded by an obscure officer whose name was Cambronne. At every discharge, the square grew less, but returned the fire. It replied to grape by bullets, narrowing in its four walls continually. Afar off the fugitives, stopping for a moment out of breath, heard in the darkness this dismal thunder decreasing.

When this legion was reduced to a handful, when their flag was reduced to a shred, when their muskets, exhausted of ammunition, were reduced to nothing but clubs, when the pile of corpses was larger than the group of the living, there spread among the conquerors a sort of sacred terror about these sublime martyrs, and the English artillery, stopping to take breath, was silent. It was a kind of respite. These combatants had about them, as it were, a swarm of spectres, the outlines of men on horseback, the black profile of the cannons, the white sky seen through the wheels and the gun-carriages; the colossal death's head which heroes always see in the smoke of the battle was advancing upon them, and glaring at them. They could hear in the gloom of the twilight the loading of the pieces, the lighted matches like tigers' eyes in the night made a circle about their heads; all the linstocks of the English batteries approached the guns, when, touched by their heroism, holding the death-moment suspended over these men, an English general, Colville, according to some, Maitland, according to others, cried to them: "Brave Frenchman, surrender!" Cambronne answered: "*Merde!*"

XV
CAMBRONNE

OUT of respect to the French reader, the finest word, perhaps, that a Frenchman ever uttered cannot be repeated to him. We are prohibited from embalming a sublimity in history.

At our own risk and peril, we violate that prohibition.

Among these giants, then, there was one Titan—Cambronne.

To speak that word, and then to die, what could be more grand! for to accept death is to die, and it is not the fault of this man, if, in the storm of grape, he survived.

The man who won the battle of Waterloo is not Napoleon put to rout nor Wellington giving way at four o'clock, desperate at five; not Blücher, who did not fight; the man who won the battle of Waterloo was Cambronne.

To fulminate such a word at the thunderbolt which kills you is victory.

To make this answer to disaster, to say this to destiny, to give this base for the future lion, to fling down this reply at the rain of the previous night, at the treacherous wall of Hougomont, at the sunken road of Ohain, at the delay of Grouchy, at the arrival of Blücher, to be ironical in the sepulchre, to act so as to remain upright after one shall have fallen, to drown in two syllables the European coalition, to offer to kings these privities already known to the Cæsars, to make the last of words the first, by associating it with the glory of France, to close Waterloo insolently by a Mardi Gras, to complete Leonidas by Rabelais, to sum up this victory in a supreme word which cannot be pronounced, to lose the field, and to preserve history, after this carnage to have the laugh on his side, is immense.

It is an insult to the thunderbolt. That attains the grandeur of Æschylus.

This word of Cambronne's gives the effect of a fracture. It is the breaking of a heart by scorn; it is an overplus of agony in explosion. Who conquered? Wellington? No. Without Blücher he would have been lost. Blücher? No. If Wellington had not commenced, Blücher could not have finished. This Cambronne, this passer at the last hour, this unknown soldier, this infinitesimal of war, feels that there is a lie in a catastrophe, doubly bitter; and at the moment when he is bursting with rage, he is offered this mockery—life? How can he restrain himself? They are there, all the kings of Europe, the fortunate generals, the thundering Joves, they have a hundred thousand victorious soldiers, and behind the hundred thousand, a million; their guns, with matches lighted, are agape; they have the Imperial Guard and the Grand Army under their feet; they have crushed

Napoleon, and Cambronne only remains; there is none but this worm of the earth to protest. He will protest. Then he seeks for a word as one seeks for a sword. He froths at the mouth, and this froth is the word. Before this mean and monstrous victory, before this victory without victors, this desperate man straightens himself up, he suffers its enormity, but he establishes its nothingness; and he does more than spit upon it; and overwhelmed in numbers and material strength he finds in the soul an expression—ordure. We repeat it, to say that, to do that, to find that, is to be the conqueror.

The soul of great days entered into this unknown man at that moment of death. Cambronne finds the word of Waterloo, as Rouget de l'Isle finds the Marseillaise, through a superior inspiration. An effluence from the divine afflatus detaches itself, and passes over these men, and they tremble, and the one sings the supreme song, and the other utters the terrible cry. This word of titanic scorn Cambronne throws down not merely to Europe, in the name of the Empire, that would be but little; he throws it down to the past, in the name of the Revolution. It is heard, and men recognise in Cambronne the old soul of the giants. It seems as if it were a speech of Danton, or a roar of Kléber.

To this word of Cambronne, the English voice replied: "Fire!" the batteries flamed, the hill trembled, from all those brazen throats went forth a final vomiting of grape, terrific; a vast smoke, dusky white in the light of the rising moon, rolled out, and when the smoke was dissipated, there was nothing left. That formidable remnant was annihilated; the guard was dead. The four walls of the living redoubt had fallen, hardly could a quivering be distinguished here and there among the corpses; and thus the French legions, grander than the Roman legions, expired at Mont Saint Jean on ground soaked in rain and blood, in the sombre wheat-fields, at the spot where now, at four o'clock in the morning, whistling, and gaily whipping up his horse, Joseph passes, who drives the mail from Nivelles.

XVI
QUOT LIBRAS IN DUCE?

THE battle of Waterloo is an enigma. It is as obscure to those who won it as to him who lost it. To Napoleon it is a panic;*

Blücher sees in it only fire; Wellington comprehends nothing of it. Look at the reports. The bulletins are confused, the commentaries are foggy. The former stammer, the latter falter. Jomini separates the battle of Waterloo into four periods; Muffling divides it into three tides of fortune; Charras alone, though upon some points our appreciation differs from his, has seized with his keen glance the characteristic lineaments of that catastrophe of human genius struggling with divine destiny. All the other historians are blinded by the glare, and are groping about in that blindness. A day of lightnings, indeed, the downfall of the military monarchy, which, to the great amazement of kings, has dragged with it all kingdoms, the fall of force, the overthrow of war.

In this event, bearing the impress of superhuman necessity, man's part is nothing.

Does taking away Waterloo from Wellington and from Blücher, detract anything from England and Germany? No. Neither illustrious England nor august Germany is in question in the problem of Waterloo. Thank heaven, nations are great aside from the dismal chances of the sword. Neither Germany, nor England, nor France, is held in a scabbard. At this day when Waterloo is only a clicking of sabres, above Blücher, Germany has Goethe, and above Wellington, England has Byron. A vast uprising of ideas is peculiar to our century, and in this aurora England and Germany have a magnificent share. They are majestic because they think. The higher plane which they bring to civilisation is intrinsic to them; it comes from themselves, and not from an accident. The advancement which they have made in the nineteenth century does not spring from Waterloo. It is only barbarous nations who have a sudden growth after a victory. It is the fleeting vanity of the streamlet swelled by the storm. Civilised nations, especially in our times, are not exalted nor abased by the good or bad fortune of a captain. Their specific gravity in the human race results from something more than a combat. Their honour, thank God, their dignity, their light, their genius, are not numbers that heroes and conquerors, those gamblers, can cast into the lottery of battles. Oftentimes a

---

* "A battle ended, a day finished, false measures repaired, greater successes assured for the morrow, all was lost by a moment of panic."—(Napoleon, *Dictations at St. Helena*)

battle lost is progress attained. Less glory, more liberty. The drum is silent, reason speaks. It is the game at which he who loses, gains. Let us speak, then, coolly of Waterloo on both sides. Let us render unto Fortune the things that are Fortune's, and unto God the things that are God's. What is Waterloo? A victory? No. A prize.

A prize won by Europe, paid by France.

It was not much to put a lion there.

Waterloo moreover is the strangest encounter in history. Napoleon and Wellington: they are not enemies, they are opposites. Never has God, who takes pleasure in antitheses, made a more striking contrast and a more extraordinary meeting. On one side, precision, foresight, geometry, prudence, retreat assured, reserves economised, obstinate composure, imperturbable method, strategy to profit by the ground, tactics to balance battalions, carnage drawn to the line, war directed watch in hand, nothing left voluntarily to intuition, inspiration, a military marvel, a superhuman instinct; a chance, ancient classic courage, absolute correctness; on the other flashing glance, a mysterious something which gazes like the eagle and strikes like the thunderbolt, prodigious art in disdainful impetuosity, all the mysteries of a deep soul, intimacy with Destiny; river, plain, forest, hill, commanded, and in some sort forced to obey, the despot going even so far as to tyrannise over the battle-field; faith in a star joined to strategic science, increasing it, but disturbing it. Wellington was the Barrême of war, Napoleon was its Michael Angelo, and this time genius was vanquished by calculation.

On both sides they were expecting somebody. It was the exact calculator who succeeded. Napoleon expected Grouchy; he did not come. Wellington expected Blücher; he came.

Wellington is classic war taking her revenge. Bonaparte, in his dawn, had met her in Italy, and defeated her superbly. The old owl fled before the young vulture. Ancient tactics had been not only thunderstruck, but had received mortal offence. What was this Corsican of twenty-six? What meant this brilliant novice who, having everything against him, nothing for him, with no provisions, no munition, no cannon, no shoes, almost without an army, with a handful of men against multitudes, rushed upon allied Europe, and absurdly gained victories that were impossible? Whence came this thundering madman who, almost without taking breath, and with the same set of the combatants in hand, pulverised one after the other the five armies of the Emperor of Germany, overthrowing Beaulieu upon Alvinzi, Wurmser upon Beaulieu, Melas upon Wurmser, Mack upon Melas? Who was this new-comer in war with the confidence of destiny? The academic military school excommunicated him as it ran away. Thence an implacable hatred of the old system of war against the new, of the correct sabre against the flashing sword, and of the chequer-board against genius. On the 18th of June, 1815, this hatred had the last word, and under Lodi, Montebello, Montenotte, Mantua, Marengo, Arcola, it wrote: Waterloo. Triumph of the commonplace, grateful to majorities. Destiny consented to this irony. In his decline, Napoleon again found Wurmser before him, but young. Indeed, to produce Wurmser, it would have been enough to whiten Wellington's hair.

Waterloo is a battle of the first rank won by a captain of the second.

What is truly admirable in the battle of Waterloo is England, English firmness, English resolution, English blood; the superb thing which England had there—may it not displease her—is herself. It is not her captain, it is her army.

Wellington, strangely ungrateful, declared in a letter to Lord Bathurst that his army, the army that fought on the 18th of June, 1815, was a "detestable army." What does this dark assemblage of bones, buried beneath the furrows of Waterloo, think of that?

England has been too modest in regard to Wellington. To make Wellington so great is to belittle England. Wellington is but a hero like the rest. These Scotch Grays, these Horse Guards, these regiments of Maitland and of Mitchell, this infantry of Pack and Kempt, this cavalry of Ponsonby and of Somerset, these Highlanders playing the bagpipe under the storm of grape, these battalions of Rylandt, these raw recruits who hardly knew how to handle a musket, holding out against the veteran bands of Essling and Rivoli—all that is grand. Wellington was tenacious, that was his merit, and we do not undervalue it, but the least of his foot-soldiers or his horsemen was quite as firm as he. The iron soldier is as good as the Iron Duke. For our part, all our glorification goes to the English soldier, the English army, the English people. If trophy there be, to England the trophy is due. The Waterloo column would be more just if, instead of the figure of a man, it lifted to the clouds the statue of a nation.

But this great England will be offended at what we say here. She has still, after her 1688 and our 1789, the feudal illusion. She believes in hereditary right, and in the hierarchy. This people, surpassed by none in might and glory, esteems itself as a nation, not as a people. So much so that as a people they subordinate themselves willingly, and take a Lord for a head. Workmen, they submit to be despised; soldiers, they submit to be whipped. We remember that at the battle of Inkerman a sergeant who, as it appeared, had saved the army, could not be mentioned by Lord Raglan, the English military hierarchy not permitting any hero below the rank of officer to be spoken of in a report.

What we admire above all, in an encounter like that of Waterloo, is the prodigious skill of fortune. The night's rain, the wall of Hougomont, the sunken road of Ohain, Grouchy deaf to cannon, Napoleon's guide who deceives him, Bulow's guide who leads him right; all this cataclysm is wonderfully carried out.

Taken as a whole, let us say, Waterloo was more of a massacre than a battle.

Of all great battles, Waterloo is that which has the shortest line in proportion to the number engaged. Napoleon, two miles, Wellington, a mile and a half; seventy-two thousand men on each side. From this density came the carnage.

The calculation has been made and this proportion established: Loss of men: at Austerlitz, French, fourteen per cent.; Russians, thirty per cent., Austrians, forty-four per cent. At Wagram, French, thirteen per cent.; Austrians, fourteen. At La Moscowa, French, thirty-seven per cent.; Russians, forty-four. At Bautzen, French, thirteen per cent.; Russians and Prussians, fourteen. At Waterloo, French, fifty-six per cent.; Allies, thirty-one. Average for Waterloo, forty-one per cent. A hundred and forty-four thousand men; sixty thousand dead.

The field of Waterloo to-day has that calm which belongs to the earth, impassive support of man; it resembles any other plain.

At night, however, a sort of visionary mist arises from it, and if some traveller be walking there, if he looks, if he listens, if he dreams like Virgil in the fatal plain of Philippi, he becomes possessed by the hallucination of the disaster. The terrible 18th of June is again before him; the artificial hill of the monument fades away, this lion, whatever it be, is dispelled; the field of battle resumes its reality; the lines of infantry undulate in the plain, furious gallops traverse the horizon; the bewildered dreamer sees the flash of sabres, the glistening of bayonets, the bursting of shells, the awful intermingling of the thunders; he hears, like a death-rattle from the depths of a tomb, the vague clamour of the phantom battle; these shadows are grenadiers; these gleams are cuirassiers; this skeleton is Napoleon; that skeleton is Wellington; all this is unreal, and yet it clashes and combats; and the ravines run red, and the trees shiver, and there is fury even in the clouds and, in the darkness, all those savage heights, Mont Saint Jean, Hougomont, Frischemont, Papelotte, Planchenoit, appear confusedly crowned with whirlwinds of spectres exterminating each other.

XVII
MUST WE APPROVE WATERLOO?

THERE exists a very respectable liberal school, which does not hate Waterloo. We are not of them. To us Waterloo is but the unconscious date of liberty. That such an eagle should come from such an egg, is certainly an unlooked-for thing.

Waterloo, if we place ourselves at the culminating point of view of the question, is intentionally a counter-revolutionary victory. It is Europe against France; it is Petersburg, Berlin, and Vienna against Paris; it is the *status quo* against the initiative; it is the 14th of June, 1789, attacked by the 20th March, 1815; it is the monarchies clearing the decks for action against indomitable French uprising. The final extinction of this vast people, for twenty-six years in eruption, such was the dream. It was the solidarity of the Brunswicks, the Nassaus, the Romanoffs, the Hohenzollerns, and the Hapsburgs, with the Bourbons. Divine right rides behind with Waterloo. It is true that the empire having been despotic, royalty, by the natural reaction of things, was forced to become liberal, and also that a constitutional order has indirectly sprung from Waterloo, to the great regret of the conquerors. The fact is, that revolution cannot be conquered, and that being providential and absolutely decreed, it reappears continually, before Waterloo in Bonaparte, throwing down the old thrones, after Waterloo in Louis XVIII., granting and submitting to the charter. Bonaparte places a postillion on the throne of Naples and a sergeant on the throne of Sweden, employing inequality to demonstrate equality; Louis XVIII. at Saint Ouen countersigns the declaration of the rights of man. Would you realise what Revolution is, call it Progress; and would you realise what Progress is, call it To-morrow. To-morrow performs its work irresistibly, and it performs it from to-day. It always reaches its aim through unexpected means. It employs Wellington to make Foy, who was only a soldier, an orator. Foy falls at Hougomont and rises again at the rostrum. Thus progress goes on. No tool comes amiss to this workman. It adjusts to its divine work without being disconcerted, the man who strode over the Alps, and the good old tottering invalid of the Père Elysée. It makes use of the cripple as well as the conqueror, the conqueror without, the cripple within. Waterloo, by cutting short the demolition of European thrones by the sword, has had no other effect than to continue the revolutionary work in another way. The saberers have gone out, the time of the thinkers has come. The age which Waterloo would have checked, has marched on and pursued its course. This inauspicious victory has been conquered by liberty.

In fine and incontestably, that which triumphed at Waterloo; that which smiled behind Wellington; that which brought him all the marshals' batons of Europe, among them, it is said, the baton of marshal of France, that which joyfully rolled barrows of earth full of bones to rear the mound of the lion; that which has written triumphantly on that pedestal this date: June 18th, 1815; that which encouraged Blücher sabering the fugitives; that which, from the height of the plateau of Mont Saint Jean, hung over France as over a prey, was Counter-revolution. It was Counter-revolution which murmured this infamous word—dismemberment. Arriving at Paris, it had a near view of the crater; it felt that these ashes were burning its feet, and took a second thought. It came back lisping of a charter.

Let us see in Waterloo only what there is in Waterloo. Of intentional liberty, nothing. The Counter-revolution was involuntarily liberal, as, by a corresponding phenomenon, Napoleon was involuntarily revolutionary. On the 18th of June, 1815, Robespierre on horseback was thrown from the saddle.

XVIII
RECRUDESCENCE OF DIVINE RIGHT

END of the dictatorship. The whole European system fell.

The empire sank into a darkness which resembled that of the expiring Roman world. It rose again from the depths, as in the time of the Barbarians. Only, the barbarism of 1815, which should be called by its special name, the counter-revolution, was short-winded, soon out of breath, and soon stopped. The empire, we must acknowledge, was wept over, and wept over by heroic eyes. If there be glory in the sceptre-sword, the empire had been glory itself. It had spread over the earth all the light which tyranny can give—a sombre light. Let us say further—an obscure light. Compared to the real day, it is night. This disappearance of night had the effect of an eclipse.

Louis XVIII. returned to Paris. The dancing in a ring of the 8th of July effaced the enthusiasm of the 20th of March. The Corsican became the antithesis of the Bearnois. The flag of the dome of the Tuileries was white. The exile mounted the throne. The fir table of Hartwell took its place before the chair decorated with fleur-de-lis of Louis XIV. Men talked of Bouvines and Fontenoy as of yesterday, Austerlitz being out of date. The altar and the throne fraternised majestically. One of the most unquestionably safe forms of society in the nineteenth century was established in France and on the Continent. Europe put on the white cockade. Trestaillon became famous. The device *non pluribus impar* reappeared in the radiations on the façade of the barracks of the quay of Orsay. Where there had been an imperial guard, there was a red house. The arc du Carrousel,—covered with awkwardly gained victories,—disowned by these new times, and a little ashamed, perhaps, of Marengo and Arcola, extricated itself from the affair by the statue of the Duke of Angoulême. The cemetery de la Madeleine, the terrible Potter's field of '93, was covered with marble and jasper, the bones of Louis XVI. and Marie-Antoinette being in this dust. In the ditch of Vincennes, a sepulchral column rose from the ground, recalling the fact that the Duke of Enghien died in the same month in which Napoleon was crowned. Pope Pius VII., who had performed this consecration very near the time of this death, tranquilly blessed the fall as he had blessed the elevation. At Schœnbrunn there was a little shadow four years old which it was seditious to call the King of Rome. And these things were done, and these kings resumed their thrones, and the master of Europe was put in a cage, and the old *régime* became the new, and all the light and shade of the earth changed place, because, in the afternoon of a summer's day, a cow-boy said to a Prussian in a wood: "Pass this way and not that!"

This 1815 was a sort of gloomy April. The old unhealthy and poisonous realities took on new shapes. Falsehood espoused 1789, divine right masked itself under a charter, fictions became constitutional, prejudices, superstitions and mental reservations, with article 14 hugged to the heart, put on a varnish of liberalism. Serpents changing their skins.

Man had been at once made greater and made less by Napoleon. The ideal, under this splendid material reign, had received the strange name of ideology. Serious recklessness of a great man, to turn the future into derision. The people, however, that food for cannon so fond of the cannoneer, looked for him. Where is he? What is he doing? "Napoleon is dead," said a visitor to an invalid of Marengo and Waterloo. "*He, dead!*" cried the soldier; "*are you sure of that?*" Imagination defied this prostrate man. The heart of Europe, after Waterloo, was gloomy. An enormous void remained long after the disappearance of Napoleon.

Kings threw themselves into this void. Old Europe profited by it to assume a new form. There was a Holy Alliance. Belle Alliance the fatal field of Waterloo had already said in advance.

In presence of and confronting this ancient Europe made over, the lineaments of a new France began to appear. The future, the jest of the emperor, made its appearance. It had on its brow this star, Liberty. The ardent eyes of rising generations turned towards it. Strange to tell, men became enamoured at the same time of this future, Liberty, and of this past, Napoleon. Defeat had magnified the vanquished. Bonaparte fallen seemed higher than Bonaparte in power. Those who had triumphed, were struck with fear. England guarded him through Hudson Lowe, and France watched him through Montchenu. His folded arms became the anxiety of thrones. Alexander called him, My Wakefulness. This terror arose from the amount of revolution he had in him. This is the explanation and excuse of Bonapartist liberalism. This phantom made the old world quake. Kings reigned ill at ease with the rock of Saint Helena in the horizon.

While Napoleon was dying at Longwood, the sixty thousand men fallen on the field of Waterloo tranquilly mouldered away, and something of their peace spread over the world. The congress of Vienna made from it the treaties of 1815, and Europe called that the Restoration.

Such is Waterloo.

But what is that to the Infinite? All this tempest, all this cloud, this war, then this peace, all this darkness, disturb not for a moment the light of that infinite Eye, before which the least of insects leaping from one blade of grass to another equals the eagle flying from spire to spire among the towers of Notre-Dame.

XIX
THE FIELD OF BATTLE AT NIGHT

WE return, for it is a requirement of this book, to the fatal field of battle.

On the 18th of June, 1815, the moon was full. Its light favoured the ferocious pursuit of Blücher, disclosed the traces of the fugitives, delivered this helpless mass to the bloodthirsty Prussian cavalry, and aided in the massacre. Night sometimes lends such tragic assistance to catastrophe.

When the last gun had been fired the plain of Mont Saint Jean remained deserted.

The English occupied the camp of the French; it is the usual verification of victory to sleep in the bed of the vanquished. They established their bivouac around Rossomme. The Prussians, let loose upon the fugitives, pushed forward. Wellington went to the village of Waterloo to make up his report to Lord Bathurst.

If ever the *sic vos non vobis* were applicable, it is surely to this village of Waterloo. Waterloo did nothing, and was two miles distant from the action. Mont Saint Jean was cannonaded, Hougomont was burned, Papelotte was burned, Planchenoit was burned, La Haie Sainte was taken by assault, La Belle Alliance witnessed the meeting of the two conquerors; these names are scarcely known, and Waterloo, which had nothing to do with the battle, has all the honour of it.

We are not of those who glorify war; when the opportunity presents itself we describe its realities. War has frightful beauties which we have not concealed; it has also, we must admit, some deformities. One of the most surprising is the eager spoliation of the dead after a victory. The day after a battle dawns upon naked corpses.

Who does this? Who thus sullies the triumph? Whose is this hideous furtive hand which glides into the pocket of victory? Who are these pickpockets following their trade in the wake of glory? Some philosophers, Voltaire among others, affirm that they are precisely those who have achieved the glory. They are the same, say they, there is no exchange; those who survive pillage those who succumb. The hero of the day is the vampire of the night. A man has a right, after all, to despoil in part a corpse which he has made.

For our part we do not believe this. To gather laurels and to steal the shoes from a dead man, seems to us impossible to the same hand.

One thing is certain, that, after the conquerors, come the robbers. But let us place the soldier, especially the soldier of to-day, beyond this charge.

Every army has a train, and there the accusation should lie. Bats, half brigand and half valet, all species of night bird engendered by this twilight which is called war, bearers of uniforms who never fight, sham invalids, formidable cripples, interloping sutlers, travelling, sometimes with their wives, on little carts and stealing what they sell, beggars offering themselves as guides to officers, army-servants, marauders; armies on the march formerly—we do not speak of the present time—were followed by all these, to such an extent that, in technical language, they are called "camp-followers." No army and no nation was responsible for these beings; they spoke Italian and followed the Germans; they spoke French and followed the English. It was by one of these wretches, a Spanish camp-follower who spoke French, that the Marquis of Fervacques, deceived by his Picardy gibberish, and taking him for one of us, was treacherously killed and robbed on the very battle-field during the night which followed the victory of Cerisoles. From marauding came the marauder. The detestable maxim, *Live on your enemy*, produced this leper, which rigid discipline alone can cure. There are reputations which are illusory; it is not always known why certain generals, though they have been great, have been so popular. Turenne was adored by his soldiers because he tolerated pillage;

the permission to do wrong forms part of kindness: Turenne was so kind that he allowed the Palatinate to be burned and put to the sword. There were seen in the wake of armies more or less of marauders according as the commander was more or less severe. Hoche and Marceau had no camp-followers; Wellington—we gladly do him this justice—had few.

However, during the night of the 18th of June, the dead were despoiled. Wellington was rigid; he ordered whoever should be taken in the act to be put to death; but rapine is persevering. The marauders were robbing in one corner of the battle-field while they were shooting them in another.

The moon was an evil genius on this plain.

Towards midnight a man was prowling or rather crawling along the sunken road of Ohain. He was, to all appearance, one of those whom we have just described, neither English nor French, peasant nor soldier, less a man than a ghoul, attracted by the scent of the corpses, counting theft for victory, coming to rifle Waterloo. He was dressed in a blouse which was in part a capote, was restless and daring, looking behind and before as he went. Who was this man? Night, probably, knew more of his doings than day! He had no knapsack, but evidently large pockets under his capote. From time to time he stopped, examined the plain around him as if to see if he were observed, stooped down suddenly, stirred on the ground something silent and motionless, then rose up and skulked away. His gliding movement, his attitudes, his rapid and mysterious gestures, made him seem like those twilight spectres which haunt ruins and which the old Norman legends call the Goers.

Certain nocturnal water-birds make such motions in marshes.

An eye which had carefully penetrated all this haze, might have noticed at some distance, standing as it were concealed behind the ruin which is on the Nivelles road at the corner of the route from Mont Saint Jean to Braine l'Alleud, a sort of little sutler's wagon, covered with tarred osiers, harnessed to a famished jade browsing nettles through her bit, and in the wagon a sort of woman seated on some trunks and packages. Perhaps there was some connection between this wagon and the prowler.

The night was serene. Not a cloud was in the zenith. What mattered it that the earth was red, the moon retained her whiteness. Such is the indifference of heaven. In the meadows, branches of trees broken by grape, but not fallen, and held by the bark, swung gently in the night wind. A breath, almost a respiration, moved the brushwood. There was a quivering in the grass which seemed like the departure of souls.

The tread of the patrols and groundsmen of the English camp could be heard dimly in the distance.

Hougomont and La Haie Sainte continued to burn, making, one in the east and the other in the west, two great flames, to which was attached, like a necklace of rubies with two carbuncles at its extremities, the cordon of bivouac fires of the English, extending in an immense semicircle over the hills of the horizon.

We have spoken of the catastrophe of the road to Ohain. The heart almost sinks with terror at the thought of such a death for so many brave men.

If anything is frightful, if there be a reality which surpasses dreams, it is this: to live, to see the sun, to be in full possession of manly vigour, to have health and joy, to laugh sturdily, to rush towards a glory which dazzlingly invites you on, to feel a very pleasure in respiration, to feel your heart beat, to feel yourself a reasoning being, to speak, to think, to hope, to love; to have mother, to have wife, to have children, to have sunlight, and suddenly, in a moment, in less than a minute, to feel yourself buried in an abyss, to fall, to roll, to crush, to be crushed, to see the grain, the flowers, the leaves, the branches, to be able to seize upon nothing, to feel your sword useless, men under you, horses over you, to strike about you in vain, your bones broken by some kick in the darkness, to feel a heel which makes your eyes leap from their sockets, to grind the horseshoes with rage in your teeth, to stifle, to howl, to twist, to be under all this, and to say: just now I was a living man!

There, where this terrible death-rattle had been, all was now silent. The cut of the sunken road was filled with horses and riders inextricably heaped together. Terrible entanglement. There were no longer slopes to the road; dead bodies filled it even with the plain and came to the edge of the banks like a well-measured bushel of barley. A mass of dead above, a river of blood below—such was this road on the evening of the 18th of June, 1815. The blood ran even to the Nivelles road, and oozed through in a large pool in front of the abattis of trees, which barred that road, at a spot which is still shown. It was, it will be remembered, at the opposite point towards the road from Genappe, that the burying of the cuirassiers took place. The thickness of the mass of bodies was proportioned to the depth of the hollow road. Towards the middle, at a spot where it became shallower, over which Delord's division had passed, this bed of death became thinner.

The night prowler which we have just introduced to the reader went in this direction. He ferreted through this immense grave. He looked about. He passed an indescribably hideous review of the dead. He walked with his feet in blood.

Suddenly he stopped.

A few steps before him, in the sunken road, at a point where the mound of corpses ended, from under this mass of men and horses appeared an open hand, lighted by the moon.

This hand had something upon a finger which sparkled: it was a gold ring.

The man stooped down, remained a moment, and when he rose again there was no ring upon that hand.

He did not rise up precisely; he remained in a sinister and startled attitude, turning his back to the pile of dead, scrutinising the horizon, on his knees, all the front of his body being supported on his two fore-fingers, his head raised just enough to peep above the edge of the hollow road. The four paws of the jackal are adapted to certain actions.

Then, deciding upon his course, he arose.

At this moment he experienced a shock. He felt that he was held from behind.

He turned; it was the open hand, which had closed, seizing the lapel of his capote.

An honest man would have been frightened. This man began to laugh.

"Oh," said he, "it's only the dead man. I like a ghost better than a gendarme."

However, the hand relaxed and let go its hold. Strength is soon exhausted in the tomb.

"Ah ha!" returned the prowler, "is this dead man alive? Let us see."

He bent over again, rummaged among the heap, removed whatever impeded him, seized the hand, laid hold of the arm, disengaged the head, drew out the body, and some moments after dragged into the shadow of the hollow road an inanimate man, at least one who was senseless. It was a cuirassier, an officer; an officer, also, of some rank; a great gold epaulette protruded from beneath his cuirass, but he had no casque. A furious sabre cut had disfigured his face, where nothing but blood was to be seen. It did not seem, however, that he had any limbs broken; and by some happy chance, if the word is possible here, the bodies were arched above him in such a way as to prevent his being crushed. His eyes were closed.

He had on his cuirass the silver cross of the Legion of Honour.

The prowler tore off this cross, which disappeared in one of the gulfs which he had under his capote.

After which he felt the officer's fob, found a watch there, and took it. Then he rummaged in his vest and found a purse, which he pocketed.

When he had reached this phase of the succour he was lending the dying man, the officer opened his eyes.

"Thanks," said he feebly.

The rough movements of the man handling him, the coolness of the night, and breathing the fresh air freely, had roused him from his lethargy.

The prowler answered not. He raised his head. The sound of a footstep could be heard on the plain; probably it was some patrol who was approaching.

The officer murmured, for there were still signs of suffering in his voice:

"Who has gained the battle?"

"The English," answered the prowler.

The officer replied:

"Search my pockets. You will there find a purse and a watch. Take them."

This had already been done.

The prowler made a pretence of executing the command, and said:

"There is nothing there."

"I have been robbed," replied the officer; "I am sorry. They should have been yours."

The step of the patrol became more and more distinct.

"Somebody is coming," said the prowler, making a movement as if he would go.

The officer, raising himself up painfully upon one arm, held him back.

"You have saved my life. Who are you?"

The prowler answered quick and low:

"I belong, like yourself, to the French army. I must go. If I am taken I shall be shot. I have saved your life. Help yourself now."

"What is your grade?"

"Sergeant."

"What is your name?"

"Thénardier."

"I shall not forget that name," said the officer. "And you, remember mine. My name is Pontmercy."

I

NUMBER 24601 BECOMES NUMBER 9430

JEAN VALJEAN has been retaken.

We shall be pardoned for passing rapidly over the painful details. We shall merely reproduce a couple of items published in the newspapers of that day, some few months after the remarkable events that occurred at M—— sur M——.

The articles referred to are somewhat laconic. It will be remembered that the *Gazette des Tribunaux* had not yet been established.

We copy the first from the *Drapeau Blanc*. It is dated the 25th of July, 1823:

"A district of the Pas-de-Calais has just been the scene of an extraordinary occurrence. A stranger in that department, known as Monsieur Madeleine, had, within a few years past, restored, by means of certain new processes, the manufacture of jet and black glass ware—a former local branch of industry. He had made his own fortune by it, and, in fact, that of the entire district. In acknowledgment of his services he had been appointed mayor. The police has discovered that Monsieur Madeleine was none other than an escaped convict, condemned in 1796 for robbery, and named Jean Valjean. This Jean Valjean has been sent back to the galleys. It appears that previous to his arrest, he succeeded in withdrawing from Laffitte's a sum amounting to more than half a million which he had deposited there, and which it is said, by the way, he had very legitimately realised in his business. Since his return to the galleys at Toulon, it has been impossible to discover where Jean Valjean concealed this money."

The second article, which enters a little more into detail, is taken from the *Journal de Paris* of the same date:

"An old convict, named Jean Valjean, has recently been brought before the Var Assizes, under circumstances calculated to attract attention. This villain had succeeded in eluding the vigilance of the police; he had changed his name, and had even been adroit enough to procure the appointment of mayor in one of our small towns in the North. He had established in this town a very considerable business, but was, at length, unmasked

and arrested, thanks to the indefatigable zeal of the public
authorities. He kept, as his mistress, a prostitute, who died of
the shock at the moment of his arrest. This wretch, who is
endowed with herculean strength, managed to escape, but, three
or four days afterwards, the police retook him, in Paris, just as
he was getting into one of the small vehicles that ply between
the capital and the village of Montfermeil (Seine-et-Oise). It is
said that he had availed himself of the interval of these three or
four days of freedom, to withdraw a considerable sum deposited
by him with one of our principal bankers. The amount is estimated at six or seven hundred thousand francs. According to
the minutes of the case, he has concealed it in some place known
to himself alone, and it has been impossible to seize it; however
that may be, the said Jean Valjean has been brought before the
assizes of the Department of the Var under indictment for an
assault and armed robbery on the high road committed some
eight years ago on the person of one of those honest lads who,
as the patriarch of Ferney has written in immortal verse,

> ... De Savoie arrivent tous les ans,
> Et dont la main légèrement essuie
> Ces longs canaux engorgés par la suie.*

This bandit attempted no defence. It was proven by the able and
eloquent representative of the crown that the robbery was
shared in by others, and that Jean Valjean formed one of a band
of robbers in the South. Consequently, Jean Valjean, being
found guilty, was condemned to death. The criminal refused to
appeal to the higher courts, and the king, in his inexhaustible
clemency, deigned to commute his sentence to that of hard
labour in prison for life. Jean Valjean was immediately forwarded to the galleys at Toulon."

It will not be forgotten that Jean Valjean had at M—— sur
M—— certain religious habits. Some of the newspapers and,
among them, the *Constitutionnel*, held up this commutation as a
triumph of the clerical party.

Jean Valjean changed his number at the galleys. He became
9430.

---

* ... Who come from Savoy every year,
  And whose hand deftly wipes out
  Those long channels choked up with soot.

While we are about it, let us remark, in dismissing the subject, that with M. Madeleine, the prosperity of M—— sur M—— disappeared; all that he had foreseen, in that night of fever and irresolution, was realised; he gone, the *soul* was gone. After his downfall, there was at M—— sur M—— that egotistic distribution of what is left when great men have fallen—that fatal carving up of prosperous enterprises which is daily going on, out of sight, in human society, and which history has noted but once, and then, because it took place after the death of Alexander. Generals crown themselves kings; the foremen, in this case, assumed the position of manufacturers. Jealous rivalries arose. The spacious workshops of M. Madeleine were closed; the building fell into ruin, the workmen dispersed. Some left the country, others abandoned the business. From that time forth, everything was done on a small, instead of on the large scale, and for gain rather than for good. No longer any centre; competition on all sides, and on all sides venom. M. Madeleine had ruled and directed everything. He fallen, every man strove for himself, the spirit of strife succeeded to the spirit of organisation, bitterness to cordiality, hatred of each against each instead of the good will of the founder towards all; the threads knitted by M. Madeleine became entangled and were broken; the workmanship was debased, the manufacturers were degraded, confidence was killed; customers diminished, there were fewer orders, wages decreased, the shops became idle, bankruptcy followed. And, then, there was nothing left for the poor. All that was there disappeared.

Even the state noticed that some one had been crushed, in some direction. Less than four years after the decree of the court of assizes establishing the identity of M. Madeleine and Jean Valjean, for the benefit of the galleys, the expense of collecting the taxes was doubled in the district of M—— sur M——, and M. de Villèle remarked the fact, on the floor of the Assembly, in the month of February, 1827.

II

IN WHICH A COUPLE OF LINES WILL BE READ WHICH CAME, PERHAPS, FROM THE EVIL ONE

BEFORE proceeding further, it will not be amiss to relate, in some detail, a singular incident which took place, about the same time, at Montfermeil, and which, perhaps, does not fall in badly with certain conjectures of the public authorities.

There exists, in the neighbourhood of Montfermeil, a very ancient superstition, all the more rare and precious from the fact that a popular superstition in the vicinity of Paris is like an aloe tree in Siberia. Now, we are of those who respect anything in the way of a rarity. Here, then, is the superstition of Montfermeil: they believe, there, that the Evil One has, from time immemorial, chosen the forest as the hiding-place for his treasure. The good wives of the vicinity affirm that it is no unusual thing to meet, at sundown, in the secluded portions of the woods, a black-looking man, resembling a wagoner or wood-cutter, shod in wooden shoes, clad in breeches and sack of coarse linen, and recognisable from the circumstance that, instead of a cap or hat, he has two immense horns upon his head. That certainly ought to render him recognisable. This man is constantly occupied in digging holes. There are three ways of dealing when you meet him.

The first mode is to approach the man and speak to him. Then you perceive that the man is nothing but a peasant, that he looks black because it is twilight, that he is digging no hole whatever, but is merely cutting grass for his cows; and that what had been taken for horns are nothing but his pitchfork which he carries on his back, and the prongs of which, thanks to the night perspective, seemed to rise from his head. You go home and die within a week. The second method is to watch him, to wait until he has dug the hole, closed it up, and gone away; then, to run quickly to the spot, to open it and get the "treasure" which the black-looking man has, of course, buried there. In this case, you die within a month. The third manner is not to speak to the dark man nor even to look at him, and to run away as fast as you can. You die within the year.

As all three of these methods have their drawbacks, the second, which, at least, offers some advantages, among others that of possessing a treasure, though it be but for a month, is the one generally adopted. Daring fellows, who never neglect a good chance, have, therefore, many times, it is asseverated, reopened the holes thus dug by the black-looking man, and tried to rob the Devil. It would appear, however, that it is not a very good business—at least, if we are to believe tradition, and, more especially, two enigmatic lines in barbarous Latin left us, on this subject, by a roguish Norman monk, named Tryphon, who dabbled in the black art. This Tryphon was buried in the abbey of St. Georges de Bocherville, near Rouen, and toads are produced from his grave.

Well then, the treasure-seeker makes tremendous efforts, for the holes referred to are dug, generally, very deep; he sweats, he digs, he works away all night, for this is done in the night-time; he gets his clothes wet, he consumes his candle, he hacks and breaks his pickaxe, and when, at length, he has reached the bottom of the hole, when he has put his hand upon the "treasure," what does he find? What is this treasure of the Evil One? A penny—sometimes a crown; a stone, a skeleton, a bleeding corpse, sometimes a spectre twice folded like a sheet of paper in a portfolio, sometimes nothing. This is what seems to be held forth to the indiscreet and prying by the lines of Tryphon:

> Fodit, et in fossa thesauros condit opaca
> As, nummos, lapides, cadaver, simulacra, nihilque.

It appears that, in our time, they find in addition sometimes a powder-horn with bullets, sometimes an old pack of brown and greasy cards which have evidently been used by the Devil. Tryphon makes no mention of these articles, as Tryphon lived in the twelfth century, and it does not appear that the Evil One had wit enough to invent powder in advance of Roger Bacon or cards before Charles VI.

Moreover, whoever plays with these cards is sure to lose all he has, and as to the powder in the flask, it has the peculiarity of bursting your gun in your face.

Now, very shortly after the time when the authorities took it into their heads that the liberated convict Jean Valjean had, during his escape of a few days' duration, been prowling about Montfermeil, it was remarked, in that village, that a certain old road-labourer named Boulatruelle had "a fancy" for the woods. People in the neighbourhood claimed to know that Boulatruelle had been in the galleys, he was under police surveillance, and, as he could find no work anywhere, the government employed him at half wages as a mender on the cross-road from Gagny to Lagny.

This Boulatruelle was a man in bad odour with the people of the neighbourhood; he was too respectful, too humble, prompt to doff his cap to everybody; he always trembled and smiled in the presence of the gendarmes, was probably in secret connection with robber-bands, said the gossips, and suspected of lying in wait in the hedge corners, at night-fall. He had nothing in his favour except that he was a drunkard.

What had been observed was this:

For some time past, Boulatruelle had left off his work at stone-breaking and keeping the road in order, very early, and had gone into the woods with his pick. He would be met towards evening in the remotest glades and the wildest thickets, having the appearance of a person looking for something and, sometimes, digging holes. The good wives who passed that way took him at first for Beelzebub, then they recognised Boulatruelle, and were by no means reassured. These chance meetings seemed greatly to disconcert Boulatruelle. It was clear that he was trying to conceal himself, and that there was something mysterious in his operations.

The village gossips said:—"It's plain that the Devil has been about, Boulatruelle has seen him and is looking for his treasure. The truth is, he is just the fellow to rob the Evil One."—The Voltairians added: "Will Boulatruelle catch the Devil or the Devil catch Boulatruelle?"—The old women crossed themselves very often.

However, the visits of Boulatruelle to the woods ceased and he recommenced his regular labour on the road. People began to talk about something else.

A few, however, retained their curiosity, thinking that there might be involved in the affair, not the fabulous treasures of the legend, but some goodly matter more substantial than the Devil's bank-bills, and that Boulatruelle had half spied out the secret. The worst puzzled of all were the schoolmaster and the tavern-keeper, Thénardier, who was everybody's friend, and who had not disdained to strike up an intimacy with even Boulatruelle.

"He has been in the galleys," said Thénardier. "Good Lord! nobody knows who is there or who may be there!"

One evening, the schoolmaster remarked that, in old times, the authorities would have inquired into what Boulatruelle was about in the woods, and that he would have been compelled to speak—even put to torture, if need were—and that Boulatruelle would not have held out, had he been put to the question by water, for example.

"Let us put him to the wine question," said Thénardier.

So they made up a party and plied the old roadsman with drink. Boulatruelle drank enormously, but said little. He combined with admirable art and in masterly proportions the thirst of a guzzler with the discretion of a judge. However, by dint of returning to the charge and by putting together and twisting the obscure expressions that he did let fall, Thénardier and the schoolmaster made out, as they thought, the following:

One morning about daybreak as he was going to his work, Boulatruelle had been surprised at seeing under a bush in a corner of the wood, a pickaxe and spade, *as one would say, hidden there*. However, he supposed that they were the pick and spade of old Six-Fours, the water-carrier, and thought no more about it. But, on the evening of the same day, he had seen, without being seen himself, for he was hidden behind a large tree, "a person who did not belong at all to that region, and whom he, Boulatruelle, knew very well"—or, as Thénardier translated it, "*an old comrade at the galleys*"—turn off from the high road towards the thickest part of the wood. Boulatruelle obstinately refused to tell the stranger's name. This person carried a package, something square, like a large box or a small trunk. Boulatruelle was surprised. Seven or eight minutes, however, elapsed before it occurred to him to follow the "person." But he was too late. The person was already in the thick woods, night had come on, and Boulatruelle did not succeed in overtaking him. Thereupon he made up his mind to watch the outskirts of the wood. "There was a moon." Two or three hours later, Boulatruelle saw this person come forth again from the wood, this time carrying now not the little trunk but a pick and a spade. Boulatruelle let the person pass unmolested, because, as he thought to himself, the other was three times as strong as he, was armed with a pickaxe, and would probably murder him, on recognising his countenance and seeing that he, in turn, was recognised. Touching display of freeling in two old companions unexpectedly meeting! But the pick and the spade were a ray of light to Boulatruelle; he hastened to the bushes, in the morning, and found neither one nor the other. He thence concluded that this person, on entering the wood, had dug a hole with his pick, had buried the chest, and had, then, filled up the hole with his spade. Now, as the chest was too small to contain a corpse, it must contain money; hence his continued searches.

Boulatruelle had explored, sounded, and ransacked the whole forest, and had rummaged every spot where the earth seemed to have been freshly disturbed. But all in vain.

He had turned up nothing. Nobody thought any more about it, at Montfermeil, excepting a few good gossips, who said: "Be sure the road-labourer of Gagny didn't make all that fuss for nothing: the devil was certainly there."

III

SHOWING THAT THE CHAIN OF THE IRON RING MUST NEEDS HAVE UNDERGONE A CERTAIN PREPARATION TO BE THUS BROKEN BY ONE BLOW OF THE HAMMER

TOWARDS the end of October, in that same year, 1823, the inhabitants of Toulon saw coming back into their port, in consequence of heavy weather, and in order to repair some damages, the ship *Orion*, which was at a later period employed at Brest as a vessel of instruction, and which then formed a part of the Mediterranean squadron. This ship, crippled as she was, for the sea had used her roughly, produced some sensation on entering the roadstead. She flew I forget what pennant, but it entitled her to a regular salute of eleven guns, which she returned shot for shot: in all twenty-two. It has been estimated that in salutes, royal and military compliments, exchanges of courteous hubbub, signals of etiquette, roadstead and citadel formalities, risings and settings of the sun saluted daily by all fortresses and all vessels of war, the opening and closing of gates, etc., etc., the civilised world, in every part of the globe, fires off, daily, one hundred and fifty thousand useless cannon shots. At six francs per shot, that would amount to nine hundred thousand francs per day, or three hundred millions per year, blown off in smoke. This is only an item. In the meanwhile, the poor are dying with hunger.

The year 1823 was what the Restoration has called the "time of the Spanish War."

That war comprised many events in one, and no small number of singular things. It was a great family affair of the Bourbons; the French branch aiding and protecting the branch at Madrid, that is to say, performing the duties of seniority; an apparent return to our national traditions, mixed up with subserviency, and cringing to the cabinets of the North; the Duc d'Angoulême, dubbed by the liberal journals *the hero of Andujar*, repressing, with a triumphal attitude—rather contradicted by his peaceful mien—the old and very real terrorism of the Holy Office, in conflict with the chimerical terrorism of the Liberals; sans-culottes revived, to the great alarm of all the old dowagers, under the name of *descamisados*; monarchists striving to impede progress, which they styled anarchy; the theories of '89 rudely interrupted in their undermining advances; a halt from all Europe, intimated to the French idea of revolution, making its tour of the globe; side by side with the son of France, general-in-chief, the Prince de Carignan, afterwards Charles Albert, enlisting in this crusade of the kings against the peoples, as a volunteer, with a grenadier's epaulettes of red wool; the soldiers of the empire again betaking themselves to the field, but after eight years of rest, grown old, gloomy, and under the white cockade; the tricolour displayed abroad by a heroic handful of Frenchmen, as the white flag had been at Coblentz, thirty years before; monks mingling with our troopers; the spirit of liberty and of innovation reduced by bayonets; principles struck dumb by cannon-shot; France undoing by her arms what she had done with her mind; to cap the climax, the leaders on the other side sold, their troops irresolute; cities besieged by millions of money; no military dangers, and yet some explosions possible, as is the case in every mine entered and taken by surprise, but little blood shed, but little honour gained; shame for a few, glory for none. Such was this war, brought about by princes who descended from Louis XIV., and carried on by generals who sprang from Napoleon. It had this wretched fate, that it recalled neither the image of a great war nor of a great policy.

A few feats of arms were serious affairs; the taking of Trocadero, among others, was a handsome military exploit; but, taken all in all, we repeat, the trumpets of this war emit a cracked and feeble sound, the general appearance of it was suspicious, and history approves the unwillingness of France to father so false a triumph. It seemed clear that certain Spanish officers intrusted with the duty of resistance, yielded too easily, the idea of bribery was suggested by a contemplation of the victory; it appeared as if the generals rather than the battles had been won, and the victorious soldier returned humiliated. It was war grown petty indeed, where you could read *Bank of France* on the folds of the flag.

Soldiers of the war of 1808, under whose feet Saragossa had so terribly crumbled, knit their brows at this ready surrender of fastness and citadels, and regretted Palafox. It is the mood of France to prefer to have before her a Rostopchine rather than a Ballesteros.

In a still graver point of view, which it is well to urge, too, this war, which broke the military spirit of France, fired the democratic spirit with indignation. It was a scheme of subjugation. In this campaign, the object held out to the French soldier, son of democracy, was the conquest of a yoke for the neck of another. Hideous contradiction. France exists to arouse the soul of the peoples, not to stifle it. Since 1792, all the revolutions of Europe have been but the French Revolution: liberty radiates on every side from France. That is a fact as clear as noonday. Blind is he who does not see it! Bonaparte has said it.

The war of 1823, an outrage on the generous Spanish nation, was, at the same time, an outrage on the French Revolution. This monstrous deed of violence France committed, but by compulsion; for, aside from wars of liberation, all that armies do they do by compulsion. The words *passive obedience* tell the tale. An army is a wondrous masterpiece of combination, in which might is the result of an enormous sum-total of utter weakness. Thus only can we explain a war waged by humanity against humanity, in despite of humanity.

As to the Bourbons, the war of 1823 was fatal to them. They took it for a success. They did not see what danger there is in attempting to kill an idea by a military watchword. In their simplicity, they blundered to the extent of introducing into their establishment, as an element of strength, the immense enfeeblement of a crime. The spirit of ambuscade and lying in wait entered into their policy. The germ of 1830 was in 1823. The Spanish campaign became in their councils an argument on behalf of violent measures and intrigues in favour of divine right. France having restored *el rey neto* in Spain, could certainly restore the absolute monarchy at home. They fell into the tremendous error of mistaking the obedience of the soldier for the acquiescence of the nation. That fond delusion ruins thrones. It will not do to fall asleep either in the shade of a upas tree or in the shadow of an army.

But let us return to the ship *Orion*.

During the operations of the army of the Prince,

commanding-in-chief, a squadron cruised in the Mediterranean. We have said that the *Orion* belonged to that squadron, and that she had been driven back by stress of weather to the port of Toulon.

The presence of a vessel of war in port has about it a certain influence which attracts and engages the multitude. It is because it is something grand, and the multitude like what is imposing.

A ship-of-the-line is one of the most magnificent struggles of human genius with the forces of nature.

A vessel of the line is composed of the heaviest, and at the same time the lightest materials, because she has to contend, at one and the same time, with the three forms of matter, the solid, the liquid, and the fluid. She has eleven claws of iron to grasp the rock at the bottom of the sea, and more wings and feelers than the butterfly to catch the breezes in the clouds. Her breath goes forth through her hundred and twenty guns as through enormous trumpets, and haughtily answers the thunderbolt. Ocean strives to lead her astray in the frightful sameness of his billows, but the ship has her compass, which is her soul, always counselling her and always pointing towards the north. In dark nights, her lanterns take the place of the stars. Thus, then, to oppose the wind, she has her ropes and canvas; against the water her timber; against the rock her iron, her copper, and her lead; against the darkness, light; against immensity, needle.

Whoever would form an idea of all these gigantic proportions, the aggregate of which constitutes a ship-of-the-line, has but to pass under one of the covered ship-houses, six stories high, at Brest or Toulon. The vessels in process of construction are seen there under glass cases, so to speak. That colossal beam is a yard; that huge column of timber lying on the ground and reaching out of sight is the mainmast. Taking it from its root in the hold to its summit in the clouds, it is sixty fathoms long, and is three feet in diameter at its base. The English mainmast rises two hundred and seventeen feet above the water-line. The navy of our fathers used cables, ours uses chains. Now the mere coil of chains of a hundred-gun ship is four feet high, twenty feet broad, and eight feet thick. And for the construction of this vessel, how much timber is required? It is a floating forest.

And yet, be it remembered, that we are here speaking only of the war vessel of some forty years ago, the mere sailing craft; steam, then in its infancy, has, since that time, added new wonders to this prodigy called a man-of-war. At the present day, for example, the mixed vessel, the screw-propeller, is a surprising piece of mechanism moved by a spread of canvas measuring four thousand square yards of surface, and by a steam-engine of twenty-five hundred horse power.

Without referring to these fresher marvels, the old-fashioned ship of Christopher Columbus and of De Ruyter is one of the noblest works of man. It is exhaustless in force as the breadth of infinitude; it gathers up the wind in its canvas, it is firmly fixed in the immense chaos of the waves, it floats and it reigns.

But a moment comes, when the white squall breaks that sixty-foot yard like a straw; and when the wind flaw bends that four-hundred-foot mast like a reed; when that anchor, weighing its tons upon tons, is twisted in the maw of the wave like the angler's hook in the jaws of a pike; when those monster guns utter plaintive and futile roarings which the tempest whirls away into space and night, when all this might and all this majesty are engulfed in a superior might and majesty.

Whenever immense strength is put forth only to end in immense weakness, it makes men meditate. Hence it is that, in seaports, the curious, without themselves knowing exactly why, throng about these wonderful instruments of war and navigation.

Every day, then, from morning till night, the quays, the wharves, and the piers of the port of Toulon were covered with a throng of saunterers and idlers, whose occupation consisted in gazing at the *Orion*.

The *Orion* was a ship that had long been in bad condition. During her previous voyages, thick layers of shellfish had gathered on her bottom to such an extent as to seriously impede her progress; she had been put on the dry-dock the year before, to be scraped, and then she had gone to sea again. But this scraping had injured her fastening.

In the latitude of the Balearic Isles, her planking had loosened and opened, and as there was in those days no copper sheathing, the ship had leaked. A fierce equinoctial came on, which had stove in the larboard bows and a porthole, and damaged the fore-chain-wales. In consequence of these injuries, the *Orion* had put back to Toulon.

She was moored near the arsenal. She was in commission, and they were repairing her. The hull had not been injured on the starboard side, but a few planks had been taken off here and there, according to custom, to admit the air to the framework.

One morning, the throng which was gazing at her witnessed an accident.

The crew was engaged in furling sail. The topman, whose duty it was to take in the starboard upper corner of the main top-sail, lost his balance. He was seen tottering; the dense throng assembled on the wharf of the arsenal uttered a cry, the man's head overbalanced his body, and he whirled over the yard, his arms outstretched towards the deep; as he went over, he grasped the man-ropes, first with one hand, and then with the other, and hung suspended in that manner. The sea lay far below him at a giddy depth. The shock of his fall had given to the man-ropes a violent swinging motion, and the poor fellow hung dangling to and fro at the end of this line, like a stone in a sling.

To go to his aid was to run a frightful risk. None of the crew, who were all fishermen of the coast recently taken into service, dared attempt it. In the meantime, the poor topman was becoming exhausted; his agony could not be seen in his countenance, but his increasing weakness could be detected in the movements of all his limbs. His arms twisted about in horrible contortions. Every attempt he made to reascend only increased the oscillations of the man-ropes. He did not cry out, for fear of losing his strength. All were now looking forward to the moment when he should let go of the rope, and, at instants, all turned their heads away that they might not see him fall. There are moments when a rope's end, a pole, the branch of a tree, is life itself, and it is a frightful thing to see a living being lose his hold upon it, and fall like a ripe fruit.

Suddenly, a man was discovered clambering up the rigging with the agility of a wildcat. This man was clad in red—it was a convict; he wore a green cap—it was a convict for life. As he reached the round top, a gust of wind blew off his cap and revealed a head entirely white: it was not a young man.

In fact, one of the convicts employed on board in some prison task, had, at the first alarm, run to the officer of the watch, and, amid the confusion and hesitation of the crew, while all the sailors trembled and shrank back, had asked permission to save the topman's life at the risk of his own. A sign of assent being given, with one blow of a hammer he broke the chain riveted to the iron ring at his ankle, then took a rope in his hand, and flung himself into the shrouds. Nobody, at the moment, noticed with what ease the chain was broken. It was only some time afterwards that anybody remembered it.

In a twinkling he was upon the yard. He paused a few seconds, and seemed to measure it with his glance. Those seconds, during which the wind swayed the sailor to and fro at the end of the rope, seemed ages to the lookers-on. At length, the convict raised his eyes to heaven, and took a step forward. The crowd drew a long breath. He was seen to run along the yard. On reaching its extreme tip, he fastened one end of the rope he had with him, and let the other hang at full length. Thereupon, he began to let himself down by his hands along this rope, and then there was an inexpressible sensation of terror; instead of one man, two were seen dangling at that giddy height.

You would have said it was a spider seizing a fly; only, in this case, the spider was bringing life, and not death. Ten thousand eyes were fixed upon the group. Not a cry; not a word was uttered; the same emotion contracted every brow. Every man held his breath, as if afraid to add the least whisper to the wind which was swaying the two unfortunate men.

However, the convict had, at length, managed to make his way down to the seaman. It was time; one minute more, and the man, exhausted and despairing, would have fallen into the deep. The convict firmly secured him to the rope to which he clung with one hand while he worked with the other. Finally, he was seen reascending to the yard, and hauling the sailor after him; he supported him there, for an instant, to let him recover his strength, and then, lifting him in his arms, carried him, as he walked along the yard, to the crosstrees, and from there to the round-top, where he left him in the hands of his mess-mates.

Then the throng applauded; old galley sergeants wept, women hugged each other on the wharves, and, on all sides, voices were heard exclaiming, with a sort of tenderly subdued enthusiasm:—"This man must be pardoned!"

He, however, had made it a point of duty to descend again immediately, and go back to his work. In order to arrive more quickly he slid down the rigging, and started to run along a lower yard. All eyes were following him. There was a certain moment when every one felt alarmed; whether it was that he felt fatigued, or because his head swam, people thought they saw him hesitate and stagger. Suddenly, the throng uttered a thrilling outcry: the convict had fallen into the sea.

The fall was perilous. The frigate *Algeciras* was moored close to the *Orion*, and the poor convict had plunged between the two ships. It was feared that he would be drawn under one or the other. Four men sprang, at once, into a boat. The people cheered them on, and anxiety again took possession of all minds. The man had not again risen to the surface. He had disappeared in the sea, without making even a ripple, as though he had fallen into a cask of oil. They sounded and dragged the place. It was in vain. The search was continued until night, but not even the body was found.

The next morning, the *Toulon Journal* published the following lines:—"November 17, 1823. Yesterday, a convict at work on board the *Orion*, on his return from rescuing a sailor, fell into the sea, and was drowned. His body was not recovered. It is presumed that it has been caught under the piles at the pier-head of the arsenal. This man was registered by the number 9430, and his name was Jean Valjean."

BOOK THIRD – FULFILMENT OF THE PROMISE TO THE DEPARTED

I

THE WATER QUESTION AT MONTFERMEIL

MONTFERMEIL is situated between Livry and Chelles, upon the southern slope of the high plateau which separates the Ourcq from the Marne. At present, it is a considerable town, adorned all the year round with stuccoed villas, and, on Sundays, with citizens in full blossom. In 1823, there were at Montfermeil neither so many white houses nor so many comfortable citizens; it was nothing but a village in the woods. You would find, indeed, here and there a few country seats of the last century, recognisable by their grand appearance, their balconies of twisted iron, and those long windows the little panes of which show all sorts of different greens upon the white of the closed shutters. But Montfermeil was none the less a village. Retired dry-goods merchants and amateur villagers had not yet discovered it. It was a peaceful and charming spot, and not upon the road to any place; the inhabitants cheaply enjoyed that rural life which is so luxuriant and so easy of enjoyment. But water was scarce there on account of the height of the plateau.

They had to go a considerable distance for it. The end of the village towards Gagny drew its water from the magnificent ponds in the forest on that side; the other end, which surrounds the church and which is towards Chelles, found drinking-water only at a little spring on the side of the hill, near the road to Chelles, about fifteen minutes' walk from Montfermeil.

It was therefore a serious matter for each household to obtain its supply of water. The great houses, the aristocracy, the Thénardier tavern included, paid a penny a bucket-full to an old man who made it his business, and whose income from the Montfermeil water-works was about eight sous per day; but this man worked only till seven o'clock in summer and five in the winter, and when night had come on, and the first-floor shutters were closed, whoever had no drinking-water went after it, or went without it.

This was the terror of the poor being whom the reader has not perhaps forgotten—little Cosette. It will be remembered that Cosette was useful to the Thénardiers in two ways, they got pay from the mother and work from the child. Thus when the mother ceased entirely to pay, we have seen why, in the preceding chapters, the Thénardiers kept Cosette. She saved them a servant. In that capacity she ran for water when it was wanted. So the child, always horrified at the idea of going to the spring at night, took good care that water should never be wanting at the house.

Christmas in the year 1823 was particularly brilliant at Montfermeil. The early part of the winter had been mild; so far there had been neither frost nor snow. Some jugglers from Paris had obtained permission from the mayor to set up their stalls in the main street of the village, and a company of pedlars had, under the same licence, put up their booths in the square before the church and even in the lane du Boulanger, upon which, as the reader perhaps remembers, the Thénardier chop-house was situated. This filled up the taverns and pot-houses, and gave to this little quiet place a noisy and joyous appearance. We ought also to say, to be a faithful historian, that, among the curiosities displayed in the square, there was a menagerie in which frightful clowns, clad in rags and come nobody knows whence, were exhibiting in 1823 to the peasants of Montfermeil one of those horrid Brazilian vultures, a specimen of which our Muséum Royal did not obtain until 1845, and the eye of which is a tricoloured cockade. Naturalists call this bird, I believe, Caracara Polyborus; it belongs to the order of the Apicidæ and the family of the vultures. Some good old retired Bonapartist soldiers in the village went to see the bird as a matter of faith. The jugglers pronounced the tri-coloured cockade a unique phenomenon, made expressly by God for their menagerie.

On that Christmas evening, several men, wagoners and pedlars were seated at table and drinking around four or five candles in the low hall of the Thénardier tavern. This room resembled all bar-rooms; tables, pewter-mugs, bottles, drinkers, smokers; little light, and much noise. The date, 1823, was, however, indicated by the two things then in vogue with the middle classes, which were on the table, a kaleidoscope and a fluted tin lamp. Thénardier, the wife, was looking to the supper, which was cooking before a bright blazing fire; the husband, Thénardier, was drinking with his guests and talking politics.

Aside from the political discussions, the principal subjects of which were the Spanish war and the Duc d'Angoulême, local interludes were heard amid the hubbub, like these, for instance:——

"Down around Nanterre and Suresnes wine is turning out well. Where they expected ten casks they are getting twelve. That is getting a good yield of juice out of the press." "But the grapes can't be ripe?" "Oh, in these parts there is no need of harvesting ripe; the wine is fat enough by spring." "It is all light wine then?" "There is a good deal lighter wines than they make hereabouts. You have to harvest green."

Etc.

Or, indeed, a miller might be bawling:——

"Are we responsible for what there is in the bags? We find a heap of little seeds there, but we can't amuse ourselves by picking out, and of course we have got to let 'em go through the stones; there's darnel, there's fennel, there's cockles, there's vetch, there's hemp, there's fox-tail, and a lot of other weeds, not counting the stones that there is in some wheat, especially Breton wheat. I don't like to grind Breton wheat, no more than carpenters like to saw boards with nails in 'em. Just think of the dirt that all that makes in the till. And then they complain of the flour. It's their own fault. We ain't to blame for the flour."

Between two windows, a mower seated at a table with a farmer, who was making a bargain for a piece of work to be done the next season, was saying:——

"There is no harm in the grass having the dew on. It cuts better. The dew is a good thing. It is all the same, that are grass o' yours is young, and pretty hard to cut. You see it is so green; you see it bends under the scythe."

Etc.

Cosette was at her usual place, seated on the cross-piece of the kitchen table, near the fire-place; she was clad in rags; her bare feet were in wooden shoes, and by the light of the fire she was knitting woollen stockings for the little Thénardiers. A young kitten was playing under the chairs. In a neighbouring room the fresh voices of two children were heard laughing and prattling; it was Eponine and Azelma.

In the chimney-corner, a cow-hide hung upon a nail.

At intervals, the cry of a very young child, which was somewhere in the house, was heard above the noise of the bar-room. This was a little boy which the woman had had some winters before—"She didn't know why," she said: "it was the cold

weather,"—and which was a little more than three years old.
The mother had nursed him, but did not love him. When the
hungry clamour of the brat became too much to hear:—"Your
boy is squalling," said Thénardier, "why don't you go and see
what he wants?" "Bah!" answered the mother; "I am sick of
him." And the poor little fellow continued to cry in the
darkness.

II
TWO PORTRAITS COMPLETED

THE Thénardiers have hitherto been seen in this book in profile
only; the time has come to turn this couple about and look at
them on all sides.

Thénardier has just passed his fiftieth year; Madame
Thénardier had reached her fortieth, which is the fiftieth for
woman, so that there was an equilibrium of age between the
husband and wife.

The reader has perhaps, since her first appearance, preserved
some remembrance of this huge Thénardiess;—for such we shall
call the female of this species,—large, blonde, red, fat, brawny,
square, enormous, and agile; she belonged, as we have said, to
the race of those colossal wild women who posturise at fairs
with paving-stones hung in their hair. She did everything about
the house, the chamber-work, the washing, the cooking, anything she pleased, and played the deuce generally. Cosette was
her only servant; a mouse in the service of an elephant. Everything trembled at the sound of her voice; windows and furniture
as well as people. Her broad face, covered with freckles, had the
appearance of a skimmer. She had a beard. She was the ideal of
a butcher's boy dressed in petticoats. She swore splendidly; she
prided herself on being able to crack a nut with her fist. Apart
from the novels she had read, which at times gave you an odd
glimpse of the affected lady under the ogress, the idea of calling
her a woman never would have occurred to anybody. This
Thénardiess seemed like a cross between a wench and a fish-
woman. If you heard her speak, you would say it is a gendarme;
if you saw her drink, you would say it is a cartman; if you saw
her handle Cosette, you would say it is the hangman. When at
rest, a tooth protruded from her mouth.

The other Thénardier was a little man, meagre, pale, angular, bony, and lean, who appeared to be sick, and whose health was excellent; here his knavery began. He smiled habitually as a matter of business, and tried to be polite to everybody, even to the beggar to whom he refused a penny. He had the look of a weasel, and the mien of a man of letters. He had a strong resemblance to the portraits of the Abbé Delille. He affected drinking with wagoners. Nobody ever saw him drunk. He smoked a large pipe. He wore a blouse, and under it an old black coat. He made pretensions to literature and materialism. There were names which he often pronounced in support of anything whatever that he might say. Voltaire, Raynal, Parny, and, oddly enough, St. Augustine. He professed to have "a system." For the rest, a great swindler. A fellow-sopher. There is such a variety. It will be remembered, that he pretended to have been in the service; he related with some pomp that at Waterloo, being sergeant in a Sixth or Ninth Light something, he alone, against a squadron of Hussars of Death, had covered with his body, and saved amid a shower of grape, "a general dangerously wounded." Hence the flaming picture on his sign, and the name of his inn, which was spoken of in the region as the "tavern of the sergeant of Waterloo." He was liberal, classical, and a Bonapartist. He had subscribed for the Champ d'Asile. It was said in the village that he had studied for the priesthood.

We believe that he had only studied in Holland to be an innkeeper. This whelp of the composite order was, according to all probability, some Fleming of Lille in Flanders, a Frenchman in Paris, a Belgian in Brussels, conveniently on the fence between the two frontiers. We understand his prowess at Waterloo. As we have seen, he exaggerated it a little. Ebb and flow, wandering, adventure, was his element; a violated conscience is followed by a loose life; and without doubt, at the stormy epoch of the 18th of June, 1815, Thénardier belonged to that species of marauding sutlers of whom we have spoken, scouring the country, robbing here and selling there, and travelling in family style, man, woman, and children, in some rickety carry-all, in the wake of marching troops, with the instinct to attach himself always to the victorious army. This campaign over, having, as he said, some "quibus," he had opened a "chophouse" at Montfermeil.

This "quibus," composed of purses and watches, gold rings and silver crosses, gathered at the harvest time in the furrows sown with corpses, did not form a great total, and had not lasted this sutler, now become a tavern-keeper, very long.

Thénardier had that indescribable stiffness of gesture which, with an oath, reminds you of the barracks, and, with a sign of the cross of the seminary. He was a fine talker. He was fond of being thought learned. Nevertheless, the schoolmaster remarked that he made mistakes in pronunciation. He made out travellers' bills in a superior style, but practised eyes sometimes found them faulty in orthography. Thénardier was sly, greedy, lounging, and clever. He did not disdain servant girls, consequently his wife had no more of them. This giantess was jealous. It seemed to her that this little, lean, and yellow man must be the object of universal desire.

Thénardier, above all a man of astuteness and poise, was a rascal of the subdued order. This is the worst species; there is hypocrisy in it.

Not that Thénardier was not on occasion capable of anger, quite as much as his wife; but that was very rare, and at such times, as if he were at war with the whole human race, as if he had in him a deep furnace of hatred, as if he were of those who are perpetually avenging themselves, who accuse everybody about them of the evils that befall them, and are always ready to throw on the first comer, as legitimate grievance, the sum-total of the deceptions, failures, and calamities of their life—as all this leaven worked in him, and boiled up into his mouth and eyes, he was frightful. Woe to him who came within reach of his fury, then!

Besides all his other qualities, Thénardier was attentive and penetrating, silent or talkative as occasion required, and always with great intelligence. He had somewhat the look of sailors accustomed to squinting the eye in looking through spy-glasses. Thénardier was a statesman.

Every new-comer who entered the chop-house said, on seeing the Thénardiess: There is the master of the house. It was an error. She was not even *the mistress*. The husband was both master and mistress. She performed, he created. He directed everything by a sort of invisible and continuous magnetic action. A word sufficed, sometimes a sign; the mastodon obeyed. Thénardier was to her, without her being really aware of it, a sort of being apart and sovereign. She had the virtues of her order of creation; never would she have differed in any detail

with "Monsieur Thénardier"—nor—impossible supposition—
would she have publicly quarrelled with her husband, on any
matter whatever. Never had she committed "before company"
that fault of which women are so often guilty, and which is called
in parliamentary language: discovering the crown. Although
their accord had no other result than evil, there was food for
contemplation in the submission of the Thénardiess to her husband. This bustling mountain of flesh moved under the little
finger of this frail despot. It was, viewed from its dwarfed and
grotesque side, this great universal fact: the homage of matter to
spirit; for certain deformities have their origin in the depths even
of eternal beauty. There was somewhat of the unknown in
Thénardier; hence the absolute empire of this man over this
woman. At times, she looked upon him as upon a lighted candle;
at others, she felt him like a claw.

This woman was a formidable creation, who loved nothing
but her children, and feared nothing but her husband. She was a
mother because she was a mammal. Her maternal feelings
stopped with her girls, and, as we shall see, did not extend to
boys. The man had but one thought—to get rich.

He did not succeed. His great talents had no adequate opportunity. Thénardier at Montfermeil was ruining himself, if ruin
is possible at zero. In Switzerland, or in the Pyrenees, this penni-
less rogue would have become a millionaire. But where fate
places the innkeeper he must browse.

It is understood that the word *innkeeper* is employed here in a
restricted sense, and does not extend to an entire class.

In this same year, 1823, Thénardier owed about fifteen
hundred francs, of pressing debts, which rendered him moody.

However obstinately unjust destiny was to him, Thénardier
was one of those men who best understood, to the greatest
depth and in the most modern style, that which is a virtue
among the barbarous, and a subject of merchandise among the
civilised—hospitality. He was, besides, an admirable poacher,
and was counted an excellent shot. He had a certain cool and
quiet laugh, which was particularly dangerous.

His theories of innkeeping sometimes sprang from him by
flashes. He had certain professional aphorisms which he incul-
cated in the mind of his wife. "The duty of the innkeeper," said
he to her one day, emphatically, and in a low voice, "is to sell to
the first comer, food, rest, light, fire, dirty linen, servants, fleas,

and smiles; to stop travellers, empty small purses, and honestly lighten large ones; to receive families who are travelling with respect: scrape the man, pluck the woman, and pick the child; to charge for the open window, the closed window, the chimney corner, the sofa, the chair, the stool, the bench, the feather bed, the mattress, and the straw bed; to know how much the mirror is worn, and to tax that; and, by the five hundred thousand devils, to make the traveller pay for everything, even to the flies that his dog eats!"

This man and this woman were cunning and rage married—a hideous and terrible pair.

While the husband calculated and schemed, the Thénardiess thought not of absent creditors, took no care either for yesterday or the morrow, and lived passionately in the present moment.

Such were these two beings. Cosette was between them, undergoing their double pressure, like a creature who is at the same time being bruised by a millstone, and lacerated with pincers. The man and the woman had each a different way. Cosette was beaten unmercifully; that came from the woman. She went barefoot in winter; that came from the man.

Cosette ran up stairs and down stairs; washed, brushed, scrubbed, swept, ran, tired herself, got out of breath, lifted heavy things, and, puny as she was, did the rough work. No pity; a ferocious mistress, a malignant master. The Thénardier chop-house was like a snare, in which Cosette had been caught, and was trembling. The ideal of oppression was realised by this dismal servitude. It was something like a fly serving spiders.

The poor child was passive and silent.

When they find themselves in such condition at the dawn of existence, so young, so feeble, among men, what passes in these souls fresh from God!

III
MEN MUST HAVE WINE AND HORSES WATER

FOUR new guests had just come in.

Cosette was musing sadly; for, though she was only eight years old, she had already suffered so much that she mused with the mournful air of an old woman.

She had a black eye from a blow of the Thénardiess's fist,

which made the Thénardiess say from time to time, "How ugly she is with her patch on her eye."

Cosette was then thinking that it was evening, late in the evening, that the bowls and pitchers in the rooms of the travellers who had arrived must be filled immediately, and that there was no more water in the cistern.

One thing comforted her a little; they did not drink much water in the Thénardier tavern. There were plenty of people there who were thirsty; but it was that kind of thirst which reaches rather towards the jug than the pitcher. Had anybody asked for a glass of water among these glasses of wine, he would have seemed a savage to all those men. However, there was an instant when the child trembled; the Thénardiess raised the cover of a kettle which was boiling on the range, then took a glass and hastily approached the cistern. She turned the faucet; the child had raised her head and followed all her movements. A thin stream of water ran from the faucet, and filled the glass half full.

"Here," said she, "there is no more water!" Then she was silent for a moment. The child held her breath.

"Pshaw!" continued the Thénardiess, examining the half-filled glass, "there is enough of it, such as it is."

Cosette resumed her work, but for more than a quarter of an hour she felt her heart leaping into her throat like a great ball.

She counted the minutes as they thus rolled away, and eagerly wished it were morning.

From time to time, one of the drinkers would look out into the street and exclaim:—"It is as black as an oven!" or, "It would take a cat to go along the street without a lantern to-night!" And Cosette shuddered.

All at once, one of the pedlars who lodged in the tavern came in, and said in a harsh voice:

"You have not watered my horse."

"Yes, we have, sure," said the Thénardiess.

"I tell you no, ma'am," replied the pedlar.

Cosette came out from under the table.

"Oh, yes, monsieur!" said she, "the horse did drink; he drank in the bucket, the bucket full, and 'twas me that carried it to him, and I talked to him."

This was not true. Cosette lied.

"Here is a girl as big as my fist, who can tell a lie as big as a house," exclaimed the pedlar. "I tell you that he has not had any water, little wench! He has a way of blowing when he has not had any water, that I know well enough."

Cosette persisted, and added in a voice stifled with anguish, and which could hardly be heard:

"But he did drink a good deal."

"Come," continued the pedlar, in a passion, "that is enough; give my horse some water, and say no more about it."

Cosette went back under the table.

"Well, of course that is right," said the Thénardiess; "if the beast has not had any water, she must have some."

Then looking about her:

"Well, what has become of that girl?"

She stooped down and discovered Cosette crouched at the other end of the table, almost under the feet of the drinkers.

"Aren't you coming?" cried the Thénardiess.

Cosette came out of the kind of hole where she had hidden. The Thénardiess continued:

"Mademoiselle Dog-without-a-name, go and carry some drink to this horse."

"But, ma'am," said Cosette feebly, "there is no water."

The Thénardiess threw the street door wide open.

"Well, go after some!"

Cosette hung her head, and went for an empty bucket that was by the chimney-corner.

The bucket was larger than she, and the child could have sat down in it comfortably.

The Thénardiess went back to her range, and tasted what was in the kettle with a wooden spoon, grumbling the while.

"There is some at the spring. She is the worst girl that ever was. I think 'twould have been better if I'd left out the onions."

Then she fumbled in a drawer where there were some pennies, pepper, and garlic.

"Here, Mamselle Toad," added she, "get a big loaf at the baker's, as you come back. Here is fifteen sous."

Cosette had a little pocket in the side of her apron; she took the piece without saying a word, and put it in that pocket.

Then she remained motionless, bucket in hand, the open door before her. She seemed to be waiting for somebody to come to her aid.

"Get along!" cried the Thénardiess.

Cosette went out. The door closed.

IV

A DOLL ENTERS UPON THE SCENE

THE row of booths extended along the street from the church, the reader will remember, as far as the Thénardier tavern. These booths, on account of the approaching passage of the citizens on their way to the midnight mass, were all illuminated with candles, burning in paper lanterns, which, as the schoolmaster of Montfermeil, who was at that moment seated at one of Thénardier's tables, said, produced a magical effect. In retaliation, not a star was to be seen in the sky.

The last of these stalls, set up exactly opposite Thénardier's door, was a toy-shop, all glittering with trinkets, glass beads, and things magnificent in tin. In the first rank, and in front, the merchant had placed, upon a bed of white napkins, a great doll nearly two feet high dressed in a robe of pink-crape with golden wheat-ears on its head, and which had real hair and enamel eyes. The whole day, this marvel had been displayed to the bewilderment of the passers under ten years of age, but there had not been found in Montfermeil a mother rich enough, or prodigal enough to give it to her child. Eponine and Azelma had passed hours in contemplating it, and Cosette herself, furtively, it is true, had dared to look at it.

At the moment when Cosette went out, bucket in hand, all gloomy and overwhelmed as she was, she could not help raising her eyes towards this wonderful doll, towards *the lady* as she called it. The poor child stopped, petrified. She had not seen this doll so near before.

This whole booth seemed a palace to her; this doll was not a doll, it was a vision. It was joy, splendour, riches, happiness, and it appeared in a sort of chimerical radiance to this unfortunate little being, buried so deeply in a cold and dismal misery. Cosette was measuring with the sad and simple sagacity of childhood the abyss which separated her from that doll. She was saying to herself that one must be a queen, or at least a princess, to have a "thing" like that. She gazed upon this beautiful pink dress, this beautiful smooth hair, and she was thinking, "How happy must be that doll!" Her eye could not turn away from this fantastic booth. The longer she looked, the more she was dazzled. She thought she saw paradise. There were other dolls behind the large one that appeared to her to be fairies and genii.

The merchant walking to and fro in the back part of his stall, suggested the Eternal Father.

In this adoration, she forgot everything, even the errand on which she had been sent. Suddenly, the harsh voice of the Thénardiess called her back to reality: "How, jade, haven't you gone yet? Hold on; I am coming for you! I'd like to know what she's doing there? Little monster, be off!"

The Thénardiess had glanced into the street, and perceived Cosette in ecstasy.

Cosette fled with her bucket, running as fast as she could.

V

THE LITTLE GIRL ALL ALONE

As the Thénardier tavern was in that part of the village which is near the church, Cosette had to go to the spring in the woods towards Chelles to draw water.

She looked no more at the displays in the booths; so long as she was in the lane Boulanger, and in the vicinity of the church, the illuminated stalls lighted the way, but soon the last gleam from the last stall disappeared. The poor child found herself in darkness. She became buried in it. Only, as she became the prey of a certain sensation, she shook the handle of the bucket as much as she could on her way. That made a noise, which kept her company.

The further she went, the thicker became the darkness. There was no longer anybody in the street. However, she met a woman who turned around on seeing her pass, and remained motionless, muttering between her teeth, "Where in the world can that child be going! Is it a phantom child?" Then the woman recognised Cosette. "Oh," said she, "it is the lark!"

Cosette thus passed through the labyrinth of crooked and deserted streets, which terminates the village of Montfermeil towards Chelles. As long as she had houses, or even walls, on the sides of the road, she went on boldly enough. From time to time, she saw the light of a candle through the cracks of a shutter; it was light and life to her; there were people there; that kept up her courage. However, as she advanced, her speed slackened as if mechanically. When she had passed the corner of the last house, Cosette stopped. To go beyond the last booth had been difficult; to go further than the last house became impossible. She put the bucket on the ground, buried her hands in her hair, and began to scratch her head slowly, a motion peculiar to terrified and hesitating children. It was Montfermeil no longer, it was the open country; dark and deserted space was before her. She looked with despair into this darkness where nobody was, where there were beasts, where there were perhaps ghosts. She looked intensely, and she heard the animals walking in the grass, and she distinctly saw the ghosts moving in the trees. Then she seized her bucket again; fear gave her boldness: "Pshaw," said she, "I will tell her there isn't any more water!" And she resolutely went back into Montfermeil.

She had scarcely gone a hundred steps when she stopped again, and began to scratch her head. Now, it was the Thénardiess that appeared to her; the hideous Thénardiess, with her hyena mouth and wrath flashing from her eyes. The child cast a pitiful glance before her and behind her. What could she do? What would become of her? Where should she go? Before her, the spectre of the Thénardiess; behind her, all the phantoms of night and of the forest. It was at the Thénardiess that she recoiled. She took the road to the spring again, and began to run. She ran out of the village; she ran into the woods, seeing nothing, hearing nothing. She did not stop running until out of breath, and even then she staggered on. She went right on, desperate.

Even while running, she wanted to cry.

The nocturnal tremulousness of the forest wrapped her about completely.

She thought no more; she saw nothing more. The immensity of night confronted this little creature. On one side, the infinite shadow; on the other, an atom.

It was only seven or eight minutes' walk from the edge of the woods to the spring. Cosette knew the road, from travelling it several times a day. Strange thing, she did not lose her way. A remnant of instinct guided her blindly. But she neither turned her eyes to the right nor to the left, for fear of seeing things in the trees and in the bushes. Thus she arrived at the spring.

It was a small natural basin, made by the water in the loamy soil, about two feet deep, surrounded with moss, and with that long figured grass called Henry Fourth's collars, and paved with a few large stones. A brook escaped from it with a gentle, tranquil murmur.

Cosette did not take time to breathe. It was very dark, but she was accustomed to come to this fountain. She felt with her left hand in the darkness for a young oak which bent over the spring and usually served her as a support, found a branch, swung herself from it, bent down and plunged the bucket in the water. She was for a moment so excited that her strength was tripled. When she was thus bent over, she did not notice that the pocket of her apron emptied itself into the spring. The fifteen-sous piece fell into the water. Cosette neither saw it nor heard it fall. She drew out the bucket almost full and set it on the grass.

This done, she perceived that her strength was exhausted. She was anxious to start at once; but the effort of filling the bucket had been so great that it was impossible for her to take a step. She was compelled to sit down. She fell upon the grass and remained in a crouching posture.

She closed her eyes, then she opened them, without knowing why, without the power of doing otherwise. At her side, the water shaken in the bucket made circles that resembled serpents of white fire.

Above her head, the sky was covered with vast black clouds which were like sheets of smoke. The tragic mask of night seemed to bend vaguely over this child.

Jupiter was setting in the depths of the horizon.

The child looked with a startled eye upon that great star which she did not know and which made her afraid. The planet, in fact, was at that moment very near the horizon and was crossing a dense bed of mist which gave it a horrid redness. The mist, gloomily empurpled, magnified the star. One would have called it a luminous wound.

A cold wind blew from the plain. The woods were dark, without any rustling of leaves, without any of those vague and fresh coruscations of summer. Great branches drew themselves up fearfully. Mean and shapeless bushes whistled in the glades. The tall grass wriggled under the north wind like eels. The brambles twisted about like long arms seeking to seize their prey in their claws. Some dry weeds driven by the wind, passed rapidly by, and appeared to flee with dismay before something that was following. The prospect was dismal.

Darkness makes the brain giddy. Man needs light, whoever plunges into the opposite of day feels his heart chilled. When the eye sees blackness, the mind sees trouble. In an eclipse, in night, in the sooty darkness, there is anxiety even to the strongest. Nobody walks alone at night in the forest without trembling. Darkness and trees, two formidable depths—a reality of chimeras appears in the indistinct distance. The Inconceivable outlines itself a few steps from you with a spectral clearness. You see floating in space or in your brain something strangely vague and unseizable as the dreams of sleeping flowers. There are fierce phantoms in the horizon. You breathe in the odours of the great black void. You are afraid, and are tempted to look behind you. The hollowness of night, the haggardness of all things, the silent profiles that fade away as you advance, the obscure dishevelments, angry clumps, livid pools, the gloomy reflected in the funereal, the sepulchral immensity of silence, the possible unknown beings, the swaying of mysterious branches, the frightful twistings of the trees, long spires of shivering grass—against all this you have no defence. There is no bravery which does not shudder and feel the nearness of anguish. You feel something hideous, as if the soul were amalgamating with the shadow. This penetration of the darkness is inexpressibly dismal for a child.

Forests are apocalypses; and the beating of the wings of a little soul makes an agonising sound under their monstrous vault.

Without being conscious of what she was experiencing, Cosette felt that she was seized by this black enormity of nature. It was not merely terror that held her, but something more terrible even than terror. She shuddered. Words fail to express the peculiar strangeness of that shudder which chilled her through and through. Her eye had become wild. She felt that perhaps she would be compelled to return there at the same hour the next night.

Then, by a sort of instinct, to get out of this singular state, which she did not understand, but which terrified her, she began to count aloud, one, two, three, four, up to ten, and when she had finished, she began again. This restored her to a real perception of things about her. Her hands, which she had wet in drawing the water, felt cold. She arose. Her fear had returned, a natural and insurmountable fear. She had only one thought, to fly; to fly with all her might, across woods, across fields, to houses, to windows, to lighted candles. Her eyes fell upon the bucket that was before her. Such was the dread with which the

Thénardiess inspired her, that she did not dare to go without the bucket of water. She grasped the handle with both hands. She could hardly lift the bucket.

She went a dozen steps in this manner, but the bucket was full, it was heavy, she was compelled to rest it on the ground. She breathed an instant then grasped the handle again, and walked on, this time a little longer. But she had to stop again. After resting a few seconds, she started on. She walked bending forward, her head down, like an old woman: the weight of the bucket strained and stiffened her thin arms. The iron handle was numbing and freezing her little wet hands; from time to time she had to stop, and every time she stopped, the cold water that splashed from the bucket fell upon her naked knees. This took place in the depth of a wood, at night, in the winter, far from all human sight; it was a child of eight years; there was none but God at that moment who saw this sad thing.

And undoubtedly her mother, alas!

For there are things which open the eyes of the dead in their grave.

She breathed with a kind of mournful rattle; sobs choked her, but she did not dare to weep; so fearful was she of the Thénardiess, even at a distance. She always imagined that the Thénardiess was near.

However, she could not make much headway in this manner, and was getting along very slowly. She tried hard to shorten her resting spells, and to walk as far as possible between them. She remembered with anguish that it would take her more than an hour to return to Montfermeil thus, and that the Thénardiess would beat her. This anguish added to her dismay at being alone in the woods at night. She was worn out with fatigue, and was not yet out of the forest. Arriving near an old chestnut tree which she knew, she made a last halt, longer than the others, to get well rested; then she gathered all her strength, took up the bucket again, and began to walk on courageously. Meanwhile the poor little despairing thing could not help crying: "Oh! my God! my God!"

At that moment she felt all at once that the weight of the bucket was gone. A hand, which seemed enormous to her, had just caught the handle and was carrying it easily. She raised her head. A large dark form, straight and erect, was walking beside her in the gloom. It was a man who had come up behind her, and whom she had not heard. This man, without saying a word, had grasped the handle of the bucket she was carrying.

There are instincts for all the crises of life.

The child was not afraid.

VI

WHICH PERHAPS PROVES THE INTELLIGENCE OF BOULATRUELLE

IN the afternoon of that same Christmas-day, 1823, a man walked a long time in the most deserted portion of the Boulevard de l'Hôpital at Paris. This man had the appearance of some one who was looking for lodgings, and seemed to stop by preference before the most modest houses of this dilapidated part of the Faubourg Saint Marceau.

We shall see further on that this man did in fact hire a room in this isolated quarter.

This man, in his dress as in his whole person, realised the type of what might be called the mendicant of good society—extreme misery being combined with extreme neatness. It is a rare coincidence which inspires intelligent hearts with this double respect that we feel for him who is very poor and for him who is very worthy. He wore a round hat, very old and carefully brushed, a long coat, completely threadbare, of coarse yellow cloth, a colour which was in nowise extraordinary at that epoch, a large waistcoat with pockets of antique style, black trousers worn grey at the knees, black woollen stockings, and thick shoes with copper buckles. One would have called him an old preceptor of a good family, returned from the emigration. From his hair, which was entirely white, from his wrinkled brow, from his livid lips, from his face in which everything breathed exhaustion and weariness of life, one would have supposed him considerably over sixty. From his firm though slow step, and the singular vigour impressed upon all his motions, one would hardly have thought him fifty. The wrinkles on his forehead were well disposed, and would have prepossessed in his favour any one who observed him with attention. His lip contracted with a strange expression, which seemed severe and yet which was humble. There was in the depths of his eye an indescribably mournful serenity. He carried in his left hand a small package tied in a handkerchief, with his right he leaned upon a sort of staff cut from a hedge. This staff had been finished with some care, and did not look very badly; the knots were smoothed down, and a coral head had been formed with red wax; it was a cudgel, and it seemed a cane.

There are few people on that boulevard, especially in winter. This man appeared to avoid them rather than seek them, but without affectation.

At that epoch the king, Louis XVIII., went almost every day to Choisy Le Roy. It was one of his favourite rides. About two o'clock, almost invariably, the carriage and the royal cavalcade were seen to pass at full-speed through the Boulevard de l'Hôpital.

This supplied the place of watch and clock to the poor women of the quarter, who would say: "It is two o'clock, there he is going back to the Tuileries."

And some ran, and others fell into line; for when a king passes by, there is always a tumult. Moreover, the appearance and disappearance of Louis XVIII. produced a certain sensation in the streets of Paris. It was rapid, but majestic. This impotent king had a taste for fast driving; not being able to walk, he wished to run; this cripple would have gladly been drawn by the lightning. He passed by, peaceful and severe, in the midst of naked sabres. His massive coach, all gilded, with great lily branches painted on the panels, rolled noisily along. One hardly had time to catch a glance of it. In the back corner on the right could be seen, upon cushions covered with white satin, a broad face, firm and red, a forehead freshly powdered à la bird of paradise, a proud eye, stern and keen, a well-read smile, two large epaulettes of bullion waving over a citizen's dress, the Golden Fleece, the cross of Saint Louis, the cross of the Legion of Honour, the silver badge of the Holy Spirit, a big belly, and a large blue ribbon; that was the king. Outside of Paris, he held his hat with white feathers upon his knees, which were inclosed in high English gaiters; when he re-entered the city, he placed his hat upon his head, bowing but little. He looked coldly upon the people, who returned his look. When he appeared for the first time in the Quartier Saint Marceau, all he succeeded in eliciting was this saying of a resident to his comrade: "It's that big fellow who is the government."

This unfailing passage of the king at the same hour was then the daily event of the Boulevard de l'Hôpital.

The promenader in the yellow coat evidently did not belong to the quarter, and probably not to Paris, for he was ignorant of this circumstance. When at two o'clock the royal carriage, surrounded by a squadron of silver-laced body-guard, turned into the boulevard, after passing La Salpêtrière, he appeared surprised, and almost frightened. There was no one else in the cross alley, and he retired hastily behind a corner of the side wall, but this did not prevent the Duke d'Havré seeing him. The Duke d'Havré, as captain of the guards in waiting that day, was seated in the carriage opposite the king. He said to his majesty: "There is a man who has a bad look." Some policemen, who were clearing the passage for the king, also noticed him; one of them was ordered to follow him. But the man plunged into the little solitary streets of the Faubourg, and as night was coming on the officer lost his track, as is established by a report addressed on the same evening to the Comte Anglès, Minister of State, Prefect of Police.

When the man in the yellow coat had thrown the officer off his track, he turned about, not without looking back many times to make sure that he was not followed. At a quarter past four, that is to say, after dark, he passed in front of the theatre of the Porte Saint Martin where the play that day was *The Two Convicts*. The poster, lit up by the reflection from the theatre, seemed to strike him, for, although he was walking rapidly, he stopped to read it. A moment after, he was in the *cul-de-sac* de la Planchette, and entered the *Pewter platter*, which was then the office of the Lagny stage. This stage started at half past four. The horses were harnessed, and the travellers, who had been called by the driver hastily, were climbing the high iron steps of the vehicle.

The man asked:

"Have you a seat?"

"Only one, beside me, on the box," said the driver.

"I will take it."

"Get up then."

Before starting, however, the driver cast a glance at the poor apparel of the traveller, and at the smallness of his bundle, and took his pay.

"Are you going through to Lagny?" asked the driver.

"Yes," said the man.

The traveller paid through to Lagny.

They started off. When they had passed the barrière, the driver tried to start a conversation, but the traveller answered only in monosyllables. The driver concluded to whistle, and swear at his horses.

The driver wrapped himself up in his cloak. It was cold. The man did not appear to notice it. In this way they passed through Gournay and Neuilly sur Marne. About six o'clock in the evening they were at Chelles. The driver stopped to let his horses breathe, in front of the wagoners' tavern established in the old buildings of the royal abbey.

"I will get down here," said the man.

He took his bundle and stick, and jumped down from the stage.

A moment afterwards he had disappeared.

He did not go into the tavern.

When, a few minutes afterwards, the stage started off for Lagny, it did not overtake him in the main street of Chelles.

The driver turned to the inside passengers:

"There," said he, "is a man who does not belong here, for I don't know him. He has an appearance of not having a sou; however, he don't stick about money; he pays to Lagny, and he only goes to Chelles. It is night, all the houses are shut, he don't go to the tavern, and we don't overtake him. He must, then, have sunk into the ground."

The man had not sunk into the ground, but he had hurried rapidly in the darkness along the main street of Chelles; then he had turned to the left, before reaching the church, into the cross-road leading to Montfermeil, like one who knew the country and had been that way before.

He followed this road rapidly. At the spot where it intersects the old road bordered with trees that goes from Gagny to Lagny, he heard footsteps approaching. He concealed himself hastily in a ditch, and waited there till the people who were passing were a good distance off. The precaution was indeed almost superfluous, for, as we have already said, it was a very dark December night. There were scarcely two or three stars to be seen in the sky.

It is at this point that the ascent of the hill begins. The man did not return to the Montfermeil road; he turned to the right, across the fields, and gained the woods with rapid strides.

When he reached the wood, he slackened his pace, and began

to look carefully at all the trees, pausing at every step, as if he were seeking and following a mysterious route known only to himself. There was a moment when he appeared to lose himself, and then he stopped, undecided. Finally he arrived, by continual groping, at a glade where there was a heap of large whitish stones. He made his way quickly towards these stones, and examined them with attention in the dusk of the night, as if he were passing them in review. A large tree, covered with these excrescences which are the warts of vegetation, was a few steps from the heap of stones. He went to this tree, and passed his hand over the bark of the trunk, as if he were seeking to recognise and to count all the warts.

Opposite this tree, which was an ash, there was a chestnut tree wounded in the bark, which had been staunched with a bandage of zinc nailed on. He rose on tip-toe and touched that band of zinc.

Then he stamped for some time upon the ground in the space between the tree and the stones, like one who would be sure that the earth had not been freshly stirred.

This done, he took his course and resumed his walk through the woods.

This was the man who had fallen in with Cosette.

As he made his way through the copse in the direction of Montfermeil, he had perceived that little shadow, struggling along with a groan, setting her burden on the ground, then taking it up and going on again. He had approached her and seen that it was a very young child carrying an enormous bucket of water. Then he had gone to the child, and silently taken hold of the handle of the bucket.

VII

COSETTE SIDE BY SIDE WITH THE UNKNOWN, IN THE DARKNESS

COSETTE, we have said, was not afraid.

The man spoke to her. His voice was serious, and was almost a whisper.

"My child, that is very heavy for you which you are carrying there."

Cosette raised her head and answered:

"Yes, monsieur."

"Give it to me," the man continued, "I will carry it for you."
Cosette let go of the bucket. The man walked along with her.
"It is very heavy, indeed," said he to himself. Then he added:
"Little girl, how old are you?"

"Eight years, monsieur."

"And have you come far in this way?"

"From the spring in the woods."

"And are you going far?"

"A good quarter of an hour from here."

The man remained a moment without speaking, then he said abruptly:

"You have no mother then?"

"I don't know," answered the child.

Before the man had had time to say a word, she added:

"I don't believe I have. All the rest have one. For my part, I have none."

And after a silence, she added:

"I believe I never had any."

The man stopped, put the bucket on the ground, stooped down and placed his hands upon the child's shoulders, making an effort to look at her and see her face in the darkness.

The thin and puny face of Cosette was vaguely outlined in the livid light of the sky.

"What is your name?" said the man.

"Cosette."

It seemed as if the man had an electric shock. He looked at her again, then letting go of her shoulders, took up the bucket, and walked on.

A moment after, he asked:

"Little girl, where do you live?"

"At Montfermeil, if you know it."

"It is there that we are going?"

"Yes, monsieur."

He made another pause, then he began:

"Who is it that has sent you out into the woods after water at this time of night?"

"Madame Thénardier."

The man resumed with a tone of voice which he tried to render indifferent, but in which there was nevertheless a singular tremor:

"What does she do, your Madame Thénardier?"

"She is my mistress," said the child. "She keeps the tavern."

"The tavern," said the man. "Well, I am going there to lodge to-night. Show me the way."

"We are going there," said the child.

The man walked very fast. Cosette followed him without difficulty. She felt fatigue no more. From time to time, she raised her eyes towards this man with a sort of tranquillity and inexpressible confidence. She had never been taught to turn towards Providence and to pray. However, she felt in her bosom something that resembled hope and joy, and which rose towards heaven.

A few minutes passed. The man spoke:

"Is there no servant at Madame Thénardier's?"

"No, monsieur."

"Are you alone?"

"Yes, monsieur."

There was another interval of silence. Cosette raised her voice:

"That is, there are two little girls."

"What little girls?"

"Ponine and Zelma."

The child simplified in this way the romantic names dear to the mother.

"What are Ponine and Zelma?"

"They are Madame Thénardier's young ladies, you might say her daughters."

"And what do they do?"

"Oh!" said the child, "they have beautiful dolls, things which there's gold in; they are full of business. They play, they amuse themselves."

"All day long?"

"Yes, monsieur."

"And you?"

"Me! I work."

"All day long?"

The child raised her large eyes in which there was a tear, which could not be seen in the darkness, and answered softly:

"Yes, monsieur."

She continued after an interval of silence:

"Sometimes, when I have finished my work and they are willing, I amuse myself also."

"How do you amuse yourself?"

"The best I can. They let me alone. But I have not many playthings. Ponine and Zelma are not willing for me to play with their dolls. I have only a little lead sword, no longer than that."

The child showed her little finger.

"And which does not cut?"

"Yes, monsieur," said the child, "it cuts lettuce and flies' heads."

They reached the village; Cosette guided the stranger through the streets. They passed by the bakery, but Cosette did not think of the bread she was to have brought back. The man questioned her no more, and now maintained a mournful silence. When they had passed the church, the man, seeing all these booths in the street, asked Cosette:

"Is it fair-time here?"

"No, monsieur, it is Christmas."

As they drew near the tavern, Cosette timidly touched his arm:

"Monsieur?"

"What, my child?"

"Here we are close by the house."

"Well?"

"Will you let me take the bucket now?"

"What for?"

"Because, if madame sees that anybody brought it for me, she will beat me."

The man gave her the bucket. A moment after they were at the door of the chop-house.

VIII

INCONVENIENCE OF ENTERTAINING A POOR MAN WHO IS PERHAPS RICH

COSETTE could not help casting one look towards the grand doll still displayed in the toy-shop, then she rapped. The door opened. The Thénardiess appeared with a candle in her hand.

"Oh! it is you, you little beggar! Lud-a-massy! you have taken your time! she has been playing, the wench!"

"Madame," said Cosette, trembling, "there is a gentleman who is coming to lodge."

The Thénardiess very quickly replaced her fierce air by her amiable grimace, a change at sight peculiar to innkeepers, and looked for the new-comer with eager eyes.

"Is it monsieur?" said she.

"Yes, madame," answered the man, touching his hat.

Rich travellers are not so polite. This gesture and the sight of the stranger's costume and baggage which the Thénardiess passed in review at a glance made the amiable grimace disappear and the fierce air reappear. She added drily:

"Enter, goodman."

The "goodman" entered. The Thénardiess cast a second glance at him, examined particularly his long coat which was absolutely threadbare, and his hat which was somewhat broken, and with a nod, a wink, and a turn of her nose, consulted her husband, who was still drinking with the wagoners. The husband answered by that imperceptible shake of the forefinger which, supported by a protrusion of the lips, signifies in such a case: "complete destitution." Upon this the Thénardiess exclaimed:

"Ah! my brave man, I am very sorry, but I have no room."

"Put me where you will," said the man, "in the garret, in the stable. I will pay as if I had a room."

"Forty sous."

"Forty sous. Well."

"In advance."

"Forty sous," whispered a wagoner to the Thénardiess, "but it is only twenty sous."

"It is forty sous for him," replied the Thénardiess in the same tone. "I don't lodge poor people for less."

"That is true," added her husband softly, "it ruins a house to have this sort of people."

Meanwhile the man, after leaving his stick and bundle on a bench, had seated himself at a table on which Cosette had been quick to place a bottle of wine and a glass. The pedlar, who had asked for the bucket of water, had gone himself to carry it to his horse. Cosette had resumed her place under the kitchen table and her knitting.

The man, who hardly touched his lips to the wine he had turned out, was contemplating the child with a strange attention.

Cosette was ugly. Happy, she might, perhaps, have been

pretty. We have already sketched this little pitiful face. Cosette was thin and pale; she was nearly eight years old, but one would hardly have thought her six. Her large eyes, sunk in a sort of shadow, were almost put out by continual weeping. The corners of her mouth had that curve of habitual anguish, which is seen in the condemned and in the hopelessly sick. Her hands were, as her mother had guessed, "covered with chilblains." The light of the fire which was shining upon her, made her bones stand out and rendered her thinness fearfully visible. As she was always shivering, she had acquired the habit of drawing her knees together. Her whole dress was nothing but a rag, which would have excited pity in the summer, and which excited horror in the winter. She had on nothing but cotton, and that full of holes; not a rag of woollen. Her skin showed here and there, and black and blue spots could be distinguished, which indicated the places where the Thénardiess had touched her. Her naked legs were red and rough. The hollows under her collar-bones would make one weep. The whole person of this child, her gait, her attitude, the sound of her voice, the intervals between one word and another, her looks, her silence, her least motion, expressed and uttered a single idea: fear.

Fear was spread all over her; she was, so to say, covered with it; fear drew back her elbows against her sides, drew her heels under her skirt, made her take the least possible room, prevented her from breathing more than was absolutely necessary, and had become what might be called her bodily habit, without possible variation, except of increase. There was in the depth of her eye an expression of astonishment mingled with terror.

This fear was such that on coming in, all wet as she was, Cosette had not dared go and dry herself by the fire, but had gone silently to her work.

The expression of the countenance of this child of eight years was habitually so sad and sometimes so tragical that it seemed, at certain moments, as if she were in the way of becoming an idiot or a demon.

Never, as we have said, had she known what it is to pray, never had she set foot within a church. "How can I spare the time?" said the Thénardiess.

The man in the yellow coat did not take his eyes from Cosette.

Suddenly, the Thénardiess exclaimed out:

"Oh! I forgot! that bread!"

Cosette, according to her custom whenever the Thénardiess raised her voice, sprang out quickly from under the table.

She had entirely forgotten the bread. She had recourse to the expedient of children who are always terrified. She lied.

"Madame, the baker was shut."

"You ought to have knocked."

"I did knock, madame."

"Well?"

"He didn't open."

"I'll find out to-morrow if that is true," said the Thénardiess, "and if you are lying you will lead a pretty dance. Meantime give me back the fifteen-sous piece."

Cosette plunged her hand into her apron pocket, and turned white. The fifteen-sous piece was not there.

"Come," said the Thénardiess, "didn't you hear me?"

Cosette turned her pocket inside out; there was nothing there. What could have become of that money? The little unfortunate could not utter a word. She was petrified.

"Have you lost it, the fifteen-sous piece?" screamed the Thénardiess, "or do you want to steal it from me?"

At the same time she reached her arm towards the cowhide hanging in the chimney-corner.

This menacing movement gave Cosette the strength to cry out:

"Forgive me! Madame! Madame! I won't do so any more!"

The Thénardiess took down the whip.

Meanwhile the man in the yellow coat had been fumbling in his waistcoat pocket, without being noticed. The other travellers were drinking or playing cards, and paid no attention to anything.

Cosette was writhing with anguish in the chimney-corner, trying to gather up and hide her poor half-naked limbs. The Thénardiess raised her arm.

"I beg your pardon, madame," said the man, "but I just now saw something fall out of the pocket of that little girl's apron and roll away. That may be it."

At the same time he stooped down and appeared to search on the floor for an instant.

"Just so, here it is," said he, rising.

And he handed a silver piece to the Thénardiess.

"Yes, that is it," said she.

That was not it, for it was a twenty-sous piece, but the Thénardiess found her profit in it. She put the piece in her pocket, and contented herself with casting a ferocious look at the child and saying:

"Don't let that happen again, ever."

Cosette went back to what the Thénardiess called "her hole," and her large eye, fixed upon the unknown traveller, began to assume an expression that it had never known before. It was still only an artless astonishment, but a sort of blind confidence was associated with it.

"O! you want supper?" asked the Thénardiess of the traveller.

He did not answer. He seemed to be thinking deeply.

"What is that man?" said she between her teeth. "It is some frightful pauper. He hasn't a penny for his supper. Is he going to pay me for his lodging only? It is very lucky, anyway, that he didn't think to steal the money that was on the floor."

A door now opened, and Eponine and Azelma came in.

They were really two pretty little girls, rather city girls than peasants, very charming, one with her well-polished auburn tresses, the other with her long black braids falling down her back and both so lively, neat, plump, fresh, and healthy, that it was a pleasure to see them. They were warmly clad, but with such maternal art, that the thickness of the stuff detracted nothing from the coquetry of the fit. Winter was provided against without effacing spring. These two little girls shed light around them. Moreover, they were regnant. In their toilet, in their gaiety, in the noise they made, there was sovereignty. When they entered, the Thénardiess said to them in a scolding tone, which was full of adoration: "Ah! you are here then, you children!"

Then, taking them upon her knees one after the other, smoothing their hair, tying over their ribbons, and finally letting them go with that gentle sort of shake which is peculiar to mothers, she exclaimed:

"Are they dowdies!"

They went and sat down by the fire. They had a doll which they turned backwards and forwards upon their knees with many pretty prattlings. From time to time, Cosette raised her eyes from her knitting, and looked sadly at them as they were playing.

Eponine and Azelma did not notice Cosette. To them she was like the dog. These three little girls could not count twenty-four years among them all, and they already represented all human society; on one side envy, on the other disdain.

The doll of the Thénardier sisters was very much faded, and very old and broken; and it appeared none the less wonderful to Cosette, who had never in her life had a doll, *a real doll*, to use an expression that all children will understand.

All at once, the Thénardiess, who was continually going and coming about the room, noticed that Cosette's attention was distracted, and that instead of working she was busied with the little girls who were playing.

"Ah! I've caught you!" cried she. "That is the way you work! I'll make you work with a cowhide, I will."

The stranger, without leaving his chair, turned towards the Thénardiess.

"Madame," said he, smiling diffidently. "Pshaw! let her play!"

On the part of any traveller who had eaten a slice of mutton, and drunk two bottles of wine at his supper, and who had not had the appearance of *a horrid pauper*, such a wish would have been a command. But that a man who wore that hat should allow himself to have a desire, and that a man who wore that coat should permit himself to have a wish, was what the Thénardiess thought ought not to be tolerated. She replied sharply:

"She must work, for she eats. I don't support her to do nothing."

"What is it she is making?" said the stranger, in that gentle voice which contrasted so strangely with his beggar's clothes and his porter's shoulders.

The Thénardiess deigned to answer.

"Stockings, if you please. Stockings for my little girls who have none, worth speaking of, and will soon be going barefooted."

The man looked at Cosette's poor red feet, and continued:

"When will she finish that pair of stockings?"

"It will take her at least three or four good days, the lazy thing."

"And how much might this pair of stockings be worth, when it is finished?"

The Thénardiess cast a disdainful glance at him.

"At least thirty sous."

"Would you take five francs for them?" said the man.

"Goodness!" exclaimed a wagoner who was listening, with a horse-laugh, "five francs? It's a humbug! five bullets!"

Thénardier now thought it time to speak.

"Yes, monsieur, if it is your fancy, you can have that pair of stockings for five francs. We can't refuse anything to travellers."

"You must pay for them now," said the Thénardiess, in her short and peremptory way.

"I will buy that pair of stockings," answered the man, "and," added he, drawing a five-franc piece from his pocket and laying it on the table, "I will pay for them."

Then he turned towards Cosette.

"Now your work belongs to me. Play, my child."

The wagoner was so affected by the five-franc piece, that he left his glass and went to look at it.

"It's so, that's a fact!" cried he, as he looked at it. "A regular hindwheel! and no counterfeit!"

Thénardier approached, and silently put the piece in his pocket.

The Thénardiess had nothing to reply. She bit her lips, and her face assumed an expression of hatred.

Meanwhile Cosette trembled. She ventured to ask:

"Madame, is it true? can I play?"

"Play!" said the Thénardiess in a terrible voice.

"Thank you, madame," said Cosette. And, while her mouth thanked the Thénardiess, all her little soul was thanking the traveller.

Thénardier returned to his drink. His wife whispered in his ear:

"What can that yellow man be?"

"I have seen," answered Thénardier, in a commanding tone, "millionaires with coats like that."

Cosette had left her knitting, but she had not moved from her place. Cosette always stirred as little as was possible. She had taken from a little box behind her a few old rags, and her little lead sword.

Eponine and Azelma paid no attention to what was going on. They had just performed a very important operation; they had caught the kitten. They had thrown the doll on the floor, and Eponine, the elder, was dressing the kitten, in spite of her mewings and contortions, with a lot of clothes and red and blue rags. While she was engaged in this serious and difficult labour, she was talking to her sister in that sweet and charming language of children, the grace of which, like the splendour of the butterfly's wings, escapes when we try to preserve it.

"Look! look, sister, this doll is more amusing than the other. She moves, she cries, she is warm. Come, sister, let us play with her. She shall be my little girl; I will be a lady. I'll come to see you, and you must look at her. By and by you must see her whiskers, and you must be surprised. And then you must see her ears, and then you must see her tail, and that will astonish you. And you must say to me: 'Oh! my stars!' and I will say to you, 'Yes, madame, it is a little girl that I have like that.' Little girls are like that now."

Azelma listened to Eponine with wonder.

Meanwhile, the drinkers were singing an obscene song, at which they laughed enough to shake the room. Thénardier encouraged and accompanied them.

As birds make a nest of anything, children make a doll of no matter what. While Eponine and Azelma were dressing up the cat, Cosette, for her part, had dressed up the sword. That done, she had laid it upon her arm, and was singing it softly to sleep.

The doll is one of the most imperious necessities, and at the same time one of the most charming instincts of female childhood. To care for, to clothe, to adorn, to dress, to undress, to dress over again, to teach, to scold a little, to rock, to cuddle, to put to sleep, to imagine that something is somebody—all the future of woman is there. Even while musing and prattling, while making little wardrobes and little baby-clothes, while sewing little dresses, little bodices, and little jackets, the child becomes a little girl, the little girl becomes a great girl, the great girl becomes a woman. The first baby takes the place of the last doll.

A little girl without a doll is almost as unfortunate and quite as impossible as a woman without children.

Cosette had therefore made a doll of her sword.

The Thénardiess, on her part, approached the *yellow man.* "My husband is right," thought she; "it may be Monsieur Laffitte. Some rich men are so odd."

She came and rested her elbow on the table at which he was sitting.

"Monsieur," said she——

At this word *monsieur*, the man turned. The Thénardiess had called him before only *brave man* or *good man*.

"You see, monsieur," she pursued, putting on her sweetest look, which was still more unendurable than her ferocious manner, "I am very willing the child should play, I am not opposed to it; it is well for once, because you are generous. But, you see, she is poor; she must work."

"The child is not yours, then?" asked the man.

"Oh dear! no, monsieur! It is a little pauper that we have taken in through charity. A sort of imbecile child. She must have water on her brain. Her head is big, as you see. We do all we can for her, but we are not rich. We write in vain to her country; for six months we have had no answer. We think that her mother must be dead."

"Ah!" said the man, and he fell back into his reverie.

"This mother was no great things," added the Thénardiess. "She abandoned her child."

During all this conversation, Cosette, as if an instinct had warned her that they were talking about her, had not taken her eyes from the Thénardiess. She listened. She heard a few words here and there.

Meanwhile the drinkers, all three-quarters drunk, were repeating their foul chorus with redoubled gaiety. It was highly spiced with jests, in which the names of the Virgin and the child Jesus were often heard. The Thénardiess had gone to take her part in the hilarity. Cosette, under the table, was looking into the fire, which was reflected from her fixed eye; she was again rocking the sort of rag baby that she had made, and as she rocked it, she sang in a low voice; "My mother is dead! my mother is dead! my mother is dead!"

At the repeated entreaties of the hostess, the yellow man, "the millionaire," finally consented to sup.

"What will monsieur have?"

"Some bread and cheese," said the man.

"Decidedly, it is a beggar," thought the Thénardiess.

The revellers continued to sing their songs, and the child, under the table, also sang hers.

All at once, Cosette stopped. She had just turned and seen the little Thénardiers' doll, which they had forsaken for the cat and left on the floor, a few steps from the kitchen table.

Then she let the bundled-up sword, that only half satisfied her, fall, and ran her eyes slowly around the room. The Thénardiess was whispering to her husband and counting some money, Eponine and Azelma were playing with the cat, the travellers were eating or drinking or singing, nobody was looking at her. She had not a moment to lose. She crept out from under the table on her hands and knees, made sure once more that nobody was watching her, then darted quickly to the doll, and seized it. An instant afterwards she was at her place, seated, motionless, only turned in such a way as to keep the doll that she held in her arms in the shadow. The happiness of playing with a doll was so rare to her that it had all the violence of rapture.

Nobody had seen her, except the traveller, who was slowly eating his meagre supper.

This joy lasted for nearly a quarter of an hour.

But in spite of Cosette's precautions, she did not perceive that one of the doll's feet *stuck out*, and that the fire of the fireplace lighted it up very vividly. This rosy and luminous foot which protruded from the shadow suddenly caught Azelma's eye, and she said to Eponine: "Oh! sister!"

The two little girls stopped, stupefied; Cosette had dared to take the doll.

Eponine got up, and without letting go of the cat, went to her mother and began to pull at her skirt.

"Let me alone," said the mother; "what do you want?"

"Mother," said the child, "look there."

And she pointed at Cosette.

Cosette, wholly absorbed in the ecstasy of her possession, saw and heard nothing else.

The face of the Thénardiess assumed the peculiar expression which is composed of the terrible mingled with the commonplace and which has given this class of women the name of furies.

This time wounded pride exasperated her anger still more. Cosette had leaped over all barriers. Cosette had laid her hands upon the doll of "those young ladies." A czarina who had seen a moujik trying on the grand cordon of her imperial son would have had the same expression.

She cried with a voice harsh with indignation:

"Cosette!"

Cosette shuddered as if the earth had quaked beneath her. She turned around.

"Cosette!" repeated the Thénardiess.

Cosette took the doll and placed it gently on the floor with a kind of veneration mingled with despair. Then, without taking away her eyes, she joined her hands, and, what is frightful to tell in a child of that age, she wrung them; then, what none of the emotions of the day had drawn from her, neither the run in the wood, nor the weight of the bucket of water, nor the loss of the money, nor the sight of the cowhide, nor even the stern words she had heard from the Thénardiess, she burst into tears. She sobbed.

Meanwhile the traveller arose.

"What is the matter?" said he to the Thénardiess.

"Don't you see?" said the Thénardiess, pointing with her finger to the *corpus delicti* lying at Cosette's feet.

"Well, what is that?" said the man.

"That beggar," answered the Thénardiess, "has dared to touch the children's doll."

"All this noise about that?" said the man. "Well, what if she did play with that doll?"

"She has touched it with her dirty hands!" continued the Thénardiess, "with her horrid hands!"

Here Cosette redoubled her sobs.

"Be still!" cried the Thénardiess.

The man walked straight to the street door, opened it, and went out.

As soon as he had gone, the Thénardiess profited by his absence to give Cosette under the table a severe kick, which made the child shriek.

The door opened again, and the man reappeared, holding in his hands the fabulous doll of which we have spoken, and which had been the admiration of all the youngsters of the village since morning; he stood it up before Cosette, saying:

"Here, this is for you."

It is probable that during the time he had been there—more than an hour—in the midst of his reverie, he had caught confused glimpses of this toy-shop, lighted up with lamps and candles so splendidly that it shone through the bar-room window like an illumination.

Cosette raised her eyes; she saw the man approach her with that doll as she would have seen the sun approach, she heard those astounding words: *This is for you.* She looked at him, she looked at the doll, then she drew back slowly, and went and hid as far as she could under the table in the corner of the room.

She wept no more, she cried no more, she had the appearance of no longer daring to breathe.

The Thénardiess, Eponine, and Azelma were so many statues. Even the drinkers stopped. There was a solemn silence in the whole bar-room.

The Thénardiess, petrified and mute, recommenced her conjectures anew: "What is this old fellow? is he a pauper? is he a millionaire? Perhaps he's both, that is a robber."

The face of the husband Thénardier presented that expressive wrinkle which marks the human countenance whenever the dominant instinct appears in it with all its brutal power. The innkeeper contemplated by turns the doll and the traveller; he seemed to be scenting this man as he would have scented a bag of money. This only lasted for a moment. He approached his wife and whispered to her:

"That machine cost at least thirty francs. No nonsense. Down on your knees before the man!"

Coarse natures have this in common with artless natures, that they have no transitions.

"Well, Cosette," said the Thénardiess in a voice which was meant to be sweet, and which was entirely composed of the sour honey of vicious women, "a'in't you going to take your doll?"

Cosette ventured to come out of her hole.

"My little Cosette," said Thénardier with a caressing air, "Monsieur gives you a doll. Take it. It is yours."

Cosette looked upon the wonderful doll with a sort of terror. Her face was still flooded with tears, but her eyes began to fill, like the sky in the breaking of the dawn, with strange radiations of joy. What she experienced at that moment was almost like what she would have felt if some one had said to her suddenly: Little girl, you are queen of France.

It seemed to her that if she touched that doll, thunder would spring forth from it.

Which was true to some extent, for she thought that the Thénardiess would scold and beat her.

However, the attraction overcame her. She finally approached and timidly murmured, turning towards the Thénardiess:

"Can I, madame?"

No expression can describe her look, at once full of despair, dismay, and transport.

"Good Lord!" said the Thénardiess, "it is yours. Since monsieur gives it to you."

"Is it true, is it true, monsieur?" said Cosette; "is the lady for me?"

The stranger appeared to have his eyes full of tears. He seemed to be at that stage of emotion in which one does not speak for fear of weeping. He nodded assent to Cosette, and put the hand of "the lady" in her little hand.

Cosette withdrew her hand hastily, as if that of *the lady* burned her, and looked down at the floor. We are compelled to add, that at that instant she thrust out her tongue enormously. All at once she turned, and seized the doll eagerly.

"I will call her Catharine," said she.

It was a strange moment when Cosette's rags met and pressed against the ribbons and the fresh pink muslins of the doll.

"Madame," said she, "may I put her in a chair?"

"Yes, my child," answered the Thénardiess.

It was Eponine and Azelma now who looked upon Cosette with envy.

Cosette placed Catharine on a chair, then sat down on the floor before her, and remained motionless, without saying a word, in the attitude of contemplation.

"Why don't you play, Cosette?" said the stranger.

"Oh! I am playing," answered the child.

This stranger, this unknown man, who seemed like a visit from Providence to Cosette, was at that moment the being which the Thénardiess hated more than aught else in the world. However, she was compelled to restrain herself. Her emotions were more than she could endure, accustomed as she was to dissimulation, by endeavouring to copy her husband in all her actions. She sent her daughters to bed immediately, then asked the yellow man's *permission* to send Cosette to bed—*who is very tired to-day*, added she, with a motherly air. Cosette went to bed, holding Catharine in her arms.

The Thénardiess went from time to time to the other end of the room, where her husband was, *to soothe her soul*, she said. She exchanged a few words with him, which were the more furious that she did not dare to speak them aloud:—

"The old fool! what has he got into his head, to come here

to disturb us! to want that little monster to play! to give her dolls! to give forty-franc dolls to a slut that I wouldn't give forty sous for. A little more, and he would say your majesty to her, as they do to the Duchess of Berry! Is he in his senses? he must be crazy, the strange old fellow!"

"Why? It is very simple," replied Thénardier. "If it amuses him! It amuses you for the girl to work; it amuses him for her to play. He has the right to do it. A traveller can do as he likes, if he pays for it. If this old fellow is a philanthropist, what is that to you? if he is crazy it don't concern you. What do you interfere for, as long as he has money?"

Language of a master and reasoning of an innkeeper, which neither in one case nor the other admits of reply.

The man had leaned his elbows on the table, and resumed his attitude of reverie. All the other travellers, pedlars, and wagoners, had drawn back a little, and sung no more. They looked upon him from a distance with a sort of respectful fear.

This solitary man, so poorly clad, who took five-franc pieces from his pocket with so much indifference, and who lavished gigantic dolls on little brats in wooden shoes, was certainly a magnificent and formidable goodman.

Several hours passed away. The midnight mass was said, the revel was finished, the drinkers had gone, the house was closed, the room was deserted, the fire had gone out, the stranger still remained in the same place and in the same posture. From time to time he changed the elbow on which he rested. That was all. But he had not spoken a word since Cosette was gone.

The Thénardiers alone, out of propriety and curiosity, had remained in the room.

"Is he going to spend the night like this?" grumbled the Thénardiess. When the clock struck two in the morning, she acknowledged herself beaten, and said to her husband: "I am going to bed, you may do as you like." The husband sat down at a table in a corner, lighted a candle, and began to read the *Courrier Français*.

A good hour passed thus. The worthy innkeeper had read the *Courrier Français* at least three times, from the date of the number to the name of the printer. The stranger did not stir.

Thénardier moved, coughed, spit, blew his nose, and creaked his chair. The man did not stir. "Is he asleep?" thought Thénardier. The man was not asleep, but nothing could arouse him.

Finally, Thénardier took off his cap, approached softly, and ventured to say:—

"Is monsieur not going to repose?"

Not going to bed would have seemed to him too much and too familiar. To *repose* implied luxury, and there was respect in it. Such words have the mysterious and wonderful property of swelling the bill in the morning. A room in which you *go to bed* costs twenty sous; a room in which you *repose* costs twenty francs.

"Yes," said the stranger, "you are right. Where is your stable?"

"Monsieur," said Thénardier, with a smile, "I will conduct monsieur."

He took the candle, the man took his bundle and his staff, and Thénardier led him into a room on the first floor, which was very showy, furnished all in mahogany, with a high-post bedstead and red calico curtains.

"What is this?" said the traveller.

"It is properly our bridal chamber," said the innkeeper. "We occupy another like this, my spouse and I; this is not open more than three or four times in a year."

"I should have liked the stable as well," said the man, bluntly.

Thénardier did not appear to hear this not very civil answer.

He lighted two entirely new wax candles, which were displayed upon the mantel; a good fire was blazing in the fireplace. There was on the mantel, under a glass case, a woman's head-dress of silver thread and orange-flowers.

"What is this?" said the stranger.

"Monsieur," said Thénardier, "it is my wife's bridal cap."

The traveller looked at the object with a look which seemed to say: "there was a moment, then, when this monster was a virgin."

Thénardier lied, however. When he hired this shanty to turn it into a chop-house, he found the room thus furnished, and bought this furniture, and purchased at second-hand these orange-flowers, thinking that this would cast a gracious light over "his spouse," and that the house would derive from them what the English call respectability.

When the traveller turned again the host had disappeared. Thénardier had discreetly taken himself out of the way without daring to say good-night, not desiring to treat with a disrespectful cordiality a man whom he proposed to skin royally in the morning.

The innkeeper retired to his room; his wife was in bed, but not asleep. When she heard her husband's step, she turned towards him and said:

"You know that I am going to kick Cosette out doors to-morrow."

Thénardier coolly answered:

"You are, indeed!"

They exchanged no further words, and in a few moments their candle was blown out.

For his part, the traveller had put his staff and bundle in a corner. The host gone, he sat down in an arm-chair, and remained some time thinking. Then he drew off his shoes, took one of the two candles, blew out the other, pushed open the door, and went out of the room, looking about him as if he were searching for something. He passed through a hall, and came to the stairway. There he heard a very soft little sound, which resembled the breathing of a child. Guided by this sound he came to a sort of triangular nook built under the stairs, or, rather, formed by the staircase itself. This hole was nothing but the space beneath the stairs. There, among all sorts of old baskets and old rubbish, in the dust and among the cobwebs, there was a bed; if a mattress so full of holes as to show the straw, and a covering so full of holes as to show the mattress, can be called a bed. There were no sheets. This was placed on the floor immediately on the tiles. In this bed Cosette was sleeping.

The man approached and looked at her.

Cosette was sleeping soundly; she was dressed. In the winter she did not undress on account of the cold. She held the doll clasped in her arms; its large open eyes shone in the obscurity. From time to time she heaved a deep sigh, as if she were about to wake, and she hugged the doll almost convulsively. There was only one of her wooden shoes at the side of her bed. An open door near Cosette's nook disclosed a large dark room. The stranger entered. At the further end, through a glass window, he perceived two little beds with very white spreads. They were those of Azelma and Eponine. Half hid behind these beds was a willow cradle without curtains, in which the little boy who had cried all the evening was sleeping.

The stranger conjectured that this room communicated with

that of the Thénardiers. He was about to withdraw when his eye fell upon the fire-place, one of those huge tavern fire-places where there is always so little fire, when there is a fire, and which are so cold to look upon. In this one there was no fire, there were not even any ashes. What there was, however, attracted the traveller's attention. It was two little children's shoes, of coquettish shape and of different sizes. The traveller remembered the graceful and immemorial custom of children putting their shoes in the fire-place on Christmas night, to wait there in the darkness in expectation of some shining gift from their good fairy. Eponine and Azelma had taken good care not to forget this, and each had put one of her shoes in the fire-place.

The traveller bent over them.

The fairy—that is to say, the mother—had already made her visit, and shining in each shoe was a beautiful new ten-sous piece.

The man rose up and was on the point of going away, when he perceived further along, by itself, in the darkest corner of the fire-place, another object. He looked, and recognised a shoe, a horrid wooden shoe of the clumsiest sort, half broken and covered with ashes and dried mud. It was Cosette's shoe. Cosette, with that touching confidence of childhood which can always be deceived without ever being discouraged, had also placed her shoe in the fire-place.

What a sublime and sweet thing is hope in a child who has never known anything but despair!

There was nothing in this wooden shoe.

The stranger fumbled in his waistcoat, bent over, and dropped into Cosette's shoe a gold louis.

Then he went back to his room with stealthy tread.

IX
THÉNARDIER MANŒUVRING

ON the following morning, at least two hours before day, Thénardier, seated at a table in the bar-room, a candle by his side with pen in hand, was making out the bill of the traveller in the yellow coat.

His wife was standing, half bent over him, following him with her eyes. Not a word passed between them. It was, on one side, a profound meditation, on the other that religious admiration with which we observe a marvel of the human mind spring up and expand. A noise was heard in the house; it was the lark, sweeping the stairs.

After a good quarter of an hour and some erasures, Thénardier produced this masterpiece.

Bill of Monsieur in No. 1.

Supper	3	frs.
Room	10	"
Candle	5	"
Fire	4	"
Service	1	"
Total.	23	frs.

Service was written *servisse*.

"Twenty-three francs!" exclaimed the woman, with an enthusiasm which was mingled with some hesitation.

Like all great artists, Thénardier was not satisfied.

"Pooh!" said he.

It was the accent of Castlereagh drawing up for the Congress of Vienna the bill which France was to pay.

"Monsieur Thénardier, you are right, he deserves it," murmured the woman, thinking of the doll given to Cosette in the presence of her daughters; "it is right! but it's too much. He won't pay it."

Thénardier put on his cold laugh, and said: "He will pay it."

This laugh was the highest sign of certainty and authority. What was thus said, must be. The woman did not insist. She began to arrange the tables; the husband walked back and forth in the room. A moment after he added:

"I owe, at least, fifteen hundred francs!"

He seated himself thoughtfully in the chimney-corner, his feet in the warm ashes.

"Ah ha!" replied the woman, "you don't forget that I kick Cosette out of the house to-day? The monster! it tears my vitals to see her with her doll! I would rather marry Louis XVIII., than keep her in the house another day!"

Thénardier lighted his pipe, and answered between two puffs:

"You'll give the bill to the man."

Then he went out.

He was scarcely out of the room when the traveller came in.

Thénardier reappeared immediately behind him, and remained motionless in the half-open door, visible only to his wife.

The yellow man carried his staff and bundle in his hand.

"Up so soon!" said the Thénardiess; "is monsieur going to leave us already?"

While speaking, she turned the bill in her hands with an embarrassed look, and made creases in it with her nails. Her hard face exhibited a shade of timidity and doubt that was not habitual.

To present such a bill to a man who had so perfectly the appearance of "a pauper" seemed too awkward to her.

The traveller appeared preoccupied and absent-minded.

He answered:

"Yes, madame, I am going away."

"Monsieur, then, had no business at Montfermeil?" replied she.

"No, I am passing through; that is all. Madame," added he, "what do I owe?"

The Thénardiess, without answering, handed him the folded bill.

The man unfolded the paper and looked at it; but his thoughts were evidently elsewhere.

"Madame," replied he, "do you do a good business in Montfermeil?"

"So-so, monsieur," answered the Thénardiess, stupefied at seeing no other explosion.

She continued in a mournful and lamenting strain:

"Oh! monsieur, the times are very hard, and then we have so few rich people around here! It is a very little place, you see. If we only had rich travellers now and then, like monsieur! We have so many expenses! Why, that little girl eats us out of house and home."

"What little girl?"

"Why, the little girl you know! Cosette! the Lark, as they call her about here!"

"Ah!" said the man.

She continued:

"How stupid these peasants are with their nicknames! She looks more like a bat than a lark. You see, monsieur, we don't ask charity, but we are not able to give it. We make nothing, and have a great deal to pay. The licence, the excise, the doors and windows, the tax on everything! Monsieur knows that the government demands a deal of money. And then I have my own girls. I have nothing to spend on other people's children."

The man replied in a voice which he endeavoured to render indifferent, and in which there was a slight tremulousness.

"Suppose you were relieved of her?"

"Who? Cosette?"

"Yes."

The red and violent face of the woman became illumined with a hideous expression.

"Ah, monsieur! my good monsieur! take her, keep her, take her away, carry her off, sugar her, stuff her, drink her, eat her, and be blessed by the holy Virgin and all the saints in Paradise!"

"Agreed."

"Really! you will take her away?"

"I will."

"Immediately?"

"Immediately. Call the child."

"Cosette!" cried the Thénardiess.

"In the meantime," continued the man, "I will pay my bill. How much is it?"

He cast a glance at the bill, and could not repress a movement of surprise.

"Twenty-three francs?"

He looked at the hostess and repeated:

"Twenty-three francs?"

There was, in the pronunciation of these two sentences, thus repeated, the accent which lies between the point of exclamation and the point of interrogation.

The Thénardiess had had time to prepare herself for the shock. She replied with assurance:

"Yes, of course, monsieur! it is twenty-three francs."

The stranger placed five five-franc pieces upon the table.

"Go for the little girl," said he.

At this moment Thénardier advanced into the middle of the room and said:

"Monsieur owes twenty-six sous."

"Twenty-six sous!" exclaimed the woman.

"Twenty sous for the room," continued Thénardier coldly,

"and six for supper. As to the little girl, I must have some talk with monsieur about that. Leave us, wife."

The Thénardiess was dazzled by one of those unexpected flashes which emanate from talent. She felt that the great actor had entered upon the scene, answered not a word, and went out.

As soon as they were alone, Thénardier offered the traveller a chair. The traveller sat down, but Thénardier remained standing and his face assumed a singular expression of good-nature and simplicity.

"Monsieur," said he, "listen, I must say that I adore this child."

The stranger looked at him steadily.

"What child?"

Thénardier continued:

"How strangely we become attached! What is all this silver? Take back your money. This child I adore."

"Who is that?" asked the stranger.

"Oh, our little Cosette! And you wish to take her away from us? Indeed, I speak frankly, as true as you are an honourable man, I cannot consent to it. I should miss her. I have had her since she was very small. It is true, she costs us money; it is true she has her faults, it is true we are not rich, it is true I paid four hundred francs for medicines at one time when she was sick. But we must do something for God. She has neither father nor mother; I have brought her up. I have bread enough for her and for myself. In fact, I must keep this child. You understand, we have affections; I am a good beast; myself, I do not reason; I love this little girl; my wife is hasty, but she loves her also. You see, she is like our own child. I feel the need of her prattle in the house."

The stranger was looking steadily at him all the while. He continued:

"Pardon me, excuse me, monsieur, but one does not give his child like that to a traveller. Isn't it true that I am right? After that, I don't say—you are rich and have the appearance of a very fine man—if it is for her advantage,—but I must know about it. You understand? On the supposition that I should let her go and sacrifice my own feelings, I should want to know where she is going. I would not want to lose sight of her, I should want to know who she was with, that I might come and see her now and then, and that she might know that her good foster-father was still watching over her. Finally, there are things which are not possible. I do not know even your name. If you should take her away, I should say, alas for the little Lark, where has she gone? I must, at least, see some poor rag of paper, a bit of a passport, something."

The stranger, without removing from him this gaze which went, so to speak, to the bottom of his conscience, answered in a severe and firm tone.

"Monsieur Thénardier, people do not take a passport to come five leagues from Paris. If I take Cosette, I take her, that is all. You will not know my name, you will not know my abode, you will not know where she goes, and my intention is that she shall never see you again in her life. Do you agree to that? Yes or no?"

As demons and genii recognise by certain signs the presence of a superior God, Thénardier comprehended that he was to deal with one who was very powerful. It came like an intuition; he understood it with his clear and quick sagacity; although during the evening he had been drinking with the wagoners, smoking, and singing bawdy songs, still he was observing the stranger all the while, watching him like a cat, and studying him like a mathematician. He had been observing him on his own account, for pleasure and by instinct, and at the same time lying in wait as if he had been paid for it. Not a gesture, not a movement of the man in the yellow coat had escaped him. Before even the stranger had so clearly shown his interest in Cosette, Thénardier had divined it. He had surprised the searching glances of the old man constantly returning to the child. Why this interest? What was this man? Why, with so much money in his purse, this miserable dress? These were questions which he put to himself without being able to answer them, and they irritated him. He had been thinking it over all night. This could not be Cosette's father. Was it a grandfather? Then why did he not make himself known at once? When a man has a right, he shows it. This man evidently had no right to Cosette. Then who was he? Thénardier was lost in conjectures. He caught glimpses of everything, but saw nothing. However it might be, when he commenced the conversation with this man, sure that there was a secret in all this, sure that the man had an interest in remaining unknown, he felt himself strong; at the stranger's clear and firm answer, when he saw that this mysterious personage was mysterious and nothing more, he felt weak. He was expecting nothing of the kind. His conjectures were put to flight. He rallied his ideas. He weighed all in a second. Thénardier was one of those men who comprehend a situation at a glance. He decided that this was the moment to advance straightforward and swiftly. He did what great captains do at that decisive instant which they alone can recognise; he unmasked his battery at once.

"Monsieur," said he, "I must have fifteen hundred francs."

The stranger took from his side-pocket an old black leather pocket-book, opened it, and drew forth three bank bills which he placed upon the table. He then rested his large thumb on these bills, and said to the tavern-keeper:

"Bring Cosette."

While this was going on what was Cosette doing?

Cosette, as soon as she awoke, had run to her wooden shoe. She had found the gold piece in it. It was not a Napoleon, but one of those new twenty-franc pieces of the Restoration, on the face of which the little Prussian queue had replaced the laurel crown. Cosette was dazzled. Her destiny began to intoxicate her. She did not know that it was a piece of gold; she had never seen one before; she hastily concealed it in her pocket as if she had stolen it. Nevertheless she felt it boded good to her. She divined whence the gift came, but she experienced a joy that was filled with awe. She was gratified; she was moreover stupefied. Such magnificent and beautiful things seemed unreal to her. The doll made her afraid, the gold piece made her afraid. She trembled with wonder before these magnificences. The stranger himself did not make her afraid. On the contrary, he reassured her. Since the previous evening, amid all her astonishment, and in her sleep, she was thinking in her little child's mind of this man who had such an old, and poor, and sad appearance, and who was so rich and so kind. Since she had met this goodman in the wood, it seemed as though all things were changed about her. Cosette, less happy than the smallest swallow of the sky, had never known what it is to take refuge under a mother's wing. For five years, that is to say, as far back as she could remember, the poor child had shivered and shuddered. She had always been naked under the biting north wind of misfortune, and now it seemed to her that she was clothed. Before her soul was cold, now it was warm. Cosette was no longer afraid of the

Thénardiers; she was no longer alone; sh
look to.

She hurriedly set herself to her morni
which she had placed in the same pocket
which the fifteen-sous piece had fallen the
tracted her attention from her work. She di
it, but she spent five minutes at a time conter
must confess, with her tongue thrust out. W ... sweeping the
stairs, she stopped and stood there, motionless, forgetting her
broom, and the whole world besides, occupied in looking at
this shining star at the bottom of her pocket.

It was in one of these reveries that the Thénardiess found her.

At the command of her husband, she had gone to look for
her. Wonderful to tell, she did not give her a slap nor even call
her a hard name. "Cosette," said she, almost gently, "come
quick."

An instant after, Cosette entered the bar-room.

The stranger took the bundle he had brought and untied it.
This bundle contained a little woollen frock, an apron, a coarse
cotton under-garment, a petticoat, a scarf, woollen stockings,
and shoes—a complete dress for a girl of seven years. It was all
in black.

"My child," said the man, "take this and go and dress yourself
quick."

The day was breaking when those of the inhabitants of
Montfermeil who were beginning to open their doors, saw pass
on the road to Paris a poorly clad goodman leading a little girl
dressed in mourning who had a pink doll in her arms. They
were going towards Livry.

It was the stranger and Cosette.

No one recognised the man; as Cosette was not now in tatters, few recognised her.

Cosette was going away. With whom? She was ignorant.
Where? She knew not. All she understood was, that she was
leaving behind the Thénardier chop-house. Nobody had
thought of bidding her good-bye, nor had she of bidding good-
bye to anybody. She went out from that house, hated and hating.

Poor gentle being, whose heart had only been crushed
hitherto.

Cosette walked seriously along, opening her large eyes, and
looking at the sky. She had put her louis in the pocket of her

on. From time to time she bent over and cast a glance
and then looked at the goodman. She felt somewhat as if
e were near God.

X

WHO SEEKS THE BEST MAY FIND THE WORST

THE Thénardiess, according to her custom, had left her husband alone. She was expecting great events. When the man and
Cosette were gone, Thénardier, after a good quarter of an hour,
took her aside, and showed her the fifteen hundred francs.

"What's that?" said she.

It was the first time, since the beginning of their housekeeping, that she had dared to criticise the act of her master.

He felt the blow.

"True you are right," said he; "I am a fool. Give me my hat."

He folded the three bank bills, thrust them into his pocket,
and started in all haste, but he missed the direction and took the
road to the right. Some neighbours of whom he inquired put
him on the track; the Lark and the man had been seen to go in
the direction of Livry. He followed this indication, walking
rapidly and talking to himself.

"This man is evidently a millionaire dressed in yellow, and as
for me, I am a brute. He first gave twenty sous, then five francs,
then fifty francs, then fifteen hundred francs, all so readily. He
would have given fifteen thousand francs. But I shall catch
him."

And then this bundle of clothes, made ready beforehand for
the little girl; all that was strange, there was a good deal of
mystery under it. When one gets hold of a mystery, he does not
let go of it. The secrets of the rich are sponges full of gold; a
man ought to know how to squeeze them. All these thoughts
were whirling in his brain. "I am a brute," said he.

On leaving Montfermeil and reaching the turn made by the
road to Livry, the route may be seen for a long distance on the
plateau. On reaching this point he counted on being able to see
the man and the little girl. He looked as far as his eye could
reach, but saw nothing. He inquired again. In the meanwhile
he was losing time. The passers-by told him that the man and
child whom he sought had travelled towards the wood in the
direction of Gagny. He hastened in this direction.

They had the start of him, but a child walks slowly, and he went rapidly. And then the country was well known to him.

Suddenly he stopped and struck his forehead like a man who has forgotten the main thing, and who thinks of retracing his steps.

"I ought to have taken my gun!" said he.

Thénardier was one of those double natures who sometimes appear among us without our knowledge, and disappear without ever being known, because destiny has shown us but one side of them. It is the fate of many men to live thus half submerged. In a quiet ordinary situation, Thénardier had all that is necessary to make—we do not say to be—what passes for an honest tradesman, a good citizen. At the same time, under certain circumstances, under the operation of certain occurrences exciting his baser nature, he had in him all that was necessary to be a villain. He was a shopkeeper in which lay hidden a monster. Satan ought for a moment to have squatted in some corner of the hole in which Thénardier lived and studied this hideous masterpiece.

After hesitating an instant:

"Bah!" thought he, "they would have time to escape!"

And he continued on his way, going rapidly forward, and almost as if he were certain, with the sagacity of the fox scenting a flock of partridges.

In fact, when he had passed the ponds, and crossed obliquely the large meadow at the right of the avenue de Bellevue, as he reached the grassy path which nearly encircles the hill, and which covers the arch of the old aqueduct of the abbey of Chelles, he perceived above a bush, the hat on which he had already built so many conjectures. It was the man's hat. The bushes were low. Thénardier perceived that the man and Cosette were seated there. The child could not be seen, she was so short, but he could see the head of the doll.

Thénardier was not deceived. The man had sat down there to give Cosette a little rest. The chop-house keeper turned aside the bushes, and suddenly appeared before the eyes of those whom he sought.

"Pardon me, excuse me, monsieur," said he, all out of breath; "but here are your fifteen hundred francs."

So saying, he held out the three bank bills to the stranger.

The man raised his eyes:

"What does that mean?"

Thénardier answered respectfully:

"Monsieur, that means that I take back Cosette."

Cosette shuddered, and hugged close to the goodman.

He answered, looking Thénardier straight in the eye, and spacing his syllables:

"You—take—back—Cosette?"

"Yes, monsieur, I take her back. I tell you I have reflected. Indeed, I haven't the right to give her to you. I am an honest man, you see. This little girl is not mine. She belongs to her mother. Her mother has confided her to me; I can only give her up to her mother. You will tell me: But her mother is dead. Well. In that case, I can only give up the child to a person who shall bring me a written order, signed by the mother, stating I should deliver the child to him. That is clear."

The man, without answering, felt in his pocket, and Thénardier saw the pocket-book containing the bank bills reappear.

The tavern-keeper felt a thrill of joy.

"Good!" thought he; "hold on. He is going to corrupt me!"

Before opening the pocket-book, the traveller cast a look about him. The place was entirely deserted. There was not a soul either in the wood, or in the valley. The man opened the pocket-book, and drew from it not the handful of bank bills which Thénardier expected, but a little piece of paper, which he unfolded and presented open to the innkeeper, saying:

"You are right. Read that!"

Thénardier took the paper and read.

"M—— sur M——, March 25, 1823.

"Monsieur Thénardier:

"You will deliver Cosette to the bearer. He will settle all small debts.

"I have the honour to salute you with consideration.

FANTINE."

"You know that signature?" replied the man.

It was indeed the signature of Fantine. Thénardier recognised it.

There was nothing to say. He felt doubly enraged, enraged at being compelled to give up the bribe which he hoped for, and enraged at being beaten. The man added:

"You can keep this paper as your receipt."

Thénardier retreated in good order.

"This signature is very well imitated," he grumbled between his teeth. "Well, so be it!"

Then he made a desperate effort.

"Monsieur," said he, "it is all right. Then you are the person. But you must settle 'all small debts.' There is a large amount due to me."

The man rose to his feet, and said at the same time, snapping with his thumb and finger some dust from his threadbare sleeve:

"Monsieur Thénardier, in January the mother reckoned that she owed you a hundred and twenty francs; you sent her in February a memorandum of five hundred francs; you received three hundred francs at the end of February, and three hundred at the beginning of March. There has since elapsed nine months which, at fifteen francs per month, the price agreed upon, amounts to a hundred and thirty-five francs. You had received a hundred francs in advance. There remain thirty-five francs due you. I have just given you fifteen hundred francs."

Thénardier felt what the wolf feels the moment when he finds himself seized and crushed by the steel jaws of the trap.

"What is this devil of a man?" thought he.

He did what the wolf does, he gave a spring. Audacity had succeeded with him once already.

"Monsieur-I-don't-know-your-name," said he resolutely, and putting aside this time all show of respect. "I shall take back Cosette or you must give me a thousand crowns."

The stranger said quietly:

"Come, Cosette."

He took Cosette with his left hand, and with the right picked up his staff, which was on the ground.

Thénardier noted the enormous size of the cudgel, and the solitude of the place.

The man disappeared in the wood with the child, leaving the chop-house keeper motionless and nonplussed.

As they walked away, Thénardier observed his broad shoulders, a little rounded, and his big fists.

Then his eyes fell back upon his own puny arms and thin hands. "I must have been a fool indeed," thought he, "not to have brought my gun, as I was going on a hunt."

However, the innkeeper did not abandon the pursuit.

"I must know where he goes," said he; and he began to follow them at a distance. There remained two things in his possession, one a bitter mockery, the piece of paper signed Fantine, and the other a consolation, the fifteen hundred francs.

The man was leading Cosette in the direction of Livry and Bondy. He was walking slowly, his head bent down, in an attitude of reflection and sadness. The winter had bereft the wood of foliage, so that Thénardier did not lose sight of them, though remaining at a considerable distance behind. From time to time the man turned, and looked to see if he were followed. Suddenly he perceived Thénardier. He at once entered a coppice with Cosette, and both disappeared from sight. "The devil!" said Thénardier. And he redoubled his pace.

The density of the thicket compelled him to approach them. When the man reached the thickest part of the wood, he turned again. Thénardier had endeavoured to conceal himself in the branches in vain, he could not prevent the man from seeing him. The man cast an uneasy glance at him, then shook his head, and resumed his journey. The innkeeper again took up the pursuit. They walked thus two or three hundred paces. Suddenly the man turned again. He perceived the innkeeper. This time he looked at him so forbiddingly that Thénardier judged it "unprofitable" to go further. Thénardier went home.

XI
NUMBER 9430 COMES UP AGAIN,
AND COSETTE DRAWS IT

JEAN VALJEAN was not dead.

When he fell into the sea, or rather when he threw himself into it, he was, as we have seen, free from his irons. He swam under water to a ship at anchor to which a boat was fastened.

He found means to conceal himself in this boat until evening. At night he betook himself again to the water, and reached the land a short distance from Cape Brun.

There, as he did not lack for money, he could procure clothes. A little public-house in the environs of Balaguier was then the place which supplied clothing for escaped convicts, a lucrative business. Then Jean Valjean, like all those joyless fugitives who are endeavouring to throw off the track the spy of the law and social fatality, followed an obscure and wandering path.

He found an asylum first in Pradeaux, near Beausset. Then he went towards Grand Villard near Briançon, in the Hautes Alpes. Groping and restless flight, threading the mazes of the mole whose windings are unknown. There were afterwards found some traces of his passage in Ain, on the territory of Civrieux, in the Pyrenees at Accons, at a place called the Grange-de-Domecq, near the hamlet of Chavailles, and in the environs of Périgneux, at Brunies, a canton of Chapelle Gonaguet. He finally reached Paris. We have seen him at Montfermeil.

His first care, on reaching Paris, had been to purchase a mourning dress for a little girl of seven years, then to procure lodgings. That done, he had gone to Montfermeil.

It will be remembered that, at the time of his former escape, or near that time, he had made a mysterious journey of which justice had had some glimpse.

Moreover, he was believed to be dead, and that thickened the obscurity which surrounded him. At Paris there fell into his hands a paper which chronicled the fact. He felt reassured, and almost as much at peace as if he really had been dead.

On the evening of the same day that Jean Valjean had rescued Cosette from the clutches of the Thénardiess, he entered Paris again. He entered the city at night-fall, with the child, by the barrière de Monceaux. There he took a cabriolet, which carried him as far as the esplanade of the Observatory. There he got out, paid the driver, took Cosette by the hand, and both in the darkness of the night, through the deserted streets in the vicinity of l'Ourcine and la Glacière, walked towards the boulevard de l'Hôpital.

The day had been strange and full of emotion for Cosette; they had eaten behind hedges bread and cheese bought at isolated chop-houses; they had often changed carriages, and had travelled short distances on foot. She did not complain; but she was tired, and Jean Valjean perceived it by her pulling more heavily at his hand while walking. He took her in his arms; Cosette, without letting go of Catharine, laid her head on Jean Valjean's shoulder, and went to sleep.

BOOK FOURTH –
THE OLD GORBEAU HOUSE

I

MASTER GORBEAU

FORTY years ago, the solitary pedestrian who ventured into the unknown regions of La Salpêtrière and went up along the Boulevard as far as the Barrière d'Italie, reached certain points where it might be said that Paris disappeared. It was no longer a solitude, for there were people passing; it was not the country, for there were houses and streets; it was not a city, the streets had ruts in them, like the highways, and grass grew along their borders; it was not a village, the houses were too lofty. What was it then? It was an inhabited place where there was nobody, it was a desert place where there was somebody; it was a boulevard of the great city, a street of Paris, wilder, at night, than a forest, and gloomier, by day, than a graveyard.

It was the old quarter of the Horse Market.

Our pedestrian, if he trusted himself beyond the four tumbling walls of this Horse Market, if willing to go even further than the Rue du Petit Banquier, leaving on his right a courtyard shut in by lofty walls, then a meadow studded with stacks of tanbark that looked like the gigantic beaver dams, then an inclosure half filled with lumber and piles of logs, sawdust and shavings, from the top of which a huge dog was baying, then a long, low, ruined wall with a small dark-coloured and decrepit gate in it, covered with moss, which was full of flowers in spring-time, then, in the loneliest spot, a frightful broken-down structure on which could be read in large letters: POST NO BILLS; this bold promenader, we say, would reach the corner of the Rue des Vignes-Saint-Marcel, a latitude not much explored. There, near a manufactory and between two garden walls, could be seen at the time of which we speak an old ruined dwelling that, at first sight, seemed as small as a cottage, yet was, in reality, as vast as a cathedral. It stood with its gable end towards the highway, and hence its apparent diminutiveness. Nearly the whole house was hidden. Only the door and one window could be seen.

This old dwelling had but one story.

On examining it, the peculiarity that first struck the beholder was that the door could never have been anything but the door of a hovel, while the window, had it been cut in freestone and not in rough material, might have been the casement of a lordly residence.

The door was merely a collection of worm-eaten boards rudely tacked together with cross-pieces that looked like pieces of firewood clumsily split out. It opened directly on a steep staircase with high steps covered with mud, plaster, and dust, and of the same breadth as the door, and which seemed from the street to rise perpendicularly like a ladder, and disappear in the shadow between two walls. The top of the shapeless opening which this door closed upon, was disguised by a narrow topscreen, in the middle of which had been sawed a three-cornered orifice that served both for skylight and ventilator when the door was shut. On the inside of the door a brush dipped in ink had, in a couple of strokes of the hand, traced the number 52, and above the screen, the same brush had daubed the number 50, so that a new-comer would hesitate, asking: Where am I?

The top of the entrance says, at number 50; the inside, how-ever, replies, No! at number 52! The dust-coloured rags that hung in guise of curtains about the three-cornered ventilator, we will not attempt to describe.

The window was broad and of considerable height, with large panes in the sashes and provided with Venetian shutters; only the panes had received a variety of wounds which were at once concealed and made manifest by ingenious strips and bandages of paper, and the shutters were so broken and dis-jointed that they menaced the passers-by more than they shielded the occupants of the dwelling. The horizontal slats were lacking, here and there, and had been very simply replaced with boards nailed across, so that what had been a Venetian, in the first instance, ended as a regular close shutter. This door with its dirty look and this window with its decent though dilapidated appearance, seen thus in one and the same building, produced the effect of two ragged beggars bound in the same direction and walking side by side, with different mien under the same rags, one having always been a pauper while the other had been a gentleman.

The staircase led up to a very spacious interior, which looked like a barn converted into a house. This structure had for its main channel of communication a long hall, on which there opened, on either side, apartments of different dimensions scarcely habitable, rather resembling booths than rooms. These chambers looked out upon the shapeless grounds of the neighbourhood. Altogether, it was dark and dull and dreary, even melancholy and sepulchral, and it was penetrated, either by the dim, cold rays of the sun or by icy draughts, according to the situation of the cracks, in the roof, or in the door. One interesting and picturesque peculiarity of this kind of tenement is the monstrous size of the spiders.

To the left of the main door, on the boulevard, a small window that had been walled up formed a square niche some six feet from the ground, which was filled with stones that passing urchins had thrown into it.

A portion of this building has recently been pulled down, but what remains, at the present day, still conveys an idea of what it was. The structure, taken as a whole, is not more than a hundred years old. A hundred years is youth to a church, but old age to a private mansion. It would seem that the dwelling of Man partakes of his brief existence, and the dwelling of God, of His eternity.

The letter-carriers called the house No. 50–52; but it was known, in the quarter, as Gorbeau House.

Let us see how it came by that title.

The "gatherers-up of unconsidered trifles" who collect anecdotes as the herbalist his simples, and prick the fleeting dates upon their memories with a pin, know that there lived in Paris, in the last century, about 1770, two attorneys of the Châtelet, one named Corbeau and the other Renard—two names, anticipated by La Fontaine. The chance for a joke was altogether too fine a one to be let slip by the goodly company of lawyers' clerks. So, very soon, the galleries of the courtrooms rang with the following parody, in rather gouty verse:

> Maître Corbeau, sur un dossier perché,
>   Tenait dans son bec une saisie exécutoire;
> Maître Renard, par l'odeur alléché,
>   Lui fit à peu près cette histoire:
> Hé! bonjour! etc.*

The two honest practitioners, annoyed by these shafts of wit, and rather disconcerted in their dignity by the roars of laughter that followed them, resolved to change their names, and, with that view applied to the king. The petition was presented to Louis XV. on the very day on which the Pope's Nuncio and the Cardinal de La Roche-Aymon in the presence of his Majesty, devoutly kneeling one on each side of Madame Du Barry, put her slippers on her naked feet, as she was getting out of bed. The king, who was laughing, continued his laugh; he passed gaily from the two bishops to the two advocates, and absolved these limbs of the law from their names almost. It was granted to Master Corbeau, by the king's good pleasure, to add a flourish to the first letter of his name, thus making it Gorbeau; Master Renard was less fortunate, as he only got permission to put a P. before the R. which made the word Prenard,† a name no less appropriate than the first one.

Now, according to tradition, this Master Gorbeau was the proprietor of the structure numbered 50–52, Boulevard de l'Hôpital. He was, likewise, the originator of the monumental window.

Hence, this building got its name of Gorbeau House.

Opposite No. 50–52 stands, among the shade-trees that line the Boulevard, a tall elm, three-quarters dead, and almost directly in front, opens the Rue de la Barrière des Gobelins—a street, at that time, without houses, unpaved, bordered with scrubby trees, grass-grown or muddy, according to the season, and running squarely up to the wall encircling Paris. An odour of vitriol ascended in puffs from the roofs of a neighbouring factory.

The Barrière was quite near. In 1832, the encircling wall yet existed.

This Barrière itself filled the mind with gloomy images. It was on the way to the Bicêtre. It was there that, under the Empire and the Restoration, condemned criminals re-entered Paris on the day of their execution. It was there, that, about the year 1829, was committed the mysterious assassination, called "the murder of the Barrière de Fontainebleau," the perpetrators

---

* Master Crow, on a document perched,
    In his beak held a fat execution,
Master Fox, with his jaws well besmirched,
    Thus spoke up, to his neighbour's confusion.
"Good day! my fine fellow," quoth he, etc.
† Prenard—a grasping fellow.

of which the authorities have never discovered—a sombre problem which has not yet been solved, a terrible enigma not yet
unravelled. Go a few steps further, and you find that fatal Rue
Croulebarbe where Ulbach stabbed the goatherd girl of Ivry, in
a thunderstorm, in the style of a melodrama. Still a few steps,
and you come to those detestable clipped elm-trees of the Barrière Saint Jacques, that expedient of philanthropists to hide the
scaffold, that pitiful and shameful Place de Brève of a cockney,
shop-keeping society which recoils from capital punishment,
yet dares neither to abolish it with lofty dignity, nor to maintain
it with firm authority.

Thirty-seven years ago, excepting this place, Saint-Jacques,
which seemed fore-doomed, and always was horrible, the
gloomiest of all this gloomy Boulevard was the spot, still so
unattractive, where stood the old building 50–52.

The city dwelling-houses did not begin to start up there
until some twenty-five years later. The place was repulsive. In
addition to the melancholy thought that seized you there, you
felt conscious of being between La Salpêtrière, the cupola of
which was in sight, and Bicêtre, the barrier of which was close
by—that is to say, between the wicked folly of woman and that
of man. Far as the eye could reach there was nothing to be seen
but the public shambles, the city wall, and here and there the
side of a factory, resembling a barrack or a monastery; on all
sides, miserable hovels and heaps of rubbish, old walls as black
as widows' weeds, and new walls as white as winding-sheets; on
all sides, parallel rows of trees, buildings in straight lines, low,
flat structures, long, cold perspectives, and the gloomy sameness
of right angles. Not a variation of the surface of the ground, not
a caprice of architecture, not a curve. Altogether, it was chilly,
regular, and hideous. Nothing stifles one like this perpetual
symmetry. Symmetry is ennui, and ennui is the very essence of
grief and melancholy. Despair yawns. Something more terrible
than a hell of suffering may be conceived; to wit, a hell of ennui.
Were there such a hell in existence, this section of the Boulevard
de l'Hôpital might well serve as the approach to it.

Then, at nightfall, at the moment when the day is dying out,
especially in winter, at that hour when the evening breeze tears
from the elms their faded and withered leaves, when the gloom
is deep, without a single star, or when the moon and the wind
make openings in the clouds, this boulevard became positively

terrifying. The dark outlines shrank together, and even lost themselves in the obscurity like fragments of the infinite. The passer-by could not keep from thinking of the innumerable bloody traditions of the spot. The solitude of this neighbourhood in which so many crimes had been committed, had something fearful about it. One felt presentiments of snares in this obscurity; all the confused outlines visible through the gloom were eyed suspiciously, and the oblong cavities between the trees seemed like graves. In the day-time it was ugly; in the evening, it was dismal; at night, it was ominous of evil. In summer, in the twilight, some old women might be seen seated, here and there, under the elms, on benches made mouldy by the rain. These good old dames were addicted to begging.

In conclusion, this quarter, which was rather superannuated than ancient, from that time began to undergo a transformation. Thenceforth, whoever would see it, must hasten. Each day, some of its details wholly passed away. Now, as has been the case for twenty years past, the terminus of the Orleans railroad lies just outside of the old suburb, and keeps it in movement. Wherever you may locate, in the outskirts of a capital, a railroad depôt, it is the death of a suburb and the birth of a city. It would seem as though around these great centres of the activity of nations, at the rumbling of these mighty engines, at the snorting of these giant draught-horses of civilisation, which devour coal and spout forth fire, the earth, teeming with germs of life, trembles and opens to swallow old dwellings of men and to bring forth new; old houses crumble, new houses spring up.

Since the depôt of the Orleans railway invaded the grounds of La Salpêtrière, the old narrow streets that adjoin the Fossés Saint Victor and the Jardin des Plantes are giving way, violently traversed, as they are, three or four times a day, by those streams of diligences, hacks and omnibuses, which, in course of time, push back the houses right and left; for there are things that sound strangely, and yet which are precisely correct; and, just as the remark is true that, in large cities, the sun causes the fronts of houses looking south to vegetate and grow, so is it undeniable that the frequent passage of vehicles widens the streets. The symptoms of a new life are evident. In that old provincial quarter, and in its wildest corners, pavement is beginning to appear, sidewalks are springing up and stretching to longer and longer distances, even in those parts where there are as yet no passers-by. One morning, a memorable morning in July, 1845, black kettles filled with bitumen were seen smoking there: on that day, one could exclaim that civilisation had reached the Rue de l'Ourcine, and that Paris had stepped across into the Faubourg Saint Marceau.

II
A NEST FOR OWL AND WREN

BEFORE this Gorbeau tenement Jean Valjean stopped. Like the birds of prey, he had chosen this lonely place to make his nest.

He fumbled in his waistcoat and took from it a sort of night-key, opened the door, entered, then carefully closed it again and ascended the stairway, still carrying Cosette.

At the top of the stairway he drew from his pocket another key, with which he opened another door. The chamber which he entered and closed again immediately was a sort of garret, rather spacious, furnished only with a mattress spread on the floor, a table, and a few chairs. A stove containing a fire, the coals of which were visible, stood in one corner. The street lamp of the boulevards shed a dim light through this poor interior. At the further extremity there was a little room containing a cot bed. On this Jean Valjean laid the child without waking her.

He struck a light with a flint and steel and lit a candle, which, with his tinder-box, stood ready, beforehand, on the table; and, as he had done on the preceding evening, he began to gaze upon Cosette with a look of ecstasy, in which the expression of goodness and tenderness went almost to the verge of insanity. The little girl, with that tranquil confidence which belongs only to extreme strength or extreme weakness, had fallen asleep without knowing with whom she was, and continued to slumber without knowing where she was.

Jean Valjean bent down and kissed the child's hand.

Nine months before, he had kissed the hand of the mother, who also had just fallen asleep.

The same mournful, pious, agonising feeling now filled his heart.

He knelt down by the bedside of Cosette.

It was broad daylight, and yet the child slept on. A pale ray from the December sun struggled through the garret window and traced upon the ceiling long streaks of light and shade.

Suddenly a carrier's wagon, heavily laden, trundled over the cobble-stones of the boulevard, and shook the old building like the rumbling of a tempest, jarring it from cellar to roof-tree.

"Yes, madame!" cried Cosette, starting up out of sleep, "here I am! here I am!"

And she threw herself from the bed, her eyelids still half closed with the weight of slumber, stretching out her hand towards the corner of the wall.

"Oh! what shall I do? Where is my broom?" said she.

By this time her eyes were fully open, and she saw the smiling face of Jean Valjean.

"Oh! yes—so it is!" said the child. "Good morning, monsieur."

Children at once accept joy and happiness with quick familiarity, being themselves naturally all happiness and joy.

Cosette noticed Catharine at the foot of the bed, laid hold of her at once, and, playing the while, asked Jean Valjean a thousand questions.—Where was she? Was Paris a big place? Was Madame Thénardier really very far away? Wouldn't she come back again, etc., etc. All at once she exclaimed, "How pretty it is here!"

It was a frightful hovel, but she felt free.

"Must I sweep?" she continued at length.

"Play!" replied Jean Valjean.

And thus the day passed by. Cosette, without troubling herself with trying to understand anything about it, was inexpressibly happy with her doll and her good friend.

III

TWO MISFORTUNES MINGLED MAKE HAPPINESS

THE dawn of the next day found Jean Valjean again near the bed of Cosette. He waited there, motionless, to see her wake.

Something new was entering his soul.

Jean Valjean had never loved anything. For twenty-five years he had been alone in the world. He had never been a father, lover, husband, or friend. At the galleys, he was cross, sullen, abstinent, ignorant, and intractable. The heart of the old convict was full of freshness. His sister and her children had left in his memory only a vague and distant impression, which had finally almost entirely vanished. He had made every exertion to find them again, and, not succeeding, had forgotten them. Human nature is thus constituted. The other tender emotions of his youth, if any such he had, were lost in an abyss.

When he saw Cosette, when he had taken her, carried her away, and rescued her, he felt his heart moved. All that he had of feeling and affection was aroused and vehemently attracted towards this child. He would approach the bed where she slept, and would tremble there with delight; he felt inward yearnings, like a mother, and knew not what they were; for it is something very incomprehensible and very sweet, this grand and strange emotion of a heart in its first love.

Poor old heart, so young!

But, as he was fifty-five and Cosette was but eight years old, all that he might have felt of love in his entire life melted into a sort of ineffable radiance.

This was the second white vision he had seen. The bishop had caused the dawn of virtue on his horizon; Cosette evoked the dawn of love.

The first few days rolled by amid this bewilderment.

On her part, Cosette, too, unconsciously underwent a change, poor little creature! She was so small when her mother left her, that she could not recollect her now. As all children do, like the young shoots of the vine that cling to everything, she had tried to love. She had not been able to succeed. Everybody had repelled her—the Thénardiers, their children, other children. She had loved the dog; it died, and after that no person and no thing would have aught to do with her. Mournful thing to tell, and one which we have already hinted, at the age of eight her heart was cold. This was not her fault; it was not the faculty of love that she lacked; alas! it was the possibility. And so, from the very first day, all that thought and felt in her began to love this kind old friend. She now felt sensations utterly unknown to her before—a sensation of budding and of growth.

Her kind friend no longer impressed as old and poor. In her eyes Jean Valjean was handsome, just as the garret had seemed pretty.

Such are the effects of the aurora-glow of childhood, youth, and joy. The newness of earth and of life has something to do with it. Nothing is so charming as the ruddy tints that happiness can shed around a garret room. We all, in the course of our lives, have had our rose-coloured sky-parlour.

Nature had placed a wide chasm—fifty years' interval of age—between Jean Valjean and Cosette. This chasm fate filled up. Fate abruptly brought together, and wedded with its resistless power, these two shattered lives, dissimilar in years, but similar in sorrow. The one, indeed, was the complement of the other. The instinct of Cosette sought for a father, as the instinct of Jean Valjean sought for a child. To meet, was to find one another. In that mysterious moment, when their hands touched, they were welded together. When their two souls saw each other, they recognised that they were mutually needed, and they closely embraced.

Taking the words in their most comprehensive and most absolute sense, it might be said that, separated from everything by the walls of the tomb, Jean Valjean was the husband bereaved, as Cosette was the orphan. This position made Jean Valjean become, in a celestial sense, the father of Cosette.

And, in truth, the mysterious impression produced upon Cosette, in the depths of the woods at Chelles, by the hand of Jean Valjean grasping her own in the darkness, was not an illusion but a reality. The coming of this man and his participation in the destiny of this child had been the advent of God.

In the meanwhile, Jean Valjean had well chosen his hiding-place. He was there in a state of security that seemed to be complete.

The apartment with the side chamber which he occupied with Cosette, was the one whose window looked out upon the boulevard. This window being the only one in the house, there was no neighbour's prying eye to fear either from that side or opposite.

The lower floor of No. 50–52 was a sort of dilapidated shed; it served as a sort of stable for market gardeners, and had no communication with the upper floor. It was separated from it by the flooring, which had neither stairway nor trap-door, and was, as it were, the diaphragm of the old building. The upper floor contained, as we have said, several rooms and a few lofts, only one of which was occupied—by an old woman, who was maid of all work to Jean Valjean. All the rest was uninhabited.

It was this old woman, honoured with the title of landlady, but, in reality, intrusted with the functions of portress, who had rented him these lodgings on Christmas Day. He had passed himself off to her as a gentleman of means, ruined by the Spanish

Bonds, who was going to live there with his grand-daughter. He had paid her for six months in advance, and engaged the old dame to furnish the chamber and the little bedroom, as we have described them. This old woman it was who had kindled the fire in the stove and made everything ready for them, on the evening of their arrival.

Weeks rolled by. These two beings led in that wretched shelter a happy life.

From the earliest dawn, Cosette laughed, prattled, and sang. Children have their morning song, like birds.

Sometimes it happened that Jean Valjean would take her little red hand, all chapped and frost-bitten as it was, and kiss it. The poor child, accustomed only to blows, had no idea what this meant, and would draw back ashamed.

At times, she grew serious and looked musingly at her little black dress. Cosette was no longer in rags; she was in mourning. She was issuing from utter poverty and was entering upon life.

Jean Valjean had begun to teach her to read. Sometimes, while teaching the child to spell, he would remember that it was with the intention of accomplishing evil that he had learned to read, in the galleys. This intention had now been changed into teaching a child to read. Then the old convict would smile with the pensive smile of angels.

He felt in this a pre-ordination from on high, a volition of some one more than man, and he would lose himself in reverie. Good thoughts as well as bad have their abysses.

To teach Cosette to read, and to watch her playing, was nearly all Jean Valjean's life. And then, he would talk to her about her mother, and teach her to pray.

She called him *Father*, and knew him by no other name.

He spent hours seeing her dress and undress her doll, and listening to her song and prattle. From that time on, life seemed full of interest to him, men seemed good and just; he no longer, in his thoughts, reproached any one with any wrong; he saw no reason, now, why he should not live to grow very old, since his child loved him. He looked forward to a long future illuminated by Cosette with charming light. The very best of us are not altogether exempt from some tinge of egotism. At times, he thought with a sort of quiet satisfaction, that she would be by no means handsome.

This is but personal opinion; but in order to express our idea thoroughly, at the point Jean Valjean had reached, when he began to love Cosette, it is not clear to us that he did not require this fresh supply of goodness to enable him to persevere in the right path. He had seen the wickedness of men and the misery of society under new aspects—aspects incomplete and, unfortunately, showing forth only one side of the truth—the lot of woman summed up in Fantine, public authority personified in Javert; he had been sent back to the galleys this time for doing good; new waves of bitterness had overwhelmed him; disgust and weariness had once more resumed their sway; the recollection of the bishop, even, was perhaps eclipsed, sure to reappear afterwards, luminous and triumphant; yet, in fact, this blessed remembrance was growing feebler. Who knows that Jean Valjean was not on the point of becoming discouraged and falling back to evil ways? Love came, and he again grew strong. Alas! he was no less feeble than Cosette. He protected her, and she gave strength to him. Thanks to him, she could walk upright in life; thanks to her, he could persist in virtuous deeds. He was the support of this child, and this child was his prop and staff. Oh, divine and unfathomable mystery of the compensations of Destiny!

IV

WHAT THE LANDLADY DISCOVERED

JEAN VALJEAN was prudent enough never to go out in the daytime. Every evening, however, about twilight, he would walk for an hour or two, sometimes alone, often with Cosette, selecting the most unfrequented side alleys of the boulevards and going into the churches at nightfall. He was fond of going to St. Médard, which is the nearest church. When he did not take Cosette, she remained with the old woman; but it was the child's delight to go out with her kind old friend. She preferred an hour with him even to her delicious tête-à-têtes with Catharine. He would walk along holding her by the hand, and telling her pleasant things.

It turned out that Cosette was very playful.

The old woman was housekeeper and cook, and did the marketing.

They lived frugally, always with a little fire in the stove, but like people in embarrassed circumstances. Jean Valjean made no change in the furniture described on the first day, excepting that he caused a solid door to be put up in place of the glass door of Cosette's little bed-chamber.

He still wore his yellow coat, his black pantaloons, and his old hat. On the street he was taken for a beggar. It sometimes happened that kind-hearted dames, in passing, would turn and hand him a penny. Jean Valjean accepted the penny and bowed humbly. It chanced sometimes, also, that he would meet some wretched creature begging alms, and then, glancing about him to be sure no one was looking, he would stealthily approach the beggar, slip a piece of money, often silver, into his hand, and walk rapidly away. This had its inconveniences. He began to be known in the quarter as *the beggar who gives alms*.

The old *landlady*, a crabbed creature, fully possessed with that keen observation as to all that concerned her neighbours, which is peculiar to the suburbs, watched Jean Valjean closely without exciting his suspicion. She was a little deaf, which made her talkative. She had but two teeth left, one in the upper and one in the lower jaw, and these she was continually rattling together. She had questioned Cosette, who, knowing nothing, could tell nothing, further than that she came from Montfermeil. One morning this old female spy saw Jean Valjean go, with an appearance which seemed peculiar to the old busybody, into one of the uninhabited apartments of the building. She followed him with the steps of an old cat, and could see him without herself being seen, through the chink of the door directly opposite. Jean Valjean had, doubtless for greater caution, turned his back towards the door in question. The old woman saw him fumble in his pocket, and take from it a needle case, scissors, and thread, and then proceed to rip open the lining of one lapel of his coat and take from under it a piece of yellowish paper, which he unfolded. The beldame remarked with dismay, that it was a bank bill for a thousand francs. It was the second or third one only that she had ever seen. She ran away very much frightened.

A moment afterwards, Jean Valjean accosted her, and asked her to get this thousand-franc bill changed for him, adding that it was the half-yearly interest on his property which he had received on the previous day. "Where?" thought the old woman. He did not go out until six o'clock, and the government treasury is certainly not open at that hour. The old woman got the note changed, all the while forming her conjectures.

This bill of a thousand francs, commented upon and multiplied, gave rise to a host of breathless conferences among the gossips of the Rue des Vignes Saint Marcel.

Some days afterwards, it chanced that Jean Valjean, in his shirt-sleeves, was sawing wood in the entry. The old woman was in his room doing the chamberwork. She was alone. Cosette was intent upon the wood he was sawing. The woman saw the coat hanging on a nail, and examined it. The lining had been sewed over. She felt it carefully and thought she could detect in the lapels and in the padding, thicknesses of paper. Other thousand-franc bills beyond a doubt!

She noticed, besides, that there were all sorts of things in the pockets. Not only were there the needles, scissors, and thread which she had already seen, but a large pocket-book, a very big knife, and, worst symptom of all, several wigs of different colours. Every pocket of this coat had the appearance of containing something to be provided with against sudden emergencies.

Thus, the occupants of the old building reached the closing days of winter.

V

A FIVE-FRANC PIECE FALLING ON THE FLOOR MAKES A NOISE

THERE was, in the neighbourhood of Saint Médard, a mendicant who sat crouching over the edge of a condemned public well near by, and to whom Jean Valjean often gave alms. He never passed this man without giving him a few pennies. Sometimes he spoke to him. Those who were envious of this poor creature said he was in the pay of the police. He was an old church beadle of seventy-five, who was always mumbling prayers.

One evening, as Jean Valjean was passing that way, unaccompanied by Cosette, he noticed the beggar sitting in his usual place, under the street lamp which had just been lighted. The man, according to custom, seemed to be praying and was bent over. Jean Valjean walked up to him, and put a piece of money in his hand, as usual. The beggar suddenly raised his eyes, gazed intently at Jean Valjean, and then quickly dropped his head. This movement was like a flash; Jean Valjean shuddered; it seemed to him that he had just seen, by the light of the street lamp, not the calm, sanctimonious face of the aged beadle, but a terrible and well-known countenance. He experienced the sensation one would feel on finding himself suddenly face to face, in the gloom, with a tiger. He recoiled, horror-stricken and petrified, daring neither to breathe nor to speak, to stay nor to fly, but gazing upon the beggar who had once more bent down his head, with its tattered covering, and seemed to be no longer conscious of his presence. At this singular moment, an instinct, perhaps the mysterious instinct of self-preservation, prevented Jean Valjean from uttering a word. The beggar had the same form, the same rags, the same general appearance as on every other day. "Pshaw!" said Jean Valjean to himself, "I am mad! I am dreaming! It cannot be!" And he went home, anxious and ill at ease.

He scarcely dared to admit, even to himself, that the countenance he thought he had seen was the face of Javert.

That night, upon reflection, he regretted that he had not questioned the man so as to compel him to raise his head a second time. On the morrow, at nightfall, he went thither, again. The beggar was in his place. "Good day! Good day!" said Jean Valjean, with firmness, as he gave him the accustomed alms. The beggar raised his head and answered in a whining voice: "Thanks, kind sir, thanks!" It was, indeed, only the old beadle.

Jean Valjean now felt fully reassured. He even began to laugh. "What the deuce was I about to fancy that I saw Javert," thought he; "is my sight growing poor already?" And he thought no more about it.

Some days after, it might be eight o'clock in the evening, he was in his room, giving Cosette her spelling lesson, which the child was repeating in a loud voice, when he heard the door of the building open and close again. That seemed odd to him. The old woman, the only occupant of the house besides himself and Cosette, always went to bed at dark to save candles. Jean Valjean made a sign to Cosette to be silent. He heard some one coming up the stairs. Possibly, it might be the old woman who had felt unwell and had been to the druggist's. Jean Valjean listened. The footstep was heavy, and sounded like a man's; but the old woman wore heavy shoes, and there is nothing so much like the step of a man as the step of an old woman. However, Jean Valjean blew out his candle.

He sent Cosette to bed, telling her in a suppressed voice to lie down very quietly—and, as he kissed her forehead, the footsteps stopped. Jean Valjean remained silent and motionless, his back turned towards the door, still seated on his chair from which he had not moved, and holding his breath in the darkness. After a considerable interval, not hearing anything more, he turned round without making any noise, and as he raised his eyes towards the door of his room, he saw a light through the key-hole. This ray of light was an evil star in the black background of the door and the wall. There was, evidently, somebody outside with a candle who was listening.

A few minutes elapsed, and the light disappeared. But he heard no sound of footsteps, which seemed to indicate that whoever was listening at the door had taken off his shoes.

Jean Valjean threw himself on his bed without undressing, but could not shut his eyes that night.

At daybreak, as he was sinking into slumber from fatigue, he was aroused, again, by the creaking of the door of some room at the end of the hall, and then he heard the same footstep which had ascended the stairs, on the preceding night. The step approached. He started from his bed and placed his eye to the keyhole, which was quite a large one, hoping to get a glimpse of the person, whoever it might be, who had made his way into the building in the night-time and had listened at his door. It was a man, indeed, who passed by Jean Valjean's room, this time without stopping. The hall was still too dark for him to make out his features; but, when the man reached the stairs, a ray of light from without made his figure stand out like a profile, and Jean Valjean had a full view of his back. The man was tall, wore a long frock-coat, and had a cudgel under his arm. It was the redoubtable form of Javert.

Jean Valjean might have tried to get another look at him through his window that opened on the boulevard, but he would have had to raise the sash, and that he dared not do.

It was evident that the man had entered by means of a key, as if at home. "Who, then, had given him the key?—and what was the meaning of this?"

At seven in the morning, when the old lady came to clear up the rooms, Jean Valjean eyed her sharply, but asked her no questions. The good dame appeared as usual.

While she was doing her sweeping, she said:——

"Perhaps monsieur heard some one come in, last night?"

At her age and on that boulevard, eight in the evening is the very darkest of the night.

"Ah! yes, by the way, I did," he answered in the most natural tone. "Who was it?"

"It's a new lodger," said the old woman, "who has come into the house."

"And his name——?"

"Well, I hardly recollect now. Dumont or Daumont.—Some such name as that."

"And what is he—this M. Daumont?"

The old woman studied him, a moment, through her little foxy eyes, and answered:

"He's a gentleman living on his income like you."

She may have intended nothing by this, but Jean Valjean thought he could make out that she did.

When the old woman was gone, he made a roll of a hundred francs he had in a drawer and put it into his pocket. Do what he would to manage this so that the clinking of the silver should not be heard, a five-franc piece escaped his grasp and rolled jingling away over the floor.

At dusk, he went to the street-door and looked carefully up and down the boulevard. No one was to be seen. The boulevard seemed to be utterly deserted. It is true that there might have been someone hidden behind a tree.

He went upstairs again.

"Come," said he to Cosette.

He took her by the hand and they both went out.

BOOK FIFTH –
A DARK CHASE NEEDS A SILENT HOUND

I

THE ZIGZAGS OF STRATEGY

In order to understand the pages immediately following, and others also which will be found further on, an observation is here necessary.

Many years have already passed away since the author of this book, who is compelled, reluctantly, to speak of himself, was in Paris. Since then, Paris has been transformed. A new city has arisen, which to him is in some sense unknown. He need not say that he loves Paris; Paris is the native city of his heart. Through demolition and reconstruction, the Paris of his youth, that Paris which he religiously treasures in his memory, has become a Paris of former times. Let him be permitted to speak of that Paris as if it still existed. It is possible that where the author is about to conduct his readers, saying: "In such a street there is such a house," there is now no longer either house or street. The reader will verify it, if he chooses to take the trouble. As to himself, the author knows not the new Paris, and writes with the old Paris before his eyes in an illusion which is precious to him. It is a sweet thing for him to imagine that there still remains something of what he saw when he was in his own country, and that all is not vanished. While we are living in our native land, we fancy that these streets are indifferent to us, that these windows, these roofs, and these doors are nothing to us, that these walls are strangers to us, that these trees are no more than other trees, that these houses which we never enter are useless to us, that this pavement on which we walk is nothing but stone. In after times, when we are there no longer, we find that those streets are very dear, that we miss those roofs, those windows, and those doors, that those walls are necessary to us, that those trees are our well-beloved, that those houses which we never entered we entered every day, and that we have left something of our affections, our life, and our heart in those streets. All those places which we see no more, which perhaps we shall never see again, but the image of which we have preserved, assume a mournful charm, return to us with the sadness of a spectre, make the holy land visible to us, and are, so to speak,

445

the very form of France; and we love them and call them up such as they are, such as they were, and hold to them, unwilling to change anything, for one clings to the form of his fatherland as to the face of his mother.

Permit us, then, to speak of the past in the present. Saying which, we beg the reader to take note of it, and we proceed.

Jean Valjean had immediately left the boulevard and began to thread the streets, making as many turns as he could, returning sometimes upon his track to make sure that he was not followed.

This manœuvre is peculiar to the hunted stag. On ground where the foot leaves a mark, it has, among other advantages, that of deceiving the hunters and the dogs by the counter-step. It is what is called in venery *false reimbushment*.

The moon was full. Jean Valjean was not sorry for that. The moon, still near the horizon, cut large prisms of light and shade in the streets. Jean Valjean could glide along the houses and the walls on the dark side and observe the light side. He did not, perhaps, sufficiently realise that the obscure side escaped him. However, in all the deserted little streets in the neighbourhood of the Rue de Poliveau, he felt sure that no one was behind him.

Cosette walked without asking any questions. The sufferings of the first six years of her life had introduced something of the passive into her nature. Besides—and this is a remark to which we shall have more than one occasion to return—she had become familiar, without being fully conscious of them, with the peculiarities of her good friend and the eccentricities of destiny. And then, she felt safe, being with him.

Jean Valjean knew, no more than Cosette, where he was going. He trusted in God, as she trusted in him. It seemed to him that he also held some one greater than himself by the hand; he believed he felt a being leading him, invisible. Finally, he had no definite idea, no plan, no project. He was not even absolutely sure that this was Javert, and then it might be Javert, and Javert not know that he was Jean Valjean. Was he not disguised? was he not supposed to be dead? Nevertheless, singular things had happened within the last few days. He wanted no more of them. He was determined not to enter Gorbeau House again. Like the animal hunted from his den, he was looking for a hole to hide in until he could find one to remain in.

Jean Valjean described many and varied labyrinths in the Quartier Mouffetard, which was asleep already as if it were still

under the discipline of the middle age and the yoke of the cur-
few; he produced different combinations, in wise strategy, with
the Rue Censier and the Rue Copeau, the Rue du Battoir Saint
Victor and the Rue du Puits l'Ermite. There are lodgings in that
region, but he did not even enter them, not finding what suited
him. He had no doubt whatever that if, perchance, they had
sought his track, they had lost it.

As eleven o'clock struck in the tower of Saint Etienne du
Mont, he crossed the Rue de Pontoise in front of the bureau of
the Commissary of Police, which is at No. 14. Some moments
afterwards, the instinct of which we have already spoken made
him turn his head. At this moment he saw distinctly—thanks to
the commissary's lamp which revealed them—three men following him quite near, pass one after another under this lamp
on the dark side of the street. One of these men entered the
passage leading to the commissary's house. The one in advance
appeared to him decidedly suspicious.

"Come, child!" said he to Cosette, and he made haste to get
out of the Rue de Pontoise.

He made a circuit, went round the arcade des Patriarches,
which was closed on account of the lateness of the hour, walked
rapidly through the Rue de l'Epée-de-Bois and the Rue de
l'Arbalète, and plunged into the Rue des Postes.

There was a square there, where the Collège Rollin now
is, and from which branches off the Rue Neuve-Sainte-
Geneviève.

(We need not say that the Rue Neuve-Sainte-Geneviève is
an old street, and that there a postchaise did not pass once in ten
years through the Rue des Postes. This Rue des Postes was in
the thirteenth century inhabited by potters, and its true name is
Rue des Pots.)

The moon lighted up this square brightly. Jean Valjean concealed himself in a doorway, calculating that if these men were
still following him, he could not fail to get a good view of them
when they crossed this lighted space.

In fact, three minutes had not elapsed when the men
appeared. There were now four of them; all were tall, dressed in
long brown coats, with round hats, and great clubs in their
hands. They were not less fearfully forbidding by their size and
their large fists than by their stealthy tread in the darkness. One
would have taken them for four spectres in citizen's dress.

They stopped in the centre of the square and formed a group like people consulting. They appeared undecided. The man who seemed to be the leader turned and energetically pointed in the direction in which Jean Valjean was; one of the others seemed to insist with some obstinacy on the contrary direction. At the instant when the leader turned, the moon shone full in his face. Jean Valjean recognised Javert perfectly.

II

IT IS FORTUNATE THAT VEHICLES CAN CROSS THE BRIDGE OF AUSTERLITZ

UNCERTAINTY was at an end for Jean Valjean; happily, it still continued with these men. He took advantage of their hesitation; it was time lost for them, gained for him. He came out from the doorway in which he was concealed, and made his way into the Rue des Postes towards the region of the Jardin des Plantes. Cosette began to be tired; he took her in his arms, and carried her. There was nobody in the streets, and the lamps had not been lighted on account of the moon.

He doubled his pace.

In a few steps, he reached the Goblet pottery, on the façade of which the old inscription stood out distinctly legible in the light of the moon:

> De Goblet fils c'est ici la fabrique;
> Venez choisir des cruches et des brocs,
> Des pots à fleurs, des tuyaux, de la brique.
> A tout venant le Cœur vend des Carreaux.

He passed through the Rue de la Clef, then by the Fontaine de Saint Victor along the Jardin des Plantes by the lower streets, and reached the quay. There he looked around. The quay was deserted. The streets were deserted. Nobody behind him. He took breath.

He arrived at the bridge of Austerlitz.

It was still a toll-bridge at this period.

He presented himself at the toll-house and gave a sou.

"It is two sous," said the toll-keeper. "You are carrying a child who can walk. Pay for two."

He paid, annoyed that his passage should have attracted observation. All flight should be gliding.

A large cart was passing the Seine at the same time, and like him was going towards the right bank. This could be made of use. He could go the whole length of the bridge in the shade of this cart.

Towards the middle of the bridge, Cosette, her feet becoming numb, desired to walk. He put her down and took her by the hand.

The bridge passed, he perceived some wood-yards a little to the right and walked in that direction. To get there, he must venture into a large clear open space. He did not hesitate. Those who followed him were evidently thrown off his track, and Jean Valjean believed himself out of danger. Sought for, he might be, but followed he was not.

A little street, the Rue de Chemin Vert Saint Antoine, opened between two wood-yards inclosed by walls. This street was narrow, obscure, and seemed made expressly for him. Before entering it, he looked back.

From the point where he was, he could see the whole length of the bridge of Austerlitz.

Four shadows, at that moment, entered upon the bridge.

These shadows were coming from the Jardin des Plantes towards the right bank.

These four shadows were the four men.

Jean Valjean felt a shudder like that of the deer when he sees the hounds again upon his track.

One hope was left him; it was that these men had not entered upon the bridge, and had not perceived him when he crossed the large square clear space leading Cosette by the hand.

In that case, by plunging into the little street before him, if he could succeed in reaching the wood-yards, the marshes, the fields, the open grounds, he could escape.

It seemed to him that he might trust himself to this silent little street. He entered it.

III

SEE THE PLAN OF PARIS OF 1727

SOME three hundred paces on, he reached a point where the street forked. It divided into two streets, the one turning off obliquely to the left, the other to the right. Jean Valjean had before him the two branches of a Y. Which should he choose?

He did not hesitate, but took the right.

Why?

Because the left branch led towards the faubourg—that is to say, towards the inhabited region, and the right branch towards the country—that is, towards the uninhabited region.

But now, they no longer walked very fast. Cosette's step slackened Jean Valjean's pace.

He took her up and carried her again. Cosette rested her head upon the goodman's shoulder, and did not say a word.

He turned, from time to time, and looked back. He took care to keep always on the dark side of the street. The street was straight behind him. The two or three first times he turned, he saw nothing; the silence was complete, and he kept on his way somewhat reassured. Suddenly, on turning again, he thought he saw in the portion of the street through which he had just passed, far in the obscurity, something which stirred.

He plunged forward rather than walked, hoping to find some side street by which to escape, and once more to elude his pursuers.

He came to a wall.

This wall, however, did not prevent him from going further; it was a wall forming the side of a cross alley, in which the street Jean Valjean was then in came to an end.

Here again he must decide; should he take the right or the left?

He looked to the right. The alley ran out to a space between some buildings that were mere sheds or barns, then terminated abruptly. The end of this blind alley was plain to be seen—a great white wall.

He looked to the left. The alley on this side was open, and, about two hundred paces further on, ran into a street of which it was an affluent. In this direction lay safety.

The instant Jean Valjean decided to turn to the left, to try to reach the street which he saw at the end of the alley, he perceived, at the corner of the alley and the street towards which he was just about going, a sort of black, motionless statue.

It was a man, who had just been posted there, evidently, and who was waiting for him, guarding the passage.

Jean Valjean was startled.

This part of Paris where Jean Valjean was, situated between the Faubourg Saint Antoine and La Râpée, is one of those which have been entirely transformed by the recent works—a change for the worse, in the opinion of some, a transfiguration, according to others. The vegetable gardens, the wood-yards, and the old buildings are gone. There are now broad new streets, amphitheatres, circuses, hippodromes, railroad depôts, a prison, Mazas; progress, as we see, with its corrective.

Half a century ago, in the common popular language, full of tradition, which obstinately calls l'Institut *Les Quartre Nations*, and l'Opera Comique *Feydeau*, the precise spot which Jean Valjean had reached was called the *Petit Picpus*. The Porte Saint Jacques, the Porte Paris, the Barrière des Sergents, the Porcherons, the Galiote, the Célestins, the Capuchins, the Mail, the Bourbe, the Arbre de Carcovie, the Petite Pologne, the Petit Picpus, these are names of the old Paris floating over into the new. The memory of the people buoys over these waifs of the past.

The Petit Picpus, which in fact hardly had a real existence, and was never more than a mere outline of a quarter, had almost the monkish aspect of a Spanish city. The roads were poorly paved, the streets were thinly built up. Beyond the two or three streets of which we are about to speak, there was nothing there but wall and solitude. Not a shop, not a vehicle, hardly a light here and there in the windows; all the lights put out after ten o'clock. Gardens, convents, wood-yards, market gardens, a few scattered low houses, and great walls as high as the houses.

Such was the quarter in the last century. The Revolution had already very much altered it. The republican authorities had pulled down buildings and run streets into and through it. Depositories of rubbish had been established there. Thirty years ago, this quarter was being gradually erased by the construction of new buildings. It is now completely blotted out. The Petit Picpus, of which no present plan retains a trace, is clearly enough indicated in the plan of 1727, published at Paris by Denis Thierry, Rue Saint Jacques, opposite the Rue du Plâtre, and at Lyons by Jean Girin, Rue Mercière, à la Prudence. The Petit Picpus had what we have just called a Y of streets, formed by the Rue du Chemin Vert Saint Antoine dividing into two branches and taking on the left the name Petite Rue Picpus and on the right the name of the Rue Polonceau. The two branches of the Y were joined at the top as by a bar. This bar was called the Rue Droit Mur. The Rue Polonceau ended there; the Petite

Rue Picpus passed beyond, rising towards the Marché Lenoir. He who, coming from the Seine, reached the extremity of the Rue Polonceau, had on his left the Rue Droit Mur turning sharply at a right angle, before him the side wall of that street, and on his right a truncated prolongation of the Rue Droit Mur, without thoroughfare, called the Cul-de-sac Genrot.

Jean Valjean was in this place.

As we have said, on perceiving the black form standing sentry at the corner of the Rue Droit Mur and the Petite Rue Picpus, he was startled. There was no doubt. He was watched by this shadow.

What should he do?

There was now no time to turn back. What he had seen moving in the obscurity some distance behind him, the moment before, was undoubtedly Javert and his squad. Javert probably had already reached the commencement of the street of which Jean Valjean was at the end. Javert, to all appearance, was acquainted with this little trap, and had taken his precautions by sending one of his men to guard the exit. These conjectures, so like certainties, whirled about wildly in Jean Valjean's troubled brain, as a handful of dust flies before a sudden blast. He scrutinised the Cul-de-sac Genrot; there were high walls. He scrutinised the Petite Rue Picpus; there was a sentinel. He saw the dark form repeated in black upon the white pavement flooded with the moonlight. To advance, was to fall upon that man. To go back, was to throw himself into Javert's hands. Jean Valjean felt as if caught by a chain that was slowly winding up. He looked up into the sky in despair.

IV

GROPING FOR ESCAPE

In order to understand what follows, it is necessary to form an exact idea of the little Rue Droit Mur, and particularly the corner which it makes at the left as you leave the Rue Polonceau to enter this alley. The little Rue Droit Mur was almost entirely lined on the right, as far as the Petite Rue Picpus, by houses of poor appearance; on the left by a single building of severe outline, composed of several structures which rose gradually a story or two, one above another, as they approached the Petite Rue Picpus, so that the building, very high on the side of the Petite

Rue Picpus, was quite low on the side of the Rue Polonceau. There, at the corner of which we have spoken, it became so low as to be nothing more than a wall. This wall did not abut squarely on the corner, which was cut off diagonally, leaving a considerable space that was shielded by the two angles thus formed from observers at a distance in either the Rue Polonceau, or the Rue Droit Mur.

From these two angles of the truncated corner, the wall extended along the Rue Polonceau as far as a house numbered 49, and along the Rue Droit Mur, where its height was much less, to the sombre-looking building of which we have spoken, cutting its gable, and thus making a new re-entering angle in the street. This gable had a gloomy aspect; there was but one window to be seen, or rather two shutters covered with a sheet of zinc, and always closed.

The situation of the places which we describe here is rigorously exact, and we certainly awaken a very precise remembrance in the minds of the old inhabitants of the locality.

This truncated corner was entirely filled by a thing which seemed like a colossal and miserable door. It was a vast shapeless assemblage of perpendicular planks, broader above than below, bound together by long transverse iron bands. At the side there was a porte-cochère of the ordinary dimensions, which had evidently been cut in within the last fifty years.

A lime-tree lifted its branches above this corner, and the wall was covered with ivy towards the Rue Polonceau.

In the imminent peril of Jean Valjean, this sombre building had a solitary and uninhabited appearance which attracted him. He glanced over it rapidly. He thought if he could only succeed in getting into it, he would perhaps be safe. Hope came to him with the idea.

Midway of the front of this building on the Rue Droit Mur, there were at all the windows of the different stories old leaden waste-pipes. The varied branchings of the tubing which was continued from a central conduit to each of these waste-pipes, outlined on the façade a sort of tree. These ramifications of the pipes with their hundred elbows seemed like those old closely-pruned grape-vines which twist about over the front of ancient farm-houses.

This grotesque espalier, with its sheet-iron branches, was the first object which Jean Valjean saw. He seated Cosette with her back against a post, and, telling her to be quiet, ran to the spot where the conduit came to the pavement. Perhaps there was some means of scaling the wall by that and entering the house. But the conduit was dilapidated and out of use, and scarcely held by its fastening. Besides, all the windows of this silent house were protected by thick bars of iron, even the dormer windows. And then the moon shone full upon this façade, and the man who was watching from the end of the street would have seen Jean Valjean making the escalade. And then what should he do with Cosette? How could he raise her to the top of a three-story house?

He gave up climbing by the conduit, and crept along the wall to the Rue Polonceau.

When he reached this flattened corner where he had left Cosette, he noticed that there no one could see him. He escaped, as we have just explained, all observation from every side. Besides, he was in the shade. Then there were two doors. Perhaps they might be forced. The wall, above which he saw the lime and the ivy, evidently surrounded a garden, where he could at least conceal himself, although there were no leaves on the trees yet, and pass the rest of the night.

Time was passing. He must act quickly.

He tried the carriage door, and found at once that it was fastened within and without.

He approached the other large door with more hope. It was frightfully decrepit, its immense size even rendering it less solid; the planks were rotten, the iron fastenings, of which there were three, were rusted. It seemed possible to pierce this worm-eaten structure.

On examining it, he saw that this door was not a door. It had neither hinges, braces, lock, nor crack in the middle. The iron bands crossed from one side to the other without a break. Through the crevices of the planks he saw the rubble-work and stones, roughly cemented, which passers-by could have seen within the last ten years. He was compelled to admit with consternation that this appearance of a door was simply an ornamentation in wood of a wall, upon which it was placed. It was easy to tear off a board, but then he would find himself face to face with a wall.

V

WHICH WOULD BE IMPOSSIBLE WERE THE STREETS LIGHTED WITH GAS

AT this moment a muffled and regular sound began to make itself heard at some distance. Jean Valjean ventured to thrust his head a little way around the corner of the street. Seven or eight soldiers, formed in platoon, had just turned into the Rue Polonceau. He saw the gleam of their bayonets. They were coming towards him.

The soldiers, at whose head he distinguished the tall form of Javert, advanced slowly and with precaution. They stopped frequently. It was plain they were exploring all the recesses of the walls and all the entrances of doors and alleys.

It was—and here conjecture could not be deceived—some patrol which Javert had met and which he had put in requisition. Javert's two assistants marched in the ranks.

At the rate at which they were marching, and the stops they were making, it would take them about a quarter of an hour to arrive at the spot where Jean Valjean was. It was a frightful moment. A few minutes separated Jean Valjean from that awful precipice which was opening before him for the third time. And the galleys now were no longer simply the galleys; they were Cosette lost for ever; that is to say, a life in death.

There was now only one thing possible.

Jean Valjean had this peculiarity, that he might be said to carry two knapsacks; in one he had the thoughts of a saint, in the other the formidable talents of a convict. He helped himself from one or the other as occasion required.

Among other resources, thanks to his numerous escapes from the galleys at Toulon, he had, it will be remembered, become master of that incredible art of raising himself, in the right angle of a wall, if need be to the height of a sixth story; an art without ladders or props, by mere muscular strength, supporting himself by the back of his neck, his shoulders, his hips, and his knees, hardly making use of the few projections of the stone, which rendered so terrible and so celebrated the corner of the yard of the Conciergerie of Paris by which, some twenty years ago, the convict Battemolle made his escape.

Jean Valjean measured with his eyes the wall above which he saw the lime-tree. It was about eighteen feet high. The angle that it made with the gable of the great building was filled in its lower part with a pile of masonry of triangular shape, probably intended to preserve this too convenient recess from a too public use. This preventive filling-up of the corners of a wall is very common in Paris.

This pile was about five feet high. From its top the space to climb to get upon the wall was hardly more than fourteen feet.

The wall was capped by a flat stone without any projection.

The difficulty was Cosette. Cosette did not know how to scale a wall. Abandon her? Jean Valjean did not think of it. To carry her was impossible. The whole strength of a man is necessary to accomplish these strange ascents. The least burden would make him lose his centre of gravity and he would fall.

He needed a cord. Jean Valjean had none. Where could he find a cord, at midnight, in the Rue Polonceau? Truly at that instant, if Jean Valjean had had a kingdom, he would have given it for a rope.

All extreme situations have their flashes which sometimes make us blind, sometimes illuminate us.

The despairing gaze of Jean Valjean encountered the lamppost in the Cul-de-sac Genrot.

At this epoch there were no gas-lights in the streets of Paris. At nightfall they lighted the street lamps, which were placed at intervals, and were raised and lowered by means of a rope traversing the street from end to end, running through the grooves of posts. The reel on which this rope was wound was inclosed below the lantern in a little iron box, the key of which was kept by the lamp-lighter, and the rope itself was protected by a casing of metal.

Jean Valjean, with the energy of a final struggle, crossed the street at a bound, entered the cul-de-sac, sprang the bolt of the little box with the point of his knife, and an instant after was back at the side of Cosette. He had a rope. These desperate inventors of expedients, in their struggles with fatality, move electrically in case of need.

We have explained that the street lamps had not been lighted that night. The lamp in the Cul-de-sac Genrot was then, as a matter of course, extinguished like the rest, and one might pass by without even noticing that it was not in its place.

Meanwhile the hour, the place, the darkness, the preoccupation of Jean Valjean, his singular actions, his going to and fro, all this began to disturb Cosette. Any other child would have uttered loud cries long before. She contented herself with pulling Jean Valjean by the skirt of his coat. The sound of the approaching patrol was constantly becoming more and more distinct.

"Father," said she, in a whisper, "I am afraid. Who is it that is coming?"

"Hush!" answered the unhappy man, "it is the Thénardiess."

Cosette shuddered. He added:

"Don't say a word; I'll take care of her. If you cry, if you make any noise, the Thénardiess will hear you. She is coming to catch you."

Then, without any haste, but without doing anything a second time, with a firm and rapid decision, so much the more remarkable at such a moment when the patrol and Javert might come upon him at any instant, he took off his cravat, passed it around Cosette's body under the arms, taking care that it should not hurt the child, attached this cravat to an end of the rope by means of the knot which seamen call a swallow-knot, took the other end of the rope in his teeth, took off his shoes and stockings and threw them over the wall, climbed upon the pile of masonry and began to raise himself in the angle of the wall and the gable with as much solidity and certainty as if he had the rounds of a ladder under his heels and his elbows. Half a minute had not passed before he was on his knees on the wall.

Cosette watched him, stupefied, without saying a word. Jean Valjean's charge and the name of the Thénardiess had made her dumb.

All at once, she heard Jean Valjean's voice calling to her in a low whisper:

"Put your back against the wall."

She obeyed.

"Don't speak, and don't be afraid," added Jean Valjean.

And she felt herself lifted from the ground.

Before she had time to think where she was she was at the top of the wall.

Jean Valjean seized her, put her on his back, took her two little hands in his left hand, lay down flat and crawled along the top of the wall as far as the cut-off corner. As he had supposed, there was a building there, the roof of which sloped from the top of the wooden casing we have mentioned very nearly to the ground, with a gentle inclination, and just reaching to the lime-tree.

A fortunate circumstance, for the wall was much higher on this side than on the street. Jean Valjean saw the ground beneath him at a great depth.

He had just reached the inclined plane of the roof, and had not yet left the crest of the wall, when a violent uproar proclaimed the arrival of the patrol. He heard the thundering voice of Javert:

"Search the cul-de-sac! The Rue Droit Mur is guarded, the Petite Rue Picpus also. I'll answer for it if he is in the cul-de-sac."

The soldiers rushed into the Cul-de-sac Genrot.

Jean Valjean slid down the roof, keeping hold of Cosette, reached the lime-tree, and jumped to the ground. Whether from terror, or from courage, Cosette had not uttered a whisper. Her hands were a little scraped.

VI
COMMENCEMENT OF AN ENIGMA

JEAN VALJEAN found himself in a sort of garden, very large and of a singular appearance; one of those gloomy gardens which seem made to be seen in the winter and at night. This garden was oblong, with a row of large poplars at the further end, some tall forest trees in the corners, and a clear space in the centre, where stood a very large isolated tree, then a few fruit trees, contorted and shaggy, like big bushes, some vegetable beds, a melon patch the glass covers of which shone in the moonlight, and an old well. There were here and there stone benches which seemed black with moss. The walks were bordered with sorry little shrubs perfectly straight. The grass covered half of them, and a green moss covered the rest.

Jean Valjean had on one side the building, down the roof of which he had come, a wood-pile, and behind the wood, against the wall, a stone statue, the mutilated face of which was now nothing but a shapeless mask which was seen dimly through the obscurity.

The building was in ruins, but some dismantled rooms could be distinguished in it, one of which was well filled, and appeared to serve as a shed.

The large building of the Rue Droit Mur which ran back on the Petite Rue Picpus, presented upon this garden two square façades. These inside façades were still more gloomy than those on the outside. All the windows were grated. No light was to be seen. On the upper stories there were shutters as in prisons. The shadow of one of these façades was projected upon the other, and fell on the garden like an immense black pall.

No other house could be seen. The further end of the garden was lost in mist and in darkness. Still, he could make out walls intersecting, as if there were other cultivated grounds beyond, as well as the low roofs of the Rue Polonceau.

Nothing can be imagined more wild and more solitary than this garden. There was no one there, which was very natural on account of the hour; but it did not seem as if the place were made for anybody to walk in, even in broad noon.

Jean Valjean's first care had been to find his shoes, and put them on; then he entered the shed with Cosette. A man trying to escape never thinks himself sufficiently concealed. The child, thinking constantly of the Thénardiess, shared his instinct, and cowered down as closely as she could.

Cosette trembled, and pressed closely to his side. They heard the tumultuous clamour of the patrol ransacking the cul-de-sac and the street, the clatter of their muskets against the stones, the calls of Javert to the watchmen he had stationed, and his imprecations mingled with words which they could not distinguish.

At the end of a quarter of an hour it seemed as though this stormy rumbling began to recede. Jean Valjean did not breathe.

He had placed his hand gently upon Cosette's mouth.

But the solitude about him was so strangely calm that that frightful din, so furious and so near, did not even cast over it a shadow of disturbance. It seemed as if these walls were built of the deaf stones spoken of in Scripture.

Suddenly, in the midst of this deep calm, a new sound arose; a celestial, divine, ineffable sound, as ravishing as the other was horrible. It was a hymn which came forth from the darkness, a bewildering mingling of prayer and harmony in the obscure and fearful silence of the night; voices of women, but voices with the pure accents of virgins, and artless accents of children; those voices which are not of earth, and which resemble those that the new-born still hear, and the dying hear already. This song came from the gloomy building which overlooked the garden. At the moment when the uproar of the demons receded, one would have said, it was a choir of angels approaching in the darkness.

Cosette and Jean Valjean fell on their knees.

They knew not what it was; they knew not where they were; but they both felt, the man and the child, the penitent and the innocent, that they ought to be on their knees.

These voices had this strange effect; they did not prevent the building from appearing deserted. It was like a supernatural song in an uninhabited dwelling.

While these voices were singing Jean Valjean was entirely absorbed in them. He no longer saw the night, he saw a blue sky. He seemed to feel the spreading of these wings which we all have within us.

The chant ceased. Perhaps it had lasted a long time. Jean Valjean could not have told. Hours of ecstasy are never more than a moment.

All had again relapsed into silence. There was nothing more in the street, nothing more in the garden. That which threatened, that which reassured, all had vanished. The wind rattled the dry grass on the top of the wall, which made a low, soft, and mournful noise.

VII
THE ENIGMA CONTINUED

THE night wind had risen, which indicated that it must be between one and two o'clock in the morning. Poor Cosette did not speak. As she had sat down at his side and leaned her head on him, Jean Valjean thought that she was asleep. He bent over and looked at her. Her eyes were wide open, and she had a look that gave Jean Valjean pain.

She was still trembling.

"Are you sleepy?" said Jean Valjean.

"I am very cold," she answered.

A moment after she added:

"Is she there yet?"

"Who?" said Jean Valjean.

"Madame Thénardier."

Jean Valjean had already forgotten the means he had employed to secure Cosette's silence.

"Oh!" said he. "She has gone. Don't be afraid any longer."

The child sighed as if a weight were lifted from her breast.

The ground was damp, the shed open on all sides, the wind freshened every moment. The goodman took off his coat and wrapped Cosette in it.

"Are you warmer, so?"

"Oh! yes, father!"

"Well, wait here a moment for me. I shall soon be back."

He went out of the ruin, and along by the large building, in search of some better shelter. He found doors, but they were all closed. All the windows of the ground-floor were barred.

As he passed the interior angle of the building, he noticed several arched windows before him, where he perceived some light. He rose on tiptoe and looked in at one of these windows. They all opened into a large hall, paved with broad slabs, and intersected by arches and pillars, he could distinguish nothing but a slight glimmer in the deep obscurity. This glimmer came from a night-lamp burning in a corner. The hall was deserted; everything was motionless. However, by dint of looking, he thought he saw something, stretched out on the pavement, which appeared to be covered with a shroud, and which resembled a human form. It was lying with the face downwards, the arms crossed, in the immobility of death. One would have said, from a sort of serpent which trailed along the pavement, that this ill-omened figure had a rope about its neck.

The whole hall was enveloped in that mist peculiar to dimly-lighted places, which always increases horror.

Jean Valjean has often said since that, although in the course of his life he had seen many funereal sights, never had he seen anything more freezing and more terrible than this enigmatical figure fulfilling some strange mystery, he knew not what, in that gloomy place, and thus dimly seen in the night. It was terrifying to suppose that it was perhaps dead, and still more terrifying to think that it might be alive.

He had the courage to press his forehead against the glass and watch to see if the thing would move. He remained what seemed to him a long time in vain; the prostrate form made no movement. Suddenly he was seized with an inexpressible dismay, and he fled. He ran towards the shed without daring to look behind him. It seemed to him that if he should turn his head he would see the figure walking behind him with rapid strides and shaking its arms.

He reached the ruin breathless. His knees gave way; a cold sweat oozed out from every pore.

Where was he? who would ever have imagined anything equal to this species of sepulchre in the midst of Paris? what was this strange house? A building full of nocturnal mystery, calling to souls in the shade with the voice of angels, and, when they came, abruptly presenting to them this frightful vision—promising to open the radiant gate of Heaven and opening the horrible door of the tomb. And that was in fact a building, a house which had its number in a street? It was not a dream? He had to touch the walls to believe it.

The cold, the anxiety, the agitation, the anguish of the night, were giving him a veritable fever, and all his ideas were jostling in his brain.

He went to Cosette. She was sleeping.

VIII

THE ENIGMA REDOUBLES

THE child had laid her head upon a stone and gone to sleep.

He sat down near her and looked at her. Little by little, as he beheld her, he grew calm, and regained possession of his clearness of mind.

He plainly perceived this truth, the basis of his life henceforth, that so long as she should be alive, so long as he should have her with him, he should need nothing except for her, and fear nothing save on her account. He did not even realise that he was very cold, having taken off his coat to cover her.

Meanwhile, through the reverie into which he had fallen, he had heard for some time a singular noise. It sounded like a little bell that some one was shaking. This noise was in the garden. It was heard distinctly though feebly. It resembled the dimly heard tinkling of cow-bells in the pastures at night.

This noise made Jean Valjean turn.

He looked, and saw that there was some one in the garden.

Something which resembled a man was walking among the glass cases of the melon patch, rising up, stooping down, stopping, with a regular motion, as if he were drawing or stretching something upon the ground. This being appeared to limp.

Jean Valjean shuddered with the continual tremor of the outcast. To them everything is hostile and suspicious. They distrust the day because it helps to discover them, and the night because it helps to surprise them. Just now he was shuddering because the garden was empty, now he shuddered because there was some one in it.

He fell again from chimerical terrors into real terrors. He said to himself that perhaps Javert and his spies had not gone away, that they had doubtless left somebody on the watch in the street; that, if this man should discover him in the garden, he would cry thief, and would deliver him up. He took the sleeping Cosette gently in his arms and carried her into the furthest corner of the shed behind a heap of old furniture that was out of use. Cosette did not stir.

From there he watched the strange motions of the man in the melon patch. It seemed very singular, but the sound of the bell followed every movement of the man. When the man approached, the sound approached; when he moved away, the sound moved away; if he made some sudden motion, a trill accompanied the motion; when he stopped, the noise ceased. It seemed evident that the bell was fastened to this man; but then what could that mean? what was this man to whom a bell was hung as to a ram or a cow?

While he was resolving these questions, he touched Cosette's hands. They were icy.

"Oh! God!" said he.

He called to her in a low voice:

"Cosette!"

She did not open her eyes.

He shook her smartly.

She did not wake.

"Could she be dead?" said he, and he sprang up, shuddering from head to foot.

The most frightful thoughts rushed through his mind in confusion. There are moments when hideous suppositions besiege us like a throng of furies and violently force the portals of our brain. When those whom we love are in danger, our solicitude invents all sorts of follies. He remembered that sleep may be fatal in the open air in a cold night.

Cosette was pallid; she had fallen prostrate on the ground at his feet, making no sign.

He listened for her breathing; she was breathing; but with a respiration that appeared feeble and about to stop.

How should he get her warm again? how rouse her? All else was banished from his thoughts. He rushed desperately out of the ruin.

It was absolutely necessary that in less than a quarter of an hour Cosette should be in bed and before a fire.

IX
THE MAN WITH THE BELL

HE walked straight to the man whom he saw in the garden. He had taken in his hand the roll of money which was in his vest-pocket.

This man had his head down, and did not see him coming. A few strides, Jean Valjean was at his side.

Jean Valjean approached him, exclaiming:

"A hundred francs!"

The man started and raised his eyes.

"A hundred francs for you," continued Jean Valjean, "if you will give me refuge to-night."

The moon shone full in Jean Valjean's bewildered face.

"What, it is you, Father Madeleine!" said the man.

This name, thus pronounced, at this dark hour, in this unknown place, by this unknown man, made Jean Valjean start back.

He was ready for anything but that. The speaker was an old man, bent and lame, dressed much like a peasant, who had on his left knee a leather knee-cap from which hung a bell. His face was in the shade, and could not be distinguished.

Meanwhile the goodman had taken off his cap, and was exclaiming, tremulously:

"Ah! my God! how did you come here, Father Madeleine? How did you get in, O Lord? Did you fall from the sky? There is no doubt, if you ever do fall, you will fall from there. And what has happened to you? You have no cravat, you have no hat, you have no coat? Do you know that you would have frightened anybody who did not know you? No coat? Merciful heavens! are the saints all crazy now? But how did you get in?"

One word did not wait for another. The old man spoke with a rustic volubility in which there was nothing disquieting. All this was said with a mixture of astonishment, and frank good nature.

"Who are you? and what is this house!" asked Jean Valjean.

"Oh! indeed, that is good now," exclaimed the old man. "I am the one you got the place for here, and this house is the one you got me the place in. What! you don't remember me?"

"No," said Jean Valjean. "And how does it happen that you know me?"

"You saved my life," said the man.

He turned, a ray of the moon lighted up his side face, and Jean Valjean recognised old Fauchelevent.

"Ah!" said Jean Valjean, "it is you? yes, I remember you."

"That is very fortunate!" said the old man, in a reproachful tone.

"And what are you doing here?" added Jean Valjean.

"Oh! I am covering my melons."

Old Fauchelevent had in his hand, indeed, at the moment when Jean Valjean accosted him, the end of a piece of awning which he was stretching out over the melon patch. He had already spread out several in this way during the hour he had been in the garden. It was this work which made him go through the peculiar motions observed by Jean Valjean from the shed.

He continued:

"I said to myself: the moon is bright, there is going to be a frost. Suppose I put their jackets on my melons? And," added he, looking at Jean Valjean, with a loud laugh, "you would have done well to do as much for yourself! but how did you come here?"

Jean Valjean, finding that he was known by this man, at least under his name of Madeleine, went no further with his precautions. He multiplied questions. Oddly enough their parts seemed reversed. It was he, the intruder, who put questions.

"And what is this bell you have on your knee?"

"That!" answered Fauchelevent, "that is so that they may keep away from me."

"How! keep away from you?"

Old Fauchelevent winked in an indescribable manner.

"Ah! Bless me! there's nothing but women in this house;

plenty of young girls. It seems that I am dangerous to meet. The bell warns them. When I come they go away."

"What is this house?"

"Why, you know very well."

"No, I don't."

"Why, you got me this place here as gardener."

"Answer me as if I didn't know."

"Well, it is the Convent of the Petit Picpus, then."

Jean Valjean remembered. Chance, that is to say, Providence, had thrown him precisely into this convent of the Quartier Saint Antoine, to which old Fauchelevent, crippled by his fall from his cart, had been admitted, upon his recommendation, two years before. He repeated as if he were talking to himself:

"The Convent of the Petit Picpus!"

"But now, really," resumed Fauchelevent, "how the deuce did you manage to get in, you, Father Madeleine? It is no use for you to be a saint, you are a man; and no men come in here."

"But you are here."

"There is none but me."

"But," resumed Jean Valjean, "I must stay here."

"Oh! my God," exclaimed Fauchelevent.

Jean Valjean approached the old man, and said to him in a grave voice:

"Father Fauchelevent, I saved your life."

"I was first to remember it," answered Fauchelevent.

"Well, you can now do for me what I once did for you."

Fauchelevent grasped in his old wrinkled and trembling hands the robust hands of Jean Valjean, and it was some seconds before he could speak; at last he exclaimed:

"Oh! that would be a blessing of God if I could do something for you, in return for that! I save your life! Monsieur Mayor, the old man is at your disposal."

A wonderful joy had, as it were, transfigured the old gardener. A radiance seemed to shine forth from his face.

"What do you want me to do?" he added.

"I will explain. You have a room?"

"I have a solitary shanty, over there, behind the ruins of the old convent, in a corner that nobody ever sees. There are three rooms."

The shanty was in fact so well concealed behind the ruins,

and so well arranged, that no one should see it—that Jean Valjean had not seen it.

"Good," said Jean Valjean. "Now I ask of you two things."

"What are they, Monsieur Madeleine?"

"First, that you will not tell anybody what you know about me. Second, that you will not attempt to learn anything more."

"As you please. I know that you can do nothing dishonourable, and that you have always been a man of God. And then, besides, it was you that put me here. It is your place, I am yours."

"Very well. But now come with me. We will go for the child."

"Ah!" said Fauchelevent, "there is a child!"

He said not a word more, but followed Jean Valjean as a dog follows his master.

In half an hour Cosette, again become rosy before a good fire, was asleep in the old gardener's bed. Jean Valjean had put on his cravat and coat; his hat, which he had thrown over the wall, had been found and brought in. While Jean Valjean was putting on his coat, Fauchelevent had taken off his knee-cap with the bell attached, which now, hanging on a nail near a shutter, decorated the wall. The two men were warming themselves, with their elbows on a table, on which Fauchelevent had set a piece of cheese, some brown bread, a bottle of wine, and two glasses, and the old man said to Jean Valjean, putting his hand on his knee:

"Ah! Father Madeleine! you didn't know me at first? You save people's lives and then you forget them? Oh! that's bad; they remember you. You are ungrateful!"

X

IN WHICH IS EXPLAINED HOW
JAVERT LOST THE GAME

THE events, the reverse of which, so to speak, we have just seen, had been brought about under the simplest conditions.

When Jean Valjean, on the night of the very day that Javert arrested him at the death-bed of Fantine, escaped from the municipal prison of M—— sur M——, the police supposed that the escaped convict would start for Paris. Paris is a maelstrom in which everything is lost; and everything disappears in

this whirlpool of the world as in the whirlpool of the sea. No
forest conceals a man like this multitude. Fugitives of all kinds
know this. They go to Paris to be swallowed up; there are swal-
lowings-up which save. The police know it also, and it is in
Paris that they search for what they have lost elsewhere. They
searched there for the ex-mayor of M——sur M——. Javert
was summoned to Paris to aid in the investigation. Javert, in
fact, was of great aid in the recapture of Jean Valjean. The zeal
and intelligence of Javert on this occasion were remarked by M.
Chabouillet, Secretary of the Prefecture, under Count Anglès.
M. Chabouillet, who had already interested himself in Javert,
secured the transfer of the inspector of M—— sur M—— to
the police of Paris. There Javert rendered himself in various
ways, and, let us say, although the word seems unusual for such
service, honourably, useful.

He thought no more of Jean Valjean—with these hounds
always upon the scent, the wolf of to-day banishes the memory
of the wolf of yesterday—when, in December, 1823, he read a
newspaper, he who never read the newspapers; but Javert, as a
monarchist, made a point of knowing the details of the triumphal entry of the "Prince generalissimo" into Bayonne. Just
as he finished the article which interested him, a name—the
name of Jean Valjean—at the bottom of the page attracted his
attention. The newspaper announced that the convict Jean Valjean was dead, and published the fact in terms so explicit, that
Javert had no doubt of it. He merely said: "*That settles it.*" Then
he threw aside the paper, and thought no more of it.

Some time afterwards it happened that a police notice was
transmitted by the Prefecture of Seine-et-Oise to the Prefecture
of Police of Paris in relation to the kidnapping of a child, which
had taken place, it was said, under peculiar circumstances in the
commune of Montfermeil. A little girl, seven or eight years old,
the notice said, who had been confided by her mother to an
innkeeper of the country, had been stolen by an unknown man;
this little girl answered to the name of Cosette, and was the
child of a young woman named Fantine, who had died at the
Hôpital, nobody knew when or where. This notice came under
the eyes of Javert, and set him to thinking.

The name of Fantine was well known to him. He remembered that Jean Valjean had actually made him—Javert—laugh
aloud by asking of him a respite of three days, in order to go for

the child of this creature. He recalled the fact that Jean Valjean had been arrested at Paris, at the moment he was getting into the Montfermeil diligence. Some indications had even led him to think then that it was the second time that he was entering this diligence, and that he had already, the night previous, made another excursion to the environs of this village, for he had not been seen in the village itself. What was he doing in this region of Montfermeil? Nobody could divine. Javert understood it. The daughter of Fantine was there. Jean Valjean was going after her. Now this child had been stolen by an unknown man! Who could this man be? Could it be Jean Valjean? But Jean Valjean was dead. Javert, without saying a word to any one, took the diligence at the Plat d'Etain, cul-de-sac de Planchette, and took a trip to Montfermeil.

He expected to find great developments there; he found great obscurity.

For the first few days, the Thénardiers, in their spite, had blabbed the story about. The disappearance of the Lark had made some noise in the village. There were soon several versions of the story, which ended by becoming a case of kidnapping. Hence the police notice. However, when the first ebullition was over, Thénardier, with admirable instinct, very soon arrived at the conclusion that it is never useful to set in motion the Procureur du Roi; that the first result of his complaints in regard to the *kidnapping* of Cosette would be to fix upon himself, and on many business troubles which he had, the keen eye of justice. The last thing that owls wish is a candle. And first of all, how should he explain the fifteen hundred francs he had received? He stopped short, and enjoined secrecy upon his wife, and professed to be astonished when anybody spoke to him of the *stolen child*. He knew nothing about it; undoubtedly he had made some complaint at the time that the dear little girl should be "taken away" so suddenly; he would have liked, for affection's sake, to keep her two or three days; but it was her "grandfather" who had come for her, the most natural thing in the world. He had added the grandfather, which sounded well. It was upon this story that Javert fell on reaching Montfermeil. The grandfather put Jean Valjean out of the question.

Javert, however, dropped a few questions like plummets into Thénardier's story. Who was this grandfather, and what was his name? Thénardier answered with simplicity: "He is a rich farmer.

I saw his passport. I believe his name is M. Guillaume Lambert."

Lambert is a very respectable reassuring name. Javert returned to Paris.

"Jean Valjean is really dead," said he, "and I am a fool."

He had begun to forget all this story, when, in the month of March, 1824, he heard an odd person spoken of who lived in the parish of Saint Médard, and who was called "the beggar who gives alms." This person was, it was said, a man living on his income whose name nobody knew exactly, and who lived alone with a little girl eight years old, who knew nothing of herself except that she came from Montfermeil. Montfermeil! This name constantly recurring, excited Javert's attention anew. An old begging police spy, formerly a beadle, to whom this person had extended his charity, added some other details. "This man was very unsociable, never going out except at night, speaking to nobody, except to the poor sometimes, and allowing nobody to get acquainted with him. He wore a horrible old yellow coat which was worth millions, being lined all over with bank bills." This decidedly piqued Javert's curiosity. That he might get a near view of this fantastic rich man without frightening him away, he borrowed one day of the beadle his old frock, and the place where the old spy squatted every night droning out his orisons and playing the spy as he prayed.

"The suspicious individual" did indeed come to Javert thus disguised, and gave him alms; at that moment Javert raised his head and the shock which Jean Valjean received, thinking that he recognised Javert, Javert received, thinking that he recognised Jean Valjean.

However, the obscurity might have deceived him, the death of Jean Valjean was officially certified; Javert had still serious doubts; and in case of doubt, Javert, scrupulous as he was, never seized any man by the collar.

He followed the old man to Gorbeau House, and set "the old woman" talking, which was not at all difficult. The old woman confirmed the story of the coat lined with millions, and related to him the episode of the thousand-franc note. She had seen it! she had touched it! Javert hired a room. That very night he installed himself in it. He listened at the door of the mysterious lodger, hoping to hear the sound of his voice, but Jean Valjean perceived his candle through the key-hole and baulked the spy by keeping silence.

The next day Jean Valjean decamped. But the noise of the five-franc piece which he dropped was noticed by the old woman, who hearing money moving, suspected that he was going to move, and hastened to forewarn Javert. At night, when Jean Valjean went out, Javert was waiting for him behind the trees of the boulevard with two men.

Javert had called for assistance from the Prefecture, but he had not given the name of the person he hoped to seize. That was his secret; and he kept it for three reasons; first, because the least indiscretion might give the alarm to Jean Valjean; next, because the arrest of an old escaped convict who was reputed dead, a criminal whom the records of justice had already classed for ever *among malefactors of the most dangerous kind*, would be a magnificent success which the old members of the Parisian police certainly would never leave to a new-comer like Javert, and he feared they would take his galley slave away from him; finally, because Javert, being an artist, had a liking for surprises. He hated these boasted successes which are deflowered by talking of them long in advance. He liked to elaborate his masterpieces in the shade, and then to unveil them suddenly afterwards.

Javert had followed Jean Valjean from tree to tree, then from street corner to street corner, and had not lost sight of him a single instant; even in the moments when Jean Valjean felt himself most secure, the eye of Javert was upon him. Why did not Javert arrest Jean Valjean? Because he was still in doubt.

It must be remembered that at that time the police was not exactly at its ease; it was cramped by a free press. Some arbitrary arrests, denounced by the newspapers, had been re-echoed even in the Chambers, and rendered the Prefecture timid. To attack individual liberty was a serious thing. The officers were afraid of making mistakes, the Prefect held them responsible; an error was the loss of their place. Imagine the effect which this brief paragraph, repeated in twenty papers, would have produced in Paris. "Yesterday, an old white-haired grandsire, a respectable person living on his income, who was taking a walk with his grand-daughter, eight years old, was arrested and taken to the Station of the Prefecture as an escaped convict!"

Let us say, in addition, that Javert had his own personal scruples; the injunctions of his conscience were added to the injunctions of the Prefect. He was really in doubt.

Jean Valjean turned his back, and walked away in the darkness.

Sadness, trouble, anxiety, weight of cares, this new sorrow of being obliged to fly by night, and to seek a chance asylum in Paris for Cosette and himself, the necessity of adapting his pace to the pace of a child, all this, without his knowing it even, had changed Jean Valjean's gait, and impressed upon his carriage such an appearance of old age that the police itself, incarnated in Javert, could be deceived. The impossibility of approaching too near, his dress of an old preceptor of the emigration, the declaration of Thénardier, who made him a grandfather; finally, the belief in his death at the galleys, added yet more to the uncertainty which was increasing in Javert's mind.

For a moment he had an idea of asking him abruptly for his papers. But if the man were not Jean Valjean and if the man were not a good old honest man of means, he was probably some sharper profoundly and skilfully adept in the obscure web of Parisian crime, some dangerous chief of bandits, giving alms to conceal his other talents, an old trick. He had comrades, accomplices, retreats on all hands, in which he would take refuge without doubt. All these windings which he was making in the streets seemed to indicate that he was not a simple honest man. To arrest him too soon would be "to kill the goose that laid the golden eggs." What inconvenience was there in waiting? Javert was very sure that he would not escape.

He walked on, therefore, in some perplexity, questioning himself continually in regard to this mysterious personage.

It was not until quite late, in the Rue de Pontoise, that, thanks to the bright light which streamed from a bar-room, he decidedly recognised Jean Valjean.

There are in this world two beings who can be deeply thrilled: the mother, who finds her child, and the tiger, who finds his prey. Javert felt this profound thrill.

As soon as he had positively recognised Jean Valjean, the formidable convict, he perceived that there were only three of them, and sent to the commissary of police, of the Rue de Pontoise, for additional aid. Before grasping a thorny stick, men put on gloves.

This delay and stopping at the Rollin square to arrange with his men made him lose the scent. However, he had very soon guessed that Jean Valjean's first wish would be to put the river between his pursuers and himself. He bowed his head and reflected, like a hound who put his nose to the ground to be sure of the way. Javert, with his straightforward power of instinct, went directly to the bridge of Austerlitz. A word to the toll-keeper set him right. "Have you seen a man with a little girl?" "I made him pay two sous," answered the tollman. Javert reached the bridge in time to see Jean Valjean on the other side of the river leading Cosette across the space lighted by the moon. He saw him enter the Rue de Chemin Vert Saint Antoine, he thought of the Cul-de-sac Genrot placed there like a trap, and of the only outlet from the Rue Droit Mur into the Petite Rue Picpus. He *put out beaters*, as hunters say; he sent one of his men hastily by a detour to guard that outlet. A patrol passing on its return to the station at the arsenal, he put it in requisition and took it along with him. In such games soldiers are trumps. Moreover, it is a maxim that, to take the boar requires the science of the hunter, and the strength of the dogs. These combinations being effected, feeling that Jean Valjean was caught between the Cul-de-sac Genrot on the right, his officer on the left, and himself, Javert, in the rear, he took a pinch of snuff.

Then he began to play. He enjoyed a ravishing and infernal moment; he let his man go before him, knowing that he had him, but desiring to put off as long as possible the moment of arresting him, delighting to feel that he was caught, and to see him free, fondly gazing upon him with the rapture of the spider which lets the fly buzz, or the cat which lets the mouse run. The paw and the talon find a monstrous pleasure in the quivering of the animal imprisoned in their grasp. What delight there is in this suffocation!

Javert was rejoicing. The links of his chain were solidly welded. He was sure of success; he had now only to close his hand.

Accompanied as he was, the very idea of resistance was impossible, however energetic, however vigorous, and however desperate Jean Valjean might be.

Javert advanced slowly, sounding and ransacking on his way all the recesses of the street as he would the pockets of a thief.

When he reached the centre of the web, the fly was no longer there.

Imagine his exasperation.

He questioned his sentinel at the corner of the Rue Droit Mur and Rue Picpus; this officer, who had remained motionless at his post, had not seen the man pass.

It happens sometimes that a stag breaks with the head covered, that is to say escapes, although the hound is upon him; then the oldest hunters know not what to say. Duvivier, Ligniville, and Desprez are at fault. On the occasion of a mishap of this sort, Artonge exclaimed: *It is not a stag, it is a sorcerer.*

Javert would fain have uttered the same cry.

His disappointment had a moment of despair and fury.

It is certain that Napoleon blundered in the campaign in Russia, that Alexander blundered in the war in India, that Cæsar blundered in the African war, that Cyrus blundered in the war in Scythia, and that Javert blundered in this campaign against Jean Valjean. He did wrong perhaps in hesitating to recognise the old galley slave. The first glance should have been enough for him. He did wrong in not seizing him without ceremony in the old building. He did wrong in not arresting him when he positively recognised him in the Rue de Pontoise. He did wrong to hold a council with his aides, in full moonlight, in the Rollin square. Certainly advice is useful, and it is well to know and to question those of the dogs which are worthy of credit; but the hunter cannot take too many precautions when he is chasing restless animals, like the wolf and the convict. Javert, by too much forethought in setting his bloodhounds on the track, alarmed his prey by giving him wind of the pursuit, and allowed him the start. He did wrong, above all, when he had regained the scent at the bridge of Austerlitz, to play the formidable and puerile game of holding such a man at the end of a thread. He thought himself stronger than he was, and believed he could play mouse with a lion. At the same time, he esteemed himself too weak when he deemed it necessary to obtain a reinforcement. Fatal precaution, loss of precious time. Javert made all these blunders, and yet he was none the less one of the wisest and most correct detectives that ever existed. He was, in the full force of the term, what in venery is called a *gentle dog*. But who is perfect?

Great strategists have their eclipses.

Great blunders are often made, like large ropes, of a multitude of fibres. Take the cable thread by thread, take separately all the little determining motives, you break them one after another, and you say: that is all. Wind them and twist them together, they become an enormity; Attila hesitating between Marcian in the East and Valentinian in the West; Hannibal delaying at Capua; Danton falling to sleep at Arcis sur Aube.

However this may be, even at the moment when he perceived that Jean Valjean had escaped him, Javert did not lose his presence of mind. Sure that the convict who had broken his ban could not be far away, he set watches, arranged traps and ambushes, and beat the quarter the night through. The first thing that he saw was the displacement of the lamp, the rope of which was cut. Precious indication, which led him astray, however, by directing all his researches towards the Cul-de-sac Genrot. There are in that cul-de-sac some rather low walls which face upon gardens the limits of which extend to some very large uncultivated grounds. Jean Valjean evidently must have fled that way. The fact is that, if he had penetrated into the Cul-de-sac Genrot a little further, he would have done so, and would have been lost. Javert explored these gardens and these grounds, as if he were searching for a needle.

At daybreak, he left two intelligent men on the watch, and returned to the Prefecture of Police, crestfallen as a spy who has been caught by a thief.

BOOK SIXTH – PETIT PICPUS

I

PETITE RUE PICPUS, No. 62

NOTHING resembled more closely, half a century ago, the commonest *porte-cochère* of the time than the *porte-cochère* of No. 62 Petite Rue Picpus. This door was usually half open in the most attractive manner, disclosing two things which have nothing very funereal about them—a court surrounded with walls bedecked with vines, and the face of a lounging porter. Above the rear wall large trees could be seen. When a beam of sunshine enlivened the court, when a glass of wine enlivened the porter, it was difficult to pass by No. 62 Petite Rue Picpus, without carrying away a pleasant idea. It was, however, a gloomy place of which you had had a glimpse.

The door smiled; the house prayed and wept.

If you succeeded, which was not easy, in passing the porter—which for almost everybody was even impossible, for there was an *open sesame* which you must know;—if, having passed the porter, you entered on the right a little vestibule which led to a stairway shut in between two walls, and so narrow that but one person could pass at a time; if you did not allow yourself to be frightened by the yellow wall paper with the chocolate surbase that extended along the stairs, if you ventured to go up, you passed by a first broad stair, then a second, and reached the second story in a hall where the yellow hue and the chocolate plinth followed you with a peaceful persistency. Staircase and hall were lighted by two handsome windows. The hall made a sudden turn and became dark. If you doubled that cape, you came, in a few steps, to a door, all the more mysterious that it was not quite closed. You pushed it open, and found yourself in a little room about six feet square, the floor tiled, scoured, neat and cold, and the walls hung with fifteen-cent paper, nankeen-coloured paper with green flowers. A dull white light came from a large window with small panes which was at the left, and which took up the whole width of the room. You looked, you saw no one; you listened, you heard no step and no human sound. The wall was bare; the room had no furniture, not even a chair.

You looked again, and you saw in the wall opposite the door

a quadrangular opening about a foot square, covered with a grate of iron bars crossing one another, black, knotted, solid, which formed squares, I had almost said meshes, less than an inch across. The little green flowers on the nankeen paper came calmly and in order to these iron bars, without being frightened or scattered by the dismal contact. In case any living being had been so marvellously slender as to attempt to get in or out by the square hole, this grate would have prevented it. It did not let the body pass, but it did let the eyes pass, that is to say, the mind. This seemed to have been cared for, for it had been doubled by a sheet of tin inserted in the wall a little behind it, and pierced with a thousand holes more microscopic than those of a skimmer. At the bottom of this plate there was an opening cut exactly like the mouth of a letter-box. A piece of broad tape attached to a bell hung at the right of the grated opening.

If you pulled this tape, a bell tinkled and a voice was heard, very near you, which startled you.

"Who is there?" asked the voice.

It was a woman's voice, a gentle voice, so gentle that it was mournful.

Here again there was a magic word which you must know. If you did not know it, the voice was heard no more, and the wall again became silent as if the wild obscurity of the sepulchre had been on the other side.

If you knew the word, the voice added:

"Enter at the right."

You then noticed at your right, opposite the window, a glazed door surmounted by a glazed sash and painted grey. You lifted the latch, you passed through the door, and you felt exactly the same impression as when you enter a grated box at the theatre before the grate is lowered and the lights are lit. You were in fact in a sort of theatre box, hardly made visible by the dim light of the glass door, narrow, furnished with two old chairs and a piece of tattered straw matting—a genuine box with its front to lean upon, upon which was a tablet of black wood. This box was grated, but it was not a grate of gilded wood as at the Opera; it was a monstrous trellis of iron bars frightfully tangled together, and bolted to the wall by enormous bolts which resembled clenched fists.

After a few minutes, when your eyes began to get accustomed to this cavernous light, you tried to look through the grate, but could not see more than six inches beyond. There you saw a barrier of black shutters, secured and strengthened by wooden cross-bars painted gingerbread colour. These shutters were jointed, divided into long slender strips, and covered the whole length of the grate. They were always closed.

In a few moments, you heard a voice calling to you from behind these shutters and saying:

"I am here. What do you want of me?"

It was a loved voice, perhaps sometimes an adored one. You saw nobody. You hardly heard a breath. It seemed as if it were a ghostly voice speaking to you across the portal of the tomb.

If you appeared under certain necessary conditions, very rare, the narrow strip of one of these shutters opened in front of you, and the ghostly voice became an apparition. Behind the grate, behind the shutter, you perceived, as well as the grate permitted, a head, of which you saw only the mouth and chin; the rest was covered with a black veil. You caught a glimpse of a black guimp and an ill-defined form covered with a black shroud. This head spoke to you, but did not look at you and never smiled at you.

The light which came from behind you was disposed in such wise that you saw her in the light, and she saw you in the shade. This light was symbolic.

Meantime your eyes gazed eagerly, through this aperture thus opened, into this place closed against all observation.

A deep obscurity enveloped this form thus clad in mourning. Your eyes strained into this obscurity, and sought to distinguish what was about the apparition. In a little while you perceived that you saw nothing. What you saw was night, void, darkness, a wintry mist mingled with a sepulchral vapour, a sort of terrifying quiet, a silence from which you distinguished nothing, not even sighs—a shade in which you discerned nothing, not even phantoms.

What you saw was the interior of a cloister.

It was the interior of that stern and gloomy house that was called the convent of the Bernardines of the Perpetual Adoration. This box where you were was the parlour. This voice, the first that spoke to you, was the voice of the portress, who was always seated, motionless and silent, on the other side of the wall, near the square aperture, defended by the iron grate and the plate with the thousand holes, as by a double visor.

The obscurity in which the grated box was sunk arose from

this, that the locutory, which had a window on the side towards the outside world, had none on the convent side. Profane eyes must see nothing of this sacred place.

There was something, however, beyond this shade, there was a light; there was a life within this death. Although this convent was more inaccessible than any other, we shall endeavour to penetrate it, and to take the reader with us, and to relate, as fully as we may, something which story-tellers have never seen, and consequently have never related.

II
THE OBEDIENCE OF MARTIN VERGA

THIS convent, which in 1824 had existed for long years in the Petite Rue Picpus, was a community of Bernardines of the Obedience of Martin Verga.

These Bernardines, consequently, were attached, not to Clairvaux, like other Bernardines, but to Cîteaux, like the Benedictines. In other words, they were subjects, not of Saint Bernard, but of Saint Benedict.

Whoever is at all familiar with old folios, knows that Martin Verga founded in 1425 a congregation of Bernardine-Benedictines, having their chief convent at Salamanca and an affiliation at Alcalá.

This congregation had put out branches in all the Catholic countries of Europe.

These grafts of one order upon another are not unusual in the Latin church. To speak only of a single order of Saint Benedict, which is here in question—to this order are attached, without counting the Obedience of Martin Verga, four congregations; two in Italy, Monte Cassino and Santa Giustina of Padua, two in France, Cluny and Saint Maur; and nine orders, Vallombrosa, Grammont, the Cœlestines, the Camaldules, the Carthusians, the Humiliati, the Olivetans, the Sylvestrines, and finally Cîteaux, for Cîteaux itself, the trunk of other orders, is only an off-shoot from Saint Benedict. Cîteaux dates from Saint Robert, Abbé of Molesme, in the diocese of Langres in 1098. Now it was in 529 that the devil, who had retired to the desert of Subiaco (he was old; had he become a hermit?), was driven from the ancient temple of Apollo where he was living with Saint Benedict, then seventeen years old.

Next to the rules of the Carmelites, who go bare-footed, wear a withe about their throat, and never sit down, the most severe rules are those of the Bernardine-Benedictines of Martin Verga. They are clothed with a black guimp, which, according to the express command of Saint Benedict, comes up to the chin. A serge dress with wide sleeves, a large woollen veil, the guimp which rises to the chin, cut square across the breast, and the fillet which comes down to the eyes, constitute their dress. It is all black, except the fillet, which is white. The novices wear the same dress, all in white. The professed nuns have in addition a rosary by their side.

The Bernardine-Benedictines of Martin Verga perform the devotion of the Perpetual Adoration, as do the Benedictines called Ladies of the Holy Sacrament, who, at the commencement of this century, had at Paris two houses, one at the Temple, the other in the Rue Neuve Sainte Geneviève. In other respects the Bernardine-Benedictines of the Petit Picpus of whom we are speaking, were an entirely separate order from the Ladies of the Holy Sacrament, whose cloisters were in the Rue Neuve Sainte Geneviève and at the Temple. There were many differences in their rules, there were some in their costume. The Bernardine-Benedictines of the Petit Picpus wore a black guimp, and the Benedictines of the Holy Sacrament and of the Rue Neuve Sainte Geneviève wore a white one and had moreover upon their breast a crucifix about three inches long in silver or copper gilt. The nuns of the Petit Picpus did not wear this crucifix. The devotion of the Perpetual Adoration, common to the house of the Petit Picpus and to the house of the Temple, left the two orders perfectly distinct. There is a similarity only in this respect between the Ladies of the Holy Sacrament and the Bernardines of Martin Verga, even as there is a similitude, in the study and the glorification of all the mysteries relative to the infancy, the life and the death of Jesus Christ, and to the Virgin, between two orders widely separated and occasionally inimical, the Oratory of Italy, established at Florence by Philip di Neri, and the Oratory of France, established at Paris by Pierre de Bérulle. The Oratory of Paris claims the precedence, Philip di Neri being only a saint, and Bérulle being a cardinal.

Let us return to the severe Spanish rules of Martin Verga.

The Bernardine-Benedictines of this Obedience abstain from meat all the year round, fast during Lent and many other days peculiar to them, rise out of their first sleep at one o'clock in the morning to read their breviary and chant matins until three, sleep in coarse woollen sheets at all seasons and upon straw, use no baths, never light any fire, scourge themselves every Friday, observe the rule of silence, speak to one another only at recreations, which are very short, and wear haircloth chemises for six months, from the fourteenth of September, the Exaltation of the Holy Cross, until Easter. These six months are a moderation—the rules say all the year; but this haircloth chemise, insupportable in the heat of summer, produced fevers and nervous spasms. It became necessary to limit its use. Even with this mitigation, after the fourteenth of September, when the nuns put on this chemise, they have three or four days of fever. Obedience, poverty, chastity, continuance in cloister; such are their vows, rendered much more difficult of fulfilment by the rules.

The prioress is elected for three years by the mothers, who are called *vocal mothers,* because they have a voice in the chapter. A prioress can be re-elected but twice, which fixes the longest possible reign of a prioress at nine years.

They never see the officiating priest, who is always concealed from them by a woollen curtain nine feet high. During the sermon, when the preacher is in the chapel, they drop their veil over their face; they must always speak low, walk with their eyes on the ground and their head bowed down. But one man can enter the convent, the archbishop of the diocese.

There is indeed one other, the gardener; but he is always an old man, and in order that he may be perpetually alone in the garden and that the nuns may be warned to avoid him, a bell is attached to his knee.

They are subject to the prioress with an absolute and passive submission. It is canonical subjection in all its abnegation. As at the voice of Christ, *ut voci Christi,* at a nod, at the first signal, *ad nutum, ad primum signum,* promptly, with pleasure, with perserverance, with a certain blind obedience, *promptè, hilariter, perserveranter, et cœcâ quâdam obedientiâ,* like the file in the workman's hands, *quasi limam in manibus, fabri,* forbidden to read or write without express permission, *legere vel scribere non addiscerit sine expressâ superioris licentiâ.*

Each one of them in turn performed what they call *the reparation.* The Reparation is prayer for all sins, for all faults, for all disorders, for all violations, for all iniquities, for all the crimes which are committed upon the earth. During twelve consecutive hours, from four o'clock in the afternoon till four o'clock in the morning, or from four o'clock in the morning till four o'clock in the afternoon, the sister who performs *the reparation* remains on her knees upon the stone before the holy sacrament, her hands clasped and a rope around her neck. When fatigue becomes insupportable, she prostrates herself, her face against the marble and her arms crossed; this is all her relief. In this attitude, she prays for all the guilty in the universe. This is grand even to sublimity.

As this act is performed before a post on the top of which a taper is burning, they say indiscriminately, *to perform the reparation* or *to be at the post*. The nuns even prefer, from humility, this latter expression, which involves an idea of punishment and of abasement.

The performance of the reparation is a process in which the whole soul is absorbed. The sister at the post would not turn were a thunderbolt to fall behind her.

Moreover, there is always a nun on her knees before the holy sacrament. They remain for an hour. They are relieved like soldiers standing sentry. That is the Perpetual Adoration.

The prioresses and the mothers almost always have names of peculiar solemnity, recalling not the saints and the martyrs, but moments in the life of Christ, like Mother Nativity, Mother Conception, Mother Presentation, Mother Passion. The names of saints, however, are not prohibited.

When you see them, you see only their mouth.

They all have yellow teeth. Never did a tooth-brush enter the convent. To brush the teeth is the top round of a ladder, the bottom round of which is—to lose the soul.

They never say *my* or *mine*. They have nothing of their own, and must cherish nothing. They say *our* of everything; thus: our veil, our chaplet; if they speak of their chemise, they say *our chemise*. Sometimes they become attached to some little object, to a prayer-book, a relic, or a sacred medal. As soon as they perceive that they are beginning to cherish this object, they must give it up. They remember the reply of Saint Theresa, to whom a great lady, at the moment of entering her order, said: permit me, mother, to send for a holy Bible which I cherish very much. "*Ah! you cherish something! In that case, do not enter our house.*"

None are allowed to shut themselves up, and to have a *home, a room*. They live in open cells. When they meet one another, one says: *Praise and adoration to the most holy sacrament of the altar!* The other responds: *Forever.* The same ceremony when one knocks at another's door. Hardly is the door touched when a gentle voice is heard from the other side hastily saying, Forever. Like all rituals, this becomes mechanical from habit; and one sometimes says *forever* before the other has had time to say, what is indeed rather lengthy, *Praise and adoration to the most holy sacrament of the altar!*

Among the Visitandines, the one who comes in says: *Ave Maria*, and the one to whose cell she comes says: *Gratiâ plena.* This is their good day, which is, in fact, "graceful."

At each hour of the day, three supplementary strokes sound from the bell of the convent church. At this signal, prioress, mothers, professed nuns, sister servants, novices, postulants, all break off from what they are saying, doing, or thinking, and say at once, if it is five o'clock, for example: *At five o'clock and at all times, praise and adoration to the most holy sacrament of the altar!* If it is eight o'clock: *At eight and at all times*, etc., and so on, according to whatever hour it may be.

This custom, which is intended to interrupt the thoughts, and to lead them back constantly to God, exists in many communities; the formula only, varies. Thus, at the Infant Jesus, they say: *At the present hour and at all hours may the love of Jesus enkindle my heart!*

The Benedictine-Bernardines of Martin Verga, cloistered fifty years ago in the Petit Picpus, chant the offices in a grave psalmody, pure plain-chant, and always in a loud voice for the whole duration of the office. Wherever there is an asterisk in the missal, they make a pause and say in a low tone: *Jesus— Mary—Joseph.* For the office for the dead, they take so low a pitch, that it is difficult for female voices to reach it. The effect is thrilling and tragical.

Those of the Petit Picpus had had a vault made under their high altar for the burial of their community. The *government*, as they call it, does not permit corpses to be deposited in this vault. They therefore were taken from the convent when they died. This was an affliction to them, and horrified them as if it were a violation.

They had obtained—small consolation—the privilege of

being buried at a special hour and in a special place in the old Vaugirard Cemetery, which was located in ground formerly belonging to the community.

On Thursday these nuns heard high mass, vespers, and all the offices the same as on Sunday. They moreover scrupulously observed all the little feast days, unknown to the people of the world of which the church was formerly lavish in France, and is still lavish in Spain and Italy. Their attendance at chapel is interminable. As to the number and duration of their prayers, we cannot give a better idea than by quoting the frank words of one of themselves: *The prayers of the postulants are frightful, the prayers of the novices worse, and the prayers of the professed nuns still worse.*

Once a week the chapter assembles; the prioress presides, the mothers attend. Each sister comes in her turn, kneels upon the stone, and confesses aloud, before all, the faults and sins which she has committed during the week. The mothers consult together after each confession, and announce the penalty aloud.

In addition to open confession, for which they reserve all serious faults, they have for venial faults what they call the *coulpe*. To perform the coulpe is to prostrate yourself on your face during the office, before the prioress until she, who is never spoken of except as *our mother*, indicates to the sufferer, by a gentle rap upon the side of her stall, that she may rise. The coulpe is performed for very petty things; a glass broken, a veil torn, an involuntary delay of a few seconds at an office, a false note in church, etc.,—these are enough for the coulpe. The coulpe is entirely spontaneous; it is the *culpable* herself (this word is here etymologically in its place) who judges herself and who inflicts it upon herself. On feast-days and Sundays there are four chorister mothers who sing the offices before a large desk with four music stands. One day a mother chorister intoned a psalm which commenced by *Ecce*, and, instead of *Ecce*, she pronounced in a loud voice these three notes: *ut, si, sol*; for this absence of mind she underwent a coulpe which lasted through the whole office. What rendered the fault peculiarly enormous was, that the chapter laughed.

When a nun is called to the locutory, be it even the prioress, she drops her veil, it will be remembered, in such a way as to show nothing but her mouth.

The prioress alone can communicate with strangers. The

others can see only their immediate family, and that very rarely. If by chance persons from without present themselves to see a nun whom they have known or loved in the world, a formal negotiation is necessary. If it be a woman, permission may be sometimes accorded; the nun comes and is spoken to through the shutters, which are never opened except for a mother or sister. It is unnecessary to say that permission is always refused to men.

Such are the rules of Saint Benedict, rendered more severe by Martin Verga.

These nuns are not joyous, rosy, and cheerful, as are often the daughters of other orders. They are pale and serious. Between 1825 and 1830 three became insane.

III
SEVERITIES

A POSTULANCY of at least two years is required, often four; a novitiate of four years. It is rare that the final vows can be pronounced under twenty-three or twenty-four years. The Bernardine-Benedictines of Martin Verga admit no widows into their order.

They subject themselves in their cells to many unknown self-mortifications of which they must never speak.

The day on which a novice makes her profession she is dressed in her finest attire, with her head decked with white roses, and her hair glossy and curled; then she prostrates herself; a great black veil is spread over her, and the office for the dead is chanted. The nuns then divide into two files, one file passes near her, saying in plaintive accents: *Our sister is dead*, and the other file responds in ringing tones: *living in Jesus Christ!*

At the period to which this history relates, a boarding-school was attached to the convent. A school of noble young girls, for the most part rich, among whom were noticeable Mesdem-oiselles De Sainte Aulaire and De Bélissen, and an English girl bearing the illustrious Catholic name of Talbot. These young girls, reared by these nuns between four walls, grew up in horror of the world and of the age. One of them said to us one day: *to see the pavement of the street made me shiver from head to foot*. They were dressed in blue with a white cap, and a Holy Spirit, in silver or copper gilt, upon their breast. On certain grand feast-days, particularly on Saint Martha's day, they were allowed, as a high favour and a supreme pleasure, to dress as nuns and perform the offices and the ritual of Saint Benedict for a whole day. At first the professed nuns lent them their black garments. That appeared profane, and the prioress forbade it. This loan was permitted only to novices. It is remarkable that these representations, undoubtedly tolerated and encouraged in the convent by a secret spirit of proselytism, and to give these children some foretaste of the holy dress, were a real pleasure and a genuine recreation for the scholars. They simply amused themselves. *It was new; it was a change.* Candid reasons of childhood, which do not succeed, however, in making us, mundane people, comprehend the felicity of holding a holy sprinkler in the hand, and remaining standing entire hours singing in quartette before a desk.

The pupils, austerities excepted, conformed to all the ritual of the convent. There are young women who, returned to the world, and after several years of marriage, have not yet succeeded in breaking off the habit of saying hastily, whenever there is a knock at the door: *Forever!* Like the nuns, the boarders saw their relatives only in the locutory. Even their mothers were not permitted to embrace them. Strictness upon this point was carried to the following extent: One day a young girl was visited by her mother accompanied by a little sister three years old. The young girl wept, for she wished very much to kiss her sister. Impossible. She begged that the child should at least be permitted to pass her little hand through the bars that she might kiss it. This was refused almost with indignation.

IV
GAIETIES

THESE young girls have none the less filled this solemn house with charming reminiscences.

At certain hours, childhood sparkled in this cloister. The hour of recreation struck. A door turned upon its hinges. The birds said good! here are the children! An irruption of youth inundated this garden, which was cut by walks in the form of a cross, like a shroud. Radiant faces, white foreheads, frank eyes full of cheerful light, auroras of all sorts scattered through this darkness. After the chants, the bell-ringing, the knells, and the offices, all at once this hum of little girls burst forth sweeter than the hum of bees. The hive of joy opened, and each one brought her honey. They played, they called to one another, they formed groups, they ran; pretty little white teeth chatted in the corners; veils from a distance watched over the laughter, shadows spying the sunshine; but what matter! They sparkled and they laughed. These four dismal walls had their moments of bewilderment. They too shared, dimly lighted up by the reflection of so much joy, in this sweet and swarming whirl. It was like a shower of roses upon this mourning. The young girls frolicked under the eyes of the nuns; the gaze of sinlessness does not disturb innocence. Thanks to these children, among so many hours of austerity, there was one hour of artlessness. The little girls skipped, the larger ones danced. In this cloister, play was mingled with heaven. Nothing was so transporting and superb, as all these fresh, blooming souls. Homer might have laughed there with Perrault and there were, in this dark garden, enough of youth, health, murmurs, cries, uproar, pleasure and happiness, to smooth the wrinkles from off all granddames, those of the epic as well as the tale, those of the throne as well as the hut, from Hecuba to Mother Goose.

In this house, more than anywhere else, perhaps, have been heard these *children's sayings*, which have so much grace, and which make one laugh with a laugh full of thought. It was within these four forbidding walls that a child of five years exclaimed one day: "*Mother, a great girl has just told me that I have only nine years and ten months more to stay here. How glad I am!*"

Here, also, that this memorable dialogue occurred:

A Mother—"What are you crying for, my child?"

The Child (six years old), sobbing—"I told Alice I knew my French history. She says I don't know it, and I do know it."

Alice, larger (nine years)—"No, she doesn't know it."

The Mother—"How is that, my child?"

Alice—"She told me to open the book anywhere and ask her any question there was in the book, and she could answer it."

"Well?"

"She didn't answer it."

"Let us see. What did you ask her?"

"I opened the book anywhere, just as she said, and I asked her the first question I found."

"And what was the question?"

"It was: *What happened next?*"

Here this profound observation was made about a rather dainty parrot, which belonged to a lady boarder:

"*Isn't she genteel! she picks off the top of her tart, like a lady.*"

From one of the tiles of the cloister, the following confession was picked up, written beforehand, so as not to be forgotten, by a little sinner seven years old.

"Father, I accuse myself of having been avaricious.

"Father, I accuse myself of having been adulterous.

"Father, I accuse myself of having raised my eyes towards the gentlemen."

Upon one of the grassy banks of this garden, the following story was improvised by a rosy mouth six years old, and listened to by blue eyes four and five years old:

"There were three little chickens who lived in a country where there were a good many flowers. They picked the flowers and they put them in their pockets. After that, they picked the leaves, and they put them in their playthings. There was a wolf in the country, and there was a good many woods; and the wolf was in the woods; and he ate up the little chickens."

And again, this other poem:

"There was a blow with a stick.

"It was Punchinello who struck the cat.

"That didn't do him any good; it did her harm.

"Then a lady put Punchinello in prison."

There, also, these sweet and heartrending words were said by a little foundling that the convent was rearing through charity. She heard the others talking about their mothers, and she murmured in her little place:

"*For my part, my mother was not there when I was born.*"

There was a fat portress, who was always to be seen hurrying about the corridors with her bunch of keys, and whose name was Sister Agatha. The *great big* girls,—over ten, called her *Agathocles.*

The refectory, a large oblong room, which received light only from a cloister window with a fluted arch opening on a level with the garden, was dark and damp, and, as the children said—full of beasts. All the surrounding places furnished it their contingents of insects. Each of its four corners had received in the language of the pupils, a peculiar and expressive name. There was the Spiders' corner, the Caterpillars' corner, the

Wood-lice's corner, and the Crickets' corner. The crickets' corner was near the kitchen, and was highly esteemed. It was not so cold as the others. From the refectory the names had passed to the school-room, and served to distinguish there, as at the old Mazarin College, four nations. Each pupil belonged to one of these four nations according to the corner of the refectory in which she sat at meals. One day, the archbishop, making his pastoral visit, saw enter the class which he was passing, a pretty little blushing girl with beautiful fair hair; and he asked another scholar, a charming fresh-cheeked brunette, who was near him:

"What is this little girl?"

"She is a spider, monseigneur."

"Pshaw!—and this other one?"

"She is a cricket."

"And that one?"

"She is a caterpillar."

"Indeed! And what are you?"

"I am a wood-louse, monseigneur."

Every house of this kind has its peculiarities. At the commencement of this century, Ecouen was one of those serene and graceful places where, in a shade which was almost august, the childhood of young girls was passed. At Ecouen, by way of rank in the procession of the Holy Sacrament, they made a distinction between the virgins and the florists. There were also "the canopies," and the "censers," the former carrying the cords of the canopy, the latter swinging censers before the Holy Sacrament. The flowers returned of right to the florists. Four "virgins" walked at the head of the procession. On the morning of the great day, it was not uncommon to hear the question in the dormitory.

"Who is a virgin?"

Madame Campan relates this saying of a "little girl" seven years old to a "great girl" of sixteen who took the head of the procession, while she, the little one, remained in the rear. "You're a virgin, you are; but I am not."

V

DISTRACTIONS

ABOVE the door of the refectory was written in large black letters this prayer, which was called *the white Paternoster*, and which possessed the virtue of leading people straight in to Paradise:

"Little white paternoster, which God made, which God said, which God laid in Paradise. At night, on going to bed, I finded (sic) three angels lying on my bed, one at the foot, two at the head, the good Virgin Mary in the middle, who to me said that I should went to bed, and nothing suspected. The good God is my father, the Holy Virgin is my mother, the three apostles are my brothers, the three virgins are my sisters. The chemise in which God was born, my body is enveloped in; the cross of Saint Marguerite on my breast is writ; Madame the Virgin goes away through the fields, weeping for God, meeted Monsieur Saint John. Monsieur Saint John, where do you come from? I come from *Ave Salus*. You have not seen the good God, have you? He is on the tree of the cross, his feet hanging, his hands nailing, a little hat of white thorns upon his head. Whoever shall say this three times at night, three times in the morning, will win Paradise in the end."

In 1827, this characteristic orison had disappeared from the wall under a triple layer of paper. It is fading away to this hour in the memory of some young girls of that day, old ladies now.

A large crucifix hanging upon the wall completed the decoration of this refectory, the only door of which, as we believe we have said, opened upon the garden. Two narrow tables, at the sides of each of which were two wooden benches, extended along the refectory in parallel lines from one end to the other. The walls were white, and the tables black; these two mourning colours are the only variety in convents. The meals were coarse, and the diet of even the children strict. A single plate, meat and vegetables together, or salt fish, constituted the fare. This brief bill of fare was, however, an exception, reserved for the scholars alone. The children ate in silence, under the watchful eyes of the mother for the week, who, from time to time, if a fly ventured to hum or to buzz contrary to rule, noisily opened and shut a wooden book. This silence was seasoned with the Lives of the Saints, read in a loud voice from a little reading desk placed at the foot of a crucifix. The reader was a large pupil, selected for the week. There were placed at intervals along the bare table, glazed earthen bowls, in which each pupil washed her cup and dish herself, and sometimes threw refuse bits, tough meat or tainted fish; this was punished. These bowls were called *water basins*.

A child who broke the silence made a "cross with her tongue." Where? On the floor. She licked the tiles. Dust, that end of all joys, was made to chastise these poor little rosebuds, when guilty of prattling.

There was a book in the convent, which is the *only copy* ever printed, and which it is forbidden to read. It is the Rules of Saint Benedict; arcana into which no profane eye must penetrate. *Nemo regulas, seu constitutiones nostras, externis communicabit.*

The scholars succeeded one day in purloining this book, and began to read it eagerly, a reading often interrupted by fears of being caught, which made them close the volume very suddenly. But from this great risk they derived small pleasure. A few unintelligible pages about the sins of young boys, were what they thought "most interesting."

They played in one walk of the garden, along which were a few puny fruit trees. In spite of the close watch and the severity of the punishments, when the wind had shaken the trees, they sometimes succeeded in furtively picking up a green apple, a half-rotten apricot, or a worm-eaten pear. But I will let a letter speak, which I have at hand; a letter written twenty-five years ago by a former pupil, now Madame the Duchess of——, one of the most elegant women of Paris. I quote verbatim:— "We hide our pear or our apple as we can. When we go up to spread the covers on our beds before supper, we put them under our pillows, and at night eat them in bed, and when we cannot do that, we eat them in the closets." This was one of their most vivid pleasures.

At another time, also on the occasion of a visit of the archbishop to the convent, one of the young girls, Mademoiselle Bouchard, a descendant of the Montmorencies, wagered that she would ask leave of absence for a day, a dreadful thing in a community so austere. The wager was accepted, but no one of those who took it believed she would dare do it. When the opportunity came, as the archbishop was passing before the scholars, Mademoiselle Bouchard, to the indescribable dismay of her companions, left the ranks, and said: "Monseigneur, leave of absence for a day." Mademoiselle Bouchard was tall and fresh-looking, with the prettiest little rosy face in the world. M. De Quélen smiled and said: *"How now, my dear child, leave of absence for a day! Three days, if you like. I grant you three days."* The prioress could do nothing; the archbishop had spoken. A scandal to the convent, but a joyful thing for the school. Imagine the effect.

This rigid cloister was not, however, so well walled in, that the life of the passions of the outside world, that drama, that romance even, did not penetrate it. To prove this, we will merely state briefly an actual, incontestable fact, which, however, has in itself no relation to our story, not being attached to it even by a thread. We mention this merely to complete the picture of the convent in the mind of the reader.

There was about that time, then, in the convent, a mysterious person, not a nun, who was treated with great respect, and who was called *Madame Albertine*. Nothing was known of her, except that she was insane, and that in the world she was supposed to be dead. There were, it was said, involved in her story, some pecuniary arrangements necessary for a great marriage.

This woman, hardly thirty years old, a beautiful brunette, stared wildly with her large black eyes. Was she looking at anything? It was doubtful. She glided along rather than walked; she never spoke; it was not quite certain that she breathed. Her nostrils were as thin and livid as if she had heaved her last sigh. To touch her hand was like touching snow. She had a strange spectral grace. Wherever she came, all were cold. One day, a sister seeing her pass, said to another, "She passes for dead." "Perhaps she is," answered the other.

Many stories were told about Madame Albertine. She was the eternal subject of curiosity of the boarders. There was in the chapel a gallery, which was called *l'Œil-de-Bœuf*. In this gallery, which had only a circular opening, an *œil-de-bœuf*, Madame Albertine attended the offices. She was usually alone there, because from this gallery, which was elevated, the preacher or the officiating priest could be seen, which was forbidden to the nuns. One day, the pulpit was occupied by a young priest of high rank, the Duke de Rohan, peer of France, who was an officer of the Mousquetaires Rouges in 1815, when he was Prince de Léon, and who died afterwards in 1830, a cardinal, and Archbishop of Besançon. This was the first time that M. de Rohan had preached in the convent of the Petit Picpus. Madame Albertine ordinarily attended the sermons and the offices with perfect calmness and complete silence. On that day, as soon as she saw M. de Rohan, she half rose, and, in all the stillness of the chapel, exclaimed: "*What? Auguste?*" The whole community were astounded, and turned their heads; the preacher raised his eyes, but Madame Albertine had fallen back into her motionless silence. A breath from the world without, a glimmer of life, had passed for a moment over that dead and icy form, then all had vanished, and the lunatic had again become a corpse.

These two words, however, set everybody in the convent who could speak to chattering. How many things there were in that *What? Auguste?* How many revelations! M. de Rohan's name was, in fact, Auguste. It was clear that Madame Albertine came from the highest society, since she knew M. de Rohan; that she had occupied a high position herself, since she spoke of so great a noble so familiarly; and that she had some connection with him, of relationship perhaps, but beyond all doubt very intimate, since she knew his "pet name."

Two very severe duchesses, Mesdames de Choiseul and de Sérent, often visited the community, to which they doubtless were admitted by virtue of the privilege of *Magnates mulieres*, greatly to the terror of the school. When the two old ladies passed, all the poor young girls trembled and lowered their eyes.

M. de Rohan was, moreover, without knowing it, the object of the attention of the school-girls. He had just at that time been made, while waiting for the episcopacy, grand-vicar of the Archbishop of Paris. He was in the habit of coming rather frequently to chant the offices in the chapel of the nuns of the Petit Picpus. None of the young recluses could see him, on account of the serge curtain, but he had a gentle, penetrating voice, which they came to recognise and distinguish. He had been a mousquetaire; and then he was said to be very agreeable, with beautiful chestnut hair, which he wore in curls, and a large girdle of magnificent moire, while his black cassock was of the most elegant cut in the world. All these girlish imaginations were very much occupied with him.

No sound from without penetrated the convent. There was, however, one year when the sound of a flute was heard. This was an event, and the pupils of the time remember it yet.

It was a flute on which somebody in the neighbourhood was playing. This flute always played the same air, an air long since forgotten: *My Zétulba, come reign o'er my soul,* and they heard it two or three times a day. The young girls passed hours in listening, the mothers were distracted, heads grew giddy, punishments were exhausted. This lasted for several months.

The pupils were all more or less in love with the unknown musician. Each one imagined herself *Zétulba*. The sound of the flute came from the direction of the Rue Droit Mur; they would have given everything, sacrificed everything, dared everything to see, were it only for a second, to catch a glimpse of the "young man" who played so deliciously on that flute, and who, without suspecting it, was playing at the same time upon all their hearts. There were some who escaped by a back door, and climbed up to the third story on the Rue Droit Mur, incurring days of suffering in the endeavour to see him. Impossible. One went so far as to reach her arm above her head through the grate and wave her white handkerchief. Two were bolder still. They found means to climb to the top of a roof, and risking themselves there, they finally succeeded in seeing the "young man." He was an old gentleman of the emigration, ruined and blind, who was playing upon the flute in his garret to while away the time.

VI

THE LITTLE CONVENT

THERE were in this inclosure of the Petit Picpus three perfectly distinct buildings, the Great Convent, in which the nuns lived, the school building, in which the pupils lodged, and finally what was called the Little Convent. This was a detached building with a garden, in which dwelt in common many old nuns of various orders, remnants of cloisters destroyed by the revolution; a gathering of all shades black, grey, and white, from all the communities and of all the varieties possible; what might be called, if such a coupling of names were not disrespectful, a sort of motley convent.

From the time of the empire, all these poor scattered and desolate maidens had been permitted to take shelter under the wings of the Benedictine-Bernardines. The government made them a small allowance; the ladies of the Petit Picpus had received them with eagerness. It was a grotesque mixture. Each followed her own rules. The school-girls were sometimes permitted, as a great recreation, to make them a visit; so that these young memories have retained among others a reminiscence of holy Mother Bazile, of holy Mother Scholastique, and of Mother Jacob.

One of these refugees found herself again almost in her own home. She was a nun of Sainte Aure, the only one of her order who survived. The ancient convent of the Ladies of Sainte Aure occupied at the beginning of the eighteenth century this same house of the Petit Picpus which afterwards belonged to the Benedictines of Martin Verga. This holy maiden, too poor to wear the magnificent dress of her order, which was a white robe with a scarlet scapula, had piously clothed a little image with it, which she showed complacently, and which at her death she bequeathed to the house. In 1824, there remained of this order only one nun; to-day there remains only a doll.

In addition to these worthy mothers, a few old women of fashion had obtained permission of the prioress, as had Madame Albertine, to retire into the Little Convent. Among the number were Madame de Beaufort, d'Hautpoul, and Madame la Marquise Dufresne. Another was known in the convent only by the horrible noise she made in blowing her nose. The pupils called her Racketini.

About 1820 or 1821, Madame de Genlis, who at that time was editing a little magazine called the *Intrépide*, asked permission to occupy a room at the convent of the Petit Picpus. Monsieur the Duke of Orleans recommended her. A buzzing in the hive; the mothers were all in a tremor; Madame de Genlis had written romances; but she declared that she was the first to detest them, and then she had arrived at her phase of fierce devotion. God aiding, and the prince also, she entered.

She went away at the end of six or eight months, giving as a reason that the garden had no shade. The nuns were in raptures. Although very old, she still played on the harp, and that very well.

On going away, she left her mark on her cell. Madame de Genlis was superstitious and fond of Latin. These two terms give a very good outline of her. There could still be seen a few years ago, pasted up in a little closet in her cell, in which she locked up her money and jewellery, these five Latin lines written in her hand with red ink upon yellow paper, and which, in her opinion, possessed the virtue of frightening away thieves:

Imparibus meritis pendent tria corpora ramis:
Dismas et Gesmas, media est divina potestas;
Alta petit Dismas, infelix, infima, Gesmas;

Nos et res nostras conservet summa potestas,
Hos versus dicas, ne tu furto tua perdas.

These lines in Latin of the Sixth Century, raise the question as to whether the names of the two thieves of Calvary were, as is commonly believed, Dimas and Gestas, or Dismas and Gesmas. The latter orthography would make against the pretensions which the Vicomte de Gestas put forth, in the last century, to be a descendant of the unrepentant thief. The convenient virtue attributed to these lines was, moreover, an article of faith in the order of the Hospitallers.

The church of the convent, which was built in such a manner as to separate as much as possible the Great Convent from the school, was, of course, common to the school, the Great Convent and the Little Convent. The public even were admitted there by a beggarly entrance opening from the street. But everything was arranged in such a way that none of the inmates of the cloister could see a face from without. Imagine a church, the choir of which should be seized by a gigantic hand, and bent round in such a way as to form, not, as in ordinary churches, a prolongation behind the altar, but a sort of room or obscure cavern at the right of the priest; imagine this room closed by the curtain seven feet high of which we have already spoken; heap together in the shade of this curtain on wooded stalls, the nuns of the choir at the left, the pupils at the right, the sister servants and the novices in the rear, and you will have some idea of the nuns of the Petit Picpus, attending divine service. This cavern, which was called the choir, communicated with the cloister by a narrow passage. The church received light from the garden. When the nuns were attending offices in which their rules commanded silence, the public was advised of their presence only by the sound of the rising and falling stall-seats.

VII
A FEW OUTLINES IN THIS SHADE

DURING the six years which separate 1819 from 1825, the prioress of the Petit Picpus was Mademoiselle De Blemeur, whose religious name was Mother Innocent. She was of the family of Marguerite De Blemeur, author of the *Lives of the Saints of the Order of St. Benedict*. She had been re-elected. A woman of about sixty, short, fat, "chanting like a cracked kettle," says the letter from which we have already quoted; but an excellent woman, the only one who was cheerful in the whole convent, and on that account adored.

Mother Innocent resembled her ancestor Marguerite, the Dacier of the Order. She was well-read, erudite, learned, skilful, curious in history, stuffed with Latin, crammed with Greek, full of Hebrew, and rather a monk than a nun.

The sub-prioress was an old Spanish nun almost blind, Mother Cineres.

The most esteemed among the mothers were Mother Sainte Honorine, the treasurer, Mother Sainte Gertrude, first mistress of the novices, Mother Sainte Ange, second mistress, Mother Annunciation, sacristan, Mother Sainte Augustin, nurse, the only nun in the convent who was ill-natured; then Mother Sainte Mechthilde (Mlle. Gauvain), quite young and having a wonderful voice; Mother Des Anges (Mlle. Drouet), who had been in the convent of the Filles-Dieu and in the convent of the Trésor, between Gisors and Magny; Mother Sainte Joseph (Mlle. de Cogolludo), Mother Sainte Adelaide (Mlle. D'Auverney), Mother Mercy (Mlle. de Cifuentes), who could not endure the austerities, Mother Compassion (Mlle. De la Miltière, received at sixty in spite of the rules, very rich); Mother Providence (Mlle. de Laudinière), Mother Presentation (Mlle. de Siguenza), who was prioress in 1847; finally, Mother Sainte Céligne (sister of the sculptor Ceracchi), since insane, Mother Sainte Chantal (Mlle. de Suzon), since insane.

There was still among the prettiest a charming girl of twenty-three, from the Isle of Bourbon, a descendant of the Chevalier Roze, who was called in the world Mademoiselle Roze, and who called herself Mother Assumption.

Mother Sainte Mechthilde, who had charge of the singing and the choir, gladly availed herself of the pupils. She usually took a complete gamut of them, that is to say, seven, from ten years old to sixteen inclusive, of graduated voice and stature, and had them sing, standing in a row, ranged according to their age from the smallest to the largest. This presented to the sight something like a harp of young girls, a sort of living pipe of Pan made of angels.

Those of the servant sisters whom the pupils liked best were Sister Sainte Euphrasie, Sister Sainte Marguerite, Sister Sainte

Marthe, who was in her dotage, and Sister Sainte Michael, whose long nose made them laugh.

All these women were gentle to all these children. The nuns were severe only to themselves. The only fires were in the school building, and the fare, compared with that of the convent, was choice. Besides that, they received a thousand little attentions. Only when a child passed near a nun and spoke to her, the nun never answered.

This rule of silence had had this effect that, in the whole convent, speech was withdrawn from human creatures and given to inanimate objects. Sometimes it was the church-bell that spoke, sometimes the gardener's. A very sonorous bell, placed beside the portress and which was heard all over the house, indicated by its variations, which were a kind of acoustic telegraph, all the acts of material life to be performed, and called to the locutory, if need were, this or that inhabitant of the house. Each person and each thing had its special ring. The prioress had one and one; the sub-prioress one and two. Six-five announced the recitation, so that the pupils never said going to recitation, but going to six-five. Four-four was Madame de Genlis' signal. It was heard very often. *It is the four deuce*, said the uncharitable. Nineteen strokes announced a great event. It was the opening of the *close door*, a fearful iron plate bristling with bolts which turned upon its hinges only before the archbishop.

He and the gardener excepted, as we have said, no man entered the convent. The pupils saw two others; one, the almoner, the Abbé Banès, old and ugly, whom they had the privilege of contemplating through a grate in the choir; the other, the drawing-master, M. Ansiaux, whom the letter from which we have already quoted a few lines, calls M. *Anciot*, and describes as a *horrid old hunchback*.

We see that all the men were select.

Such was this rare house.

VIII
POST CORDA LAPIDES

After sketching its moral features, it may not be useless to point out in a few words its material configuration. The reader has already some idea of it.

The convent of the Petit Picpus Saint Antoine almost entirely

filled the large trapezium which was formed by the intersection
of the Rue Polonceau, the Rue Droit Mur, the Petite Rue
Picpus, and the built-up alley called in the old plans Rue Aumarais. These four streets surrounded this trapezium like a ditch.
The convent was composed of several buildings and a garden.
The principal building, taken as a whole, was an aggregation of
hybrid constructions which, in a bird's-eye view, presented with
considerable accuracy the form of a gibbet laid down on the
ground.

The long arm of the gibbet extended along the whole portion of the Rue Droit Mur comprised between the Petite Rue
Picpus and the Rue Polonceau; the short arm was a high, grey,
severe, grated façade which overlooked the Petite Rue Picpus;
the *porte-cochère*, No. 62, marked the end of it. Towards the
middle of this façade, the dust and ashes had whitened an old
low-arched door where the spiders made their webs, and which
was opened only for an hour or two on Sunday and on the rare
occasions when the corpse of a nun was taken out of the convent. It was the public entrance of the church. The elbow of the
gibbet was a square hall which served as pantry, and which
the nuns called the *expense*. In the long arm were the cells of the
mothers, sisters and novices. In the short arm were the kitchens,
the refectory, lined with cells, and the church. Between the
door, No. 62, and the corner of the closed alley Aumarais, was
the school, which could not be seen from the outside. The rest
of the trapezium formed the garden, which was much lower
than the level of the Rue Polonceau, so that the walls were
considerably higher on the inside than on the outside. The
garden, which was slightly convex, had in the centre, on the top
of a knoll, a beautiful fir, pointed and conical, from which
parted, as from the centre of a buckler, four broad walks, and,
arranged two by two between the broad walks, eight narrow
ones, so that, if the inclosure had been circular, the geometrical
plan of the walks would have resembled a cross placed over a
wheel. The walks, all extending to the very irregular walls of
the garden, were of unequal length. They were bordered with
gooseberry bushes. At the further end of the garden a row of
large poplars extended from the ruins of the old convent, which
was at the corner of the Rue Droit Mur, to the house of the
Little Convent, which was at the corner of the alley Aumarais.
Before the Little Convent, was what was called the Little

Garden. Add to this outline a courtyard, all manner of angles
made by detached buildings, prison walls, no prospect and no
neighbourhood, but the long black line of roofs which ran along
the other side of the Rue Polonceau, and you can form a complete image of what was, forty-five years ago, the house of the
Bernardines of the Petit Picpus. This holy house had been built
on the exact site of a famous tennis-court, which existed from
the fourteenth to the sixteenth century, and which was called
the *court of the eleven thousand devils*.

All these streets, moreover, were among the most ancient in
Paris. These names, Droit Mur and Aumarais, are very old; the
streets which bear them are much older still. The alley Aumarais
was called the alley Maugout; the Rue Droit Mur was called the
Rue des Eglantiers, for God opened the flowers before man cut
stone.

IX
A CENTURY UNDER A GUIMP

SINCE we are dealing with the details of what was formerly the
convent of the Petit Picpus, and have dared to open a window
upon that secluded asylum, the reader will pardon us another
little digression, foreign to the object of this book, but characteristic and useful, as it teaches us that the cloister itself has its
original characters.

There was in the Little Convent a centenarian who came
from the Abbey of Fontevrault. Before the revolution she had
even been in society. She talked much of M. de Miromesnil,
keeper of the seals under Louis XVI., and of the lady of a President Duplat whom she had known very well. It was her pleasure
and her vanity to bring forward these names on all occasions.
She told wonders of the Abbey of Fontevrault, that it was like a
city, and that there were streets within the convent.

She spoke with a Picardy accent which delighted the pupils.
Every year she solemnly renewed her vows, and, at the moment
of taking the oath, she would say to the priest: Monseigneur St.
Francis gave it to Monseigneur St. Julian, Monseigneur St. Julian gave it to Monseigneur St. Eusebius, Monseigneur St. Eusebius gave it to Monseigneur St. Procopius, etc., etc.; so I give it
to you, my father. And the pupils would laugh, not in their

sleeves, but in their veils, joyous little stifled laughs which made the mothers frown.

At one time, the centenarian was telling stories. She said that in *her youth the Bernardines did not yield the precedence to the Mousquetaires*. It was a century which was speaking, but it was the eighteenth century. She told of the custom in Champagne and Burgundy before the revolution, of the four wines. When a great personage, a marshal of France, a prince, a duke or peer, passed through a city of Burgundy or Champagne, the corporation of the city waited on him, delivered an address, and presented him with four silver goblets in which were four different wines. Upon the first goblet he read this inscription: *Monkey wine*, upon the second: *lion wine*, upon the third: *sheep wine*, upon the fourth: *swine wine*. These four inscriptions expressed the four descending degrees of drunkenness: the first that which enlivens; the second, that which irritates; the third, that which stupefies; finally the last, that which brutalises.

She had in a closet, under key, a mysterious object, which she cherished very highly. The rules of Fontevrault did not prohibit it. She would not show this object to anybody. She shut herself up, which her rules permitted, and hid herself whenever she wished to look at it. If she heard a step in the hall, she shut the closet as quickly as she could with her old hands. As soon as anybody spoke to her about this, she was silent, although she was so fond of talking. The most curious were foiled by her silence, and the most persevering by her obstinacy. This also was a subject of comment for all who were idle or listless in the convent. What then could this thing be, so secret and so precious, which was the treasure of the centenarian? Doubtless, some sacred book, or some unique chaplet? or some proven relic? They lost themselves in conjecture. On the death of the poor old woman they ran to the closet sooner, perhaps, than was seemly, and opened it. The object of their curiosity was found under triple cloths, like a blessed patine. It was a Faenza plate, representing Loves in flight, pursued by apothecaries' boys, armed with enormous syringes. The pursuit is full of grimaces and comic postures. One of the charming little Loves is already spitted. He struggles, shakes his little wings, and still tries to fly away, but the lad capering about, laughs with a Satanic laughter. Moral:—love conquered by colic. This plate, very curious, moreover, and which had the honour, perhaps, of giving an idea to Molière, was still in existence in September, 1845; it was for sale in a second-hand store in the Boulevard Beaumarchais.

This good old woman would receive no visit from the outside world, *because*, said she, *the locutory is too gloomy*.

X
ORIGIN OF THE PERPETUAL ADORATION

THAT almost sepulchral locutory, of which we have endeavoured to give an idea, is an entirely local feature, which is not reproduced with the same severity in other convents. At the convent of the Rue du Temple in particular, which, indeed, was of another order, the black shutters were replaced by brown curtains, and the locutory itself was a nicely floored parlour, the windows of which were draped with white muslin, while the walls admitted a variety of pictures, a portrait of a Benedictine nun, with uncovered face, flower-pieces, and even a Turk's head.

It was in the garden of the convent of the Rue du Temple, that that horse-chestnut tree stood, which passed for the most beautiful and the largest in France, and which, among the good people of the eighteenth century, had the name of being *the father of all the horse-chestnuts in the kingdom*.

As we have said, this convent of the Temple was occupied by the Benedictines of the Perpetual Adoration, Benedictines quite distinct from those who spring from Citeaux. This order of the Perpetual Adoration is not very ancient, and does not date back more than two hundred years. In 1649, the Holy Sacrament was profaned twice, within a few days, in two churches in Paris, at Saint Sulpice and at Saint Jean en Grève—a rare and terrible sacrilege, which shocked the whole city. The Prior Grand-vicar of Saint Germain des Prés ordained a solemn procession of all his clergy, in which the Papal Nuncio officiated. But this expiation was not sufficient for two noble women, Madame Courtin, Marquise de Boucs, and the Countess of Châteauvieux. This outrage, committed before the "most august sacrament of the altar," although transient, did not pass away from these two holy souls, and it seemed to them that it could be atoned for only by a "Perpetual Adoration" in some convent. They both, one in 1652, the other in 1653, made donations of

considerable sums to Mother Catharine de Bar, surnamed of the
Holy Sacrament, a Benedictine nun, to enable her to found,
with that pious object, a monastery of the order of Saint Benedict; the first permission for this foundation was given to
Mother Catharine de Bar, by M. de Metz, Abbé of Saint Germain, "with the stipulation that no maiden shall be received
unless she brings three hundred livres of income, which is six
thousand livres of principal." After the Abbé of Saint Germain,
the king granted letters patent, and the whole, abbatial charter
and letters royal, was confirmed in 1654, by the Chamber of
Accounts and by the Parlement.

Such is the origin and the legal consecration of the establish-
ment of Benedictines of the Perpetual Adoration of the Holy
Sacrament at Paris. Their first convent was "built new," Rue
Cassette, with the money of Mesdames de Boucs and de
Châteauvieux.

This order, as we see, is not to be confounded with the Bene-
dictines called Cistercians. It sprang from the Abbé of Saint
Germain des Prés, in the same manner as the Ladies of the
Sacred Heart spring from the General of the Jesuits and the
Sisters of Charity from the General of the Lazarists.

It is also entirely different from the Bernardines of the Petit
Picpus, whose interior life we have been exhibiting. In 1657,
Pope Alexander VII., by special bull, authorised the Bernardines
of the Petit Picpus to practise the Perpetual Adoration like the
Benedictines of the Holy Sacrament. But the two orders, none
the less, remained distinct.

XI

END OF THE PETIT PICPUS

FROM the time of the restoration, the convent of the Petit
Picpus had been dwindling away; this was a portion of the general death of the order, which, since the eighteenth century, has
been going the way of all religious orders. Meditation is, as well
as prayer, a necessity of humanity; but, like everything which
the revolution has touched, it will transform itself, and, from
being hostile to social progress, will become favourable to it.

The house of the Petit Picpus dwindled rapidly. In 1840, the
little convent had disappeared; the school had disappeared.
There were no longer either the old women, or the young girls;

the former were dead, the latter had gone away. *Volaverunt*.

The rules of the Perpetual Adoration are so rigid that they inspire dismay; inclinations recoil, the order gets no recruits. In 1845, it still gathered here and there a few sister servants; but no nuns of the choir. Forty years ago there were nearly a hundred nuns, fifteen years ago there were only twenty-eight. How many are there to-day? In 1847 the prioress was young, a sign that the opportunity for choice was limited. She was not forty. As the number diminishes the fatigue increases; the service of each becomes more difficult, thenceforth they saw the moment approaching when there should be only a dozen sorrowful and bowed shoulders to bear the hard rules of Saint Benedict. The burden is inflexible, and remains the same for the few as for the many. It weighs down, it crushes. Thus they died. Since the author of this book lived in Paris, two have died. One was twenty-five, the other twenty-three. The latter might say with Julia Alpinula: *Hic jaceo, Vixi annos viginti et tres*. It was on account of this decay that the convent abandoned the education of girls.

We could not pass by this extraordinary, unknown, obscure house without entering and leading in those who accompany us, and who listen as we relate, for the benefit of some, perhaps, the melancholy history of Jean Valjean. We have penetrated into that community full of its old practices which seem so novel to-day. It is the closed garden. *Hortus conclusus*. We have spoken of this singular place with minuteness, but with respect, as much at least as respect and minuteness are reconcilable. We do not comprehend everything, but we insult nothing. We are equally distant from the hosannahs of Joseph De Maistre, who goes so far as to sanctify the executioner, and the mockery of Voltaire, who goes so far as to rail at the crucifix.

Illogicalness of Voltaire, be it said by the way; for Voltaire would have defended Jesus as he defended Calas; and, for those even who deny the superhuman incarnation, what does the crucifix represent? The assassinated sage.

In the nineteenth century the religious idea is undergoing a crisis. We are unlearning certain things, and we do well, provided that while unlearning one thing we are learning another. No vacuum in the human heart! Certain forms are torn down, and it is well that they should be, but on condition that they are followed by reconstructions.

In the meantime let us study the things which are no more. It is necessary to understand them, were it only to avoid them. The counterfeits of the past take assumed names, and are fond of calling themselves the future. That spectre, the past, not unfrequently falsifies its passport. Let us be ready for the snare. Let us beware. The past has a face, superstition, and a mask, hypocrisy. Let us denounce the face and tear off the mask.

As to convents, they present a complex question. A question of civilisation, which condemns them; a question of liberty, which protects them.

BOOK SEVENTH – A PARENTHESIS

I
THE CONVENT AS AN ABSTRACT IDEA

THIS book is a drama the first character of which is the Infinite. Man is the second.

This being the case, when a convent was found on our path, we were compelled to penetrate it. Why so? Because the convent, which is common to the East as well as to the West, to ancient as well as to modern times, to Paganism as well as to Buddhism, to Mahometanism as well as to Christianity, is one of the optical appliances turned by man upon the Infinite.

This is not the place for the development at length of certain ideas; however, while rigidly maintaining our reservations, our limits of expression, and even our impulses of indignation; whenever we meet with the Infinite in man, whether well or ill understood, we are seized with an involuntary feeling of respect. There in the synagogue, in the mosque, a hideous side that we detest, and in the pagoda and in the wigwam, a sublime aspect that we adore. What a subject of meditation for the mind, and what a limitless source of reverie is this reflection of God upon the human wall!

II
THE CONVENT AS A HISTORICAL FACT

IN THE light of history, reason, and truth, monastic life stands condemned.

Monasteries, when they are numerous in a country, are knots in the circulation; encumbrances, centres of indolence, where there should be centres of industry. Monastic communities are to the great social community what the ivy is to the oak, what the wart is to the human body. There prosperity and fatness are the impoverishment of the country. The monastic system, useful as it is in the dawn of civilisation, in effecting the abatement of brutality by the development of the spiritual, is injurious in the manhood of nations. Especially when it relaxes and enters upon its period of disorganisation, the period in which we now see it, does it become baneful, for every reason that made it salutary, in its period of purity.

These withdrawals into convents and monasteries have had their day. Cloisters, although beneficial in the first training of modern civilisation, cramped its growth, and are injurious to its development. Regarded as an institution, and as a method of culture for man, monasteries, good in the tenth century, were open to discussion in the fifteenth, and are detestable in the nineteenth. The leprosy of monasticism has gnawed, almost to a skeleton, two admirable nations, Italy and Spain, one the light, and the other the glory of Europe, for centuries; and, in our time, the cure of these two illustrious peoples is beginning, thanks only to the sound and vigorous hygiene of 1789.

The convent, the old style convent especially, such as it appeared on the threshold of this century, in Italy, Austria, and Spain, is one of the gloomiest concretions of the Middle Ages. The cloister, the cloister as there beheld, was the intersecting point of multiplied horrors. The Catholic cloister, properly so-called, is filled with the black effulgence of death.

The Spanish convent is dismal above all the rest. There, rise in the obscurity, beneath vaults filled with mist, beneath domes dim with thick shadow, massive Babel-like altars, lofty as cathedrals; there, hang by chains in the deep gloom, immense white emblems of the crucifixion; there, are extended, naked on the ebon wood, huge ivory images of Christ—more than bloody, bleeding—hideous and magnificent, their bones protruding from the elbows, their knee-pans disclosing the strained integuments, their wounds revealing the raw flesh—crowned with thorns of silver, nailed with nails of gold, with drops of blood in rubies on their brows, and tears of diamonds in their eyes. The diamonds and the rubies seem real moisture; and down below there, in the shadow, make veiled ones weep, whose loins are scratched and torn with haircloth, and scourges set thick with iron points, whose breasts are bruised with wicker pads, and whose knees are lacerated by the continual attitude of prayer; women who deem themselves wives; spectres that fancy themselves seraphim. Do these women think? No. Have they a will? No. Do they love? No. Do they live? No. Their nerves have become bone; their bones have become rock. Their veil is the enwoven night. Their breath, beneath that veil, is like some indescribable, tragic respiration of death itself. The abbess, a phantom, sanctifies and terrifies them. The immaculate is there, austere to behold. Such are the old convents of Spain—dens of terrible devotion, lairs inhabited by virgins, wild and savage places.

Catholic Spain was more Roman than Rome herself. The Spanish convent was the model of the Catholic convent. The air was redolent of the East. The archbishop, as officiating kislar-aga of heaven, locked in, and zealously watched this seraglio of souls set apart for God. The nun was the odalisque, the priest was the eunuch. The fervently devout were, in their dreams, the chosen ones, and were possessed of Christ. At night, the lovely naked youth descended from the cross, and became the rapture of the cell. Lofty walls guarded from all the distractions of real life the mystic Sultana, who had the Crucified for Sultan. A single glance without was an act of perfidy. The *in pace* took the place of the leather sack. What they threw into the sea in the East, they threw into the earth in the West. On either side, poor women wrung their hands; the waves to those—to these the pit; there the drowned and here the buried alive. Monstrous parallelism!

In our day, the champions of the Past, unable to deny these things, have adopted the alternative of smiling at them. It has become the fashion, a convenient and a strange one, to suppress the revelations of history, to invalidate the comments of philosophy, and to draw the pen across all unpleasant facts and all gloomy inquiries. "*Topics for declamation*," throw in the skilful. "*Declamation*," echo the silly. Jean Jacques, a declaimer; Diderot, a declaimer; Voltaire on Calas, Labarre, and Sirven, a declaimer! I forget who it is who has lately made out Tacitus, too, a declaimer, Nero a victim, and "that poor Holophernes" a man really to be pitied.

Facts, however, are stubborn, and hard to baffle. The author of this book has seen, with his own eyes, about twenty miles from Brussels, a specimen of the Middle Ages, within everybody's reach, at the Abbey of Villars—the orifices of the secret dungeons in the middle of the meadow which was once the courtyard of the cloister and, on the banks of the Dyle, four stone cells, half underground and half under water. These were *in pace*. Each of these dungeons has a remnant of an iron wicket, a closet, and a barred skylight, which, on the outside, is two feet above the surface of the river, and from the inside is six feet above the ground. Four feet in depth of the river flows along the outer face of the wall; the ground near by is constantly wet.

This saturated soil was the only bed of the *in pace* occupant. In one of these dungeons there remains the stump of an iron collar fixed in the wall; in another may be seen a kind of square box, formed of four slabs of granite, too short for a human being to lie down in, too low to stand in erect. Now, in this was placed a creature like ourselves, and then a lid of stone was closed above her head. There it is. You can see it; you can touch it. These *in pace*; these dungeons; these iron hinges; these metal collars; this lofty skylight, on a level with which the river runs; this box of stone, covered by its lid of granite, like a sepulchre, with this difference, that it shut in the living and not the dead; this soil of mud, this cess-pool; these oozing walls. Oh! what declaimers!

III
UPON WHAT CONDITIONS WE CAN RESPECT THE PAST

MONASTICISM, such as it was in Spain, and such as it is in Thibet, is for civilisation a kind of consumption. It stops life short. It, in one word, depopulates. Monastic incarceration is castration. In Europe, it has been a scourge. Add to that, the violence so often done to conscience; the ecclesiastical calling so frequently compulsory; the feudal system leaning on the cloister; primogeniture emptying into the monastery the surplus of the family; the ferocious cruelties which we have just described; the *in pace*; mouths closed, brains walled-up, so many hapless intellects incarcerated in the dungeons of eternal vows; the assumption of the gown, the burial of souls alive. Add these individual torments to the national degradation, and, whoever you may be, you will find yourself shuddering at the sight of the frock and the veil, those two winding sheets of human invention.

However, on certain points and in certain places, in spite of philosophy, and in spite of progress, the monastic spirit perseveres in the full blaze of the nineteenth century, and a singular revival of asceticism, at this very moment, amazes the civilised world. The persistence of superannuated institutions in striving to perpetuate themselves is like the obstinacy of a rancid odour clinging to the hair; the pretension of spoiled fish that insists on being eaten, the tenacious folly of a child's garment trying to clothe a man, or the tenderness of a corpse returning to embrace the living.

"Ingrates!" exclaims the garment. "I shielded you in weakness. Why do you reject me now?" "I come from the depths of the sea," says the fish; "I was once a rose," cries the odour; "I loved you," murmurs the corpse; "I civilised you," says the convent.

To this there is but one reply: "In the past."

To dream of the indefinite prolongation of things dead and the government of mankind by embalming; to restore dilapidated dogmas, regild the shrines, replaster the cloisters, reconsecrate the reliquaries, revamp old superstitions, replenish fading fanaticism, put new handles in worn-out sprinkling brushes, reconstitute monasticism; to believe in the salvation of society by the multiplication of parasites; to foist the past upon the present, all this seems strange. There are, however, advocates for such theories as these. These theorists, men of mind too, in other things, have a very simple process; they apply to the past a coating of what they term divine right, respect for our forefathers, time-honoured authority, sacred tradition, legitimacy; and they go about, shouting, "Here! take this, good people!" This kind of logic was familiar to the ancients; their soothsayers practised it. Rubbing over a black heifer with chalk, they would exclaim, "She is white." *Bos cretatus*.

As for ourselves, we distribute our respect, here and there, and spare the past entirely, provided it will but consent to be dead. But, if it insist upon being alive, we attack it and endeavour to kill it.

Superstitions, bigotries, hypocrisies, prejudices, these phantoms, phantoms though they be, are tenacious of life; they have teeth and nails in their shadowy substance, and we must grapple with them, body to body, and make war upon them and that, too, without cessation; for it is one of the fatalities of humanity to be condemned to eternal struggle with phantoms. A shadow is hard to seize by the throat and dash upon the ground.

A convent in France, in the high noon of the nineteenth century, is a college of owls confronting the day. A cloister in the open act of asceticism in the full face of the city, of '89, of 1830 and of 1848, Rome blooming forth in Paris, is an anachronism. In ordinary times, to disperse an anachronism and cause it to vanish, one has only to make it spell the year of our Lord. But, we do not live in ordinary times.

Let us attack, then.

Let us attack, but let us distinguish. The characteristic of truth is never to run into excess. What need has she of exaggeration? Some things must be destroyed, and some things must be merely cleared up and investigated. What power there is in a courteous and serious examination! Let us not therefore carry flame where light alone will suffice.

Well, then, assuming that we are in the nineteenth century, we are opposed, as a general proposition, and in every nation, in Asia as well as in Europe, in Judea as well as in Turkey, to ascetic seclusion in monasteries. He who says "convent" says "marsh." Their putrescence is apparent, their stagnation is baleful, their fermentation fevers and infects the nations, and their increase becomes an Egyptian plague. We cannot, without a shudder, think of those countries where Fakirs, Bonzes, Santons, Caloyers, Marabouts, and Talapoins multiply in swarms, like vermin.

Having said this much, the religious question still remains. This question has some mysterious aspects, and we must ask leave to look it steadily in the face.

IV
THE CONVENT VIEWED IN THE LIGHT OF PRINCIPLE

MEN come together and live in common. By what right? By virtue of the right of association.

They shut themselves up. By what right? Every man has to open or to shut his door.

They do not go out. By what right? By virtue of the right to go and come which implies the right to stay at home.

And what are they doing there, at home?

They speak in low tones; they keep their eyes fixed on the ground; they work. They give up the world, cities, sensual enjoyments, pleasures, vanities, pride, interest. They go clad in coarse woollen or coarse linen. Not one of them possesses any property whatever. Upon entering, he who was rich becomes poor. What he had, he gives to all. He who was what is called a nobleman, a man of rank, a lord, is the equal of him who was a peasant. The cell is the same for all. All undergo the same tonsure, wear the same frock, eat the same black bread, sleep on the same straw, and die on the same ashes. The same sack-cloth is on every back, the same rope about every waist. If it be the rule to go bare-footed, all go with naked feet. There may be a prince among them; the prince is a shadow like all the rest. Titles there are none. Family names even have disappeared. They answer only to Christian names. All are bowed beneath the equality of their baptismal names. They have dissolved the family of the flesh, and have formed, in their community, the family of the spirit. They have no other relatives than all mankind. They succour the poor, they tend the sick. They choose out those whom they are to obey, and they address one another by the title: "Brother!"

You stop me, exclaiming: "But, that is the ideal monastery!"

It is enough that it is a possible monastery, for me to take it into consideration.

Hence it is that, in the preceding book, I spoke of a convent with respect. The Middle Ages aside, Asia aside, and the historical and political question reserved, in the purely philosophical point of view, beyond the necessities of militant polemics, on condition that the monastery be absolutely voluntary and contain none but willing devotees, I should always look upon the monastic community with a certain serious, and, in some respects, deferential attention. Where community exists, there likewise exists the true body politic, and where the latter is, there too is justice. The monastery is the product of the formula: "Equality, Fraternity." Oh! how great is liberty! And how glorious the transfiguration! Liberty suffices to transform the monastery into a republic!

Let us proceed.

These men or women who live within those four walls, and dress in haircloth, are equal in condition and call each other brother and sister. It is well, but do they do aught else?

Yes.

What?

They gaze into the gloom, they kneel, and they join their hands.

What does that mean?

V
PRAYER

THEY PRAY.

To whom?

To God.

Pray to God, what is meant by that?

Is there an infinite outside of us? Is this infinite, one, inherent, permanent; necessarily substantial, because it is infinite, and because, if matter were wanting to it, it would in that respect be limited; necessarily intelligent, because it is infinite, and because if it lacked intelligence, it would be to that extent, finite? Does this infinite awaken in us the idea of essence, while we are able to attribute to ourselves the idea of existence only? In other words, is it not the absolute of which we are the relative?

At the same time, while there is an infinite outside of us, is there not an infinite within us? These two infinites (fearful plural!) do they not rest super-posed on one another? Does not the second infinite underlie the first, so to speak? Is it not the mirror, the reflection, the echo of the first, an abyss concentric with another abyss? Is this second infinite, intelligent also? Does it think? Does it love? Does it will? If the two infinites be intelligent, each one of them has a will principle, and there is a "me" in the infinite above, as there is a "me" in the infinite below. The "me" below is the soul; the "me" above is God.

To place, by process of thought, the infinite below in contact with the infinite above, is called "prayer."

Let us not take anything away from the human mind; suppression is evil. We must reform and transform. Certain faculties of man are directed towards the Unknown; thought, meditation, prayer. The Unknown is an ocean. What is conscience? It is the compass of the Unknown. Thought, meditation, prayer, these are the great, mysterious pointings of the needle. Let us respect them. Whither tend these majestic irradiations of the soul? into the shadow, that is, towards the light.

The grandeur of democracy is that it denies nothing and renounces nothing of humanity. Close by the rights of Man, side by side with them, at least, are the rights of the Soul.

To crush out fanaticisms and revere the Infinite, such is the law. Let us not confine ourselves to falling prostrate beneath the tree of Creation and contemplating its vast ramifications full of stars. We have a duty to perform, to cultivate the human soul, to defend mystery against miracle, to adore the incomprehensible and reject the absurd; to admit nothing that is inexplicable excepting what is necessary, to purify faith and obliterate superstition from the face of religion, to remove the vermin from the garden of God.

VI

ABSOLUTE EXCELLENCE OF PRAYER

As to methods of prayer, all are good, if they be but sincere. Turn your book over and be in the infinite.

There is, we are aware, a philosophy that denies the infinite. There is also a philosophy classed pathologically, which denies the sun; this philosophy is called blindness.

To set up a sense we lack as a source of truth, is a fine piece of blind man's assurance.

And the rarity of it consists in the haughty air of superiority and compassion which is assumed towards the philosophy that sees God, by this philosophy that has to grope its way. It makes one think of a mole exclaiming: "How they excite my pity with their prate about a sun!"

There are, we know, illustrious and mighty atheists. These men, in fact, led round again towards truth by their very power, are not absolutely sure of being atheists; with them, the matter is nothing but a question of definitions, and, at all events, if they do not believe in God, being great minds, they prove God.

We hail, in them, philosophers, while, at the same time, inexorably disputing their philosophy.

But, let us proceed.

An admirable thing, too, is the facility of settling everything to one's satisfaction with words. A metaphysical school at the North, slightly impregnated with the fogs, has imagined that it effected a revolution in the human understanding by substituting for the word "Force" the word "Will."

To say, "the plant wills," instead of "the plant grows," would be indeed pregnant with meaning if you were to add, "the universe wills." Why? Because this would flow from it: the plant wills, then it has a "me;" the universe wills, then it has a God.

To us, however, who, in direct opposition to this school, reject nothing *a priori*, a will in the plant, which is accepted by this school, appears more difficult to admit, than a will in the universe, which it denies.

To deny the will of the infinite, that is to say God, can be done only on condition of denying the infinite itself. We have demonstrated that.

Denial of the infinite leads directly to nihilism. Everything becomes "a conception of the mind."

With nihilism no discussion is possible. For the logical nihilist doubts the existence of his interlocutor, and is not quite sure that he exists himself.

From his point of view it is possible that he may be to himself only a "conception of his mind."

However, he does not perceive that all he has denied he admits in a mass by merely pronouncing the word "mind."

To sum up, no path is left open for thought by a philosophy that makes everything come to but one conclusion, the monosyllable "No."

To "No," there is but one reply: "Yes."

Nihilism has no scope. There is no nothing. Zero does not exist. Everything is something. Nothing is nothing.

Man lives by affirmation even more than he does by bread.

To behold and to show forth, even these will not suffice. Philosophy should be an energy; it should find its aim and its effect in the amelioration of mankind. Socrates should enter into Adam and produce Marcus Aurelius—in other words, bring forth from the man of enjoyment, the man of wisdom—and change Eden into the Lyceum. Science should be a cordial. Enjoyment! What wretched aim, and what pitiful ambition! The brute enjoys. Thought, this is the true triumph of the soul. To proffer thought to the thirst of men, to give to all, as an elixir, the idea of God, to cause conscience and science to fraternise in them, and to make them good men by this mysterious confrontation—such is the province of true philosophy. Morality is truth in full bloom. Contemplation leads to action. The absolute should be practical. The ideal must be made air and food and drink to the human mind. It is the ideal which has the right to say: *Take of it, this is my flesh, this is my blood.* Wisdom is a sacred communion. It is upon that condition that it ceases to be a sterile love of science, and becomes the one and supreme method by which to rally humanity; from philosophy it is promoted to religion.

Philosophy should not be a mere watch-tower, built upon mystery, from which to gaze at ease upon it, with no other result than to be a convenience for the curious.

For ourselves, postponing the development of our thought to some other occasion, we will only say that we do not comprehend either man as a starting-point, or progress as the goal, without those two forces which are the two great motors, faith and love.

Progress is the aim, the ideal is the model.

What is the ideal? It is God.

Ideal, absolute, perfection, the infinite—these are identical words.

VII
PRECAUTIONS TO BE TAKEN IN CENSURE

HISTORY and philosophy have eternal duties, which are, at the same time, simple duties—to oppose Caiaphas as bishop, Draco as judge, Trimalcion as legislator, and Tiberius as emperor. This is clear, direct, and limpid, and presents no obscurity. But the right to live apart, even with its inconveniences and abuses, must be verified and dealt with carefully. The life of the cenobite is a human problem.

When we speak of convents, those seats of error but of innocence, of mistaken views but of good intentions, of ignorance but of devotion, of torment but of martyrdom, we must nearly always have "Yes" and "No" upon our lips.

A convent is a contradiction,—its object salvation, its means self-sacrifice. The convent is supreme egotism resulting in supreme self-denial.

"Abdicate that you may reign" seems to be the device of monasticism.

In the cloister they suffer that they may enjoy—they draw a bill of exchange on death—they discount the celestial splendour in terrestrial night. In the cloister, hell is accepted as the charge made in advance on the future inheritance of heaven.

The assumption of the veil or the frock is a suicide reimbursed by an eternity.

It seems to us that, in treating such a subject, raillery would be quite out of place. Everything relating to it is serious, the good as well as the evil.

The good man knits his brows, but never smiles with the bad man's smile. We can understand anger but not malignity.

VIII
FAITH—LAW

A few words more.

We blame the Church when it is saturated with intrigues; we despise the spiritual when it is harshly austere to the temporal; but we honour everywhere, the thoughtful man.

We bow to the man who kneels.

A faith is a necessity to man. Woe to him who believes nothing.

A man is not idle, because he is absorbed in thought. There is a visible labour and there is an invisible labour.

To meditate is to labour; to think is to act.

Folded arms work, closed hands perform, a gaze fixed on heaven is a toil.

Thales remained motionless for four years. He founded philosophy.

In our eyes, cenobites are not idlers, nor is the recluse a sluggard.

To think of the Gloom is a serious thing.

Without at all invalidating what we have just said, we believe that a perpetual remembrance of the tomb is proper for the living. On this point, the priest and the philosopher agree: *We must die*. The Abbé of La Trappe answers Horace.

To mingle with one's life a certain presence of the sepulchre is the law of the wise man, and it is the law of the ascetic. In this relation, the ascetic and the sage tend towards a common centre.

There is a material advancement; we desire it. There is, also, a moral grandeur; we hold fast to it.

Unreflecting, headlong minds say:

"Of what use are those motionless figures by the side of mystery? What purpose do they serve? What do they effect?"

Alas! in the presence of that obscurity which surrounds us and awaits us, not knowing what the vast dispersion of all things will do with us, we answer: There is, perhaps, no work more sublime than that which is accomplished by these souls; and we add, There is no labour, perhaps, more useful.

Those who pray always are necessary to those who never pray.

In our view, the whole question is in the amount of thought that is mingled with prayer.

Leibniz, praying, is something grand; Voltaire, worshipping, is something beautiful. *Deo erexit Voltaire.*

We are for religion against the religions.

We are of those who believe in the pitifulness of orisons, and in the sublimity of prayer.

Besides, in this moment through which we are passing, a moment which happily will not leave its stamp upon the nineteenth century; in this hour which finds so many with their brows abased so low and their souls so little uplifted, among so many of the living whose motto is happiness, and who are occupied with the brief, mis-shapen things of matter, whoever is self-exiled seems venerable to us. The monastery is a renunciation. Self-sacrifice, even when misdirected, is still self-sacrifice. To assume as duty an uninviting error has its peculiar grandeur.

Considered in itself, ideally, and holding it up to truth, until it is impartially and exhaustively examined in all its aspects, the monastery, and particularly the convent—for woman suffers most under our system of society, and in this exile of the cloister there is an element of protest—the convent, we repeat, has, unquestionably, a certain majesty.

This monastic existence, austere and gloomy as it is, of which we have delineated a few characteristics, is not life, is not liberty: for it is not the grave, for it is not completion: it is that singular place, from which, as from the summit of a lofty mountain, we perceive, on one side, the abyss in which we are, and, on the other, the abyss wherein we are to be: it is a narrow and misty boundary, that separates two worlds, at once illuminated and obscured by both, where the enfeebled ray of life commingles with the uncertain ray of death; it is the twilight of the tomb.

For ourselves, we, who do not believe what these women believe, but live, like them, by faith, never could look without a species of tender and religious awe, a kind of pity full of envy, upon those devoted beings, trembling yet confident—those humble yet august souls, who dare to live upon the very confines of the great mystery, waiting between the world closed to them and heaven not yet opened; turned towards the daylight not yet seen, with only the happiness of thinking that they know where it is; their aspirations directed towards the abyss and the unknown, their gaze fixed on the motionless gloom, kneeling, dismayed, stupefied, shuddering, and half borne away at certain times by the deep pulsations of Eternity.

BOOK EIGHTH –
CEMETERIES TAKE WHAT IS GIVEN THEM

I

WHICH TREATS OF THE MANNER OF
ENTERING THE CONVENT

INTO this house it was that Jean Valjean had, as Fauchelevent said, "fallen from heaven."

He had crossed the garden wall at the corner of the Rue Polonceau. That angels' hymn which he had heard in the middle of the night, was the nuns chanting matins; that hall of which he had caught a glimpse in the obscurity, was the chapel; that phantom which he had seen extended on the floor was the sister performing the reparation; that bell the sound of which had so strangely surprised him was the gardener's bell fastened to old Fauchelevent's knee.

When Cosette had been put to bed, Jean Valjean and Fauchelevent had, as we have seen, taken a glass of wine and a piece of cheese before a blazing fire; then, the only bed in the shanty being occupied by Cosette, they had thrown themselves each upon a bundle of straw. Before closing his eyes, Jean Valjean had said: "Henceforth I must remain here." These words were chasing one another through Fauchelevent's head the whole night.

To tell the truth, neither of them had slept.

Jean Valjean, feeling that he was discovered and Javert was upon his track, knew full well that he and Cosette were lost should they return into the city. Since the new blast which had burst upon him had thrown him into this cloister, Jean Valjean had but one thought, to remain there. Now, for one in his unfortunate position, this convent was at once the safest and the most dangerous place, the most dangerous, for, no man being allowed to enter, if he should be discovered, it was a flagrant crime, and Jean Valjean would take but one step from the convent to prison; the safest, for if he succeeded in getting permission to remain, who would come there to look for him? To live in an impossible place; that would be safety.

For his part, Fauchelevent was racking his brains. He began by deciding that he was utterly bewildered. How did Monsieur Madeleine come there, with such walls! The walls of a cloister are not so easily crossed. How did he happen to be with a child? A man does not scale a steep wall with a child in his arms. Who was this child? Where did they both come from? Since Fauchelevent had been in the convent, he had not heard a word from M—— sur M——, and he knew nothing of what had taken place. Father Madeleine wore that air which discourages questions; and moreover, Fauchelevent said to himself: "One does not question a saint." To him Monsieur Madeleine had preserved all his prestige. From some words that escaped from Jean Valjean, however, the gardener thought he might conclude that Monsieur Madeleine had probably failed on account of the hard times, and that he was pursued by his creditors; or it might be that he was compromised in some political affair and was concealing himself; which did not at all displease Fauchelevent, who, like many of our peasants of the north, had an old Bonapartist heart. Being in concealment, Monsieur Madeleine had taken the convent for an asylum, and it was natural that he should wish to remain there. But the mystery to which Fauchelevent constantly returned and over which he was racking his brains was, that Monsieur Madeleine should be there, and that this little girl should be with him. Fauchelevent saw them, touched them, spoke to them, and yet did not believe it. An incomprehensibility had made its way into Fauchelevent's hut. Fauchelevent was groping amid conjectures, but saw nothing clearly except this: Monsieur Madeleine has saved my life. This single certainty was sufficient, and determined him. He said aside to himself: It is my turn now. He added in his conscience: Monsieur Madeleine did not deliberate so long when the question was about squeezing himself under the wagon to draw me out. He decided that he would save Monsieur Madeleine.

He however put several questions to himself and made several answers: "After what he has done for me, if he were a thief, would I save him? just the same. If he were an assassin, would I save him? just the same. Since he is a saint, shall I save him? just the same."

But to have him remain in the convent, what a problem was that! Before that almost chimerical attempt, Fauchelevent did not recoil; this poor Picardy peasant, with no other ladder than his devotion, his goodwill, a little of that old country cunning, engaged for once in the service of a generous intention, undertook to scale the impossibilities of the cloister and the craggy escarpments of the rules of Saint Benedict. Fauchelevent was an old man who had been selfish throughout his life, and who, near the end of his days, crippled, infirm, having no interest longer in the world, found it sweet to be grateful, and seeing a virtuous action to be done, threw himself into it like a man who, at the moment of death, finding at hand a glass of some good wine which he had never tasted, should drink it greedily. We might add that the air which he had been breathing now for several years in this convent had destroyed his personality, and had at last rendered some good action necessary to him.

He formed his resolution then: to devote himself to Monsieur Madeleine.

We have just described him as a *poor Picardy peasant*. The description is true, but incomplete. At the point of this story at which we now are, a closer acquaintance with Fauchelevent becomes necessary. He was a peasant, but he had been a notary, which added craft to his cunning, and penetration to his simplicity. Having, from various causes, failed in his business, from a notary he had fallen to a cartman and labourer. But, in spite of the oaths and blows which seem necessary with horses, he had retained something of the notary. He had some natural wit; he said neither I is nor I has; he could carry on a conversation, a rare thing in a village; and the other peasants said of him: he talks almost like a gentleman. Fauchelevent belonged in fact to that class which the flippant and impertinent vocabulary of the last century termed *half-yeoman*, *half-clown*; and which the metaphors falling from the castle to the hovel, label in the distribution of the commonalty: *half-rustic*, *half-citizen*, *pepper-and-salt*. Fauchelevent, although sorely tried and sorely used by Fortune, a sort of poor old soul worn threadbare, was nevertheless an impulsive man, and had a very willing heart; a precious quality, which prevents one from ever being wicked. His faults and his vices, for such he had, were superficial; and finally, his physiognomy was one of those which attract the observer. That old face had none of those ugly wrinkles in the upper part of the forehead which indicate wickedness or stupidity.

At daybreak, having dreamed enormously, old Fauchelevent opened his eyes, and saw Monsieur Madeleine, who, seated upon his bunch of straw, was looking at Cosette as she slept. Fauchelevent half arose, and said:——

"Now that you are here, how are you going to manage to come in?"

This question summed up the situation, and wakened Jean Valjean from his reverie.

The two men took counsel.

"To begin with," said Fauchelevent, "you will not set foot outside of this room, neither the little girl nor you. One step in the garden, we are ruined."

"That is true."

"Monsieur Madeleine," resumed Fauchelevent, "you have arrived at a very good time; I mean to say very bad; there is one of these ladies dangerously sick. On that account they do not look this way much. She must be dying. They are saying the forty-hour prayers. The whole community is in derangement. That takes up their attention. She who is about departing is a saint. In fact, we are all saints here; all the difference between them and me is, that they say: our cell, and I say: my shanty. They are going to have the orison for the dying, and then the orison for the dead. For to-day we shall be quiet here; and I do not answer for to-morrow."

"However," observed Jean Valjean, "this shanty is under the corner of the wall; it is hidden by a sort of ruin; there are trees; they cannot see it from the convent."

"And I add, that the nuns never come near it."

"Well?" said Jean Valjean.

The interrogation point which followed that well, meant: it seems to me that we can remain here concealed. This interrogation point Fauchelevent answered:——

"There are the little girls."

"What little girls?" asked Jean Valjean.

As Fauchelevent opened his mouth to explain the words he had just uttered, a single stroke of a bell was heard.

"The nun is dead," said he. "There is the knell."

And he motioned to Jean Valjean to listen.

The bell sounded a second time.

"It is the knell, Monsieur Madeleine. The bell will strike every minute, for twenty-four hours, until the body goes out of the church. You see they play. In their recreations, if a ball rolls here, that is enough for them to come after it, in spite of the rules, and rummage all about here. Those cherubs are little devils."

"Who?" asked Jean Valjean.

"The little girls. You would be found out very soon. They would cry, 'What! a man!' But there is no danger to-day. There will be no recreation. The day will be all prayers. You hear the bell. As I told you, a stroke every minute. It is the knell."

"I understand, Father Fauchelevent. There are boarding scholars."

And Jean Valjean thought within himself:——

"Here, then, Cosette can be educated, too."

Fauchelevent exclaimed:——

"Zounds! they are the little girls for you! And how they would scream at sight of you! and how they would run! Here, to be a man, is to have the plague. You see how they fasten a bell to my leg, as they would to a wild beast."

Jean Valjean was studying more and more deeply. "The convent would save us," murmured he. Then he raised his voice:

"Yes, the difficulty is in remaining."

"No," said Fauchelevent, "it is to get out."

Jean Valjean felt his blood run cold.

"To get out?"

"Yes, Monsieur Madeleine, in order to come in, it is necessary that you should get out."

And, after waiting for a sound from the tolling bell to die away, Fauchelevent pursued:——

"It would not do to have you found here like this. Whence do you come? for me you have fallen from heaven because I know you; but for the nuns you must come in at the door."

Suddenly they heard a complicated ringing upon another bell.

"Oh!" said Fauchelevent, "that is the ring for the mothers. They are going to the chapter. They always hold a chapter when anybody dies. She died at daybreak. It is usually at daybreak that people die. But cannot you go out the way you came in? Let us see; this is not to question you, but where did you come in?"

Jean Valjean became pale; the bare idea of climbing down again into that formidable street, made him shudder. Make your way out of a forest full of tigers, and when out, fancy yourself advised by a friend to return. Jean Valjean imagined all the police still swarming in the quarter, officers on the watch, sentries everywhere, frightful fists stretched out towards his collar,—Javert, perhaps, at the corner of the square.

"Impossible," said he. "Father Fauchelevent, let it go that I fell from on high."

"Ah! I believe it, I believe it," replied Fauchelevent. "You have no need to tell me so. God must have taken you into his hand, to have a close look at you, and then put you down. Only he meant to put you into a monastery; he made a mistake. Hark? another ring; that is to warn the porter to go and notify the municipality, so that they may go and notify the death-physician, so that he may come and see that there is really a dead woman. All that is the ceremony of dying. These good ladies do not like this visit very much. A physician believes in nothing. He lifts the veil. He even lifts some thing else, sometimes. How soon they have notified the inspector, this time! What can be the matter? Your little one is asleep yet. What is her name?"

"Cosette."

"She is your girl? that is to say: you should be her grandfather?"

"Yes."

"For her, to get out will be easy. I have my door, which opens into the court. I knock; the porter opens. I have my basket on my back; the little girl is inside; I go out. Father Fauchelevent goes out with his basket—that is all simple. You will tell the little girl to keep very still. She will be under cover. I will leave her as soon as I can, with a good old friend of mine, a fruiteress, in the Rue du Chemin Vert, who is deaf, and who has a little bed. I will scream into the fruiteress's ear that she is my niece, and she must keep her for me till to-morrow. Then the little girl will come back with you; for I shall bring you back. It must be done. But how are you going to manage to get out?"

Jean Valjean shook his head.

"Let nobody see me, that is all, Father Fauchelevent. Find some means to get me out, like Cosette, in a basket, and under cover."

Fauchelevent scratched the tip of his ear with the middle finger of his left hand—a sign of serious embarrassment.

A third ring made a diversion.

"That is the death-physician going away," said Fauchelevent. "He has looked, and said she is dead; it is right. When the inspector has visaed the passport for paradise, the undertaker sends a coffin. If it is a mother, the mothers lay her out; if it is a sister, the sisters lay her out. After which, I nail it up. That's a part of my gardening. A gardener is something of a gravedigger. They put her in a low room in the church which communicates with the street, and where no man can enter except the death-physician. I do not count the bearers and myself for men. In that room I nail the coffin. The bearers come and take her, and whip-up, driver: that is the way they go to heaven. They bring in a box with nothing in it, they carry it away with something inside. That is what an interment is. *De profundis.*"

A ray of the rising sun beamed upon the face of the sleeping Cosette, who half-opened her mouth dreamily, seeming like an angel drinking in the light. Jean Valjean was looking at her. He no longer heard Fauchelevent.

Not being heard is no reason for silence. The brave old gardener quietly continued his garrulous rehearsal.

"The grave is at the Vaugirard cemetery. They pretend that this Vaugirard cemetery is going to be suppressed. It is an ancient cemetery, which is not according to the regulations, which does not wear the uniform, and which is going to be retired. I am sorry for it, for it is convenient. I have a friend there—Father Mestienne, the gravedigger. The nuns here have the privilege of being carried to that cemetery at night-fall. There is an order of the Préfecture, expressly for them. But what events since yesterday? Mother Crucifixion is dead, and Father Madeleine"——

"Is buried," said Jean Valjean, sadly smiling.

Fauchelevent echoed the word.

"Really, if you were here for good, it would be a genuine burial."

A fourth time the bell rang out. Fauchelevent quickly took down the knee-piece and bell from the nail, and buckled it on his knee.

"This time, it is for me. The mother prioress wants me. Well! I am pricking myself with the tongue of my buckle. Monsieur Madeleine, do not stir, but wait for me. There is something new. If you are hungry, there is the wine, and bread and cheese."

And he went out of the hut, saying: "I am coming, I am coming."

Jean Valjean saw him hasten across the garden, as fast as his crooked leg would let him, with side glances at his melons the while.

In less than ten minutes, Father Fauchelevent, whose bell put the nuns to flight as he went along, rapped softly at a door, and a gentle voice answered—*Forever, Forever!* that is to say, *Come in*.

This door was that of the parlour allotted to the gardener, for use when it was necessary to communicate with him. This parlour was near the hall of the chapter. The prioress, seated in the only chair in the parlour, was waiting for Fauchelevent.

II
FAUCHELEVENT FACING THE DIFFICULTY

A SERIOUS and troubled bearing is peculiar, on critical occasions, to certain characters and certain professions, especially priests and monastics. At the moment when Fauchelevent entered, this double sign of preoccupation marked the countenance of the prioress, the charming and learned Mademoiselle de Blemeur, Mother Innocent, who was ordinarily cheerful.

The gardener made a timid bow, and stopped at the threshold of the cell. The prioress, who was saying her rosary, raised her eyes and said:

"Ah! it is you, Father Fauvent."

This abbreviation had been adopted in the convent.

Fauchelevent again began his bow.

"Father Fauvent, I have called you."

"I am here, reverend mother."

"I wish to speak to you."

"And I, for my part," said Fauchelevent, with a boldness at which he was alarmed himself, "I have something to say to the most reverend mother."

The prioress looked at him.

"Ah, you have a communication to make to me."

"A petition!"

"Well, what is it?"

Goodman Fauchelevent, ex-notary, belonged to that class of peasants who are never disconcerted. A certain combination of ignorance and skill is very effective; you do not suspect it, and you accede to it. Within little more than two years that he had lived in the convent, Fauchelevent had achieved a success in the community. Always alone, and even while attending to his garden, he had hardly anything to do but to be curious. Being, as he was, at a distance from all these veiled women, going to and fro, he saw before him hardly more than a fluttering of shadows. By dint of attention and penetration, he had succeeded in clothing all these phantoms with flesh, and these dead were alive to him. He was like a deaf man whose sight is extended, and like a blind man whose hearing is sharpened. He had applied himself to unravelling the meaning of the various rings, and had made them out; so that in this enigmatic and taciturn cloister, nothing was hidden from him; this sphynx blabbed all her secrets in his ear. Fauchelevent, knowing everything, concealed everything. That was his art. The whole convent thought him stupid—a great merit in religion. The mothers prized Fauchelevent. He was a rare mute. He inspired confidence. Moreover, he was regular in his habits, and never went out except when it was clearly necessary on account of the orchard and the garden. This discretion in his conduct was counted to his credit. He had, nevertheless, learned the secrets of two men; the porter of the convent, who knew the peculiarities of the parlour, and the gravedigger of the cemetery, who knew the singularities of burial: in this manner, he had a double-light in regard to these nuns—one upon their life, the other upon their death. But he did not abuse it. The congregation thought much of him, old, lame, seeing nothing, probably a little deaf—how many good qualities! It would have been difficult to replace him.

The goodman, with the assurance of one who feels that he is appreciated, began before the reverend prioress a rustic harangue, quite diffuse and very profound. He spoke at length of his age, his infirmities, of the weight of years henceforth doubly heavy upon him, of the growing demands of his work, of the size of the garden, of the nights to be spent, like last night for example, when he had to put awnings over the melons on account of the moon; and finally ended with this: "that he had a brother—(the prioress gave a start)—a brother not young—(second start of the prioress, but a reassured start)—that if it was desired, this brother could come and live with him and help him; that he was an excellent gardener; that the community would get good services from him, better than his own; that, otherwise, if his brother were not admitted, as he, the oldest, felt that he was broken down, and unequal to the labour, he would be obliged to leave, though with much regret; and that his brother had a little girl that he would bring with him, who

would be reared under God in the house, and who, perhaps,—
who knows?—would some day become a nun."

When he had finished, the prioress stopped the sliding of her
rosary through her fingers, and said:

"Can you, between now and night, procure a strong iron
bar?"

"For what work?"

"To be used as a lever."

"Yes, reverend mother," answered Fauchelevent.

The prioress, without adding a word, arose, and went into
the next room, which was the hall of the chapter, where the
vocal mothers were probably assembled: Fauchelevent remained
alone.

III
MOTHER INNOCENT

ABOUT a quarter of an hour elapsed. The prioress returned and
resumed her seat.

Both seemed preoccupied. We report as well as we can the
dialogue that followed.

"Father Fauvent?"

"Reverend mother?"

"You are familiar with the chapel?"

"I have a little box there to go to mass, and the offices."

"And you have been in the choir about your work?"

"Two or three times."

"A stone is to be raised."

"Heavy?"

"The slab of the pavement at the side of the altar."

"The stone that covers the vault?"

"Yes."

"That is a piece of work where it would be well to have two
men."

"Mother Ascension, who is as strong as a man, will help you."

"A woman is never a man."

"We have only a woman to help you. Everybody does what
he can. Because Dom Mabillon gives four hundred and seventeen epistles of St. Bernard, and Merlonus Horstius gives only
three hundred and sixty-seven, I do not despise Merlonus
Horstius."

"Nor I either."

"Merit consists in work according to our strength. A cloister is not a ship-yard."

"And a woman is not a man. My brother is very strong."

"And then you will have a lever."

"That is the only kind of key that fits that kind of door."

"There is a ring in the stone."

"I will pass the lever through it."

"And the stone is arranged to turn on a pivot."

"Very well, reverend mother, I will open the vault."

"And the four mother choristers will assist you."

"And when the vault is opened?"

"It must be shut again."

"Is that all?"

"No."

"Give me your orders, most reverend mother."

"Fauvent, we have confidence in you."

"I am here to do everything."

"And to keep silent about everything."

"Yes, reverend mother."

"When the vault is opened——"

"I will shut it again."

"But before——"

"What, reverend mother?"

"Something must be let down."

There was silence. The prioress, after a quivering of the underlip which resembled hesitation, spoke:

"Father Fauvent?"

"Reverend mother?"

"You know that a mother died this morning."

"No."

"You have not heard the bell then?"

"Nothing is heard at the further end of the garden."

"Really?"

"I can hardly distinguish my ring."

"She died at daybreak."

"And then, this morning, the wind didn't blow my way."

"It is Mother Crucifixion. One of the blest."

The prioress was silent, moved her lips a moment as in a mental orison, and resumed:

"Three years ago, merely from having seen Mother Crucifixion at prayer, a Jansenist, Madame de Béthune, became orthodox."

"Ah! yes, I hear the knell now, reverend mother."

"The mothers have carried her into the room of the dead, which opens into the church."

"I know."

"No other man than you can or must enter that room. Be watchful. It would not look well for a man to enter the room of the dead!"

"Oftener."

"Eh?"

"Oftener?"

"What do you say?"

"I say oftener."

"Oftener than what?"

"Reverend mother, I don't say oftener than what; I say oftener."

"I do not understand you. Why do you say oftener?"

"To say as you do, reverend mother."

"But I did not say oftener."

"You did not say it; but I said it to say as you did."

The clock struck nine.

"At nine o'clock in the morning, and at all hours, praise and adoration to the most holy sacrament of the altar," said the prioress.

"Amen!" said Fauchelevent.

The clock struck in good time. It cut short that Oftener. It is probable, that without it the prioress and Fauchelevent would never have got out of the snarl.

Fauchelevent wiped his forehead.

The prioress again made a little low murmur, probably sacred, then raised her voice.

"During her life, Mother Crucifixion worked conversions; after her death, she will work miracles."

"She will!" answered Fauchelevent, correcting his step, and making an effort not to blunder again.

"Father Fauvent, the community has been blessed in Mother Crucifixion. Doubtless, it is not given to everybody to die like Cardinal de Bérulle, saying the holy mass, and to breathe out his soul to God, pronouncing these words: *Hanc igitur oblationem.* But without attaining to so great happiness, Mother Crucifixion had a very precious death. She had her consciousness to the last. She spoke to us, then she spoke to the angels. She gave us her last commands. If you had a little more faith, and if you could have been in her cell, she would have cured your leg by touching it. She smiled. We felt that she was returning to life in God. There was something of Paradise in that death."

Fauchelevent thought that he had been listening to a prayer.

"Amen!" said he.

"Father Fauvent, we must do what the dead wish."

The prioress counted a few beads on her chaplet. Fauchelevent was silent. She continued:

"I have consulted upon this question several ecclesiastics labouring in Our Lord, who are engaged in the exercise of clerical functions, and with admirable results."

"Reverend mother, we hear the knell much better here than in the garden."

"Furthermore, she is more than a departed one; she is a saint."

"Like you, reverend mother."

"She slept in her coffin for twenty years, by the express permission of our Holy Father, Pius VII."

"He who crowned the Emp—— Buonaparte."

For a shrewd man like Fauchelevent, the reminiscence was untoward. Luckily the prioress, absorbed in her thoughts, did not hear him. She continued:

"Father Fauvent?"

"Reverend mother?"

"St. Diodorus, Archbishop of Cappadocia, desired that this single word might be written upon his tomb: *Acarus*, which signifies a worm of the dust; that was done. Is it true?"

"Yes, reverend mother."

"The blessed Mezzocane, Abbé of Aquila, desired to be buried under the gibbet; that was done."

"It is true."

"St. Terence, Bishop of Ostia, at the mouth of the Tiber, requested to have engraved upon his tomb the mark which was put upon the graves of parricides, in the hope that travellers would spit upon his grave. That was done. We must obey the dead."

"So be it."

"The body of Bernard Guidonis, who was born in France

near Roche Abeille, was, as he has ordered, and in spite of the king of Castile, brought to the church of the Dominicans at Limoges, although Bernard Guidonis was Bishop of Tuy, in Spain. Can this be denied?"

The fact is attested by Plantavit de la Fosse.

"No, indeed, reverend mother."

A few beads of her chaplet were told over silently. The prioress went on:

"Father Fauvent, Mother Crucifixion will be buried in the coffin in which she has slept for twenty years."

"That is right."

"It is a continuation of sleep."

"I shall have to nail her up then in that coffin."

"Yes."

"And we will put aside the undertaker's coffin?"

"Precisely."

"I am at the disposal of the most reverend community."

"The four mother choristers will help you."

"To nail up the coffin I don't need them."

"No. To let it down."

"Where?"

"Into the vault."

"What vault?"

"Under the altar."

Fauchelevent gave a start.

"The vault under the altar!"

"Under the altar."

"But——"

"You will have an iron bar."

"Yes, but——"

"You will lift the stone with the bar by means of the ring."

"But——"

"We must obey the dead. To be buried in the vault under the altar of the chapel, not to go into profane ground, to remain in death where she prayed in life; this was the last request of Mother Crucifixion. She has asked it, that is to say, commanded it."

"But it is forbidden."

"Forbidden by men, enjoined by God."

"If it should come to be known?"

"We have confidence in you."

"Oh! as for me, I am like a stone in your wall."

"The chapter has assembled. The vocal mothers, whom I have just consulted again and who are now deliberating, have decided that Mother Crucifixion should be, according to her desire, buried in her coffin under our altar. Think, Father Fauvent, if there should be miracles performed here! what glory under God for the community! Miracles spring from tombs."

"But, reverend mother, if the agent of the Health Commission——"

"St. Benedict II., in the matter of burial, resisted Constantine Pogonatus."

"However, the Commissary of Police——"

"Chonodemaire, one of the seven German kings who entered Gaul in the reign of Constantius, expressly recognised the right of conventuals to be inhumed in religion, that is to say, under the altar."

"But the Inspector of the Prefecture——"

"The world is nothing before the cross. Martin, eleventh general of the Carthusians, gave to his order this device: *Stat crux dum volvitur orbis.*"

"Amen," said Fauchelevent, imperturbable in this method of extricating himself whenever he heard any Latin.

Any audience whatever is sufficient for one who has been too long silent. On the day that the rhetorician Gymnastoras came out of prison, full of suppressed dilemmas and syllogisms, he stopped before the first tree he met with, harangued it, and put forth very great efforts to convince it. The prioress, habitually subject to the constraint of silence, and having a surplus in her reservoir, rose, and exclaimed with the loquacity of an opened mill-sluice:

"I have on my right Benedict, and on my left Bernard. What is Bernard? he is the first Abbot of Clairvaux. Fontaines in Burgundy is blessed for having been his birthplace. His father's name was Tecelin, and his mother's Alethe. He began at Citeaux, and ended at Clairvaux; he was ordained abbot by the Bishop of Chalons-sur-Saône, Guillaume de Champeaux; he had seven hundred novices, and founded a hundred and sixty monasteries; he overthrew Abeilard at the Council of Sens in 1140, and Peter de Bruys and Henry his disciple, and another heterodox set called the Apostolicals; he confounded Arnold of Brescia, struck monk Ralph dumb, the slayer of the Jews, presided in 1148 over the Council of Rheims, caused Gilbert de la Porée, Bishop of Poitiers, to be condemned, caused Eon de l'Etoile to be condemned, arranged the differences of princes, advised the King, Louis the Young, counselled Pope Eugenius III., regulated the Temple, preached the Crusade, performed two hundred and fifty miracles in his lifetime, and as many as thirty-nine in one day. What is Benedict? he is the patriarch of Monte Cassino; he is the second founder of the Claustral Holiness, he is the Basil of the West. His order has produced forty popes, two hundred cardinals, fifty patriarchs, sixteen hundred archbishops, four thousand six hundred bishops, four emperors, twelve empresses, forty-six kings, forty-one queens, three thousand six hundred canonised saints, and has existed for fourteen hundred years. On one side, St. Bernard; on the other the agent of the Health Commission! On one side, St. Benedict; on the other the sanitary inspector! The state, Health Department, funeral regulations, rules, the administration, do we recognise these things? Anybody would be indignant to see how we are treated. We have not even the right to give our dust to Jesus Christ! Your sanitary commission is an invention of the revolution. God subordinated to the commissary of police; such is this age. Silence, Fauvent!"

Fauchelevent, beneath this douche, was not quite at ease. The prioress continued:

"The right of the convent to burial cannot be doubted by anybody. There are none to deny it save fanatics and those who have gone astray. We live in times of terrible confusion. People are ignorant of what they ought to know, and know those things of which they ought to be ignorant. They are gross and impious. There are people in these days who do not distinguish between the great St. Bernard and the Bernard entitled des Pauvres Catholiques, a certain good ecclesiastic who lived in the thirteenth century. Others blaspheme so far as to couple the scaffold of Louis XVI. with the cross of Jesus Christ. Louis XVI. was only a king. Let us then take heed for God! There are no longer either just or unjust. Voltaire's name is known, and the name of Cæsar de Bus is not known. Nevertheless Cæsar de Bus is in bliss and Voltaire is in torment. The last archbishop, the Cardinal of Perigord, did not even know that Charles de Gondren succeeded Bérulle, and Francis Bourgoin, Gondren, and Jean François Senault, Bourgoin, and Father de Sainte-Marthe, Jean

François Senault. The name of Father Cotton is known, not because he was one of the three who laboured in the foundation of the Oratory, but because he was the subject of an oath for the Huguenot King Henry IV. St. François de Sales is popular with the world, because he cheated at play. And then religion is attacked. Why? Because there have been wicked priests, because Sagittaire, Bishop of Gap, was a brother of Salone, Bishop of Embrun, and both were followers of Mammon. What does that amount to? Does that prevent Martin de Tours from being a saint and having given half his cloak to a poor man? The saints are persecuted. Men shut their eyes to the truth. Darkness becomes habitual. The most savage beasts are blind beasts. Nobody thinks of hell in earnest. Oh! the wicked people! By the king, now means, by the revolution. Men no longer know what is due to the living or the dead. Holy death is forbidden. The sepulchre is a civil affair. This is horrible. St. Leo II. wrote two letters expressly, one to Peter Notaire, the other to the King of the Visigoths, to combat and overthrow, upon questions touching the dead, the authority and the supremacy of the emperor. Walter, Bishop of Châlons, in this matter made opposition to Otho, Duke of Burgundy. The ancient magistracy acceded to it. Formerly we had votes in the chapter concerning secular affairs. The Abbot of Citeaux, general of the order, was hereditary counsellor of the Parlement of Burgundy. We do with our dead as we please. Is not the body of St. Benedict himself in France in the Abbey of Fleury, called St. Benedict sur Loire, though he died in Italy, at Monte Cassino, on a Saturday, the 21st of the month of March in the year 543! All this is incontestable. I abhor the Psallants, I hate the Prayers, I execrate heretics, but I should detest still more whoever might sustain the contrary of what I have said. You have only to read Arnold Wion Gabriel Bucelin, Trithemius, Maurolicus, and Dom Luke d'Achery."

The prioress drew breath, then turning towards Fauchelevent:

"Father Fauvent, is it settled?"

"It is settled, reverend mother."

"Can we count upon you?"

"I shall obey."

"It is well."

"I am entirely devoted to the convent."

"It is understood, you will close the coffin. The sisters will carry it into the chapel. The office for the dead will be said. Then they will return to the cloister. Between eleven o'clock and midnight, you will come with your iron bar. All will be done with the greatest secrecy. There will be in the chapel only the four mother choristers, Mother Ascension, and you."

"And the sister who will be at the post."

"She will not turn."

"But she will hear."

"She will not listen; moreover, what the cloister knows the world does not know."

There was a pause again. The prioress continued:

"You will take off your bell. It is needless that the sister at the post should perceive that you are there."

"Reverend mother?"

"What, Father Fauvent?"

"Has the death-physician made his visit?"

"He is going to make it at four o'clock to-day. The bell has been sounded which summons the death-physician. But you do not hear any ring then?"

"I only pay attention to my own."

"That is right, Father Fauvent."

"Reverend mother, I shall need a lever at least six feet long."

"Where will you get it?"

"Where there are gratings there are always iron bars. I have my heap of old iron at the back of the garden."

"About three-quarters of an hour before midnight; do not forget."

"Reverend mother?"

"What?"

"If you should ever have any other work like this, my brother is very strong. A Turk."

"You will do it as quickly as possible."

"I cannot go very fast. I am infirm; it is on that account I need help. I limp."

"To limp is not a crime, and it may be a blessing. The Emperor Henry II., who fought the Antipope Gregory, and re-established Benedict VIII., has two surnames: the Saint and the Lame."

"Two surtouts are very good," murmured Fauchelevent, who, in reality, was a little hard of hearing.

"Father Fauvent, now I think of it, we will take a whole hour. It is not too much. Be at the high altar with the iron bar at eleven o'clock. The office commences at midnight. It must all be finished a good quarter of an hour before."

"I will do everything to prove my zeal for the community. This is the arrangement. I shall nail up the coffin. At eleven o'clock precisely I will be in the chapel. The mother choristers will be there. Mother Ascension will be there. Two men would be better. But no matter! I shall have my lever. We shall open the vault, let down the coffin, and close the vault again. After which, there will be no trace of anything. The government will suspect nothing. Reverend mother, is this all so?"

"No."

"What more is there, then?"

"There is still the empty coffin."

This brought them to a stand. Fauchelevent pondered. The prioress pondered.

"Father Fauvent, what shall be done with the coffin?"

"It will be put in the ground."

"Empty?"

Another silence. Fauchelevent made with his left hand that peculiar gesture, which dismisses an unpleasant question.

"Reverend mother, I nail up the coffin in the lower room in the church, and nobody can come in there except me, and I will cover the coffin with the pall."

"Yes, but the bearers, in putting it into the hearse and in letting it down into the grave, will surely perceive that there is nothing inside."

"Ah! the de——!" exclaimed Fauchelevent.

The prioress began to cross herself, and looked fixedly at the gardener. *Vil* stuck in his throat.

He made haste to think of an expedient to make her forget the oath.

"Reverend mother, I will put some earth into the coffin. That will have the effect of a body."

"You are right. Earth is the same thing as man. So you will prepare the empty coffin?"

"I will attend to that."

The face of the prioress, till then dark and anxious, became again serene. She made him the sign of a superior dismissing an inferior. Fauchelevent moved towards the door. As he was going out, the prioress gently raised her voice.

"Father Fauvent, I am satisfied with you; to-morrow after the burial, bring your brother to me, and tell him to bring his daughter."

IV

IN WHICH JEAN VALJEAN HAS QUITE THE APPEARANCE OF HAVING READ AUSTIN CASTILLEJO

THE strides of the lame are like the glances of the one-eyed: they do not speedily reach their aim. Furthermore, Fauchelevent was perplexed. It took him nearly a quarter of an hour to get back to the shanty in the garden. Cosette was awake. Jean Valjean had seated her near the fire. At the moment when Fauchelevent entered, Jean Valjean was showing her the gardener's basket hanging on the wall and saying to her:

"Listen attentively to me, my little Cosette. We must go away from this house, but we shall come back, and we shall be very well off here. The good man here will carry you out on his back inside there. You will wait for me at a lady's. I shall come and find you. Above all, if you do not want the Thénardiess to take you back, obey and say nothing."

Cosette nodded her head with a serious look.

At the sound of Fauchelevent opening the door, Jean Valjean turned.

"Well?"

"All is arranged, and nothing is," said Fauchelevent. "I have permission to bring you in; but before bringing you in, it is necessary to get you out. That is where the cart is blocked! For the little girl, it is easy enough."

"You will carry her out?"

"And she will keep quiet?"

"I will answer for it."

"But you, Father Madeleine?"

And, after an anxious silence, Fauchelevent exclaimed:

"But why not go out the way you came in?"

Jean Valjean, as before, merely answered: "Impossible."

Fauchelevent, talking more to himself than to Jean Valjean, grumbled:

"There is another thing that torments me. I said I would put in some earth. But I think that earth inside, instead of a body, will not be like it; that will not do, it will shake about; it will move. The men will feel it. You understand, Father Madeleine, the government will find it out."

Jean Valjean stared at him, and thought that he was raving.

Fauchelevent resumed:

"How the d—ickens are you going to get out? For all this must be done to-morrow. To-morrow I am to bring you in. The prioress expects you."

Then he explained to Jean Valjean that this was a reward for a service that he, Fauchelevent, was rendering to the community. That it was a part of his duties to assist in burials, that he nailed up the coffins, and attended the gravedigger at the cemetery. That the nun who died that morning had requested to be buried in the coffin which she had used as a bed, and interred in the vault under the altar of the chapel. That this was forbidden by the regulations of the police, but that she was one of those departed ones to whom nothing is refused. That the prioress and the vocal mothers intended to carry out the will of the deceased. So much the worse for the government. That he, Fauchelevent, would nail up the coffin in the cell, raise the stone in the chapel, and let down the body into the vault. And that, in return for this, the prioress would admit his brother into the house as gardener and his niece as boarder. That his brother was M. Madeleine, and that his niece was Cosette. That the prioress had told him to bring his brother the next evening, after the fictitious burial at the cemetery. But that he could not bring M. Madeleine from the outside, if M. Madeleine were not outside. That that was the first difficulty. And then that he had another difficulty; the empty coffin.

"What is the empty coffin?" asked Jean Valjean.

Fauchelevent responded:

"The coffin from the administration."

"What coffin? and what administration?"

"A nun dies. The municipality physician comes and says: there is a nun dead. The government sends a coffin. The next day it sends a hearse and some bearers to take the coffin and carry it to the cemetery. The bearers will come and take up the coffin; there will be nothing in it."

"Put somebody in it."

"A dead body? I have none."

"No."

"What then?"

"A living body."

"What living body?"

"Me," said Jean Valjean.

Fauchelevent, who had taken a seat, sprang up as if a cracker had burst under his chair.

"You!"

"Why not?"

Jean Valjean had one of those rare smiles which came over him like the aurora in a winter sky.

"You know, Fauchelevent, that you said: Mother Crucifix-ion is dead, and that I added: and Father Madeleine is buried. It will be so."

"Ah! good, you are laughing, you are not talking seriously."

"Very seriously. I must get out!"

"Undoubtedly."

"And I told you to find a basket and a cover for me also."

"Well!"

"The basket will be of pine, and the cover will be of black cloth."

"In the first place, a white cloth. The nuns are buried in white."

"Well, a white cloth."

"You are not like other men, Father Madeleine."

To see such devices, which are nothing more than the savage and foolhardy inventions of the galleys, appear in the midst of the peaceful things that surrounded him and mingled with what he called the "little jog-jog of the convent" was to Fauchelevent an astonishment comparable to that of a person who should see a seamew fishing in the brook in the Rue St. Denis.

Jean Valjean continued:

"The question is, how to get out without being seen. This is the means. But in the first place tell me, how is it done? where is this coffin?"

"The empty one?"

"Yes."

"Down in what is called the dead-room. It is on two trestles and under the pall."

"What is the length of the coffin?"

"Six feet."

"What is the dead-room?"

"It is a room on the ground floor, with a grated window towards the garden, closed on the outside with a shutter, and two doors; one leading to the convent, the other to the church."

"What church?"

"The church on the street, the church for everybody."

"Have you the keys of those two doors?"

"No. I have the key of the door that opens into the convent; the porter has the key of the door that opens into the church."

"When does the porter open that door?"

"Only to let in the bearers, who come after the coffin; as soon as the coffin goes out, the door is closed again."

"Who nails up the coffin?"

"I do."

"Who puts the cloth on it?"

"I do."

"Are you alone?"

"No other man, except the police physician, can enter the dead-room. That is even written upon the wall."

"Could you, to-night, when all are asleep in the convent, hide me in that room?"

"No. But I can hide you in a little dark closet which opens into the dead-room, where I keep my burial tools, and of which I have the care and the key."

"At what hour will the hearse come after the coffin to-morrow?"

"About three o'clock in the afternoon. The burial takes place at the Vaugirard cemetery, a little before night. It is not very near."

"I shall remain hidden in your tool-closet all night and all the morning. And about eating? I shall be hungry."

"I will bring you something."

"You can come and nail me up in the coffin at two o'clock."

Fauchelevent started back, and began to snap his fingers.

"But it is impossible!"

"Pshaw! to take a hammer and drive some nails into a board?"

What seemed unheard-of to Fauchelevent was, we repeat, simple to Jean Valjean. Jean Valjean had been in worse straits. He who has been a prisoner knows the art of making himself small acording to the dimensions of the place for escape. The prisoner is subject to flight as the sick man is to the crisis which cures or kills him. An escape is a cure. What does not one undergo to be cured? To be nailed up and carried out in a chest like a bundle, to live a long time in a box, to find air where there is none, to economise the breath for entire hours, to know how to be stifled without dying—that was one of the gloomy talents of Jean Valjean.

Moreover, a coffin in which there is a living being, that convict's expedient, is also an emperor's expedient. If we can believe the monk Austin Castillejo, this was the means which Charles V., desiring after his abdication to see La Plombes again a last time, employed to bring her into the monastery of St. Juste and to take her out again.

Fauchelevent, recovering a little, exclaimed:

"But how will you manage to breathe?"

"I shall breathe."

"In that box? Only to think of it suffocates me."

"You surely have a gimlet, you can make a few little holes about the mouth here and there, and you can nail it without drawing the upper board tight."

"Good! But if you happen to cough or sneeze?"

"He who is escaping never coughs and never sneezes."

And Jean Valjean added:

"Father Fauchelevent, I must decide: either to be taken here, or to be willing to go out in the hearse."

Everybody has noticed the taste which cats have for stopping and loitering in a half-open door. Who has not said to a cat: Why don't you come in? There are men who, with an opportunity half-open before them, have a similar tendency to remain undecided between two resolutions, at the risk of being crushed by destiny abruptly closing the opportunity. The over prudent, cats as they are, and because they are cats, sometimes run more danger than the bold. Fauchelevent was of this hesitating nature. However, Jean Valjean's coolness won him over in spite of himself. He grumbled:

"It is true, there is no other way."

Jean Valjean resumed:

"The only thing that I am anxious about, is what will be done at the cemetery."

"That is just what does not embarrass me," exclaimed Fauchelevent. "If you are sure of getting yourself out of the coffin, I am sure of getting you out of the grave. The grave-

digger is a drunkard and a friend of mine. He is Father Mestienne. An old son of the old vine. The gravedigger puts the dead
in the grave, and I put the gravedigger in my pocket. I will tell
you what will take place. We shall arrive a little before dusk,
three-quarters of an hour before the cemetery gates are closed.
The hearse will go to the grave. I shall follow: that is my business. I will have a hammer, a chisel, and some pincers in my
pocket. The hearse stops, the bearers tie a rope around your
coffin and let you down. The priest says the prayers, makes the
sign of the cross, sprinkles the holy water, and is off. I remain
alone with Father Mestienne. He is my friend, I tell you. One
of two things; either he will be drunk, or he will not be drunk.
If he is not drunk, I say to him: come and take a drink before
the *Good Quince* is shut. I get him away, I fuddle him; Father
Mestienne is not long in getting fuddled, he is always half way.
I lay him under the table, I take his card from him to return to
the cemetery with! and I come back without him. You will have
only me to deal with. If he is drunk, I say to him: be off. I'll do
your work. He goes away, and I pull you out of the hole."

Jean Valjean extended his hand, upon which Fauchelevent
threw himself with a rustic outburst of touching devotion.

"It is settled, Father Fauchelevent. All will go well."

"Provided nothing goes amiss," thought Fauchelevent.
"How terrible that would be!"

V

IT IS NOT ENOUGH TO BE A DRUNKARD
TO BE IMMORTAL

NEXT day, as the sun was declining, the scattered passers on the
Boulevard du Maine took off their hats at the passage of an old-
fashioned hearse, adorned with death's-heads, cross-bones, and
tear-drops. In this hearse there was a coffin covered with a white
cloth upon which was displayed a large black cross like a great
dummy with hanging arms. A draped carriage, in which might
be seen a priest in a surplice, and a choir-boy in a red calotte,
followed. Two bearers in grey uniform with black trimmings
walked on the right and left of the hearse. In the rear came an
old man dressed like a labourer, who limped. The procession
moved towards the Vaugirard cemetery.

Sticking out of the man's pocket were the handle of a

hammer, the blade of a cold chisel, and the double handles of a pair of pincers.

The Vaugirard cemetery was an exception among the cemeteries of Paris. It had its peculiar usages, so far that it had its porte-cochère, and its small door which, in the quarter, old people tenacious of old words, called the cavalier door, and the pedestrian door. The Bernardine-Benedictines of the Petit Picpus had obtained the right, as we have said, to be buried in a corner apart and at night, this ground having formerly belonged to their community. The gravediggers, having thus to work in the cemetery in the evening in summer, and at night in winter, were subject to a peculiar discipline. The gates of the cemeteries of Paris closed at that epoch at sunset, and, this being a measure of municipal order, the Vaugirard cemetery was subject to it like the rest. The cavalier door and the pedestrian door were two contiguous gratings; near which was a pavilion built by the architect Perronet, in which the door-keeper of the cemetery lived. These gratings therefore inexorably turned upon their hinges the instant the sun disappeared behind the dome of the Invalides. If any gravedigger, at that moment, was belated in the cemetery his only resource for getting out was his gravedigger's card, given him by the administration of funeral ceremonies. A sort of letter-box was arranged in the shutter of the gate-keeper's window. The gravedigger dropped his card into this box, the gate-keeper heard it fall, pulled the string, and the pedestrian door opened. If the gravedigger did not have his card, he gave his name; the gate-keeper, sometimes in bed and asleep, got up, went to identify the gravedigger, and open the door with the key; the gravedigger went out, but paid fifteen francs fine.

This cemetery, with its peculiarities over breaking the rules, disturbed the symmetry of the administration. It was suppressed shortly after 1830. The Mont Parnasse Cemetery, called the Cemetery of the East, has succeeded it, and has inherited this famous drinking house let into the Vaugirard cemetery, which was surmounted by a quince painted on a board, which looked on one side upon the tables of the drinkers, and on the other upon graves, with this inscription: *The Good Quince.*

The Vaugirard cemetery was what might be called a decayed cemetery. It was falling into disuse. Mould was invading it, flowers were leaving it. The well-to-do citizens little cared to be buried at Vaugirard; it sounded poor. Père Lachaise is very fine!

to be buried in Père Lachaise is like having mahogany furniture. Elegance is understood by that. The Vaugirard cemetery was a venerable inclosure, laid out like an old French garden. Straight walks, box, evergreens, hollies, old tombs under old yews, very high grass. Night there was terrible. There were some very dismal outlines there.

The sun had not yet set when the hearse with the white pall and the black cross entered the avenue of the Vaugirard cemetery. The lame man who followed it was no other than Fauchelevent.

The burial of Mother Crucifixion in the vault under the altar, the departure of Cosette, the introduction of Jean Valjean into the dead-room, all had been carried out without obstruction, and nothing had gone wrong.

We will say, by the way, the inhumation of Mother Crucifixion under the convent altar is, to us, a perfectly venial thing. It is one of those faults which resemble a duty. The nuns had accomplished it, not only without discomposure, but with an approving conscience. In the cloister, what is called the "government" is only an interference with authority, an interference which is always questionable. First the rules; as to the code, we will see. Men, make as many laws as you please, but keep them for yourselves. The tribute to Cæsar is never more than the remnant of the tribute to God. A prince is nothing in presence of a principle.

Fauchelevent limped behind the hearse, very well satisfied. His two twin plots, one with the nuns, the other with M. Madeleine, one for the convent, the other against it, had succeeded equally well. Jean Valjean's calmness had that powerful tranquillity which is contagious. Fauchelevent had now no doubt of success. What remained to be done was nothing. Within two years he had fuddled the gravedigger ten times, good Father Mestienne, a rubicund old fellow. Father Mestienne was play for him. He did what he liked with him. He got him drunk at will and at his fancy. Mestienne saw through Fauchelevent's eyes. Fauchelevent's security was complete.

At the moment the convoy entered the avenue leading to the cemetery, Fauchelevent, happy, looked at the hearse and rubbed his big hands together, saying in an undertone:

"Here's a farce!"

Suddenly the hearse stopped; they were at the gate. It was

necessary to exhibit the burial permit. The undertaker whispered with the porter of the cemetery. During this colloquy, which always causes a delay of a minute or two, somebody, an unknown man, came and placed himself behind the hearse at Fauchelevent's side. He was a working-man, who wore a vest with large pockets, and had a pick under his arm.

Fauchelevent looked at this unknown man.

"Who are you?" he asked.

The man answered:

"The gravedigger."

Should a man survive a cannon-shot through his breast, he would present the appearance that Fauchelevent did.

"The gravedigger?"

"Yes."

"You!"

"Me."

"The gravedigger is Father Mestienne."

"He was."

"How! he was?"

"He is dead."

Fauchelevent was ready for anything but this, that a gravedigger could die. It is, however, true; gravediggers themselves die. By dint of digging graves for others, they open their own.

Fauchelevent remained speechless. He had hardly the strength to stammer out:

"But it's not possible!"

"It is so."

"But," repeated he, feebly, "the gravedigger is Father Mestienne."

"After Napoleon, Louis XVIII. After Mestienne, Gribier. Peasant, my name is Gribier."

Fauchelevent grew pale; he stared at Gribier.

He was a long, thin, livid man, perfectly funereal. He had the appearance of a broken-down doctor turned gravedigger.

Fauchelevent burst out laughing.

"Ah! what droll things happen! Father Mestienne is dead. Little Father Mestienne is dead, but hurrah for little Father Lenoir! You know what little Father Lenoir is? It is the mug of red for a six spot. It is the mug of Surêne, zounds! real Paris Surêne. So he is dead, old Mestienne! I am sorry for it; he was a jolly fellow. But you too, you are a jolly fellow. Isn't that so, comrade? we will go and take a drink together, right away."

The man answered: "I have studied, I have graduated. I never drink."

The hearse had started, and was rolling along the main avenue of the cemetery.

Fauchelevent had slackened his pace. He limped still more from anxiety than from infirmity.

The gravedigger walked before him.

Fauchelevent again scrutinised the unexpected Gribier.

He was one of those men who, though young, have an old appearance, and who, though thin, are very strong.

"Comrade!" cried Fauchelevent.

The man turned.

"I am the gravedigger of the convent."

"My colleague," said the man.

Fauchelevent, illiterate, but very keen, understood that he had to do with a very formidable species, a good talker.

He mumbled out:

"Is it so, Father Mestienne is dead?"

The man answered:

"Perfectly. The good God consulted his list of bills payable. It was Father Mestienne's turn. Father Mestienne is dead."

Fauchelevent repeated mechanically:

"The good God."

"The good God," said the man authoritatively. "What the philosophers call the Eternal Father; the Jacobins, the Supreme Being."

"Are we not going to make each other's acquaintance?" stammered Fauchelevent.

"It is made. You are a peasant, I am a Parisian."

"We are not acquainted as long as we have not drunk together. He who empties his glass empties his heart. Come and drink with me. You can't refuse."

"Business first."

Fauchelevent said to himself: I am lost.

They were now only a few rods from the path that led to the nuns' corner.

The gravedigger continued:

"Peasant, I have seven youngsters that I must feed. As they must eat, I must not drink."

And he added with the satisfaction of a serious being who is making a sententious phrase:

"Their hunger is the enemy of my thirst."

The hearse turned a huge cypress, left the main path, took a little one, entered upon the grounds, and was lost in a thicket. This indicated the immediate proximity of the grave. Fauchelevent slackened his pace, but could not slacken that of the hearse. Luckily the mellow soil, wet by the winter rains, stuck to the wheels, and made the track heavy.

He approached the gravedigger.

"They have such a good little Argenteuil wine," suggested Fauchelevent.

"Villager," continued the man, "I ought not to be a gravedigger. My father was porter at the Prytanée. He intended me for literature. But he was unfortunate. He met with losses at the Bourse, I was obliged to renounce the condition of an author. However, I am still a public scribe."

"But then you are not the gravedigger?" replied Fauchelevent, catching at a straw, feeble as it was.

"One does not prevent the other. I cumulate."

Fauchelevent did not understand this last word.

"Let us go and drink," said he.

Here an observation is necessary. Fauchelevent, whatever was his anguish, proposed to drink, but did not explain himself on one point; who should pay? Ordinarily Fauchelevent proposed, and Father Mestienne paid. A proposal to drink resulted evidently from the new situation produced by the fact of the new gravedigger, and this proposal he must make; but the old gardener left, not unintentionally, the proverbial quarter of an hour of Rabelais in the shade. As for him, Fauchelevent, however excited he was, he did not care about paying.

The gravedigger went on, with a smile of superiority:

"We must live. I accepted the succession of Father Mestienne. When one has almost finished his classes, he is a philosopher. To the labour of my hand, I have added the labour of my arm. I have my little writer's shop at the Market in the Rue de Sèvre. You know? the market of the Parapluies. All the cooks of the Croix Rouge come to me; I patch up their declarations to their true loves. In the morning I write love letters; in the evening I dig graves. Such is life, countryman."

The hearse advanced; Fauchelevent, full of anxiety, looked

about him on all sides. Great drops of sweat were falling from his forehead.

"However," continued the gravedigger, "one cannot serve two mistresses; I must choose between the pen and the pick. The pick hurts my hand."

The hearse stopped.

The choir-boy got out of the mourning carriage, then the priest.

One of the forward wheels of the hearse mounted on a little heap of earth, beyond which was seen an open grave.

"Here is a farce!" repeated Fauchelevent in consternation.

VI

IN THE NARROW HOUSE

WHO was in the coffin? We know. Jean Valjean.

Jean Valjean had arranged it so that he could live in it, and could breathe a very little.

It is a strange thing to what extent an easy conscience gives calmness in other respects. The entire combination pre-arranged by Jean Valjean had been executed, and executed well, since the night before. He counted, as did Fauchelevent, upon Father Mestienne. He had no doubt of the result. Never was a situation more critical, never calmness more complete.

The four boards of the coffin exhaled a kind of terrible peace. It seemed as if something of the repose of the dead had entered into the tranquillity of Jean Valjean.

From within that coffin he had been able to follow, and he had followed, all the phases of the fearful drama which he was playing with Death.

Soon after Fauchelevent had finished nailing down the upper board, Jean Valjean had felt himself carried out, then wheeled along. By the diminished jolting, he had felt that he was passing from the pavement to the hard ground; that is to say, that he was leaving the streets and entering upon the boulevards. By a dull sound, he had divined that they were crossing the bridge of Austerlitz. At the first stop he had comprehended that they were entering the cemetery; at the second stop he had said: here is the grave.

He felt that hands hastily seized the coffin, then a harsh scraping upon the boards; he concluded that that was a rope which they were tying around the coffin to let it down into the excavation.

Then he felt a kind of dizziness.

Probably the bearer and the gravedigger had tipped the coffin and let the head down before the feet. He returned fully to himself on feeling that he was horizontal and motionless. He had touched the bottom.

He felt a certain chill.

A voice arose above him, icy and solemn. He heard pass away, some Latin words which he did not understand, pronounced so slowly that he could catch them one after another:

"*Qui dormiunt in terræ pulvere, evigilabunt; alii in vitam æternam, et alii in opprobrium, ut videant semper.*"

A child's voice said:

"*De profundis.*"

The deep voice recommenced:

"*Requiem æternam dona ei, Domine.*"

The child's voice responded:

"*Et lux perpetua luceat ei.*"

He heard upon the board which covered him something like the gentle patter of a few drops of rain. It was probably the holy water.

He thought: "This will soon be finished. A little more patience. The priest is going away. Fauchelevent will take Mestienne away to drink. They will leave me. Then Fauchelevent will come back alone, and I shall get out. That will take a good hour."

The deep voice resumed.

"*Requiescat in pace.*"

And the child's voice said:

"*Amen.*"

Jean Valjean, intently listening, perceived something like receding steps.

"Now there they go," thought he. "I am alone."

All at once he heard a sound above his head which seemed to him like a clap of thunder.

It was a spadeful of earth falling upon the coffin.

A second spadeful of earth fell.

One of the holes by which he breathed was stopped up.

A third spadeful of earth fell.

Then a fourth.

There are things stronger than the strongest man. Jean Valjean lost consciousness.

VII
IN WHICH WILL BE FOUND THE ORIGIN OF THE SAYING: DON'T LOSE YOUR CARD

LET us see what occurred over the coffin in which Jean Valjean lay.

When the hearse had departed and the priest and the choir-boy had got into the carriage, and were gone, Fauchelevent, who had never taken his eyes off the gravedigger, saw him stoop, and grasp his spade, which was standing upright in the heap of earth.

Hereupon, Fauchelevent formed a supreme resolve.

Placing himself between the grave and the gravedigger, and folding his arms, he said:

"I'll pay for it!"

The gravedigger eyed him with amazement, and replied:

"What, peasant?"

Fauchelevent repeated:

"I'll pay for it!"

"For what?"

"For the wine."

"What wine?"

"The Argenteuil."

"Where's the Argenteuil?"

"At the Good Quince."

"Go to the devil!" said the gravedigger.

And he threw a spadeful of earth upon the coffin.

The coffin gave back a hollow sound. Fauchelevent felt himself stagger, and nearly fell into the grave. In a voice in which the strangling sound of the death-rattle began to be heard he cried:

"Come, comrade, before the Good Quince closes!"

The gravedigger took up another spadeful of earth. Fauchelevent continued:

"I'll pay," and he seized the gravedigger by the arm.

"Hark ye, comrade," he said, "I am the gravedigger of the convent, and have come to help you. It's a job we can do at night. Let us take a drink first."

And as he spoke, even while clinging desperately to this urgent effort, he asked himself, with some misgiving: "And even should he drink—will he get tipsy?"

"Good rustic," said the gravedigger, "if you insist, I consent. We'll have a drink, but after my work, never before it."

And he tossed his spade again. Fauchelevent held him.

"It is Argenteuil at six sous the pint!"

"Ah, bah!" said the gravedigger, "you're a bore. Ding-dong, ding-dong, the same thing over and over again; that's all you can say. Be off, about your business."

And he threw in the second spadeful.

Fauchelevent had reached that point where a man knows no longer what he is saying.

"Oh! come on, and take a glass, since I'm the one to pay," he again repeated.

"When we've put the child to bed," said the gravedigger.

He tossed in the third spadeful: then, plunging his spade into the earth, he added:

"You see, now, it's going to be cold to-night, and the dead one would cry out after us, if we were to plant her there without good covering."

At this moment, in the act of filling his spade, the gravedigger stooped low and the pocket of his vest gaped open.

The bewildered eye of Fauchelevent rested mechanically on this pocket, and remained fixed.

The sun was not yet hidden behind the horizon, and there was still light enough to distinguish something white in the gaping pocket.

All the lightning which the eye of a Picardy peasant can contain flashed into the pupils of Fauchelevent. A new idea had struck him.

Without the gravedigger, who was occupied with his spadeful of earth, perceiving him, he slipped his hand from behind into the pocket, and took from him the white object it contained.

The gravedigger flung into the grave the fourth spadeful.

Just as he was turning to take the fifth, Fauchelevent, looking at him with imperturbable calmness, asked:

"By the way, my new friend, have you your card?"

The gravedigger stopped.

"What card?"

"The sun is setting."

"Well, let him put on his night-cap."

"The cemetery-gate will be closed."

"Well, what then?"

"Have you your card?"

"Oh! my card!" said the gravedigger, and he felt in his pocket.

Having rummaged one pocket, he tried another. From these, he proceeded to try his watch-fobs, exploring the first, and turning the second inside out.

"No!" said he, "no! I haven't got my card. I must have forgotten it."

"Fifteen francs fine!" said Fauchelevent.

The gravedigger turned green. Green is the paleness of people naturally livid.

"Oh, good-gracious God, what a fool I am!" he exclaimed. "Fifteen francs fine!"

"Three hundred-sou pieces," said Fauchelevent.

The gravedigger dropped his spade.

Fauchelevent's turn had come.

"Come! come, recruit," said Fauchelevent, "never despair; there's nothing to kill oneself about, and feed the worms. Fifteen francs are fifteen francs, and besides, you may not have them to pay. I am an old hand, and you a new one. I know all the tricks and traps and turns and twists of the business. I'll give you a friend's advice. One thing is clear—the sun is setting—and the graveyard will be closed in five minutes."

"That's true," replied the gravedigger.

"Five minutes is not time enough for you to fill the grave—it's as deep as the very devil—and get out of this before the gate is shut."

"You're right."

"In that case, there is fifteen francs fine."

"Fifteen francs!"

"But you have time. . . . Where do you live?"

"Just by the barrière. Fifteen minutes' walk. Number 87 Rue de Vaugirard."

"You have time, if you will hang your toggery about your neck, to get out at once."

"That's true."

"Once outside of the gate, you scamper home, get your card,

come back, and the gatekeeper will let you in again. Having your card, there's nothing to pay. Then you can bury your dead man. I'll stay here, and watch him while you're gone, to see that he doesn't run away."

"I owe you my life, peasant!"

"Be off, then, quick!" said Fauchelevent.

The gravedigger, overcome with gratitude, shook his hands, and started at a run.

When the gravedigger had disappeared through the bushes, Fauchelevent listened until his footsteps died away, and then, bending over the grave, called out in a low voice:

"Father Madeleine!"

No answer.

Fauchelevent shuddered. He dropped rather than clambered down into the grave, threw himself upon the head of the coffin, and cried out:

"Are you there?"

Silence in the coffin.

Fauchelevent, no longer able to breathe for the shiver that was on him, took his cold chisel and hammer, and wrenched off the top board. The face of Jean Valjean could be seen in the twilight, his eyes closed and his cheeks colourless.

Fauchelevent's hair stood erect with alarm; he rose to his feet, and then tottered with his back against the side of the grave, ready to sink down upon the coffin. He looked upon Jean Valjean.

Jean Valjean lay there pallid and motionless.

Fauchelevent murmured in a voice low as a whisper:

"He is dead!"

Then straightening himself, and crossing his arms so violently that his clenched fists sounded against his shoulders, he exclaimed:

"This is the way I have saved him!"

Then the poor old man began to sob, talking aloud to himself the while, for it is a mistake to think that talking to one's self is not natural. Powerful emotions often speak aloud.

"It's Father Mestienne's fault. What did he die for, the fool? What was the use of going off in that way, just when no one expected it? It was he who killed poor M. Madeleine. Father Madeleine! He is in the coffin. He's settled. There's an end of it. Now, what's the sense of such things? Good God! he's dead!

Yes, and his little girl—what am I to do with her? What will the fruit-woman say? That such a man could die in that way. Good Heaven, is it possible! When I think that he put himself under my cart! ... Father Madeleine! Father Madeleine! Mercy, he's suffocated, I said so—but, he wouldn't believe me. Now, here's a pretty piece of business! He's dead—one of the very best men God ever made; aye, the best, the very best! And his little girl! I'm not going back there again. I'm going to stay here. To have done such a thing as this! It's well worth while to be two old greybeards, in order to be two old fools. But, to begin with, how did he manage to get into the convent—that's where it started. Such things shouldn't be done. Father Madeleine! Father Madeleine! Father Madeleine! Madeleine! Monsieur Madeleine! Monsieur Mayor! He doesn't hear me. Get yourself out of this now, if you please."

And he tore his hair.

At a distance, through the trees, a harsh grating sound was heard. It was the gate of the cemetery closing.

Fauchelevent again bent over Jean Valjean, but suddenly started back with all the recoil that was possible in a grave. Jean Valjean's eyes were open, and gazing at him.

To behold death is terrifying, and to see a sudden restoration is nearly as much so. Fauchelevent became cold and white as a stone, haggard and utterly disconcerted by all these powerful emotions, and not knowing whether he had the dead or the living to deal with, stared at Jean Valjean, who in turn stared at him.

"I was falling asleep," said Jean Valjean.

And he rose to a sitting posture.

Fauchelevent dropped on his knees.

"Oh, blessed Virgin! How you frightened me!"

Then, springing again to his feet, he cried:

"Thank you, Father Madeleine!"

Jean Valjean had merely swooned. The open air had revived him.

Joy is the reflex of terror. Fauchelevent had nearly as much difficulty as Jean Valjean in coming to himself.

"Then you're not dead! Oh, what good sense you have! I called you so loudly that you got over it. When I saw you with your eyes shut, I said, 'Well, there now! he's suffocated!' I should have gone raving mad—mad enough for a strait-jacket. They'd have put me in the Bicêtre. What would you have had me do, if you had been dead? And your little girl! the fruit-woman would have understood nothing about it! A child plumped into her lap, and its grandfather dead! What a story to tell! By all the saints in heaven, what a story! Ah! but you're alive—that's the best of it."

"I am cold," said Jean Valjean.

These words recalled Fauchelevent completely to the real state of affairs, which were urgent. These two men, even when restored, felt without knowing it, a peculiar agitation and a strange inward trouble, which was but the sinister bewilderment of the place.

"Let us get away from here at once," said Fauchelevent.

He thrust his hand into his pocket, and drew from it a flask with which he was provided.

"But a drop of this first!" said he.

The flask completed what the open air had begun. Jean Valjean took a swallow of brandy, and felt thoroughly restored.

He got out of the coffin, and assisted Fauchelevent to nail down the lid again. Three minutes afterwards, they were out of the grave.

After this, Fauchelevent was calm enough. He took his time. The cemetery was closed. There was no fear of the return of Gribier the gravedigger. That recruit was at home, hunting up his "card," and rather unlikely to find it, as it was in Fauchelevent's pocket. Without his card, he could not get back into the cemetery.

Fauchelevent took the spade and Jean Valjean the pick, and together they buried the empty coffin.

When the grave was filled, Fauchelevent said to Jean Valjean: "Come, let us go; I'll keep the spade, and you take the pick."

Night was coming on rapidly.

Jean Valjean found it hard to move and walk. In the coffin he had stiffened considerably, somewhat in reality like a corpse. The anchylosis of death had seized him in that narrow wooden box. He had, in some sort, to thaw himself out of the sepulchre.

"You are benumbed," said Fauchelevent; "and what a pity that I'm bandy-legged, or we'd run a bit."

"No matter!" replied Jean Valjean, "a few steps will put my legs into walking order."

They went out by the avenues the hearse had followed.

When they reached the closed gate and the porter's lodge, Fauchelevent, who had the gravedigger's card in his hand, dropped it into the box, the porter drew the cord, the gate opened, and they went through.

"How well everything goes!" said Fauchelevent; "what a good plan that was of yours, Father Madeleine!"

They passed the Barrière Vaugirard in the easiest way in the world. In the neighbourhood of a graveyard, a pick and spade are two passports.

The Rue de Vaugirard was deserted.

"Father Madeleine," said Fauchelevent, as he went along, looking up at the houses, "you have better eyes than mine—which is number 87?"

"Here it is, now," said Jean Valjean.

"There's no one in the street," resumed Fauchelevent. "Give me the pick, and wait for me a couple of minutes."

Fauchelevent went in at number 87, ascended to the topmost flight, guided by the instinct which always leads the poor to the garret, and knocked, in the dark, at the door of a little attic room. A voice called:

"Come in!"

It was Gribier's voice.

Fauchelevent pushed open the door. The lodging of the gravedigger was, like all these shelters of the needy, an unfurnished but much littered loft. A packing-case of some kind—a coffin, perhaps—supplied the place of a bureau, a straw pallet the place of a bed, a butter-pot the place of a water-cooler, and the floor served alike for chairs and table. In one corner, on a ragged old scrap of carpet, was a haggard woman, and a number of children were huddled together. The whole of this wretched interior bore the traces of recent overturn. One would have said that there had been an earthquake served up there "for one." The coverlets were displaced, the ragged garments scattered about, the pitcher broken, the mother had been weeping, and the children probably beaten; all traces of a headlong and violent search. It was plain that the gravedigger had been looking, wildly, for his card, and had made everything in the attic, from his pitcher to his wife, responsible for the loss. He had a desperate appearance.

But Fauchelevent was in too great a hurry for the end of his adventure, to notice this gloomy side of his triumph.

As he came in, he said:

"I've brought your spade and pick."

Gribier looked at him with stupefaction.

"What, it is you, peasant?"

"And, to-morrow morning, you will find your card with the gate-keeper of the cemetery."

And he set down the pick and the spade on the floor.

"What does all this mean?" asked Gribier.

"Why, it means that you let your card drop out of your pocket; that I found it on the ground when you had gone; that I buried the corpse; that I filled in the grave; that I finished your job; that the porter will give you your card, and that you will not have to pay the fifteen francs. That's what it means, recruit!"

"Thanks, villager!" exclaimed Gribier in amazement. "The next time I will treat."

VIII
SUCCESSFUL EXAMINATION

An hour later, in the depth of night, two men and a child stood in front of No. 62, Petite Rue Picpus. The elder of the men lifted the knocker and rapped.

It was Fauchelevent, Jean Valjean, and Cosette.

The two men had gone to look for Cosette at the shop of the fruiteress of the Rue de Chemin Vert, where Fauchelevent had left her on the preceding evening. Cosette had passed the twenty-four hours wondering what it all meant and trembling in silence. She trembled so much that she had not wept, nor had she tasted food nor slept. The worthy fruit-woman had asked her a thousand questions without obtaining any other answer than a sad look that never varied. Cosette did not let a word of all she had heard and seen, in the last two days, escape her. She divined that a crisis had come. She felt, in her very heart, that she must be "good." Who has not experienced the supreme effect of these two words pronounced in a certain tone in the ear of some little frightened creature, "Don't speak!" Fear is mute. Besides, no one ever keeps a secret so well as a child.

But when, after those mournful four-and-twenty hours, she again saw Jean Valjean, she uttered such a cry of joy that any thoughtful person hearing her would have divined in it an escape from some yawning gulf.

Fauchelevent belonged to the convent and knew all the pass-words. Every door opened before him.

Thus was that doubly fearful problem solved of getting out and getting in again.

The porter, who had his instructions, opened the little side door which served to communicate between the court and the garden, and which, twenty years ago, could still be seen from the street, in the wall at the extremity of the court, facing the porte-cochère. The porter admitted all three by this door, and from that point they went to this private inner parlour, where Fauchelevent had, on the previous evening, received the orders of the prioress.

The prioress, rosary in hand, was awaiting them. A mother, with her veil down, stood near her. A modest taper lighted, or one might almost say, pretended to light up the parlour.

The prioress scrutinised Jean Valjean. Nothing scans so care-fully as a downcast eye.

Then she proceeded to question:

"You are the brother?"

"Yes, reverend mother," replied Fauchelevent.

"What is your name?"

Fauchelevent replied:

"Ultimus Fauchelevent!"

He had, in reality, had a brother named Ultimus, who was dead.

"From what part of the country are you?"

Fauchelevent answered:

"From Picquigny, near Amiens."

"What is your age?"

Fauchelevent answered:

"Fifty."

"What is your business?"

Fauchelevent answered:

"Gardener."

"Are you a true Christian?"

Fauchelevent answered:

"All of our family are such."

"Is this your little girl?"

Fauchelevent answered:

"Yes, reverend mother."

"You are her father?"

Fauchelevent answered:

"Her grandfather."

The mother said to the prioress in an undertone:

"He answers well."

Jean Valjean had not spoken a word.

The prioress looked at Cosette attentively, and then said, aside to the mother——

"She will be homely."

The two mothers talked together very low for a few minutes in a corner of the parlour, and then the prioress turned and said——

"Father Fauvent, you will have another knee-cap and bell. We need two, now."

So, next morning, two little bells were heard tinkling in the garden and the nuns could not keep from lifting a corner of their veils. They saw two men digging side by side, in the lower part of the garden under the trees—Fauvent and another. Immense event! The silence was broken, so far as to say——

"It's an assistant-gardener!"

The mothers added:

"He is Father Fauvent's brother."

In fact, Jean Valjean was regularly installed; he had the leather knee-cap and the bell; henceforth he had his commission. His name was Ultimus Fauchelevent.

The strongest recommendation for Cosette's admission had been the remark of the prioress: *She will be homely.*

The prioress having uttered this prediction, immediately took Cosette into her friendship and gave her a place in the school building as a charity pupil.

There is nothing not entirely logical in this.

It is all in vain to have no mirrors in convents; women are conscious of their own appearance; young girls who know that they are pretty do not readily become nuns; the inclination to the calling being in inverse proportion to good looks, more is expected from the homely than from the handsome ones. Hence a marked preference for the homely.

This whole affair elevated good old Fauchelevent greatly; he had achieved a triple success;—in the eyes of Jean Valjean whom he had rescued and sheltered; with the gravedigger, Gribier, who said he had saved him from a fine; and, at the convent, which, thanks to him, in retaining the coffin of Mother Crucifixion under the altar, eluded Cæsar and satisfied God. There was a coffin with a body in it at the Petit Picpus, and a coffin without a body in the Vaugirard cemetery. Public order was greatly disturbed thereby, undoubtedly, but nobody perceived it. As for the convent, its gratitude to Fauchelevent was deep. Fauchelevent became the best of servants and the most precious of gardeners.

At the next visit of the archbishop the prioress related the affair to his grace, half by way of a confession and half as a boast.

The archbishop, on returning from the convent, spoke of it with commendation and very quietly to M. de Latil, the Confessor of Monsieur, and, subsequently, Archbishop of Rheims and a cardinal. This praise and admiration for Fauchelevent travelled far, for it went to Rome. We have seen a note addressed by the then reigning pope, Leo XII., to one of his relatives, Monsignore of the Papal Embassy at Paris, who bore the same name as his own, Della Genga. It contained these lines: "It seems that there is in a convent in Paris, an excellent gardener who is a holy man, named Fauvent." Not a whisper of all this fame reached Fauchelevent in his shanty; he continued to weed and graft and cover his melon-beds without being, in the least, aware of his excellence and holiness. He had no more suspicion of his splendid reputation than any Durham or Surrey ox whose picture is published in the *London Illustrated News* with this inscription: "*The ox which won the premium at the cattle show.*"

IX
THE CLOSE

COSETTE, at the convent, still kept silent. She very naturally thought herself Jean Valjean's daughter. Moreover, knowing nothing, there was nothing she could tell, and then, in any case, she would not have told anything. As we have remarked, nothing habituates children to silence like misfortune. Cosette had suffered so much that she was afraid of everything, even to speak, even to breathe. A single word had so often brought down an avalanche on her head! She had hardly begun to feel re-assured since she had been with Jean Valjean. She soon became accustomed to the convent. Still, she longed for Catharine, but dared not say so. One day, however, she said to Jean Valjean, "If I had known it, father, I would have brought her with me."

Cosette, in becoming a pupil at the convent, had to assume the dress of the school girls. Jean Valjean succeeded in having the garments which she laid aside given to him. It was the same mourning suit he had carried for her to put on when she left the Thénardiers. It was not much worn. Jean Valjean rolled up these garments, as well as the woollen stockings and shoes, with much camphor and other aromatic substances of which there is such an abundance in convents, and packed them in a small valise which he managed to procure. He put this valise in a chair near his bed, and always kept the key of it in his pocket.

"Father," Cosette one day asked him, "what is that box there that smells so good?"

Father Fauchelevent, besides the "glory" we have just described, and of which he was unconscious, was recompensed for his good deed; in the first place it made him happy, and then he had less work to do, as it was divided. Finally, as he was very fond of tobacco, he found the presence of M. Madeleine advantageous in another point of view; he took three times as much tobacco as before and that too in a manner infinitely more voluptuous, since M. Madeleine paid for it. The nuns did not adopt the name of *Ultimus*; they called Jean Valjean *the other Fauvent*.

If those holy women had possessed aught of the discrimination of Javert, they might have remarked, in course of time, that when there was any little errand to run outside for on account of the garden, it was always the elder Fauchelevent, old, infirm, and lame as he was, who went, and never the other; but, whether it be that eyes continually fixed upon God cannot play the spy, or whether they were too constantly employed in watching one another, they noticed nothing.

However, Jean Valjean was well satisfied to keep quiet and still. Javert watched the quarter for a good long month.

The convent was to Jean Valjean like an island surrounded by wide waters. These four walls were, henceforth, the world to him. Within them he could see enough of the sky to be calm, and enough of Cosette to be happy.

A very pleasant life began again for him.

He lived with Fauchelevent in the out-building at the foot of the garden. This petty structure, built of rubbish, which was still standing in 1845, consisted, as we have already stated, of three rooms, all of which were bare to the very walls. The principal one had been forcibly pressed upon M. Madeleine by Fauchelevent, for Jean Valjean had resisted in vain. The wall of this room, besides the two nails used for hanging up the knee-leather and the hoe, was decorated with a royalist specimen of paper-money of '93, pasted above the fire-place, of which the following is a counterpart:

✕	✕	✕	✕	*Armée Catholique*	✕	✕	✕	✕
✕								✕
✕				*De par le Roi*				✕
				***Bon commercable de* dix** LIVRES				
✕				*pour objets fournis à l'armée*				✕
				remboursable à la paix.				
✕				Série 3. No. 10390				✕
✕				*Stofflet.*				✕
✕	✕	✕	✕	*et Royale*	✕	✕	✕	✕

This Vendean assignat had been tacked to the wall by the preceding gardener, a former member of the Chouan party, who had died at the convent, and whom Fauchelevent had succeeded.

Jean Valjean worked every day in the garden, and was very useful there. He had formerly been a pruner, and now found it quite in his way to be a gardener. It may be remembered that he knew all kinds of receipts and secrets of field-work. These he turned to account. Nearly all the orchard trees were wild stock; he grafted them and made them bear excellent fruit.

Cosette was allowed to come every day, and pass an hour with him. As the sisters were melancholy, and he was kind, the child compared him with them, and worshipped him. Every day, at the hour appointed, she would hurry to the little building. When she entered the old place, she filled it with Paradise. Jean Valjean basked in her presence and felt his own happiness increase by reason of the happiness he conferred on Cosette. The delight we inspire in others has this enchanting peculiarity that, far from being diminished like every other reflection, it returns to us more radiant than ever. At the hours of recreation, Jean Valjean from a distance watched her playing and romping, and he could distinguish her laughter from the laughter of the rest.

For, now, Cosette laughed.

Even Cosette's countenance had, in a measure, changed. The gloomy cast had disappeared. Laughter is sunshine; it chases winter from the human face.

When the recreation was over and Cosette went in, Jean Valjean watched the windows of her schoolroom, and, at night, would rise from his bed to take a look at the windows of the room in which she slept.

God has his own ways. The convent contributed, like Cosette, to confirm and complete, in Jean Valjean, the work of the bishop. It cannot be denied that one of virtue's phases ends in pride. Therein is a bridge built by the Evil One. Jean Valjean was, perhaps, without knowing it, near that very phase of virtue, and that very bridge, when Providence flung him into the convent of the Petit Picpus. So long as he compared himself only with the bishop, he found himself unworthy and remained humble; but, for some time past, he had been comparing himself with the rest of men, and pride was springing up in him. Who knows? He might have finished by going gradually back to hate.

The convent stopped him on this descent.

It was the second place of captivity he had seen. In his youth, in what had been for him the commencement of life, and, later, quite recently too, he had seen another, a frightful place, a terrible place, the severities of which had always seemed to him to be the iniquity of public justice and the crime of the law. Now, after having seen the galleys, he saw the cloister, and reflecting that he had been an inmate of the galleys, and that he now was, so to speak, a spectator of the cloister, he anxiously compared them in his meditations with anxiety.

Sometimes he would lean upon his spade and descend slowly along the endless rounds of reverie.

He recalled his former companions, and how wretched they were. They rose at dawn and toiled until night. Scarcely allowed to sleep they lay on camp-beds, and were permitted to have mattresses but two inches thick in halls which were warmed only during the most inclement months. They were attired in hideous red sacks, and had given to them, as a favour, a pair of canvas pantaloons in the heats of midsummer, and a square of woollen stuff to throw over their shoulders, during the bitterest frosts of winter. They had no wine to drink, no meat for food excepting when sent upon "extra hard work." They lived without names, distinguished solely by numbers, and reduced, as it were, to ciphers, lowering their eyes, lowering their voices, with their hair cropped close, under the rod, and plunged in shame.

Then, his thoughts reverted to the beings before his eyes.

These beings, also, lived with their hair cut close, their eyes bent down, their voices hushed, not in shame indeed, but amid the scoffs of the world; not with their backs bruised by the gaoler's staff, but with their shoulders lacerated by self-inflicted penance. Their names, too, had perished from among men, and they now existed under austere designations alone. They never ate meat and never drank wine; they often remained until evening without food. They were attired not in red sacks, but in black habits of woollen, heavy in summer, light in winter, unable to increase or diminish them, without even the privilege, according to the season, of substituting a linen dress or a woollen cloak, and then, for six months of the year, they wore under-clothing of serge which fevered them. They dwelt not in dormitories warmed only in the bitterest frost of winter, but in cells where fire was never kindled. They slept not on mattresses two inches thick, but upon straw. Moreover, they were not even allowed to sleep, for, every night, after a day of labour, they were, when whelmed beneath the weight of the first sleep, at the moment when they were just beginning to slumber, and, with difficulty, to collect a little warmth, required to waken, rise and assemble for prayers in an icy-cold and gloomy chapel, with their knees on the stone pavement.

On certain days, each one of these beings, in her turn, had to remain twelve hours in succession kneeling upon the flags, or prostrate on her face, with her arms crossed.

The others were men, these were women. What had these men done? They had robbed, ravished, plundered, killed, assassinated. They were highwaymen, forgers, poisoners, incendiaries, murderers, parricides. What had these women done? They had done nothing.

On one side, robbery, fraud, imposition, violence, lust, homicide, every species of sacrilege, every description of offence; on the other, one thing only,—innocence.

A perfect innocence almost borne upwards in a mysterious Assumption, clinging still to Earth through virtue, already touching Heaven through holiness.

On the one hand, the mutual avowal of crimes detailed with bated breath; on the other, faults confessed aloud. And oh! what crimes! and oh! what faults!

On one side foul miasma, on the other, ineffable perfume. On the one side, a moral pestilence, watched day and night, held in subjection at the cannon's mouth, and slowly consuming its infected victims; on the other, chaste kindling of every soul together on the same hearthstone. There, utter gloom; here, the shadow, but a shadow full of light, and the light full of glowing radiations.

Two seats of slavery; but, in the former, rescue possible, a legal limit always in view, and, then, escape. In the second, perpetuity, the only hope at the most distant boundary of the future, that gleam of liberty which men call death.

In the former, the captives were enchained by chains only; in the other, they were enchained by faith alone.

What resulted from the first? One vast curse, the gnashing of teeth, hatred, desperate depravity, a cry of rage against human society, sarcasm against heaven.

What issued from the second? Benediction and love.

And, in these two places, so alike and yet so different, these two species of beings so dissimilar were performing the same work of expiation.

Jean Valjean thoroughly comprehended the expiation of the first; personal expiation, expiation for oneself. But, he did not understand that of the others, of these blameless, spotless creatures, and he asked himself with a tremor: "Expiation of what? What expiation?"

A voice responded in his conscience: the most divine of all human generosity, expiation for others.

Here we withhold all theories of our own: we are but the narrator; at Jean Valjean's point of view we place ourselves and we merely reproduce his impressions.

He had before his eyes the sublime summit of self-denial, the loftiest possible height of virtue; innocence forgiving men their sins and expiating them in their stead; servitude endured, torture accepted, chastisement and misery invoked by souls that had not sinned in order that these might not fall upon souls which had; the love of humanity losing itself in the love of God, but remaining there, distinct and suppliant; sweet, feeble beings supporting all the torments of those who are punished, yet retaining the smile of those who are rewarded. And then he remembered that he had dared to complain.

Often, in the middle of the night, he would rise from his bed to listen to the grateful anthem of these innocent beings thus overwhelmed with austerities, and he felt the blood run cold in his veins as he reflected that they who were justly punished never raised their voices towards Heaven excepting to blaspheme, and that he, wretch that he was, had uplifted his clenched fist against God.

Another strange thing which made him muse and meditate profoundly seemed like an intimation whispered in his ear by Providence itself: the scaling of walls, the climbing over inclosures, the risk taken in defiance of danger or death, the difficult and painful ascent—all those very efforts that he had made to escape from the other place of expiation, he had made to enter this one. Was this an emblem of his destiny?

This house, also, was a prison, and bore dismal resemblance to the other from which he had fled, and yet he had never conceived anything like it.

He once more saw gratings, bolts and bars of iron—to shut in whom? Angels.

Those lofty walls which he had seen surrounding tigers, he now saw encircling lambs.

It was a place of expiation, not of punishment; and yet it was still more austere, more sombre and more pitiless than the other. These virgins were more harshly bent down than the convicts. A harsh, cold blast, the blast that had frozen his youth, careered across that grated moat and manacled the vultures; but a wind still more biting and more cruel beat upon the dove cage.

And why?

When he thought of these things, all that was in him gave way before this mystery of sublimity. In these meditations, pride vanished. He reverted, again and again, to himself; he felt his own pitiful unworthiness, and often wept. All that had occurred in his existence, for the last six months, led him back towards the holy injunctions of the bishop; Cosette through love, the convent through humility.

Sometimes, in the evening, about dusk, at the hour when the garden was solitary, he was seen kneeling, in the middle of the walk that ran along the chapel, before the window through which he had looked, on the night of his first arrival, turned towards the spot where he knew that the sister who was performing the reparation was prostrate in prayer. Thus he prayed kneeling before this sister.

It seemed as though he dared not kneel directly before God.

Everything around him, this quiet garden, these balmy flowers, these children, shouting with joy, these meek and simple women, this silent cloister, gradually entered into all his being, and, little by little, his soul subsided into silence like this cloister, into fragrance like these flowers, into peace like this garden, into simplicity like these women, into joy like these children. And then he reflected that two houses of God had received him in succession at the two critical moments of his life, the first when every door was closed and human society repelled him; the second, when human society again howled upon his track, and the galleys once more gaped for him; and that, had it not been for the first, he should have fallen back into crime, and had it not been for the second, into punishment.

His whole heart melted in gratitude, and he loved more and more. Several years passed thus. Cosette was growing.

MARIUS

MARIUS
BOOK FIRST – PARIS ATOMISED

I
PARVULUS

PARIS has a child and the forest has a bird; the bird is called the sparrow; the child is called the gamin.

Couple these two ideas, the one containing all the heat of the furnace, the other all the light of the dawn; strike together these two sparks, Paris and infancy; and there leaps forth from them a little creature. Homuncio, Plautus would say.

This little creature is full of joy. He has not food to eat every day, yet he goes to the show every evening, if he sees fit. He has no shirt to his back, no shoes to his feet, no roof over his head; he is like the flies in the air who have none of all these things. He is from seven to thirteen years of age, lives in troops, ranges the streets, sleeps in the open air, wears an old pair of his father's pantaloons down about his heels, an old hat of some other father, which covers his ears, and a single suspender of yellow listing, runs about, is always on the watch and on the search, kills time, colours pipes, swears like an imp, hangs about the wine-shop, knows thieves and robbers, is hand in glove with the street-girls, rattles off slang, sings smutty songs, and, withal, has nothing bad in his heart. This is because he has a pearl in his soul, innocence; and pearls do not dissolve in mire. So long as man is a child, God wills that he be innocent.

If one could ask of this vast city: what is that creature? She would answer: "it is my bantling."

II
SOME OF HIS PRIVATE MARKS

THE gamin of Paris is the dwarf of the giantess.

We will not exaggerate. This cherub of the gutter sometimes has a shirt, but then he has only one; sometimes he has shoes, but then they have no soles; sometimes he has a shelter, and he loves it, for there he finds his mother; but he prefers the street, for there he finds his liberty. He has sports of his own, roguish tricks of his own, of which a hearty hatred of the bourgeois is the basis; he has his own metaphors; to be dead he calls eating dandelions by the root; he has his own occupations, such as running for hacks, letting down carriage-steps, sweeping the crossings in rainy weather, which he styles making ponts des arts, crying the speeches often made by the authorities on behalf of the French people, and digging out the streaks between the flags of the pavement; he has his own kind of money, consisting of all the little bits of wrought copper that can be found on the public thoroughfares. This curious coin, which takes the name of scraps, has an unvarying and well-regulated circulation throughout this little gipsy-land of children.

He has a fauna of his own, which he studies carefully in the corners; the good God's bug, the death's head grub, the mower, the devil, a black insect that threatens you by twisting about its tail which is armed with two horns. He has his fabulous monster which has scales on its belly, and yet is not a lizard, has warts on its back, and yet is not a toad, which lives in the crevices of old lime-kilns and dry-cisterns, a black, velvety, slimy, crawling creature, sometimes swift and sometimes slow of motion, emitting no cry, but which stares at you, and is so terrible that nobody has ever seen it; this monster he calls the "deaf thing." Hunting for deaf things among the stones is a pleasure which is thrillingly dangerous. Another enjoyment is to raise a flag of the pavement suddenly and see the wood-lice. Every region of Paris is famous for the discoveries which can be made in it. There are earwigs in the wood-yards of the Ursulines, there are wood-lice at the Pantheon, and tadpoles in the ditches of the Champ-de-Mars.

In repartee, this youngster is as famous as Talleyrand. He is equally cynical, but he is more sincere. He is gifted with an odd kind of unpremeditated jollity; he stuns the shopkeeper with his wild laughter. His gamut slides merrily from high comedy to farce.

A funeral is passing. There is a doctor in the procession. "Hullo!" shouts a gamin, "how long is it since the doctors began to take home their work?"

Another happens to be in a crowd. A grave-looking man, who wears spectacles and trinkets, turns upon him indignantly: "You scamp, you've been seizing my wife's waist!"

"I, sir! search me!"

III

HE IS AGREEABLE

In the evening, by means of a few pennies which he always manages to scrape together, the *homuncio* goes to some theatre. By the act of passing that magic threshold, he becomes transfigured; he was a *gamin*, he becomes a *titi*. Theatres are a sort of vessel turned upside down with the hold at the top; in this hold the *titi* gather in crowds. The *titi* is to the *gamin* what the butterfly is to the grub; the same creature on wings and sailing through the air. It is enough for him to be there with his radiance of delight, his fulness of enthusiasm and joy and his clapping of hands like the clapping of wings, to make that hold, close, dark, fœtid, filthy, unwholesome, hideous, and detestable, as it is, a very Paradise.

Give to a being the useless, and deprive him of the needful, and you have the *gamin*.

The *gamin* is not without a certain inclination towards literature. His tendency, however—we say it with the befitting quantum of regret—would not be considered as towards the classic. He is, in his nature, but slightly academic. For instance, the popularity of Mademoiselle Mars among this little public of children was spiced with a touch of irony. The *gamin* called her Mademoiselle *Muche*.

This being jeers, wrangles, sneers, jangles, has frippery like a baby and rags like a philosopher, fishes in the sewer, hunts in the drain, extracts gaiety from filth, lashes the street-corners with his wit, fleers and bites, hisses and sings, applauds and hoots, tempers Hallelujah with turalural, psalmodises all sorts of rhythms from De Profundis to the Chie-en-lit, finds without searching, knows what he does not know, is Spartan even to roguery, is witless even to wisdom, is lyric even to impurity, would squat upon Olympus, wallows in the dung-heap and comes out of it covered with stars. The gamin of Paris is an urchin Rabelais.

He is never satisfied with his pantaloons unless they have a watch-fob.

He is seldom astonished, is frightened still less frequently, turns superstitions into doggerel verses and sings them, collapses exaggerations, makes light of mysteries, sticks out his tongue at ghosts, dismounts everything that is on stilts, and introduces caricature into all epic pomposities. This is not because he is

prosaic, far from it; but he substitutes the phantasmagoria of fun
for solemn dreams. Were Adamaster to appear to him, he would
shout out: "Hallo, there, old Bug-a-boo!"

IV
HE MAY BE USEFUL

PARIS begins with the cockney and ends with the *gamin*, two
beings of which no other city is capable; passive acceptation
satisfied with merely looking on, and exhaustless enterprise;
Prudhomme and Fouillou. Paris alone comprises this in its
natural history. All monarchy is comprised in the cockney; all
anarchy in the *gamin*.

This pale child of the Paris suburbs lives, develops, and gets
into and out of "scrapes," amid suffering, a thoughtful witness
of our social realities and our human problems. He thinks himself careless, but he is not. He looks on, ready to laugh; ready,
also, for something else. Whoever ye are who call yourselves
Prejudice, Abuse, Ignominy, Oppression, Iniquity, Despotism,
Injustice, Fanaticism, Tyranny, beware of the gaping *gamin*.

This little fellow will grow.

Of what clay is he made? Of the first mud of the street. A
handful of common soil, a breath and, behold, Adam! It is
enough that a God but pass. A God always has passed where the
gamin is. Chance works in the formation of this little creature.
By this word chance we mean, in some degree, hazard. Now,
will this pigmy, thoroughly kneaded with the coarse common
earth, ignorant, illiterate, wild, vulgar, mobbish, as he is,
become an Ionian, or a Bœotian? Wait, *currit rota*, the life of
Paris, that demon which creates the children of chance and the
men of destiny, reversing the work of the Latin potter, makes of
the jug a costly vase.

V
HIS FRONTIERS

THE *gamin* loves the city, he loves solitude also, having something of the sage in him. *Urbis amator*, like Fuscus; *ruris amator*,
like Flaccus.

To rove about, musing, that is to say loitering, is, for a philosopher, a good way of spending time; especially in that kind of

mock rurality, ugly but odd, and partaking of two natures, which surrounds certain large cities, particularly Paris. To study the banlieue is to study the amphibious. End of trees, beginning of houses, end of grass, beginning of pavement, end of furrows, beginning of shops, end of ruts, beginning of passions, end of the divine murmur, beginning of the human hubbub; hence, the interest is extraordinary.

Hence, it is that in these by no means inviting spots which are always termed *gloomy*, the dreamer selects his apparently aimless walks.

He who writes these lines has long been a loiterer about the Barrière of Paris, and to him it is a source of deepest remembrances. That close-clipped grass, those stony walks, that chalk, that clay, that rubbish, those harsh monotones of open lots and fallow land, those early plants of the market gardeners suddenly descried in some hollow of the ground, that mixture of wild nature with the urban landscape, those wide unoccupied patches where the drummers of the garrison hold their noisy school and imitate, as it were, the lighter din of battle, those solitudes by day and ambuscades by night, the tottering old mill turning with every breeze the hoisting-wheels of the stone-quarries, the drinking shops at the corners of the cemeteries, the mysterious charm of those dark high walls, which divide into squares immense grounds, dimly seen in the distance, but bathed in sunshine and alive with butterflies—all these attracted him.

There is hardly anybody but knows those singular places, the Glacière, the Cunette, the hideous wall of Grenelle spotted with balls, the Mont Parnasse, the Fosse-aux-Loups, the white hazel trees on the high banks of the Marne, Mont-Souris, the Tombe-Issoire, the Pierre Plate de Chatillon where there is an old exhausted quarry which is of no further use but as a place for the growth of mushrooms, and is closed on a level with the ground by a trap-door of rotten boards. The Campagna of Rome is one idea; the banlieue of Paris is another; to see in whatever forms our horizon, nothing but fields, houses, or trees, is to be but superficial; all the aspects of things are thoughts of God. The place where an open plain adjoins a city always bears the impress of some indescribable, penetrating melancholy. There, nature and humanity address you at one and the same moment. There, the originalities of place appear.

He who, like ourselves, has rambled through these solitudes contiguous to our suburbs, which one might term the limbo of Paris, has noticed dotted about, here and there, always in the most deserted spot and at the most unexpected moment, beside some straggling hedge or in the corner of some dismal wall, little helter-skelter groups of children, filthy, muddy, dusty, uncombed, dishevelled, playing mumble-peg crowned with violets. These are all the runaway children of poor families. The outer boulevard is their breathing medium, and the banlieue belongs to them. There, they play truant, continually. There they sing, innocently, their collection of low songs. They are, or rather, they live there, far from every eye, in the soft radiance of May or June, kneeling around a hole in the ground, playing marbles, squabbling for pennies, irresponsible, birds flown, let loose and happy; and, the moment they see you, remembering that they have a trade and must make their living, they offer to sell you an old woollen stocking full of May-bugs, or a bunch of lilacs. These meetings with strange children are among the seductive but at the same time saddening charms of the environs of Paris.

Sometimes among this crowd of boys, there are a few little girls—are they their sisters?—almost young women, thin, feverish, freckled, gloved with sunburn, with head-dresses of rye-straw and poppies, gay, wild, bare-footed. Some of them are seen eating cherries among the growing grain. In the evening, they are heard laughing. These groups, warmly lighted up by the full blaze of noon-day, or seen dimly in the twilight, long occupy the attention of the dreamer, and these visions mingle with his reveries.

Paris, the centre; the banlieue, the circumference; to these children, this is the whole world. They never venture beyond it. They can no more live out of the atmosphere of Paris than fish can live out of water. To them, beyond two leagues from the barrières there is nothing more. Ivry, Gentilly, Arcueil, Belleville, Aubervilliers, Menilmontant, Choisy-le-Roi, Billancourt, Meudon, Issy, Vanvre, Sèvres, Puteaux, Neuilly, Gennevilliers, Colombes, Romainville, Chatou, Asnières, Bougival, Nanterre, Enghien, Noisy-le-Sec, Nogent, Gournay, Drancy, Gonesse; these are the end of the world.

VI
A SCRAP OF HISTORY

AT the period, although it is almost contemporaneous, in which the action of this story is laid, there was not, as there now is, a police officer at every street-corner (an advantage we have no time to enlarge upon); truant children abounded in Paris. The statistics gave an average of two hundred and sixty homeless children, picked up annually by the police on their rounds, in open lots, in houses in process of building, and under the arches of bridges. One of these nests, which continues famous, produced "the swallows of the bridge of Arcola." This, moreover, is the most disastrous of our social symptoms. All the crimes of man begin with the vagrancy of childhood.

We must except Paris, however. To a considerable degree, and notwithstanding the reminiscence we have just recalled, the exception is just. While in every other city, the truant boy is the lost man; while, almost everywhere, the boy given up to himself is, in some sort, devoted and abandoned to a species of fatal immersion in public vices which eat out of him all that is respectable, even conscience itself, the *gamin* of Paris, we must insist, chipped and spotted as he is on the surface, is almost intact within. A thing magnificent to think of, and one that shines forth resplendently in the glorious probity of our popular revolutions; a certain incorruptibility results from the mental fluid which is to the air of Paris what salt is to the water of the ocean. To breathe the air of Paris preserves the soul.

What we here say alleviates, in no respect, that pang of the heart which we feel whenever we meet one of these children, around whom we seem to see floating the broken ties of the disrupted family. In our present civilisation, which is still so incomplete, it is not a very abnormal thing to find these disruptions of families, separating in the darkness, scarcely knowing what has become of their children—dropping fragments of their life, as it were, upon the public highway. Hence arise dark destinies. This is called, for the sad chance has coined its own expression, "being cast upon the pavement of Paris."

These abandonments of children, be it said, in passing, were not discouraged by the old monarchy. A little of Egypt and of Bohemia in the lower strata, accommodated the higher spheres, and answered the purpose of the powerful. Hatred to the instruction of the children of the people was a dogma. What was the use of "a little learning"? Such was the password. Now the truant child is the corollary of the ignorant child. Moreover, the monarchy sometimes had need of children, and then it skimmed the street.

Under Louis XIV., not to go any further back, the king, very wisely, desired to build up a navy. The idea was a good one. But let us look at the means. No navy could there be, if, side by side with the sailing vessel, the sport of the wind, to tow it along, in case of need, there were not another vessel capable of going where it pleased, either by the oar or by steam; the galleys were to the navy, then, what steamers now are. Hence, there must be galleys; but galleys could be moved only by galley slaves, and therefore there must be galley slaves. Colbert, through the provincial intendants and the parlements, made as many galley slaves as possible. The magistracy set about the work with good heart. A man kept his hat on before a procession, a Huguenot attitude; he was sent to the galleys. A boy was found in the street; if he had no place to sleep in, and was fifteen years old, he was sent to the galleys. Great reign, great age.

Under Louis XV. children disappeared in Paris; the police carried them off—nobody knows for what mysterious use. People whispered with affright horrible conjectures about the purple baths of the king. Barbier speaks ingenuously of these things. It sometimes happened that the officers, running short of children, took some who had fathers. The fathers, in despair, rushed upon the officers. In such cases, the parlement interfered and hung—whom? The officers? No; the fathers.

VII

THE GAMIN WILL HAVE HIS PLACE AMONG THE CLASSIFICATIONS OF INDIA

THE Parisian order of *gamins* is almost a caste. One might say: nobody wants to have anything to do with them.

This word *gamin* was printed for the first time, and passed from the popular language into that of literature, in 1834. It was in a little work entitled *Claude Gueux* that the word first appeared. It created a great uproar. The word was adopted.

The elements that go to make up respectability among the gamins are very varied. We knew and had to do with one who was greatly respected and admired, because he had seen a man fall from the towers of Notre Dame; another, because he had succeeded in making his way into the rear inclosure where the statues intended for the dome of the Invalides were deposited, and had scraped off some of the lead; a third because he had seen a diligence upset; and still another, because he knew a soldier who had almost knocked out the eye of a bourgeois.

This explains that odd exclamation of a Parisian gamin, a depth of lamentation which the multitude laugh at without comprehending. "*Oh, Lordy, Lordy! a'nt I unlucky! Only think I never even saw anybody fall from a fifth story*;"—the words pronounced with an inexpressible twang of his own.

What a rich saying for a peasant was this! "Father so-and-so, your wife's illness has killed her; why didn't you send for a doctor?" "What are you thinking about, friend?" says the other. "Why, we poor people *we haves to die ourselves*." But, if all the passiveness of the peasant is found in this saying, all the rollicking anarchy of the urchin of the suburbs is contained in the following:——A poor wretch on his way to the gallows was listening to his confessor, who sat beside him in the cart. A Paris boy shouted out: "*He's talking to his long-gown. Oh, the sniveller!*"

A certain audacity in religious matters sets off the gamin. It is a great thing to be strong-minded.

To be present at executions is a positive duty. These imps point at the guillotine and laugh. They give it all kinds of nicknames: "End of the Soup"—"Old Growler"—"Sky-Mother"—"The Last Mouthful," etc., etc. That they may lose nothing of the sight, they scale walls, hang on to balconies, climb trees, swing to gratings, crouch into chimneys. The *gamin* is a born slater as he is a born sailor. A roof inspires him with no more fear than a mast. No festival is equal to the execution-ground,—La Grève. Samson and the Abbé Montes are the really popular names. They shout to the victim to encourage him. Sometimes, they admire him. The *gamin* Lacenaire, seeing the horrible Dautun die bravely, used an expression which was full of future: "*I was jealous of him!*" In the order of *gamins* Voltaire is unknown, but they are acquainted with Papavoine. They mingle in the same recital, "the politicals" with murderers. They have traditions of the last clothes worn by them all. They know that Tolleron had on a forge-man's cap, and that Avril wore one of otter skin; that Louvel had on a round hat, that old

Delaporte was bald and bareheaded, that Castaing was ruddy and good-looking, that Bories had a sweet little beard, that Jean Martin kept on his suspenders, and that Lecouffé and his mother quarrelled. *Don't be finding fault now with your basket*, shouted a *gamin* to the latter couple. Another, to see Debacker pass, being too short in the crowd, began to climb a lamp-post on the quay. A gendarme on that beat scowled at him. "Let me get up, Mister Gendarme," said the gamin. And then, to soften the official, he added: "I won't fall." "Little do I care about your falling," replied the gendarme.

In the order of *gamins*, a memorable accident is greatly prized. One of their number reaches the very pinnacle of distinction, if he happen to cut himself badly, "into the bone," as they say.

The fist is by no means an inferior element of respect. One of the things the gamin is fondest of saying is, "I'm jolly strong, I am!" To be left-handed makes you an object of envy. Squinting is highly esteemed.

VIII

IN WHICH WILL BE FOUND A PLEASANTRY
OF THE LATE KING

IN summer, he transforms himself into a frog; and in the evening, at night-fall, opposite the bridges of Austerlitz and Jena, from the coal rafts and washerwomen's boats, he plunges head-foremost into the Seine, and into all sorts of infractions of the laws of modesty and the police. However, the policemen are on the look-out, and there results from this circumstance a highly dramatic situation which, upon one occasion, gave rise to a fraternal and memorable cry. This cry, which was quite famous about 1830, is a strategic signal from *gamin* to *gamin*; it is scanned like a verse of Homer, with a style of notation almost as inexplicable as the Eleusinian melody of the Panathenæans recalling once more the ancient "Evohe!" It is as follows: "*Ohé! Titi, ohé! lookee yonder! they're comin' to ketch ye! Grab yer clothes and cut through the drain!*"

Sometimes this gnat—it is thus that he styles himself—can read; sometimes he can write; he always knows how to scrawl. He gets by some unknown and mysterious mutual instruction, all talents which may be useful in public affairs; from 1815 to

1830, he imitated the call of the turkey; from 1830 to 1848, he scratched a pear on the walls. One summer evening, Louis Philippe returning to the palace on foot, saw one of them, a little fellow, so high, sweating and stretching upon tiptoe, to make a charcoal sketch of a gigantic pear, on one of the pillars of the Neuilly gateway; the king, with that good nature which he inherited from Henry IV., helped the boy, completed the pear, and gave the youngster a gold louis, saying: *"The pear's on that too!"* The *gamin* loves uproar. Violence and noise please him. He execrates "the curés". One day, in the Rue de l'Université, one of these young scamps was making faces at the porte-cochère of No. 69. "Why are you doing that at this door?" asked a passer-by. The boy replied: "There's a curé there." It was, in fact, the residence of the Papal Nuncio. Nevertheless, whatever may be the Voltairian tendencies of the *gamin*, should an occasion present itself to become a choir-boy, he would, very likely, accept, and in such case would serve the mass properly. There are two things of which he is the Tantalus, which he is always wishing for, but never attains—to overthrow the government, and to get his trousers mended.

The *gamin*, in his perfect state, possesses all the policemen of Paris, and, always, upon meeting one, can put a name to the countenance. He counts them off on his fingers. He studies their ways, and has special notes of his own upon each one of them. He reads their souls as an open book. He will tell you off-hand and without hesitating—Such a one is a *traitor*; such a one is *very cross*; such a one is *great*, such a one is *ridiculous*; (all these expressions, traitor, cross, great and ridiculous, have in his mouth a peculiar signification)—"That chap thinks the Pont Neuf belongs to him, and hinders people from walking on the cornice outside of the parapets; that other one has a mania for pulling *persons'* ears;" etc. etc.

IX
THE ANCIENT SOUL OF GAUL

THERE was something of this urchin in Poquelin, the son of the market-place; there was something of him in Beaumarchais. The *gamin* style of life is a shade of the Gallic mind. Mingled with good sense, it sometimes gives it additional strength, as alcohol does to wine. Sometimes, it is a defect; Homer nods;

one might say Voltaire plays *gamin*. Camille Desmoulins was a suburban. Championnet, who brutalised miracles, was a child of the Paris streets; he had when a little boy *besprinkled the porticoes* of St. Jean de Beauvais and St. Etienne du Mont; he had chatted with the shrine of St. Geneviève enough to throw into convulsions the sacred vial of St. Januarius.

The Paris *gamin* is respectful, ironical, and insolent. He has bad teeth, because he is poorly fed, and his stomach suffers, and fine eyes because he has genius. In the very presence of Jehovah, he would go hopping and jumping up the steps of Paradise. He is very good at boxing with both hands and feet. Every description of growth is possible to him. He plays in the gutter and rises from it by revolt; his effrontery is not cured by grape; he was a blackguard, lo! he is a hero! like the little Theban, he shakes the lion's skin; Barra the drummer was a Paris *gamin*; he shouts "Forward!" as the charger of Holy Writ says "Ha! ha!" and in a moment, he passes from the urchin to the giant.

This child of the gutter is, also, the child of the ideal. Measure this sweep of wing which reaches from Molière to Barra.

As sum total, and to embrace all in a word, the *gamin* is a being who amuses himself because he is unfortunate.

X
ECCE PARIS, ECCE HOMO

To sum up all once more, the *gamin* of Paris of the present day, is as the *græulus* of Rome was in ancient times, the people as a child, with the wrinkles of the old world on its brow.

The *gamin* is a beauty and, at the same time, a disease of the nation—a disease that must be cured. How? By light.

Light makes whole.

Light enlightens.

All the generous irradiations of society spring from science, letters, the arts, and instruction. Make men, make men. Give them light, that they may give you warmth. Soon or late, the splendid question of universal instruction will take its position with the irresistible authority of absolute truth; and then those who govern under the superintendence of the French idea will have to make this choice: the children of France or the *gamins* of Paris; flames in the light or will o' the wisps in the gloom.

The *gamin* is the expression of Paris, and Paris is the expression of the world.

For Paris is a sum total. Paris is the ceiling of the human race. All this prodigious city is an epitome of dead and living manners and customs. He who sees Paris, seems to see all history through with sky and constellations in the intervals. Paris has a Capitol, the Hôtel de Ville; a Parthenon, Notre Dame; a Mount Aventine, the Faubourg St. Antoine; an Asinarium, the Sorbonne; a Pantheon, the Pantheon; a Viâ Sacra, the Boulevard des Italiens; a tower of the Winds, public opinion—and supplies the place of the Gemoniæ by ridicule. Its *majo* is the "faraud," its *Trasteverino* is the suburban; its *hammal* is the strong man of the market-place; its *lazzarone* is the pègre; its cockney is the *gandin*. All that can be found anywhere can be found in Paris. The fish-woman of Dumarsais can hold her own with the herb-woman of Euripides, the discobolus Vejanus lives again in Forioso the rope-dancer, Therapontigonus Miles might go arm in arm with the grenadier Vadeboncœur, Damasippus the curiosity broker would be happy among the old curiosity shops, Vincennes would lay hold of Socrates just as the whole Agora would clap Diderot into a strong box; Grimod de la Reynière discovered roast-beef cooked with its own fat as Curtillus had invented roast hedgehog; we see, again, under the balloon of the Arc de l'Etoile the trapezium mentioned in Plautus; the sword-eater of the Poecilium met with by Apuleius is the swallower of sabres on the Pont-Neuf; the nephew of Rameau and Curculion the parasite form a pair; Ergasilus would get himself presented to Cambacérès by d'Aigrefeuille; the four dandies of Rome, Alcesimarchus, Phoedromus, Diabolus, and Argyrippe, may be seen going down la Courtille in the Labutat post-coach; Aulus Gellius did not stop longer in front of Congrio than Charles Nodier before Punch and Judy; Marton is not a tigress, but Pardalisca was not a dragon; Pantolabus the buffoon chaffs Nomentanus the fast-liver at the Café Anglais; Hermogenus is a tenor in the Champs-Elysées, and, around him, Thrasius the beggar in the costume of Bobèche plies his trade; the bore who buttonholes you in the Tuileries makes you repeat, after the lapse of two thousand years, the apostrophe of Thesprion: *quis properantem me prehendit pallio?* The wine of Surêne parodies the wine of Alba; the red rim of Desaugiers balances the huge goblet of Balatron, Père Lachaise exhales, under the nocturnal rains, the same lurid emanations that were seen in the Esquilies, and the grave of the poor purchased for five years, is about the equivalent of the hired coffin of the slave.

Ransack your memory for something which Paris has not. The vat of Trophonius contains nothing that is not in the washtub of Mesmer; Ergaphilas is resuscitated in Cagliostro; the Brahmin Vâsaphantâ is in the flesh again in the Count Saint Germain; the cemetery of St. Médard turns out quite as good miracles as the Oumoumié mosque at Damascus.

Paris has an Æsop in Mayeux, and a Canidia in Mademoiselle Lenormand. It stands aghast like Delphos at the blinding realities of visions; it tips tables as Dodona did tripods. It enthrones the grisette as Rome did the courtesan; and, in fine, if Louis XV. is worse than Claudius, Madame Dubarry is better than Messalina. Paris combines in one wonderful type which has had real existence, and actually elbowed us, the Greek nudity, the Hebrew ulcer, the Gascon jest. It mingles Diogenes, Job, and Paillasse, dresses up a ghost in old numbers of the *Constitutionnel*, and produces Shadrac Duclos.

Although Plutarch may say: *the tyrant never grows old*, Rome, under Sylla as well as under Domitian, resigned herself and of her own accord put water in her wine. The Tiber was a Lethe, if we may believe the somewhat doctrinal eulogy pronounced upon it by Varus Vibiscus: *Contra Gracchos Tiberim habemus. Bibere Tiberim, id est seditionem oblivisci.* Paris drinks a quarter of a million of gallons of water per day, but that does not prevent it upon occasion from beating the alarm and sounding the tocsin.

With all that, Paris is a good soul. It accepts everything right royally; it is not difficult in the realms of Venus; its Callipyge is of the Hottentot stamp; if it but laughs, it pardons, ugliness makes it merry; deformity puts it in good humour, vice diverts its attention; be droll and you may venture to be a scamp; even hypocrisy, that sublimity of cynicism, it does not revolt at; it is so literary that it does not hold its nose over Basilius, and is no more shocked at the prayer of Tartuffe than Horace was at the hiccough of Priapus. No feature of the universal countenance is wanting in the profile of Paris. The Mabile dancing garden is not the polyhymnian dance of the Janiculum, but the costume-hirer devours the lorette there with her eyes exactly as the procuress Staphyla watched the virgin Planesium. The Barrière du Combat is not a Coliseum, but there is as much ferocity exhibited as though Cæsar were a spectator. The Syrian hostess has more grace than Mother Saguet, but, if Virgil haunted the Roman wine shop, David d'Angers, Balzac, and Charlet have sat down in the drinking-places of Paris. Paris is regnant. Geniuses blaze on all sides, and red perukes flourish. Adonaïs passes by in his twelve-wheeled car of thunder and lightning; Silenus makes his entry upon his tun. For Silenus read Ramponneau.

Paris is a synonym of Cosmos. Paris is Athens, Rome, Sybaris, Jerusalem, Pantin. All the eras of civilisation are there in abridged edition, all the epochs of barbarism also. Paris would be greatly vexed, had she no guillotine.

A small admixture of the Place de Grève is good. What would all this continual merrymaking be without that seasoning? Our laws have wisely provided for this, and, thanks to them, this relish turns its edge upon the general carnival.

XI
RIDICULE AND REIGN

Of bounds and limits, Paris has none. No other city ever enjoyed that supreme control which sometimes derides those whom it reduces to submission. *To please you, O Athenians!* exclaimed Alexander. Paris does more than lay down the law; it lays down the fashion; Paris does more than lay down the fashion; it lays down the routine. Paris may be stupid if it please; sometimes it allows itself this luxury; then, the whole universe is stupid with it. Upon this Paris awakes, rubs its eyes, and says: "Am I stupid!" and bursts out laughing in the face of mankind. What a marvel is such a city! how strange a thing that all this mass of what is grand and what is ludicrous should be so harmonious, that all this majesty is not disturbed by all this parody, and that the same mouth can to-day blow the trump of the last judgment and to-morrow a penny whistle; Paris possesses an all-commanding joviality. Its gaiety is of the thunderbolt, and its frolicking holds a sceptre. Its hurricanes spring sometimes from a wry face. Its outbursts, its great days, its masterpieces, its prodigies, its epics fly to the ends of the universe, and so do its cock and bull stories also. Its laughter is the mouth of a volcano that bespatters the whole earth. Its jokes are sparks that kindle. It forces upon the nations its caricatures as well as its ideal; the loftiest monuments of human civilisation accept its sarcasms and lend their eternity to its waggeries. It is superb; it has a marvellous Fourteenth of July that delivers the globe; it makes all the nations take the oath of the tennis-court; its night of the Fourth of August disperses in three hours a thousand years of feudalism; it makes of its logic the muscle of the unanimous will; it multiplies itself under all the forms of the sublime; it fills with its radiance Washington, Kosciusko, Bolivar, Botzaris, Riego, Bem, Manin, Lopez, John Brown, Garibaldi; it is everywhere, where the future is being enkindled at Boston in 1779, at the Isle de St. Leon in 1820, at Pesth in 1848, at Palermo in 1860; it whispers the mighty watchword *Liberty* in the ears of the American Abolitionists grouped together in the boat at Harper's Ferry, and also in the ears of the patriots of Ancona assembled in the gloom at the Archi, in front of the Gozzi tavern, on the seaside; it creates Canaris; it creates Quiroga; it creates Pisicane; it radiates greatness over the earth; it is in going whither its breath impels, that Byron dies at Missolonghi, and Mazet at Barcelona; it is a rostrum beneath the feet of Mirabeau, and a crater beneath the feet of Robespierre; its books, its stage, its art, its science, its literature, its philosophy are the manuals of the human race, to it belong Pascal, Regnier, Corneille, Descartes, Jean Jacques; Voltaire for every moment, Molière for every century; it makes the universal mouth speak its language, and that language becomes the Word; it builds up in every mind the idea of progress; the liberating dogmas which it forges are swords by the pillows of the generations and with the soul of its thinkers and poets have all the heroes of all nations since 1789 been made; but that does not prevent it from playing the gamin, and this enormous genius called Paris, even while transfiguring the world with its radiance, draws the nose of Bouginier in charcoal on the wall of the Temple of Theseus, and writes *Crédeville the robber* on the Pyramids.

Paris is always showing its teeth; when it is not scolding, it is laughing.

Such is Paris. The smoke of its roofs is the ideas of the universe. A heap of mud and stone, if you will, but above all, a moral being. It is more than great, it is immense. Why? Because it dares.

To dare; progress is at this price.

All sublime conquests are, more or less, the rewards of daring. That the revolution should come, it was not enough that

Montesquieu should foresee it, that Diderot should preach it, that Beaumarchais should announce it, that Condorcet should calculate it, that Arouet should prepare it, that Rousseau should premeditate it; Danton must dare it.

That cry, *"Audace,"* is a *Fiat Lux!* The onward march of the human race requires that the heights around it should be ablaze with noble and enduring lessons of courage. Deeds of daring dazzle history, and form one of the guiding lights of man. The dawn dares when it rises. To strive, to brave all risks, to persist, to persevere, to be faithful to yourself, to grapple hand to hand with destiny, to surprise defeat by the little terror it inspires, at one time to confront unrighteous power, at another to defy intoxicated triumph, to hold fast, to hold hard—such is the example which the nations need, and the light that electrifies them. The same puissant lightning darts from the torch of Prometheus and the clay-pipe of Cambronne.

XII
THE FUTURE LATENT IN THE PEOPLE

As to the people of Paris, even when grown to manhood, it is, always, the *gamin*; to depict the child is to depict the city, and therefore it is that we have studied this eagle in this open-hearted sparrow.

It is in the suburbs especially, we insist, that the Parisian race is found; there is the pure blood; there is the true physiognomy; there this people works and suffers, and suffering and toil are the two forms of men. There are vast numbers of unknown beings teeming with the strangest types of humanity, from the stevedore of the Rapée to the horsekiller of Montfaucon. *Fex urbis*, exclaims Cicero; *mob*, adds the indignant Burke; the herd, the multitude, the populace. Those words are quickly said. But if it be so, what matters it? What is it to me that they go barefoot? They cannot read. So much the worse. Will you abandon them for that? Would you make their misfortune their curse? Cannot the light penetrate these masses? Let us return to that cry: Light! and let us persist in it! Light! light! Who knows but that these opacities will become transparent? are not revolutions transfigurations? Proceed, philosophers, teach, enlighten, enkindle, think aloud, speak aloud, run joyously towards the broad daylight, fraternise in the public squares, announce the glad tidings, scatter plenteously your alphabets, proclaim human rights, sing your Marseillaises, sow enthusiasms broadcast, tear off green branches from the oak-trees. Make thought a whirl-wind. This multitude can be sublimated. Let us learn to avail ourselves of this vast combustion of principles and virtues, which sparkles, crackles, and thrills at certain periods. These bare feet, these naked arms, these rags, these shades of ignorance, these depths of abjectness, these abysses of gloom may be employed in the conquest of the ideal. Look through the medium of the people, and you shall discern the truth. This lowly sand which you trample beneath your feet, if you cast it into the furnace, and let it melt and seethe, shall become resplendent crystal, and by means of such as it a Galileo and a Newton shall discover stars.

XIII
LITTLE GAVROCHE

ABOUT eight or nine years after the events narrated in the second part of this story, there was seen, on the Boulevard du Temple, and in the neighbourhood of the Château d'Eau, a little boy of eleven or twelve years of age, who would have realised with considerable accuracy the ideal of the *gamin* previously sketched, if, with the laughter of his youth upon his lips, his heart had not been absolutely dark and empty. This child was well muffled up in a man's pair of pantaloons, but he had not got them from his father, and in a woman's chemise, which was not an inheritance from his mother. Strangers had clothed him in these rags out of charity. Still, he had a father and a mother. But his father never thought of him, and his mother did not love him. He was one of those children so deserving of pity from all, who have fathers and mothers, and yet are orphans.

This little boy never felt so happy as when in the street. The pavement was not so hard to him as the heart of his mother.

His parents had thrown him out into life with a kick.

He had quite ingenuously spread his wings, and taken flight.

He was a boisterous, pallid, nimble, wide-awake, roguish urchin, with an air at once vivacious and sickly. He went, came, sang, played pitch and toss, scraped the gutters, stole a little, but he did it gaily like the cats and the sparrows, laughed when people called him an errand-boy, and got angry when they called him a ragamuffin. He had no shelter, no food, no fire, no love, but he was light-hearted because he was free.

When these poor creatures are men, the millstone of our social system almost always comes in contact with them, and grinds them, but while they are children they escape because they are little. The smallest hole saves them.

However, deserted as this lad was, it happened sometimes, every two or three months, that he would say to himself: "Come, I'll go and see my mother!" Then he would leave the Boulevard, the Cirque, the Porte Saint Martin, go down along the quays, cross the bridges, reach the suburbs, walk as far as the Salpêtrière, and arrive—where? Precisely at that double number, 50–52, which is known to the reader, the Gorbeau building.

At the period referred to, the tenement No. 50–52, usually empty, and permanently decorated with the placard "Rooms to let," was, for a wonder, tenanted by several persons who, in all other respects as is always the case at Paris, had no relation to or connection with each other. They all belonged to that indigent class which begins with the small bourgeois in embarrassed circumstances, and descends, from grade to grade of wretchedness, through the lower strata of society, until it reaches those two beings in whom all the material things of civilisation terminate, the scavenger and the ragpicker.

The "landlady" of the time of Jean Valjean was dead, and had been replaced by another exactly like her. I do not remember what philosopher it was who said: "There is never any lack of old women."

The new old woman was called Madame Bougon, and her life had been remarkable for nothing except a dynasty of three paroquets, which had in succession wielded the sceptre of her affections.

Among those who lived in the building, the wretchedest of all were a family of four persons, father, mother, and two daughters nearly grown, all four lodging in the same garret room, one of those cells of which we have already spoken.

This family at first sight presented nothing very peculiar but its extreme destitution; the father, in renting the room, had given his name as Jondrette. Some time after his moving in, which had singularly resembled, to borrow the memorable expression of the landlady, the entrance of nothing at all, this Jondrette said to the old woman, who, like her predecessor, was, at the same time, portress and swept the stairs: "Mother So-and-So, if anybody should come and ask for a Pole or an Italian or, perhaps, a Spaniard, that is for me."

Now, this family was the family of our sprightly little bare-footed urchin. When he came there, he found distress and, what is sadder still, no smile; a cold hearthstone and cold hearts. When he came in, they would ask: "Where have you come from?" He would answer: "From the street." When he was going away they would ask him: "Where are you going to?" He would answer: "Into the street." His mother would say to him: "What have you come here for?"

The child lived, in this absence of affection, like those pale plants that spring up in cellars. He felt no suffering from this mode of existence, and bore no ill-will to anybody. He did not know how a father and mother ought to be.

But yet his mother loved his sisters.

We had forgotten to say that on the Boulevard du Temple this boy went by the name of little Gavroche. Why was his name Gavroche? Probably because his father's name was Jondrette.

To break all links seems to be the instinct of some wretched families.

The room occupied by the Jondrettes in the Gorbeau tene-ment was the last at the end of the hall. The adjoining cell was tenanted by a very poor young man who was called Monsieur Marius.

Let us see who and what Monsieur Marius was.

BOOK SECOND – THE GRAND BOURGEOIS

I

NINETY YEARS OLD AND THIRTY-TWO TEETH

IN the Rue Boucherat, Rue de Normandie, and Rue de Saintonge, there still remain a few old inhabitants who preserve a memory of a fine old man named M. Gillenormand, and who like to talk about him. This man was old when they were young. This figure, to those who look sadly upon that vague swarm of shadows which they call the past, has not yet entirely disappeared from the labyrinth of streets in the neighbourhood of the Temple, to which, under Louis XIV., were given the names of all the provinces of France, precisely as in our days the names of all the capitals of Europe have been given to the streets in the new Quartier Tivoli; an advance, be it said by the way, in which progress is visible.

M. Gillenormand, who was as much alive as any man can be, in 1831, was one of those men who have become curiosities, simply because they have lived a long time; and who are strange, because formerly they were like everybody else, and now they are no longer like anybody else. He was a peculiar old man, and very truly a man of another age—the genuine bourgeois of the eighteenth century, a very perfect specimen, a little haughty, wearing his good old bourgeoisie as marquises wear their marquisates. He had passed his ninetieth year, walked erect, spoke in a loud voice, saw clearly, drank hard, ate, slept, and snored. He had every one of his thirty-two teeth. He wore glasses only when reading. He was of an amorous humour, but said that for ten years past he had decidedly and entirely renounced women. He was no longer pleasing, he said; he did not add: "I am too old," but, "I am too poor." He would say: "If I were not ruined, he! he!" His remaining income in fact was only about fifteen thousand livres. His dream was of receiving a windfall, and having an income of a hundred thousand francs, in order to keep mistresses. He did not belong, as we see, to that sickly variety of octogenarians who, like M. de Voltaire, are dying all their life; it was not a milk and water longevity; this jovial old man was always in good health. He was superficial, hasty, easily angered. He got into a rage on all occasions, most frequently when most unseasonable. When anybody contradicted him he raised his cane; he beat his servants as in the time of Louis XIV. He had an unmarried daughter over fifty years old, whom he belaboured severely when he was angry, and whom he would gladly have horsewhipped. She seemed to him about eight years old. He cuffed his domestics vigorously and would say: Ah! slut! One of his oaths was: *By the big slippers of big slipperdom!* In some respects he was of a singular tranquillity: he was shaved every day by a barber who had been crazy and who hated him, being jealous of M. Gillenormand on account of his wife, a pretty coquettish woman. M. Gillenormand admired his own discernment in everything, and pronounced himself very sagacious; this is one of his sayings: "I have indeed some penetration; I can tell when a flea bites me, from what woman it comes." The terms which he oftenest used were: *sensible men*, and *nature*. He did not give to this last word the broad acceptation which our epoch has assigned to it. But he twisted it into his own use in his little chimney-corner satires: "Nature," he would say, "in order that civilisation may have a little of everything, gives it even some specimens of amusing barbarism. Europe has samples of Asia and Africa, in miniature. The cat is a drawing-room tiger, the lizard is a pocket crocodile. The danseuses of the opera are rosy savagesses. They do not eat men, they feed upon them. Or rather, the little magicians change them into oysters, and swallow them. The Caribs leave nothing but the bones, they leave nothing but the shells. Such are our customs. We do not devour, we gnaw; we do not exterminate, we clutch."

II
LIKE MASTER, LIKE DWELLING

HE lived in the Marais, Rue des Filles de Calvaire, No. 6. The house was his own. This house has been torn down, and rebuilt since, and its number has probably been changed in the revolutions of numbering to which the streets of Paris are subject. He occupied an ancient and ample apartment on the first story, between the street and the gardens, covered to the ceiling with fine Gobelin and Beauvais tapestry representing pastoral scenes; the subjects of the ceiling and the panels were repeated in miniature upon the arm-chairs. He surrounded his bed with a large screen with nine leaves varnished with Coromandel lac. Long, full curtains hung at the windows, and made great, magnificent broken folds. The garden, which was immediately beneath his windows, was connected with the angle between them by means of a staircase of twelve or fifteen steps, which the old man ascended and descended very blithely. In addition to a library adjoining his room, he had a boudoir which he thought very much of, a gay retreat, hung with magnificent straw-colour tapestry, covered and ordered by M. de Vivonne from his convicts for his mistress. M. Gillenormand had inherited this from a severe maternal great-aunt, who died at the age of a hundred. He had had two wives. His manners held a medium between the courtier which he had never been, and the counsellor which he might have been. He was gay, and kind when he wished to be. In his youth, he had been one of those men who are always deceived by their wives and never by their mistresses, because they are at the same time the most disagreeable husbands and the most charming lovers in the world. He was a connoisseur in painting. He had in his room a wonderful portrait of nobody knows who, painted by Jordaens, done in great dabs with the brush, with millions of details, in a confused manner and as if by chance. M. Gillenormand's dress was not in the fashion of Louis XV., nor even in the fashion of Louis XVI.; he wore the costume of the *incroyables* of the Directory. He had thought himself quite young until then, and had kept up with the fashions. His coat was of light cloth, with broad facings, a long swallow tail, and large steel buttons. Add to this short breeches and shoe buckles. He always carried his hands in his pockets. He said authoritatively: *The French Revolution is a mess of scamps.*

III
LUKE ESPRIT

WHEN sixteen years old, one evening, at the opera, he had had the honour of being stared at, at the same time, by two beauties then mature and celebrated and besung by Voltaire, La Camargo and La Sallé. Caught between two fires, he had made a heroic retreat towards a little danseuse, a girl named Nahenry, who was sixteen years old, like him obscure as a cat, and with whom he fell in love. He was full of reminiscences. He would exclaim: "How pretty she was, that Guimard Guimardin Guimardinette, the last time I saw her at Longchamps, frizzled in lofty sentiments, with her curious trinkets in turquoise, her dress the colour of a new-born child, and her muff in agitation!" He had worn in his youth a vest of London short, of which he talked frequently and fluently. "I was dressed like a Turk of the Levantine Levant," said he. Madame de Boufflers, having accidentally seen him when he was twenty years old, described him as a "charming fool." He ridiculed all the names which he saw in politics or in power, finding them low and vulgar. He read the journals, *the newspapers, the gazettes*, as he said, stifling with bursts of laughter. "Oh!" said he, "what are these people! Corbière! Humann! Casimir Perier! those are ministers for you. I imagine I see this in a journal: M. Gillenormand, Minister; that would be a joke. Well! they are so stupid that it would go!" He called everything freely by its name, proper or improper, and was never restrained by the presence of women. He would say coarse, obscene, and indecent things with an inexpressible tranquillity and coolness which was elegant. It was the off-hand way of his time. It is worthy of remark that the age of periphrases in verse was the age of crudities in prose. His godfather had predicted that he would be a man of genius, and gave him these two significant names: Luke Esprit.

IV

AN INSPIRING CENTENARIAN

He had taken several prizes in his youth at the college at Moulins, where he was born, and had been crowned by the hands of the Duke de Nivernais, whom he called the Duke de Nevers. Neither the Convention, nor the death of Louis XVI., nor Napoleon, nor the return of the Bourbons, had been able to efface the memory of this coronation. The *Duke de Nevers* was to him the great figure of the century. "What a noble, great lord," said he, "and what a fine air he had with his blue ribbon!" In Monsieur Gillenormand's eyes, Catharine II. had atoned for the crime of the partition of Poland by buying the secret of the elixir of gold from Bestuchef, for three thousand roubles. Over this he grew animated. "The elixir of gold," exclaimed he, "Bestuchef's yellow dye, General Lamotte's drops, these were in the eighteenth century, at a louis for a half ounce flask, the great remedy for the catastrophes of love, the panacea against Venus. Louis XV. sent two hundred flasks to the Pope." He would have been greatly exasperated and thrown off his balance if anybody had told him that the elixir of gold was nothing but the perchloride of iron. Monsieur Gillenormand worshipped the Bourbons and held 1789 in horror; he was constantly relating how he saved himself during the Reign of Terror, and how, if he had not had a good deal of gaiety and a good deal of wit, his head would have been cut off. If any young man ventured to eulogise the republic in his presence, he turned black in the face, and was angry enough to faint. Sometimes he would allude to his ninety years of age, and say, *I really hope that I shall not see ninety-three twice*. At other times he intimated to his people that he intended to live a hundred years.

V

BASQUE AND NICOLETTE

HE had his theories. Here is one of them: "When a man passionately loves women, and has a wife of his own for whom he cares but little, ugly, cross, legitimate, fond of asserting her rights, roosting on the code and jealous on occasion, he has but one way to get out of it and keep the peace, that is to let his wife have the purse-strings. This abdication makes him free. The wife keeps herself busy then, devotes herself to handling specie, verdigrises her fingers, takes charge of the breeding of the tenants, the bringing up of the farmers, convokes lawyers, presides over notaries, harangues justices, visits pettifoggers, follows up lawsuits, writes out leases, dictates contracts, feels herself sovereign, sells, buys, regulates, promises and compromises, binds and cancels, cedes, concedes, and retrocedes, arranges, deranges, economises, wastes; she does foolish things, a magisterial and personal pleasure, and this consoles her. While her husband disdains her, she has the satisfaction of ruining her husband." This theory, Monsieur Gillenormand had applied to himself, and it had become his history. His wife, the second one, had administered his fortune in such wise that there remained to Monsieur Gillenormand, when one fine day he found himself a widower, just enough to obtain, by turning almost everything into an annuity, an income of fifteen thousand francs, three-quarters of which would expire with himself. He had no hesitation, little troubled with the care of leaving an inheritance. Moreover, he had seen that patrimonies met with adventures, and, for example, became *national property*; he had been present at the avatars of the consolidated thirds, and he had little faith in the ledger. "*Rue Quincampoix for all that!*" said he. His house in Rue des Filles du Calvaire, we have said, belonged to him. He had two domestics, "a male and a female." When a domestic entered his service, Monsieur Gillenormand rebaptised him. He gave to the men the name of their province: Nîmois, Comtois, Poitevin, Picard. His last valet was a big, pursy, wheezy man of fifty-five, incapable of running twenty steps, but as he was born at Bayonne, Monsieur Gillenormand called him Basque. As for female servants, they were all called Nicolette in his house (even Magnon, who will reappear as we proceed). One day a proud cook, with a blue sash, of the lofty race of porters, presented herself. "How much do you want a month?" asked Monsieur Gillenormand. "Thirty francs." "What is your name?" "Olympie." "You shall have fifty francs, and your name shall be Nicolette."

VI

IN WHICH WE SEE LA MAGNON
AND HER TWO LITTLE ONES

At Monsieur Gillenormand's grief was translated into anger; he was furious at being in despair. He had every prejudice, and took every licence. One of the things of which he made up his external relief and his internal satisfaction was, we have just indicated, that he was still a youthful gallant, and that he passed for such energetically. He called this having "royal renown." His royal renown sometimes attracted singular presents. One day there was brought to his house in a basket, something like an oyster basket, a big boy, new-born, crying like the deuce, and duly wrapped in swaddling clothes, which a servant girl turned away six months before attributed to him. Monsieur Gillenormand was at that time fully eighty-four years old. Indignation and clamour on the part of the bystanders. And who did this bold wench think would believe this? What effrontery! What an abominable calumny! Monsieur Gillenormand, however, manifested no anger. He looked upon the bundle with the amiable smile of a man who is flattered by a calumny, and said aside: "Well, what? what is it? what is the matter there? what have we here? you are in a pretty state of amazement, and indeed seem like any ignorant people. The

Duke d'Angoulême, natural son of his majesty Charles IX., married at eighty-five a little hussy of fifteen; Monsieur Virginal, Marquis d'Alhuye, brother of Cardinal de Sourdis, Archbishop of Bordeaux, at eighty-three, had, by a chambermaid of the wife of President Jacquin, a son, a true love son, who was a Knight of Malta, and knighted Councillor of State; one of the great men of this century, Abbé Tabarand, was the son of a man eighty-seven years old. These things are anything but uncommon. And then the Bible! Upon that, I declare that this little gentleman is not mine. But take care of him. It is not his fault." This process was too easy. The creature, she whose name was Magnon, made him a second present the year after. It was a boy again. This time Monsieur Gillenormand capitulated. He sent the two brats back to the mother, engaging to pay eighty francs a month for their support, upon condition that the said mother should not begin again. He added, "I wish the mother to treat them well. I will come to see them from time to time." Which he did. He had had a brother, a priest, who had been for thirty-three years rector of the Academy of Poitiers, and who died at seventy-nine. "*I lost him young*," said he. This brother, of whom hardly a memory is left, was a quiet miser, who, being a priest, felt obliged to give alms to the poor whom he met, but never gave them anything more than coppers or worn-out sous, finding thus the means of going to Hell by the road to Paradise. As to Monsieur Gillenormand, the elder, he made no trade of alms-giving, but gave willingly and nobly. He was benevolent, abrupt, charitable, and had he been rich, his inclination would have been to be magnificent. He wished that all that concerned him should be done in a large way, even rascalities. One day, having been swindled in an inheritance by a business man, in a gross and palpable manner, he uttered this solemn exclamation: "Fie! this is not decent! I am really ashamed of these petty cheats. Everything is degenerate in this century, even the rascals. 'Sdeath! this is not the way to rob a man like me. I am robbed as if in a wood, but meanly robbed. *Silvæ sint consul dignæ!*" He had had, we have said, two wives; by the first a daughter, who had remained unmarried, and by the second another daughter, who died when about thirty years old, and who had married for love, or luck, or otherwise, a soldier of fortune, who had served in the armies of the republic and the empire, had won the cross at Austerlitz, and been made colonel at Waterloo. "*This is the disgrace of my family,"* said the old bourgeois. He took a great deal of snuff, and had a peculiar skill in ruffling his lace frill with the back of his hand. He had very little belief in God.

VII
RULE:—NEVER RECEIVE ANYBODY EXCEPT IN THE EVENING

SUCH was M. Luke Esprit Gillenormand, who had not lost his hair, which was rather grey than white, and always combed in dog's-ears. To sum up, and with all this, a venerable man.

He was of the eighteenth century, frivolous and great.

In 1814, and in the early years of the Restoration, Monsieur Gillenormand, who was still young—he was only seventy-four—had lived in the Faubourg Saint Germain, Rue Servandoni, near Saint Sulpice. He had retired to the Marais only upon retiring from society, after his eighty years were fully accomplished.

And in retiring from society, he had walled himself up in his habits; the principal one, in which he was invariable, was to keep his door absolutely closed by day, and never to receive anybody whatever, on any business whatever, except in the evening. He dined at five o'clock, then his door was open. This was the custom of his century, and he would not swerve from it. "The day is vulgar," said he, "and only deserves closed shutters. People who are anybody light up their wit when the zenith lights up its stars." And he barricaded himself against everybody, were it even the king. The old elegance of his time.

VIII
TWO DO NOT MAKE A PAIR

AS to the two daughters of Monsieur Gillenormand, we have just spoken of them. They were born ten years apart. In their youth they resembled each other very little; and in character as well as in countenance, were as far from being sisters as possible. The younger was a cheerful soul, attracted towards everything that is bright, busy with flowers, poetry, and music, carried away into the glories of space, enthusiastic, ethereal, affianced from childhood in the ideal to a dim heroic figure. The elder had also her chimera; in the azure depth she saw a contractor, some good, coarse commissary, very rich, a husband splendidly stupid, a million-made man, or even a prefect; receptions at the prefecture, an usher of the ante-chamber, with the chain on his neck, official bails, harangues at the mayor's, to be "*Madame la préfète*," this whirled in her imagination. The two sisters wandered thus, each in her own fancy, when they were young girls. Both had wings, one like an angel, the other like a goose.

No ambition is fully realised, here below at least. No paradise becomes terrestrial at the period in which we live. The younger had married the man of her dreams, but she was dead. The elder was not married.

At the moment she makes her entry into the story which we are relating, she was an old piece of virtue, an incombustible prude, one of the sharpest noses and one of the most obtuse minds which could be discovered. A characteristic incident. Outside of the immediate family nobody had ever known her first name. She was called *Mademoiselle Gillenormand the elder*.

In cant, Mademoiselle Gillenormand the elder could have given odds to an English miss. She was immodestly modest. She had one frightful reminiscence in her life: one day a man had seen her garter.

Age had only increased this pitiless modesty. Her dress front was never thick enough, and never rose high enough. She multiplied hooks and pins where nobody thought of looking. The peculiarity of prudery is to multiply sentinels, in proportion as the fortress is less threatened.

However, explain who can these ancient mysteries of innocence, she allowed herself to be kissed without displeasure, by an officer of lancers who was her grand-nephew and whose name was Théodule.

Spite of this favoured lancer, the title *Prude*, under which we have classed her, fitted her absolutely. Mademoiselle Gillenormand was a kind of twilight soul. Prudery is half a virtue and half a vice.

To prudery she added bigotry, a suitable lining. She was of the fraternity of the Virgin, wore a white veil on certain feast-days, muttered special prayers, revered "the holy blood," venerated "the sacred heart," remained for hours in contemplation before an old-fashioned Jesuit altar in a chapel closed to the vulgar faithful, and let her soul fly away among the little marble clouds and along the grand rays of gilded wood.

She had a chapel friend, an old maid like herself, called Mademoiselle Vaubois, who was perfectly stupid, and in comparison with whom Mademoiselle Gillenormand had the happiness of being an eagle. Beyond her Agnus Deis and her Ave Marias, Mademoiselle Vaubois had no light except upon the different modes of making sweetmeats. Mademoiselle Vaubois, perfect in her kind, was the ermine of stupidity without a single stain of intelligence.

We must say that in growing old, Mademoiselle Gillenormand had rather gained than lost. This is the case with passive natures. She had never been peevish, which is a relative goodness; and then, years wear off angles, and the softening of time had come upon her. She was sad with an obscure sadness of which she had not the secret herself. There was in her whole person the stupor of a life ended but never commenced.

She kept her father's house. Monsieur Gillenormand had his daughter with him as we have seen Monseigneur Bienvenu have his sister with him. These households of an old man and an old maid are not rare, and always have the touching aspect of two feeblenesses leaning upon each other.

There was besides in the house, between this old maid and this old man, a child, a little boy, always trembling and mute before M. Gillenormand. M. Gillenormand never spoke to this child but with stern voice, and sometimes with uplifted cane: "*Here! Monsieur—rascal, blackguard, come here! Answer me, rogue! Let me see you, scape-grace!*" etc. etc. He idolised him.

It was his grandson. We shall see this child again.

BOOK THIRD –
THE GRANDFATHER AND THE GRANDSON

I
AN OLD MAN

WHEN M. Gillenormand lived in the Rue Servandoni, he frequented several very fine and very noble salons. Although a bourgeois, M. Gillenormand was welcome. As he was twice witty, first with his own wit, then with the wit which was attributed to him, he was even sought after and lionised. He went nowhere save on condition of ruling there. There are men who at any price desire influence and to attract the attention of others; where they cannot be oracles, they make themselves laughing-stocks. Monsieur Gillenormand was not of this nature; his dominance in the royalist salons which he frequented cost him none of his self-respect. He was an oracle everywhere. It was his fortune to have as an antagonist, Monsieur de Bonald, and even Monsieur Bengy-Puy-Vallée.

About 1817, he always spent two afternoons a week at a house in his neighbourhood, in the Rue Férou, that of the Baroness of T——, a worthy and venerable lady, whose husband had been, under Louis XVI., French Ambassador at Berlin. The Baron of T., who, during his life, had devoted himself passionately to ecstasies and magnetic visions, died in the emigration, ruined, leaving no fortune but ten manuscript volumes bound in red morocco with gilt edges, of very curious memoirs upon Mesmer and his trough. Madame de T. had not published the memoirs from motives of dignity, and supported herself on a small income, which had survived the flood nobody knows how. Madame de T. lived far from the court,—*a very mixed society*, said she,—in a noble, proud, and poor isolation. A few friends gathered about her widow's hearth twice a week, and this constituted a pure royalist salon. They took tea, and uttered, as the wind set towards elegy or dithyrambic, groans or cries of horror over the century, over the charter, over the Buonapartists, over the prostitution of the blue ribbon to bourgeois, over the Jacobinism of Louis XVIII.; and they amused themselves in whispers with hopes which rested upon Monsieur, since Charles X.

They hailed the vulgar songs in which Napoleon was called *Nicolas* with transports of joy. Duchesses, the most delicate and the most charming women in the world, went into ecstasies over couplets like this addressed "to the federals:"

> Renforcez dans vos culottes
> Le bout d'chemis' qui vous pend.
> Qu'on n' dis pas qu' les patriotes
> Ont arboré l'drapeau blanc!

They amused themselves with puns which they thought terrible, with innocent plays upon words which they supposed to be venomous, with quatrains and even distiches; thus upon the Dessolles ministry, a moderate cabinet of which MM. Decazes and Deserre were members:

> Pour raffermir le trône ébranlé sur sa base,
> Il faut changer de sol, et de serre et de case.

Or sometimes they drew up the list of the Chamber of Peers, "Chamber abominably jacobin," and in this list they arranged the names, so as to make, for example, phrases like this: *Damas. Sabran. Gouvion Saint Cyr.* All this gaily.

In this little world they parodied the revolution. They had some inclinations or other which sharpened the same anger in the inverse sense. They sang their little *ça ira*:

> Ah! ça ira! ça ira! ça ira!
> Les buonapartist' à la lanterne!

Songs are like the guillotine; they cut indifferently, to-day this head, to-morrow that. It is only a variation.

In the Fualdès affair, which belongs to this time, 1816, they took sides with Bastide and Jausion, because Fualdès was a "Buonapartist." They called the liberals, *the brothers and friends*; this was the highest degree of insult.

Like certain menageries, the Baroness de T——'s salon had two lions. One was M. Gillenormand, the other was Count de Lamothe Valois, of whom it was whispered, with a sort of consideration: "*Do you know? He is the Lamothe of the necklace affair.*" Partisans have such singular amnesties as these.

We will add also: "Among the bourgeois, positions of honour are lowered by too easy intercourse; you must take care whom you receive; just as there is a loss of caloric in the neighbourhood of those who are cold, there is a diminution of consideration in the approach of people who are despised. The old highest society held itself above this law as it did above all others, Marigny, La Pompadour's brother, is a visitor of the Prince de Soubise. Although? no, because. Du Barry, godfather of La Vaubernier, is very welcome at the Marshal de Richelieu's. This society is Olympus. Mercury and the Prince de Gueménée are at home there. A thief is admitted, provided he be a lord."

The Count de Lamothe, who, in 1815, was a man of seventy-five, was remarkable for nothing save his silent and sententious air, his cold, angular face, his perfectly polished manners, his coat buttoned up to his cravat, and his long legs, always crossed in long, loose pantaloons, of the colour of burnt sienna. His face was of the colour of his pantaloons.

This M. de Lamothe was "esteemed" in this salon, on account of his "celebrity," and, strange to say, but true, on account of the name of Valois.

As to M. Gillenormand, his consideration was absolutely for himself alone. He made authority. He had, sprightly as he was, and without detriment to his gaiety, a certain fashion of being, which was imposing, worthy, honourable, and genteelly lofty; and his great age added to it. A man is not a century for nothing. Years place at last a venerable crown upon a head.

He gave, moreover, some of those repartees which certainly have in them the genuine sparkle. Thus when the King of Prussia, after having restored Louis XVIII., came to make him a visit under the name of Count de Ruppin, he was received by the descendant of Louis XIV. somewhat like a Marquis of Brandenburg, and with the most delicate impertinence. Monsieur Gillenormand approved this. "*All kings who are not the King of France,*" said he, "*are kings of a province.*" The following question and answer were uttered one day in his presence: "What is the sentence of the editor of the *Courier Français*?" "To be hung up for awhile." "*Up* is superfluous," observed Monsieur Gillenormand. Sayings of this kind make position for a man.

At an anniversary *Te Deum* for the return of the Bourbons, seeing Monsieur de Talleyrand pass, he said: *There goes His Excellency the Bad*.

M. Gillenormand was usually accompanied by his daughter, this long mademoiselle, then past forty, and seeming fifty, and by a beautiful little boy of seven, white, rosy, fresh-looking, with happy and trustful eyes, who never appeared in this salon without hearing a buzz about him: "How pretty he is! What a pity! poor child!" This child was the boy to whom we have but just alluded. They called him "poor child," because his father was "a brigand of the Loire."

This brigand of the Loire was M. Gillenormand's son-in-law, already mentioned, and whom M. Gillenormand called *the disgrace of his family*.

II
ONE OF THE RED SPECTRES OF THAT TIME

WHOEVER, at that day, had passed through the little city of Vernon, and walked over that beautiful monumental bridge which will be very soon replaced, let us hope, by some horrid wire bridge, would have noticed, as his glance fell from the top of the parapet, a man of about fifty, with a leather casque on his head, dressed in pantaloons and waistcoat of coarse grey cloth, to which something yellow was stitched which had been a red ribbon, shod in wooden shoes, browned by the sun, his face almost black and his hair almost white, a large scar upon his forehead extending down his cheek, bent, bowed down, older than his years, walking nearly every day with a spade and a pruning knife in his hand, in one of those walled compartments, in the vicinity of the bridge, which, like a chain of terraces border the left bank of the Seine,—charming inclosures full of flowers of which one would say, if they were much larger, they are gardens, and if they were a little smaller, they are bouquets. All these inclosures are bounded by the river on one side and by a house on the other. The man in the waistcoat and wooden shoes of whom we have just spoken lived, about the year 1817, in the smallest of these inclosures and the humblest of these houses. He lived there solitary and alone, in silence and in poverty, with a woman who was neither young nor old, neither beautiful nor ugly, neither peasant nor bourgeois, who waited upon him. The square of earth which he called his garden was celebrated in the town for the beauty of the flowers which he cultivated in it. Flowers were his occupation.

By dint of labour, perseverance, attention, and pails of water, he had succeeded in creating after the Creator, and had invented certain tulips and dahlias which seemed to have been forgotten by Nature. He was ingenious; he anticipated Soulange Bodin in the formation of little clumps of heather earth for the culture of rare and precious shrubs from America and China. By break of day, in summer, he was in his walks, digging, pruning, weeding, watering, walking in the midst of his flowers with an air of kindness, sadness, and gentleness, sometimes dreamy and motionless for whole hours listening to the song of a bird in a tree, the prattling of a child in a house, or oftener with his eyes fixed on some drop of dew at the end of a spear of grass, of which the sun was making a carbuncle. His table was very frugal, and he drank more milk than wine. An urchin would make him yield, his servant scolded him. He was timid, so much so as to seem unsociable, he rarely went out, and saw nobody but the poor who rapped at his window, and his curé, Abbé Mabeuf, a good old man. Still, if any of the inhabitants of the city or strangers, whoever they might be, curious to see his tulips and roses, knocked at his little house, he opened his door with a smile. This was the brigand of the Loire.

Whoever, at the same time, had read the military memoirs, the biographies, the *Moniteur*, and the bulletins of the Grand Army, would have been struck by a name which appears rather often, the name of George Pontmercy. When quite young, this George Pontmercy was a soldier in the regiment of Saintonge. The revolution broke out. The regiment of Saintonge was in the Army of the Rhine. For the old regiments of the monarchy kept their province names even after the fall of the monarchy, and were not brigaded until 1794. Pontmercy fought at Spires, at Worms, at Neustadt, at Turkheim, at Alzey, at Mayence where he was one of the two hundred who formed Houchard's rear-guard. He with eleven others held their ground against the Prince of Hesse's corps behind the old rampart of Andernach, and only fell back upon the bulk of the army when the hostile cannon had effected a breach from the top of the parapet to the slope of the glacis. He was under Kleber at Marchiennes, and at the battle of Mont Palissel, where he had his arm broken by a musket-ball. Then he passed to the Italian frontier, and he was one of the thirty grenadiers who defended the Col di Tende with Joubert. Joubert was made Adjutant-General, and Pontmercy Second-Lieutenant. Pontmercy was by the side of Berthier in the midst of the storm of balls on that day of Lodi of which Bonaparte said: *Berthier was cannoneer, cavalier, and grenadier.* He saw his old general, Joubert, fall at Novi, at the moment when, with uplifted sword, he was crying: Forward! Being embarked with his company, through the necessities of the campaign, in a pinnace, which was on the way from Genoa to some little port on the coast, he fell into a wasp's-nest of seven or eight English vessels. The Genoese captain wanted to throw the guns into the sea, hide the soldiers in the hold, and slip through in the dark like a merchantman. Pontmercy had the colours seized to the halyards of the ensign-staff, and passed proudly under the guns of the British frigates. Fifty miles further on, his boldness increasing, he attacked with his pinnace and captured a large English transport carrying troops to Sicily, so loaded with men and horses that the vessel was full to the hatches. In 1805, he was in that division of Malher which captured Günzburg from the Archduke Ferdinand. At Weltingen he received in his arms under a shower of balls Colonel Maupetit, who was mortally wounded at the head of the 9th Dragoons. He distinguished himself at Austerlitz in that wonderful march in echelon under the enemy's fire. When the cavalry of the Russian Imperial Guard crushed a battalion of the 4th of the Line, Pontmercy was one of those who revenged the repulse, and overthrew the Guard. The emperor gave him the cross. Pontmercy successively saw Wurmser made prisoner in Mantua, Melas in Alexandria, and Mack in Ulm. He was in the eighth corps, of the Grand Army, which Mortier commanded, and which took Hamburg. Then he passed into the 55th of the Line which was the old Flanders regiment. At Eylau, he was in the churchyard where the heroic captain Louis Hugo, uncle of the author of this book, sustained alone with his company of eighty-three men, for two hours, the whole effort of the enemy's army. Pontmercy was one of the three who came out of that churchyard alive. He was at Friedland. Then he saw Moscow, then the Beresina, then Lutzen, Bautzen, Dresden, Wachau, Leipsig, and the defiles of Glenhausen, then Montmirail, Château-Thierry, Caron, the banks of the Marne, the banks of the Aisne, and the formidable position at Laon. At Arney le Duc, a captain, he sabred ten cossacks, and saved, not his general, but his corporal. He was wounded on that occasion, and twenty-seven splinters were extracted from his left arm alone. Eight days before the capitulation of Paris, he exchanged with a comrade, and entered the cavalry. He had what was called under the old régime *the double-*

hand, that is to say, equal skill in managing, as a soldier, the sabre or the musket, as an officer, a squadron or a battalion. It is this skill, perfected by military education, which gives rise to certain special arms, the dragoons, for instance, who are both cavalry and infantry. He accompanied Napoleon to the island of Elba. At Waterloo he led a squadron of cuirassiers in Dubois' brigade. He it was who took the colours from the Lunenburg battalion. He carried the colours to the emperor's feet. He was covered with blood. He had received, in seizing the colours, a sabre stroke across his face. The emperor, well pleased, cried to him: *You are a Colonel, you are a Baron, you are an Officer of the Legion of Honour!* Pontmercy answered: *Sire, I thank you for my widow.* An hour afterwards, he fell in the ravine of Ohain. Now who was this George Pontmercy? He was that very brigand of the Loire.

We have already seen something of his history. After Waterloo, Pontmercy, drawn out, as will be remembered, from the sunken road of Ohain, succeeded in regaining the army, and was passed along from ambulance to ambulance to the cantonments of the Loire.

The Restoration put him on half-pay, then sent him to a residence, that is to say under surveillance at Vernon. The king, Louis XVIII., ignoring all that had been done in the Hundred Days, recognised neither his position of officer of the Legion of Honour, nor his rank of colonel, nor his title of baron. He, on his part, neglected no opportunity to sign himself *Colonel Baron Pontmercy.* He had only one old blue coat, and he never went out without putting on the rosette of an officer of the Legion of Honour. The *procureur du roi* notified him that he would be prosecuted for "illegally" wearing this decoration. When this notice was given to him by a friendly intermediary, Pontmercy answered with a bitter smile: "I do not know whether it is that I no longer understand French, or you no longer speak it; but the fact is I do not understand you." Then he went out every day for a week with his rosette. Nobody dared to disturb him. Two or three times the minister of war or the general commanding the department wrote to him with this address: *Monsieur Commandant Pontmercy.* He returned the letters unopened. At the same time, Napoleon at St. Helena was treating Sir Hudson Lowe's missives addressed to General Bonaparte in the same way. Pontmercy at last, excuse the word, came to have in his mouth the same saliva as his emperor.

So too, there were in Rome a few Carthaginian soldiers, taken prisoners, who refused to bow to Flaminius, and who had a little of Hannibal's soul.

One morning, he met the *procureur du roi* in one of the streets of Vernon, went up to him and said: "Monsieur *procureur du roi*, am I allowed to wear my scar?"

He had nothing but his very scanty half-pay as chief of squadron. He hired the smallest house he could find in Vernon. He lived there alone; how we have just seen. Under the empire, between two wars he had found time to marry Mademoiselle Gillenormand. The old bourgeois, who really felt outraged, consented with a sigh, saying: "*The greatest families are forced to it.*" In 1815, Madame Pontmercy, an admirable woman in every respect, noble and rare, and worthy of her husband, died, leaving a child. This child would have been the colonel's joy in his solitude; but the grandfather had imperiously demanded his grandson, declaring that, unless he were given up to him, he would disinherit him. The father yielded for the sake of the little boy, and not being able to have his child he set about loving flowers.

He had moreover given up everything, making no movement nor conspiring with others. He divided his thoughts between the innocent things he was doing, and the grand things he had done. He passed his time hoping for a pink or remembering Austerlitz.

M. Gillenormand had no intercourse with his son-in-law. The colonel was to him "a bandit," and he was to the colonel "a blockhead." M. Gillenormand never spoke of the colonel, unless sometimes to make mocking allusions to "his barony." It was expressly understood that Pontmercy should never endeavour to see his son or speak to him, under pain of the boy being turned away, and disinherited. To the Gillenormands, Pontmercy was pestiferous. They intended to bring up the child to their liking. The colonel did wrong perhaps to accept these conditions, but he submitted to them, thinking that he was doing right, and sacrificing himself alone.

The inheritance from the grandfather Gillenormand was a small affair, but the inheritance from Mlle. Gillenormand the elder was considerable. This aunt, who had remained single, was very rich from the maternal side, and the son of her sister was her natural heir. The child, whose name was Marius, knew that he had a father, but nothing more. Nobody spoke a word to him about him. However, in the society into which his grandfather took him, the whisperings, the hints, the winks, enlightened the little boy's mind at length; he finally comprehended something of it, and as he naturally imbibed by a sort of infiltration and slow penetration the ideas and opinions which formed, so to say, the air he breathed, he came little by little to think of his father only with shame and with a closed heart.

While he was thus growing up, every two or three months the colonel would escape, come furtively to Paris like a fugitive from justice breaking his ban, and go to Saint Sulpice, at the hour when Aunt Gillenormand took Marius to mass. There, trembling lest the aunt should turn round, concealed behind a pillar, motionless, not daring to breathe, he saw his child. The scarred veteran was afraid of the old maid.

From this, in fact, came his connection with the curé of Vernon, Abbé Mabeuf.

This worthy priest was the brother of a warden of Saint Sulpice, who had several times noticed this man gazing upon his child, and the scar on his cheek, and the big tears in his eyes. This man, who had so really the appearance of a man, and who wept like a woman, had attracted the warden's attention. This face remained in his memory. One day, having gone to Vernon to see his brother, he met Colonel Pontmercy on the bridge, and recognised the man of Saint Sulpice. The warden spoke of it to the curé, and the two, under some pretext, made the colonel a visit. This visit led to others. The colonel, who at first was very reserved, finally unbosomed himself, and the curé and the warden came to know the whole story, and how Pontmercy was sacrificing his own happiness to the future of his child. The result was that the curé felt a veneration and tenderness for him, and the colonel, on his part, felt an affection for the curé. And, moreover, when it happens that both are sincere and good, nothing will mix and amalgamate more easily than an old priest and an old soldier. In reality, they are the same kind of man. One has devoted himself to his country upon earth, the other to his country in heaven; there is no other difference.

Twice a year, on the first of January and on St. George's Day, Marius wrote filial letters to his father, which his aunt dictated, and which, one would have said, were copied from some Complete Letter Writer; this was all that M. Gillenormand allowed;

and the father answered with very tender letters, which the grandfather thrust into his pocket without reading.

III
REQUIESCANT

The salon of Madame de T. was all that Marius Pontmercy knew of the world. It was the only opening by which he could look out into life. This opening was sombre, and through this porthole there came more cold than warmth, more night than day. The child, who was nothing but joy and light on entering this strange world, in a little while became sad, and, what is still more unusual at his age, grave. Surrounded by all these imposing and singular persons, he looked about him with a serious astonishment. Everything united to increase his amazement. There were in Madame de T.'s salon some very venerable noble old ladies whose names were Mathan, Noah, Lévis which was pronounced Lévi, Cambis which was pronounced Cambyse. These antique faces and these biblical names mingled in the child's mind with his Old Testament, which he was learning by heart, and when they were all present, seated in a circle about a dying fire, dimly lighted by a green-shaded lamp, with their stern profiles, their grey or white hair, their long dresses of another age, in which mournful colours only could be distinguished, at rare intervals dropping a few words which were at once majestic and austere, the little Marius looked upon them with startled eyes thinking that he saw, not women, but patriarchs and magi, not real beings, but phantoms.

Among these phantoms were scattered several priests, who frequented this old salon, and a few gentlemen; the Marquis de Sass——, secretary of commands to Madame de Berry, the Viscount de Val——, who published some monorhymed odes under the pseudonym of *Charles Antoine*, the Prince de Beauff——, who, quite young, was turning grey, and had a pretty and witty wife whose dress of scarlet velvet with gold trimmings, worn very low in the neck, startled this darkness, the Marquis de C—— d'E——, the man in all France who best understood "proportioned politeness," the Count d'Am——, the goodman with the benevolent chin, and the Chevalier de Port de Guy, a frequenter of the library of the Louvre, called the king's cabinet. M. de Port de Guy, bald and rather old than aged, related that in 1793, when sixteen years of age, he was sent to the galleys as "refractory," and chained with an octogenarian, the Bishop of Mirepoix, refractory also, but as a priest, while he was so as a soldier. This was at Toulon. Their business was to go to the scaffold at night, and gather up the heads and bodies of those that had been guillotined during the day; they carried these dripping trunks upon their backs, and their red galley caps were encrusted behind with blood, dry in the morning, wet at night. These tragic anecdotes abounded in Madame de T.'s salon; and by dint of cursing Marat, they came to applaud Trestaillon. A few deputies of the undiscoverable kind played their whist there, M. Thibord du Chalard, M. Lemarchant de Gomicourt, and the celebrated jester of the Right, M. Cornet Dincourt. The Bailli de Ferrette, with his short breeches and his thin legs, sometimes passed through this salon on the way to M. de Talleyrand's. He had been the pleasure companion of the Count d'Artois, and reversing Aristotle cowering before Campaspe, he had made La Guimard walk on all fours, and in this manner shown to the centuries a philosopher avenged by a bailli.

As for the priests, there was Abbé Halma, the same to whom M. Larose, his assistant on *La Foudre*, said: *Pshaw! who is there that is not fifty years old? a few greenhorns perhaps?* Abbé Letourneur, the king's preacher, Abbé Frayssinous, was not yet either count, or bishop, or minister, or peer, and who wore an old cassock short of buttons, and Abbé Keravenant, curé de Saint Germain des Prés; besides these the Pope's Nuncio, at that time Monsignor Macchi, Archbishop of Nisibi, afterwards cardinal, remarkable for his long pensive nose, and another monsignor with the following titles: Abbate Palmieri, Domestic Prelate, one of the seven participating prothonotaries of the Holy See, canon of the Insignia of the Liberian Basilicate, advocate of the Saints, *postulatore di santi*, which relates to the business of canonisation and signifies very nearly: master of requests for the section of paradise. Finally, two cardinals, M. de la Luzerne and Monsieur de Cl—— T——. The Cardinal de la Luzerne was a writer, and was to have, some years later, the honour of signing articles in the *Conservateur* side by side with Chateaubriand; Monsieur de Cl—— T—— was Archbishop of Toul——, and often came to rusticate at Paris with his nephew the Marquis of T——, who has been Minister of Marine and of War. The

Cardinal de Cl——— T——— was a little, lively old man, showing his red stockings under his turned-up cassock; his peculiarities were hate of the Encyclopedia and desperate play at billiards, and people who, at that time, on summer evenings passed along the Rue M———, where the Hôtel de Cl——— T——— was at that time, stopped to hear the clicking of the balls and the sharp voice of the cardinal crying to his fellow conclavist, Monseigneur Cottret, Bishop *in partibus* of Carysta: *Mark, Abbé, I have caromed.* The Cardinal de Cl——— T——— had been brought to Madame de T.'s by his most intimate friend, M. de Roquelaure, formerly Bishop of Senlis and one of the Forty. M. de Roquelaure was noteworthy for his tall stature and his assiduity at the Academy; through the glass door of the hall near the Library in which the French Academy then held its sessions, the curious could every Friday gaze upon the old Bishop of Senlis, usually standing, freshly powdered, with violet stockings, and turning his back to the door, apparently to show his little collar to better advantage. All these ecclesiastics, though for the most part courtiers as well as churchmen, added to the importance of the T. salon, the lordly aspect of which was emphasised by five peers of France, the Marquis de Vib———, the Marquis de Tal———, the Marquis d'Herb———, the Viscount Damo———, and the Duke de Val———. This Duke de Val———, although Prince de Mon———, that is to say, a foreign sovereign prince, had so high an idea of France and the peerage that he saw everything through their medium. He it was who said: *The cardinals are the French peers of Rome; the Lords are the French peers of England.* Finally, since, in this century, the revolution must make itself felt everywhere, this feudal salon was, as we have said, ruled by a bourgeois. Monsieur Gillenormand reigned there.

There was the essence and the quintessence of Parisian Legitimatist society. People of renown, even though royalists, were held in quarantine. There is always anarchy in renown. Chateaubriand, had he entered there, would have had the same effect as Père Duchêne. Some repentant back-sliders, however, penetrated, by sufferance, into this orthodox world. Count Beug——— was received there by favour.

The "noble" salons of the present day bear no resemblance to those salons. The Faubourg Saint Germain of the present smells of heresy. The royalists of this age are demagogues, we must say it to their praise.

At Madame de T.'s, the society being superior, there was exquisite and haughty taste under a full bloom of politeness. Their manners comported with all sorts of involuntary refinements which were the ancient régime itself, buried, but living. Some of these peculiarities, in language especially, seemed grotesque. Superficial observers would have taken for provincial what was only ancient. They called a woman *madame la générale.* *Madame la colonelle* was not entirely out of use. The charming Madame de Léon, in memory doubtless of the Duchesses de Longueville and de Chevreuse, preferred this appellation to her title of Princess. The Marchioness of Créquy also called herself *madame la colonelle.*

It was this little lofty world which invented at the Tuileries the refinement of always saying, when speaking to the king in person, *the king,* in the third person, and never, *your majesty,* the title *your majesty* having been "sullied by the usurper."

Facts and men were judged there. They ridiculed the century, which dispensed with comprehending it. They assisted one another in astonishment. Each communicated to the rest the quantity of light he had. Methuselah instructed Epimenides. The deaf kept the blind informed. They declared, that the time since Coblentz had not elapsed. Just as Louis XVIII. was, by the grace of God, in the twenty-fifth year of his reign, the emigrees were, in reality, in the twenty-fifth year of their youth.

All was harmonious; nothing was too much alive; speech was hardly a breath; the journal, suiting the salon, seemed a papyrus. There were young people there, but they were slightly dead. In the ante-chamber, the liveries were old. These personages, completely out of date, were served by domestics of the same kind. Altogether they had the appearance of having lived a long time ago, and of being obstinate with the sepulchre. Conserve, Conservatism, Conservative, was nearly all the dictionary; *to be in good odour,* was the point. There was in fact something aromatic in the opinions of these venerable groups, and their ideas smelt of Indian herbs. It was a mummy world. The masters were embalmed, the valets were stuffed.

A worthy old marchioness, a ruined emigree, having now but one servant, continued to say: *My people.*

What was done in Madame de T.'s parlour? They were ultra.

To be ultra; this word, although what it represents has not

perhaps disappeared,—this word has now lost its meaning. Let us explain it.

To be ultra is to go beyond. It is to attack the sceptre in the name of the throne, and the mitre in the name of the altar; it is to maltreat the thing you support; it is to kick in the traces; it is to cavil at the stake for under-cooking heretics; it is to reproach the idol with a lack of idolatry; it is to insult by excess of respect; it is to find in the pope too little papistry, in the king too little royalty, and too much light in the night; it is to be dissatisfied with the albatross, with snow, with the swan, and the lily in the name of whiteness; it is to be the partisan of things to the point of becoming their enemy; it is to be so very pro, that you are con.

The ultra spirit is a peculiar characteristic of the first phase of the Restoration.

There was never anything in history like this little while, beginning in 1814, and ending about 1820, on the advent of Monsieur de Villèle, the practical man of the Right. These six years were an extraordinary moment; at once brilliant and gloomy, smiling and sombre, lighted as by the radiance of dawn, and at the same time enveloped in the darkness of the great catastrophes which still filled the horizon, though they were slowly burying themselves in the past. There was there, in that light and that shade, a little world by itself, new and old, merry and sad, juvenile and senile, rubbing its eyes; nothing resembles an awaking so much as a return; a group which looked upon France whimsically, and upon which France looked with irony; streets full of good old owl marquises returned and returning, "ci-devants," astounded at everything, brave and noble gentlemen smiling at being in France, and weeping over it also; delighted to see their country again, in despair at finding their monarchy no more; the nobility of the crusades spitting upon the nobility of the empire, that is to say the nobility of the sword; historic races losing the meaning of history; sons of the companions of Charlemagne disdaining the companions of Napoleon. Swords, as we have said, insulted each other; the sword of Fontenoy was ridiculous, and nothing but rust; the sword of Marengo was hateful, and nothing but a sabre. Formerly disowned Yesterday. The sense of the grand was lost as well as the sense of the ridiculous. There was somebody who called Bonaparte Scapin. That word is no more. Nothing, we repeat, now remains of it. When we happen to draw some form from it, and endeavour to make it live again in our thought, it seems as strange to us as an antediluvian world. It also, in fact, has been swallowed up by a deluge. It has disappeared under two revolutions. What floods are ideas! How quickly they cover all that they are commissioned to destroy and to bury, and how rapidly they create frightful abysses!

Such was the character of the salons in those far-off and simple ages when M. Martainville was wittier than Voltaire.

These salons had a literature and politics of their own. They believed in Fiévée. M. Agier gave laws to them. They criticised M. Colnet, the publicist of the bookstall of the Quai Malaquais. Napoleon was nothing but the Corsican Ogre. At a later day the introduction into history of M. the Marquis de Buonaparte, Lieutenant-General of the armies of the king, was a concession to the spirit of the century.

These salons did not long maintain their purity. As early as 1818, doctrinaires began to bud out in them, a troublesome species. Their style was to be royalists, and to apologise for it. Just where the ultras were proudest, the doctrinaires were a little ashamed. They were witty; they were silent; their political dogmas were suitably starched with pride; they ought to have been successful. They indulged in what was moreover convenient, an excess of white cravat and close-buttoned coat. The fault, or the misfortune of the doctrinaire-party was the creation of an old youth. They assumed the postures of sages. Their dream was to engraft upon an absolute and excessive principle a limited power. They opposed, and sometimes with a rare intelligence, destructive liberalism by conservative liberalism. We heard them say: "Be considerate towards royalism; it has done much real service. It has brought us back tradition, worship, religion, respect. It is faithful, brave, chivalric, loving, devoted. It comes to associate, although with regret, to the new grandeur of the nation the old grandeur of the monarchy. It is wrong in not comprehending the revolution, the empire, glory, liberty, new ideas, new generations, the century. But this wrong which it does us, have we not sometimes done it the same? The revolution, whose heirs we are, ought to comprehend all. To attack royalism is a misconception of liberalism. What a blunder, and what blindness? Revolutionary France is wanting in respect for historic France, that is to say for her mother, that is to say for herself. After the 5th of September, the nobility of the monarchy is treated as the nobility of the empire was treated after the 8th of July. They were unjust towards the eagle, we are unjust towards the fleur-de-lis. Must we then always have something to proscribe? Of what use is it to deface the crown of Louis XIV., or to scratch off the escutcheon of Henry IV.? We rail at Monsieur de Vaublanc who effaced the N's. from the Bridge of Jena? But what did he do? What we are doing. Bouvines belongs to us as well as Marengo. The fleurs-de-lis are ours as well as the N's. They are our patrimony. What is gained by diminishing it? We must not disown our country in the past more than in the present. Why not desire our whole history? Why not love all of France?"

This is the way in which the doctrinaires criticised and patronised royalism, which was displeased at being criticised and furious at being patronised.

The ultras marked the first period of royalism; the assemblage characterised the second. To fervency succeeded skill. Let us not prolong this sketch.

In the course of this narrative, the author of this book found in his path this strange moment of contemporary history; he was obliged to glance at it in passing, and to trace some of the singular lineaments of that society now unknown. But he does it rapidly and without any bitter or derisive intention. Reminiscences, affectionate and respectful, for they relate to his mother, attach him to this period. Besides, we must say, that same little world has its greatness. We may smile at it, but we can neither despise it nor hate it. It was the France of former times.

Marius Pontmercy went, like all children, through various studies. When he left the hands of Aunt Gillenormand, his grandfather entrusted him to a worthy professor, of the purest classic innocence. This young, unfolding soul passed from a prude to a pedant. Marius had his years at college, then he entered the law-school. He was royalist, fanatical, and austere. He had little love for his grandfather, whose gaiety and cynicism wounded him, and the place of his father was a dark void.

For the rest, he was an ardent but cool lad, noble, generous, proud, religious, lofty; honourable even to harshness, pure even to unsociableness.

IV
END OF THE BRIGAND

THE completion of Marius' classical studies was coincident with M. Gillenormand's retirement from the world. The old man bade farewell to the Faubourg Saint Germain, and to Madame de T.'s salon, and established himself in the Marais, at his house in the Rue des Filles du Calvaire. His servants were, in addition to the porter, this chambermaid Nicolette who had succeeded Magnon, and this short-winded and pursy Basque whom we have already mentioned.

In 1827, Marius had just attained his eighteenth year. On coming in one evening, he saw his grandfather with a letter in his hand.

"Marius," said M. Gillenormand, "you will set out to-morrow for Vernon."

"What for?" said Marius.

"To see your father."

Marius shuddered. He had thought of everything but this, that a day might come, when he would have to see his father. Nothing could have been more unlooked for, more surprising, and, we must say, more disagreeable. It was aversion compelled to intimacy. It was not chagrin; no, it was pure drudgery.

Marius, besides his feelings of political antipathy, was convinced that his father, the sabrer, as M. Gillenormand called him in the gentler moments, did not love him; that was clear, since he had abandoned him and left him to others. Feeling that he was not loved at all, he had no love. Nothing more natural, said he to himself.

He was so astounded that he did not question M. Gillenormand. The grandfather continued:

"It appears that he is sick. He asks for you."

And after a moment of silence he added:

"Start to-morrow morning. I think there is at the Cour des Fontaines a conveyance which starts at six o'clock and arrives at night. Take it. He says the case is urgent."

Then he crumpled up the letter and put it in his pocket. Marius could have started that evening and been with his father the next morning. A diligence then made the trip to Rouen from the Rue du Bouloi by night passing through Vernon. Neither M. Gillenormand nor Marius thought of inquiring.

The next day at dusk, Marius arrived at Vernon. Candles were just beginning to be lighted. He asked the first person he met for *the house of Monsieur Pontmercy.* For in his feelings he agreed with the Restoration, and he, too, recognised his father neither as baron nor as colonel.

The house was pointed out to him. He rang; a woman came and opened the door with a small lamp in her hand.

"Monsieur Pontmercy?" said Marius.

The woman remained motionless.

"Is it here?" asked Marius.

The woman gave an affirmative nod of the head.

"Can I speak with him?"

The woman gave a negative sign.

"But I am his son!" resumed Marius. "He expects me."

"He expects you no longer," said the woman.

Then he perceived that she was in tears.

She pointed to the door of a low room; he entered.

In this room, which was lighted by a tallow candle on the mantel, there were three men, one of them standing, one on his knees, and one stripped to his shirt and lying at full length upon the floor. The one upon the floor was the colonel.

The two others were a physician and a priest who was praying.

The colonel had been three days before attacked with a brain fever. At the beginning of the sickness, having a presentiment of ill, he had written to Monsieur Gillenormand to ask for his son. He had grown worse. On the very evening of Marius' arrival at Vernon, the colonel had had a fit of delirium; he sprang out of his bed in spite of the servant, crying: "My son has not come! I am going to meet him!" Then he had gone out of his room and fallen upon the floor of the hall. He had but just died.

The doctor and the curé had been sent for. The doctor had come too late, the curé had come too late. The son also had come too late.

By the dim light of the candle, they could distinguish upon the cheek of the pale and prostrate colonel a big tear which had fallen from his death-stricken eye. The eye was glazed, but the tear was not dry. This tear was for his son's delay.

Marius looked upon this man, whom he saw for the first time, and for the last—this venerable and manly face, these open eyes which saw not this white hair, these robust limbs upon which he distinguished here and there brown lines which were sabre-cuts, and a species of red stars which were bullet-holes. He looked upon that gigantic scar which imprinted heroism upon this face on which God had impressed goodness. He thought that this man was his father and that this man was dead, and he remained unmoved.

The sorrow which he experienced was the sorrow which he would have felt before any other man whom he might have seen stretched out in death.

Mourning, bitter mourning was in that room. The servant was lamenting by herself in a corner, the curé was praying, and his sobs were heard; the doctor was wiping his eyes; the corpse itself wept.

This doctor, this priest, and this woman, looked at Marius through their affliction without saying a word; it was he who was the stranger. Marius, too little moved, felt ashamed and embarrassed at his attitude; he had his hat in his hand, he let it fall to the floor, to make them believe that grief deprived him of strength to hold it.

At the same time he felt something like remorse, and he despised himself for acting thus. But was it his fault? He did not love his father, indeed!

The colonel left nothing. The sale of his furniture hardly paid for his burial. The servant found a scrap of paper which she handed to Marius. It contained this in the handwriting of the colonel:

"*For my Son.*—The emperor made me a baron upon the battle-field of Waterloo. Since the Restoration contests this title which I have bought with my blood, my son will take it and bear it. I need not say that he will be worthy of it." On the back, the colonel had added: "At this same battle of Waterloo, a sergeant saved my life. This man's name is Thénardier. Not long ago, I believe he was keeping a little tavern in a village in the suburbs of Paris, at Chelles or at Montfermeil. If my son meets him, he will do Thénardier all the service he can."

Not from duty towards his father, but on account of that vague respect for death which is always so imperious in the heart of man, Marius took this paper and pressed it.

No trace remained of the colonel. Monsieur Gillenormand had his sword and uniform sold to a second-hand dealer. The neighbours stripped the garden and carried off the rare flowers. The other plants became briery and scraggy, and died.

Marius remained only forty-eight hours at Vernon. After the burial, he returned to Paris and went back to his law, thinking no more of his father than if he had never lived. In two days the colonel had been buried, and in three days forgotten. Marius wore crape on his hat. That was all.

V

THE UTILITY OF GOING TO MASS, TO BECOME REVOLUTIONARY

MARIUS had preserved the religious habits of his childhood. One Sunday he had gone to hear mass at Saint Sulpice, at this same chapel of the Virgin to which his aunt took him when he was a little boy, and being that day more absent-minded and dreamy than usual, he took his place behind a pillar and knelt down, without noticing it, before a Utrecht velvet chair, on the back of which this name was written: *Monsieur Mabeuf, church-warden*. The mass had hardly commenced when an old man presented himself and said to Marius:

"Monsieur, this is my place."

Marius moved away readily, and the old man took his chair.

After mass, Marius remained absorbed in thought a few steps distant; the old man approached him again and said: "I beg your pardon, monsieur, for having disturbed you a little while ago, and for disturbing you again now; but you must have thought me impertinent, and I must explain myself."

"Monsieur," said Marius, "it is unnecessary."

"Yes!" resumed the old man; "I do not wish you to have a bad opinion of me. You see I think a great deal of that place. It seems to me that the mass is better there. Why? I will tell you. To that place I have seen for ten years, regularly, every two or three months, a poor, brave father come, who had no other opportunity and no other way of seeing his child, being prevented through some family arrangements. He came at the hour when he knew his son was brought to mass. The little one never suspected that his father was here. He did not even know, perhaps, that he had a father, the innocent boy! The father, for his part, kept behind a pillar, so that nobody should see him. He looked at his child, and wept. This poor man worshipped this little boy. I saw that. This place has become sanctified, as it were, for me, and I have acquired the habit of coming here to hear mass. I prefer it to the bench, where I have a right to be as a warden. I was even acquainted slightly with this unfortunate gentleman. He had a father-in-law, a rich aunt, relatives, I do not remember exactly, who threatened to disinherit the child if he, the father, should see him. He had sacrificed himself that his son might some day be rich and happy. They were separated by political opinions. Certainly I approve of political opinions, but there are people who do not know where to stop. Bless me! because a man was at Waterloo he is not a monster; a father is not separated from his child for that. He was one of Bonaparte's colonels. He is dead, I believe. He lived at Vernon, where my brother is curé, and his name is something like Pontmarie, Montpercy. He had a handsome sabre-cut."

"Pontmercy," said Marius, turning pale.

"Exactly; Pontmercy. Did you know him?"

"Monsieur," said Marius, "he was my father."

The old churchwarden clasped his hands, and exclaimed——

"Ah! you are the child! Yes, that is it; he ought to be a man now. Well! poor child, you can say that you had a father who loved you well."

Marius offered his arm to the old man, and walked with him to his house. Next day he said to Monsieur Gillenormand:——

"We have arranged a hunting party with a few friends. Will you permit me to be absent for three days?"

"Four," answered the grandfather; "go; amuse yourself."

And, with a wink he whispered to his daughter——

"Some love affair!"

VI
WHAT IT IS TO HAVE MET A CHURCHWARDEN

WHERE Marius went we shall see a little further on.

Marius was absent three days, then he returned to Paris, went straight to the library of the law-school, and asked for the file of the *Moniteur*.

He read the *Moniteur*; he read all the histories of the republic and the empire; the *Memorial de Sainte-Hélène*; all the memoirs, journals, bulletins, proclamations; he devoured everything. The first time he met his father's name in the bulletins of the grand army he had a fever for a whole week. He went to see the generals under whom George Pontmercy had served—among others, Count H. The churchwarden, Mabeuf, whom he had gone to see again, gave him an account of the life at Vernon, the colonel's retreat, his flowers and his solitude. Marius came to understand fully this rare, sublime, and gentle man, this sort of lion-lamb who was his father.

In the meantime, engrossed in this study, which took up all his time, as well as all his thoughts, he hardly saw the Gillenormands more. At the hours of meals he appeared; then when they looked for him, he was gone. The aunt grumbled. The grandfather smiled. "Poh, poh! it is the age for the lasses!" Sometimes the old man added: "The devil! I thought that it was some gallantry. It seems to be a passion."

It was a passion, indeed. Marius was on the way to adoration for his father.

At the same time an extraordinary change took place in his ideas. The phases of this change were numerous and gradual. As this is the history of many minds of our time, we deem it useful to follow these phases step by step and to indicate them all.

This history on which he had now cast his eyes, startled him.

The first effect was bewilderment.

The republic, the empire, had been to him, till then, nothing but monstrous words. The republic, a guillotine in a twilight; the empire, a sabre in the night. He had looked into them, and there, where he expected to find only a chaos of darkness, he had seen, with a sort of astounding surprise, mingled with fear and joy, stars shining, Mirabeau, Vergniaud, Saint-Just, Robespierre, Camille Desmoulins, Danton, and a sun rising, Napoleon. He knew not where he was. He recoiled blinded by the splendours. Little by little, the astonishment passed away, he accustomed himself to this radiance; he looked upon acts without dizziness, he examined personages without error; the revolution and the empire set themselves in luminous perspective before his straining eyes; he saw each of these two groups of events and men arrange themselves into two enormous facts: the republic into the sovereignty of the civic right restored to the masses, the empire into the sovereignty of the French idea imposed upon Europe; he saw spring out of the revolution the grand figure of the people, and out of the empire the grand figure of France. He declared to himself that all that had been good.

What his bewilderment neglected in this first far too syn-
thetic appreciation, we do not think it necessary to indicate
here. We are describing the state of a mind upon the march.
Progress is not accomplished at a bound. Saying this, once for
all, for what precedes as well as for what is to follow, we
continue.

He perceived then that up to that time he had comprehended
his country no more than he had his father. He had known
neither one nor the other, and he had had a sort of voluntary
night over his eyes. He now saw, and on the one hand he
admired, on the other he worshipped.

He was full of regret and remorse and he thought with despair that all he had in his soul he could say now only to a tomb.
Oh! if his father were living, if he had had him still, if God in
his mercy and in his goodness had permitted that his father
might be still alive, how he would have run, how he would
have plunged headlong, how he would have cried to his father:
"Father! I am here! it is I! my heart is the same as yours! I am
your son!" How he would have embraced his white head, wet
his hair with tears, gazed upon his scar, pressed his hands, worshipped his garments, kissed his feet! oh! why had this father
died so soon, before the adolescence, before the justice, before
the love of his son! Marius had a continual sob in his heart which
said at every moment: "Alas!" At the same time he became more
truly serious, more truly grave, surer of his faith and his thought.
Gleams of the true came at every instant to complete his
reasoning. It was like an interior growth. He felt a sort of natural
aggrandisement which these two new things, his father and his
country, brought to him.

As when one has a key, everything opened; he explained to
himself what he had hated, he penetrated what he had abhorred;
he saw clearly henceforth the providential, divine, and human
meaning of the great things which he had been taught to detest,
and the great men whom he had been instructed to curse. When
he thought of his former opinions, which were only of yesterday, but which seemed so ancient to him already, he became
indignant at himself, and he smiled. From the rehabilitation
of his father he had naturally passed to the rehabilitation of
Napoleon.

This, however, we must say, was not accomplished without
labour.

From childhood he had been imbued with the judgment of the party of 1814 in regard to Bonaparte. Now, all the prejudices of the Restoration, all its interests, all its instincts, tended to the disfigurement of Napoleon. It execrated him still more than it did Robespierre. It made skilful use of the fatigue of the nation and the hatred of mothers. Bonaparte had become a sort of monster almost fabulous, and to depict him to the imagination of the people, which, as we have already said, resembles the imagination of children, the party of 1814 present in succession every terrifying mask, from that which is terrible, while yet it is grand, to that which is terrible in the grotesque, from Tiberius to Bugaboo. Thus, in speaking of Bonaparte, you might either weep, or burst with laughter, provided hatred was the basis. Marius had never had—about that man, as he was called—any other ideas in his mind. They had grown together with the tenacity of his nature. There was in him a complete little man who was devoted to hatred of Napoleon.

On reading his history, especially in studying it in documents and materials, the veil which covered Napoleon from Marius' eyes gradually fell away. He perceived something immense, and suspected that he had been deceiving himself up to that moment about Bonaparte as well as about everything else; each day he saw more clearly; and he began to mount slowly, step by step, in the beginning almost with regret, afterwards with rapture, and as if drawn by an irresistible fascination, at first the sombre stages, then the dimly lighted stages, finally the luminous and splendid stages of enthusiasm.

One night he was alone in his little room next the roof. His candle was lighted; he was reading, leaning on his table by the open window. All manner of reveries came over him from the expanse of space and mingled with his thought. What a spectacle is night! We hear dull sounds, not knowing whence they come, we see Jupiter, twelve hundred times larger than the earth, glistening like an ember, the welkin is black, the stars sparkle, it is terror-inspiring.

He was reading the bulletins of the Grand Army, those heroic strophes written on the battle-field; he saw there at intervals his father's name, the emperor's name everywhere; the whole of the grand empire appeared before him, he felt as if a tide were swelling and rising within him; it seemed to him at moments that his father was passing by him like a breath, and whispering in his ear; gradually he grew wandering; he thought he heard the drums, the cannon, the trumpets, the measured tread of the battalions, the dull and distant gallop of the cavalry; from time to time he lifted his eyes to the sky and saw the colossal constellations shining in the limitless abysses, then they fell back upon the book, and saw there other colossal things moving about confusedly. His heart was full. He was transported, trembling, breathless; suddenly, without himself knowing what moved him, or what he was obeying, he arose, stretched his arms out of the window, gazed fixedly into the gloom, the silence, the darkling infinite, the eternal immensity and cried: Vive l'empereur!

From that moment it was all over; the Corsican Ogre—the usurper—the tyrant—the monster who was the lover of his sisters—the actor who took lessons from Talma—the poisoner of Jaffa—the tiger—Buonaparté—all this vanished, and gave place in his mind to a suffused and brilliant radiance in which shone out from an inaccessible height the pale marble phantom of Cæsar. The emperor had been to his father only the beloved captain, whom one admires, and for whom one devotes himself; to Marius he was something more. He was the predestined constructor of the French group, succeeding the Roman group in the mastery of the world. He was the stupendous architect of a downfall, the successor of Charlemagne, of Louis XI., of Henry IV., of Richelieu, of Louis XIV., and of the Committee of Public Safety, having doubtless his blemishes, his faults, and even his crimes, that is to say being man; but august in his faults, brilliant in his blemishes, mighty in his crimes.

He was the man foreordained to force all nations to say: the Grand Nation. He was better still; he was the very incarnation of France, conquering Europe by the sword which he held, and the world by the light which he shed. Marius saw in Bonaparte the flashing spectre which will always rise upon the frontier, and which will guard the future. Despot, but dictator; despot resulting from a republic and summing up a revolution. Napoleon became to him the people-man as Jesus is the God-man.

We see, like all new converts to a religion, his conversion intoxicated him, he plunged headlong into adhesion, and he went too far. His nature was such; once upon a descent it was almost impossible for him to hold back. Fanaticism for the sword took possession of him, and became complicated in his mind with enthusiasm for the idea. He did not perceive that along with genius, and indiscriminately, he was admiring force, that is to say that he was installing in the two compartments of his idolatry, on one side what is divine, and on the other what is brutal. In several respects he began to deceive himself in other matters. He admitted everything. There is a way of meeting error while on the road of truth. He had a sort of wilful implicit faith which swallowed everything in mass. On the new path upon which he had entered, in judging the crimes of the ancient régime as well as in measuring the glory of Napoleon, he neglected the attenuating circumstances.

However this might be, a great step had been taken. Where he had formerly seen the fall of the monarchy, he now saw the advent of France. His pole-star was changed. What had been the setting, was now the rising of the sun. He had turned around.

All these revolutions were accomplished in him without a suspicion of it in his family.

When, in this mysterious labour, he had entirely cast off his old Bourbon and ultra skin, when he had shed the aristocrat, the jacobite, and the royalist, when he was fully revolutionary, thoroughly democratic, and almost republican, he went to an engraver on the Quai des Orfèvres, and ordered a hundred cards bearing this name: *Baron Marius Pontmercy.*

This was but a very logical consequence of the change which had taken place in him, a change in which everything gravitated about his father.

However, as he knew nobody, and could not leave his cards at anybody's door, he put them in his pocket.

By another natural consequence, in proportion as he drew nearer to his father, his memory, and the things for which the colonel had fought for twenty-five years, he drew off from his grandfather. As we have mentioned, for a long time M. Gillenormand's capriciousness had been disagreeable to him. There was already between them all the distaste of a serious young man for a frivolous old man. Geront's gaiety shocks and exasperates Werther's melancholy. So long as the same political opinions and the same ideas had been common to them, Marius had met M. Gillenormand by means of them as if upon a bridge. When this bridge fell, the abyss appeared. And then, above all, Marius felt inexpressibly revolted when he thought that M. Gillenormand, from stupid motives, had pitilessly torn him from the colonel, thus depriving the father of the child, and the child of the father.

Through affection and veneration for his father, Marius had almost reached aversion for his grandfather.

Nothing of this, however, as we have said, was betrayed externally. Only he was more and more frigid; laconic at meals, and scarcely ever in the house. When his aunt scolded him for it, he was very mild, and gave as an excuse his studies, courts, examinations, dissertations, etc. The grandfather did not change his infallible diagnosis: "In love? I understand it."

Marius was absent for a while from time to time.

"Where can he go to?" asked the aunt.

On one of these journeys, which were always very short, he went to Montfermeil in obedience to the injunction which his father had left him, and sought for the former sergeant of Waterloo, the innkeeper Thénardier. Thénardier had failed, the inn was closed, and nobody knew what had become of him. While making these researches, Marius was away from the house four days.

"Decidedly," said the grandfather, "he is going astray."

They thought they noticed that he wore something, upon his breast and under his shirt, hung from his neck by a black ribbon.

VII
SOME PETTICOAT

WE have spoken of a lancer.

He was a grand-nephew of M. Gillenormand's on the paternal side, who passed his life away from his family, and far from all domestic hearths in garrison. Lieutenant Théodule Gillenormand fulfilled all the conditions required for what is called a handsome officer. He had "the waist of a girl," a way of trailing the victorious sabre, and a curling moustache. He came to Paris very rarely, so rarely that Marius had never seen him. The two cousins knew each other only by name. Théodule was, we think we have mentioned, the favourite of Aunt Gillenormand, who preferred him because she did not see him. Not seeing people permits us to imagine in them every perfection.

One morning, Mlle. Gillenormand the elder had retired to her room as much excited as her placidity allowed. Marius had asked his grandfather again for permission to make a short journey, adding that he intended to set out that evening. "Go!" the grandfather had answered, and M. Gillenormand had added aside, lifting his eyebrows to the top of his forehead: "He is getting to be an old offender." Mlle. Gillenormand had returned to her room very much perplexed, dropping this exclamation point on the stairs: "That is pretty!" and this interrogation point: "But where can he be going?" She imagined some more or less illicit affair of the heart, a woman in the shadow, a rendezvous, a mystery, and she would not have been sorry to thrust her spectacles into it. The taste of a mystery resembles the first freshness of a slander; holy souls never despise that. There is in the secret compartments of bigotry some curiosity for scandal.

She was therefore a prey to a blind desire for learning a story.

As a diversion from this curiosity which was giving her a little more agitation than she allowed herself, she took refuge in her talents, and began to festoon cotton upon cotton, in one of those embroideries of the time of the empire and the restoration in which a great many cab wheels appear. Clumsy work, crabbed worker. She had been sitting in her chair for some hours when the door opened. Mlle. Gillenormand raised her eyes; Lieutenant Théodule was before her making the regulation bow. She uttered a cry of pleasure. You may be old, you may be a prude, you may be a bigot, you may be his aunt, but it is always pleasant to see a lancer enter your room.

"You here, Théodule!" exclaimed she.

"On my way, aunt."

"Embrace me then."

"Here goes!" said Théodule.

And he embraced her. Aunt Gillenormand went to her secretary, and opened it.

"You stay with us at least all the week?"

"Aunt, I leave this evening."

"Impossible!"

"Mathematically."

"Stay, my dear Théodule, I beg you."

"The heart says yes, but my orders say no. The story is simple. Our station is changed, we were at Melun, we are sent to Gaillon. To go from the old station to the new, we must pass through Paris. I said: I am going to go and see my aunt."

"Take this for your pains."

She put ten louis into his hand.

"You mean for my pleasure, dear aunt."

Théodule embraced her a second time, and she had the happiness of having her neck a little chafed by the braid of his uniform.

"Do you make the journey on horseback with your regiment?" she asked.

"No, aunt. I wanted to see you. I have a special permit. My servant takes my horse; I go by the diligence. And, speaking of that, I have a question to ask you."

"What?"

"My cousin, Marius Pontmercy, is travelling also, is he?"

"How do you know that?" exclaimed the aunt, her curiosity suddenly excited to the quick.

"On my arrival, I went to the diligence to secure my place in the coupé."

"Well?"

"A traveller had already secured a place on the impériale. I saw his name on the book."

"What name?"

"Marius Pontmercy."

"The wicked fellow!" exclaimed the aunt. "Ah! your cousin is not a steady boy like you. To think that he is going to spend the night in a diligence."

"Like me."

"But for you, it is from duty; for him, it is from dissipation."

"What is the odds?" said Théodule.

Here, an event occurred in the life of Mademoiselle Gillenormand the elder; she had an idea. If she had been a man, she would have slapped her forehead. She apostrophised Théodule:

"Are you sure that your cousin does not know you?"

"Yes. I have seen him; but he has never deigned to notice me."

"And you are going to travel together so?"

"He on the impériale, I in the coupé."

"Where does this diligence go?"

"To Les Andelys."

"Is there where Marius is going?"

"Unless, like me, he stops on the road. I get off at Vernon to take the branch for Gaillon. I know nothing of Marius' route."

"Marius! what an ugly name! What an idea it was to name him Marius! But you at least—your name is Théodule!"

"I would rather it were Alfred," said the officer.

"Listen, Théodule."

"I am listening, aunt."

"Pay attention."

"I am paying attention."

"Are you ready?"

"Yes."

"Well, Marius is often away."

"Eh! eh!"

"He travels."

"Ah! ah!"

"He sleeps away."

"Oh! oh!"

"We want to know what is at the bottom of it."

Théodule answered with the calmness of a man of bronze:

"Some petticoat."

And with that stifled chuckle which reveals certainty, he added:

"A lass."

"That is clear," exclaimed the aunt, who thought she heard Monsieur Gillenormand speak, and who felt her conviction spring irresistibly from this word *lass*, uttered almost in the same tone by the grand-uncle and the grand-nephew. She resumed:

"Do us a kindness. Follow Marius a little way. He does not know you, it will be easy for you. Since there is a lass, try to see the lass. You can write us the account. It will amuse grandfather."

Théodule had no excessive taste for this sort of watching; but he was much affected by the ten louis, and he thought he saw a possible succession of them. He accepted the commission and said: "As you please, aunt." And he added aside: "There I am, a duenna."

Mademoiselle Gillenormand embraced him.

"You would not play such pranks, Théodule. You are obedient to discipline, you are the slave of your orders, you are a scrupulous and dutiful man, and you would not leave your family to go to see such a creature."

The lancer put on the satisfied grimace of Cartouche praised for his honesty.

Marius, on the evening which followed this dialogue, mounted the diligence without suspecting that he was watched. As to the watchman, the first thing that he did, was to fall asleep. His slumber was sound and indicated a clear conscience. Argus snored all night.

At daybreak, the driver of the diligence shouted: "Vernon! Vernon relay! passengers for Vernon?" And Lieutenant Théodule awoke.

"Good," growled he, half asleep, "here I get off."

Then, his memory clearing up by degrees, an effect of awakening, he remembered his aunt, the ten louis, and the account he was to render of Marius' acts and deeds. It made him laugh.

"Perhaps he has left the coach," thought he, while he buttoned up his undress waistcoat. "He may have stopped at Poissy; he may have stopped at Triel; if he did not get off at Meuluan, he may have got off at Mantes, unless he got off at Rolleboise, or unless he only came to Pacy, with the choice of turning to the left towards Evreux, or to the right towards Laroche Guyon. Run after him, aunt. What the devil shall I write to her, the good old woman?"

At this moment a pair of black pantaloons getting down from the impériale, appeared before the window of the coupé.

"Can that be Marius?" said the lieutenant.

It was Marius.

A little peasant girl, beside the coach, among the horses and postillions, was offering flowers to the passengers. "Flowers for your ladies," cried she.

Marius approached her and bought the most beautiful flowers in her basket.

"Now," said Théodule leaping down from the coach, "there is something that interests me. Who the deuce is he going to carry those flowers to? It ought to be a mighty pretty woman for so fine a bouquet. I would like to see her."

And, no longer now by command, but from personal curiosity, like those dogs who hunt on their own account, he began to follow Marius.

Marius paid no attention to Théodule. Some elegant women got out of the diligence; he did not look at them. He seemed to see nothing about him.

"Is he in love?" thought Théodule.

Marius walked towards the church.

"All right," said Théodule to himself. "The church! that is it. These rendezvous which are spiced with a bit of mass are the best of all. Nothing is so exquisite as an ogle which passes across the good God."

Arriving at the church, Marius did not go in, but went behind the building. He disappeared at the corner of one of the buttresses of the apsis.

"The rendezvous is outside," said Théodule. "Let us see the lass."

And he advanced on tiptoe towards the corner which Marius had turned.

On reaching it, he stopped, astounded.

Marius, his face hid in his hands, was kneeling in the grass, upon a grave. He had scattered his bouquet. At the end of the grave, at an elevation which marked the head, there was a black wooden cross with this name in white letters: COLONEL BARON PONTMERCY. He heard Marius sobbing.

The lass was a tomb.

VIII
MARBLE AGAINST GRANITE

IT was here that Marius had come the first time that he absented himself from Paris. It was here that he returned every time that M. Gillenormand said: he sleeps out.

Lieutenant Théodule was absolutely disconcerted by this unexpected encounter with a sepulchre; he experienced a disagreeable and singular sensation which he was incapable of analysing, and which was made up of respect for a tomb mingled with respect for a colonel. He retreated, leaving Marius alone in the churchyard, and there was something of discipline in this retreat. Death appeared to him with huge epaulettes, and he gave him almost a military salute. Not knowing what to write to his aunt, he decided to write nothing at all; and probably nothing would have resulted from the discovery made by Théodule in regard to Marius' amours, had not, by one of those mysterious arrangements so frequently accidental, the scene at Vernon been almost immediately followed by a sort of counter-blow at Paris.

Marius returned from Vernon early in the morning of the third day, was set down at his grandfather's, and, fatigued by the two nights passed in the diligence, feeling the need of making up for his lack of sleep by an hour at the swimming school, ran quickly up to his room, took only time enough to lay off his travelling coat and the black ribbon which he wore about his neck, and went away to the bath.

M. Gillenormand, who had risen early like all old persons who are in good health, had heard him come in, and hastened as fast as he could with his old legs, to climb to the top of the stairs where Marius' room was, that he might embrace him, question him while embracing him, and find out something about where he came from.

But the youth had taken less time to go down than the octogenarian to go up, and when Grandfather Gillenormand entered the garret room, Marius was no longer there.

The bed was not disturbed, and upon the bed were displayed without distrust the coat and the black ribbon.

"I like that better," said M. Gillenormand.

And a moment afterwards he entered the parlour where Mademoiselle Gillenormand the elder was already seated, embroidering her cab wheels.

The entrance was triumphal.

M. Gillenormand held in one hand the coat and in the other the neck ribbon, and cried:

"Victory! We are going to penetrate the mystery! we shall know the end of the end, we shall feel of the libertinism of our trickster! here we are with the romance even. I have the portrait!"

In fact, a black shagreen box, much like to a medallion, was fastened to the ribbon.

The old man took this box and looked at it some time without opening it, with that air of desire, ravishment, and anger, with which a poor, hungry devil sees an excellent dinner pass under his nose, when it is not for him.

"For it is evidently a portrait. I know all about that. This is worn tenderly upon the heart. What fools they are! Some abominable quean, enough to make one shudder probably! Young folks have such bad taste in these days!"

"Let us see, father," said the old maid.

The box opened by pressing a spring. They found nothing in it but a piece of paper carefully folded.

"*From the same to the same,*" said M. Gillenormand, bursting with laughter. "I know what that is. A love-letter!"

"Ah! then let us read it!" said the aunt.

And she put on her spectacles. They unfolded the paper and read this:

"*For my son.*—The emperor made me a baron upon the battle-field of Waterloo. Since the Restoration contests this title which I have bought with my blood, my son will take it and bear it. I need not say that he will be worthy of it."

The feelings of the father and daughter cannot be described. They felt chilled as by the breath of a death's head. They did not exchange a word. M. Gillenormand, however, said in a low voice, and as if talking to himself:

"It is the handwriting of that sabrer."

The aunt examined the paper, turned it on all sides, then put it back in the box.

Just at that moment, a little oblong package, wrapped in blue paper, fell from a pocket of the coat. Mademoiselle Gillenormand picked it up and unfolded the blue paper. It was Marius' hundred cards. She passed one of them to M. Gillenormand, who read: *Baron Marius Pontmercy.*

The old man rang. Nicolette came. M. Gillenormand took the ribbon, the box, and the coat, threw them all on the floor in the middle of the parlour, and said:

"Take away those things."

A full hour passed in complete silence. The old man and the old maid sat with their backs turned to one another, and were probably, each on their side, thinking over the same things. At the end of that hour, Aunt Gillenormand said:

"Pretty!"

A few minutes afterwards, Marius made his appearance. He came in. Even before crossing the threshold of the parlour, he perceived his grandfather holding one of his cards in his hand, who, on seeing him, exclaimed with his crushing air of sneering, bourgeois superiority:

"Stop! stop! stop! stop! stop! you are a baron now. I present you my compliments. What does this mean?"

Marius coloured slightly, and answered:

"It means that I am my father's son."

M. Gillenormand checked his laugh, and said harshly:

"Your father; I am your father."

"My father," resumed Marius with downcast eyes and stern manner, "was a humble and heroic man, who served the

Republic and France gloriously, who was great in the greatest history that men have ever made, who lived a quarter of a century in the camp, by day under grape and under balls, by night in the snow, in the mud, and in the rain, who captured colours, who received twenty wounds, who died forgotten and abandoned, and who had but one fault; that was in loving too dearly two ingrates, his country and me."

This was more than M. Gillenormand could listen to. At the word, *Republic*, he rose, or rather, sprang to his feet. Every one of the words which Marius had pronounced, had produced the effect upon the old royalist's face, of a blast from a bellows upon a burning coal. From dark he had become red, from red purple, and from purple glowing.

"Marius!" exclaimed he, "abominable child! I don't know what your father was! I don't want to know! I know nothing about him and I don't know him! but what I do know is, that there was never anything but miserable wretches among all that rabble! that they were all beggars, assassins, red caps, thieves! I say all! I say all! I know nobody! I say all! do you hear, Marius? Look you, indeed, you are as much a baron as my slipper! they were all bandits who served Robespierre! all brigands who served B-u-o-naparte! all traitors who betrayed, betrayed, betrayed! their legitimate king! all cowards who ran from the Prussians and English at Waterloo! That is what I know. If your father is among them I don't know him, I am sorry for it, so much the worse, your servant!"

In his turn, Marius now became the coal, and M. Gillenormand the bellows. Marius shuddered in every limb, he knew not what to do, his head burned. He was the priest who sees all his wafers thrown to the winds, the fakir who sees a passer-by spit upon his idol. He could not allow such things to be said before him unanswered. But what could he do? His father had been trodden under foot and stamped upon in his presence, but by whom? by his grandfather. How should he avenge the one without outraging the other? It was impossible for him to insult his grandfather, and it was equally impossible for him not to avenge his father. On one hand a sacred tomb, on the other white hairs. He was for a few moments dizzy and staggering with all this whirlwind in his head; then he raised his eyes, looked straight at his grandfather, and cried in a thundering voice:

"Down with the Bourbons, and the great hog Louis XVIII.!"

Louis XVIII. had been dead for four years; but it was all the same to him.

The old man, scarlet as he was, suddenly became whiter than his hair. He turned towards a bust of the Duke de Berry which stood upon the mantel, and bowed to it profoundly with a sort of peculiar majesty. Then he walked twice, slowly and in silence, from the fire-place to the window and from the window to the fire-place, traversing the whole length of the room and making the floor crack as if an image of stone were walking over it. The second time, he bent towards his daughter, who was enduring the shock with the stupor of an aged sheep, and said to her with a smile that was almost calm:

"A baron like Monsieur and a bourgeois like me cannot remain under the same roof."

And all at once straightening up, pallid, trembling, terrible, his forehead swelling with the fearful radiance of anger, he stretched his arm towards Marius and cried to him:

"Be off."

Marius left the house.

The next day, M. Gillenormand said to his daughter:

"You will send sixty pistoles every six months to this blood-drinker, and never speak of him to me again."

Having an immense residuum of fury to expend, and not knowing what to do with it, he spoke to his daughter with coldness for more than three months.

Marius, for his part, departed in indignation. A circumstance, which we must mention, had aggravated his exasperation still more. There are always such little fatalities complicating domestic dramas. Feelings are embittered by them, although in reality the faults are none the greater. In hurriedly carrying away, at the old man's command, Marius' "things" to his room, Nicolette had, without perceiving it, dropped, probably on the garret stairs, which were dark, the black shagreen medallion which contained the paper written by the colonel. Neither the paper nor the medallion could be found. Marius was convinced that "Monsieur Gillenormand"—from that day forth he never named him otherwise—had thrown "his father's will" into the fire. He knew by heart the few lines written by the colonel, and consequently nothing was lost. But the paper, the writing, that

sacred relic, all that was his heart itself. What had been done
with it?

Marius went away without saying where he was going, and
without knowing where he was going, with thirty francs, his
watch, and a few clothes in a carpet-bag. He hired a cabriolet
by the hour, jumped in, and drove at random towards the Latin
quarter.

What was Marius to do?

BOOK FOURTH –
THE FRIENDS OF THE A B C

I

A GROUP WHICH ALMOST BECAME HISTORIC

At that period, apparently indifferent, something of a revolutionary thrill was vaguely felt. Whispers coming from the depths of '89 and of '92 were in the air. Young Paris was, excuse the expression, in the process of moulting. People were transformed almost without suspecting it, by the very movement of the time. The hand which moves over the dial moves also among souls. Each one took the step forward which was before him. Royalists became liberals, liberals became democrats.

It was like a rising tide, complicated by a thousand ebbs; the peculiarity of the ebb is to make mixtures; thence very singular combinations of ideas; men worshipped at the same time Napoleon and liberty. We are now writing history. These were the mirages of that day. Opinions pass through phases. Voltairian royalism, a grotesque variety, had a fellow not less strange, Bonapartist liberalism.

Other groups of minds were more serious. They fathomed principle; they attached themselves to right. They longed for the absolute, they caught glimpses of the infinite realisations; the absolute by its very rigidity, pushes the mind towards the boundless, and makes it float in the illimitable. There is nothing like dream to create the future. Utopia to-day, flesh and blood to-morrow.

Advanced opinions had double foundations. The appearance of mystery threatened "the established order of things," which was sullen and suspicious—a sign in the highest degree revolutionary. The reservations of power meet the reservations of the people in the sap. The incubation of insurrections replies to the plotting of *coups d'état*.

At that time there were not yet in France any of those underlying organisations like the German Tugendbund and the Italian Carbonari; but here and there obscure excavations were branching out. La Cougourde was assuming form at Aix; there was in Paris, among other affiliations of this kind, the Society of the Friends of the A B C.

Who were the Friends of the A B C? A society having as its

aim, in appearance, the education of children; in reality, the elevation of men.

They declared themselves the Friends of the A B C.* The *abaissé* [the abased] were the people. They wished to raise them up. A pun at which you should not laugh. Puns are sometimes weighty in politics, witness the *Castratus ad castra*, which made Narses a general of an army; witness, *Barbari et Barbarini*; witness, *Fueros y Fuegos*; witness, *Tu es Petrus et super hanc Petram*, etc., etc.

The Friends of the A B C were not numerous, it was a secret society in the embryonic state; we should almost say a coterie, if coteries produced heroes. They met in Paris, at two places, near the Halles, in a wine shop called *Corinthe*, which will be referred to hereafter, and near the Pantheon, in a little coffeehouse on the Place Saint Michel, called *Le Café Musain*, now torn down; the first of these two places of rendezvous was near the working-men, the second near the students.

The ordinary conventicles of the Friends of the A B C were held in a back room of the Café Musain.

This room, quite distant from the café, with which it communicated by a very long passage, had two windows, and an exit by a private stairway upon the little Rue des Grès. They smoked, drank, played, and laughed there. They talked very loud about everything, and in whispers about something else. On the wall was nailed, an indication sufficient to awaken the suspicion of a police officer, an old map of France under the republic.

Most of the Friends of the A B C were students, in thorough understanding with a few working-men. The names of the principal are as follows. They belong to a certain extent to history; Enjolras, Combeferre, Jean Prouvaire, Feuilly, Courfeyrac, Bahorel, Lesgle or Laigle, Joly, Grataire.

These young men constituted a sort of family among themselves, by force of friendship. All except Laigle were from the South.

This was a remarkable group. It has vanished into the invisible depths which are behind us. At the point of this drama which we have now reached, it may not be useless to throw a ray of light upon these young heads before the reader sees them sink into the shadow of a tragic fate.

*A B C in French, is pronounced ah-bay-say, exactly like the French word, *abaissé*.

Enjolras, whom we have named first, the reason why will be seen by-and-by, was an only son and was rich.

Enjolras was a charming young man, who was capable of being terrible. He was angelically beautiful. He was Antinous wild. You would have said, to see the thoughtful reflection of his eye, that he had already, in some preceding existence, passed through the revolutionary apocalypse. He had the tradition of it like an eye-witness. He knew all the little details of the grand thing, a pontifical and warrior nature, strange in a youth. He was officiating and militant; from the immediate point of view, a soldier of democracy; above the movement of the time, a priest of the ideal. He had a deep eye, lids a little red, thick under lip, easily becoming disdainful, and a high forehead. Much forehead in a face is like much sky in a horizon. Like certain young men of the beginning of this century and the end of the last century, who became illustrious in early life, he had an exceedingly youthful look, as fresh as a young girl's, although he had hours of pallor. He was now a man, but he seemed a child still. His twenty-two years of age appeared seventeen; he was serious, he did not seem to know that there was on the earth a being called woman. He had but one passion, the right; but one thought, to remove all obstacles. Upon Mount Aventine, he would have been Gracchus; in the Convention, he would have been Saint Just. He hardly saw the roses, he ignored the spring, he did not hear the birds sing; Evadne's bare bosom would have moved him no more than Aristogeiton; to him, as to Harmodius, flowers were good only to hide the sword. He was severe in his pleasures. Before everything but the republic, he chastely dropped his eyes. He was the marble lover of liberty. His speech was roughly inspired and had the tremor of a hymn. He astonished you by his soaring. Woe to the love affair that should venture to intrude upon him! Had any grisette of the Place Cambrai or the Rue Saint Jean de Beauvais, seeing this college boy's face, this form of a page, those long fair lashes, those blue eyes, that hair flying in the wind, those rosy cheeks, those pure lips, those exquisite teeth, felt a desire to taste all this dawn, and tried her beauty upon Enjolras, a surprising and terrible look would have suddenly shown her the great gulf, and taught her not to confound with the gallant cherubim of Beaumarchais the fearful cherubim of Ezekiel.

Beside Enjolras who represented the logic of the revolution,

Combeferre represented its philosophy. Between the logic of the revolution and its philosophy, there is this difference—that its logic could conclude with war, while its philosophy could only end in peace. Combeferre completed and corrected Enjolras. He was lower and broader. His desire was to instil into all minds the broad principles of general ideas; he said "Revolution, but civilisation;" and about the steep mountain he spread the vast blue horizon. Hence, in all Combeferre's views, there was something attainable and practicable. Revolution with Combeferre was more respirable than with Enjolras. Enjolras expressed its divine right, and Combeferre its natural right. The first went as far as Robespierre; the second stopped at Condorcet. Combeferre more than Enjolras lived the life of the world generally. Had it been given to these two young men to take a place in history, one would have been the upright man, the other would have been the wise man. Enjolras was more manly. Combeferre was more humane. *Homo* and *Vir* indeed express the exact shade of difference. Combeferre was gentle, as Enjolras was severe, from natural purity. He loved the word citizen, but he preferred the word man. He would have gladly said: *Hombre*, like the Spaniards. He read everything, went to the theatres, attended the public courts, learned the polarisation of light from Arago, was enraptured with a lecture in which Geoffroy Saint-Hilaire had explained the double function of the exterior carotid artery and the interior carotid artery, one of which supplies the face, the other the brain; he kept pace with the times, followed science step by step, confronted Saint Simon with Fourier, deciphered hieroglyphics, broke the pebbles which he found and talked about geology, drew a moth-butterfly from memory, pointed out the mistakes in French in the dictionary of the Academy, studied Puységur and Deleuze, affirmed nothing, not even miracles; denied nothing, not even ghosts; looked over the files of the *Moniteur*, reflected. He declared the future was in the hands of the schoolmaster, and busied himself with questions of education. He desired that society should work without ceasing at the elevation of the intellectual and moral level; at the coming of knowledge, at bringing ideas into circulation, at the growth of the mind in youth; and he feared that the poverty of the methods then in vogue, the meanness of a literary world which was circumscribed by two or three centuries, called classical, the tyrannical dogmatism of official pedants, scholastic prejudices and routine, would result in making artificial oyster-beds of our colleges. He was learned, purist, precise, universal, a hard student, and at the same time given to musing, "even chimerical," said his friends. He believed in all the dreams: railroads, the suppression of suffering in surgical operations, the fixing of the image in the camera obscura, the electric telegraph, the steering of balloons. Little dismayed, moreover, by the citadels built upon all sides against the human race by superstitions, despotisms, and prejudices, he was one of those who think that science will at last turn the position. Enjolras was a chief; Combeferre was a guide. You would have preferred to fight with the one and march with the other. Not that Combeferre was not capable of fighting; he did not refuse to close with an obstacle, and to attack it by main strength and by explosion, but to put, gradually, by the teaching of axioms and the promulgation of positive laws, the human race in harmony with its destinies, pleased him better; and of the two lights, his inclination was rather for illumination than for conflagration. A fire would cause a dawn, undoubtedly, but why not wait for the break of day? A volcano enlightens, but the morning enlightens still better. Combeferre, perhaps, preferred the pure radiance of the beautiful to the glory of the sublime. A light disturbed by smoke, an advance purchased by violence, but half satisfied this tender and serious mind. A headlong plunge of a people into the truth, a '93, startled him; still stagnation repelled him yet more, in it he felt putrefaction and death; on the whole, he liked foam better than miasma and he preferred the torrent to the cess pool, and the Falls of Niagara to the Lake of Montfaucon. In short, he desired neither halt nor haste. While his tumultuous friends, chivalrously devoted to the absolute, adored and asked for splendid revolutionary adventures, Combeferre inclined to let progress do her work,—the good progress; cold, perhaps, but pure, methodical, but irreproachable! phlegmatic, but imperturbable. Combeferre would have knelt down and clasped his hands, asking that the future might come in all its radiant purity and that nothing might disturb the unlimited virtuous development of the people. "*The good must be innocent*," he repeated incessantly. And in fact, if it is the grandeur of the revolution to gaze steadily upon the dazzling ideal, and to fly to it through the lightnings, with blood and fire in its talons, it is the beauty of progress to be without a stain;

and there is between Washington, who represents the one, and
Danton, who incarnates the other, the difference which separates the angel with the wings of a swan, from the angel with
the wings of an eagle.

Jean Prouvaire was yet a shade more subdued than Combeferre. He called himself Jehan, from that little momentary fanci-
fulness which mingled with the deep and powerful movement
from which arose the Middle Ages, then so necessary. Jean Prouvaire was addicted to love; he cultivated a pot of flowers, played
on the flute, made verses, loved the people, mourned over
woman, wept over childhood, confounded the future and God
in the same faith and blamed the revolution for having cut off a
royal head, that of André Chénier. His voice was usually delicate
but at times suddenly became masculine. He was well read, even
to erudition, and almost an orientalist. Above all, he was good,
and, a very natural thing to one who knows how near goodness
borders upon grandeur, in poetry he preferred the grand. He
understood Italian, Latin, Greek, and Hebrew; and that served
him only to read four poets: Dante, Juvenal, Æschylus, and
Isaiah. In French he preferred Corneille to Racine, and Agrippa
d'Aubigné to Corneille. He was fond of strolling in fields of
wild oats and blue-bells, and paid almost as much attention to
the clouds as to passing events. His mind had two attitudes—one
towards man, the other towards God; he studied, or he contemplated. All day he pondered over social questions: wages, capital,
credit, marriage, religion, liberty of thought, liberty of love,
education, punishment, misery, association, property, production and distribution, the lower enigma which covers the
human ant-hill with a shadow; and at night he gazed upon the
stars, those enormous beings. Like Enjolras, he was rich and an
only son. He spoke gently, bent his head, cast down his eyes,
smiled with embarrassment, dressed badly, had an awkward air,
blushed at nothing, was very timid, still intrepid.

Feuilly was a fan-maker, an orphan, who with difficulty
earned three francs a day, and who had but one thought, to
deliver the world. He had still another desire—to instruct himself, which he also called deliverance. He had taught himself to
read and write; all that he knew, he had learned alone. Feuilly
was a generous heart. He had an immense embrace. This orphan
had adopted the people. Being without a mother, he had meditated upon his mother country. He was not willing that there

should be any man upon the earth without a country. He nurtured within himself, with the deep divination of the man of the people, what we now call *the idea of nationality*. He had learned history expressly that he might base his indignation upon a knowledge of its cause. In this new upper room of utopists particularly interested in France, he represented the foreign nations. His speciality was Greece, Poland, Hungary, the Danubian Provinces, and Italy. He uttered these names incessantly, in season and out of season, with the tenacity of the right. Turkey upon Greece and Thessaly, Russia upon Warsaw, Austria upon Venice, these violations exasperated him. The grand highway robbery of 1772 excited him above all. There is no more sovereign eloquence than the truth in indignation; he was eloquent with this eloquence. He was never done with that infamous date, 1772, that noble and valiant people blotted out by treachery, that threefold crime, that monstrous ambuscade, prototype and pattern of all those terrible suppressions of states which, since, have stricken several noble nations, and have, so to say, erased the record of their birth. All the contemporary assaults upon society date from the partition of Poland. The partition of Poland is a theorem of which all the present political crimes are corollaries. Not a despot, not a traitor, for a century past, who has not visaed, confirmed, counter-signed, and set his initials to, *ne varietur*, the partition of Poland. When you examine the list of modern treasons, that appears first of all. The Congress of Vienna took advice of this crime before consummating its own. The halloo was sounded by 1772, 1815 is the quarry. Such was the usual text of Feuilly. This poor workingman had made himself a teacher of justice, and she rewarded him by making him grand. For there is in fact eternity in the right. Warsaw can no more be Tartar than Venice can be Teutonic. The kings lose their labour at this, and their honour. Sooner or later, the submerged country floats to the surface and reappears. Greece again becomes Greece, Italy again becomes Italy. The protest of the right against the fact, persists forever. The robbery of a people never becomes prescriptive. These lofty swindles have no future. You cannot pick the mark out of a nation as you can out of a handerkerchief.

Courfeyrac had a father whose name was M. de Courfeyrac. One of the false ideas of the restoration in point of aristocracy and nobility was its faith in the particle. The particle, we know, has no significance. But the bourgeois of the time of *La Minerve* considered this poor *de* so highly that men thought themselves obliged to renounce it. M. de Chauvelin called himself M. Chauvelin, M. de Caumartin, M. Caumartin, M. de Constant de Rebecque, Benjamin Constant, M. de Lafayette, M. Lafayette. Courfeyrac did not wish to be behind, and called himself briefly Courfeyrac.

We might almost, in what concerns Courfeyrac, stop here, and content ourselves with saying as to the remainder: Courfeyrac, see Tholomyès.

Courfeyrac had in fact that youthful animation which we might call the diabolic beauty of mind. In later life, this dies out, like the playfulness of the kitten, and all that grace ends, on two feet in the bourgeois, and on four paws in the mouser.

This style of mind is transmitted from generation to generation of students, passed from hand to hand by the successive growths of youth, *quasi cursores*, nearly always the same: so that, as we have just indicated, any person who has listened to Courfeyrac in 1828, would have thought he was hearing Tholomyès in 1817. Courfeyrac only was a brave fellow. Beneath the apparent similarities of the exterior mind, there was great dissimilarity between Tholomyès and him. The latent man which existed in each, was in the first altogether different from what it was in the second. There was in Tholomyès an attorney, and in Courfeyrac a paladin.

Enjolras was the chief, Combeferre was the guide, Courfeyrac was the centre. The others gave more light, he gave more heat; the truth is, that he had all the qualities of a centre, roundness and radiance.

Bahorel had figured in the bloody tumult of June, 1822, on the occasion of the burial of young Lallemand.

Bahorel was a creature of good humour and bad company, brave, a spendthrift, prodigal almost to generosity, talkative almost to eloquence, bold almost to effrontery; the best possible devil's-pie; with fool-hardy waistcoats and scarlet opinions; a wholesale blusterer, that is to say, liking nothing so well as a quarrel unless it were émeute, and nothing so well as an émeute unless it were a revolution; always ready to break a paving-stone, then to tear up a street, then to demolish a government, to see the effect of it; a student of the eleventh year. He had adopted for his motto: *never a lawyer,* and for his coat of arms a bedroom table on which you might discern a square cap. Whenever he passed by the law-school, which rarely happened, he buttoned up his overcoat, the paletot was not yet invented, and he took hygienic precautions. He said of the portal of the school: what a fine old man! and of the dean, M. Delvincourt: what a monument! He saw in his studies subjects for ditties, and in his professors opportunities for caricatures. He ate up in doing nothing a considerable allowance, something like three thousand francs. His parents were peasants, in whom he had succeeded in inculcating a respect for their son.

He said of them: "They are peasants and not bourgeois; which explains their intelligence."

Bahorel, a capricious man, was scattered over several cafés; the others had habits, he had none. He loafed. To err is human. To loaf is Parisian. At bottom, a penetrating mind and more of a thinker than he seemed.

He served as a bond between the Friends of the A B C and some other groups which were without definite shape, but which were to take form afterwards.

In this conclave of young heads there was one bald member.

The Marquis d'Avaray, whom Louis XVIII. made a duke for having helped him into a cab the day that he emigrated, related that in 1814, on his return to France, as the king landed at Calais, a man presented a petition to him.

"What do you want?" said the king.

"Sire, a post-office."

"What is your name?"

"L'Aigle." [The eagle].

The king scowled, looked at the signature of the petition and saw the name written thus: LESGLE. This orthography, anything but Bonapartist, pleased the king, and he began to smile. "Sire," resumed the man with the petition, "my ancestor was a dog-trainer surnamed Lesgueules [The Chaps]. This surname has become my name. My name is Lesgueules, by contraction Lesgle, and by corruption L'Aigle." This made the king finish his smile. He afterwards gave the man the post-office at Meaux, either intentionally or inadvertently.

The bald member of the club was son of this Lesgle, or Lègle, and signed his name Lègle (de Meaux). His comrades, for the sake of brevity, called him Bossuet.

Bossuet was a cheery fellow who was unlucky. His speciality

was to succeed in nothing. On the other hand, he laughed at everything. At twenty-five he was bald. His father had died owning a house and some land, but he, the son, had found nothing more urgent than to lose this house and land in a bad speculation. He had nothing left. He had considerable knowledge and wit, but he always miscarried. Everything failed him, everything deceived him; whatever he built up fell upon him. If he split wood, he cut his finger. If he had a mistress, he very soon discovered that he had also a friend. Every moment some misfortune happened to him; hence his joviality. He said: *I live under the roof of the falling tiles.* Rarely astonished since he was always expecting some accident, he took ill luck with serenity and smiled at the vexations of destiny like one who hears a jest. He was poor, but his fund of good-humour was inexhaustible. He soon reached his last sou, never his last burst of laughter. When met by adversity, he saluted that acquaintance cordially, he patted catastrophes on the back; he was so familiar with fatality as to call it by its nick-name. "Good morning, old Genius," he would say.

These persecutions of fortune had made him inventive. He was full of resources. He had no money, but he found means, when it seemed good to him, to go to "reckless expenses." One night, he even spent a hundred francs on a supper with a quean, which inspired him in the midst of the orgy with this memorable saying: "*Daughter of five louis, pull off my boots.*"

Bossuet was slowly making his way towards the legal profession; he was doing his law, in the manner of Bahorel. Bossuet had never much domicile, sometimes none at all. He lodged sometimes with one, sometimes with another, oftenest with Joly. Joly was studying medicine. He was two years younger than Bossuet.

Joly was a young Malade Imaginaire. What he had learned in medicine was rather to be a patient than a physician. At twenty-three, he thought himself a valetudinarian, and passed his time in looking at his tongue in a mirror. He declared that man is a magnet, like the needle, and in his room he placed his bed with the head to the south and the foot to the north, so that at night the circulation of the blood should not be interfered with by the grand magnetic current of the globe. In stormy weather, he felt his pulse. Nevertheless, the gayest of all. All these incoherences, young, notional, sickly, joyous, got along very well together, and the result was an eccentric and agreeable person whom his comrades, prodigal of consonants, called Jolllly. "You can fly upon four L's," [*ailes*, wings] said Jean Prouvaire.

Joly had the habit of rubbing his nose with the end of his cane, which is an indication of a sagacious mind.

All these young men, diverse as they were, and of whom, as a whole we ought only to speak seriously, had the same religion: Progress.

All were legitimate sons of the French Revolution. The lightest became solemn when pronouncing this date: '89. Their fathers according to the flesh, were, or had been Feuillants, Royalists, Doctrinaires; it mattered little; this hurly-burly which antedated them, had nothing to do with them; they were young; the pure blood of principles flowed in their veins. They attached themselves without an intermediate shade to incorruptible right and to absolute duty.

Affiliated and initiated, they secretly sketched out their ideas.

Among all these passionate hearts and all these undoubting minds there was one sceptic. How did he happen to be there? from juxtaposition. The name of this sceptic was Grantaire, and he usually signed with the rebus: R [*grand R*, great R]. Grantaire was a man who took good care not to believe anything. He was, moreover, one of the students who had learned most during their course in Paris; knew that the best coffee was at the Café Lemblin, and the best billiard table at the Café Voltaire; that you could find good rolls and good girls at the hermitage on the Boulevard du Maine, broiled chickens at Mother Saguet's, excellent chowders at the Barrière de la Cunette, and a peculiar light white wine at the Barrière du Combat. He knew the good places for everything; furthermore, boxing, tennis, a few dances, and he was a profound cudgel-player. A great drinker to boot. He was frightfully ugly; the prettiest shoebinder of that period, Irma Boissy, revolting at his ugliness, had uttered this sentence: "Grantaire is impossible," but Grantaire's self-conceit was not disconcerted. He looked tenderly and fixedly upon every woman, appearing to say of them all: *if I only would*; and trying to make his comrades believe that he was in general demand.

All these words: rights of the people, rights of man, social contract, French Revolution, republic, democracy, humanity, civilisation, religion, progress, were, to Grantaire, very nearly meaningless. He smiled at them. Scepticism, that cries of the intellect, had not left one entire idea in his mind. He lived in irony. This was his axiom: There is only one certainty, my full glass. He ridiculed all devotion, under all circumstances, in the brother as well as the father, in Robespierre the younger as well as Loizerolles. "They were very forward to be dead," he exclaimed. He said of the cross: "There is a gibbet which has made a success." A rover, a gambler, a libertine, and often drunk, he displeased these young thinkers by singing incessantly: "*I loves the girls and I loves good wine.*" Air: Vive Henri IV.

Still, this sceptic had a fanaticism. This fanaticism was neither an idea, nor a dogma, nor an art, nor a science; it was a man: Enjolras. Grantaire admired, loved, and venerated Enjolras. To whom did this anarchical doubter ally himself in this phalanx of absolute minds? To the most absolute. In what way did Enjolras subjugate him? By ideas? No. By a character. A phenomenon often seen. A sceptic adhering to a believer; that is as simple as the law of the complementary colours. What we lack attracts us. Nobody loves the light like the blind man. The dwarf adores the drum-major. The toad is always looking up at the sky; why? To see the bird fly. Grantaire, in whom doubt was creeping, loved to see faith soaring in Enjolras. He had need of Enjolras. Without understanding it himself clearly, and without trying to explain it, that chaste, healthy, firm, direct, hard, candid nature charmed him. He admired, by instinct, his opposite. His soft, wavering, disjointed, diseased, deformed ideas, attached themselves to Enjolras as to a backbone. His moral spine leaned upon that firmness. Grantaire, by the side of Enjolras, became somebody again. He was himself, moreover, composed of two apparently incompatible elements. He was ironical and cordial. His indifference was loving. His mind dispensed with belief, yet his heart could not dispense with friendship. A thorough contradiction; for an affection is a conviction. His nature was so. There are men who seem born to be the opposite, the reverse, the counterpart. They are Pollux, Patroclus, Nisus, Eudamidas, Hephæstion, Pechméja. They live only upon condition of leaning on another; their names are continuations, and are only written preceded by the conjunction *and*; their existence is not their own; it is the other side of a destiny which is not theirs. Grantaire was one of these men. He was the reverse of Enjolras.

We might almost say that affinities commence with the letters of the alphabet. In the series, O and P are inseparable. You can, as you choose, pronounce O and P, or Orestes and Pylades.

Grantaire, a true satellite of Enjolras, lived in this circle of young people; he dwelt in it; he took pleasure only in it; he followed them everywhere. His delight was to see these forms coming and going in the fumes of the wine. He was tolerated for his good-humour.

Enjolras, being a believer, disdained this sceptic, and being sober, scorned this drunkard. He granted him a little haughty pity. Grantaire was an unaccepted Pylades. Always rudely treated by Enjolras, harshly repelled, rejected, yet returning, he said of Enjolras: "What a fine statue!"

II

FUNERAL ORATION UPON BLONDEAU, BY BOSSUET

ON a certain afternoon, which had, as we shall see, some coincidence with events before related, Laigle de Meaux was leaning lazily back against the doorway of the Café Musain. He had the appearance of a caryatid in vacation; he was supporting nothing but his reverie. He was looking at the Place Saint Michel. Leaning back is a way of lying down standing which is not disliked by dreamers. Laigle de Meaux was thinking, without melancholy, of a little mishap which had befallen him the day before at the law-school, and which modified his personal plans for the future—plans which were, moreover, rather indefinite.

Reverie does not hinder a cabriolet from going by, nor the dreamer from noticing the cabriolet. Laigle de Meaux, whose eyes were wandering in a sort of general stroll, perceived, through all his somnambulism, a two-wheeled vehicle turning into the square, which was moving at a walk, as if undecided. What did this cabriolet want? why was it moving at a walk? Laigle looked at it. There was inside, beside the driver, a young man, and before the young man, a large carpet-bag. The bag exhibited to the passers this name, written in big black letters upon a card sewed to the cloth: MARIUS PONTMERCY.

This name changed Laigle's attitude. He straightened up and addressed this apostrophe to the young man in the cabriolet:

"Monsieur Marius Pontmercy?"

The cabriolet, thus called upon, stopped.

The young man, who also seemed to be profoundly musing, raised his eyes.

"Well?" said he.

"You are Monsieur Marius Pontmercy?"

"Certainly."

"I was looking for you," said Laigle de Meaux.

"How is that?" inquired Marius; for he it was, in fact he had just left his grandfather's, and he had before him a face which he saw for the first time. "I do not know you."

"Nor I either. I do not know you," answered Laigle.

Marius thought he had met a buffoon, and that this was the beginning of a mystification in the middle of the street. He was not in a pleasant humour just at that moment. He knit his brows; Laigle de Meaux, imperturbable, continued:

"You were not at school yesterday."

"It is possible."

"It is certain."

"You are a student?" inquired Marius.

"Yes, Monsieur. Like you. The day before yesterday I happened to go into the school. You know, one sometimes has such notions. The professor was about to call the roll. You know that they are very ridiculous just at that time. If you miss the third call, they erase your name. Sixty francs gone."

Marius began to listen. Laigle continued:

"It was Blondeau who was calling the roll. You know Blondeau; he has a very sharp and very malicious nose, and delights in smelling out the absent. He slily commenced with the letter P. I was not listening, not being concerned in that letter. The roll went on well, no erasure, the universe was present, Blondeau was sad. I said to myself, Blondeau, my love, you won't do the slightest execution to-day. Suddenly, Blondeau calls *Marius Pontmercy*; nobody answers. Blondeau, full of hope, repeats louder: *Marius Pontmercy?* And he seizes his pen. Monsieur, I have bowels. I said to myself rapidly: Here is a brave fellow who is going to be erased. Attention. This is a real live fellow who is not punctual. He is not a good boy. He is not a book-worm, a student who studies, a white-billed pedant strong on science, letters, theology, and wisdom, one of those numskulls drawn out with four pins, a pin for each faculty. He is an honourable idler who loafs, who likes to rusticate, who cultivates the grisette, who pays his court to beauty, who is perhaps, at this very moment, with my mistress. Let us save him. Death to Blondeau! At that moment Blondeau dipped his pen, black with erasures into the ink, cast his tawny eye over the room, and repeated for the third time: *Marius Pontmercy!* I answered: *Present!* In that way you were not erased."

"Monsieur!—" said Marius.

"And I was," added Laigle de Meaux.

"I do not understand you," said Marius.

Laigle resumed:

"Nothing more simple. I was near the chair to answer, and near the door to escape. The professor was looking at me with a certain fixedness. Suddenly, Blondeau, who must be the malignant nose of which Boileau speaks, leaps to the letter L. L is my letter; I am of Meaux, and my name is Lesgle."

"L'Aigle!" interrupted Marius, "what a fine name."

"Monsieur, the Blondeau re-echoes this fine name and cries: '*Laigle!*' I answer: *Present!* Then Blondeau looks at me with the gentleness of a tiger, smiles, and says: *If you are Pontmercy, you are not Laigle.* A phrase which is uncomplimentary to you, but which brought me only to grief. So saying, he erases me."

Marius exclaimed:

"Monsieur, I am mortified——"

"First of all," interrupted Laigle, "I beg leave to embalm Blondeau in a few words of feeling eulogy. I suppose him dead. There wouldn't be much to change in his thinness, his paleness, his coldness, his stiffness, and his odour. And I say: *Erudimini qui judicatis terram.* Here lies Blondeau, Blondeau the Nose, Blondeau Nasica, the ox of discipline, *bos disciplinæ*, the Molossus of his orders, the angel of the roll, who was straight, square, exact, rigid, honest, and hideous. God has erased him as he erased me."

Marius resumed:

"I am very sorry——"

"Young man," said Laigle of Meaux, "let this be a lesson to you. In future, be punctual."

"I really must give a thousand excuses."

"Never expose yourself again to having your neighbour erased."

"I am very sorry."

Laigle burst out laughing.

"And I, in raptures; I was on the brink of being a lawyer. This rupture saves me. I renounce the triumphs of the bar. I shall not defend the widow, and I shall not attack the orphan.

No more toga, no more probation. Here is my erasure obtained. It is to you that I owe it, Monsieur Pontmercy. I intend to pay you a solemn visit of thanks. Where do you live?"

"In this cabriolet," said Marius.

"A sign of opulence," replied Laigle calmly. "I congratulate you. You have here rent of nine thousand francs a year."

Just then Courfeyrac came out of the café.

Marius smiled sadly.

"I have been paying this rent for two hours, and I hope to get out of it; but, it is the usual story, I do not know where to go."

"Monsieur," said Courfeyrac, "come home with me."

"I should have priority," observed Laigle, "but I have no home."

"Silence, Bossuet," replied Courfeyrac.

"Bossuet," said Marius, "but I thought you called yourself Laigle."

"Of Meaux," answered Laigle; "metaphorically, Bossuet."

Courfeyrac got into the cabriolet.

"Driver," said he, "Hôtel de la Porte Saint Jacques."

And that same evening, Marius was installed in a room at the Hôtel de la Porte Saint Jacques, side by side with Courfeyrac.

III

THE ASTONISHMENTS OF MARIUS

In a few days, Marius was the friend of Courfeyrac. Youth is the season of prompt weldings and rapid cicatrisations. Marius, in Courfeyrac's presence, breathed freely, a new thing for him. Courfeyrac asked him no questions. He did not even think of it. At that age, the countenance tells all at once. Speech is useless. There are some young men of whom we might say their physiognomies are talkative. They look at one another, they know one another.

One morning, however, Courfeyrac abruptly put this question to him.

"By the way, have you any political opinions?"

"What do you mean?" said Marius, almost offended at the question.

"What are you?"

"Bonapartist democrat."

"Grey shade of quiet mouse colour," said Courfeyrac.

The next day, Courfeyrac introduced Marius to the Café Musain. Then he whispered in his ear with a smile: "I must give you your admission into the revolution." And he took him into the room of the Friends of the A B C. He presented him to the other members, saying in an undertone this simple word which Marius did not understand: "A pupil."

Marius had fallen into a mental wasps' nest. Still, although silent and serious, he was not the less winged, nor the less armed.

Marius, up to this time solitary and inclined to soliloquy and privacy by habit and by taste, was a little bewildered at this flock of young men about him. All these different progressives attacked him at once, and perplexed him. The tumultuous sweep and sway of all these minds at liberty and at work set his ideas in a whirl. Sometimes, in the confusion, they went so far from him that he had some difficulty in finding them again. He heard talk of philosophy, of literature, of art, of history, of religion, in a style he had not looked for. He caught glimpses of strange appearances; and, as he did not bring them into perspective, he was not sure that it was not a chaos that he saw. On abandoning his grandfather's opinions for his father's he had thought himself settled; he now suspected, with anxiety, and without daring to confess it to himself, that he was not. The angle under which he saw all things was beginning to change anew. A certain oscillation shook the whole horizon of his brain. A strange internal moving-day. He almost suffered from it.

It seemed that there were to these young men no "sacred things." Marius heard, upon every subject, a singular language annoying to his still timid mind.

A theatre poster presented itself, decorated with the title of a tragedy of the old repertory, called classic: "Down with tragedy dear to the bourgeois!" cried Bahorel. And Marius heard Combeferre reply.

"You are wrong, Bahorel. The bourgeoisie love tragedy, and upon that point we must let the bourgeoisie alone. Tragedy in a wig has its reason for being, and I am not one of those who, in the name of Æschylus, deny it the right of existence. There are rough drafts in nature; there are, in creation, ready-made parodies; a bill which is not a bill, wings which are not wings, fins which are not fins, claws which are not claws, a mournful cry which inspires us with the desire to laugh, there is the duck. Now, since the fowl exists along with the bird, I do not see why classic tragedy should not exist in the face of antique tragedy."

At another time Marius happened to be passing through the Rue Jean Jacques Rousseau between Enjolras and Courfeyrac.

Courfeyrac took his arm:

"Give attention. This is the Rue Plâtrière, now called Rue Jean Jacques Rousseau, on account of a singular household which lived on it sixty years ago. It consisted of Jean Jacques and Thérèse. From time to time, little creatures were born in it. Thérèse brought them forth. Jean Jacques turned them forth."

And Enjolras replied with severity:

"Silence before Jean Jacques! I admire that man. He disowned his children; very well; but he adopted the people."

None of these young men uttered this word: the emperor. Jean Prouvaire alone sometimes said Napoleon; all the rest said Bonaparte. Enjolras pronounced *Buonaparte*.

Marius became confusedly astonished. *Initium sapientæ.*

IV

THE BACK ROOM OF THE CAFÉ MUSAIN

OF the conversations among these young men which Marius frequented and in which he sometimes took part, one shocked him severely.

This was held in the back room of the Café Musain. Nearly all the Friends of the A B C were together that evening. The large lamp was ceremoniously lighted. They talked of one thing and another without passion and with noise. Save Enjolras and Marius, who were silent, each one harangued a little at random. The talk of comrades does sometimes amount to these harmless tumults. It was a play and a fracas as much as a conversation. One threw out words which another caught up. They were talking in each of the four corners.

No woman was admitted into this back room, except Louison, the dish-washer of the café, who passed through it from time to time to go from the washroom to the "laboratory."

Grantaire, perfectly boozy, was deafening the corner of which he had taken possession, he was talking sense and nonsense with all his might; he cried:

"I am thirsty. Mortals, I have a dream: that the tun of Heidelberg has an attack of apoplexy, and that I am the dozen leeches which is to be applied to it. I would like a drink. I desire to forget life. Life is a hideous invention of somebody I don't know who. It doesn't last, and it is good for nothing. You break your neck to live. Life is a stage scene in which there is little that is practical. Happiness is an old sash painted on one side. The ecclesiast says: all is vanity; I agree with that goodman who perhaps never existed. Zero, not wishing to go entirely naked, has clothed himself in vanity. O vanity! the patching up of everything with big words! a kitchen is a laboratory, a dancer is a professor, a mountebank is a gymnast, a boxer is a pugilist, an apothecary is a chemist, a hod-carrier is an architect, a jockey is a sportsman, a wood-louse is a pterygoranchiate. Vanity has a right side and a wrong side; the right side is stupid, it is the negro with his beads; the wrong side is silly, it is the philosopher with his rags. I weep over one and I laugh over the other. That which is called honours and dignities, and even honour and dignity, is generally pinchbeck. Kings make a plaything of human pride. Caligula made a horse consul; Charles II. made a sirloin a knight. Now parade yourselves then between the consul Incitatus and the baronet Roast-beef. As to the intrinsic value of people, it is hardly respectable any longer. Listen to the panegyric which neighbours pass upon each other. White is ferocious upon white; should the lily speak, how it would fix out the dove? a bigot gossiping about a devotee is more venomous than the asp and the blue viper. It is a pity that I am ignorant, for I would quote you a crowd of things, but I don't know anything. For instance, I always was bright; when I was a pupil with Gros, instead of daubing pictures, I spent my time in pilfering apples. So much for myself; as for the rest of you, you are just as good as I am. I make fun of your perfections, excellences, and good qualities. Every good quality runs into a defect; economy borders on avarice, the generous are not far from the prodigal, the brave man is close to the bully; he who says very pious says slightly sanctimonious; there are just as many vices in virtue as there are holes in the mantle of Diogenes. Which do you admire, the slain or the slayer, Cæsar or Brutus? People generally are for the slayer. Hurrah for Brutus! he slew. That is virtue. Virtue, if it may be, but folly also. There are some queer stains on these great men. The Brutus who slew Cæsar was in love with a statue of a little boy. This statue was by the Greek sculptor Strongylion, who also designed that statue of an amazon called the Beautiful-limbed, Euknemos, which Nero carried with him on his journeys. This Strongylion left nothing but two statues which put Brutus and Nero in harmony. Brutus was in love with one and Nero with the other. All history is only a long repetition. One century plagiarises another. The battle of Marengo copies the battle of Pydna; the Tolbach of Clovis and the Austerlitz of Napoleon are as like as two drops of blood. I make little account of victory. Nothing is so stupid as to vanquish; the real glory is to convince. But try now to prove something! you are satisfied with succeeding, what mediocrity! and with conquering, what misery! Alas, vanity and cowardice everywhere. Everything obeys success, even grammar. *Si volet usus*, says Horace. I despise therefore the human race. Shall we descend from the whole to a part? Will you have me set about admiring the peoples? what people, if you please? Greece? The Athenians, those Parisians of old times, killed Phocion, as if we should say Coligny, and fawned upon the tyrants to such a degree that Anacephoras said of Pisistratus: His water attracts the bees. The most considerable man in Greece for fifty years was that grammarian Philetas, who was so small and so thin that he was obliged to put lead on his shoes so as not to be blown away by the wind. There was in the grand square of Corinth a statue by the sculptor Silanion, catalogued by Pliny; this statue represented Episthates. What did Episthates do? He invented the trip in wrestling. This sums up Greece and glory. Let us pass to others. Shall I admire England? Shall I admire France? France? what for? on account of Paris. I have just told you my opinion of Athens. England? for what? on account of London? I hate Carthage. And then, London, the metropolis of luxury, is the capital of misery. In the single parish of Charing Cross, there are a hundred deaths a year from starvation. Such is Albion. I add, as a completion, that I have seen an English girl dance with a crown of roses and blue spectacles. A groan then for England. If I do not admire John Bull, shall I admire Brother Jonathan then? I have little taste for this brother with his slaves. Take away *time is money*, and what is left of England? take away *cotton is king*, and what is left of America? Germany is the lymph; Italy is the bile. Shall we go into ecstasies over Russia? Voltaire admired her. He admired China also. I confess that Russia has her beauties, among others a strong despotism; but I am sorry for the despots. They have very delicate health. An Alexis decapitated, a Peter stabbed, a Paul strangled, another Paul trampled down by blows from the heel of a boot, divers Ivans butchered, several Nicholases and Basils poisoned, all that indicates that the palace of the Emperors of Russia is in an alarming condition of insalubrity. All civilised nations offer to the admiration of the thinker this circumstance: war; but war, civilised war, exhausts and sums up every form of banditism, from the brigandage of the Trabucaires of the gorges of Mount Jaxa to the marauding of the Camanche Indians in the Doubtful Pass. Pshaw! will you tell me Europe is better than Asia for all that? I admit that Asia is ridiculous; but I do not quite see what right you have to laugh at the Grand Lama, you people of the Occident who have incorporated into your fashions and your elegancies all the multifarious ordures of majesty, from Queen Isabella's dirty chemise to the chamberchair of the dauphin. Messieurs humans, I tell you, not a bit of it! It is at Brussels that they consume the most brandy, at Madrid the most chocolate, at Amsterdam the most gin, at London the most wine, at Constantinople the most coffee, at Paris the most absinthe; those are all the useful notions. Paris takes the palm on the whole. In Paris, the rag-pickers even are Sybarites; Diogenes would have much rather been a rag-picker in the Place Maubert than a philosopher in the Piræus. Learn this also: the wine-shops of the rag-pickers are called *bibines*; the most celebrated are the *Saucepan* and the *Slaughter-house*. Therefore, O drinking-shops, eating-shops, tavern signs, barrooms, tea parties, meat markets, dance houses, brothels, rag-pickers' tippling-shops, caravanserai of the caliphs, I swear to you, I am a voluptuary, I eat at Richard's at forty sous a head, I must have Persian carpets on which to roll Cleopatra naked! Where is Cleopatra? Ah! it is you, Louison! Good morning."

Thus Grantaire, more than drunk, spread himself out in words catching up the dish-washer on her way, in his corner of the Musain back room.

Bossuet, extending his hand, endeavoured to impose silence upon him, and Grantaire started again still more beautifully:

"Eagle of Meaux, down with your claws. You have no effect upon me with your gesture of Hippocrates refusing his drugs to Artaxerxes. I dispense you from quieting me. Moreover, I am sad. What would you have me tell you? Man is wicked, man is deformed; the butterfly has succeeded, man has missed fire. God failed on this animal. A crowd gives you nothing but choice of ugliness. The first man you meet will be a wretch. *Femme* [woman] rhymes with *infâme* [infamous]. Yes, I have the spleen, in addition to melancholy, with nostalgia, besides hypochondria, and I sneer, and I rage, and I yawn, and I am tired, and I am knocked in the head, and I am tormented! Let God go to the Devil!"

"Silence, capital R!" broke in Bossuet, who was discussing a point of law aside, and who was more than half buried in a string of judicial argot, of which here is the conclusion:

"———And as for me, although I am hardly a legist, and at best an amateur attorney, I maintain this: that by the terms of the common law of Normandy, at St. Michael's, and for every year, an equivalent must be paid for the benefit of the seigneur, saving the rights of others, by each and every of them, as well proprietaries as those seized by inheritance, and this for all terms of years, leases, freeholds, contracts domainiary and domainial, of mortgagees and mortgagors———"

"Echo, plaintive nymph," muttered Grantaire.

Close beside Grantaire, at a table which was almost silent, a sheet of paper, an inkstand and a pen between two wine glasses, announced that a farce was being sketched out. This important business was carried on in a whisper, and the two heads at work touched each other.

"We must begin by finding the names. When we have found the names, we will find a subject."

"That is true. Dictate: I will write."

"Monsieur Dorimon."

"Wealthy?"

"Of course."

"His daughter Celestine."

"———tine. What next?"

"Colonel Sainval."

"Sainval is old. I would say Valsin."

Besides these dramatic aspirants, another group, who also were taking advantage of the confusion to talk privately, were discussing a duel. An old man, of thirty, was advising a young one, of eighteen, and explaining to him what sort of an adversary he had to deal with.

"The devil! Look out for yourself. He is a beautiful sword.

His play is neat. He comes to the attack, no lost feints, a pliant wrist, sparkling play, a flash, step exact, and ripostes mathematical. Zounds! and he is left-handed, too."

In the corner opposite to Grantaire, Joly and Bahorel were playing dominoes and talking of love.

"You are lucky," said Joly; "you have a mistress who is always laughing."

"That is a fault of hers," answered Bahorel. "Your mistress does wrong to laugh. It encourages you to deceive her. Seeing her gay takes away your remorse; if you see her sad, your conscience troubles you."

"Ingrate! A laughing woman is so good a thing! And you never quarrel!"

"That is a part of the treaty we have made. When we made our little Holy Alliance, we assigned to each our own boundary which we should never pass. What is situated towards the north belongs to Vaud, towards the south to Gex. Hence our peace."

"Peace is happiness digesting."

"And you, Jolllly, how do you come on in your falling out with Mamselle—you know who I mean?"

"She sulks with cruel patience."

"So you are a lover pining away."

"Alas!"

"If I were in your place, I would get rid of her."

"That is easily said."

"And done. Isn't it Musichetta that she calls herself?"

"Yes. Ah! my poor Bahorel, she is a superb girl, very literary with small feet, small hands, dresses well, white, plump, and has eyes like a fortune-teller. I am crazy about her."

"My dear fellow, then you must please her, be fashionable, and show off your legs. Buy a pair of doeskin pantaloons at Staub's. They yield."

"At what rate?" cried Grantaire.

The third corner had fallen a prey to a poetical discussion. The Pagan mythology was wrestling with the Christian mythology. The subject was Olympus, for which Jean Prouvaire, by very romanticism, took sides. Jean Prouvaire was timid only in repose. Once excited, he burst forth, a sort of gaiety characterised his enthusiasm, and he was at once laughing and lyric.

"Let us not insult the gods," said he. "The gods, perhaps, have not left us. Jupiter does not strike me as dead. The gods are dreams, say you. Well, even in nature, such as it now is, we find all the grand old pagan myths again. Such a mountain with the profile of a citadel, like the Vignemarle, for instance, is still to me the head-dress of Cybele; it is not proved that Pan does not come at night to blow into the hollow trunks of the willows, while he stops the holes with his fingers one after another; and I have always believed that Io had something to do with the cascade of Pissevache."

In the last corner, politics was the subject. They were abusing the Charter of Louis XVIII. Combeferre defended it mildly, Courfeyrac was energetically battering it to a breach. There was on the table an unlucky copy of the famous Touquet Charter. Courfeyrac caught it up and shook it, mingling with his arguments the rustling of that sheet of paper.

"First, I desire no kings; were it only from the economical point of view, I desire none; a king is a parasite. We do not have kings gratis. Listen to this: cost of kings. At the death of Francis I., the public debt of France was thirty thousand livres de rente; at the death of Louis XIV., it was two thousand six hundred millions at twenty-eight livres the mark, which was equivalent in 1760, according to Desmarest, to four thousand five hundred millions, and which is equivalent to-day to twelve thousand millions. Secondly, no offence to Combeferre, a charter granted is a vicious expedient of civilisation. To avoid the transition, to smoothe the passage, to deaden the shock, to make the nation pass insensibly from monarchy to democracy by the practice of constitutional fictions, these are all detestable arguments! No! no! never give the people a false light. Principles wither and grow pale in your constitutional cave. No half measures, no compromises, no grant from the king, to the people. In all these grants, there is an Article 14. Along with the hand which gives 'there is the claw which takes back.' I wholly refuse your charter. A charter is a mask; the lie is beneath it. A people who accept a charter, abdicate. Right is right only when entire. No! no charter!"

It was winter; two logs were crackling in the fire-place. It was tempting, and Courfeyrac could not resist. He crushed the poor Touquet Charter in his hand, and threw it into the fire. The paper blazed up. Combeferre looked philosophically upon the burning of Louis XVIII.'s masterpiece, and contented himself with saying:

"The charter metamorphosed in flames."

And the sarcasms, the sallies, the jests, that French thing which is called high spirits, that English thing which is called humour, good taste and bad taste, good reasons and bad reasons, all the commingled follies of dialogue, rising at once and crossing from all points of the room, made above their heads a sort of joyous bombardment.

V

ENLARGEMENT OF THE HORIZON

THE jostlings of young minds against each other have this wonderful attribute, that one can never foresee the spark, nor predict the flash. What may spring up in a moment? Nobody knows. A burst of laughter follows a scene of tenderness. In a moment of buffoonery, the serious makes its entrance. Impulses depend upon a chance word. The spirit of each is sovereign. A jest suffices to open the door to the unlooked for. Theirs are conferences with sharp turns, where the perspective suddenly changes. Chance is the director of these conversations.

A stern thought, oddly brought out of a clatter of words, suddenly crossed the tumult of speech in which Grantaire, Bahorel, Prouvaire, Bossuet, Combeferre, and Courfeyrac were confusedly fencing.

How does a phrase make its way into a dialogue? whence comes it that it makes its mark all at once upon the attention of those who hear it? We have just said, nobody knows. In the midst of the uproar Bossuet suddenly ended some apostrophe to Combeferre with this date:

"The 18th of June, 1815: Waterloo."

At this name, Waterloo, Marius, who was leaning on a table with a glass of water by him, took his hand away from under his chin and began to look earnestly about the room.

"Pardieu," exclaimed Courfeyrac (*Parbleu*, at that period, was falling into disuse), "that number 18 is strange, and striking to me. It is the fatal number of Bonaparte. Put Louis before and Brumaire behind, you have the whole destiny of the man, with this expressive peculiarity, that the beginning is hard pressed by the end."

Enjolras, till now dumb, broke the silence, and thus addressed Courfeyrac:

"You mean the crime by the expiation."

This word, *crime*, exceeded the limits of the endurance of Marius, already much excited by the abrupt evocation of Waterloo.

He rose, he walked slowly towards the map of France spread out upon the wall, at the bottom of which could be seen an island in a separate compartment; he laid his finger upon this compartment and said:

"Corsica. A little island which has made France truly great."

This was a breath of freezing air. All was silent. They felt that now something was to be said.

Bahorel, replying to Bossuet, was just assuming a pet attitude. He gave it up to listen.

Enjolras, whose blue eye was not fixed upon anybody, and seemed staring into space, answered without looking at Marius:

"France needs no Corsica to be great. France is great because she is France. *Quia nominor leo.*"

Marius felt no desire to retreat, he turned towards Enjolras, and his voice rang with a vibration which came from the quivering of his nerves:

"God forbid that I should lessen France! but it is not lessening her to join her with Napoleon. Come, let us talk then. I am a new-comer among you, but I confess that you astound me. Where are we? who are we? who are you? who am I? Let us explain ourselves about the emperor. I hear you say Buonaparte, accenting the *u* like the royalists. I can tell you that my grandfather does better yet; he says Buonaparté. I thought you were young men. Where is your enthusiasm then? and what do you do with it? whom do you admire, if you do not admire the emperor? and what more must you have? If you do not like that great man, what great men would you have? He was everything. He was complete. He had in his brain the cube of human faculties. He made codes like Justinian, he dictated like Cæsar, his conversation joined the lightning of Pascal to the thunderbolt of Tacitus, he made history and he wrote it, his bulletins are Iliads, he combined the figures of Newton with the metaphors of Mahomet, he left behind him in the Orient words as grand as the pyramids, at Tilsit he taught majesty to emperors, at the Academy of Sciences he replied to Laplace, in the Council of State he held his ground with Merlin, he gave a soul to the geometry of those and to the trickery of these, he was legal with the attorneys and sidereal with the astronomers; like Cromwell blowing out one candle when two were lighted, he went to the Temple to cheapen a curtain tassel; he saw everything; he knew everything; which did not prevent him from laughing a good-man's laugh by the cradle of his little child; and all at once, startled Europe listened, armies set themselves in march, parks of artillery rolled along, bridges of boats stretched over the rivers, clouds of cavalry galloped in the hurricane, cries, trumpets, a trembling of thrones everywhere, the frontiers of the kingdoms oscillated upon the map, the sound of a superhuman blade was heard leaping from its sheath, men saw him, him, standing erect in the horizon with a flame in his hands and a resplendence in his eyes, unfolding in the thunder his two wings, the Grand Army and the Old Guard, and he was the archangel of war!"

All were silent, and Enjolras bowed his head. Silence always has something of the effect of an acquiescence or of a sort of pushing to the wall. Marius, almost without taking breath, continued with a burst of enthusiasm:

"Be just, my friends! to be the empire of such an emperor, what a splendid destiny for a people, when that people is France, and when it adds its genius to the genius of such a man! To appear and to reign, to march and to triumph, to have every capital for a magazine, to take his grenadiers and make kings of them, to decree the downfall of dynasties, to transfigure Europe at a double quickstep, so that men feel, when you threaten, that you lay your hand on the hilt of the sword of God, to follow, in a single man, Hannibal, Cæsar, and Charlemagne, to be the people of one who mingles with your every dawn the glorious announcement of a battle gained, to be wakened in the morning by the cannon of the Invalides, to hurl into the vault of day mighty words which blaze for ever, Marengo, Arcola, Austerlitz, Jena, Wagram! to call forth at every moment constellations of victories in the zenith of the centuries, to make the French Empire, the successor of the Roman Empire, to be the grand nation and to bring forth the grand army, to send your legions flying over the whole earth as a mountain sends its eagles upon all sides, to vanquish, to rule, to thunderstrike, to be in Europe a kind of gilded people through much glory, to sound through history a Titan trumpet call, to conquer the world twice, by conquest and by resplendence, this is sublime, and what can be more grand?"

"To be free," said Combeferre.

Marius in his turn bowed his head: these cold and simple words had pierced his epic effusion like a blade of steel, and he felt it vanish within him. When he raised his eyes, Combeferre was there no longer. Satisfied probably with his reply to the apotheosis, he had gone out, and all, except Enjolras, had followed him. The room was empty. Enjolras, remaining alone with Marius, was looking at him seriously. Marius, meanwhile, having rallied his ideas a little, did not consider himself beaten; there was still something left of the ebullition within him, which doubtless was about to find expression in syllogisms arrayed against Enjolras, when suddenly they heard somebody singing as he was going downstairs. It was Combeferre, and what he was singing is this:

> Si César m'avait donné
>   La gloire et la guerre,
> Et qu'il me fallût quitter
>   L'amour de ma mère,
>   Je dirais au grand César:
> Reprends ton sceptre et ton char,
>   J'aime mieux ma mère, ô gué!
>   J'aime mieux ma mère.*

The wild and tender accent with which Combeferre sang, gave to this stanza a strange grandeur. Marius, thoughtful and with his eyes directed to the ceiling, repeated almost mechanically: "my mother——"

At this moment, he felt Enjolras' hand on his shoulder.

"Citizen," said Enjolras to him, "my mother is the republic."

VI
RES ANGUSTA

THAT evening left Marius in a profound agitation, with a sorrowful darkness in his soul. He was experiencing what

---

* If Cæsar had given me
    Glory and war
And if I must abandon
    The love of my mother,
I would say to great Cæsar:
Take thy sceptre and car,
    I prefer my mother, ah me!
    I prefer my mother.

perhaps the earth experiences at the moment when it is furrowed with the share that the grains of wheat may be sown; it feels the wound alone; the thrill of the germ and the joy of the fruit do not come until later.

Marius was gloomy. He had but just attained a faith; could he so soon reject it? He decided within himself that he could not. He declared to himself that he would not doubt, and he began to doubt in spite of himself. To be between two religions, one which you have not yet abandoned, and another which you have not yet adopted, is insupportable; and twilight is pleasant only to bat-like souls. Marius was an open eye, and he needed the true light. To him the dusk of doubt was harmful. Whatever might be his desire to stop where he was, and to hold fast there, he was irresistibly compelled to continue, to advance, to examine, to think, to go forward. Where was that going to lead him? he feared, after having taken so many steps which had brought him nearer to his father, to take now any steps which should separate them. His dejection increased with every reflection which occurred to him. Steep cliffs rose about him. He was on good terms neither with his grandfather nor with his friends; rash towards the former, backward towards the others; and he felt doubly isolated, from old age, and also from youth. He went no more to the Café Musain.

In this trouble in which his mind was plunged he scarcely gave a thought to certain serious phases of existence. The realities of life do not allow themselves to be forgotten. They came and jogged his memory sharply.

One morning, the keeper of the house entered Marius' room, and said to him:

"Monsieur Courfeyrac is responsible for you."

"Yes."

"But I am in need of money."

"Ask Courfeyrac to come and speak with me," said Marius.

Courfeyrac came; the host left them. Marius related to him what he had not thought of telling him before, that he was, so to speak, alone in the world, without any relatives.

"What are you going to become?" said Courfeyrac.

"I have no idea," answered Marius.

"What are you going to do?"

"I have no idea."

"Have you any money?"

"Fifteen francs."

"Do you wish me to lend you some?"

"Never."

"Have you any clothes?"

"What you see."

"Have you any jewellery?"

"A watch."

"A silver one?"

"Gold, here it is."

"I know a dealer in clothing who will take your overcoat and one pair of trousers."

"That is good."

"You will then have but one pair of trousers, one waistcoat, one hat, and one coat."

"And my boots."

"What? you will not go barefoot? what opulence!"

"That will be enough."

"I know a watchmaker who will buy your watch."

"That is good."

"No, it is not good. What will you do afterwards?"

"What I must. Anything honourable at least."

"Do you know English?"

"No."

"Do you know German?"

"No."

"That is bad."

"Why?"

"Because a friend of mine, a bookseller, is making a sort of encyclopædia, for which you could have translated German or English articles. It is poor pay, but it gives a living."

"I will learn English and German."

"And in the meantime?"

"In the meantime I will eat my coats and my watch."

The clothes dealer was sent for. He gave twenty francs for the clothes. They went to the watchmaker. He gave forty-five francs for the watch.

"That is not bad," said Marius to Courfeyrac, on returning to the house; "with my fifteen francs, this makes eighty francs."

"The hotel bill?" observed Courfeyrac.

"Ah! I forgot," said Marius.

The host presented his bill, which must be paid on the spot. It amounted to seventy francs.

"I have ten francs left," said Marius.

"The devil," said Courfeyrac, "you will have five francs to eat while you are learning English, and five francs while you are learning German. That will be swallowing a language very rapidly or a hundred-sous piece very slowly. "

Meanwhile Aunt Gillenormand, who was really a kind person on sad occasions, had finally unearthed Marius' lodgings.

One morning when Marius came home from the school, he found a letter from his aunt, and the *sixty pistoles*, that is to say, six hundred francs in gold, in a sealed box.

Marius sent the thirty louis back to his aunt, with a respectful letter, in which he told her that he had the means of living, and that he could provide henceforth for all his necessities. At that time he had three francs left.

The aunt did not inform the grandfather of this refusal, lest she should exasperate him. Indeed, had he not said: "Let nobody ever speak to me of this blood-drinker?"

Marius left the Porte Saint Jacques Hôtel, unwilling to contract debt.

BOOK FIFTH –
THE EXCELLENCE OF MISFORTUNE

I
MARIUS NEEDY

LIFE became stern to Marius. To eat his coats and his watch was nothing. He chewed that inexpressible thing which is called *the cud of bitterness*. A horrible thing, which includes days without bread, nights without sleep, evenings without a candle, a hearth without a fire, weeks without labour, a future without hope, a coat out at the elbows, an old hat which makes young girls laugh, the door found shut against you at night because you have not paid your rent, the insolence of the porter and the landlord, the jibes of neighbours, humiliations, self-respect outraged, any drudgery acceptable, disgust, bitterness, prostration—Marius learned how one swallows down all these things, and how they are often the only things that one has to swallow. At that period of existence, when man has need of pride, because he has need of love, he felt that he was mocked at because he was badly dressed, and ridiculed because he was poor. At the age when youth swells the heart with an imperial pride, he more than once dropped his eyes upon his worn-out boots, and experienced the undeserved shame and the poignant blushes of misery. Wonderful and terrible trial, from which the feeble come out infamous, from which the strong come out sublime. Crucible into which destiny casts a man whenever she desires a scoundrel or a demi-god.

For there are many great deeds done in the small struggles of life. There is a determined though unseen bravery, which defends itself foot to foot in the darkness against the fatal invasions of necessity and of baseness. Noble and mysterious triumphs which no eye sees, which no renown rewards, which no flourish of triumph salutes. Life, misfortunes, isolation, abandonment, poverty, are battle-fields which have their heroes; obscure heroes, sometimes greater than the illustrious heroes.

Strong and rare natures are thus created; misery, almost always a stepmother, is sometimes a mother; privation gives birth to power of soul and mind; distress is the nurse of self-respect; misfortune is a good breast for great souls.

There was a period in Marius' life when he swept his own

hall, when he bought a pennyworth of Brie cheese at the market-woman's, when he waited for nightfall to make his way to the baker's and buy a loaf of bread, which he carried furtively to his garret, as if he had stolen it. Sometimes there was seen to glide into the corner meat-market, in the midst of the jeering cooks who elbowed him, an awkward young man, with books under his arm, who had a timid and frightened appearance, and who, as he entered, took off his hat from his forehead, which was dripping with sweat, made a low bow to the astonished butcher, another bow to the butcher's boy, asked for a mutton cutlet, paid six or seven sous for it, wrapped it up in paper, put it under his arm between two books, and went away. It was Marius. On this cutlet, which he cooked himself, he lived three days.

The first day he ate the meat; the second day he ate the fat; the third day he gnawed the bone. On several occasions, Aunt Gillenormand made overtures, and sent him the sixty pistoles. Marius always sent them back, saying that he had no need of anything.

He was still in mourning for his father, when the revolution which we have described was accomplished in his ideas. Since then, he had never left off black clothes. His clothes left him, however. A day came, at last, when he had no coat. His trousers were going also. What was to be done? Courfeyrac, for whom he also had done some good turns, gave him an old coat. For thirty sous, Marius had it turned by some porter or other, and it was a new coat. But this coat was green. Then Marius did not go out till after nightfall. That made his coat black. Desiring always to be in mourning, he clothed himself with night.

Through all this, he procured admission to the bar. He was reputed to occupy Courfeyrac's room, which was decent, and where a certain number of law books, supported and filled out by some odd volumes of novels, made up the library required by the rules.

When Marius had become a lawyer, he informed his grandfather of it, in a letter which was frigid, but full of submission and respect. M. Gillenormand took the letter with trembling hands, read it, and threw it torn in pieces, into the basket. Two or three days afterwards, Mademoiselle Gillenormand overheard her father, who was alone in his room, talking aloud. This was always the case when he was much excited. She listened: the old man said: "If you were not a fool, you would know that a man cannot be a baron and a lawyer at the same time."

II
MARIUS POOR

IT is with misery as with everything else. It gradually becomes endurable. It ends by taking form and becoming fixed. You vegetate, that is to say you develop in some wretched fashion, but sufficient for existence. This is the way in which Marius Pontmercy's life was arranged.

He had got out of the narrowest place; the pass widened a little before him. By dint of hard work, courage, perseverance, and will, he had succeeded in earning by his labour about seven hundred francs a year. He had learned German and English; thanks to Courfeyrac, who introduced him to his friend the publisher, Marius filled, in the literary department of the book-house, the useful rôle of *utility*. He made out prospectuses, translated from the journals, annotated republications, compiled biographies, etc., net result, year in and year out, seven hundred francs. He lived on this. How? Not badly. We are going to tell.

Marius occupied, at an annual rent of thirty francs, a wretched little room in the Gorbeau tenement, with no fireplace, called a cabinet, in which there was no more furniture than was indispensable. The furniture was his own. He gave three francs a month to the old woman who had charge of the building, for sweeping his room and bringing him every morning a little warm water, a fresh egg, and a penny loaf of bread. On this loaf and this egg he breakfasted. His breakfast varied from two or four sous, as eggs were cheap or dear. At six o'clock in the evening he went down into the Rue Saint Jacques, to dine at Rousseau's, opposite Basset's the print dealer's, at the corner of the Rue des Mathurins. He ate no soup. He took a sixpenny plate of meat, a threepenny half-plate of vegetables, and a threepenny dessert. For three sous, as much bread as he liked. As for wine, he drank water. On paying at the counter, where Madame Rousseau was seated majestically, still plump and fresh also in those days, he gave a sou to the waiter, and Madame Rousseau gave him a smile. Then he went away. For sixteen sous, he had a smile and a dinner.

This Rousseau restaurant, where so few bottles and so many

pitchers were emptied, was rather an appeasant than a restorant. It is not kept now. The master had a fine title; he was called Rousseau the Aquatic.

Thus, breakfast four sous, dinner sixteen sous, his food cost him twenty sous a day, which was three hundred and sixty-five francs a year. Add the thirty francs for his lodging, and the thirty-six francs to the old woman, and a few other trifling expenses, and for four hundred and fifty francs, Marius was fed, lodged, and waited upon. His clothes cost him a hundred francs, his linen fifty francs, his washing fifty francs; the whole did not exceed six hundred and fifty francs. This left him fifty francs. He was rich. He occasionally lent ten francs to a friend. Courfeyrac borrowed sixty francs of him once. As for fire, having no fire-place, Marius had "simplified" it.

Marius always had two complete suits, one old "for every day," the other quite new, for special occasions. Both were black. He had but three shirts, one he had on, another in the drawer, the third at the washer-woman's. He renewed them as they wore out. They were usually ragged, so he buttoned his coat to his chin.

For Marius to arrive at this flourishing condition had required years. Hard years, and difficult ones; those to get through, these to climb. Marius had never given up for a single day. He had undergone everything, in the shape of privation; he had done everything, except get into debt. He gave himself this credit, that he had never owed a sou to anybody. For him a debt was the beginning of slavery. He felt even that a creditor is worse than a master; for a master owns only your person, a creditor owns your dignity and can belabour that. Rather than borrow, he did not eat. He had had many days of fasting. Feeling that all extremes meet and that if we do not take care, abasement of fortune may lead to baseness of soul, he watched jealously over his pride. Such a habit or such a carriage as, in any other condition, would have appeared deferential, seemed humiliating, and he braced himself against it. He risked nothing, not wishing to take a backward step. He had a kind of stern blush upon his face. He was timid even to rudeness.

In all his trials he felt encouraged and sometimes even upborne by a secret force within. The soul helps the body, and at certain moments uplifts it. It is the only bird which sustains its cage.

By the side of his father's name, another name was engraven upon Marius' heart, the name of Thénardier. Marius, in his enthusiastic yet serious nature, surrounded with a sort of halo the man to whom, as he thought, he owed his father's life, that brave sergeant who had saved the colonel in the midst of the balls and bullets of Waterloo. He never separated the memory of this man from the memory of his father, and he associated them in his veneration. It was a sort of worship with two steps, the high altar for the colonel, the low one for Thénardier. The idea of the misfortune into which he knew that Thénardier had fallen and been engulfed, intensified his feeling of gratitude. Marius had learned at Montfermeil of the ruin and bankruptcy of the unlucky innkeeper. Since then, he had made untold effort to get track of him, and to endeavour to find him, in that dark abyss of misery in which Thénardier had disappeared. Marius had beaten the whole country; he had been to Chelles, to Bondy, to Gournay, to Nogent, to Lagny. For three years he had been devoted to this, spending in these explorations what little money he could spare. Nobody could give him any news of Thénardier; it was thought he had gone abroad. His creditors had sought for him, also, with less love than Marius, but with as much zeal, and had not been able to put their hands on him. Marius blamed and almost hated himself for not succeeding in his researches. This was the only debt which the colonel had left him, and Marius made it a point of honour to pay it. "What," thought he, "when my father lay dying on the field of battle, Thénardier could find him through the smoke and the grape, and bring him off on his shoulders, and yet he owed him nothing; while I, who owe so much to Thénardier, I cannot reach him in that darkness in which he is suffering, and restore him, in my turn, from death to life. Oh! I will find him!" Indeed, to find Thénardier, Marius would have given one of his arms, and to save him from his wretchedness, all his blood. To see Thénardier, to render some service to Thénardier, to say to him—"You do not know me, but I do know you. Here I am, dispose of me!" This was the sweetest and most magnificent dream of Marius.

III
MARIUS A MAN

MARIUS was now twenty years old. It was three years since he had left his grandfather. They remained on the same terms on both sides, without attempting a reconciliation, and without seeking to meet. And, indeed, what was the use of meeting? to come in conflict? Which would have had the best of it? Marius was a vase of brass, but M. Gillenormand was an iron pot.

To tell the truth, Marius was mistaken as to his grandfather's heart. He imagined that M. Gillenormand had never loved him, and that this crusty and harsh yet smiling old man, who swore, screamed, stormed, and lifted his cane, felt for him at most only the affection, at once slight and severe, of the old men of comedy. Marius was deceived. There are fathers who do not love their children; there is no grandfather who does not adore his grandson. In reality, we have said, M. Gillenormand worshipped Marius. He worshipped him in his own way, with an accompaniment of cuffs, and even of blows; but, when the child was gone, he felt a dark void in his heart; he ordered that nobody should speak of him again, and regretted that he was so well obeyed. At first he hoped that this Buonapartist, this Jacobin, this terrorist, this Septembrist, would return. But weeks passed away, months passed away, years passed away; to the great despair of M. Gillenormand, the blood-drinker did not reappear! "But I could not do anything else than turn him away," said the grandfather, and he asked himself: "If it were to be done again, would I do it?" His pride promptly answered Yes, but his old head, which he shook in silence, sadly answered, No. He had his hours of dejection. He missed Marius. Old men need affection as they do sunshine. It is warmth. However strong his nature might be, the absence of Marius had changed something in him. For nothing in the world would he have taken a step towards the "little rogue;" but he suffered. He never inquired after him, but he thought of him constantly. He lived, more and more retired, in the Marais. He was still, as formerly, gay and violent, but his gaiety had a convulsive harshness as if it contained grief and anger, and his bursts of violence always terminated by a sort of placid and gloomy exhaustion. He said sometimes: "Oh! if he would come back, what a good box of the ear I would give him."

As for the aunt, she thought too little to love very much; Marius was now nothing to her but a sort of dim, dark outline; and she finally busied herself a good deal less about him than with the cat or the paroquet which she probably had. What increased the secret suffering of Grandfather Gillenormand, was that he shut her entirely out, and let her suspect nothing of it. His chagrin was like those newly invented furnaces which consume their own smoke. Sometimes it happened that some blundering, officious body would speak to him of Marius, and ask: "What is your grandson doing, or what has become of him?" The old bourgeois would answer, with a sigh if he was too sad, or giving his ruffle a tap, if he wished to seem gay: "Monsieur the Baron Pontmercy is pettifogging in some hole."

While the old man was regretting, Marius was rejoicing. As with all good hearts, suffering had taken away his bitterness. He thought of M. Gillenormand only with kindness, but he had determined to receive nothing more from the man *who had been cruel to his father.* This was now the softened translation of his first indignation. Moreover, he was happy in having suffered, and in suffering still. It was for his father. His hard life satisfied him, and pleased him. He said to himself with a sort of pleasure that—*it was the very least;* that it was—an expiation; that—save for this, he would have been punished otherwise and later, for his unnatural indifference towards his father, and towards such a father;—that it would not have been just that his father should have had all the suffering, and himself none;—what were his efforts and his privation, moreover, compared with the heroic life of the colonel? that finally his only way of drawing near his father, and becoming like him, was to be valiant against indigence as he had been brave against the enemy; and that this was doubtless what the colonel meant by the words: "*He will be worthy of it.*" Words which Marius continued to bear, not upon his breast, the colonel's paper having disappeared, but in his heart.

And then, when his grandfather drove him away, he was but a child; now he was a man. He felt it. Misery, we must insist, had been good to him. Poverty in youth, when it succeeds, is so far magnificent that it turns the whole will towards effort, and the whole soul towards aspiration. Poverty strips the material life entirely bare, and makes it hideous; thence arise inexpressible yearnings towards the ideal life. The rich young man has a hundred brilliant and coarse amusements, racing, hunting, dogs, cigars, gaming, feasting, and the rest; busying the lower portions of the soul at the expense of its higher and delicate portions. The poor young man must work for his bread; he eats; when he has eaten, he has nothing more but reverie. He goes free to the play which God gives; he beholds the sky, space, the stars, the flowers, the children, the humanity in which he suffers, the creation in which he shines. He looks at humanity so much that he sees the soul, he looks at creation so much that he sees God. He dreams, he feels that he is great; he dreams again, and he feels that he is tender. From the egotism of the suffering man, he passes to the compassion of the contemplating man. A wonderful feeling springs up within him, forgetfulness of self, and pity for all. In thinking of the numberless enjoyments which nature offers, gives, and gives lavishly to open souls, and refuses to closed souls, he, a millionaire of intelligence, comes to grieve for the millionaires of money. All hatred goes out of his heart in proportion as all light enters his mind. And then is he unhappy? No. The misery of a young man is never miserable. The first lad you meet, poor as he may be, with his health, his strength, his quick step, his shining eyes, his blood which circulates warmly, his black locks, his fresh cheeks, his rosy lips, his white teeth, his pure breath, will always be envied by an old emperor. And then every morning he sets about earning his bread; and while his hands are earning his living, his backbone is gaining firmness, his brain is gaining ideas. When his work is done, he returns to ineffable ecstasies, to contemplation, to joy; he sees his feet in difficulties, in obstacle, on the pavement, in thorns, sometimes in the mire; his head is in the light. He is firm, serene, gentle, peaceful, attentive, serious, content with little, benevolent; and he blesses God for having given him these two estates which many of the rich are without; labour which makes him free, and thought which makes him noble.

This is what had taken place in Marius. He had even, to tell the truth, gone a little too far on the side of contemplation. The day on which he had arrived at the point of being almost sure of earning his living, he stopped there, preferring to be poor, and retrenching from labour to give to thought. That is to say, he passed sometimes whole days in thinking, plunged and swallowed up like a visionary, in the mute joys of ecstasy and interior radiance. He had put the problem of his life thus: to work as little as possible at material labour, that he might work as much as possible at impalpable labour; in other words, to give a few hours to real life, and to cast the rest into the infinite. He did not perceive, thinking that he lacked nothing, that contemplation thus obtained comes to be one of the forms of sloth, that he was content with subduing the primary necessities of life, and that he was resting too soon.

It was clear that, for his energetic and generous nature, this could only be a transitory state, and that at the first shock against the inevitable complications of destiny, Marius would arouse.

Meantime, although he was a lawyer, and whatever Grandfather Gillenormand might think, he was not pleading, he was not even pettifogging. Reverie had turned him away from the law. To consort with attorneys, to attend courts, to hunt up cases, was wearisome. Why should he do it? He saw no reason for changing his business. This cheap and obscure book-making had procured him sure work, work with little labour, which, as we have explained, was sufficient for him.

One of the booksellers for whom he worked, M. Magimel, I think, had offered to take him home, give him a good room, furnish him regular work, and pay him fifteen hundred francs a year. To have a good room! fifteen hundred francs! Very well. But to give up his liberty! to work for a salary, to be a kind of literary clerk! In Marius' opinion, to accept would make his position better and worse at the same time; he would gain in comfort and lose in dignity; it was a complete and beautiful misfortune given up for an ugly and ridiculous constraint; something like a blind man who should gain one eye. He refused.

Marius' life was solitary. From his taste for remaining outside of everything, and also from having been startled by its excesses, he had decided not to enter the group presided over by Enjolras. They had remained good friends; they were ready to help one another, if need were, in all possible ways; but nothing more. Marius had two friends, one young, Courfeyrac, and one old, M. Mabeuf. He inclined towards the old one. First he was indebted to him for the revolution through which he had gone; he was indebted to him for having known and loved his father. "*He operated upon me for the cataract*," said he.

Certainly, this churchwarden had been decisive.

M. Mabeuf was not, however, on that occasion anything

more than the calm and passive agent of providence. He had enlightened Marius accidentally and without knowing it, as a candle does which somebody carries; he had been the candle and not the somebody.

As to the interior political revolution in Marius, M. Mabeuf was entirely incapable of comprehending it, desiring it, or directing it.

As we shall meet M. Mabeuf hereafter, a few words will not be useless.

IV

M. MABEUF

THE day that M. Mabeuf said to Marius: "*Certainly, I approve of political opinions,*" he expressed the real condition of his mind. All political opinions were indifferent to him, and he approved them all without distinction, provided they left him quiet, as the Greeks called the Furies, "the beautiful, the good, the charming," the *Eumenides*. M. Mabeuf's political opinion was a passionate fondness for plants, and a still greater one for books. He had, like everybody else, his termination in *ist*, without which nobody could have lived in those times, but he was neither a royalist, nor a Bonapartist, nor a chartist, nor an Orleanist, nor an anarchist; he was an old-bookist.

He did not understand how men could busy themselves with hating one another about such bubbles as the charter, democracy, legitimacy, the monarchy, the republic, etc., when there were in this world all sorts of mosses, herbs and shrubs, which they could look at, and piles of folios and even of 32mos which they could pore over. He took good care not to be useless; having books did not prevent him from reading, being a botanist did not prevent him from being a gardener. When he knew Pontmercy, there was this sympathy between the colonel and himself, that what the colonel did for flowers, he did for fruits. M. Mabeuf had succeeded in producing seedling pears as highly flavoured as the pears of Saint Germain; to one of his combinations, as it appears, we owe the October Mirabelle, now famous, and not less fragrant than the Summer Mirabelle. He went to mass rather from good-feeling than from devotion, and because he loved the faces of men, but hated their noise, and he found them, at church only, gathered together and silent. Feeling that he ought to be something in the government, he had chosen the career of a churchwarden. Finally, he had never succeeded in loving any woman as much as a tulip bulb, or any man as much as an Elzevir. He had long passed his sixtieth year, when one day somebody asked him: "Were you never married?" "I forget," said he. When he happened sometimes—to whom does it not happen?—to say: "Oh! if I were rich," it was not upon ogling a pretty girl, like M. Gillenormand, but upon seeing an old book. He lived alone, with an old governess. He was a little gouty, and when he slept, his old fingers, stiffened with rheumatism, were clenched in the folds of the clothes. He had written and published a *Flora of the Environs of Cauteretz* with coloured illustrations, a highly esteemed work, the plates of which he owned and which he sold himself. People came two or three times a day and rang his bell, in the Rue Mézières, for it. He received fully two thousand francs a year for it; this was nearly all his income. Though poor, he had succeeded in gathering together, by means of patience, self-denial, and time, a valuable collection of rare copies on every subject. He never went out without a book under his arm, and he often came back with two. The only decoration of the four ground-floor rooms which, with a small garden, formed his dwelling, were some framed herbariums and a few engravings of old masters. The sight of a sword or a gun chilled him. In his whole life, he had never been near a cannon, even at the Invalides. He had a passable stomach, a brother who was a curé, hair entirely white, no teeth left either in his mouth or in his mind, a tremor of the whole body, a Picard accent, a childlike laugh, weak nerves, and the appearance of an old sheep. With all that, no other friend nor any other intimate acquaintance among the living, but an old bookseller of the Porte Saint Jacques named Royol. His mania was the naturalisation of indigo in France.

His servant was, also, a peculiar variety of innocence. The poor good old woman was a maid. Sultan, her cat, who could have mewed the Miserere of Allegri at the Sistine Chapel, had filled her heart and sufficed for the amount of passion which she possessed. None of her dreams went as far as man. She had never got beyond her cat. She had, like him, moustaches. Her glory was in the whiteness of her caps. She spent her time on Sunday after mass in counting her linen in her trunk, and in spreading out upon her bed the dresses in the piece which she had bought and never made up. She could read. Monsieur Mabeuf had given her the name of *Mother Plutarch*.

Monsieur Mabeuf took Marius into favour, because Marius, being young and gentle, warmed his old age without arousing his timidity. Youth, with gentleness, has upon old men the effect of sunshine without wind. When Marius was full of military glory, gunpowder, marches, and countermarches, and all those wonderful battles in which his father had given and received such huge sabre strokes, he went to see Monsieur Mabeuf, and Monsieur Mabeuf talked with him about the hero from the floricultural point of view.

Towards 1830, his brother the curé died, and almost immediately after, as at the coming on of night, the whole horizon of Monsieur Mabeuf was darkened. By a failure—of a notary—he lost ten thousand francs, which was all the money that he possessed in his brother's name and his own. The revolution of July brought on a crisis in bookselling. In hard times, the first thing that does not sell is a *Flora*. *The Flora of the Environs of Cauteretz* stopped short. Weeks went by without a purchaser. Sometimes Monsieur Mabeuf would start at the sound of the bell. "Monsieur," Mother Plutarch would say sadly, "it is the water-porter." In short, Monsieur Mabeuf left the Rue Mézières one day, resigned his place as churchwarden, gave up Saint Sulpice, sold a part, not of his books, but of his prints—what he prized the least—and installed himself in a little house on the Boulevard Montparnasse, where however he remained but one quarter, for two reasons; first, the ground floor and the garden let for three hundred francs, and he did not dare to spend more than two hundred francs for his rent; secondly, being near the Fatou shooting gallery, he heard pistol shots; which was insupportable to him.

He carried off his *Flora*, his plates, his herbariums, his portfolios and his books, and established himself near La Saltpêtrière in a sort of cottage in the village of Austerlitz, where at fifty crowns a year he had three rooms, a garden inclosed with a hedge, and a well. He took advantage of this change to sell nearly all his furniture. The day of his entrance into this new dwelling, he was very gay, and drove nails himself on which to hang the engravings and the herbariums; he dug in his garden the rest of the day, and in the evening, seeing that Mother Plutarch had a gloomy and thoughtful air, he tapped her on the shoulder and said with a smile: "We have the indigo."

Only two visitors, the bookseller of the Porte Saint Jacques and Marius, were admitted to his cottage at Austerlitz, a tumultuous name which was, to tell the truth, rather disagreeable to him.

However, as we have just indicated, brains absorbed in wisdom, or in folly, or, as often happens, in both at once, are but very slowly permeable by the affairs of life. Their own destiny is far from them. There results from such concentrations of mind a passivity which, if it were due to reason, would resemble philosophy. We decline, we descend, we fall, we are even overthrown, and we hardly perceive it. This always ends, it is true, by an awakening, but a tardy one. In the meantime, it seems as though we were neutral in the game which is being played between our good and our ill fortune. We are the stake, yet we look upon the contest with indifference.

Thus it was that amid this darkness which was gathering about him, all his hopes going out one after another, Monsieur Mabeuf had remained serene, somewhat childishly, but very thoroughly. His habits of mind had the swing of a pendulum. Once wound up by an illusion, he went a very long time, even when the illusion had disappeared. A clock does not stop at the very moment you lose the key.

Monsieur Mabeuf had some innocent pleasures. These pleasures were cheap and unlooked-for; the least chance furnished them. One day Mother Plutarch was reading a romance in one corner of the room. She read aloud, as she understood better so. To read aloud, is to assure yourself of what you are reading. There are people who read very loud, and who appear to be giving their words of honour for what they are reading.

It was with that kind of energy that Mother Plutarch was reading the romance she held in her hand. Monsieur Mabeuf heard, but was not listening.

As she read, Mother Plutarch came to this passage. It was about an officer of dragoons and a belle:

"The belle *bouda* [pouted], and the *dragon* [dragoon]———"

Here she stopped to wipe her spectacles.

"Bouddha and the Dragon," said Monsieur Mabeuf in an undertone. "Yes, it is true, there was a dragon who, from the depth of his cave, belched forth flames from his jaws and was burning up the sky. Several stars had already been set on fire by this monster, who, besides, had claws like a tiger. Bouddha went into his cave and succeeded in converting the dragon. That is a good book which you are reading there, Mother Plutarch. There is no more beautiful legend."

And Monsieur Mabeuf fell into a delicious reverie.

V

POVERTY A GOOD NEIGHBOUR OF MISERY

MARIUS had a liking for this open-hearted old man, who saw that he was being slowly seized by indigence, and who had come gradually to be astonished at it, without, however, as yet becoming sad. Marius met Courfeyrac, and went to see Monsieur Mabeuf. Very rarely, however; once or twice a month, at most.

It was Marius' delight to take long walks alone on the outer boulevards, or in the Champ de Mars, or in the less frequented walks of the Luxembourg. He sometimes spent half a day in looking at a vegetable garden, at the beds of salad, the fowls on the dung-heap and the horse turning the wheel of the pump. The passers-by looked at him with surprise, and some thought that he had a suspicious appearance and an ill-omened manner. He was only a poor young man, dreaming without an object.

It was in one of these walks that he had discovered the Gorbeau tenement, and its isolation and cheapness being an attraction to him, he had taken a room in it. He was only known in it by the name of Monsieur Marius.

All passions, except those of the heart, are dissipated by reverie. Marius' political fevers were over. The revolution of 1830, by satisfying him, and soothing him, had aided in this. He remained the same, with the exception of his passionateness. He had still the same opinions. But they were softened. Properly speaking, he held opinions no longer; he had sympathies. Of what party was he? of the party of humanity. Out of humanity he chose France; out of the nation he chose the people; out of the people he chose woman. To her, above all, his pity went out. He now preferred an idea to a fact, a poet to a hero, and he admired a book like Job still more than an event like Marengo. And then, when, after a day of meditation, he returned at night along the boulevards, and saw through the branches of the trees the fathomless space, the nameless lights, the depths, the darkness, the mystery, all that which is only human seemed to him very pretty.

Marius thought he had, and he had perhaps in fact arrived at the truth of life and of human philosophy, and he had finally come hardly to look at anything but the sky, the only thing that truth can see from the bottom of her well.

This did not hinder him from multiplying plans, combinations, scaffoldings, projects for the future. In this condition of reverie, an eye which could have looked into Marius' soul would have been dazzled by its purity. In fact, were it given to our eye of flesh to see into the consciences of others, we should judge a man much more surely from what he dreams than from what he thinks. There is will in the thought, there is none in the dream. The dream, which is completely spontaneous, takes and keeps, even in the gigantic and the ideal, the form of our mind. Nothing springs more directly and more sincerely from the very bottom of our souls than our unreflected and indefinite aspirations towards the splendours of destiny. In these aspirations, much more than in ideas which are combined, studied, and compared, we can find the true character of each man. Our chimeras are what most resemble ourselves. Each one dreams the unknown and the impossible according to his own nature.

Towards the middle of this year, 1831, the old woman who waited upon Marius told him that his neighbours, the wretched Jondrette family, were to be turned into the street. Marius, who passed almost all his days out of doors, hardly knew that he had any neighbours.

"Why are they turned out?" said he.

"Because they do not pay their rent; they owe for two terms."

"How much is that?"

"Twenty francs," said the old woman.

Marius had thirty francs in reserve in a drawer.

"Here," said he to the old woman, "there are twenty-five francs. Pay for these poor people, give them five francs, and do not tell them that it is from me."

VI

THE SUPPLANTER

IT happened that the regiment to which Lieutenant Théodule belonged came to be stationed at Paris. This was the occasion of a second idea occurring to Aunt Gillenormand. She had, the first time, thought she would have Marius watched by Théodule; she plotted to have Théodule supplant Marius.

At all events, and in case the grandfather should feel a vague need of a young face in the house—these rays of dawn are sometimes grateful to ruins—it was expedient to find another Marius. "Yes," thought she, "it is merely an erratum such as I see in the books; for Marius read Théodule."

A grandnephew is almost a grandson; for want of a lawyer a lancer will do.

One morning, as Monsieur Gillenormand was reading something like *La Quotidienne*, his daughter entered, and said in her softest voice, for the matter concerned her favourite:

"Father, Théodule is coming this morning to present his respects to you."

"Who is that,—Théodule?"

"Your grandnephew."

"Ah!" said the grandfather.

Then he resumed his reading, thought no more of the grandnephew who was nothing more than any Théodule, and very soon was greatly excited, as was almost always the case when he read. The "sheet" which he had, royalist indeed—that was a matter of course,—announced for the next day, without any mollification, one of the little daily occurrences of the Paris of that time; that the students of the schools of Law and Medicine would meet in the square of the Pantheon at noon—to deliberate. The question was one of the topics of the moment; the artillery of the National Guard, and a conflict between the Minister of War and "the citizen militia" on the subject of the cannon planted in the court of the Louvre. The students were to "deliberate" thereupon. It did not require much more to enrage Monsieur Gillenormand.

He thought of Marius, who was a student, and who, probably, would go, like the others, "to deliberate, at noon, in the square of the Pantheon."

While he was dwelling upon this painful thought, Lieutenant

Théodule entered, in citizen's dress, which was adroit, and was discreetly introduced by Mademoiselle Gillenormand. The lancer reasoned thus: "The old druid has not put everything into an annuity. It is well worth while to disguise oneself in taffeta occasionally."

Mademoiselle Gillenormand said aloud to her father:

"Théodule, your grandnephew."

And, in a whisper, to the lieutenant:

"Say yes to everything."

And she retired.

The lieutenant, little accustomed to such venerable encounters, stammered out with some timidity: "Good morning, uncle," and made a mixed bow composed of the involuntary and mechanical awkwardness of the military salute finished off with the bow of the bourgeois.

"Ah! it is you; very well, take a seat," said the old man.

And then, he entirely forgot the lancer.

Théodule sat down, and Monsieur Gillenormand got up.

Monsieur Gillenormand began to walk up and down with his hands in his pockets, talking aloud, and rubbing with his nervous old fingers the two watches which he carried in his two waistcoat pockets.

"This mess of snivellers! they meet together in the square of the Pantheon. Virtue of my quean. Scapegraces yesterday at nurse! If their noses were squeezed, the milk would run out! And they deliberate at noon to-morrow! What are we coming to? what are we coming to? It is clear that we are going to the pit. That is where the descamisados have led us! The citizen artillery! To deliberate about the citizen artillery! To go out and jaw in the open air about the blowing of the National Guard! And whom will they find themselves with there! Just see where jacobinism leads to. I will bet anything you please, a million against a fig, that they will all be fugitives from justice and discharged convicts. Republicans and galley slaves, they fit like a nose and a handkerchief. Carnot said: 'Where would you have me go, traitor?' Fouché answered: 'Wherever you like, fool!' That is what republicans are."

"It is true," said Théodule.

Monsieur Gillenormand turned his head half around, saw Théodule, and continued.

"Only to think that this rogue has been so wicked as to turn carbonaro! Why did you leave my house? To go out and be a republican. Pish! in the first place the people do not want your republic, they do not want it, they have good sense, they know very well that there always have been kings, and that there always will be, they know very well that the people, after all, is nothing but the people, they laugh at your republic, do you understand, idiot? Is not that caprice of yours horrible? To fall in love with Père Duchesne, to cast sheep's eyes at the guillotine, to sing ditties and play the guitar under the balcony of '93, we must spit upon all these young folks, they are so stupid! They are all in a heap. Not one is out of it. It is enough to breathe the air that blows down the street to make them crazy. The nineteenth century is poison. The first blackguard you will meet wears his goat's beard, thinks he is very clever and discards his old relatives. That is republican, that is romantic. What is that indeed, romantic? have the kindness to tell me what that is! Every possible folly. A year ago you went to *Hernani*. I want to know, *Hernani*! antitheses! abominations which are not written in French! And then they have cannon in the court of the Louvre. Such is the brigandage of these things."

"You are right, uncle," said Théodule.

M. Gillenormand resumed:

"Cannon in the court of the Museum! what for? Cannon, what do you want? Do you want to shoot down the Apollo Belvedere? What have cartridges to do with Venus de' Medici? Oh! these young folks nowadays, all scamps! What a small affair is their Benjamin Constant! And those who are not scoundrels are boobies! They do all they can to be ugly, they are badly dressed, they are afraid of women, they appear like beggars about petticoats, which makes the wenches burst out laughing; upon my word, you would say the poor fellows are ashamed of love. They are homely, and they finish themselves off by being stupid; they repeat the puns of Tiercelin and Potier, they have sackcoats, horse-jockeys' waistcoats, coarse cotton shirts, coarse cloth trousers, coarse leather boots, and their jabber is like their feathers. Their jargon would serve to sole their old shoes with. And all these foolish brats have political opinions. They ought to be strictly forbidden to have any political opinions. They fabricate systems, they reform society, they demolish monarchy, they upset all laws, they put the garret into the cellar, and my porter in place of the king, they turn Europe topsy-turvy, they rebuild the world, and the favours they get are sly peeps at washerwomen's legs when they are getting into their carts! Oh! Marius! Oh! you beggar! going to bawl in a public place! to discuss, to debate, to take measures! they call them measures, just gods! disorder shrinks and becomes a ninny. I have seen chaos, I see a jumble. Scholars deliberating about the National Guard, you would not see that among the Ojibways or among the Cadodaches! The savages who go naked, their pates looking like shuttlecocks, with clubs in their paws, are not so wild as these bachelors. Fourpenny monkeys! they pass for learned and capable! they deliberate and reason! it is the world's end. It is evidently the end of this miserable terraqueous globe. It needed some final hiccough, France is giving it. Deliberate, you rogues. Such things will happen as long as they go and read the papers under the arches of the Odeon. That costs them a sou, and their good sense, and their intelligence, and their heart, and their soul, and their mind. They come away from there, and they bring the camp into their family. All these journals are a pest; all, even the *Drapeau Blanc*! at bottom Martainville was a jacobin. Oh! just heavens! you can be proud of having thrown your grandfather into despair, you can!"

"That is evident," said Théodule.

And taking advantage of M. Gillenormand's drawing breath, the lancer added magisterially: "There ought to be no journal but the *Moniteur* and no book but the *Annuaire Militaire*."

M. Gillenormand went on.

"He is like their Sieyès! a regicide ending off as a senator; that is always the way they end. They slash themselves with thee-and-thouing, and citizen, so that they may come to be called Monsieur the Count, Monsieur the Count as big as my arm, the butchers of September. The philosopher Sieyès! I am happy to say that I never made any more account of the philosophies of all these philosophers than of the spectacles of the clown of Tivoli. I saw the senators one day passing along the Quai Malaquais in mantles of violet velvet sprinkled with bees, and hats in the style of Henri IV. They were hideous. You would have said they were the monkeys of the tiger's court. Citizens, I tell you that your progress is a lunacy, that your humanity is a dream, that your revolution is a crime, that your republic is a monster, that your young maiden France comes from the brothel, and I maintain it before you all, whoever you are, be you publicists, be you economists, be you legists, be you greater connoisseurs in liberty, equality, and fraternity than the axe of the guillotine! I tell you that, my goodmen!"

"Zounds," cried the lieutenant, "that is wonderfully true."

M. Gillenormand broke off a gesture which he had begun, turned, looked the lancer Théodule steadily in the eyes, and said:

"You are a fool."

BOOK SIXTH –
THE CONJUNCTION OF TWO STARS

I

THE NICKNAME: MODE OF FORMATION
OF FAMILY NAMES

MARIUS was now a fine-looking young man, of medium height, with heavy jet black hair, a high intelligent brow, large and passionate nostrils, a frank and calm expression, and an indescribable something beaming from every feature, which was at once lofty, thoughtful and innocent. His profile, all the lines of which were rounded, but without loss of strength, possessed that Germanic gentleness which has made its way into French physiognomy through Alsace and Lorraine, and that entire absence of angles which rendered the Sicambri so recognisable among the Romans, and which distinguishes the leonine from the aquiline race. He was at that season of life at which the mind of men who think, is made up in nearly equal proportions of depth and simplicity. In a difficult situation he possessed all the essentials of stupidity; another turn of the screw, and he could become sublime. His manners were reserved, cold, polished, far from free. But as his mouth was very pleasant, his lips the reddest and his teeth the whitest in the world, his smile corrected the severity of his physiognomy. At certain moments there was a strange contrast between this chaste brow and this voluptuous smile. His eye was small, his look great.

At the time of his most wretched poverty, he noticed that girls turned when he passed, and with a deathly feeling in his heart he fled or hid himself. He thought they looked at him on account of his old clothes, and that they were laughing at him; the truth is, that they looked at him because of his graceful appearance, and that they dreamed over it.

This wordless misunderstanding between him and the pretty girls he met, had rendered him hostile to society. He attached himself to none, for the excellent reason that he fled before all. Thus he lived without aim—like a beast, said Courfeyrac.

Courfeyrac said to him also: "Aspire not to be a sage (they used familiar speech; familiarity of speech is characteristic of youthful friendships). My dear boy, a piece of advice. Read not so much in books, and look a little more upon the Peggies. The little rogues are good for thee, O Marius! By continual flight and blushing thou shalt become a brute."

At other times Courfeyrac met him with: "Good day, Monsieur Abbé."

When Courfeyrac said anything of this kind to him, for the next week Marius avoided women, old as well as young, more than ever, and especially did he avoid the haunts of Courfeyrac.

There were, however, in all the immensity of creation, two women from whom Marius never fled, and whom he did not at all avoid. Indeed he would have been very much astonished had anybody told him that they were women. One was the old woman with the beard, who swept his room, and who gave Courfeyrac an opportunity to say: "As his servant wears her beard, Marius does not wear his." The other was a little girl that he saw very often, and that he never looked at.

For more than a year Marius had noticed in a retired walk of the Luxembourg, the walk which borders the parapet of the Pépinière, a man and a girl quite young, nearly always sitting side by side, on the same seat, at the most retired end of the walk, near the Rue de l'Ouest. Whenever that chance which controls the promenades of men whose eye is turned within, led Marius to this walk, and it was almost every day, he found this couple there. The man might be sixty years old; he seemed sad and serious; his whole person presented the robust but wearied appearance of a soldier retired from active service. Had he worn a decoration, Marius would have said: it is an old officer. His expression was kind, but it did not invite approach, and he never returned a look. He wore a blue coat and pantaloons, and a broad-brimmed hat, which always appeared to be new, a black cravat, and Quaker linen, that is to say, brilliantly white, but of coarse texture. A grisette passing near him one day, said: There is a very nice widower. His hair was perfectly white.

The first time the young girl that accompanied him sat down on the seat which they seemed to have adopted, she looked like a girl of about thirteen or fourteen, puny to the extent of being almost ugly, awkward, insignificant, yet promising, perhaps, to have rather fine eyes. But they were always looking about with a disagreeable assurance. She wore the dress at once aged and childish, peculiar to the convent school-girl, an ill-fitting garment of coarse black merino. They appeared to be father and daughter.

For two or three days Marius scrutinised this old man, who was not yet an aged man, and this little girl, not yet a woman; then he paid no more attention to them. For their part they did not even seem to see him. They talked with each other peacefully, and with indifference to all else. The girl chatted incessantly and gaily. The old man spoke little, and at times looked upon her with an unutterable expression of fatherliness.

Marius had acquired a sort of mechanical habit of promenading on this walk. He always found them there.

It was usually thus:

Marius would generally reach the walk at the end opposite their seat, promenade the whole length of it, passing before them, then return to the end by which he entered, and so on. He performed this turn five or six times in his promenade, and this promenade five or six times a week, but they and he had never come to exchange bows. This man and this young girl, though they appeared, and perhaps because they appeared, to avoid observation, had naturally excited the attention of the five or six students, who, from time to time, took their promenades along the Pépinière; the studious after their lecture, the others after their game of billiards. Courfeyrac, who belonged to the latter, had noticed them at some time or other, but finding the girl homely, had very quickly and carefully avoided them. He had fled like a Parthian, launching a nickname behind him. Struck especially by the dress of the little girl and the hair of the old man, he had named the daughter *Mademoiselle Lanoire* [Black] and the father *Monsieur Leblanc* [White]; and so, as nobody knew them otherwise, in the absence of a name, this surname had become fixed. The students said: "Ah! Monsieur Leblanc is at his seat!" and Marius, like the rest, had found it convenient to call this unknown gentleman M. Leblanc.

We shall do as they did, and say M. Leblanc for the convenience of this story.

Marius saw them thus nearly every day at the same hour during the first year. He found the man very much to his liking, but the girl rather disagreeable.

II
LUX FACTA EST

THE second year, at the precise point of this history to which the reader has arrived, it so happened that Marius broke off this habit of going to the Luxembourg, without really knowing why himself, and there were nearly six months during which he did not set foot in his walk. At last he went back there again one day; it was a serene summer morning, Marius was as happy as one always is when the weather is fine. It seemed to him as if he had in his heart all the bird songs which he heard, and all the bits of blue sky which he saw through the trees.

He went straight to "his walk," and as soon as he reached it, he saw, still on the same seat, this well known pair. When he came near them, however, he saw that it was indeed the same man, but it seemed to him that it was no longer the same girl. The woman whom he now saw was a noble, beautiful creature, with all the most bewitching outlines of woman, at the precise moment at which they are yet combined with all the most charming graces of childhood,—that pure and fleeting moment which can only be translated by these two words: sweet fifteen. Beautiful chestnut hair, shaded with veins of gold, a brow which seemed chiselled marble, cheeks which seemed made of roses, a pale incarnadine, a flushed whiteness, an exquisite mouth, whence came a smile like a gleam of sunshine, and a voice like music, a head which Raphael would have given to Mary, on a neck which Jean Goujon would have given to Venus. And that nothing might be wanting to this ravishing form, the nose was not beautiful, it was pretty; neither straight nor curved, neither Italian nor Greek; it was the Parisian nose; that is, something sprightly, fine, irregular, and pure, the despair of painters and the charm of poets.

When Marius passed near her, he could not see her eyes, which were always cast down. He saw only her long chestnut lashes, eloquent of mystery and modesty.

But that did not prevent the beautiful girl from smiling as she listened to the white-haired man who was speaking to her, and nothing was so transporting as this maidenly smile with these downcast eyes.

At the first instant Marius thought it was another daughter of the same man, a sister doubtless of her whom he had seen before. But when the invariable habit of his promenade led him for the second time near the seat, and he had looked at her attentively, he recognised that she was the same. In six months the little girl had become a young woman; that was all. Nothing is more frequent than this phenomenon. There is a moment when girls bloom out in a twinkling and become roses all at once. Yesterday we left them children, to-day we find them dangerous.

She had not only grown; she had become idealised. As three April days are enough for certain trees to put on a covering of flowers, so six months had been enough for her to put on a mantle of beauty.

We sometimes see people, poor and mean, who seem to awaken, pass suddenly from indigence to luxury, incur expenses of all sorts, and become all at once splendid, prodigal, and magnificent. That comes from interest received; yesterday was payday. The young girl had received her dividend.

And then she was no longer the school-girl with her plush hat, her merino dress, her shapeless shoes, and her red hands; taste had come to her with beauty. She was a woman well dressed, with a sort of simple and rich elegance without any particular style. She wore a dress of black damask, a mantle of the same, and a white crape hat. Her white gloves showed the delicacy of her hand which played with the Chinese ivory handle of her parasol, and her silk boot betrayed the smallness of her foot. When you passed near her, her whole toilet exhaled the penetrating fragrance of youth.

As to the man, he was still the same.

The second time that Marius came near her, the young girl raised her eyes; they were of a deep celestial blue, but in this veiled azure was nothing yet beyond the look of a child. She looked at Marius with indifference, as she would have looked at any little monkey playing under the sycamores, or the marble vase which cast its shadow over the bench; and Marius also continued his promenade thinking of something else.

He passed four or five times more by the seat where the young girl was, without even turning his eyes towards her.

On the following days he came as usual to the Luxembourg, as usual he found "the father and daughter" there, but he paid no attention to them. He thought no more of this girl now that she was handsome than he had thought of her when she was homely. He passed very near the bench on which she sat, because that was his habit.

III
EFFECT OF SPRING

ONE day the air was mild, the Luxembourg was flooded with sunshine and shadow, the sky was as clear as if the angels had washed it in the morning, the sparrows were twittering in the depths of the chestnut trees, Marius had opened his whole soul to nature, he was thinking of nothing, he was living and breathing, he passed near this seat, the young girl raised her eyes, their glances met.

But what was there now in the glance of the young girl? Marius could not have told. There was nothing, and there was everything. It was a strange flash.

She cast down her eyes and he continued on his way.

What he had seen was not the simple, artless eye of a child; it was a mysterious abyss, half opened, then suddenly closed.

There is a time when every young girl looks thus. Woe to him upon whom she looks!

This first glance of a soul which does not yet know itself is like the dawn in the sky. It is the awakening of something radiant and unknown. Nothing can express the dangerous chasm of this unlooked-for gleam which suddenly suffuses adorable mysteries, and which is made up of all the innocence of the present and of all the passion of the future. It is a kind of irresolute lovingness which is revealed by chance, and which is waiting. It is a snare which Innocence unconsciously spreads, and in which she catches hearts without intending to, and without knowing it. It is a maiden glancing like a woman.

It is rare that deep reverie is not born of this glance wherever it may fall. All that is pure, and all that is vestal, is concentrated in this celestial and mortal glance, which more than the most studied ogling of the coquette, has the magic power of suddenly forcing into bloom in the depths of a heart this flower of the shade full of perfumes and poisons, which is called love.

At night, on returning to his garret, Marius cast a look upon his dress, and for the first time perceived that he had the slovenliness, the indecency, and the unheard-of stupidity, to promenade in the Luxembourg with his "every-day" suit, a hat broken

near the band, coarse teamsters' boots, black pantaloons shiny
at the knees, and a black coat threadbare at the elbows.

IV
COMMENCEMENT OF A GREAT DISTEMPER

THE next day, at the usual hour, Marius took from his closet his
new coat, his new pantaloons, his new hat, and his new boots;
he dressed himself in this panoply complete, put on his gloves,
prodigious prodigality, and went to the Luxembourg.

On the way, he met Courfeyrac, and pretended not to see
him. Courfeyrac, on his return home, said to his friends:

"I have just met Marius' new hat and coat, with Marius
inside. Probably he was going to an examination. He looked
stupid enough."

On reaching the Luxembourg, Marius took a turn round the
fountain and looked at the swans; then he remained for a long
time in contemplation before a statue, the head of which was
black with moss, and which was minus a hip. Near the fountain
was a big-bellied bourgeois of forty, holding a little boy of five
by the hand, to whom he was saying: "Beware of extremes,
my son. Keep thyself equally distant from despotism and from
anarchy." Marius listened to this good bourgeois. Then he took
another turn around the fountain. Finally, he went towards "his
walk;" slowly, and as if with regret. One would have said that
he was at once compelled to go and prevented from going. He
was unconscious of all this, and thought he was doing as he did
every day.

When he entered the walk he saw M. Leblanc and the young
girl at the other end "on their seat." He buttoned his coat,
stretched it down that there might be no wrinkles, noticed with
some complaisance the lustre of his pantaloons, and marched
upon the seat. There was something of attack in this march, and
certainly a desire of conquest. I say, then, he marched upon the
seat, as I would say: Hannibal marched upon Rome.

Beyond this there was nothing which was not mechanical in
all his movements, and he had in no wise interrupted the customary preoccupations of his mind and his labour. He was
thinking at that moment that the *Manual du Baccalauréat* was a
stupid book, and that it must have been compiled by rare old
fools, to give an analysis, as of masterpieces of the human mind,

of three tragedies of Racine and only one of Molière's comed-ies. He had a sharp singing sound in his ear. While approaching the seat, he was smoothing the wrinkles out of his coat, and his eyes were fixed on the young girl. It seemed to him as though she filled the whole extremity of the walk with a pale, bluish light.

As he drew nearer, his step became slower and slower. At some distance from the seat, long before he had reached the end of the walk, he stopped, and he did not know himself how it happened, but he turned back. He did not even say to himself that he would not go to the end. It was doubtful if the young girl could see him so far off, and notice his fine appearance in his new suit. However, he held himself very straight, so that he might look well, in case anybody who was behind should hap-pen to notice him.

He reached the opposite end and then returned, and this time he approached a little nearer to the seat. He even came to within about three trees of it, but there he felt an indescribable lack of power to go further, and he hesitated. He thought he had seen the young girl's face bent towards him. Still he made a great and manly effort, conquered his hesitation, and continued his advance. In a few seconds, he was passing before the seat, erect and firm, blushing to his ears, without daring to cast a look to the right or the left, and with his hand in his coat like a statesman. At the moment he passed under the guns of the fort-ress, he felt a frightful palpitation of the heart. She wore, as on the previous day, her damask dress and her crape hat. He heard the sound of an ineffable voice, which might be "her voice." She was talking quietly. She was very pretty. He felt it, though he made no effort to see her. "She could not, however," thought he, "but have some esteem and consideration for me, if she knew that I was the real author of the dissertation on Marcos Obregon de la Ronda, which Monsieur François de Neuf-château has put, as his own, at the beginning of his edition of *Gil Blas*!"

He passed the seat, went to the end of the walk, which was quite near, then turned and passed again before the beautiful girl. This time he was very pale. Indeed, he was experiencing nothing that was not very disagreeable. He walked away from the seat and from the young girl, and although his back was turned, he imagined that she was looking at him, and that made him stumble.

He made no effort to approach the seat again, he stopped midway of the walk, and sat down there—a thing which he never did—casting many side glances, and thinking, in the most indistinct depths of his mind, that after all it must be difficult for persons whose white hat and black dress he admired, to be absolutely insensible to his glossy pantaloons and his new coat.

At the end of a quarter of an hour, he rose, as if to recommence his walk towards this seat, which was encircled by a halo. He, however, stood silent and motionless. For the first time in fifteen months, he said to himself, that this gentleman, who sat there every day with his daughter, had undoubtedly noticed him, and probably thought his assiduity very strange.

For the first time, also, he felt a certain irreverence in designating this unknown man, even in the silence of his thought, by the nickname of M. Leblanc.

He remained thus for some minutes with his head down tracing designs on the ground with a little stick which he had in his hand.

Then he turned abruptly away from the seat, away from Monsieur Leblanc and his daughter, and went home.

That day he forgot to go to dinner. At eight o'clock in the evening he discovered it, and as it was too late to go down to the Rue Saint Jacques, "No matter," said he, and he ate a piece of bread.

He did not retire until he had carefully brushed and folded his coat.

V

SUNDRY THUNDERBOLTS FALL UPON MA'AM BOUGON

NEXT day, Ma'am Bougon (Ma'am "Grumpy"),—thus Courfeyrac designated the old portress-landlady of the Gorbeau tenement;—her name was in reality Madame Burgon, but as we have stated, this terrible fellow Courfeyrac respected nothing,— Ma'am Bougon was stupefied with astonishment to see Monsieur Marius go out again with his new coat.

He went again to the Luxembourg, but did not get beyond his seat midway of the walk. He sat down there as on the day previous, gazing from a distance and seeing distinctly the white hat, the black dress, and especially the bluish light. He did not stir from the seat, and did not go home until the gates of the

Luxembourg were shut. He did not see Monsieur Leblanc and his daughter retire. He concluded from that that they left the garden by the gate on the Rue de l'Ouest. Later, some weeks afterwards, when he thought of it, he could not remember where he had dined that night.

The next day, for the third time, Ma'am Bougon was thunderstruck. Marius went out with his new suit. "Three days running!" she exclaimed.

She made an attempt to follow him, but Marius walked briskly and with immense strides; it was a hippopotamus undertaking to catch a chamois. In two minutes she lost sight of him, and came back out of breath three quarters choked by her asthma, and furious. "The silly fellow," she muttered, "to put on his handsome clothes every day and make people run like that!"

Marius had gone to the Luxembourg.

The young girl was there with Monsieur Leblanc. Marius approached as near as he could, seeming to be reading a book, but he was still very far off, then he returned and sat down on his seat, where he spent four hours watching the artless little sparrows as they hopped along the walk; they seemed to him to be mocking him.

Thus a fortnight rolled away. Marius went to the Luxembourg, no longer to promenade, but to sit down, always in the same place, and without knowing why. Once there he did not stir. Every morning he put on his new suit, not to be conspicuous, and he began again the next morning.

She was indeed of a marvellous beauty. The only remark which could be made, that would resemble a criticism, is that the contradiction between her look, which was sad, and her smile, which was joyous, gave to her countenance something a little wild, which produced this effect, that at certain moments this sweet face became strange without ceasing to be charming.

VI
TAKEN PRISONER

On one of the last days of the second week, Marius was as usual sitting on his seat, holding in his hand an open book of which he had not turned a leaf for two hours. Suddenly he trembled. A great event was commencing at the end of the walk. Monsieur

Leblanc and his daughter had left their seat, the daughter had taken the arm of the father, and they were coming slowly towards the middle of the walk where Marius was. Marius closed his book, then he opened it, then he made an attempt to read. He trembled. The halo was coming straight towards him. "O dear!" thought he, "I shall not have time to take an attitude." However, the man with the white hair and the young girl were advancing. It seemed to him that it would last a century, and that it was only a second. "What are they coming by here for?" he asked himself. "What! is she going to pass this place! Are her feet to press this ground in this walk, but a step from me?" He was overwhelmed, he would gladly have been very handsome, he would gladly have worn the cross of the Legion of Honour. He heard the gentle and measured sound of their steps approaching. He imagined that Monsieur Leblanc was hurling angry looks upon him. "Is he going to speak to me?" thought he. He bowed his head; when he raised it they were quite near him. The young girl passed, and in passing she looked at him. She looked at him steadily, with a sweet and thoughtful look which made Marius tremble from head to foot. It seemed to him that she reproached him for having been so long without coming to her, and that she said: "It is I who come." Marius was bewildered by these eyes full of flashing light and fathomless abysses.

He felt as though his brain were on fire. She had come to him, what happiness! And then, how she had looked at him! She seemed more beautiful than she had ever seemed before. Beautiful with a beauty which combined all of the woman with all of the angel, a beauty which would have made Petrarch sing and Dante kneel. He felt as though he was swimming in the deep blue sky. At the same time he was horribly disconcerted, because he had a little dust on his boots.

He felt sure that she had seen his boots in this condition.

He followed her with his eyes till she disappeared, then he began to walk in the Luxembourg like a madman. It is probable that at times he laughed, alone as he was, and spoke aloud. He was so strange and dreamy when near the child's nurses that every one thought he was in love with her.

He went out of the Luxembourg to find her again in some street.

He met Courfeyrac under the arches of the Odeon, and said:

"Come and dine with me." They went to Rousseau's and spent six francs. Marius ate like an ogre. He gave six sous to the waiter. At dessert he said to Courfeyrac: "Have you read the paper? What a fine speech Audry de Puyraveau has made!"

He was desperately in love.

After dinner he said to Courfeyrac, "Come to the theatre with me." They went to the Porte Saint Martin to see Frederick in *L'Auberge des Adrets*. Marius was hugely amused.

At the same time he became still more strange and incomprehensible. On leaving the theatre, he refused to look at the garter of a little milliner who was crossing a gutter, and when Courfeyrac said: "*I would not object to putting that woman in my collection*," it almost horrified him.

Courfeyrac invited him to breakfast next morning at the Café Voltaire. Marius went and ate still more than the day before. He was very thoughtful, and yet very gay. One would have said that he seized upon all possible occasions to burst out laughing. To every country-fellow who was introduced to him he gave a tender embrace. A circle of students gathered round the table, and there was talk of the flummery paid for by the government which was retailed at the Sorbonne; then the conversation fell upon the faults and gaps in the dictionaries and prosodies of Quicherat. Marius interrupted the discussion by exclaiming: "However, it is a very pleasant thing to have the Cross."

"He is a comical fellow!" said Courfeyrac, aside to Jean Prouvaire.

"No," replied Jean Prouvaire, "he is serious."

He was serious, indeed. Marius was in this first vehement and fascinating period which the grand passion commences.

One glance had done all that.

When the mine is loaded, and the match is ready, nothing is simpler. A glance is a spark.

It was all over with him. Marius loved a woman. His destiny was entering upon the unknown.

The glances of women are like certain apparently peaceful but really formidable machines. You pass them every day quietly, with impunity, and without suspicion of danger. There comes a moment when you forget even that they are there. You come and go, you muse, and talk, and laugh. Suddenly you feel that you are seized! it is done. The wheels have caught you, the glance has captured you. It has taken you, no matter how or where, by any portion whatever of your thought which was trailing, through any absence of mind. You are lost. You will be drawn in entirely. A train of mysterious forces has gained possession of you. You struggle in vain. No human succour is possible. You will be drawn down from wheel to wheel, from anguish to anguish, from torture to torture. You, your mind, your fortune, your future, your soul; and you will not escape from the terrible machine, until, according as you are in the power of a malevolent nature, or a noble heart, you shall be disfigured by shame or transfigured by love.

VII

ADVENTURES OF THE LETTER *U* ABANDONED TO CONJECTURE

ISOLATION, separation from all things, pride, independence, a taste for nature, lack of everyday material activity, life in one's self, the secret struggles of chastity, and an ecstasy of goodwill towards the whole creation, had prepared Marius for this possession which is called love. His worship for his father had become almost a religion, and, like all religion, had retired into the depths of his heart. He needed something above that. Love came.

A whole month passed during which Marius went every day to the Luxembourg. When the hour came, nothing could keep him away. "He is out at service," said Courfeyrac. Marius lived in transports. It is certain that the young girl looked at him.

He finally grew bolder, and approached nearer to the seat. However he passed before it no more, obeying at once the instinct of timidity and the instinct of prudence, peculiar to lovers. He thought it better not to attract the "attention of the father." He formed his combinations of stations behind trees and the pedestals of statues, with consummate art, so as to be seen as much as possible by the young girl and as little as possible by the old gentleman. Sometimes he would stand for half an hour motionless behind some Leonidas or Spartacus with a book in his hand, over which his eyes, timidly raised, were looking for the young girl, while she, for her part, was turning her charming profile towards him, suffused with a smile. While yet talking in the most natural and quiet way in the world with the white-haired man, she rested upon Marius all the dreams of a maidenly and passionate eye. Ancient and immemorial art which Eve knew from the first day of the world, and which every woman knows from the first day of her life! Her tongue replied to one and her eyes to the other.

We must, however, suppose that M. Leblanc perceived something of this at last, for often when Marius came, he would rise and begin to promenade. He had left their accustomed place, and had taken the seat at the other end of the walk, near the Gladiator, as if to see whether Marius would follow them. Marius did not understand it, and committed that blunder. "The father" began to be less punctual and did not bring "his daughter" every day. Sometimes he came alone. Then Marius did not stay. Another blunder.

Marius took no note of these symptoms. From the phase of timidity he had passed, a natural and inevitable progress, to the phase of blindness. His love grew. He dreamed of her every night. And then there came to him a good fortune for which he had not even hoped, oil upon the fire, double darkness upon his eyes. One night, at dusk, he found on the seat, which "M. Leblanc and his daughter" had just left, a handkerchief, a plain handkerchief without embroidery, but white, fine, and which appeared to him to exhale ineffable odours. He seized it in transport. This handkerchief was marked with the letters U. F.: Marius knew nothing of this beautiful girl, neither her family, nor her name, nor her dwelling; these two letters were the first thing he had caught of her, adorable initials upon which he began straightway to build his castle. It was evidently her first name. Ursula, thought he, what a sweet name! He kissed the handkerchief, inhaled its perfume, put it over his heart, on his flesh in the day-time, and at night went to sleep with it on his lips.

"I feel her whole soul in it!" he exclaimed.

This handkerchief belonged to the old gentleman, who had simply let it fall from his pocket.

For days and days after this piece of good fortune, he always appeared at the Luxembourg kissing this handkerchief and placing it on his heart. The beautiful child did not understand this at all, and indicated it to him by signs, which he did not perceive.

"Oh, modesty!" said Marius.

VIII
EVEN THE INVALIDES MAY BE LUCKY

SINCE we have pronounced the word *modesty*, and since we conceal nothing, we must say that once, however, through all his ecstasy "his Ursula" gave him a very serious pang. It was upon one of the days when she prevailed upon M. Leblanc to leave the seat and to promenade on the walk. A brisk north wind was blowing, which swayed the tops of the plane trees. Father and daughter, arm in arm, had just passed before Marius' seat. Marius had risen behind them and was following them with his eyes, as it was natural that he should in this desperate situation of his heart.

Suddenly a gust of wind, rather more lively than the rest, and probably intrusted with the little affairs of Spring, flew down from La Pépinière, rushed upon the walk, enveloped the young girl in a transporting tremor worthy of the nymphs of Virgil and the fauns of Theocritus, and raised her skirt, this skirt more sacred than that of Isis, almost to the height of the garter. A limb of exquisite mould was seen. Marius saw it. He was exasperated and furious.

The young girl had put down her dress with a divinely startled movement, but he was outraged none the less. True, he was alone in the walk. But there might have been somebody there. And if anybody had been there! could one conceive of such a thing? what she had done was horrible! Alas, the poor child had done nothing; there was but one culprit, the wind; and yet Marius in whom all the Bartholo which there is in Cherubin was confusedly trembling, was determined to be dissatisfied, and was jealous of his shadow. For it is thus that is awakened in the human heart, and imposed upon man, even unjustly, the bitter and strange jealousy of the flesh. Besides, and throwing this jealousy out of consideration, there was nothing that was agreeable to him in the sight of that beautiful limb; the white stocking of the first woman that came along would have given him more pleasure.

When "his Ursula," reaching the end of the walk, returned with M. Leblanc, and passed before the seat on which Marius had again sat down, Marius threw at her a cross and cruel look. The young girl slightly straightened back, with that elevation of the eyelids, which says: "Well, what is the matter with him?"

That was "their first quarrel."

Marius had hardly finished this scene with her when somebody came down the walk. It was an Invalide, very much bent, wrinkled and pale with age, in the uniform of Louis XV., with the little oval patch of red cloth with crossed swords on his back, the soldier's Cross of Saint Louis, and decorated also by a coat sleeve in which there was no arm, a silver chin, and a wooden leg. Marius thought he could discern that this man appeared to be very much pleased. It seemed to him even that the old cynic, as he hobbled along by him, had addressed to him a very fraternal and very merry wink, as if by some chance they had been put into communication and had enjoyed some dainty bit of good fortune together. What had he seen to be so pleased, this relic of Mars? What had happened between this leg of wood and the other? Marius had a paroxysm of jealousy. "Perhaps he was by!" said he; "perhaps he saw!" And he would have been glad to exterminate the Invalide.

Time lending his aid, every point is blunted. This anger of Marius against "Ursula," however just and proper it might be, passed away. He forgave her at last; but it was a great effort; he pouted at her three days.

Meanwhile, in spite of all that, and because of all that, his passion was growing, and was growing mad.

IX
AN ECLIPSE

WE have seen how Marius discovered, or thought he discovered, that her name was Ursula.

Hunger comes with love. To know that her name was Ursula had been much; it was little. In three or four weeks Marius had devoured this piece of good fortune. He desired another. He wished to know where she lived.

He had committed one blunder in falling into the snare of the seat by the Gladiator. He had committed a second by not remaining at the Luxembourg when Monsieur Leblanc came there alone. He committed a third, a monstrous one. He followed "Ursula."

She lived in the Rue de l'Ouest, in the least frequented part of it, in a new three-story house, of modest appearance.

From that moment Marius added to his happiness in seeing

her at the Luxembourg, the happiness of following her home.

His hunger increased. He knew her name, her first name, at least, the charming name, the real name of a woman; he knew where she lived; he desired to know who she was.

One night after he had followed them home, and seen them disappear at the porte-cochère, he entered after them, and said boldly to the porter:——

"Is it the gentleman on the first floor who has just come in?"

"No," answered the porter. "It is the gentleman on the third."

Another fact. This success made Marius still bolder.

"In front?" he asked.

"Faith!" said the porter, "the house is only built on the street."

"And what is this gentleman?"

"He lives on his income, monsieur. A very kind man, who does a great deal of good among the poor, though not rich."

"What is his name?" continued Marius.

The porter raised his head, and said:——

"Is monsieur a detective?"

Marius retired, much abashed, but still in great transports. He was getting on.

"Good," thought he. "I know that her name is Ursula, that she is the daughter of a retired gentleman, and that she lives there, in the third story, in the Rue de l'Ouest."

Next day Monsieur Leblanc and his daughter made but a short visit to the Luxembourg; they went away while it was yet broad daylight. Marius followed them into the Rue de l'Ouest, as was his custom. On reaching the porte-cochère, Monsieur Leblanc passed his daughter in, and then stopped, and before entering himself, turned and looked steadily at Marius. The day after that they did not come to the Luxembourg. Marius waited in vain all day.

At nightfall he went to the Rue de l'Ouest, and saw a light in the windows of the third story. He walked beneath these windows until the light was put out.

The next day nobody at the Luxembourg. Marius waited all day, and then went to perform his night duty under the windows. That took him till ten o'clock in the evening. His dinner took care of itself. Fever supports the sick man, and love the lover.

He passed a week in this way. Monsieur Leblanc and his

daughter appeared at the Luxembourg no more. Marius made melancholy conjectures; he dared not watch the porte-cochère during the day. He limited himself to going at night to gaze upon the reddish light of the windows. At times he saw shadows moving, and his heart beat high.

On the eighth day when he reached the house, there was no light in the windows. "What!" said he, "the lamp is not yet lighted. But yet it is dark. Or they have gone out?" He waited till ten o'clock. Till midnight. Till one o'clock in the morning. No light appeared in the third story windows, and nobody entered the house. He went away very gloomy.

On the morrow—for he lived only from morrow to morrow; there was no longer any to-day, so to speak, to him—on the morrow he found nobody at the Luxembourg, he waited; at dusk he went to the house. No light in the windows; the blinds were closed; the third story was entirely dark.

Marius knocked at the porte-cochère; went in and said to the porter:——

"The gentleman of the third floor?"

"Moved," answered the porter.

Marius tottered, and said feebly:

"Since when?"

"Yesterday."

"Where does he live now?"

"I don't know anything about it."

"He has not left his new address, then?"

"No."

And the porter, looking up, recognised Marius.

"What! it is you!" said he, but decidedly now, "you do keep bright look-out."

BOOK SEVENTH – PATRON-MINETTE

I
THE MINES AND THE MINERS

EVERY human society has what is called in the theatres a *third substage*. The social soil is mined everywhere, sometimes for good, sometimes for evil. These works are in strata; there are upper mines and lower mines. There is a top and a bottom in this dark sub-soil which sometimes sinks beneath civilisation, and which our indifference and our carelessness trample underfoot. The Encyclopædia, in the last century, was a mine almost on the surface. The dark caverns, these gloomy protectors of primitive Christianity, were awaiting only an opportunity to explode beneath the Cæsars, and to flood the human race with light. For in these sacred shades there is latent light. Volcanoes are full of a blackness, capable of flashing flames. All lava begins at midnight. The catacombs, where the first mass was said, were not merely the cave of Rome; they were the cavern of the world.

There is under the social structure, this complex wonder of a mighty burrow,—of excavations of every kind. There is the religious mine, the philosophic mine, the political mine, the economic mine, the revolutionary mine. This pick with an idea, that pick with a figure, the other pick with a vengeance. They call and they answer from one catacomb to another. Utopias travel under ground in the passages. They branch out in every direction. They sometimes meet there and fraternise. Jean Jacques lends his pick to Diogenes, who lends him his lantern. Sometimes they fight. Calvin takes Socinius by the hair. But nothing checks or interrupts the tension of all these energies towards their object. The vast simultaneous activity which goes to and fro, and up and down, and up again, in these dusky regions, and which slowly transforms the upper through the lower, and the outer through the inner; vast unknown swarming of workers. Society has hardly a suspicion of this work of undermining which, without touching its surface, changes its substance. So many subterranean degrees, so many differing labours, so many varying excavations. What comes from all this deep delving? The future.

The deeper we sink, the more mysterious are the workers.

To a degree which social philosophy can recognise, the work is good; beyond this degree it is doubtful and mixed; below, it becomes terrible. At a certain depth, the excavations become impenetrable to the soul of civilisation, the respirable limit of man is passed; the existence of monsters becomes possible.

The descending ladder is a strange one; each of its rounds corresponds to a step whereupon philosophy can set foot, and where we discover some one of her workers, sometimes divine, sometimes monstrous. Below John Huss is Luther; below Luther is Descartes; below Descartes is Voltaire; below Voltaire is Condorcet; below Condorcet is Robespierre; below Robespierre is Marat; below Marat is Babeuf. And that continues. Lower still, in dusky confusion, at the limit which separates the indistinct from the invisible, glimpses are caught of other men in the gloom, who perhaps no longer exist. Those of yesterday are spectres; those of to-morrow are goblins. The embryonary work of the future is one of the visions of the philosopher.

A fœtus world in limbo, what a wonderful profile!

Saint Simon, Owen, Fourier, are there also, in lateral galleries.

Indeed, although an invisible divine chain links together all these subterranean pioneers, who almost always believe they are alone, yet are not, their labours are very diverse, and the glow of some is in contrast with the flame of others. Some are paradisaic, others are tragic. Nevertheless, be the contrast what it may, all these workers, from the highest to the darkest, from the wisest to the silliest, have one thing in common, and that is disinterestedness. Marat, like Jesus, forgets himself. They throw self aside; they omit self, they do not think of self. They see something other than themselves. They have a light in their eyes, and this light is searching for the absolute. The highest has all heaven in his eyes; the lowest, enigmatical as he may be, has yet beneath his brows the pale glow of the infinite. Venerate him, whatever he may do, who has this sign, the star-eye.

The shadow-eye is the other sign.

With it evil commences. Before him whose eye has no light, reflect and tremble. Social order has its black miners.

There is a point where undermining becomes burial, and where light is extinguished.

Below all these mines which we have pointed out, below all these galleries, below all this immense underground venous system of progress and of utopia, far deeper in the earth, lower than Marat, lower than Babeuf, lower, much lower, and without any connection with the upper galleries, is the last sap. A fear-inspiring place. This is what we have called the third substage. It is the grave of the depths. It is the cave of the blind *Inferi*.

This communicates with the gulfs.

II
THE LOWEST DEPTH

THERE disinterestedness vanishes. The demon is dimly rough-hewn; every one for himself. The eyeless I howls, searches, gropes, and gnaws. The social Ugolino is in this gulf.

The savage outlines which prowl over this grave, half brute, half phantom, have no thought for universal progress, they ignore ideas and words, they have no care but for individual glut. They are almost unconscious, and there is in them a horrible defacement. They have two mothers, both stepmothers, ignorance and misery. They have one guide, want; and their only form of satisfaction is appetite. They are voracious as beasts, that is to say ferocious, not like the tyrant but like the tiger. From suffering these goblins pass to crime; fated filiation, giddy procreation, the logic of darkness. What crawls in the third substage is no longer the stifled demand for the absolute, it is the protest of matter. Man there becomes dragon. Hunger and thirst are the point of departure: Satan is the point of arrival. From this cave comes Lacenaire.

We have just seen, in the fourth book, one of the compartments of the upper mine, the great political, revolutionary, and philosophic sap. There, as we have said, all is noble, pure, worthy, and honourable. There, it is true, men may be deceived and are deceived, but there error is venerable, so much heroism does it imply. For the sum of all work which is done there, there is one name: Progress.

The time has come to open other depths, the depths of horror.

There is beneath society, we must insist upon it, and until the day when ignorance shall be no more, there will be, the great cavern of evil.

This cave is beneath all, and is the enemy of all. It is hate universal. This cave knows no philosophers; its poniard has never made a pen. Its blackness has no relation to the sublime blackness of script. Never have the fingers of night, which are clutching beneath this asphyxiating vault, turned the leaves of a book, or unfolded a journal. Babeuf is a speculator to Cartouche; Marat is an aristocrat to Schinderhannes. The object of this cave is the ruin of all things.

Of all things. Including therein the upper saps, which it execrates. It does not undermine, in its hideous crawl, merely the social order of the time; it undermines philosophy, it undermines science, it undermines law, it undermines human thought, it undermines civilisation, it undermines revolution, it undermines progress. It goes by the naked names of theft, prostitution, murder, and assassination. It is darkness, and it desires chaos. It is vaulted in with ignorance.

All the others, those above it, have but one object—to suppress it. To that end philosophy and progress work through all their organs at the same time, through amelioration of the real as well as through contemplation of the absolute. Destroy the cave Ignorance, and you destroy the mole Crime.

We will condense in a few words a portion of what we have just said. The only social peril is darkness.

Humanity is identity. All men are the same clay. No difference, here below at least, in predestination. The same darkness before, the same flesh during, the same ashes after life. But ignorance, mixed with the human composition, blackens it. This incurable ignorance possesses the heart of man, and there becomes Evil.

III
BABET, GUEULEMER, CLAQUESOUS,
AND MONTPARNASSE

A QUARTETTE of bandits, Claquesous, Gueulemer, Babet, and Montparnasse, ruled from 1830 to 1835 over the third substage of Paris.

Gueulemer was a Hercules without a pedestal. His cave was the Arche-Marion sewer. He was six feet high, and had a marble chest, brazen biceps, cavernous lungs, a colossus' body, and a bird's skull. You would think you saw the Farnese Hercules dressed in duck pantaloons and a cotton-velvet waistcoat. Gueulemer, built in this sculptural fashion, could have subdued monsters; he found it easier to become one. Low forehead, large temples, less than forty, the foot of a goose, coarse short hair, a bushy cheek, a wild boar's beard; from this you see the man. His muscles asked for work, his stupidity would have none. This was a huge lazy force. He was an assassin through nonchalance. He was thought to be a creole. Probably there was a little of Marshal Brown in him, he having been a porter at Avignon in 1815. After this he had become a bandit.

The diaphaneity of Babet contrasted with the meatiness of Gueulemer. Babet was thin and shrewd. He was transparent, but impenetrable. You could see the light through his bones, but nothing through his eye. He professed to be a chemist. He had been bar-keeper for Bobèche, and clown for Bobino. He had played vaudeville at Saint Mihiel. He was an affected man, a great talker, who italicised his smiles and quoted his gestures. His business was to sell plaster busts and portraits of the "head of the Government" in the street. Moreover, he pulled teeth. He had exhibited monstrosities at fairs, and had a booth with a trumpet and this placard: "Babet, dental artist, member of the Academies, physical experimenter on metals and metal-loids, extirpates teeth, removes stumps left by other dentists. Price: one tooth, one franc fifty centimes; two teeth, two francs; three teeth, two francs fifty centimes. Improve your opportunity." (This "improve your opportunity," meant: "get as many pulled as possible.") He had been married, and had had children. What had become of his wife and children, he did not know. He had lost them as one loses his pocket handkerchief. A remarkable exception in the obscure world to which he belonged, Babet read the papers. One day during the time he had his family with him in his travelling booth he had read in the *Messenger* that a woman had been delivered of a child, likely to live, which had the face of a calf, and he had exclaimed: "*There is a piece of good luck! My wife hasn't the sense to bring me a child like that.*" Since then, he had left everything, "to take Paris in hand." His own expression.

What was Claquesous? He was night. Before showing himself he waited till the sky was daubed with black. At night he came out of a hole, which he went into again before day. Where was this hole? Nobody knew. In the most perfect obscurity, and to his accomplices he always turned his back when he spoke. Was his name Claquesous? No. He said: "My name is Nothing-at-all." If a candle was brought he put on a mask. He was a ventriloquist. Babet said: "*Claquesous is a night-bird with two voices.*" Claquesous was restless, roving, terrible. It was not certain that he had a name, Claquesous being a nickname; it was not certain that he had a voice, his chest speaking oftener than his mouth; it was not certain that he had a face, nobody having ever seen anything but this mask. He disappeared as if he sank into the ground; he came like an apparition.

A mournful sight was Montparnasse. Montparnasse was a child; less than twenty, with a pretty face, lips like cherries, charming black locks, the glow of spring in his eyes; he had all the vices and aspired to all the crimes. The digestion of what was bad gave him an appetite for what was worse. He was the *gamin* turned vagabond and the vagabond become an assassin. He was genteel, effeminate, graceful, robust, weak, and ferocious. He wore his hat turned up on the left side, to make room for the tuft of hair, according to the fashion of 1829. He lived by robbery. His coat was the most fashionable cut, but threadbare. Montparnasse was a fashion plate living in distress and committing murders. The cause of all the crimes of this young man was his desire to be well dressed. The first grisette who had said to him: "You are handsome," had thrown the stain of darkness into his heart, and had made a Cain of this Abel. Thinking that he was handsome, he had desired to be elegant; now the first of elegances is idleness: idleness for a poor man is crime. Few prowlers were so much feared as Montparnasse. At eighteen, he had already left several corpses on his track. More than one traveller lay in the shadow of this wretch, with extended arms and with his face in a pool of blood. Frizzled, pomaded, with slender waist, hips like a woman, the bust of a Prussian officer, a buzz of admiration about him from the girls of the boulevard, an elaborately-tied cravat, a sling-shot in his pocket, a flower in his button-hole; such was this charmer of the sepulchre.

IV
COMPOSITION OF THE BAND

THESE four bandits formed a sort of Proteus, winding through the police and endeavouring to escape from the indiscreet glances of Vidocq "under various form, tree, flame, and fountain," lending each other their names and their tricks, concealing themselves in their own shadow, each a refuge and a hiding-place for the others, throwing off their personalities, as one takes off a false nose at a masked ball, sometimes simplifying themselves till they are but one, sometimes multiplying themselves till Coco Lacour himself took them for a multitude.

These four men were not four men; it was a sort of mysterious robber with four heads preying upon Paris by wholesale; it was the monstrous polyp of evil which inhabits the crypt of society.

By means of their ramifications and the underlying network of their relations, Babet, Gueulemer, Claquesous, and Montparnasse, controlled the general lying-in-wait business of the Department of the Seine. Originators of ideas in this line, men of midnight imagination came to them for the execution. The four villains being furnished with the single draft, they took charge of putting it on the stage. They worked upon scenario. They were always in condition to furnish a company proportioned and suitable to any enterprise which stood in need of aid, and was sufficiently lucrative. A crime being in search of arms, they sublet accomplices to it. They had a company of actors of darkness at the disposition of every cavernous tragedy.

They usually met at nightfall, their waking hour, in the waste grounds near La Salpêtrière. There they conferred. They had the twelve dark hours before them; they allotted their employ.

Patron-Minette, such was the name which was given in subterranean society to the association of these four men. In the old, popular, fantastic language, which now is dying out every day, *Patron-Minette* means morning, just as *entre chien et loup* [between dog and wolf], means night. This appellation, Patron-Minette, probably came from the hour at which their work ended, the dawn being the moment for the disappearance of phantoms and the separation of bandits. These four were known by this title. When the Chief Judge of the Assizes visited Lacenaire in prison, he questioned him in relation to some crime which Lacenaire denied. "Who did do it?" asked the judge. Lacenaire made this reply, enigmatical to the magistrate, but clear to the police: "Patron-Minette, perhaps."

Sometimes a play may be imagined from the announcement of the characters: so, too, we may almost understand what a band is from the list of the bandits. We give, for these names are preserved in the documents, the appellations to which the principal subordinates of Patron-Minette responded:

Panchaud, alias Printanier, alias Bigrenaille.

Brujon. (There was a dynasty of Brujons; we shall say something about it hereafter.)

Boulatruelle, the road-mender, already introduced.

Laveuve.

Finistère.

Homer Hogu, negro.

Mardisoir.

Dépêche.

Fauntleroy, alias Bouquetière.

Glorieux, a liberated convict.

Barrecarrosse, alias Monsieur Dupont.

L'esplanade-du-Sud.

Poussagrive.

Carmagnolet.

Kruideniers, alias Bizarro.

Mangedentelle.

Les-pieds-en-l'air.

Demi-liard, alias Deux-milliards.

Etc., etc.

We pass over some of them, and not the worst. These names have faces. They express not only beings, but species. Each of these names answers to a variety of these shapeless toadstools of the cellars of civilisation.

These beings, by no means free with their faces, were not of those whom we see passing in the streets. During the day, wearied out by their savage nights, they went away to sleep, sometimes in the parget-kilns, sometimes in the abandoned quarries of Montmartre or Montrouge, sometimes in the sewers. They burrowed.

What has become of these men? They still exist. They have always existed. Horace speaks of them: *Ambubaiarum collegia, pharmacopolæ, mendici, mimæ*; and so long as society shall be what it is, they will be what they are. Under the dark vault of their cave, they are for ever reproduced from the ooze of society. They return, spectres, always the same; but they bear the same name no longer, and they are no longer in the same skins.

The individuals extirpated, the tribe still exists.

They have always the same faculties. From beggar to the prowler the race preserves its purity. They divine purses in pockets, they scent watches in fobs. Gold and silver to them are odorous. There are simple bourgeois of whom you might say that they have a robbable appearance. These men follow these bourgeois patiently. When a foreigner or a countryman passes by they have spider thrills.

Such men, when, towards midnight, on a lone boulevard, you meet them or catch a glimpse of them, are terrifying. They seem not men, but forms fashioned of the living dark; you would say that they are generally an integral portion of the darkness, that they are not distinct from it, that they have no other soul than the gloom, and that it is only temporarily and to live for a few minutes a monstrous life, that they are dis-aggregated from the night.

What is required to exorcise these goblins? Light. Light in floods. No bat resists the dawn. Illuminate the bottom of society.

BOOK EIGHTH – THE NOXIOUS POOR

I
MARIUS, LOOKING FOR A GIRL WITH A HAT, MEETS A MAN WITH A CAP

SUMMER passed, then autumn; winter came. Neither M. Leblanc nor the young girl had set foot in the Luxembourg. Marius had now but one thought, to see that sweet, that adorable face again. He searched continually; he searched everywhere: he found nothing. He was no longer Marius the enthusiastic dreamer, the resolute man, ardent yet firm, the bold challenger of destiny, the brain which projected and built future upon future, the young heart full of plans, projects, prides, ideas, and desires; he was a lost dog. He fell into a melancholy. It was all over with him. Work disgusted him, walking fatigued him, solitude wearied him, vast nature, once so full of forms, of illuminations, of voices, of counsels, of perspectives, of horizons, of teachings, was now a void before him. It seemed to him that everything had disappeared.

He was still full of thought, for he could not be otherwise; but he no longer found pleasure in his thoughts. To all which they were silently but incessantly proposing to him, he answered in the gloom: What is the use?

He reproached himself a hundred times. Why did I follow her? I was so happy in seeing her only! She looked upon me; was not that infinite? She had the appearance of loving me. Was not that everything? I desired to have what? There is nothing more after that. I was a fool. It is my fault, etc., etc. Courfeyrac, to whom he confided nothing; that was his nature; but who found cut a little of everything; that was his nature also; had begun by felicitating him upon being in love, and wondering at it withal; then seeing Marius fallen into this melancholy, he had at last said to him: "I see that you have been nothing but an animal. Here, come to the Cabin."

Once, confiding in a beautiful September sun, Marius allowed himself to be taken to the Bal de Sceaux, by Courfeyrac, Bossuet, and Grantaire, hoping, what a dream! that he might possibly find her there. We need not say that he did not see her whom he sought. "But yet it is here that all the lost women are to be found," muttered Grantaire. Marius left his friends at the ball, and went back on foot, alone, tired, feverish, with sad and troubled eyes, in the night, overcome by the noise and dust of the joyous coaches full of singing parties who passed by him returning from the festival, while he, discouraged, was breathing in the pungent odour of the walnut trees by the wayside, to restore his brain.

He lived more and more alone, bewildered, overwhelmed, given up to his inward anguish, walking to and fro in his grief like a wolf in a cage, seeking everywhere for the absent, stupefied with love.

At another time, an accidental meeting produced a singular effect upon him. In one of the little streets in the neighbourhood of the Boulevard des Invalides, he saw a man dressed like a labourer, wearing a cap with a long visor, from beneath which escaped a few locks of very white hair. Marius was struck by the beauty of this white hair, and noticed the man who was walking with slow steps and seemed absorbed in painful meditation. Strangely enough, it appeared to him that he recognised M. Leblanc. It was the same hair, the same profile, as far as the cap allowed him to see, the same manner, only sadder. But why these working-man's clothes? what did that mean? what did this disguise signify? Marius was astounded. When he came to himself, his first impulse was to follow the man; who knows but he had at last caught the trace which he was seeking? At all events, he must see the man again nearer, and clear up the enigma. But this idea occurred to him too late, the man was now gone. He had taken some little side street, and Marius could not find him again. This adventure occupied his mind for a few days, and then faded away. "After all," said he to himself, "it is probably only a resemblance."

II
A WAIF

MARIUS still lived in the Gorbeau tenement. He paid no attention to anybody there.

At this time, it is true, there were no occupants remaining in the house but himself and those Jondrettes whose rent he had once paid, without having ever spoken, however, either to the father, or to the mother, or to the daughters. The other tenants had moved away or died, or had been turned out for not paying their rent.

One day, in the course of this winter, the sun shone a little in the afternoon, but it was the second of February, that ancient Candlemas-day whose treacherous sun, the precursor of six weeks of cold, inspired Matthew Laensberg with these two lines, which have deservedly become classic:

> Qu'il luise ou qu'il luiserne,
> L'ours rentre en sa caverne.*

Marius had just left his; night was falling. It was his dinner hour; for it was still necessary for him to go to dinner, alas! oh, infirmity of the ideal passions.

He had just crossed his door-sill which Ma'am Bougon was sweeping at that very moment, muttering at the same time this memorable monologue:

"What is there that is cheap now? everything is dear. There is nothing but people's trouble that is cheap; that comes for nothing, people's trouble."

Marius went slowly up the boulevard towards the barrière, on the way to the Rue Saint Jacques. He was walking thoughtfully, with his head down.

Suddenly he felt that he was elbowed in the dusk; he turned, and saw two young girls in rags, one tall and slender, the other a little shorter, passing rapidly by, breathless, frightened, and apparently in flight; they had met him, had not seen him, and had jostled him in passing. Marius could see in the twilight their livid faces, their hair tangled and flying, their frightful bonnets, their tattered skirts, and their naked feet. As they ran they were talking to each other. The taller one said in a very low voice:

"The *cognes* came. They just missed *pincer* me at the *demi-cercle*."

The other answered: "I saw them. I *cavalé, cavalé, cavalé.*"

Marius understood, through this dismal argot, that the gendarmes, or the city police, had not succeeded in seizing these two girls, and that the girls had escaped.

They plunged in under the trees of the boulevard behind

---

* Let it gleam or let it glimmer,
  The bear returns into his cave.

him, and for a few seconds made a kind of dim whiteness in the obscurity which soon faded out.

Marius stopped for a moment.

He was about to resume his course when he perceived a little greyish packet on the ground at his feet. He stooped down and picked it up. It was a sort of envelope which appeared to contain papers.

"Good," said he, "those poor creatures must have dropped this!"

He retraced his steps, he called, he did not find them; he concluded they were already beyond hearing, put the packet in his pocket and went to dinner.

On his way, in an alley on the Rue Mouffetard, he saw a child's coffin covered with a black cloth, placed upon three chairs and lighted by a candle. The two girls of the twilight returned to his mind.

"Poor mothers," thought he. "There is one thing sadder than to see their children die—to see them lead evil lives."

Then these shadows which had varied his sadness went out from his thoughts, and he fell back into his customary train. He began to think of his six months of love and happiness in the open air and the broad daylight under the beautiful trees of the Luxembourg.

"How dark my life has become!" said he to himself. "Young girls still pass before me. Only formerly they were angels; now they are ghouls."

III
QUADRIFRONS

IN the evening, as he was undressing to go to bed, he happened to feel in his coat-pocket the packet which he had picked up on the boulevard. He had forgotten it. He thought it might be well to open it, and that the packet might perhaps contain the address of the young girls, if, in reality, it belonged to them, or at all events the information necessary to restore it to the person who had lost it.

He opened the envelope.

It was unsealed and contained four letters, also unsealed.

The addresses were upon them.

All four exhaled an odour of wretched tobacco.

The first letter was addressed: *To Madame, Madame the Marchioness de Grucheray, Square opposite the Chamber of Deputies, No.——*

Marius said to himself that he should probably find in this letter the information of which he was in search, and that, moreover, as the letter was not sealed, probably it might be read without impropriety.

It was in these words:

"Madame the Marchioness:

"The virtue of kindness and piety is that which binds society most closely. Call up your christian sentiment, and cast a look of compassion upon this unfortunate Spanish victim of loyalty and attachment to the sacred cause of legitimacy, which he has paid for with his blood, consecrated his fortune, wholy, to defend this cause, and to-day finds himself in the greatest missery. He has no doubt that your honourable self will furnish him assistance to preserve an existence extremely painful for a soldier of education and of honour full of wounds, reckons in advance upon the humanity which animmates you and upon the interest which Madame the Marchioness feels in a nation so unfortunate. Their prayer will not be in vain, and their memory will retain herr charming souvenir.

"From my respectful sentiments with which I have the honour to be

"Madame,

   "DON ALVARÈS, Spanish captain of cabalry, royalist refuge in France, who finds himself traveling for his country and ressources fail him to continue his travells."

No address was added to the signature. Marius hoped to find the address in the second letter, the superscription of which ran: *to Madame, Madame the Countess de Montvernet, Rue Cassette, No. 9.* Marius read as follows:

"Madame the Comtess,

"It is an unfortunate mothur of a family of six children the last of whom is only eight months old. Me sick since my last lying-in, abandoned by my husband for five months haveing no ressources in the world the most frightful indigance.

"In the hope of Madame the Comtesse, she has the honour to be, Madame, with a profound respect,

"Mother BALIZARD."

Marius passed to the third letter, which was, like the preceding, a begging one; it read:

"Monsieur Pabourgeot, elector, wholesale merchant-milliner, Rue Saint Denis, corner of the Rue aux Fers.

"I take the liberty to address you this letter to pray you to accord me the pretious favour of your simpathies and to interest you in a man of letters who has just sent a drama to the Théatre Français. Its subject is historical, and the action takes place in Auvergne in the time of the empire: its style, I believe, is natural, laconic and perhaps has some merit. There are verses to be sung in four places. The comic, the serious, the unforeseen, mingle themselves with the variety of the characters and with a tint of romance spread lightly over all the plot which advances misteriously, and by striking terns, to a denouement in the midst of several hits of splendid scenes.

"My principal object is to satisfie the desire which animates progressively the man of our century, that is to say, fashion, that caprisious and grotesque weathercock which changes almost with every new wind.

"In spite of these qualities I have reason to fear that jealousy, the selfishness of the privileged authors, may secure my exclusion from the theatre, for I am not ignorant of the distaste with which new-comers are swollowed.

"Monsieur Pabourgeot, your just reputation as an enlightened protector of literary fokes emboldens me to send my daughter to you, who will expose to you our indignant situation, wanting bread and fire in this wynter season. To tell you that I pray you to accept the homage which I desire to offer you in my drama and in all those which I make, is to prove to you how ambicious I am of the honour of sheltering myself under your aegis, and of adorning my writings with your name. If you deign to honour me with the most modest offering, I shall occupy myself immediately a piese of verse for you to pay my tribut of recognition. This piese, which I shall endeavour to render as perfect as possible, will be sent to you before being inserted in the beginning of the drama and given upon the stage.

"To Monsieur and Madame Pabourgeot,
            My most respectful homage,
                                    "GENFLOT, man of letters.

"P.S. Were it only forty sous.

"Excuse me for sending my daughter and for not presenting myself, but sad motives of dress do not permit me, alas! to go out——"

Marius finally opened the fourth letter. There was on the address: *To the beneficent gentleman of the church of Saint Jaques du Haut Pas.* It contained these few lines:

"Beneficent man.

"If you will deign to accompany my daughter, you will see a misserable calamity, and I will show you my certificates.

"At the sight of these writings your generous soul will be moved with a sentiment of lively benevolence, for true philosophers always experience vivid emotions.

"Agree, compassionate man, that one must experience the most cruel necessity, and that it is very painful, to obtain relief, to have it attested by authority, as if we were not free to suffer and to die of inanition while waiting for some one to relieve our missery. The fates are very cruel to some and too lavish or too careful to others.

"I await your presence or your offering, if you deign to make it, and I pray you to have the kindness to accept the respectful sentiments with which I am proud to be,

"Truly magnanimous man,
        "Your very humble
            And very obedient servant,
                    "P. FABANTOU, dramatic artist."

After reading these four letters, Marius did not find himself much wiser than before.

In the first place none of the signers gave his address.

Then they seemed to come from four different individuals, Don Alvarès, Mother Balizard, the poet Genflot, and the dramatic artist Fabantou; but, strangely enough, these letters were all four written in the same hand.

What was the conclusion from that, unless that they came from the same person?

Moreover, and this rendered the conjecture still more probable, the paper, coarse and yellow, was the same in all four, the odour of tobacco was the same, and although there was an evident endeavour to vary the style, the same faults of orthography were reproduced with a very quiet certainty, and Genflot, the man of letters, was no more free from them than the Spanish captain.

To endeavour to unriddle this little mystery was a useless labour. If it had not been a waif, it would have had the appearance of a mystification. Marius was too sad to take a joke kindly even from chance, or to lend himself to the game which the street pavement seemed to wish to play with him. It appeared to him that he was like Colin Maillard among the four letters, which were mocking him.

Nothing, however, indicated that these letters belonged to the girls whom Marius had met on the boulevard. After all, they were but waste paper evidently without value.

Marius put them back into the envelope, threw it into a corner, and went to bed.

About seven o'clock in the morning, he had got up and breakfasted, and was trying to set about his work when there was a gentle rap at his door.

As he owned nothing, he never locked his door, except sometimes, and that very rarely, when he was about some pressing piece of work. And, indeed, even when absent, he left his key in the lock. "You will be robbed," said Ma'am Bougon. "Of what?" said Marius. The fact is, however, that one day somebody had stolen an old pair of boots, to the great triumph of Ma'am Bougon.

There was a second rap, very gentle like the first.

"Come in," said Marius.

The door opened.

"What do you want, Ma'am Bougon?" asked Marius, without raising his eyes from the books and papers which he had on his table.

A voice, which was not Ma'am Bougon's, answered:

"I beg your pardon, Monsieur——"

It was a hollow, cracked, smothered, rasping voice, the voice of an old man, roughened by brandy and by liquors.

Marius turned quickly and saw a young girl.

IV
A ROSE IN MISERY

A GIRL who was quite young, was standing in the half-opened door. The little round window through which the light found its way into the garret was exactly opposite the door, and lit up this form with a pallid light. It was a pale, puny, meagre creature, nothing but a chemise and a skirt covered a shivering and chilly nakedness. A string for a belt, a string for a head-dress, sharp shoulders protruding from the chemise, a blonde and lymphatic pallor, dirty shoulder-blades, red hands, the mouth open and sunken, some teeth gone, the eyes dull, bold, and drooping, the form of an unripe young girl and the look of a corrupted old woman; fifty years joined with fifteen; one of those beings who are both feeble and horrible at once, and who make those shudder whom they do not make weep.

Marius arose and gazed with a kind of astonishment upon this being, so much like the shadowy forms which pass across our dreams.

The most touching thing about it was that this young girl had not come into the world to be ugly. In her early childhood, she must have even been pretty. The grace of her youth was still struggling against the hideous old age brought on by debauchery and poverty. A remnant of beauty was dying out upon this face of sixteen, like the pale sun which is extinguished by frightful clouds at the dawn of a winter's day.

The face was not absolutely unknown to Marius. He thought he remembered having seen it somewhere.

"What do you wish, mademoiselle?" asked he.

The young girl answered with her voice like a drunken galley slave's:

"Here is a letter for you, Monsieur Marius."

She called Marius by his name; he could not doubt that her business was with him; but what was this girl? how did she know his name?

Without waiting for an invitation, she entered. She entered resolutely, looking at the whole room and the unmade bed with a sort of assurance which chilled the heart. She was barefooted. Great holes in her skirt revealed her long limbs and her sharp knees. She was shivering.

She had really in her hand a letter which she presented to Marius.

Marius, in opening this letter, noticed that the enormously large wafer was still wet. The message could not have come far. He read:

"My amiable neighbour, young man!

"I have lerned your kindness towards me, that you have paid my rent six months ago. I bless you, young man. My eldest daughter will tell you that we have been without a morsel of bread for two days, four persons, and my spouse sick. If I am not desseived by my thoughts, I think I may hope that your generous heart will soften at this exposure and that the desire will subjugate you of being propitious to me by deigning to lavish upon me some light gift.

"I am with the distinguished consideration which is due to the benefactors of humanity,

"JONDRETTE

"P.S. My daughter will await your orders, dear Monsieur Marius."

This letter, in the midst of the obscure accident which had occupied Marius' thoughts since the previous evening, was a candle in a cave. Everything was suddenly cleared up.

This letter came from the same source as the other four. It was the same writing, the same style, the same orthography, the same paper, the same odour of tobacco.

There were five missives, five stories, five names, five signatures and a single signer. The Spanish Captain Don Alvarès, the unfortunate mother Balizard, the dramatic poet Genflot, the old comedy writer Fabantou, were all four named Jondrette, if indeed the name of Jondrette himself was Jondrette.

During the now rather long time that Marius had lived in the tenement, he had had, as we have said, but very few opportunities to see, or even catch a glimpse of his very poor neighbours. His mind was elsewhere, and where the mind is, thither the eyes are directed. He must have met the Jondrettes in the passage and on the stairs, more than once, but to him they were only shadows; he had taken so little notice that on the previous evening he had brushed against the Jondrette girls upon the boulevard without recognising them; for it was evidently they;

and it was with great difficulty that this girl, who had just come into his room, had awakened in him beneath his disgust and pity, a vague remembrance of having met with her elsewhere.

Now he saw everything clearly. He understood that the occupation of his neighbour Jondrette in his distress was to work upon the sympathies of benevolent persons; that he procured their addresses, and that he wrote under assumed names letters to people whom he deemed rich and compassionate, which his daughters carried, at their risk and peril; for this father was one who risked his daughters; he was playing a game with destiny, and he put them into the stake. Marius understood, to judge by their flight in the evening, by their breathlessness, by their terror, by those words of argot which he had heard, that probably these unfortunate things were carrying on also some of the secret trades of darkness, and that from all this the result was, in the midst of human society constituted as it is, two miserable beings who were neither children, nor girls, nor women, a species of impure yet innocent monsters produced by misery.

Sad creatures without name, without age, without sex, to whom neither good nor evil were any longer possible, and for whom, on leaving childhood, there is nothing more in this world, neither liberty, nor virtue, nor responsibility. Souls blooming yesterday, faded to-day, like those flowers which fall in the street and are bespattered by the mud before a wheel crushes them.

Meantime, while Marius fixed upon her an astonished and sorrowful look, the young girl was walking to and fro in the room with the boldness of a spectre. She bustled about regardless of her nakedness. At times, her chemise, unfastened and torn, fell almost to her waist. She moved the chairs, she disarranged the toilet articles on the bureau, she felt of Marius' clothes, she searched over what there was in the corners.

"Ah," said she, "you have a mirror!"

And she hummed, as if she had been alone, snatches of songs, light refrains which were made dismal by her harsh and guttural voice. Beneath this boldness could be perceived an indescribable constraint, restlessness, and humility. Effrontery is a shame.

Nothing was more sorrowful than to see her amusing herself, and, so to speak, fluttering about the room with the movements of a bird which is startled by the light, or which has a wing broken. You feel that under other conditions of education and of destiny, the gay and free manner of this young girl might have been something sweet and charming. Never among animals does the creature which is born to be a dove change into an osprey. That is seen only among men.

Marius was reflecting, and let her go on.

She went to the table.

"Ah!" said she, "books!"

A light flashed through her glassy eye. She resumed, and her tone expressed that happiness of being able to boast of something, to which no human creature is insensible:

"I can read, I can."

She hastily caught up the book which lay open on the table, and read fluently:

"——General Bauduin received the order to take five battalions of his brigade and carry the château of Hougomont, which is in the middle of the plain of Waterloo——"

She stopped:

"Ah, Waterloo! I know that. It is a battle in old times. My father was there; my father served in the armies. We are jolly good Bonapartists at home, that we are. Against English, Waterloo is."

She put down the book, took up a pen, and exclaimed:

"And I can write, too!"

She dipped the pen in the ink, and turning towards Marius:

"Would you like to see? Here, I am going to write a word to show."

And before he had had time to answer, she wrote upon a sheet of blank paper which was on the middle of the table: "*The Cognes are here.*"

Then, throwing down the pen:

"There are no mistakes in spelling. You can look. We have received an education, my sister and I. We have not always been what we are. We were not made——"

Here she stopped, fixed her faded eye upon Marius, and burst out laughing, saying in a tone which contained complete anguish stifled by complete cynicism:

"Bah!"

And she began to hum these words, to a lively air:

J'ai faim, mon père.
Pas de fricot.

> J'ai froid, ma mère.
> Pas de tricot.
> Grelotte,
> Lolotte!
> Sanglote,
> Jacquot!

Hardly had she finished this stanza when she exclaimed:

"Do you ever go to the theatre, Monsieur Marius? I do. I have a little brother who is a friend of some artists, and who gives me tickets sometimes. Now, I do not like the seats in the galleries. You are crowded, you are uncomfortable. There are sometimes coarse people there; there are also people who smell bad."

Then she looked at Marius, put on a strange manner, and said to him:

"Do you know, Monsieur Marius, that you are a very pretty boy?"

And at the same time the same thought occurred to both of them, which made her smile and made him blush.

She went to him, and laid her hand on his shoulder: "You pay no attention to me, but I know you, Monsieur Marius. I meet you here on the stairs, and then I see you visiting a man named Father Mabeuf, who lives out by Austerlitz, sometimes, when I am walking that way. That becomes you very well, your tangled hair."

Her voice tried to be very soft, but succeeded only in being very low. Some of her words were lost in their passage from the larynx to the lips, as upon a key-board in which some notes are missing.

Marius had drawn back quietly.

"Mademoiselle," said he, with his cold gravity, "I have here a packet, which is yours, I think. Permit me to return it to you."

And he handed her the envelope, which contained the four letters.

She clapped her hands and exclaimed:

"We have looked everywhere!"

Then she snatched the packet, and opened the envelope, saying:

"Lordy, Lordy, haven't we looked, my sister and I? And you have found it! on the boulevard, didn't you? It must have been on the boulevard? You see, this dropped when we ran. It was my brat of a sister who made the stupid blunder. When we got home we could not find it. As we did not want to be beaten, since that is needless, since that is entirely needless, since that is absolutely needless, we said at home that we had carried the letters to the persons, and that they told us: Nix! Now here they are, these poor letters. And how did you know they were mine? Ah, yes! by the writing! It was you, then, that we knocked against last evening. We did not see you, really! I said to my sister: Is that a gentleman. My sister said:—I think it is a gentleman!"

Meanwhile she had unfolded the petition addressed "to the beneficent gentleman of the church Saint Jacques du Haut Pas."

"Here!" said she, "this is for the old fellow who goes to mass. And this too is the hour. I am going to carry it to him. He will give us something perhaps for breakfast."

Then she began to laugh, and added:

"Do you know what it will be if we have breakfast to-day? It will be that we shall have had our breakfast for day before yesterday, our dinner for day before yesterday, our breakfast for yesterday, our dinner for yesterday, all that at one time this morning. Yes! zounds! if you're not satisfied, stuff till you burst, dogs!"

This reminded Marius of what the poor girl had come to his room for.

He felt in his waistcoat, he found nothing there.

The young girl continued, seeming to talk as if she were no longer conscious that Marius was there present.

"Sometimes I go away at night. Sometimes I do not come back. Before coming to this place, the other winter, we lived under the arches of the bridges. We hugged close to each other so as not to freeze. My little sister cried. How chilly the water is! When I thought of drowning myself, I said: No; it is too cold. I go all alone when I want to, I sleep in the ditches sometimes. Do you know, at night, when I walk on the boulevards, I see the trees like gibbets, I see all the great black houses like the towers of Notre Dame, I imagine that the white walls are the river, I say to myself: Here, there is water there! The stars are like illumination lamps, one would say that they smoke, and that the wind blows them out, I am confused, as if I had horses breathing in my ear; though it is night, I hear hand-organs and spinning wheels, I don't know what. I think that somebody is throwing stones at me, I run without knowing it, it is all a whirl, all a whirl. When one has not eaten, it is very queer."

And she looked at him with a wandering eye.

After a thorough exploration of his pockets, Marius had at last got together five francs and sixteen sous. This was at the time all that he had in the world. "That is enough for my dinner to-day," thought he, "to-morrow we will see." He took the sixteen sous, and gave the five francs to the young girl.

She took the piece eagerly.

"Good," said she, "there is some sunshine!"

And as if the sun had had the effect to loosen an avalanche of argot in her brain, she continued:

"Five francs! a shiner! a monarch! in this *piolle*! it is *chenâtre*! You are a good *mion*. I give you my *palpitant*. Bravo for the *fanandels*! Two days of *pivois*! and of *viandemuche*! and of *frictomar*! we shall *pitancer chenument*! and *bonne mouise*!"

She drew her chemise up over her shoulders, made a low bow to Marius, then a familiar wave of the hand, and moved towards the door, saying:

"Good morning, monsieur. It is all the same. I am going to find my old man."

On her way she saw on the bureau a dry crust of bread moulding there in the dust; she sprang upon it, and bit it, muttering:

"That is good! it is hard! it breaks my teeth!"

Then she went out.

V

THE JUDAS OF PROVIDENCE

FOR five years Marius had lived in poverty, in privation, in distress even, but he perceived that he had never known real misery. Real misery he had just seen. It was this sprite which had just passed before his eyes. In fact, he who has seen the misery of man only has seen nothing, he must see the misery of woman; he who has seen the misery of woman only has seen nothing, he must see the misery of childhood.

When man has reached the last extremity, he comes, at the same time, to the last expedients. Woe to the defenceless beings who surround him! Work, wages, bread, fire, courage, willingness, all fail him at once. The light of day seems to die away without, the moral light dies out within: in this gloom, man meets the weakness of woman and childhood, and puts them by force to ignominious uses.

Then all horrors are possible. Despair is surrounded by fragile walls which all open into vice or crime.

Health, youth, honour, the holy and passionate delicacies of the still tender flesh, the heart, virginity, modesty, that epidermis of the soul, are fatally disposed of by that blind groping which seeks for aid, which meets degradation, and which accommodates itself to it. Fathers, mothers, children, brothers, sisters, men, women, girls, cling together, and almost grow together like a mineral formation, in that dark promiscuity of sexes, of relationships, of ages, of infancy, of innocence. They crouch down, back to back, in a kind of fate-hovel. They glance at one another sorrowfully. Oh, the unfortunate! how pallid they are! how cold they are! It seems as though they were on a planet much further from the sun than we.

This young girl was to Marius a sort of messenger from the night.

She revealed to him an entire and hideous aspect of the darkness.

Marius almost reproached himself with the fact that he had been so absorbed in his reveries and passion that he had not until now cast a glance upon his neighbours. Paying their rent was a mechanical impulse; everybody would have had that impulse; but he, Marius, should have done better. What! a mere wall separated him from these abandoned beings, who lived by groping in the night without the pale of the living; he came in contact with them, he was in some sort the last link of the human race which they touched, he heard them live or rather breathe beside him, and he took no notice of them! every day at every moment, he heard them through the wall, walking, going, coming, talking, and he did not lend his ear! and in these words there were groans, and he did not even listen, his thoughts were elsewhere, upon dreams, upon impossible glimmerings, upon loves in the sky, upon infatuations; and all the while human beings, his brothers in Jesus Christ, his brothers in the people, were suffering death agonies beside him! agonising uselessly; he even caused a portion of their suffering, and aggravated it. For had they had another neighbour, a less chimerical and more observant neighbour, an ordinary and charitable man, it was clear that their poverty would have been noticed, their signals of distress would have been seen, and long ago perhaps they would have been gathered up and saved! Undoubtedly they seemed very depraved, very corrupt, very vile, very hateful, even, but those are rare who fall without becoming degraded; there is a point, moreover, at which the unfortunate and the infamous are associated and confounded in a single word, a fatal word, *Les Misérables*; whose fault is it? And then, is it not when the fall is lowest that charity ought to be greatest?

While he thus preached to himself, for there were times when Marius, like all truly honest hearts, was his own monitor, and scolded himself more than he deserved, he looked at the wall which separated him from the Jondrettes, as if he could send his pitying glance through that partition to warn those unfortunate beings. The wall was a thin layer of plaster, upheld by laths and joists, through which, as we have just seen, voices and words could be distinguished perfectly. None but the dreamer, Marius, would not have perceived this before. There was no paper hung on this wall either on the side of the Jondrettes, or on Marius' side; its coarse construction was bare to the eye. Almost unconsciously, Marius examined this partition; sometimes reverie examines, observes, and scrutinises, as thought would do. Suddenly he arose, he noticed towards the top, near the ceiling, a triangular hole, where three laths left a space between them. The plaster which should have stopped this hole was gone, and by getting upon the bureau he could see through that hole into the Jondrettes' garret. Pity has and should have its curiosity. This hole was a kind of Judas. It is lawful to look upon misfortune like a betrayer for the sake of relieving it. "Let us see what these people are," thought Marius, "and to what they are reduced."

He climbed upon the bureau, put his eye to the crevice, and looked.

VI
THE WILD MAN IN HIS LAIR

CITIES, like forests, have their dens in which hide all their vilest and most terrible monsters. But in cities, what hides thus is ferocious, unclean, and petty, that is to say, ugly; in forests, what hides is ferocious, savage, and grand, that is to say, beautiful.

Den for den, those of beasts are preferable to those of men. Caverns are better than the wretched holes which shelter humanity.

What Marius saw was a hole.

Marius was poor and his room was poorly furnished, but even as his poverty was noble, his garret was clean. The den into which his eyes were at that moment directed, was abject, filthy, fetid, infectious, gloomy, unclean. All the furniture was a straw chair, a rickety table, a few old broken dishes, and in two of the corners two indescribable pallets; all the light came from a dormer window of four panes, curtained with spiders' webs. Just enough light came through that loophole to make a man's face appear like the face of a phantom. The walls had a leprous look, and were covered with seams and scars like a face disfigured by some horrible malady; a putrid moisture oozed from them. Obscene pictures could be discovered upon them coarsely sketched in charcoal.

The room which Marius occupied had a broken brick pavement; this one was neither paved nor floored; the inmates walked immediately upon the old plastering of the ruinous tenement, which had grown black under their feet. Upon this uneven soil where the dust was, as it were, incrusted, and which was virgin soil in respect only of the broom, were grouped at random constellations of socks, old shoes, and hideous rags; however, this room had a fire-place; so it rented for forty francs a year. In the fire-place there was a little of everything, a chafing-dish, a kettle, some broken boards, rags hanging on nails, a bird cage, some ashes, and even a little fire. Two embers were smoking sullenly.

The size of this garret added still more to its horror. It had projections, angles, black holes, recesses under the roof, bays, and promontories. Beyond were hideous, unfathomable corners, which seemed as if they must be full of spiders as big as one's fist, centipedes as large as one's foot, and perhaps even some unknown monsters of humanity.

One of the pallets was near the door, the other near the window. Each had one end next the chimney and both were opposite Marius. In a corner near the opening through which Marius was looking, hanging upon the wall in a black wooden frame, was a coloured engraving at the bottom of which was written in large letters: THE DREAM. It represented a sleeping woman and a sleeping child, the child upon the woman's lap, an eagle in a cloud with a crown in his beak, and the woman putting away the crown from the child's head, but without waking; in the background Napoleon in a halo, leaning against a large blue column with a yellow capital adorned with this inscription:

MARINGO
AUSTERLITS
IENA
WAGRAMME
ELOT

Below this frame a sort of wooden panel longer than it was wide was standing on the floor and leaning at an angle against the wall. It had the appearance of a picture set against the wall, of a frame probably daubed on the other side, of a pier glass taken down from a wall and forgotten to be hung again.

By the table, upon which Marius saw a pen, ink, and paper, was seated a man of about sixty, small, thin, livid, haggard, with a keen, cruel, and restless air; a hideous harpy.

Lavater, if he could have studied this face, would have found in it a mixture of vulture and pettifogger; the bird of prey and the man of tricks rendering each other ugly and complete, the man of tricks making the bird of prey ignoble, the bird of prey making the man of tricks horrible.

This man had a long grey beard. He was dressed in a woman's chemise, which showed his shaggy breast and his naked arms bristling with grey hairs. Below this chemise were a pair of muddy pantaloons and boots from which the toes stuck out.

He had a pipe in his mouth, and was smoking. There was no more bread in the den, but there was tobacco.

He was writing, probably some such letter as those which Marius had read.

On one corner of the table was an old odd volume with a reddish cover, the size of which, the old duodecimo of series of books, betrayed that it was a novel. On the cover was displayed the following title, printed in huge capitals: GOD, THE KING, HONOUR AND THE LADIES, BY DUCRAY DUMINIL, 1814.

As he wrote, the man talked aloud, and Marius heard his words:

"To think that there is no equality even when we are dead! Look at Père Lachaise! The great, those who are rich, are in the upper part, in the avenue of the acacias, which is paved. They can go there in a carriage. The low, the poor, the unfortunate, they are put in the lower part, where there is mud up to the knees, in holes, in the wet. They are put there so that they may rot sooner! You cannot go to see them without sinking into the ground."

Here he stopped, struck his fist on the table, and added, gnashing his teeth:

"Oh! I could eat the world!"

A big woman, who might have been forty years old or a hundred, was squatting near the fire-place, upon her bare feet.

She also was dressed only in a chemise and a knit skirt patched with pieces of old cloth. A coarse tow apron covered half the skirt. Although this woman was bent and drawn up into herself, it could be seen that she was very tall. She was a kind of giantess by the side of her husband. She had hideous hair, light red sprinkled with grey, that she pushed back from time to time with her huge shining hands which had flat nails.

Lying on the ground, at her side, wide open, was a volume of the same appearance as the other, and probably of the same novel.

Upon one of the pallets Marius could discern a sort of slender little wan girl seated, almost naked, with her feet hanging down, having the appearance neither of listening, nor of seeing, nor of living.

The younger sister, doubtless, of the one who had come to his room.

She appeared to be eleven or twelve years old. On examining her attentively, he saw that she must be fourteen. It was the child who, the evening before, on the boulevard, said: "I *cavalé, cavalé, cavalé!*"

She was of that sickly species which long remains backward, then pushes forward rapidly, and all at once. These sorry human plants are produced by want. These poor creatures have neither childhood nor youth. At fifteen they appear to be twelve; at sixteen they appear to be twenty. To-day a little girl, to-morrow a woman. One would say that they leap through life, to have done with it sooner.

This being now had the appearance of a child.

Nothing, moreover, indicated the performance of any labour in this room; not a loom, not a wheel, not a tool. In one corner a few scraps of iron of an equivocal appearance. It was that gloomy idleness which follows despair, and which precedes the death-agony.

Marius looked for some time into that funereal interior, more fearful than the interior of a tomb; for here were felt the movements of a human soul, and the palpitation of life.

The garret, the cellar, the deep ditch, in which some of the wretched crawl at the bottom of the social edifice, are not the sepulchre itself, they are its ante-chamber; but like those rich men who display their greatest magnificence at the entrance of their palace, death, who is close at hand, seems to display his greatest wretchedness in this vestibule.

The man became silent, the woman did not speak, the girl did not seem to breathe. Marius could hear the pen scratching over the paper.

The man muttered out, without ceasing to write:—"Rabble! rabble! all is rabble!"

This variation upon the ejaculation of Solomon drew a sigh from the woman.

"My darling, be calm," said she. "Do not hurt yourself, dear. You are too good to write to all those people, my man."

In poverty bodies hug close to each other as in the cold, but hearts grow distant. This woman, according to all appearance, must have loved this man with as much love as was in her; but probably, in the repeated mutual reproaches which grew out of the frightful distress that weighed upon them all, this love had become extinguished. She now felt towards her husband nothing more than the ashes of affection. Still the words of endearment, as often happens, had survived. She said to him: *Dear*; *my darling*; *my man*, etc., with her lips, her heart was silent.

The man returned to his writing.

VII
STRATEGY AND TACTICS

MARIUS, with a heavy heart, was about to get down from the sort of observatory which he had extemporised, when a sound attracted his attention, and induced him to remain in his place.

The door of the garret was hastily opened. The eldest

daughter appeared upon the threshold. On her feet she had coarse men's shoes, covered with mud, which had been spattered as high as her red ankles, and she was wrapped in a ragged old gown which Marius had not seen upon her an hour before, but which she had probably left at his door that she might inspire the more pity, and which she must have put on upon going out. She came in, pushed the door to behind her, stopped to take breath, for she was quite breathless, then cried with an expression of joy and triumph:

"He is coming!"

The father turned his eyes, the woman turned her head, the younger sister did not stir.

"Who?" asked the father.

"The gentleman!"

"The philanthropist?"

"Yes."

"Of the church of Saint Jacques?"

"Yes."

"That old man?"

"Yes."

"He is going to come?"

"He is behind me."

"You are sure?"

"I am sure."

"There, true, he is coming?"

"He is coming in a fiacre."

"In a fiacre. It is Rothschild?"

The father arose.

"How are you sure? if he is coming in a fiacre, how is it that you get here before him? you gave him the address, at least? you told him the last door at the end of the hall on the right? provided he does not make a mistake? you found him at the church then? did he read my letter? what did he say to you?"

"Tut, tut, tut!" said the girl, "how you run on, goodman! I'll tell you: I went into the church, he was at his usual place, I made a curtsey to him, and I gave him the letter, he read it and said to me: Where do you live, my child? I said: Monsieur, I will show you. He said to me: No, give me your address; my daughter has some purchases to make, I am going to take a carriage and I will get to your house as soon as you do. I gave him the address. When I told him the house, he appeared surprised and hesitated an instant, then he said: It is all the same, I will go. When mass was over, I saw him leave the church with his daughter. I saw them get into a fiacre. And I told him plainly the last door at the end of the hall on the right."

"And how do you know that he will come?"

"I just saw the fiacre coming into the Rue du Petit Banquier. That is what made me run."

"How do you know it is the same fiacre?"

"Because I had noticed the number."

"What is the number?"

"Four hundred and forty."

"Good, you are a clever girl."

The girl looked resolutely at her father, and showing the shoes which she had on, said:

"A clever girl that may be, but I tell you that I shall never put on these shoes again, and that I will not do it, for health first, and then for decency's sake. I know nothing more provoking than soles that squeak and go ghee, ghee, ghee, all along the street. I would rather go barefoot."

"You are right," answered the father, in a mild tone which contrasted with the rudeness of the young girl, "but they would not let you go into the churches; the poor must have shoes. People do not go to God's house barefooted," added he bitterly. Then returning to the subject which occupied his thoughts——

"And you are sure then, sure that he is coming?"

"He is at my heels," said she.

The man sprang up. There was a sort of illumination on his face.

"Wife!" cried he, "you hear. Here is the philanthropist. Put out the fire."

The astounded woman did not stir.

The father, with the agility of a mountebank, caught a broken pot which stood on the mantel, and threw some water upon the embers.

Then turning to his elder daughter:

"You! unbottom the chair!"

His daughter did not understand him at all.

He seized the chair, and with a kick he ruined the seat. His leg went through it.

As he drew out his leg, he asked his daughter:

"Is it cold?"

"Very cold. It snows."

The father turned towards the younger girl, who was on the pallet near the window, and cried in a thundering voice:

"Quick! off the bed, good-for-nothing! will you never do anything? break a pane of glass!"

The little girl sprang off the bed trembling.

"Break a pane of glass!" said he again.

The child was speechless.

"Do you hear me?" repeated the father, "I tell you to break a pane!"

The child, with a sort of terrified obedience, rose upon tip-toe and struck her fist into a pane. The glass broke and fell with a crash.

"Good," said the father.

He was serious, yet rapid. His eye ran hastily over all the nooks and corners of the garret.

You would have said he was a general, making his final pre-parations at the moment when the battle was about to begin.

The mother, who had not yet said a word, got up and asked in a slow, muffled tone, her words seeming to come out as if curdled:

"Dear, what is it you want to do?"

"Get into bed," answered the man.

His tone admitted of no deliberation. The mother obeyed, and threw herself heavily upon one of the pallets.

Meanwhile a sob was heard in a corner.

"What is that?" cried the father.

The younger daughter, without coming out of the darkness into which she had shrunk, showed her bleeding fist. In breaking the glass she had cut herself; she had gone to her mother's bed, and she was weeping in silence.

It was the mother's turn to rise and cry out.

"You see now! what stupid things you are doing? breaking your glass, she has cut herself!"

"So much the better!" said the man. "I knew she would."

"How! so much the better?" resumed the woman.

"Silence!" replied the father. "I suppress the liberty of the press."

Then tearing the chemise which he had on, he made a band-age with which he hastily wrapped up the little girl's bleeding wrist.

That done, his eye fell upon the torn chemise with satisfaction. "And the chemise too," said he, "all this has a good appearance."

An icy wind whistled at the window and came into the room. The mist from without entered and spread about like a whitish wadding picked apart by invisible fingers. Through the broken pane the falling snow was seen. The cold promised the day before by the Candlemas sun had come indeed.

The father cast a glance about him as if to assure himself that he had forgotten nothing. He took an old shovel and spread ashes over the moistened embers in such a way as to hide them completely.

Then rising and standing with his back to the chimney:

"Now," said he, "we can receive the philanthropist."

VIII

THE SUNBEAM IN THE HOLE

THE large girl went to her father and laid her hand on his.

"Feel how cold I am," said she.

"Pshaw!" answered the father. "I am a good deal colder than that."

The mother cried impetuously:

"You always have everything better than the rest, even pain."

"Down!" said the man.

The mother, after a peculiar look from the man, held her peace.

There was a moment of silence in the den. The eldest daughter was scraping the mud off the bottom of her dress with a careless air, the young sister continued to sob; the mother had taken her head in both hands and was covering her with kisses, saying to her in a low tone:

"My treasure, I beg of you, it will be nothing, do not cry, you will make your father angry."

"No!" cried the father, "on the contrary! sob! sob! that does finely."

Then turning to the eldest:

"Ah! but he does not come! if he was not coming, I shall have put out my fire, knocked the bottom out of my chair, torn my chemise, and broken my window for nothing."

"And cut the little girl!" murmured the mother.

"Do you know," resumed the father, "that it is as cold as a dog in this devilish garret? If this man should not come! Oh! that is it! he makes us wait for him! he says: Well! they will wait for me! that is what they are for!—Oh! how I hate them, and how I would strangle them with joy and rejoicing, enthusiasm and satisfaction, these rich men! all the rich! these professed charitable men, who make their plums, who go to mass, who follow the priesthood, preachy, preachy, who give in to the cowls, and who think themselves above us, and who come to humiliate us, and to bring us clothes! as they call them! rags which are not worth four sous, and bread! that is not what I want of the rabble! I want money! But money, never! because they say that we would go and drink it, and that we are drunkards and do-nothings! And what then are they, and what have they been in their time? Thieves! they would not have got rich without that! Oh! somebody ought to take society by the four corners of the sheet and toss it all into the air! Everything would be crushed, it is likely, but at least nobody would have anything, there would be so much gained! But what now is he doing, your mug of a benevolent gentleman? is he coming? The brute may have forgotten the address! I will bet that the old fool——"

Just then there was a light rap at the door, the man rushed forward and opened it, exclaiming with many low bows and smiles of adoration:

"Come in, monsieur! deign to come in, my noble bene-factor, as well as your charming young lady."

A man of mature age and a young girl appeared at the door of the garret.

Marius had not left his place. What he felt at that moment escapes human language.

It was She.

Whoever has loved, knows all the radiant meaning contained in the three letters of this word: She.

It was indeed she. Marius could hardly discern her through the luminous vapour which suddenly spread over his eyes. It was that sweet absent being, that star which had been his light, for six months, it was that eye, that brow, that mouth, that beautiful vanished face which had produced night when it went away. The vision had been in an eclipse, it was reappearing.

She appeared again in this gloom, in this garret, in this shape-less den, in this horror!

Marius shuddered desperately. What! it was she! the beating of his heart disturbed his sight. He felt ready to melt into tears. What! at last he saw her again after having sought for her so long! it seemed to him that he had just lost his soul and that he had just found it again.

She was still the same, a little paler only; her delicate face was set in a violet velvet hat, her form was hidden under a black satin pelisse, below her long dress he caught a glimpse of her little foot squeezed into a silk buskin.

She was still accompanied by Monsieur Leblanc.

She stepped into the room and laid a large package on the table.

The elder Jondrette girl had retreated behind the door and was looking upon that velvet hat, that silk dress, and that charming happy face, with an evil eye.

IX

JONDRETTE WEEPS ALMOST

THE den was so dark that people who came from outdoors felt as if they were entering a cellar on coming in. The two newcomers stepped forward, therefore, with some hesitation, hardly discerning the dim forms about them, while they were seen and examined with perfect ease by the tenants of the garret, whose eyes were accustomed to this twilight.

Monsieur Leblanc approached with his kind and compassionate look, and said to the father:

"Monsieur, you will find in this package some new clothes, some stockings, and some new coverlids."

"Our angelic benefactor overwhelms us," said Jondrette, bowing down to the floor. Then, stooping to his eldest daughter's ear, while the two visitors were examining this lamentable abode, he added rapidly in a whisper:

"Well! what did I tell you? rags? no money. They are all alike! Tell me, how was the letter to this old blubber-lip signed?"

"Fabantou," answered the daughter.

"The dramatic artist, good!"

This was lucky for Jondrette, for at that very moment Monsieur Leblanc turned towards him and said to him, with the appearance of one who is trying to recollect a name:

"I see that you are indeed to be pitied, Monsieur——"

"Fabantou," said Jondrette quickly.

"Monsieur Fabantou, yes, that is it. I remember."

"Dramatic artist, monsieur, and who has had his successes."

Here Jondrette evidently thought the moment come to make an impression upon the "philanthropist." He exclaimed in a tone of voice which belongs to the braggadocio of the juggler at a fair, and, at the same time, to the humility of a beggar on the highway: "Pupil of Talma! Monsieur! I am a pupil of Talma! Fortune once smiled on me. Alas! now it is the turn of misfortune. Look, my benefactor, no bread, no fire. My poor darlings have no fire! My only chair unseated! A broken window! in such weather as is this! My spouse in bed! sick!"

"Poor woman!" said Monsieur Leblanc.

"My child injured!" added Jondrette.

The child, whose attention had been diverted by the arrival of the strangers, was staring at "the young lady," and had ceased her sobbing.

"Why don't you cry? why don't you scream?" said Jondrette to her in a whisper.

At the same time he pinched her injured hand. All this with the skill of a juggler.

The little one uttered loud cries.

The adorable young girl whom Marius in his heart called "his Ursula" went quickly to her:

"Poor, dear child!" said she.

"Look, my beautiful young lady," pursued Jondrette, "her bleeding wrist! It is an accident which happened in working at a machine by which she earned six sous a day. It may be necessary to cut off her arm."

"Indeed!" said the old gentleman, alarmed.

The little girl, taking this seriously, began to sob again beautifully.

"Alas, yes, my benefactor!" answered the father.

For some moments, Jondrette had been looking at "the philanthropist" in a strange manner. Even while speaking, he seemed to scrutinise him closely as if he were trying to recall some reminiscence. Suddenly, taking advantage of a moment when the new-comers were anxiously questioning the smaller girl about her mutilated hand, he passed over to his wife who was lying in her bed, appearing to be overwhelmed and stupid, and said to her quickly and in a very low tone:

"Notice that man!"

Then turning towards M. Leblanc, and continuing his lamentation:

"You see, monsieur! my whole dress is nothing but a chemise of my wife's! and that all torn! in the heart of winter. I cannot go out, for lack of a coat. If I had a sign of a coat, I should go to see Mademoiselle Mars, who knows me, and of whom I am a great favourite. She is still living in the Rue de la Tour des Dames, is not she? You know, monsieur, we have played together in the provinces. I shared her laurels. Celimène would come to my relief, monsieur! Elmira would give alms to Belisarius! But no, nothing! And not a sou in the house! My wife sick, not a sou! My daughter dangerously injured, not a sou! My spouse has choking fits. It is her time of life, and then the nervous system has something to do with it. She needs aid, and my daughter also! But the doctor! but the druggist! how can I pay them! not a penny! I would fall on my knees before a penny, monsieur! You see how the arts are fallen! And do you know, my charming young lady, and you, my generous patron, do you know, you who breathe virtue and goodness, and who perfume that church where my daughter, in going to say her prayers, sees you every day? For I bring up my daughters religiously, monsieur. I have not allowed them to take to the theatre. Ah! the rogues! that I should see them tripping! I do not jest! I fortify them with sermons about honour, about morals, about virtue! Ask them! They must walk straight. They have a father. They are none of those unfortunates, who begin by having no family, and who end by marrying the public. They are Mamselle Nobody, and become Madame Everybody. Thank heaven! none of that in the Fabantou family! I mean to educate them virtuously, and that they may be honest, and that they may be genteel, and that they may believe in God's sacred name! Well, monsieur, my worthy monsieur, do you know what is going to happen to-morrow? To-morrow is the 4th of February, the fatal day, the last delay that my landlord will give me; if I do not pay him this evening, to-morrow my eldest daughter, myself, my spouse with her fever, my child with her wound, we shall all four be turned out of doors, and driven off into the street, upon the boulevard, without shelter, into the rain, upon the snow. You see, monsieur, I owe four quarters, a year! that is sixty francs."

Jondrette lied. Four quarters would have made but forty francs, and he could not have owed for four, since it was not six months since Marius had paid for two.

M. Leblanc took five francs from his pocket and threw them on the table.

Jondrette had time to mutter into the ear of his elder daughter:

"The whelp! what does he think I am going to do with his five francs? That will not pay for my chair and my window! I must make my expenses!"

Meantime, M. Leblanc had taken off a large brown overcoat, which he wore over his blue surtout, and hung it over the back of the chair.

"Monsieur Fabantou," said he, "I have only these five francs with me; but I am going to take my daughter home, and I will return this evening; is it not this evening that you have to pay?"

Jondrette's face lighted up with a strange expression. He answered quickly:

"Yes, my noble monsieur. At eight o'clock, I must be at my landlord's."

"I will be here at six o'clock, and I will bring you the sixty francs."

"My benefactor!" cried Jondrette, distractedly.

And he added in an undertone:

"Take a good look at him, wife!"

M. Leblanc took the arm of the beautiful young girl, and turned towards the door:

"Till this evening, my friends," said he.

"Six o'clock," said Jondrette.

"Six o'clock precisely."

Just then the overcoat on the chair caught the eye of the elder daughter.

"Monsieur," said she, "you forget your coat."

Jondrette threw a crushing glance at his daughter, accompanied by a terrible shrug of the shoulders.

M. Leblanc turned and answered with a smile:

"I do not forget it, I leave it."

"O my patron," said Jondrette, "my noble benefactor, I am melting into tears! Allow me to conduct you to your carriage."

"If you go out," replied M. Leblanc, "put on this overcoat. It is really very cold."

Jondrette did not make him say it twice. He put on the brown overcoat very quickly.

And they went out all three, Jondrette preceding the two strangers.

X

PRICE OF PUBLIC CABRIOLETS: TWO FRANCS AN HOUR

MARIUS had lost nothing of all this scene, and yet in reality he had seen nothing of it. His eyes had remained fixed upon the young girl, his heart had, so to speak, seized upon her and enveloped her entirely, from her first step into the garret. During the whole time she had been there, he had lived that life of ecstasy which suspends material perceptions and precipitates the whole soul upon a single point. He contemplated, not that girl, but that light in a satin pelisse and a velvet hat. Had the star Sirius entered the room he would not have been more dazzled.

While the young girl was opening the bundle, unfolding the clothes and the coverlids, questioning the sick mother kindly and the little injured girl tenderly, he watched all her motions, he endeavoured to hear her words. He knew her eyes, her forehead, her beauty, her stature, her gait, he did not know the sound of her voice. He thought he had caught a few words of it once at the Luxembourg, but he was not absolutely sure. He would have given ten years of his life to hear it, to be able to carry a little of that music in his soul. But all was lost in the wretched displays and trumpet blasts of Jondrette. This added a real anger to the transport of Marius. He brooded her with his eyes. He could not imagine that it really was that divine creature which he saw in the midst of the misshapen beings of this monstrous den. He seemed to see a humming-bird among toads.

When he went out, he had but one thought, to follow her, not to give up her track, not to leave her without knowing where she lived, not to lose her again, at least, after having so miraculously found her! He leaped down from the bureau and took his hat. As he was putting his hand on the bolt, and was just going out, he reflected and stopped. The hall was long, the stairs steep, Jondrette a great talker, M. Leblanc doubtless had not yet got into his carriage; if he should turn round in the passage, or on the stairs, or on the doorstep, and perceive him,

Marius, in that house, he would certainly be alarmed and would find means to escape him anew, and it would be all over at once. What was to be done? wait a little? but during the delay the carriage might go. Marius was perplexed. At last he took the risk and went out of his room.

There was nobody in the hall. He ran to the stairs. There was nobody on the stairs. He hurried down, and reached the boulevard in time to see a fiacre turn the corner of the Rue du Petit Banquier and return into the city.

Marius rushed in that direction. When he reached the corner of the boulevard, he saw the fiacre again going rapidly down the Rue Mouffetard; the fiacre was already at a long distance, there was no means of reaching it, what should he do? run after it? impossible; and then from the carriage they would certainly notice a man running at full speed in pursuit of them, and the father would recognise him. Just at this moment, marvellous and unheard-of good fortune, Marius saw a public cab passing along the boulevard, empty. There was but one course to take, to get into this cab, and follow the fiacre. That was sure, effectual, and without danger.

Marius made a sign to the driver to stop, and cried to him:

"Right away!"

Marius had no cravat, he had on his old working coat, some of the buttons of which were missing, and his shirt was torn in one of the plaits of the bosom.

The driver stopped, winked, and reached his left hand towards Marius, rubbing his forefinger gently with his thumb.

"What?" said Marius.

"Pay in advance," said the driver.

Marius remembered that he had only sixteen sous with him.

"How much?" he asked.

"Forty sous."

"I will pay when I get back."

The driver made no reply, but to whistle an air from La Palisse and whip up his horse.

Marius saw the cab move away with a bewildered air. For the want of twenty-four sous he was losing his joy, his happiness, his love! he was falling back into night! he had seen, and he was again becoming blind. He thought bitterly, and it must indeed be said, with deep regret, of the five francs he had given that very morning to that miserable girl. Had he had those five francs he would have been saved, he would have been born again, he would have come out of limbo and darkness, he would have come out of his isolation, his spleen, his bereavement; he would have again knotted the black thread of his destiny with that beautiful golden thread which had just floated before his eyes and broken off once more. He returned to the old tenement in despair.

He might have thought that M. Leblanc had promised to return in the evening, and that he had only to take better care to follow him then; but in his wrapt contemplation he had hardly understood it.

Just as he went up the stairs, he noticed on the other side of the boulevard, beside the deserted wall of the Rue de la Barrière des Gobelins, Jondrette in the "philanthropist's" overcoat, talking to one of those men of dangerous appearance, who, by common consent, are called *prowlers of the barrières*; men of equivocal faces, suspicious speech, who have an appearance of evil intentions, and who usually sleep by day, which leads us to suppose that they work by night.

These two men quietly talking while the snow was whirling about them in its fall made a picture which a policeman certainly would have observed, but which Marius hardly noticed.

Nevertheless, however mournful was the subject of his reflections, he could not help saying to himself that this prowler of the barrières with whom Jondrette was talking, resembled a certain Panchaud, alias Printanier, alias Bigrenaille, whom Courfeyrac had once pointed out to him, and who passed in the quartier for a very dangerous night-wanderer. We have seen this man's name in the preceding book. This Panchaud, alias Printanier, alias Bigrenaille, figured afterwards in several criminal trials, and has since become a celebrated scoundrel. He was still at that time only a notorious scoundrel. He is now a matter of tradition among bandits and assassins. He was the head of a school near the close of the last reign. And in the evening, at nightfall, at the hour when crowds gather and speak low, he was talked about at La Force in La Fosse aux Lions. You might even in that prison, just at the spot where that privy sewer, which served for the astonishing escape of thirty prisoners in broad day in 1843, passes under the encircling passage-way; you might, above the flagging of that sewer, read his name, PANCHAUD, audaciously cut by himself upon the outer wall in one of his attempts to escape. In 1832, the police already had him under their eye, but he had not yet really made his début.

XI
OFFERS OF SERVICE BY MISERY TO GRIEF

MARIUS mounted the stairs of the old tenement with slow steps; just as he was going into his cell, he perceived in the hall behind him the elder Jondrette girl, who was following him. This girl was odious to his sight; it was she who had his five francs, it was too late to ask her for them, the cab was there no longer, the fiacre was far away. Moreover she would not give them back to him. As to questioning her about the address of the people who had just come, that was useless; it was plain that she did not know, since the letter signed Fabantou was addressed *to the beneficent gentleman of the Church Saint Jacques du Haut Pas*.

Marius went into his room and pushed to his door behind him.

It did not close; he turned and saw a hand holding the door partly open.

"What is it?" he asked, "who is there?"

It was the Jondrette girl.

"Is it you?" said Marius almost harshly, "you again? What do you want of me?"

She seemed thoughtful and did not look at him. She had lost the assurance which she had had in the morning. She did not come in but stopped in the dusky hall, where Marius perceived her through the half-open door.

"Come now, will you answer?" said Marius. "What is it you want of me?"

She raised her mournful eyes, in which a sort of confused light seemed to shine dimly, and said to him:

"Monsieur Marius, you look sad. What is the matter with you?"

"With me?"

"Yes, you."

"There is nothing the matter with me."

"Yes!"

"No."

"I tell you there is!"

"Let me be quiet!"

Marius pushed the door anew, she still held it back.

"Stop," said she, "you are wrong. Though you may not be rich, you were good this morning. Be so again now. You gave me something to eat, tell me now what ails you. You are troubled at something, that is plain. I do not want you to be troubled. What must be done for that? Can I serve you in anything? Let me. I do not ask your secrets, you need not tell them to me, but yet I may be useful. I can certainly help you, since I help my father. When it is necessary to carry letters, go into houses, inquire from door to door, find out an address, follow somebody, I do it. Now, you can certainly tell me what is the matter with you. I will go and speak to the persons; sometimes for somebody to speak to the persons is enough to understand things, and it is all arranged. Make use of me."

An idea came into Marius' mind. What straw do we despise when we feel that we are sinking?

He approached the girl.

"Listen," said he to her, kindly.

She interrupted him with a flash of joy in her eyes.

"Oh! yes, talk softly to me! I like that better."

"Well," resumed he, "you brought this old gentleman here with his daughter."

"Yes."

"Do you know their address?"

"No."

"Find it for me."

The girl's eyes, which had been gloomy, had become joyful; they now became dark.

"Is that what you want?" she asked.

"Yes."

"Do you know them?"

"No."

"That is to say," said she hastily, "you do not know her, but you want to know her."

This *them* which had become *her* had an indescribable significance and bitterness.

"Well, can you do it?" said Marius.

"You shall have the beautiful young lady's address."

There was again, in these words "the beautiful young lady," an expression which made Marius uneasy. He continued:

"Well, no matter! the address of the father and daughter. Their address, yes!"

She looked steadily at him.

"What will you give me?"

"Anything you wish!"

"Anything I wish?"

"Yes."

"You shall have the address."

She looked down, and then with a hasty movement closed the door.

Marius was alone.

He dropped into a chair, with his head and both elbows on the bed, swallowed up in thoughts which he could not grasp, and as if he were in a fit of vertigo. All that had taken place since morning, the appearance of the angel, her disappearance, what this poor creature had just said to him, a gleam of hope floating in an ocean of despair,—all this was confusedly crowding his brain.

Suddenly he was violently awakened from his reverie.

He heard the loud, harsh voice of Jondrette pronounce these words for him, full of the strangest interest:

"I tell you that I am sure of it, and that I recognised him!"

Of whom was Jondrette talking? he had recognised whom? M. Leblanc? the father of "his Ursula"? What! did Jondrette know him? was Marius just about to get in this sudden and unexpected way all the information the lack of which made his life obscure to himself? was he at last to know whom he loved, who that young girl was? who her father was? was the thick shadow which enveloped them to be rolled away? was the veil to be rent? Oh! heavens!

He sprang, rather than mounted, upon the bureau, and resumed his place near the little aperture in the partition.

He again saw the interior of the Jondrette den.

XII
USE OF M. LEBLANC'S FIVE-FRANC PIECE

NOTHING had changed in the appearance of the family, except that the wife and daughters had opened the package, and put on the woollen stockings and underclothes. Two new coverlids were thrown over the two beds.

Jondrette had evidently just come in. He had not yet recovered his regular breathing. His daughters were sitting on the floor near the fire-place, the elder binding up the hand of the younger. His wife lay as if exhausted upon the pallet near the fire-place with an astonished countenance. Jondrette was walking up and down the garret with rapid strides. His eyes had an extraordinary look.

The woman, who seemed timid and stricken with stupor before her husband, ventured to say to him:

"What, really? you are sure?"

"Sure! It was eight years ago! but I recognise him! Ah! I recognise him! I recognised him immediately. What! it did not strike you?"

"No."

"And yet I told you to pay attention. But it is the same height, the same face, hardly any older; there are some men who do not grow old; I don't know how they do it; it is the same tone of voice. He is better dressed, that is all! Ah! mysterious old devil, I have got you, all right!"

He checked himself, and said to his daughters:

"You go out! It is queer that it did not strike your eye."

They got up to obey.

The mother stammered out:

"With her sore hand?"

"The air will do her good," said Jondrette. "Go along."

It was clear that this man was one of those to whom there is no reply. The two girls went out.

Just as they were passing the door, the father caught the elder by the arm, and said with a peculiar tone:

"You will be here at five o'clock precisely. Both of you. I shall need you."

Marius redoubled his attention.

Alone with his wife, Jondrette began to walk the room again, and took two or three turns in silence. Then he spent a few minutes in tucking the bottom of the woman's chemise which he wore into the waist of his trousers.

Suddenly he turned towards the woman, folded his arms, and exclaimed:

"And do you want I should tell you one thing? the young lady——"

"Well, what?" said the woman, "the young lady?"

Marius could doubt no longer, it was indeed of her that they were talking. He listened with an intense anxiety. His whole life was concentrated in his ears.

But Jondrette stooped down, and whispered to his wife. Then he straightened up and finished aloud:

"It is she!"

"That girl?" said the wife.

"That girl!" said the husband.

No words could express what there was in the *that girl* of the mother. It was surprise, rage, hatred, anger, mingled and combined in a monstrous intonation. The few words that had been spoken, some name, doubtless, which her husband had whispered in her ear had been enough to rouse this huge drowsy woman and to change her repulsiveness to hideousness.

"Impossible!" she exclaimed, "when I think that my daughters go barefoot and have not a dress to put on! What! a satin pelisse, a velvet hat, buskins, and all! more than two hundred francs' worth! one would think she was a lady! no, you are mistaken! why, in the first place she was horrid, this one is not bad! she is really not bad! it cannot be she!"

"I tell you it is she. You will see."

At this absolute affirmation, the woman raised her big red and blonde face and looked at the ceiling with a hideous expression. At that moment she appeared to Marius still more terrible than her husband. She was a swine with the look of a tigress.

"What!" she resumed, "this horrible beautiful young lady who looked at my girls with an appearance of pity, can she be that beggar! Oh, I would like to stamp her heart out!"

She sprang off the bed, and remained a moment standing, her hair flying, her nostrils distended, her mouth half open, her fists clenched and drawn back. Then she fell back upon the pallet. The man still walked back and forth, paying no attention to his female.

After a few moments of silence, he approached her and stopped before her, with folded arms, as before.

"And do you want I should tell you one thing?"

"What?" she asked.

He answered in a quick and low voice:

"My fortune is made."

The woman stared at him with that look which means: Has the man who is talking to me gone crazy?

He continued:

"Thunder! it is a good long time now that I have been a parishioner of the die-of-hunger-if-you-have-any-fire-and-die-of-cold-if-you-have-any-bread parish! I have had misery enough! my yoke and the yoke of other people! I jest no longer, I find it comic no longer, enough of puns, good God! No more farces, Father Eternal! I want food for my hunger, I want drink for my thirst! to stuff! to sleep! to do nothing! I want to have my turn, I do! before I burst! I want to be a bit of a millionaire!"

He took a turn about the garret and added:

"Like other people."

"What do you mean?" asked the woman.

He shook his head, winked and lifted his voice like a street doctor about to make a demonstration:

"What do I mean? listen!"

"Hist!" muttered the woman, "not so loud! if it means business nobody must hear."

"Pshaw! who is there to hear? our neighbour? I saw him go out just now. Besides, does he hear, the great stupid? and then I tell you that I saw him go out."

Nevertheless, by a sort of instinct, Jondrette lowered his voice, not enough, however, for his words to escape Marius. A favourable circumstance, and one which enabled Marius to lose nothing of this conversation, was that the fallen snow deafened the sound of the carriages on the boulevard.

Marius heard this:

"Listen attentively. He is caught, the Crœsus! it is all right. It is already done. Everything is arranged. I have seen the men. He will come this evening at six o'clock. To bring his sixty francs, the rascal! did you see how I got that out, my sixty francs, my landlord, my 4th of February! it is not even a quarter! was that stupid! He will come then at six o'clock! our neighbour is gone to dinner then. Mother Bougon is washing dishes in the city. There is nobody in the house. Our neighbour never comes back before eleven o'clock. The girls will stand watch. You shall help us. He will be his own executor."

"And if he should not be his own executor," asked the wife.

Jondrette made a sinister gesture and said:

"We will execute him."

And he burst into a laugh.

It was the first time that Marius had seen him laugh. This laugh was cold and feeble, and made him shudder.

Jondrette opened a closet near the chimney, took out an old cap and put it on his head after brushing it with his sleeve.

"Now," said he, "I am going out. I have still some men to see. Some good ones. You will see how it is going to work. I shall be back as soon as possible, it is a great hand to play, look out for the house."

And with his two fists in the two pockets of his trousers, he stood a moment in thought, then exclaimed:

"Do you know that it is very lucky indeed that he did not recognise me? If he had been the one to recognise me he would not have come back. He would escape us! It is my beard that saved me! my romantic beard! my pretty little romantic beard!"

And he began to laugh again.

He went to the window. The snow was still falling, and blotted out the grey sky.

"What villainous weather!" said he.

Then folding his coat:

"The skin is too large. It is all the same," added he, "he did devilish well to leave it for me, the old scoundrel! Without this I should not have been able to go out and the whole thing would have been spoiled! But on what do things hang!"

And pulling his cap over his eyes, he went out.

Hardly had he had time to take a few steps in the hall, when the door opened and his tawny and cunning face again appeared.

"I forgot," said he. "You will have a charcoal fire."

And he threw into his wife's apron the five-franc piece which the "philanthropist" had left him.

"A charcoal fire?" asked the woman.

"Yes."

"How many bushels?"

"Two good ones."

"That will be thirty sous. With the rest, I will buy something for dinner."

"The devil, no."

"Why?"

"The piece of a hundred sous is not to be spent."

"Why?"

"Because I shall have something to buy."

"What?"

"Something."

"How much will you need?"

"Where is there a tool store near here?"

"Rue Mouffetard."

"Oh! yes, at the corner of some street; I see the shop."

"But tell me now how much you will need for what you have to buy?"

"Fifty sous or three francs."

"There won't be much left for dinner."

"Don't bother about eating to-day. There is better business."

"That is enough, my jewel."

At this word from his wife, Jondrette closed the door, and Marius heard his steps recede along the hall and go rapidly down the stairs.

Just then the clock of Saint Médard struck one.

XIII

SOLUS CUM SOLO, IN LOCO REMOTO, NON COGITABANTUR ORARE PATER NOSTER

MARIUS, all dreamer as he was, was, as we have said, of a firm and energetic nature. His habits of solitary meditation, while developing sympathy and compassion in him, had perhaps diminished his liability to become irritated, but left intact the faculty of indignation; he had the benevolence of a brahmin and the severity of a judge; he would have pitied a toad, but he would have crushed a viper. Now it was into a viper's hole that he had just been looking; it was a nest of monsters that he had before his eyes.

"I must put my foot on these wretches," said he.

None of the enigmas which he hoped to see unriddled was yet cleared up; on the contrary, all had perhaps become still darker; he knew nothing more of the beautiful child of the Luxembourg or of the man whom he called M. Leblanc, except that Jondrette knew them. Across the dark words which had been uttered, he saw distinctly but one thing, that an ambuscade was preparing, an ambuscade obscure, but terrible; that they were both running a great risk, she probably, her father certainly; that he must foil the hideous combinations of the Jondrettes and break the web of these spiders.

He looked for a moment at the female Jondrette. She had pulled an old sheet-iron furnace out of a corner and she was fumbling among the old iron.

He got down from the bureau as quietly as he could, taking care to make no noise.

In the midst of his dread at what was in preparation, and the horror with which the Jondrettes had inspired him, he felt a sort of joy at the idea that it would perhaps be given to him to render so great a service to her whom he loved.

But what was he to do? warn the persons threatened? where should he find them? He did not know their address. They had reappeared to his eyes for an instant, then they had again plunged into the boundless depths of Paris. Wait at the door for M. Leblanc at six o'clock in the evening, the time when he would arrive, and warn him of the plot? But Jondrette and his men would see him watching, the place was solitary, they would be stronger than he, they would find means to seize him or get him out of the way, and he whom Marius wished to save would be lost. One o'clock had just struck, the ambuscade was to be carried out at six. Marius had five hours before him.

There was but one thing to be done.

He put on his presentable coat, tied a cravat about his neck, took his hat, and went out, without making any more noise than if he had been walking barefooted upon moss.

Besides the Jondrette woman was still fumbling over her old iron.

Once out of the house, he went to the Rue du Petit Banquier.

He was about midway of that street near a very low wall which he could have stepped over in some places and which bordered a broad field, he was walking slowly, absorbed in his thoughts as he was, and the snow deafened his steps; all at once he heard voices talking very near him. He turned his head, the street was empty, there was nobody in it, it was broad daylight, and yet he heard voices distinctly.

It occurred to him to look over this wall.

There were in fact two men there with their backs to the wall, seated in the snow, and talking in a low tone.

These two forms were unknown to him, one was a bearded man in a blouse, and the other a long-haired man in tatters. The bearded man had on a Greek cap, the other was bare-headed, and there was snow in his hair.

By bending his head over above them, Marius could hear.

The long-haired one jogged the other with his elbow, and said:

"With Patron-Minette, it can't fail."

"Do you think so?" said the bearded one; and the long-haired one replied:

"It will be a *fafiot* of five hundred *balles* for each of us, and the worst that can happen: five years, six years, ten years at most!"

The other answered hesitatingly, shivering under his Greek cap:

"Yes, it is a real thing. We can't go against such things."

"I tell you that the affair can't fail," replied the long-haired one. "Father What's-his-name's *maringotte* will be harnessed."

Then they began to talk about a melodrama which they had seen the evening before at La Gaîté.

Marius went on his way.

It seemed to him that the obscure words of these men, so strangely hidden behind that wall, and crouching down in the snow, were not perhaps without some connection with Jondrette's terrible projects. That must be *the affair*.

He went towards the Faubourg Saint Marceau, and asked at the first shop in his way where he could find a commissary of police.

Number 14, Rue de Pontoise, was pointed out to him.

Marius went thither.

Passing a baker's shop, he bought a two-sou loaf and ate it, foreseeing that he would have no dinner.

On his way he rendered to Providence its due. He thought that if he had not given his five francs to the Jondrette girl in the morning, he would have followed M. Leblanc's fiacre, and consequently known nothing of this, so that there would have been no obstacle to the ambuscade of the Jondrettes, and M. Leblanc would have been lost, and doubtless his daughter with him.

XIV

IN WHICH A POLICE OFFICER GIVES A LAWYER TWO FISTICUFFS

On reaching Number 14, Rue de Pontoise, he went upstairs and asked for the commissary of police.

"The commissary of police is not in," said one of the office boys; "but there is an inspector who answers for him. Would you like to speak to him? is it urgent?"

"Yes," said Marius.

The office boy introduced him into the commissary's private room. A man of tall stature was standing there, behind a railing, in front of a stove, and holding up with both hands the flaps of a huge overcoat with three capes. He had a square face, a thin and firm mouth, very fierce, bushy, greyish whiskers, and an eye that would turn your pockets inside out. You might have said of this eye, not that it penetrated, but that it ransacked.

This man's appearance was not much less ferocious or formidable than Jondrette's; it is sometimes no less startling to meet the dog than the wolf.

"What do you wish?" said he to Marius, without adding monsieur.

"The commissary of police?"

"He is absent. I answer for him."

"It is a very secret affair."

"Speak, then."

"And very urgent."

"Then speak quickly."

This man, calm and abrupt, was at the same time alarming and reassuring. He inspired fear and confidence. Marius related his adventure.—That a person whom he only knew by sight was to be drawn into an ambuscade that very evening; that occupying the room next the place, he, Marius Pontmercy, attorney, had heard the whole plot through the partition; that the scoundrel who had contrived the plot was named Jondrette; that he had accomplices, probably prowlers of the barrières, among others a certain Panchaud, alias Printanier, alias Bigrenaille; that Jondrette's daughters would stand watch; that there was no means of warning the threatened man, as not even his name was known; and finally, that all this was to be done at six o'clock that evening, at the most desolate spot on the Boulevard de l'Hôpital, in the house numbered 50–52.

At that number the inspector raised his head, and said coolly:

"It is then in the room at the end of the hall?"

"Exactly," said Marius, and he added, "Do you know that house?"

The inspector remained silent a moment, then answered, warming the heel of his boot at the door of the stove:

"It seems so."

He continued between his teeth, speaking less to Marius than to his cravat.

"There ought to be a dash of Patron-Minette in this."

That word struck Marius.

"Patron-Minette," said he. "Indeed, I heard that word pronounced."

And he related to the inspector the dialogue between the long-haired man and the bearded man in the snow behind the wall on the Rue du Petit Banquier.

The inspector muttered:

"The long-haired one must be Brujon, and the bearded one must be Demi-Liard, alias Deux-Milliards."

He had dropped his eyes again, and was considering.

"As to the Father What's-his-name, I have a suspicion of who he is. There, I have burnt my coat. They always make too much fire in these cursed stoves. Number 50—52. Old Gorbeau property."

Then he looked at Marius:

"You have seen only this bearded man and this long-haired man?"

"And Panchaud."

"You did not see a sort of little devilish rat prowling about there?"

"No."

"Nor a great, big, clumsy heap, like the elephant in the Jardin des Plantes?"

"No."

"Nor a villain who has the appearance of an old red cue?"

"No."

"As to the fourth nobody sees him, not even his helpers, clerks, and agents. It is not very surprising that you did not see him."

"No. What are all these beings?" inquired Marius.

The inspector answered:

"And then it is not their hour."

He relapsed into silence, then resumed:

"No. 50—52. I know the shanty. Impossible to hide ourselves in the interior without the artists perceiving us, then they would leave and break up the play. They are so modest! the public annoys them. None of that, none of that. I want to hear them sing, and make them dance."

This monologue finished, he turned towards Marius and asked him, looking steadily at him:

"Will you be afraid?"

"Of what?" said Marius.

"Of these men?"

"No more than you!" replied Marius rudely, who began to notice that this police spy had not yet called him monsieur.

The inspector looked at Marius still more steadily and continued with a sententious solemnity:

"You speak now like a brave man and an honest man. Courage does not fear crime, and honesty does not fear authority."

Marius interrupted him:

"That is well enough; but what are you going to do?"

The inspector merely answered:

"The lodgers in that house have latch-keys to get in with at night. You must have one?"

"Yes," said Marius.

"Have you it with you?"

"Yes."

"Give it to me," said the inspector.

Marius took his key from his waistcoat, handed it to the inspector, and added:

"If you trust me you will come in force."

The inspector threw a glance upon Marius such as Voltaire would have thrown upon a provincial academician who had proposed a rhyme to him; with a single movement he plunged both his hands, which were enormous, into the two immense pockets of his overcoat, and took out two small steel pistols, of the kind called fisticuffs. He presented them to Marius, saying hastily and abruptly:

"Take these. Go back home. Hide yourself in your room; let them think you have gone out. They are loaded. Each with two balls. You will watch; there is a hole in the wall, as you have told me. The men will come. Let them go on a little. When you deem the affair at a point, and when it is time to stop it, you will fire off a pistol. Not too soon. The rest is my affair. A pistol shot in the air, into the ceiling, no matter where. Above all, not too soon. Wait till the consummation is commenced; you are a lawyer, you know what that is."

Marius took the pistols and put them in the side pocket of his coat.

"They make a bunch that way, they show," said the inspector. "Put them in your fobs rather."

Marius hid the pistols in his fobs.

"Now," pursued the inspector, "there is not a minute to be lost by anybody. What time is it? Half past two. It is at seven?"

"Six o'clock," said Marius.

"I have time enough," continued the inspector, "but I have only enough. Forget nothing of what I have told you. Bang. A pistol shot."

"Be assured," answered Marius.

And as Marius placed his hand on the latch of the door to go out, the inspector called to him:

"By the way, if you need me between now and then, come or send here. You will ask for Inspector Javert."

XV

JONDRETTE MAKES HIS PURCHASE

A FEW moments afterwards, towards three o'clock, Courfeyrac happened to pass along the Rue Mouffetard in company with Bossuet. The snow was falling still faster, and filled the air. Bossuet was just saying to Courfeyrac:

"To see all these snowflakes falling, one would say that there is a swarm of white butterflies in the sky." All at once Bossuet perceived Marius, who was going up the street towards the barrière with a very peculiar appearance.

"Hold on, Marius," said Bossuet.

"I saw him," said Courfeyrac. "Don't speak to him."

"Why?"

"He is busy."

"At what?"

"Don't you see how he looks?"

"What look?"

"He has the appearance of a man who is following somebody."

"That is true," said Bossuet.

"And see what eyes he is making!" added Courfeyrac.

"But who the devil is he following?"

"Some deary-sweety-flowery-bonnet! he is in love."

"But," observed Bossuet, "I do not see any deary, nor any sweety, nor any flowery bonnet in the street. There is no woman."

Courfeyrac looked and exclaimed:

"He is following a man!"

In fact a man, with a cap on his head, and whose grey beard they distinguished although only his back could be seen, was walking some twenty paces in advance of Marius.

This man was dressed in a new overcoat, which was too large for him, and a horrid pair of pantaloons in tatters and black with mud.

Bossuet burst out laughing.

"Who is that man?"

"He?" replied Courfeyrac, "he is a poet. Poets are fond of wearing the trousers of a rabbit-skin pedlar, and the coat of a peer of France."

"Let us see where Marius is going," said Bossuet, "let us see where this man is going, let us follow them, eh?"

"Bossuet!" exclaimed Courfeyrac, "Eagle of Meaux! you are a prodigious fool. Follow a man who is following a man!"

They went on their way.

Marius had in fact seen Jondrette passing along the Rue Mouffetard and was watching him.

Jondrette went straight on without suspecting that there was now an eye fixed upon him.

He left the Rue Mouffetard, and Marius saw him go into one of the most wretched places on the Rue Gracieuse; he stayed there about a quarter of an hour, and then returned to the Rue Mouffetard. He stopped at a hardware store, which there was in those times at the corner of the Rue Pierre Lombard, and, a few minutes afterwards, Marius saw him come out of the shop holding in his hand a large cold chisel with a white wooden handle which he concealed under his coat. At the upper end of the Rue de Petit Gentilly, he turned to the left and walked rapidly to the Rue du Petit Banquier. Night was falling; the snow which had ceased to fall for a moment was beginning again; Marius hid just at the corner of the Rue du Petit Banquier, which was solitary, as usual, and did not follow Jondrette further. It was fortunate that he did, for, on reaching the low wall where Marius had heard the long-haired man and the bearded man talking, Jondrette turned around, made sure that nobody was following him or saw him, then stepped over the wall, and disappeared.

The grounds which this wall bounded communicated with the rear court of an old livery stable-keeper of bad repute, who had failed, but who had still a few old vehicles under his sheds.

Marius thought it best to take advantage of Jondrette's absence to get home; besides it was getting late; every evening, Ma'am Bougon, on going out to wash her dishes in the city, was in the habit of closing the house door, which was always locked at dusk; Marius had given his key to the inspector of police; it was important, therefore, that he should make haste.

Evening had come; night had almost closed in; there was now but one spot in the horizon or in the whole sky which was lighted by the sun; that was the moon.

She was rising red behind the low dome of La Salpêtrière.

Marius returned to No. 50–52 with rapid strides. The door was still open, when he arrived. He ascended the stairs on tip-toe, and glided along the wall of the hall as far as his room. This hall, it will be remembered, was lined on both sides by garrets, which were all at that time empty and to let. Ma'am Bougon usually left the doors open. As he passed by one of these doors, Marius thought he perceived in the unoccupied cell four motionless heads, which were made dimly visible by a remnant of daylight falling through the little window. Marius, not wishing to be seen, did not endeavour to see. He succeeded in getting into his room without being perceived and without any noise. It was time. A moment afterwards, he heard Ma'am Bougon going out and closing the door of the house.

XVI

IN WHICH WILL BE FOUND THE SONG TO AN ENGLISH AIR IN FASHION IN 1832

MARIUS sat down on his bed. It might have been half-past five o'clock. A half-hour only separated him from what was to come. He heard his arteries beat as one hears the ticking of a watch in the dark. He thought of this double march that was going on that moment in the darkness, crime advancing on the one hand, justice coming on the other. He was not afraid, but he could not think without a sort of shudder of the things which were so soon to take place. To him, as to all those whom some surprising adventure has suddenly befallen, this whole day seemed but a dream; and, to assure himself that he was not the prey of a nightmare, he had to feel the chill of the two steel pistols in his fob-pockets.

It was not now snowing; the moon, growing brighter and brighter, was getting clear of the haze, and its light, mingled with the white reflection from the fallen snow, gave the room a twilight appearance.

There was a light in the Jondrette den. Marius saw the hole in the partition shine with a red gleam which appeared to him bloody.

He was sure that this gleam could hardly be produced by a candle. However, there was no movement in their room, nobody was stirring there, nobody spoke, not a breath, the stillness was icy and deep, and save for that light he could have believed that he was beside a sepulchre.

Marius took his boots off softly, and pushed them under his bed.

Some minutes passed. Marius heard the lower door turn on its hinges; a heavy and rapid step ascended the stairs and passed along the corridor, the latch of the garret was noisily lifted; Jondrette came in.

Several voices were heard immediately. The whole family was in the garret. Only they kept silence in the absence of the master, like the cubs in the absence of the wolf.

"It is me," said he.

"Good evening, *pèremuche*," squeaked the daughters.

"Well!" said the mother.

"All goes to a charm," answered Jondrette, "but my feet are as cold as a dog's. Good, that is right, you are dressed up. You must be able to inspire confidence."

"All ready to go out."

"You will forget nothing of what I told you! you will do the whole of it?"

"Rest assured about that."

"Because—" said Jondrette. And he did not finish his sentence. Marius heard him put something heavy on the table, probably the chisel which he had bought.

"Ah, ha!" said Jondrette, "have you been eating here?"

"Yes," said the mother, "I have had three big potatoes and some salt. I took advantage of the fire to cook them."

"Well," replied Jondrette, "to-morrow I will take you to dine with me. There will be a duck and the accompaniments. You shall dine like Charles X.; everything is going well?"

Then he added, lowering his voice:

"The mouse-trap is open. The cats are ready."

He lowered his voice still more, and said:

"Put that into the fire."

Marius heard a sound of charcoal, as if somebody was striking it with pincers or some iron tool, and Jondrette continued:

"Have you greased the hinges of the door, so that they shall not make any noise?"

"Yes," answered the mother.

"What time is it?"

"Six o'clock, almost. The half has just struck on Saint Médard."

"The devil!" said Jondrette, "the girls must go and stand watch. Come here, you children, and listen to me."

There was a whispering.

Jondrette's voice rose again:

"Has Bougon gone out?"

"Yes," said the mother.

"Are you sure there is nobody at home in our neighbour's room?"

"He has not been back to-day, and you know that it is his dinner time."

"You are sure?"

"Sure."

"It is all the same," replied Jondrette; "there is no harm in going to see whether he is at home. Daughter, take the candle and go."

Marius dropped on his hands and knees, and crept noiselessly under the bed.

Hardly had he concealed himself, when he perceived a light through the cracks of his door.

"P'pa," cried a voice, "he has gone out."

He recognised the voice of the elder girl.

"Have you gone in?" asked the father.

"No," answered the girl; "but as his key is in the door, he has gone out."

The father cried:

"Go in just the same."

The door opened, and Marius saw the tall girl come in with a candle. She had the same appearance as in the morning, except that she was still more horrible in this light.

She walked straight towards the bed. Marius had a moment of inexpressible anxiety, but there was a mirror nailed on the wall near the bed; it was to that she was going. She stretched up on tiptoe and looked at herself in it. A sound of old iron rattling was heard in the next room.

She smoothed her hair with the palm of her hand, and smiled at the mirror, singing the while in her broken sepulchral voice:

> Nos amours ont duré toute une semaine,
> Mais que du bonheur les instants sont courts!
> S'adorer huit jours, c'était bien la peine!
> Le temps des amours devrait durer toujours!
> Devrait durer toujours! devrait durer toujours!

Meanwhile Marius was trembling. It seemed impossible to him that she should not hear his breathing.

She went to the window and looked out, speaking aloud in her half-crazy way.

"How ugly Paris is when he puts a white shirt on!" said she.

She returned to the mirror and renewed her grimaces, taking alternately front and the three-quarter views of herself.

"Well," cried her father, "what are you doing now?"

"I am looking under the bed and the furniture," answered she, continuing to arrange her hair; "there is nobody here."

"Booby!" howled the father. "Here immediately, and let us lose no time."

"I am coming! I am coming!" said she. "One has no time for anything in their shanty."

She hummed:

> Vous me quittez pour aller à la gloire,
> Mon triste cœur suivra partout vos pas.

She cast a last glance at the mirror, and went out, shutting the door after her.

A moment afterwards, Marius heard the sound of the bare feet of the two young girls in the passage, and the voice of Jondrette crying to them.

"Pay attention, now! one towards the barrière, the other at the corner of the Rue du Petit Banquier. Don't lose sight of the house door a minute, and if you see the least thing, here immediately! tumble along! You have a key to come in with."

The elder daughter muttered:

"To stand sentry barefoot in the snow!"

"To-morrow you shall have boots of beetle colour silk!" said the father.

They went down the stairs, and, a few seconds afterwards, the sound of the lower door shutting announced that they had gone out.

There were now in the house only Marius and the Jondrettes, and probably also the mysterious beings of whom Marius had caught a glimpse in the twilight behind the door of the un-tenanted garret.

XVII

USE OF MARIUS' FIVE-FRANC PIECE

MARIUS judged that the time had come to resume his place at his observatory. In a twinkling, and with the agility of his age, he was at the hole in the partition.

He looked in.

The interior of the Jondrette apartment presented a singular appearance, and Marius found the explanation of the strange light which he had noticed. A candle was burning in a verdi-grised candlestick, but it was not that which really lighted the room. The entire den was, as it were, illuminated by the reflec-tion of a large sheet iron furnace in the fire-place, which was filled with lighted charcoal. The fire which the female Jondrette had made ready in the daytime. The charcoal was burning and the furnace was red hot, a blue flame danced over it and helped to show the form of the chisel bought by Jondrette in the Rue Pierre Lombard, which was growing ruddy among the coals. In a corner near the door, and arranged as if for anticipated use, were two heaps which appeared to be, one a heap of old iron, the other a heap of ropes. All this would have made one, who had known nothing of what was going forward, waver between a very sinister idea and a very simple idea. The room thus lighted up seemed rather a smithy than a mouth of hell; but Jondrette, in that glare, had rather the appearance of a demon than of a blacksmith.

The heat of the glowing coals was such that the candle upon the table melted on the side towards the furnace and was burning fastest on that side. An old copper dark lantern, worthy of Diogenes turned Cartouche, stood upon the mantel.

The furnace, which was set into the fire-place, beside the almost extinguished embers, sent its smoke into the flue of the chimney and exhaled no odour.

The moon, shining through the four panes of the window, threw its whiteness into the ruddy and flaming garret; and to Marius' poetic mind, a dreamer even in the moment of action, it was like a thought of heaven mingled with the shapeless night-mares of earth.

A breath of air, coming through the broken square, helped to dissipate the charcoal odour and to conceal the furnace.

The Jondrette lair was, if the reader remembers what we have said of the Gorbeau house, admirably chosen for the theatre of a deed of darkness and violence, and for the concealment of a crime. It was the most retired room of the most isolated house of the most solitary boulevard in Paris. If ambuscade had not existed, it would have been invented there.

The whole depth of a house and a multitude of untenanted rooms separated this hole from the boulevard and its only window opened upon waste fields inclosed with walls and palisade fences.

Jondrette had lighted his pipe, sat down on the dismantled chair, and was smoking. His wife was speaking to him in a low tone.

If Marius had been Courfeyrac, that is to say, one of those men who laugh at every opportunity in life, he would have burst with laughter when his eye fell upon this woman. She had on a black hat with plumes somewhat similar to the hats of the heralds-at-arms at the consecration of Charles X., an immense tartan shawl over her knit skirt, and the man's shoes which her daughter had disdained in the morning. It was this toilet which had drawn from Jondrette the exclamation: *Good! you are dressed up! you have done well! You must be able to inspire confidence!*

As to Jondrette, he had not taken off the new surtout, too large for him, which M. Leblanc had given him, and his costume continued to offer that contrast between the coat and pantaloons which constituted in Courfeyrac's eyes the ideal of a poet.

Suddenly Jondrette raised his voice:

"By the way, now, I think of it. In such weather as this he will come in a fiacre. Light the lantern, take it, and go down. You will stay there behind the lower door. The moment you hear the carriage stop, you will open immediately, he will come up, you will light him up the stairs and above the hall, and when he comes in here, you will go down again immediately, pay the driver, and send the fiacre away."

"And the money?" asked the woman.

Jondrette fumbled in his trousers, and handed her five francs.

"What is that?" she exclaimed.

Jondrette answered with dignity:——

"It is the monarch which our neighbour gave this morning." And he added:——

"Do you know? we must have two chairs here."

"What for?"

"To sit in."

Marius felt a shiver run down his back on hearing the woman make this quiet reply:——

"Pardieu! I will get our neighbour's."

And with rapid movement she opened the door of the den, and went out into the hall.

Marius physically had not the time to get down from the bureau, and go and hide himself under the bed.

"Take the candle," cried Jondrette.

"No," said she, "that would bother me; I have two chairs to bring. It is moonlight."

Marius heard the heavy hand of mother Jondrette groping after his key in the dark. The door opened. He stood nailed to his place by apprehension and stupor.

The woman came in.

The gable window let in a ray of moonlight, between two great sheets of shadow. One of these sheets of shadow entirely covered the wall against which Marius was leaning, so as to conceal him.

The mother Jondrette raised her eyes, did not see Marius, took the two chairs, the only chairs which Marius had, and went out, slamming the door noisily behind her.

She went back into the den.

"Here are the two chairs."

"And here is the lantern," said the husband. "Go down quick."

She hastily obeyed, and Jondrette was left alone.

He arranged the two chairs on the two sides of the table, turned the chisel over in the fire, put an old screen in front of the fire-place, which concealed the furnace, then went to the corner where the heap of ropes was, and stooped down, as if to examine something. Marius then perceived that what he had taken for a shapeless heap, was a rope ladder, very well made, with wooden rounds, and two large hooks to hang it by.

This ladder and a few big tools, actual masses of iron, which were thrown upon the pile of old iron heaped up behind the door, were not in the Jondrette den in the morning, and had evidently been brought there in the afternoon, during Marius' absence.

"Those are smith's tools," thought Marius.

Had Marius been a little better informed in this line, he would have recognised, in what he took for smith's tools, certain instruments capable of picking a lock or forcing a door and others capable of cutting or hacking,—the two families of sinister tools, which thieves call *cadets* and *fauchants*.

The fire-place and the table, with the two chairs, were exactly opposite Marius. The furnace was hidden; the room was now lighted only by the candle; the least thing upon the table or the mantel made a great shadow. A broken water-pitcher masked the half of one wall. There was in the room a calm which was inexpressibly hideous and threatening. The approach of some appalling thing could be felt.

Jondrette had let his pipe go out—a sure sign that he was intensely absorbed—and had come back and sat down. The candle made the savage ends and corners of his face stand out prominently. There were contractions of his brows, and abrupt openings of his right hand, as if he were replying to the last counsels of a dark interior monologue. In one of these obscure replies which he was making to himself, he drew the table drawer out quickly towards him, took out a long carving knife which was hidden there, and tried its edge on his nail. This done, he put the knife back into the drawer, and shut it.

Marius, for his part, grasped the pistol which was in his right fob pocket, took it out, and cocked it.

The pistol in cocking gave a little, clear, sharp sound.

Jondrette started, and half rose from his chair.

"Who is there?" cried he.

Marius held his breath; Jondrette listened a moment, then began to laugh, saying:——

"What a fool I am! It is the partition cracking."

Marius kept the pistol in his hand.

XVIII

MARIUS' TWO CHAIRS FACE EACH OTHER

JUST then the distant and melancholy vibration of a bell shook the windows. Six o'clock struck on Saint Médard.

Jondrette marked each stroke with a nod of his head. At the sixth stroke, he snuffed the candle with his fingers.

Then he began to walk about the room, listened in the hall, walked, listened again: "Provided he comes!" muttered he; then he returned to his chair.

He had hardly sat down when the door opened.

The mother Jondrette had opened it, and stood in the hall making a horrible, amiable grimace, which was lighted up from beneath by one of the holes of the dark lantern.

"Walk in," said she.

"Walk in, my benefactor," repeated Jondrette, rising precipitately.

Monsieur Leblanc appeared.

He had an air of serenity which made him singularly venerable.

He laid four louis upon the table.

"Monsieur Fabantou," said he, "that is for your rent and your pressing wants. We will see about the rest."

"God reward you, my generous benefactor!" said Jondrette, and rapidly approaching his wife:

"Send away the fiacre!"

She slipped away, while her husband was lavishing bows and offering a chair to Monsieur Leblanc. A moment afterwards she came back and whispered in his ear:

"It is done."

The snow which had been falling ever since morning, was so deep that they had not heard the fiacre arrive, and did not hear it go away.

Meanwhile Monsieur Leblanc had taken a seat.

Jondrette had taken possession of the other chair opposite Monsieur Leblanc.

Now, to form an idea of the scene which follows, let the reader call to mind the chilly night, the solitudes of La Salpêtrière covered with snow, and white in the moonlight, like immense shrouds, the flickering light of the street lamps here and there reddening these tragic boulevards and the long rows of black elms, not a passer perhaps within a mile around, the Gorbeau tenement at its deepest degree of silence, horror, and night, in that tenement, in the midst of these solitudes, in the midst of this darkness, the vast Jondrette garret lighted by a candle, and in this den two men seated at a table, Monsieur Leblanc tranquil, Jondrette smiling and terrible, his wife, the wolf dam, in a corner, and, behind the partition, Marius, invisible, alert, losing no word, losing no movement, his eye on the watch, the pistol in his grasp.

Marius, moreover, was experiencing nothing but an emotion of horror, not fear. He clasped the butt of the pistol, and felt reassured. "I shall stop this wretch when I please," thought he.

He felt that the police was somewhere near by in ambush, awaiting the signal agreed upon, and all ready to stretch out its arm.

He hoped, moreover, that from this terrible meeting between Jondrette and Monsieur Leblanc some light would be thrown upon all that he was interested to know.

XIX
THE DISTRACTIONS OF DARK CORNERS

No sooner was Monsieur Leblanc seated than he turned his eyes towards the empty pallets.

"How does the poor little injured girl do?" he inquired.

"Badly," answered Jondrette with a doleful yet grateful smile, "very badly, my worthy monsieur. Her eldest sister has taken her to the Bourbe to have her arm dressed. You will see them, they will be back directly."

"Madame Fabantou appears to me much better?" resumed Monsieur Leblanc, casting his eyes upon the grotesque accoutrement of the female Jondrette, who, standing between him and the door, as if she were already guarding the exit, was looking at him in a threatening and almost a defiant posture.

"She is dying," said Jondrette. "But you see, monsieur! she has so much courage, that woman! She is not a woman, she is an ox."

The woman, touched by the compliment, retorted with the smirk of a flattered monster:

"You are always too kind to me, Monsieur Jondrette."

"Jondrette!" said M. Leblanc, "I thought that your name was Fabantou?"

"Fabantou or Jondrette!" replied the husband hastily. "Sobriquet as an artist!"

And, directing a shrug of the shoulders towards his wife, which M. Leblanc did not see, he continued with an emphatic and caressing tone of voice:

"Ah! how long we have always got along together, this poor dear and I! What would be left to us, if it were not for that? We are so unfortunate, my respected monsieur! We have arms, no labour! We have courage, no work! I do not know how the government arranges it, but, upon my word of honour, I am no jacobin, monsieur, I am no brawler, I wish them no harm, but if I were the ministers, upon my most sacred word, it would go differently. Now, for example, I wanted to have my girls learn the trade of making card boxes. You will say: What! a trade? Yes! a trade! a simple trade! a living! What a fall, my benefactor! What a degradation, when one has been what we were! Alas! we have nothing left from our days of prosperity! Nothing but one single thing, a painting, to which I cling, but yet which I shall have to part with, for we must live! item, we must live!"

While Jondrette was talking, with an apparent disorder which detracted nothing from the crafty and cunning expression of his physiognomy, Marius raised his eyes, and perceived at the back of the room somebody whom he had not before seen. A man had come in so noiselessly that nobody had heard the door turn on its hinges. This man had a knit woollen waistcoat of violet colour, old, worn-out, stained, cut, and showing gaps at all its folds, full trousers of cotton velvet, socks on his feet, no shirt, his neck bare, his arms bare and tattooed, and his face stained black. He sat down in silence and with folded arms on the nearest bed, and as he kept behind the woman, he was distinguished only with difficulty.

That kind of magnetic instinct which warns the eye made M. Leblanc turn almost at the same time with Marius. He could not help a movement of surprise, which did not escape Jondrette:

"Ah! I see!" exclaimed Jondrette, buttoning up his coat with a complacent air, "you are looking at your overcoat. It's a fit! my faith, it's a fit!"

"Who is that man?" said M. Leblanc.

"That man?" said Jondrette, "that is a neighbour. Pay no attention to him."

The neighbour had a singular appearance. However, factories of chemical products abound in Faubourg Saint Marceau. Many machinists might have their faces blacked. The whole person of M. Leblanc, moreover, breathed a candid and intrepid confidence. He resumed:

"Pardon me; what were you saying to me, Monsieur Fabantou?"

"I was telling you, monsieur and dear patron," replied Jondrette, leaning his elbows on the table, and gazing at M. Leblanc with fixed and tender eyes, similar to the eyes of a boa constrictor, "I was telling you that I had a picture to sell."

A slight noise was made at the door. A second man entered, and sat down on the bed behind the female Jondrette. He had his arms bare, like the first, and a mask of ink or of soot.

Although this man had, literally, slipped into the room, he could not prevent M. Leblanc from perceiving him.

"Do not mind them," said Jondrette. "They are people of the house. I was telling you, then, that I have a valuable painting left. Here, monsieur, look."

He got up, went to the wall, at the foot of which stood the panel of which we have spoken, and turned it round, still leaving it resting against the wall. It was something, in fact, that resembled a picture, and which the candle scarcely revealed. Marius could make nothing out of it, Jondrette being between him and the picture; he merely caught a glimpse of a coarse daub, with a sort of principal personage, coloured in the crude and glaring style of strolling panoramas and paintings upon screens.

"What is that?" asked M. Leblanc.

Jondrette exclaimed:

"A painting by a master; a picture of great price, my benefactor! I cling to it as to my two daughters, it calls up memories to me! but I have told you, and I cannot unsay it, I am so unfortunate that I would part with it."

Whether by chance, or whether there was some beginning of distrust, while examining the picture, M. Leblanc glanced towards the back of the room. There were now four men there, three seated on the bed, one standing near the door-casing; all four bare-armed, motionless, and with blackened faces. One of those who were on the bed was leaning against the wall, with his eyes closed, and one would have said he was asleep. This one was old; his white hair over his black face was horrible. The two others appeared young; one was bearded, the other had long hair. None of them had shoes on; those who did not have socks were barefooted.

Jondrette noticed that M. Leblanc's eye was fixed upon these men.

"They are friends. They live near by," said he. "They are dark because they work in charcoal. They are chimney doctors. Do not occupy your mind with them, my benefactor, but buy my picture. Take pity on my misery. I shall not sell it to you at a high price. How much do you estimate it worth?"

"But," said M. Leblanc, looking Jondrette full in the face and like a man who puts himself on his guard, "this is some tavern sign, it is worth about three francs."

Jondrette answered calmly:

"Have you your pocket-book here? I will be satisfied with a thousand crowns."

M. Leblanc rose to his feet, placed his back to the wall, and ran his eye rapidly over the room. He had Jondrette at his left on the side towards the window, and his wife and the four men at his right on the side towards the door. The four men did not stir, and had not even the appearance of seeing him; Jondrette had begun again to talk in a plaintive key, with his eyes so wild and his tones so mournful that M. Leblanc might have thought that he had before his eyes nothing more nor less than a man gone crazy from misery.

"If you do not buy my picture, dear benefactor," said Jondrette, "I am without resources, I have only to throw myself into the river. When I think that I wanted to have my two girls learn to work on cardboard demi-fine, cardboard work for gift-boxes. Well! they must have a table with a board at the bottom so that the glasses shall not fall on the ground, they must have a furnace made on purpose, a pot with three compartments for the different degrees of strength which the paste must have according to whether it is used for wood, for paper, or for cloth, a knife to cut the pasteboard, a gauge to adjust it, a hammer for the stamps, pincers, the devil, how do I know what else? and all this to earn four sous a day! and work fourteen hours! and every box passes through the girl's hands thirteen times! and wetting the paper! and to stain nothing! and to keep the paste warm! the devil! I tell you! four sous a day! how do you think one can live?"

While speaking Jondrette did not look at M. Leblanc, who was watching him. M. Leblanc's eye was fixed upon Jondrette, and Jondrette's eye upon the door, Marius' breathless attention went from one to the other. M. Leblanc appeared to ask himself, "Is this an idiot?" Jondrette repeated two or three times with all sorts of varied inflections in the drawling and begging style: "I can only throw myself into the river! I went down three steps for that the other day by the side of the bridge of Austerlitz!"

Suddenly his dull eye lighted up with a hideous glare, this little man straightened up and became horrifying, he took a step towards M. Leblanc and cried to him in a voice of thunder:

"But all this is not the question! do you know me?"

XX
THE AMBUSCADE

THE door of the garret had been suddenly flung open, disclosing three men in blue blouses with black paper masks. The first was spare and had a long iron-bound cudgel; the second, who was a sort of colossus, held by the middle of the handle, with the axe down, a butcher's pole-axe. The third, a broad-shouldered man, not so thin as the first, nor so heavy as the second, held in his clenched fist an enormous key stolen from some prison door.

It appeared that it was the arrival of these men for which Jondrette was waiting. A rapid dialogue commenced between him and the man with the cudgel, the spare man.

"Is everything ready?" said Jondrette.

"Yes," answered the spare man.

"Where is Montparnasse then?"

"The young primate stopped to chat with your daughter."

"Which one?"

"The elder."

"Is there a fiacre below?"

"Yes."

"The *maringotte* is ready?"

"Ready."

"With two good horses?"

"Excellent."

"It is waiting where I said it should wait?"

"Yes."

"Good," said Jondrette

M. Leblanc was very pale. He looked over everything in the room about him like a man who understands into what he has fallen, and his head, directed in turn towards all the heads which surrounded him, moved on his neck with an attentive and astonished slowness, but there was nothing in his manner which resembled fear. He had made an extemporised intrenchment of the table; and this man who, the moment before, had the appearance only of a good old man, had suddenly become a sort of athlete, and placed his powerful fist upon the back of his chair with a surprising and formidable gesture.

This old man, so firm and so brave before so great a peril, seemed to be one of those natures who are courageous as they are good, simply and naturally. The father of a woman that we love is never a stranger to us. Marius felt proud of this unknown man.

Three of the men of whom Jondrette had said: they are *chimney doctors*, had taken from the heap of old iron, one a large pair of shears, another a steelyard bar, the third a hammer, and placed themselves before the door without saying a word. The old man was still on the bed, and had merely opened his eyes. The woman Jondrette was sitting beside him.

Marius thought that in a few seconds more the time would come to interfere, and he raised his right hand towards the ceiling, in the direction of the hall, ready to let off his pistol-shot.

Jondrette, after his colloquy with the man who had the cudgel, turned again towards M. Leblanc and repeated his question, accompanying it with that low, smothered, and terrible laugh of his:

"You do not recognise me, then?"

M. Leblanc looked him in the face, and answered:

"No."

Then Jondrette came up to the table. He leaned forward over the candle, folding his arms, and pushing his angular and ferocious jaws up towards the calm face of M. Leblanc, as nearly as he could without forcing him to draw back, and in that posture, like a wild beast just about to bite, he cried:

"My name is not Fabantou, my name is not Jondrette, my name is Thénardier! I am the innkeeper of Montfermeil! do you understand me? Thénardier! now do you know me?"

An imperceptible flush passed over M. Leblanc's forehead, and he answered without a tremor or elevation of voice, and with his usual placidness:

"No more than before."

Marius did not hear this answer. Could anybody have seen him at that moment in that darkness, he would have seen that he was haggard, astounded, and thunderstruck. When Jondrette had said: *My name is Thénardier*, Marius had trembled in every limb, and supported himself against the wall as if he had felt the chill of a swordblade through his heart. Then his right arm, which was just ready to fire the signal shot, dropped slowly down, and at the moment that Jondrette had repeated: *Do you understand me, Thénardier?* Marius' nerveless fingers had almost dropped the pistol. Jondrette, in unveiling who he was, had not moved M. Leblanc, but he had completely unnerved Marius. That name of Thénardier, which M. Leblanc did not seem to know, Marius knew. Remember what that name was to him! that name he had worn on his heart, written in his father's will! he carried it in the innermost place of his thoughts, in the holiest spot of his memory, in that sacred command: "A man named Thénardier saved my life. If my son should meet him, he will do him all the good he can." That name, we remember, was one of the devotions of his soul; he mingled it with the name of his father in his worship. What! here was Thénardier, here was that Thénardier, here was that innkeeper of Montfermeil, for whom he had so long and so vainly sought! He had found him at last, and how? this saviour of his father was a bandit! this man, to whom he, Marius, burned to devote himself, was a monster! this deliverer of Colonel Pontmercy was in the actual commission of a crime, the shape of which Marius did not yet see very distinctly, but which looked like an assassination! and upon whom, Great God! what a fatality! what a bitter mockery of

Fate! His father from the depths of his coffin commanded him to do all the good he could to Thénardier; for four years Marius had had no other thought than to acquit this debt of his father, and the moment that he was about to cause a brigand to be seized by justice, in the midst of a crime, destiny called to him: that is Thénardier! his father's life, saved in a storm of grape upon the heroic field of Waterloo, he was at last about to reward this man for, and to reward him with the scaffold! He had resolved, if ever he found this Thénardier, to accost him in no other wise than by throwing himself at his feet, and now he found him indeed, but to deliver him to the executioner! his father said to him: Aid Thénardier! and he was answering that adored and holy voice by crushing Thénardier! presenting as a spectacle to his father in his tomb, the man who had snatched him from death at the peril of his life, executed in the Place St. Jacques by the act of his son, this Marius to whom he had bequeathed this man! And what a mockery to have worn so long upon his breast the last wishes of his father, written by his hand, only to act so frightfully contrary to them! but on the other hand, to see him ambuscade and not prevent it! to condemn the victim and spare the assassin, could he be bound to any gratitude towards such a wretch? all the ideas which Marius had had for the last four years were, as it were, pierced through and through by this unexpected blow. He shuddered. Everything depended upon him. He held in his hand, they all unconscious, those beings who were moving there before his eyes. If he fired the pistol, M. Leblanc was saved and Thénardier was lost; if he did not, M. Leblanc was sacrificed, and, perhaps, Thénardier escaped. To hurl down the one or to let the other fall! remorse on either hand. What was to be done? which should he choose? be wanting to his most imperious memories, to so many deep resolutions, to his most sacred duty, to that most venerated paper! be wanting to his father's will, or suffer a crime to be accomplished? He seemed on the one hand to hear "his Ursula" entreating him for her father, and on the other the colonel commending Thénardier to him. He felt that he was mad. His knees gave way beneath him; and he had not even time to deliberate, with such fury was the scene which he had before his eyes rushing forward. It was like a whirlwind, which he had thought himself master of, and which was carrying him away. He was on the point of fainting.

Meanwhile Thénardier, we will call him by no other name henceforth, was walking to and fro before the table in a sort of bewilderment and frenzied triumph.

He clutched the candle and put it on the mantel with such a shock that the flame was almost extinguished and the tallow was spattered upon the wall.

Then he turned towards M. Leblanc, and with a frightful look, spit out this:

"Singed! smoked! basted! spitted!"

And he began to walk again, in full explosion.

"Ha!" cried he, "I have found you again at last, monsieur philanthropist! monsieur threadbare millionaire! monsieur giver of dolls! old marrow-bones! ha! you do not know me? no, it was not you who came to Montfermeil, to my inn, eight years ago, the night of Christmas, 1823! it was not you who took away Fantine's child from my house! the Lark! it was not you who had a yellow coat! no! and a package of clothes in your hand just as you came here this morning! say now, wife! it is his mania it appears, to carry packages of woollen stockings into houses! old benevolence, get out! Are you a hosier, monsieur millionaire? you give the poor your shop sweepings, holy man! what a charlatan! Ha! you do not know me? Well, I knew you! I knew you immediately as soon as you stuck your nose in here. Ah! you are going to find out at last that it is not all roses to go into people's houses like that, under pretext of their being inns, with worn-out clothes, with the appearance of a pauper, to whom anybody would have given a sou, to deceive persons, to act the generous, take their help away, and threaten them in the woods, and that you do not get quit of it by bringing back afterwards, when people are ruined, an overcoat that is too large and two paltry hospital coverlids, old beggar, child-stealer!"

He stopped, and appeared to be talking to himself for a moment. One would have said that his fury dropped like the Rhone into some hole; then, as if he were finishing aloud something that he had been saying to himself, he struck his fist on the table and cried:

"With his honest look!"

And apostrophising M. Leblanc:

"Zounds! you made a mock of me once! You are the cause of all my misfortunes! For fifteen hundred francs you got a girl that I had and who certainly belonged to rich people, and who had already brought me in a good deal of money, and from whom I ought to have got enough to live on all my life! A girl who would have made up all that I lost in that abominable chop-house where they had such royal sprees and where I devoured my all like a fool! Oh! I wish that all the wine that was drunk in my house had been poison to those who drank it! But no matter! Say, now! you must have thought me green when you went away with the Lark? you had your club in the woods! you were the strongest! Revenge! The trumps are in my hand to-day. You are skunked, my good man! Oh! but don't I laugh! Indeed, I do! Didn't he fall into the trap? I told him that I was an actor, that my name was Fabantou, that I had played comedy with Mamselle Mars, with Mamselle Muche, that my landlord must be paid to-morrow the 4th of February, and he did not even think that the 8th of January is quarter day and not the 4th of February! The ridiculous fool! And these four paltry philippes that he brings me! Rascal! He had not even heart enough to go up to a hundred francs! And how he swallowed my platitudes! The fellow amused me. I said to myself: Blubber-lips! Go on, I have got you, I lick your paws this morning! I will gnaw your heart to-night!"

Thénardier stopped. He was out of breath. His little narrow chest was blowing like a blacksmith's bellows. His eye was full of the base delight of a feeble, cruel, and cowardly animal, which can finally prostrate that of which it has stood in awe, and insult what it has flattered, the joy of a dwarf putting his heel upon the head of Goliath, the joy of a jackal beginning to tear a sick bull, dead enough to not be able to defend himself, alive enough yet to suffer.

M. Leblanc did not interrupt him but said when he stopped:

"I do not know what you mean. You are mistaken. I am a very poor man and anything but a millionaire. I do not know you; you mistake me for another."

"Ha!" screamed Thénardier, "good mountebank! You stick to that joke yet! You are in the fog, my old boy! Ah! you do not remember! You do not see who I am!"

"Pardon me, monsieur," answered M. Leblanc, with a tone of politeness which, at such a moment, had a peculiarly strange and powerful effect, "I see that you are a bandit."

Who has not noticed it, hateful beings have their tender points; monsters are easily annoyed. At this word bandit, the

Thénardiess sprang off the bed. Thénardier seized his chair as if he were going to crush it in his hands: "Don't you stir," cried he to his wife, and turning towards M. Leblanc:

"Bandit! Yes, I know that you call us so, you rich people! Yes! it is true I have failed; I am in concealment, I have no bread; I have not a sou, I am a bandit. Here are three days that I have eaten nothing, I am a bandit! Ah! you warm your feet; you have Sacoski pumps, you have wadded overcoats like arch-bishops, you live on the first floor in houses with a porter, you eat truffles, you eat forty-franc bunches of asparagus in the month of January, and green peas, you stuff yourselves, and when you want to know if it is cold you look in the news-paper to see at what degree the thermometer of the inventor, Chevalier, stands. But we are our own thermometers! We have no need to go to the quai at the corner of the Tour de l'Horloge, to see how many degrees below zero it is; we feel the blood stiffen in our veins and the ice reach our hearts, and we say 'There is no God!' And you come into our caverns, yes, into our caverns, and call us bandits. But we will eat you! but we will devour you, poor little things! Monsieur Millionaire! know this:—I have been a man established in business, I have been licensed, I have been an elector, I am a citizen, I am! And you, perhaps, are not one?"

Here Thénardier took a step towards the men who were before the door, and added with a shudder:

"When I think that he dares to come and talk to me, as if I were a cobbler!"

Then addressing M. Leblanc with a fresh burst of frenzy:

"And know this, too, monsieur philanthropist! I am no doubtful man. I am not a man whose name nobody knows, and who comes into houses to carry off children. I am an old French soldier; I ought to be decorated. I was at Waterloo, I was, and in that battle I saved a general, named the Comte de Pontmercy. This picture which you see, and which was painted by David at Bruqueselles, do you know who it represents? It represents me. David desired to immortalise that feat of arms. I have General Pontmercy on my back, and I am carrying him through the storm of grape. That is history. He has never done anything at all for me, this general; he is no better than other people. But, nevertheless, I saved his life at the risk of my own, and I have my pockets full of certificates. I am a soldier at Waterloo—name of a thousand names! And now that I have had the goodness to tell you all this, let us make an end of it; I must have some money; I must have a good deal of money, I must have an immense deal of money, or I will exterminate you, by the thunder of God!"

Marius had regained some control over his distress, and was listening. The last possibility of doubt had now vanished. It was indeed the Thénardier of the will. Marius shuddered at that reproach of ingratitude flung at his father, and which he was on the point of justifying so fatally. His perplexities were redoubled. Moreover, there was in all these words of Thénardier, in his tone, in his gestures, in his look which flashed out flames at every word, there was in this explosion of an evil nature exposing its entire self, in this mixture of braggadocio and abjectness, of pride and pettiness, of rage and folly in this chaos of real grievances and false sentiments, in this shamelessness of a wicked man tasting the sweetness of violence, in this brazen nakedness of a deformed soul, in this conflagration of every suffering combined with every hatred, something which was as hideous as evil and as sharp and bitter as the truth.

The picture by a master, the painting by David, the purchase of which he had proposed to M. Leblanc, was, the reader has guessed, nothing more than the sign of his chop-house, painted, as will be remembered, by himself, the only relic which he had saved from his shipwreck at Montfermeil.

As he had ceased to intercept Marius' line of vision, Marius could now look at the thing, and in this daub he really made out a battle, a background of smoke, and one man carrying off another. It was the group of Thénardier and Pontmercy; the saviour sergeant, the colonel saved. Marius was as it were intoxicated; this picture in some sort restored his father to life; it was not now the sign of the Montfermeil inn, it was a resurrection; in it a tomb half opened, from it a phantom arose. Marius heard his heart ring in his temples, he had the cannon of Waterloo sounding in his ears; his bleeding father dimly painted upon this dusky panel startled him, and it seemed to him that that shapeless shadow was gazing steadily upon him.

When Thénardier had taken breath he fixed his bloodshot eyes upon Monsieur Leblanc, and said in a low and abrupt tone:

"What have you to say before we begin to dance with you?"

Monsieur Leblanc said nothing. In the midst of this silence a hoarse voice threw in this ghastly sarcasm from the hall:

"If there is any wood to split, I am on hand!"

It was the man with the pole-axe who was making merry.

At the same time a huge face, bristly and dirty, appeared in the doorway, with a hideous laugh, which showed not teeth, but fangs.

It was the face of the man with the pole-axe.

"What have you taken off your mask for?" cried Thénardier, furiously.

"To laugh," replied the man.

For some moments, Monsieur Leblanc had seemed to follow and to watch all the movements of Thénardier, who, blinded and bewildered by his own rage, was walking to and fro in the den with the confidence inspired by the feeling that the door was guarded, having armed possession of a disarmed man, and being nine to one, even if the Thénardiess should count but for one man. In his apostrophe to the man with the pole-axe, he turned his back to Monsieur Leblanc.

Monsieur Leblanc seized this opportunity, pushed the chair away with his foot, the table with his hand, and at one bound, with a marvellous agility, before Thénardier had had time to turn around he was at the window. To open it, get up and step through it, was the work of a second. He was half outside when six strong hands seized him, and drew him forcibly back into the room. The three "chimney doctors" had thrown themselves upon him. At the same time the Thénardiess had clutched him by the hair.

At the disturbance which this made, the other bandits ran in from the hall. The old man, who was on the bed, and who seemed overwhelmed with wine, got off the pallet, and came tottering along with a road-mender's hammer in his hand.

One of the "chimney doctors," whose blackened face was lighted up by the candle, and in whom Marius, in spite of this colouring, recognised Panchaud, alias Printanier, alias Bigrenaille, raised a sort of loaded club made of a bar of iron with a knob of lead at each end, over Monsieur Leblanc's head.

Marius could not endure this sight. "Father," thought he, "pardon me!" And his finger sought the trigger of the pistol. The shot was just about to be fired, when Thénardier's voice cried:

"Do him no harm!"

This desperate attempt of the victim, far from exasperating Thénardier, had calmed him. There were two men in him, the ferocious man and the crafty man. Up to this moment, in the first flush of triumph, before his prey stricken down and motionless, the ferocious man had been predominant; when the victim resisted, and seemed to desire a struggle, the crafty man reappeared and resumed control.

"Do him no harm!" he repeated, and without suspecting it, the first result of this was to stop the pistol which was just ready to go off, and paralyse Marius, to whom the urgency seemed to disappear, and who, in view of this new phase of affairs, saw no impropriety in waiting longer. Who knows but some chance may arise which will save him from the fearful alternative of letting the father of Ursula perish, or destroying the saviour of the colonel!

A herculean struggle had commenced. With one blow full in the chest M. Leblanc had sent the old man sprawling into the middle of the room, then with two back strokes had knocked down two other assailants, whom he held one under each knee; the wretches screamed under the pressure as if they had been under a granite mill-stone; but the four others had seized the formidable old man by the arms and the back, and held him down over the two prostrate "chimney doctors." Thus, master of the latter and mastered by the former, crushing those below him and suffocating under those above him, vainly endeavouring to shake off all the violence and blows which were heaped upon him, M. Leblanc disappeared under the horrible group of the bandits, like a wild boar under a howling pack of hounds and mastiffs.

They succeeded in throwing him over upon the bed nearest to the window and held him there in awe. The Thénardiess had not let go of his hair.

"Here," said Thénardier, "let it alone. You will tear your shawl."

The Thénardiess obeyed, as the she-wolf obeys her mate, with a growl.

"Now, the rest of you," continued Thénardier, "search him."

M. Leblanc seemed to have given up all resistance. They searched him. There was nothing upon him but a leather purse which contained six francs, and his handkerchief.

Thénardier put the handkerchief in his pocket.

"What! no pocket-book?" he asked.

"Nor any watch," answered one of the "chimney doctors."

"It is all the same," muttered, with the voice of a ventriloquist, the masked man who had the big key, "he is an old rough."

Thénardier went to the corner by the door and took a bundle of ropes which he threw to them.

"Tie him to the foot of the bed," said he, and perceiving the old fellow who lay motionless, when he was stretched across the room by the blow of M. Leblanc's fist:

"Is Boulatruelle dead?" asked he.

"No," answered Bigrenaille, "he is drunk."

"Sweep him into a corner," said Thénardier.

Two of the "chimney doctors" pushed the drunkard up to the heap of old iron with their feet.

"Babet, what did you bring so many for?" said Thénardier in a low tone to the man with the cudgel, "it was needless."

"What would you have?" replied the man with the cudgel, "they all wanted to be in. The season is bad. There is nothing doing."

The pallet upon which M. Leblanc had been thrown was a sort of hospital bed supported by four big roughly squared wooden posts. M. Leblanc made no resistance. The brigands bound him firmly, standing, with his feet to the floor, by the bed-post furthest from the window and nearest to the chimney.

When the last knot was tied, Thénardier took a chair and came and sat down nearly in front of M. Leblanc. Thénardier looked no longer like himself, in a few seconds the expression of his face had passed from unbridled violence to tranquil and crafty mildness. Marius hardly recognised in that polite, clerkly smile, the almost beastly mouth which was foaming a moment before; he looked with astonishment upon this fantastic and alarming metamorphosis, and he experienced what a man would feel who should see a tiger change itself into an attorney.

"Monsieur," said Thénardier.

And with a gesture dismissing the brigands who still had their hands upon M. Leblanc:

"Move off a little, and let me talk with monsieur."

They all retired towards the door. He resumed:

"Monsieur, you were wrong in trying to jump out the

window. You might have broken your leg. Now, if you please, we will talk quietly. In the first place I must inform you of a circumstance I have noticed, which is that you have not yet made the least outcry."

Thénardier was right; this incident was true, although it had escaped Marius in his anxiety. M. Leblanc had only uttered a few words without raising his voice, and, even in his struggle by the window with the six bandits, he had preserved the most profound and the most remarkable silence. Thénardier continued:

"Indeed! you might have cried thief a little, for I should not have found it inconvenient. Murder! that is said upon occasion, and, as far as I am concerned, I should not have taken it in bad part. It is very natural that one should make a little noise when he finds himself with persons who do not inspire him with as much confidence as they might; you might have done it, and we should not have disturbed you. We would not even have gagged you. And I will tell you why. It is because this room is very deaf. That is all I can say for it, but I can say that. It is a cave. We could fire a bomb here, and at the nearest guardhouse it would sound like a drunkard's snore. Here a cannon would go boom, and thunder would go puff. It is a convenient apartment. But, in short, you did not cry out, that was better, I make you my compliments for it, and I will tell you what I conclude from it: my dear monsieur, when a man cries out, who is it that comes? The police. And after the police? Justice. Well! you did not cry out; because you were no more anxious than we to see justice and the police come. It is because,—I suspected as much long ago,—you have some interest in concealing something. For our part we have the same interest. Now we can come to an understanding."

While speaking thus, it seemed as though Thénardier, with his gaze fixed upon Monsieur Leblanc, was endeavouring to thrust the daggers which he looked, into the very conscience of his prisoner. His language, moreover, marked by a sort of subdued and sullen insolence, was reserved and almost select, and in this wretch who was just before nothing but a brigand, one could now perceive the man who studied to be a priest.

The silence which the prisoner had preserved, this precaution which he had carried even to the extent of endangering his life, this resistance to the first impulse of nature, which is to utter a cry, all this, it must be said, since it had been remarked, was annoying to Marius, and painfully astonished him.

The observation of Thénardier, well founded as it was, added in Marius' eyes still more to the obscurity of the mysterious cloud that enveloped this strange and serious face to which Courfeyrac had given the nickname of Monsieur Leblanc. But whatever he might be, bound with ropes, surrounded by assassins, half buried so to speak, in a grave which was deepening beneath him every moment, before the fury as well as before the mildness of Thénardier, this man remained impassable; and Marius could not repress at such a moment his admiration for that superbly melancholy face.

Here was evidently a soul inaccessible to fear, and ignorant of dismay. Here was one of those men who are superior to astonishment in desperate situations. However extreme the crisis, however inevitable the catastrophe, there was nothing there of the agony of the drowning man, staring with horrified eyes as he sinks to the bottom.

Thénardier quietly got up, went to the fire-place, took away the screen which he leaned against the nearest pallet, and thus revealed the furnace full of glowing coals in which the prisoner could plainly see the chisel at a white heat, spotted here and there with little scarlet stars.

Then Thénardier came back and sat down by Monsieur Leblanc.

"I continue," said he. "Now we can come to an understanding. Let us arrange this amicably. I was wrong to fly into a passion just now. I do not know where my wits were, I went much too far, I talked extravagantly. For instance, because you are a millionaire, I told you that I wanted money, a good deal of money, an immense deal of money. That would not be reasonable. My God, rich as you may be, you have your expenses; who does not have them? I do not want to ruin you, I am not a catch-poll, after all. I am not one of those people who, because they have the advantage in position, use it to be ridiculous. Here, I am willing to go half way and make some sacrifice on my part. I need only two hundred thousand francs."

Monsieur Leblanc did not breathe a word. Thénardier went on:

"You see that I water my wine pretty well. I do not know the state of your fortune, but I know that you do not care much for money and a benevolent man like you can certainly give two hundred thousand francs to a father of a family who is unfortunate. Certainly you are reasonable also, you do not imagine that I would take the trouble I have to-day, and that I would organise the affair of this evening, which is a very fine piece of work in the opinion of these gentlemen, to end off by asking you for enough to go and drink fifteen-sou red wine and eat veal at Desnoyers'. Two hundred thousand francs, it is worth it. That trifle once out of your pocket, I assure you that all is said, and that you need not fear a snap of the finger. You will say: but I have not two hundred thousand francs with me. Oh! I am not exacting. I do not require that, I only ask one thing. Have the goodness to write what I shall dictate."

Here Thénardier paused, then he added, emphasising each word and casting a smile towards the furnace:

"I give you notice that I shall not admit that you cannot write."

A grand inquisitor might have envied that smile.

Thénardier pushed the table close up to Monsieur Leblanc, and took the inkstand, a pen, and a sheet of paper from the drawer, which he left partly open, and from which gleamed the long blade of the knife.

He laid the sheet of paper before Monsieur Leblanc.

"Write," said he.

The prisoner spoke at last:

"How do you expect me to write? I am tied."

"That is true, pardon me!" said Thénardier, "you are quite right."

And turning towards Bigrenaille:

"Untie monsieur's right arm."

Panchaud, alias Printanier, alias Bigrenaille, executed Thénardier's order. When the prisoner's right hand was free, Thénardier dipped the pen into the ink, and presented it to him.

"Remember, monsieur, that you are in our power, at our discretion, that no human power can take you away from here, and that we should be really grieved to be obliged to proceed to unpleasant extremities. I know neither your name nor your address, but I give you notice that you will remain tied until the person whose duty it will be to carry the letter which you are about to write, has returned. Have the kindness now to write."

"What?" asked the prisoner.

"I will dictate."

M. Leblanc took the pen.

Thénardier began to dictate:

"My daughter——"

The prisoner shuddered and lifted his eyes to Thénardier.

"Put 'my dear daughter,'" said Thénardier. M. Leblanc obeyed. Thénardier continued:

"Come immediately——"

He stopped.

"You call her daughter, do you not?"

"Who?" asked M. Leblanc.

"Zounds!" said Thénardier, "the little girl, the Lark."

M. Leblanc answered without the least apparent emotion:

"I do not know what you mean."

"Well, go on," said Thénardier, and he began to dictate again.

"'Come immediately, I have imperative need of you. The person who will give you this note is directed to bring you to me. I am waiting for you. Come with confidence.'"

M. Leblanc had written the whole. Thénardier added:

"Ah! strike out *come with confidence*, that might lead her to suppose that the thing is not quite clear and that distrust is possible."

M. Leblanc erased the three words.

"Now," continued Thénardier, "sign it. What is your name?"

The prisoner laid down the pen and asked:

"For whom is this letter?"

"You know very well," answered Thénardier, "for the little girl, I have just told you."

It was evident that Thénardier avoided naming the young girl in question. He said "the Lark," he said "the little girl," but he did not pronounce the name. The precaution of a shrewd man preserving his own secret before his accomplices. To speak the name would have been to give up the whole "affair" to them, and to tell them more than they needed to know.

He resumed:

"Sign it. What is your name?"

"Urbain Fabre," said the prisoner.

Thénardier, with the movement of a cat, thrust his hand into his pocket and pulled out the handkerchief taken from

M. Leblanc. He looked for the mark upon it and held it up to the candle.

"U. F. That is it. Urbain Fabre. Well, sign U. F."

The prisoner signed.

"As it takes two hands to fold the letter, give it to me, I will fold it."

This done, Thénardier resumed:

"Put on the address, *Mademoiselle Fabre*, at your house. I know that you live not very far from here, in the neighbourhood of Saint Jacques du Haut Pas, since you go there to mass every day, but I do not know in what street. I see that you understand your situation. As you have not lied about your name, you will not lie about your address. Put it on yourself."

The prisoner remained thoughtful for a moment, then he took the pen and wrote:

"Mademoiselle Fabre, at Monsieur Urbain Fabre's, Rue Saint Dominique d'Enfer, No. 17."

Thénardier seized the letter with a sort of feverish convulsive movement.

"Wife!" cried he.

The Thénardiess sprang forward.

"Here is the letter. You know what you have to do. There is a fiacre below. Go right away, and come back ditto."

And addressing the man with the pole-axe:

"Here, since you have taken off your hide-your-nose, go with the woman. You will get up behind the fiacre. You know where you left the *maringotte*."

"Yes," said the man.

And, laying down his pole-axe in a corner, he followed the Thénardiess.

As they were going away, Thénardier put his head through the half-open door and screamed into the hall:

"Above all things do not lose the letter! remember that you have two hundred thousand francs with you."

The harsh voice of the Thénardiess answered:

"Rest assured, I have put it in my bosom."

A minute had not passed when the snapping of a whip was heard, which grew fainter and rapidly died away.

"Good!" muttered Thénardier. "They are going good speed. At that speed the bourgeoise will be back in three quarters of an hour."

He drew a chair near the fire-place and sat down, folding his arms and holding his muddy boots up to the furnace.

"My feet are cold," said he.

There were now but five bandits left in the den with Thénardier and the prisoner. These men, through the masks or the black varnish which covered their faces and made of them, as fear might suggest, charcoal men, negroes, or demons, had a heavy and dismal appearance, and one felt that they would execute a crime as they would any drudgery, quietly, without anger and without mercy, with a sort of irksomeness. They were heaped together in a corner like brutes, and were silent. Thénardier was warming his feet. The prisoner had relapsed into his taciturnity. A gloomy stillness had succeeded the savage tumult which filled the garret a few moments before.

The candle, in which a large thief had formed, hardly lighted up the enormous den, the fire had grown dull, and all their monstrous heads made huge shadows on the walls and on the ceiling.

No sound could be heard save the quiet breathing of the drunken old man, who was asleep.

Marius was waiting in an anxiety which everything increased. The riddle was more impenetrable than ever. Who was this "little girl," whom Thénardier had also called the Lark? was it his "Ursula"? The prisoner had not seemed to be moved by this word, the Lark, and answered in the most natural way in the world: I do not know what you mean. On the other hand, the two letters U. F. were explained; it was Urbain Fabre, and Ursula's name was no longer Ursula. This Marius saw most clearly. A sort of hideous fascination held him spellbound to the place from which he observed and commanded the whole scene. There he was, almost incapable of reflection and motion, as if annihilated by such horrible things in so close proximity. He was waiting, hoping for some movement, no matter what, unable to collect his ideas and not knowing what course to take.

"At all events," said he, "if the Lark is she, I shall certainly see her, for the Thénardiess is going to bring her here. Then all will be plain. I will give my blood and my life if need be, but I will deliver her. Nothing shall stop me."

Nearly half an hour passed thus. Thénardier appeared absorbed in a dark meditation, the prisoner did not stir. Nevertheless Marius thought he had heard at intervals and for some moments a little dull noise from the direction of the prisoner.

Suddenly Thénardier addressed the prisoner:

"Monsieur Fabre, here, so much let me tell you at once."

These few words seemed to promise a clearing up. Marius listened closely. Thénardier continued:

"My spouse is coming back, do not be impatient. I think the Lark is really your daughter, and I find it quite natural that you should keep her. But listen a moment; with your letter, my wife is going to find her. I told my wife to dress up, as you saw, so that your young lady would follow her without hesitation. They will both get into the fiacre with my comrade behind. There is somewhere outside one of the barriers a *maringotte* with two very good horses harnessed. They will take your young lady there. She will get out of the carriage. My comrade will get into the *maringotte* with her, and my wife will come back here to tell us: 'It is done.' As to your young lady, no harm will be done her; the *maringotte* will take her to a place where she will be quiet, and as soon as you have given me the little two hundred thousand francs, she will be sent back to you. If you have me arrested, my comrade will give the Lark a pinch, that is all."

The prisoner did not utter a word. After a pause, Thénardier continued:

"It is very simple, as you see. There will be no harm done unless you wish there should be. That is the whole story. I tell you in advance so that you may know."

He stopped; the prisoner did not break the silence, and Thénardier resumed:

"As soon as my spouse has got back and said: 'The Lark is on her way,' we will release you, and you will be free to go home to bed. You see that we have no bad intentions."

Appalling images passed before Marius' mind. What! this young girl whom they were kidnapping, they were not going to bring her here? One of those monsters was going to carry her off into the gloom? where?—And if it were she! And it was clear that it was she. Marius felt his heart cease to beat. What was he to do? Fire off the pistol? put all these wretches into the hands of justice? But the hideous man of the pole-axe would none the less be out of all reach with the young girl, and Marius remembered these words of Thénardier, the bloody signification of which he divined: *If you have me arrested, my comrade will give the Lark a pinch.*

Now it was not by the colonel's will alone, it was by his love itself, by the peril of her whom he loved, that he felt himself held back.

This fearful situation, which had lasted now for more than an hour, changed its aspect at every moment. Marius had the strength to pass in review successively all the most heart-rending conjectures, seeking some hope and finding more. The tumult of his thoughts strangely contrasted with the deathly silence of the den.

In the midst of this silence they heard the sound of the door of the stairway which opened, then closed.

The prisoner made a movement in his bonds.

"Here is the bourgeoise," said Thénardier.

He had hardly said this, when in fact the Thénardiess burst into the room, red, breathless, panting, with glaring eyes, and cried, striking her hands upon her hips both at the same time:

"False address!"

The bandit whom she had taken with her, came in behind her and picked up his pole-axe again:

"False address?" repeated Thénardier.

She continued:

"Nobody! Rue Saint Dominique, number seventeen, no Monsieur Urbain Fabre! They do not know who he is!"

She stopped for lack of breath, then continued:

"Monsieur Thénardier! this old fellow has cheated you! you are too good, do you see! I would have cut up the *Margoulette* for you in quarters, to begin with! and if he had been ugly, I would have cooked him alive! Then he would have had to talk, and had to tell where the girl is, and had to tell where the rhino is! That is how I would have fixed it! No wonder that they say men are stupider than women! Nobody! number seventeen! It is a large porte-cochère! No Monsieur Fabre! Rue Saint Dominique, full gallop, and drink-money to the driver, and all! I spoke to the porter and the portress, who is a fine stout woman, they did not know the fellow."

Marius breathed. She, Ursula or the Lark, she whom he no longer knew what to call, was safe.

While his exasperated wife was vociferating, Thénardier had seated himself on the table; he sat a few seconds without saying a word, swinging his right leg, which was hanging down, and gazing upon the furnace with a look of savage reverie.

At last he said to the prisoner with a slow and singularly ferocious inflexion:

"A false address! what did you hope for by that?"

"To gain time!" cried the prisoner with a ringing voice.

And at the same moment he shook off his bonds; they were cut. The prisoner was no longer fastened to the bed save by one leg.

Before the seven men had had time to recover themselves and spring upon him he had bent over to the fire-place, reached his hand towards the furnace, then rose up, and now Thénardier, the Thénardiess, and the bandits, thrown by the shock into the back part of the room, beheld him with stupefaction, holding above his head the glowing chisel, from which fell an ominous light, almost free and in a formidable attitude.

At the judicial inquest, to which the ambuscade in the Gorbeau tenement gave rise in the sequel, it appeared that a big sou, cut and worked in a peculiar fashion, was found in the garret, when the police made a descent upon it; this big sou was one of those marvels of labour which the patience of the galleys produces in the darkness and for the darkness, marvels which are nothing else but instruments of escape. These hideous and delicate products of a wonderful art are to jewellery what the metaphors of argot are to poetry. There are Benvenuto Cellinis in the galleys, even as there are Villons in language. The unhappy man who aspires to deliverance, finds the means, sometimes without tools, with a folding knife, with an old case knife, to split a sou into two thin plates, to hollow out these two plates without touching the stamp of the mint, and to cut a screwthread upon the edge of the sou, so as to make the plates adhere anew. This screws and unscrews at will; it is a box. In this box, they conceal a watch-spring, and this watch-spring, well handled, cuts off rings of some size and bars of iron. The unfortunate convict is supposed to possess only a sou; no, he possesses liberty. A big sou of this kind, on subsequent examination by the police, was found open and in two pieces in the room under the pallet near the window. There was also discovered a little saw of blue steel which could be concealed in the big sou. It is probable that when the bandits were searching the prisoner's pockets, he had this big sou upon him and succeeded in hiding it in his hand; and that afterwards, having his right hand free, he unscrewed it and used the saw to cut the ropes by which he was fastened, which would explain the slight noise and the imperceptible movements which Marius had noticed.

Being unable to stoop down for fear of betraying himself, he had not cut the cords on his left leg.

The bandits had recovered their first surprise.

"Be easy," said Bigrenaille to Thénardier. "He holds yet by one leg, and he will not go off, I answer for that. I tied that shank for him."

The prisoner now raised his voice:

"You are pitiable, but my life is not worth the trouble of so long a defence. As to your imagining that you could make me speak, that you could make me write what I do not wish to write, that you could make me say what I do not wish to say——"

He pulled up the sleeve of his left arm, and added:

"Here."

At the same time he extended his arm, and laid upon the naked flesh the glowing chisel, which he held in his right hand, by the wooden handle.

They heard the hissing of the burning flesh; the odour peculiar to chambers of torture spread through the den. Marius staggered lost in horror; the brigands themselves felt a shudder; the face of the wonderful old man hardly contracted, and while the red iron was sinking into the smoking, impassable, and almost august wound, he turned upon Thénardier his fine face, in which there was no hatred, and in which suffering was swallowed up in a serene majesty.

With great and lofty natures the revolt of the flesh and the senses against the assaults of physical pain, brings out the soul, and makes it appear on the countenance, in the same way as mutinies of the soldiery force the captain to show himself.

"Wretches," said he, "have no more fear for me than I have of you."

And drawing the chisel out of the wound, he threw it through the window, which was still open; the horrible glowing tool disappeared, whirling into the night, and fell in the distance, and was quenched in the snow.

The prisoner resumed:

"Do with me what you will."

He was disarmed.

"Lay hold of him," said Thénardier.

Two of the brigands laid their hands upon his shoulders, and the masked man with the ventriloquist's voice placed himself in front of him, ready to knock out his brains with a blow of the key, at the least motion.

At the same time Marius heard beneath him, at the foot of the partition, but so near that he could not see those who were talking, this colloquy, exchanged in a low voice:

"There is only one thing more to do."

"To kill him!"

"That is it."

It was the husband and wife who were holding counsel.

Thénardier walked with slow steps towards the table, opened the drawer, and took out the knife.

Marius was tormenting the trigger of his pistol. Unparalleled perplexity! For an hour there had been two voices in his conscience, one telling him to respect the will of his father, the other crying to him to succour the prisoner. These two voices, without interruption, continued their struggle, which threw him into agony. He had vaguely hoped up to that moment to find some means of reconciling these two duties, but no possible way had arisen. The peril was now urgent, the last limit of hope was passed; at a few steps from the prisoner, Thénardier was reflecting, with the knife in his hand.

Marius cast his eyes wildly about him; the last mechanical resource of despair.

Suddenly he started.

At his feet, on the table, a clear ray of the full moon illuminated and seemed to point out to him a sheet of paper. Upon that sheet he read this line, written in large letters that very morning, by the elder of the Thénardier girls:

"THE COGNES ARE HERE."

An idea, a flash crossed Marius' mind; that was the means which he sought; the solution of this dreadful problem which was torturing him, to spare the assassin and to save the victim. He knelt down upon his bureau, reached out his arm, caught up the sheet of paper, quietly detached a bit of plaster from the partition, wrapped it in the paper, and threw the whole through the crevice into the middle of the den.

It was time. Thénardier had conquered his last fears, or his last scruples, and was moving towards the prisoner.

"Something fell!" cried the Thénardiess.

"What is it?" said the husband.

The woman had sprung forward, and picked up the piece of plaster wrapped in the paper. She handed it to her husband.

"How did this come in?" asked Thénardier.

"Egad!" said the woman, "how do you suppose it got in? It came through the window."

"I saw it pass," said Bigrenaille.

Thénardier hurriedly unfolded the paper, and held it up to the candle.

"It is Eponine's writing. The devil!"

He made a sign to his wife, who approached quickly, and he showed her the line written on the sheet of paper; then he added in a hollow voice:

"Quick! the ladder! leave the meat in the trap, and clear the camp!"

"Without cutting the man's throat?" asked the Thénardiess.

"We have not the time."

"Which way?" inquired Bigrenaille.

"Through the window," answered Thénardier. "As Ponine threw the stone through the window, that shows that the house is not watched on that side."

The mask with the ventriloquist's voice laid down his big key, lifted both arms into the air, and opened and shut his hands rapidly three times, without saying a word. This was like the signal to clear the decks in a fleet. The brigands, who were holding the prisoner, let go of him; in the twinkling of an eye, the rope ladder was unrolled out of the window, and firmly fixed to the casing by the two iron hooks.

The prisoner paid no attention to what was passing about him. He seemed to be dreaming or praying.

As soon as the ladder was fixed, Thénardier cried:

"Come, bourgeoise!"

And he rushed towards the window.

But as he was stepping out, Bigrenaille seized him roughly by the collar.

"No; say now, old joker! after us."

"After us!" howled the bandits.

"You are children," said Thénardier. "We are losing time. The *railles* are at our heels."

"Well," said one of the bandits, "let us draw lots who shall go out first."

Thénardier exclaimed:

"Are you fools? are you cracked? You are a mess *of jobards*! Losing time, isn't it? drawing lots, isn't it? with a wet finger! for the short straw! write our names! put them in a cap!——"

"Would you like my hat?" cried a voice from the door.

They all turned round. It was Javert.

He had his hat in his hand, and was holding it out smiling.

XXI
THE VICTIMS SHOULD ALWAYS BE ARRESTED FIRST

JAVERT, at nightfall, had posted his men and hid himself behind the trees on the Rue de la Barrière des Gobelins, which fronts the Gorbeau tenement on the other side of the boulevard. He commenced by opening "his pocket," to put into it the two young girls, who were charged with watching the approaches to the den. But he only "bagged" Azelma. As for Eponine, she was not at her post; she had disappeared and he could not take her. Then Javert put himself in rest, and listened for the signal agreed upon. The going and coming of the fiacre fretted him greatly. At last, he became impatient, and, *sure that there was a nest there*, sure of being "*in good luck*," having recognised several of the bandits who had gone in, he finally decided to go up without waiting for the pistol shot.

It will be remembered that he had Marius' pass-key.

He had come at the right time.

The frightened bandits rushed for the arms which they had thrown down anywhere when they had attempted to escape. In less than a second, these seven men, terrible to look upon, were grouped in a posture of defence; one with his pole-axe, another with his key, a third with his club, the others with the shears, the pincers, and the hammers, Thénardier grasping his knife. The Thénardiess seized a huge paving-stone which was in the corner of the window, and which served her daughters for a footstool.

Javert put on his hat again, and stepped into the room, arms folded, his cane under his arm, his sword in its sheath.

"Halt there," said he. "You will not pass out through the window, you will pass out through the door. It is less unwholesome. There are seven of you, fifteen of us. Don't let us collar you like Auvergnats. Be genteel."

Bigrenaille took a pistol which he had concealed under his blouse, and put it into Thénardier's hand, whispering in his ear:

"It is Javert. I dare not fire at that man. Dare you?"

"*Parbleu!*" answered Thénardier.

"Well, fire."

Thénardier took the pistol, and aimed at Javert.

Javert, who was within three paces, looked at him steadily, and contented himself with saying:

"Don't fire, now! It will flash in the pan."

Thénardier pulled the trigger. The pistol flashed in the pan.

"I told you so!" said Javert.

Bigrenaille threw his tomahawk at Javert's feet.

"You are the emperor of the devils! I surrender."

"And you?" asked Javert of the other bandits.

They answered:

"We, too."

Javert replied calmly:

"That is it, that is well, I said so, you are genteel."

"I only ask one thing," said Bigrenaille, "that is, that I shan't be refused tobacco while I am in solitary."

"Granted," said Javert.

And turning round and calling behind him:

"Come in now!"

A squad of sergents de ville with drawn swords, and officers armed with axes and clubs, rushed in at Javert's call. They bound the bandits. This crowd of men, dimly lighted by a candle, filled the den with shadow.

"Handcuffs on all!" cried Javert.

"Come on, then!" cried a voice which was not a man's voice, but of which nobody could have said: "It is the voice of a woman."

The Thénardiess had intrenched herself in one of the corners of the window, and it was she who had just uttered this roar.

The sergents de ville and officers fell back.

She had thrown off her shawl, but kept on her hat; her husband, crouched down behind her, was almost hidden beneath the fallen shawl, and she covered him with her body, holding the paving-stone with both hands above her head with the poise of a giantess who is going to hurl a rock.

"Take care!" she cried.

They all crowded back towards the hall. A wide space was left in the middle of the garret.

The Thénardiess cast a glance at the bandits who had allowed themselves to be tied, and muttered in a harsh and guttural tone:

"The cowards!"

Javert smiled, and advanced into the open space which the Thénardiess was watching with all her eyes.

"Don't come near! get out," cried she, "or I will crush you!"

"What a grenadier!" said Javert; "mother, you have a beard like a man, but I have claws like a woman."

And he continued to advance.

The Thénardiess, her hair flying wildly and terrible, braced her legs, bent backwards, and threw the paving-stone wildly at Javert's head. Javert stooped, the stone passed over him, hit the wall behind, from which it knocked down a large piece of the plastering, and returned, bounding from corner to corner across the room, luckily almost empty, finally stopping at Javert's heels.

At that moment Javert reached the Thénardier couple. One of his huge hands fell upon the shoulder of the woman, and the other upon her husband's head.

"The handcuffs!" cried he.

The police officers returned in a body, and in a few seconds Javert's order was executed.

The Thénardiess, completely crushed, looked at her manacled hands and those of her husband, dropped to the floor and exclaimed, with tears in her eyes:

"My daughters!"

"They are provided for," said Javert.

Meanwhile the officers had found the drunken fellow who was asleep behind the door, and shook him. He awoke stammering.

"Is it over, Jondrette?"

"Yes," answered Javert.

The six manacled bandits were standing; however, they still retained their spectral appearance, three blackened, three masked.

"Keep on your masks," said Javert.

And, passing them in review with the eye of a Frederic II. at parade at Potsdam, he said to the three "chimney doctors":

"Good day, Bigrenaille. Good day, Brujon. Good day, Deux Milliards."

Then, turning towards the three masks, he said to the man of the pole-axe:

"Good day, Gueulemer."

And to the man of the cudgel:

"Good day, Babet."

And to the ventriloquist:

"Your health, Claquesous."

Just then he perceived the prisoner of the bandits, who, since the entrance of the police, had not uttered a word, and had held his head down.

"Untie monsieur!" said Javert, "and let nobody go out."

This said, he sat down with authority before the table, on which the candle and the writing materials still were, drew a stamped sheet from his pocket, and commenced his procès verbal.

When he had written the first lines, a part of the formula, which is always the same, he raised his eyes:

"Bring forward the gentleman whom these gentlemen had bound."

The officers looked about them.

"Well," asked Javert, "where is he now?"

The prisoner of the bandits, M. Leblanc, M. Urbain Fabre, the father of Ursula, or the Lark, had disappeared.

The door was guarded, but the window was not. As soon as he saw that he was unbound, and while Javert was writing, he had taken advantage of the disturbance, the tumult, the confusion, the obscurity, and a moment when their attention was not fixed upon him, to leap out of the window.

An officer ran to the window, and looked out; nobody could be seen outside.

The rope ladder was still trembling.

"The devil!" said Javert, between his teeth, "that must have been the best one."

XXII

THE LITTLE BOY WHO CRIED IN PART SECOND

THE day following that in which these events took place in the house on the Boulevard de l'Hôpital, a child, who seemed to come from somewhere near the bridge of Austerlitz, went up by the cross-alley on the right in the direction of the Barrière de Fontainebleau. Night had closed in. This child was pale, thin, dressed in rags, with tow trousers in the month of February, and was singing with all his might.

At the corner of the Rue du Petit Banquier, an old crone was fumbling in a manure-heap by the light of a street lamp; the child knocked against her as he passed, then drew back, exclaiming:

"Why! I took that for an enormous, enormous dog!"

He pronounced the word enormous the second time with a pompous and sneering voice which capitals would express very well: an enormous, ENORMOUS dog!

The old woman rose up furious.

"Jail-bird!" muttered she. "If I had not been stooping over, I know where I would have planted my foot!"

The child was now at a little distance.

"K'sss! k'sss!" said he. "After all, perhaps I was not mistaken."

The old woman, choking with indignation, sprang up immediately, and the red glare of the lantern fully illuminating her livid face, all hollowed out with angles and wrinkles, with crows' feet at the corners of her mouth. Her body was lost in the shadow, and only her head could be seen. One would have said it was the mask of Decrepitude shrivelled by a flash in the night. The child looked at her.

"Madame," said he, "has not the style of beauty that suits me."

He went on his way and began to sing again:

> Le roi Coupdesabot
> S'en allait à la chasse
> A la chasse aux corbeaux——

At the end of these three lines he stopped. He had reached No. 50–52, and finding the door locked, had begun to batter it with kicks, heroic and re-echoing kicks, that revealed rather the men's shoes which he wore, than the child's feet which he had.

Meantime, this same old woman, whom he had met with at the corner of the Rue du Petit Banquier, was running after him with much clamour and many crazy gestures. What's the matter? what's the matter? Good God! They are staving the door down! They are breaking into the house!

The kicks continued.

The old woman exhausted her lungs.

"Is that the way they use houses nowadays?"

Suddenly she stopped. She had recognised the *gamin*.

"What! it is that Satan!"

"Hullo, it is the old woman," said the child. "Good day, Burgonmuche. I have come to see my ancestors."

The old woman responded, with a composite grimace, an admirable extemporisation of hatred making the most of decay and ugliness, which was unfortunately lost in the obscurity:

"There is nobody there, nosey."

"Pshaw!" said the child, "where is my father, then?"

"At La Force."

"Heigho! and my mother?"

"At Saint Lazare."

"Well! and my sisters?"

"At Les Madelonnettes."

The child scratched the back of his ear, looked at Ma'am Bougon and said:

"Ah!"

Then he turned on his heel, and a moment afterwards, the old woman, who stopped on the doorstep, heard him sing with his clear, fresh voice, as he disappeared under the black elms shivering in the wintry winds:

> Le roi Coupdesabot
> S'en allait à la chasse,
> A la chasse aux corbeaux,
> Monté sur des échasses.
> Quand on passait dessous,
> On lui payait deux sous.

SAINT DENIS
AND IDYLL OF THE RUE PLUMET

SAINT DENIS
BOOK FIRST – A FEW PAGES OF HISTORY

I
WELL CUT

THE years 1831 and 1832, the two years immediately connected with the Revolution of July, constitute one of the most peculiar and most striking periods in history. These two years, among those which precede and those which follow them, are like two mountains. They have the revolutionary grandeur. In them we discern precipices. In them the social masses, the very strata of civilisation, the consolidated group of superimposed and cohering interests, the venerable profile of the old French formation, appear and disappear at every instant through the stormy clouds of systems, passions, and theories. These appearances and disappearances have been named resistance and movement. At intervals we see truth gleaming forth, that daylight of the human soul.

This remarkable period is short enough, and is beginning to be far enough from us, so that it is henceforth possible to catch its principal outlines.

We will make the endeavour.

The Restoration had been one of those intermediate phases, difficult of definition, in which there are fatigue, buzzings, murmurs, slumber, tumult, and which are nothing more nor less than the arrival of a great nation at a halting-place. These periods are peculiar, and deceive the politicians who would take advantage of them. At first, the nation asks only for repose; men have but one thirst, for peace; they have but one ambition, to be little. That is a translation of being quiet. Great events, great fortunes, great ventures, great men, thank God, they have seen enough of them; they have been overhead in them. They would exchange Cæsar for Prusias, and Napoleon for the king of Yvetot. "What a good little king he was!" They have walked since daybreak, it is the evening of a long and rough day; they made the first relay with Mirabeau, the second with Robespierre, the third with Bonaparte, they are thoroughly exhausted. Every one of them asks for a bed.

Devotions wearied out, heroisms grown old, ambitions full-fed, fortunes made, all seek, demand, implore, solicit, what? A place to lie down? They have it. They take possession of peace, quietness, and leisure; they are content. At the same time, however, certain facts arise, compel recognition and knock at the door on their side, also. These facts have sprung from revolutions and wars; they exist, they live, they have a right to instal themselves in society, and they do instal themselves; and most of the time the facts are pioneers and quartermasters that merely prepare the ground for principles.

Then, that is what appears to the political philosopher.

At the same time that weary men demand repose, accomplished facts demand guarantees. Guarantees to facts are the same thing as repose to men.

This is what England demanded of the Stuarts after the Protector; this is what France demanded of the Bourbons after the empire.

These guarantees are a necessity of the times. They must be accorded. The princes "grant" them, but in reality it is the force of circumstances which gives them. A profound truth, and a piece of useful knowledge, of which the Stuarts had no suspicion in 1662, and of which the Bourbons had not even a glimpse in 1814.

The predestined family which returned to France when Napoleon fell, had the fatal simplicity to believe that it was it that gave, and that what it had given it could take back; that the house of Bourbon possessed Divine Right, that France possessed nothing, and that the political rights conceded in the Charter of Louis XVIII. were only a branch of the divine right, detached by the House of Bourbon and graciously given to the people until such day as it should please the king to take it back again. Still, by the regret which the gift cost them, the Bourbons should have felt that it did not come from them.

They were surly with the nineteenth century. They made a sour face at every development of the nation. To adopt a trivial word, that is to say, a popular and a true one, they looked glum. The people saw it.

They believed that they were strong, because the empire had been swept away before them like a scene at a theatre. They did not perceive that they themselves had been brought in in the same way. They did not see that they also were in that hand which had taken off Napoleon.

They believed that they were rooted because they were the

past. They were mistaken; they were a portion of the past, but the whole past was France. The roots of French society were not in Bourbons but in the nation. These obscure and undying roots did not constitute the right of a family, but the history of a people. They were everywhere except under the throne.

The house of Bourbon was to France the illustrious and bloodstained knot of her history, but it was not the principal element of her destiny, or the essential basis of her politics. She could do without the Bourbons; she had done without them for twenty-two years; there had been a solution of continuity; they did not suspect it. And how should they suspect it, they who imagined that Louis XVII. reigned on the 9th of Thermidor, and that Louis XVIII. reigned on the day of Marengo. Never, since the beginning of history, have princes been so blind in the presence of facts, and of the portion of divine authority which facts contain and promulgate. Never had that earthly pretension which is called the right of kings, denied the divine right to such an extent.

A capital error which led that family to lay its hand upon the guarantees "granted" in 1814, upon the concessions, as it called them. Sad thing! what they called their concessions were our conquests; what they called our encroachments were our rights.

When its hour seemed come, the Restoration, supposing itself victorious over Bonaparte, and rooted in the country, that is to say, thinking itself strong and thinking itself deep, took its resolution abruptly and risked its throw. One morning it rose in the face of France, and, lifting up its voice, it denied the collect-ive title and the individual title, sovereignty to the nation, liberty to the citizen. In other words, it denied to the nation what made it a nation, and to the citizen what made him a citizen.

This is the essence of those famous acts which are called the ordinances of July.

The Restoration fell.

It fell justly. We must say, however, that it had not been absolutely hostile to all forms of progress. Some grand things were done in its presence.

Under the Restoration the nation became accustomed to discussion with calmness, which was wanting in the republic; and to grandeur in peace, which was wanting in the empire. France, free and strong, had been an encouraging spectacle to the other peoples of Europe. The Revolution had had its say under Robespierre; the cannon had had its say under Bonaparte; under Louis XVIII. and Charles X. intelligence in its turn found speech. The wind ceased, the torch was relighted. The pure light of mind was seen trembling upon the serene summits. A magnificent spectacle, full of use and charm. For fifteen years there were seen at work, in complete peace, and openly in pub- lic places, these great principles, so old to the thinker, so new to the statesman: equality before the law, freedom of conscience, freedom of speech, freedom of the press, the accessibility of every function to every aptitude. This went on thus until 1830. The Bourbons were an instrument of civilisation, which broke in the hands of Providence.

The fall of the Bourbons was full of grandeur, not on their part but on the part of the nation. They left the throne with gravity, but without authority; their descent into the night was not one of those solemn disappearances which leave a dark emotion to history; it was neither the spectral calmness of Charles I., nor the eagle cry of Napoleon. They went away, that is all. They laid off the crown, and did not keep the halo. They were worthy, but they were not august. They fell short, to some extent, of the majesty of their misfortune. Charles X., during the voyage from Cherbourg, having a round table cut into a square table, appeared more solicitous of imperilled etiquette than of the falling monarchy. This pettiness saddened the devoted men who loved them, and the serious men who hon- oured their race. The people, for its part, was wonderfully noble. The nation, attacked one morning by force and arms, by a sort of royal insurrection, felt so strong that it had no anger. It defended itself, restrained itself, put things into their places, the government into the hands of the law, the Bourbons into exile, alas! and stopped. It took the old king, Charles X., from under that dais which had sheltered Louis XVIII., and placed him gently on the ground. It touched the royal personages sadly and with precaution. It was not a man, it was not a few men, it was France, all France, France victorious and intoxicated with her victory, seeming to remember herself, and putting in practice before the eyes of the whole world these grave words of Guil- laume du Vair after the day of the barricades: "It is easy for those who are accustomed to gather the favours of the great, and to leap, like a bird, from branch to branch, from a grievous to a flourishing fortune, to show themselves bold towards their prince in his adversity; but to me the fortune of my kings will always be venerable, and principally when they are in grief."

The Bourbons carried with them respect, but not regret. As we have said, their misfortune was greater than they. They faded away in the horizon.

The Revolution of July immediately found friends and enemies throughout the world. The former rushed towards it with enthusiasm and joy, the latter turned away; each according to his own nature. The princes of Europe, at the first moment, owls in this dawn, closed their eyes, shocked and stupefied, and opened them only to threaten. A fright which can be understood, an anger which can be excused. This strange revolution had hardly been a shock; it did not even do vanquished royalty the honour of treating it as an enemy and shedding its blood. In the eyes of the despotic governments, always interested that liberty should calumniate herself, the Revolution of July had the fault of being formidable and yet being mild. Nothing, however, was attempted, or plotted against it. The most dissatisfied, the most irritated, the most horrified, bowed to it; whatever may be our selfishness and our prejudices, a mysterious respect springs from events in which we feel the intervention of a hand higher than that of man.

The Revolution of July is the triumph of the Right prostrating the fact. A thing full of splendour.

The right prostrating the fact. Thence the glory of the Revolution of 1830, thence its mildness also. The right, when it triumphs, has no need to be violent.

The right is the just and the true.

The peculiarity of the right is that it is always beautiful and pure. The fact, even that which is most necessary in appearance, even that most accepted by its contemporaries, if it exist only as fact, and if it contain too little of the right, or none at all, is destined infallibly to become, in the lapse of time, deformed, unclean, perhaps even monstrous. If you would ascertain at once what degree of ugliness the fact may reach, seen in the distance of the centuries, look at Machiavelli. Machiavelli is not an evil genius, nor a demon, nor a cowardly and miserable writer; he is nothing but the fact. And he is not merely the Italian fact, he is the European fact, the fact of the sixteenth century. He seems hideous, and he is so, in presence of the moral idea of the nineteenth.

This conflict of the right and the fact endures from the origin of society. To bring the duel to an end, to amalgamate the pure ideal with the human reality, to make the right peacefully inter-penetrate the fact, and the fact the right, this is the work of the wise.

II
BADLY SEWED

BUT the work of the wise is one thing, the work of the able another.

The Revolution of 1830 soon grounded.

As soon as the revolution strikes the shore, the able carve up the wreck.

The able, in our age, have decreed to themselves the title of statesmen, so that this word, statesman, has come to be, in some sort, a word of argot. Indeed, let no one forget, wherever there is ability only, there is necessarily pettiness. To say "the able," amounts to saying, "mediocrity."

Just as saying, "statesmen," is sometimes equivalent to saying "traitors."

According to the able, therefore, revolutions such as the Revolution of July, are arteries cut; a prompt ligature is needed. The right, too grandly proclaimed, is disquieting. So, the right once affirmed, the state must be reaffirmed. Liberty being assured, we must take thought for power.

Thus far the wise do not separate from the able, but they begin to distrust. Power, very well. But, first, what is power? Secondly, whence comes it?

The able seem not to hear the murmurs of objection, and they continue their work.

According to these politicians, ingenious in putting a mask of necessity upon profitable fictions, the first need to a people after a revolution, if this people forms part of a monarchical continent, is to procure a dynasty. In this way, say they, it can have peace after its revolution, that is to say, time to staunch its wounds and to repair its house. The dynasty hides the scaffold-ing and covers the ambulance.

Now, it is not always easy to procure a dynasty.

In case of necessity, the first man of genius, or even the first adventurer you meet, suffices for a king. You have in the first place Bonaparte, and in the second Iturbide.

But the first family you meet with does not suffice to make a dynasty. There must be a certain amount of antiquity in a race, and the wrinkles of centuries are not extemporised.

If we place ourselves at the statesmen's point of view, of course with every reservation, after a revolution, what are the qualities of the king who springs from it? He may be, and it is well that he should be, revolutionary, that is to say, a participant in his own person in this revolution, that he should have taken part in it, that he should be compromised in it, or made illustrious, that he should have touched the axe or handled the sword.

What are the qualities of a dynasty? It should be national; that is to say, revolutionary at a distance, not by acts performed, but by ideas accepted. It should be composed of the past and be historic, of the future and be sympathetic.

All this explains why the first revolutions content themselves with finding a man, Cromwell or Napoleon; and why the second absolutely insists on finding a family, the house of Brunswick or the house of Orleans.

Royal houses resemble those banyan trees of India, each branch of which, by bending to the ground, takes root there and becomes a banyan. Each branch may become a dynasty. On the sole condition that it bend to the people.

Such is the theory of the able.

This, then, is the great art, to give a success something of the sound of a catastrophe, in order that those who profit by it may tremble also, to moderate a step in advance with fear, to enlarge the curve of transition to the extent of retarding progress, to tame down this work, to denounce and restrain the ardencies of enthusiasm, to cut off the corners and the claws, to clog triumph, to swaddle the right, to wrap up the people-giant in flannel and hurry him to bed, to impose a diet upon this excess of health, to put Hercules under convalescent treatment, to hold back the event within the expedient, to offer to minds thirsting for the ideal this nectar extended from barley-water, to take precautions against too much success, to furnish the revolution with a skylight.

The year 1830 carried out this theory, already applied to England by 1688.

The year 1830 is a revolution arrested in mid career. Half progress, quasi right. Now logic ignores the Almost, just as the sun ignores the candle.

Who stops revolutions half way? The bourgeoisie.

Why?

Because the bourgeoisie is the interest which has attained to satisfaction. Yesterday it was appetite, to-day it is fulness, to-morrow it will be satiety.

The phenomenon of 1814 after Napoleon, was reproduced in 1830 after Charles X.

There has been an attempt, an erroneous one, to make a special class of the bourgeoisie. The bourgeoisie is simply the contented portion of the people. The bourgeois is the man who has now time to sit down. A chair is not a caste.

But, by wishing to sit down, we may stop the progress even of the human race. That has often been the fault of the bourgeois.

The commission of a fault does not constitute a class. Egotism is not one of the divisions of the social order.

Moreover, we must be just even towards egotism. The state to which, after the shock of 1830, that part of the nation which is called bourgeoisie aspired, was not inertia, which is a complication of indifference and idleness, and which contains something of shame; it was not slumber, which supposes a momentary forgetfulness accessible to dreams; it was a halt.

Halt is a word formed with a singular and almost contradictory double meaning: a troop on the march, that is to say, movement; a stopping, that is to say, repose.

Halt is the regaining of strength, it is armed and watchful repose; it is the accomplished fact which plants sentinels and keeps itself upon its guard. Halt supposes battle yesterday and battle to-morrow.

This is the interval between 1830 and 1848.

What we here call battle may also be called progress.

The bourgeoisie, then, as well as the statesmen, felt the need of a man who should express this word: Halt! An Although Because. A composite individuality, signifying revolution and signifying stability; in other words, assuring the present through the evident compatibility of the past with the future.

This man was "found at hand." His name was Louis Philippe d'Orleans.

The 221 made Louis Philippe king. Lafayette undertook the coronation. He called it *the best of republics*. The Hotel de Ville of Paris replaced the Cathedral of Rheims.

This substitution of a demi-throne for the complete throne was "the work of 1830."

When the able had finished their work, the immense viciousness of their solution became apparent. All this was done without reference to absolute right. The absolute right cried "I protest!" then, a fearful thing, it went back into the obscurity.

III
LOUISE PHILIPPE

REVOLUTIONS have a terrible arm and a fortunate hand; they strike hard and choose well. Even when incomplete, even degenerate and abused, and reduced to the condition of revolution junior, like the Revolution of 1830, they almost always retain enough of the light of providence to prevent a fatal fall. Their eclipse is never an abdication.

Still, let us not boast too loudly; revolutions, even, are deceived, and disclose grave mistakes.

Let us return to 1830. The year 1830 was fortunate in its deviation. In the establishment which called itself order after the Revolution was cut short, the king was better than the royalty. Louis Philippe was a rare man.

Son of a father to whom history will certainly allow attenuating circumstances, but as worthy of esteem as that father had been worthy of blame; having all private virtues and many public virtues; careful of his health, his fortune, his person, his business, knowing the value of a minute, though not always the value of a year; sober, serene, peaceful, patient; good man and good prince; sleeping with his wife and having lackeys in his palace whose business it was to exhibit the conjugal bed to the bourgeois, an ostentation of domestic regularity which had its use after the former illegitimate displays of the elder branch; knowing all the languages of Europe, and, what is rarer, all the languages of all interests, and speaking them; admirable representative of "the middle class," but surpassing it, and in every way greater than it; having the excellent sense, even while appreciating the blood from which he sprang, to estimate himself above all at his own intrinsic worth, and, about the question of his race even, very particular, declaring himself Orleans and not Bourbon; really first Prince of the Blood, while he had only been Most Serene Highness, but a frank bourgeois the day he was Majesty; diffuse in public, concise in private; a declared, but not proven miser; in reality one of those economical persons who are prodigal in matters of fancy or their duty; well read, but not very appreciative of letters; a gentleman, but not chivalrous; simple, calm, and strong; worshipped by his family and by his house; a seductive talker, an undeceived statesman, interiorly cold, ruled by the present interest, governing always by the nearest convenience, incapable of malice or of gratitude, pitilessly wearing out superiorities upon mediocrities, able in opposing through parliamentary majorities those mysterious unanimities which mutter almost inaudibly beneath thrones; expansive, sometimes imprudent in his expansion, but with marvellous address in that imprudence; fertile in expedients, in faces, in masks; making France afraid of Europe and Europe of France; loving his country incontestably, but preferring his family; prizing domination more than authority, and authority more than dignity; a disposition which is to this extent fatal, that, turning everything towards success, it admits of ruse, and does not absolutely repudiate baseness; but which is profitable to this extent, that it preserves politics from violent shocks, the state from fractures, and society from catastrophes; minute, correct, vigilant, attentive, sagacious, indefatigable; contradicting himself sometimes, and giving himself the lie; bold against Austria at Ancona, obstinate against England in Spain, bombarding Antwerp and paying Pritchard; singing the Marseillaise with conviction; inaccessible to depression, to weariness, to taste for the beautiful and the ideal, to foolhardy generosity, to Utopia, to chimeras, to anger, to vanity, to fear; having every form of personal bravery; general at Valmy, soldier at Jemappes, his life attempted eight times by regicides, yet always smiling; brave as a grenadier, courageous as a thinker; anxious merely before the chances of a European disturbance, and unfit for great political adventures; always ready to risk his life, never his work; disguising his pleasure in the form of influence that he might be obeyed rather as an intelligence than as a king; endowed with observation and not with divination, paying little attention to minds, but able to read the character of men, that is to say, needing to see in order to judge; prompt and penetrating good sense, practical wisdom, ready speech, prodigious memory; digging incessantly into that memory, his only point of resemblance with Cæsar, Alexander, and Napoleon, knowing facts, details, dates, proper names, ignorant of tendencies, passions, the diverse genii of the multitude, interior aspirations, the hidden and obscure uprisings of souls, in one word, all that might be called the invisible currents of conscience; accepted by the surface, but little in accord with the under-France; making his way by craft; governing too much and not reigning enough; his own prime minister; excelling in making of the pettiness of realities an obstacle to the immensity of ideas; adding to a true creative faculty for civilisation, order, and organisation, an indescribable spirit of routine and chicanery, founder and attorney of a dynasty; possessing something of Charlemagne and something of a lawyer; to sum up, a lofty and original figure, a prince who knew how to gain powers in spite of the restlessness of France, and power in spite of the jealousy of Europe. Louis Philippe will be classed among the eminent men of his century and would be ranked among the most illustrious rulers of history if he had had a little love of glory, and had appreciated what is great to the same extent that he appreciated what is useful.

Louis Philippe had been handsome, and, when old, was still fine looking; not always agreeable to the nation, he always was to the multitude; he pleased. He had this gift, a charm. Majesty he lacked; he neither wore the crown, though king, nor white hair, though an old man. His manners were of the old régime, and his habits of the new, a mixture of the noble and the bourgeois which was befitting to 1830; Louis Philippe was regnant transition; he had preserved the ancient pronunciation and the ancient orthography which he put into the service of modern opinions; he loved Poland and Hungary, but he wrote *les polonois*, and pronounced *les hongrais*. He wore the dress of the National Guard like Charles X., and the cordon of the Legion of Honour like Napoleon.

He went rarely to chapel, not at all to the chase, never to the opera. Incorruptible by priests, dog-keepers, and danseuses; this entered into his popularity with the bourgeoisie. He had no court. He went out with his umbrella under his arm, and this umbrella for a long time was a portion of his glory. He was something of a mason, something of a gardener, and something of a doctor; he bled a postillion who fell from his horse; Louis

Philippe no more went without his lancet than Henry III. without his poniard. The royalists laughed at this ridiculous king, the first who had spilled blood to save.

In the complaints of history against Louis Philippe, there is a deduction to be made, there is what is to be charged to the royalty, what is to be charged to the reign, and what is to be charged to the king; three columns, each of which gives a different total. The right of democracy confiscated, progress made the second interest, the protests of the street violently repressed, the military execution of insurrections, émeutes passed over by arms, the Rue Transnonain, the councils of war, the absorption of the real country by the legal country, the theory of the government but half carried out, with three hundred thousand privileged persons, are the acts of the royalty; Belgium refused, Algeria too harshly conquered, and, like India by the English, with more of barbarism than civilisation, the breach of faith with Abd-el-Kader, Blaye, Deutz purchased, Pritchard paid, are the acts of the reign, the policy, which looked rather to the family than to the nation, is the act of the king.

As we see, when the deduction is made, the charge against the king is diminished.

His great fault was this: He was modest in the name of France.

Whence comes this fault?

We must tell.

Louis Philippe was a too fatherly king; this incubation of a family which is to be hatched into a dynasty is afraid of everything, and cannot bear disturbance; hence excessive timidity, annoying to a people who have the 14th of July in their civil traditions, and Austerlitz in their military traditions.

Moreover, if we throw aside public duties, which first demand to be fulfilled, this deep tenderness of Louis Philippe for his family, the family deserved. This domestic group was wonderful. Their virtues emulated their talents. One of Louis Philippe's daughters, Maria d'Orleans, put the name of her race among artists as Charles d'Orleans had put it among poets. Out of her soul she made a statue which she called Jeanne d'Arc. Two of Louis Philippe's sons drew from Metternich this eulogy of a demagogue: *They are young men such as we rarely see and princes such as we never see.*

This is, without keeping anything back, but also without aggravating anything, the truth about Louis Philippe.

To be Prince Equality, to bear within himself the contradiction of the Restoration and the Revolution, to have this threatening aspect of the revolutionist which becomes reassuring in the ruler, such was the fortune of Louis Philippe in 1830; never was there a more complete adaptation of a man to an event; the one entered into the other, and there was an incarnation. Louis Philippe is 1830 made man. Moreover, he had in his favour that grand designation for the throne, exile. He had been proscribed, a wanderer, poor. He had lived by his labour. In Switzerland, this heir to the richest princely domains in France had sold an old horse, to procure food. At Reichenau he had given lessons in mathematics, while his sister Adelaide did sewing and embroidery. These memories associated with a king, rendered the bourgeoisie enthusiastic. He had with his own hands demolished the last iron cage of Mont Saint Michel, built by Louis XI. and used by Louis XV. He was the companion of Dumouriez, he was the friend of Lafayette; he had belonged to the Jacobin Club; Mirabeau had slapped him on the shoulder; Danton had said to him, "Young man!" At twenty-four years of age, in '93, being M. de Chartres, from the back of an obscure bench in the convention, he had been present at the trial of Louis XVI., so well named *that poor tyrant*. The blind clairvoyance of the Revolution, crushing royalty in the king, and the king with the royalty, almost without noticing the man in the savage overthrow of the idea, the vast storm of the tribunal-assembly, the public wrath questioning, Capet not knowing what to answer, the fearful stupefied vacillation of this royal head under that terrible blow, the relative innocence of all in that catastrophe, of those who condemned as well as of him who was condemned; he had seen these things, he had looked upon this mad whirl; he had seen the centuries appear at the bar of the Convention; he had seen behind Louis XVI., that hapless, responsible by-passer, rising up in the darkness, the fear-inspiring criminal, the monarchy; and there was still in his soul a respectful fear before this limitless justice of the people, almost as impersonal as the justice of God.

The effect which the Revolution produced upon him was tremendous. His memory was like a living impression of those grand years, minute by minute. One day, before a witness whom it is impossible for us to doubt, he corrected from memory the whole letter A of the alphabetic list of the constituent assembly.

Louis Philippe was a king in broad day. While he reigned the press was free, the tribune was free, conscience and speech were free! The laws of September are clear and open. Knowing well the corroding power of light on privileges, he left his throne exposed to the light. History will acknowledge this loyalty.

Louis Philippe, like all historic men who have left the scene, is now to be put upon his trial by the human conscience. He is as yet only before the grand jury.

The hour in which history speaks with its free and venerable accent, has not yet struck for him; the time has not come to pronounce final judgment upon this king; that austere and illustrious historian Louis Blanc, has himself recently modified his first verdict: Louis Philippe was the elect of those two almosts which are called the 221 and 1830, that is to say, of a demi-parliament and a demi-revolution; and at all events, from the superior point of view in which philosophy ought to place herself, we could judge him here, as we have before intimated, only under certain reservations in the name of the absolute democratic principle; in the eyes of the absolute, beyond these rights: the rights of man first, the rights of the people afterwards, all is usurpation; but we can say at present, having made these reservations, that, to sum up, and in whatever way he is considered, Louis Philippe, taken by himself, and from the point of view of human goodness, will remain, to use the old language of ancient history, one of the best princes that ever sat upon a throne.

What is there against him? That throne. Take from Louis Philippe the king, there remains the man. And the man is good. He is sometimes so good as to be admirable. Often, in the midst of the gravest cares, after a day of struggle against the whole diplomacy of the continent, he retired at evening into his apartment, and there, exhausted with fatigue, bowed down with sleep, what did he do? He took a bundle of documents, and passed the night in reviewing a criminal prosecution, feeling that it was something to make head against Europe, but that it was a much grander thing still to save a man from the executioner. He was obstinate against his keeper of the seals; he disputed inch by inch the ground of the guillotine with the attorney-generals, *those babblers of the law*, as he called them.

Sometimes the heaped-up documents covered his table; he examined them all; it was anguish to him to give up those wretched condemned heads. One day he said to the same witness whom we have just now referred to: *Last night I saved seven*. During the early years of his reign, the death penalty was abolished and the re-erected scaffold was a severe blow to the king. La Grève having disappeared with the elder branch a bourgeois Grève was instituted under the name of Barrière Saint Jacques; "practical men" felt the need of a quasi-legitimate guillotine; and this was one of the victories of Casimir Perier, who represented the more conservative portions of the bourgeoisie, over Louis Philippe, who represented its more liberal portions. Louis Philippe annotated Beccaria with his own hand. After the Fieschi machine, he exclaimed: *What a pity that I was not wounded! I could have pardoned him*. At another time, alluding to the resistance of his ministers, he wrote concerning a political convict, who is one of the noblest figures of our times: *His pardon is granted, it only remains for me to obtain it*. Louis Philippe was as gentle as Louis IX., and as good as Henry IV.

Now, to us, in history where goodness is the pearl of great price, he who has been good stands almost above him who has been great.

Louis Philippe having been estimated with severity by some, harshly, perhaps, by others, it is very natural that a man, now himself a phantom, who knew this king, should come forward to testify for him before history; this testimony, whatever it may be, is evidently and above all disinterested; an epitaph written by a dead man is sincere; one shade may console another shade; the sharing of the same darkness gives the right to praise; and there is little fear that it will ever be said of two tombs in exile: This one flattered the other.

IV
CREVICES UNDER THE FOUNDATION

At the moment the drama which we are relating is about to penetrate into the depths of one of the tragic clouds which cover the first years of the reign of Louis Philippe, we could not be ambiguous, and it was necessary that this book should be explicit in regard to this king.

Louis Philippe entered into the royal authority without

violence, without direct action on his part, by the action of a revolutionary transfer, evidently very distinct from the real aim of the revolution, but in which he, the Duke d'Orleans, had no personal initiative. He was a born prince, and believed himself elected king. He had not given himself this command; he had not taken it; it had been offered to him and he had accepted it; convinced, wrongly in our opinion, but convinced, that the offer was consistent with right, and that the acceptance was consistent with duty. Hence a possession in good faith. Now, we say it in all conscience, Louis Philippe being in good faith in his possession, and the democracy being in good faith in their attack, the terror which arises from social struggles is chargeable neither to the king nor to the democracy. A shock of principles resembles a shock of the elements. The ocean defends the water, the hurricane defends the air; the king defends royalty, the democracy defends the people; the relative, which is the monarchy, resists the absolute, which is the republic; society bleeds under this struggle, but what is its suffering to-day will be its safety hereafter; and, at all events, there is no censure due to those who struggle; one of the two parties is evidently mistaken; right is not like the colossus of Rhodes, upon two shores at once, one foot in the republic, one foot in royalty; it is indivisible, and all on one side; but those who are mistaken are sincerely mistaken; a blind man is no more a criminal than a Vendéen is a brigand. Let us, then, impute these terrible collisions only to the fatality of things. Whatever these tempests may be, human responsibility is not mingled with them.

Let us complete this exposition.

The government of 1830 had from the first a hard life. Born yesterday, it was obliged to fight to-day.

It was hardly installed when it began to feel on all sides vague movements directed against the machinery of July, still so newly set up, and so far from secure.

Resistance was born on the morrow, perhaps even it was born on the eve.

From month to month the hostility increased, and from dumb it became outspoken.

The Revolution of July, tardily accepted, as we have said, outside of France by the kings, had been diversely interpreted in France.

God makes visible to men his will in events, an obscure text written in a mysterious language. Men make their translations of it forthwith; hasty translations, incorrect, full of faults, omissions, and misreadings. Very few minds comprehend the divine tongue. The most sagacious, the most calm, the most profound, decipher slowly, and, when they arrive with their text, the need has long gone by; there are already twenty translations in the public square. From each translation a party is born, and from each misreading a faction; and each party believes it has the only true text, and each faction believes that it possesses the light.

Often the government itself is a faction.

There are in revolutions some swimmers against the stream, these are the old parties.

To the old parties, who are attached to hereditary right by the grace of God, revolutions having arisen from the right of revolt, there is a right of revolt against them. An error. For in revolutions the revolted party is not the people, it is the king. Revolution is precisely the opposite of revolt. Every revolution, being a normal accomplishment, contains in itself its own legitimacy, which false revolutionists sometimes dishonour, but which persists, even when sullied, which survives, even when stained with blood. Revolutions spring, not from an accident, but from necessity. A revolution is a return from the factitious to the real. It is, because it must be.

The old legitimist parties none the less assailed the Revolution of 1830 with all the violence which springs from false reasoning. Errors are excellent projectiles. They struck it skilfully just where it was vulnerable, at the defect in its cuirass, its want of logic; they attacked this revolution in its royalty. They cried to it: Revolution, why this king? Factions are blind men who aim straight.

This cry was uttered also by the republicans. But, coming from them, this cry was logical. What was blindness with the legitimists was clear-sightedness with the democrats. The year 1830 had become bankrupt with the people. The democracy indignantly reproached it with its failure.

Between the attack of the past and the attack of the future, the establishment of July was struggling. It represented the moment, in conflict on the one hand with the monarchical centuries, on the other hand with the eternal right.

Moreover, externally, being no longer the revolution, and becoming the monarchy, 1830 was obliged to keep step with

Europe. To preserve peace, an increase of complication. A harmony required in the wrong way is often more onerous than a war. From this sullen conflict, always muzzled but always muttering, is born armed peace, that ruinous expedient of civilisation suspected by herself. The royalty of July reared, in spite of the lash, in the harness of the European cabinets. Metternich would have been glad to put it in kicking-straps. Pushed upon in France by progress, it pushed upon the monarchies in Europe, those tardigrades. Towed, it towed.

Meanwhile, within the country, pauperism, proletariat, wages, education, punishment, prostitution, the lot of woman, riches, misery, production, consumption, distribution, exchange, money, credit, rights of capital, rights of labour, all these questions multiplied over society; a terrible steep.

Outside of the political parties properly speaking, another movement manifested itself. To the democratic fermentation, the philosophic fermentation responded. The élite felt disturbed as well as the multitude; otherwise, but as much.

Thinkers were meditating, while the soil, that is to say, the people, traversed by the revolutionary currents, trembled beneath them with mysterious epileptic shocks. These thinkers, some isolated, others gathered into families and almost into communion, were turning over social questions, peacefully, but profoundly; impassible miners, who were quietly pushing their galleries into the depths of a volcano, scarcely disturbed by the sullen commotions and the half-seen glow of lava.

This tranquillity was not the least beautiful spectacle of that agitated period.

These men left to political parties the question of rights, they busied themselves with the question of happiness.

The well-being of man was what they wished to extract from society.

They raised the material questions, questions of agriculture, of industry, of commerce, almost to the dignity of a religion. In civilisation such as it is constituted to small extent by God, to great by man, interests are combined, aggregated, and amalgamated in such a manner as to form actual hard rock, according to a dynamic law patiently studied by the economists, those geologists of politics.

These men who grouped themselves under different appellations but who may all be designated by the generic title of socialists, endeavoured to pierce this rock and to make the living waters of human felicity gush forth from it.

From the question of the scaffold to the question of war, their labours embraced everything. To the rights of man, proclaimed by the French Revolution, they added the rights of woman and the rights of childhood.

No one will be astonished that, for various reasons, we do not here treat fundamentally, from the theoretic point of view, the questions raised by socialism. We limit ourselves to indicating them.

All the problems which the socialists propounded, aside from the cosmogonic visions, dreams, and mysticism, may be reduced to two principal problems.

First problem:

To produce wealth.

Second problem:

To distribute it.

The first problem contains the question of labour.

The second contains the question of wages.

In the first problem the question is of the employment of force.

In the second of the distribution of enjoyment.

From the good employment of force results public power.

From the good distribution of enjoyment results individual happiness.

By good distribution, we must understand not equal distribution, but equitable distribution. The highest equality is equity.

From these two things combined, public power without, individual happiness within, results social prosperity.

Social prosperity means, man happy, the citizen free, the nation great.

England solves the first of these two problems. She creates wealth wonderfully; she distributes it badly. This solution, which is complete only on one side, leads her inevitably to these two extremes: monstrous opulence, monstrous misery. All the enjoyment to a few, all the privation to the rest, that is to say, to the people; privilege, exception, monopoly, feudality, springing from labour itself, a false and dangerous situation which founds public power upon private misery, which plants the grandeur of the state in the suffering of the individual. A grandeur ill constituted, in which all the material elements are combined, and into which no moral element enters.

Communism and agrarian law think they have solved the second problem. They are mistaken. Their distribution kills production. Equal partition abolishes emulation. And consequently labour. It is a distribution made by the butcher, who kills what he divides. It is therefore impossible to stop at these professed solutions. To kill wealth is not to distribute it.

The two problems must be solved together to be well solved. The two solutions must be combined and form but one.

Solve the first only of the two problems, you will be Venice, you will be England. You will have like Venice an artificial power, or like England a material power; you will be the evil rich man, you will perish by violence, as Venice died, or by bankruptcy, as England will fall, and the world will let you die and fall, because the world lets everything fall and die which is nothing but selfishness, everything which does not represent a virtue or an idea for the human race.

It is of course understood that by these words, Venice, England, we designate not the people, but the social constructions; the oligarchies superimposed upon the nations, and not the nations themselves. The nations always have our respect and our sympathy. Venice, the people, will be reborn; England, the aristocracy, will fall, but England, the nation, is immortal. This said, we proceed.

Solve the two problems, encourage the rich, and protect the poor, suppress misery, put an end to the unjust speculation upon the weak by the strong, put a bridle upon the iniquitous jealousy of him who is on the road, against him who has reached his end, adjust mathematically and fraternally wages to labour, join gratuitous and obligatory instruction to the growth of childhood, and make science the basis of manhood, develop the intelligence while you occupy the arm, be at once a powerful people and a family of happy men, democratise property, not by abolishing it, but by universalising it, in such a way that every citizen without exception may be a proprietor, an easier thing than it is believed to be; in two words, learn to produce wealth and learn to distribute it, and you shall have material grandeur and moral grandeur combined; and you shall be worthy to call yourselves France.

This, above and beyond a few sects which ran wild, is what

socialism said; that is what it sought to realise; this is what it outlined in men's minds.

Admirable efforts! sacred attempts!

These doctrines, these theories, these resistances, the unforeseen necessity for the statesman to consult with the philosopher, confused evidences half seen, a new politics to create, accordant with the old world, and yet not too discordant with the ideal of the revolution; a state of affairs in which Lafayette must be used to oppose Polignac, the intuition of progress transparent in the émeute, the chambers, and the street, competitions to balance about him, his faith in the revolution, perhaps some uncertain eventual resignation arising from the vague acceptance of a definitive superior right, his desire to remain in his race, his family pride, his sincere respect for the people, his own honesty, preoccupied Louis Philippe almost painfully, and at moments, strong and as courageous as he was, overwhelmed him under the difficulties of being king.

He felt beneath his feet a terrible disaggregation which was not, however, a crumbling into dust—France being more France than ever.

Dark drifts covered the horizon. A strange shadow approaching nearer and nearer, was spreading little by little over men, over things, over ideas; a shadow which came from indignations and from systems. All that had been hurriedly stifled was stirring and fermenting. Sometimes the conscience of the honest man caught its breath, there was so much confusion in that air in which sophisms were mingled with truths. Minds trembled in the social anxiety like leaves at the approach of the storm. The electric tension was so great that at certain moments any chance-comer, though unknown, flashed out. Then the twilight obscurity fell again. At intervals, deep and sullen mutterings enabled men to judge of the amount of lightning in the cloud.

Twenty months had hardly rolled away since the revolution of July, the year 1832 had opened with an imminent and menacing aspect. The distress of the people; labourers without bread; the last Prince de Condé lost in the darkness; Brussels driving away the Nassaus, as Paris had driven away the Bourbons; Belgium offering herself to a French prince, and given to an English prince; the Russian hatred of Nicholas; in our rear two demons of the south, Ferdinand in Spain, Miguel in Portu-

gal; the earth quaking in Italy; Metternich extending his hand
over Bologna; France bluntly opposing Austria at Ancona; in
the north a mysterious ill-omened sound of a hammer nailing
Poland again into its coffin; throughout Europe angry looks
keeping watch over France; England a suspicious ally, ready to
push over whoever might bend, and to throw herself upon
whoever might fall; the peerage sheltering itself behind Beccaria, to refuse four heads to the law; the *fleur-de-lys* erased from
the king's carriage; the cross torn down from Notre Dame;
Lafayette in decay; Laffitte ruined; Benjamin Constant dead in
poverty; Casimir Perier dead from loss of power; the political
disease and the social disease breaking out in the two capitals of
the realm, one the city of thought, the other the city of labour;
at Paris civil war, at Lyons servile war; in the two cities the same
furnace glare; the flush of the crater on the forehead of the
people; the South fanatical, the West disturbed; the Duchess of
Berry in La Vendée; plots, conspiracies, uprisings, the cholera,
added to the dismal tumult of ideas, the dismal uproar of events.

V

FACTS FROM WHICH HISTORY SPRINGS,
AND WHICH HISTORY IGNORES

TOWARDS the end of April everything was worse. The
fermentation became a boiling. Since 1830 there had been here
and there some little partial émeutes, quickly repressed, but
again breaking out, signs of a vast underlying conflagration.
Something terrible was brooding. Glimpses were caught of the
lineaments, still indistinct and scarcely visible, of a possible
revolution. France looked to Paris; Paris looked to the Faubourg
Saint Antoine.

The Faubourg Saint Antoine sullenly warmed up, was beginning to boil.

The wine-shops of the Rue de Charonne, although the junction of the two epithets seems singular, applied to wine-shops,
were serious and stormy.

In them the simple existence of the government was brought
in question. The men there publicly discussed whether it were
the thing to fight or to remain quiet. There were back shops where
all oath was administered to working-men, that they would be
in the streets at the first cry of alarm, and "that they would fight

without counting the number of the enemy." The engagement once taken, a man seated in a corner of the wine-shop "made a sonorous voice," and said: "*You understand it! you have sworn it!*" Sometimes they went upstairs into a closed room, and there scenes occurred which were almost masonic. Oaths were administered *to the initiated to render service to them as they would to their own fathers.* That was the formula.

In the lower rooms they read "subversive" pamphlets. *They pelted the government,* says a secret report of the times.

Such words as these were heard.—"*I don't know the names of the chiefs. As for us, we shall only know the day two hours beforehand.*" A working-man said: "*There are three hundred of us, let us put in ten sous each, that will make a hundred and fifty francs to manufacture powder and ball.*" Another said: "*I don't ask six months, I don't ask two. In less than a fortnight we shall meet the government face to face. With twenty-five thousand men we can make a stand.*" Another said: "*I don't go to bed, because I am making cartridges all night.*" From time to time, men "like bourgeois, and in fine coats" came, "causing embarrassment," and having the air "of command," gave a grip of the hand *to the most important,* and went away. They never stayed more than ten minutes. Significant words were exchanged in a low voice: "*The plot is ripe, the thing is complete.*" "This was buzzed by all who were there," to borrow the very expression of one of the participants. The exaltation was such, that one day, in a public wine-shop, a working-man exclaimed: *We have no arms!* One of his comrades answered: *The soldiers have!* thus parodying, without suspecting it, Bonaparte's proclamation to the army of Italy. "When they have anything more secret," adds a report, "they do not communicate it in those places." One can hardly comprehend what they could conceal after saying what they did.

The meetings were sometimes periodical. At some, there were never more than eight or ten, and always the same persons. In others, anybody who chose entered, and the room was so full that they were forced to stand. Some were there from enthusiasm and passion; others because *it was on their way to their work.* As in the time of the revolution, there were in these wine-shops some female patriots, who embraced the new-comers.

Other expressive facts came to light.

A man entered a shop, drank, and went out, saying: "*Wine-merchant, what is due, the revolution will pay.*"

At a wine-shop opposite the Rue de Charonne, revolution-ary officers were elected. The ballots were gathered in caps.

Some working-men met at a fencing-master's, who gave lessons in the Rue de Cotte. There was a trophy of arms there, formed of wooden swords, canes, clubs, and foils. One day they took the buttons off the foils. A working-man said: "*We are twenty-five; but they don't count on me, because they look upon me as a machine.*" This machine was afterwards Quénisset.

All the little things which were premeditated, gradually acquired some strange notoriety. A woman sweeping her door-step said to another woman: *For a long time they have been hard at work making cartridges.* Proclamations were read in the open street, addressed to the National Guards of the Departments. One of these proclamations was signed: *Burtot, wine-merchant.*

One day at a liquor-dealer's door in the Lenoir market, a man with a heavy beard and an Italian accent mounted on a block and read aloud a singular writing which seemed to emanate from a secret power. Groups formed about him and applauded. The passages which stirred the crowd most were caught and noted down. ". . . Our doctrines are trammelled, our proclamations are torn down, our posters are watched and thrown into prison . . ." ". . . The recent fall in cottons has converted many moder-ates . . ." "The future of the peoples is being worked out in our obscure ranks." ". . . Behold the statement of the matter: action or reaction, revolution or counter-revolution. For, in our times, there is no belief longer in inertia or in immobility. For the people or against the people, that is the question. There is no other." ". . . The day that we no longer suit you, crush us, but until then help us to go forward." All this in broad day.

Other acts, bolder still, were suspected by the people on account of their very boldness. On the 4th of April, 1832, a passer-by mounted the block at the corner of the Rue Sainte Marguerite, and cried: *I am a Babouvist!* But under Babeuf the people scented Gisquet.

Among other things, this man said:

"Down with property! The opposition of the left are cowards and traitors. When they want to be right, they preach revolu-tion. They are democrats that they may not be beaten, and royalists that they may not fight. The republicans are feathered beasts. Distrust the republicans, citizen labourers."

"Silence, citizen spy!" cried a working-man.

This put an end to the discourse.

Mysterious incidents occurred.

At nightfall, a working-man met "a well-dressed man" near the canal, who said to him: "Where are you going, citizen?" "Monsieur," said the working-man, "I have not the honour of knowing you." "I know you very well." And the man added: "Don't be afraid. I am the officer of the Committee. They are suspicious that you are not very sure. You know that if you reveal anything, we have an eye upon you." Then he gave the working-man a grip of the hand and went away, saying: "We shall meet again soon."

The police, on the scout, overheard, not merely in the wine-shops, but in the street, singular dialogues: "Get yourself admitted very quick," said a weaver to a cabinet-maker.

"Why?"

"There is going to be some shooting."

Two passers in rags exchanged these remarkable phrases, big with apparent Jacquerie.

"Who governs us?"

"Monsieur Philippe."

"No, it's the bourgeoisie."

You would be mistaken if you supposed that we used the word Jacquerie in bad part. The Jacques were the poor.

Another time, two men were heard passing by, one of whom said to the other: "We have a good plan of attack."

Of a private conversation between four men crouching in a ditch at the fork of the road by the Barrière du Trône, there was caught only this:

"All that is possible will be done that he may promenade in Paris no more."

Who was *he*? Threatening obscurity.

"The principal chiefs," as they said in the Faubourg, kept out of sight. They were believed to meet to concert together, in a wine-shop near Point Saint Eustache. One named Aug——, chief of the Tailors' Benevolent Society, Rue Mondétour, was thought to act as principal intermediary between the chiefs and the Faubourg Saint Antoine. Nevertheless, there was always much obscurity about these chiefs, and no actual fact could weaken the singular boldness of the response afterwards made by a prisoner before the Court of Peers.

"Who was your chief?"

"*I knew none, and I recognised none.*"

Still it was hardly more than words, transparent, but vague; sometimes rumours in the air, they-says, hearsay. Other indications were discovered.

A carpenter, engaged on the Rue de Reuilly in nailing the boards of a fence about a lot on which a house was building, found in the lot a fragment of a torn letter, on which the following lines were still legible.

"... The Committee must take measures to prevent recruiting in the sections for the different societies..."

And in a postscript:

"We have learned that there are muskets at No. 5 (bis) Rue du Faubourg Poissonière, to the number of five or six thousand, at an armourer's in that court. The section has no arms."

What excited the carpenter and made him show the thing to his neighbours was that a few steps further on he picked up another paper also torn, but still more significant, the form of which we reproduce on account of the historic interest of these strange documents:

Q	C	D	S	
				Learn this list by heart. Afterwards, tear it up. Men who are admitted will do the same when you have transmitted them their orders. Health and fraternity. *u og a' fe.* L.

Those who were at the time in the secret of this discovery, did not know till afterwards the meaning of these four capitals; *quinturions*, *centurions*, *decurions*, *scouts*, and the sense of those letters: *u og a' fe* which was a date, and which meant *this 15th April, 1832.* Under each capital were inscribed names followed by very characteristic indications. Thus: Q. *Baunerel.* 8 muskets. 83 cartridges. Sure man. C. *Boubière.* 1 pistol. 40 cartridges. D. *Rollet.* 1 foil. 1 pistol. 1 pound of powder. S. *Teissier.* 1 sabre. 1 cartridge-box. Exact. *Terreur.* 8 muskets. Brave, etc.

Finally this carpenter found, in the same inclosure also, a third paper on which was written in pencil, but very legibly, this enigmatic list:

Unity. Blanchard: dry-tree. 6.

Barra. Soize. Salle au Comte.
Kosciusko. Aubry the butcher?
J. J. R.
Caius Gracchus.
Right of revision. Dufond. Four.
Fall of the Girondins. Derbac. Maubuée.
Washington. Pinson. 1 pist. 86 cart.
Marseillaise.
Sover. of the people. Michel. Quincampoix. Sabre.
Hoche.
Marceau. Plato. Dry-tree.
Warsaw. Tilly, crier of *Le Populaire*.

The honest bourgeois who finally came into possession of this list knew its signification. It appeared that this list gave the complete nomenclature of the sections of the Fourth Arrondissernent of the Society of the Rights of Man, with the names and residences of the chiefs of sections. At this day, when all these facts then unknown are matter of history only, they can be published. It should be added that the foundation of the Society of the Rights of Man seems to have been posterior to the time when this paper was found. Perhaps it was merely a draft.

Meanwhile, after rumours and speeches, after written indications, material facts began to leak out.

In the Rue Popincourt, at an old curiosity shop, there were seized in a bureau drawer seven sheets of grey paper all evenly folded in quarto; these sheets inclosed twenty-six squares of the same grey paper folded in the form of cartridges, and a card upon which was written:

Saltpetre,	12 ounces.
Sulphur,	2 ounces.
Charcoal,	2 ounces and a half.
Water,	2 ounces.

The official report of the seizure stated that the drawer exhaled a strong odour of powder.

A mason going home, after his day's work, forgot a little package on a bench near the Bridge of Austerlitz. This package was carried to the guardhouse. It was opened and disclosed two printed dialogues, signed *Lahautière*, a song entitled: *Working-men, associate*, and a tin box full of cartridges.

A working-man, drinking with a comrade, made him put his

hand on him to see how warm he was; the other felt a pistol under his vest.

In a ditch on the boulevard, between Père Lachaise and the Barrière du Trône, at the most solitary spot, some children, playing, discovered under a heap of chips and rubbish a bag which contained a bullet-mould, a wooden mandrel for making cartridges, a wooden mortar in which there were some grains of hunting powder, and a little melting pot the interior of which showed unmistakable traces of melted lead.

Some policemen, penetrating suddenly at five o'clock in the morning into the house of a man, named Pardon, who was afterwards sectionary of the section of the Barricade Merry, and was killed in the insurrection of April, 1834, found him standing not far from his bed, with cartridges in his hands, which he was in the act of making.

About the hour when working-men rest, two men were seen to meet between the Barrière Picpus and the Barrière Charenton in a little cross-alley between two walls near a wine-dealer's who had a card-table before his door. One took a pistol from under his blouse and handed it to the other. At the moment of handing it to him he perceived that the perspiration from his breast had communicated some moisture to the powder. He primed the pistol, and added some powder to that which was already in the pan. Then the two men went away.

A man named Gallais, afterwards killed in the Rue Beaubourg in the affair of April, boasted that he had seven hundred cartridges and twenty-four gun-flints at home.

The government received word one day that arms had just been distributed in the Faubourg and two hundred thousand cartridges. The week afterwards thirty thousand cartridges were distributed. A remarkable thing, the police could not seize one. An intercepted letter contained: "The day is not distant when in four hours by the clock, eighty thousand patriots will be under arms."

All this fermentation was public, we might almost say tranquil. The imminent insurrection gathered its storm calmly in the face of the government. No singularity was wanting in this crisis, still subterranean, but already perceptible. Bourgeois talked quietly with working-men about the preparations. They would say: "How is the émeute coming on?" in the same tone in which they would have said: "How is your wife?"

A furniture dealer, Rue Moreau, asked: "Well, when do you attack?"

Another shopkeeper said:

"You will attack very soon, I know. A month ago there were fifteen thousand of you, now there are twenty-five thousand of you." He offered his gun, and a neighbour offered a little pistol which he wanted to sell for seven francs.

The revolutionary fever, however, was increasing. No point of Paris or of France was exempt from it. The artery pulsated everywhere. Like those membranes which are born of certain inflammations and formed in the human body, the network of the secret societies began to spread over the country. From the Association of the Friends of the People, public and secret at the same time, sprang the Society of the Rights of Man, which dated one of its orders of the day thus: *Pluviôse, year 40 of the Republican Era*, which was to survive even the decrees of the Court of Assizes pronouncing its dissolution, and which had no hesitation in giving its sections such significant names as these:

The Pikes.	The Vagrants.
Tocsin.	Forward march.
Alarm Gun.	Robespierre.
Phrygian Cap.	Level.
21st January.	Ça ira.
The Beggars.	

The Society of the Rights of Man produced the Society of Action. These were the more impatient who left it and ran forward. Other associations sought to recruit from the large mother societies. The sectionaries complained of being pestered by this. Thus arose *The Gallic Society* and *the Organising Committee of the Municipalities*. Thus the associations for *the Freedom of the Press*, for *Individual Freedom*, for *the Instruction of the People, against Direct Taxes*. Then the society of the Equalitist Workingmen which divided into three fractions, the Equalitists, the Communists and the Reformers. Then the Army of the Bastilles, a sort of cohort with a military organisation, four men commanded by a corporal, ten by a sergeant, twenty by a second lieutenant, forty by a lieutenant; there were never more than five hundred men who knew each other. A creation in which precaution was combined with boldness, and which seems marked with the genius of Venice. The central committee, which was the head, had two arms, the Society of Action and the Army of the Bastilles. A legitimist association, the Chevaliers of Fidelity, moved among these republican affiliations. But it was denounced and repudiated.

The Parisian societies ramified into the principal cities. Lyons, Nantes, Lisle, and Marseilles had their Society of the Rights of Man, the Carbonari, the Free Men. Aix had a revolutionary society which was called the Cougourde. We have already pronounced this word.

At Paris the Faubourg Saint Marceau was hardly less noisy than the Faubourg Saint Antoine, and the schools not less excited than the Faubourgs. A café in the Rue St. Hyacinthe, and the drinking and smoking room of the Seven Billiards, Rue des Mathurin St. Jacques, served as rallying places for the students. The Society of the Friends of the A B C, affiliated with the Mutualists of Angers and with the Cougourde of Aix, met, as we have seen, at the Café Musain. These same young people also gathered, as we have said, in a restaurant wine-shop near the Rue Mondétour which was called Corinthe. These meetings were secret, others were as public as possible, and we may judge of their boldness by this fragment of an interrogatory during one of the subsequent trials: "Where was this meeting held?" "Rue de la Paix." "In whose house?" "In the street." "What sections were there?" "But one." "Which one?" "The Manual section." "Who was the chief?" "I." "You are too young to have formed alone the grave resolution of attacking the government. Whence came your instructions?" "From the central committee."

The army was mined at the same time as the population, as was proved afterwards by the movements of Béford, Lunéville, and Epinal. They counted on the fifty-second regiment, the fifth, the eighth, the thirty-seventh, and the twentieth light. In Burgundy and in the cities of the South *the tree of Liberty* was planted. That is to say, a pole surmounted by a red cap.

Such was the situation.

This situation was, as we said in the beginning, rendered tangible and emphatic by the Faubourg Saint Antoine more than by any other portion of the population. There was the stitch in the side.

This old Faubourg, populous as an ant-hill, industrious, courageous, and choleric as a hive, was thrilling with the expectation and the desire for a commotion. Everything was in agitation, and yet labour was not interrupted on that account. Nothing can give an idea of that vivid yet dark phase of affairs. There are in that Faubourg bitter distresses hidden under garret roofs; there are there also ardent and rare intelligencies. And it is especially in reference to distress and intelligence that it is dangerous for extremes to meet.

The Faubourg Saint Antoine had still other causes of excitement, for it felt the rebound of the commercial crises of the failures, the strikes, and stoppages, inherent in great political disturbances. In time of revolution misery is at once cause and effect. The blow which it strikes returns upon itself. This population, full of proud virtue, filled with latent caloric to the highest point, always ready for an armed contest, prompt to explode, irritated, deep, mined, seemed only waiting for the fall of a spark. Whenever certain sparks are floating over the horizon, driven by the wind of events, we cannot but think of the Faubourg Saint Antoine and the terrible chance which has placed that powder-mill of sufferings and ideas at the gates of Paris.

The wine-shops of the *Faubourg Antoine*, more than once referred to in the preceding sketch, have a notoriety which is historic. In times of trouble their words are more intoxicating than their wine. A sort of prophetic spirit and an odour of the future circulates in them, swelling hearts and enlarging souls. The wine-shops of the Faubourg Antoine resemble those taverns of Mount Aventine, over the Sybil's cave, and communicating with the deep and sacred afflatus; taverns whose tables were almost tripods, and where men drank what Ennius calls *the sibylline wine*.

The Faubourg Saint Antoine is a reservoir of people. Revolutionary agitation makes fissures in it through which flows popular sovereignty. This sovereignty may do harm; it makes mistakes like everything else; but, even when led astray, it is still grand. We may say of it as of the blind Cyclops, *Ingens*.

In '93, according as the idea which was afloat was good or bad, according as it was the day of fanaticism or of enthusiasm, there came from the Faubourg Saint Antoine sometimes savage legions, sometimes heroic bands.

Savage. We must explain this word. What was the aim of those bristling men who in the demiurgic days of revolutionary chaos, ragged, howling, wild, with tomahawk raised, and pike aloft, rushed over old overturned Paris? They desired the end of oppressions, the end of tyrannies, the end of the sword, labour for man, instruction for children, social gentleness for woman, liberty, equality, fraternity, bread for all, ideas for all. The Edenisation of the world, Progress; and this holy, good, and gentle thing, progress, pushed to the wall and beside themselves, they demanded, terrible, half naked, a club in their grasp, and a roar in their mouth. They were savages, yes; but the savages of civilisation.

They proclaimed the right furiously; they desired, were it through fear and trembling, to force the human race into paradise. They seemed barbarians, and they were saviours. With the mask of night they demanded the light.

In contrast with these men, wild, we admit, and terrible, but wild and terrible for the good, there are other men, smiling, embroidered, gilded, beribboned, bestarred, in silk stockings, in white feathers, in yellow gloves, in varnished shoes, who, leaning upon a velvet table by the corner of a marble mantel, softly insist upon the maintenance and the preservation of the past, the middle ages, divine right, fanaticism, ignorance, slavery, the death penalty, and war, glorifying politely and in mild tones the sabre, the stake, and the scaffold. As for us, if we were compelled to choose between the barbarians of civilisation, and the civilisees of barbarism, we would choose the barbarians.

But, thanks to heaven, other choice is possible. No abrupt fall is necessary, forward more than backward. Neither despotism, nor terrorism. We desire progress with gentle slope.

God provides for this. The smoothing of acclivities is the whole policy of God.

VI

ENJOLRAS AND HIS LIEUTENANTS

NOT far from this period, Enjolras, in view of possible events, took a sort of mysterious account of stock.

All were in conventicle at the Café Musain.

Enjolras said, mingling with his words a few semi-enigmatic but significant metaphors:

"It is well to know where we are and on whom we can rely. If we desire fighting men, we must make them. Have the wherewith to strike. That can do no harm. Travellers have a better chance of catching a thrust of a horn when there are bulls in the road than when there are none. Let us then take a little account of the herd. How many are there of us? We cannot put this work off till to-morrow. Revolutionists ought always to be ready; progress has no time to lose. Let us not trust to the moment. Let us not be taken unprepared. We must go over all the seams which we have made, and see if they hold. This business should be probed to the bottom to-day. Courfeyrac, you will see the Polytechnicians. It is their day out. To-day, Wednesday. Feuilly, will you not see the men of the Glacière? Combeferre has promised me to go to Picpus. There is really an excellent swarm there. Bahorel will visit the Estrapade. Prouvaire, the masons are growing lukewarm; you will bring us news from the lodge in the Rue de Grenelle Saint Honoré. Joly will go to Dupuytren's clinique and feel the pulse of the Medical School. Bossuet will make a little tour in the Palace of Justice and chat with the young lawyers. I will take charge of the Cougourde."

"Then it is all arranged," said Courfeyrac.

"No."

"What more is there then?"

"A very important thing."

"What is it?" inquired Combeferre.

"The Barrière du Maine," answered Enjolras.

Enjolras remained a moment, as it were, absorbed in his reflections, then resumed:

"At the Barrière du Maine there are marble cutters, painters, assistants in sculptors' studios. It is an enthusiastic family but subject to chills. I do not know what has ailed them for some time. They are thinking of other things. They are fading out. They spend their time in playing dominoes. Somebody must go and talk to them a little, and firmly too. They meet at Richefeu's They can be found there between noon and one o'clock. We must blow upon these embers. I had counted on that absent-minded Marius for this, for on the whole he is good, but he does not come any more. I must have somebody for the Barrière du Maine. I have nobody left."

"I," said Grantaire, "I am here."

"You?"

"I."

"You to indoctrinate republicans! you, to warm up, in the name of principles, hearts that have grown cold!"

"Why not?"

"Is it possible that you can be good for anything?"

"Yes, I have a vague ambition for it," said Grantaire.

"You don't believe in anything."

"I believe in you."

"Grantaire, do you want to do me a service?"

"Anything. Polish your boots."

"Well, don't meddle with our affairs. Sleep off your bitters."

"You are an ingrate, Enjolras."

"You would be a fine man to go to the Barrière du Maine! you would be capable of it!"

"I am capable of going down the Rue des Grès, of crossing the Place Saint Michel, of striking off through the Rue Monsieur le Prince, of taking the Rue de Vaugirard, of passing the Carmes, of turning into the Rue d'Assas, of reaching the Rue du Cherche Midi, of leaving behind me the Conseil de Guerre, of hurrying through the Rue des Vieilles Tuileries, of striding through the Boulevard, of following the Chaussée du Maine, of crossing over the Barrière, and of entering Richefeu's. I am capable of that. My shoes are capable of it."

"Do you know anything about these comrades at Richefeu's?"

"Not much. We are on good terms, though."

"What will you say to them?"

"I will talk to them about Robespierre, faith. About Danton, about principles."

"You!"

"I. But you don't do me justice. When I am about it, I am terrible. I have read Prudhomme, I know the Contrat Social, I know my Constitution of the year Two by heart. 'The Liberty of the citizen ends where the Liberty of another citizen begins.' Do you take me for a brute? I have an old assignat in my drawer. The Rights of Man, the sovereignty of the people, zounds! I am even a little of a Hébertist. I can repeat, for six hours at a time, watch in hand, superb things."

"Be serious," said Enjolras.

"I am savage," answered Grantaire.

Enjolras thought for a few seconds, and made the gesture of a man who forms his resolution.

"Grantaire," said he gravely, "I consent to try you. You shall go to the Barrière du Maine."

Grantaire lived in a furnished room quite near the Café Musain. He went out, and came back in five minutes. He had been home to put on a Robespierre waistcoat.

"Red," said he as he came in, looking straight at Enjolras.

Then, with the flat of his huge hand, he smoothed the two scarlet points of his waistcoat over his breast.

And, approaching Enjolras, he whispered in his ear:

"Set your mind at ease."

He jammed down his hat, resolutely, and went out.

A quarter of an hour later, the back room of the Café Musain was deserted. All the Friends of the A B C had gone, each his own way, to their business. Enjolras, who had reserved the Cougourde for himself, went out last.

Those of the Courgourde of Aix who were at Paris met at that time on the Plain of Issy, in one of the abandoned quarries so numerous on that side of Paris.

Enjolras, on his way towards this place of rendezvous, passed the situation in review. The gravity of events was plainly visible. When events, premonitory of some latent social malady, are moving heavily along, the least complication stops them and shackles them. A phenomenon whence come overthrows and new births. Enjolras caught glimpses of a luminous uprising under the dark skirts of the future. Who knows? the moment was perhaps approaching. The people seizing their rights again, what a beautiful spectacle! the Revolution majestically resuming possession of France, and saying to the world: to be continued to-morrow! Enjolras was content. The furnace was heating. He had, at that very instant, a powder-train of friends extended over Paris. He was composing in his thoughts, with the philosophic and penetrating eloquence of Combeferre, the cosmopolitan enthusiasm of Feuilly, Courfeyrac's animation, Bahorel's laughter, Jean Prouvaire's melancholy, Joly's science, and Bossuet's sarcasms, a sort of electric spark taking fire in all directions at once. All in the work. Surely, the result would answer to the effort. This was well. This led him to think of Grantaire. "Stop," said he to himself, "the Barrière du Maine hardly takes me out of my way. Suppose I go as far as Richefeu's? Let us get a glimpse of what Grantaire is doing, and how he is getting along."

One o'clock sounded from the belfry of Vaugirard when Enjolras reached the Richefeu smoking-room. He pushed open the door, went in, folded his arms, letting the door swing to so that it hit his shoulders, and looked into the room full of tables, men, and smoke.

A voice was ringing out in the mist, sharply answered by another voice. It was Grantaire talking with an adversary whom he had found.

Grantaire was seated, opposite another figure, at a table of Saint Anne marble strewed with bran, and dotted with dominoes: he was striking the marble with his fist, and what Enjolras heard was this:

"Double six."

"Four."

"The beast! I can't play."

"You are done for. Two."

"Six."

"Three."

"Ace."

"It is my lay."

"Four points."

"Hardly."

"Yours."

"I made an awful blunder."

"You are doing well."

"Fifteen."

"Seven more."

"That makes me twenty-two. (Musing.) Twenty-two!"

"You didn't expect the double six. If I had laid it in the beginning, it would have changed the whole game."

"Two again."

"Ace."

"Ace! Well, five."

"I haven't any."

"You laid, I believe?"

"Yes."

"Blank."

"Has he any chance! Ah! you have one chance! (Long reverie.) Two."

"Ace."

"Neither a five, nor an ace. That is bothering for you."

"Domino."

"Dogs on it!"

BOOK SECOND – EPONINE

I

THE FIELD OF THE LAKE

MARIUS had seen the unexpected dénouement of the ambuscade upon the track of which he had put Javert; but hardly had Javert left the old ruin, carrying away his prisoners in three coaches, when Marius also slipped out of the house. It was only nine o'clock in the evening. Marius went to Courfeyrac's. Courfeyrac was no longer the imperturbable inhabitant of the Latin Quarter; he had gone to live in the Rue de la Verrerie "for political reasons;" this quarter was one of those in which the insurrection was fond of installing itself in those days. Marius said to Courfeyrac: "I have come to sleep with you." Courfeyrac drew a mattress from his bed, where there were two, laid it on the floor, and said: "There you are."

The next day, by seven o'clock in the morning, Marius went back to the tenement, paid his rent, and what was due to Ma'am Bougon, had his books, bed, table, bureau, and his two chairs loaded upon a hand-cart, and went off without leaving his address, so that when Javert came back in the forenoon to question Marius about the events of the evening, he found only Ma'am Bougon, who answered him, "moved!"

Ma'am Bougon was convinced that Marius was somehow an accomplice of the robbers seized the night before. "Who would have thought so?" she exclaimed among the portresses of the quarter, "a young man who had so much the appearance of a girl!"

Marius had two reasons for his prompt removal. The first was, that he now had a horror of that house, where he had seen, so near at hand, and in all its most repulsive and most ferocious development, a social deformity perhaps still more hideous than the evil rich man: the evil poor. The second was, that he did not wish to figure in the trial which would probably follow, and be brought forward to testify against Thénardier.

Javert thought that the young man, whose name he had not retained, had been frightened and had escaped, or, perhaps, had not even returned home at the time of the ambuscade; still he made some effort to find him, but he did not succeed.

A month rolled away, then another. Marius was still with

847

Courfeyrac. He knew from a young attorney, an habitual attendant in the ante-rooms of the court, that Thénardier was in solitary confinement. Every Monday Marius sent to the clerk of La Force five francs for Thénardier.

Marius, having now no money, borrowed the five francs of Courfeyrac. It was the first time in his life that he had borrowed money. This periodical five francs was a double enigma, to Courfeyrac who furnished them, and to Thénardier who received them. "To whom can it go?" thought Courfeyrac. "Where can it come from?" Thénardier asked himself.

Marius, moreover, was in sore affliction. Everything had relapsed into darkness. He no longer saw anything before him; his life was again plunged into that mystery in which he had been blindly groping. He had for a moment seen close at hand in that obscurity, the young girl whom he loved, the old man who seemed her father, these unknown beings who were his only interest and his only hope in this world; and at the moment he had thought to hold them fast, a breath had swept all those shadows away. Not a spark of certainty or truth had escaped even from that most fearful shock. No conjecture was possible. He knew not even the name which he had thought he knew. Certainly it was no longer Ursula. And the Lark was a nick-name. And what should he think of the old man? Was he really hiding from the police? The white-haired working-man whom Marius had met in the neighbourhood of the Invalides recurred to his mind. It now became probable that that working-man and M. Leblanc were the same man. He disguised himself then? This man had heroic sides and equivocal sides. Why had he not called for help? why had he escaped? was he, yes or no, the father of the young girl? Finally, was he really the man whom Thénardier thought he recognised? Could Thénardier have been mistaken? So many problems without issue. All this, it is true, detracted nothing from the angelic charms of the young girl of the Luxembourg. Bitter wretchedness; Marius had a pas-sion in his heart, and night over his eyes. He was pushed, he was drawn, and he could not stir. All had vanished, except love. Even of love, he had lost the instincts and the sudden illumina-tions. Ordinarily, this flame which consumes us, illumines us also a little, and sheds some useful light without. Those vague promptings of passion, Marius no longer even heard. Never did he say to himself: Suppose I go there? Suppose I try this? She whom he could no longer call Ursula was evidently somewhere; nothing indicated to Marius the direction in which he must seek for her. His whole life was now resumed in two words: an absolute uncertainty in an impenetrable mist. To see her again, Her; he aspired to this continually; he hoped for it no longer.

To crown all, want returned. He felt close upon him, behind him, that icy breath. During all these torments, and now for a long time, he had discontinued his work, and nothing is more dangerous than discontinued labour; it is habit lost. A habit easy to abandon, difficult to resume.

A certain amount of reverie is good, like a narcotic in discreet doses. It soothes the fever, sometimes high, of the brain at work and produces in the mind a soft and fresh vapour which corrects the too angular contours of pure thought, fills up the gaps and intervals here and there, binds them together, and blunts the sharp corners of ideas. But too much reverie submerges and drowns. Woe to the brain-worker who allows himself to fall entirely from thought into reverie! He thinks that he shall rise again easily, and he says that after all, it is the same thing. An error!

Thought is the labour of the intellect, reverie is its pleasure. To replace thought by reverie is to confound poison with nourishment.

Marius, we remember, had begun in this way. Passion supervened, and had at last precipitated him into bottomless and aimless chimeras. One no longer goes out of the house except to walk and dream. Sluggish birth. A tumultuous and stagnant gulf. And, as work diminishes, necessities increase. This is the law. Man, in the dreamy state, is naturally prodigal and luxurious; the relaxed mind cannot lead a severe life. There is, in this way of living, some good mingled with the evil, for if the softening be fatal, the generosity is wholesome and good. But the poor man who is generous and noble, and who does not work, is lost. His resources dry up, his necessities mount up.

Fatal slope, down which the firmest and the noblest are drawn, as well as the weakest and the most vicious, and which leads to one of these two pits, suicide or crime.

By continually going out for reverie, there comes a day when you go to throw yourself into the water.

The excess of reverie produces men like Escousse and Lebras.

Marius was descending this slope with slow steps, his eyes

fixed upon her whom he saw no more. What we have here written seems strange, and still it is true. The memory of an absent being grows bright in the darkness of the heart; the more it has disappeared the more radiant it is; the despairing and gloomy soul sees that light in its horizon; star of the interior night. She, this was all the thought of Marius. He dreamed of nothing else; he felt confusedly that his old coat was becoming an impossible coat and that his new coat was becoming an old coat, that his shirts were wearing out, that his hat was wearing out, that his boots were wearing out, that is to say, that his life was wearing out, and he said to himself, "If I could only see her again before I die."

A single sweet idea remained to him, that she had loved him, that her eyes had told him so, that she did not know his name but that she knew his soul, and that, perhaps, where she was, whatever that mysterious place might be, she loved him still. Who knows but she was dreaming of him as he was dreaming of her? Sometimes in the inexplicable hours, such as every heart has which loves, having reasons for sorrow only, yet feeling nevertheless a vague thrill of joy, he said to himself: It is her thoughts which come to me! Then he added, my thoughts reach her also, perhaps!

This illusion, at which he shook his head the moment afterwards, succeeded notwithstanding in casting some ray into his soul, which occasionally resembled hope. From time to time, especially at that evening hour which saddens dreamers most of all, he dropped upon a quire of paper, which he devoted to that purpose, the purest, the most impersonal, the most ideal of the reveries with which love filled his brain. He called that "writing to her."

We must not suppose that his reason was disordered. Quite the contrary. He had lost the capability of work, and of moving firmly towards a definite end, but he was more clear-sighted and correct than ever. Marius saw, in a calm and real light, although a singular one, what was going on under his eyes, even the most indifferent facts of men; he said the right word about everything with a sort of honest languor and candid disinterestedness. His judgment, almost detached from hope, soared and floated aloft.

In this situation of mind nothing escaped him, nothing deceived him, and he saw at every moment the bottom of life, humanity, and destiny. Happy, even in anguish, is he to whom

God has given a soul worthy of love and of grief! He who has not seen the things of this world, and the hearts of men by this double light, has seen nothing, and knows nothing of the truth.

The soul which loves and which suffers is in the sublime state.

The days passed, however, one after another, and there was nothing new. It seemed to him, merely, that the dreary space which remained for him to run through was contracting with every instant. He thought that he already saw distinctly the brink of the bottomless precipice.

"What!" he repeated to himself, "shall I never see her again before!"

If you go up the Rue Saint Jacques, leave the barrière at your side, and follow the old interior boulevard to the left for some distance, you come to the Rue de la Santé, then La Glacière, and, a little before reaching the small stream of the Gobelins, you find a sort of field, which is, in the long and monotonous circuit of the boulevards of Paris, the only spot where Ruysdael would be tempted to sit down.

That indescribable something from which grace springs is there, a green meadow crossed by tight drawn ropes, on which rags are drying in the wind, an old market-garden farm-house built in the time of Louis XIII., with its large roof grotesquely pierced with dormer windows, broken palisade fences, a small pond between the poplars, women, laughter, voices; in the horizon the Pantheon, the tree of the Deaf-mutes, the Val de Grâce, black, squat, fantastic, amusing, magnificent, and in the background the severe square summits of the towers of Notre Dame.

As the place is worth seeing, nobody goes there. Hardly a cart or a wagon once in a quarter of an hour.

It happened one day that Marius' solitary walks conducted him to this spot near this pond. That day there was a rarity on the boulevard, a passer. Marius, vaguely struck with the almost sylvan charm of the spot, asked this traveller: "What is the name of this place?"

The traveller answered: "It is the Field of the Lark."

And he added: "It was here that Ulbach killed the shepherd-ess of Ivry."

But after that word, "the Lark," Marius had heard nothing more. There are such sudden congelations in the dreamy state, which a word is sufficient to produce. The whole mind condenses abruptly about one idea, and ceases to be capable of any other perception.

The Lark was the appellation which, in the depths of Marius' melancholy, had replaced Ursula. "Yes," said he in the kind of unreasoning stupor peculiar to these mysterious asides, "this is her field. I shall learn here where she lives."

This was absurd, but irresistible.

And he came every day to this Field of the Lark.

II

EMBRYONIC FORMATION OF CRIMES IN THE INCUBATION OF PRISONS

JAVERT'S triumph in the Gorbeau tenement had seemed complete, but it was not so.

In the first place, and this was his principal regret, Javert had not made the prisoner prisoner. The victim who slips away is more suspicious than the assassin; and it was probable that this personage, so precious a capture to the bandits, would be a not less valuable prize to the authorities.

And then, Montparnasse had escaped Javert.

He must await another occasion to lay his hand upon "that devilish dandy." Montparnasse, in fact, having met Eponine, who was standing sentry under the trees of the boulevard, had led her away, liking rather to be Némorin with the daughter than to be Schinderhannes with the father. Well for him that he did so. He was free. As to Eponine, Javert "nabbed" her; trifling consolation. Eponine had rejoined Azelma at Les Madelonnettes.

Finally, on the trip from the Gorbeau tenement to La Force, one of the principal prisoners, Claquesous, had been lost. Nobody knew how it was done, the officers and sergeants "didn't understand it," he had changed into vapour, he had glided out of the handcuffs, he had slipped through the cracks of the carriage, the fiacre was leaky, and had fled; nothing could be said, save that on reaching the prison there was no Claquesous. There were either fairies or police in the matter. Had Claquesous melted away into the darkness like a snowflake in the water? Was there some secret connivance of the officers? Did this man belong to the double enigma of disorder and of order? Was he concentric with infraction and with repression?

Had this sphinx forepaws in crime and hind-paws in authority? Javert in no wise accepted these combinations, and his hair rose on end in view of such an exposure; but his squad contained other inspectors besides himself, more deeply initiated, perhaps, than himself, although his subordinates, in the secrets of the prefecture, and Claquesous was so great a scoundrel that he might be a very good officer. To be on such intimate juggling relations with darkness is excellent for brigandage and admirable for the police. There are such two-edged rascals. However it might be, Claquesous was lost, and was not found again. Javert appeared more irritated than astonished at it.

As to Marius, "that dolt of a lawyer," who was "probably frightened," and whose name Javert had forgotten, Javert cared little for him. Besides he was a lawyer, they are always found again. But was he a lawyer merely?

The trial commenced.

The police judge thought it desirable not to put one of the men of the Patron-Minette band into solitary confinement, hoping for some blabbing. This was Brujon, the long-haired man of the Rue du Petit Banquier. He was left in the Charlemagne court, and the watchmen kept their eyes upon him.

This name, Brujon, is one of the traditions of La Force. In the hideous court called the Bâtiment Neuf, which the administration named Court Saint Bernard, and which the robbers named La Fosse aux Lions, upon that wall covered with filth and with mould, which rises on the left to the height of the roofs, near an old rusty iron door which leads into the former chapel of the ducal hotel of La Force, now become a dormitory for brigands, a dozen years ago there could still be seen a sort of bastille coarsely cut in the stone with a nail, and below it this signature:

BRUJON, 1811.

The Brujon of 1811 was the father of the Brujon of 1832.

This last, of whom only a glimpse was caught in the Gorbeau ambuscade, was a sprightly young fellow, very cunning and very adroit, with a flurried and plaintive appearance. It was on account of this flurried air that the judge had selected him, thinking that he would be of more use in the Charlemagne court than in a solitary cell.

Robbers do not cease operations because they are in the

hands of justice. They are not disconcerted so easily. Being in prison for one crime does not prevent the commencement of another crime. They are artists who have a picture in the parlour, and who labour none the less for that on a new work in their studio.

Brujon seemed stupefied by the prison. He was sometimes seen whole hours in the Charlemagne court, standing near the sutler's window, and staring like an idiot at that dirty list of prices of supplies which began with: *garlic, 62 centimes*, and ended with: *cigars, cinq centimes*. Or instead, he would pass his time in trembling and making his teeth chatter, saying that he had a fever, and inquiring if one of the twenty-eight beds in the fever ward was not vacant.

Suddenly, about the second fortnight in February, 1832, it was discovered that Brujon, that sleepy fellow, had sent out, through the agents of the house, not in his own name, but in the name of three of his comrades, three different commissions, which had cost him in all fifty sous, a tremendous expense which attracted the attention of the prison brigadier.

He inquired into it, and by consulting the price list of commissions hung up in the convicts' waiting-room, he found that the fifty sous were made up thus: three commissions; one to the Pantheon, ten sous; one to the Val de Grâce, fifteen sous; and one to the Barrière de Grenelle, twenty-five sous. This was the dearest of the whole list. Now the Pantheon, the Val de Grâce, and the Barrière de Grenelle happened to be the residences of three of the most dreaded prowlers of the barriers, Kruideniers alias Bizarro, Glorieux, a liberated convict, and Barrecarrosse, upon whom this incident fixed the eyes of the police. They thought they divined that these men were affiliated with Patron-Minette, two of whose chiefs, Babet and Gueulemer, were secured. It was supposed that Brujon's messages sent, not addressed to any houses, but to persons who were waiting for them in the street, must have been notices of some projected crime. There were still other indications; they arrested the three prowlers, and thought they had foiled Brujon's machination whatever it was.

About a week after these measures were taken, one night, a watchman, who was watching the dormitory in the lower part of the New Building, at the instant of putting his chestnut into the chestnut-box—this is the means employed to make sure that the watchmen do their duty with exactness; every hour a chestnut must fall into every box nailed on the doors of the dormitories—a watchman then saw through the peep-hole of the dormitory, Brujon sitting up in his bed and writing something by the light of the reflector. The warden entered, Brujon was put into the dungeon for a month, but they could not find what he had written. The police knew nothing more.

It is certain, however, that the next day "a postillion" was thrown from the Charlemagne court into the Fosse aux Lions, over the five-story building which separates the two courts.

Prisoners call a ball of bread artistically kneaded, which is sent *into Ireland*, that is to say, over the roof of a prison from one court to the other, a postillion. Etymology: over England; from one county to the other; *into Ireland*. This ball falls in the court. He who picks it up opens it, and finds a letter in it addressed to some prisoner in the court. If it be a convict who finds it, he hands the letter to its destination; if it be a warden, or one of those secretly bribed prisoners who are called sheep in the prisons and foxes in the galleys, the letter is carried to the office and delivered to the police.

This time the postillion reached its address, although he for whom the message was destined was then *in solitary*. Its recipient was none other than Babet, one of the four heads of Patron-Minette.

The postillion contained a paper rolled up, on which there were only these two lines:

"Babet, there is an affair on hand in the Rue Plumet. A grating in a garden."

This was the thing that Brujon had written in the night.

In spite of spies, both male and female, Babet found means to send the letter from La Force to La Salpêtrière to "a friend" of his who was shut up there. This girl in her turn transmitted the letter to another whom she knew, named Magnon, who was closely watched by the police, but not yet arrested. This Magnon, whose name the reader has already seen, had some relations with the Thénardiers which will be related hereafter, and could, by going to see Eponine, serve as a bridge between La Salpêtrière and Les Madelonnettes.

It happened just at that very moment, the proofs in the prosecution of Thénardier failing in regard to his daughters, that Eponine and Azelma were released.

When Eponine came out, Magnon, who was watching for her at the door of Les Madelonnettes, handed her Brujon's note to Babet, charging her to find out about the affair.

Eponine went to the Rue Plumet, reconnoitred the grating and the garden, looked at the house, spied, watched, and, a few days after, carried to Magnon, who lived in the Rue Clocheperce, a biscuit, which Magnon transmitted to Babet's mistress at La Salpêtrière. A biscuit, in the dark symbolism of the prisons, signifies: *nothing to do.*

So that in less than a week after that, Babet and Brujon, meeting on the way from La Force, as one was going "to examination," and the other was returning from it: "Well," asked Brujon, "the Rue P.?" "Biscuit," answered Babet.

This was the end of that fœtus of crime, engendered by Brujon in La Force.

This abortion, however, led to results entirely foreign to Brujon's programme. We shall see them.

Often, when thinking to knot one thread, we tie another.

III

AN APPARITION TO FATHER MABEUF

MARIUS now visited nobody, but he sometimes happened to meet Father Mabeuf.

While Marius was slowly descending those dismal steps, which one might call cellar stairs, and which lead into places without light where we hear the happy walking above us, M. Mabeuf also was descending.

The Flora of Cauteretz had absolutely no sale more. The experiments upon indigo had not succeeded in the little garden of Austerlitz, which was very much exposed. M. Mabeuf could only cultivate a few rare plants which like moisture and shade. He was not discouraged, however. He had obtained a bit of ground in the Jardin des Plantes, with a good exposure, to carry on, "at his own cost," his experiments upon indigo. For this he had put the plates of his *Flora* into pawn. He had reduced his breakfast to two eggs, and he left one of them for his old servant, whose wages he had not paid for fifteen months. And often his breakfast was his only meal. He laughed no more with his child-like laugh, he had become morose, and he now received no visits. Marius was right in not thinking to come. Sometimes, at the hour when M. Mabeuf went to the Jardin des Plantes, the old man and the young man met on the Boulevard de l'Hôpital. They did not speak, but sadly nodded their heads. It is a bitter thing that there should be a moment when misery unbinds! They had been two friends, they were two passers.

The bookseller, Royol, was dead. M. Mabeuf now knew only his books, his garden, and his indigo; those were to him the three forms which happiness, pleasure, and hope had taken. This fed his life. He said to himself: "When I have made my blue balls, I shall be rich, I will take my plates out of pawn, I will bring my *Flora* into vogue through charlatanism, by big payments and by announcements in the journals, and I will buy, I well know where, a copy of Pierre de Médine's *Art de Naviguer*, with woodcuts, edition of 1559." In the meantime he worked all day on his indigo bed, and at night returned home to water his garden, and read his books. M. Mabeuf was at this time very nearly eighty years old.

One night he saw a singular apparition.

He had come home while it was still broad day. Mother Plutarch, whose health was poor, was sick and gone to bed. He had dined on a bone on which a little meat was left, and a bit of bread which he had found on the kitchen table, and had sat down on a block of stone, which took the place of a seat in his garden.

Near this seat there rose in the fashion of the old orchard-gardens, a sort of hut, in a ruinous condition, of joists and boards, a warren on the ground floor, a fruit-house above. There were no rabbits in the warren, but there were a few apples in the fruit-house. A remnant of the winter's store.

M. Mabeuf had begun to look through, reading by the way, with the help of his spectacles, two books which enchanted him, and in which he was even absorbed, a more serious thing at his age. His natural timidity fitted him, to a certain extent, to accept superstitions. The first of these books was the famous treatise of President Delancre, *On the inconstancy of Demons*, the other was the quarto of Mutor de la Rubaudière, *On the devils of Vauvert and the goblins of La Biévé*. This last book interested him the more, since his garden was one of the spots formerly haunted by goblins. Twilight was beginning to whiten all above and to blacken all below. As he read, Father Mabeuf was looking over the book which he held in his hand, at his plants, and among others at a magnificent rhododendron which was one of his consolations; there had been four days of drought, wind, and sun, without a drop of rain; the stalks bent over, the buds hung down, the leaves were falling, they all needed to be watered; the rhododendron especially was a sad sight. Father Mabeuf was one of those to whom plants have souls. The old man had worked all day on his indigo bed, he was exhausted with fatigue, he got up nevertheless, put his books upon the bench, and walked, bent over and with tottering steps, to the well, but when he had grasped the chain, he could not even draw it far enough to unhook it. Then he turned and looked with a look of anguish towards the sky which was filling with stars.

The evening had that serenity which buries the sorrows of man under a strangely dreary yet eternal joy. The night promised to be as dry as the day had been.

"Stars everywhere!" thought the old man; "not the smallest cloud! not a drop of water."

And his head, which had been raised for a moment, fell back upon his breast.

He raised it again and looked at the sky, murmuring:

"A drop of dew! a little pity!"

He endeavoured once more to unhook the well-chain, but he could not.

At this moment he heard a voice which said:

"Father Mabeuf, would you like to have me water your garden?"

At the same time he heard a sound like that of a passing deer in the hedge, and he saw springing out of the shrubbery a sort of tall, slender girl, who came and stood before him, looking boldly at him. She had less the appearance of a human being than of a form which had just been born of the twilight.

Before Father Mabeuf, who was easily startled, and who was, as we have said, subject to fear, could answer a word, this being, whose motions seemed grotesquely abrupt in the obscurity, had unhooked the chain, plunged in and drawn out the bucket, and filled the watering-pot, and the goodman saw this apparition with bare feet and a ragged skirt running along the beds, distributing life about her. The sound of the water upon the leaves filled Father Mabeuf's soul with transport. It seemed to him that now the rhododendron was happy.

When the first bucket was emptied, the girl drew a second, then a third. She watered the whole garden.

Moving thus along the walks, her outline appearing entirely black, shaking her torn shawl over her long angular arms, she seemed something like a bat.

When she had ended, Father Mabeuf approached her with tears in his eyes, and laid his hand upon her forehead.

"God will bless you," said he, "you are an angel, since you care for flowers."

"No," she answered, "I am the devil, but that is all the same to me."

The old man exclaimed, without waiting for and without hearing her answer:

"What a pity that I am so unfortunate and so poor, and that I cannot do anything for you!"

"You can do something," said she.

"What?"

"Tell me where M. Marius lives."

The old man did not understand.

"What Monsieur Marius?"

He raised his glassy eye and appeared to be looking for something that had vanished.

"A young man who used to come here."

Meanwhile M. Mabeuf had fumbled in his memory.

"Ah! yes,—" he exclaimed, "I know what you mean. Listen, now! Monsieur Marius—the Baron Marius Pontmercy, yes! he lives—or rather he does not live there now—ah! well, I don't know."

While he spoke, he had bent over to tie up a branch of the rhododendron, and he continued:

"Ah! I remember now. He passes up the boulevard very often, and goes toward La Glacière, Rue Croulebarbe. The Field of the Lark. Go that way. He isn't hard to find."

When M. Mabeuf rose up, there was nobody there; the girl had disappeared.

He was decidedly a little frightened.

"Really," thought he, "if my garden was not watered, I should think it was a spirit."

An hour later when he had gone to bed, this returned to him, and, as he was falling asleep, at that troubled moment when thought, like that fabulous bird which changes itself into fish to pass through the sea, gradually takes the form of dream to pass through sleep, he said to himself confusedly:

"Indeed, this much resembles what Rubaudière relates of the goblins. Could it be a goblin?"

IV

AN APPARITION TO MARIUS

A FEW days after this visit of a "spirit" to Father Mabeuf, one morning—it was Monday, the day on which Marius borrowed the hundred-sous piece of Courfeyrac for Thénardier—Marius had put this hundred-sous piece into his pocket and before carrying it to the prison once, he had gone "to take a little walk," hoping that it would enable him to work on his return. It was eternally so. As soon as he rose in the morning, he sat down before a book and a sheet of paper to work upon some translation; the work he had on hand at that time was the translation into French of a celebrated quarrel between two Germans, the controversy between Gans and Savigny; he took Savigny, he took Gans, read four lines, tried to write one of them, could not, saw a star between his paper and his eyes, and rose from his chair, saying: "I will go out. That will put me in trim."

And he would go to the Field of the Lark.

There he saw the star more than ever, and Savigny and Gans less than ever.

He returned, tried to resume his work, and did not succeed; he found no means of tying a single one of the broken threads in his brain; then he would say: "I will not go out to-morrow. It prevents my working." Yet he went out every day.

He lived in the Field of the Lark rather than in Courfeyrac's room. This was his real address: Boulevard de la Santé, seventh tree from the Rue Croulebarbe.

That morning, he had left this seventh tree, and sat down on the bank of the brook of the Gobelins. The bright sun was gleaming through the new and glossy leaves.

He was thinking of "Her!" And his dreaminess, becoming reproachful, fell back upon himself, he thought sorrowfully of the idleness, the paralysis of the soul, which was growing up within him, and of that night which was thickening before him hour by hour so rapidly that he had already ceased to see the sun.

Meanwhile, through this painful evolution of indistinct ideas which were not even a soliloquy, so much had action become enfeebled within him, and he no longer had even strength to develop his grief—through this melancholy distraction, the sensations of the world without reached him. He heard behind and below him, on both banks of the stream, the washer-women of the Gobelins beating their linen; and over his head, the birds chattering and singing in the elms. On the one hand the sound of liberty, of happy unconcern, of winged leisure; on the other, the sound of labour. A thing which made him muse profoundly, and almost reflect, these two joyous sounds.

All at once, in the midst of his ecstasy of exhaustion, he heard a voice which was known to him, say:

"Ah! there he is!"

He raised his eyes and recognised the unfortunate child who had come to his room one morning, the elder of the Thénardier girls, Eponine; he now knew her name. Singular fact, she had become more wretched and more beautiful, two steps which seemed impossible. She had accomplished a double progress towards the light, and towards distress. She was barefooted and in rags, as on the day when she had so resolutely entered his room, only her rags were two months older; the holes were larger, the tatters dirtier. It was the same rough voice, the same forehead tanned and wrinkled by exposure; the same free, wild, and wandering gaze. She had, in addition to her former expression, that mixture of fear and sorrow which the experience of a prison adds to misery.

She had spears of straw and grass in her hair, not like Ophelia from having gone mad through the contagion of Hamlet's madness but because she had slept in some stable loft.

And with all this, she was beautiful. What a star thou art, O youth!

Meantime, she had stopped before Marius, with an expression of pleasure upon her livid face, and something which resembled a smile.

She stood for a few seconds, as if she could not speak.

"I have found you, then?" said she at last. "Father Mabeuf was right; it was on this boulevard. How I have looked for you! if you only knew! Do you know? I have been in the jug. A fortnight! They have let me out! seeing that there was nothing against me and then I was not of the age of discernment. It lacked two months. Oh! how I have looked for you! it is six weeks now. You don't live down there any longer?"

"No," said Marius.

"Oh! I understand. On account of the affair. Such scares are disagreeable. You have moved. What! why do you wear such an old hat as that? a young man like you ought to have fine clothes. Do you know, Monsieur Marius? Father Mabeuf calls you Baron Marius, I forget what more. It's not true that you are a baron? barons are old fellows, they go to the Luxembourg in front of the château where there is the most sun, they read the *Quotidienne* for a sou. I went once for a letter to a baron's like that. He was more than a hundred years old. But tell me, where do you live now?"

Marius did not answer.

"Ah!" she continued, "you have a hole in your shirt. I must mend it for you."

She resumed with an expression which gradually grew darker:

"You don't seem to be glad to see me?"

Marius said nothing; she herself was silent for a moment, then exclaimed:

"But if I would, I could easily make you glad!"

"How?" inquired Marius. "What does that mean?"

"Ah! you used to speak more kindly to me!" replied she.

"Well, what is it that you mean?"

She bit her lip; she seemed to hesitate, as if passing through a kind of interior struggle. At last, she appeared to decide upon her course.

"So much the worse, it makes no difference. You look sad, I want you to be glad. But promise me that you will laugh, I want to see you laugh and hear you say: Ah, well! that is good. Poor Monsieur Marius! you know, you promised me that you would give me whatever I should ask——"

"Yes! but tell me!"

She looked into Marius' eyes and said:

"I have the address."

Marius turned pale. All his blood flowed back to his heart.

"What address?"

"The address you asked me for."

She added as if she were making an effort:

"The address—you know well enough!"

"Yes!" stammered Marius.

"Of the young lady!"

Having pronounced this word, she sighed deeply.

Marius sprang up from the bank on which he was sitting, and took her wildly by the hand.

"Oh! come! show me the way, tell me! ask me for whatever you will! Where is it?"

"Come with me," she answered. "I am not sure of the street and the number; it is away on the other side from here, but I know the house very well. I will show you."

She withdrew her hand and added in a tone which would have pierced the heart of an observer, but which did not even touch the intoxicated and transported Marius:

"Oh! how glad you are!"

A cloud passed over Marius' brow. He seized Eponine by the arm:

"Swear to me one thing!"

"Swear?" said she, "what does that mean? Ah! you want me to swear?"

And she laughed.

"Your father! promise me, Eponine! swear to me that you will not give this address to your father!"

She turned towards him with an astounded appearance.

"Eponine! How do you know that my name is Eponine?"

"Promise what I ask you!"

But she did not seem to understand.

"That is nice! you called me Eponine!"

Marius caught her by both arms at once.

"But answer me now, in heaven's name! pay attention to what I am saying, swear to me that you will not give the address you know to your father!"

"My father?" said she. "Oh! yes, my father! Do not be concerned on his account. He is in solitary. Besides, do I busy myself about my father!"

"But you don't promise me!" exclaimed Marius.

"Let me go then!" said she, bursting into a laugh, "how you shake me! Yes! yes! I promise you that! I swear to you that! What is it to me? I won't give the address to my father. There! will that do? is that it?"

"Nor to anybody?" said Marius.

"Nor to anybody."

"Now," added Marius, "show me the way."

"Right away?"

"Right away."

"Come. Oh! how glad he is!" said she.

After a few steps, she stopped.

"You follow too near me, Monsieur Marius. Let me go forward, and follow me like that, without seeming to. It won't do for a fine young man, like you, to be seen with a woman like me."

No tongue could tell all that there was in that word, woman, thus uttered by this child.

She went on a few steps, and stopped again; Marius rejoined her. She spoke to him aside and without turning:

"By the way, you know you have promised me something?"

Marius fumbled in his pocket. He had nothing in the world but the five francs intended for Thénardier. He took it, and put it into Eponine's hand.

She opened her fingers and let the piece fall on the ground, and, looking at him with a gloomy look:

"I don't want your money," said she.

BOOK THIRD –
THE HOUSE IN THE RUE PLUMET

I
THE SECRET HOUSE

TOWARDS the middle of the last century, a velvet-capped president of the Parlement of Paris having a mistress and concealing it, for in those days the great lords exhibited their mistresses and the bourgeois concealed theirs, had *"une petite maison"* built in the Faubourg Saint Germain, in the deserted Rue de Blomet, now called the Rue Plumet, not far from the spot which then went by the name of the *Combat des Animaux*.

This was a summer-house of but two stories; two rooms on the ground floor, two chambers in the second story, a kitchen below, a boudoir above, a garret next the roof, the whole fronted by a garden with a large iron grated gate opening on the street. This garden contained about an acre. This was all that the passers-by could see; but in the rear of the house there was a small yard, at the further end of which there was a low building, two rooms only and a cellar, a convenience intended to conceal a child and nurse in case of need. This building communicated, from the rear, by a masked door opening secretly, with a long narrow passage, paved, winding, open to the sky, bordered by two high walls, and which, concealed with wonderful art, and as it were lost between the inclosures of the gardens and fields, all the corners and turnings of which it followed, came to an end at another door, also concealed, which opened a third of a mile away, almost in another quartier, upon the unbuilt end of the Rue de Babylone.

The president came in this way, so that those even who might have watched and followed him, and those who might have observed that the president went somewhere mysteriously every day, could not have suspected that going to the Rue de Babylone was going to the Rue Blomet. By skilful purchases of land, the ingenious magistrate was enabled to have this secret route to his house made upon his own ground, and consequently without supervision. He had afterwards sold off the lots of ground bordering on the passage in little parcels for flower and vegetable gardens, and the proprietors of these lots of ground supposed on both sides that what they saw was a partition wall, and did

865

not even suspect the existence of that long ribbon of pavement winding between two walls among their beds and fruit trees. The birds alone saw this curiosity. It is probable that the larks and the sparrows of the last century had a good deal of chattering about the president.

The house, built of stone in the Mansard style, wainscoted, and furnished in the Watteau style, rock-work within, peruke without, walled about with a triple hedge of flowers, had a discreet, coquettish, and solemn appearance about it, suitable to a caprice of love and of magistracy.

This house and this passage, which have since disappeared, were still in existence fifteen years ago. In '93, a coppersmith bought the house to pull it down, but not being able to pay the price for it, the nation sent him into bankruptcy. So that it was the house that pulled down the coppersmith. Thereafter the house remained empty, and fell slowly into ruin, like all dwellings to which the presence of man no longer communicates life. It remained, furnished with its old furniture, and always for sale or to let, and the ten or twelve persons who passed through the Rue Plumet in the course of a year were notified of this by a yellow and illegible piece of paper which had hung upon the railing of the garden since 1810.

Towards the end of the Restoration, these same passers might have noticed that the paper had disappeared, and that, also, the shutters of the upper story were open. The house was indeed occupied. The windows had "little curtains," a sign that there was a woman there.

In the month of October, 1829, a man of a certain age had appeared and hired the house as it stood, including, of course, the building in the rear, and the passage which ran out to the Rue de Babylone. He had the secret openings of the two doors of this passage repaired. The house, as we have just said, was still nearly furnished with the president's old furniture. The new tenant had ordered a few repairs, added here and there what was lacking, put in a few flags in the yard, a few bricks in the basement, a few steps in the staircase, a few tiles in the floors, a few panes in the windows, and finally came and installed himself with a young girl and an aged servant, without any noise, rather like somebody stealing in than like a man who enters his own house. The neighbours did not gossip about it, for the reason that there were no neighbours.

This tenant, to partial extent, was Jean Valjean; the young girl was Cosette. The servant was a spinster named Toussaint, whom Jean Valjean had saved from the hospital and misery, and who was old, stuttering, and a native of a province, three qualities which had determined Jean Valjean to take her with him. He hired the house under the name of Monsieur Fauchelevent, gentleman. In what has been related hitherto, the reader doubtless recognised Jean Valjean even before Thénardier did.

Why had Jean Valjean left the convent of the Petit Picpus? What had happened?

Nothing had happened.

As we remember, Jean Valjean was happy in the convent, so happy that his conscience at last began to be troubled. He saw Cosette every day, he felt paternity springing up and developing within him more and more, he brooded this child with his soul, he said to himself that she was his, that nothing could take her from him, that this would be so indefinitely, that certainly she would become a nun, being every day gently led on towards it, that thus the convent was henceforth the universe to her as well as to him, that he would grow old there and she would grow up there, that she would grow old there and he would die there; that finally, ravishing hope, no separation was possible. In reflecting upon this, he at last began to find difficulties. He questioned himself. He asked himself if all this happiness were really his own, if it were not made up of the happiness of another, of the happiness of this child whom he was appropriating and plundering, he, an old man; if this was not a robbery? He said to himself that this child had a right to know what life was before renouncing it; that to cut her off, in advance, and, in some sort, without consulting her, from all pleasure, under pretence of saving her from all trial, to take advantage of her ignorance and isolation to give her an artificial vocation, was to outrage a human creature and to lie to God. And who knows but, thinking over all this some day, and being a nun with regret, Cosette might come to hate him? a final thought, which was almost selfish and less heroic than the others, but which was insupportable to him. He resolved to leave the convent.

He resolved it, he recognised with despair that it must be done. As to objections, there were none. Five years of sojourn between those four walls, and of absence from among men, had necessarily destroyed or dispersed the elements of alarm. He might return tranquilly among men. He had grown old, and all had changed. Who would recognise him now? And then, to look at the worst, there was no danger save for himself, and he had no right to condemn Cosette to the cloister for the reason that he had been condemned to the galleys. What, moreover, is danger in presence of duty? Finally, nothing prevented him from being prudent, and taking proper precautions.

As to Cosette's education, it was almost finished and complete.

His determination once formed, he awaited an opportunity. It was not slow to present itself. Old Fauchelevent died.

Jean Valjean asked an audience of the reverend prioress, and told her that having received a small inheritance on the death of his brother, which enabled him to live henceforth without labour, he would leave the service of the convent, and take away his daughter; but that, as it was not just that Cosette, not taking her vows, should have been educated gratuitously, he humbly begged the reverend prioress to allow him to offer the community, as indemnity for the five years which Cosette had passed there, the sum of five thousand francs.

Thus Jean Valjean left the convent of the Perpetual Adoration.

On leaving the convent, he took in his own hands, and would not entrust to any assistant, the little box, the key of which he always had about him. This box puzzled Cosette, on account of the odour of embalming which came from it.

Let us say at once, that henceforth this box never left him more. He always had it in his room. It was the first, and sometimes the only thing that he carried away in his changes of abode. Cosette laughed about it, and called this box *the inseparable*, saying: "I am jealous of it."

Jean Valjean nevertheless did not appear again in the open city without deep anxiety.

He discovered the house in the Rue Plumet, and buried himself in it. He was henceforth in possession of the name of Ultimus Fauchelevent.

At the same time he hired two other lodgings in Paris, in order to attract less attention than if he always remained in the same quartier, to be able to change his abode on occasion, at the slightest anxiety which he might feel, and finally, that he might not again find himself in such a strait as on the night when he had so miraculously escaped from Javert. These two lodgings were two very humble dwellings, and of a poor appearance, in two quartiers widely distant from each other, one in the Rue de l'Ouest, the other in the Rue de l'Homme Armé.

He went from time to time, now to the Rue de l'Homme Armé and now to the Rue de l'Ouest, to spend a month or six weeks, with Cosette, without taking Toussaint. He was waited upon by the porters, and gave himself out for a man of some means of the suburbs, having a foothold in the city. This lofty virtue had three domiciles in Paris in order to escape from the police.

II
JEAN VALJEAN A NATIONAL GUARD

STILL, properly speaking, he lived in the Rue Plumet, and he had ordered his life there in the following manner:

Cosette with the servant occupied the house; she had the large bedroom with painted piers, the boudoir with gilded mouldings, the president's parlour furnished with tapestry and huge arm-chairs; she had the garden. Jean Valjean had a bed put into Cosette's chamber with a canopy of antique damask in three colours, and an old and beautiful Persian carpet, bought at Mother Gaucher's in the Rue du Figuier Saint Paul, and, to soften the severity of these magnificent relics, he had added to this curiosity shop all the little lively and graceful pieces of furniture used by young girls, an étagère, a bookcase and gilt books, a writing-case, a blotting-case, a work-table inlaid with pearl, a silver-gilt dressing-case, a dressing table in Japan porcelain. Long damask curtains of three colours, on a red ground, matching those of the bed, hung at the second story windows. On the first floor, tapestry curtains. All winter Cosette's Petite Maison was warmed from top to bottom. For his part, he lived in the sort of porter's lodge in the back-yard, with a mattress on a cot bedstead, a white wood table, two straw chairs, an earthen water-pitcher, a few books upon a board, his dear box in a corner, never any fire. He dined with Cosette, and there was a black loaf on the table for him. He said to Toussaint, when she entered their service: "Mademoiselle is the mistress of the house." "And you, m-monsieur?" replied Toussaint, astounded. "Me I am much better than the master, I am the father."

Cosette had been trained to housekeeping in the convent, and she regulated the expenses, which were very moderate. Every day Jean Valjean took Cosette's arm, and went to walk with her. They went to the least frequented walk of the Luxembourg, and every Sunday to mass, always at Saint Jacques du Haut Pas, because it was quite distant. As that is a very poor quartier, he gave much alms there, and the unfortunate surrounded him in the church, which had given him the title of the superscription of the epistle of the Thénardiers: *To the benevolent gentleman of the church of Saint Jacques du Haut Pas.* He was fond of taking Cosette to visit the needy and the sick. No stranger came into the house in the Rue Plumet. Toussaint brought the provisions, and Jean Valjean himself went after the water to a watering trough which was near by on the boulevard. They kept the wood and the wine in a kind of semi-subterranean vault covered with rock-work, which was near the door on the Rue de Babylone, and which had formerly served the president as a grotto; for, in the time of the Folies and the Petites Maisons, there was no love without a grotto.

There was on the Rue de Babylone door a box for letters and papers; but the three occupants of the summer-house on the Rue Plumet receiving neither papers nor letters, the entire use of the box, formerly the agent of amours and the confidant of a legal spark, was now limited to the notices of the receiver of taxes and the Guard warnings. For M. Fauchelevent belonged to the National Guard: he had not been able to escape the close meshes of the enrollment of 1831. The municipal investigation made at that time had extended even to the convent of the Petit Picpus, a sort of impenetrable and holy cloud from which Jean Valjean had come forth venerable in the eyes of his magistracy, and, in consequence, worthy of mounting guard.

Three or four times a year, Jean Valjean donned his uniform, and performed his duties; very willingly moreover; it was a good disguise for him, which associated him with everybody else while leaving him solitary. Jean Valjean had completed his sixtieth year, the age of legal exemption; but he did not appear more than fifty; moreover, he had no desire to escape from his sergeant-major and to cavil with the Count de Lobau; he had no civil standing; he was concealing his name, he was concealing his identity, he was concealing his age, he was concealing everything; and, we have just said, he was very willingly a National

Guard. To resemble the crowd who pay their taxes, this was his whole ambition. This man had for his ideal within, the angel—without, the bourgeois.

We must note one incident, however. When Jean Valjean went out with Cosette, he dressed as we have seen, and had much the air of an old officer. When he went out alone, and this was most usually in the evening, he was always clad in the waistcoat and trousers of a working-man, and wore a cap which hid his face. Was this precaution, or humility? Both at once. Cosette was accustomed to the enigmatic aspect of her destiny, and hardly noticed her father's singularities. As for Toussaint, she venerated Jean Valjean, and thought everything good that he did. One day, her butcher, who had caught sight of Jean Valjean, said to her: "That is a funny body." She answered: "He is a s-saint!"

Neither Jean Valjean, nor Cosette, nor Toussaint, ever came in or went out except by the gate on the Rue de Babylone. Unless one had seen them through the grated gate of the garden, it would have been difficult to guess that they lived in the Rue Plumet. This gate always remained closed. Jean Valjean had left the garden uncultivated, that it might not attract attention.

In this, he deceived himself, perhaps.

III

FOLIIS AC FRONDIBUS

THIS garden, thus abandoned to itself for more than half a century, had become very strange and very pleasant. The passers-by of forty years ago stopped in the street to look at it, without suspecting the secrets which it concealed behind its fresh green thickets. More than one dreamer of that day has many a time allowed his eyes and his thoughts indiscreetly to penetrate through the bars of the ancient gate which was padlocked, twisted, tottering; secured by two green and mossy pillars, and grotesquely crowned with a pediment of indecipherable arabesque.

There was a stone seat in a corner, one or two mouldy statues, some trellises loosened by time and rotting upon the wall; no walks, moreover, nor turf, dog-grass everywhere. Horticulture had departed, and nature had returned. Weeds were abundant, a wonderful hap for a poor bit of earth. The heyday

of the gilliflowers was splendid. Nothing in this garden opposed
the sacred effort of things towards life; venerable growth was at
home there. The trees bent over towards the briers, the briers
mounted towards the trees, the shrub had climbed, the branch
had bowed, that which runs upon the ground had attempted to
find that which blooms in the air, that which floats in the wind
had stooped towards that which trails in the moss; trunks,
branches, leaves, twigs, tufts, tendrils, shoots, thorns, were
mingled, crossed, married, confounded; vegetation, in a close
and strong embrace, had celebrated and accomplished there
under the satisfied eye of the Creator, in this inclosure of three
hundred feet square, the sacred mystery of its fraternity, symbol
of human fraternity. This garden was no longer a garden; it was
a colossal bush, that is to say, something which is as impenetrable
as a forest, populous as a city, tremulous as a nest, dark as a
cathedral, odorous as a bouquet, solitary as a tomb, full of life as
a multitude.

In Floréal, this enormous shrub, free behind its grating and
within its four walls, warmed into the deep labour of universal
germination, thrilled at the rising sun almost like a stag which
inhales the air of universal love and feels the April sap mounting
and boiling in his veins, and shaking its immense green antlers
in the wind, scattered over the moist ground, over the broken
statues, over the sinking staircase of the summer-house, and
even over the pavement of the deserted street, flowers in stars,
dew in pearls, fecundity, beauty, life, joy, perfume. At noon, a
thousand white butterflies took refuge in it, and it was a heavenly sight to see this living snow of summer whirling about in
flakes in the shade. There, in this gay darkness of verdure, a
multitude of innocent voices spoke softly to the soul, and what
the warbling had forgotten to say, the humming completed. At
night, a dreamy vapour arose from the garden and wrapped it
around; a shroud of mist, a calm and celestial sadness, covered
it; the intoxicating odour of honeysuckles and bindweed rose
on all sides like an exquisite and subtle poison; you heard the
last appeals of the woodpecker, and the wagtails drowsing under
the branches; you felt the sacred intimacy of bird and tree; by
day the wings rejoiced the leaves; by night the leaves protected
the wings.

In winter, the bush was black, wet, bristling, shivering, and
let the house be seen in part. You perceived, instead of the

flowers in the branches and the dew in the flowers, the long silver ribbons of the snails upon the thick and cold carpet of yellow leaves; but in every way, under every aspect, in every season, spring, winter, summer, autumn, this little inclosure exhaled melancholy, contemplation, solitude, liberty, the absence of man, the presence of God, and the old rusty grating appeared to say: "This garden is mine!"

In vain was the pavement of Paris all about it, the classic and splendid residences of the Rue de Varennes within a few steps, the dome of the Invalides quite near, the Chamber of Deputies not far off; in vain did the carriages of the Rue de Bourgogne and the Rue Saint Dominique roll pompously in its neighbour-hood, in vain did the yellow, brown, white, and red omnibuses pass each other in the adjoining square, the Rue Plumet was a solitude; and the death of the old proprietors, the passage of a revolution, the downfall of ancient fortunes, absence, oblivion, forty years of abandonment and of widowhood, had sufficed to call back into this privileged place the ferns, the mulleins, the hemlocks, the milfoils, the tall weeds, the great flaunting plants with large leaves of a pale greenish drab, the lizards, the beetles, the restless and rapid insects; to bring out of the depths of the earth, and display within these four walls, an indescribably wild and savage grandeur; and that nature, who disavows the mean arrangements of man, and who always gives her whole self where she gives herself at all, as well in the ant as in the eagle, should come to display herself in a poor little Parisian garden with as much severity and majesty as in a virgin forest of the New World.

Nothing is really small; whoever is open to the deep pene-tration of nature knows this. Although indeed no absolute satisfaction may be vouchsafed to philosophy, no more in circumscribing the cause than in limiting the effect, the con-templator falls into unfathomable ecstasies in view of all these decompositions of forces resulting in unity. All works for all.

Algebra applies to the clouds; the radiance of the star benefits the rose; no thinker would dare to say that the perfume of the hawthorn is useless to the constellations. Who then can calcu-late the path of the molecule? how do we know that the crea-tions of worlds are not determined by the fall of grains of sand? Who then understands the reciprocal flux and reflux of the infinitely great and the infinitely small, the echoing of causes in the abysses of being, and the avalanches of creation? A flesh-worm is of account; the small is great, the great is small; all is in equilibrium in necessity; fearful vision for the mind. There are marvellous relations between beings and things; in this inexhaustible whole, from sun to grub, there is no scorn; all need each other. Light does not carry terrestrial perfumes into the azure depths without knowing what it does with them; night distributes the stellar essence to the sleeping plants. Every bird which flies has the thread of the infinite in its claw. Germination includes the hatching of a meteor and the tap of a swallow's bill breaking the egg, and it leads forward the birth of an earthworm and the advent of Socrates. Where the telescope ends, the microscope begins. Which of the two has the grander view? Choose. A bit of mould is a pleiad of flowers; a nebula is an ant-hill of stars. The same promiscuity, and still more wonderful, between the things of the intellect and the things of matter. Elements and principles are mingled, combined, espoused, multiplied one by another, to such a degree as to bring the material world and the moral world into the same light. Phenomena are perpetually folded back upon themselves. In the vast cosmical changes, the universal life comes and goes in unknown quantities, rolling all in the invisible mystery of the emanations, losing no dream from no single sleep, sowing an animalcule here, crumbling a star there, oscillating and winding, making a force of light and an element of thought, disseminated and indivisible, dissolving all, save that geometrical point, the me; reducing everything to the soul-atom; making everything blossom into God, entangling, from the highest to the lowest, all activities in the obscurity of a dizzying mechanism, hanging the flight of an insect upon the movement of the earth, subordinating, who knows? were it only by the identity of the law, the evolutions of the comet in the firmament to the circling of the infusoria in the drop of water. A machine made of mind. Enormous gearing, whose first motor is the gnat, and whose last wheel is the zodiac.

IV
CHANGE OF GRATING

It seemed as if this garden, first made to conceal licentious mysteries, had been transformed and rendered fit for the shelter of chaste mysteries. There were no longer in it either bowers, or lawns, or arbours, or grottoes; there was a magnificent dishevelled obscurity falling like a veil upon all sides; Paphos had become Eden again. Some secret repentance had purified this retreat. This flower-girl now offered its flowers to the soul. This coquettish garden, once so very free, had returned to virginity and modesty. A president assisted by a gardener, a goodman who thought he was a second Lamoignon, and another goodman who thought he was a second Lenôtre, had distorted it, pruned it, crumpled it, bedizened it, fashioned it for gallantry; nature had taken it again, had filled it with shade, and had arranged it for love.

There was also in this solitude a heart which was all ready. Love had only to show himself; there was a temple there composed of verdure, of grass, of moss, of the sighs of birds, of soft shade, of agitated branches, and a soul made up of gentleness, of faith, of candour, of hope, of aspiration, and of illusion.

Cosette had left the convent, still almost a child; she was a little more than fourteen years old, and she was "at the ungrateful age;" as we have said, apart from her eyes, she seemed rather homely than pretty; she had, however, no ungraceful features, but she was awkward, thin, timid, and bold at the same time, a big child in short.

Her education was finished; that is to say, she had been taught religion, and also, and above all, devotion; then "history," that is, the thing which they call thus in the convent, geography, grammar, the participles, the kings of France, a little music, to draw profiles, etc., but further than this she was ignorant of everything, which is a charm and a peril. The soul of a young girl ought not to be left in obscurity; in after life there spring up too sudden and too vivid mirages, as in a camera obscura. She should be gently and discreetly enlightened, rather by the reflection of realities than by their direct and stern light. A useful and graciously severe half-light which dissipates puerile fear and prevents a fall. Nothing but the maternal instinct, a wonderful intuition into which enter the memories of the maiden and the experience of the woman, knows how this half-light should be applied, and of what it should be formed. Nothing supplies this instinct. To form the mind of a young girl, all the nuns in the world are not equal to one mother.

Cosette had had no mother. She had only had many mothers, in the plural.

As to Jean Valjean, there was indeed within him all manner of tenderness and all manner of solicitude; but he was only an old man who knew nothing at all.

Now, in this work of education, in this serious matter of the preparation of a woman for life, how much knowledge is needed to struggle against that ignorance which we call innocence.

Nothing prepares a young girl for passions like the convent. The convent turns the thoughts in the direction of the unknown. The heart, thrown back upon itself, makes for itself a channel, being unable to overflow, and deepens, being unable to expand. From thence visions, suppositions, conjectures, romances sketched out, longings for adventures, fantastic constructions, whole castles built in the interior obscurity of the mind, dark and secret dwellings where the passions find an immediate lodging as soon as the grating is crossed and they are permitted to enter. The convent is a compression which, in order to triumph over the human heart, must continue through the whole life.

On leaving the convent, Cosette could have found nothing more grateful and more dangerous than the house on the Rue Plumet. It was the continuation of solitude with the beginning of liberty; an inclosed garden, but a sharp, rich, voluptuous, and odorous nature; the same dreams as in the convent, but with glimpses of young men; a grating, but upon the street.

Still, we repeat, when she came there she was but a child. Jean Valjean gave her this uncultivated garden. "Do whatever you like with it," said he to her. It delighted Cosette; she ransacked every thicket and turned over every stone, she sought for "animals," she played while she dreamed; she loved this garden for the insects which she found in the grass under her feet, while she loved it for the stars which she saw in the branches over her head.

And then she loved her father, that is to say, Jean Valjean, with all her heart, with a frank filial passion which made the goodman a welcome and very pleasant companion for her. We remember that M. Madeleine was a great reader; Jean Valjean continued it; through this he had come to talk very well; he had the secret wealth and the eloquence of a humble and earnest intellect which has secured its own culture. He retained just enough harshness to flavour his goodness; he had a rough mind and a gentle heart. At the Luxembourg in their conversations, he gave long explanations of everything, drawing from what he had read, drawing also from what he had suffered. As she listened, Cosette's eyes wandered dreamily.

This simple man was sufficient for Cosette's thought, even as this wild garden was to her eyes. When she had had a good chase after the butterflies, she would come up to him breathless and say, "Oh! how I have run!" He would kiss her forehead.

Cosette adored the goodman. She was always running after him. Where Jean Valjean was, was happiness. As Jean Valjean did not live in the summer-house or the garden, she found more pleasure in the paved back-yard than in the inclosure full of flowers, and in the little bedroom furnished with straw chairs than in the great parlour hung with tapestry, where she could recline on silken arm-chairs. Jean Valjean sometimes said to her, smiling with the happiness of being teased: "Why don't you go home? why don't you leave me alone?"

She would give him those charming little scoldings which are so full of grace coming from the daughter to the father.

"Father, I am very cold in your house; why don't you put in carpet and a stove here?"

"Dear child, there are many people who are better than I, who have not even a roof over their heads."

"Then why do I have a fire and all things comfortable?"

"Because you are a woman and a child."

"Pshaw! men then ought to be cold and uncomfortable?"

"Some men."

"Well, I will come here so often that you will be obliged to have a fire."

Again she said to him:

"Father, why do you eat miserable bread like that?"

"Because, my daughter."

"Well, if you eat it, I shall eat it."

Then, so that Cosette should not eat black bread, Jean Valjean ate white bread.

Cosette had but vague remembrance of her childhood. She prayed morning and evening for her mother, whom she had never known. The Thénardiers had remained to her like two hideous faces of some dream. She remembered that she had been "one day, at night," sent into a wood after water. She thought that that was very far from Paris. It seemed to her that she had commenced life in an abyss, and that Jean Valjean had drawn her out of it. Her childhood impressed her as a time when there were only centipedes, spiders, and snakes about her. When she was dozing at night, before going to sleep, as she had no very clear idea of being Jean Valjean's daughter, and that he was her father, she imagined that her mother's soul had passed into this goodman and come to live with her.

When he sat down, she would rest her cheek on his white hair and silently drop a tear, saying to herself: "This is perhaps my mother, this man!"

Cosette, although this may be a strange statement, in her profound ignorance as a girl brought up in a convent, maternity moreover being absolutely unintelligible to virginity, had come to imagine that she had had as little of a mother as possible. She did not even know her name. Whenever she happened to ask Jean Valjean what it was, Jean Valjean was silent. If she repeated her question, he answered by a smile. Once she insisted; the smile ended with a tear.

This silence of Jean Valjean's covered Fantine with night.

Was this prudence? was it respect? was it a fear to give up that name to the chances of another memory than his own?

While Cosette was a little girl, Jean Valjean had been fond of talking with her about her mother; when she was a young maiden, this was impossible for him. It seemed to him that he no longer dared. Was this on account of Cosette? was it on account of Fantine? He felt a sort of religious horror at introducing that shade into Cosette's thoughts, and at bringing in the dead as a third sharer of their destiny. The more sacred that shade was to him, the more formidable it seemed to him. He thought of Fantine and felt overwhelmed with silence. He saw dimly in the darkness something which resembled a finger on a mouth. Had all that modesty which had once been Fantine's and which, during her life, had been forced out of her by violence, returned after her death to take its place over her, to watch, indignant, over the peace of the dead woman, and to guard her fiercely in her tomb? Did Jean Valjean, without knowing it, feel its influence? We who believe in death are not of those who would reject this mysterious explanation. Hence the impossibility of pronouncing, even at Cosette's desire, this name: Fantine.

One day Cosette said to him:

"Father, I saw my mother in a dream last night. She had

two great wings. My mother must have attained to sanctity in her life."

"Through martyrdom," answered Jean Valjean.

Still, Jean Valjean was happy.

When Cosette went out with him, she leaned upon his arm, proud, happy, in the fulness of her heart. Jean Valjean, at all these marks of a tenderness so exclusive and so fully satisfied with him alone, felt his thought melt into delight. The poor man shuddered, overflowed with an angelic joy; he declared in his transport that this would last through life; he said to himself that he really had not suffered enough to deserve such radiant happiness, and he thanked God, in the depths of his soul, for having permitted that he, a miserable man, should be so loved by this innocent being.

V

THE ROSE DISCOVERS THAT SHE IS AN ENGINE OF WAR

ONE day Cosette happened to look in her mirror, and she said to herself: "What!" It seemed to her almost that she was pretty. This threw her into strange anxiety. Up to this moment she had never thought of her face. She had seen herself in her glass, but she had not looked at herself. And then, she had often been told that she was homely; Jean Valjean alone would quietly say: "Why no! why! no!" However that might be, Cosette had always thought herself homely, and had grown up in that idea with the pliant resignation of childhood. And now suddenly her mirror said like Jean Valjean: "Why no!" She had no sleep that night. "If I were pretty!" thought she, "how funny it would be if I should be pretty!" And she called to mind those of her companions whose beauty had made an impression in the convent and said: "What! I should be like Mademoiselle Such-a-one!"

The next day she looked at herself, but not by chance, and she doubted. "Where were my wits gone?" said she, "no, I am homely." She had merely slept badly, her eyes were dark and she was pale. She had not felt very happy the evening before, in the thought that she was beautiful, but she was sad at thinking so no longer. She did not look at herself again, and for more than a fortnight she tried to dress her hair with her back to the mirror.

In the evening after dinner, she regularly made tapestry or did some convent work in the parlour, while Jean Valjean read by her side. Once, on raising her eyes from her work, she was very much surprised at the anxious way in which her father was looking at her.

At another time, she was passing along the street, and it seemed to her that somebody behind her, whom she did not see, said: "Pretty woman! but badly dressed." "Pshaw!" thought she, "that is not me. I am well dressed and homely." She had on at the time her plush hat and merino dress.

At last, she was in the garden one day, and heard poor old Toussaint saying: "Monsieur, do you notice how pretty mademoiselle is growing?" Cosette did not hear what her father answered. Toussaint's words threw her into a sort of commotion. She ran out of the garden, went up to her room, hurried to the glass, it was three months since she had looked at herself, and uttered a cry. She was dazzled by herself.

She was beautiful and handsome; she could not help being of Toussaint's and her mirror's opinion. Her form was complete, her skin had become white, her hair had grown lustrous, an unknown splendour was lighted up in her blue eyes. The consciousness of her beauty came to her entire, in a moment, like broad daylight when it bursts upon us; others noticed it moreover, Toussaint said so, it was of her evidently that the passer had spoken, there was no more doubt; she went down into the garden again, thinking herself a queen, hearing the birds sing, it was in winter, seeing the sky golden, the sunshine in the trees, flowers among the shrubbery, wild, mad, in an inexpressible rapture.

For his part, Jean Valjean felt a deep and undefinable anguish in his heart.

He had in fact, for some time past, been contemplating with terror that beauty which appeared every day more radiant upon Cosette's sweet face. A dawn, charming to all others, dreary to him.

Cosette had been beautiful for some time before she perceived it. But, from the first day, this unexpected light which slowly rose and by degrees enveloped the young girl's whole person, wounded Jean Valjean's gloomy eyes. He felt that it was a change in a happy life, so happy that he dared not stir for fear of disturbing something. This man who had passed through every distress, who was still all bleeding from the lacerations of his destiny, who had been almost evil, and who had become almost holy, who, after having dragged the chain of the galleys, now dragged the invisible but heavy chain of indefinite infamy, this man whom the law had not released, and who might be at any instant retaken, and led back from the obscurity of his virtue to the broad light of public shame, this man accepted all, excused all, pardoned all, blessed all, wished well to all, and only asked of Providence, of men, of the laws, of society, of nature, of the world, this one thing, that Cosette should love him!

That Cosette should continue to love him! That God would not prevent the heart of this child from coming to him, and remaining his! Loved by Cosette, he felt himself healed, refreshed, soothed, satisfied, rewarded, crowned. Loved by Cosette, he was content! he asked nothing more. Had anybody said to him: "Do you desire anything better?" he would have answered: "No." Had God said to him: "Do you desire heaven?" he would have answered: "I should be the loser."

Whatever might affect this condition, were it only on the surface, made him shudder as if it were the commencement of another. He had never known very clearly what the beauty of a woman was; but, by instinct, he understood, that it was terrible.

This beauty which was blooming out more and more triumphant and superb beside him, under his eyes, upon the ingenuous and fearful brow of this child—he looked upon it, from the depths of his ugliness, his old age, his misery, his reprobation, and his dejection, with dismay.

He said to himself: "How beautiful she is! What will become of me?"

Here in fact was the difference between his tenderness and the tenderness of a mother. What he saw with anguish, a mother would have seen with delight.

The first symptoms were not slow to manifest themselves.

From the morrow of the day on which she had said: "Really, I am handsome!" Cosette gave attention to her dress. She recalled the words of the passer: "Pretty, but badly dressed," breath of an oracle which had passed by her and vanished after depositing in her heart one of the two germs which must afterwards fill the whole life of the woman, coquetry. Love is the other.

With faith in her beauty, the entire feminine soul blossomed within her. She was horrified at the merino and ashamed of the plush. Her father had never refused her anything. She knew at once the whole science of the hat, the dress, the cloak, the boot, the cuff, the stuff which sits well, the colour which is becoming, that science which makes the Parisian woman something so charming, so deep, and so dangerous. The phrase *heady woman* was invented for her.

In less than a month little Cosette was, in that Thebaid of the Rue de Babylone, not only one of the prettiest women, which is something, but one of "the best dressed" in Paris, which is much more. She would have liked to meet "her passer" to hear what he would say, and "to show him!" The truth is that she was ravishing in every point, and that she distinguished marvellously well between a Gérard hat and an Herbaut hat.

Jean Valjean beheld these ravages with anxiety. He, who felt that he could never more than creep, or walk at the most, saw wings growing on Cosette.

Still, merely by simple inspection of Cosette's toilette, a woman would have recognised that she had no mother. Certain little proprieties, certain special conventionalities, were not observed by Cosette. A mother, for instance, would have told her that a young girl does not wear damask.

The first day that Cosette went out with her dress and mantle of black damask and her white crape hat she came to take Jean Valjean's arm, gay, radiant, rosy, proud, and brilliant. "Father," said she, "how do you like this?" Jean Valjean answered in a voice which resembled the bitter voice of envy: "Charming!" He seemed as usual during the walk. When they came back he asked Cosette:

"Are you not going to wear your dress and hat any more?"

This occurred in Cosette's room. Cosette turned towards the wardrobe where her boarding-school dress was hanging.

"That disguise!" said she. "Father, what would you have me do with it? Oh! to be sure, no, I shall never wear those horrid things again. With that machine on my head, I look like Madame Mad-dog."

Jean Valjean sighed deeply.

From that day, he noticed that Cosette, who previously was always asking to stay in, saying: "Father, I enjoy myself better here with you," was now always asking to go out. Indeed, what is the use of having a pretty face and a delightful dress, if you do not show them?

He also noticed that Cosette no longer had the same taste for the back-yard. She now preferred to stay in the garden, walking even without displeasure before the grating. Jean Valjean, ferocious, did not set his foot in the garden. He stayed in his back-yard, like a dog.

Cosette, by learning that she was beautiful, lost the grace of not knowing it; an exquisite grace, for beauty heightened by artlessness is ineffable, and nothing is so adorable as dazzling innocence, going on her way, and holding in her hand, all unconscious, the key of a paradise. But what she lost in ingenuous grace, she gained in pensive and serious charm. Her whole person, pervaded by the joys of youth, innocence, and beauty, breathed a splendid melancholy.

It was at this period that Marius, after the lapse of six months, saw her again at the Luxembourg.

VI
THE BATTLE COMMENCES

COSETTE, in her seclusion, like Marius in his, was all ready to take fire. Destiny, with its mysterious and fatal patience, was slowly bringing these two beings near each other, fully charged and all languishing with the stormy electricities of passion,— these two souls which held love as two clouds hold lightning, and which were to meet and mingle in a glance like clouds in a flash.

The power of a glance has been so much abused in love stories, that it has come to be disbelieved in. Few people dare now to say that two beings have fallen in love because they have looked at each other. Yet it is in this way that love begins, and in this way only. The rest is only the rest, and comes afterwards. Nothing is more real than these great shocks which two souls give each other in exchanging this spark.

At that particular moment when Cosette unconsciously looked with this glance which so affected Marius, Marius had no suspicion that he also had a glance which affected Cosette.

She received from him the same harm and the same blessing.

For a long time now she had seen and scrutinised him as young girls scrutinise and see, while looking another way.

Marius still thought Cosette ugly, while Cosette already began to think Marius beautiful. But as he paid no attention to her, this young man was quite indifferent to her.

Still she could not help saying to herself that he had beautiful hair, beautiful eyes, beautiful teeth, a charming voice, when she heard him talking with his comrades; that he walked with an awkward gait, if you will, but with a grace of his own; that he didn't appear altogether stupid; that his whole person was noble, gentle, natural, and proud, and finally that he had a poor appearance, but that he had a good appearance.

On the day their eyes met and at last said abruptly to both those first obscure and ineffable things which the glance stammers out, Cosette at first did not comprehend. She went back pensively to the house in the Rue de l'Ouest, to which Jean Valjean, according to his custom, had gone to spend six weeks. The next day, on waking, she thought of this unknown young man, so long indifferent and icy, who now seemed to give some attention to her, and it did not seem to her that this attention was in the least degree pleasant. She was rather a little angry at this disdainful beau. An under-current of war was excited in her. It seemed to her, and she felt a pleasure in it still altogether childish, that at last she should be avenged.

Knowing that she was beautiful, she felt thoroughly, although in an indistinct way, that she had a weapon. Women play with their beauty as children do with their knives. They wound themselves with it.

We remember Marius' hesitations, his palpitations, his terrors. He remained at his seat and did not approach, which vexed Cosette. One day she said to Jean Valjean: "Father, let us walk a little this way." Seeing that Marius was not coming to her, she went to him. In such a case, every woman resembles Mahomet. And then, oddly enough, the first symptom of true love in a young man is timidity, in a young woman, boldness. This is surprising, and yet nothing is more natural. It is the two sexes tending to unite, and each acquiring the qualities of the other.

That day Cosette's glance made Marius mad, Marius' glance made Cosette tremble. Marius went away confident, and Cosette anxious. From that day onward, they adored each other.

The first thing that Cosette felt was a vague yet deep sadness. It seemed to her that since yesterday her soul had become black. She no longer recognised herself. The whiteness of soul of young girls, which is composed of coldness and gaiety, is like snow. It melts before love, which is its sun.

Cosette did not know what love was. She had never heard the word uttered in its earthly sense. In the books of profane music which came into the convent, *amour* was replaced by *tambour*, or *Pandour*. This made puzzles which exercised the imagination of the great girls, such as: *Oh! how delightful is the tambour!* or: *Pity is not a Pandour!* But Cosette had left while yet too young to be much concerned about the "tambour." She did not know, therefore, what name to give to what she now experienced. Is one less sick for not knowing the name of the disease?

She loved with so much the more passion as she loved with ignorance. She did not know whether it were good or evil, beneficent or dangerous, necessary or accidental, eternal or transitory, permitted or prohibited: she loved. She would have been very much astonished if anybody had said to her: "You are sleepless; that is forbidden! You do not eat! that is very wrong! You have sinkings and palpitations of the heart! that is not right. You blush and you turn pale when a certain being dressed in black appears at the end of a certain green walk! that is abominable!" She would not have understood it, and she would have answered: "How can I be to blame in a thing in which I can do nothing, and of which I know nothing?"

It proved that the love which presented itself was precisely that which best suited the condition of her soul. It was a sort of far-off worship, a mute contemplation, a deification by an unknown votary. It was the apprehension of adolescence by adolescence, the dream of her nights become a romance and remaining a dream, the wished-for phantom realised at last, and made flesh, but still having neither name, nor wrong, nor stain, nor need, nor defect; in a word, a lover distant and dwelling in the ideal, a chimera having a form. Any closer and more palpable encounter would at this first period have terrified Cosette, still half buried in the magnifying mirage of the cloister. She had all the terrors of children and all the terrors of nuns commingled. The spirit of the convent, with which she had been imbued for five years, was still slowly evaporating from her whole person, and made everything tremulous about her. In this condition, it was not a lover that she needed, it was not even an admirer, it was a vision. She began to adore Marius as something charming, luminous, and impossible.

As extreme artlessness meets extreme coquetry, she smiled upon him, very frankly.

She awaited impatiently every day the hour for her walk, she found Marius there, she felt herself inexpressibly happy, and sincerely believed that she uttered her whole thought when she said to Jean Valjean: "What a delightful garden the Luxembourg is!"

Marius and Cosette were in the dark in regard to each other. They did not speak, they did not bow, they were not acquainted; they saw each other, and, like the stars in the sky separated by millions of leagues, they lived by gazing upon each other.

Thus it was that Cosette gradually became a woman, and beautiful and loving, grew with consciousness of her beauty, and in ignorance of her love. Coquettish withal, through innocence.

VII

TO SADNESS, SADNESS AND A HALF

EVERY condition has its instinct. The old and eternal mother, Nature, silently warned Jean Valjean of the presence of Marius. Jean Valjean shuddered in the darkest of his mind. Jean Valjean saw nothing, knew nothing, but still gazed with persistent fixedness at the darkness which surrounded him, as if he perceived on one side something which was building, and on the other something which was falling down. Marius, also warned, and, according to the deep law of God, by this same mother, Nature, did all that he could to hide himself from the "father." It happened, however, that Jean Valjean sometimes perceived him. Marius' ways were no longer at all natural. He had an equivocal prudence and an awkward boldness. He ceased to come near them as formerly; he sat down at a distance, and remained there in an ecstasy; he had a book and pretended to be reading; why did he pretend? Formerly he came with his old coat, now he had his new coat on every day; it was not very certain that he did not curl his hair, he had strange eyes, he wore gloves; in short, Jean Valjean cordially detested this young man.

Cosette gave no ground for suspicion. Without knowing exactly what affected her, she had a very definite feeling that it was something, and that it must be concealed.

There was between the taste for dress which had arisen in Cosette and the habit of wearing new coats which had grown upon this unknown man, a parallelism which made Jean Valjean anxious. It was an accident perhaps, doubtless, certainly, but a threatening accident.

He had never opened his mouth to Cosette about the unknown man. One day, however, he could not contain himself, and with that uncertain despair which hastily drops the plummet into its unhappiness, he said to her: "What a pedantic air that young man has!"

Cosette, a year before, an unconcerned little girl, would have answered: "Why no, he is charming." Ten years later, with the love of Marius in her heart, she would have answered: "Pedantic and insupportable to the sight! you are quite right!" At the period of life and of heart in which she then was, she merely answered with supreme calmness: "That young man!"

As if she saw him for the first time in her life.

"How stupid I am!" thought Jean Valjean. "She had not even noticed him. I have shown him to her myself."

O simplicity of the old! depth of the young!

There is another law of these young years of suffering and care, of these sharp struggles of the first love against the first obstacles, the young girl does not allow herself to be caught in any toil, the young man falls into all. Jean Valjean had commenced a sullen war against Marius, which Marius, with the sublime folly of his passion and his age, did not guess. Jean Valjean spread around him a multitude of snares; he changed his hours, he changed his seat, he forgot his handkerchief, he went to the Luxembourg alone; Marius fell headlong into every trap; and to all these interrogation points planted upon his path by Jean Valjean he answered ingenuously, yes. Meanwhile Cosette was still walled in in her apparent unconcern and her imperturbable tranquillity, so that Jean Valjean came to this conclusion: "This booby is madly in love with Cosette, but Cosette does not even know of his existence!"

There was nevertheless a painful tremor in the heart. The moment when Cosette would fall in love might come at any instant. Does not everything begin by indifference?

Once only Cosette made a mistake, and startled him. He rose from the seat to go, after sitting there three hours, and she said: "So soon!"

Jean Valjean had not discontinued the promenades in the Luxembourg, not wishing to do anything singular, and above all dreading to excite any suspicion in Cosette; but during those hours so sweet to the two lovers, while Cosette was sending her smile to the intoxicated Marius, who perceived nothing but that, and now saw nothing in the world save one radiant, adored face, Jean Valjean fixed upon Marius glaring and terrible eyes. He who had come to believe that he was no longer capable of a malevolent feeling, had moments in which, when Marius was there, he thought that he was again becoming savage and ferocious, and felt opening and upheaving against this young man those old depths of his soul where there had once been so much wrath. It seemed to him almost as if the unknown craters were forming within him again.

What? he was there, that creature. What did he come for? He came to pry, to scent, to examine, to attempt: he came to say, "Eh, why not?" he came to prowl about his, Jean Valjean's life!—to prowl about his happiness, to clutch it and carry it away!

Jean Valjean added: "Yes, that is it! what is he looking for? an adventure? What does he want? an amour! An amour!—and as for me! What! I, after having been the most miserable of men, shall be the most unfortunate; I shall have spent sixty years of life upon my knees; I shall have suffered all that a man can suffer; I shall have grown old without having been young; I shall have lived with no family, no relatives, no friends, no wife, no children! I shall have left my blood on every stone, on every thorn, on every post, along every wall; I shall have been mild, although the world was harsh to me, and good, although it was evil; I shall have become an honest man in spite of all; I shall have repented of the wrong which I have done, and pardoned the wrongs which have been done to me and the moment that I am rewarded, the moment that it is over, the moment that I reach the end, the moment that I have what I desire, rightfully and justly; I have paid for it, I have earned it; it will all disappear, it will all vanish, and I shall lose Cosette, and I shall lose my life, my joy, my soul, because a great booby has been pleased to come and lounge about the Luxembourg."

Then his eyes filled with a strange and dismal light. It was no longer a man looking upon a man; it was not an enemy looking upon an enemy. It was a dog looking upon a robber.

We know the rest. The insanity of Marius continued. One day he followed Cosette to the Rue de l'Ouest. Another day he spoke to the porter; the porter in his turn spoke, and said to Jean Valjean: "Monsieur, who is that curious young man who has been asking for you?" The next day, Jean Valjean cast that glance at Marius which Marius finally perceived. A week after, Jean Valjean had moved. He resolved that he would never set his foot again either in the Luxembourg, or in the Rue de l'Ouest. He returned to the Rue Plumet.

Cosette did not complain, she said nothing, she asked no questions, she did not seek to know any reason; she was already at that point at which one fears discovery and self-betrayal. Jean Valjean had no experience of this misery, the only misery which is charming, and the only misery which he did not know; for this reason, he did not understand the deep significance of Cosette's silence. He noticed only that she had become sad, and he became gloomy. There was on either side an armed inexperience.

Once he made a trial. He asked Cosette:

"Would you like to go to the Luxembourg?"

A light illumined Cosette's pale face.

"Yes," said she.

They went. Three months had passed. Marius went there no longer. Marius was not there.

The next day, Jean Valjean asked Cosette again:

"Would you like to go to the Luxembourg?"

She answered sadly and quietly:

"No!"

Jean Valjean was hurt by this sadness, and harrowed by this gentleness.

What was taking place in this spirit so young, and already so impenetrable? What was in course of accomplishment in it? what was happening to Cosette's soul? Sometimes, instead of going to bed, Jean Valjean sat by his bedside with his head in his hands, and he spent whole nights asking himself: "What is there in Cosette's mind?" and thinking what things she could be thinking about.

Oh! in those hours, what mournful looks he turned towards the cloister, that chaste summit, that abode of angels, that inaccessible glacier of virtue! With what despairing rapture he contemplated that convent garden, full of unknown flowers and secluded maidens, where all perfumes and all souls rose straight towards Heaven! How he worshipped that Eden, now closed for ever, from which he had voluntarily departed, and from which he had foolishly descended! How he regretted his self-denial, his madness in having brought Cosette back to the world, poor hero of sacrifice, caught and thrown to the ground by his very devotedness! How he said to himself: "What have I done?"

Still nothing of this was exhibited towards Cosette: neither capriciousness nor severity. Always the same serene and kind face. Jean Valjean's manner was more tender and more paternal than ever. If anything could have raised a suspicion that there was less happiness, it was the greater gentleness.

For her part, Cosette was languishing. She suffered from the absence of Marius, as she had rejoiced in his presence, in a peculiar way, without really knowing it. When Jean Valjean ceased to take her on their usual walk, her woman's instinct murmured confusedly in the depths of her heart, that she must not appear to cling to the Luxembourg; and that if it were indifferent to her, her father would take her back there. But days, weeks, and months passed away. Jean Valjean had tacitly accepted Cosette's tacit consent. She regretted it. It was too late. The day she returned to the Luxembourg, Marius was no longer there. Marius then had disappeared; it was all over, what could she do? Would she ever find him again? She felt a constriction of her heart, which nothing relaxed, and which was increasing every day; she no longer knew whether it was winter or summer, sunshine or rain, whether the birds sang, whether it was the season for dahlias or daisies, whether the Luxembourg was more charming than the Tuileries, whether the linen which the washer-woman brought home was starched too much, or not enough, whether Toussaint did "her marketing" well or ill, and she became dejected, absorbed, intent upon a single thought, her eye wild and fixed, as when one looks into the night at the deep black place where an apparition has vanished.

Still she did not let Jean Valjean see anything, except her paleness. She kept her face sweet for him.

This paleness was more than sufficient to make Jean Valjean anxious. Sometimes he asked her:

"What is the matter with you?"

She answered:

"Nothing."

And after a silence, as she felt that he was sad also, she

continued: "And you, father, is not something the matter with you?"

"Me? nothing," said he.

These two beings, who had loved each other so exclusively, and with so touching a love, and who had lived so long for each other, were now suffering by each other and through each other; without speaking of it, without harsh feeling, and smiling the while.

VIII
THE CHAIN

THE more unhappy of the two was Jean Valjean. Youth, even in its sorrows, always has a brilliancy of its own.

At certain moments, Jean Valjean suffered so much that he became puerile. It is the peculiarity of grief to bring out the childish side of man. He felt irresistibly that Cosette was escaping him. He would have been glad to put forth an effort, to hold her fast, to rouse her enthusiasm by something external and striking. These ideas, puerile, as we have just said, and at the same time senile, gave him by their very childishness a just idea of the influence of gewgaws over the imagination of young girls. He chanced once to see a general pass in the street on horseback in full uniform, Count Coutard, Commandant of Paris. He envied this gilded man, he thought what happiness it would be to be able to put on that coat which was an incontestable thing, that if Cosette saw him thus it would dazzle her, that when he should give his arm to Cosette and pass before the gate of the Tuileries they would present arms to him and that that would so satisfy Cosette that it would destroy her inclination to look at the young men.

An unexpected shock came to him in the midst of these sad thoughts.

In the isolated life which they were leading, and since they had come to live in the Rue Plumet, they had formed a habit. They sometimes made a pleasure excursion to go and see the sun rise, a gentle joy suited to those who are entering upon life and those who are leaving it.

A walk at early dawn, to him who loves solitude, is equivalent to a walk at night, with the gaiety of nature added. The streets are empty and the birds are singing. Cosette, herself a bird, usually awoke early. These morning excursions were arranged the evening before. He proposed, she accepted. They were planned as a conspiracy, they went out before day, and these were so many pleasant hours for Cosette. Such innocent eccentricities have a charm for the young.

Jean Valjean's inclination was, we know, to go to unfrequented spots, to solitary nooks, to neglected places. There were at that time in the neighbourhood of the barrières of Paris some poor fields, almost in the city, where there grew in summer a scanty crop of wheat, and which in autumn, after this was gathered, appeared not to have been harvested, but stripped. Jean Valjean had a predilection for these fields. Cosette did not dislike them. To him it was solitude, to her it was liberty. There she became a little girl again, she could run and almost play, she took off her hat, laid it on Jean Valjean's knees, and gathered flowers. She looked at the butterflies upon the blossoms, but did not catch them; gentleness and tenderness are born with love, and the young girl who has in her heart a trembling and fragile idea, feels pity for a butterfly's wing. She wove garlands of wild poppies which she put upon her head and which, lit up and illuminated in the sunshine, and blazing like a flame, made a crown of fire for her fresh and rosy face.

Even after their life had been saddened, they continued their habit of morning walks.

So one October morning, tempted by the deep serenity of the autumn of 1831, they had gone out, and found themselves at daybreak near the Barrière du Maine. It was not day, it was dawn, a wild and ravishing moment. A few constellations here and there in the deep pale heavens, the earth all black, the sky all white, a shivering in the spears of grass, everywhere the mysterious thrill of the twilight. A lark, which seemed among the stars, was singing at this enormous height, and one would have said that this hymn from littleness to the infinite was calming the immensity. In the east the Val de Grâce carved out upon the clear horizon, with the sharpness of steel, its obscure mass; Venus was rising in splendour behind that dome like a soul escaping from a dark edifice.

All was peace and silence; nobody upon the highway; on the footpaths a few scattered working-men, hardly visible, going to their work.

Jean Valjean was seated in the side walk, upon some timbers

lying by the gate of a lumber-yard. He had his face turned towards the road, and his back towards the light; he had forgotten the sun which was just rising; he had fallen into one of those deep meditations in which the whole mind is absorbed, which even imprison the senses, and which are equivalent to four walls. There are some meditations which may be called vertical; when one is at the bottom it takes time to return to the surface of the earth. Jean Valjean had descended into one of these reveries. He was thinking of Cosette, of the happiness possible if nothing came between her and him, of that light with which she filled his life, a light which was the atmosphere of his soul. He was almost happy in his reverie. Cosette, standing near him, was watching the clouds as they became ruddy.

Suddenly, Cosette exclaimed: "Father, I should think somebody was coming down there." Jean Valjean looked up.

Cosette was right.

The highway which leads to the ancient Barrière du Maine is a prolongation, as everybody knows, of the Rue de Sèvres, and is intersected at a right angle by the interior boulevard. At the corner of the highway and the boulevard, at the point where they diverge, a sound was heard, difficult of explanation at such an hour, and a kind of moving confusion appeared. Some shapeless thing which came from the boulevard was entering upon the highway.

It grew larger, it seemed to move in order, still it was bristling and quivering; it looked like a wagon; but they could not make out the load. There were horses, wheels, cries; whips were cracking. By degrees the features became definite, although enveloped in darkness. It was in fact a wagon which had just turned out of the boulevard into the road, and which was making its way towards the barrière, near which Jean Valjean was; a second, of the same appearance, followed it, then a third, then a fourth; seven vehicles turned in in succession, the horses' heads touching the rear of the wagons. Dark forms were moving upon these wagons, flashes were seen in the twilight as if of drawn swords, a clanking was heard which resembled the rattling of chains; it advanced, the voices grew louder, and it was as terrible a thing as comes forth from the cavern of dreams.

As it approached it took form, and outlined itself behind the trees with the pallor of an apparition; the mass whitened; daylight, which was rising little by little, spread a palid gleam over this crawling thing, which was at once sepulchral and alive, the heads of the shadows became the faces of corpses, and it was this:

Seven wagons were moving in file upon the road. Six of them were of a peculiar structure. They resembled coopers' drays; they were a sort of long ladder placed upon two wheels, forming thills at the forward end. Each dray, or better, each ladder, was drawn by four horses tandem. Upon these ladders strange clusters of men were carried. In the little light that there was, these men were not seen, they were only guessed. Twenty-four on each wagon, twelve on each side, back to back, their faces towards the passers-by, their legs hanging down, these men were travelling thus; and they had behind them something which clanked and which was a chain, and at their necks something which shone and which was an iron collar. Each had his collar, but the chain was for all; so that these twenty-four men, if they should chance to get down from the dray and walk, would be made subject to a sort of inexorable unity, and have to wiggle over the ground with the chain for a backbone, very much like centipedes. In front and rear of each wagon, two men, armed with muskets, stood, each having an end of the chain under his foot. The collars were square. The seventh wagon, a huge cart with racks, but without a cover, had four wheels and six horses, and carried a resounding pile of iron kettles, melting pots, furnaces, and chains, over which were scattered a number of men, who were bound and lying at full length, and who appeared to be sick. This cart, entirely exposed to view, was furnished with broken hurdles which seemed to have served in the ancient punishments.

These wagons kept the middle of the street. At either side marched a row of guards of infamous appearance, wearing three-pronged hats like the soldiers of the Directory, stained, torn, filthy, muffled up in Invalides' uniforms and hearse-boys' trousers, half grey and half blue, almost in tatters, with red epaulettes, yellow cross-belts, sheath-knives, muskets, and clubs: a species of servant-soldiers. These sbirri seemed a compound of the abjectness of the beggar and the authority of the executioner. The one who appeared to be their chief had a horsewhip in his hand. All these details, blurred by the twilight, were becoming clearer and clearer in the growing light. At the head and the rear of the convoy, gendarmes marched on horseback, solemn, and with drawn swords.

This cortège was so long that when the first wagon reached the barrière, the last had hardly turned out of the boulevard.

A crowd, come from nobody knows where, and gathered in a twinkling, as is frequently the case in Paris, were pushing along the two sides of the highway and looking on. In the neighbouring lanes there were heard people shouting and calling each other, and the wooden shoes of the market gardeners who were running to see.

The men heaped upon the drays were silent as they were jolted along. They were livid with the chill of the morning. They all had tow trousers, and their bare feet were in wooden shoes. The rest of their costume was according to the fancy of misery. Their dress was hideously variegated: nothing is more dismal than the harlequin of rags. Felt hats jammed out of shape, glazed caps, horrible cloth caps, and beside the linen monkey-jacket, the black coat out at the elbows; several had women's hats; others had baskets on their heads, hairy breasts could be seen, and through the holes in their clothing tattooings could be discerned; temples of love, burning hearts, cupids; eruptions, and red sores could also be seen. Two or three had a rope of straw fixed to the bars of the dray, and hung beneath them like a stirrup, which sustained their feet. One of them held in his hand and carried to his mouth something which looked like a black stone, which he seemed to be gnawing; it was bread which he was eating. There were none but dry eyes among them; they were rayless, or lighted with an evil light. The troop of escort was cursing, the chained did not whisper; from time to time there was heard the sound of the blow of a club upon their shoulders or their heads; some of these men were yawning; their rags were terrible; their feet hung down, their shoulders swung, their heads struck together, their irons rattled, their eyes glared fiercely, their fists were clenched or open inertly like the hands of the dead; behind the convoy a troop of children were bursting with laughter.

This file of wagons, whatever it was, was dismal. It was evident that to-morrow, that in an hour, a shower might spring up, that it would be followed by another, and another, and that the worn-out clothing would be soaked through, that once wet, these men would never get dry, that once chilled, they would never get warm again, that their tow trousers would be fastened to their skin by the rain, that water would fill their wooden shoes, that blows of the whip could not prevent the chattering of their jaws, that the chain would continue to hold them by the neck, that their feet would continue to swing; and it was impossible not to shudder at seeing these human creatures thus bound and passive under the chilling clouds of autumn, and given up to the rain, to the wind, to all the fury of the elements, like trees and stones.

The clubs did not spare even the sick, who lay tied with ropes and motionless in the seventh wagon, and who seemed to have been thrown there like sacks filled with misery.

Suddenly, the sun appeared; the immense radiance of the Orient burst forth, and one would have said that it set all these savage heads on fire. Their tongues were loosed, a conflagration of sneers, of oaths, and songs burst forth. The broad horizontal light cut the whole file in two, illuminating their heads and their bodies, leaving their feet and the wheels in the dark. Their thoughts appeared upon their faces; the moment was appalling; demons visible with their masks fallen off, ferocious souls laid bare. Lighted up, this group was still dark. Some, who were gay, had quills in their mouths from which they blew vermin among the crowd, selecting the women; the dawn intensified these mournful profiles by the blackness of the shade; not one of these beings who was not deformed by misery; and it was so monstrous that one would have said that it changed the sunbeams into the gleam of the lightning's flash. The wagon load which led the cortège had struck up and were singing at the top of their voices with a ghastly joviality a medley of Desaugiers, then famous, *la Vestale*; the trees shivered drearily on the side walks, the bourgeois listened with faces of idiotic bliss to these obscenities chanted by spectres.

Every form of distress was present in this chaos of a cortège; there was the facial angle of every beast, old men, youths, bald heads, grey beards, cynical monstrosities, dogged resignation, savage grimaces, insane attitudes, snouts set off with caps, heads like those of young girls with corkscrews over their temples, child faces horrifying on that account, thin skeleton faces which lacked nothing but death. On the first wagon was a negro, who, perhaps, had been a slave and could compare chains. The fearful leveller, disgrace, had passed over these brows; at this degree of abasement the last transformation had taken place in all of its utmost degree; and ignorance, changed into stupidity, was the equal of intelligence changed into despair. No possible choice among these men who seemed by their appearance the élite of the mire. It was clear that the marshal, whoever he was, of this foul procession had not classified them. These beings had been bound and coupled pell-mell, probably in alphabetic disorder, and loaded haphazard upon these wagons. The aggregation of horrors, however, always ends by evolving a resultant; every addition of misfortune gives a total; there came from each chain a common soul, and each cartload had its own physiognomy. Beside the one which was singing, there was one which was howling; a third was begging; one was seen gnashing his teeth; another was threatening the bystanders, another blaspheming God; the last was silent as the tomb. Dante would have thought he saw the seven circles of Hell on their passage.

A passage from condemnation towards punishment, made drearily, not upon the formidable flashing car of the Apocalypse, but more dismal still upon a hangman's cart.

One of the guard, who had a hook on the end of his club, from time to time made a semblance of stirring up this heap of human ordure. An old woman in the crowd pointed them out with her finger to a little boy five years old and said: "*Whelp, that will teach you!*"

As the songs and the blasphemy increased, he who seemed the captain of the escort cracked his whip, and upon that signal, a fearful, sullen, and promiscuous cudgelling, which sounded like hail, fell upon the seven wagons; many roared and foamed; which redoubled the joy of the gamins who had collected, a swarm of flies upon these wounds.

Jean Valjean's eye had become frightful. It was no longer an eye; it was that deep window, which takes the place of the look in certain unfortunate beings, who seem unconscious of reality, and from which flashes out the reflection of horrors and catastrophes. He was not looking upon a sight; a vision was appearing to him. He endeavoured to rise, to flee, to escape; he could not move a limb. Sometimes things which you see, clutch you and hold you. He was spell-bound, stupefied, petrified, asking himself, through a vague unutterable anguish, what was the meaning of this sepulchral persecution, and whence came this pandemonium which was pursuing him. All at once he raised his hand to his forehead, a common gesture with those to whom memory suddenly returns; he remembered that this was really the route, that this detour was usual to avoid meeting the king, which was always possible on the Fontainebleau road, and that, thirty-five years before, he had passed through this barrière.

Cosette, though from another cause, was equally terrified. She did not comprehend; her breath failed her; what she saw did not seem possible to her; at last she exclaimed:

"Father! what can there be in those wagons?"

Jean Valjean answered:

"Convicts."

"And where are they going?"

"To the galleys."

At this moment the cudgelling, multiplied by a hundred hands, reached its climax; blows with the flat of the sword joined in; it was a fury of whips and clubs; the galley slaves crouched down, a hideous obedience was produced by the punishment, and all were silent with the look of chained wolves. Cosette trembled in every limb; she continued:

"Father, are they still men?"

"Sometimes," said the wretched man.

It was in fact the chain which, setting out before day from Bicêtre, took the Mans road to avoid Fontainebleau, where the king then was. This detour made the terrible journey last three or four days longer; but to spare the royal person the sight of the punishment, it may well be prolonged.

Jean Valjean returned home overwhelmed. Such encounters are shocks, and the memory which they leave resembles a convulsion.

Jean Valjean, however, on the way back to the Rue de Babylone with Cosette, did not notice that she asked him other questions regarding what they had just seen; perhaps he was himself too much absorbed in his own dejection to heed her words or to answer them. But at night, as Cosette was leaving him to go to bed, he heard her say in an undertone, and as if talking to herself: "It seems to me that if I should meet one of those men in my path, O my God, I should die just from seeing him near me!"

Fortunately it happened that on the morrow of this tragic day there were, in consequence of some official celebration, fêtes in Paris, a review in the Champ de Mars, rowing matches upon the Seine, theatricals in the Champs-Elysées, fireworks at l'Etoile, illuminations everywhere. Jean Valjean, doing violence to his habits, took Cosette to these festivities, for the purpose of diverting her mind from the memories of the day before, and of effacing under the laughing tumult of all Paris, the abominable thing which had passed before her. The review, which enlivened the fête, made the display of uniforms quite natural; Jean Valjean put on his National Guard uniform with the vague interior feeling of a man who is taking refuge. Yet the object of this walk seemed attained. Cosette, whose law it was to please her father, and for whom, moreover, every sight was new, accepted the diversion with the easy and blithe grace of youth, and did not look too disdainfully upon that promiscuous bowl of joy which is called a public fête; so that Jean Valjean could believe that he had succeeded, and that no trace remained of the hideous vision.

Some days later, one morning, when the sun was bright, and they were both upon the garden steps, another infraction of the rules which Jean Valjean seemed to have imposed upon himself, and of the habit of staying in her room which sadness had imposed upon Cosette, Cosette, in her dressing-gown, was standing in that undress of the morning hour which is charmingly becoming to young girls, and which has the appearance of a cloud upon a star; and, with her head in the light, rosy from having slept well, under the tender gaze of the gentle goodman, she was picking a daisy in pieces. Cosette was ignorant of the transporting legend, *I love thee a little, passionately,* etc.; who should have taught it to her? She was fingering this flower, by instinct, innocently, without suspecting that to pick a daisy in pieces is to pluck a heart. Were there a fourth Grace named Melancholy, and were it smiling, she would have seemed that Grace.

Jean Valjean was fascinated by the contemplation of her slender fingers upon that flower, forgetting everything in the radiance of this child. A redbreast was twittering in the shrubbery beside them. White clouds were crossing the sky so gaily that one would have said they had just been set at liberty. Cosette continued picking her flower attentively; she seemed to be thinking of something; but that must have been pleasant. Suddenly she turned her head over her shoulder with the delicate motion of the swan, and said to Jean Valjean: "Father, what are they then, the galley slaves?"

BOOK FOURTH – AID FROM BELOW
MAY BE AID FROM ABOVE

I

WOUND WITHOUT, CURE WITHIN

THUS their life gradually darkened.

There was left to them but one distraction, and this had formerly been a pleasure: that was to carry bread to those who were hungry, and clothing to those who were cold. In these visits to the poor, in which Cosette often accompanied Jean Valjean, they found some remnant of their former lightheartedness; and, sometimes, when they had had a good day, when many sorrows had been relieved and many little children revived and made warm, Cosette, in the evening, was a little gay. It was at this period that they visited the Jondrette den.

The day after that visit, Jean Valjean appeared in the cottage in the morning, with his ordinary calmness, but with a large wound on his left arm, very much inflamed and very venomous, which resembled a burn, and which he explained in some fashion. This wound confined him within doors more than a month with fever. He would see no physician. When Cosette urged it: "Call the dog-doctor," said he.

Cosette dressed it night and morning with so divine a grace and so angelic a pleasure in being useful to him, that Jean Valjean felt all his old happiness return, his fears and his anxieties dissipate, and he looked upon Cosette, saying: "Oh! the good wound! Oh! the kind hurt!"

Cosette, as her father was sick, had deserted the summerhouse and regained her taste for the little lodge and the backyard. She spent almost all her time with Jean Valjean, and read to him the books which he liked. In general, books of travels. Jean Valjean was born anew; his happiness revived with inexpressible radiance; the Luxembourg, the unknown young prowler, Cosette's coldness, all these clouds of his soul faded away. He now said to himself: "I imagined all that. I am an old fool."

His happiness was so great, that the frightful discovery of the Thénardiers, made in the Jondrette den, and so unexpectedly, had in some sort glided over him. He had succeeded in escaping; his trace was lost, what mattered the rest! he thought of it only to grieve over those wretches. "They are now in prison, and can do no harm in future," thought he, "but what a pitiful family in distress!"

As to the hideous vision of the Barrière du Maine, Cosette had never mentioned it again.

At the convent, Sister Sainte Mechthilde had taught Cosette music. Cosette had the voice of a warbler with a soul, and sometimes in the evening, in the humble lodging of the wounded man, she sang plaintive songs which rejoiced Jean Valjean.

Spring came, the garden was so wonderful at that season of the year, that Jean Valjean said to Cosette: "You never go there, I wish you would walk in it." "As you will, father," said Cosette.

And, out of obedience to her father, she resumed her walks in the garden, oftenest alone, for, as we have remarked, Jean Valjean, who probably dreaded being seen through the gate, hardly ever went there.

Jean Valjean's wound had been a diversion.

When Cosette saw that her father was suffering less, and that he was getting well, and that he seemed happy, she felt a contentment that she did not even notice, so gently and naturally did it come upon her. It was then the month of March, the days were growing longer, winter was departing, winter always carries with it something of our sadness; then April came, that daybreak of summer, fresh like every dawn, gay like every childhood; weeping a little sometimes like the infant that it is. Nature in this month has charming gleams which pass from the sky, the clouds, the trees, the fields, and the flowers, into the heart of man.

Cosette was still too young for this April joy, which resembled her, not to find its way to her heart. Insensibly, and without a suspicion on her part, the darkness passed away from her mind. In the spring it becomes light in sad souls, as at noon it becomes light in cellars. And Cosette was not now very sad. So it was, however, but she did not notice it. In the morning, about ten o'clock, after breakfast, when she had succeeded in enticing her father into the garden for a quarter of an hour, and while she was walking in the sun in front of the steps, supporting his wounded arm, she did not perceive that she was laughing every moment, and that she was happy.

Jean Valjean saw her, with intoxication, again become fresh and rosy.

"Oh! the blessed wound!" repeated he in a whisper.

And he was grateful to the Thénardiers.

As soon as his wound was cured, he resumed his solitary and twilight walks.

It would be a mistake to believe that one can walk in this way alone in the uninhabited regions of Paris, and not meet with some adventure.

II

MOTHER PLUTARCH IS NOT EMBARRASSED ON THE EXPLANATION OF A PHENOMENON

ONE evening little Gavroche had had no dinner; he remembered that he had had no dinner also the day before; this was becoming tiresome. He resolved that he would try for some supper. He went wandering about beyond La Salpêtrière, in the deserted spots; those are the places for good luck; where there is nobody, can be found something. He came to a settlement which appeared to him to be the village of Austerlitz.

In one of his preceding strolls, he had noticed an old garden there haunted by an old man and an old woman, and in this garden a passable apple tree. Beside this apple tree, there was a sort of fruit-loft poorly inclosed where the conquest of an apple might be made. An apple is a supper; an apple is life. What ruined Adam might save Gavroche. The garden was upon a solitary lane unpaved and bordered with bushes for lack of houses; a hedge separated it from the lane.

Gavroche directed his steps towards the garden; he found the lane, he recognised the apple tree, he verified the fruit-loft, he examined the hedge; a hedge is a stride. Day was declining, not a cat in the lane, the time was good. Gavroche sketched out the escalade, then suddenly stopped. Somebody was talking in the garden. Gavroche looked through one of the openings of the hedge.

Within two steps of him, at the foot of the hedge on the other side, precisely at the point where the hole he was meditating would have taken him, lay a stone which made a kind of seat, and on this seat the old man of the garden was sitting with the old woman standing before him. The old woman was muttering. Gavroche, who was anything but discreet, listened.

"Monsieur Mabeuf!" said the old woman.

"Mabeuf!" thought Gavroche, "that is a funny name."

The old man who was addressed made no motion. The old woman repeated:

"Monsieur Mabeuf."

The old man, without raising his eyes from the ground, determined to answer:

"What, Mother Plutarch?"

"Mother Plutarch!" thought Gavroche, "another funny name."

Mother Plutarch resumed, and the old man was forced to enter into the conversation:

"The landlord is dissatisfied."

"Why so?"

"There are three quarters due."

"In three months there will be four."

"He says he will turn you out of doors to sleep."

"I shall go."

"The grocery woman wants to be paid. She holds on to her wood. What will you keep warm with this winter? We shall have no wood."

"There is the sun."

"The butcher refuses credit, he will not give us any more meat."

"That is all right. I do not digest meat well. It is too heavy."

"What shall we have for dinner?"

"Bread."

"The baker demands something on account, and says no money, no bread."

"Very well."

"What will you eat?"

"We have the apples from the apple tree."

"But, monsieur, we can't live like that without money."

"I have not any."

The old woman went away, the old man remained alone. He began to reflect. Gavroche was reflecting on his side. It was almost night.

The first result of Gavroche's reflection was that instead of climbing over the hedge he crept under. The branches separated a little at the bottom of the bushes.

"Heigho," exclaimed Gavroche internally, "an alcove!" and he hid in it. He almost touched Father Mabeuf's seat. He heard the octogenarian breathe.

Then, for dinner, he tried to sleep.

Sleep of a cat, sleep with one eye. Even while crouching there Gavroche kept watch.

The whiteness of the twilight sky blanched the earth, and the lane made a livid line between two rows of dusky bushes.

Suddenly, upon that whitened band two dim forms appeared. One came before—the other, at some distance, behind.

"There are two fellows," growled Gavroche.

The first form seemed some old bourgeois bent and thoughtful, dressed more than simply, walking with the slow pace of an aged man, and taking his ease in the starry evening.

The second was straight, firm, and slight. It regulated its step by the step of the first; but in the unwonted slowness of the gait, dexterity and agility were manifest. This form had, in addition to something wild and startling, the whole appearance of what was then called a dandy; the hat was of the latest style, the coat was black, well cut, probably of fine cloth, and closely fitted to the form. The head was held up with a robust grace, and, under the hat, could be seen in the twilight the pale profile of a young man. This profile had a rose in its mouth. The second form was well known to Gavroche: it was Montparnasse.

As to the other, he could have said nothing about it, except that it was an old goodman.

Gavroche immediately applied himself to observation.

One of these two passers evidently had designs upon the other. Gavroche was well situated to see the issue. The alcove had very conveniently become a hiding-place.

Montparnasse hiding, at such an hour, in such a place—it was threatening. Gavroche felt his *gamin*'s heart moved with pity for the old man.

What could he do? intervene? one weakness in aid of another? That would be ludicrous to Montparnasse. Gavroche could not conceal it from himself that, to this formidable bandit of eighteen, the old man first, the child afterwards, would be but two mouthfuls.

While Gavroche was deliberating, the attack was made, sharp and hideous. The attack of a tiger on a wild ass, a spider on a fly. Montparnasse, on a sudden, threw away the rose, sprang upon the old man, collared him, grasped him and fastened to him, and Gavroche could hardly restrain a cry. A moment afterwards, one of these men was under the other, exhausted, panting, struggling, with a knee of marble upon his breast. Only it was not altogether as Gavroche had expected. The one on the ground was Montparnasse; the one above was the goodman. All this happened a few steps from Gavroche.

The old man had received the shock and had returned it, and returned it so terribly that in the twinkling of an eye the assailant and assailed had changed parts.

"There is a brave Invalide!" thought Gavroche.

And he could not help clapping his hands. But it was a clapping of hands thrown away. It did not reach the two combatants, absorbed and deafened by each other, and mingling their breath in the contest.

There was silence. Montparnasse ceased to struggle. Gavroche said this aside: "Can he be dead?"

The goodman had not spoken a word, nor uttered a cry. He arose, and Gavroche heard him say to Montparnasse:

"Get up."

Montparnasse got up, but the goodman held him. Montparnasse had the humiliated and furious attitude of a wolf caught by a sheep.

Gavroche looked and listened, endeavouring to double his eyes by his ears. He was enormously amused.

He was rewarded for his conscientious anxiety as a spectator. He was able to seize upon the wing the following dialogue, which borrowed a strangely tragic tone from the darkness. The goodman questioned. Montparnasse responded.

"How old are you?"

"Nineteen."

"You are strong and well. Why don't you work?"

"It is fatiguing."

"What is your business?"

"Loafer."

"Speak seriously. Can I do anything for you? What would you like to be?"

"A robber."

There was a silence. The old man seemed to be thinking deeply. He was motionless, yet did not release Montparnasse.

From time to time the young bandit, vigorous and nimble, made the efforts of a beast caught in a snare. He gave a spring, attempted a trip, twisted his limbs desperately, endeavoured to escape. The old man did not appear to perceive it, and with a single hand held his two arms with the sovereign indifference of absolute strength.

The old man's reverie continued for some time, then, looking steadily upon Montparnasse, he gently raised his voice and addressed to him, in that obscurity in which they were, a sort of solemn allocution of which Gavroche did not lose a syllable:

"My child, you are entering by laziness into the most laborious of existences. Ah! you declare yourself a loafer! prepare to labour. Have you seen a terrible machine called the rolling-mill? Beware of it, it is a cunning and ferocious thing; if it but catch the skirt of your coat, you are drawn in entirely. This machine is idleness. Stop, while there is yet time, and save yourself! otherwise, it is all over; you will soon be between the wheels. Once caught, hope for nothing more. To fatigue, idler! no more rest. The implacable iron hand of labour has seized you. Earn a living, have a task, accomplish a duty, you do not wish it! To be like others is tiresome! Well! you will be different. Labour is the law; he who spurns it as tiresome will have it as a punishment. You are unwilling to be a working-man, you will be a slave. Labour releases you on the one hand only to retake you on the other; you are unwilling to be her friend, you will be her negro. Ah! you have refused the honest weariness of men, you shall have the sweat of the damned. While others sing, you will rave. You will see from afar, from below, other men at work; it will seem to you that they are at rest. The labourer, the reaper, the sailor, the blacksmith, will appear to you in the light like the blessed in a paradise. What a radiance in the anvil! To drive the plough, to bind the sheaf, is happiness. The bark free before the wind, what a festival! You, idler, dig, draw, roll, march! Drag your halter, you are a beast of burden in the train of hell! Ah! to do nothing, that is your aim. Well! not a week, not a day, not an hour, without crushing exhaustion. You can lift nothing but with anguish. Every minute which elapses will make your muscles crack. What will be a feather for others will be a rock for you. The simplest things will become steep. Life will make itself a monster about you. To go, to come, to breathe, so many terrible labours. Your lungs will feel like a hundred-pound weight. To go here rather than there will be a problem to solve. Any other man who wishes to go out, opens his door, it is done, he is out of doors. You, if you wish to go out, must pierce your wall. To go into the street, what does everybody do? Everybody goes down the staircase! but you, you will tear up your bed clothes, you will make a rope of them strip by strip, then you will pass through your window and you will hang on that thread over an abyss, and it will be at night, in the storm, in the rain, in the tempest, and, if the rope is too short, you will have but one way to descend, to fall. To fall at a venture, into the abyss, from whatever height, upon what? Upon whatever is below, upon the unknown. Or you will climb through the flue of a chimney, at the risk of burning yourself; or you will crawl through a sewer, at the risk of being drowned. I do not speak of the holes which you must conceal, of the stones which you must take out and put back twenty times a day, of the mortar which you must hide in your mattress. A lock presents itself, the bourgeois has in his pocket his key, made by a locksmith. You, if you want to pass out, are condemned to make a frightful masterpiece; you will take a big sou, you will cut it into two slices; with what tools? You will invent them. That is your business. Then you will hollow out the interior of these two slices, preserving the outside carefully, and you will cut all around the edge a screwthread, so that they will fit closely one upon the other, like a bottom and a cover. The bottom and the top thus screwed together, nobody will suspect anything. To the watchmen, for you will be watched, it will be a big sou; to you, it will be a box. What will you put in this box? A little bit of steel. A watch-spring in which you will cut teeth, and which will be a saw. With this saw, as long as a pin, and hidden in this sou, you will have to cut the bolt of the lock, the slide of the bolt, the clasp of the padlock, and the bar which you will have at your window, and the iron ring which you will have on your leg. This masterpiece finished, this prodigy accomplished, all those miracles of art, of address, of skill, of patience, executed, if it comes to be known that you are the author, what will be your reward? the dungeon. Behold your future. Idleness, pleasure, what abysses! To do nothing is a dreary course to take, be sure of it. To live idle upon the substance of society! To be useless, that is to say, noxious! This leads straight to the lowest depth of misery.

"Woe to him who would be a parasite! he will be vermin. Ah! it is not pleasant to you to work? Ah! you will have but one thought; to eat, and drink, and sleep in luxury. You will drink water, you will eat black bread, you will sleep upon a board,

with irons riveted to your limbs, the chill of which you will feel
at night upon your flesh! You will break those irons, you will
flee. Very well. You will drag yourself on your belly in the
bushes, and eat grass like the beasts of the forest. And you will be
retaken. And then you will spend years in a dungeon, fastened to
a wall, groping for a drink from your pitcher, gnawing a frightful loaf of darkness which the dogs would not touch, eating
beans which the worms have eaten before you. You will be a
wood-louse in a cellar. Oh! take pity on yourself, miserable
child, young thing, a suckling not twenty years ago, who doubtless have a mother still alive! I conjure you, listen to me. You
desire fine black clothes, shining pumps, to curl your hair, to
put sweet-scented oil upon your locks, to please your women,
to be handsome. You will be close shorn, with a red coat and
wooden shoes. You wish a ring on your finger, you will have an
iron collar on your neck. And if you look at a woman, a blow
of the club. And you will go in there at twenty, and you will
come out at fifty! You will enter young, rosy, fresh, with your
eyes bright and all your teeth white, and your beautiful youthful
hair; you will come out broken, bent, wrinkled, toothless, horrible, with white hair! Oh! my child, you are taking a mistaken
road, laziness is giving you bad advice; the hardest of all labour
is robbery. Trust me, do not undertake this dreadful drudgery
of being an idler. To become a rascal is not comfortable. It is
not so hard to be an honest man. Go, now, and think of what I
have said to you. And now, what did you want of me? my purse?
here it is."

And the old man, releasing Montparnasse, put his purse in
his hand, which Montparnasse weighed for a moment, after
which, with the same mechanical precaution as if he had stolen
it, Montparnasse let it glide gently into the back pocket of his
coat.

All this said and done, the goodman turned his back and
quietly resumed his walk.

"Blockhead!" murmured Montparnasse.

Who was this goodman? the reader has doubtless guessed.

Montparnasse, in stupefaction, watched him till he disappeared in the twilight. This contemplation was fatal to him.

While the old man was moving away, Gavroche was
approaching.

Gavroche, with a side glance, made sure that Father Mabeuf,

perhaps asleep, was still sitting on the seat. Then the urchin came out of his bushes, and began to creep along in the shade, behind the motionless Montparnasse. He reached Montparnasse thus without being seen or heard, gently insinuated his hand into the back pocket of the fine black cloth coat, took the purse, withdrew his hand, and, creeping off again, glided away like an adder into the darkness. Montparnasse, who had no reason to be upon his guard, and who was reflecting for the first time in his life, perceived nothing of it. Gavroche, when he had reached the point where Father Mabeuf was, threw the purse over the hedge, and fled at full speed.

The purse fell on the foot of Father Mabeuf. This shock awoke him. He stooped down, and picked up the purse. He did not understand it at all, and he opened it. It was a purse with two compartments; in one there were some small coins; in the other, there were six napoleons.

M. Mabeuf, very much startled, carried the thing to his governess.

"This falls from the sky," said Mother Plutarch.

BOOK FIFTH –
THE END OF WHICH IS UNLIKE THE BEGINNING

I

SOLITUDE AND THE BARRACKS

COSETTE'S grief, so poignant still, and so acute four or five months before, had, without her knowledge even, entered upon convalescence. Nature, Spring, her youth, her love for her father, the gaiety of the birds and the flowers, were filtering little by little, day by day, drop by drop, into this soul so pure and so young, something which almost resembled oblivion. Was the fire dying out entirely? or was it merely becoming a bed of embers? The truth is, that she had scarcely anything left of that sorrowful and consuming feeling.

One day she suddenly thought of Marius: "What!" said she, "I do not think of him now."

In the course of that very week she noticed, passing before the grated gate of the garden, a very handsome officer of lancers, waist like a wasp, ravishing uniform, cheeks like a young girl's, sabre under his arm, waxed moustaches, polished schapska. Moreover, fair hair, full blue eyes, plump, vain, insolent and pretty face; the very opposite of Marius. A cigar in his mouth. Cosette thought that this officer doubtless belonged to the regiment in barracks on the Rue de Babylone.

The next day, she saw him pass again. She noticed the hour.

Dating from this time, was it chance? she saw him pass almost every day.

The officer's comrades perceived that there was, in this garden so "badly kept," behind that wretched old-fashioned grating, a pretty creature that always happened to be visible on the passage of the handsome lieutenant, who is not unknown to the reader, and whose name was Théodule Gillenormand.

"Stop!" said they to him. "Here is a little girl who has her eye upon you; why don't you look at her?"

"Do you suppose I have the time," answered the lancer, "to look at all the girls who look at me?"

This was the very time when Marius was descending gloomily towards agony, and saying: "If I could only see her again before I die!" Had his wish been realised, had he seen Cosette at that moment looking at a lancer, he would not have been able to utter a word, and would have expired of grief.

Whose fault was it? Nobody's.

Marius was of that temperament which sinks into grief, and remains there; Cosette was of that which plunges in, and comes out again.

Cosette indeed was passing that dangerous moment, the fatal phase of feminine reverie abandoned to itself, when the heart of an isolated young girl resembles the tendrils of a vine which seize hold, as chance determines, of the capital of a column or the sign-post of a tavern. A hurried and decisive moment, critical for every orphan, whether she be poor or whether she be rich, for riches do not defend against a bad choice; misalliances are formed very high; the real misalliance is that of souls and, even as more than one unknown young man, without name, or birth, or fortune, is a marble column which sustains a temple of grand sentiments and grand ideas, so you may find a satisfied and opulent man of the world, with polished boots and varnished speech, who, if you look, not at the exterior but the interior, that is to say at what is reserved for the wife, is nothing but a stupid joist, darkly haunted by violent, impure, and debauched passions; the sign-post of a tavern.

What was there in Cosette's soul? A soothed or sleeping passion; love in a wavering state; something which was limpid, shining, disturbed to a certain depth, gloomy below. The image of the handsome officer was reflected from the surface. Was there a memory at the bottom? deep at the bottom? Perhaps, Cosette did not know.

A singular incident followed.

II
FEARS OF COSETTE

IN the first fortnight in April, Jean Valjean went on a journey. This, we know, happened with him from time to time, at very long intervals. He remained absent one or two days at the most. Where did he go? nobody knew, not even Cosette. Once only, on one of these trips, she had accompanied him in a fiacre as far as the corner of a little cul-de-sac, on which she read: *Impasse de la Planchette*. There he got out, and the fiacre took Cosette back to the Rue de Babylone. It was generally when money was needed for the household expenses that Jean Valjean made these little journeys.

Jean Valjean then was absent. He had said: "I shall be back in three days."

In the evening, Cosette was alone in the parlour. To amuse herself, she had opened her piano and began to sing, playing an accompaniment, the chorus from *Euryanthe: Hunters wandering in the woods!* which is perhaps the finest piece in all music.

All at once it seemed to her that she heard a step in the garden.

It could not be her father, he was absent; it could not be Toussaint, she was in bed. It was ten o'clock at night.

She went to the window shutter which was closed and put her ear to it.

It appeared to her that it was a man's step, and that he was treading very softly.

She ran immediately up to the first story, into her room, opened a slide in her blind, and looked into the garden. The moon was full. She could see as plainly as in broad day.

There was nobody there.

She opened the window. The garden was absolutely silent and all that she could see of the street was as deserted as it always was.

Cosette thought she had been mistaken. She had imagined she heard this noise. It was a hallucination produced by Weber's sombre and majestic chorus, which opens before the mind startling depths, which trembles before the eye like a bewildering forest, and in which we hear the crackling of the dead branches beneath the anxious step of the hunters dimly seen in the twilight.

She thought no more about it.

Moreover, Cosette by nature was not easily startled. There was in her veins the blood of the gipsy and of the adventuress who goes barefoot. It must be remembered she was rather a lark than a dove. She was wild and brave at heart.

The next day, not so late, at nightfall, she was walking in the garden. In the midst of the confused thoughts which filled her mind, she thought she heard for a moment a sound like the sound of the evening before, as if somebody were walking in the darkness under the trees, not very far from her, but she said to herself that nothing is more like a step in the grass than the rustling of two limbs against each other, and she paid no attention to it. Moreover, she saw nothing.

She left "the bush;" she had to cross a little green grass-plot to reach the steps. The moon, which had just risen behind her, projected, as Cosette came out from the shrubbery, her shadow before her upon this grass-plot.

Cosette stood still, terrified.

By the side of her shadow, the moon marked out distinctly upon the sward another shadow singularly frightful and terrible, a shadow with a round hat.

It was like the shadow of a man who might have been standing in the edge of the shrubbery, a few steps behind Cosette.

For a moment she was unable to speak, or cry, or call, or stir, or turn her head.

At last she summoned up all her courage and resolutely turned round.

There was nobody there.

She looked upon the ground. The shadow had disappeared.

She returned into the shrubbery, boldly hunted through the corners, went as far as the gate, and found nothing.

She felt her blood run cold. Was this also a hallucination? What! two days in succession? One hallucination may pass, but two hallucinations? What made her most anxious was that the shadow was certainly not a phantom. Phantoms never wear round hats.

The next day Jean Valjean returned. Cosette narrated to him what she thought she had heard and seen. She expected to be reassured, and that her father would shrug his shoulders and say: "You are a foolish little girl."

Jean Valjean became anxious.

"It may be nothing," said he to her.

He left her under some pretext and went into the garden, and she saw him examining the gate very closely.

In the night she awoke; now she was certain, and she distinctly heard somebody walking very near the steps under her window. She ran to her slide and opened it. There was in fact a man in the garden with a big club in his hand. Just as she was about to cry out, the moon lighted up the man's face. It was her father!

She went back to bed saying: "So he is really anxious"!

Jean Valjean passed that night in the garden and the two

nights following. Cosette saw him through the hole in her shutter.

The third night the moon was smaller and rose later, it might have been one o'clock in the morning, she heard a loud burst of laughter and her father's voice calling her:

"Cosette!"

She sprang out of bed, threw on her dressing-gown, and opened her window.

Her father was below on the grass-plot.

"I woke you up to show you," said he. "Look, here is your shadow in a round hat."

And he pointed to a shadow on the sward made by the moon, and which really bore a close resemblance to the appearance of a man in a round hat. It was a figure produced by a sheet-iron stove-pipe with a cap, which rose above a neighbouring roof.

Cosette also began to laugh, all her gloomy suppositions fell to the ground, and the next day, while breakfasting with her father, she made merry over the mysterious garden haunted by shadows of stove-pipes.

Jean Valjean became entirely calm again; as to Cosette, she did not notice very carefully whether the stove-pipe was really in the direction of the shadow which she had seen, or thought she saw, and whether the moon was in the same part of the sky. She made no question about the oddity of a stove-pipe which is afraid of being caught in the act, and which retires when you look at its shadow, for the shadow had disappeared when Cosette turned round, and Cosette had really believed that she was certain of that. Cosette was fully reassured. The demonstration appeared to her complete, and the idea that there could have been anybody walking in the garden that evening, or that night, no longer entered her head.

A few days afterwards, however, a new incident occurred.

III
ENRICHED BY THE COMMENTARIES OF TOUSSAINT

In the garden, near the grated gate, on the street, there was a stone seat protected from the gaze of the curious by a hedge, but which, nevertheless, by an effort, the arm of a passer could reach through the grating and the hedge.

One evening in this same month of April, Jean Valjean had

gone out; Cosette, after sunset, had sat down on this seat. The wind was freshening in the trees, Cosette was musing; a vague sadness was coming over her little by little, that invincible sadness which evening gives and which comes perhaps, who knows? from the mystery of the tomb half-opened at that hour.

Fantine was perhaps in that shadow.

Cosette rose, slowly made the round of the garden, walking in the grass which was wet with dew, and saying to herself through the kind of melancholy somnambulism in which she was enveloped: "One really needs wooden shoes for the garden at this hour. I shall catch cold."

She returned to the seat.

Just as she was sitting down, she noticed in the place she had left a stone of considerable size which evidently was not there the moment before.

Cosette reflected upon this stone, asking herself what it meant. Suddenly, the idea that this stone did not come upon the seat of itself, that somebody had put it there, that an arm had passed through that grating, this idea came to her and made her afraid. It was a genuine fear this time; there was the stone. No doubt was possible, she did not touch it, fled without daring to look behind her, took refuge in the house, and immediately shut the glass-door of the stairs with shutter, bar, and bolt. She asked Toussaint:

"Has my father come in?"

"Not yet, mademoiselle."

(We have noticed once for all Toussaint's stammering. Let us be permitted to indicate it no longer. We dislike the musical notation of an infirmity.)

Jean Valjean, a man given to thought and a night-walker, frequently did not return till quite late.

"Toussaint," resumed Cosette, "you are careful in the evening to bar the shutters well, upon the garden at least, and to really put the little iron things into the little rings which fasten?"

"Oh! never fear, mademoiselle."

Toussaint did not fail, and Cosette well knew it, but she could not help adding:

"Because it is so solitary about here!"

"For that matter," said Toussaint, "that is true. We would be assassinated before we would have time to say Boo! And then, monsieur doesn't sleep in the house. But don't be afraid, mademoiselle, I fasten the windows like Bastilles. Lone women! I am sure it is enough to make us shudder! Just imagine it! to see men come into the room at night and say to you: Hush! and set themselves to cutting your throat. It isn't so much the dying, people die, that is all right, we know very well that we must die, but it is the horror of having such people touch you. And then their knives, they must cut badly! O God!"

"Be still," said Cosette. "Fasten everything well."

Cosette, dismayed by the melodrama improvised by Toussaint, and perhaps also by the memory of the apparitions of the previous week which came back to her, did not even dare to say to her: "Go and look at the stone which somebody has laid on the seat!" for fear of opening the garden door again, and lest "the men" would come in. She had all the doors and windows carefully closed, made Toussaint go over the whole house from cellar to garret, shut herself up in her room, drew her bolts, looked under her bed, lay down, and slept badly. All night she saw the stone big as a mountain and full of caves.

At sunrise—the peculiarity of sunrise is to make us laugh at all our terrors of the night, and our laugh is always proportioned to the fear we have had—at sunrise Cosette, on waking, looked upon her fright as upon a nightmare and said to herself: "What have I been dreaming about? This is like those steps which I thought I heard at night last week in the garden! It is like the shadow of the stove-pipe! And am I going to be a coward now!"

The sun, which shone through the cracks of her shutters, and made the damask curtains purple, reassured her to such an extent that it all vanished from her thoughts, even the stone.

"There was no stone on the bench, any more than there was a man with a round hat in the garden; I dreamed the stone as I did the rest."

She dressed herself, went down to the garden, ran to the bench, and felt a cold sweat. The stone was there.

But this was only for a moment. What is fright by night is curiosity by day.

"Pshaw!" said she, "now let us see."

She raised the stone, which was pretty large. There was something underneath which resembled a letter.

It was a white paper envelope. Cosette seized it; there was no address on the one side, no wafer on the other. Still the envelope, although open, was not empty. Papers could be seen in it.

Cosette examined it. There was no more fright, there was curiosity no more; there was a beginning of anxious interest.

Cosette took out of the envelope what it contained, a quire of paper, each page of which was numbered and contained a few lines written in a rather pretty hand-writing, thought Cosette, and very fine.

Cosette looked for a name, there was none; a signature, there was none. To whom was it addressed? to her probably, since a hand had placed the packet upon her seat. From whom did it come? An irresistible fascination took possession of her, she endeavoured to turn her eyes away from these leaves which trembled in her hand, she looked at the sky, the street, the acacias all steeped in light, some pigeons which were flying about a neighbouring roof, then all at once her eye eagerly sought the manuscript, and she said to herself that she must know what there was in it.

This is what she read:

IV
A HEART UNDER A STONE

THE reduction of the universe to a single being, the expansion of a single being even to God, this is love.

Love is the salutation of the angel to the stars.

How sad is the soul when it is sad from love!

What a void is the absence of the being who alone fills the world! Oh! how true it is that the beloved being becomes God! One would conceive that God would be jealous if the Father of all had not evidently made creation for the soul, and the soul for love!

A glimpse of a smile under a white crape hat with a lilac coronet is enough, for the soul to enter into the palace of dreams.

God is behind all things, but all things hide God. Things are black, creatures are opaque. To love a being, is to render her transparent.

Certain thoughts are prayers. There are moments when, whatever be the attitude of the body, the soul is on its knees.

———————

Separated lovers deceive absence by a thousand chimerical things which still have their reality. They are prevented from seeing each other, they cannot write to each other; they find a multitude of mysterious means of correspondence. They commission the song of the birds, the perfume of flowers, the laughter of children, the light of the sun, the sighs of the wind, the beams of the stars, the whole creation. And why not? All the works of God were made to serve love. Love is powerful enough to charge all nature with its messages.

O Spring! thou art a letter which I write to her.

———————

The future belongs still more to the heart than to the mind. To love is the only thing which can occupy and fill up eternity. The infinite requires the inexhaustible.

———————

Love partakes of the soul itself. It is of the same nature. Like it, it is a divine spark; like it, it is incorruptible, indivisible, imperishable. It is a point of fire which is within us, which is immortal and infinite, which nothing can limit and which nothing can extinguish. We feel it burn even in the marrow of our bones, and we see it radiate even to the depths of the sky.

———————

O love! adorations! light of two minds which comprehend each other, of two hearts which are interchanged, of two glances which interpenetrate! You will come to me, will you not, happiness? Walks together in the solitudes! days blessed and radiant! I have sometimes dreamed that from time to time hours detached themselves from the life of the angels and came here below to pass through the destiny of men.

———————

God can add nothing to the happiness of those who love one another, but to give them unending duration. After a life of love, an eternity of love is an augmentation indeed; but to increase in its intensity the ineffable felicity which love gives to the soul in this world, is impossible, even with God. God is the plenitude of heaven; love is the plenitude of man.

———————

You look at a star from two motives, because it is luminous

and because it is impenetrable. You have at your side a softer radiance and a greater mystery, woman.

We all, whoever we may be, have our respirable beings. If they fail us, the air fails us, we stifle, then we die. To die for lack of love is horrible. The asphyxia of the soul.

When love has melted and mingled two beings into an angelic and sacred unity, the secret of life is found for them; they are then but the two terms of a single destiny; they are then but the two wings of a single spirit. Love, soar!

The day that a woman who is passing before you sheds a light upon you as she goes, you are lost, you love. You have then but one thing to do: to think of her so earnestly that she will be compelled to think of you.

What love begins can be finished only by God.

True love is in despair and in raptures over a glove lost or a handkerchief found, and it requires eternity for its devotion and its hopes. It is composed at the same time of the infinitely great and the infinitely small.

If you are stone, be loadstone, if you are plant, be sensitive, if you are man, be love.

Nothing suffices love. We have happiness, we wish for paradise; we have paradise, we wish for Heaven.

O ye who love each other, all this is in love. Be wise enough to find it. Love has, as much as Heaven, contemplation, and more than Heaven, passionate delight.

"Does she still come to the Luxembourg?" "No, monsieur." "She hears mass in this church, does she not?" "She comes here no more." "Does she still live in this house?" "She has moved away!" "Whither has she gone to live?" "She did not say!"

What a gloomy thing, not to know the address of one's soul!

Love has its childlikenesses, the other passions have their littlenesses. Shame on the passions which render man little! Honour to that which makes him a child!

There is a strange thing, do you know it? I am in the night. There is a being who has gone away and carried the heavens with her.

Oh! to be laid side by side in the same tomb, hand clasped in hand, and from time to time, in the darkness, to caress a finger gently, that would suffice for my eternity.

You who suffer because you love, love still more. To die of love, is to live by it.

Love. A sombre starry transfiguration is mingled with this crucifixion. There is ecstasy in the agony.

O joy of the birds! it is because they have their nest that they have their song.

Love is a celestial respiration of the air of paradise.

Deep hearts, wise minds take life as God has made it; it is a long trial, an unintelligible preparation for the unknown destiny. This destiny, the true one, begins for man at the first step in the interior of the tomb. Then something appears to him, and he begins to discern the definite. The definite, think of this word. The living see the infinite; the definite reveals itself only to the dead. Meantime, love and suffer, hope and contemplate. Woe, alas! to him who shall have loved bodies, forms, appearances only. Death will take all from him. Try to love souls, you shall find them again.

I met in the street a very poor young man who was in love. His hat was old, his coat was threadbare—there were holes at his elbows; the water passed through his shoes and the stars through his soul.

What a grand thing, to be loved! What a grander thing still, to love! The heart becomes heroic through passion. It is no longer composed of anything but what is pure; it no longer rests upon anything but what is elevated and great. An unworthy thought can no more spring up in it than a nettle upon a glacier. The soul lofty and serene, inaccessible to common passions and common emotions, rising above the clouds and the shadows of this world, its follies, its falsehoods, its hates, its vanities, its miseries, inhabits the blue of the skies, and only feels more the deep and subterranean commotions of destiny, as the summit of the mountains feels the quaking of the earth.

———————

Were there not someone who loved, the sun would be extinguished.

V

COSETTE AFTER THE LETTER

DURING the reading, Cosette entered gradually into reverie. At the moment she raised her eyes from the last line of the last page, the handsome officer, it was his hour, passed triumphant before the grating. Cosette thought him hideous.

She began again to contemplate the letter. It was written in a ravishing hand-writing, thought Cosette; in the same hand, but with different inks, sometimes very black, sometimes pale, as ink is put into the inkstand, and consequently on different days. It was then a thought which had poured itself out there, sigh by sigh, irregularly, without order, without choice, without aim, at hazard. Cosette had never read anything like it. This manuscript, in which she found still more clearness than obscurity, had the effect upon her of a half-opened sanctuary. Each of these mysterious lines was resplendent to her eyes, and flooded her heart with a strange light. The education which she had received had always spoken to her of the soul and never of love, almost like one who should speak of the brand and not of the flame. This manuscript of fifteen pages revealed to her suddenly and sweetly the whole of love, the sorrow, the destiny, the life, the eternity, the beginning, the end. It was like a hand which had opened and thrown suddenly upon her a handful of sunbeams. She felt in these few lines a passionate, ardent, generous, honest nature, a consecrated will, an immense sorrow and a boundless hope, an oppressed heart, a glad ecstasy. What was this manuscript? a letter. A letter with no address, no name, no date, no signature, intense and disinterested, an enigma composed of truths, a message of love made to be brought by an angel and read by a virgin, a rendezvous given beyond the earth, a love-letter from a phantom to a shade. He was a calm yet exhausted absent one, who seemed ready to take refuge in death, and who sent to the absent Her the secret of destiny, the key of life, love. It had been written with the foot in the grave and the finger in Heaven. These lines, fallen one by one upon the paper, were what might be called drops of soul.

Now these pages, from whom could they come? Who could have written them?

Cosette did not hesitate for a moment. One single man.

He!

Day had revived in her mind; all had appeared again. She felt a wonderful joy and deep anguish. It was he! he who wrote to her! he who was there! he whose arm had passed through that grating! While she was forgetting him, he had found her again! But had she forgotten him? No, never! She was mad to have thought so for a moment. She had always loved him, always adored him. The fire had been covered and had smouldered for a time, but she clearly saw it had only sunk in the deeper, and now it burst out anew and fired her whole being. This letter was like a spark dropped from that other soul into hers. She felt the conflagration rekindling. She was penetrated by every word of the manuscript: "Oh, yes!" said she, "how I recognise all this! This is what I had already read in his eyes."

As she finished it for the third time, Lieutenant Théodule returned before the grating, and rattled his spurs on the pavement. Cosette mechanically raised her eyes. She thought him flat, stupid, silly, useless, conceited, odious, impertinent, and very ugly. The officer thought it his duty to smile. She turned away insulted and indignant. She would have been glad to have thrown something at his head.

She fled, went back to the house and shut herself up in her room to read over the manuscript again, to learn it by heart, and to muse. When she had read it well, she kissed it, and put it in her bosom.

It was done. Cosette had fallen back into the profound seraphic love. The abyss of Eden had reopened.

All that day Cosette was in a sort of stupefaction. She could hardly think, her ideas were like a tangled skein in her brain. She could really conjecture nothing, she hoped while yet trembling, what? vague things. She dared to promise herself nothing, and she would refuse herself nothing. Pallors passed over her face and chills over her body. It seemed to her at moments that she was entering the chimerical; she said to herself, "is it real?" then she felt of the beloved paper under her dress, she pressed it against her heart, she felt its corners upon her flesh, and if Jean Valjean had seen her at that moment, he would have shuddered before that luminous and unknown joy which flashed from her eyes. "Oh, yes!" thought she, "it is indeed he! this comes from him for me!"

And she said to herself, that an intervention of angels, that a celestial chance had restored him to her.

O transfigurations of love! O dreams! this celestial chance, this intervention of angels, was that bullet of bread thrown by one robber to another robber, from the Charlemagne court to La Fosse aux Lions, over the roofs of La Force.

VI

THE OLD ARE MADE TO GO OUT WHEN CONVENIENT

WHEN evening came, Jean Valjean went out; Cosette dressed herself. She arranged her hair in the manner which best became her, and she put on a dress the neck of which, as it had received one cut of the scissors too much, and as, by this slope, it allowed the turn of the neck to be seen, was, as young girls say, "a little immodest." It was not the least in the world immodest, but it was prettier than otherwise. She did all this without knowing why.

Did she expect a visit? no.

At dusk, she went down to the garden. Toussaint was busy in her kitchen, which looked out upon the back-yard.

She began to walk under the branches, putting them aside with her hand from time to time, because there were some that were very low.

She thus reached the seat.

The stone was still there.

She sat down, and laid her soft white hand upon that stone as if she would caress it and thank it.

All at once, she had that indefinable impression which we feel, though we see nothing, when there is somebody standing behind us.

She turned her head and arose.

It was he.

He was bareheaded. He appeared pale and thin. She hardly discerned his black dress. The twilight dimmed his fine forehead, and covered his eyes with darkness. He had, under a veil of incomparable sweetness, something of death and of night.

His face was lighted by the light of a dying day, and by the thought of a departing soul.

It seemed as if he was not yet a phantom, and was now no longer a man.

His hat was lying a few steps distant in the shrubbery.

Cosette, ready to faint, did not utter a cry. She drew back slowly, for she felt herself attracted forward. He did not stir. Through the sad and ineffable something which enwrapped him, she felt the look of his eyes, which she did not see.

Cosette, in retreating, encountered a tree, and leaned against it. But for this tree, she would have fallen.

Then she heard his voice, that voice which she had never really heard, hardly rising above the rustling of the leaves, and murmuring:

"Pardon me, I am here. My heart is bursting, I could not live as I was, I have come. Have you read what I placed there, on this seat? do you recognise me at all? do not be afraid of me. It is a long time now, do you remember the day when you looked upon me? it was at the Luxembourg, near the Gladiator. And the day when you passed before me? it was the 16th of June and the 2nd of July. It will soon be a year. For a very long time now, I have not seen you at all. I asked the chairkeeper, she told me that she saw you no more. You lived in the Rue de l'Ouest, on the third floor front, in a new house, you see that I know! I followed you. What was I to do? And then you disappeared. I thought I saw you pass once when I was reading the papers under the arches of the Odéon. I ran. But no. It was a person who had a hat like yours. At night, I come here. Do not be afraid, nobody sees me. I come for a near look at your windows. I walk very softly that you may not hear, for perhaps you would be afraid. The other evening I was behind you, you turned round, I fled. Once I heard you sing. I was happy. Does it disturb you that I should hear you sing through the shutter? it can do you no harm. It cannot, can it? See, you are my angel, let me come sometimes; I believe I am going to die. If you but knew! I adore you! Pardon me, I am talking to you, I do not know what I am saying to you, perhaps I annoy you, do I annoy you?"

"O mother!" said she.

And she sank down upon herself as if she were dying.

He caught her, she fell, he caught her in his arms, he grasped her tightly, unconscious of what he was doing. He supported her even while tottering himself. He felt as if his head were enveloped in smoke; flashes of light passed through his eyelids; his ideas vanished; it seemed to him that he was performing a religious act, and that he was committing a profanation. Moreover, he did not feel one passionate emotion for this ravishing woman, whose form he felt against his heart. He was lost in love.

She took his hand and laid it on her heart. He felt the paper there, and stammered:

"You love me, then?"

She answered in a voice so low that it was no more than a breath which could scarcely be heard:

"Hush! you know it!"

And she hid her blushing head in the bosom of the proud and intoxicated young man.

He fell upon the seat, she by his side. There were no more words. The stars were beginning to shine. How was it that their lips met? How is it that the birds sing, that the snow melts, that the rose opens, that May blooms, that the dawn whitens behind the black trees on the shivering summit of the hills?

One kiss, and that was all.

Both trembled, and they looked at each other in the darkness with brilliant eyes.

They felt neither the fresh night, nor the cold stone, nor the damp ground, nor the wet grass, they looked at each other, and their hearts were full of thought. They had clasped hands, without knowing it.

She did not ask him, she did not even think of it, in what way and by what means he had succeeded in penetrating into the garden. It seemed so natural to her that he should be there.

From time to time Marius' knee touched Cosette's knee, which gave them both a thrill.

At intervals, Cosette faltered out a word. Her soul trembled upon her lips like a drop of dew upon a flower.

Gradually they began to talk. Overflow succeeded to silence, which is fulness. The night was serene and splendid above their heads. These two beings, pure as spirits, told each other all their dreams, their frenzies, their ecstasies, their chimeras, their despondencies, how they had adored each other from afar, how they had longed for each other, their despair when they had ceased to see each other. They confided to each other in an intimacy of the ideal, which even now nothing could have increased, all that was most hidden and most mysterious of themselves. They related to each other, with a candid faith in their illusions, all that love, youth, and that remnant of childhood which was theirs, suggested to their thought. These two hearts poured themselves out into each other, so that at the end of an hour, it was the young man who had the young girl's soul and the young girl who had the soul of the young man. They inter-penetrated, they enchanted, they dazzled each other.

When they had finished, when they had told each other everything, she laid her head upon his shoulder, and asked him:

"What is your name?"

"My name is Marius," said he. "And yours?"

"My name is Cosette."

BOOK SIXTH – LITTLE GAVROCHE

I

A MALEVOLENT TRICK OF THE WIND

SINCE 1823, and while the Montfermeil chop-house was gradually foundering and being swallowed up, not in the abyss of a bankruptcy, but in the sink of petty debts, the Thénardier couple had had two more children; both male. This made five; two girls and three boys. It was a good many.

The Thénardiess had disembarrassed herself of the two last, while yet at an early age and quite small, with singular good fortune.

Disembarrassed is the word. There was in this woman but a fragment of nature. A phenomenon, moreover, of which there is more than one example. Like Madame la Maréchale de La Mothe Houdancourt, the Thénardiess was a mother only to her daughters. Her maternity ended there. Her hatred of the human race began with her boys. On the side towards her sons, her malignity was precipitous, and her heart had at that spot a fearful escarpment. As we have seen, she detested the eldest; she execrated the two others. Why? Because. The most terrible of motives and the most unanswerable of responses: Because. "I have no use for a squalling pack of children," said this mother.

We must explain how the Thénardiers had succeeded in disencumbering themselves of their two youngest children, and even in deriving a profit from them.

This Magnon girl, spoken of some pages back, was the same who had succeeded in getting her two children endowed by goodman Gillenormand. She lived on the Quai des Célestins, at the corner of that ancient Rue du Petit Musc which has done what it could to change its evil renown into good odour. Many will remember that great epidemic of croup which desolated, thirty-five years ago, the quarters bordering on the Seine at Paris, and of which science took advantage to experiment on a large scale as to the efficacy of insufflations of alum, now so happily replaced by the tincture of iodine externally applied. In that epidemic, Magnon lost her two boys, still very young, on the same day, one in the morning, the other at night. This was a blow. These children were precious to their mother; they represented eighty francs a month. These eighty francs were paid with great exactness, in the name of M. Gillenormand, by his rent-agent, M. Barge, retired constable, Rue du Roi de Sicile. The children dead, the income was buried. Magnon sought for an expedient. In that dark masonry of evil of which she was a part, everything is known, secrets are kept, and each aids the other. Magnon needed two children! the Thénardiess had two. Same sex, same age. Good arrangement for one, good investment for the other. The little Thénardiers became the little Magnons. Magnon left the Quai des Célestins and went to live in the Rue Clocheperce. In Paris, the identity which binds an individual to himself is broken from one street to another.

The government, not being notified, did not object, and the substitution took place in the most natural way in the world. Only Thénardier demanded, for this loan of children, ten francs a month, which Magnon promised, and even paid. It need not be said that Monsieur Gillenormand continued to pay. He came twice a year to see the little ones. He did not perceive the change. "Monsieur," said Magnon to him, "how much they look like you."

Thénardier, to whom avatars were easy, seized this opportunity to become Jondrette. His two girls and Gavroche had hardly had time to perceive that they had two little brothers. At a certain depth of misery, men are possessed by a sort of spectral indifference, and look upon their fellow beings as upon goblins. Your nearest relatives are often but vague forms of shadow for you, hardly distinct from the nebulous background of life, and easily reblended with the invisible.

On the evening of the day she had delivered her two little ones to Magnon, expressing her willingness freely to renounce them forever, the Thénardiess had, or feigned to have, a scruple. She said to her husband: "But this is abandoning one's children!" Thénardier, magisterial and phlegmatic, cauterised the scruple with this phrase: "Jean Jacques Rousseau did better!" From scruple the mother passed to anxiety: "But suppose the police come to torment us? What we have done here, Monsieur Thénardier, say now, is it lawful?" Thénardier answered: "Everything is lawful. Nobody will see it but the sky. Moreover, with children who have not a sou, nobody has any interest to look closely into it."

Magnon had a kind of elegance in crime. She made a toilette. She shared her rooms, furnished in a gaudy yet wretched style, with a shrewd Frenchified English thief. This naturalised Parisian English woman, recommendable by very rich connections, intimately acquainted with the medals of the Bibliothèque and the diamonds of Mademoiselle Mars, afterwards became famous in the judicial records. She was called *Mamselle Miss.*

The two little ones who had fallen to Magnon had nothing to complain of. Recommended by the eighty francs, they were taken care of, as everything is which is a matter of business; not badly clothed, not badly fed, treated almost like "little gentlemen," better with the false mother than with the true. Magnon acted the lady and did not talk argot before them.

They passed some years thus: Thénardier augured well of it. It occurred to him one day to say to Magnon who brought him his monthly ten francs, "*The father* must give them an education."

Suddenly, these two poor children, till then well cared for, even by their ill fortune, were abruptly thrown out into life, and compelled to begin it.

A numerous arrest of malefactors like that of the Jondrette garret, necessarily complicated with ulterior searches and seizures, is really a disaster for this hideous occult counter-society which lives beneath public society; an event like this involves every description of misfortune in that gloomy world. The catastrophe of the Thénardiers produced the catastrophe of Magnon.

One day, a short time after Magnon handed Eponine the note relative to the Rue Plumet, there was a sudden descent of the police in the Rue Clocheperce. Magnon was arrested as well as Mamselle Miss, and the whole household, which was suspicious, was included in the haul. The two little boys were playing at the time in a back-yard, and saw nothing of the raid. When they wanted to go in, they found the door closed and the house empty. A cobbler, whose shop was opposite, called them and handed them a paper which "their mother" had left for them. On the paper there was an address: M. Barge, rent-agent, Rue du Roi de Sicile, No. 8. The man of the shop said to them: "You don't live here any more. Go there—it is near by—the first street to the left. Ask your way with this paper."

The children started, the elder leading the younger, and holding in his hand the paper which was to be their guide. He was cold, and his benumbed little fingers had but an awkward grasp, and held the paper loosely. As they were turning out of the Rue Clocheperce, a gust of wind snatched it from him, and, as night was coming on, the child could not find it again.

They began to wander, as chance led them, in the streets.

II

IN WHICH LITTLE GAVROCHE TAKES ADVANTAGE OF NAPOLEON THE GREAT

SPRING in Paris is often accompanied with keen and sharp north winds, by which one is not exactly frozen, but frost-bitten; these winds, which mar the most beautiful days, have precisely the effect of those currents of cold air which enter a warm room through the cracks of an ill-closed window or door. It seems as if the dreary door of winter were partly open and the wind were coming in at it. In the spring of 1832, the time when the first great epidemic of this century broke out in Europe, these winds were sharper and more piercing than ever. A door still more icy than that of winter was ajar. The door of the sepulchre. The breath of the cholera was felt in those winds.

In the meteorological point of view, these cold winds had this peculiarity, that they did not exclude a strong electric tension. Storms accompanied by thunder and lightning were frequent during this time.

One evening when these winds were blowing harshly, to that degree that January seemed returned, and the bourgeois had resumed their cloaks, little Gavroche, always shivering cheerfully under his rags, was standing, as if in ecstasy, before a wig-maker's shop in the neighbourhood of the Orme Saint Gervais. He was adorned with a woman's woollen shawl, picked up nobody knows where, of which he had made a muffler. Little Gavroche appeared to be intensely admiring a wax bride, with bare neck and a head-dress of orange flowers, which was revolving behind the sash, exhibiting between two lamps its smile to the passers; but in reality he was watching the shop to see if he could not "chiper" a cake of soap from the front, which he would afterwards sell for a sou to a hairdresser in the banlieue. It often happened that he breakfasted upon one of these cakes. He called this kind of work, for which he had some talent, "shaving the barbers."

As he was contemplating the bride and squinting at the cake

of soap, he muttered between his teeth: "Tuesday. It isn't Tuesday. Is it Tuesday? Perhaps it is Tuesday. Yes, it is Tuesday."

Nobody ever discovered to what this monologue related.

If, perchance, this soliloquy referred to the last time he had dined, it was three days before, for it was then Friday.

The barber in his shop, warmed by a good stove, was shaving a customer and casting from time to time a look towards this enemy, this frozen and brazen *gamin*, who had both hands in his pockets, but his wits evidently out of their sheath.

While Gavroche was examining the bride, the windows, and the Windsor soap, two children of unequal height, rather neatly dressed, and still smaller than he, one appearing to be seven years old, the other five, timidly turned the knob of the door and entered the shop, asking for something, charity, perhaps, in a plaintive manner which rather resembled a groan than a prayer. They both spoke at once and their words were unintelligible because sobs choked the voice of the younger, and the cold made the elder's teeth chatter. The barber turned with a furious face, and without leaving his razor, crowding back the elder with his left hand and the little one with his knee, pushed them into the street and shut the door saying:

"Coming and freezing people for nothing!"

The two children went on, crying. Meanwhile a cloud had come up; it began to rain.

Little Gavroche ran after them and accosted them:

"What is the matter with you, little brats?"

"We don't know where to sleep," answered the elder.

"Is that all?" said Gavroche. "That is nothing. Does anybody cry for that? Are they canaries then?"

And assuming, through his slightly bantering superiority, a tone of softened authority and gentle protection:

"*Momacques*, come with me."

"Yes, monsieur," said the elder.

And the two children followed him as they would have followed an archbishop. They had stopped crying.

Gavroche led them up the Rue Saint Antoine in the direction of the Bastille.

Gavroche, as he travelled on, cast an indignant and retrospective glance at the barber's shop.

"He has no heart, that *merlan*," he muttered. "He is an *Angliche*."

A girl, seeing them all three marching in a row, Gavroche at the head, broke into a loud laugh. This laugh was lacking in respect for the group.

"Good day, Mamselle Omnibus," said Gavroche to her.

A moment afterwards, the barber recurring to him, he added:

"I am mistaken in the animal; he isn't a *merlan*, he is a snake. Wig-maker, I am going after a locksmith, and I will have a rattle made for your tail."

This barber had made him aggressive. He apostrophised, as he leaped across a brook, a portress with a beard fit to meet Faust upon the Brocken, who had her broom in her hand.

"Madame," said he to her, "you have come out with your horse, have you?"

And upon this, he splashed the polished boots of a passer with mud.

"Whelp!" cried the man, furious.

Gavroche lifted his nose above his shawl.

"Monsieur complains?"

"Of you!" said the passer.

"The bureau is closed," said Gavroche. "I receive no more complaints."

Meanwhile, continuing up the street, he saw, quite frozen under a porte-cochère, a beggar girl of thirteen or fourteen, whose clothes were so short that her knees could be seen. The little girl was beginning to be too big a girl for that. Growth plays you such tricks. The skirt becomes short at the moment that nudity becomes indecent.

"Poor girl!" said Gavroche. "She hasn't even any breeches. But here, take this."

And, taking off all that good woollen which he had about his neck, he threw it upon the bony and purple shoulders of the beggar girl, where the muffler became a shawl.

The little girl looked at him with an astonished appearance, and received the shawl in silence. At a certain depth of distress, the poor, in their stupor, groan no longer over evil, and are no longer thankful for good.

This done:

"Brrr!" said Gavroche, shivering worse than St. Martin, who, at least, kept half his cloak.

At this brrr! the storm, redoubling its fury, became violent. These malignant skies punish good actions.

"Ah," exclaimed Gavroche, "what does this mean? It rains again! Good God, if this continues, I withdraw my subscription."

And he continued his walk.

"It's all the same," added he, casting a glance at the beggar girl who was cuddling herself under the shawl, "there is somebody who has a famous peel."

And, looking at the cloud, he cried:

"Caught!"

The two children limped along behind him.

As they were passing by one of those thick grated lattices which indicate a baker's shop, for bread like gold is kept behind iron gratings, Gavroche turned:

"Ah, ha, *mômes*, have we dined?"

"Monsieur," answered the elder, "we have not eaten since early this morning."

"You are then without father or mother?" resumed Gavroche, majestically.

"Excuse us, monsieur, we have a papa and mamma, but we don't know where they are."

"Sometimes that's better than knowing," said Gavroche, who was a thinker.

"It is two hours now," continued the elder, "that we have been walking; we have been looking for things in every corner, but we can find nothing."

"I know," said Gavroche. "The dogs eat up everything."

He resumed, after a moment's silence:

"Ah! we have lost our authors. We don't know now what we have done with them. That won't do, *gamins*. It is stupid to get lost like that for people of any age. Ah, yes, we must *licher* for all that."

Still he asked them no questions. To be without a home, what could be more natural?

The elder of the two *mômes*, almost entirely restored to the quick unconcern of childhood, made this exclamation:

"It is very queer for all that. Mamma, who promised to take us to look for some blessed box, on Palm Sunday."

"Neurs," answered Gavroche.

"Mamma," added the elder, "is a lady who lives with Mamselle Miss."

"Tanflûte," replied Gavroche.

Meanwhile he had stopped, and for a few minutes he had been groping and fumbling in all sorts of recesses which he had in his rags.

Finally he raised his head with an air which was only intended for one of satisfaction, but which was in reality triumphant.

"Let us compose ourselves, *momignards*. Here is enough for supper for three."

And he took a sou from one of his pockets.

Without giving the two little boys time for amazement, he pushed them both before him into the baker's shop, and laid his sou on the counter, crying:

"Boy! five centimes' worth of bread."

The man, who was the master baker himself, took a loaf and a knife.

"In three pieces, boy!" resumed Gavroche, and he added with dignity:

"There are three of us."

And seeing that the baker, after having examined the three costumes, had taken a black loaf, he thrust his finger deep into his nose with a respiration as imperious as if he had had the great Frederick's pinch of snuff at the end of his thumb, and threw full in the baker's face this indignant apostrophe:

"Whossachuav?"

Those of our readers who may be tempted to see in this summons of Gavroche to the baker a Russian or Polish word, or one of those savage cries which the Iowas and the Botocudos hurl at each other from one bank of a stream to the other in their solitudes, are informed that it is a phrase which they use every day (they, our readers), and which takes the place of this phrase: what is that you have? The baker understood perfectly well, and answered:

"Why! it is bread, very good bread of the second quality."

"You mean *larton brutal*,"* replied Gavroche, with a calm cold disdain. "white bread, boy! *larton savonné*! I am treating."

The baker could not help smiling, and while he was cutting the white bread, he looked at them in a compassionate manner which offended Gavroche.

"Come, paper cap!" said he, "what are you fathoming us like that for?"

---

*Black bread.

All three placed end to end would hardly have made a fathom.

When the bread was cut, the baker put the sou in his drawer, and Gavroche said to the two children:

"*Morfilez.*"

The little boys looked at him confounded.

Gavroche began to laugh:

"Ah! stop, that is true, they don't know yet, they are so small."

And he added:

"Eat."

At the same time he handed each of them a piece of bread.

And, thinking that the elder, who appeared to him more worthy of his conversation, deserved some special encouragement and ought to be relieved of all hesitation in regard to satisfying his appetite, he added, giving him the largest piece:

"Stick that in your gun."

There was one piece smaller than the other two; he took it for himself.

The poor children were starving, Gavroche included. While they were tearing the bread with their fine teeth, they encumbered the shop of the baker who, now that he had received his pay, was regarding them ill-humouredly.

"Come into the street," said Gavroche.

They went on in the direction of the Bastille.

From time to time when they were passing before a lighted shop the smaller one stopped to look at the time by a leaden watch suspended from his neck by a string.

"Here is decidedly a real canary," said Gavroche.

Then he thoughtfully muttered between his teeth:

"It's all the same, if I had any *mômes*, I would hug them tighter than this."

As they finished their pieces of bread and reached the corner of that gloomy Rue des Ballets, at the end of which the low and forbidding wicket of La Force is seen:

"Hullo, is that you, Gavroche?" said somebody.

"Hullo, is that you, Montparnasse?" said Gavroche.

A man had just accosted the *gamin*, and this man was none other than Montparnasse, disguised with blue eye-glasses, but recognisable by Gavroche.

"Mastiff!" continued Gavroche, "you have a peel the colour of a flaxseed poultice and blue spectacles like a doctor. You are in style, 'pon the word of an old man."

"Hush!" said Montparnasse, "not so loud."

And he hastily drew Gavroche out of the light of the shops.

The two little boys followed mechanically, holding each other by the hand.

When they were under the black arch of a porte-cochère, sheltered from sight and from the rain:

"Do you know where I am going?" inquired Montparnasse.

"To the Abbey of Monte à Regret,"* said Gavroche.

"Joker!"

And Montparnasse continued:

"I am going to find Babet."

"Ah!" said Gavroche, "her name is Babet."

Montparnasse lowered his voice.

"Not her, his."

"Ah, Babet!"

"Yes, Babet."

"I thought he was buckled."

"He has slipped the buckle," answered Montparnasse.

And he rapidly related to the *gamin* that, on the morning of that very day, Babet, having been transferred to the Conciergerie, had escaped by turning to the left instead of turning to the right in "the vestibule of the Examination hall."

Gavroche admired the skill.

"What a dentist!" said he.

Montparnasse added a few particulars in regard to Babet's escape and finished with:

"Oh! that is not all."

Gavroche, while listening, had caught hold of a cane which Montparnasse had in his hand; he had pulled mechanically on the upper part, and the blade of a dagger appeared.

"Ah!" said he, pushing the dagger back hastily, "you have brought your gendarme disguised as a bourgeois."

Montparnasse gave him a wink.

"The deuce!" resumed Gavroche, "then you are going to have a tussle with the *cognes*?"

"We don't know," answered Montparnasse with an indifferent air. "It is always well to have a pin about you."

Gavroche insisted:

"What is it you are going to do to-night?"

* To the scaffold.

Montparnasse took up the serious line anew and said, biting his syllables:

"Several things."

And abruptly changing the conversation:

"By the way!"

"What?"

"A story of the other day. Just think of it. I meet a bourgeois. He makes me a present of a sermon and his purse. I put that in my pocket. A minute afterwards I feel in my pocket. There is nothing there."

"Except the sermon," said Gavroche.

"But you," resumed Montparnasse, "where are you going now?"

Gavroche showed his two protégés and said:

"I am going to put these children to bed."

"Where do they sleep?"

"At my house."

"Your house. Where is that?"

"At my house."

"You have a room then?"

"Yes, I have a room."

"And where is your room?"

"In the elephant," said Gavroche.

Montparnasse, although by nature not easily astonished, could not restrain an exclamation:

"In the elephant?"

"Well, yes, in the elephant," replied Gavroche, "whossematruthat?"

This is also a word in the language which nobody writes and which everybody uses. Whossematruthat, signifies what is the matter with that?

The profound observation of the *gamin* recalled Montparnasse to calmness and to good sense. He appeared to return to more respectful sentiments for Gavroche's lodging.

"Indeed!" said he, "yes, the elephant. Are you well off there?"

"Very well," said Gavroche. "There, really *chenument*. There are no draughts of wind as there are under the bridges."

"How do you get in?"

"I get in."

"There is a hole then?" inquired Montparnasse.

"Zounds! But it musn't be told. It is between the forelegs. The *coqueurs** haven't seen it."

"And you climb up? Yes, I understand."

"In a twinkling, crick, crack, it is done, all alone."

After a moment, Gavroche added:

"For these little boys I shall have a ladder."

Montparnasse began to laugh:

"Where the devil did you get these brats?"

Gavroche simply answered:

"They are some *momichards* a wig-maker made me a present of."

Meanwhile Montparnasse had become thoughtful.

"You recognised me very easily," he murmured.

He took from his pocket two little objects which were nothing but two quills wrapped in cotton and introduced one into each nostril. This made him a new nose.

"That changes you," said Gavroche, "you are not so ugly, you ought to keep so all the time."

Montparnasse was a handsome fellow, but Gavroche was a scoffer.

"Joking aside," asked Montparnasse, "how do you like that?"

It was also another sound of voice. In the twinkling of an eye, Montparnasse had become unrecognisable.

"Oh! play us Punchinello!" exclaimed Gavroche.

The two little ones, who had not been listening till now, they had themselves been so busy in stuffing their fingers into their noses, were attracted by this name and looked upon Montparnasse with dawning joy and admiration.

Unfortunately Montparnasse was anxious.

He laid his hand on Gavroche's shoulder and said to him, dwelling upon his words:

"Listen to a digression, boy, if I were on the Square, with my *dogue*, my *dague*, and my *digue*, and if you were so prodigal as to offer me twenty great sous, I shouldn't refuse to *goupiner*† for them, but we are not on Mardi Gras."

This grotesque phrase produced a singular effect upon the *gamin*. He turned hastily, cast his small sparkling eyes about him with intense attention, and perceived, within a few steps, a

---

* Spies, policemen.
† To labour.

sergent de ville, whose back was turned to them. Gavroche let an "ah, yes!" escape him, which he suppressed upon the spot, and shaking Montparnasse's hand:

"Well, good night," said he, "I am going to my elephant with my *mômes*. On the supposition that you should need me some night, you will come and find me there. I live in the second story. There is no porter. You will ask for Monsieur Gavroche."

"All right," said Montparnasse.

And they separated, Montparnasse making his way towards the Grève and Gavroche towards the Bastille. The little five-year-old drawn along by his brother, whom Gavroche was drawing along, turned his head back several times to see "Punchinello" going away.

The unintelligent phrase by which Montparnasse had warned Gavroche of the presence of the sergent de ville, contained no other talisman than the syllable *dig* repeated five or six times under various forms. This syllable *dig*, not pronounced singly, but artistically mingled with the words of a phrase, means: *Take care, we cannot talk freely.* There was furthermore in Montparnasse's phrase a literary beauty which escaped Gavroche, that is *my dogue, my dague, and my digue*, an expression of the argot of the Temple, which signifies *my dog, my knife, and my wife*, very much used among the Pitres and the Queues Rouges of the age of Louis XIV., when Molière wrote and Callot drew.

Twenty years ago, there was still to be seen in the southeast corner of the Place de la Bastille, near the canal basin dug in the ancient ditch of the prison citadel, a grotesque monument which has now faded away from the memory of Parisians, and which is worthy to leave some trace, for it was an idea of the "member of the Institute, General-in-Chief of the Army of Egypt."

We say monument, although it was only a rough model. But this rough model itself, a huge plan, a vast carcass of an idea of Napoleon which two or three successive gusts of wind had carried away and thrown each time further from us, had become historical, and had acquired a definiteness which contrasted with its provisional aspect. It was an elephant, forty feet high, constructed of framework and masonry, bearing on its back its tower, which resembled a house, formerly painted green by some house-painter, now painted black by the sun, the rain, and the weather. In that open and deserted corner of the Square, the broad front of the colossus, his trunk, his tusks, his size, his enormous rump, his four feet like columns, produced at night, under the starry sky, a startling and terrible outline. One knew not what it meant. It was a sort of symbol of the force of the people. It was gloomy, enigmatic, and immense. It was a mysterious and mighty phantom, visibly standing by the side of the invisible spectre of the Bastille.

Few strangers visited this edifice, no passer-by looked at it. It was falling into ruin; every season, the mortar which was detached from its sides made hideous wounds upon it. "The ædiles," as they say in fashionable dialect, had forgotten it since 1814. It was there in its corner, gloomy, diseased, crumbling, surrounded by a rotten railing, continually besmeared by drunken coachmen; crevices marked up the belly, a lath was sticking out from the tail, the tall grass came far up between its legs; and as the level of the Square had been rising for thirty years all about it, by that slow and continuous movement which insensibly raises the soil of great cities, it was in a hollow, and it seemed as if the earth sank under it. It was huge, condemned, repulsive, and superb; ugly to the eye of the bourgeois, melancholy to the eye of the thinker. It partook, to some extent, of a filth soon to be swept away, and, to some extent, of a majesty soon to be decapitated.

As we have said, night changed its appearance. Night is the true medium for everything which is shadowy. As soon as twilight fell, the old elephant became transfigured; he assumed a tranquil and terrible form in the fearful serenity of the darkness. Being of the past, he was of the night; and this obscurity was fitting to his greatness.

This monument, rude, squat, clumsy, harsh, severe, almost deformed, but certainly majestic, and impressed with a sort of magnificent and savage seriousness, has disappeared, leaving a peaceable reign to the kind of gigantic stove, adorned with its stove-pipe, which has taken the place of the forbidding nine-towered fortress, almost as the bourgeoisie replaces feudality. It is very natural that a stove should be the symbol of an epoch of which a tea-kettle contains the power. This period will pass away, it is already passing away; we are beginning to understand that, if there may be force in a boiler, there can be power only in a brain; in other words, that what leads and controls the world, is not locomotives, but ideas. Harness the locomotives to the ideas, very well; but do not take the horse for the horseman.

However this may be, to return to the Place de la Bastille, the architect of the elephant had succeeded in making something grand with plaster; the architect of the stove-pipe has succeeded in making something petty with bronze.

This stove-pipe, which was baptised with a sonorous name, and called the Column of July, this would-be monument of an abortive revolution, was still, in 1832, enveloped in an immense frame-work covering, which we for our part still regret, and by a large board inclosure, which completed the isolation of the elephant.

It was towards this corner of the square, dimly lighted by the reflection of a distant lamp, that the *gamin* directed the two "*mômes.*"

We must be permitted to stop here long enough to declare that we are within the simple reality, and that twenty years ago the police tribunals would have had to condemn upon a complaint for vagrancy and breach of a public monument, a child who should have been caught sleeping in the interior even of the elephant of the Bastille. This fact stated, we continue.

As they came near the colossus, Gavroche comprehended the effect which the infinitely great may produce upon the infinitely small, and said:

"Brats! don't be frightened."

Then he entered through a gap in the fence into the inclosure of the elephant, and helped the *mômes* to crawl through the breach. The two children, a little frightened, followed Gavroche without saying a word, and trusted themselves to that little Providence in rags who had given them bread and promised them a lodging.

Lying by the side of the fence was a ladder, which, by day, was used by the working-men of the neighbouring wood-yard. Gavroche lifted it with singular vigour, and set it up against one of the elephant's forelegs. About the point where the ladder ended, a sort of black hole could be distinguished in the belly of the colossus.

Gavroche showed the ladder and the hole to his guests, and said to them:

"Mount and enter."

The two little fellows looked at each other in terror.

"You are afraid, *mômes*!" exclaimed Gavroche.

And he added:

"You shall see."

He clasped the elephant's wrinkled foot, and in a twinkling, without deigning to make use of the ladder, he reached the crevice. He entered it as an adder glides into a hole, and disappeared, and a moment afterwards the two children saw his pallid face dimly appearing like a faded and wan form, at the edge of the hole full of darkness.

"Well," cried he, "why don't you come up, *momignards*? you'll see how nice it is! Come up," said he, to the elder, "I will give you a hand."

The little ones urged each other forward. The *gamin* made them afraid and reassured them at the same time, and then it rained very hard. The elder ventured. The younger, seeing his brother go up, and himself left all alone between the paws of this huge beast, had a great desire to cry, but he did not dare.

The elder clambered up the rounds of the ladder. He tottered badly. Gavroche, while he was on his way, encouraged him with the exclamations of a fencing master to his scholars, or of a muleteer to his mules:

"Don't be afraid!"

"That's it!"

"Come on!"

"Put your foot there!"

"Your hand here!"

"Be brave!"

And when he came within his reach he caught him quickly and vigorously by the arm and drew him up.

"Gulped!" said he.

The *môme* had passed through the crevice.

"Now," said Gavroche, "wait for me. Monsieur, have the kindness to sit down."

And, going out by the crevice as he had entered, he let himself glide with the agility of a monkey along the elephant's leg, he dropped upon his feet in the grass, caught the little five-year-old by the waist and set him half way up the ladder, then he began to mount up behind him, crying to the elder:

"I will push him; you pull him."

In an instant the little fellow was lifted, pushed, dragged,

pulled, stuffed, crammed into the hole without having had time
to know what was going on. And Gavroche, entering after him,
pushing back the ladder with a kick so that it fell upon the grass,
began to clap his hands, and cried:

"Here we are! Hurrah for General Lafayette!"

This explosion over, he added:

"Brats, you are in my house."

Gavroche was in fact at home.

O unexpected utility of the useless! charity of great things!
goodness of giants! This monstrous monument which had contained a thought of the emperor, had become the box of a *gamin*.
The *môme* had been accepted and sheltered by the colossus. The
bourgeois in their Sunday clothes, who passed by the elephant
of the Bastille, frequently said, eyeing it scornfully with their
goggle eyes: "What's the use of that?" The use of it was to save
from the cold, the frost, the hail, the rain, to protect from the
wintry wind, to preserve from sleeping in the mud, which
breeds fever, and from sleeping in the snow, which breeds death,
a little being with no father or mother, with no bread, no clothing, no asylum. The use of it was to receive the innocent whom
society repelled. The use of it was to diminish the public crime.
It was a den open for him to whom all doors were closed. It
seemed as if the miserable old mastodon, invaded by vermin
and oblivion, covered with warts, mould, and ulcers, tottering,
worm-eaten, abandoned, condemned, a sort of colossal beggar
asking in vain the alms of a benevolent look in the middle of the
Square, had taken pity itself on this other beggar, the poor
pigmy who went with no shoes to his feet, no roof over his
head, blowing his fingers, clothed in rags, fed upon what is
thrown away. This was the use of the elephant of the Bastille.
This idea of Napoleon, disdained by men, had been taken up by
God. That which had been illustrious only, had become august.
The emperor must have had, to realise what he meditated, por-
phyry, brass, iron, gold, marble; for God the old assemblage of
boards, joists, and plaster was enough. The emperor had had a
dream of genius; in this titanic elephant, armed, prodigious,
brandishing his trunk, bearing his tower, and making the joyous
and vivifying waters gush out on all sides about him, he desired
to incarnate the people. God had done a grander thing with it,
he lodged a child.

The hole by which Gavroche had entered was a break hardly

visible from the outside, concealed as it was, and as we have said under the belly of the elephant, and so narrow that hardly anything but cats and *mômes* could have passed through.

"Let us begin," said Gavroche, "by telling the porter that we are in."

And plunging into the obscurity with certainty, like one who is familiar with his room, he took a board and stopped the hole.

Gavroche plunged again into the obscurity. The children heard the sputtering of the taper plunged into the phosphoric bottle. The chemical taper was not yet in existence; the Fumade tinder-box represented progress at that period.

A sudden light made them wink; Gavroche had just lighted one of those bits of string soaked in resin which are called cellar-rats. The cellar-rats, which made more smoke than flame, rendered the inside of the elephant dimly visible.

Gavroche's two guests looked about them, and felt something like what one would feel who should be shut up in the great tun of Heidelberg, or better still, what Jonah must have felt in the Biblical belly of the whale. An entire and gigantic skeleton appeared to them, and enveloped them. Above, a long dusky beam, from which projected at regular distances massive encircling timbers, represented the vertebral column with its ribs, stalactites of plaster hung down like the viscera, and from one side to the other huge spider-webs made dusty diaphragms. Here and there in the corners great blackish spots were seen, which had the appearance of being alive, and which changed their places rapidly with a wild and startled motion.

The debris fallen from the elephant's back upon his belly had filled up the concavity, so that they could walk upon it as upon a floor.

The smaller one hugged close to his brother and said in a low tone:

"It is dark."

This word made Gavroche cry out. The petrified air of the two *mômes* rendered a shock necessary.

"What is that you are driving at?" he exclaimed. "Are we humbugging? are we becoming the disgusted? Must you have the Tuileries? would you be fools? Say, I inform you that I do not belong to the regiment of ninnies. Are you the brats of the pope's headwaiter?"

A little roughness is good for alarm. It is reassuring. The two children came close to Gavroche.

Gavroche, paternally softened by this confidence, passed "from the grave to the gentle," and addressing himself to the smaller:

"Goosy," said he to him, accenting the insult with a caressing tone, "it is outside that it is dark. Outside it rains, here it doesn't rain; outside it is cold, here there isn't a speck of wind; outside there are heaps of folks, here there isn't anybody; outside there isn't even a moon, here there is my candle, by jinks!"

The two children began to regard the apartment with less fear; but Gavroche did not allow them much longer leisure for contemplation.

"Quick," said he.

And he pushed them towards what we are very happy to be able to call the bottom of the chamber.

His bed was there.

Gavroche's bed was complete. That is to say, there was a mattress, a covering, and an alcove with curtains.

The mattress was a straw mat, the covering a large blanket of coarse grey wool, very warm and almost new. The alcove was like this:

Three rather long laths, sunk and firmly settled into the rubbish of the floor, that is to say of the belly of the elephant, two in front and one behind, and tied together by a string at the top, so as to form a pyramidal frame. This frame supported a fine trellis of brass wire which was simply hung over it, but artistically applied and kept in place by fastenings of iron wire, in such a way that it entirely enveloped the three laths. A row of large stones fixed upon the ground all about this trellis so as to let nothing pass. This trellis was nothing more nor less than a fragment of those copper nettings which are used to cover the bird-houses in menageries. Gavroche's bed under this netting was as if in a cage. Altogether it was like an Esquimaux tent.

It was this netting which took the place of curtains.

Gavroche removed the stones a little which kept down the netting in front, and the two folds of the trellis which lay one over the other opened.

"*Mômes*, on your hands and knees!" said Gavroche.

He made his guests enter into the cage carefully, then he went in after them, creeping, pulled back the stones, and hermetically closed the opening.

They were all three stretched upon the straw.

Small as they were, none of them could have stood up in the alcove. Gavroche still held the cellar-rat in his hand.

"Now," said he, "*pioncez!* I am going to suppress the candelabra."

"Monsieur," inquired the elder of the two brothers, of Gavroche, pointing to the netting, "what is that?"

"That," said Gavroche, "is for the rats, *pioncez!*"

However he felt it incumbent upon him to add a few words for the instruction of these beings of a tender age, and he continued:

"They are things from the Jardin des Plantes. They are used for ferocious animals. Tsaol (it is a whole) magazine full of them. Tsony (it is only) to mount over a wall, climb by a window and pass under a door. You get as much as you want."

While he was talking, he wrapped a fold of the coverlid about the smaller one, who murmured:

"Oh! that is good! it is warm!"

Gavroche looked with satisfaction upon the coverlid.

"That is also from the Jardin des Plantes," said he. "I took that from the monkeys."

And, showing the elder the mat upon which he was lying, a very thick mat and admirably made, he added:

"That was the giraffe's."

After a pause, he continued:

"The beasts had all this. I took it from them. They didn't care. I told them: It is for the elephant."

He was silent again and resumed:

"We get over the walls and we make fun of the government. That's all."

The two children looked with a timid and stupefied respect upon this intrepid and inventive being, a vagabond like them, isolated like them, wretched like them, who was something wonderful and all-powerful, who seemed to them supernatural, and whose countenance was made up of all the grimaces of an old mountebank mingled with the most natural and most pleasant smile.

"Monsieur," said the elder timidly, "you are not afraid then of the sergents de ville?"

Gavroche merely answered:

"*Môme!* we don't say sergents de ville, we say *cognes*."

The smaller boy had his eyes open, but he said nothing. As he was on the edge of the mat, the elder being in the middle, Gavroche tucked the coverlid under him as a mother would have done, and raised the mat under his head with some old rags in such a way as to make a pillow for the *môme*. Then he turned towards the elder:

"Eh! we are pretty well off here!"

"Oh, yes," answered the elder, looking at Gavroche with the expression of a rescued angel.

The two poor little soaked children were beginning to get warm.

"Ah, now," continued Gavroche, "what in the world were you crying for?"

And pointing out the little one to his brother:

"A youngster like that, I don't say, but a big boy like you to cry is silly; it makes you look like a calf."

"Well," said the child, "we had no room, no place to go."

"Brat!" replied Gavroche, "we don't say a room, we say a *piolle.*"

"And then we were afraid to be all alone like that in the night."

"We don't say night, we say *sorgue.*"

"Thank you, monsieur," said the child.

"Listen to me," continued Gavroche, "you must never whine any more for anything. I will take care of you. You will see what fun we have. In summer we will go to the Glacière with Navet, a comrade of mine, we will go swimming in the Basin, we will run on the track before the Bridge of Austerlitz all naked, that makes the washer-women mad. They scream, they scold, if you only knew how funny they are! We will go to see the skeleton man. He is alive. At the Champs-Elysées. That parishioner is as thin as anything. And then I will take you to the theatre. I will take you to Frederick Lemaître's. I have tickets, I know the actors, I even played once in a piece. We were *mômes* so high, we ran about under a cloth, that made the sea. I will have you engaged at my theatre. We will go and see the savages. They're not real, those savages. They have red tights which wrinkle, and you can see their elbows darned with white thread. After that we will go to the Opera. We will go in with the claqueurs. The claque at the Opera is very select. I wouldn't go with the claque on the boulevards. At the Opera, just think, there are some who pay twenty sous, but they are fools. They call them dish-clouts. And then we will go to see the guillotining. I will show you the executioner. He lives in the Rue des Marais. Monsieur Sanson. There is a letter-box on his door. Oh! we have famous fun!"

At this moment, a drop of wax fell upon Gavroche's finger, and recalled him to the realities of life.

"The deuce!" said he, "there's the match used up. Attention! I can't spend more than a sou a month for my illumination. When we go to bed, we must go to sleep. We haven't time to read the romances of Monsieur Paul de Kock. Besides the light might show through the cracks of the porte-cochère, and the *cognes* couldn't help seeing."

"And then," timidly observed the elder who alone dared to talk with Gavroche and reply to him, "a spark might fall into the straw, we must take care not to burn the house up."

"We don't say burn the house," said Gavroche, "we say *riffauder* the *bocard*."

The storm redoubled. They heard, in the intervals of the thunder, the tempest beating against the back of the colossus.

"Pour away, old rain!" said Gavroche. "It does amuse me to hear the decanter emptying along the house's legs. Winter is a fool; he throws away his goods, he loses his trouble, he can't wet us, and it makes him grumble, the old water-porter!"

This allusion to thunder, all the consequences of which Gavroche accepted as a philosopher of the nineteenth century, was followed by a very vivid flash, so blinding that something of it entered by the crevice into the belly of the elephant. Almost at the same instant the thunder burst forth very furiously. The two little boys uttered a cry, and rose so quickly that the trellis was almost thrown out of place; but Gavroche turned his bold face towards them, and took advantage of the clap of thunder to burst into a laugh.

"Be calm, children. Don't upset the edifice. That was fine thunder; give us some more. That wasn't any fool of a flash. Bravo God! by jinks! that is most as good as it is at the theatre."

This said, he restored order in the trellis, gently pushed the two children to the head of the bed, pressed their knees to stretch them out at full length, and exclaimed:

"As God is lighting his candle, I can blow out mine. Children, we must sleep, my young humans. It is very bad not to sleep. It would make you *schlinguer* in your strainer, or, as the big bugs say, stink in your jaws. Wind yourselves up well in the peel! I'm going to extinguish. Are you all right?"

"Yes," murmured the elder, "I am right. I feel as if I had feathers under my head."

"We don't say head," cried Gavroche, "we say *tronche*."

The two children hugged close to each other. Gavroche finished arranging them upon the mat, and pulled the coverlid up to their ears, then repeated for the third time the injunction in hieratic language:

"*Pioncez!*"

And he blew out the taper.

Hardly was the light extinguished when a singular tremor began to agitate the trellis under which the three children were lying. It was a multitude of dull rubbings, which gave a metallic sound, as if claws and teeth were grinding the copper wire. This was accompanied by all sorts of little sharp cries.

The little boy of five, hearing this tumult over his head, and shivering with fear, pushed the elder brother with his elbow, but the elder brother had already "*pioncé*," according to Gavroche's order. Then the little boy, no longer capable of fearing him, ventured to accost Gavroche, but very low, and holding his breath:

"Monsieur?"

"Hey?" said Gavroche, who had just closed his eyes.

"What is that?"

"It is the rats," answered Gavroche.

And he laid his head again upon the mat.

The rats, in fact, which swarmed by thousands in the carcass of the elephant, and which were those living black spots of which we have spoken, had been held in awe by the flame of the candle so long as it burned, but as soon as this cavern, which was, as it were, their city, had been restored to night, smelling there what the good storyteller Perrault calls "some fresh meat," they had rushed in en masse upon Gavroche's tent, climbed to the top, and were biting its meshes as if they were seeking to get through this new-fashioned mosquito bar.

Still the little boy did not go to sleep.

"Monsieur!" he said again.

"Hey?" said Gavroche.

"What are the rats?"

"They are mice."

This explanation reassured the child a little. He had seen some white mice in the course of his life, and he was not afraid of them. However, he raised his voice again:

"Monsieur?"

"Hey?" replied Gavroche.

"Why don't you have a cat?"

"I had one," answered Gavroche, "I brought one here, but they ate her up for me."

This second explanation undid the work of the first, and the little fellow again began to tremble. The dialogue between him and Gavroche was resumed for the fourth time.

"Monsieur!"

"Hey?"

"Who was it that was eaten up?"

"The cat."

"Who was it that ate the cat?"

"The rats."

"The mice?"

"Yes, the rats."

The child, dismayed by these mice who ate cats, continued:

"Monsieur, would those mice eat us?"

"Golly!" said Gavroche.

The child's terror was complete. But Gavroche added:

"Don't be afraid! they can't get in. And when I am here. Here, take hold of my hand. Be still and *pioncez*!"

Gavroche at the same time took the little fellow's hand across his brother. The child clasped his hand against his body, and felt safe. Courage and strength have such mysterious communications. It was once more silent about them, the sound of voices had startled and driven away the rats; in a few minutes they might have returned and done their worst in vain, the three *mômes*, plunged in slumber, heard nothing more.

The hours of the night passed away. Darkness covered the immense Place de la Bastille; a wintry wind, which mingled with the rain, blew in gusts, the patrolmen ransacked the doors, alleys, yards and dark corners, and, looking for nocturnal vagabonds, passed silently by the elephant; the monster, standing, motionless, with open eyes in the darkness, appeared to be in reverie and well satisfied with his good deeds, and he sheltered from the heavens and from men the three poor sleeping children.

To understand what follows, we must remember that at that period the guardhouse of the Bastille was situated at the other extremity of the Square, and that what occurred near the elephant could neither be seen nor heard by the sentinel.

Towards the end of the hour which immediately precedes daybreak, a man turned out of the Rue Saint Antoine, running, crossed the Square, turned the great inclosure of the Column of July, and glided between the palisades under the belly of the elephant. Had any light whatever shone upon this man, from his thoroughly wet clothing, one would have guessed that he had passed the night in the rain. When under the elephant he raised a grotesque call, which belongs to no human language and which a parrot alone could reproduce. He twice repeated this call, of which the following orthography gives but a very imperfect idea:

"Kirikikiou!"

At the second call, a clear, cheerful young voice answered from the belly of the elephant:

"Yes!"

Almost immediately the board which closed the hole moved away, and gave passage to a child, who descended along the elephant's leg and dropped lightly near the man. It was Gavroche. The man was Montparnasse.

As to this call, *kirikikiou*, it was undoubtedly what the child meant by, *You will ask for Monsieur Gavroche.*

On hearing it he had waked with a spring, crawled out of his "alcove," separating the netting a little, which he afterwards carefully closed again, then he had opened the trap and descended.

The man and the child recognised each other silently in the dark; Montparnasse merely said:

"We need you. Come and give us a lift."

The *gamin* did not ask any other explanation.

"I'm on hand," said he.

And they both took the direction of the Rue Saint Antoine, whence Montparnasse came, winding their way rapidly through the long file of market wagons which go down at that hour towards the market.

The market gardeners, crouching among the salads and vegetables, half asleep, buried up to the eyes in the boots of their
wagons on account of the driving rain, did not even notice these
strange passengers.

III

THE FORTUNES AND MISFORTUNES OF ESCAPE

WHAT had taken place that same night at La Force was this:

An escape had been concerted between Babet, Brujon,
Gueulemer, and Thénardier, although Thénardier was in solitary. Babet had done the business for himself during the day, as
we have seen from the account of Montparnasse to Gavroche.
Montparnasse was to help them from without.

Brujon, having spent a month in a chamber of punishment,
had had time, first, to twist a rope, secondly, to perfect a plan.
Formerly these stern cells in which the discipline of the prison
delivers the condemned to himself, were composed of four
stone walls, a ceiling of stone, a pavement of tiles, a camp bed, a
grated air-hole, a double iron door, and were called dungeons;
but the dungeon has been thought too horrible; now it is composed of an iron door, a grated air-hole, a camp bed, a pavement
of tiles, a ceiling of stone, four stone walls, and it is called chamber of punishment. There is a little light in them about noon.
The inconvenience of these chambers which, as we see, are not
dungeons, is that they allow beings to reflect who should be
made to work.

Brujon then had reflected, and he had gone out of the chamber of punishment with a rope. As he was reputed very dangerous in the Charlemagne Court, he was put into the Bâtiment
Neuf. The first thing which he found in the Bâtiment Neuf was
Gueulemer, the second was a nail; Gueulemer, that is to say
crime, a nail, that is to say liberty.

Brujon, of whom it is time to give a complete idea, was,
with an appearance of delicate complexion and a profoundly
premeditated languor, a polished, gallant, intelligent robber,
with an enticing look and an atrocious smile. His look was a
result of his will, and his smile of his nature. His first studies
in his art were directed towards roofs; he had made a great
improvement in the business of the lead strippers who despoil
roofings and distrain eaves by the process called: *the double fat.*

What rendered the moment peculiarly favourable for an attempt at escape, was that some workmen were taking off and relaying, at that very time, a part of the slating of the prison. The Cour Saint Bernard was not entirely isolated from the Charlemagne Court and the Cour Saint Louis. There were scaffoldings and ladders up aloft; in other words, bridges and stairways leading towards deliverance.

Bâtiment Neuf, the most cracked and decrepit affair in the world, was the weak point of the prison. The walls were so much corroded by saltpetre that they had been obliged to put a facing of wood over the arches of the dormitories, because the stones detached themselves and fell upon the beds of the prisoners. Notwithstanding this decay, the blunder was committed of shutting up in the Bâtiment Neuf the most dangerous of the accused, of putting "the hard cases" in there, as they say in prison language.

The Bâtiment Neuf contained four dormitories one above the other and an attic which was called the Bel Air. A large chimney, probably of some ancient kitchen of the Dukes de La Force, started from the ground floor, passed through the four stories, cutting in two all the dormitories in which it appeared to be a kind of flattened pillar, and went out through the roof.

Gueulemer and Brujon were in the same dormitory. They had been put into the lower story by precaution. It happened that the heads of their beds rested against the flue of the chimney.

Thénardier was exactly above them in the attic known as the Bel Air.

The passer who stops in the Rue Culture Sainte Catherine beyond the barracks of the firemen, in front of the porte-cochère of the bath-house, sees a yard full of flowers and shrubs in boxes, at the further end of which is a little white rotunda with two wings enlivened by green blinds, the bucolic dream of Jean Jacques. Not more than ten years ago, above this rotunda there arose a black wall, enormous, hideous, and bare, against which it was built. This was the encircling wall of La Force.

This wall, behind this rotunda, was Milton seen behind Berquin.

High as it was, this wall was over-topped by a still blacker roof which could be seen behind. This was the roof of the Bâtiment Neuf. You noticed in it four dormer windows with gratings; these were the windows of the Bel Air. A chimney pierced the roof, the chimney which passed through the dormitories.

The Bel Air, this attic of the Bâtiment Neuf, was a kind of large garret hall, closed with triple gratings and double sheet iron doors studded with monstrous nails. Entering at the north end, you had on your left the four windows, and on your right, opposite the windows, four large square cages, with spaces between, separated by narrow passages, built breast-high of masonry with bars of iron to the roof.

Thénardier had been in solitary in one of these cages since the night of the 3rd of February. Nobody has ever discovered how, or by what contrivance, he had succeeded in procuring and hiding a bottle of that wine invented, it is said, by Desrues, with which a narcotic is mixed, and which the band of the Endormeurs has rendered celebrated.

There are in many prisons treacherous employees, half jailers and half thieves, who aid in escapes, who sell a faithless service to the police, and who make much more than their salary.

On this same night, then, on which little Gavroche had picked up the two wandering children, Brujon and Gueulemer, knowing that Babet, who had escaped that very morning, was waiting for them in the street as well as Montparnasse, got up softly and began to pierce the flue of the chimney which touched their beds with the nail which Brujon had found. The fragments fell upon Brujon's bed, so that nobody heard them. The hail storm and the thunder shook the doors upon their hinges, and made a frightful and convenient uproar in the prison. Those of the prisoners who awoke made a feint of going to sleep again, and let Gueulemer and Brujon alone. Brujon was adroit; Gueulemer was vigorous. Before any sound had reached the watchman who was lying in the grated cell with a window opening into the sleeping room, the wall was pierced, the chimney scaled, the iron trellis which closed the upper orifice of the flue forced, and the two formidable bandits were upon the roof. The rain and the wind redoubled, the roof was slippery.

"What a good *sorgue* for a *crampe*,"* said Brujon.

A gulf of six feet wide and eighty feet deep separated them from the encircling wall. At the bottom of this gulf they saw a

---

*What a good night for an escape.

sentinel's musket gleaming in the obscurity. They fastened one end of the rope which Brujon had woven in his cell, to the stumps of the bars of the chimney which they had just twisted off, threw the other end over the encircling wall, cleared the gulf at a bound, clung to the coping of the wall, bestrode it, let themselves glide one after the other down along the rope upon a little roof which adjoined the bath-house, pulled down their rope, leaped into the bath-house yard, crossed it, pushed open the porter's slide, near which hung the cord, pulled the cord, opened the porte-cochère, and were in the street.

It was not three-quarters of an hour since they had risen to their feet on their beds in the darkness, their nail in hand, their project in their heads.

A few moments afterwards they had rejoined Babet and Montparnasse, who were prowling about the neighbourhood.

In drawing down their rope, they had broken it, and there was a piece remaining fastened to the chimney on the roof. They had received no other damage than having pretty thoroughly skinned their hands.

That night Thénardier had received a warning, it never could be ascertained in what manner, and did not go to sleep.

About one o'clock in the morning, the night being very dark, he saw two shadows passing on the roof, in the rain and in the raging wind, before the window opposite his cage. One stopped at the window long enough for a look. It was Brujon. Thénardier recognised him, and understood. That was enough for him. Thénardier, described as an assassin, and detained under the charge of lying in wait by night with force and arms, was kept constantly in sight. A sentinel, who was relieved every two hours, marched with loaded gun before his cage. The Bel Air was lighted by a reflector. The prisoner had irons on his feet weighing fifty pounds. Every day, at four o'clock in the afternoon, a warden, escorted by two dogs—this was customary at that period—entered his cage, laid down near his bed a two pound loaf of black bread, a jug of water, and a dish full of very thin soup in which a few beans were swimming, examined his irons, and struck upon the bars. This man, with his dogs, returned twice in the night.

Thénardier had obtained permission to keep a kind of an iron spike which he used to nail his bread into a crack in the wall, "in order," said he, "to preserve it from the rats." As

Thénardier was constantly in sight, they imagined no danger from this spike. However, it was remembered afterwards that a warden had said: "It would be better to let him have nothing but a wooden pike."

At two o'clock in the morning, the sentinel, who was an old soldier, was relieved, and his place was taken by a conscript. A few moments afterwards, the man with the dogs made his visit, and went away without noticing anything, except the extreme youth and the "peasant air" of the "greenhorn." Two hours afterwards, at four o'clock, when they came to relieve the conscript, they found him asleep, and lying on the ground like a log near Thénardier's cage. As to Thénardier, he was not there. His broken irons were on the floor. There was a hole in the ceiling of his cage, and above, another hole in the roof. A board had been torn from his bed, and doubtless carried away, for it was not found again. There was also seized in the cell a half empty bottle, containing the rest of the drugged wine with which the soldier had been put to sleep. The soldier's bayonet had disappeared.

At the moment of this discovery, it was supposed that Thénardier was out of all reach. The reality is, that he was no longer in the Bâtiment Neuf, but that he was still in great danger.

Thénardier, on reaching the roof of the Bâtiment Neuf, found the remnant of Brujon's cord hanging on to the bars of the upper trap of the chimney, but this broken end being much too short, he was unable to escape over the sentry's path as Brujon and Gueulemer had done.

On turning from the Rue des Ballets into the Rue du Roi de Sicile, on the right you meet almost immediately with a dirty recess. There was a house there in the last century, of which only the rear wall remains, a genuine ruin wall which rises to the height of the third story among the neighbouring buildings. This ruin can be recognised by two large square windows which may still be seen; the one in the middle, nearer the right gable, is crossed by a worm-eaten joist fitted like a cap-piece for a shore. Through these windows could formerly be discerned a high and dismal wall, which was a part of the encircling wall of La Force.

The void which the demolished house left upon the street is half filled by a palisade fence of rotten boards, supported by five stone posts. Hidden in this inclosure is a little shanty built against that part of the ruin which remains standing. The fence has a gate which a few years ago was fastened only by a latch.

Thénardier was upon the crest of this ruin a little after three o'clock in the morning.

How had he got there? That is what nobody has ever been able to explain or understand. The lightning must have both confused and helped him. Did he use the ladders and the scaffoldings of the slaters to get from roof to roof, from inclosure to inclosure, from compartment to compartment, to the buildings of the Charlemagne court, then the buildings of the Cour Saint Louis, the encircling wall, and from thence to the ruin on the Rue du Roi de Sicile? But there were gaps in this route which seemed to render it impossible. Did he lay down the plank from his bed as a bridge from the roof of the Bel Air to the encircling wall, and did he crawl on his belly along the coping of the wall, all round the prison as far as the ruin? But the encircling wall of La Force followed an indented and uneven line, it rose and fell, it sank down to the barracks of the firemen, it rose up to the bathing-house, it was cut by buildings, it was not of the same height on the Hotel Lamoignon as on the Rue Pavée, it had slopes and right angles everywhere; and then the sentinels would have seen the dark outline of the fugitive; on this supposition again, the route taken by Thénardier is still almost inexplicable. By either way, an impossible flight. Had Thénardier, illuminated by that fearful thirst for liberty which changes precipices into ditches, iron gratings into osier screens, a cripple into an athlete, an old gouty into a bird, stupidity into instinct, instinct into intelligence, and intelligence into genius, had Thénardier invented and extemporised a third method? It has never been known.

One cannot always comprehend the marvels of escape. The man who escapes, let us repeat, is inspired; there is something of the star and the lightning in the mysterious gleam of flight; the effort towards deliverance is not less surprising than the flight towards the sublime; and we say of an escaped robber: How did he manage to scale that roof? just as it is said of Corneille: Where did he learn *that he would die*?

However this may be, dripping with sweat, soaked through by the rain, his clothes in strips, his hands skinned, his elbows bleeding, his knees torn, Thénardier had reached what children, in their figurative language, call the edge of the wall of the ruin, he had stretched himself on it at full length, and there his strength failed him. A steep escarpment, three stories high, separated him from the pavement of the street.

The rope which he had was too short.

He was waiting there, pale, exhausted, having lost all the hope which he had had, still covered by night, but saying to himself that day was just about to dawn, dismayed at the idea of hearing in a few moments the neighbouring clock of Saint Paul's strike four, the hour when they would come to relieve the sentinel and would find him asleep under the broken roof, gazing with a kind of stupor through the fearful depth, by the glimmer of the lamps, upon the wet and black pavement, that longed for yet terrible pavement which was death yet which was liberty.

He asked himself if his three accomplices in escape had succeeded, if they had heard him, and if they would come to his aid. He listened. Except a patrolman, nobody had passed through the street since he had been there. Nearly all the travel of the gardeners of Montreuil Charonne, Vincennes, and Bercy to the Market, is through the Rue Saint Antoine.

The clock struck four. Thénardier shuddered. A few moments afterwards, that wild and confused noise which follows upon the discovery of an escape, broke out in the prison. The sounds of doors opening and shutting, the grinding of gratings upon their hinges, the tumult in the guardhouse, the harsh calls of the gate-keepers, the sound of the butts of muskets upon the pavement of the yards reached him. Lights moved up and down in the grated windows of the dormitories, a torch ran along the attic of the Bâtiment Neuf, the firemen of the barracks alongside had been called. Their caps, which the torches lighted up in the rain, were going to and fro along the roofs. At the same time Thénardier saw in the direction of the Bastille a whitish cloud throwing a dismal pallor over the lower part of the sky.

He was on the top of a wall ten inches wide, stretched out beneath the storm, with two precipices, at the right and at the left, unable to stir, giddy at the prospect of falling, and horror-stricken at the certainty of arrest, and his thoughts, like the pendulum of a clock, went from one of these ideas to the other: "Dead if I fall, taken if I stay."

In this anguish, he suddenly saw, the street being still

wrapped in obscurity, a man who was gliding along the walls, and who came from the direction of the Rue Pavée, stop in the recess above which Thénardier was as it were suspended. This man was joined by a second, who was walking with the same precaution, then by a third, then by a fourth. When these men were together, one of them lifted the latch of the gate in the fence, and they all four entered the inclosure of the shanty. They were exactly under Thénardier. These men had evidently selected this recess so as to be able to talk without being seen by the passers or by the sentinel who guards the gate of La Force a few steps off. It must also be stated that the rain kept this sentinel blockaded in his sentry-box. Thénardier, not being able to distinguish their faces, listened to their words with the desperate attention of a wretch who feels that he is lost.

Something which resembled hope passed before Thénardier's eyes; these men spoke argot.

The first said, in a low voice, but distinctly:

"*Décarrons*. What is it we *maquillons icigo*?"*

The second answered:

"*Il lansquine* enough to put out the *riffe* of the *rabouin*. And then the *coqueurs* are going by, there is a *grivier* there who carries a *gaffe*, shall we let them *emballer* us *icicaille*?"†

These two words, *icigo* and *icicaille*, which both mean ici [here], and which belong, the first to the argot of the Barrières, the second to the argot of the Temple, were revelations to Thénardier. By *icigo* he recognised Brujon, who was a prowler of the Barrières, and by *icicaille* Babet, who, among all his other trades, had been a second-hand dealer at the Temple.

The ancient argot of the age of Louis XIV., is now spoken only at the Temple, and Babet was the only one who spoke it quite purely. Without icicaille, Thénardier would not have recognised him, for he had entirely disguised his voice.

Meanwhile the third put in a word:

"Nothing is urgent yet, let us wait a little. How do we know that he doesn't need our help?"

By this, which was only French, Thénardier recognised

---

* Let us go, what are we doing here?

† It rains enough to put out the devil's fire. And then the police are going by. There is a soldier there who is standing sentinel. Shall we let them arrest us here?

Montparnasse, whose elegance consisted in understanding all argots and speaking none.

As to the fourth, he was silent, but his huge shoulders betrayed him. Thénardier had no hesitation. It was Gueulemer.

Brujon replied almost impetuously, but still in a low voice:

"What is it you *bonnez* us there? The *tapissier* couldn't draw his *crampe*. He don't know the *trus*, indeed! Bouliner his *limace* and *faucher* his *empaffes*, *maquiller* a *tortouse*, *caler boulins* in the *lourdes*, *braser* the *taffes*, *maquiller caroubles*, *faucher* the Bards, balance his *tortouse* outside, *panquer* himself, *camoufler* himself, one must be a *mariol*? The old man couldn't do it, he don't know how to *goupiner*! *

Babet added, still in that prudent, classic argot which was spoken by Poulailler and Cartouche, and which is to the bold, new, strongly-coloured, and hazardous argot which Brujon used, what the language of Racine is to the language of André Chénier:

"Your *orgue tapissier* must have been made *marron* on the stairs. One must be *arcasien*. He is a *galifard*. He has been played the *harnache* by a *roussin*, perhaps even by a *roussi*, who has beaten him *comtois*. Lend your *oche*, Montparnasse, do you hear those *criblements* in the college? You have seen all those *camoufles*. He has *tombé*, come! He must be left to draw his twenty *longes*. I have no *taf*, I am no *taffeur*, that is *colombé*, but there is nothing more but to make the *lezards*, or otherwise they will make us *gambiller* for it. Don't *renauder*, come with *nousiergue*. Let us go and *picter* a *rouillarde encible*."†

"Friends are not left in difficulty," muttered Montparnasse.

"I *bonnis* you that he is *malade*," replied Brujon. "At the hour which *toque*, the *tapissier* isn't worth a *broque*! We can do nothing

* What is it you tell us there? The innkeeper couldn't escape. He don't know the trade, indeed! Tear up his shirt and cut up his bedclothes to make a rope, to make holes in the doors, to forge false papers, to make false keys, to cut his irons, to hang his rope outside, to hide himself, to disguise himself, one must be a devil! The old man couldn't do it, he don't know how to work.

† Your innkeeper must have been caught in the act. One must be a devil. He is an apprentice. He has been duped by a spy, perhaps even by a sheep, who made him his gossip. Listen, Montparnasse, do you hear those cries in the prison? You have seen all those lights. He is retaken, come! He must be left to get his twenty years. I have no fear, I am no coward, that is known; but there is nothing more to be done, or otherwise they will make us dance. Don't be angry, come with us. Let us go and drink a bottle of old wine together.

here. *Décarrons*. I expect every moment that a *cogne* will *cintrer* me in *pogne!*" *

Montparnasse resisted now but feebly; the truth is, that these four men, with that faithfulness which bandits exhibit in never abandoning each other, had been prowling all night about La Force at whatever risk, in hope of seeing Thénardier rise above some wall. But the night which was becoming really too fine, it was storming enough to keep all the streets empty, the cold which was growing upon them, their soaked clothing, their wet shoes, the alarming uproar which had just broken out in the prison, the passing hours, the patrolmen they had met, hope departing, fear returning, all this impelled them to retreat. Montparnasse himself, who was, perhaps, to some slight extent a son-in-law of Thénardier, yielded. A moment more, they were gone. Thénardier gasped upon his wall like the shipwrecked sailors of the *Méduse* on their raft when they saw the ship which had appeared, vanish in the horizon.

He dared not call them, a cry overheard might destroy all; he had an idea, a final one, a flash of light; he took from his pocket the end of Brujon's rope, which he had detached from the chimney of the Bâtiment Neuf, and threw it into the inclosure.

This rope fell at their feet.

"A widow!"† said Babet.

"My tortouse!"‡ said Brujon.

"There is the innkeeper," said Montparnasse.

They raised their eyes. Thénardier advanced his head a little.

"Quick!" said Montparnasse, "have you the other end of the rope, Brujon?"

"Yes."

"Tie the two ends together, we will throw him the rope, he will fasten it to the wall, he will have enough to get down."

Thénardier ventured to speak:

"I am benumbed."

"We will warm you."

"I can't stir."

"Let yourself slip down, we will catch you."

---

* I tell you that he is retaken. At the present time, the innkeeper isn't worth a penny. We can do nothing here. Let us go. I expect every moment that a sergent de ville will have me in his hand.

† A rope (argot of the Temple).

‡ My rope (argot of the Barrières).

"My hands are stiff."

"Only tie the rope to the wall."

"I can't."

"One of us must get up," said Montparnasse.

"Three stories!" said Brujon.

An old plaster flue, which had served for a stove which had formerly been in use in the shanty, crept along the wall, rising almost to the spot at which they saw Thénardier. This flue, then very much cracked and full of seams, has since fallen, but its traces can still be seen. It was very small.

"We could get up by that," said Montparnasse.

"By that flue!" exclaimed Babet, "an *orgue*,* never! it would take a *mion*."†

"It would take a *môme*,"‡ added Brujon.

"Where can we find a brat?" said Gueulemer.

"Wait," said Montparnasse, "I have the thing."

He opened the gate of the fence softly, made sure that nobody was passing in the street, went out carefully, shut the door after him, and started on a run in the direction of the Bastille.

Seven or eight minutes elapsed, eight thousand centuries to Thénardier; Babet, Brujon, and Gueulemer kept their teeth clenched; the door at last opened again, and Montparnasse appeared, out of breath, with Gavroche. The rain still kept the street entirely empty.

Little Gavroche entered the inclosure and looked upon these bandit forms with a quiet air. The water was dripping from his hair. Gueulemer addressed him:

"Brat, are you a man?"

Gavroche shrugged his shoulders and answered:

"A *môme* like *mézig* is an *orgue*, and *orgues* like *vousailles* are *mômes*."§

"How the *mion* plays with the spittoon!"¶ exclaimed Babet.

"The *môme pantinois* isn't *maquillé* of *fertille lansquinée*,"‖ added Brujon.

---

* A man.
† A child (argot of the Temple).
‡ A child (argot of the Barrières).
§ A child like me is a man, and men like you are children.
¶ How well the child's tongue is hung!
‖ The Parisian child isn't made of wet straw.

"What is it you want?" said Gavroche.

Montparnasse answered:

"To climb up by this flue."

"With this widow,"*said Babet.

"And *ligoter* the *tortouse*,"† continued Brujon.

"To the *monté* of the *montant*."‡ resumed Babet.

"To the *pieu* of the *vanterne*,"§ added Brujon.

"And then?" said Gavroche.

"That's all!" said Gueulemer.

The *gamin* examined the rope, the flue, the wall, the windows, and made that inexpressible and disdainful sound with the lips which signifies:

"What's that?"

"There is a man up there whom you will save," replied Montparnasse.

"Will you?" added Brujon.

"Goosy!" answered the child, as if the question appeared to him absurd; and he took off his shoes.

Gueulemer caught up Gavroche with one hand, put him on the roof of the shanty, the worm-eaten boards of which bent beneath the child's weight, and handed him the rope which Brujon had tied together during the absence of Montparnasse. The *gamin* went towards the flue, which it was easy to enter, thanks to a large hole at the roof. Just as he was about to start, Thénardier, who saw safety and life approaching, bent over the edge of the wall; the first gleam of day lighted up his forehead reeking with sweat, his livid cheeks, his thin and savage nose, his grey bristly beard, and Gavroche recognised him:

"Hold on!" said he, "it is my father!—Well, that don't hinder!"

And taking the rope in his teeth, he resolutely commenced the ascent.

He reached the top of the ruin, bestrode the old wall like a horse, and tied the rope firmly to the upper cross-bar of the window.

A moment afterwards Thénardier was in the street.

As soon as he had touched the pavement, as soon as he felt

* This rope.
† Fasten the rope.
‡ To the top of the wall.
§ To the cross-bar of the window.

himself out of danger, he was no longer either fatigued, benumbed, or trembling; the terrible things through which he had passed vanished like a whiff of smoke, all that strange and ferocious intellect awoke, and found itself erect and free, ready to march forward. The man's first words were these:

"Now, who are we going to eat?"

It is needless to explain the meaning of this frightfully transparent word, which signifies all at once to kill, to assassinate, and to plunder. Eat, real meaning: *devour.*

"Let us hide first," said Brujon, "finish in three words and we will separate immediately. There was an affair which had a good look in the Rue Plumet, a deserted street, an isolated house, an old rusty grating upon a garden, some lone women."

"Well, why not?" inquired Thénardier.

"Your *fée** Eponine, has been to see the thing," answered Babet.

"And she brought a biscuit to Magnon," added Gueulemer, "nothing to *maquiller* there."†

"The *fée* isn't *loffe,*" ‡ said Thénardier. "Still we must see."

"Yes, yes," said Brujon, "we must see."

Meantime none of these men appeared longer to see Gavroche who, during this colloquy, had seated himself upon one of the stone supports of the fence; he waited a few minutes, perhaps for his father to turn towards him, then he put on his shoes, and said:

"It is over? you have no more use for me? men! you are out of your trouble. I am going. I must go and get my *mômes* up."

And he went away.

The five men went out of the inclosure one after another.

When Gavroche had disappeared at the turn of the Rue des Ballets, Babet took Thénardier aside.

"Did you notice that *mion?*" he asked him.

"What *mion?*"

"The *mion* who climbed up the wall and brought you the rope."

"Not much."

"Well, I don't know, but it seems to me that it is your son."

"Pshaw!" said Thénardier, "do you think so?"

---

* Your daughter.
† Nothing to do there.
‡ Stupid.

I
ORIGIN

PIGRITIA is a terrible word.

It engenders a world, *la pègre*, read *robbery*, and a hell, *la pègrenne*, read *hunger*.

So idleness is a mother.

She has a son, robbery, and a daughter, hunger.

Where are we now? In argot.

What is argot? It is at the same time the nation and the idiom, it is robbery under its two aspects; people and language.

When thirty-four years ago the narrator of this grave and gloomy story introduced into a work written with the same aim as the present* a robber talking argot, there was amazement and clamour. "What! how! argot! But argot is hideous! why, it is the language of convicts, of the galleys, of the prisons, of all that is most abominable in society!" etc., etc., etc.

We have never comprehended this sort of objection.

Since then two powerful romancers, one of whom is a profound observer of the human heart, the other an intrepid friend of the people, Balzac and Eugène Sue, having made bandits talk in their natural tongue as the author of *Le Dernier Jour d'un condamné* had done in 1828, the same outcry was made. It was repeated: "What do these writers mean by this revolting patois? Argot is horrid! argot makes us shudder!"

Who denies it? Undoubtedly.

Where the purpose is to probe a wound, an abyss, or a society, since when has it been a crime to descend too far, to go to the bottom? We had always thought that it was sometimes an act of courage, and at the very least a simple and useful act, worthy of the sympathetic attention which is merited by a duty accomplished and accepted. Not explore the whole, not study the whole, stop by the way, why? To stop is the part of the lead and not of the leadsman.

Certainly, to go into the lowest depths of the social order, where the earth ends and the mire begins, to search in those thick waters to pursue, to seize and to throw out still throbbing

---

* *Le Dernier Jour d'un condamné.*

upon the pavement this abject idiom which streams with filth as it is thus drawn to the light, this pustulous vocabulary in which each word seems a huge ring from some monster of the slime and the darkness, is neither an attractive task nor an easy task. Nothing is more mournful than to contemplate thus bare, by the light of thought, the fearful crawl of argot. It seems indeed as if it were a species of horrible beast made for the night, which has just been dragged from its cess-pool. We seem to see a frightful living and bristling bush which trembles, moves, quivers, demands its darkness again, menaces, and stares. This word resembles a fang, that a quenched and bleeding eye; this phrase seems to move like the claw of a crab. All this is alive with the hideous vitality of things which are organised in disorganisation.

Now, since when has horror excluded study? Since when has the sickness driven away the physician? Imagine a naturalist who should refuse to study the viper, the bat, the scorpion, the scolopendra, the tarantula, and who should cast them back into their darkness, saying: Oh! how ugly they are! The thinker who should turn away from argot would be like a surgeon who should turn away from an ulcer or a wart. He would be a philologist hesitating to examine a fact of language, a philosopher hesitating to scrutinise a fact of humanity. For, it must indeed be said to those who know it not, argot is both a literary phenomenon and a social result. What is argot; properly speaking? Argot is the language of misery.

Here we may be stopped; facts may be generalised, which is sometimes a method of extenuating them; it may be said that all trades, all professions, one might almost add all the accidents of the social hierarchy and all the forms of the intellect, have their argot. The merchant who says: *merchantable London stout, fine quality Marseilles*, the stockbroker who says: *seller sixty, dividend off*, the gambler who says: *I'll see you ten better, will you fight the tiger?* the huissier of the Norman Isles who says: *the enfeoffor restricted to his lands cannot claim the fruits of these grounds during the heritable seisin of the renouncer's fixtures*, the philosopher who says: *phenomenal triplicity*, the whale-hunter who says: *there she blows, there she breaches*, the phrenologist who says: *amativeness, combativeness, secretiveness*, the fencing-master who says: *tierce, quarte, retreat*, the compositor who says: *a piece of pie*, all, compositor, fencing-master, phrenologist, whale-hunter, philosopher, huissier, gambler, stockbroker, merchant, speak argot. The cobbler who says: *my kid*, the shop-keeper who says: *my counter-jumper*, the barber who says: *my clerk*, the printer who says: *my devil*, speak argot. In strictness, and if we will be absolute, all the various methods of saying right and left, the sailor's *larboard* and *starboard*, the machinist's *court side* and *garden side*, the beadle's *Epistle side* and *Gospel side*, are argot. There is an argot of the affected as there was the argot of the *Précieuses*. The Hôtel de Rambouillet bordered to some extent upon the Cour des Miracles. There is an argot of duchesses, witness this phrase written in a love-letter by a very great lady and a very pretty woman of the Restoration: "You will find in these postings a multitude of reasons why I should libertise."* Diplomatic ciphers are argot; the Pontifical Chancellory, in saying 26 for *Rome, grkztntgzyal* for *packet*, and *abfxustgrnogrkzu tu xi* for *Duke of Modena*, speaks argot. The physicians of the Middle Ages who, to say carrot, radish, and turnip, said: *opoponach, perfroschinum, reptitalmus, dracatholicum angelorum, postmegorum* spoke argot. The sugar manufacturer who says: "*Rectified, loaf, clarified, crushed, lump, molasses, mixed common, burned, caked,*" this honest manufacturer talks argot. A certain critical school of twenty years ago which said: "*The half of Shakespeare is plays upon words and puns*"—spoke argot. The poet and the artist who, with deep significance, will describe M. de Montmorency as "bourgeois, if he is not familiar with poetry and statues," speak argot. The classic Academician who calls flowers *Flora*, fruits *Pomona*, the sea *Neptune*, love *the fires*, beauty *the attractions*, a horse *a courser*, the white or the tricoloured cockade *the rose of Bellona*, the three-cornered hat *the triangle of Mars*, the classic Academician speaks argot. Algebra, medicine, botany, have their argot. The language which is employed afloat, that wonderful language of the sea, so complete and so picturesque, which was spoken by Jean Bart, Duquesne, Suffren, and Duperré, which mingles with the whistling of the rigging, with the sound of the speaking trumpet, with the clash of the boarding-axe, with the rolling, with the wind, with the squall, with the cannon, is all a heroic and splendid argot which is to the savage argot of crime what the lion is to the jackal.

Undoubtedly. But, whatever can be said about it, this

---

* You will find in this gossip a multitude of reasons why I should take my liberty.

method of understanding the word argot is an extension, which
even people in general will not admit. As for us, we continue to
this word its old acceptation, precise, circumscribed, and definite and we limit argot to argot. The real argot, the argot *par
excellence*, if these words can be joined, the immemorial argot
which was a realm, is nothing more nor less, we repeat, than the
ugly, restless, sly, treacherous, venomous, cruel, crooked, vile,
deep, deadly language of misery. There is, at the extremity of all
debasements and all misfortunes, a last wretchedness which
revolts and determines to enter into a struggle against the whole
mass of fortunate things and reigning rights; a hideous struggle
in which, sometimes by fraud, sometimes by force, at the same
time sickly and fierce, it attacks social order with pin-thrusts
through vice and with club strokes through crime. For the
necessities of this struggle, misery has invented a language of
battle which is argot.

To buoy up and to sustain above oblivion, above the abyss,
were it only a fragment of any language whatever which man
has spoken and which would otherwise be lost, that is to say one
of the elements, good or evil, of which civilisation is composed
or with which it is complicated, is to extend the data of social
observation; it is to serve civilisation itself. This service, Plautus
rendered, intentionally or unintentionally, by making two
Carthaginian soldiers speak Phœnician; this service Molière
rendered, by making so many of his personages speak Levantine
and all manner of patois. Here objections are revived; the
Phœnician, perfectly right! the Levantine, well and good! even
patois, so be it! these are languages which have belonged to
nations or provinces; but argot? what is the use of preserving
argot? what is the use of "buoying up" argot?

To this we shall answer but a word. Certainly, if the language
which a nation or a province has spoken is worthy of interest,
there is something still more worthy of attention and study in
the language which a misery has spoken.

It is the language which has been spoken in France, for
example, for more than four centuries, not merely by a particular form of misery, but by misery, every possible human misery.

And then, we insist, the study of social deformities and
infirmities and their indication in order to cure them, is not a
work in which choice is permissible. The historian of morals
and ideas has a mission no less austere than that of the historian

of events. The latter has the surface of civilisation, the struggles of the crowns, the births of princes, the marriages of kings, the battles, the assemblies, the great public men, the revolutions in the sunlight, all the exterior; the other historian has the interior, the foundation, the people who work, who suffer, and who wait, overburdened woman, agonising childhood, the dumb wars of man with man, the obscure ferocities, the prejudices, the established iniquities, the subterranean reactions of the law, the secret evolutions of souls, the vague shudderings of the multitudes, the starving, the barefooted, the bare-armed, the disinherited, the orphans, the unfortunate and the infamous, all the goblins that wander in darkness. He must descend with a heart at the same time full of charity and of severity, as a brother and as a judge, to those impenetrable casemates where crawl in confusion those who bleed and those who strike, those who weep and those who curse, those who fast and those who devour, those who suffer wrong, and those who commit it. Have these historians of hearts and souls lesser duties than the historians of exterior facts? Do you think that Dante has fewer things to say than Machiavelli? Is the under-world of civilisation, because it is deeper and more gloomy, less important than the upper? Do we really know the mountain when we do not know the cavern?

We must say, however, by the way, from some words of what precedes, a decided separation between the two classes of historians might be inferred, which does not exist in our mind. No man is a good historian of the open, visible, signal, and public life of the nations, if he is not, at the same time, to a certain extent, the historian of their deeper and hidden life; and no man is a good historian of the interior if he know not to be, whenever there is need, the historian of the exterior. The history of morals and ideas interpenetrates the history of events, and vice versa. They are two orders of different facts which answer to each other, which are always linked with and often produce each other. All the lineaments which Providence traces upon the surface of a nation have their dark but distinct parallels, in the bottom, and all the convulsions of the bottom produce upheavals at the surface. True history dealing with all, the true historian deals with all.

Man is not a circle with a single centre; he is an ellipse with two foci. Facts are one, ideas are the other.

Argot is nothing more nor less than a wardrobe in which language, having some bad deed to do, disguises itself. It puts on word-masks and metaphoric rags.

In which way it becomes horrible.

We can hardly recognise it. Is it really the French tongue, the great human tongue? There it is ready to enter upon the scene and give the cue to crime, and fitted for all the employments of the repertory of evil. It walks no more, it hobbles, it limps upon the crutch of the Cour des Miracles, a crutch which can be metamorphosed into a club; it gives itself the name of vagrancy; all the spectres, its dressing-maids, have begrimed it; it drags itself along and rears its head, the two characteristics of the reptile. It is apt for all parts henceforth, made squint-eyed by the forger, verdigrised by the poisoner, charcoaled by the incendiary's soot; and the murderer puts on his red.

When we listen, on the side of honest people, at the door of society, we overhear the dialogue of those who are without. We distinguish questions and answers. We perceive, without understanding, a hideous murmur, sounding almost like human tones, but nearer a howling than speech. This is argot. The words are uncouth, and marked by an indescribably fantastic beastliness. We think we hear hydras talking.

It is the unintelligible in the dark. It gnashes and it whispers, completing twilight by enigma. It grows black in misfortune, it grows blacker still in crime; these two blacknesses amalgamated make argot. Darkness in the atmosphere, darkness in the deeds, darkness in the voices. Appalling toad language, which comes and goes, hops, crawls, drivels, and moves monstrously in that boundless grey mist made up of rain, night, hunger, vice, lying, injustice, nakedness, asphyxia, and winter, the broad noonday of the miserable.

Let us have compassion on the chastened. Who, alas! are we ourselves? who am I who speak to you? who are you who listen to me? whence do we come? and is it quite certain that we did nothing before we were born? The earth is not without resemblance to a jail? Who knows that man is not a prisoner of Divine Justice?

Look closely into life. It is so constituted that we feel punishment everywhere.

Are you what is called a fortunate man? Well, you are sad every day. Each day has its great grief or its little care. Yesterday you were trembling for the health of one who is dear to you, to-day you fear for your own; to-morrow it will be an anxiety about money, the next day the slanders of a calumniator, the day after the misfortune of a friend; then the weather, then something broken or lost, then a pleasure for which you are reproached by your conscience or your vertebral column reproaches you; another time, the course of public affairs. Without counting heart troubles. And so on. One cloud is dissipated, another gathers. Hardly one day in a hundred of unbroken joy and of unbroken sunshine. And you are of that small number who are fortunate! As to other men, stagnant night is upon them.

Reflecting minds make little use of this expression: the happy and the unhappy. In this world, the vestibule of another evidently, there is none happy.

The true division of humanity is this: the luminous and the dark.

To diminish the number of the dark, to increase the number of the luminous, behold the aim. This is why we cry: education, knowledge! to learn to read is to kindle a fire; every syllable spelled sparkles.

But he who says light does not necessarily say joy. There is suffering in the light; in excess it burns. Flame is hostile to the wing. To burn and yet to fly, this is the miracle of genius.

When you know and when you love you shall suffer still. The day dawns in tears. The luminous weep, were it only over the dark.

II
ROOTS

ARGOT is the language of the dark.

Thought is aroused in its gloomiest depths, social philosophy is excited to its most poignant meditations, before this enigmatic dialect which is at once withered and rebellious. Here is chastisement visible. Each syllable has a branded look. The words of the common language here appear as if wrinkled and shrivelled under the red-hot iron of the executioner. Some seem still smoking. A phrase affects you like the branded shoulder of a robber suddenly laid bare. Ideas almost refuse to be expressed by these substantives condemned of justice. Its metaphor is some-times so shameless that we feel it has worn the iron collar.

Still, in spite of all that and because of all that, this strange dialect has of right its compartment in that great impartial col-lection in which there is place for the rusty farthing as well as for the gold medal, and which is called literature. Argot, whether we consent to it or not, has its syntax and its poesy. It is a language. If, by the deformity of certain terms, we recognise that it was mumbled by Mandrin, by the splendour of certain metonymies, we feel that it was spoken by Villon.

This verse so exquisite and so famous:

> Mais où sont les neiges d'antan?*

is a verse of argot. *Antan—ante annum*—is a word of the argot of Thunes which signifies the past year, and by extension *formerly*. There might still be read thirty-five years ago, at the time of the departure of the great chain in 1827, in one of the dungeons of Bicêtre, this maxim engraved on the wall with a nail by a king of Thunes condemned to the galleys: *Les dabs d'antan trimaient siempre pour la pierre du Cöesre*. Which means: *the kings of old time always went to be consecrated*. In the mind of that king, consecra-tion was the galleys.

The word *decarade*, which expresses the departure of a heavy wagon at a gallop, is attributed to Villon, and it is worthy of him. This word, which strikes fire with four feet, resumes in a masterly onomatopœia the whole of La Fontaine's admirable verse:

> Six forts chevaux tiraient un coche.†

In a purely literary point of view, few studies would be more curious and more prolific than that of argot. It is a complete language within a language, a sort of diseased excrescence, a sickly graft which has produced a vegetation, a parasite which has its roots in the old Gallic trunk, the sinister foliage of which creeps over an entire side of the language. This is what may be called the primary aspect, the general aspect of argot. But to those who study language as it should be studied, that is to say as geologists study the earth, argot appears, as it were, a true

---

* But where are the snows of yesteryear?
† Six sturdy horses drew a coach.

alluvium. According as we dig more or less deep, we find in argot, beneath the old popular French, Provençal, Spanish, Italian, Levantine, this language of the Mediterranean ports, English and German, Romance in its three varieties, French Romance, Italian Romance, Romance Romance, Latin, and finally Basque and Celtic. A deep and grotesque formation. A subterranean edifice built in common by all the miserable. Each accursed race has deposited its stratum, each suffering has dropped its stone, each heart has given its pebble. A multitude of evil, low, or embittered souls, who have passed through life and vanished in eternity, are preserved here almost entire and in some sort still visible under the form of a monstrous word.

Will you have Spanish? the old Gothic argot swarms with it. Here is *boffette*, blow, which comes from *bofeton*; *vantane*, window (afterwards *vanterne*), which comes from *vantana*; *gat*, cat, which comes from *gato*; *acite*, oil, which comes from *aceyte*. Will you have Italian? Here is *spade*, sword, which comes from *spada*; *carvel*, boat, which comes from *caravella*. Will you have English? Here is *bichot*, bishop; *raille*, spy, which comes from *rascal*, *rascallion*; *pilche*, box, which comes from *pilcher*. Will you have German? Here is *caleur*, waiter, *kellner*; *hers*, master, *herzog* (duke). Will you have Latin? Here is *frangir*, to break, *frangere*; *affurer*, to rob, *fur*; *cadène*, chain, *catena*; there is a word which appears in all the languages of the continent with a sort of mysterious power and authority, the word *magnus*; the Scotchman makes of it his *mac*, which designates the chief of the clan, Mac Farlane, Mac Callummore, the great Farlane, the great Callummore;* argot makes of it the *meck*, and afterwards, the *meg*, that is to say God. Will you have Basque? Here is *gahisto*, the devil, which comes from *gaïztoa*, evil; *sorgabon*, a good night, which comes from *gabon*, good evening. Will you have Celtic? Here is *blavin*, handkerchief, which comes from *blavet*, gushing water; *mènesse*, woman (in a bad sense), which comes from *meinec*, full of stones; *barant*, brook, from *baranton*, fountain; *goffeur*, locksmith, from *goff*, blacksmith; *guedouze*, death, which comes from *guenn-du*, white-black. Finally, will you have history? argot calls crowns *maltèses*, a reminiscence of the coins which circulated on the galleys of Malta.

Besides the philological origins which we have just pointed

---

* It should, however, be observed that *mac* in Celtic means son.

out, argot has other still more natural roots, which spring, so to speak, from the mind of man itself.

First, the direct creation of words. In this is the mystery of languages. To paint by words which have forms, we know not how nor why. This is the primitive foundation of all human language—what might be called the granite. Argot swarms with words of this kind, root-words, made out of whole cloth, we know not where nor by whom, without etymology, without analogy, without derivation, solitary, barbarous, sometimes hideous words which have a singular power of expression, and which are all alive. The executioner, *the taule*; the forest, *the sabri*; fear, flight, *taf*; the lackey, *the larbin*, the general, the préfet, the minister, *pharos*; the devil, *the rabouin*. There is nothing stranger than these words, which mask and yet reveal. Some of them, *the rabouin*, for example, are at the same time grotesque and terrible, and produce the effect of a cyclopian grimace.

Secondly, metaphor. It is the peculiarity of a language, the object of which is to tell everything and conceal everything, to abound in figures. Metaphor is an enigma which offers itself as a refuge to the robber who plots a blow, to the prisoner who plans an escape. No idiom is more metaphorical than argot, *to unscrew the coco*,* to wring the neck; *to wind up*,† to eat; *to be sheaved*,‡ to be judged; *a rat*,§ a bread thief, *il lansquine*, it rains, an old and striking figure, which in some sort carries its date with it, which assimilates the long slanting lines of the rain with the thick and driving pikes of the lansquenets, and which includes in a single word the popular metonymy, *it rains pitchforks*. Sometimes, in proportion as argot passes from the first period to the second, words pass from the savage and primitive state to the metaphorical sense. The devil ceases to be *the rabouin* and becomes *the baker*, he who puts into the oven. This is more witty, but not so grand; something like Racine after Corneille, like Euripedes after Æschylus. Certain phrases of argot which partake of both periods, and have at the same time the barbaric and the metaphorical character, resemble phantasmagorias. *Les sorgueurs vont sollicer des gails à la lune* (the prowlers are going to

---

* *Devisser le coco.*
† *Tortiller.*
‡ *Etre gerbé.*
§ *Un rat.*

steal some horses by night). This passes before the mind like a group of spectres. We know not what we see.

Thirdly, expedient. Argot lives upon the language. It uses it at its caprice, it takes from it by chance, and contents itself often, when the necessity arises, with summarily and grossly distorting it. Sometimes with common words thus deformed, and mystified with words of pure argot, it forms picturesque expressions in which we feel the mixture of the two preceding elements, direct creation and metaphor: *Le cab jaspine, je marronne que la roulotte de Pantin trime dans la sabri*, the dog barks, I suspect that the Paris diligence is passing in the woods. *Le dab est sinve, la dabuge est merlouis sière, la fée est bative*, the bourgeois is stupid, the bourgeoise is cunning, the daughter is pretty. Most commonly, in order to mislead listeners, argot contents itself with adding promiscuously to all the words of the language a sort of ignoble tail, a termination in *aille*, in *orgue*, in *iergue*, or in *uche*. Thus: *Vouzierque trouvaille bonorgue ce gigotmuche?** Do you like this leg of mutton? A phrase addressed by Cartouche to a turnkey, to know whether the amount offered for an escape satisfied him. The termination in *mar* is of modern date.

Argot, being the idiom of corruption, is easily corrupted. Moreover, as it always seeks disguise so soon as it perceives it is understood, it transforms itself. Unlike all other vegetation, every ray of light upon it kills what it touches. Thus argot goes on decomposed and recomposed incessantly; an obscure and rapid process which never ceases. It changes more in ten years than the language in ten centuries. Thus the *larton*† becomes the *lartif*; the *gail*‡ becomes the *gaye*; the *fertauche*,§ the *fertille*; the *momignard*, the *momacque*; the *fiques*,¶ the *frusques*; the *chique*,‖ the *égrugeoir*; the *colabre*,♮ the *colas*. The devil is first *gahisto*, then the *rabouin*, then the baker; the priest is the *ratichon*, then the boar; the dagger is the twenty-two, then the *surin*, then the *lingre*; police officers are *railles*, then *roussins*, then *rousses*, then lacing merchants, then *couqueurs*, then *cognes*; the executioner is the

---

* *Triovez-vous ce gigot bon?*
† Bread.
‡ Horse.
§ Straw.
¶ Clothes.
‖ The church.
♮ The neck.

Taule, then *Charlot*, then the *atigeur*, then the *becquilard*. In the seventeenth century, to fight was *to take some tobacco*, in the nineteenth it is *to chew the jaws*. Twenty different expressions have passed between these two extremes. Cartouche would speak Hebrew to Lacenaire. All the words of this language are perpetually in flight like the men who use them.

From time to time, however, and because of this very change, the ancient argot reappears and again becomes new. It has its centres in which it is continuous. The temple preserves the argot of the seventeenth century; Bicêtre, when it was a prison, preserved the argot of Thunes. There was heard the termination in *anche* of the old Thuners. *Boyanches tu?** (do you drink?), *il croyanche†* (he believes). But perpetual movement, nevertheless, is the law.

If the philosopher succeeds in fixing for a moment for the observer this language, which is incessantly evaporating, he falls into painful yet useful meditations. No study is more efficacious and more prolific in instruction. Not a metaphor, not an etymology of argot which does not contain its lesson. Among these men, *to beat* means *to feign*; they beat a sickness; craft is their strength.

To them the idea of man is inseparable from the idea of shade. The night is called *sorgue*; man, *orgue*. Man is a derivative of night.

They have acquired the habit of considering society as an atmosphere which kills them, as a fatal force, and they speak of their liberty as one would of his health. A man arrested is *sick*; a man condemned is *dead*.

What is most terrible to the prisoner in the four stone walls which enshroud him is a sort of icy chastity; he calls the dungeon the *castus*. In this funereal place, life without is always under its most cheerful aspect. The prisoner has irons on his feet; you might suppose that he would be thinking that people walk with their feet? no, he is thinking that people dance with their feet; so, let him succeed in sawing through his irons, his first idea is that now he can dance, and he calls the saw a *fandango*. A *name* is a *centre*; a deep assimilation. The bandit has two heads, one which regulates his actions and controls him

* *Bois-tu.*
† *Il croit.*

during his whole life, another which he has on his shoulders on the day of his death; he calls the head which counsels him to crime the *sorbonne*, and the head which expiates it the *tronche*. When a man has nothing but rags on his body and vices in his heart, when he has reached that double degradation, material as well as moral, which characterises, in its two acceptations, the word beggarly, he is at an edge for crime; he is like a well-whetted knife; he has two edges, his distress and his wickedness; so argot does not say "a vagabond;" it says a *réguisé*. What are the galleys? a brazier of damnation, a Hell. The convict calls himself a *fagot*. Finally, what name do the malefactors give to the prison? *the college*. A whole penitentiary system might spring from this word.

Would you know where most of the songs of the galleys have originated, those refrains called in special phrase the *lirlonfa*? Listen to this.

There was at the Châtelet de Paris a broad long cellar. This cellar was eight feet deep below the level of the Seine. It had neither windows nor ventilators, the only opening was the door; men could enter, but not air. The cellar had for a ceiling a stone arch, and for a floor, ten inches of mud. It had been paved with tiles, but, under the oozing of the waters, the pavement had rotted and broken up. Eight feet above the floor, a long massive beam crossed this vault from side to side; from this beam there hung, at intervals, chains three feet in length, and at the end of these chains were iron collars. Men condemned to the galleys were put into this cellar until the day of their departure for Toulon. They were pushed under this timber, where each had his iron swinging in the darkness, waiting for him. The chains, those pendent arms, and the collars, those open hands, seized these wretches by the neck. They were riveted, and they were left there. The chain being too short, they could not lie down. They remained motionless in this cave, in this blackness, under this timber, almost hung, forced to monstrous exertions to reach their bread or their pitcher, the arch above their heads, the mud up to their knees, their ordure running down their legs, collapsing with fatigue, their hips and knees giving way, hanging by their hands to the chain to rest themselves, unable to sleep except standing, and awakened every moment by the strangling of the collar: some did not awake. In order to eat, they had to draw their bread, which was thrown into the mire, up the leg with the heel, within reach of the hand. How long did they continue thus? A month, two months, six months sometimes; one remained a year. It was the antechamber of the galleys. Men were put there for stealing a hare from the king. In this hell-sepulchre what did they do? What can be done in a sepulchre, they agonised, and what can be done in a hell, they sang. For where there is no more hope, song remains. In the waters of Malta, when a galley was approaching, they heard the song before they heard the oars. The poor poacher, Survincent, who had passed through the cellar-prison of the Châtelet said: *it was the rhymes which sustained me*. Uselessness of poetry. Of what use is rhyme? In this cellar almost all the argot songs took birth. It is from the dungeon of the Grand Châtelet de Paris that the melancholy galley refrain of Montgomery comes: *Timaloumisaine, timoulamaison*. Most of these songs are dreary; some are cheerful; one is tender:

> Icicaille est le théâtre
> Du petit dardant.*

The endeavour is vain, you cannot annihilate that eternal relic of the human heart, love.

In this world of dark deeds secrecy is preserved. Secrecy is the interest of all. Secrecy to these wretches is the unity which serves as a basis of union. To violate secrecy is to tear from each member of this savage community something of himself. To inform against, in the energetic language of argot, is called: *Manger le morceau*.† As if the informer seized a bit of the substance of all, and fed upon a morsel of the flesh of each.

What is to receive a blow? The hackneyed metaphor responds: *C'est voir trente-six chandelles*.‡ Here argot intervenes and says: *chandelle, camoufle*. Upon this, the common language gives as a synonym for blow, *camouflet*. Thus, by a sort of upward penetration, through the aid of a metaphor, that incalculable trajectory, argot rises from the cavern to the Academy; and Poulailler saying: "I light my *camoufle*," makes Voltaire write: "Langleviel La Beaumelle deserves a hundred *camouflets*!"

---

* Here we have the theatre
  Of the little archer (Cupid).
† To eat the morsel.
‡ It is to see thirty-six candles; English, to see stars.

A search into argot is a discovery at every step. Study and research into this strange idiom lead to the mysterious point of intersection between popular society and outcast society.

The robber also has his food for powder, his matter for plunder, you, me, the world in general; the *pantre*. (*Pan*, everybody.)

Argot is speech become a convict.

That the thinking principle of man can be trampled down so low, that it can be bound and dragged there by the obscure tyrannies of fatality, that it can be tied with unknown fastenings in that gulf, this is appalling.

Oh, pitiful thought of the miserable!

Alas! will none come to the help of the human soul in this gloom? Is it its destiny for ever to await the mind, the liberator, the huge rider of Pegasus and the hippogriffs, the aurora-hued combatant who descends from the skies with wings, the radiant Knight of the future? Shall it always call to its aid the gleaming lance of the ideal in vain? is it condemned to hear the Evil coming terribly through the depths of the abyss, and to see nearer and nearer at hand, under the hideous water, that dragon-head, those jaws reeking with foam, that serpentine waving of claws, distensions, and rings? Must it remain there, with no ray, no hope, abandoned to that horrible approach, vaguely scented by the monster, shuddering, dishevelled, wringing its hands, for ever chained to the rock of night, hopeless Andromeda, white and naked in the darkness?

III

ARGOT WHICH WEEPS AND ARGOT WHICH LAUGHS

As we see, all argot, the argot of four hundred years ago as well as the argot of the present, is pervaded with that sombre spirit of symbolism which gives to its every word, sometimes an appearance of grief, sometimes an air of menace. We feel in it the old, savage gloom of those vagabonds of the Cour des Miracles who played cards with packs peculiar to themselves, some of which have been preserved. The eight of clubs, for instance, represented a large tree bearing eight enormous clover leafs, a sort of fantastic personification of the forest. At the foot of this tree a fire was seen at which three hares were roasting a hunter on a spit, and in the background, over another fire, was a smoking pot from which the head of a dog projected. Nothing can be more mournful than these pictured reprisals, upon a pack of cards, in the days of the stake for roasting contrabandists, and the cauldron for boiling counterfeiters. The various forms which thought assumed in the realm of argot, even song, even raillery, even menace, all had this impotent and exhausted character. All the songs, some melodies of which have been preserved, were humble and lamentable unto weeping. The *pègre* calls itself *the poor pègre*, and it is always the hare hiding, the mouse escaping, the bird flying. Scarcely does it complain, it contents itself with a sigh; one of its groans has come down to us: "*Je n'entrave que le dail comment meck, le daron des orgues, peut atiger ses mômes et ses momignards et les locher criblant sans être agité lui-même.*"* The miserable being, whenever he has time to reflect, imagines himself mean before the law and wretched before society; he prostrates himself, he begs, he turns towards pity; we feel that he recognises that he is wrong.

Towards the middle of the last century, there was a change. The prison songs, the robbers' ritornels acquired, so to speak, an insolent and jovial expression. The plaintive *maluré* was supplanted by the *larifla*. We find in the eighteenth century, in almost all the songs of the galleys, the chain-gangs, and the prisons, a diabolical and enigmatic gaiety. We hear this boisterous and ringing refrain, which one would say was lighted with a phosphorescent gleam, and which seems as if it were thrown forth upon the forest by a will-o'-the-wisp playing the fife:

> Mirlababi surlababo
> Mirliton ribonribette
> Surlababi mirlababo
> Mirliton ribonribo.

This was sung while cutting a man's throat in a cave or in the edge of a forest.

A serious symptom. In the eighteenth century the old melancholy of these gloomy classes is dissipated. They began to laugh. They ridicule the great *meg* and the great *dab*. Speaking of Louis XV. they call the King of France "the Marquis of Pantin." They are almost cheerful. A sort of flickering light comes from these wretches, as if conscience ceased to weigh upon them. These

---

* I do not understand how God, the father of men, can torture his children and his grandchildren, and hear them cry without being tortured himself.

pitiful tribes of the darkness have no longer the desperate audacity of deeds merely, they have the reckless audacity of mind. A
sign that they are losing the perception of their criminality, and
that they feel even among thinkers and dreamers some mysterious support which is unconsciously given. A sign that pillage
and robbery are beginning to infiltrate even into doctrines and
sophisms, in such a way as to lose something of their ugliness by
giving much of it to the sophisms and the doctrines. A sign in
short, if no diversion arises, of some prodigious and speedy
outburst.

Let us pause for a moment. Whom are we accusing here? is
it the eighteenth century? is it its philosophy? Certainly not.
The work of the eighteenth century is sound and good. The
Encyclopædists, Diderot at their head, the physiocratists, Turgot
at their head, the philosophers, Voltaire at their head, the utopists, Rousseau at their head: these are four sacred legions. To
them the immense advance of humanity towards the light is due.
They are the four vanguards of the human race going to the
four cardinal points of progress, Diderot towards the beautiful,
Turgot towards the useful, Voltaire towards the true, Rousseau
towards the just. But beside and beneath the philosophers, there
were the sophists, a poisonous vegetation mingled with the
healthy growth, hemlock in the virgin forest. While the executioner was burning upon the chief staircase of the Palais de Justice the grand liberating books of the century, writers now
forgotten were publishing, with the privilege of the king, many
strangely disorganising writings greedily read by the outcast.
Some of these publications, strange to say, patronised by a
prince, are still in the *Bibliothèque Secrète*. These facts, deep
rooted, but ignored, were unperceived on the surface. Sometimes the very obscurity of a fact is its danger. It is obscure
because it is subterranean. Of all the writers, he perhaps who
dug the most unwholesome gallery through the masses was
Restif de La Bretonne.

This work, adapted to all Europe, committed greater ravages
in Germany than anywhere else. In Germany, during a certain
period, summed up by Schiller in his famous drama, *The Robbers*, robbery and plunder, elevated into a protest against property and labour, appropriated certain elementary, specious, and
false ideas, just in appearance, absurd in reality, enwrapped
themselves in these ideas, disappeared in them in some sort,

took an abstract name, and passed into the state of theory, and in this wise circulated among the labouring, suffering, and honest multitudes, unknown even to the imprudent chemists who had prepared the mixture, unknown even to the masses who accepted it. Whenever a thing of this kind occurs, it is serious. Suffering engenders wrath; and while the prosperous classes blind themselves, or fall asleep, which also is to close the eyes, the hatred of the unfortunate classes lights its torch at some fretful or ill-formed mind which is dreaming in a corner, and begins to examine society. Examination by hatred, a terrible thing.

Hence, if the misfortune of the time so wills, those frightful commotions which were formerly called *Jacqueries*, in comparison with which purely political agitations are child's play, and which are not merely the struggle of the oppressed against the oppressor, but the revolt of discomfort against well-being. All falls then.

Jacqueries are people-quakes.

This danger, imminent perhaps in Europe towards the end of the eighteenth century, was cut short by the French Revolution, that immense act of probity.

The French Revolution, which is nothing more nor less than the ideal armed with the sword, started to its feet, and by the very movement, closed the door of evil and opened the door of good.

It cleared up the question, promulgated truth, drove away miasma, purified the century, crowned the people.

We may say of it that it created man a second time, in giving him a second soul, his rights.

The nineteenth century inherits and profits by its work, and today the social catastrophe which we just now indicated is simply impossible. Blind is he who prophesies it! Silly is he who dreads it! Revolution is vaccination for Jacquerie.

Thanks to the Revolution, social conditions are changed. The feudal and monarchical diseases are no longer in our blood. There is nothing more of the Middle Ages in our constitution. We live no longer in the times when frightful interior swarms made eruption, when men heard beneath their feet the obscure course of a sullen sound, when there appeared on the surface of civilisation some mysterious uprising of molehills, when the soil cracked, when the mouths of caverns opened, and when men saw monstrous heads spring suddenly from the earth.

The revolutionary sense is a moral sense. The sentiment of rights, developed, develops the sentiment of duty. The law of all is liberty, which ends where the liberty of others begins, according to Robespierre's admirable definition. Since '89, the entire people has been expanding in the sublimated individual; there is no poor man, who, having his rights, has not his ray; the starving man feels within himself the honour of France; the dignity of the citizen is an interior armour; he who is free is scrupulous; he who votes reigns. Hence incorruptibility; hence the abortion of unnoxious lusts; hence the eyes heroically cast down before temptations. The revolutionary purification is such that on a day of deliverance, a 14th of July, or a 10th of August, there is no longer a mob. The first cry of the enlightened and enlarging multitudes is: death to robbers! Progress is an honest man; the ideal and the absolute pick no pockets. By whom in 1848 were the chests escorted which contained the riches of the Tuileries? by the rag-pickers of the Faubourg Saint Antoine. The rag mounted guard over the treasure. Virtue made these tatters resplendent. There was there, in those chests, in boxes hardly closed, some even half open, amid a hundred dazzling caskets, that old crown of France all in diamonds, surmounted by the regent's carbuncle of royalty, which was worth thirty millions. Barefooted they guarded that crown.

No more Jacquerie then. I regret it on account of the able. That is the old terror which has had its last effect, and which can never henceforth be employed in politics. The great spring of the red spectre is broken. Everybody knows it now. The scarecrow no longer scares. The birds take liberties with the puppet, the beetles make free with it, the bourgeois laugh at it.

IV
THE TWO DUTIES: TO WATCH AND TO HOPE

THIS being so, is all social danger dissipated? Certainly not. No Jacquerie. Society may be reassured on that account; the blood will rush to its head no more, but let it take thought as to the manner of its breathing. Apoplexy is no longer to be feared, but consumption is there. The consumption of society is called misery.

We die undermined as well as stricken down.

Let us not weary of repeating it, to think first of all of the outcast and sorrowful multitudes, to solace them, to give them air, to enlighten them, to love them, to enlarge their horizon magnificently, to lavish upon them education in all its forms, to offer them the example of labour, never the example of idleness, to diminish the weight of the individual burden by intensifying the idea of the universal object, to limit poverty without limiting wealth, to create vast fields of public and popular activity, to have, like Briareus, a hundred hands to stretch out on all sides to the exhausted and the feeble, to employ the collective power in the great duty of opening workshops for all arms, schools for all aptitudes and laboratories for all intelligences, to increase wages, to diminish suffering, to balance the ought and the have, that is to say, to proportion enjoyment to effort and gratification, to need, in one word, to evolve from the social structure, for the benefit of those who suffer and those who are ignorant, more light and more comfort; this is, let sympathetic souls forget it not, the first of fraternal obligations, this is, let selfish hearts know it, the first of political necessities.

And, we must say, all that is only a beginning. The true statement is this: labour cannot be a law without being a right.

We do not dwell upon it; this is not the place.

If nature is called providence, society should be called foresight.

Intellectual and moral growth is not less indispensable than material amelioration. Knowledge is a viaticum, thought is of primary necessity, truth is nourishment as well as wheat. A reason, by fasting from knowledge and wisdom, becomes puny. Let us lament as over stomachs, over minds which do not eat. If there is anything more poignant than a body agonising for want of bread, it is a soul which is dying of hunger for light.

All progress is tending towards the solution. Some day we shall be astounded. The human race rising, the lower strata will quite naturally come out from the zone of distress. The abolition of misery will be brought about by a simple elevation of level.

This blessed solution, we should do wrong to distrust.

The past, it is true, is very strong at the present hour. It is reviving. This revivification of a corpse is surprising. Here it is walking and advancing. It seems victorious; this dead man is a conqueror. He comes with his legion, the superstitions, with his sword, despotism, with his banner, ignorance; within a little time he has won ten battles. He advances, he threatens, he laughs, he is at our doors. As for ourselves, we shall not despair. Let us sell the field whereon Hannibal is camped.

We who believe, what can we fear?

There is no backward flow of ideas more than of rivers.

But let those who desire not the future, think of it. In saying no to progress, it is not the future which they condemn, but themselves. They give themselves a melancholy disease; they inoculate themselves with the past. There is but one way of refusing to-morrow, that is to die.

Now, no death, that of the body as late as possible, that of the soul never, is what we desire.

Yes, the enigma shall say its word, the sphinx shall speak, the problem shall be resolved. Yes, the people, rough-hewn by the eighteenth century, shall be completed by the nineteenth. An idiot is he who doubts it! The future birth, the speedy birth of universal well-being, is a divinely fatal phenomenon.

Immense pushings together rule human affairs and lead them all in a given time to the logical condition, that is to say, to equilibrium; that is to say, to equity. A force composite of earth and of Heaven results from humanity and governs it; this force is a worker of miracles; miraculous issues are no more difficult to it than extraordinary changes. Aided by science which comes from man, and by the event which comes from Another, it is little dismayed by those contradictions in the posture of problems, which seem impossibilities to the vulgar. It is no less capable of making a solution leap forth from the comparison of ideas than a teaching from the comparison of facts, and we may expect everything from this mysterious power of progress, which some fine day confronts the Orient with the Occident in the depths of a sepulchre, and makes the Imaums talk with Bonaparte in the interior of the great pyramid.

In the meantime, no halt, no hesitation, no interruption in the grand march of minds. Social philosophy is essentially science and peace. Its aim is, and its result must be, to dissolve angers by the study of antagonisms. It examines, it scrutinises, it analyses; then it recomposes. It proceeds by way of reduction, eliminating hatred from all.

That a society may be swamped in a gale which breaks loose over men has been seen more than once; history is full of ship-wrecks of peoples and of empires; customs, laws, religions, some fine day, the mysterious hurricane passes by and sweeps them all away. The civilisations of India, Chaldea, Persia, Assyria, Egypt, have disappeared, one after the other. Why? we know not. What are the causes of these disasters? we do not know. Could these societies have been saved? was it their own fault? did they persist in some vital vice which destroyed them? how much of suicide is there in these terrible deaths of a nation and of a race? Questions without answer. Darkness covers the condemned civilisations. They were not seaworthy, for they were swallowed up; we have nothing more to say; and it is with a sort of bewilderment that we behold, far back in that ocean which is called the past, behind those colossal billows, the centuries, the foundering of those huge ships, Babylon, Nineveh, Tarsus, Thebes, Rome, under the terrible blast which comes from all the mouths of darkness. But darkness there, light here. We are ignorant of the diseases of the ancient civilisations, we know the infirmities of our own. We have everywhere upon it the rights of light; we contemplate its beauties and we lay bare its deformities. Where it is unsound we probe; and, once the disease is determined, the study of the cause leads to the discovery of the remedy. Our civilisation, the work of twenty centuries, is at once their monster and their prodigy; it is worth saving. It will be saved. To relieve it, is much already; to enlighten it, is something more. All the labours of modern social philosophy ought to converge towards this end. The thinker of to-day has a great duty, to auscultate civilisation.

We repeat it, this auscultation is encouraging; and it is by this persistence in encouragement that we would finish these few pages, austere interlude of a sorrowful drama. Beneath the mortality of society we feel the imperishability of humanity. Because it was here and there those wounds, craters, and those ringworms, solfataras, because of a volcano which breaks, and which throws out its pus, the globe does not die. The diseases of a people do not kill man.

And nevertheless, he who follows the social clinic shakes his head at times. The strongest, the tenderest, the most logical have their moments of fainting.

Will the future come? It seems that we may almost ask this question when we see such terrible shadow. Sullen face-to-face of the selfish and the miserable. On the part of the selfish, prejudices, the darkness of the education of wealth, appetite increasing through intoxication, a stupefaction of prosperity which deafens, a dread of suffering which, with some, is carried even to aversion for sufferers, an implacable satisfaction, the me so puffed up that it closes the soul; on the part of the miserable, covetousness, envy, hatred of seeing others enjoy, the deep yearnings of the human animal towards the gratifications, hearts full of gloom, sadness, want, fatality, ignorance impure and simple.

Must we continue to lift our eyes towards heaven? is the luminous point which we there discern of those which are quenched? The ideal is terrible to see, thus lost in the depths, minute, isolated, imperceptible, shining, but surrounded by all those great black menaces monstrously massed about it; yet in no more danger than a star in the jaws of the clouds.

BOOK EIGHTH –
ENCHANTMENTS AND DESOLATIONS

I
SUNSHINE

THE reader has understood that Eponine, having recognised through the grating the inhabitant of that Rue Plumet, to which Magnon had sent her, had begun by diverting the bandits from the Rue Plumet, had then conducted Marius thither, and that after several days of ecstasy before that grating, Marius, drawn by that force which pushes the iron towards the magnet and the lover towards the stones of which the house of her whom he loves is built, had finally entered Cosette's garden as Romeo did the garden of Juliet. It had even been easier for him than for Romeo; Romeo was obliged to scale a wall, Marius had only to push aside a little one of the bars of the decrepit grating, which was loosened in its rusty socket, like the teeth of old people. Marius was slender, and easily passed through.

As there was never anybody in the street, and as, moreover, Marius entered the garden only at night, he ran no risk of being seen.

From that blessed and holy hour when a kiss affianced these two souls, Marius came every evening. If, at this period of her life, Cosette had fallen into the love of a man who was unscrupulous and a libertine, she would have been ruined; for there are generous natures which give themselves, and Cosette was one. One of the magnanimities of woman is to yield. Love, at that height at which it is absolute, is associated with an inexpressibly celestial blindness of modesty. But what risks do you run, O noble souls! Often, you give the heart, we take the body. Your heart remains to you, and you look upon it in the darkness, and shudder. Love has no middle term; either it destroys, or it saves. All human destiny is this dilemma. This dilemma, destruction or salvation, no fatality proposes more inexorably than love. Love is life, if it be not death. Cradle; coffin also. The same sentiment says yes and no in the human heart. Of all the things which God has made, the human heart is that which sheds most light, and, alas! most night.

God willed that the love which Cosette met, should be one of those loves which save.

Through all the month of May of that year 1832, there were there, every night, in that poor, wild garden, under that shrubbery each day more odorous and more dense, two beings composed of every chastity and every innocence, overflowing with all the felicities of Heaven, more nearly archangels than men, pure, noble, intoxicated, radiant, who were resplendent to each other in the darkness. It seemed to Cosette that Marius had a crown, and to Marius that Cosette had a halo. They touched each other, they beheld each other, they clasped each other's hands, they pressed closely to each other; but there was a distance which they did not pass. Not that they respected it; they were ignorant of it. Marius felt a barrier, the purity of Cosette, and Cosette felt a support, the loyalty of Marius. The first kiss was the last also. Marius, since, had not gone beyond touching Cosette's hand, or her neckerchief, or her ringlets, with his lips. Cosette was to him a perfume, and not a woman. He breathed her. She refused nothing and he asked nothing. Cosette was happy, and Marius was satisfied. They lived in that ravishing condition which might be called the dazzling of a soul by a soul. It was that ineffable first embrace of two virginities in the ideal. Two swans meeting upon the Jungfrau.

At that hour of love, an hour when passion is absolutely silent under the omnipotence of ecstasy, Marius, the pure and seraphic Marius, would have been capable rather of visiting a public woman than of lifting Cosette's dress to the height of her ankle. Once, on a moonlight night, Cosette stooped to pick up something from the ground, her dress loosened and displayed the rounding of her bosom. Marius turned away his eyes.

What passed between these two beings? Nothing. They were adoring each other.

At night, when they were there, this garden seemed a living and sacred place. All the flowers opened about them, and proffered them their incense; they too opened their souls and poured them forth to the flowers: the lusty and vigorous vegetation trembled full of sap and intoxication about these two innocent creatures, and they spoke words of love at which the trees thrilled.

What were these words? Whispers, nothing more. These whispers were enough to arouse and excite all this nature. A magic power, which one can hardly understand by this prattle, which is made to be borne away and dissipated like whiffs of smoke by the wind under the leaves. Take from these murmurs of two lovers that melody which springs from the soul, and which accompanies them like a lyre, what remains is only a shade. You say: What! is that all? Yes, childish things, repetitions, laughs about nothing, inutilities, absurdities, all that is deepest and most sublime in the world! the only things which are worth being said and listened to.

These absurdities, these poverties, the man who has never heard them, the man who has never uttered them, is an imbecile and a wicked man.

Cosette said to Marius:

"Do you know my name is Euphrasie?"

"Euphrasie? Why no, your name is Cosette."

"Oh! Cosette is such an ugly name that they gave me somehow when I was little. But my real name is Euphrasie. Don't you like that name, Euphrasie?"

"Yes—but Cosette is not ugly."

"Do you like it better than Euphrasie?"

"Why—yes."

"Then I like it better, too. It is true it is pretty, Cosette. Call me Cosette."

And the smile which she added made of this dialogue an idyl worthy of a celestial grove.

At another time she looked at him steadily and exclaimed:

"Monsieur, you are handsome, you are beautiful, you are witty, you are not stupid in the least, you are much wiser than I, but I defy you with this word: I love you!"

And Marius, in a cloudless sky, thought he heard a strophe sung by a star.

Or again, she gave him a little tap because he coughed, and said to him:

"Do not cough, monsieur. I do not allow coughing here without permission. It is very naughty to cough and disturb me. I want you to be well, because, in the first place, if you were not well, I should be very unhappy. What will you have me do for you!"

And that was all purely divine.

Once Marius said to Cosette:

"Just think, I thought at one time that your name was Ursula."

This made them laugh the whole evening.

In the midst of another conversation, he happened to exclaim:

"Oh! one day at the Luxembourg I would have been glad to break the rest of the bones of an Invalide!"

But he stopped short and went no further. He would have been obliged to speak to Cosette of her garter, and that was impossible for him. There was an unknown coast there, the flesh, before which this immense innocent love recoiled with a kind of sacred awe.

Marius imagined life with Cosette like this, without anything else: to come every evening to the Rue Plumet, to put aside the complaisant old bar of the president's grating, to sit side by side upon this seat, to behold through the trees the scintillation of the commencing night, to make the fold of the knee of his pantaloons intimate with the fulness of Cosette's dress, to caress her thumb nail, to say dearest to her, to inhale one after the other the odour of the same flower, for ever, indefinitely. During this time the clouds were passing above their heads. Every breath of wind bears away more dreams from man than clouds from the sky.

That this chaste, almost severe, love was absolutely without gallantry, we will not say. "To pay compliments" to her whom we love is the first method of caressing, a demi-audacity venturing. A compliment is something like a kiss through a veil. Pleasure sets her soft seal there, even while hiding herself. Before pleasure the heart recoils, to love better. Marius' soft words, all saturated as they were with chimera, were, so to speak, sky-blue. The birds, when they are flying on high beside the angels, must hear such words. There was mingled with them, however, life, humanity, all the positiveness of which Marius was capable. It was what is said in the grotto, a prelude to what will be said in the alcove: a lyrical effusion, the strophe and the sonnet mingled, the gentle hyperboles of cooing, all the refinements of adoration arranged in a bouquet and exhaling a subtle celestial perfume, an ineffable warbling of heart to heart.

"Oh!" murmured Marius, "how beautiful you are! I dare not look at you. That is why I stare at you. You are a grace. I do not know what is the matter with me. The hem of your dress, when the tip of your shoe appears, completely overwhelms me. And then what enchanting glow when I see a glimpse of your thought. You reason astonishingly. It seems to me at times that you are a dream. Speak, I am listening to you, I am wondering at you. O Cosette! how strange and charming it is! I am really mad. You are adorable, mademoiselle. I study your feet with the microscope and your soul with the telescope."

And Cosette answered:

"I have been loving you a little more every minute since this morning."

Questions and answers fared as they might in this dialogue, always falling naturally at last upon love, like those loaded toys which always fall upon their base.

Cosette's whole person was alertness, ingenuousness, transparency, whiteness, candour, radiance. We might say of Cosette that she was pellucid. She gave to him who saw her a sensation of April and of dawn. There was dew in her eyes. Cosette was a condensation of auroral light in womanly form.

It was quite natural that Marius, adoring her, should admire her. But the truth is that this little schoolgirl, fresh from the convent mill, talked with an exquisite penetration and said at times all manner of true and delicate words. Her prattle was conversation. She made no mistakes, and saw clearly. Woman feels and speaks with the tender instinct of the heart, that infallibility. Nobody knows like a woman how to say things at the same time sweet and profound. Sweetness and depth, this is all of woman; this is all of Heaven.

In this fulness of felicity, at every instant tears came to their eyes. An insect trodden upon, a feather falling from a nest, a twig of hawthorn broken, moved their pity, and their ecstasy, sweetly drowned in melancholy, seemed to ask nothing better than to weep. The most sovereign symptom of love, is a tenderness sometimes almost insupportable.

And, by the side of this—all these contradictions are the lightning play of love—they were fond of laughing, and laughed with a charming freedom, and so familiarly that they sometimes seemed almost like two boys. Nevertheless, though hearts intoxicated with chastity may be all unconscious, nature, who can never be forgotten, is always present. There she is, with her aim, animal yet sublime; and whatever may be the innocence of souls, we feel, in the most modest intercourse, the adorable and mysterious shade which separates a couple of lovers from a pair of friends.

They worshipped each other.

The permanent and the immutable continue. There is loving, there is smiling and laughing, and little pouts with the lips, and interlacing of the fingers, and fondling speech, yet that does not hinder eternity. Two lovers hide in the evening, in the twilight, in the invisible with the birds, with the roses, they fascinate each other in the shadow with their hearts which they throw into their eyes, they murmur, they whisper, and during all this time immense librations of stars fill infinity.

II
THE STUPEFACTION OF COMPLETE HAPPINESS

THEIR existence was vague, bewildered with happiness. They did not perceive the cholera which decimated Paris that very month. They had been as confidential with each other as they could be, but this had not gone very far beyond their names. Marius had told Cosette that he was an orphan, that his name was Marius Pontmercy, that he was a lawyer, that he lived by writing things for publishers, that his father was a colonel, that he was a hero, and that he, Marius, had quarrelled with his grandfather who was rich. He had also said something about being a baron; but that had produced no effect upon Cosette. Marius baron! She did not comprehend. She did not know what that word meant. Marius was Marius. On her part she had confided to him that she had been brought up at the Convent of the Petit Picpus, that her mother was dead as well as his, that her father's name was M. Fauchelevent, that he was very kind, that he gave much to the poor, but that he was poor himself, and that he deprived himself of everything while he deprived her of nothing.

Strange to say, in the kind of symphony in which Marius had been living since he had seen Cosette, the past, even the most recent, had become so confused and distant to him that what Cosette told him satisfied him fully. He did not even think to speak to her of the night adventure at the Gorbeau tenement, the Thénardiers, the burning, and the strange attitude and the singular flight of her father. Marius had temporarily forgotten all that; he did not even know at night what he had done in the morning, nor where he had breakfasted, nor who had spoken to him; he had songs in his ear which rendered him deaf to every other thought; he existed only during the hours in which he saw Cosette. Then, as he was in Heaven, it was quite natural that he should forget the earth. They were both supporting with languor the undefinable burden of the immaterial pleasures. Thus live these somnambulists called lovers.

Alas! who has not experienced all these things? why comes there an hour when we leave this azure, and why does life continue afterwards?

Love almost replaces thought. Love is a burning forgetfulness of all else. Ask logic then of passion. There is no more an absolute logical chain in the human heart than there is a perfect geometrical figure in the celestial mechanics. To Cosette and Marius there was nothing in being beyond Marius and Cosette. The universe about them had fallen out of sight. They lived in a golden moment. There was nothing before, nothing after. It is doubtful if Marius thought whether Cosette had a father. He was so dazzled that all was effaced from his brain. Of what then did they talk, these lovers? We have seen, of the flowers, the swallows, the setting sun, the rising of the moon, of all important things. They had told all, except everything. The all of lovers is nothing. But the father, the realities, the garret, those bandits, that adventure, what was the use? and was he quite certain that that nightmare was real? They were two, they adored each other, there was nothing but that. Everything else was not. It is probable that this oblivion of the hell behind us is a part of arrival at paradise. Have we seen demons? are there any? have we trembled? have we suffered? We know nothing now about that. A rosy cloud rests upon it all.

These two beings, then, were living thus, very high, with all the improbability of nature; neither at the nadir nor at the zenith, between man and the seraph, above earth, below the ether, in the cloud; scarcely flesh and bone, soul and ecstasy from head to foot; too sublimated already to walk upon the earth, and yet too much weighed down with humanity to disappear in the sky, in suspension like atoms which are awaiting precipitation; apparently outside of destiny; ignoring that beaten track yesterday, to-day, to-morrow; astounded, swooping, floating; at times, light enough to soar into the infinity; almost ready for the eternal flight.

They were sleeping awake in this rocking cradle. O splendid lethargy of the real overwhelmed by the ideal!

Sometimes, beautiful as was Cosette, Marius closed his eyes

before her. With closed eyes is the best way of looking at the soul.

Marius and Cosette did not ask where this would lead them. They looked upon themselves as arrived. It is a strange demand for men to ask that love should anywhither.

III
SHADOW COMMENCES

JEAN VALJEAN suspected nothing.

Cosette, a little less dreamy than Marius, was cheerful, and that was enough to make Jean Valjean happy. The thoughts of Cosette, her tender preoccupations, the image of Marius which filled her soul, detracted nothing from the incomparable purity of her beautiful, chaste, and smiling forehead. She was at the age when the maiden bears her love as the angel bears her lily. And then when two lovers have an understanding they always get along well; any third person who might disturb their love, is kept in perfect blindness by a very few precautions, always the same for all lovers. Thus never any objections from Cosette to Jean Valjean. Did he wish to take a walk? yes, my dear father. Did he wish to remain at home? very well. Would he spend the evening with Cosette? she was in raptures. As he always retired at ten o'clock, at such times Marius would not come to the garden till after that hour, when from the street he would hear Cosette open the glass-door leading out on the steps. We need not say that Marius was never met by day. Jean Valjean no longer even thought that Marius was in existence. Once, only, one morning, he happened to say to Cosette: "Why, you have something white on your back!" The evening before, Marius, in a transport, had pressed Cosette against the wall.

Old Toussaint who went to bed early, thought of nothing but going to sleep, once her work was done, and was ignorant of all, like Jean Valjean.

Never did Marius set foot into the house. When he was with Cosette they hid themselves in a recess near the steps, so that they could neither be seen nor heard from the street, and they sat there, contenting themselves often, by way of conversation, with pressing each other's hands twenty times a minute while looking into the branches of the trees. At such moments, a thunderbolt might have fallen within thirty paces of them, and they would not have suspected it, so deeply was the reverie of the one absorbed and buried in the reverie of the other.

Limpid purities. Hours all white, almost all alike. Such loves as these are a collection of lily leaves and dove-down.

The whole garden was between them and the street. Whenever Marius came in and went out, he carefully replaced the bar of the grating in such a way that no derangement was visible.

He went away commonly about midnight, returning to Courfeyrac's. Courfeyrac said to Bahorel:

"Would you believe it? Marius comes home nowadays at one o'clock in the morning."

Bahorel answered:

"What would you expect? every young person has his wild oats."

At times Courfeyrac folded his arms, assumed a serious air, and said to Marius:

"You are getting dissipated, young man!"

Courfeyrac, a practical man, was not pleased at this reflection of an invisible paradise upon Marius; he had little taste for unpublished passions, he was impatient at them, and he occasionally would serve Marius with a summons to return to the real.

One morning, he threw out this admonition:

"My dear fellow, you strike me at present as being situated in the moon, kingdom of dream, province of illusion, capital Soap-Bubble. Come, be a good boy, what is her name?"

But nothing could make Marius "confess." You might have torn his nails out sooner than one of the two sacred syllables which composed that ineffable name, *Cosette*. True love is luminous as the dawn, and silent as the grave. Only there was, to Courfeyrac, this change in Marius, that he had a radiant taciturnity.

During this sweet month of May, Marius and Cosette knew these transcendent joys:

To quarrel and to say monsieur and mademoiselle, merely to say Marius and Cosette better afterwards;

To talk at length, and with most minute detail, of people who did not interest them in the least; a further proof that, in this ravishing opera which is called love, the libretto is almost nothing;

For Marius, to listen to Cosette talking dress;

For Cosette, to listen to Marius talking politics;

To hear, knee touching knee, the wagons roll along the Rue de Babylone;

To gaze upon the same planet in space, or the same worm glow in the grass;

To keep silence together; a pleasure still greater than to talk; Etc., etc.

Meanwhile various complications were approaching.

One evening Marius was making his way to the rendezvous by the Boulevard des Invalides; he usually walked with his head bent down; as he was just turning the corner of the Rue Plumet, he heard some one saying very near him:

"Good evening, Monsieur Marius."

He looked up, and recognised Eponine.

This produced a singular effect upon him. He had not thought even once of this girl since the day she brought him to the Rue Plumet, he had not seen her again, and she had completely gone out of his mind. He had motives of gratitude only towards her; he owed his present happiness to her, and still it was annoying to him to meet her.

It is a mistake to suppose that passion, when it is fortunate and pure, leads man to a state of perfection; it leads him simply, as we have said, to a state of forgetfulness. In this situation man forgets to be bad, but he also forgets to be good. Gratitude, duty, necessary and troublesome memories, vanish. At any other time Marius would have felt very differently towards Eponine. Absorbed in Cosette he had not even clearly in his mind that this Eponine's name was Eponine Thénardier, and that she bore a name written in his father's will, that name to which he would have been, a few months before, so ardently devoted. We show Marius just as he was. His father himself, disappeared somewhat from his soul beneath the splendour of his love.

He answered with some embarrassment:

"What! is it you, Eponine?"

"Why do you speak to me so sternly? Have I done anything to you?"

"No," answered he.

Certainly, he had nothing against her. Far from it. Only, he felt that he could not do otherwise, now that he had whispered to Cosette, than speak coldly to Eponine.

As he was silent, she exclaimed:

"Tell me now—"

Then she stopped. It seemed as if words failed this creature, once so reckless and so bold. She attempted to smile and could not. She resumed:

"Well?—"

Then she was silent again, and stood with her eyes cast down.

"Good evening, Monsieur Marius," said she all at once abruptly, and she went away.

IV

CAB ROLLS IN ENGLISH AND YELPS IN ARGOT

THE next day, it was the 3rd of June, the 3rd of June, 1832, a date which must be noted on account of the grave events which were at that time suspended over the horizon of Paris like thunder-clouds. Marius, at nightfall, was following the same path as the evening before, with the same rapturous thoughts in his heart, when he perceived, under the trees of the boulevard, Eponine approaching him. Two days in succession, this was too much. He turned hastily, left the boulevard, changed his route, and went to the Rue Plumet through the Rue Monsieur.

This caused Eponine to follow him to the Rue Plumet, a thing which she had not done before. She had been content until then to see him on his way through the boulevard without even seeking to meet him. The evening previous, only, had she tried to speak to him.

Eponine followed him then, without a suspicion on his part. She saw him push aside the bar of the grating, and glide into the garden.

"Why!" said she, "he is going into the house."

She approached the grating, felt of the bars one after another, and easily recognised the one which Marius had displaced.

She murmured in an undertone, with a mournful accent:

"None of that, Lisette!"

She sat down upon the surbase of the grating, close beside the bar, as if she were guarding it. It was just at the point at which the grating joined the neighbouring wall. There was an obscure corner there, in which Eponine was entirely hidden.

She remained thus for more than an hour, without stirring and without breathing, a prey to her own thoughts.

About ten o'clock in the evening, one of the two or three

passers in the Rue Plumet, a belated old bourgeois who was hurrying through this deserted and ill-famed place, keeping along the garden grating, on reaching the angle which the grating made with the wall, heard a sullen and threatening voice which said:

"I wouldn't be surprised if he came every evening!"

He cast his eyes about him, saw nobody, dared not look into that dark corner, and was very much frightened. He doubled his pace.

This person had reason to hasten, for a very few moments afterwards six men, who were walking separately and at some distance from each other along the wall, and who might have been taken for a tipsy patrol, entered the Rue Plumet.

The first to arrive at the grating of the garden stopped and waited for the others; in a second they were all six together.

These men began to talk in a low voice.

"It is *icicaille*," said one of them.

"Is there a *cab** in the garden?" asked another.

"I don't know. At all events I have *levé*† a bullet which we will make him *morfiler*." ‡

"Have you some mastic to *frangir* the *vanterne*?" §

"Yes."

"The grating is old," added a fifth, who had a voice like a ventriloquist.

"So much the better," said the second who had spoken. "It will not *criblera*¶ under the *bastringue*,‖ and will not be so hard to *faucher*." ♮

The sixth, who had not yet opened his mouth, began to examine the grating as Eponine had done an hour before, grasping each bar successively and shaking it carefully. In this way he came to the bar which Marius had loosened. Just as he was about to lay hold of this bar, a hand, starting abruptly from the shadow, fell upon his arm, he felt himself pushed sharply back by the

---

* Dog.
† Brought. From the Spanish *llevar*.
‡ Eat.
§ To break a pane by means of a plaster of mastic, which, sticking to the window, holds the glass and prevents noise.
¶ Cry.
‖ Saw.
♮ Cut.

middle of his breast, and a roughened voice said to him without crying out:

"There is a *cab*."

At the same time he saw a pale girl standing before him.

The man felt that commotion which is always given by the unexpected. He bristled up hideously; nothing is so frightful to see as ferocious beasts which are startled, their appearance when terrified is terrifying. He recoiled, and stammered:

"What is this creature?"

"Your daughter."

It was indeed Eponine who was speaking to Thénardier.

On the appearance of Eponine the five others, that is to say, Claquesous, Gueulemer, Babet, Montparnasse, and Brujon, approached without a sound, without haste, without saying a word, with the ominous slowness peculiar to these men of the night.

In their hands might be distinguished some strangely hideous tools. Gueulemer had one of those crooked crowbars which the prowlers call *fanchons*.

"Ah, there, what are you doing here? what do you want of us? are you crazy?" exclaimed Thénardier, as much as one can exclaim in a whisper. "What do you come and hinder us in our work for?"

Eponine began to laugh and sprang to his neck.

"I am here, my darling father, because I am here. Is there any law against sitting upon the stones in these days? It is you who shouldn't be here. What are you coming here for, since it is a biscuit? I told Magnon so. There is nothing to do here. But embrace me now, my dear good father! What a long time since I have seen you! You are out then?"

Thénardier tried to free himself from Eponine's arms, and muttered:

"Very well. You have embraced me. Yes, I am out. I am not in. Now, be off."

But Eponine did not loose her hold and redoubled her caresses.

"My darling father, how did you do it? You must have a good deal of wit to get out of that! Tell me about it! And my mother? where is my mother? Give me some news of mamma."

Thénardier answered:

"She is well, I don't know, let me alone, I tell you to be off."

"I don't want to go away just now," said Eponine, with the pettishness of a spoiled child, "you send me away when here it is four months that I haven't seen you, and when I have hardly had time to embrace you."

And she caught her father again by the neck.

"Ah! come now, this is foolish," said Babet.

"Let us hurry!" said Gueulemer, "the *coqueurs* may come along."

The ventriloquist sang this distich:

> Nous n' sommes pas le jour de l'an,
> A bécoter papa maman.*

Eponine turned towards the five bandits.

"Why, this is Monsieur Brujon. Good-day, Monsieur Babet. Good-day, Monsieur Claquesous. Don't you remember me, Monsieur Gueulemer? How goes it, Montparnasse?"

"Yes, they recognise you," said Thénardier. "But good-day, good-night, keep off! don't disturb us!"

"It is the hour for foxes, and not for pullets," said Montparnasse.

"You see well enough that we are going to *goupiner icigo*,"† added Babet.

Eponine took Montparnasse's hand.

"Take care," said he, "you will cut yourself, I have a *lingre*‡ open."

"My darling Montparnasse," answered Eponine very gently, "we must have confidence in people. I am my father's daughter, perhaps. Monsieur Babet, Monsieur Gueulemer, it is I who was charged with finding out about this affair."

It is remarkable that Eponine did not speak argot. Since she had known Marius, that horrid language had become impossible to her.

She pressed in her little hand, as bony and weak as the hand of a corpse, the great rough fingers of Gueulemer, and continued:

"You know very well that I am not a fool. Ordinarily you believe me. I have done you service on occasion. Well, I have

---

* 'Tis not the first of the new year,
    To hug papa and mamma dear.
† To work here.
‡ Knife.

learned all about this, you would expose yourself uselessly, do you see. I swear to you that there is nothing to be done in that house."

"There are lone women," said Gueulemer.

"No. The people have moved away."

"The candles have not, anyhow!" said Babet.

And he showed Eponine, through the top of the trees, a light which was moving about in the garret of the cottage. It was Toussaint, who had sat up to hang out her clothes to dry.

Eponine made a final effort.

"Well," said she, "they are very poor people, and it is a shanty where there isn't a sou."

"Go to the devil!" cried Thénardier. "When we have turned the house over, and when we have put the cellar at the top and the garret at the bottom, we will tell you what there is inside, and whether it is *balles*, *ronds*, or *broques*."*

And he pushed her to pass by.

"My good friend Monsieur Montparnasse," said Eponine, "I beg you, you who are a good boy, don't go in!"

"Take care, you will cut yourself," replied Montparnasse.

Thénardier added, with his decisive tone:

"Clear out, *fée*, and let men do their work!"

Eponine let go of Montparnasse's hand, which she had taken again, and said:

"You will go into that house then?"

"Just a little!" said the ventriloquist, with a sneer.

Then she placed her back against the grating, faced the six bandits who were armed to the teeth, and to whom the night gave faces of demons, and said in a low and firm voice:

"Well, I, I won't have it."

They stopped astounded. The ventriloquist, however, finished his sneer. She resumed.

"Friends! listen to me. That isn't the thing. Now I speak. In the first place, if you go into the garden, if you touch this grating, I shall cry out, I shall rap on doors, I shall wake everybody up, I shall have all six of you arrested, I shall call the sergents de ville."

"She would do it," said Thénardier in a low tone to Brujon and the ventriloquist.

* Francs, sous, or farthings.

She shook her head, and added:

"Beginning with my father!"

Thénardier approached.

"Not so near, goodman!" said she.

He drew back, muttering between his teeth: "Why, what is the matter with her?" and he added:

"Slut!"

She began to laugh in a terrible way:

"As you will, you shall not go in, I am not the daughter of a dog, for I am the daughter of a wolf. There are six of you, what is that to me? You are men. Now, I am a woman. I am not afraid of you, not a bit. I tell you that you shall not go into this house, because it does not please me. If you approach, I shall bark. I told you so, I am the *cab*, I don't care for you. Go your ways, you annoy me. Go where you like, but don't come here, I forbid it! You have knives, I have feet and hands. That makes no difference, come on now!"

She took a step towards the bandits, she was terrible, she began to laugh.

"The devil! I am not afraid. This summer, I shall be hungry; this winter, I shall be cold. Are they fools, these geese of men, to think that they can make a girl afraid! Of what! afraid? Ah, pshaw, indeed! Because you have hussies of mistresses who hide under the bed when you raise your voice, it won't do here! I, I am not afraid of anything!"

She kept her eye fixed upon Thénardier, and said:

"Not even you, father!"

Then she went on, casting her ghastly bloodshot eyes over the bandits:

"What is it to me whether somebody picks me up to-morrow on the pavement of the Rue Plumet, beaten to death with a club by my father, or whether they find me in a year in the ditches of Saint Cloud, or at the Ile de Cygnes, among the old rotten rubbish and the dead dogs?"

She was obliged to stop; a dry cough seized her, her breath came like a rattle from her narrow and feeble chest.

She resumed:

"I have but to cry out, they come, bang! You are six; but I am everybody."

Thénardier made a movement towards her.

" 'Proach not!" cried she.

He stopped, and said to her mildly:

"Well, no; I will not approach, but don't speak so loud. Daughter, you want then to hinder us in our work? Still we must earn our living. Have you no love for your father now?"

"You bother me," said Eponine.

"Still we must live, we must eat——"

"Die."

Saying which, she sat down on the surbase of the grating, humming:

> Mon bras si dodu,
> Ma jambe bien faite,
> Et le temps perdu.*

She had her elbow on her knee and her chin in her hand, and she was swinging her foot with an air of indifference. Her dress was full of holes, and showed her sharp shoulder-blades. The neighbouring lamp lit up her profile and her attitude. Nothing could be more resolute or more surprising.

The six assassins, sullen and abashed at being held in check by a girl, went under the protecting shade of the lantern and held counsel, with humiliated and furious shrugs of their shoulders.

She watched them the while with a quiet yet indomitable air.

"Something is the matter with her," said Babet. "Some reason. Is she in love with the *cab*? But it is a pity to lose it. Two women, an old fellow who lodges in a back-yard, there are pretty good curtains at the windows. The old fellow must be a *guinal*.† I think it is a good thing."

"Well, go in the rest of you," exclaimed Montparnasse. "Do the thing. I will stay here with the girl, and if she trips——"

He made the open knife which he had in his hand gleam in the light of the lantern.

Thénardier said not a word and seemed ready for anything.

Brujon, who was something of an oracle, and who had, as we know, "got up the thing," had not yet spoken. He appeared thoughtful. He had a reputation for recoiling from nothing, and

---

* So plump is my arm,
  My leg so well formed,
  Yet my time has no charm.
† A Jew.

they knew that he had plundered, from sheer bravado, a police station. Moreover he made verses and songs, which gave him a great authority.

Babet questioned him.

"You don't say anything, Brujon?"

Brujon remained silent a minute longer, then he shook his head in several different ways, and at last decided to speak.

"Here: I met two sparrows fighting this morning; to-night, I run against a woman quarrelling. All this is bad. Let us go away."

They went away.

As they went, Montparnasse murmured:

"No matter, if they had said so, I would have made her feel the weight of my hand."

Babet answered:

"Not I. I don't strike a lady."

At the corner of the street, they stopped and exchanged this enigmatic dialogue in a smothered voice:

"Where are we going to sleep to-night?"

"Under *Patin*."*

"Have you the key of the grating with you, Thénardier?"

"Humph."

Eponine, who had not taken her eyes off from them, saw them turn back the way they had come. She rose and began to creep along the walls and houses behind them. She followed them as far as the boulevard. There, they separated, and she saw these men sink away in the obscurity into which they seemed to melt.

V
THINGS OF THE NIGHT

AFTER the departure of the bandits, the Rue Plumet resumed its quiet night appearance.

What had just taken place in this street would not have astonished a forest. The trees, the copse, the heath, the branches roughly intertangled, the tall grass, have a darkly mysterious existence; this wild multitude sees there sudden apparitions of the invisible; there what is below man distinguishes through the dark what is above man; and there in the night meet things

* Pantin, Paris.

unknown by us living men. Nature, bristling and tawny, is startled at certain approaches in which she seems to feel the supernatural. The forces of the shadow know each other, and have mysterious balancings among themselves. Teeth and claws dread the intangible. Bloodthirsty brutality, voracious and starving appetites in quest of prey, instincts armed with nails and jaws which find in the belly their origin and their object behold and snuff with anxiety the impassive spectral figure prowling beneath a shroud, standing in its dim shivering robe, and seeming to them to live with a dead and terrible life. These brutalities, which are matter only, confusedly dread having to do with the infinite dark condensed into an unknown being. A black figure barring the passage stops the wild beast short. That which comes from the graveyard intimidates and disconcerts that which comes from the den; the ferocious is afraid of the sinister: wolves recoil before a ghoul.

VI

MARIUS BECOMES SO REAL AS TO GIVE COSETTE HIS ADDRESS

WHILE this species of dog in human form was mounting guard over the grating, and the six bandits were slinking away before a girl, Marius was with Cosette.

Never had the sky been more studded with stars, or more charming, the trees more tremulous, the odour of the shrubs more penetrating; never had the birds gone to sleep in the leaves with a softer sound; never had all the harmonies of the universal serenity better responded to the interior music of love; never had Marius been more enamoured, more happy, more in ecstasy. But he had found Cosette sad. Cosette had been weeping. Her eyes were red.

It was the first cloud in this wonderful dream.

Marius' first word was:

"What is the matter?"

"See."

Then she sat down on the seat near the stairs, and as he took his place all trembling beside her, she continued:

"My father told me this morning to hold myself in readiness, that he had business, and that perhaps we should go away."

Marius shuddered from head to foot.

When we are at the end of life, to die means to go away; when we are at the beginning, to go away means to die.

For six weeks Marius, gradually, slowly, by degrees, had been each day taking possession of Cosette. A possession entirely ideal, but thorough. As we have entirely explained, in the first love, the soul is taken far before the body; afterwards the body is taken far before the soul; sometimes the soul is not taken at all; the Faublas and the Prudhommes add: because there is none; but the sarcasm is fortunately a blasphemy. Marius then possessed Cosette, as minds possess; but he wrapped her in his whole soul, and clasped her jealously with an incredible conviction. He possessed her smile, her breath, her perfume, the deep radiance of her blue eyes, the softness of her skin when he touched her hand, the charming mark that she had on her neck, all her thoughts. They had agreed never to go to sleep without dreaming of each other, and they had kept their word. He possessed all Cosette's dreams. He beheld untiringly, and he sometimes touched with his breath, the short hairs at the back of her neck, and he declared to himself that there was not one of those little hairs which did not belong to him, Marius. He gazed upon and adored the things which she wore, her knot of ribbon, her gloves, her cuffs, her slippers, as sacred objects of which he was master. He thought that he was lord of those pretty shell-combs which she had in her hair, and he said to himself even, dim and confused stammerings of dawning desire, that there was not a thread of her dress, not a mesh in her stockings, not a fold of her corset, which was not his. At Cosette's side, he felt near his wealth, near his property, near his despot, and near his slave. It seemed as if they so mingled their souls, that if they desired to take them back again, it would have been impossible to identify them. "This one is mine." "No, it is mine." "I assure you that you are mistaken. This is really I." "What you take for you, is I." Marius was something which was a part of Cosette, and Cosette was something which was a part of Marius. Marius felt Cosette living within him. To have Cosette, to possess Cosette, this to him was not separable from breathing. Into the midst of this faith, of this intoxication, of this virginal possession, marvellous and absolute, of this sovereignty, these words: "We are going away," fell all at once, and the sharp voice of reality cried to him: "Cosette is not yours!"

Marius awoke. For six weeks Marius had lived, as we have

said, outside of life; this word, going away, brought him roughly back to it.

He could not find a word. She said to him in her turn:

"What is the matter?"

He answered so low that Cosette hardly heard him:

"I don't understand what you have said."

She resumed:

"This morning my father told me to arrange all my little affairs and to be ready, that he would give me his clothes to pack, that he was obliged to take a journey, that we were going away, that we must have a large trunk for me and a small one for him, to get all that ready within a week from now, and that we should go perhaps to England."

"But it is monstrous!" exclaimed Marius.

It is certain that at that moment, in Marius' mind, no abuse of power, no violence, no abomination of the most cruel tyrants, no action of Busiris, Tiberius, or Henry VIII., was equal in ferocity to this: M. Fauchelevent taking his daughter to England because he has business.

He asked in a feeble voice:

"And when would you start?"

"He didn't say when."

"And when should you return?"

"He didn't say when."

Marius arose, and said coldly:

"Cosette, shall you go?"

Cosette turned upon him her beautiful eyes full of anguish and answered with a sort of bewilderment:

"Where?"

"To England? shall you go?"

"Why do you speak so to me?"

"I ask you if you shall go?"

"What would you have me do?" said she, clasping her hands.

"So, you will go?"

"If my father goes."

"So, you will go?"

Cosette took Marius' hand and pressed it without answering.

"Very well," said Marius. "Then I shall go elsewhere."

Cosette felt the meaning of this word still more than she understood it. She turned so pale that her face became white in the darkness. She stammered:

"What do you mean?"

Marius looked at her, then slowly raised his eyes towards heaven and answered:

"Nothing."

When his eyes were lowered, he saw Cosette smiling upon him. The smile of the woman whom we love has a brilliancy which we can see by night.

"How stupid we are! Marius, I have an idea."

"What?"

"Go if we go! I will tell you where! Come and join me where I am!"

Marius was now a man entirely awakened. He had fallen back into reality. He cried to Cosette:

"Go with you? are you mad? But it takes money, and I have none! Go to England? Why I owe now, I don't know, more than ten louis to Courfeyrac, one of my friends whom you do not know! Why I have an old hat which is not worth three francs, I have a coat from which some of the buttons are gone in front, my shirt is all torn, my elbows are out, my boots let in the water; for six weeks I have not thought of it, and I have not told you about it. Cosette! I am a miserable wretch. You only see me at night, and you give me your love; if you should see me by day, you would give me a sou! Go to England? Ah! I have not the means to pay for a passport!"

He threw himself against a tree which was near by, standing with his arms above his head, his forehead against the bark, feeling neither the tree which was chafing his skin, nor the fever which was hammering his temples, motionless, and ready to fall, like a statue of Despair.

He was a long time thus. One might remain through eternity in such abysses. At last he turned. He heard behind him a little stifled sound, soft and sad.

It was Cosette sobbing.

She had been weeping more than two hours while Marius had been thinking.

He came to her, fell on his knees, and, prostrating himself slowly, he took the tip of her foot which peeped from under her dress and kissed it.

She allowed it in silence. There are moments when woman accepts, like a goddess sombre and resigned, the religion of love.

"Do not weep," said he.

She murmured:

"Because I am perhaps going away, and you cannot come!"

He continued:

"Do you love me?"

She answered him by sobbing out that word of Paradise which is never more enrapturing than when it comes through tears:

"I adore you."

He continued with a tone of voice which was an inexpressible caress:

"Do not weep. Tell me, will you do this for me, not to weep?"

"Do you love me, too?" said she.

He caught her hand.

"Cosette, I have never given my word of honour to anybody, because I stand in awe of my word of honour. I feel that my father is at my side. Now, I give you my most sacred word of honour that, if you go away, I shall die."

There was in the tone with which he pronounced these words a melancholy so solemn and so quiet, that Cosette trembled. She felt that chill which is given by a stern and true fact passing over us. From the shock she ceased weeping.

"Now listen," said he, "do not expect me to-morrow."

"Why not?"

"Do not expect me till the day after to-morrow!"

"Oh! why not?"

"You will see."

"A day without seeing you! Why, that is impossible."

"Let us sacrifice one day to gain perhaps a whole life."

And Marius added in an under tone, and aside:

"He is a man who changes none of his habits, and he has never received anybody till evening."

"What man are you speaking of?" inquired Cosette.

"Me? I said nothing."

"What is it you hope for, then?"

"Wait till the day after to-morrow."

"You wish it?"

"Yes, Cosette."

She took his head in both her hands, rising on tiptoe to reach his height, and striving to see his hope in his eyes.

Marius continued:

"It occurs to me, you must know my address, something

may happen, we don't know; I live with that friend named Courfeyrac, Rue de la Verrerie, number 16."

He put his hand in his pocket, took out a penknife, and wrote with the blade upon the plastering of the wall:

16, Rue de la Verrerie.

Cosette, meanwhile, began to look into his eyes again.

"Tell me your idea. Marius, you have an idea. Tell me. Oh! tell me, so that I may pass a good night!"

"My idea is this: that it is impossible that God should wish to separate us. Expect me the day after to-morrow."

"What shall I do till then?" said Cosette. "You, you are out doors, you go, you come! How happy men are. I have to stay alone. Oh! how sad I shall be! What is it you are going to do to-morrow evening, tell me?"

"I shall try a plan."

"Then I will pray God, and I will think of you from now till then, that you may succeed. I will not ask any more questions, since you wish me not to. You are my master. I shall spend my evening to-morrow singing that music of Euryanthe which you love, and which you came to hear one evening behind my shutter. But the day after to-morrow you will come early; I shall expect you at night, at nine o'clock precisely. I forewarn you. Oh, dear! how sad it is that the days are long! You understand; ——when the clock strikes nine, I shall be in the garden."

"And I too."

And without saying it, moved by the same thought, drawn on by those electric currents which put two lovers in continual communication, both intoxicated with pleasure even in their grief, they fell into each other's arms, without perceiving that their lips were joined, while their uplifted eyes, overflowing with ecstasy and full of tears, were fixed upon the stars.

When Marius went out, the street was empty. It was the moment when Eponine was following the bandits to the boulevard.

While Marius was thinking with his head against the tree, an idea had passed through his mind; an idea, alas! which he himself deemed senseless and impossible. He had formed a desperate resolution.

VII

THE OLD HEART AND YOUNG HEART IN PRESENCE

GRANDFATHER Gillenormand had, at this period, fully completed his ninety-first year. He still lived with Mademoiselle Gillenormand, Rue des Filles du Calvaire, No. 6, in that old house which belonged to him. He was, as we remember, one of those antique old men who await death still erect, whom age loads without making them stoop, and whom grief itself does not bend.

Still, for some time, his daughter had said: "My father is failing." He no longer beat the servants; he struck his cane with less animation on the landing of the stairs, when Basque was slow in opening the door. The revolution of July had hardly exasperated him for six months. He had seen almost tranquilly in the *Moniteur* this coupling of words: M. Humblot Conté, peer of France. The fact is, that the old man was filled with dejection. He did not bend, he did not yield; that was no more a part of his physical than of his moral nature; but he felt himself interiorly failing. Four years he had been waiting for Marius, with his foot down, that is just the word, in the conviction that that naughty little scapegrace would ring at his door some day or other: now he had come, in certain gloomy hours, to say to himself that even if Marius should delay, but little longer—It was not death that was insupportable to him; it was the idea that perhaps he should never see Marius again. Never see Marius again,—that had not, even for an instant, entered into his thought until this day; now this idea began to appear to him, and it chilled him. Absence, as always happens when feelings are natural and true, had only increased his grandfather's love for the ungrateful child who had gone away like that. It is on December nights, with the thermometer at zero, that we think most of the sun. M. Gillenormand was, or thought himself, in any event, incapable of taking a step, he the grandfather, towards his grandson; "I would die first," said he. He acknowledged no fault on his part; but he thought of Marius only with a deep tenderness and the mute despair of an old goodman who is going away into the darkness.

He was beginning to lose his teeth, which added to his sadness.

M. Gillenormand, without however acknowledging it to

himself for he would have been furious and ashamed at it, had never loved a mistress as he loved Marius.

He had had hung in his room, at the foot of his bed, as the first thing which he wished to see on awaking, an old portrait of his other daughter, she who was dead, Madame Pontmercy, a portrait taken when she was eighteen years old. He looked at this portrait incessantly. He happened one day to say, while looking at it:

"I think it looks like the child."

"Like my sister?" replied Mademoiselle Gillenormand. "Why yes."

The old man added:

"And like him also."

Once, as he was sitting, his knees pressed together, and his eyes almost closed, in a posture of dejection, his daughter ventured to say to him:

"Father, are you still so angry with him?"

She stopped, not daring to go further.

"With whom?" asked he.

"With that poor Marius?"

He raised his old head, laid his thin and wrinkled fist upon the table, and cried in his most irritated and quivering tone:

"Poor Marius, you say? That gentleman is a rascal, a worthless knave, a little ungrateful vanity, with no heart, no soul, a proud, a wicked man!"

And he turned away that his daughter might not see the tear he had in his eyes.

Three days later, after a silence which had lasted for four hours, he said to his daughter snappishly:

"I have had the honour to beg Mademoiselle Gillenormand never to speak to me of him."

Aunt Gillenormand gave up all attempts and came to this profound diagnosis: "My father never loved my sister very much after her folly. It is clear that he detests Marius."

"After her folly" meant: after she married the colonel.

Still, as may have been conjectured, Mademoiselle Gillenormand had failed in her attempt to substitute her favourite, the officer of lancers, for Marius. The supplanter Théodule had not succeeded. Monsieur Gillenormand had not accepted the *quid pro quo*. The void in the heart does not accommodate itself to a proxy. Théodule, for his part, even while snuffing the inheritance, revolted at the drudgery of pleasing. The goodman wearied the lancer, and the lancer shocked the goodman. Lieutenant Théodule was lively doubtless, but a babbler; frivolous, but vulgar; a good liver, but of bad company; he had mistresses, it is true, and he talked about them a good deal, that is also true; but he talked about them badly. All his qualities had a defect. Monsieur Gillenormand was wearied out with hearing him tell of all the favours that he had won in the neighbourhood of his barracks, Rue de Babylone. And then Lieutenant Théodule sometimes came in his uniform with the tricolour cockade. This rendered him altogether insupportable. Grandfather Gillenormand, at last, said to his daughter: "I have had enough of him, your Théodule. I have little taste for warriors in time of peace. Entertain him yourself, if you like. I am not sure, but I like the sabrers even better than the trailers of the sabre. The clashing of blades in battle is not so wretched, after all, as the rattling of the sheaths on the pavement. And then, to harness himself like a bully, and to strap himself up like a flirt, to wear a corset under a cuirass, is to be ridiculous twice over. A genuine man keeps himself at an equal distance from swagger and roguery. Neither hector, nor heartless. Keep your Théodule for yourself."

It was of no use for his daughter to say: "Still he is your grandnephew," it turned out that Monsieur Gillenormand, who was grandfather to the ends of his nails, was not granduncle at all.

In reality, as he had good judgment and made the comparison, Théodule only served to increase his regret for Marius.

One evening, it was the 4th of June, which did not prevent Monsieur Gillenormand from having a blazing fire in his fireplace, he had said good-night to his daughter who was sewing in the adjoining room. He was alone in his room with the rural scenery, his feet upon the andirons, half enveloped in his vast coromandel screen with nine folds, leaning upon his table on which two candles were burning under a green shade, buried in his tapestried arm-chair, a book in his hand, but not reading. He was dressed, according to his custom, *en incroyable*, and resembled an antique portrait of Garat. This would have caused him to be followed in the streets, but his daughter always covered him when he went out, with a huge bishop's doublet, which hid his dress. At home, except in getting up and going to bed, he never wore a dressing-gown. "*It gives an old look*," said he.

Monsieur Gillenormand thought of Marius lovingly and bitterly; and, as usual, the bitterness predominated. An increase of tenderness always ended by boiling over and turning into indignation. He was at that point where we seek to adopt a course, and to accept what rends us. He was just explaining to himself that there was now no longer any reason for Marius to return, that if he had been going to return, he would have done so already, that he must give him up. He endeavoured to bring himself to the idea that it was over with and that he would die without seeing "that gentleman" again. But his whole nature revolted; his old paternity could not consent to it. "What?" said he, this was his sorrowful refrain, "he will not come back!" His bald head had fallen upon his breast, and he was vaguely fixing a lamentable and irritated look upon the embers on his hearth.

In the deepest of this reverie, his old domestic, Basque, came in and asked:

"Can monsieur receive Monsieur Marius?"

The old man straightened up, pallid and like a corpse which rises under a galvanic shock. All his blood had flown back to his heart. He faltered:

"Monsieur Marius what?"

"I don't know," answered Basque, intimidated and thrown out of countenance by his master's appearance. "I have not seen him. Nicolette just told me: There is a young man here, say that it is Monsieur Marius."

M. Gillenormand stammered out in a whisper:

"Show him in."

And he remained in the same attitude, his head shaking, his eyes fixed on the door. It opened. A young man entered. It was Marius.

Marius stopped at the door, as if waiting to be asked to come in.

His almost wretched dress was not perceived in the obscurity produced by the green shade. Only his face, calm and grave, but strangely sad, could be distinguished.

M. Gillenormand, as if congested with astonishment and joy, sat for some moments without seeing anything but a light, as when one is in the presence of an apparition. He was almost fainting; he perceived Marius through a blinding haze. It was indeed he, it was indeed Marius!

At last! after four years! He seized him, so to speak, all over at a glance. He thought him beautiful, noble, striking, adult, a complete man, with graceful attitude and pleasing air. He would gladly have opened his arms, called him, rushed upon him, his heart melted in rapture, affectionate words welled and overflowed in his breast; indeed, all his tenderness started up and came to his lips, and, through the contrast which was the groundwork of his nature, there came forth a harsh word. He said abruptly:

"What is it you come here for?"

Marius answered with embarrassment:

"Monsieur——"

M. Gillenormand would have had Marius throw himself into his arms. He was displeased with Marius and with himself. He felt that he was rough, and that Marius was cold. It was to the goodman an insupportable and irritating anguish, to feel himself so tender and so much in tears within, while he could only be harsh without. The bitterness returned. He interrupted Marius with a sharp tone:

"Then what do you come for?"

This then signified: *If you don't come to embrace me.* Marius looked at his grandfather, whose pallor had changed to marble.

"Monsieur——"

The old man continued, in a stern voice:

"Do you come to ask my pardon? have you seen your fault?"

He thought to put Marius on the track, and that "the child" was going to bend. Marius shuddered; it was the disavowal of his father which was asked of him; he cast down his eyes and answered:

"No, monsieur."

"And then," exclaimed the old man impetuously, with a grief which was bitter and full of anger, "what do you want with me?"

Marius clasped his hands, took a step, and said in a feeble and trembling voice:

"Monsieur, have pity on me."

This word moved M. Gillenormand; spoken sooner, it would have softened him, but it came too late. The grandfather arose; he supported himself upon his cane with both hands, his lips were white, his forehead quivered, but his tall stature commanded the stooping Marius.

"Pity on you, monsieur! The youth asks pity from the old

man of ninety-one! You are entering life, I am leaving it; you go to the theatre, the ball, the café, the billiard-room; you have wit, you please the women, you are a handsome fellow, while I cannot leave my chimney-corner in midsummer; you are rich, with the only riches there are, while I have all the poverties of old age; infirmity, isolation. You have your thirty-two teeth, a good stomach, a keen eye, strength, appetite, health, cheerfulness, a forest of black hair, while I have not even white hair left; I have lost my teeth, I am losing my legs, I am losing my memory, there are three names of streets which I am always confounding, the Rue Charlot, the Rue du Chaume, and the Rue Saint Claude, there is where I am; you have the whole future before you full of sunshine, while I am beginning not to see another drop of it, so deep am I getting into the night; you are in love, of course, I am not loved by anybody in the world; and you ask pity of me. Zounds, Molière forgot this. If that is the way you jest at the Palais, Messieurs Lawyers, I offer you my sincere compliments. You are funny fellows."

And the octogenarian resumed in an angry and stern voice:

"Come now, what do you want of me?"

"Monsieur," said Marius, "I know that my presence is displeasing to you, but I come only to ask one thing of you, and then I will go away immediately."

"You are a fool!" said the old man. "Who tells you to go away?"

This was the translation of those loving words which he had deep in his heart: *Come, ask my pardon now! Throw yourself on my neck!* M. Gillenormand felt that Marius was going to leave him in a few moments, that his unkind reception repelled him, that his harshness was driving him away; he said all this to himself, and his anguish increased; and as his anguish immediately turned into anger, his harshness augmented. He would have had Marius comprehend, and Marius did not comprehend; which rendered the goodman furious. He continued:

"What! you have left me! me, your grandfather, you have left my house to go nobody knows where; you have afflicted your aunt, you have been, that is clear, it is more pleasant, leading the life of a bachelor, playing the elegant, going home at all hours, amusing yourself, you have not given me a sign of life; you have contracted debts without even telling me to pay them; you have made yourself a breaker of windows and a rioter, and, at the end of four years, you come to my house, and have nothing to say but that!"

This violent method of pushing the grandson to tenderness produced only silence on the part of Marius. M. Gillenormand folded his arms, a posture which with him was particularly imperious, and apostrophised Marius bitterly.

"Let us make an end of it. You have come to ask something of me, say you? Well what? what is it? speak!"

"Monsieur," said Marius, with the look of a man who feels that he is about to fall into an abyss, "I come to ask your permission to marry."

M. Gillenormand rang. Basque half opened the door.

"Send my daughter in."

A second later—the door opened again. Mademoiselle Gillenormand did not come in, but showed herself. Marius was standing mute, his arms hanging down, with the look of a criminal. M. Gillenormand was coming and going up and down the room. He turned towards his daughter and said to her:

"Nothing. It is Monsieur Marius. Bid him good evening. Monsieur wishes to marry. That is all. Go."

The crisp, harsh tones of the old man's voice announced a strange fulness of feeling. The aunt looked at Marius with a bewildered air, appeared hardly to recognise him, allowed neither a motion nor a syllable to escape her, and disappeared at a breath from her father, quicker than a dry leaf before a hurricane.

Meanwhile Grandfather Gillenormand had returned and stood with his back to the fire-place.

"You marry! at twenty-one! You have arranged that! You have nothing but a permission to ask! a formality. Sit down, monsieur. Well, you have had a revolution since I had the honour to see you. The Jacobins have had the upper hand. You ought to be satisfied. You are a republican, are you not, since you are a baron? You arrange that. The republic is sauce to the barony. Are you decorated by July?—did you take a bit of the Louvre, monsieur? There is close by here, in the Rue Saint Antoine, opposite the Rue des Nonaindières, a ball incrusted in the wall of the third story of a house with this inscription: July 28th, 1830. Go and see that. That produces a good effect. Ah! Pretty things those friends of yours do. By the way, are they not making a fountain in the square of the monument of M. the

Duke de Berry? So you want to marry? Whom? can the question be asked without indiscretion?"

He stopped, and, before Marius had had time to answer, he added violently:

"Come now, you have a business? your fortune made? how much do you earn at your lawyer's trade?"

"Nothing," said Marius, with a firmness and resolution which were almost savage.

"Nothing? you have nothing to live on but the twelve hundred livres which I send you?"

Marius made no answer. M. Gillenormand continued:

"Then I understand the girl is rich?"

"As I am."

"What! no dowry?"

"No."

"Some expectations?"

"I believe not."

"With nothing to her back! and what is the father?"

"I do not know."

"What is her name?"

"Mademoiselle Fauchelevent."

"Fauchewhat?"

"Fauchelevent."

"Pttt!" said the old man.

"Monsieur!" exclaimed Marius.

M. Gillenormand interrupted him with the tone of a man who is talking to himself.

"That is it, twenty-one, no business, twelve hundred livres a year, Madame the Baroness Pontmercy will go to the market to buy two sous' worth of parsley."

"Monsieur," said Marius, in the desperation of the last vanishing hope, "I supplicate you! I conjure you, in the name of heaven, with clasped hands, monsieur, I throw myself at your feet, allow me to marry her!"

The old man burst into a shrill, dreary laugh, through which he coughed and spoke.

"Ha, ha, ha! you said to yourself, 'The devil! I will go and find that old wig, that silly dolt! What a pity that I am not twenty-five! how I would toss him a good respectful notice! how I would give him the go-by. Never mind, I will say to him: Old idiot, you are too happy to see me, I desire to marry, I desire to espouse mamselle no matter whom, daughter of monsieur no matter what, I have no shoes, she has no chemise, all right; I desire to throw to the dogs my career, my future, my youth, my life; I desire to make a plunge into misery with a wife at my neck, that is my idea, you must consent to it! and the old fossil will consent.' Go, my boy, as you like, tie your stone to yourself, espouse your Pousselevent, your Couplevent—Never, monsieur! never!"

"Father!"

"Never!"

At the tone in which this "never" was pronounced Marius lost all hope. He walked the room with slow steps, his head bowed down, tottering, more like a man who is dying than like one who is going away. M. Gillenormand followed him with his eyes, and, at the moment the door opened and Marius was going out, he took four steps with the senile vivacity of impetuous and self-willed old men, seized Marius by the collar, drew him back forcibly into the room, threw him into an arm-chair, and said to him:

"Tell me about it!"

It was that single word, *father*, dropped by Marius, which had caused this revolution.

Marius looked at him in bewilderment. The changing countenance of M. Gillenormand expressed nothing now but a rough and ineffable good-nature. The guardian had given place to the grandfather.

"Come, let us see, speak, tell me about your love scrapes, jabber, tell me all! Lord! how foolish these young folks are!"

"Father," resumed Marius——

The old man's whole face shone with an unspeakable radiance.

"Yes! that is it! call me father, and you shall see!"

There was now something so kind, so sweet, so open, so paternal in this abruptness, that Marius, in this sudden passage from discouragement to hope, was, as it were, intoxicated, stupefied. He was sitting near the tables, the light of the candle made the wretchedness of his dress apparent, and the grandfather gazed at it in astonishment.

"Well, father," said Marius——

"Come now," interrupted M. Gillenormand, "then you really haven't a sou? you are dressed like a robber."

He fumbled in a drawer and took out a purse, which he laid upon the table:

"Here, there is a hundred louis, buy yourself a hat."

"Father," pursued Marius, "my good father, if you knew. I love her. You don't realise it; the first time that I saw her was at the Luxembourg, she came there; in the beginning I did not pay much attention to her, and then I do not know how it came about, I fell in love with her. Oh! how wretched it has made me! Now at last I see her every day, at her own house, her father does not know it, only think that they are going away, we see each other in the garden in the evening, her father wants to take her to England, then I said to myself: I will go and see my grandfather and tell him about it. I should go crazy in the first place, I should die, I should make myself sick, I should throw myself into the river. I must marry her because I should go crazy. Now, that is the whole truth, I do not believe that I have forgotten anything. She lives in a garden where there is a railing, in the Rue Plumet. It is near the Invalides."

Grandfather Gillenormand, radiant with joy, had sat down by Marius' side. While listening to him and enjoying the sound of his voice, he enjoyed at the same time a long pinch of snuff. At that word, Rue Plumet, he checked his inspiration and let the rest of his snuff fall on his knees.

"Rue Plumet!—you say Rue Plumet?—Let us see now! —Are there not some barracks down there? Why yes, that is it. Your cousin Théodule has told me about her. The lancer, the officer.—A lassie, my good friend, a lassie!—Lord yes, Rue Plumet. That is what used to be called Rue Blomet. It comes back to me now. I have heard tell about this little girl of the grating in the Rue Plumet. In a garden, a Pamela. Your taste is not bad. They say she is nice. Between ourselves, I believe that ninny of a lancer has paid his court to her a little. I do not know how far it went. After all that does not amount to anything. And then, we must not believe him. He is a boaster. Marius! I think it is very well for a young man like you to be in love. It belongs to your age. I like you better in love than as a Jacobin. I like you better taken by a petticoat, Lord! by twenty petticoats, than by Monsieur de Robespierre. For my part, I do myself this justice that in the matter of *sansculottes*, I have never liked anything but women. Pretty women are pretty women, the devil! there is no objection to that. As to the little girl, she receives you unknown to papa. That is all right. I have had adventures like that myself. More than one. Do you know how we do? we don't take the thing ferociously; we don't rush into the tragic; we don't conclude with marriage and with Monsieur the Mayor and his scarf. We are altogether a shrewd fellow. We have good sense. Slip over it, mortals, don't marry. We come and find grandfather who is a goodman at heart, and who almost always has a few rolls of louis in an old drawer; we say to him: 'Grandfather, that's how it is.' And grandfather says: 'That is all natural. Youth must fare and old age must wear. I have been young, you will be old. Go on, my boy, you will repay this to your grandson. There are two hundred pistoles. Amuse yourself, roundly! Nothing better! that is the way the thing should be done. We don't marry, but that doesn't hinder.' You understand me?"

Marius, petrified and unable to articulate a word, shook his head.

The goodman burst into a laugh, winked his old eye, gave him a tap on the knee, looked straight into his eyes with a significant and sparkling expression, and said to him with the most amorous shrug of the shoulders:

"Stupid! make her your mistress."

Marius turned pale. He had understood nothing of all that his grandfather had been saying. This rigmarole of Rue Blomet, of Pamela, of barracks, of a lancer, had passed before Marius like a phantasmagoria. Nothing of all could relate to Cosette, who was a lily. The goodman was wandering. But this wandering had terminated in a word which Marius did understand, and which was a deadly insult to Cosette. That phrase, *make her your mistress*, entered the heart of the chaste young man like a sword.

He rose, picked up his hat which was on the floor, and walked towards the door with a firm and assured step. There he turned, bowed profoundly before his grandfather, raised his head again and said:

"Five years ago you outraged my father; to-day you have outraged my wife. I ask nothing more of you, monsieur. Adieu."

Grandfather Gillenormand, astounded, opened his mouth, stretched out his arms, attempted to rise, but before he could utter a word, the door closed and Marius had disappeared.

The old man was for a few moments motionless, and as it were thunder-stricken, unable to speak or breathe, as if a hand were clutching his throat. At last he tore himself from his chair, ran to the door as fast as a man who is ninety-one can run, opened it and cried:

"Help! help!"

His daughter appeared, then the servants. He continued with a pitiful rattle in his voice:

"Run after him! catch him! what have I done to him! he is mad! he is going away! Oh! my God! oh! my God!—this time he will not come back!"

He went to the window which looked upon the street, opened it with his tremulous old hands, hung more than half his body outside, while Basque and Nicolette held him from behind, and cried:

"Marius! Marius! Marius! Marius!"

But Marius was already out of hearing, and was at that very moment turning the corner of the Rue Saint Louis.

The octogenarian carried his hands to his temples two or three times, with an expression of anguish, drew back tottering, and sank into an arm-chair, pulseless, voiceless, tearless, shaking his head, and moving his lips with a stupid air, having now nothing in his eyes or in his heart but something deep and mournful, which resembled night.

BOOK NINTH – WHERE ARE THEY GOING?

I

JEAN VALJEAN

THAT very day, towards four o'clock in the afternoon, Jean Valjean was sitting alone upon the reverse of one of the most solitary embankments of the Champ de Mars. Whether from prudence, or from a desire for meditation, or simply as a result of one of those insensible changes of habits which creep little by little into all lives, he now rarely went out with Cosette. He wore his working-man's waistcoat, brown linen trousers, and his cap with the long visor hid his face. He was now calm and happy in regard to Cosette; what had for some time alarmed and disturbed him was dissipated; but within a week or two anxieties of a different nature had come upon him. One day, when walking on the boulevard, he had seen Thénardier; thanks to his disguise, Thénardier had not recognised him; but since then Jean Valjean had seen him again several times, and he was now certain that Thénardier was prowling about the quartier. This was sufficient to make him take a serious step. Thénardier there! this was all dangers at once. Moreover, Paris was not quiet: the political troubles had this inconvenience for him who had anything in his life to conceal, that the police had become very active, and very secret, and that in seeking to track out a man like Pépin or Morey, they would be very likely to discover a man like Jean Valjean. Jean Valjean had decided to leave Paris, and even France, and to pass over to England. He had told Cosette. In less than a week he wished to be gone. He was sitting on the embankment in the Champ de Mars, revolving all manner of thoughts in his mind, Thénardier, the police, the journey, and the difficulty of procuring a passport.

On all these points he was anxious.

Finally, an inexplicable circumstance which had just burst upon him, and with which he was still warm, had added to his alarm. On the morning of that very day, being the only one up in the house, and walking in the garden before Cosette's shutters were open, he had suddenly come upon this line scratched upon the wall, probably with a nail.

16, Rue de la Verrerie.

1024

It was quite recent, the lines were white in the old black mortar, a tuft of nettles at the foot of the wall was powdered with fresh fine plaster. It had probably been written during the night. What was it? an address? a signal for others? a warning for him? At all events, it was evident that the garden had been violated, and that some persons unknown had penetrated into it. He recalled the strange incidents which had already alarmed the house. His mind worked upon this canvas. He took good care not to speak to Cosette of the line written on the wall, for fear of frightening her.

In the midst of these meditations, he perceived, by a shadow which the sun had projected, that somebody had just stopped upon the crest of the embankment immediately behind him. He was about to turn round, when a folded paper fell upon his knees, as if a hand had dropped it from above his head. He took the paper, unfolded it, and read on it this word, written in large letters with a pencil:

REMOVE.

Jean Valjean rose hastily, there was no longer anybody on the embankment; he looked about him, and perceived a species of being larger than a child, smaller than a man, dressed in a grey blouse and trousers of dirt-coloured cotton velvet, which jumped over the parapet and let itself slide into the ditch of the Champ de Mars.

Jean Valjean returned home immediately, full of thought.

II

MARIUS

MARIUS had left M. Gillenormand's desolate. He had entered with a very small hope; he came out with an immense despair.

Still, and those who have observed the beginnings of the human heart will understand it, the lancer, the officer, the ninny, the cousin Théodule, had left no shadow in his mind. Not the slightest. The dramatic poet might apparently hope for some complications from this revelation, made in the very teeth of the grandson by the grandfather. But what the drama would gain, the truth would lose. Marius was at that age when we believe no ill; later comes the age when he believes all. Suspicions are nothing more nor less than wrinkles. Early youth has none. What overwhelms Othello, glides over Candide. Suspect

Cosette! There are a multitude of crimes which Marius could have more easily committed.

He began to walk the streets, the resource of those who suffer. He thought of nothing which he could ever remember. At two o'clock in the morning he returned to Courfeyrac's, and threw himself, dressed as he was, upon his mattress. It was broad sunlight when he fell asleep, with that frightful, heavy slumber in which the ideas come and go in the brain. When he awoke, he saw standing in the room, their hats upon their heads, all ready to go out, very busy, Courfeyrac, Enjolras, Feuilly, and Combeferre.

Courfeyrac said to him:

"Are you going to the funeral of General Lamarque?"

It seemed to him that Courfeyrac was speaking Chinese.

He went out some time after them. He put into his pocket the pistols which Javert had confided to him at the time of the adventure of the 3rd of February, and which had remained in his hands. These pistols were still loaded. It would be difficult to say what obscure thought he had in his mind in taking them with him.

He rambled about all day without knowing where; it rained at intervals, he did not perceive it; for his dinner he bought a penny roll at a baker's, put it in his pocket, and forgot it. It would appear that he took a bath in the Seine without being conscious of it. There are moments when a man has a furnace in his brain. Marius was in one of those moments. He hoped nothing more, he feared nothing more; he had reached this condition since the evening before. He waited for night with feverish impatience, he had but one clear idea; that was, that at nine o'clock he should see Cosette. This last happiness was now his whole future; afterwards, darkness. At intervals, while walking along the most deserted boulevards, he seemed to hear strange sounds in Paris. He roused himself from his reverie and said: "Are they fighting?"

At nightfall, at precisely nine o'clock, as he had promised Cosette, he was in the Rue Plumet. When he approached the grating he forgot everything else. It was forty-eight hours since he had seen Cosette, he was going to see her again, every other thought faded away, and he felt now only a deep and wonderful joy. Those minutes in which we live centuries always have this sovereign and wonderful peculiarity, that for the moment while they are passing, they entirely fill the heart.

Marius displaced the grating, and sprang into the garden. Cosette was not at the place where she usually waited for him. He crossed the thicket and went to the recess near the steps. "She is waiting for me there," said he. Cosette was not there. He raised his eyes, and saw the shutters of the house were closed. He took a turn around the garden, the garden was deserted. Then he returned to the house, and, mad with love, intoxicated, dismayed, exasperated with grief and anxiety, like a master who returns home in an untoward hour, he rapped on the shutters. He rapped, he rapped again, at the risk of seeing the window open and the forbidding face of the father appear and ask him: "What do you want?" This was nothing compared with what he now began to see. When he had rapped, he raised his voice and called Cosette. "Cosette!" cried he. "Cosette!" repeated he imperiously. There was no answer. It was settled. Nobody in the garden; nobody in the house.

Marius fixed his despairing eyes upon that dismal house, as black, as silent, and more empty than a tomb. He looked at the stone seat where he had passed so many adorable hours with Cosette. Then he sat down upon the steps, his heart full of tenderness and resolution, he blessed his love in the depths of his thought, and he said to himself that since Cosette was gone, there was nothing more for him but to die.

Suddenly he heard a voice which appeared to come from the street, and which cried through the trees:

"Monsieur Marius!"

He arose.

"Hey?" said he.

"Monsieur Marius, is it you?"

"Yes."

"Monsieur Marius," added the voice, "your friends are expecting you at the barricade, in the Rue de la Chanvrerie."

This voice was not entirely unknown to him. It resembled the harsh and roughened voice of Eponine. Marius ran to the grating, pushed aside the movable bar, passed his head through, and saw somebody who appeared to him to be a young man rapidly disappearing in the twilight.

III
M. MABEUF

JEAN VALJEAN'S purse was useless to M. Mabeuf. M. Mabeuf,
in his venerable childlike austerity, had not accepted the gift of
the stars; he did not admit that a star could coin itself into gold
louis. He did not guess that what fell from the sky came from
Gavroche. He carried the purse to the Commissary of Police of
the quartier, as a lost article, placed by the finder at the disposition of claimants. The purse was lost, in fact. We need not say
that nobody reclaimed it, and it did not help M. Mabeuf.

For the rest, M. Mabeuf had continued to descend.

The experiments upon indigo had succeeded no better at the
Jardin des Plantes than in his garden at Austerlitz. The year
before, he owed his housekeeper her wages; now, we have seen,
he owed three quarters of his rent. The pawnbroker, at the
expiration of thirteen months, had sold the plates of his *Flora*.
Some coppersmith had made saucepans of them. His plates
gone, being no longer able even to complete the broken sets of
his *Flora* which he still possessed, he had given up engravings
and text at a wretched price to a secondhand bookseller, as *odd
copies*. He had now nothing left of the work of his whole life.
He began to eat up the money from these copies. When he
saw that this slender resource was failing him, he renounced his
garden and left it uncultivated. Before this, and for a long time
before, he had given up the two eggs and the bit of beef which
he used to eat from time to time. He dined on bread and potatoes. He had sold his last furniture, then all his spare bedding
and clothing, then his collections of plants and his pictures; but
he still had his most precious books, several of which were of
great rarity, among others *Les Quadrins Historiques de la Bible*,
edition of 1560, *La Concordance des Bibles* of Pierre de Besse, *Les
Marguerites de la Marguerite* of Jean de la Haye with a dedication
to the Queen of Navarre, the book *On the charge and dignity of
the Ambassador* by the Sieur de Villiers Hotman, a *Florilegium
Rabbinicum* of 1644, a Tibullus of 1567 with this splendid
inscription: *Venetiis, in ædibus Manutianis*; finally a Diogenes
Laertius, printed at Lyons in 1644, containing the famous variations of the manuscript 411, of the thirteenth century, in the
Vatican, and those of the two manuscripts of Venice, 393 and
394, so fruitfully consulted by Henri Estienne, and all the

passages in the Doric dialect which are found only in the celebrated manuscript of the twelfth century of the library of Naples. M. Mabeuf never made a fire in his room, and went to bed by daylight so as not to burn a candle. It seemed that he had now no neighbours, he was shunned when he went out; he was aware of it. The misery of a child is interesting to a mother, the misery of a young man is interesting to a young woman, the misery of an old man is interesting to nobody. This is of all miseries the coldest. Still Father Mabeuf had not entirely lost his childlike serenity. His eye regained some vivacity when it was fixed upon his books, and he smiled when he thought of the Diogenes Laertius, which was a unique copy. His glass bookcase was the only piece of furniture which he had preserved beyond what was indispensable.

One day Mother Plutarch said to him:

"I have nothing to buy the dinner with."

What she called the dinner was a loaf of bread and four or five potatoes.

"On credit?" said M. Mabeuf.

"You know well enough that they refuse me."

M. Mabeuf opened his library, looked long at all his books one after another, as a father, compelled to decimate his children, would look at them before choosing, then took one of them hastily, put it under his arm, and went out. He returned two hours afterwards with nothing under his arm, laid thirty sous on the table, and said:

"You will get some dinner."

From that moment, Mother Plutarch saw settling over the old man's white face a dark veil which was never lifted again.

The next day, the day after, every day, he had to begin again. M. Mabeuf went out with a book and came back with a piece of money. As the bookstall keepers saw that he was forced to sell, they bought from him for twenty sous what he had paid twenty francs for, sometimes to the same booksellers. Volume by volume, the whole library passed away. He said at times: "I am eighty years old however," as if he had some lingering hope of reaching the end of his days before reaching the end of his books. His sadness increased. Once, however, he had a pleasure. He went out with a Robert Estienne which he sold for thirty-five sous on the Quai Malaquais and returned with an Aldine which he had bought for forty sous in the Rue des Grès. "I owe five sous," said he to Mother Plutarch, glowing with joy.

That day he did not dine.

He belonged to the Society of Horticulture. His poverty was known there. The president of this society came to see him, promised to speak to the Minister of Agriculture and Commerce about him, and did so. "Why, how now!" exclaimed the minister. "I do believe! An old philosopher! a botanist! an inoffensive man! We must do something for him!" The next day M. Mabeuf received an invitation to dine at the minister's. Trembling with joy, he showed the letter to Mother Plutarch. "We are saved!" said he. On the appointed day, he went to the minister's. He perceived that his ragged cravat, his large, old, square coat, and his shoes polished with egg, astonished the ushers. Nobody spoke to him, not even the minister. About ten o'clock in the evening, as he was still expecting a word, he heard the minister's wife, a beautiful lady in a low-necked dress, whom he had not dared to approach, asking: "What can that old gentleman be?" He returned home on foot, at midnight, in a driving rain. He had sold an Elzevir to pay for a fiacre to go with.

He had acquired the habit, every evening before going to bed, of reading a few pages in his Diogenes Laertius. He knew Greek well enough to enjoy the peculiarities of the text which he possessed. He had now no other joy. Some weeks rolled by. Suddenly Mother Plutarch fell sick. There is one thing sadder than having nothing with which to buy bread from the baker; that is, having nothing with which to buy drugs from the apothecary. One night, the doctor had ordered a very dear potion. And then, the sickness was growing worse, a nurse was needed. M. Mabeuf opened his bookcase; there was nothing more there. The last volume had gone. The Diogenes Laertius alone remained.

He put the unique copy under his arm and went out; it was the 4th of June, 1832; he went to the Porte Saint Jacques, to Royol's Successor's, and returned with a hundred francs. He laid the pile of five-franc pieces on the old servant's bedroom table, and went back to his room without saying a word.

The next day, by dawn, he was seated on the stone post in the garden, and he might have been seen from over the hedge all the morning motionless, his head bowed down, his eye vaguely fixed upon the withered beds. At intervals he wept; the old man did not seem to perceive it. In the afternoon, extraordinary sounds broke out in Paris. They resembled musket shots, and the clamour of a multitude.

Father Mabeuf raised his head. He saw a gardener going by, and asked:

"What is that?"

The gardener answered, his spade upon his shoulder, and in the most quiet tone:

"It's the émeutes."

"What émeutes?"

"Yes. They are fighting."

"What are they fighting for?"

"Oh! Lordy!" said the gardener.

"Whereabouts?" continued M. Mabeuf.

"Near the Arsenal."

Father Mabeuf went into the house, took his hat, looked mechanically for a book to put under his arm, did not find any, said: "Ah! it is true!" and went away with a bewildered air.

BOOK TENTH – JUNE 5TH, 1832

I
THE SURFACE OF THE QUESTION

OF what is the émeute composed? of nothing and of everything. Of an electricity gradually evolved, of a flame suddenly leaping forth, of a wandering force, of a passing wind. This wind meets talking tongues, dreaming brains, suffering souls, burning passions, howling miseries, and sweeps them away.

Whither?

At hazard. Across the state, across the laws, across the prosperity and the insolence of others.

Irritated convictions, eager enthusiasms, excited indignations, the repressed instincts of war, exalted young courage, noble impulses; curiosity, the taste for change, the thirst for the unexpected, that sentiment which gives us pleasure in reading the bill of a new play, and which makes the ringing of the prompter's bell at the theatre a welcome sound; vague hatreds, spites, disappointments, every vanity which believes that destiny has caused it to fail; discomforts, empty dreams, ambitions shut in by high walls, whoever hopes for an issue from a downfall; finally, at the very bottom, the mob, that mud which takes fire, such are the elements of the émeute.

Whatever is greatest and whatever is most infamous; the beings who prowl about outside of everything, awaiting an opportunity, bohemians, people without occupation, loafers about the street-corners, those who sleep at night in a desert of houses, with no other roof than the cold clouds of the sky, those who ask their bread each day from chance and not from labour, the unknown ones of misery and nothingness, the bare arms, the bare feet, belong to the émeute.

Whoever feels in his soul a secret revolt against any act whatever of the state, of life or of fate, borders on the émeute, and, so soon as it appears, begins to shiver, and to feel himself uplifted by the whirlwind.

The émeute is a sort of waterspout in the social atmosphere which suddenly takes form in certain conditions of temperature, and which, in its whirling, mounts, runs, thunders, tears up, razes, crushes, demolishes, uproots, dragging with it the grand natures and the paltry, the strong man and the feeble mind, the trunk of the tree and the blade of straw.

Woe to him whom it sweeps away, as well as to him whom it comes to smite! It breaks them one against the other.

It communicates to those whom it seizes a mysterious and extraordinary power. It fills the first comer with the force of events; it makes projectiles of everything. It makes a bullet of a pebble, and a general of a street porter.

If we may believe certain oracles of crafty politics, from the governmental point of view, something of the émeute is desirable. System: the émeute strengthens those governments which it does not overthrow. It tests the army, it concentrates the bourgeoisie; it calls out the muscles of the police; it determines the strength of the social frame. It is a gymnastic training; it is almost hygienic. Power is healthier after an émeute, as a man is after a rubbing.

The émeute, thirty years ago, was looked upon from still other points of view.

There is a theory for everything which proclaims itself "common sense;" Philinte against Alceste; mediation offered between the true and the false; explanation, admonition, a somewhat haughty extenuation which, because it is a mixture of blame and excuse, thinks itself wisdom, and is often only pedantry. An entire political school, called the compromise school, has sprung from this. Between cold water and warm water, this is the party of tepid water. This school, with its pretended depth, wholly superficial, which dissects effect without going back to the causes, from the height of a half-science, chides the agitations of the public square.

To hear this school: "The émeutes with which the achievement of 1830 was complicated, robbed that great event of a portion of its purity. The revolution of July had been a fine breeze of the popular wind, quickly followed by blue sky. They brought back the cloudy sky. They degraded that revolution, at first so remarkable for unanimity, into a quarrel. In the revolution of July, as in all sudden progress, there were some secret fractures; the émeute rendered them sensible. We might say; 'Ah! this is broken.' After the revolution of July, the deliverance only was felt; after the émeutes, the catastrophe was felt.

"Every émeute closes the shops, depresses the funds, terrifies the stockboard, suspends commerce, shackles business, precipitates failures; no more money, private fortunes shaken, the public credit disturbed, manufactures disconcerted, capital hoarded, labour depreciated, fear everywhere; reactions in all the cities. Hence yawning gulfs. It has been calculated that the first day of an émeute costs France twenty millions, the second forty, the third sixty. An émeute of three days costs a hundred and twenty millions, that is to say, looking only at the financial result, is equivalent to a disaster, a shipwreck, or the loss of a battle, which should annihilate a fleet of sixty vessels of the line.

"Beyond a doubt, historically, émeutes had their beauty; the war of the pavements is no less grand and no less pathetic than the war of the thickets; in the one there is the soul of forests; in the other the heart of cities; one has Jean Chouan, the other has Jeanne. The émeutes illuminated, with red light, but splendidly, all the most original outgrowths of the Parisian character, generosity, devotion, stormy gaiety, students proving that bravery is part of intelligence, the National Guard unwavering, bivouacs of shopkeepers, fortresses of *gamins*, scorn of death among the people on the street. Schools and legions came in conflict. After all, between the combatants, there was only a difference of age; they were the same race; they are the same stoical men who die at twenty for their ideas, at forty for their families. The army, always sad in civil wars, opposed prudence to audacity. The émeutes, at the same time that they manifested the intrepidity of the people, effected the education of the courage of the bourgeois.

"Very well. But is it all worth the bloodshed? And to the bloodshed add the future darkened, progress incriminated, anxiety among the best men, noble liberals despairing, foreign absolutism delighted with these wounds inflicted on the revolution by itself, the vanquished of 1830 triumphing and saying: 'We told you so!' Add Paris enlarged perhaps, but France surely diminished. Add, for we must tell all, the massacres which too often dishonoured the victory of order grown ferocious over liberty grown mad. Taken altogether, émeutes have been disastrous."

Thus speaks this almost wisdom with which the bourgeoisie, that almost people, so gladly contents itself.

As for us, we reject this too broad and consequently too convenient word, émeute. Between a popular movement and a popular movement, we make a distinction. We do not ask whether an émeute cost as much as a battle. In the first place wherefore a battle? Here arises the question of war. Is war less a scourge than the émeute a calamity? And then, are all émeutes calamities? And what if the 14th of July did cost a hundred and twenty millions? The establishment of Philip V. in Spain cost France two thousand millions. Even at the same price, we should prefer the 14th of July. Moreover, we put aside these figures, which seem to be reasons, and which are only words. An émeute given, we examine it in itself. In all that is said by the theoretic objection above set forth, only the effect is in question, we seek for the cause.

We specify.

II
THE BOTTOM OF THE QUESTION

THERE is the émeute, there is the insurrection; they are two angers; one is wrong, the other is right. In democratic states, the only governments founded in justice, it sometimes happens that a fraction usurps; then the whole rises up, and the necessary vindication of its right may go so far as to take up arms. In all questions which spring from the collective sovereignty, the war of the whole against the fraction is insurrection; the attack of the fraction against the whole is an émeute; according as the Tuileries contain the King or contain the Convention, they are justly or unjustly attacked. The same cannon pointed against the multitude is wrong the 10th of August, and right the 14th of Vendémiaire. Similar in appearance, different at bottom; the Swiss defend the false, Bonaparte defends the true. What universal suffrage has done in its freedom and its sovereignty cannot be undone by the street. So, in the affairs of pure civilisation; the instinct of the masses, yesterday clear-sighted, may to-morrow be clouded. The same fury is lawful against Terray, and absurd against Turgot. The breaking of machines, the pillaging of store-houses, the tearing up of rails, the demolition of docks, the false means of the multitudes, the denials of justice by the people to progress, Ramus assassinated by the students, Rousseau driven out of Switzerland with stones, is the émeute. Israel against Moses, Athens against Phocion, Rome against Scipio, is the émeute; Paris against the Bastille is insurrection. The soldiers against Alexander, the sailors against Christopher Columbus, this is the same revolt; an impious revolt; why? Because Alexander does for Asia with the sword what Christopher Columbus does for America with the compass; Alexander, like Columbus, finds a world. These gifts of a world to civilisation are such extensions of light that all resistance to them is criminal. Sometimes the people counterfeits fidelity to itself. The mob is traitor to the people. Is there, for instance, anything more strange than that long and bloody protest of the contraband saltmakers, a legitimate chronic revolt, which, at the decisive moment, on the day of safety, at the hour of the people's victory, espouses the throne, turns Chouan, and from insurrection against makes itself an émeute for! Dreary masterpieces of ignorance! The contraband saltmaker escapes the royal gallows, and, with a bit of rope at his neck, mounts the white cockade. Death to the excise gives birth to Vive le Roi. Saint Bartholomew assassins, September murderers, Avignon massacres, assassins of Coligny, assassins of Madame de Lamballe, assassins of Brune, Miquelets, Verdets, Cadenettes, companions of Jéhu, Chevaliers du Brassard, such is émeute. La Vendée is a great Catholic émeute. The sound of the advancing right knows itself, it does not always get clear of the quaking of the overthrown masses; there are foolish rages, there are cracked bells; every tocsin does not ring with the ring of bronze. The clash of passions and of ignorances is different from the shock of progress. Rise, if you will, but to grow. Show me to which side you are going. There is no insurrection but forward. Every other rising is evil; every violent step backwards is an émeute; to retreat is an act of violence against the human race. Insurrection is the Truth's access of fury; the paving stones which insurrection tears up, throw off the spark of right. These stones leave to the émeute only their mud. Danton against Louis XVI. is insurrection, Hébert against Danton is émeute.

Hence it is that, if insurrection, in given cases, may be, as Lafayette said, the most sacred of duties, an émeute may be the most deadly of crimes.

There is also some difference in the intensity of caloric; the insurrection is often a volcano, the émeute is often a fire of straw.

The revolt, as we have said, is sometimes on the part of power. Polignac is an émeuter; Camille Desmoulins is a governor.

Sometimes, insurrection is resurrection.

The solution of everything by universal suffrage being a fact entirely modern, and all history anterior to that fact being, for four thousand years, filled with violated right and the suffering of the people, each period of history brings with it such protest as is possible to it. Under the Cæsars there was no insurrection, but there was Juvenal.

The *facit indignatio* replaces the Gracchi.

Under the Cæsars there is the exile of Syene; there is also the man of the *Annales*.

We do not speak of the sublime exile of Patmos, who also overwhelms the real world with a protest in the name of the ideal, makes of a vision a tremendous satire, and throws upon Nineveh-Rome, upon Babylon-Rome, upon Sodom-Rome, the flaming reverberation of the Apocalypse.

John upon his rock is the Sphinx upon her pedestal; we cannot comprehend him; he is a Jew, and it is Hebrew; but the man who wrote the *Annales* is a Latin, let us rather say he is a Roman.

As the Neros reign darkly, they should be pictured so. Work with the graver only would be pale; into the grooves should be poured a concentrated prose which bites.

Despots are an aid to thinkers. Speech enchained is speech terrible. The writer doubles and triples his style when silence is imposed by a master upon the people. There springs from this silence a certain mysterious fulness which filters and freezes into brass in the thoughts. Compression in the history produces conciseness in the historian. The granitic solidity of some celebrated prose is only a condensation produced by the tyrant. Tyranny constrains the writer to shortenings of diameter which are increases of strength. The Ciceronian period, hardly sufficient upon Verres, would lose its edge upon Caligula. Less roundness in the phrase, more intensity in the blow. Tacitus thinks with his arm drawn back.

The nobility of a great heart, condensed into justice and truth, strikes like a thunderbolt.

Be it said in passing, it is noteworthy that Tacitus was not historically superimposed upon Cæsar. The Tiberii were reserved for him. Cæsar and Tacitus are two successive phenomena whose meeting seems mysteriously avoided by Him who, in putting the centuries on the stage, rules the entrances and the exits. Cæsar is grand, Tacitus is grand; God spares these two grandeurs by not dashing them against each other. The judge, striking Cæsar, might strike too hard, and be unjust. God did not will it. The great wars of Africa and Spain, the destruction of the Cilician pirates, civilisation introduced into Gaul, into Britain, into Germany, all this glory covers the Rubicon. There is a delicacy of divine justice here, hesitating to let loose the terrible historian upon the illustrious usurper, saving Cæsar from Tacitus, and according to the genius the extenuating circumstances.

Certainly, despotism is always despotism, even under the despot of genius. There is corruption under illustrious tyrants, but the moral pestilence is more hideous still under infamous tyrants. In these reigns nothing veils the shame; and makers of examples, Tacitus as well as Juvenal, belabour to best purpose in presence of ignominy without excuse.

Rome smells worse under Vitellius than under Sylla. Under Claudius and under Domitian, there is a deformity of baseness corresponding to the ugliness of the tyrant. The foulness of the slaves is a direct result of the despot; a miasma exhales from these crouching consciences which reflect the master; the public powers are unclean; hearts are small, consciences are sunken, souls are puny; this is so under Caracalla, this is so under Commodus, this is so under Heliogabalus, while there comes from the Roman Senate under Cæsar only the rank odour peculiar to the eagle's eyrie.

Hence the coming, apparently late, of the Tacituses and of the Juvenals; it is at the hour of evidence that the demonstrator appears.

But Juvenal and Tacitus, even like Isaiah in the biblical times, even like Dante in the Middle Ages, are men; the émeute and the insurrection are the multitude, which sometimes is wrong, sometimes is right.

In the most usual cases émeute springs from a material fact; insurrection is always a moral phenomenon. The émeute is Masaniello, the insurrection is Spartacus. Insurrection borders on the mind, émeute on the stomach; Gaster is irritated; but Gaster, certainly, is not always wrong. In cases of famine, émeute, Buzançais, for instance, has a true, pathetic, and just point of departure. Still it remains émeute. Why? because having reason at bottom, it was wrong in form. Savage, although right, violent, although strong, it struck at hazard; it marched like the blind elephant, crushing; it left behind it the corpses of old men, women, and children; it poured out, without knowing why, the blood of the inoffensive and the innocent. To nurture the people is a good end; to massacre it is an evil means.

Every armed protest, even the most legitimate, even the 10th of August, even the 14th of July, ends with the same trouble. Before the right is evolved, there is tumult and foam. In the beginning insurrection is an émeute, even as the river is a torrent. Ordinarily it ends in this ocean, revolution. Sometimes, however, coming from those high mountains which rule the moral horizon, justice, wisdom, reason, right, made of the purest snow of the ideal, after a long fall from rock to rock, after having reflected the sky in its transparency and been swollen by a hundred affluents in the majestic path of triumph, insurrection suddenly loses itself in some bourgeois quagmire, like the Rhine in a marsh.

All this is of the past, the future is different. Universal suffrage is so far admirable that it dissolves the émeute in its principle, and by giving a vote to insurrection, it takes away its arms. The vanishing of war, of the war of the streets as well as the war of the frontiers, such is inevitable progress. Whatever may be To-day, peace is To-morrow.

However, insurrection, émeute, in what the first differs from the second, the bourgeois, properly speaking, knows little of these shades. To him, all is sedition, rebellion pure and simple, revolt of the dog against the master, attempt to bite which must be punished by chain and kennel, barking, yelping, till the day when the dog's head, suddenly enlarged, stands out dimly in the darkness with a lion's face.

Then the bourgeois cries: *Vive le peuple!*

This explanation given, what, for history, is the movement of June, 1832? is it an émeute? is it an insurrection?

It is an insurrection.

We may happen, in this presentation of a fearful event, sometimes to say the émeute, but only to denote the surface facts, and always maintaining the distinction between the form émeute and the substance insurrection.

This movement of 1832 had, in its rapid explosion and in its dismal extinction, so much grandeur that those even who see in it only an émeute do not speak of it without respect. To them it is like a remnant of 1830. "Excited imaginations," say they, "do not calm down in a day. A revolution is not cut off square. It has always some necessary undulations before returning to the condition of peace like a mountain on descending towards the plain. There are no Alps without their Jura nor Pyrenees without Asturias."

This pathetic crisis of contemporary history, which the memory of Parisians calls the *epoch of émeutes*, is surely a characteristic period amid the stormy periods of this century. A last word before resuming the narrative.

The events which we are about to relate belong to that dramatic and living reality which the historian sometimes neglects, for lack of time and space. In them, however, we insist, in them is the life, the palpitation, the quivering of humanity. Little incidents, we believe we have said, are, so to speak, the foliage of great events and are lost in the distance of history. The epoch known as that *of émeutes* abounds in details of this kind. The judicial investigations, for other reasons than history, did not reveal everything, nor perhaps get to the bottom of everything. We shall therefore bring to light, among the known and public circumstances, some things which have never been known, deeds, over some of which oblivion has passed; over others, death. Most of the actors in those gigantic scenes have disappeared; from the morrow they were silent; but what we shall relate, we can say that we saw. We shall change some names, for history relates and does not inform against, but we shall paint reality. From the nature of the book which we are writing, we only show one side and an episode, and that certainly the least known, of the days of the 5th and 6th of June, 1832; but we shall do it in such a way that the reader may catch a glimpse, under the gloomy veil which we are about to lift, of the real countenance of that fearful public tragedy.

III
A BURIAL: OPPORTUNITY FOR REBIRTH

IN the spring of 1832, although for three months the cholera had chilled all hearts and thrown over their agitation an inexpressibly mournful calm, Paris had for a long time been ready for a commotion. As we have said, the great city resembles a piece of artillery; when it is loaded the falling of a spark is enough, the shot goes off. In June, 1832, the spark was the death of General Lamarque.

Lamarque was a man of renown and of action. He had had successively, under the Empire and under the Restoration, the two braveries necessary to the two epochs, the bravery of the battle-field and the bravery of the rostrum. He was eloquent as he had been valiant; men felt a sword in his speech. Like Foy, his predecessor, after having upheld command, he upheld liberty. He sat between the left and the extreme left, loved by the people because he accepted the chances of the future, loved by the masses because he had served the emperor well. He was, with Counts Gérard and Drouet, one of Napoleon's marshals *in petto*. The treaties of 1815 regarded him as a personal offence. He hated Wellington with a direct hatred which pleased the multitude; and for seventeen years, hardly noticing intermediate events, he had majestically preserved the sadness of Waterloo. In his death-agony, at his latest hour, he had pressed against his breast a sword which was presented to him by the officers of the Hundred Days. Napoleon died pronouncing the word *armée*, Lamarque pronouncing the word *patrie*.

His death, which had been looked for, was dreaded by the people as a loss, and by the government as an opportunity. This death was a mourning. Like everything which is bitter, mourning may turn into revolt. This is what happened.

The eve and the morning of the 5th of June, the day fixed for the funeral of Lamarque, the Faubourg Saint Antoine, through the edge of which the procession was to pass, assumed a formidable aspect. That tumultuous network of streets was full of rumour. Men armed themselves as they could. Some joiners carried their bench-claw "to stave in the doors." One of them had made a dagger of a shoe-hook by breaking off the hook and sharpening the stump. Another, in the fever "to attack," had slept for three nights without undressing. A carpenter named Lombier met a comrade, who asked him: "Where are you going?" "Well! I have no arms." "What then?" "I am going to my yard to look for my compasses." "What for?" "I don't know," said Lombier. A certain Jacqueline, a man of business, hailed every working-man who passed by with: "Come, you!" He bought ten sous' worth of wine, and said: "Have you any work?" "No." "Go to Filspierre's, between the Barrière Montreuil and the Barrière Charonne, you will find work." They found at Filspierre's cartridges and arms. Certain known chiefs *did the post*; that is to say, ran from one house to another to assemble their people. At Barthélemy's, near the Barrière du Trône, and at Capet's, at the Petit Chapeau, the drinkers accosted each other seriously. They were heard to say: "*Where is your pistol?*" "*Under my blouse.*" "*And yours?*" "*Under my shirt.*" On the Rue Traversière, in front of the Roland workshop, and in the Cour de la Maison Brûlée, in front of Bernier's machine-shop, groups were whispering. Among the most ardent a certain Mavot was noticed, who never worked more than a week in one shop, the masters sending him away, "because they had to dispute with him every day." Mavot was killed the next day in the barricade, in the Rue Ménilmontant. Pretot, who was also to die in the conflict, seconded Mavot, and to this question: "What is your object?" answered: "*Insurrection.*" Some working-men, gathered at the corner of the Rue de Bercy, were waiting for a man named Lemarin, revolutionary officer for the Faubourg Saint Marceau. Orders were passed about almost publicly.

On the 5th of June, then, a day of mingled rain and sunshine, the procession of General Lamarque passed through Paris with the official military pomp, somewhat increased by way of precaution. Two battalions, drums muffled, muskets reversed, ten thousand National Guards, their sabres at their sides, the batteries of artillery of the National Guard, escorted the coffin. The hearse was drawn by young men. The officers of the Invalides followed immediately bearing branches of laurel. Then came a countless multitude, strange and agitated, the sectionaries of the Friends of the People, the Law School, the Medical School, refugees from all nations, Spanish, Italian, German, Polish flags, horizontal tri-coloured flags, every possible banner, children waving green branches, stone-cutters and carpenters, who were on a strike at that very moment, printers recognisable by their paper caps, walking two by two, three by three, uttering cries, almost all brandishing clubs, a few swords, without order, and yet with a single soul, now a rout, now a column. Some platoons chose chiefs; a man, armed with a pair of pistols openly worn, seemed to be passing others in review as they filed off before him. On the cross-alleys of the boulevards, in the branches of the trees, on the balconies, at the windows, on the roofs, were swarms of heads, men, women, children; their eyes were full of anxiety. An armed multitude was passing by, a terrified multitude was looking on.

The government also was observing. It was observing, with

its hand upon the hilt of the sword. One might have seen, all ready to march, with full cartridge-boxes, guns and musquetoons loaded, in the Place Louis XV., four squadrons of carbineers, in the saddle, trumpets at their heads, in the Latin Quarter and at the Jardin des Plantes, the Municipal Guard, en échelon from street to street, at the Halle aux Vins a squadron of dragoons, at La Grève one half of the 12th Light, the other half at the Bastille, the 6th dragoons at the Célestins, the Court of the Louvre full of artillery. The rest of the troops were stationed in the barracks, without counting the regiments in the environs of Paris. Anxious authority held suspended over the threatening multitude twenty-four thousand soldiers in the city, and thirty thousand in the banlieue.

Divers rumours circulated in the cortège. They talked of legitimist intrigues; they talked of the Duke of Reichstadt, whom God was marking for death at that very moment when the populace was designating him for empire. A personage still unknown announced that at the appointed hour two foremen who had been won over, would open to the people the doors of a manufactory of arms. The dominant expression on the uncovered foreheads of most of those present, was one of subdued enthusiasm. Here and there in this multitude, a prey to so many violent, but noble, emotions, could also be seen some genuine faces of malefactors and ignoble mouths, which said "pillage!" There are certain agitations which stir up the bottom of the marsh, and which make clouds of mud rise in the water. A phenomenon to which "well-regulated" police are not strangers.

The cortège made its way, with a feverish slowness, from the house of death along the boulevards as far as the Bastille. It rained from time to time; the rain had no effect upon that throng. Several incidents, the coffin drawn around the Vendôme column, the stones thrown at the Duke de Fitz-James who was seen on a balcony with his hat on, the Gallic cock torn from a popular flag and dragged in the mud, a sergent de ville wounded by a sword thrust at the Porte Saint Martin, an officer of the 12th Light saying aloud: "I am a republican," the Polytechnic School unlooked for after its forced countersign, the cries: *Vive l'école polytechnique! Vive la république!* marked the progress of the procession. At the Bastille, long and formidable files of the curious from the Faubourg Saint Antoine made their junction with the cortège, and a certain terrible ebullition began to upheave the multitude.

One man was heard saying to another: "Do you see that man with the red beard? it is he who will say when we must draw." It would appear that the same red beard was found afterwards with the same office in another émeute; the Quénisset affair.

The hearse passed the Bastille, followed the canal, crossed the little bridge, and reached the esplanade of the Bridge of Auster-litz. There it stopped. At this moment a bird's-eye view of this multitude would have presented the appearance of a comet, the head of which was at the esplanade, while the tail, spreading over the Quai Bourdon, covered the Bastille, and stretched along the boulevard as far as the Porte Saint Martin. A circle was formed about the hearse. The vast assemblage became silent. Lafayette spoke and bade farewell to Lamarque. It was a touch-ing and august moment, all heads were uncovered, all hearts throbbed. Suddenly a man on horseback, dressed in black, appeared in the midst of the throng with a red flag, others say with a pike surmounted by a red cap. Lafayette turned away his head. Exelmans left the cortège.

This red flag raised a storm and disappeared in it. From the Boulevard Bourdon to the Bridge of Austerlitz one of those shouts which resemble billows moved the multitude. Two pro-digious shouts arose: *Lamarque to the Pantheon! Lafayette to the Hôtel de Ville!* Some young men, amid the cheers of the throng, harnessed themselves, and began to draw Lamarque in the hearse over the bridge of Austerlitz, and Lafayette in a fiacre along the Quai Morland.

In the crowd which surrounded and cheered Lafayette, was noticed and pointed out a German, named Ludwig Snyder, who afterwards died a centenarian, who had also been in the war of 1776 and who had fought at Trenton under Washington, and under Lafayette at Brandywine.

Meanwhile, on the left bank, the municipal cavalry was in motion, and had just barred the bridge, on the right bank the dragoons left the Célestins and deployed along the Quai Mor-land. The men who were drawing Lafayette suddenly perceived them at the corner of the Quai, and cried: "the dragoons!" The dragoons were advancing at a walk, in silence, their pistols in their holsters, their sabres in their sheaths, their musketoons in their rests, with an air of gloomy expectation.

At two hundred paces from the little bridge, they halted. The fiacre in which Lafayette was, made its way up to them, they opened their ranks, let it pass, and closed again behind it. At that moment the dragoons and the multitude came together. The women fled in terror.

What took place in that fatal moment? nobody could tell. It was the dark moment when two clouds mingle. Some say that a trumpet-flourish sounding the charge was heard from the direction of the Arsenal, others that a dagger-thrust was given by a child to a dragoon. The fact is that three shots were suddenly fired, the first killed the chief of the squadron, Cholet, the second killed an old deaf woman who was closing her window in the Rue Contrescarpe, the third singed the epaulette of an officer; a woman cried: "They are beginning too soon!" and all at once there was seen, from the side opposite the Quai Morland, a squadron of dragoons which had remained in barracks turning out on the gallop, with swords drawn, from the Rue Bassompierre and the Boulevard Bourdon, and sweeping all before them.

There are no more words, the tempest breaks loose, stones fall like hail, musketry bursts forth, many rush headlong down the bank and cross the little arm of the Seine now filled up, the yards of the Ile Louviers, that vast ready-made citadel, bristle with combatants, they tear up stakes, they fire pistol-shots, a barricade is planned out, the young men crowd back, pass the Bridge of Austerlitz with the hearse at a run, and charge on the Municipal Guard, the carbineers rush up, the dragoons ply the sabre, the mass scatters in every direction, a rumour of war flies to the four corners of Paris, men cry: "To arms!" they run, they tumble, they fly, they resist. Wrath sweeps along the émeute as the wind sweeps along a fire.

IV
THE EBULLITIONS OF FORMER TIMES

NOTHING is more extraordinary than the first swarming of an émeute. Everything bursts out everywhere at once. Was it foreseen? yes. Was it prepared? no. Whence does it spring? from the pavements. Whence does it fall? from the clouds. Here the insurrection has the character of a plot; there of an improvisation. The first comer takes possession of a current of the multitude and leads it whither he will. A beginning full of terror with which is mingled a sort of frightful gaiety. At first there are clamours, the shops close, the displays of the merchants disappear; then some isolated shots; people flee; butts of guns strike against porte-cochères; you hear the servant girls laughing in the yards of the houses and saying: *There is going to be a row!*

A quarter of an hour had not elapsed and here is what had taken place nearly at the same time at twenty different points in Paris.

In the Rue Sainte Croix de la Bretonnerie, some twenty young men, with beards and long hair, entered a smoking-room and came out again a moment afterwards, bearing a horizontal tricolour flag covered with crape, and having at their head three men armed, one with a sword, another with a gun, the third with a pike.

In the Rue des Nonaindières, a well-dressed bourgeois, who was pursy, had a sonorous voice, a bald head, a high forehead, a black beard, and one of those rough moustaches which cannot be smoothed down, offered cartridges publicly to the passers-by.

In the Rue Saint Pierre Montmartre, some men with bare arms paraded a black flag on which these words could be read in white letters: *Republic or death.* In the Rue des Jeûneurs, the Rue du Cadran, the Rue Montorgueil, and the Rue Mandar, appeared groups waving flags on which were visible in letters of gold, the word *section* with a number. One of these flags was red and blue with an imperceptible white stripe between.

A manufactory of arms was rifled, on the Boulevard Saint Martin, and three armourer's shops, the first in the Rue Beaubourg, the second in the Rue Michel le Comte, the third in the Rue du Temple. In a few minutes the thousand hands of the multitude seized and carried off two hundred and thirty muskets nearly all double-barrelled, sixty-four swords, eighty-three pistols. To arm more people, one took the gun, another the bayonet.

Opposite the Quai de la Grève, young men armed with muskets installed themselves with the women to shoot. One of them had a musket with a match-lock. They rang, entered, and set to making cartridges. One of these women said: "*I did not know what cartridges were, my husband told me to.*"

A throng broke into a curiosity shop in the Rue des Vieilles Haudriettes and took some yataghans and Turkish arms.

The corpse of a mason killed by a musket shot was lying in the Rue de la Perle.

And then, right bank, left bank, on the quais, on the boulevards, in the Latin quartier, in the region of the markets, breathless men, working-men, students, sectionaries, read proclamations, cried: "To arms!" broke the street lamps, unharnessed wagons, tore up the pavements, broke in the doors of the houses, uprooted the trees, ransacked the cellars, rolled hogsheads, heaped up paving stones, pebbles, pieces of furniture, boards, made barricades.

They forced the bourgeois to help them. They went into the women's houses, they made them give up the sword and the gun of their absent husbands, and wrote over the door with Spanish white: "*the arms are delivered.*" Some signed "with their names" receipts for the gun and sword, and said: "*send for them to-morrow to the mairie.*" They disarmed the solitary sentinels in the streets and the National Guards going to their municipality. They tore off the officers' epaulettes. In the Rue du Cimetière Saint Nicolas, an officer of the National Guard, pursued by a troop armed with clubs and foils, took refuge with great difficulty in a house which he was able to leave only at night, and in disguise.

In the Quartier St. Jacques, the students came out of their hotels in swarms, and went up the Rue Saint Hyacinthe to the café Du Progrès or down to the café Des Sept Billards, on the Rue des Mathurins. There, before the doors, some young men standing upon the posts distributed arms. They pillaged the lumberyard on the Rue Transnonain to make barricades. At a single point, the inhabitants resisted, at the corner of the Rues Sainte Avoye and Simon le Franc where they destroyed the barricade themselves. At a single point, the insurgents gave way; they abandoned a barricade commenced in the Rue du Temple after having fired upon a detachment of the National Guard, and fled through the Rue de la Corderie. The detachment picked up in the barricade a red flag, a package of cartridges, and three hundred pistol balls. The National Guards tore up the flag and carried the shreds at the point of their bayonets.

All that we are here relating slowly and successively took place at once in all points of the city in the midst of a vast tumult, like a multitude of flashes in a single peal of thunder.

In less than an hour twenty-seven barricades rose from the

ground in the single quartier of the markets. At the centre was that famous house, No. 50, which was the fortress of Jeanne and her hundred and six companions, and which, flanked on one side by a barricade at Saint Merry, and on the other by a barricade on the Rue Maubuée, commanded three streets, the Rue des Arcis, the Rue Saint Martin, and the Rue Aubry le Boucher on which it fronted. Two barricades at right angles ran back, one from the Rue Montorgueil to the Grande Truanderie, the other from the Rue Geoffroy Langevin to the Rue Sainte Avoye. Without counting innumerable barricades in twenty other quartiers of Paris, in the Marais, at Mount Sainte Geneviève; one, on the Rue Ménilmontant, where could be seen a porte-cochère torn from its hinges; another near the little bridge of the Hôtel Dieu made with an écossaise unhitched and overturned, within three hundred yards of the prefecture of police.

At the barricade on the Rue des Ménétriers, a well-dressed man distributed money to the labourers. At the barricade on the Rue Grenetat a horseman appeared and handed to him who appeared to be the chief of the barricade a roll which looked like a roll of money. "*This*," said he, "*is to pay the expenses, wine, et cætera.*" A young man of a light complexion, without a cravat, went from one barricade to another carrying orders. Another, with drawn sword and a blue police cap on his head, was stationing sentinels. In the interior, within the barricades, wine-shops and porters' lodges were converted into guardhouses. Moreover, the émeute was conducted according to the soundest military tactics. The narrow, uneven, sinuous streets, full of turns and corners, were admirably chosen; the environs of the markets in particular, a network of streets more intricate than a forest. The Society of the Friends of the People, it was said, had assumed the direction of the insurrection in the Quartier Sainte Avoye. A man, killed in Rue du Ponceau, who was searched, had a plan of Paris upon him.

What had really assumed the direction of the émeute was a sort of unknown impetuosity which was in the atmosphere. The insurrection, abruptly, had built the barricades with one hand, and with the other seized nearly all the posts of the garrison. In less than three hours, like a train of powder which takes fire, the insurgents had invaded and occupied on the right bank, the Arsenal, the Mayor's office of the Place Royale, all the Marais, the Popincourt manufactory of arms, the Galiote, the Château d'Eau, all of the streets near the markets; on the left bank, the barracks of the Vétérans, Sainte Pélagie, the Place Maubert, the powder-mill of the Deux Moulins, all the Barrières. At five o'clock in the afternoon they were masters of the Bastille, the Lingerie, the Blancs Manteaux; their scouts touched the Place des Victoires, and threatened the Bank, the barracks of the Petits Pères, and the Hôtel des Postes. The third of Paris was in the émeute.

At all points the struggle had commenced on a gigantic scale; and from the disarmings, from the domiciliary visits, from the armourers' shops hastily invaded, there was this result, that the combat which was commenced by throwing stones, was continued by throwing balls.

About six o'clock in the afternoon, the arcade Du Saumon became a field of battle. The émeute was at one end, the troops at the end opposite. They fired from one grating to the other. One observer, a dreamer, the author of this book, who had gone to get a near view of the volcano, found himself caught in the arcade between the two fires. He had nothing but the projection of the pilasters which separate the shops to protect him from the balls; he was nearly half an hour in this delicate situation.

Meanwhile the drums beat the long roll, the National Guards dressed and armed themselves in haste, the legions left the mairies, the regiments left their barracks. Opposite the arcade De l'Ancre, a drummer received a thrust from a dagger. Another, on the Rue du Cygne, was assailed by some thirty young men, who destroyed his drum and took away his sword. Another was killed in the Rue Grenier Saint Lazare. In the Rue Michel le Comte three officers fell dead one after another. Several Municipal Guards, wounded in the Rue des Lombards, turned back.

In front of the Cour Batave, a detachment of National Guards found a red flag bearing this inscription: *Republican revolution, No. 127.* Was it a revolution, in fact?

The insurrection had made the centre of Paris a sort of inextricable, tortuous, colossal citadel.

There was the focus, there was evidently the question. All the rest were only skirmishes. What proved that there all would be decided, was that they were not yet fighting there.

In some regiments, the soldiers were doubtful, which added to the frightful obscurity of the crisis. They remembered the popular ovation which in July, 1830, had greeted the neutrality of the 53rd of the line. Two intrepid men, who had been proved by the great wars, Marshal de Lobau and General Bugeaud, commanded, Bugeaud under Lobau. Enormous patrols, composed of battalions of the line surrounded by entire companies of the National Guard, and preceded by a commissary of police with his badge, went out reconnoitring the insurgent streets. On their side, the insurgents placed pickets at the corners of the streets and boldly sent patrols ouside of the barricades. They kept watch on both sides. The government, with an army in its hand, hesitated; night was coming on, and the tocsin of Saint Merry began to be heard. The Minister of War of the time, Marshal Soult, who had seen Austerlitz, beheld this with gloomy countenance.

These old sailors, accustomed to correct manœuvring, and having no resource or guide, save tactics, that compass of battles, are completely lost in presence of that immense foam which is called the wrath of the people. The wind of revolutions is not tractable.

The National Guard of the banlieue hurried together in disorder. A battalion of the 12th Light ran down from Saint Denis, the 14th of the Line arrived from Courbevoie, the batteries of the Military School had taken position at the Carrousel; artillery came from Vincennes.

Solitude reigned at the Tuileries. Louis Philippe was full of serenity.

V
ORIGINALITY OF PARIS

WITHIN two years, as we have said, Paris had seen more than one insurrection. Outside of the insurgent quartiers, nothing is usually more strangely calm than the physiognomy of Paris during an émeute. Paris accustoms itself very quickly to everything—it is only an émeute—and Paris is so busy that it does not trouble itself for so slight a thing. These colossal cities alone can contain at the same time a civil war, and an indescribably strange tranquillity. Usually, when the insurrection begins; when the drum, the long-roll, the genérale, are heard, the shopkeeper merely says:

"It seems there is some squabble in the Rue Saint Martin."
Or:

"Faubourg Saint Antoine."

Often he adds with unconcern:

"Somewhere down that way."

Afterwards when he distinguishes the dismal and thrilling uproar of musketry and the firing of platoons, the shopkeeper says:

"It is getting warm, then! Hullo, it is getting warm!"

A moment afterwards, if the émeute approaches and increases, he precipitately shuts his shop, and hastily puts on his uniform; that is to say, places his goods in safety and risks his person.

There is firing at the street corners, in an arcade, in a cul-de-sac; barricades are taken, lost, and retaken; blood flows, the fronts of the houses are riddled with grape, balls kill people in their beds, corpses encumber the pavement. A few streets off, you hear the clicking of billiard balls in the cafés.

The theatres open their doors and play comedies; the curious chat and laugh two steps from these streets full of war. The fiacres jog along; passers are going to dine in the city. Sometimes in the very quartier where there is fighting. In 1831 a fusillade was suspended to let a wedding party pass by.

At the time of the insurrection of the 12th of May, 1839, in the Rue Saint Martin, a little infirm old man, drawing a handcart surmounted by a tri-coloured rag, in which there were decanters filled with some liquid, went back and forth from the barricade to the troops and from the troops to the barricade, impartially offering glasses of cocoa—now to the government, now to the anarchy.

Nothing is more strange; and this is the peculiar characteristic of the émeutes of Paris, which is not found in any other capital. Two things are requisite for it, the greatness of Paris and its gaiety. It requires the city of Voltaire and of Napoleon.

This time, however, in the armed contest of the 5th of June, 1832, the great city felt something which was, perhaps, stronger than herself. She was afraid. You saw everywhere, in the most distant and the most "disinterested" quartiers, doors, windows, and shutters closed in broad day. The courageous armed, the poltroons hid. The careless and busy wayfarer disappeared. Many streets were as empty as at four o'clock in the morning. Alarming stories were circulated, ominous rumours were spread. "That *they* were masters of the Bank;" "that, merely at the cloisters of Saint Merry, there were six hundred, intrenched and fortified in the church;" "that the Line was doubtful;" "that Armand Carrel had been to see Marshal Clausel and that the marshal had said: *Have one regiment in the place first*;" "that Lafayette was sick, but that he had said to them notwithstanding: *I am with you. I will follow you anywhere where there is room for a chair*;" "that it was necessary to keep on their guard; that in the night there would be people who would pillage the isolated houses in the deserted quartiers of Paris (in this the imagination of the police was recognised, that Anne Radcliffe mixed with government);" "that a battery had been planted in the Rue Aubry le Boucher;" "that Lobau and Bugeaud were consulting; and that at midnight, or at daybreak at the latest, four columns would march at once upon the centre of the émeute, the first coming from the Bastille, the second from the Porte Saint Martin, the third from La Grève, the fourth from the markets;" "that perhaps also the troops would evacuate Paris and retire to the Champ de Mars;" "that nobody knew what might happen, but that certainly, this time, it was serious." They were concerned about Marshal Soult's hesitation. "Why doesn't he attack right away?" It is certain that he was deeply absorbed. The old lion seemed to scent in that darkness some unknown monster.

Evening came, the theatres did not open; the patrols made their round spitefully; passers were searched; the suspicious were arrested. At nine o'clock there were more than eight hundred persons under arrest; the prefecture of police was crowded, the Conciergerie was crowded, La Force was crowded. At the Conciergerie, in particular, the long vault which is called the Rue de Paris was strewn with bundles of straw, on which lay a throng of prisoners, whom the man of Lyons, Lagrange, harangued valiantly. The rustling of all this straw, stirred by all these men, was like the sound of a shower. Elsewhere the prisoners lay in the open air in the prison yards, piled one upon another. Anxiety was everywhere, and a certain tremor, little known to Paris.

People barricaded themselves in their houses; wives and mothers were terrified; you heard only this: *Oh! my God! he has not come back!* In the distance there was heard very rarely the rumbling of a wagon. People listened, on their door-sills, to the rumours, the cries, the tumults, the dull and indistinct sounds, things of which they said: *That is the cavalry*, or: *Those are the ammunition wagons galloping down*, the trumpets, the drums, the musketry, and above all, that mournful tocsin of Saint Merry. They expected the first cannon-shot. Men rose up at the corners of the streets and disappeared, crying: "Go home!" And they hastened to bolt their doors. They said: "How will it end?" From moment to moment, as night fell, Paris seemed coloured more dismally with the fearful flame of the émeute.

BOOK ELEVENTH – THE ATOM
FRATERNISES WITH THE HURRICANE

I
SOME INSIGHT INTO THE ORIGIN OF GAVROCHE'S POETRY—INFLUENCE OF AN ACADEMICIAN UPON THAT POETRY

AT the moment the insurrection, springing up at the shock of the people with the troops in front of the Arsenal, determined a backward movement in the multitude which was following the hearse and which, for the whole length of the boulevards, weighed, so to say, upon the head of the procession, there was a frightful reflux. The mass wavered, the ranks broke, all ran, darted, slipped away, some with cries of attack, others with the pallor of flight. The great river which covered the boulevards divided in a twinkling, overflowed on the right and on the left, and poured in torrents into two hundred streets at once with the rushing of an opened mill-sluice. At this moment a ragged child who was coming down the Rue Ménilmontant, holding in his hand a branch of laburnum in bloom, which he had just gathered on the heights of Belleville, caught sight, before a second-hand dealer's shop, of an old horse pistol. He threw his flowering branch upon the pavement, and cried:

"Mother What's-your-name, I'll borrow your machine."

And he ran off with the pistol.

Two minutes later, a flood of terrified bourgeois who were fleeing through the Rue Amelot and the Rue Basse, met the child who was brandishing his pistol and singing:

> La nuit on ne voit rien,
> Le jour on voit très bien,
> D'un écrit apocryphe
> Le bourgeois s'ébouriffe,
> Pratiquez la vertu,
> Tutu chapeau pointu!

It was little Gavroche going to war.

On the boulevard he perceived that the pistol had no hammer.

Whose was this refrain which served him to time his march, and all the other songs which, on occasion, he was fond of singing? we do not know. Who knows? his own perhaps. Gavroche besides kept up with all the popular airs in circulation, and mingled with them his own warbling. A sprite and a devil, he made a medley of the voices of nature and the voices of Paris. He combined the repertory of the birds with the repertory of the workshops. He knew some painters' boys, a tribe contiguous to his own. He had been, as it appears, three months a printer's apprentice. He had done an errand one day for Monsieur Baour-Lormian, one of the Forty. Gavroche was a *gamin* of letters.

Gavroche moreover had no suspicion that on that wretched rainy night when he had offered the hospitality of his elephant to two brats, it was for his own brothers that he had acted the part of Providence. His brothers in the evening, his father in the morning; such had been his night. On leaving the Rue des Ballets at early dawn, he had returned in haste to the elephant, artistically extracted the two *mômes*, shared with them such breakfast as he could invent, then went away, confiding them to that good mother, the street, who had almost brought him up himself. On leaving them, he had given them rendezvous for the evening at the same place, and left them this discourse as a farewell: "*I cut stick, otherwise spoken, I esbigne, or, as they say at the court, I haul off; Brats, if you don't find papa and mamma, come back here tonight. I will strike you up some supper and put you to bed.*" The two children, picked up by some sergent de ville and put in the retreat, or stolen by some mountebank, or simply lost in the immense Chinese Parisian turmoil, had not returned. The lower strata of the existing social world are full of these lost traces. Gavroche had not seen them since. Ten or twelve weeks had elapsed since that night. More than once he had scratched the top of his head and said: "Where the devil are my two children?"

Meanwhile he had reached, pistol in hand, the Rue du Pont aux Choux. He noticed that there was now, in that street, but one shop open, and, a matter worthy of reflection, a pastry-cook's shop. This was a providential opportunity to eat one more apple-puff before entering the unknown. Gavroche stopped, fumbled in his trousers, felt in his fob, turned out his pockets, found nothing in them, not a sou, and began to cry: "Help!"

It is hard to lack the final cake.

Gavroche none the less continued on his way.

Two minutes later, he was in the Rue Saint Louis. While passing through the Rue du Parc Royal he felt the need of some compensation for the impossible apple-puff, and he gave himself the immense pleasure of tearing down the theatre posters in broad day.

A little further along, seeing a group of well-to-do persons pass by, who appeared to him to be men of property, he shrugged his shoulders, and spit out at random this mouthful of philosophic bile:

"These rich men, how fat they are! they stuff themselves. They wallow in good dinners. Ask them what they do with their money. They don't know anything about it. They eat it, they do! How much of it the belly carries away."

II
GAVROCHE ON THE MARCH

THE brandishing of a pistol without a hammer, holding it in one's hand in the open street, is such a public function that Gavroche felt his spirits rise higher with every step. He cried, between the snatches of the Marseillaise which he was singing:

"It's all going well. I suffer a good deal in my left paw, I am broken with my rheumatism, but I am content, citizens. The bourgeois have nothing to do but to behave themselves, I am going to sneeze subversive couplets at them. What are the detectives? they are dogs. By jinks! don't let us fail in respect for dogs. Now I wish I had one to my pistol.* I come from the boulevard, my friends, it is getting hot, it is boiling over a little, it is simmering. It is time to skim the pot. Forward, men! let their impure blood water the furrows! I give my days for my country. I shall never see my concubine again, n-e-ver, over, yes. Never! but it's all the same, let us be joyful! let us fight, egad! I have had enough of despotism."

At that moment, the horse of a lancer of the National Guard, who was passing, having fallen down, Gavroche laid his pistol on the pavement, and raised up the man, then he helped to raise the horse. After which he picked up his pistol, and resumed his way.

---

*The French call the hammer of a pistol, the *dog* of it.

In the Rue de Thorigny, all was peace and silence. This apathy, suited to the Marais, contrasted with the vast surrounding uproar. Four gossips were chatting upon a doorstep. Scotland has her trios of witches, but Paris has her quartettes of gossips; and the "thou shalt be king," would be quite as ominously cast at Bonaparte in the Baudoyer Square as at Macbeth in the heath of Armuyr. It would be almost the same croaking.

The gossips of the Rue de Thorigny were busy only with their own affairs. They were three portresses and a rag-picker with her basket and hook.

The four seemed standing at the four corners of old age, which are decay, decrepitude, ruin, and sorrow.

The rag-picker was humble. In this out-door society, the rag-picker bows, the portress patronises. That is a result of the sweepings which are, as the portresses will, fat or lean, according to the fancy of her who makes the head. There may be kindness in the broom.

This rag-picker was a grateful basket, and she smiled, what a smile! to the three portresses. Such things as this were said:

"Ah, now, your cat is always spiteful, is she?"

"Luddy! cats, you know, are nat'rally the enemies of dogs. It is the dogs that complain."

"And folks, too."

"Still, cats' fleas don't get on folks."

"That's not the trouble, dogs are dangerous. I remember one year there was so many dogs they had to put it in the papers. It was the time they had the big sheep at the Tuileries to draw the King of Rome's little wagon. Do you remember the King of Rome?"

"Me, I liked the Duke of Bourdeaux better."

"For my part, I knew Louis XVII. I like Louis XVII. better."

"How dear meat is, Ma'am Patagon!"

"Oh! don't speak of it, the butchering is horrid. Horridly horrid. They have nothing but tough meat nowadays."

Here the rag-picker intervened!

"Ladies, business is very dull. The garbage heaps are shabby. Folks don't throw anything away in these days. They eat everything."

"There are poorer people than you, Vargoulême."

"Oh, that is true!" replied the rag-picker, with deference, "for my part I have an occupation."

There was a pause, and the rag-picker, yielding to that necessity for display which lies deepest in the human heart, added:

"In the morning when I get home, I pick over the basketful, I make my sorties (probably sortings). That makes heaps in my room. I put the rags in a basket, the cores in a tub, the linens in my closet, the woollens in my bureau, the old papers in the corner of the window, the things good to eat into my plate, the bits of glass in the fire-place, the old shoes behind the door, and the bones under my bed."

Gavroche, who had stopped behind, was listening.

"Old women," said he, "what business have you now talking politics?"

A volley assailed him, composed of a quadruple hoot.

"There is another scoundrel!"

"What has he got in his stump? A pistol."

"I want to know, that beggar of a *môme!*"

"They are never quiet if they are not upsetting the government."

Gavroche, in disdain, made no other reply than merely to lift the end of his nose with his thumb while he opened his hand to its full extent.

The rag-picker cried:

"Spiteful go-bare-paws!"

She who answered to the name of Ma'am Patagon clapped her hands in horror.

"There is going to be troubles, that's sure. That rascal over there with a beard, I used to see him go by every morning with a young thing in a pink cap under his arm; to-day I see him go by, he was giving his arm to a musket. Ma'am Bacheux says that there was a revolution last week at—at—at—where is the place?—at Pontoise. And then see him there with his pistol, that horrid blackguard? It seems the Célestins are all full of cannon. What would you have the government do with the scapegraces who do nothing but invent ways to disturb people, when we are beginning to be a little quiet, after all the troubles we have had, good Lord God, that poor queen that I see go by in the cart! And all this is going to make snuff dearer still. It is infamous! and surely I will go to see you guillotined, you scoundrel."

"You sniffle, my ancient," said Gavroche. "Blow your promontory."

And he passed on.

When he reached the Rue Pavée, the rag-picker recurred to his mind, and he soliloquised thus:

"You do wrong to insult the Revolutionists, Mother Heap-in-the-corner. This pistol is in your interest. It is so that you may have more things good to eat in your basket."

Suddenly he heard a noise behind him: it was the portress Patagon who had followed him, and who, from a distance, was shaking her fist at him, crying:

"You are nothing but a bastard!"

"Yes," said Gavroche, "I amuse myself at that in a profound manner."

Soon after, he passed the Hôtel Lamoignon. There he shouted out his appeal:

"En route for battle!"

And he was seized with a fit of melancholy. He looked at his pistol with a reproachful air, which seemed an endeavour to soften it:

"I go off," said he to it, "but you do not go off."

One dog may distract attention from another. A very lean cur was passing. Gavroche was moved to pity.

"My poor bow-wow," said he, "have you swallowed a barrel, then, that all the hoops show?"

Then he bent his steps towards the Orme Saint Gervais.

III
JUST INDIGNATION OF A BARBER

THE worthy barber, who drove away the two little boys to whom Gavroche opened the paternal intestines of the elephant, was at this moment in his shop, busy shaving an old legionary soldier who had served under the empire. They were chatting. The barber had naturally spoken to the veteran of the émeute, then of General Lamarque and from Lamarque they had come to the emperor. Hence a conversation between a barber and a soldier, which Prudhomme, if he had been present, would have enriched with arabesques, and which he would have entitled: *Dialogue of the razor and the sabre.*

"Monsieur," said the wig-maker, "how did the emperor mount on horseback?"

"Badly. He didn't know how to fall. So he never fell."

"Did he have fine horses? he must have had fine horses!"

"The day he gave me the cross, I noticed his animal. She was a running mare, perfectly white. Her ears were very wide apart, saddle deep, head fine, marked with a black star, neck very long, knees strongly jointed, ribs protruding, shoulders sloping, hind quarters powerful. A little more than fifteen hands high."

"A pretty horse," said the barber.

"It was the animal of his majesty."

The barber felt that after this word a little silence was proper, he conformed to it, then resumed:

"The emperor was never wounded but once, was he, monsieur?"

The old soldier answered with the calm and sovereign tone of a man who was there:

"In the heel. At Ratisbon. I never saw him so well dressed as he was that day. He was as neat as a penny."

"And you, Monsieur Veteran, you must have been wounded often?"

"I?" said the soldier, "ah! no great thing. I got two sabre slashes in my neck at Marengo, a ball in my right arm at Auster-litz, another in my left hip at Jena, at Friedland a bayonet thrust—there—at Moscow seven or eight lance thrusts, no matter where, at Lutzen a shell burst which crushed my finger—Ah! and then at Waterloo a bullet in my leg. That is all."

"How beautiful it is," exclaimed the barber with a pindaric accent, "to die on the field of battle! Upon my word, rather than die in my bed, of sickness, slowly, a little every day, with drugs, plasters, syringes, and medicine, I would prefer a cannon ball in my belly."

"You are not fastidious," said the soldier.

He had hardly finished when a frightful crash shook the shop. A pane of the window had been suddenly shattered.

The barber became pallid.

"O God!" cried he, "there is one!"

"What?"

"A cannon ball."

"Here it is," said the soldier.

And he picked up something which was rolling on the floor. It was a stone.

The barber ran to the broken window and saw Gavroche, who was running with all his might towards the Saint Jean market. On passing the barber's shop, Gavroche, who had the two *mômes* on his mind, could not resist the desire to bid him good-day, and had sent a stone through his sash.

"See!" screamed the barber, who from white had become blue, "he makes mischief for the sake of mischief. What has anybody done to that *gamin*?"

IV
THE CHILD WONDERS AT THE OLD MAN

MEANWHILE Gavroche at the Saint Jean market where the guard was already disarmed, had just—effected his junction—with a band led by Enjolras, Courfeyrac, Combeferre, and Feuilly. They were almost armed. Bahorel and Jean Prouvaire had joined them and enlarged the group. Enjolras had a double-barrelled fowling piece, Combeferre a National Guard's musket bearing the number of the legion, and at his waist two pistols which could be seen, his coat being unbuttoned, Jean Prouvaire an old cavalry musketoon, Bahorel a carbine; Courfeyrac was brandishing an unsheathed sword-cane. Feuilly, a drawn sabre in his hand, marched in the van, crying: "Poland for ever!"

They came from the Quai Morland cravatless, hatless, breathless, soaked by the rain, lightning in their eyes. Gavroche approached them calmly:

"Where are we going?"

"Come on," said Courfeyrac.

Behind Feuilly marched, or rather bounded, Bahorel, a fish in the water of the émeute. He had a crimson waistcoat, and those words which crush everything. His waistcoat overcame a passer, who cried out in desperation:

"There are the reds!"

"The reds, the reds!" replied Bahorel. "A comical fear, bourgeois. As for me, I don't tremble before a red poppy, the little red hood inspires me with no dismay. Bourgeois, believe me, leave the fear of red to horned cattle."

He caught sight of a piece of wall on which was placarded the most peaceful sheet of paper in the world, a permission to eat eggs, a charge for Lent, addressed by the Archbishop of Paris to his "ouailles" [flock].

Bahorel exclaimed:

"*Ouailles*; polite way of saying *oies*" [geese].

And he tore the charge from the wall. This conquered

Gavroche. From that moment, Garoche began to study Bahorel.

"Bahorel," observed Enjolras, "you are wrong. You should have let that charge alone, it is not with it that we have to do. You are expending your wrath uselessly. Economise your ammunition. We don't fire out of rank,—no more with the soul than with the gun."

"Each in his own way, Enjolras," retorted Bahorel. "This bishop's prosing annoys me, I want to eat eggs without any-body's permission. You have the cold burning style; I amuse myself. Besides, I am not exhausting myself, I am gaining new energy; and if I tore down that charge, by Hercules! it was to give me an appetite."

This word *Hercules*, struck Gavroche. He sought every opportunity to instruct himself, and this tearer-down of posters had his esteem. He asked him:

"What does that mean, *Hercules*?"

Bahorel answered:

"It means holy name of a dog in Latin."

Here Bahorel recognised at a window a pale young man with a black beard, who was looking at them as they were passing, probably a Friend of the A B C. He cried to him:

"Quick, cartridges! *para bellum*."

"*Bel homme!* [Handsome man!] that is true," said Gavroche, who now understood Latin.

A tumultuous cortège accompanied them, students, artists, young men affiliated to the Cougourde d'Aix, working-men, rivermen, armed with clubs and bayonets; a few, like Combeferre, with pistols thrust into their waistbands. An old man, who appeared very old, was marching with this band. He was not armed, and he was hurrying, that he should not be left behind, although he had a thoughtful expression. Gavroche perceived him:

"Whossat?" said he to Courfeyrac.

"That is an old man."

It was M. Mabeuf.

V

THE OLD MAN

WE must tell what had happened.

Enjolras and his friends were on the Boulevard Bourdon,

near the warehouses, at the moment the dragoons charged. Enjolras, Courfeyrac, and Combeferre were among those who took to the Rue Bassomipierre, crying: "To the barricades!" In the Rue Lesdiguières they met an old man trudging along. What attracted their attention was, that this goodman was walking zigzag, as if he were drunk. Moreover, he had his hat in his hand, although it had been raining all the morning, and was raining hard at that very moment. Courfeyrac recognised Father Mabeuf. He knew him from having seen him many times accompanying Marius to the door. Knowing the peaceful and more than timid habits of the old church-warden-book-worm, and astounded at seeing him in the midst of this tumult, within two steps of the cavalry charges, almost in the midst of a fusillade, bareheaded in the rain, and walking among the bullets, he went up to him, and the émeuter of five-and-twenty and the octogenarian exchanged this dialogue:

"Monsieur Mabeuf, go home."

"What for?"

"There is going to be a row."

"Very well."

"Sabre-strokes, musket shots, Monsieur Mabeuf."

"Very well."

"Cannon shots."

"Very well. Where are you going, you boys?"

"We are going to pitch the government over."

"Very well."

And he followed them. From that moment he had not uttered a word. His step had suddenly become firm; some working-men had offered him an arm, he refused with a shake of the head. He advanced almost to the front rank of the column, having at once the motion of a man who is walking, and the countenance of a man who is asleep.

"What a desperate goodman!" murmured the students. The rumour ran through the assemblage that he was—an ancient Conventionist—an old regicide. The company had turned into the Rue de la Verrerie.

Little Gavroche marched on with all his might with this song, which made him a sort of clarion. He sang:

Voici la lune qui paraît,
Quand irons-nous dans la forêt?

> Demandait Charlot à Charlotte.
>> Tou tou tou
>> Pour Chatou.
> Je n'ai qu'un Dieu, qu'un roi, qu'un liard et qu'une botte.
>> Pour avoir bu de grand matin
>> La rosée à même le thym,
>> Deux moineaux étaient en ribote.
>>> Zi zi zi
>>> Pour Passy
> Je n'ai qu'un Dieu, qu'un roi, qu'un liard et qu'une botte.
>> Et ces deux pauvres petits loups
>> Comme deux grives étaient soûls;
>> Un tigre en riait dans sa grotte.
>>> Don don don
>>> Pour Meudon.
> Je n'ai qu'un Dieu, qu'un roi, qu'un liard et qu'une botte.
>> L'un jurait et l'autre sacrait
>> Quand irons-nous dans la forêt?
>> Demandait Charlot à Charlotte.
>>> Tin tin tin
>>> Pour Pantin.
> Je n'ai qu'un Dieu, qu'un roi, qu'un liard et qu'une botte.*

They made their way towards Saint Merry.

---

*See the moon is shining, when shall we go into the woods? asked Charley of Charlotte.

Too, too, too, for Chatou. I have but one God, one king, one farthing, and one boot.

For having drunk in early morn, dew and thyme, two sparrows were in a fuddle.

Zi, zi, zi, for Passy. I have but one God, one king, one farthing, and one boot.

And these two poor little wolves were as drunk as two thrushes; a tiger laughed at it in his cave.

Don, don, don, for Meudon. I have but one God, one king, one farthing, and one boot.

One swore and the other cursed. When shall we go into the woods? asked Charley of Charlotte.

Tin, tin, tin, for Pantin. I have but one God, one king, one farthing, and one boot.

VI
RECRUITS

THE band increased at every moment. Towards the Rue des Billettes a man of tall stature, who was turning grey, whose rough and bold mien Courfeyrac, Enjolras, and Combeferre noticed, but whom none of them knew, joined them. Gavroche, busy singing, whistling, humming, going forward and rapping on the shutters of the shops with the butt of his hammerless pistol, paid no attention to this man.

It happened that, in the Rue de la Verrerie, they passed by Courfeyrac's door.

"That is lucky," said Courfeyrac, "I have forgotten my purse and I have lost my hat." He left the company and went up to his room, four stairs at a time. He took an old hat and his purse. He took also a large square box, of the size of a big valise, which was hidden among his dirty clothes. As he was running down again, the portress hailed him:

"Monsieur de Courfeyrac?"

"Portress, what is your name?" responded Courfeyrac.

The portress stood aghast.

"Why, you know it very well; I am the portress, my name is Mother Veuvain."

"Well, if you call me Monsieur de Courfeyrac again, I shall call you Mother de Veuvain. Now, speak, what is it? What do you want?"

"There is somebody who wishes to speak to you."

"Who is it?"

"I don't know."

"Where is he?"

"In my lodge."

"The devil!" said Courfeyrac.

"But he has been waiting more than an hour for you to come home!" replied the portress.

At the same time, a sort of young working-man, thin, pale, small, freckled, dressed in a torn blouse and patched pantaloons of ribbed velvet, and who had rather the appearance of a girl in boy's clothes than of a man, came out of the lodge and said to Courfeyrac in a voice which, to be sure, was not the least in the world like a woman's voice.

"Monsieur Marius, if you please?"

"He is not in."

"Will he be in this evening?"

"I don't know anything about it."

And Courfeyrac added: "As for myself, I shall not be in."

The young man looked fixedly at him, and asked him:

"Why so?"

"Because."

"Where are you going then?"

"What is that to you?"

"Do you want me to carry your box?"

"I am going to the barricades."

"Do you want me to go with you?"

"If you like," answered Courfeyrac. "The road is free; the streets belong to everybody."

And he ran off to rejoin his friends. When he had rejoined them, he gave the box to one of them to carry. It was not until a quarter of an hour afterwards that he perceived that the young man had in fact followed them.

A mob does not go precisely where it wishes. We have explained that a gust of wind carries it along. They went beyond Saint Merry and found themselves, without really knowing how, in the Rue Saint Denis.

I

HISTORY OF CORINTH FROM ITS FOUNDATION

THE Parisians who, to-day, upon entering the Rue Rambuteau from the side of the markets, notice on their right, opposite the Rue Mondétour, a basket-maker's shop, with a basket for a sign, in the shape of the Emperor Napoleon the Great, with this inscription:

NAPOLÉON EST FAIT
TOUT EN OSIER,*

do not suspect the terrible scenes which this very place saw thirty years ago.

Here were the Rue de la Chanvrerie, which the old signs spelled Chanverrerie, and the celebrated wine-shop called Corinth.

The reader will remember all that has been said about the barricade erected on this spot and eclipsed elsewhere by the barricade of Saint Merry. Upon this famous barricade of the Rue de la Chanvrerie, now fallen into deep obscurity, we are about to throw some little light.

Permit us to recur, for the sake of clearness, to the simple means already employed by us for Waterloo. Those who would picture to themselves with sufficient exactness the confused blocks of houses which stood at that period near the Pointe Saint Eustache, at the northeast corner of the markets of Paris, where is now the mouth of the Rue Rambuteau, have only to figure to themselves, touching the Rue Saint Denis at its summit, and the markets at its base, an N, of which the two vertical strokes would be the Rue de la Grande Truanderie and the Rue de la Chanvrerie, and the Rue de la Petite Truanderie would make the transverse stroke. The old Rue Mondétour cut the three strokes at the most awkward angles. So that the labyrinthine entanglement of these four streets sufficed to make, in a space of four hundred square yards, between the markets and the Rue Saint Denis, in one direction, and between the Rue du

---

* NAPOLEON IS MADE,
  ALL OF WILLOW BRAID.

Cygne and the Rue des Prêcheurs in the other direction, seven islets of houses, oddly intersecting, of various sizes, placed crosswise and as if by chance, and separated but slightly, like blocks of stone in a stone yard, by narrow crevices.

We say narrow crevices, and we cannot give a more just idea of those obscure, contracted, angular lanes, bordered by ruins eight stories high. These houses were so dilapidated, that in the Rues de la Chanvrerie and de la Petite Truanderie, the fronts were shored up with beams, reaching from one house to another. The street was narrow and the gutter wide, the passer walked along a pavement which was always wet, beside shops that were like cellars, great stone blocks encircled with iron, immense garbage heaps, and alley gates armed with enormous and venerable gratings. The Rue Rambuteau has devastated all this.

The name Mondétour pictures marvellously well the windings of all this route. A little further along you found them still better expressed by the *Rue Pirouette*, which ran into the Rue Mondétour.

The passer who came from the Rue Saint Denis into the Rue de la Chanvrerie saw it gradually narrow away before him as if he had entered an elongated funnel. At the end of the street, which was very short, he found the passage barred on the market side, and he would have thought himself in a cul-de-sac, if he had not perceived on the right and on the left two black openings by which he could escape. These were the Rue Mondétour, which communicated on the one side with the Rue des Prêcheurs, on the other with the Rues du Cygne and Petite Truanderie. At the end of this sort of cul-de-sac, at the corner of the opening on the right, might be seen a house lower than the rest, and forming a kind of cape on the street.

In this house, only two stories high, had been festively installed for three hundred years an illustrious wine-shop. This wine-shop raised a joyful sound in the very place which old Théophile has rendered famous in these two lines:

> Là branle le squelette horrible
> D'un pauvre amant qui se pendit.*

---

* There rattles the horrible skeleton of a poor lover who hanged himself.

The location was good. The proprietorship descended from father to son.

In the times of Mathurin Régnier, this wine-shop was called the *Pot aux Roses* (the Pot of Roses), and as rebuses were in fashion, it had for a sign a post (*poteau*) painted rose colour. In the last century, the worthy Natoire, one of the fantastic masters now held in disdain by the rigid school, having got tipsy several times in this wine-shop at the same table where Régnier had got drunk, out of gratitude painted a bunch of Corinth grapes upon the rose-coloured post. The landlord, from joy, changed his sign and had gilded below the bunch these words: *The Grape of Corinth*. Hence the name Corinth. Nothing is more natural to drinkers than an ellipsis. The ellipsis is the zigzag of phrase. Corinth gradually dethroned the *Pot aux Roses*. The last landlord of the dynasty, Father Hucheloup, not even knowing the tradition, had the post painted blue.

A basement-room in which was the counter, a room on the first floor in which was the billiard-table, a spiral wooden staircase piercing the ceiling, wine on the tables, smoke on the walls, candles in broad day, such was the wine-shop. A stairway with a trap-door in the basement-room led to the cellar. On the second floor were the rooms of the Hucheloups. You ascended by a stairway, which was rather a ladder than a stairway, the only entrance to which was by a back door in the large room on the first floor. In the attic, two garret rooms, with dormer windows, nests for servants. The kitchen divided the ground-floor with the counting-room.

Father Hucheloup was perhaps a born chemist, he was certainly a cook; people not only drank in his wine-shop, they ate there. Hucheloup had invented an excellent dish which was found only at his house; it was stuffed carps which he called *carpes au gras*. This was eaten by the light of a tallow candle or a lamp of the time of Louis XVI., upon tables on which an oil-cloth was nailed for a tablecloth. Men came there from a distance. Hucheloup, one fine morning, thought proper to advertise by-passers of his "speciality;" he dipped a brush in a pot of blacking, and as he had an orthography of his own, even as he had a cuisine of his own, he improvised upon his wall this remarkable inscription:

CARPES HO GRAS.

One winter, the showers and the storms took a fancy to efface the S which terminated the first word and the G which commenced the third; it was left like this:

CARPE HO RAS.

Time and the rain aiding, a humble gastronomic advertisement had become a profound piece of advice.

So that it happened that, not knowing French, Father Hucheloup had known Latin, that he had brought philosophy out of his kitchen and that, desiring simply to eclipse Carême, he had equalled Horace. And what was striking was that this also meant: Enter my wine-shop.

Nothing of all this is at present in existence. The Mondétour labyrinth was ripped up and opened wide in 1847, and probably is now no more. The Rue de la Chanvrerie and Corinth have disappeared under the pavements of the Rue Rambuteau.

As we have said, Corinth was one of the meeting, if not rallying places, of Courfeyrac and his friends. It was Grantaire who had discovered Corinth. He had entered on account of *Carpe Horas*, and he returned on account of *Carpes au Gras*. They drank there, they ate there, they shouted there; they paid little, they paid poorly, they did not pay at all, they were always welcome. Father Hucheloup was a goodman.

Hucheloup, a goodman, we have just said, was a cook with moustaches: an amusing variety. He had always an ill-humoured face, seemed to wish to intimidate his customers, grumbled at people who came to his house, and appeared more disposed to pick a quarrel with them than to serve them their soup. And still, we maintain, they were always welcome. This oddity had brought custom to his shop, and led young men to him, saying to each other: "Come and hear Father Hucheloup grumble." He had been a fencing-master. He would suddenly burst out laughing. Coarse voice, good devil. His was a comic heart, with a tragic face; he asked nothing better than to frighten you, much like those snuff-boxes which have the shape of a pistol. The discharge is a sneeze.

His wife was Mother Hucheloup, a bearded creature, and very ugly.

Towards 1830, Father Hucheloup died. With him the secret of the *carpes au gras* was lost. His widow, scarcely consolable, continued the wine-shop. But the cuisine degenerated and became execrable, the wine, which had always been bad, became frightful. Courfeyrac and his friends continued to go to Corinth, however—"from pity," said Bossuet.

Widow Hucheloup was short-winded and deformed, with memories of the country. She relieved their tiresomeness by her pronunciation. She had a way of her own of saying things which spiced her village and spring-time reminiscences. It had once been her fortune, she affirmed, to hear "the lead-breasts sing in the hawkthorns."

The room on the first floor, in which was "the restaurant," was a long and wide room, encumbered with stools, crickets, chairs, benches, and tables, and a rickety old billiard-table. It was reached by the spiral staircase which terminated at the corner of the room in a square hole like the hatchway of a ship.

This room, lighted by a single narrow window and by a lamp which was always burning, had the appearance of a garret. All the pieces of furniture on four legs behaved as if they had but three. The whitewashed walls had no ornament except this quatrain in honour of Ma'am Hucheloup:

Elle étonne à dix pas, elle épouvante à deux,
Une verrue habite en son nez hasardeux;
On tremble à chaque instant qu'elle ne vous la mouche,
Et qu'un beau jour son nez ne tombe dans a bouche.*

This was written in charcoal upon the wall.

Ma'am Hucheloup, the original, went back and forth from morning till night before this quatrain in perfect tranquillity. Two servants, called Chowder and Fricassee, and for whom nobody had ever known any other names, helped Ma'am Hucheloup to put upon the tables the pitchers of blue wine and the various broths which were served to the hungry in earthen dishes. Chowder, fat, round, red, and boisterous, former favourite sultana of the defunct Hucheloup, was uglier than any mythological monster; still, as it is fitting that the servant should always keep behind the mistress, she was less ugly than Ma'am Hucheloup. Fricassee, long, delicate, white with a lymphatic whiteness, rings around her eyes, eyelids drooping, always

---

* She astounds at ten paces, she terrifies at two, a wart inhabits her dangerous nose, you tremble every moment lest she blow it you, and lest some fine day her nose may fall into her mouth.

exhausted and dejected, subject to what might be called chronic weariness, up first, in bed last, served everybody, even the other servant, mildly and in silence, smiling through fatigue with a sort of vague sleepy smile.

Before entering the restaurant room, you might read upon the door this line written in chalk by Courfeyrac:

> Régale si tu peux et mange si tu l'oses.*

II
PRELIMINARY GAIETY

LAIGLE DE MEAUX, we know, lived more with Joly than else-where. He had a lodging as the bird has a branch. The two friends lived together, ate together, slept together. Everything was in common with them, even Musichetta a little. They were what, among the Chapeau Brothers, are called *bini*. On the morning of the 5th of June, they went to breakfast at Corinth. Joly, whose head was stopped up, had a bad cold, which Laigle was beginning to share. Laigle's coat was threadbare, but Joly was well dressed.

It was about nine o'clock in the morning when they opened the door of Corinth.

They went up to the first floor.

Chowder and Fricassee received them: "Oysters, cheese, and ham," said Laigle.

And they sat down at a table.

The wine-shop was empty; they two only were there.

Fricassee, recognising Joly and Laigle, put a bottle of wine on the table.

As they were at their first oysters, a head appeared at the hatchway of the stairs, and a voice said:

"I was passing. I smelt in the street a delicious odour of Brie cheese. I have come in."

It was Grantaire.

Grantaire took a stool and sat down at the table.

Fricassee, seeing Grantaire, put two bottles of wine on the table.

That made three.

---

* Feast if you can and eat if you dare.

"Are you going to drink those two bottles?" inquired Laigle of Grantaire.

Grantaire answered:

"All are ingenious, you alone are ingenuous. Two bottles never astonished a man."

The others had begun by eating. Grantaire began by drinking. A half bottle was quickly swallowed.

"Have you a hole in your stomach?" resumed Laigle.

"You surely have one in your elbow," said Grantaire.

And, after emptying his glass, he added:

"Ah, now, Laigle of the funeral orations, your coat is old."

"I hope so," replied Laigle. "That makes us agree so well, my coat and I. It has got all my wrinkles, it doesn't bind me anywhere, it has fitted itself to all my deformities, it is complaisant to all my motions; I feel it only because it keeps me warm. Old coats are the same thing as old friends."

"That's true," exclaimed Joly, joining in the dialogue, "an old *habit* [coat] is an old *abi* [friend]."

"Especially," said Grantaire, "in the mouth of a man whose head is stopped up."

"Grantaire," asked Laigle, "do you come from the boulevard?"

"No."

"We just saw the head of the procession pass, Joly and I."

"It is a barvellous spectacle," said Joly.

"How quiet this street is!" exclaimed Laigle. "Who would suspect that Paris is all topsy-turvy? You see this was formerly all monasteries about here! Du Breul and Sauval give the list of them, and the Abbé Lebeuf. They were all around here, they swarmed, the shod, the unshod, the shaven, the bearded, the greys, the blacks, the whites, the Franciscans, the Minimi, the Capuchins, the Carmelites, the Lesser Augustines, the Greater Augustines, the Old Augustines. They littered."

"Don't talk about monks," interrupted Grantaire, "it makes me want to scratch."

Then he exclaimed:

"Peugh! I have just swallowed a bad oyster. Here's the hypochondria upon me again. The oysters are spoiled, the servants are ugly. I hate human kind. I passed just now in the Rue Richelieu before the great public library. This heap of oyster shells, which they call a library, disgusts me to think of. How much paper! how much ink! how much scribbling! Somebody has written all that!

What booby was it who said that man is a biped with feathers? And then, I met a pretty girl whom I knew, beautiful as Spring, worthy to be called Floréal, and delighted, transported, happy, with the angels, the poor creature, because yesterday a horrid banker, pitted with small-pox, deigned to fancy her. Alas! woman watches the publican no less than the fop; cats chase mice as well as birds. This damsel, less than two months ago, was a good girl in a garret, she fixed the little ring of copper in the eyelets of corsets, how do you call it? She sewed, she had a bed, she lived with a flower-pot, she was contented. Now she is a bankeress. This transformation was wrought last night. I met the victim this morning, full of joy. The hideous part of it is, that the wench was quite as pretty to-day as yesterday. Her financier didn't appear on her face. Roses have this much more or less than women, that the traces which worms leave on them are visible. Ah! there is no morality upon the earth; I call to witness the myrtle, the symbol of love, the laurel, the symbol of war, the olive, that goose, the symbol of peace, the apple, which almost strangled Adam with its seed, and the fig, the grandfather of petticoats. As to rights, do you want to know what rights are? The Gauls covet Clusium, Rome protects Clusium, and asks them what Clusium has done to them. Brennus answers: 'What Alba did to you, what Fidenæ did to you, what the Æqui, the Volsci, and the Sabines did to you. They were your neighbours. The Clusians are ours. We understand neighbourhood as you do. You stole Alba, we take Clusium.' Rome says: 'You will not take Clusium.' Brennus took Rome. Then he cried: '*Væ victis!*' That is what rights are. Ah! in this world, what beasts of prey! what eagles! it makes me crawl all over."

He reached his glass to Joly, who filled it again, then he drank, and proceeded, almost without having been interrupted by this glass of wine, which nobody perceived, not even himself.

"Brennus, who takes Rome, is an eagle; the banker, who takes the grisette, is an eagle. No more shame here than there. Then let us believe in nothing. There is but one reality: to drink. Whatever may be your opinion, whether you are for the lean cock like the Canton of Uri, or for the fat cock, like the Canton of Glaris, matters little, drink. You talk to me of the boulevard, of the procession, et cætera. Ah, now, there is going to be a revolution again, is there? This poverty of means on the part of God astonishes me. He has to keep greasing the grooves of events continually. It hitches, it does not go. Quick, a revolution. God has his hands black with this villainous cart-grease all the time. In his place, I would work more simply, I wouldn't be winding up my machine every minute, I would lead the human race smoothly, I would knit the facts stitch to stitch, without breaking the thread, I would have no emergency, I would have no extraordinary repertory. What you fellows call progress moves by two springs, men and events. But sad to say, from time to time the exceptional is necessary. For events as well as for men, the stock company is not enough; geniuses are needed among men, and revolutions among events. Great accidents are the law; the order of things cannot get along without them; and, to see the apparitions of comets one would be tempted to believe that Heaven itself is in need of star actors. At the moment you least expect it, God placards a meteor on the wall of the firmament. Some strange star comes along, underlined by an enormous tail. And that makes Cæsar die. Brutus strikes him with a knife, and God with a comet. Crack, there is an aurora borealis, there is a revolution, there is a great man; '93 in big letters. Napoleon with a line to himself, the comet of 1811 at the top of the poster. Ah! the beautiful blue poster, all studded with unexpected flourishes! Boom! boom! extraordinary spectacle. Look up, loungers. All is dishevelled, the star as well as the drama. Good God, it is too much, and it is not enough. These resources, used in emergency, seem magnificence, and are poverty. My friends, Providence is put to his trumps. A revolution, what does that prove? That God is hard up. He makes a *coup d'état*, because there is a solution of continuity between the present and the future, and because he, God, is unable to join the two ends. In fact, that confirms me in my conjectures about the condition of Jehovah's fortune; and to see so much discomfort above and below, so much rascality and odiousness and stinginess and distress in the heavens and on the earth, from the bird which has not a grain of millet to me who have not a hundred thousand livres of income, to see human destiny, which is very much worn out, and even royal destiny, which shows the warp, witness the Prince of Condé hung, to see winter, which is nothing but a rent in the zenith through which the wind blows, to see so many tatters even in the brand new purple of the morning on the tops of the hills, to see the dew drops, those false pearls, to see the frost, that paste, to see humanity ripped, and events patched, and so many spots on the sun, and so many holes in the moon, to see so much misery everywhere, I suspect that God is not rich. He keeps up appearances, it is true, but I feel the pinch. He gives a revolution as a merchant, whose credit is low, gives a ball. We must not judge the gods from appearances. Beneath the gilding of the sky I catch a glimpse of a poor universe. Creation is bankrupt. That is why I am a malcontent. See, it is the fifth of June, it is very dark: since morning I have been waiting for the daybreak, it has not come, and I will bet that it won't come all day. It is a negligence of a badly paid clerk. Yes, everything is badly arranged, nothing fits anything, this old world is all rickety, I range myself with the opposition. Everything goes crossgrained; the universe is a tease. It is like children, those who want it haven't it, those who don't want it have it. Total: I scoff. Besides, Laigle de Meaux, that bald-head, afflicts my sight. It humiliates me to think that I am the same age as that knee. Still, I criticise, but I don't insult. The universe is what it is. I speak here without malice, and to ease my conscience. Receive, Father Eternal, the assurance of my distinguished consideration. Oh! by all saints of Olympus and by all the gods of Paradise, I was not made to be a Parisian, that is to say, to ricochet for ever, like a shuttlecock between two battledores, from the company of loafers to the company of rioters! I was made to be a Turk looking all day long at Oriental jades executing those exquisite dances of Egypt, as lascivious as the dreams of a chaste man, or a Beauce peasant, or a Venetian gentleman surrounded by gentledames, or a little German prince, furnishing the half of a foot soldier to the Germanic Confederation, and occupying his leisure in drying his socks upon his hedge, that is to say, upon his frontier! Such is the destiny for which I was born! Yes, I said Turk, and I don't unsay it. I don't understand why the Turks are commonly held in bad repute; there is some good in Mahomet; respect for the inventor of seraglios with houris, and paradises with odalisques! Let us not insult Mahometanism, the only religion that is adorned with a hen-roost! On that, I insist upon drinking. The earth is a great folly. And it appears that they are going to fight, all these idiots, to get their heads broken, to massacre one another, in midsummer, in the month of June, when they might go off with some creature under their arm, to scent in the fields the huge cup of tea of the new mown hay! Really, they are too silly. An old broken lamp which I saw just now at a second-hand shop suggests me a reflection. It is time to enlighten the human race. Yes, here I am again sad. What a thing it is to swallow an oyster or a revolution the wrong way! I am getting dismal. Oh! the frightful old world! They strive with one another, they plunder one another, they prostitute one another, they kill one another, they get used to one another!"

And Grantaire, after this fit of eloquence, had a fit of coughing, which he deserved.

"Speakig of revolutiod," said Joly, "it appears that Barius is decidedly aborous."

"Does anybody know of whom?" inquired Laigle.

"Do."

"No?"

"Do! I tell you."

"Marius' amours!" exclaimed Grantaire, "I see them now. Marius is a fog, and he must have found a vapour. Marius is of the race of poets. He who says poet, says fool. *Tymbræs Apollo*. Marius and his Mary, or his Maria, or his Marietta, or his Marion, they must make droll lovers. I imagine how it is. Ecstasies where they forget to kiss. Chaste upon the earth, but coupling in the infinite. They are souls which have senses. They sleep together in the stars."

Grantaire was entering on his second bottle, and perhaps his second harangue, when a new actor emerged from the square hole of the stairway. It was a boy of less than ten years, ragged, very small, yellow, a mug of a face, a keen eye, monstrous long hair, wet to the skin, a complacent look.

The child, choosing without hesitation among the three, although he evidently knew none of them, addressed himself to Laigle de Meaux.

"Are you Monsieur Bossuet?" asked he.

"That is my nickname," answered Laigle. "What do you want of me?"

"This is it. A big light-complexioned fellow on the boulevard said to me: Do you know Mother Hucheloup? I said: Yes, Rue de la Chanvrerie, the widow of the old man. He said to me: Go there. You will find Monsieur Bossuet there, and you will tell him from me: A—B—C. It is a joke that somebody is playing on you, isn't it? He gave me ten sous."

"Joly, lend me ten sous," said Laigle, and turning towards Grantaire: "Grantaire, lend me ten sous."

This made twenty sous which Laigle gave the child.

"Thank you, monsieur," said the little fellow.

"What is your name?" asked Laigle.

"Navet, Gavroche's friend."

"Stop with us," said Laigle.

"Breakfast with us," said Grantaire.

The child answered:

"I can't, I am with the procession, I am the one to cry, Down with Polignac."

And giving his foot a long scrape behind him, which is the most respectful of all possible bows, he went away.

The child gone, Grantaire resumed:

"This is the pure *gamin*. There are many varieties in the *gamin* genus. The notary *gamin* is called *saute-ruisseau*, the cook *gamin* is called *marimiton*, the baker *gamin* is called *mitron*, the lackey *gamin* is called *groom*, the sailor *gamin* is called *mousse*, the soldier *gamin* is called *tapin*, the painter *gamin* is called *rapin*, the trader *gamin* is called *trottin*, the courtier *gamin* is called *menin*, the king *gamin* is called *dauphin*, the god *gamin* is called *bambino*."

Meanwhile Laigle was meditating; he said in an under tone:

"A—B—C, that is to say: Lamarque's funeral."

"The big light-complexioned man," observed Grantaire, "is Enjolras, who sent to notify you."

"Shall we go?" said Bossuet.

"It raids," said Joly. "I have sword to go through fire, dot water. I dod't wadt to catch cold."

"I stay here," said Grantaire. "I prefer a breakfast to a hearse."

"Conclusion: we stay," resumed Laigle. "Well, let us drink then. Besides we can miss the funeral, without missing the émeute."

"Ah, the ébeute, I am id for that." exclaimed Joly.

Laigle rubbed his hands:

"Now they are going to retouch the Revolution of 1830. In fact, it binds the people in the armholes."

"It don't make much difference with me, your revolution," said Grantaire. "I don't execrate this government. It is the crown tempered with the night-cap. It is a sceptre terminating in an umbrella. In fact, to-day, I should think, in this weather Louis Philippe could make good use of his royalty at both ends, extend the sceptre end against the people, and open the umbrella end against the sky."

The room was dark, great clouds were completing the suppression of the daylight. There was nobody in the wine-shop, nor in the street, everybody having gone "to see the events."

"Is it noon or midnight?" cried Bossuet. "We can't see a speck. Fricassee, a light."

Grantaire, melancholy, was drinking.

"Enjolras despises me," murmured he. "Enjolras said Joly is sick. Grantaire is drunk. It was to Bossuet that he sent Navet. If he had come for me I would have followed him. So much the worse for Enjolras! I won't go to his funeral."

This resolution taken, Bossuet, Joly, and Grantaire did not stir from the wine-shop. About two o'clock in the afternoon, the table on which they were leaning was covered with empty bottles. Two candles were burning, one in a perfectly green copper candlestick, the other in the neck of a cracked decanter. Grantaire had drawn Joly and Bossuet towards wine; Bossuet and Joly had led Grantaire towards joy.

As for Grantaire, since noon, he had got beyond wine, an indifferent source of dreams. Wine, with serious drunkards, has only a quiet success. There is, in point of inebriety, black magic and white magic, wine is only white magic. Grantaire was a daring drinker of dreams. The blackness of a fearful drunkenness yawning before him, far from checking him, drew him on. He had left the bottle behind and taken to the jug. The jug is the abyss. Having at his hand neither opium nor hashish, and wishing to fill his brain with mist, he had had recourse to that frightful mixture of brandy, stout, and absinthe, which produces such terrible lethargy. It is from these three vapours, beer, brandy, and absinthe, that the lead of the soul is formed. They are three darknesses; the celestial butterfly is drowned in them; and there arise, in a membranous smoke vaguely condensed into bat wings, three dumb furies, nightmare, night, death, flitting above the sleeping Psyche.

Grantaire was not yet at this dreary phase; far from it. He was extravagantly gay, and Bossuet and Joly kept pace with him. They touched glasses. Grantaire added to the eccentric accentuation of his words and ideas incoherency of gesture; he rested his left wrist upon his knee with dignity, his arms a-kimbo, and his cravat untied, bestriding a stool, his full glass in his right hand, he threw out to the fat servant Chowder these solemn words:

"Let the palace doors be opened! Let everybody belong

to the Académie Française, and have the right of embracing
Madame Hucheloup! let us drink."

And turning towards Ma'am Hucheloup he added:

"Antique woman consecrated by use, approach that I may
gaze upon thee!"

And Joly exclaimed:

"Chowder add Fricassee, dod't give Gradtaire ady bore to
drigk. He spedds his bodey foolishly. He has already devoured
sidce this bordigg in desperate prodigality two fragcs didety-five
cedtibes."

And Grantaire replied:

"Who has been unhooking the stars without my permission
to put them on the table in the shape of candles?"

Bossuet, very drunk, had preserved his calmness.

He sat in the open window, wetting his back with the falling
rain, and gazed at his two friends.

Suddenly he heard a tumult behind him, hurried steps, cries
to arms! He turned, and saw in the Rue Saint Denis, at the end
of the Rue de la Chanvrerie, Enjolras passing, carbine in hand,
and Gavroche with his pistol, Feuilly with his sabre, Courfeyrac
with his sword, Jean Prouvaire with his musketoon, Combeferre
with his musket, Bahorel with his musket, and all the armed and
stormy gathering which followed them.

The Rue de la Chanvrerie was hardly as long as the range of
a carbine. Bossuet improvised a speaking trumpet with his two
hands, and shouted:

"Courfeyrac! Courfeyrac! ahoy!"

Courfeyrac heard the call, perceived Bossuet, and came a few
steps into the Rue de la Chanvrerie, crying a "what do you
want?" which was met on the way by a "where are you going?"

"To make a barricade," answered Courfeyrac.

"Well, here! This is a good place! make it here!"

"That is true, Eagle," said Courfeyrac.

And at a sign from Courfeyrac, the band rushed into the Rue
de la Chanvrerie.

III

NIGHT BEGINS TO GATHER OVER GRANTAIRE

THE place was indeed admirably chosen, the entrance of the
street wide, the further end contracted and like a cul-de-sac,

Corinth throttling it, Rue Mondétour easy to bar at the right and left, no attack possible except from the Rue Saint Denis, that is from the front, and without cover. Bossuet tipsy had the *coup d'œil* of Hannibal fasting.

At the irruption of the mob, dismay seized the whole street, not a passer but had gone into eclipse. In a flash, at the end, on the right, on the left, shops, stalls, alley gates, windows, blinds, dormer-windows, shutters of every size, were closed from the ground to the roofs. One frightened old woman had fixed a mattress before her window on two clothes poles, as a shield against the musketry. The wine-shop was the only house which remained open; and that for a good reason, because the band had rushed into it. "Oh my God! Oh my God!" sighed Ma'am Hucheloup.

Bossuet had gone down to meet Courfeyrac.

Joly, who had come to the window, cried:

"Courfeyrac, you bust take ad ubbrella. You will catch cold."

Meanwhile, in a few minutes, twenty iron bars had been wrested from the grated front of the wine-shop, twenty yards of pavement had been torn up, Gavroche and Bahorel had seized on its passage and tipped over the dray of a lime merchant named Anceau, this dray contained three barrels full of lime, which they had placed under the piles of paving stones; Enjolras had opened the trap-door of the cellar and all the widow Hucheloup's empty casks had gone to flank the lime barrels; Feuilly, with his fingers accustomed to colour the delicate folds of fans, had buttressed the barrels and the dray with two massive heaps of stones. Stones improvised like the rest, and obtained nobody knows where. Some shoring-timbers had been pulled down from the front of a neighbouring house and laid upon the casks. When Bossuet and Courfeyrac turned round, half the street was already barred by a rampart higher than a man. There is nothing like the popular hand to build whatever can be built by demolishing.

Chowder and Fricassee had joined the labourers. Fricassee went back and forth loaded with rubbish. Her weariness contributed to the barricade. She served paving stones, as she would have served wine, with a sleepy air.

An omnibus with two white horses passed at the end of the street.

Bossuet sprang over the pavement, ran, stopped the driver,

made the passengers get down, gave his hand "to the ladies," dismissed the conductor, and came back with the vehicle, leading the horses by the bridle.

"An omnibus," said he, "doesn't pass by Corinth. *Non licet omnibus adire Corinthum.*"

A moment later the horses were unhitched and going off at will through the Rue Mondétour, and the omnibus, lying on its side, completed the barring of the street.

Ma'am Hucheloup, completely upset, had taken refuge in the first story.

Her eyes were wandering, and she looked without seeing, crying in a whisper. Her cries were dismayed and dared not come out of her throat.

"It is the end of the world," she murmured.

Joly deposited a kiss upon Ma'am Hucheloup's coarse, red, and wrinkled neck, and said to Grantaire: "My dear fellow, I have always considered a woman's neck an infinitely delicate thing."

But Grantaire was attaining the highest regions of dithyramb. Chowder having come up to the first floor, Grantaire seized her by the waist and pulled her towards the window with long bursts of laughter.

"Chowder is ugly!" cried he; "Chowder is the dream of ugliness! Chowder is a chimera. Listen to the secret of her birth: a Gothic Pygmalion who was making cathedral waterspouts, fell in love with one of them one fine morning, the most horrible of all. He implored Love to animate her, and that made Chowder. Behold her, citizens! her hair is the colour of chromate of lead, like that of Titian's mistress, and she is a good girl. I warrant you that she will fight well. Every good girl contains a hero. As for Mother Hucheloup, she is an old brave. Look at her moustaches! she inherited them from her husband. A hussaress, indeed, she will fight too. They two by themselves will frighten the banlieue. Comrades, we will overturn the government, as true as there are fifteen acids intermediate between margaric acid and formic acid, which I don't care a fig about. Messieurs, my father always detested me, because I could not understand mathematics. I only understand love and liberty. I am Grantaire, a good boy. Never having had any money, I have never got used to it, and by that means I have never felt the need of it, but if I had been rich, there would have been no more poor! you should have seen. Oh! if the good hearts had the fat purses, how much better everything would go! I imagine Jesus Christ with Rothschild's fortune! How much good he would have done! Chowder, embrace me! you are voluptuous and timid! you have cheeks which call for the kiss of a sister, and lips which demand the kiss of a lover."

"Be still, wine-cask!" said Courfeyrac.

Grantaire answered:

"I am Capitoul and Master of Floral Games!"

Enjolras, who was standing on the crest of the barricade, musket in hand, raised his fine austere face. Enjolras, we know, had something of the Spartan and of the Puritan. He would have died at Thermopylæ with Leonidas, and would have burned Drogheda with Cromwell.

"Grantaire," cried he, "go sleep yourself sober away from here. This is the place for intoxication and not for drunkenness. Do not dishonour the barricade!"

This angry speech produced upon Grantaire a singular effect. One would have said that he had received a glass of cold water in his face. He appeared suddenly sobered. He sat down, leaned upon a table near the window, looked at Enjolras with an inexpressible gentleness, and said to him:

"Let me sleep here."

"Go sleep elsewhere," cried Enjolras.

But Grantaire, keeping his tender and troubled eyes fixed upon him, answered:

"Let me sleep here—until I die here."

Enjolras regarded him with a disdainful eye:

"Grantaire, you are incapable of belief, of thought, of will, of life, and of death."

He stammered out a few more unintelligible words, then his head fell heavily upon the table, and, a common effect of the second stage of inebriety into which Enjolras had rudely and suddenly pushed him, a moment later he was asleep.

IV

ATTEMPT AT CONSOLATION UPON THE WIDOW HUCHELOUP

BAHOREL, in ecstasies with the barricade, cried:

"There is the street in a low neck, how well it looks!"

Courfeyrac, even while helping to demolish the wine-shop, sought to console the widowed landlady.

"Mother Hucheloup, were you not complaining the other day that you had been summoned and fined because Fricassee had shaken a rug out of your window?"

"Yes, my good Monsieur Courfeyrac. Oh! my God! are you going to put that table also into your horror? And besides that, for the rug, and also for a flower-pot which fell from the attic into the street, the government fined me a hundred francs. If that isn't an abomination!"

"Well, Mother Hucheloup, we are avenging you."

Mother Hucheloup, in this reparation which they were making her, did not seem to very well understand her advantage. She was satisfied after the manner of that Arab woman who, having received a blow from her husband, went to complain to her father, crying for vengeance and saying: "Father, you owe my husband affront for affront." The father asked: "Upon which cheek did you receive the blow?" "Upon the left cheek." The father struck the right cheek, and said: "Now you are satisfied. Go and tell your husband that he has struck my daughter, but that I have struck his wife."

The rain had ceased. Recruits had arrived. Some working-men had brought under their blouses a keg of powder, a hamper containing bottles of vitriol, two or three carnival torches, and a basket full of lamps, "relics of the king's fête," which fête was quite recent, having taken place the 1st of May. It was said that these supplies came from a grocer of the Faubourg Saint Antoine, named Pépin. They broke the only lamp in the Rue de la Chanvrerie, the lamp opposite the Rue Saint Denis, and all the lamps in the surrounding streets, Mondétour, du Cygne, des Prêcheurs, and de la Grande and de la Petite Truanderie.

Enjolras, Combeferre, and Courfeyrac, directed everything. Two barricades were now building at the same time, both resting on the house of Corinth and making a right angle; the larger one closed the Rue de la Chanvrerie, the other closed the Rue Mondétour in the direction of the Rue du Cygne. This last barricade, very narrow, was constructed only of casks and paving stones. There were about fifty labourers there, some thirty armed with muskets, for, on their way, they had effected a wholesale loan from an armourer's shop.

Nothing could be more fantastic and more motley than this

band. One had a short-jacket, a cavalry sabre, and two horse-pistols; another was in shirt sleeves, with a round hat, and a powder-horn hung at his side; a third had a breast-plate of nine sheets of brown paper, and was armed with a saddler's awl. There was one of them who cried: "*Let us exterminate to the last man, and die on the point of our bayonets!*" This man had no bayonet. Another displayed over his coat a cross-belt and cartridge-box of the National Guard, with the box cover adorned with this inscription in red cloth: *Public Order.* Many muskets bearing the numbers of their legions, few hats, no cravats, many bare arms, some pikes. Add to this all ages, all faces, small pale young men, bronzed wharfmen. All were hurrying, and, while helping each other, they talked about the possible chances—that they would have help by three o'clock in the morning—that they were sure of one regiment—that Paris would rise. Terrible subjects, with which were mingled a sort of cordial joviality. One would have said they were brothers, they did not know each other's names. Great perils have this beauty, that they bring to light the fraternity of strangers.

A fire had been kindled in the kitchen, and they were melting pitchers, dishes, forks, all the pewter ware of the wine-shop into bullets. They drank through it all. Percussion-caps and buck-shot rolled pell-mell upon the tables with glasses of wine. In the billiard-room, Ma'am Hucheloup, Chowder, and Fricassee, variously modified by terror, one being stupefied, another breathless, the third alert, were tearing up old linen and making lint; three insurgents assisted them, three long-haired, bearded, and moustached wags who tore up the cloth with the fingers of a linen draper, and who made them tremble.

The man of tall stature whom Courfeyrac, Combeferre, and Enjolras had noticed, at the moment he joined the company at the corner of the Rue des Billettes, was working on the little barricade, and making himself useful there. Gavroche worked on the large one. As for the young man who had waited for Courfeyrac at his house, and had asked him for Monsieur Marius, he had disappeared very nearly at the moment the omnibus was overturned.

Gavroche, completely carried away and radiant, had charged himself with making all ready. He went, came, mounted, descended, remounted, bustled, sparkled. He seemed to be there for the encouragement of all. Had he a spur? yes, certainly, his misery; had he wings? yes, certainly, his joy. Gavroche was a whirlwind. They saw him incessantly, they heard him constantly. He filled the air, being everywhere at once. He was a kind of stimulating ubiquity; no stop possible with him. The enormous barricade felt him on its back. He vexed the loungers, he excited the idle, he reanimated the weary, he provoked the thoughtful, kept some in cheerfulness, others in breath, others in anger, all in motion, piqued a student, was biting to a working-man; took position, stopped, started on, flitted above the tumult and the effort, leaped from these to those, murmured, hummed, and stirred up the whole train; the fly on the revolutionary coach.

Perpetual motion was in his little arms, and perpetual clamour in his little lungs.

"Cheerly? more paving stones? more barrels? more machines? where are there any? A basket of plaster, to stop that hole. It is too small, your barricade. It must go higher. Pile on everything, brace it with everything. Break up the house. A barricade is Mother Gibou's tea-party. Hold on, there is a glass-door."

This made the labourers exclaim:

"A glass-door? what do you want us to do with a glass-door, tubercle?"

"Hercules yourselves?" retorted Gavroche. "A glass-door in a barricade is excellent. It doesn't prevent attacking it, but it bothers them in taking it. Then you have never hooked apples over a wall with broken bottles on it? A glass-door, it will cut the corns of the National Guards, when they try to climb over the barricade. Golly! glass is the devil. Ah, now, you haven't an unbridled imagination, my comrades."

Still, he was furious at his pistol without a hammer. He went from one to another, demanding: "A musket? I want a musket! Why don't you give me a musket?"

"A musket for you?" said Combeferre.

"Well?" replied Gavroche, "why not? I had one in 1830, in the dispute with Charles X."

Enjolras shrugged his shoulders.

"When there are enough for the men, we will give them to the children."

Gavroche turned fiercely, and answered him:

"If you are killed before me, I will take yours."

"*Gamin!*" said Enjolras.

"Smooth-face!" said Gavroche.

A stray dandy who was lounging at the end of the street made a diversion.

Gavroche cried to him:

"Come with us, young man? Well, this poor old country, you won't do anything for her then?"

The dandy fled.

V

THE PREPARATIONS

THE journal of the time which said that the barricade of the Rue de la Chanvrerie, that *almost inexpugnable construction*, as they call it, attained the level of a second story, were mistaken. The fact is, that it did not exceed an average height of six or seven feet. It was built in such a manner that the combatants could, at will, either disappear behind the wall, or look over it, and even scale the crest of it by means of a quadruple range of paving stones superposed and arranged like steps on the inner side. The front of the barricade on the outside, composed of piles of paving stones and of barrels bound together by timbers and boards which were interlocked in the wheels of the Anceau cart and the overturned omnibus, had a bristling and inextricable aspect.

An opening sufficient for a man to pass through had been left between the wall of the houses and the extremity of the barricade furthest from the wine-shop; so that a sortie was possible. The pole of the omnibus was turned directly up and held with ropes, and a red flag fixed to this pole floated over the barricade.

The little Mondétour barricade, hidden behind the wine-shop, was not visible. The two barricades united formed a staunch redoubt. Enjolras and Courfeyrac had not thought proper to barricade the other end of the Rue Mondétour which opens a passage to the markets through the Rue des Prêcheurs, wishing doubtless to preserve a possible communication with the outside, and having little dread of being attacked from the dangerous and difficult alley des Prêcheurs.

Except this passage remaining free, which constituted what Folard, in his strategic style, would have called a branch-trench, and bearing in mind also the narrow opening arranged on the Rue de la Chanvrerie, the interior of the barricade, where the wine-shop made a salient angle, presented an irregular quadrilateral closed on all sides. There was an interval of about twenty yards between the great barricade and the tall houses which formed the end of the street, so that we might say that the barricade leaned against these houses all inhabited, but closed from top to bottom.

All this labour was accomplished without hindrance in less than an hour, and without this handful of bold men seeing a bearskin-cap or a bayonet arise. The few bourgeois who still ventured at that period of the émeute into the Rue Saint Denis cast a glance down the Rue de la Chanvrerie, perceived the barricade, and redoubled their pace.

The two barricades finished, the flag run up, a table was dragged out of the wine-shop; and Courfeyrac mounted upon the table. Enjolras brought the square box and Courfeyrac opened it. This box was filled with cartridges. When they saw the cartridges, there was a shudder among the bravest, and a moment of silence.

Courfeyrac distributed them with a smile.

Each one received thirty cartridges. Many had powder and set about making others with the balls which they were moulding. As for the keg of powder, it was on a table by itself near the door, and it was reserved.

The long roll which was running through all Paris was not discontinued, but it had got to be only a monotonous sound to which they paid no more attention, with melancholy undulations.

They loaded their muskets and their carbines all together, without precipitation, with a solemn gravity. Enjolras placed three sentinels outside the barricades, one in the Rue de la Chanvrerie, the second in the Rue des Prêcheurs, the third at the corner of la Petite Truanderie.

Then, the barricades built, the posts assigned, the muskets loaded, the videttes placed, alone in these fearful streets in which there were now no passers, surrounded by these dumb, and as it were dead houses, which throbbed with no human motion, enwrapped by the deepening shadows of the twilight, which was beginning to fall, in the midst of this obscurity and this silence, through which they felt the advance of something inexpressibly tragical and terrifying, isolated, armed, determined, tranquil, they waited.

VI
WHILE WAITING

In these hours of waiting what did they do? This we must tell—for this is history.

While the men were making cartridges and the women lint, while a large frying-pan, full of melted pewter and lead, destined for the bullet-mould, was smoking over a burning furnace, while the videttes were watching the barricades with arms in their hands, while Enjolras, whom nothing could distract, was watching the videttes, Combeferre, Courfeyrac, Jean Prouvaire, Feuilly, Bossuet, Joly, Bahorel, a few others besides, sought each other and got together, as in the most peaceful days of their student-chats, and in a corner of this wine-shop changed into a casemate, within two steps of the redoubt which they had thrown up, their carbines primed and loaded resting on the backs of their chairs, these gallant young men, so near their last hour, began to sing love-rhymes.

What rhymes? Here they are:

Vous rappelez-vous notre douce vie,
Lorsque nous étions si jeunes tous deux,
Et que nous n'avions au cœur d'autre envie
Que d'être bien mis et d'être amoureux.

Lorsqu'en ajoutant votre âge à mon âge,
Nous ne comptions pas à deux quarante ans,
Et que, dans notre humble et petit ménage,
Tout, même l'hiver, nous était printemps!

Beaux jours! Manuel était fier et sage,
Paris s'asseyait à de saints banquets,
Foy lançait la foudre, et votre corsage
Avait une épingle où je me piquais.

Tout vous contemplait. Avocat sans causes,
Quand je vous menais au Prado dîner,
Vous étiez jolie au point que les roses
Me faisaient l'effet de se retourner.

Je les entendais dire: Est-elle belle!
Comme elle sent bon! quels cheveux à flots!
Sous son mantelet elle cache une aile;
Son bonnet charmant est à peine éclos.

J'errais avec toi, pressant ton bras souple.
Les passants croyaient que l'amour charmé
Avait marié, dans notre heureux couple,
Le doux mois d'avril au beau mois de mai.

Nous vivions cachés, contents, porte close,
Dévorant l'amour, bon fruit défendu;
Ma bouche n'avait pas dit une chose
Que déjà ton cœur avait répondu.

La Sorbonne était l'endroit bucolique
Où je t'adorais du soir au matin.
C'est ainsi qu'une âme amoureuse applique
La carte du Tendre au pays latin.

O place Maubert! O place Dauphine!
Quand, dans le taudis frais et printanier,
Tu tirais ton bas sur ta jambe fine,
Je voyais un astre au fond du grenier.

J'ai fort lu Platon, mais rien ne m'en reste;
Mieux que Malebranche et que Lamennais;
Tu me démontrais la bonté céleste
Avec une fleur que tu me donnais.

Je t'obéissais, tu m'étais soumise.
O grenier doré! te lacer! te voir!
Aller et venir dès l'aube en chemise,
Mirant ton front jeune à ton vieux miroir!

Et qui donc pourrait perdre la mémoire
De ces temps d'aurore et de firmament,
De rubans, de fleurs, de gaze et de moire,
Où l'amour bégaye un argot charmant!

Nos jardins étaient un pot de tulipe;
Tu masquais la vitre avec un jupon;
Je prenais le bol de terre de pipe,
Et je te donnais la tasse en japon.

Et ces grands malheurs qui nous faisaient rire!
Ton manchon brûlé, ton boa perdu!
Et ce cher portrait du divin Shakspeare
Qu'un soir pour souper nous avons vendu!

J'étais mendiant, et toi charitable;
Je baisais au vol tes bras frais et ronds.
Dante in-folio nous servait de table
Pour manger gaîment un cent de marrons.

Le première fois qu'en mon joyeux bouge
Je pris un baiser à ta lèvre en feu,
Quand tu t'en allas décoiffée et rouge,
Je restai tout pâle et je crus en Dieu!

Te rappelles-tu nos bonheurs sans nombre,
Et tous ces fichus changés en chiffons!
Oh! que de soupirs, de nos cœurs pleins d'ombre,
Se sont envolés dans les cieux profonds!

The hour, the place, these memories of youth recalled, the few stars which began to shine in the sky, the funereal repose of these deserted streets, the imminence of the inexorable event, gave a pathetic charm to these rhymes, murmured in a low tone in the twilight by Jean Prouvaire, who, as we have said, was a sweet poet.

Meanwhile they had lighted a lamp at the little barricade, and at the large one, one of those wax torches which are seen on Mardi Gras in front of the wagons loaded with masks, which are going to the Comtille. These torches, we have seen, came from the Faubourg Saint Antoine.

The torch had been placed in a kind of cage, closed in with paving stones on three sides, to shelter it from the wind, and disposed in such a manner that all the light fell upon the flag. The street and the barricade remained plunged in obscurity, and nothing could be seen but the red flag, fearfully lighted up, as if by an enormous dark lantern.

This light gave to the scarlet of the flag an indescribably terrible purple.

VII

THE MAN RECRUITED IN THE RUE DES BILLETTES

It was now quite night, nothing came. There were only confused sounds, and at intervals volleys of musketry; but rare, illsustained, and distant. This respite, which was thus prolonged, was a sign that the government was taking its time, and massing its forces. These fifty men were awaiting sixty thousand.

Enjolras felt himself possessed by that impatience which seizes strong souls on the threshold of formidable events. He went to find Gavroche, who had set himself to making cartridges in the basement-room by the doubtful light of two candles placed upon the counter through precaution on account of the powder scattered over the tables. These two candles threw no rays outside. The insurgents moreover had taken care not to have any lights in the upper stories.

Gavroche at this moment was very much engaged, not exactly with his cartridges.

The man from the Rue des Billettes had just entered the basement-room and had taken a seat at the table which was least lighted. An infantry musket of large model had fallen to his lot, and he held it between his knees. Gavroche hitherto, distracted by a hundred "amusing" things, had not even seen this man.

When he came in, Gavroche mechanically followed him with his eyes, admiring his musket, then, suddenly, when the man had sat down, the *gamin* arose. Had any one watched this man up to this time, he would have seen him observe everything in the barricade and in the band of insurgents with a singular attention; but since he had come into the room, he had fallen into a kind of meditation and appeared to see nothing more of what was going on. The *gamin* approached this thoughtful personage, and began to turn about him on the points of his toes as one walks when near somebody whom he fears to awake. At the same time, over his childish face, at once so saucy and so serious, so flighty and so profound, so cheerful and so touching, there passed all those grimaces of the old which signify: "Oh, bah! impossible! I am befogged! I am dreaming! can it be? no, it isn't! why yes! why no!" etc. Gavroche balanced himself upon his heels, clenched both fists in his pockets, twisted his neck like a bird, expended in one measureless pout all the sagacity of his lower lip. He was stupefied, uncertain, credulous, convinced, bewildered. He had the appearance of the chief of the eunuchs in the slave market discovering a Venus among dumpies, and the air of an amateur recognising a Raphael in a heap of daubs. Everything in him was at work, the instinct which scents and the intellect which combines. It was evident that an event had occurred with Gavroche.

It was in the deepest of this meditation that Enjolras accosted him.

"You are small," said Enjolras, "nobody will see you. Go out of the barricades, glide along by the houses, look about the streets a little, and come and tell me what is going on."

Gavroche straightened himself up.

"Little folks are good for something then! that is very lucky! I will go! meantime, trust the little folks, distrust the big——" And Gavroche, raising his head and lowering his voice, added, pointing to the man of the Rue des Billettes:

"You see that big fellow there?"

"Well?"

"He is a spy."

"You are sure?"

"It isn't a fortnight since he pulled me by the ear off the cornice of the Pont Royal where I was taking the air."

Enjolras hastily left the *gamin*, and murmured a few words very low to a working-man from the wine docks who was there. The working-man went out of the room and returned almost immediately, accompanied by three others. The four men, four broad-shouldered porters, placed themselves, without doing anything which could attract his attention, behind the table on which the man of the Rue des Billettes was leaning. They were evidently ready to throw themselves upon him.

Then Enjolras approached the man and asked him:

"Who are you?"

At this abrupt question, the man gave a start. He looked straight to the bottom of Enjolras' frank eye and appeared to catch his thought. He smiled with a smile which, of all things in the world, was the most disdainful, the most energetic, and the most resolute, and answered with a haughty gravity:

"I see how it is——Well, yes!"

"You are a spy?"

"I am an officer of the government."

"Your name is?"

"Javert."

Enjolras made a sign to the four men. In a twinkling, before Javert had had time to turn around, he was collared, thrown down, bound, searched.

They found upon him a little round card framed between two glasses, and bearing on one side the arms of France, engraved with this legend: *Surveillance et vigilance*, and on the other side this endorsement: JAVERT, inspector of police, aged fifty-two, and the signature of the prefect of police of the time, M. Gisquet.

He had besides his watch and his purse, which contained a few gold pieces. They left him his purse and his watch. Under the watch, at the bottom of his fob, they felt and seized a paper in an envelope, which Enjolras opened, and on which he read these six lines, written by the prefect's own hand.

"As soon as his political mission is fulfilled, Inspector Javert will ascertain, by a special examination, whether it be true that malefactors have resorts on the slope of the right bank of the Seine, near the bridge of Jena."

The search finished, they raised Javert, tied his arms behind his back, fastened him in the middle of the basement-room to that celebrated post which had formerly given its name to the wine-shop.

Gavroche, who had witnessed the whole scene and approved the whole by silent nods of his head, approached Javert and said to him:

"The mouse has caught the cat."

All this was executed so rapidly that it was finished as soon as it was perceived about the wine-shop. Javert had not uttered a cry. Seeing Javert tied to the post, Courfeyrac, Bossuet, Joly, Combeferre, and the men scattered about the two barricades, ran in.

Javert, backed up against the post, and so surrounded with ropes that he could make no movement, held up his head with the intrepid serenity of the man who has never lied.

"It is a spy," said Enjolras.

And turning towards Javert:

"You will be shot ten minutes before the barricade is taken."

Javert replied in his most imperious tone:

"Why not immediately?"

"We are economising powder."

"Then do it with a knife."

"Spy," said the handsome Enjolras, "we are judges, not assassins."

Then he called Gavroche.

"You! go about your business! Do what I told you."

"I am going," cried Gavroche.

And stopping just as he was starting:

"By the way, you will give me his musket!" And he added: "I leave you the musician, but I want the clarionet."

The *gamin* made a military salute, and sprang gaily through the opening in the large barricade.

VIII

SEVERAL INTERROGATION POINTS CONCERNING ONE LE CABUC, WHO PERHAPS WAS NOT LE CABUC

THE tragic picture which we have commenced would not be complete, the reader would not see in their exact and real relief these grand moments of social parturition and of revolutionary birth in which there is convulsion mingled with effort, were we to omit, in the outline here sketched, an incident full of epic and savage horror which occurred almost immediately after Gavroche's departure.

Mobs, as we know, are like snowballs, and gather a heap of tumultuous men as they roll. These men do not ask one another whence they come. Among the passers who had joined themselves to the company led by Enjolras, Combeferre, and Courfeyrac, there was a person wearing a porter's waistcoat worn out at the shoulders, who gesticulated and vociferated and had the appearance of a sort of savage drunkard. This man, who was named or nicknamed Le Cabuc, and who was moreover entirely unknown to those who attempted to recognise him, very drunk, or feigning to be, was seated with a few others at a table which they had brought outside of the wine-shop. This Cabuc, while inciting those to drink who were with him, seemed to gaze with an air of reflection upon the large house at the back of the barricade, the five stories of which overlooked the whole street and faced towards the Rue Saint Denis. Suddenly he exclaimed:

"Comrades, do you know? it is from that house that we must

fire. If we are at the windows, devil a one can come into the street."

"Yes, but the house is shut up," said one of the drinkers.

"Knock!"

"They won't open."

"Stave the door in!"

Le Cabuc runs to the door, which had a very massive knocker, and raps. The door does not open. He raps a second time. Nobody answers. A third rap. The same silence.

"Is there anybody here?" cries Le Cabuc.

Nothing stirs.

Then he seizes a musket and begins to beat the door with the butt. It was an old alley door, arched, low, narrow, solid, entirely of oak, lined on the inside with sheet-iron and with iron braces, a genuine postern of a bastille. The blows made the house tremble, but did not shake the door.

Nevertheless it is probable that the inhabitants were alarmed, for they finally saw a little square window on the third story light up and open, and there appeared at this window a candle, and the pious and frightened face of a grey-haired goodman who was the porter.

The man who was knocking, stopped.

"Messieurs," asked the porter, "what do you wish?"

"Open!" said Le Cabuc.

"Messieurs, that cannot be."

"Open, I tell you!"

"Impossible, messieurs!"

Le Cabuc took his musket and aimed at the porter's head; but as he was below, and it was very dark, the porter did not see him.

"Yes, or no, will you open?"

"No, messieurs!"

"You say no?"

"I say no, my good——"

The porter did not finish. The musket went off; the ball entered under his chin and passed out at the back of the neck, passing through the jugular. The old man sank down without a sigh. The candle fell and was extinguished, and nothing could now be seen but an immovable head lying on the edge of the window, and a little whitish smoke floating towards the roof.

"That's it!" said Le Cabuc, letting the butt of his musket drop on the pavement.

Hardly had he uttered these words when he felt a hand pounce upon his shoulder with the weight of an eagle's talons, and heard a voice which said to him:

"On your knees."

The murderer turned and saw before him the white cold face of Enjolras. Enjolras had a pistol in his hand.

At the explosion, he had come up.

He had grasped with his left hand Le Cabuc's collar, blouse, shirt, and suspenders.

"On your knees," repeated he.

And with a majestic movement the slender young man of twenty bent the broad-shouldered and robust porter like a reed and made him kneel in the mud. Le Cabuc tried to resist, but he seemed to have been seized by a superhuman grasp.

Pale, his neck bare, his hair flying, Enjolras, with his woman's face, had at that moment an inexpressible something of the ancient Themis. His distended nostrils, his downcast eyes, gave to his implacable Greek profile that expression of wrath and that expression of chastity which from the point of view of the ancient world belonged to justice.

The whole barricade ran up, then all ranged in a circle at a distance, feeling that it was impossible to utter a word in presence of the act which they were about to witness.

Le Cabuc, vanquished, no longer attempted to defend himself but trembled in every limb. Enjolras let go of him and took out his watch.

"Collect your thoughts," said he. "Pray or think. You have one minute."

"Pardon!" murmured the murderer, then he bowed his head and mumbled some inarticulate oaths.

Enjolras did not take his eyes off his watch; he let the minute pass, then he put his watch back into his fob. This done, he took Le Cabuc, who was writhing against his knees and howling, by the hair, and placed the muzzle of his pistol at his ear. Many of those intrepid men, who had so tranquilly entered upon the most terrible of enterprises, turned away their heads.

They heard the explosion, the assassin fell face forward on the pavement, and Enjolras straightened up and cast about him his look determined and severe.

Then he pushed the body away with his foot, and said:

"Throw that outside."

Three men lifted the body of the wretch, which was quivering with the last mechanical convulsions of the life that had flown, and threw it over the small barricade into the little Rue Mondétour.

Enjolras had remained thoughtful. Shadow, mysterious and grand, was slowly spreading over his fearful serenity. He suddenly raised his voice. There was a silence.

"Citizens," said Enjolras, "what that man did is horrible, and what I have done is terrible. He killed, that is why I killed him. I was forced to do it, for the insurrection must have its discipline. Assassination is a still greater crime here than elsewhere; we are under the eye of the revolution, we are the priests of the republic, we are the sacramental host of duty, and none must be able to calumniate our combat. I therefore judged and condemned that man to death. As for myself, compelled to do what I have done, but abhorring it, I have judged myself also, and you shall soon see to what I have sentenced myself."

Those who heard shuddered.

"We will share your fate," cried Combeferre.

"So be it," added Enjolras. "A word more. In executing that man, I obeyed necessity; but necessity is a monster of the old world, the name of necessity is Fatality. Now the law of progress is, that monsters disappear before angels, and that Fatality vanish before Fraternity. This is not a moment to pronounce the word love. No matter, I pronounce it, and I glorify it. Love, thine is the future. Death, I use thee, but I hate thee. Citizens, there shall be in the future neither darkness nor thunderbolts; neither ferocious ignorance nor blood for blood. As Satan shall be no more, so Michael shall be no more. In the future no man shall slay his fellow, the earth shall be radiant, the human race shall love. It will come, citizens, that day when all shall be concord, harmony, light, joy, and life; it will come, and it is that it may come that we are going to die."

Enjolras was silent. His virgin lips closed; and he remained some time standing on the spot where he had spilled blood, in marble immobility. His fixed eye made all about him speak low.

Jean Prouvaire and Combeferre silently grasped hands, and, leaning upon one another in the corner of the barricade, considered, with an admiration not unmingled with compassion, this severe young man, executioner and priest, luminous like the crystal, and rock also.

Let us say right here that later, after the action, when the corpses were carried to the Morgue and searched, there was a police officer's card found on Le Cabuc. The author of this book had in his own hands, in 1848, the special report made on that subject to the prefect of police in 1832.

Let us add that, if we are to believe a police tradition, strange, but probably well founded, Le Cabuc was Claquesous. The fact is, that after the death of Le Cabuc, nothing more was heard of Claquesous. Claquesous left no trace of his disappearance, he would seem to have been amalgamated with the invisible. His life had been darkness, his end was night.

The whole insurgent group were still under the emotion of this tragic trial, so quickly instituted and so quickly terminated, when Courfeyrac again saw in the barricade the small young man who in the morning had called at his house for Marius.

This boy, who had a bold and reckless air, had come at night to rejoin the insurgents.

I

FROM THE RUE PLUMET TO THE
QUARTIER SAINT DENIS

THAT voice which through the twilight had called Marius to
the barricade of the Rue de la Chanvrerie, sounded to him like
the voice of destiny. He wished to die, the opportunity presented itself, he was knocking at the door of the tomb, a hand
in the shadow held out the key. These dreary clefts in the darkness before despair are tempting. Marius pushed aside the bar
which had let him pass so many times, came out of the garden,
and said: "Let us go!"

Mad with grief, feeling no longer anything fixed or solid in
his brain, incapable of accepting anything henceforth from fate,
after these two months passed in the intoxications of youth and
of love, whelmed at once beneath all the reveries of despair, he
had now but one desire: to make an end of it very quick.

He began to walk rapidly. It happened that he was armed,
having Javert's pistols with him.

The young man whom he thought he had seen was lost from
his eyes in the streets.

Marius, who had left the Rue Plumet by the boulevard,
crossed the Esplanade and the Bridge of the Invalides, the
Champs-Elysées, the Place Louis XV., and entered the Rue de
Rivoli. The stores were open, the gas was burning under the
arches, women were buying in the shops, people were taking
ices at the Café Laiter, they were eating little cakes at the Patis-
serie Anglaise. However, a few post chaises were setting off at a
gallop from the Hôtel des Princes and the Hôtel Meurice.

Marius entered through the Delorme arcade into the Rue
Saint Honoré. The shops here were closed, the merchants were
chatting before their half-open doors, people were moving
about, the lamps were burning, above the first stories all the
windows were lighted as usual. There was cavalry in the square
of the Palais Royal.

Marius followed the Rue St. Honoré. As he receded from
the Palais Royal, there were fewer lighted windows; the shops
were entirely closed, nobody was chatting in the doors, the

street grew gloomy, and at the same time the throng grew dense. For the passers now were a throng. Nobody was seen to speak in this throng, and still there came from it a deep and dull hum.

Towards the Fontaine de l'Arbre Sec, there were "gatherings," immovable and sombre groups, which, among the comers and goers, were like stones in the middle of a running stream.

At the entrance of the Rue des Prouvaires, the throng no longer moved. It was a resisting, massive, solid, compact, almost impenetrable bloc of people, heaped together and talking in whispers. Black coats and round hats had almost disappeared. Frocks, blouses, caps, bristly and dirty faces. This multitude undulated confusedly in the misty night. Its whispering had the harsh sound of a roar. Although nobody was walking, a trampling was heard in the mud. Beyond this dense mass, in the Rue du Roule, in the Rue des Prouvaires, and in the prolongation of the Rue Saint Honoré, there was not a single window in which a candle was burning. In those streets the files of the lamps were seen stretching away solitary and decreasing. The lamps of that day resembled great red stars hanging from ropes, and threw a shadow on the pavement which had the form of a large spider. These streets were not empty. Muskets could be distinguished in stacks, bayonets moving and troops bivouacking. The curious did not pass this bound. There circulation ceased. There the multitude ended and the army began.

Marius willed with the will of a man who no longer hopes. He had been called, he must go. He found means to pass through the multitude and to pass through the bivouac of the troops, he avoided the patrols, evaded the sentinels. He made a detour, reached the Rue de Béthisy, and made his way towards the markets. At the corner of the Rue des Bourdonnais the lamps ended.

After having crossed the belt of the multitude and passed the fringe of troops, he found himself in the midst of something terrible. Not a passer more, not a soldier, not a light; nobody. Solitude, silence, night; a mysterious chill which seized upon him. To enter a street was to enter a cellar.

He continued to advance.

He took a few steps. Somebody passed near him running. Was it a man? a woman? were there several? He could not have told. It had passed and had vanished.

By a circuitous route, he came to a little street which he

judged to be the Rue de la Poterie; about the middle of this
alley he ran against some obstacle. He put out his hands. It was
an overturned cart; his foot recognised puddles of water, mud-
holes, paving stones, scattered and heaped up. A barricade had
been planned there and abandoned. He climbed over the stones
and found himself on the other side of the obstruction. He
walked very near the posts and guided himself by the walls of
the houses. A little beyond the barricade, he seemed to catch a
glimpse of something white in front of him. He approached, it
took form. It was two white horses! the omnibus horses unharnessed by Bossuet in the morning, which had wandered at
chance from street to street all day long, and had finally stopped
there, with the exhausted patience of brutes, who no more
comprehended the ways of man than man comprehends the
ways of Providence.

Marius left the horses behind him. As he came to a street
which struck him as being the Rue du Contrat Social, a shot
from a musket coming nobody knows whence, passing at random through the obscurity, whistled close by him, and the ball
pierced a copper shaving-dish suspended before a barber's shop.
This shaving-dish with the bullet-hole could still be seen, in
1846, in the Rue du Contrat Social, at the corner of the pillars
of the markets.

This musket-shot was life still. From that moment he met
nothing more.

This whole route resembled a descent down dark stairs.

Marius none the less went forward.

II
PARIS—AN OWL'S EYE VIEW

A BEING who could have soared above Paris at that moment
with the wing of the bat or the owl would have had a gloomy
spectacle beneath his eyes.

All that old quartier of the markets, which is like a city within
the city, which is traversed by the Rues Saint Denis and Saint
Martin, where a thousand little streets cross each other, and of
which the insurgents had made their stronghold and their field
of arms, would have appeared to him like an enormous black
hole dug out in the centre of Paris. There the eye fell into an
abyss. Thanks to the broken lamps, thanks to the closed

windows, there ceased all radiance, all life, all sound, all motion. The invisible police of the émeute watched everywhere, and maintained order, that is night. To drown the smallness of their number in a vast obscurity and to multiply each combatant by the possibilities which that obscurity contains, are the necessary tactics of insurrection. At nightfall, every window in which a candle was lighted had received a ball. The light was extinguished, sometimes the inhabitant killed. Thus nothing stirred. There was nothing there but fright, mourning, stupor in the houses; in the streets a sort of sacred horror. Even the long ranges of windows and of stories were not perceptible, the notching of the chimneys and the roofs, the dim reflections which gleam on the wet and muddy pavement. The eye which might have looked from above into that mass of shade would have caught a glimpse here and there perhaps, from point to point, of indistinct lights, bringing out broken and fantastic lines, outlines of singular constructions, something like ghostly gleams, coming and going among ruins; these were the barricades. The rest was a lake of obscurity, misty, heavy, funereal, above which rose, motionless and dismal silhouettes, the tower Saint Jacques, the church Saint Merry, and two or three others of those great buildings of which man makes giants and of which night makes phantoms.

All about this deserted and disquieted labyrinth, in the quartiers where the circulation of Paris was not stopped, and where a few rare lamps shone out, the aerial observer might have distinguished the metallic scintillation of sabres and bayonets, the sullen rumbling of artillery, and the swarming of silent battalions augmenting from moment to moment; a formidable girdle which was tightening and slowly closing about the émeute.

The invested quartier was now only a sort of monstrous cavern; everything in it appeared to be sleeping or motionless, and, as we have just seen, none of the streets on which you might have entered, offered anything but darkness.

A savage darkness, full of snares, full of unknown and formidable encounters, where it was fearful to penetrate and appalling to stay, where those who entered shuddered before those who were awaiting them, where those who waited trembled before those who were to come. Invisible combatants intrenched at every street-corner; the grave hidden in ambush in the thickness of the night. It was finished. No other light to be hoped for there henceforth save the flash of musketry, no other meeting save the sudden and rapid apparition of death. Where? how? when? nobody knew; but it was certain and inevitable. There, in that place marked out for the contest, the government and the insurrection, the National Guard and the popular societies, the bourgeoisie and the émeute were to grope their way. For those as for these, the necessity was the same. To leave that place slain or victors, the only possible issue henceforth. A situation so extreme, an obscurity so overpowering, that the most timid felt themselves filled with resolution and the boldest with terror.

Moreover, on both sides, fury, rancour, equal determination. For those to advance was to die, and nobody thought of retreat; for those to stay was to die, and nobody thought of flight.

All must be decided on the morrow, the triumph must be on this side or on that, the insurrection must be a revolution or a blunder. The government understood it as well as the factions; the least bourgeois felt it. Hence a feeling of anguish which mingled with the impenetrable darkness of this quartier where all was to be decided, hence a redoubling of anxiety about this silence whence a catastrophe was to issue. But one sound could be heard, a sound heart-rending as a death rattle, menacing as a malediction, the tocsin of Saint Merry. Nothing was so blood-chilling as the clamour of this wild and desperate bell wailing in the darkness.

As often happens, nature seemed to have put herself in accord with what men were about to do. Nothing disturbed the funereal harmonies of that whole. The stars had disappeared, heavy clouds filled the whole horizon with their melancholy folds. There was a black sky over those dead streets, as if an immense pall had unfolded itself over that immense tomb.

While a battle as yet entirely political was preparing in this same locality, which had already seen so many revolutionary events, while the youth, the secret associations, the schools, in the name of principles, and the middle class, in the name of interests, were approaching to dash against each other, to close with and to overthrow each other while each was hurrying and calling the final and decisive hour of the crisis, afar off and outside of that fatal quartier, in the deepest of the unfathomable caverns of that old, miserable Paris, which is disappearing under the splendour of the happy and opulent Paris, the gloomy voice of the people was heard sullenly growling.

A fearful and sacred voice, which is composed of the roar of the brute and the speech of God, which terrifies the feeble and which warns the wise, which comes at the same time from below like the voice of the lion and from above like the voice of the thunder.

III
THE EXTREME LIMIT

MARIUS had arrived at the markets.

There all was more calm, more obscure, and more motionless still than in the neighbouring streets. One would have said that the icy peace of the grave had come forth from the earth and spread over the sky.

A red glare, however, cut out upon this dark background the high roofs of the houses which barred the Rue de la Chanvrerie on the side towards Saint Eustache. It was the reflection of the torch which was blazing in the barricade of Corinth. Marius directed his steps towards this glare. It led him to the Beet Market, and he dimly saw the dark mouth of the Rue des Prêcheurs. He entered it. The vidette of the insurgents who was on guard at the other end did not perceive him. He felt that he was very near what he had come to seek, and he walked upon tiptoe. He reached in this way the elbow of that short end of the Rue Mondétour, which was, as we remember, the only communication preserved by Enjolras with the outside. Round the corner of the last house on his left, cautiously advancing his head, he looked into this end of the Rue Mondétour.

A little beyond the black corner of the alley and the Rue de la Chanvrerie, which threw a broad shadow, in which he was himself buried, he perceived a light upon the pavement, a portion of the wine-shop, and behind, a lamp twinkling in a kind of shapeless wall, and men crouching down with muskets on their knees. All this was within twenty yards of him. It was the interior of the barricade.

The houses on the right of the alley hid from him the rest of the wine-shop, the great barricade, and the flag.

Marius had but one step more to take.

Then the unhappy young man sat down upon a stone, folded his arms, and thought of his father.

He thought of that heroic Colonel Pontmercy who had been so brave a soldier, who had defended the frontier of France under the republic, and reached the frontier of Asia under the emperor, who had seen Genoa, Alessandria, Milan, Turin, Madrid, Vienna, Dresden, Berlin, Moscow, who had left upon every field of victory in Europe drops of that same blood which he, Marius, had in his veins, who had grown grey before his time in discipline and in command, who had lived with his sword-belt buckled, his epaulettes falling on his breast, his cockade blackened by powder, his forehead wrinkled by the cap, in the barracks, in the camp, in the bivouac, in the ambulance, and who after twenty years had returned from the great wars with his cheek scarred, his face smiling, simple, tranquil, admirable, pure as a child, having done everything for France and nothing against her.

He said to himself that his day had come to him also, that his hour had at last struck, that after his father, he also was to be brave, intrepid, bold, to run amidst bullets, to bare his breast to the bayonets, to pour out his blood, to seek the enemy, to seek death, that he was to wage war in his turn and to enter upon the field of battle, and that that field of battle upon which he was about to enter, was the street, and that war which he was about to wage, was civil war!

He saw civil war yawning like an abyss before him, and that in it he was to fall.

Then he shuddered.

He thought of that sword of his father which his grandfather had sold to a junk-shop, and which he himself had so painfully regretted. He said to himself that it was well that that chaste and valiant sword had escaped from him, and gone off in anger into the darkness; that if it had fled thus, it was because it was intelligent and because it foresaw the future; because it foreboded the émeute, the war of the gutters, the war of the pavements, the firing from cellar windows, blows given and received from behind; because, coming from Marengo and Friedland, it would not go to the Rue de la Chanvrerie, because after what it had done with the father, it would not do with the son! He said to himself that if that sword were there, if having received it from the bedside of his dead father, he had dared to take it and bring it away for this night combat between Frenchmen at the street-corners, most surely it would have burned his hands, and flamed before him like the sword of the angel! He said to himself that it was fortunate that it was not there and that it had disappeared, that it was well, that it was just, that his grandfather had been the true guardian of his father's glory, and that it was better that the colonel's sword had been cried at auction, sold to a dealer, thrown among old iron, than that it should be used to-day to pierce the side of the country.

And then he began to weep bitterly.

It was horrible. But what could he do? Live without Cosette, he could not. Since she had gone away, he must surely die. Had he not given her his word of honour that he should die? She had gone away knowing that; therefore it pleased her that Marius should die. And then it was clear that she no longer loved him, since she had gone away thus, without notifying him, without a word, without a letter, and she knew his address! What use in life and why live longer? And then, indeed! to have come so far, and to recoil! to have approached the danger, and to flee! to have come and looked into the barricade, and to slink away! to slink away all trembling, saying: "in fact, I have had enough of this, I have seen, that is sufficient, it is civil war, I am going away!" To abandon his friends who were expecting him! who perhaps had need of him! who were a handful against an army! To fail in all things at the same time, in his love, his friendship, his word! To give his poltroonery the pretext of patriotism! But this was impossible, and if his father's ghost were there in the shadow and saw him recoil, he would strike him with the flat of his sword and cry to him: "Advance, coward!"

A prey to the swaying of his thoughts, he bowed his head.

Suddenly he straightened up. A sort of splendid rectification was wrought in his spirit. There was an expansion of thought fitted to the confinity of the tomb; to be near death makes us see the truth. The vision of the act upon which he felt himself, perhaps on the point of entering, appeared to him no longer lamentable, but superb. The war of the street was suddenly transfigured by some indescribable interior throe of the soul, before the eye of his mind. All the tumultuous interrogation points of his reverie thronged upon him, but without troubling him. He left none without an answer.

Let us see, why should his father be indignant? are there not cases when insurrection rises to the dignity of duty? what would there be then belittling to the son of Colonel Pontmercy in the impending combat? It is no longer Montmirail or Champaubert; it is something else. It is no longer a question of a sacred territory, but of a holy idea. The country laments, so be it; but humanity applauds. Besides is it true that the country mourns? France bleeds, but liberty smiles; and before the smile of liberty, France forgets her wound. And then, looking at the matter from a still higher stand, why do men talk of civil war?

Civil war? What does this mean? Is there any foreign war? Is not every war between men, war between brothers? War is modified only by its aim. There is neither foreign war, nor civil war; there is only unjust war and just war. Until the day when the great human concordat shall be concluded, war, that at least which is the struggle of the hurrying future against the lingering past, may be necessary. What reproach can be brought against such war! War becomes shame, the sword becomes a dagger, only when it assassinates right, progress, reason, civilisation, truth. Then, civil war or foreign war, it is iniquitous; its name is crime. Outside of that holy thing, justice, by what right does one form of war despise another? by what right does the sword of Washington disown the pike of Camille Desmoulins? Leonidas against the foreigner, Timoleon against the tyrant, which is the greater? one is the defender, the other is the liberator. Shall we brand, without troubling ourselves with the object, every resort to arms in the interior of a city? then mark with infamy Brutus, Marcel, Arnold of Blankenheim, Coligny. War of the thickets? war of the streets? Why not? it was the war of Ambiorix, of Artaveld, of Marnix, of Pelagius. But Ambiorix fought against Rome, Artaveld against France, Marnix against Spain, Pelagius against the Moors; all against the foreigner. Well, monarchy is the foreigner; oppression is the foreigner; divine right is the foreigner. Despotism violates the moral frontier, as invasion violates the geographical frontier. To drive out the tyrant or to drive out the English is, in either case, to retake your territory. There comes an hour when protest no longer suffices; after philosophy there must be action; the strong hand finishes what the idea has planned; *Prometheus Bound* begins, Aristogeiton completes; the *Encyclopédie* enlightens souls, the 10th of August electrifies them. After Æschylus, Thrasybulus; after Diderot, Danton. The multitudes have a tendency to accept a master. Their mass deposits apathy. A mob easily totalises itself into obedience. Men must be aroused, pushed, shocked by the very benefits of their deliverance, their eyes wounded with the truth, light thrown them in terrible handfuls. They should be blinded a little for their own safety; this dazzling wakens them. Hence the necessity for tocsins and for wars. Great warriors must arise, illuminate the nations by boldness, and shake free this sad humanity which is covered with shadow by divine right. Cæsarean glory, force, fanaticism, irresponsible power, and absolute dominion, a mob stupidly occupied with gazing, in their twilight splendour, at these gloomy triumphs of the night. Down with the tyrant! But what? of whom do you speak? do you call Louis Philippe the tyrant? no; no more than Louis XVI. They are both what history is accustomed to call good kings; but principles cannot be parcelled out, the logic of the true is rectilinear, the peculiarity of truth is to be without complaisance; no compromise, then; all encroachment upon man must be repressed; there is divine right in Louis XVI., there is *parce que Bourbon* in Louis Philippe; both represent in a certain degree the confiscation of the right; and to wipe out the universal usurpation, it is necessary to fight them; it is necessary, France always taking the initiative. When the master falls in France, he falls everywhere. In short, to re-establish social truth, to give back to liberty her throne, to give back the people to the people, to give back sovereignty to man, to replace the purple upon the head of France, to restore in their fulness reason and equity, to suppress every germ of antagonism by restoring every man to himself, to abolish the obstacle which royalty opposes to the immense universal concord, to replace the human race on a level with right, what cause more just, and, consequently, what war more grand? These wars construct peace. An enormous fortress of prejudices, of privileges, of superstitions, of lies, of exactions, of abuses, of violence, of iniquity, of darkness, is still standing upon the world with its towers of hatred. It must be thrown down. This monstrous pile must be made to fall. To conquer at Austerlitz is grand; to take the Bastille is immense.

There is nobody who has not remarked it in himself, the soul, and this is the marvel of its complicate unity and ubiquity, has the wonderful faculty of reasoning almost coolly in the most desperate extremities; and it often happens that disconsolate passion and deep despair, in the very agony of their darkest soliloquies, weigh subjects and discuss theses. Logic is mingled with convulsion, and the thread of a syllogism floats unbroken in the dreary storm of thought. This was Marius' state of mind.

Even while thinking thus, overwhelmed but resolute, hesitating, however, and, indeed, shuddering in view of what he was about to do, his gaze wandered into the interior of the barricade. The insurgents were chatting in under tone, without moving about; and that quasi-silence was felt which marks the last phase of delay. Above them, at a third story window, Marius distinguished a sort of spectator or witness who seemed to him singularly attentive. It was the porter killed by Le Cabuc. From below, by the reflection of the torch hidden among the paving stones, this head was dimly perceptible. Nothing was more strange in that gloomy and uncertain light, than that livid, motionless, astonished face with its bristling hair, its staring eyes, and its gaping mouth, leaning over the street in an attitude of curiosity. One would have said that he who was dead was gazing at those who were about to die. A long trail of blood which had flowed from his head, descended in ruddy streaks from the window to the height of the first story, where it stopped.

BOOK FOURTEENTH –
THE GRANDEURS OF DESPAIR

I
THE FLAG: FIRST ACT

NOTHING came yet. The clock of Saint Merry had struck ten. Enjolras and Combeferre had sat down, carbine in hand, near the opening of the great barricade. They were not talking, they were listening; seeking to catch even the faintest and most distant sound of a march.

Suddenly, in the midst of this dismal calm, a clear, young, cheerful voice, which seemed to come from the Rue Saint Denis, arose and began to sing distinctly to the old popular air, *Au clair de la lune*, these lines which ended in a sort of cry similar to the crow of cock:

> Mon nez est en larmes,
> Mon ami Bugeaud,
> Prêt-moi tes gendarmes
> Pour leur dire un mot.
> Encapote bleue,
> La poule au shako,
> Voici la banlieue!
> Co-cocorico!*

They grasped each other by the hand:

"It is Gavroche," said Enjolras.

"He is warning us," said Combeferre.

A headlong run startled the empty street; they saw a creature nimbler than a clown climb over the omnibus, and Gavroche bounded into the barricade all breathless, saying:

"My musket! Here they are."

* My nose is in tears,
   My good friend Bugeaud,
   Just lend me your spears
   To tell them my woe.
   In blue cassimere,
   And feathered shako,
   The banlieue is here!
   Co-cocorico!

An electric thrill ran through the whole barricade, and a moving of hands was heard, feeling for their muskets.

"Do you want my carbine?" said Enjolras to the *gamin*.

"I want the big musket," answered Gavroche.

And he took Javert's musket.

Two sentinels had been driven back, and had come in almost at the same time as Gavroche. They were the sentinel from the end of the street, and the vidette from de la Petite Truanderie. The vidette in the little Rue des Prêcheurs remained at his post, which indicated that nothing was coming from the direction of the bridges and the markets.

The Rue de la Chanvrerie, in which a few paving stones were dimly visible by the reflection of the light which was thrown upon the flag, offered to the insurgents the appearance of a great black porch opening into a cloud of smoke.

Every man had taken his post for the combat.

Forty-three insurgents, among them Enjolras, Combeferre, Courfeyrac, Bossuet, Joly, Bahorel, and Gavroche, were on their knees in the great barricade, their heads even with the crest of the wall, the barrels of their muskets and their carbines pointed over the paving stones as through loopholes, watchful, silent, ready to fire. Six, commanded by Feuilly, were stationed with their muskets at their shoulders, in the windows of the two upper stories of Corinth.

A few moments more elapsed, then a sound of steps, measured, heavy, numerous, was distinctly heard from the direction of Saint Leu. This sound, at first faint, then distinct, then heavy and sonorous, approached slowly, without halt, without interruption, with a tranquil and terrible continuity. Nothing but this could be heard. It was at once the silence and the sound of the statue of the Commander, but this stony tread was so indescribably enormous and so multiplex, that it called up at the same time the idea of a throng and of a spectre. You would have thought you heard the stride of the fearful statue Legion. This tread approached; it approached still nearer, and stopped. They seemed to hear at the end of the street the breathing of many men. They saw nothing, however, only they discovered at the very end, in that dense obscurity, a multitude of metallic threads, as fine as needles and almost imperceptible, which moved about like those indescribable phosphoric networks which we perceive under our closed eyelids at the moment of going to sleep, in the first mists of slumber. They were bayonets and musket barrels dimly lighted up by the distant reflection of the torch.

There was still a pause, as if on both sides they were waiting. Suddenly, from the depth of that shadow, a voice, so much the more ominous, because nobody could be seen, and because it seemed as if it were the obscurity itself which was speaking, cried:

"Who is there?"

At the same time they heard the click of the levelled muskets. Enjolras answered in a lofty and ringing tone:

"French Revolution!"

"Fire!" said the voice.

A flash empurpled all the façades on the street, as if the door of a furnace were opened and suddenly closed.

A fearful explosion burst over the barricade. The red flag fell. The volley had been so heavy and so dense that it had cut the staff, that is to say, the very point of the pole of the omnibus. Some balls, which ricocheted from the cornices of the houses, entered the barricade and wounded several men.

The impression produced by this first charge was freezing. The attack was impetuous, and such as to make the boldest ponder. It was evident that they had to do with a whole regiment at least.

"Comrades," cried Courfeyrac, "don't waste the powder. Let us wait to reply till they come into the street."

"And first of all," said Enjolras, "let us hoist the flag again!"

He picked up the flag which had fallen just at his feet.

They heard from without the rattling of the ramrods in the muskets: the troops were reloading.

Enjolras continued:

"Who is there here who has courage? who replants the flag on the barricade?"

Nobody answered. To mount the barricade at the moment when without doubt it was aimed at anew, was simply death. The bravest hesitates to sentence himself, Enjolras himself felt a shudder. He repeated:

"Nobody volunteers?"

II
THE FLAG: SECOND ACT

SINCE they had arrived at Corinth and had commenced building the barricade, hardly any attention had been paid to Father Mabeuf. M. Mabeuf, however, had not left the company. He had entered the ground floor of the wine-shop and sat down behind the counter. There he had been, so to speak, annihilated in himself. He no longer seemed to look or to think. Courfeyrac and others had accosted him two or three times, warning him of the danger, entreating him to withdraw, but he had not appeared to hear them. When nobody was speaking to him, his lips moved as if he were answering somebody, and as soon as anybody addressed a word to him, his lips became still and his eyes lost all appearance of life. Some hours before the barricade was attacked, he had taken a position which he had not left since, his hands upon his knees and his head bent forward as if he were looking into an abyss. Nothing had been able to draw him out of this attitude; it appeared as if his mind were not in the barricade. When everybody had gone to take his place for the combat, there remained in the basement-room only Javert tied to the post, an insurgent with drawn sabre watching Javert, and he, Mabeuf. At the moment of the attack, at the discharge, the physical shock reached him, and, as it were, awakened him; he rose suddenly, crossed the room, and at the instant when Enjolras repeated his appeal: "Nobody volunteers?" they saw the old man appear in the doorway of the wine-shop.

His presence produced some commotion in the group. A cry arose:

"It is the Voter! it is the Conventionist! it is the Representative of the people!"

It is probable that he did not hear.

He walked straight to Enjolras, the insurgents fell back before him with a religious awe, he snatched the flag from Enjolras, who drew back petrified, and then, nobody daring to stop him, or to aid him, this old man of eighty, with shaking head but firm foot, began to climb slowly up the stairway of paving stones built into the barricade. It was so gloomy and so grand that all about him cried: "Hats off!" At each step it was frightful; his white hair, his decrepit face, his large forehead bald and wrinkled, his hollow eyes, his quivering and open mouth, his old arm raising the red banner, surged up out of the shadow and grew grand in the bloody light of the torch, and they seemed to see the ghost of '93 rising out of the earth, the flag of terror in its hand.

When he was on the top of the last step, when this trembling and terrible phantom, standing upon that mound of rubbish before twelve hundred invisible muskets, rose up, in the face of death and as if he were stronger than it, the whole barricade had in the darkness a supernatural and colossal appearance.

There was one of those silences which occur only in the presence of prodigies.

In the midst of this silence the old man waved the red flag and cried:

"*Vive la révolution! vive la république!* fraternity! equality! and death!"

They heard from the barricade a low and rapid muttering like the murmur of a hurried priest dispatching a prayer. It was probably the commissary of police who was making the legal summons at the other end of the street.

Then the same ringing voice which had cried: 'Who is there?" cried:

"Disperse!"

M. Mabeuf, pallid, haggard, his eyes illumined by the mournful fires of insanity, raised the flag above his head and repeated:

"*Vive la république!*"

"Fire!" said the voice.

A second discharge, like a shower of grape, beat against the barricade.

The old man fell upon his knees, then rose up, let the flag drop, and fell backwards upon the pavement within, like a log, at full length with his arms crossed.

Streams of blood ran from beneath him. His old face, pale and sad, seemed to behold the sky.

One of those emotions superior to man, which make us forget even to defend ourselves, seized the insurgents, and they approached the corpse with a respectful dismay.

"What men these regicides are!" said Enjolras.

Courfeyrac bent over to Enjolras' ear.

"This is only for you, and I don't wish to diminish the enthusiasm. But he was anything but a regicide. I knew him. His

name was Father Mabeuf. I don't know what ailed him to-day.
But he was a brave blockhead. Just look at his head."

"Blockhead and Brutus heart," answered Enjolras.

Then he raised his voice:

"Citizens! This is the example which the old give to the
young. We hesitated, he came! we fell back, he advanced!
Behold what those who tremble with old age teach those who
tremble with fear! This patriarch is august in the sight of the
country. He has had a long life and a magnificent death! Now
let us protect his corpse, let every one defend this old man dead
as he would defend his father living, and let his presence among
us make the barricade impregnable!"

A murmur of gloomy and determined adhesion followed
these words.

Enjolras stooped down, raised the old man's head, and
timidly kissed him on the forehead, then separating his arms,
and handling the dead with a tender care, as if he feared to hurt
him, he took off his coat, showed the bleeding holes to all,
and said:

"There now is our flag."

III

GAVROCHE WOULD HAVE DONE BETTER TO
ACCEPT ENJOLRAS' CARBINE

THEY threw a long black shawl belonging to the widow
Hucheloup over Father Mabeuf. Six men made a barrow of
their muskets, they laid the corpse upon it, and they bore it,
bareheaded, with solemn slowness, to the large table in the
basement-room.

These men, completely absorbed in the grave and sacred
thing which they were doing, no longer thought of the perilous
situation in which they were.

When the corpse passed near Javert, who was still impassible,
Enjolras said to the spy:

"You! directly."

During this time little Gavroche, who alone had not left his
post and had remained on the watch, thought he saw some
men approaching the barricade with a stealthy step. Suddenly
he cried:

"Take care!"

Courfeyrac, Enjolras, Jean Prouvaire, Combeferre, Joly, Bahorel, Bossuet, all sprang tumultuously from the wine-shop. There was hardly a moment to spare. They perceived a sparkling breadth of bayonets undulating above the barricade. Municipal Guards of tall stature were penetrating, some by climbing over the omnibus, others by the opening, pushing before them the *gamin*, who fell back, but did not fly.

The moment was critical. It was that first fearful instant of the inundation, when the stream rises to the level of the bank and when the water begins to infiltrate through the fissures in the dyke. A second more, and the barricade had been taken.

Bahorel sprang upon the first Municipal Guard who entered, and killed him at the very muzzle of his carbine; the second killed Bahorel with his bayonet. Another had already prostrated Courfeyrac, who was crying "Help!" The largest of all, a kind of colossus, marched upon Gavroche with fixed bayonet. The *gamin* took Javert's enormous musket in his little arms, aimed it resolutely at the giant, and pulled the trigger. Nothing went off. Javert had not loaded his musket. The Municipal Guard burst into a laugh and raised his bayonet over the child.

Before the bayonet touched Gavroche the musket dropped from the soldier's hands, a ball had struck the Municipal Guard in the middle of the forehead, and he fell on his back. A second ball struck the other Guard, who had assailed Courfeyrac, full in the breast, and threw him upon the pavement.

It was Marius who had just entered the barricade.

IV
THE KEG OF POWDER

MARIUS, still hidden in the corner of the Rue Mondétour, had watched the first phase of the combat, irresolute and shuddering. However, he was not able long to resist that mysterious and sovereign infatuation which we may call the appeal of the abyss. Before the imminence of the danger, before the death of M. Mabeuf, that fatal enigma, before Bahorel slain, Courfeyrac crying "Help!" that child threatened, his friends to succour or to avenge, all hesitation had vanished, and he had rushed into the conflict, his two pistols in his hands. By the first shot he had saved Gavroche and by the second delivered Courfeyrac.

At the shots, at the cries of the wounded Guards, the assailants had scaled the intrenchment, upon the summit of which could now be seen thronging Municipal Guards, soldiers of the Line, National Guards of the banlieue, musket in hand. They already covered more than two-thirds of the wall, but they did not leap into the inclosure; they seemed to hesitate, fearing some snare. They looked into the obscure barricade as one would look into a den of lions. The light of the torch only lighted up their bayonets, their bearskin caps, and the upper part of their anxious and angry faces.

Marius had now no arms, he had thrown away his discharged pistols, but he had noticed the keg of powder in the basement room near the door.

As he turned half round, looking in that direction, a soldier aimed at him. At the moment the soldier aimed at Marius, a hand was laid upon the muzzle of the musket, and stopped it. It was somebody who had sprung forward, the young working-man with velvet pantaloons. The shot went off, passed through the hand, and perhaps also through the working-man, for he fell, but the ball did not reach Marius. All this in the smoke, rather guessed than seen. Marius, who was entering the basement-room, hardly noticed it. Still he had caught a dim glimpse of that musket directed at him, and that hand which had stopped it, and he had heard the shot. But in moments like that the things which we see, waver and rush headlong, and we stop for nothing. We feel ourselves vaguely pushed towards still deeper shadow, and all is cloud.

The insurgents, surprised, but not dismayed, had rallied. Enjolras had cried: "Wait! don't fire at random!" In the first confusion, in fact, they might hit one another. Most of them had gone up to the window of the second story and to the dormer windows, whence they commanded the assailants. The most determined, with Enjolras, Courfeyrac, Jean Prouvaire, and Combeferre, had haughtily placed their backs to the houses in the rear, openly facing the ranks of soldiers and guards which crowded the barricade.

All this was accomplished without precipitation, with that strange and threatening gravity which precedes mêlées. On both sides they were taking aim, the muzzles of the guns almost touching; they were so near that they could talk with each other in an ordinary tone. Just as the spark was about to fly, an officer in a gorget and with huge epaulettes, extended his sword and said:

"Take aim!"

"Fire!" said Enjolras.

The two explosions were simultaneous, and everything disappeared in the smoke.

A stinging and stifling smoke amid which writhed, with dull and feeble groans, the wounded and the dying.

When the smoke cleared away, on both sides the combatants were seen, thinned out, but still in the same places, and reloading their pieces in silence.

Suddenly, a thundering voice was heard, crying:

"Begone, or I'll blow up the barricade!"

All turned in the direction whence the voice came.

Marius had entered the basement-room, and had taken the keg of powder, then he had profited by the smoke and the kind of obscure fog which filled the intrenched inclosure, to glide along the barricade as far as that cage of paving stones in which the torch was fixed. To pull out the torch, to put the keg of powder in its place, to push the pile of paving stones upon the keg, which stove it in, with a sort of terrible self-control—all this had been for Marius the work of stooping down and rising up; and now all, National Guards, Municipal Guards, officers, soldiers, grouped at the other extremity of the barricade, beheld him with horror, his foot upon the stones, the torch in his hand, his stern face lighted by a deadly resolution, bending the flame of the torch towards that formidable pile in which they discerned the broken barrel of powder, and uttering that terrific cry:

"Begone, or I'll blow up the barricade!"

Marius upon this barricade, after the octogenarian, was the vision of the young revolution after the apparition of the old.

"Blow up the barricade!" said a sergeant, "and yourself also!"

Marius answered:

"And myself also."

And he approached the torch to the keg of powder.

But there was no longer anybody on the wall. The assailants, leaving their dead and wounded, fled pell-mell and in disorder towards the extremity of the street, and were again lost in the night. It was a rout.

The barricade was redeemed.

V

END OF JEAN PROUVAIRE'S RHYME

ALL flocked round Marius. Courfeyrac sprang to his neck.

"You here!"

"How fortunate!" said Combeferre.

"You came in good time!" said Bossuet.

"Without you I should have been dead!" continued Courfeyrac.

"Without you I'd been gobbled!" added Gavroche.

Marius inquired:

"Where is the chief?"

"You are the chief," said Enjolras.

Marius had all day had a furnace in his brain, now it was a whirlwind. This whirlwind which was within him, affected him as if it were without, and were sweeping him along. It seemed to him that he was already at an immense distance from life. His two luminous months of joy and of love, terminating abruptly upon this frightful precipice, Cosette lost to him, this barricade, M. Mabeuf dying for the republic, himself a chief of insurgents, all these things appeared a monstrous nightmare. He was obliged to make a mental effort to assure himself that all this which surrounded him was real. Marius had lived too little as yet to know that nothing is more imminent than the impossible, and that what we must always foresee is the unforeseen. He was a spectator of his own drama, as of a play which one does not comprehend.

In this mist in which his mind was struggling, he did not recognise Javert who, bound to his post, had not moved his head during the attack upon the barricade, and who beheld the revolt going on about him with the resignation of a martyr and the majesty of a judge. Marius did not even perceive him.

Meanwhile the assailants made no movement, they were heard marching and swarming at the end of the street, but they did not venture forward, either that they were awaiting orders, or that before rushing anew upon that impregnable redoubt, they were awaiting reinforcements. The insurgents had posted sentinels, and some who were students in medicine had set about dressing the wounded.

They had thrown the tables out of the wine-shop, with the exception of two reserved for lint and cartridges, and that on which lay Father Mabeuf; they added them to the barricade, and had replaced them in the basement-room by the mattresses from the beds of the widow Hucheloup, and the servants. Upon these mattresses they had laid the wounded; as for the three poor creatures who lived in Corinth, nobody knew what had become of them. They found them at last, however, hidden in the cellar.

A bitter emotion came to darken their joy over the redeemed barricade.

They called the roll. One of the insurgents was missing. And who? One of the dearest. One of the most valiant, Jean Prouvaire. They sought him among the wounded, he was not there. They sought him among the dead, he was not there. He was evidently a prisoner.

Combeferre said to Enjolras:

"They have our friend; we have their officer. Have you set your heart on the death of this spy?"

"Yes," said Enjolras; "but less than on the life of Jean Prouvaire."

This passed in the basement-room near Javert's post.

"Well," replied Combeferre, "I am going to tie my handkerchief to my cane, and go with a flag of truce to offer to give them their man for ours."

"Listen," said Enjolras, laying his hand on Combeferre's arm.

There was a significant clicking of arms at the end of the street.

They heard a manly voice cry:

"*Vive la France! Vive l'avenir!*"

They recognised Prouvaire's voice.

There was a flash and an explosion.

Silence reigned again.

"They have killed him," exclaimed Combeferre.

Enjolras looked at Javert and said to him:

"Your friends have just shot you."

VI

THE AGONY OF DEATH AFTER THE AGONY OF LIFE

A PECULIARITY of this kind of war is that the attack on the barricades is almost always made in front, and that in general the assailants abstain from turning the positions, whether it be that they dread ambuscades, or that they fear to become entangled in the crooked streets. The whole attention of the insurgents therefore was directed to the great barricade, which was evidently the point still threatened, and where the struggle must infallibly recommence. Marius, however, thought of the little barricade and went to it. It was deserted, and was guarded only by the lamp which flickered between the stones. The little Rue Mondétour, moreover, and the branch streets de la Petite Truanderie and du Cygne, were perfectly quiet.

As Marius, the inspection made, was retiring, he heard his name faintly pronounced in the obscurity:

"Monsieur Marius!"

He shuddered, for he recognised the voice which had called him two hours before, through the grating in the Rue Plumet.

Only this voice now seemed to be but a breath.

He looked about him and saw nobody.

Marius thought he was deceived, and that it was an illusion added by his mind to the extraordinary realities which were thronging about him. He started to leave the retired recess in which the barricade was situated.

"Monsieur Marius!" repeated the voice.

This time he could not doubt, he had heard distinctly; he looked, and saw nothing.

"At your feet," said the voice.

He stooped and saw a form in the shadow, which was dragging itself towards him. It was crawling along the pavement. It was this that had spoken to him.

The lamp enabled him to distinguish a blouse, a pair of torn pantaloons of coarse velvet, bare feet, and something which resembled a pool of blood. Marius caught a glimpse of a pale face which rose towards him and said to him:

"You do not know me?"

"No."

"Eponine."

Marius bent down quickly. It was indeed that unhappy child. She was dressed as a man.

"How came you here? what are you doing there?"

"I am dying," said she.

There are words and incidents which rouse beings who are crushed. Marius exclaimed, with a start:

"You are wounded! Wait, I will carry you into the room!

They will dress your wounds! Is it serious? how shall I take you up so as not to hurt you? Where are you hurt? Help! my God! But what did you come here for?"

And he tried to pass his arm under her to lift her.

In lifting her he touched her hand.

She uttered a feeble cry.

"Have I hurt you?" asked Marius.

"A little."

"But I have only touched your hand."

She raised her hand into Marius' sight, and Marius saw in the centre of that hand a black hole.

"What is the matter with your hand?" said he.

"It is pierced."

"Pierced?"

"Yes."

"By what?"

"By a ball."

"How?"

"Did you see a musket aimed at you?"

"Yes, and a hand which stopped it."

"That was mine."

Marius shuddered.

"What madness! Poor child! But that is not so bad, if that is all, it is nothing, let me carry you to a bed. They will care for you, people don't die from a shot in the hand."

She murmured:

"The ball passed through my hand, but it went out through my back. It is useless to take me from here. I will tell you how you can care for me, better than a surgeon. Sit down by me on that stone."

He obeyed; she laid her head on Marius' knees, and without looking at him, she said:

"Oh! how good it is! How kind he is! That is it! I don't suffer any more!"

She remained a moment in silence, then she turned her head with effort and looked at Marius.

"Do you know, Monsieur Marius? It worried me that you should go into that garden, it was silly, since it was I who had shown you the house, and then indeed I ought surely to have known that a young man like you—"

She stopped, and, leaping over the gloomy transitions which

were doubtless in her mind, she added with a heartrending smile:

"You thought me ugly, didn't you?"

She continued:

"See, you are lost! Nobody will get out of the barricade, now. It was I who led you into this, it was! You are going to die, I am sure. And still when I saw him aiming at you, I put up my hand upon the muzzle of the musket. How droll it is! But it was because I wanted to die before you. When I got this ball, I dragged myself here, nobody saw me, nobody picked me up. I waited for you, I said: He will not come then? Oh! if you knew, I bit my blouse, I suffered so much! Now I am well. Do you remember the day when I came into your room, and when I looked at myself in your mirror, and the day when I met you on the boulevard near some work-women? How the birds sang! It was not very long ago. You gave me a hundred sous, and I said to you: I don't want your money. Did you pick up your piece? You are not rich; I didn't think to tell you to pick it up. The sun shone bright, I was not cold. Do you remember, Monsieur Marius? Oh! I am happy! We are all going to die."

She had a wandering, grave, and touching air. Her torn blouse showed her bare throat. While she was talking she rested her wounded hand upon her breast where there was another hole, from which there came with each pulsation a flow of blood like a jet of wine from an open bung.

Marius gazed upon this unfortunate creature with profound compassion.

"Oh!" she exclaimed suddenly, "it is coming back. I am stifling!"

She seized her blouse and bit it, and her legs writhed upon the pavement.

At this moment the chicken voice of little Gavroche resounded through the barricade. The child had mounted upon a table to load his musket and was gaily singing the song then so popular:

En voyant Lafayette
Le gendarme répète
Sauvons-nous! sauvons-nous! sauvons-nous!

Eponine raised herself up, and listened, then she murmured: "It is he."

And turning towards Marius:

"My brother is here. He must not see me. He would scold me."

"Your brother?" asked Marius, who thought in the bitterest and most sorrowful depths of his heart, of the duties which his father had bequeathed him towards the Thénardiers, "who is your brother?"

"That little boy."

"The one who is singing?"

"Yes."

Marius started.

"Oh! don't go away!" said she, "it will not be long now!"

She was sitting almost upright, but her voice was very low and broken by hiccoughs. At intervals the death-rattle interrupted her. She approached her face as near as she could to Marius' face. She added with a strange expression:

"Listen, I don't want to deceive you. I have a letter in my pocket for you. Since yesterday. I was told to put it in the post. I kept it. I didn't want it to reach you. But you would not like it of me perhaps when we meet again so soon. We do meet again, don't we? Take your letter."

She grasped Marius' hand convulsively with her wounded hand, but she seemed no longer to feel the pain. She put Marius' hand into the pocket of her blouse. Marius really felt a paper there.

"Take it," said she.

Marius took the letter.

She made a sign of satisfaction and of consent.

"Now for my pains, promise me——"

And she hesitated.

"What?" asked Marius.

"Promise me!"

"I promise you."

"Promise to kiss me on the forehead when I am dead. I shall feel it."

She let her head fall back upon Marius' knees and her eyelids closed. He thought that poor soul had gone. Eponine lay motionless; but just when Marius supposed her for ever asleep, she slowly opened her eyes in which the gloomy deepness of death appeared, and said to him with an accent the sweetness of which already seemed to come from another world:

"And then, do you know, Monsieur Marius, I believe I was a little in love with you."

She essayed to smile again and expired.

VII

GAVROCHE A PROFOUND CALCULATOR OF DISTANCES

MARIUS kept his promise. He kissed that livid forehead from which oozed an icy sweat. This was not infidelity to Cosette; it was a thoughtful and gentle farewell to an unhappy soul.

He had not taken the letter which Eponine had given him without a thrill. He had felt at once the presence of an event. He was impatient to read it. The heart of man is thus made; the unfortunate child had hardly closed her eyes when Marius thought to unfold this paper. He laid her gently upon the ground, and went away. Something told him that he could not read that letter in sight of this corpse.

He went to a candle in the basement-room. It was a little note, folded and sealed with the elegant care of a woman. The address was in a woman's hand, and ran:

"To Monsieur, Monsieur Marius Pontmercy, at M. Courfeyrac's, Rue de la Verrerie, No. 16."

He broke the seal and read:

"My beloved, alas! my father wishes to start immediately. We shall be to-night in the Rue de l'Homme Armé, No. 7. In a week we shall be in England. COSETTE June 4th."

Such was the innocence of this love that Marius did not even know Cosette's handwriting.

What happened may be told in a few words. Eponine had done it all. After the evening of the 3rd of June, she had had a double thought, to thwart the projects of her father and the bandits upon the house in the Rue Plumet, and to separate Marius from Cosette. She had changed rags with the first young rogue who thought it amusing to dress as a woman while Eponine disguised herself as a man. It was she who, in the Champ de Mars, had given Jean Valjean the expressive warning: *Remove*. Jean Valjean returned home, and said to Cosette: *we start to-night, and we are going to the Rue de l'Homme Armé with Toussaint. Next week we shall be in London*. Cosette, prostrated by this unexpected blow, had hastily written two lines to Marius. But how should she get the letter to the post? She did not go out alone, and Toussaint, surprised at such an errand, would surely show the letter to M. Fauchelevent. In this anxiety, Cosette saw, through the grating, Eponine in men's clothes, who was now prowling continually about the garden. Cosette called "this young working-man" and handed him five francs and the letter, saying to him: "carry this letter to its address right away." Eponine put the letter in her pocket. The next day, June 5th, she went to Courfeyrac's to ask for Marius, not to give him the letter, but, a thing which every jealous and loving soul will understand, "to see." There she waited for Marius, or, at least, for Courfeyrac—still to see. When Courfeyrac said to her: we are going to the barricades, an idea flashed across her mind. To throw herself into that death as she would have thrown herself into any other, and to push Marius into it. She followed Courfeyrac, made sure of the post where they were building the barricade; and very sure, since Marius had received no notice, and she had intercepted the letter, that he would at nightfall be at his usual evening rendezvous, she went to the Rue Plumet, waited there for Marius, and sent him, in the name of his friends, that appeal which must, she thought, lead him to the barricade. She counted upon Marius' despair when he should not find Cosette; she was not mistaken. She returned herself to the Rue de la Chanvrerie. We have seen what she did there. She died with that tragic joy of jealous hearts which drag the being they love into death with them, saying: nobody shall have him!

Marius covered Cosette's letter with kisses. She loved him then? He had for a moment the idea that now he need not die. Then he said to himself: "She is going away. Her father takes her to England and my grandfather refuses to consent to the marriage. Nothing is changed in the fatality." Dreamers, like Marius, have these supreme depressions, and paths hence are chosen in despair. The fatigue of life is insupportable; death is sooner over. Then he thought that there were two duties remaining for him to fulfil: to inform Cosette of his death and to send her a last farewell, and to save from the imminent catastrophe which was approaching, this poor child, Eponine's brother and Thénardier's son.

He had a pocket-book with him; the same that had contained the pages upon which he had written so many thoughts of love for Cosette. He tore out a leaf and wrote with a pencil these few lines:

"Our marriage was impossible. I have asked my grandfather, he has refused; I am without fortune, and you also. I ran to your house, I did not find you, you know the promise that I gave you? I keep it, I die, I love you. When you read this, my soul will be near you, and will smile upon you."

Having nothing to seal this letter with, he merely folded the paper, and wrote upon it this address:

"*To Mademoiselle Cosette Fauchelevent, at M. Fauchelevent's, Rue de l'Homme Armé, No. 7.*"

The letter folded, he remained a moment in thought, took his pocket-book again, opened it, and wrote these four lines on the first page with the same pencil:

"My name is Marius Pontmercy. Carry my corpse to my grandfather's, M. Gillenormand, Rue des Filles du Calvaire, No. 6, in the Marais."

He put the book into his coat-pocket, then he called Gavroche. The *gamin*, at the sound of Marius' voice, ran up with his joyous and devoted face:

"Will you do something for me?"

"Anything," said Gavroche. "God of the good God! without you I should have been cooked, sure."

"You see this letter?"

"Yes."

"Take it. Go out of the barricade immediately" (Gavroche, disturbed, began to scratch his ear), "and to-morrow morning you will carry it to its address, to Mademoiselle Cosette, at M. Fauchelevent's, Rue de l'Homme Armé, No. 7."

The heroic boy answered:

"Ah, well, but in that time they'll take the barricade, and I shan't be here."

"The barricade will not be attacked again before daybreak, according to all appearance, and will not be taken before to-morrow noon."

The new respite which the assailants allowed the barricade was, in fact, prolonged. It was one of those intermissions, frequent in night combats, which are always followed by a redoubled fury.

"Well," said Gavroche, "suppose I go and carry your letter in the morning?"

"It will be too late. The barricade will probably be blockaded; all the streets will be guarded, and you cannot get out; Go, right away!"

Gavroche had nothing more to say; he stood there, undecided, and sadly scratching his ear. Suddenly, with one of his birdlike motions, he took the letter:

"All right," said he.

And he started off on a run by the little Rue Mondétour.

Gavroche had an idea which decided him, but which he did not tell, for fear Marius would make some objection to it.

That idea was this:

"It is hardly midnight, the Rue de l'Homme Armé is not far, I will carry the letter right away, and I shall get back in time."

BOOK FIFTEENTH –
THE RUE DE L'HOMME ARMÉ

I
BLOTTER, BLABBER

WHAT are the convulsions of a city compared with the émeutes of the soul? Man is a still deeper depth than the people. Jean Valjean, at that very moment, was a prey to a frightful uprising. All the gulfs were reopened within him. He also, like Paris, was shuddering on the threshold of a formidable and obscure revolution. A few hours had sufficed. His destiny and his conscience were suddenly covered with shadow. Of him also, as of Paris, we might say: the two principles are face to face. The angel of light and the angel of darkness are to wrestle on the bridge of the abyss. Which of the two shall hurl down the other? which shall sweep him away?

On the eve of that same day, June 5th, Jean Valjean, accompanied by Cosette and Toussaint, had installed himself in the Rue de l'Homme Armé. A sudden turn of fortune awaited him there.

Cosette had not left the Rue Plumet without an attempt at resistance. For the first time since they had lived together, Cosette's will and Jean Valjean's will had shown themselves distinct, and had been, if not conflicting, at least contradictory. There was objection on one side and inflexibility on the other. The abrupt advice: *remove*, thrown to Jean Valjean by an unknown hand, had so far alarmed him as to render him absolute. He believed himself tracked out and pursued. Cosette had to yield.

They both arrived in the Rue de l'Homme Armé without opening their mouths or saying a word, absorbed in their personal meditations; Jean Valjean so anxious that he did not perceive Cosette's sadness, Cosette so sad that she did not perceive Jean Valjean's anxiety.

Jean Valjean had brought Toussaint, which he had never done in his preceding absences. He saw that possibly he should not return to the Rue Plumet, and he could neither leave Toussaint behind, nor tell her his secret. Besides he felt that she was devoted and safe. Between domestic and master, treason begins with curiosity. But Toussaint, as if she had been predestined to be the servant of Jean Valjean, was not curious. She said through her stuttering, in her Barneville peasant's speech: "I am from same to same; I think my act; the remainder is not my labour." (I am so; I do my work! the rest is not my affair.)

In this departure from the Rue Plumet, which was almost a flight, Jean Valjean carried nothing but the little embalmed valise christened by Cosette the *inseparable*. Full trunks would have required porters, and porters are witnesses. They had a coach come to the door on the Rue de Babylone, and they went away.

It was with great difficulty that Toussaint obtained permission to pack up a little linen and clothing and a few toilet articles. Cosette herself carried only her writing-desk and her blotter.

Jean Valjean, to increase the solitude and mystery of this disappearance, had arranged so as not to leave the cottage on the Rue Plumet till the close of the day, which left Cosette time to write her note to Marius. They arrived in the Rue de l'Homme Armé after nightfall.

They went silently to bed.

The lodging in the Rue de l'Homme Armé was situated in a rear court on the second story, and consisted of two bedrooms, a dining-room, and a kitchen adjoining the dining-room, with a loft where there was a cot-bed which fell to Toussaint. The dining-room was at the same time the antechamber, and separated the two bedrooms. The apartments contained all necessary furniture.

We are reassured almost as foolishly as we are alarmed; human nature is so constituted. Hardly was Jean Valjean in the Rue de l'Homme Armé, before his anxiety grew less, and by degrees was dissipated. There are quieting spots which act in some sort mechanically upon the mind. Obscure street, peaceful inhabitants. Jean Valjean felt some strange contagion of tranquillity in that lane of the ancient Paris, so narrow that it was barred to carriages by a transverse joist laid upon two posts, dumb and deaf in the midst of the noisy city, twilight in broad day, and so to speak, incapable of emotions between its two rows of lofty, century-old houses which are silent like the patriarchs that they are. There is stagnant oblivion in this street. Jean Valjean breathed there. By what means could anybody find him there?

His first care was to place the *inseparable* by his side.

He slept well. Night counsels; we may add: night calms. Next morning he awoke almost cheerful. He thought the dining-room charming, although it was hideous, furnished with an old round table, a low sideboard surmounted by a hanging mirror, a worm-eaten arm-chair, and a few other chairs loaded down with Toussaint's bundles. Through an opening in one of these bundles, Jean Valjean's National Guard uniform could be seen.

As for Cosette, she had Toussaint bring a bowl of soup to her room, and did not make her appearance till evening.

About five o'clock, Toussaint, who was coming and going, very busy with this little removal, set a cold fowl on the dining-room table, which Cosette, out of deference to her father, consented to look at.

This done, Cosette, upon pretext of a severe headache, said good-night to Jean Valjean, and shut herself in her bedroom. Jean Valjean ate a chicken's wing with a good appetite, and, leaning on the table, clearing his brow little by little, was regaining his sense of security.

While he was making this frugal dinner, he became confusedly aware, on two or three occasions, of the stammering of Toussaint, who said to him: "Monsieur, there is a row; they are fighting in Paris." But, absorbed in a multitude of interior combinations, he paid no attention to it. To tell the truth, he had not heard.

He arose and began to walk from the window to the door, and from the door to the window, growing calmer and calmer.

With calmness, Cosette, his single engrossing care, returned to his thoughts. Not that he was troubled about this headache, a petty derangement of the nerves, a young girl's pouting, the cloud of a moment, in a day or two it would be gone; but he thought of the future, and, as usual, he thought of it pleasantly. After all, he saw no obstacle to their happy life resuming its course. At certain hours, everything seems impossible; at other hours, everything appears easy; Jean Valjean was in one of those happy hours. They come ordinarily after the evil ones, like day after night, by that law of succession and contrast which lies at the very foundation of nature, and which superficial minds call antithesis. In this peaceful street, in which he had taken refuge, Jean Valjean was relieved from all that had troubled him for some time past. From the very fact that he had seen a good deal of darkness, he began to perceive a little blue sky. To have left the Rue Plumet without complication and without accident, was already a piece of good fortune. Perhaps it would be prudent to leave the country, were it only for a few months, and go to London. Well, they would go. To be in France, to be in England, what did that matter, if he had Cosette with him? Cosette was his nation. Cosette sufficed for his happiness; the idea that perhaps he did not suffice for Cosette's happiness, this idea, once his fever and his bane, did not even present itself to his mind. All his past griefs had disappeared, and he was in full tide of optimism. Cosette, being near him, seemed to belong to him; an optical effect which everybody has experienced. He arranged in his own mind and with every possible facility, the departure for England with Cosette, and he saw his happiness reconstructed, no matter where, in the perspective of his reverie.

While yet walking up and down, with slow steps, his eye suddenly met something strange.

He perceived facing him, in the inclined mirror which hung above the sideboard, and he distinctly read the lines which follow:

"My beloved, alas! my father wishes to start immediately. We shall be to-night in the Rue de l'Homme Armé, No. 7. In a week we shall be in London. COSETTE. June 4th."

Jean Valjean stood aghast.

Cosette, on arriving, had laid her blotter on the sideboard before the mirror, and, wholly absorbed in her sorrowful anguish, had forgotten it there, without even noticing that she left it wide open, and open exactly at the page upon which she had dried the five lines written by her, and which she had given in charge to the young workman passing through the Rue Plumet. The writing was imprinted upon the blotter.

The mirror reflected the writing.

There resulted what is called in geometry the symmetrical image; so that the writing reversed on the blotter was corrected by the mirror, and presented its original form; and Jean Valjean had beneath his eyes the letter written in the evening by Cosette to Marius.

It was simple and withering.

Jean Valjean went to the mirror. He read the five lines again, but he did not believe it. They produced upon him the effect of an apparition in a flash of lightning. It was a hallucination. It was impossible. It was not.

Little by little his perception became more precise; he looked at Cosette's blotter, and the consciousness of the real fact returned to him. He took the blotter and said: "It comes from that." He feverishly examined the five lines imprinted on the blotter, the reversal of the letters made a fantastic scrawl of them, and he saw no sense in them. Then he said to himself: "But that does not mean anything, there is nothing written there." And he drew a long breath, with an inexpressible sense of relief. Who has not felt these silly joys in moments of horror? The soul does not give itself up to despair until it has exhausted all illusions.

He held the blotter in his hand and gazed at it, stupidly happy, almost laughing at the hallucination of which he had been the dupe. All at once his eyes fell upon the mirror, and he saw the vision again. This time it was not a mirage. The second sight of a vision is a reality, it was palpable, it was the writing restored by the mirror. He understood.

Jean Valjean tottered, let the blotter fall, and sank down into the old arm-chair by the sideboard, his head drooping, his eyes glassy, bewildered. He said to himself that it was clear, and that the light of the world was for ever eclipsed, and that Cosette had written that to somebody. Then he heard his soul, again become terrible, give a sullen roar in the darkness. Go, then, and take from the lion the dog which he has in his cage.

A circumstance strange and sad, Marius at that moment had not yet Cosette's letter; chance had brought it, like a traitor, to Jean Valjean before delivering it to Marius.

Jean Valjean till this day had never been vanquished when put to the proof. He had been subjected to fearful trials; no violence of ill fortune had been spared him; the ferocity of fate, armed with every vengeance and with every scorn of society, had taken him for a subject and had greedily pursued him. He had neither recoiled nor flinched before anything. He had accepted, when he must, every extremity; he had sacrificed his reconquered inviolability of manhood, given up his liberty, risked his head, lost all, suffered all, and he had remained so disinterested and stoical that at times one might have believed him translated, like a martyr. His conscience, inured to all possible assaults of adversity, might seem for ever impregnable. Well, he who could have seen his inward monitor would have been compelled to admit that at this hour it was growing feeble.

For, of all the tortures which he had undergone in that inquisition of destiny, this was the most fearful. Never had such pincers seized him. He felt the mysterious quiver of every latent sensibility. He felt the laceration of the unknown fibre. Alas, the supreme ordeal, let us say rather, the only ordeal, is the loss of the beloved being.

Poor old Jean Valjean did not, certainly, love Cosette otherwise than as a father; but, as we have already mentioned, into this paternity the very bereavement of his life had introduced every love; he loved Cosette as his daughter, and he loved her as his mother, and he loved her as his sister; and, as he had never had either sweetheart or wife, as nature is a creditor who accepts no protest, that sentiment, also, the most indestructible of all, was mingled with the others, vague, ignorant, pure with the purity of blindness, unconscious, celestial, angelic, divine; less like a sentiment than like an instinct, less like an instinct than like an attraction, imperceptible and invisible, but real; and love, properly speaking, existed in his enormous tenderness for Cosette as does the vein of gold in the mountain, dark and virgin.

Remember that condition of heart which we have already pointed out. No marriage was possible between them, not even that of souls; and still it was certain that their destinies were espoused. Except Cosette, that is to say, except a childhood, Jean Valjean, in all his long life, had known nothing of those objects which man can love. The passions and the loves which succeed one another, had not left on him those successive greens, a light green over a dark green, which we notice upon leaves that pass the winter, and upon men who pass their fifty years. In short, and we have more than once insisted upon it, all that interior fusion, all that whole, the resultant of which was a lofty virtue, ended in making of Jean Valjean a father for Cosette. A strange father forged out of the grandfather, the son, the brother, and the husband, which there was in Jean Valjean; a father in whom there was even a mother; a father who loved Cosette, and who adored her, and to whom that child was light, was home, was family, was country, was paradise.

So, when he saw that it was positively ended, that she escaped him, that she glided from his hands, that she eluded him, that it was cloud, that it was water, when he had before his eyes this crushing evidence; another is the aim of her heart, another is the desire of her life, there is a beloved; I am only the father; I no longer exist; when he could no more doubt when he said to himself: "She is going away out of me!" the grief which he felt surpassed the possible. To have done all that he had done to come to this! and, what! to be nothing! Then, as we have just said, he felt from head to foot a shudder of revolt. He felt even to the roots of his hair the immense awakening of selfishness, and the Me howled in the abyss of his soul.

There are interior subsoilings. The penetration of a torturing certainty into man does not occur without breaking up and pulverising certain deep elements which are sometimes the man himself. Grief, when it reaches this stage, is a panic of all the forces of the soul. These are fatal crises. Few among us come through them without change, and firm in duty. When the limit of suffering is overpassed, the most imperturbable virtue is disconcerted. Jean Valjean took up the blotter, and convinced himself anew; he bent as if petrified over the five undeniable lines, with eye fixed; and such a cloud formed within him that one might have believed the whole interior of that soul was crumbling.

He examined this revelation, through the magnifying powers of reverie, with an apparent and frightful calmness, for it is a terrible thing when the calmness of man reaches the rigidity of the statue.

He measured the appalling step which his destiny had taken without a suspicion on his part; he recalled his fears of the previous summer, so foolishly dissipated: he recognised the precipice; it was still the same; only Jean Valjean was no longer on the brink, he was at the bottom.

A bitter and monstrous thing, he had fallen without perceiving it. All the light of his life had gone out, he believing that he constantly saw the sun.

His instinct did not hesitate. He put together certain circumstances, certain dates, certain blushes, and certain pallors of Cosette, and he said to himself: "It is he." The divination of despair is a sort of mysterious bow which never misses its aim. With his first conjecture, he hit Marius. He did not know the name, but he found the man at once. He perceived distinctly, at the bottom of the implacable evocation of memory, the unknown prowler of the Luxembourg, that wretched seeker of amours, that romantic idler, that imbecile, that coward, for it is cowardice to come and make sweet eyes at girls who are beside their father who loves them.

After he had fully determined that that young man was at the bottom of this state of affairs, and that it all came from him, he, Jean Valjean, the regenerated man, the man who had laboured so much upon his soul, the man who had made so many efforts to resolve all life, all misery, and all misfortune into love; he looked within himself, and there he saw a spectre, Hatred.

Great griefs contain dejection. They discourage existence. The man into whom they enter feels something go out of him. In youth, their visit is dismal; in later years it is ominous. Alas! when the blood is hot, when the hair is black, when the head is erect upon the body like the flame upon the torch, when the sheaf of destiny is still full, when the heart, filled with a fortunate love, still has pulsations which can be responded to, when we have before us the time to retrieve, when all women are before us, and all smiles, and all the future, and all the horizon, when the strength of life is complete, if despair is a fearful thing, what is it then in old age, when the years rush along, growing bleaker and bleaker, at the twilight hour, when we begin to see the stars of the tomb!

While he was thinking, Toussaint entered. Jean Valjean arose, and asked her:

"In what direction is it? Do you know?"

Toussaint, astonished, could only answer:

"If you please?"

Jean Valjean resumed:

"Didn't you tell me just now that they were fighting?"

"Oh! yes, monsieur," answered Toussaint. "It is over by Saint Merry."

There are some mechanical impulses which come to us, without our knowledge even, from our deepest thoughts. It was doubtless under the influence of an impulse of this kind, and of which he was hardly conscious, that Jean Valjean five minutes afterwards found himself in the street.

He was bare-headed, seated upon the stone block by the door of his house. He seemed to be listening.

The night had come.

II
THE GAMIN AN ENEMY OF LIGHT

How much time did he pass thus? What were the ebbs and the flows of that tragic meditation? did he straighten up? did he remain bowed? had he been bent so far as to break? could he yet straighten himself, and regain a foothold in his conscience upon something solid? He himself probably could not have told.

The street was empty. A few anxious bourgeois; who were rapidly returning home, hardly perceived him. Every man for himself in times of peril. The lamplighter came as usual to light the lamp which hung exactly opposite the door of No. 7, and went away. Jean Valjean, to one who had examined him in that shadow, would not have seemed a living man. There he was, seated upon the block by his door, immovable as a goblin of ice. There is congelation in despair. The tocsin was heard, and vague stormy sounds were heard. In the midst of all this convulsive clamour of the bell mingled with the émeute, the clock of St. Paul's struck eleven, gravely and without haste, for the tocsin is man; the hour is God. The passing of the hour had no effect upon Jean Valjean; Jean Valjean did not stir. However, almost at that very moment, there was a sharp explosion in the direction of the markets, a second followed, more violent still; it was probably that attack on the barricade of the Rue de la Chanvrerie which we have just seen repulsed by Marius. At this double discharge, the fury of which seemed increased by the stupor of the night, Jean Valjean was startled; he looked up in the direction whence the sound came; then he sank down upon the block, folded his arms, and his head dropped slowly upon his breast.

He resumed his dark dialogue with himself.

Suddenly he raised his eyes, somebody was walking in the street, he heard steps near him, he looked, and, by the light of the lamp, in the direction of the Archives, he perceived a livid face, young and radiant.

Gavroche had just arrived in the Rue de l'Homme Armé.

Gavroche was looking in the air, and appeared to be searching for something. He saw Jean Valjean perfectly, but he took no notice of him.

Gavroche, after looking into the air, looked on the ground; he raised himself on tiptoe and felt of the doors and windows of the ground floors; they were all closed, bolted, and chained. After having found five or six houses barricaded in this way, the *gamin* shrugged his shoulders, and took counsel with himself in these terms:

"Golly!"

Then he began to look into the air again.

Jean Valjean, who, the instant before, in the state of mind in which he was, would not have spoken nor even replied to any-body, felt irresistibly impelled to address a word to this child.

"Small boy," said he, "what is the matter with you?"

"The matter is that I am hungry," answered Gavroche tartly. And he added: "Small yourself."

Jean Valjean felt in his pocket and took out a five-franc piece.

But Gavroche, who was of the wagtail species, and who passed quickly from one action to another, had picked up a stone. He had noticed a lamp.

"Hold on," said he, "you have your lamps here still. You are not regular, my friends. It is disorderly. Break me that."

And he threw the stone into the lamp, the glass from which fell with such a clatter that some bourgeois, hid behind their curtains in the opposite house, cried: "There is 'Ninety-three!"

The lamp swung violently and went out. The street became suddenly dark.

"That's it, old street," said Gavroche, "put on your nightcap."

And turning towards Jean Valjean:

"What do you call that gigantic monument that you have got there at the end of the street? That's the Archives, isn't it? They ought to chip off these big fools of columns slightly, and make a genteel barricade of them."

Jean Valjean approached Gavroche.

"Poor creature," said he, in an under tone, and speaking to himself, "he is hungry."

And he put the hundred-sous piece into his hand.

Gavroche cocked up his nose, astonished at the size of this big sou; he looked at it in the dark, and the whiteness of the big sou dazzled him. He knew five-franc pieces by hearsay; their reputation was agreeable to him; he was delighted to see one so near. He said: "let us contemplate the tiger."

He gazed at it for a few moments in ecstasy; then, turning towards Jean Valjean, he handed him the piece and said majestically:

"Bourgeois, I prefer to break lamps. Take back your wild beast. You don't corrupt me. It has five claws; but it don't scratch me."

"Have you a mother?" inquired Jean Valjean.

Gavroche answered:

"Perhaps more than you have."

"Well," replied Jean Valjean, "keep this money for your mother."

Gavroche felt softened. Besides he had just noticed that the man who was talking to him, had no hat, and that inspired him with confidence.

"Really," said he, "it isn't to prevent my breaking the lamps?"

"Break all you like."

"You are a fine fellow," said Gavroche.

And he put the five-franc piece into one of his pockets.

His confidence increasing, he added:

"Do you belong in the street?"

"Yes; why?"

"Could you show me number seven?"

"What do you want with number seven?"

Here the boy stopped; he feared that he had said too much; he plunged his nails vigorously into his hair, and merely answered:

"Ah! that's it."

An idea flashed across Jean Valjean's mind. Anguish has such lucidities. He said to the child:

"Have you brought the letter I am waiting for?"

"You?" said Gavroche. "You are not a woman."

"The letter is for Mademoiselle Cosette; isn't it?"

"Cosette?" muttered Gavroche, "yes, I believe it is that funny name."

"Well," resumed Jean Valjean, "I am to deliver the letter to her. Give it to me."

"In that case you must know that I am sent from the barricade?"

"Of course," said Jean Valjean.

Gavroche thrust his hand into another of his pockets, and drew out a folded paper.

Then he gave a military salute.

"Respect for the despatch," said he. "It comes from the provisional government."

"Give it to me," said Jean Valjean.

Gavroche held the paper raised above his head.

"Don't imagine that this is a love-letter. It is for a woman; but it is for the people. We men, we are fighting and we respect the sex. We don't do as they do in high life, where there are lions who send love-letters to camels."

"Give it to me."

"The fact is," continued Gavroche, "you look to me like a fine fellow."

"Give it to me quick."

"Take it."

And he handed the paper to Jean Valjean.

"And hurry yourself, Monsieur What's-your-name, for Mamselle What's-her-name is waiting."

Gavroche was proud of having produced this word.

Jean Valjean asked:

"Is it to Saint Merry that the answer is to be sent?"

"In that case," exclaimed Gavroche, "you would make one of those cakes vulgarly called blunders. That letter comes from the barricade in the Rue de la Chanvrerie, and I am going back there. Good night, citizen."

This said, Gavroche went away, or rather, resumed his flight like an escaped bird towards the spot whence he came. He replunged into the obscurity as if he made a hole in it, with the rapidity and precision of a projectile; the little Rue de l'Homme Armé again became silent and solitary; in a twinkling, this strange child, who had within him shadow and dream, was buried in the dusk of those rows of black houses, and was lost there in like smoke in the darkness; and one might have thought him dissipated and vanished, if, a few minutes after his disappearance, a loud crashing of glass and the splendid patatras of a lamp falling upon the pavement had not abruptly reawakened the indignant bourgeois. It was Gavroche passing along the Rue du Chaume.

III

WHILE COSETTE AND TOUSSAINT SLEEP

JEAN VALJEAN went in with Marius' letter.

He groped his way upstairs, pleased with the darkness like an owl which holds his prey, opened and softly closed the door, listened to see if he heard any sound, decided that, according to all appearances, Cosette and Toussaint were asleep, plunged three or four matches into the bottle of the Fumade tinder-box before he could raise a spark, his hand trembled so much; there was theft in what he was about to do. At last, his candle was lighted, he leaned his elbows on the table, unfolded the paper, and read.

In violent emotions, we do not read, we prostrate the paper which we hold, so to speak, we strangle it like a˙victim, we crush the paper, we bury the nails of our wrath or of our delight in it; we run to the end, we leap to the beginning; the attention has a fever; it comprehends by wholesale, almost, the essential; it seizes a point, and all the rest disappears. In Marius' note to Cosette, Jean Valjean saw only these words.

"——I die. When you read this, my soul will be near you."

Before these two lines, he was horribly dazzled; he sat a moment as if crushed by the change of emotion which was wrought within him, he looked at Marius' note with a sort of drunken astonishment; he had before his eyes that splendour, the death of the hated being.

He uttered a hideous cry of inward joy. So, it was finished. The end came sooner than he had dared to hope. The being who encumbered his destiny was disappearing. He was going away of himself, freely, of his own accord. Without any intervention on his, Jean Valjean's part, without any fault of his, "that man" was about to die. Perhaps even he was already dead.—Here his fever began to calculate.—No. He is not dead yet. The letter was evidently written to be read by Cosette in the morning; since those two discharges which were heard between eleven o'clock and midnight, there had been nothing; the barricade will not be seriously attacked till daybreak; but it is all the same, for the moment "that man" meddled with this war, he was lost; he is caught in the net. Jean Valjean felt that he was delivered. He would then find himself once more alone with Cosette. Rivalry ceased; the future recommenced. He had only to keep the note in his pocket. Cosette would never know what had become of "that man." "I have only to let things take their course. That man cannot escape. If he is not dead yet, it is certain that he will die. What happiness!"

All this said within himself, he became gloomy.

Then he went down and waked the porter;

About an hour afterwards, Jean Valjean went out in the full dress of a National Guard, and armed. The porter had easily found in the neighbourhood what was necessary to complete his equipment. He had a loaded musket and a cartridge-box full of cartridges. He went in the direction of the markets.

IV
THE EXCESS OF GAVROCHE'S ZEAL ·

MEANWHILE an adventure had just befallen Gavroche.

Gavroche, after having conscientiously stoned the lamp in the Rue du Chaume, came to the Rue des Vieilles Haudriettes, and not seeing "a cat" there, thought it a good opportunity to strike up all the song of which he was capable. His march, far from being slackened by the singing, was accelerated. He began to scatter along the sleeping or terrified houses these incendiary couplets:

> L'oiseau médit dans les charmilles,
> Et prétend qu'hier Atala
> Avec un Russe s'en alla.
>   Où vont les belles filles,
>   Lon la.
> Mon ami pierrot, tu babilles,
> Parce que l'autre jour Mila
> Cogna sa vitre, et m'appela.   Où vont, etc.
> Les drôlesses sont fort gentilles;
> Leur poison qui m'ensorcela
> Griserait monsieur Orfila.   Où vont etc.
> J'aime l'amour et ses bisbilles,
> J'aime Agnès, j'aime Paméla,
> Lise en m'allumant se brûla.   Où vont, etc.
> Jadis, quand je vis les mantilles
> De Suzette et de Zéila,
> Mon âme à leurs plis se mêla.   Où vont, etc.
> Amour, quand, dans l'ombre où tu brilles,
> Tu coiffes de roses Lola,
> Je me damnerais pour cela.   Où vont, etc.
> Jeanne, à ton miroir tu t'habilles!
> Mon cœur un beau jour s'envola;
> Je crois que c'est Jeanne qui l'a.   Où vont, etc.

Le soir, en sortant des quadrilles,
Je morte aux étoiles Stella
Et je leur dis: regardez-la.   Où vont, etc.

Gavroche, while yet singing, was lavish of pantomime. Action is the foundation of the refrain. His face, an inexhaustible repertory of masks, made more convulsive and more fantastic grimaces than the mouths of a torn cloth in a heavy wind. Unfortunately, as he was alone and in the night, it was neither seen nor visible. There are such lost riches.

Suddenly he stopped short. "Let us interrupt the romance," said he.

His cat-like eye had just distinguished in the recess of a porte-cochère what is called in painting a harmony: that is to say, a being and a thing; the thing was a hand-cart, the being was an Auvergnat who was sleeping in it.

The arms of the cart rested on the pavement and the Auvergnat's head rested on the tail-board of the cart. His body was curled up on the inclined plane and his feet touched the ground.

Gavroche, with his experience of the things of this world, recognised a drunken man. It was some corner-porter who had drunk too much and who was sleeping too much.

"This," thought Gavroche, "is what summer nights are good for. The Auvergnat is asleep in his cart. We take the cart for the republic and we leave the Auvergnat to the monarchy."

His mind had just received this illumination:

"That cart would go jolly well on our barricade."

The Auvergnat was snoring.

Gavroche drew the cart softly by the back end and the Auvergnat by the forward end, that is to say, by the feet, and, in a minute, the Auvergnat, imperturbable, was lying flat on the pavement. The cart was delivered.

Gavroche, accustomed to face the unforeseen on all sides, always had everything about him. He felt in one of his pockets, and took out a scrap of paper and an end of a red pencil pilfered from some carpenter.

He wrote:

"*French Republic*

"Received your cart."

And he signed; "GAVROCHE."

This done, he put the paper into the pocket of the still

snoring Auvergnat's velvet waistcoat, seized the cross-piece with both hands, and started off in the direction of the markets, pushing the cart before him at a full gallop with a glorious triumphal uproar.

This was perilous. There was a post at the Imprimerie Royale. Gavroche did not think of it. This post was occupied by the National Guards of the banlieue. A certain watchfulness began to excite the squad, and their heads were lifted from their camp-beds. Two lamps broken one after another, that song sung at the top of the voice, it was a good deal for streets so cowardly, which long to go to sleep at sunset, and put their extinguisher upon their candle so early. For an hour the *gamin* had been making, in this peaceful district, the uproar of a fly in a bottle. The sergeant of the banlieue listened. He waited. He was a prudent man.

The furious rolling of the cart filled the measure of possible delay, and determined the sergeant to attempt a reconnaissance.

"There is a whole band here," said he, "we must go softly."

It was clear that the hydra of anarchy had got out of its box, and was raging in the quartier.

And the sergeant ventured out of the post with stealthy tread.

All at once, Gavroche, pushing his cart, just as he was going to turn out of the Rue des Vieilles Haudriettes, found himself face to face with a uniform, a shako, a plume, and a musket.

For the second time, he stopped short.

"Hold on," said he, "that's him. Good morning, public order."

Gavroche's astonishments were short and quickly thawed.

"Where are you going, vagabond?" cried the sergeant.

"Citizen," said Gavroche, "I haven't called you bourgeois yet. What do you insult me for?"

"Where are you going, rascal?"

"Monsieur," resumed Gavroche, "may have been a man of wit yesterday, but you were discharged this morning."

"I want to know where you are going, scoundrel?"

Gavroche answered:

"You talk genteelly. Really, nobody would guess your age. You ought to sell all your hairs at a hundred francs apiece. That would make you five hundred francs."

"Where are you going? where are you going? where are you going, bandit?"

Gavroche replied:

"Those are naughty words. The first time anybody gives you a suck, they should wipe your mouth better."

The sergeant crossed his bayonet.

"Will you tell me where you are going, at last, wretch?"

"My general," said Gavroche, "I am going after the doctor for my wife, who is put to bed."

"To arms!" cried the sergeant.

To save yourself by means of that which has ruined you is the masterpiece of a great man; Gavroche measured the entire situation at a glance. It was the cart which had compromised him; it was for the cart to protect him.

At the moment the sergeant was about to rush upon Gavroche the cart became a projectile, and, hurled with all the *gamin*'s might, ran against him furiously, and the sergeant, struck full in the stomach, fell backwards into the gutter while his musket went off in the air.

At the sergeant's cry, the men of the post had rushed out pell-mell; the sound of the musket produced a general discharge at random, after which they reloaded and began again.

This musketry at blindman's buff lasted a full quarter of an hour, and killed several squares of glass.

Meanwhile Gavroche, who had run back desperately, stopped five or six streets off, and sat down breathless upon the block at the corner of the Enfants Rouges.

He listened attentively.

After breathing a few moments, he turned in the direction in which the firing was raging, raised his left hand to the level of his nose, and threw it forward three times, striking the back of his head with his right hand at the same time: a sovereign gesture into which the Parisian *gamin* has condensed French irony, and which is evidently effective, since it has lasted already for a half century.

This cheerfulness was marred by a bitter reflection:

"Yes," said he, "I grin, I twist myself, I run over with joy; but I am losing my way. I shall have to make a detour. If I only get to the barricade in time."

Thereupon, he resumed his course.

And, while yet running:

"Ah, yes, where was I?" said he.

He began again to sing his song, as he plunged rapidly through the streets, and this receded into the darkness:

Mais il reste encor des bastilles,
Et je vais mettre le holà
Dans l'ordre public que voilà
    · Où vont les belles filles.
        Lon la.
Quelqu'un veut-il jouer aux quilles?
Tout l'ancien monde s'écroula
Quand la grosse boule roula   Où vont, etc.
Vieux bon peuple, à coups de béquilles,
Cassons ce Louvre où s'étala
La monarchie en falbala.   Où vont, etc.
Nous en avons forcé les grilles;
Le roi Charles-Dix ce jour-là
Tenait mal et se décolla.   Où vont, etc.

The taking up of arms at the post was not without result.
The cart was conquered, the drunkard was taken prisoner. One
was put on the wood-pile; the other afterwards tried before a
court-martial, as an accomplice. The public ministry of the time
availed itself of this circumstance to show its indefatigable zeal
for the defence of society.

Gavroche's adventure, preserved among the traditions of the
quartier of the Temple, is one of the most terrible reminiscences
of the old bourgeois of the Marais, and is entitled in their
memory: Nocturnal attack on the post of the Imprimerie
Royale.

JEAN VALJEAN

JEAN VALJEAN
BOOK FIRST – WAR BETWEEN FOUR WALLS

I

THE CHARYBDIS OF THE FAUBOURG SAINT ANTOINE
AND THE SCYLLA OF THE FAUBOURG DU TEMPLE

THE two most memorable barricades which the observer of social diseases might mention do not belong to the period in which the action of this book is placed. These two barricades, symbols both, under two different aspects, of a terrible situation, rose from the earth at the time of the fatal insurrection of June, 1848, the grandest street war which history has seen.

It sometimes happens that, even against principles, even against liberty, equality, and fraternity, even against universal suffrage, even against the government of all by all, from the depths of its anguish, of its discouragements, of its privations, of its fevers, of its distresses, of its miasmas, of its ignorance, of its darkness, that great madman, the rabble, protests, and the populace gives battle to the people.

The vagabonds attack the common right; the ochlocracy rises against the demos.

Those are mournful days; for there is always a certain amount of right even in this madness, there is suicide in this duel, and these words, which are intended for insults, vagabonds, rabble, ochlocracy, populace, indicate, alas! rather the fault of those who reign than the fault of those who suffer; rather the fault of the privileged than the fault of the outcasts.

As for us, we never pronounce these words save with sorrow and with respect, for when philosophy fathoms the facts to which they correspond, it often finds in them many grandeurs among the miseries. Athens was an ochlocracy; the vagabonds made Holland; the populace more than once saved Rome; and the rabble followed Jesus Christ.

There is no thinker who has not sometimes contemplated the nether magnificences.

It was of this rabble, doubtless, that St. Jerome thought, and of all those poor people, and of all those vagabonds, and of all those wretches, whence sprang the apostles and the martyrs, when he uttered those mysterious words: *Fex urbis, lex orbis.*

The exasperations of this multitude which suffers and which

1151

bleeds, its violences in misconstruction of the principles which are its life, its forcible resistance to the law, are popular *coups d'état*, and must be repressed. The honest man devotes himself to it, and, for very love for that multitude, he battles against it. But how excusable he feels it, even while opposing it; now he venerates it, even while resisting it! It is one of those rare moments when, in doing what we have to do, we feel something which disconcerts and which almost dissuades from going further; we persist, we are compelled to; but the conscience, though satisfied, is sad, and the performance of the duty is marred by an oppression of heart.

June, 1848, was, let us hasten to say, a thing apart, and almost impossible to class in the philosophy of history. All that we have just said must be set aside when we consider that extraordinary émeute in which was felt the sacred anxiety of labour demanding its rights. It must be put down, and that was duty, for it attacked the republic. But, at bottom, what was June, 1848? A revolt of the people against itself.

When the subject is not lost sight of, there is no digression; let us then be permitted for a moment to arrest the reader's attention upon the two absolutely unique barricades of which we have just spoken, and which characterised that insurrection.

One obstructed the entrance to the Faubourg Saint Antoine, the other defended the approaches of the Faubourg du Temple; those before whom arose, under the bright blue sky of June, these two frightful masterpieces of civil war, will never forget them.

The barricade Saint Antoine was monstrous; it was three stories high and seven hundred feet long. It barred from one corner to the other the vast mouth of the Faubourg, that is to say, three streets; ravined, jagged, notched, abrupt, indented with an immense rent, buttressed with mounds which were themselves bastions, pushing out capes here and there, strongly supported by the two great promontories of houses of the Faubourg, it rose like a cyclopean embankment at the foot of the terrible square which saw the 14th of July. Nineteen barricades stood at intervals along the streets in the rear of this mother barricade. Merely from seeing it, you felt in the Faubourg the immense agonising suffering which had reached that extreme moment when distress rushes into catastrophe. Of what was this barricade made? Of the ruins of three six-story houses, torn

down for the purpose, said some. Of the prodigy of all passions
said others. It had the woeful aspect of all the works of hatred:
Ruin. You might say: who built that? You might also say: who
destroyed that? It was the improvisation of ebullition. Here! that
door! that grating! that shed! that casement! that broken furnace!
that cracked pot! Bring all! throw on all! push, roll, dig, dis-
mantle, overturn, tear down all! It was the collaboration of the
pavement, the pebble, the timber, the iron bar, the chip, the
broken square, the stripped chair, the cabbage stump, the scrap,
the rag, and the malediction. It was great and it was little. It was
the bottomless pit parodied upon the spot by chaos come again.
The mass with the atom; the side wall thrown down and the
broken dish; a menacing fraternisation of all rubbish. Sisyphus
had cast in his rock and Job his potsherd. Upon the whole,
terrible. It was the acropolis of the ragamuffins. Carts overturned roughened the slope; an immense dray was displayed
there, crosswise, the axle pointing to the sky, and seemed a scar
upon that tumultuous façade; an omnibus, cheerily hoisted by
main strength to the very top of the pile, as if the architects of
that savagery would add sauciness to terror, presented its unharnessed pole to unknown horses of the air. This gigantic mass,
the alluvium of émeute, brought before the mind an Ossa upon
Pelion of all the revolutions; '93 upon '89, the 9th Thermidor
upon the 10th of August, the 18th Brumaire upon the 21st of
January, Vendémaire upon Prairial, 1848 upon 1830. The place
deserved the pains, and that barricade was worthy to appear on
the very spot where the Bastille had disappeared. Were the
ocean to make dykes, it would build them thus. The fury of the
flood was imprinted upon that misshapen obstruction. What
flood? The multitude. You would have thought you saw uproar
petrified. You would have thought you heard, upon that barricade, as if there they had been upon their hive, the humming of
the enormous black bees of progress by force. Was it a thicket?
was it a Bacchanal? was it a fortress? Dizziness seemed to have
built it by flappings of its wing. There was something of the
cloaca in this redoubt and something of Olympus in this jumble.
You saw there, in a chaos full of despair, rafters from roofs,
patches from garrets with their wall paper, window sashes with
all their glass planted in the rubbish, awaiting artillery, chimneys
torn down, wardrobes, tables, benches, a howling topsy-turvy,
and those thousand beggarly things, the refuse even of the

mendicant, which contain at once fury and nothingness. One would have said that it was the tatters of a people, tatters of wood, of iron, of bronze, of stone, and that the Faubourg Saint Antoine had swept them there to its door by one colossal sweep of the broom, making of its misery its barricade. Logs shaped like chopping blocks, dislocated chains, wooden frames with brackets having the form of gibbets, wheels projecting horizontally from the rubbish, amalgamated with this edifice of anarchy the forbidding form of the old tortures suffered by the people. The barricade Saint Antoine made a weapon of everything; all that civil war can throw at the head of society came from it; it was not battle, it was paroxysm; the carbines which defended that stronghold, among which were some blunderbusses, scattered bits of delftware, knuckle-bones, coat buttons, even table castors, dangerous projectiles on account of the copper. This barricade was furious; it threw up to the clouds an inexpressible clamour; at certain moments defying the army, it covered itself with multitude and with tempest; a mob of flaming heads crowned it; a swarming filled it; its crest was thorny with muskets, with swords, with clubs, with axes, with pikes, and with bayonets; a huge red flag fluttered in the wind; there were heard cries of command, songs of attack, the roll of the drum, the sobs of women, and the dark wild laughter of the starving. It was huge and living; and, as from the back of an electric beast there came from it a crackling of thunders. The spirit of revolution covered with its cloud that summit whereon growled this voice of the people which is like the voice of God; a strange majesty emanated from that titanic hodful of refuse. It was a garbage heap and it was Sinaï.

As we have before said, it attacked in the name of the Revolution, what? the Revolution. This barricade, chance, disorder, bewilderment, misunderstanding, the unknown, had opposed to it the Constituent Assembly, the sovereignty of the people, universal suffrage, the nation, the republic; and it was the Carmagnole defying the Marseillaise.

An insane, but heroic defiance, for this old Faubourg is a hero.

The Faubourg and its redoubt lent each other aid. The Faubourg put its shoulder to the redoubt, the redoubt braced itself upon the Faubourg. The huge barricade extended like a cliff upon which broke the strategy of the generals of Africa. Its caverns, its excrescences, its warts, its humps, made grimaces, so to speak, and sneered beneath the smoke. Grape vanished there in the shapeless; shells sank in, were swallowed up, were engulfed; bullets succeeded only in boring holes; of what use to cannonade chaos? And regiments, accustomed to the most savage sights of war, looked with anxious eye upon this kind of wild beast redoubt, by its bristling, a wild boar, and by its enormity, a mountain.

A mile from there, at the corner of the Rue du Temple which runs into the boulevard near the Château d'Eau, if you advanced your head boldly beyond the point formed by the front of the Dallemagne warehouse, you perceived in the distance, beyond the canal, in the street which mounts the slopes of Belleville, at the culminating point of the hill, a strange wall reaching the second story of the house fronts, a sort of hyphen between the houses on the right and the houses on the left, as if the street had folded back its highest wall to shut itself abruptly in. This wall was built of paving stones. It was straight, correct, cold, perpendicular, levelled with the square, built by the line, aligned by the plummet. Cement doubtless there was none, but as in certain Roman walls, that did not weaken its rigid architecture. From its height its depth could be guessed. The entablature was mathematically parallel to the base. Here and there could be distinguished, on the grey surface, loopholes almost invisible, which resembled black threads. These loopholes were separated from each other by equal intervals. The street was deserted as far as could be seen. Every window and every door closed. In the background rose this obstruction, which made of the street a cul-de-sac; an immovable and quiet wall; nobody could be seen, nothing could be heard, not a cry, not a sound, not a breath. A sepulchre.

The dazzling June sun flooded this terrible thing with light.

This was the barricade of the Faubourg du Temple.

As soon as the ground was reached and it was seen, it was impossible, even for the boldest, not to become thoughtful before this mysterious apparition. It was fitted, dovetailed, imbricated, rectilinear, symmetrical, and deathly. There was in it science and darkness. You felt that the chief of that barricade was a geometer or a spectre. You beheld it and you spoke low.

From time to time, if anybody, soldier, officer, or representative of the people, ventured to cross the solitary street, a sharp and low whistling was heard, and the passer fell wounded or dead, or, if he escaped, a ball was seen to bury itself in some closed shutter, in a space between the stores, in the plastering of a wall. Sometimes a large ball. For the men of the barricade had made of two pieces of cast-iron gas-pipe, stopped at one end with oakum and fire-clay, two small guns. No useless expenditure of powder. Almost every shot told. There were a few corpses here and there, and pools of blood upon the pavement. I recollect a white butterfly flying back and forth in the street. Summer does not abdicate.

In the vicinity, the pavements of the porte-cochères were covered with wounded.

You felt yourself beneath the eye of somebody whom you did not see, and that the whole length of the street was held under aim.

Massed behind the sort of saddleback which the narrow bridge over the canal makes at the entrance to the Faubourg du Temple, the soldiers of the attacking column, calm and collected, looked upon this dismal redoubt, this immobility, this impassability, whence death came forth. Some crept on the ground as far as the top of the curve of the bridge, taking care that their shakos did not show over it.

The valiant Colonel Monteynard admired this barricade with a shudder. "*How that is built!*" said he to a representative. "*Not one stone projects beyond another. It is porcelain.*" At that moment a ball broke the cross on his breast, and he fell.

"The cowards!" it was said. "But let them show themselves! let us see them! they dare not? they hide?" The barricade of the Faubourg du Temple, defended by eighty men, attacked by ten thousand, held out three days. On the fourth day, they did as at Zaatcha and at Constantine; they pierced through the houses, they went along the roofs, the barricade was taken. Not one of the eighty cowards thought of flight; all were killed, except the chief, Barthélemy, of whom we shall speak presently.

The barricade St. Antoine was the tumult of thunders; the barricade du Temple was silence. There was between these two redoubts the difference between the terrible and the ominous. The one seemed a gaping mouth; the other a mask.

Admitting that the gloomy and gigantic insurrection of June was composed of an anger and an enigma; you felt in the first barricade the dragon, and behind the second the sphinx.

These two fortresses were built by two men, one named Cournet, the other Barthélemy. Cournet made the barricade Saint Antoine; Barthélemy the barricade du Temple. Each was the image of him who built it.

Cournet was a man of tall stature; he had broad shoulders, a red face, a muscular arm, a bold heart, a loyal soul, a sincere and terrible eye. Intrepid, energetic, irascible, stormy, the most cordial of men, the most formidable of warriors. War, conflict, the mêlée, were the air he breathed, and put him in good-humour. He had been a naval officer, and, from his carriage and his voice, you would have guessed that he sprang from the ocean, and that he came from the tempest; he continued the hurricane in battle. Save in genius, there was in Cournet something of Danton, as, save in divinity, there was in Danton something of Hercules.

Barthélemy, thin, puny, pale, taciturn, was a kind of tragic *gamin* who, struck by a sergent de ville, watched for him, waited for him, and killed him, and, at seventeen, was sent to the galleys. He came out, and built this barricade.

Later, a terrible thing, at London, both outlaws, Barthélemy killed Cournet. It was a mournful duel. Some time after, caught in the meshes of one of those mysterious fatalities in which passion is mingled, catastrophes in which French justice sees extenuating circumstances, and in which English justice sees only death, Barthélemy was hanged. The gloomy social edifice is so constructed, that, thanks to material privation, thanks to moral darkness, this unfortunate being who contained an intelligence, firm certainly, great perhaps, began with the galleys in France, and ended with the gallows in England. Barthélemy, on all occasions, hoisted but one flag; the black flag.

II
WHAT CAN BE DONE IN THE ABYSS BUT TO TALK

Sixteen years tell in the subterranean education of the émeute, and June, 1848, understood it far better than June, 1832. Thus the barricade of the Rue de la Chanvrerie was only a rough draught and an embryo compared with the two colossal barricades which we have just sketched; but, for the period, it was formidable.

The insurgents, under the eye of Enjolras, for Marius no

longer looked to anything, turned the night to advantage. The barricade was not only repaired, but made larger. They raised it two feet. Iron bars planted in the paving stones resembled lances in rest. All sorts of rubbish added, and brought from all sides, increased the exterior intricacy. The redoubt was skilfully made over into a wall within and a thicket without.

They rebuilt the stairway of paving stones, which permitted ascent, as upon a citadel wall.

They put the barricade in order, cleared up the basement-room, took the kitchen for a hospital, completed the dressing of the wounds; gathered up the powder scattered over the floor and the tables, cast bullets, made cartridges, scraped lint, distributed the arms of the fallen, cleaned the interior of the redoubt, picked up the fragments, carried away the corpses.

They deposited the dead in a heap in the little Rue Mondét-our, of which they were still masters. The pavement was red for a long time at that spot. Among the dead were four National Guards of the banlieue. Enjolras had their uniforms laid aside.

Enjolras advised two hours of sleep. Advice from Enjolras was an order. Still, three or four only profited by it. Feuilly employed these two hours in engraving this inscription on the wall which fronted the wine-shop:

"VIVENT LES PEUPLES!"

These three words, graven in the stone with a nail, were still legible on that wall in 1848.

The three women took advantage of the night's respite to disappear finally, which made the insurgents breathe more freely.

They found refuge in some neighbouring house.

Most of the wounded could and would still fight. There were, upon a straw mattress and some bunches of straw, in the kitchen now become a hospital, five men severely wounded, two of whom were Municipal Guards. The wounds of the Municipal Guards were dressed first.

Nothing now remained in the basement-room but Mabeuf, under his black cloth, and Javert bound to the post.

"This is the dead-room," said Enjolras.

In the interior of this room, feebly lighted by a candle, at the very end the funereal table being behind the post like a horizontal bar, a sort of large dim cross was produced by Javert standing, and Mabeuf lying.

The pole of the omnibus, although maimed by the musketry, was still high enough for them to hang a flag upon it.

Enjolras, who had this quality of a chief, always to do as he said, fastened the pierced and bloody coat of the slain old man to this pole.

No meals could now be had. There was neither bread nor meat. The fifty men of the barricade, in the sixteen hours that they had been there, had very soon exhausted the meagre provisions of the wine-shop. In a given time, every barricade which holds out, inevitably becomes the raft of le Méduse. They must resign themselves to famine. They were in the early hours of that Spartan day of the 6th of June, when, in the barricade Saint Merry, Jeanne, surrounded by insurgents who were asking for bread, to all those warriors, crying: "Something to eat!" answered: "What for? it is three o'clock. At four o'clock we shall be dead."

As they could eat nothing, Enjolras forbade drinking. He prohibited wine, and put them on allowance of brandy.

They found in the cellar some fifteen bottles, full and hermetically sealed. Enjolras and Combeferre examined them. As they came up Combeferre said: "It is some of the old stock of Father Hucheloup who began as a grocer."

"It ought to be genuine wine," observed Bossuet. "It is lucky that Grantaire is asleep. If he were on his feet, we should have hard work to save those bottles." Enjolras, in spite of the murmurs, put his veto upon the fifteen bottles, and in order that no one should touch them, and that they might be as it were consecrated, he had them placed under the table on which Father Mabeuf lay.

About two o'clock in the morning, they took a count. There were left thirty-seven of them.

Day was beginning to dawn. They had just extinguished the torch which had been replaced in its socket of paving stones. The interior of the barricade, that little court taken in on the street, was drowned in darkness, and seemed, through the dim twilight horror, the deck of a disabled ship. The combatants going back and forth, moved about in it like black forms. Above this frightful nest of shadow, the stories of the mute houses were lividly outlined; at the very top the wan chimneys appeared.

The sky had that charming undecided hue, which is perhaps white, and perhaps blue. Some birds were flying with joyful notes. The tall house which formed the rear of the barricade, being towards the east, had a rosy reflection upon its roof. At the window on the third story, the morning breeze played with the grey hairs on the dead man's head.

"I am delighted that the torch is extinguished," said Courfeyrac to Feuilly. "That torch, startled in the wind, annoyed me. It appeared to be afraid. The light of a torch resembles the wisdom of a coward; it is not clear, because it trembles."

The dawn awakens minds as well as birds: all were chatting.

Joly, seeing a cat prowling about a water-spout, extracted philosophy therefrom.

"What is the cat?" he exclaimed. "It is a correction. God, having made the mouse, said: 'Hold here, I have made a blunder.' And he made the cat. The cat is the erratum of the mouse. The mouse, plus the cat, is the revised and corrected proof of creation."

Combeferre, surrounded by students and workmen, spoke of the dead, of Jean Prouvaire, of Bahorel, of Mabeuf, and even of Le Cabuc, and of the stern sadness of Enjolras. He said:

"Harmodius and Aristogeiton, Brutus, Chereas, Stephanus, Cromwell, Charlotte Corday, Sand—all, after the blow, had their moment of anguish. Our hearts are so fluctuating, and human life is such a mystery that, even in a civic murder, even in a liberating murder, if there be such, the remorse of having stricken a man surpasses the joy of having served the human race."

And, such is the course of conversation, a moment afterwards by a transition from Jean Prouvaire's rhymes, Combeferre was comparing the translators of the Georgics, Raux with Cournand, Cournand with Delille, pointing out the few passages translated by Malfilâtre, particularly the prodigies at the death of Cæsar; and from this word, Cæsar, they came to Brutus.

"Cæsar," said Combeferre, "fell justly. Cicero was severe upon Cæsar, and he was right. This severity is not diatribe. When Zoïlus insults Homer, when Mævius insults Virgil, when Visé insults Molière, when Pope insults Shakspeare, when Fréron insults Voltaire, it is an old law of envy and hatred which is at work; genius attracts insult, great men are always barked at more or less. But Zoïlus and Cicero are two. Cicero is a judge through the soul, even as Brutus is a judge through the sword. I condemn, for my own part, that final justice, the sword; but antiquity admitted it. Cæsar, the violator of the Rubicon, conferring, as coming from himself, the dignities which came from the people, not rising upon the entrance of the senate, acted, as Eutropius says, the part of a king and almost of a tyrant, *regia ac penè tyrannica*. He was a great man; so much the worse, or so much the better; the lesson is the greater. His twenty-three wounds touch me less than the spittle in the face of Jèsus Christ. Cæsar was stabbed by senators; Christ was slapped by lackeys. In the greater outrage, we feel the God."

Bossuet, overlooking the talkers from the top of the heap of paving stones, exclaimed, carbine in hand:

"O Cydathenæum, O Myrrhinus, O Probalinthe, O graces of Æantides. Oh! who will give me to pronounce the verses of Homer like a Greek of Laurium or of Edapteon?"

III
LIGHT AND DARKNESS

ENJOLRAS had gone to make a reconnaissance. He went out by the Little Rue Mondétour, creeping along by the houses.

The insurgents, we must say, were full of hope. The manner in which they had repelled the attack during the night, had led them almost to contempt in advance for the attack at daybreak. They awaited it, and smiled at it. They had no more doubt of their success than of their cause. Moreover, help was evidently about to come. They counted on it. With that facility for triumphant prophecy which is a part of the strength of the fighting Frenchman, they divided into three distinct phases the day which was opening: at six o'clock in the morning a regiment, "which had been laboured with," would come over. At noon, insurrection of all Paris; at sundown, revolution.

They heard the tocsin of Saint Merry, which had not been silent a moment since the evening; a proof that the other barricade, the great one, that of Jeanne, still held out.

All these hopes were communicated from one to another in a sort of cheerful yet terrible whisper, which resembled the buzz of a hive of bees at war.

Enjolras reappeared. He returned from his gloomy eagle's walk in the obscurity without. He listened for a moment to all this joy with folded arms, one hand over his mouth. Then, fresh and rosy in the growing whiteness of the morning, he said:

"The whole army of Paris fights. A third of that army is pressing upon the barricade in which you are. Besides the National Guard, I distinguished the shakos of the Fifth of the line and the colours of the Sixth Legion. You will be attacked in an hour. As for the people, they were boiling yesterday, but this morning they do not stir. Nothing to expect, nothing to hope. No more from a Faubourg than from a regiment. You are abandoned."

These words fell upon the buzzing of the groups, and wrought the effect which the first drops of the tempest produce upon the swarm. All were dumb. There was a moment of inexpressible silence, when you might have heard the flight of death.

This moment was short.

A voice, from the most obscure depths of the groups, cried to Enjolras:

"So be it. Let us make the barricade twenty feet high, and let us all stand by it. Citizens, let us offer the protest of corpses. Let us show that, if the people abandon the republicans, the republicans do not abandon the people."

These words relieved the minds of all from the painful cloud of personal anxieties. They were greeted by an enthusiastic acclamation.

The name of the man who thus spoke was never known; it was some obscure blouse-wearer, an unknown, a forgotten man, a passing hero, that great anonymous always found in human crises and in social births, who, at the proper instant, speaks the decisive word supremely, and who vanishes into the darkness after having for a moment represented, in the light of a flash, the people and God.

This inexorable resolution so filled the air of June 6, 1832, that, almost at the same hour, in the barricade of Saint Merry, the insurgents raised this shout which was proved on the trial, and which has become historical: "Let them come to our aid or let them not come, what matter? Let us die here to the last man."

As we see, the two barricades, although essentially isolated, communicated.

IV

FIVE LESS, ONE MORE

AFTER the man of the people, who decreed "the protest of corpses," had spoken and given the formula of the common soul, from all lips arose a strangely satisfied and terrible cry, funereal in meaning and triumphant in tone:

"Long live death! Let us all stay! "

"Why all?" said Enjolras.

"All! all!"

Enjolras resumed:

"The position is good, the barricade is fine. Thirty men are enough. Why sacrifice forty?"

They replied:

"Because nobody wants to go away."

"Citizens," cried Enjolras, and there was in his voice almost an angry tremor, "the republic is not rich enough in men to incur useless expenditures. Vainglory is a squandering. If it is the duty of some to go away, that duty should be performed as well as any other."

Enjolras, the man of principle, had over his co-religionists that sort of omnipotence which emanates from the absolute. Still, notwithstanding this omnipotence, there was a murmur.

Chief to his finger-ends, Enjolras, seeing that they murmured, insisted. He resumed haughtily:

"Let those who fear to be one of but thirty, say so."

The murmurs redoubled.

"Besides," observed a voice from one of the groups, "to go away is easily said. The barricade is hemmed in."

"Not towards the markets," said Enjolras. "The Rue Mondétour is open, and by the Rue des Prêcheurs one can reach the Marché des Innocents."

"And there," put in another voice from the group, "he will be taken. He will fall upon some grand guard of the line or the banlieue. They will see a man going by in cap and blouse. 'Where do you come from, fellow? you belong to the barricade, don't you?' And they look at your hands. You smell of powder. Shot."

Enjolras, without answering, touched Combeferre's shoulder, and they both went into the basement-room.

They came back a moment afterwards. Enjolras held out in

his hands the four uniforms which he had reserved. Combeferre followed him, bringing the cross belts and shakos.

"With this uniform," said Enjolras, "you can mingle with the ranks and escape. Here are enough for four."

And he threw the four uniforms upon the unpaved ground.

No wavering in the stoical auditory. Combeferre spoke:

"Come," said he, "we must have a little pity. Do you know what the question is now? It is a question of women. Let us see. Are there any wives, yes or no? are there any children, yes or no? Are there, yes or no, any mothers, who rock the cradle with their foot and who have heaps of little ones about them? Let him among you who has never seen the breast of a nursing-woman hold up his hand. Ah! you wish to die, I wish it also, I, who am speaking to you, but I do not wish to feel the ghosts of women wringing their hands about me. Die, so be it, but do not make others die. Suicides like those which will be accomplished here are sublime; but suicide is strict, and can have no extension; and as soon as it touches those next you, the name of suicide is murder. Think of the little flaxen heads, and think of the white hairs. Listen, but a moment ago, Enjolras, he just told me of it, saw at the corner of the Rue du Cygne a lighted casement, a candle in a poor window, in the fifth story, and on the glass the quivering shadow of the head of an old woman who appeared to have passed the night in watching and to be still waiting. She is perhaps the mother of one of you. Well, let that man go away, and let him hasten to say to his mother: 'Mother, here I am!' Let him feel at ease, the work here will be done just as well. When a man supports his relatives by his labour, he has no right to sacrifice himself. That is deserting his family. And those who have daughters, and those who have sisters! Do you think of it? You get killed, here you are dead, very well, and to-morrow? Young girls who have no bread, that is terrible. Man begs, woman sells. Ah! those charming beings, so graceful and so sweet, who have bonnets of flowers, who fill the house with chastity, who sing, who prattle, who are like a living perfume, who prove the existence of angels in heaven by the purity of maidens on the earth, that Jeanne, that Lise, that Mimi, those adorable and noble creatures who are your benediction and your pride, oh, God, they will be hungry! What would you have me say to you? There is a market for human flesh; and it is not with your shadowy hands, fluttering about them, that you can prevent them from entering it! Think of the street, think of the pavement covered with passers, think of the shops before which women walk to and fro with bare shoulders, through the mud. Those women also have been pure. Think of your sisters, those who have them. Misery, prostitution, the sergents de ville, Saint Lazare, such will be the fall of those delicate beautiful girls, those fragile wonders of modesty, grace, and beauty, fresher than the lilacs of the month of May. Ah! you are killed! ah! you are no longer with them! Very well; you desired to deliver the people from monarchy, you give your maidens to the police. Friends, beware, have compassion. Women, hapless women, are not in the habit of reflecting much. We boast that women have not received the education of men, we prevent them from reading, we prevent them from thinking, we prevent them from interesting themselves in politics; will you prevent them from going tonight to the Morgue and identifying your corpses? Come, those who have families must be good fellows and give us a grasp of the hand and go away, and leave us to the business here all alone. I know well that it requires courage to go, it is difficult; but the more difficult it is, the more praiseworthy. You say: I have a musket, I am at the barricade, come the worst, I stay. Come the worst, that is very soon said. My friends, there is a morrow; you will not be here on that morrow, but your families will. And what suffering! See, a pretty, healthy child that has cheeks like an apple, that babbles, that prattles, that jabbers, that laughs, that smells sweet under the kiss, do you know what becomes of him when he is abandoned? I saw one, very small, no taller than that. His father was dead. Some poor people had taken him in from charity, but they had no bread for themselves. The child was always hungry. It was winter. He did not cry. They saw him go up to the stove where there was never any fire, and the pipe of which, you know, was plastered with yellow clay. The child picked off some of that clay with his little fingers and ate it. His breathing was hard, his face livid, his legs soft, his belly big. He said nothing. They spoke to him, he did not answer. He died. He was brought to the Necker Hospital to die, where I saw him. I was surgeon at that hospital. Now, if there are any fathers among you, fathers whose delight it is to take a walk on Sunday holding in their great strong hand the little hand of their child, let each of those fathers imagine that that child is his own. That poor bird, I remember him well, it seems to me that I see him now, when he lay naked upon the dissecting table, his ribs projecting under his skin like graves under the grass of a church-yard. We found a kind of mud in his stomach. There were ashes in his teeth. Come, let us search our conscience and take counsel with our hearts. Statistics show that the mortality of abandoned children is fifty-five per cent. I repeat it, it is a question of wives, it is a question of mothers, it is a question of young girls, it is a question of babes. Do I speak to you for yourselves? We know very well what you are; we know very well that you are all brave, good heavens! we know very well that your souls are filled with joy and glory at giving your life for the great cause; we know very well that you feel that you are elected to die usefully and magnificently, and that each of you clings to his share of the triumph. Well and good. But you are not alone in this world. There are other beings of whom we must think. We must not be selfish."

All bowed their heads with a gloomy air.

Strange contradictions of the human heart in its most sublime moments! Combeferre, who spoke thus, was not an orphan. He remembered the mothers of others, and he forgot his own. He was going to be killed. He was "selfish."

Marius, fasting, feverish, successively driven from every hope, stranded upon grief, most dismal of shipwrecks, saturated with violent emotions and feeling the end approach, was sinking deeper and deeper into that visionary stupor which always precedes the fatal hour when voluntarily accepted.

A physiologist might have studied in him the growing symptoms of that febrile absorption known and classified by science, and which is to suffering what ecstasy is to pleasure. Despair also has its ecstasy. Marius had reached that point. He witnessed it all as from without; as we have said, the things which were occurring before him, seemed afar off; he perceived the whole, but did not distinguish the details. He saw the comers and goers through a bewildering glare. He heard the voices speak as from the depth of an abyss.

Still this moved him. There was one point in this scene which pierced through to him, and which woke him. He had now but one idea, to die, and he would not be diverted from it; but he thought, in his funereal somnambulism, that while destroying oneself it is not forbidden to save another.

He raised his voice:

"Enjolras and Combeferre are right," said he; "no useless sacrifice. I add my voice to theirs, and we must hasten. Combeferre has given the criteria. There are among you some who have families, mothers, sisters, wives, children. Let those leave the ranks."

Nobody stirred.

"Married men and supports of families, out of the ranks!" repeated Marius.

His authority was great. Enjolras was indeed the chief of the barricade, but Marius was its saviour.

"I order it," cried Enjolras.

"I beseech you," said Marius.

Then, roused by the words of Combeferre, shaken by the order of Enjolras, moved by the prayer of Marius, those heroic men began to inform against each other. "That is true," said a young man to a middle-aged man. "You are the father of a family. Go away." "It is you rather," answered the man, "you have two sisters whom you support." And an unparalleled conflict broke out. It was as to which should not allow himself to be laid at the door of the tomb.

"Make haste," said Courfeyrac, "in a quarter of an hour it will be too late."

"Citizens," continued Enjolras, "this is the republic, and universal suffrage reigns. Designate yourselves those who ought to go."

They obeyed. In a few minutes five were unanimously designated and left the ranks.

"There are five!" exclaimed Marius.

There were only four uniforms.

"Well," resumed the five, "one must stay."

And it was who should stay, and who should find reasons why the others should not stay. The generous quarrel recommenced.

"You, you have a wife who loves you." "As for you, you have your old mother." "You have neither father nor mother, what will become of your three little brothers?" "You are the father of five children." "You have a right to live, you are seventeen, it is too soon."

These grand revolutionary barricades were rendezvous of heroisms. The improbable there was natural. These men were not astonished at each other.

"Be quick," repeated Courfeyrac.

Somebody cried out from the group, to Marius:

"Designate yourself, which must stay."

"Yes," said the five, "choose. We will obey you."

Marius now believed no emotion possible. Still at this idea: to select a man for death, all his blood flowed back towards his heart. He would have turned pale if he could have been paler.

He advanced towards the five, who smiled upon him, and each, his eye full of that grand flame which we see in the depth of history over the Thermopylæs, cried to him:

"Me! me! me!"

And Marius, in a stupor, counted them; there were still five! Then his eyes fell upon the four uniforms.

At this moment a fifth uniform dropped, as if from heaven, upon the four others.

The fifth man was saved.

Marius raised his eyes and saw M. Fauchelevent.

Jean Valjean had just entered the barricade.

Whether by information obtained, or by instinct, or by chance, he came by the little Rue Mondétour. Thanks to his National Guard dress, he had passed easily.

The sentry placed by the insurgents in the Rue Mondétour, had not given the signal of alarm for a single National Guard. He permitted him to get into the street, saying to himself: "he is a reinforcement, probably, and at the very worst a prisoner." The moment was too serious for the sentinel to be diverted from his duty and his post of observation.

At the moment Jean Valjean entered the redoubt, nobody had noticed him, all eyes being fixed upon the five chosen ones and upon the four uniforms. Jean Valjean, himself, saw and understood, and silently, he stripped off his coat, and threw it upon the pile with the others.

The commotion was indescribable.

"Who is this man?" asked Bossuet.

"He is," answered Combeferre, "a man who saves others."

Marius added in a grave voice:

"I know him."

This assurance was enough for all.

Enjolras turned towards Jean Valjean:

"Citizen, you are welcome."

And he added:

"You know that we are going to die."

Jean Valjean, without answering, helped the insurgent whom he saved to put on his uniform.

V

WHAT HORIZON IS VISIBLE FROM THE TOP OF THE BARRICADE

THE situation of all, in this hour of death and in this inexorable place, found its resultant and summit in the supreme melancholy of Enjolras.

Enjolras had within himself the plenitude of revolution; he was incomplete notwithstanding, as much as the absolute can be; he clung too much to Saint Just, and not enough to Anacharsis Clootz; still his mind, in the society of the Friends of the A B C, had at last received a certain polarisation from the ideas of Combeferre; for some time, he had been leaving little by little the narrow form of dogma, and allowing himself to tread the broad paths of progress and he had come to accept, as its definitive and magnificent evolution, the transformation of the great French Republic into the immense human republic. As to the immediate means, in a condition of violence, he wished them to be violent; in that he had not varied; and he was still of that epic and formidable school, which is summed up in this word: 'Ninety-three.

Enjolras was standing on the paving-stone steps, his elbow upon the muzzle of his carbine. He was thinking; he started, as at the passing of a gust; places where death is have such tripodal effects. There came from his eyes, full of the interior sight, a kind of stifled fire. Suddenly he raised his head, his fair hair waved backwards like that of the angel upon his sombre car of stars, it was the mane of a startled lion flaming with a halo, and Enjolras exclaimed:

"Citizens, do you picture to yourselves the future? The streets of the cities flooded with light, green branches upon the thresholds, the nations sisters, men just, the old men blessing the children, the past loving the present, thinkers in full liberty, believers in full equality, for religion the heavens; God priest direct, human conscience become the altar, no more hatred, the fraternity of the workshop and the school, for reward and for penalty notoriety, to all, labour, for all, law, over all, peace, no more bloodshed, no more war, mothers happy! To subdue matter is the first step; to realise the ideal is the second. Reflect upon what progress has already done. Once the early human races looked with terror upon the hydra which blew upon the waters, the dragon which vomited fire, the griffin monster of the air, which flew with the wings of an eagle and the claws of a tiger; fearful animals which were above man. Man, however, has laid his snares, the sacred snares of intelligence, and has at last caught the monsters. We have tamed the hydra, and he is called the steamer; we have tamed the dragon, and he is called the locomotive; we are on the point of taming the griffin, we have him already, and he is called the balloon. The day when this promethean work shall be finished, and when man shall have definitely harnessed to his will the triple chimera of the ancients, the hydra, the dragon, and the griffin, he will be the master of the water, the fire, and the air, and he will be to the rest of the animated creation what the ancient gods were formerly to him. Courage, and forward! Citizens, whither are we tending? To science made government, to the force of things, recognised as the only public force, to the natural law having its sanction and its penalty in itself and promulgated by its self-evidence, to a dawn of truth, corresponding with the dawn of the day. We are tending towards the union of the peoples; we are tending towards the unity of man. No more fictions; no more parasites. The real governed by the true, such is the aim. Civilisation will hold its courts on the summit of Europe, and later at the centre of the continents, in a grand parliament of intelligence. Something like this has been seen already. The Amphictyons had two sessions a year, one at Delphi, place of the gods, the other at Thermopylæ, place of the heroes. Europe will have her Amphictyons; the globe will have its Amphictyons. France bears within her the sublime future. This is the gestation of the nineteenth century. That which was sketched by Greece is worth being finished by France. Listen to me, then, Feuilly, valiant working-man, man of the people, man of the peoples, I venerate thee. Yes, thou seest clearly future ages; yes, thou art right. Thou hadst neither father nor mother, Feuilly; thou hast adopted humanity for thy mother, and the right for thy father. Thou art going to die here; that is, to triumph. Citizens, whatever may happen to-day, through our defeat as well as through our victory, we are going to effect a revolution. Just as conflagrations light up the whole city, revolutions light up the whole human race. And what revolution shall we effect? I have just said, the revolution of the True. From the political point of view, there is but one single principle: the sovereignty of man over himself. This sovereignty of myself over myself is called Liberty. Where two or several of these sovereignties associate the state begins. But in this association there is no abdication. Each sovereignty gives up a certain portion of itself to form the common right. That portion is the same for all. This identity of concession which each makes to all, is Equality. The common right is nothing more or less than the protection of all radiating upon the right of each. This protection of all over each is called Fraternity. The point of intersection of all these aggregated sovereignties is called Society. This intersection being a junction, this point is a knot. Hence what is called the social tie. Some say social contract; which is the same thing, the word contract being etymologically formed with the idea of tie. Let us understand each other in regard to equality; for, if liberty is the summit, equality is the base. Equality, citizens, is not all vegetation on a level, a society of big spears of grass and little oaks; a neighbourhood of jealousies emasculating each other; it is, civilly, all aptitudes having equal opportunity; politically, all votes having equal weight; religiously, all consciences having equal rights. Equality has an organ: gratuitous and obligatory instruction. The right to the alphabet, we must begin by that. The primary school obligatory upon all, the higher school offered to all, such is the law. From the identical school springs equal society. Yes, instruction! Light! Light! all comes from light, and all returns to it. Citizens, the nineteenth century is grand, but the twentieth century will be happy. Then there will be nothing more like old history. Men will no longer have to fear, as now, a conquest, an invasion, a usurpation, a rivalry of nations with the armed hand, an interruption of civilisation depending on a marriage of kings, a birth in the hereditary tyrannies, a partition of the peoples by a Congress, a dismemberment by the downfall of a dynasty, a combat of two religions meeting head to head, like two goats of darkness, upon the bridge of the infinite; they will no longer have to fear famine, speculation, prostitution from distress, misery from lack of work, and the scaffold, and the sword, and the battle, and all the brigandages of chance in the forest of events. We might almost say: there will be no events more. Men will be happy. The human race will fulfil its law as the terrestrial globe fulfils its; harmony will be re-established between the soul and the star; the soul will gravitate about the truth like the star about the light. Friends, the hour in which we live, and in which I speak to you, is a gloomy hour, but of such is the terrible price of the future. A revolution is a toll-gate. Oh! the human race shall be delivered, uplifted, and consoled! We affirm it on this barricade. Whence shall arise the shout of love, if it be not from the summit of sacrifice? O my brothers, here is the place of junction between those who think and those who suffer; this barricade is made neither of paving stones, nor of timbers, nor of iron; it is made of two mounds, a mound of ideas and a mound of sorrows. Misery here encounters the ideal. Here day embraces night, and says: I will die with thee and thou shalt be born again with me. From the pressure of all desolations faith gushes forth. Sufferings bring their agony here, and ideas their immortality. This agony and this immortality are to mingle and compose our death. Brothers, he who dies here dies in the radiance of the future, and we are entering a grave illuminated by the dawn."

Enjolras broke off rather than ceased, his lips moved noiselessly, as if he were continuing to speak to himself, and they looked at him with attention, endeavouring still to hear. There was no applause; but they whispered for a long time. Speech being breath, the rustling of intellects resembles the rustling of leaves.

VI
MARIUS HAGGARD, JAVERT LACONIC

LET us tell what was passing in Marius' thoughts.

Remember the condition of his mind. As we have just mentioned, all was now to him a dream. His understanding was troubled. Marius, we must insist, was under the shadow of the great black wings which open above the dying. He felt that he had entered the tomb, it seemed to him that he was already on the other side of the wall and he no longer saw the faces of the living save with the eyes of one dead.

How came M. Fauchelevent there? Why was he there? What did he come to do? Marius put none of these questions. Besides, our despair having this peculiarity that it enwraps others as well as ourselves, it seemed logical to him that everybody should come to die.

Only he thought of Cosette with an oppression of the heart.

Moreover M. Fauchelevent did not speak to him, did not look at him, and had not even the appearance of hearing him when Marius said: I know him.

As for Marius, this attitude of M. Fauchelevent was a relief to him, and if we might employ such a word for such impressions, we should say, pleased him. He had always felt it absolutely impossible to address a word to that enigmatic man, who to him was at once equivocal and imposing. It was also a very long time since he had seen him; which, with Marius' timid and reserved nature, increased the impossibility still more.

The five men designated went out of the barricade by the little Rue Mondétour; they resembled National Guards perfectly; one of them went away weeping. Before starting, they embraced those who remained.

When the five men sent away into life had gone, Enjolras thought of the one condemned to death. He went into the basement-room. Javert, tied to the pillar, was thinking.

"Do you need anything?" Enjolras asked him.

Javert answered:

"When shall you kill me?"

"Wait. We need all our cartridges at present."

"Then, give me a drink," said Javert.

Enjolras presented him with a glass of water himself, and, as Javert was bound, he helped him to drink.

"Is that all?" resumed Enjolras.

"I am uncomfortable at this post," answered Javert. "It was not affectionate to leave me to pass the night here. Tie me as you please, but you can surely lay me on a table. Like the other."

And with a motion of his head he indicated M. Mabeuf's body.

There was, it will be remembered, at the back of the room, a long wide table, upon which they had cast balls and made cartridges. All the cartridges being made and all the powder used up, this table was free.

At Enjolras' order, four insurgents untied Javert from the post. While were untying him, a fifth held a bayonet to his breast. They left his hands tied behind his back, they put a small yet strong whipcord about his feet, which permitted him to take fifteen-inch steps like those who are mounting the scaffold, and they made him walk to the table at the back of the room, on which they extended him, tightly bound by the middle of his body.

For greater security, by means of a rope fixed to his neck, they added to the system of bonds which rendered all escape impossible, that species of ligature, called in the prisons a martingale, which, starting from the back of the neck, divides over the stomach, and is fastened to the hands after passing between the legs.

While they were binding Javert, a man, on the threshold of the door, gazed at him with singular attention. The shade which this man produced made Javert turn his head. He raised his eyes and recognised Jean Valjean. He did not even start, he haughtily dropped his eyelids, and merely said: "It is very natural."

VII
THE SITUATION GROWS SERIOUS

IT was growing light rapidly. But not a window was opened, not a door stood ajar; it was the dawn, not the hour of awakening. The extremity of the Rue de la Chanvrerie opposite the barricade had been evacuated by the troops, as we have said; it seemed free, and lay open for wayfarers with an ominous tranquillity. The Rue Saint Denis was as silent as the avenue of the Sphinxes at Thebes. Not a living being at the corners, which were whitening in a reflection of the sun. Nothing is so dismal as this brightness of deserted streets.

They saw nothing, but they heard. A mysterious movement was taking place at some distance. It was evident that the critical moment was at hand. As in the evening the sentries were driven in; but this time all.

The barricade was stronger than at the time of the first attack. Since the departure of the five, it had been raised still higher.

On the report of the sentry who had been observing the region of the markets, Enjolras, for fear of a surprise from the rear, formed an important resolution. He had barricaded the little passage of the Rue Mondétour, which till then had been open. For this purpose they unpaved the length of a few more houses. In this way, the barricade, walled in upon three streets, in front upon the Rue de la Chanvrerie, at the left upon the Rue du Cygne and la Petite Truanderie, at the right upon the Rue Mondétour, was really almost impregnable; it is true that they were fatally shut in. It had three fronts, but no longer an outlet. "A fortress, but mousetrap," said Courfeyrac with a laugh.

Enjolras had piled up near the door of the wine-shop some thirty paving stones, "torn up uselessly," said Bossuet.

The silence was now so profound on the side from which the attack must come, that Enjolras made each man resume his post for combat.

A ration of brandy was distributed to all.

Nothing is more singular than a barricade which is preparing for an assault. Each man chooses his place, as at a play. They lean on their sides, their elbows, their shoulders. There are some who make themselves stalls with paving stones. There is a corner of a wall which is annoying, they move away from it; here is a redan which may be a protection, they take shelter in it. The left-handed are precious; they take places which are inconvenient for the rest. Many make arrangements to fight sitting down. They wish to be at their ease in killing, and comfortable in dying. In the deadly war of June, 1848, an insurgent, who had a terrible aim, and who fought from the top of a terrace, on a roof, had a Voltaire arm-chair carried up there; a charge of grape found him in it.

As soon as the chief has ordered the decks cleared for the fight, all disorderly movements cease; no more skirmishing with one another; no more coteries; no more asides; no more standing apart; that which is in all minds converges, and changes into expectation of the assailant. A barricade before danger, chaos; in danger, discipline. Peril produces order.

As soon as Enjolras had taken his double-barrelled carbine, and placed himself on a kind of battlement which he had reserved, all were silent. A little dry snapping sound was heard confusedly along the wall of paving stones. They were cocking their muskets.

Moreover, their bearing was firmer and more confident than ever; excess of sacrifice is a support; they had hope no longer, but they had despair. Despair, final arm, which sometimes gives victory; Virgil has said so. Supreme resources spring from extreme resolutions. To embark in death is sometimes the means of escaping a shipwreck; and the coffin-lid becomes a plank of safety.

As on the evening before, the attention of all was turned, and we might almost say threw its weight upon the end of the street, now lighted and visible.

They had not long to wait. Activity distinctly recommenced in the direction of Saint Leu, but it did not resemble the movement of the first attack. A rattle of chains, the menacing jolt of a mass, a clicking of brass bounding over the pavement, a sort of solemn uproar, announced that an ominous body of iron was approaching. There was a shudder in the midst of those peaceful old streets, cut through and built up for the fruitful circulation of interests and ideas, and which were not made for the monstrous rumbling of the wheels of war.

The stare of all the combatants upon the extremity of the street became wild.

A piece of artillery appeared.

The gunners pushed forward the piece; it was all ready to be loaded; the forewheels had been removed; two supported the carriage, four were at the wheels, others followed with the caisson. The smoke of the burning match was seen.

"Fire!" cried Enjolras.

The whole barricade flashed fire, the explosion was terrible; an avalanche of smoke covered and effaced the gun and the men; in a few seconds the cloud dissipated, and the cannon and the men reappeared; those in charge of the piece placed it in position in front of the barricade, slowly, correctly, and without haste. Not a man had been touched. Then the gunner, bearing his weight on the breech, to elevate the range, began to point the cannon with the gravity of an astronomer adjusting a telescope.

"Bravo for the gunners!" cried Bossuet.

And the whole barricade clapped hands.

A moment afterwards, placed squarely in the very middle of the street, astride of the gutter, the gun was in battery. A formidable mouth was opened upon the barricade.

"Come, be lively!" said Courfeyrac. "There is the brute. After the fillip, the knock-down. The army stretches out its big paw to us. The barricade is going to be seriously shaken. The musketry feels, the artillery takes."

"It is a bronze eight-pounder, new model," added Combeferre. "Those pieces, however little they exceed the proportion of ten parts of tin to a hundred of copper, are liable to burst.

The excess of tin makes them too tender. In that case they have hollows and chambers in the vent. To obviate this danger, and to be able to force out the load, it would be necessary, perhaps, to return to the process of the fourteenth century, hooping, and to strengthen the piece exteriorly, by a succession of steel rings unsoldered, from the breech to the trunnion. In the meanwhile, they remedy the defect as they can; they find out where the holes and the hollows in the bore of a cannon are by means of a searcher. But there is a better way, that is the movable star of Gribeauval."

"In the sixteenth century," observed Bossuet, "they rifled their cannon."

"Yes," answered Combeferre, "that augments the ballistic power, but diminishes the accuracy of the aim. In a short range, the trajectory has not the stiffness desirable, the parabola is exaggerated, the path of the projectile is not rectilinear enough to permit it to hit the intermediate objects, a necessity of combat, however, the importance of which increases with the proximity of the enemy and the rapidity of the firing. This want of tension in the curve of the projectile, in the rifled cannon of the sixteenth century, is due to the feebleness of the charge; feeble charges, for this kind of arm, are required by the necessities of ballistics, such as, for instance, the preservation of the carriages. Upon the whole, artillery, that despot, cannot do all it would; strength is a great weakness. A cannon ball makes only two thousand miles an hour; light makes two hundred thousand miles a second. Such is the superiority of Jesus Christ over Napoleon."

"Reload arms," said Enjolras.

How was the facing of the barricade going to behave under fire? would the shot make a breach? That was the question. While the insurgents were reloading their muskets, the gunners loaded the cannon.

There was intense anxiety in the redoubt.

The gun went off; the detonation burst upon them.

"Present!" cried a cheerful voice.

And at the same time with the ball, Gavroche tumbled into the barricade.

He came by way of the Rue du Cygne, and he had nimbly clambered over the minor barricade, which fronted upon the labyrinth of the Petite Truanderie.

Gavroche produced more effect in the barricade than the ball.

The ball lost itself in the jumble of the rubbish. At the very utmost it broke a wheel of the omnibus, and finished the old Anceau cart. Seeing which, the barricade began to laugh.

"Proceed," cried Bossuet to the gunners.

VIII

THE GUNNERS PRODUCE A SERIOUS IMPRESSION

THEY surrounded Gavroche.

But he had no time to tell anything; Marius, shuddering, took him aside.

"What have you come here for?"

"Hold on!" said the boy. "What have you come for?"

And he looked straight at Marius with his epic effrontery. His eyes grew large with the proud light which was in them.

Marius continued, in a stern tone:

"Who told you to come back? At least you carried my letter to its address?"

Gavroche had some little remorse in relation to that letter. In his haste to return to the barricade, he had got rid of it rather than delivered it. He was compelled to acknowledge to himself that he had intrusted it rather rashly to that stranger, whose face even he could not distinguish. True, this man was bareheaded, but that was not enough. On the whole, he had some little interior remonstrances on this subject, and he feared Marius' reproaches. He took, to get out of the trouble, the simplest course; he lied abominably.

"Citizen, I carried the letter to the porter. The lady was asleep. She will get the letter when she wakes up."

Marius, in sending this letter, had two objects: to say farewell to Cosette, and to save Gavroche. He was obliged to be content with the half of what he intended.

The sending of his letter, and the presence of M. Fauchelevent in the barricade, this coincidence occurred to his mind. He pointed out M. Fauchelevent to Gavroche.

"Do you know that man?"

"No," said Gavroche.

Gavroche, in fact, as we have just mentioned, had only seen Jean Valjean in the night.

The troubled and sickly conjectures which had arisen in Marius' mind were dissipated. Did he know M. Fauchelevent's opinions? M. Fauchelevent was a republican, perhaps. Hence his very natural presence in this conflict.

Meanwhile Gavroche was already at the other end of the barricade, crying: "My musket!"

Courfeyrac ordered it to be given him.

Gavroche warned his "comrades," as he called them, that the barricade was surrounded. He had had great difficulty in getting through. A battalion of the line whose muskets were stacked in la Petite Truanderie, were observing the side on the Rue du Cygne; on the opposite side the municipal guard occupied the Rue des Prêcheurs. In front, they had the bulk of the army.

This information given, Gavroche added:

"I authorise you to give them a dose of pills."

Meanwhile Enjolras, on his battlement, was watching, listening with intense attention.

The assailants, dissatisfied doubtless with the effect of their fire, had not repeated it.

A company of infantry of the line had come in and occupied the extremity of the street, in the rear of the gun. The soldiers tore up the pavement, and with the stones constructed a little low wall, a sort of breastwork, which was hardly more than eighteen inches high, and which fronted the barricade. At the corner on the left of this breastwork, they saw the head of the column of a battalion of the banlieue massed in the Rue St. Denis.

Enjolras, on the watch, thought he distinguished the peculiar sound which is made when canisters of grape are taken from the caisson, and he saw the gunner change the aim and incline the piece slightly to the left. Then the cannoneers began to load. The gunner seized the linstock himself and brought it near the touch-hole.

"Heads down, keep close to the wall!" cried Enjolras, "and all on your knees along the barricade!"

The insurgents, who were scattered in front of the wine-shop, and who had left their posts of combat on Gavroche's arrival, rushed pell-mell towards the barricade; but before Enjolras' order was executed, the discharge took place with the fearful rattle of grapeshot. It was so in fact.

The charge was directed at the opening of the redoubt, it

ricocheted upon the wall, and this terrible ricochet killed two men and wounded three.

If that continued, the barricade was no longer tenable. It was not proof against grape.

There was a sound of consternation.

"Let us prevent the second shot, at any rate," said Enjolras.

And, lowering his carbine, he aimed at the gunner, who, at that moment, bending over the breech of the gun, was correcting and finally adjusting the aim.

This gunner was a fine-looking sergeant of artillery, quite young, of fair complexion, with a very mild face, and the intelligent air peculiar to that predestined and formidable arm which, by perfecting itself in horror, must end in killing war.

Combeferre, standing near Enjolras, looked at this young man.

"What a pity!" said Combeferre. "What a hideous thing these butcheries are! Come, when there are no more kings, there will be no more war. Enjolras, you are aiming at that sergeant, you are not looking at him. Just think that he is a charming young man; he is intrepid; you see that he is a thinker; these young artillery-men are well educated; he has a father, a mother, a family; he is in love probably; he is at most twenty-five years old; he might be your brother;"

"He is," said Enjolras.

"Yes," said Combeferre, "and mine also. Well, don't let us kill him."

"Let me alone. We must do what we must."

And a tear rolled slowly down Enjolras' marble cheek.

At the same time he pressed the trigger of his carbine. The flash leaped forth. The artillery-man turned twice round, his arms stretched out before him, and his head raised as if to drink the air, then he fell over on his side upon the gun, and lay there motionless. His back could be seen, from the centre of which a stream of blood gushed upwards. The ball had entered his breast and passed through his body. He was dead.

It was necessary to carry him away and to replace him. It was indeed some minutes gained.

IX

USE OF THAT OLD POACHER SKILL, AND THAT
INFALLIBLE SHOT WHICH INFLUENCED THE
CONVICTION OF 1796

THERE was confusion in the counsel of the barricade. The gun was about to be fired again. They could not hold out a quarter of an hour in that storm of grape. It was absolutely necessary to deaden the blows.

Enjolras threw out his command:

"We must put a mattress there."

"We have none," said Combeferre, "the wounded are on them."

Jean Valjean, seated apart on a block, at the corner of the wine-shop, his musket between his knees, had, up to this moment, taken no part in what was going on. He seemed not to hear the combatants about him say: "There is a musket which is doing nothing."

At the order given by Enjolras, he got up.

It will be remembered that on the arrival of the company in the Rue de la Chanvrerie, an old woman, foreseeing bullets, had put her mattress before her window. This window, a garret window, was on the roof of a house of six stories standing a little outside of the barricade. The mattress, placed crosswise, rested at the bottom upon two clothes-poles, and was sustained above by two ropes which, in the distance, seemed like threads, and which were fastened to nails driven into the window casing. These two ropes could be seen distinctly against the sky like hairs.

"Can somebody lend me a double-barrelled carbine?" said Jean Valjean.

Enjolras, who had just reloaded his, handed it to him.

Jean Valjean aimed at the window and fired.

One of the two ropes of the mattress was cut.

The mattress now hung only by one thread.

Jean Valjean fired the second barrel. The second rope struck the glass of the window. The mattress slid down between the two poles and fell into the street.

The barricade applauded.

All cried:

"There is a mattress."

"Yes," said Combeferre, "but who will go after it?"

The mattress had, in fact, fallen outside of the barricade, between the besieged and the besiegers. Now, the death of the gunner having exasperated the troops, the soldiers, for some moments, had been lying on their faces behind the line of paving stones which they had raised, and, to make up for the compulsory silence of the gun, which was quiet while its service was being reorganised, they had opened fire on the barricade. The insurgents made no response to this musketry, to spare their ammunition. The fusillade was broken against the barricade; but the street, which it filled with balls, was terrible.

Jean Valjean went out at the opening, entered the street, passed through the storm of balls, went to the mattress, picked it up, put it on his back, and returned to the barricade.

He put the mattress into the opening himself. He fixed it against the wall in such a way that the artillery-men did not see it.

This done, they awaited the charge of grape.

They had not long to wait.

The cannon vomited its package of shot with a roar. But there was no ricochet. The grape miscarried upon the mattress. The desired effect was obtained. The barricade was preserved.

"Citizen," said Enjolras to Jean Valjean, "the republic thanks you."

Bossuet admired and laughed. He exclaimed:

"It is immoral that a mattress should have so much power. Triumph of that which yields over that which thunders. But it is all the same; glory to the mattress which nullifies a cannon."

X
DAWN

AT that moment Cosette awoke.

Her room was small, neat, retired, with a long window to the east, looking upon the back-yard of the house.

Cosette knew nothing of what was going on in Paris. She had not been out of her room in the evening, and she had already withdrawn to it when Toussaint said: "It appears that there is a row."

Cosette had slept few hours, but well. She had had sweet dreams which was partly owing perhaps to her little bed being very white. Somebody who was Marius had appeared to her surrounded by a halo. She awoke with the sun in her eyes, which at first produced the effect of a continuation of her dream.

Her first emotion, on coming out of this dream, was joyous. Cosette felt entirely reassured. She was passing through, as Jean Valjean had done a few hours before, that reaction of the soul which absolutely refuses woe. She began to hope with all her might without knowing why. Then came an oppression of the heart. Here were three days now that she had not seen Marius. But she said to herself that he must have received her letter, that he knew where she was, and that he had so much tact, that he would find means to reach her. And that certainly to-day, and perhaps this very morning. It was broad day, but the rays of light were very horizontal, she thought it was very early; that she must get up, however, to receive Marius.

She felt that she could not live without Marius, and that consequently, that was enough, and that Marius would come. No objection was admissible. All that was certain. It was monstrous enough already to have suffered three days. Marius absent three days, it was horrible in the good God. Now this cruel sport of Heaven was an ordeal that was over. Marius was coming, and would bring good news. Thus is youth constituted; it quickly wipes its eyes; it believes sorrow useless and does not accept it. Youth is the smile of the future before an unknown being which is itself. It is natural for it to be happy. It seems as though it breathed hope.

Besides, Cosette could not succeed in recalling what Marius had said to her on the subject of this absence which was to last but one day, or what explanation he had given her about it. Everybody has noticed with what address a piece of money which you drop on the floor, runs and hides, and what art it has in rendering itself undiscoverable. There are thoughts which play us the same trick; they hide in a corner of our brain; it is all over; they are lost; impossible to put the memory back upon them. Cosette was a little vexed at the useless petty efforts which her recollection made. She said to herself that it was very naughty of her and very wicked to have forgotten words uttered by Marius.

She got up and performed the two ablutions, of the soul and the body, her prayer and her toilette.

We may, in extreme cases, introduce the reader into a nuptial chamber, not into a maiden's chamber. Verse would hardly dare, prose ought not.

It is the interior of a flower yet unblown, it is a whiteness in the shade, it is the inmost cell of a closed lily which ought not to be looked upon by man, while yet it has not been looked upon by the sun. Woman in the bud is sacred. The innocent bed which is thrown open, the adorable semi-nudity which is afraid of itself, the white foot which takes refuge in a slipper, the bosom which veils itself before a mirror as if that mirror were an eye; the chemise which hastens up to hide the shoulder at the snapping of a piece of furniture, or at the passing of a wagon, the ribbons tied, the clasps hooked, the lacings drawn, the starts, the shivers of cold and of modesty, the exquisite shyness in every movement, the almost winged anxiety where there is no cause for fear; the successive phases of the dress as charming as the clouds of the dawn; it is not fitting that all this should be described, and it is too much, indeed, to refer to it.

The eye of man should be more religious still before the rising of a young maiden than before the rising of a star. The possibility of touch should increase respect. The down of peach, the dust of the plum, the radiated crystal of the snow, the butterfly's wing powdered with feathers, are gross things in presence of that chastity which does not even know that it is chaste. The young maiden is only the gleam of a dream, and is not yet statue. Her alcove is hidden in the shadows of the ideal. The indiscreet touch of the eye defaces this dim penumbra. Here, to gaze is to profane.

We will show nothing, then, of all that pleasant little confusion on Cosette's awakening.

An Eastern tale relates that the rose was made white by God but that Adam having looked at it at the moment it was half opened, it was ashamed and blushed. We are of those who feel themselves speechless before young maidens and flowers, finding them venerable.

Cosette dressed herself very quickly, combed and arranged her hair, which was a very simple thing at that time, when women did not puff out their ringlets and plaits with cushions and rolls, and did not put crinoline in their hair. Then she opened the window and looked all about, hoping to discover something of the street, a corner of a house, a patch of pavement, and to be able to watch for Marius there. But she could see nothing of the street. The back-yard was surrounded with high walls, and a few gardens only were in view. Cosette pronounced these gardens hideous; for the first time in her life she found flowers ugly. The least bit of a street gutter would have been more to her mind. She finally began to look at the sky, as if she thought that Marius might come that way also.

Suddenly, she melted into tears. Not that it was fickleness of soul; but, hopes cut off by faintness of heart, such was her situation. She vaguely felt some indefinable horror. Things float in the air in fact. She said to herself that she was not sure of anything; that to lose from sight, was to lose; and the idea that Marius might indeed return to her from the sky, appeared no longer charming, but dismal.

Then, such are these clouds, calmness returned to her, and hope, and a sort of smile, unconscious, but trusting in God.

Everybody was still in bed in the house. A rural silence reigned. No shutter had been opened. The porter's box was closed. Toussaint was not up, and Cosette very naturally thought that her father was asleep. She must have suffered indeed, and she must have been still suffering, for she said to herself that her father had been unkind; but she counted on Marius. The eclipse of such a light was entirely impossible. At intervals she heard at some distance a kind of sullen jar, and she said: "It is singular that people are opening and shutting porte-cochères so early." It was the cannon battering the barricade.

There was, a few feet below Cosette's window, in the old black cornice of the wall, a nest of martins; the corbel of this nest made a little projection beyond the cornice, so that the inside of this little paradise could be seen from above. The mother was there, opening her wings like a fan over her brood; the father flew about, went away, then returned, bringing in his bill food and kisses. The rising day gilded this happy thing, the great law Multiply was there, smiling and august, and this sweet mystery was blossoming in the glory of the morning. Cosette, her hair in the sunshine, her soul in chimera, made luminous by love within, and the dawn without, bent over as if mechanically, and, almost without daring to acknowledge to herself that she was thinking of Marius at the same time, began to look at these birds, this family, this male and this female, this mother and these little ones, with the deep restlessness which a nest gives to a maiden.

XI
THE SHOT WHICH MISSES NOTHING
AND KILLS NOBODY

THE fire of the assailants continued. The musketry and the grape alternated, without much damage indeed. The top of the façade of Corinth alone suffered; the window of the first story and the dormer windows on the roof, riddled with shot and ball, were slowly demolished. The combatants who were posted there, had to withdraw. Besides, this is the art of attacking barricades; to tease for a long time, in order to exhaust the ammunition of the insurgents if they commit the blunder of replying. When it is perceived, from the slackening of their fire, that they have no longer either balls or powder, the assault is made. Enjolras did not fall into this snare; the barricade did not reply.

At each platoon fire, Gavroche thrust out his cheek with his tongue, a mark of lofty disdain:

"That's right," said he, "tear up the cloth. We want lint."

Courfeyrac jested with the grape about its lack of effect, and said to the cannon:

"You are getting diffuse, my goodman."

In a battle people force themselves upon acquaintance, as at a ball. It is probable that this silence of the redoubt began to perplex the besiegers, and make them fear some unlooked-for accident, and that they felt the need of seeing through that heap of paving stones and knowing what was going on behind that impassable wall, which was receiving their fire without answering it. The insurgents suddenly perceived a casque shining in the sun upon a neighbouring roof. A sapper was backed up against a tall chimney, and seemed to be there as a sentinel. He looked directly into the barricade.

"There is a troublesome overseer," said Enjolras.

Jean Valjean had returned his carbine to Enjolras, but he had his musket.

Without saying a word, he aimed at the sapper, and, a second afterwards, the casque, struck by a ball, fell noisily into the street. The startled soldier hastened to disappear.

A second observer took his place. This was an officer. Jean Valjean, who had reloaded his musket, aimed at the new-comer, and sent the officer's casque to keep company with the soldier's. The officer was not obstinate, and withdrew very quickly. This time the warning was understood. Nobody appeared upon the roof again, and they gave up watching the barricade.

"Why didn't you kill the man?" asked Bossuet of Jean Valjean.

Jean Valjean did not answer.

XII
DISORDER A PARTISAN OF ORDER

BOSSUET murmured in Combeferre's ear:

"He has not answered my question."

"He is a man who does kindness by musket shots," said Combeferre.

Those who retain some recollection of that now distant period know that the National Guard of the banlieue was valiant against the insurrections. It was particularly eager and intrepid in the days of June, 1832. Many a good wine-shopkeeper of Pantin, of the Vertus or of La Cunette, whose "establishment" was without custom in consequence of the émeute, became leonine on seeing his dancing-hall deserted, and died to preserve order represented by the tavern. In those days, at once bourgeois and heroic, in presence of ideas which had their knights, interests had their paladins. The prosaic motive detracted nothing from the bravery of the action. The decrease of a pile of crowns made bankers sing the Marseillaise. They poured out their blood lyrically for the counter; and with a Lacedæmonian enthusiasm they defended the shop, that immense diminutive of one's native land.

In reality we must say, there was nothing in all this which was not very serious. It was the social elements entering into conflict while awaiting the day when they shall enter into equilibrium.

Another sign of that time was anarchy mingled with governmentalism (barbarous name of the correct party). Men were for order without discipline. The drum beat unawares, at the command of some colonel of the National Guard, capricious roll-calls; many a captain went to the fire by inspiration; many a National Guard fought "from fancy," and on his own account. In the critical moments, on the "days," they took counsel less of their chiefs than of their instincts. There were in the army of order genuine guerrillas, some of the sword like Fannicot; others of the pen, like Henri Fonfrède.

Civilisation, unfortunately represented at that epoch rather by an aggregation of interests than by a group of principles, was, or thought itself in peril; it raised the cry of alarm; every man making himself a centre, defended it, aided it, and protected it, in his own way; and anybody and everybody took it upon himself to save society.

Zeal sometimes goes to the extent of extermination. Such a platoon of National Guards constituted themselves, of their own private authority, a court-martial, and condemned and executed an insurgent prisoner in five minutes. It was an improvisation of this kind which had killed Jean Prouvaire. Ferocious Lynch law, with which no party has the right to reproach others, for it is applied by the republic in America as well as by monarchy in Europe. This Lynch law is liable to mistakes. During an émeute, a young poet, named Paul Aimé Garnier, was pursued in the Place Royale at the point of the bayonet, and only escaped by taking refuge under the porte-cochère of Number 6. The cry was: *There is another of those Saint Simonians!* and there was an attempt to kill him. Now, he had under his arm a volume of the memoirs of the Duke de Saint Simon. A National Guard had read upon this book the name: *Saint Simon*, and cried: "Kill him."

On the 6th of June, 1832, a company of National Guards of the banlieue, commanded by Captain Fannicot, before mentioned, got themselves, through whim and for sport's sake, decimated in the Rue de la Chanvrerie. The fact, singular as it may seem, was proven by the judicial investigation entered upon after the insurrection of 1832. Captain Fannicot, a bold and impatient bourgeois, a kind of condottiere of the order of those we have just characterised, a fanatical and insubordinate governmentalist, could not resist the impulse to open fire before the hour, and the ambition of taking the barricade by himself all alone, that is, with his company. Exasperated by the successive appearance of the red flag and the old coat which he took for the black flag, he loudly blamed the generals and chiefs of corps, who were holding counsel, and did not deem that the moment for the decisive assault had come, and were leaving, according to a celebrated expression of one of them, "the insurrection to cook in its own juice." As for him, he thought the barricade ripe, and, as what is ripe ought to fall, he made the attempt.

He commanded men as resolute as himself, "madmen," said

a witness. His company, the same which had shot the poet Jean Prouvaire, was the first of the battalion posted at the corner of the street. At the moment when it was least expected, the captain hurled his men against the barricade. This movement, executed with more zeal than strategy, cost the Fannicot company dear. Before it had passed over two-thirds of the street, it was greeted by a general discharge from the barricade. Four, the most daring, who were running in advance, were shot down at the muzzles of the muskets, at the very foot of the redoubt; and this courageous mob of National Guards, very brave men, but who had no military tenacity, had to fall back, after some hesitation, leaving fifteen dead upon the pavement. The moment of hesitation gave the insurgents time to reload, and a second discharge, very murderous, reached the company before it was able to regain the corner of the street, its shelter. At one moment it was taken between two storms of balls, and it received the volley of the piece in battery which, receiving no orders, had not discontinued its fire. The intrepid and imprudent Fannicot was one of those killed by this volley. He was slain by the cannon, that is to say, by order.

This attack, more furious than serious, irritated Enjolras.

"The fools!" said he. "They are getting their men killed and using up our ammunition, for nothing."

Enjolras spoke like the true general of émeute that he was. Insurrection and repression do not contend with equal arms. Insurrection, readily exhaustible, has but a certain number of shots to fire, and but a certain number of combatants to expend. A cartridge-box emptied, a man killed, are not replaced. Repression, having the army, does not count men, and, having Vincennes, does not count shots. Repression has as many regiments as the barricade has men, and as many arsenals as the barricade has cartridge-boxes. Thus they are struggles of one against a hundred, which always end in the destruction of the barricade; unless revolution, abruptly appearing, casts into the balance its flaming archangel's sword. That happens. Then everything rises, the pavements begin to ferment, the redoubts of the people swarm, Paris thrills sovereignly, the *quid divinum* is set free, a 10th of August is in the air, a 29th of July is in the air, a marvellous light appears, the yawning jaws of force recoil, and the army, that lion, sees before it, erect and tranquil, this prophet, France.

XIII
GLEAMS WHICH PASS

In the chaos of sentiments and passions which defend a barricade, there is something of everything; there is bravery, youth, honour, enthusiasm, the ideal, conviction, the eager fury of the gamester, and above all, intervals of hope.

One of those intervals, one of those vague thrills of hope, suddenly crossed, at the most unexpected moment, the barricade of the Rue de la Chanvrerie.

"Hark!" abruptly exclaimed Enjolras, who was constantly on the alert, "it seems to me that Paris is waking."

It is certain that on the morning of the 6th of June the insurrection had, for an hour or two, a certain recrudescence. The obstinacy of the tocsin of Saint Merry reanimated some dull hopes. In the Rue du Poirier, in the Rue des Gravilliers, barricades were planned out. In front of the Porte Saint Martin, a young man, armed with a carbine, attacked singly a squadron of cavalry. Without any shelter, in the open boulevard, he dropped on one knee, raised his weapon to his shoulder, fired, killed the chief of the squadron, and turned round saying: "*There is another who will do us no more harm.*" He was sabred. In the Rue Saint Denis, a woman fired upon the Municipal Guard from behind a Venetian blind. The slats of the blind were seen to tremble at each report. A boy of fourteen was arrested in the Rue de la Cossonerie with his pockets full of cartridges. Several posts were attacked. At the entrance of the Rue Bertin Poiree, a very sharp and entirely unexpected fusillade greeted a regiment of cuirassiers at the head of which marched General Cavaignac de Baragne. In the Rue Planche Mibray they threw upon the troops, from the roofs, old fragments of household vessels and utensils; a bad sign; and when this fact was reported to Marshal Soult, the old lieutenant of Napoleon grew thoughtful, remembering the saying of Suchet at Saragossa: "*We are lost when the old women empty their pots upon our heads.*"

These general symptoms which were manifested just when it was supposed the émeute was localised, this fever of wrath which was regaining the upper hand, these sparks which flew here and there above those deep masses of combustible material which are called the Faubourgs of Paris, all taken together rendered the military chiefs anxious. They hastened to extinguish these beginnings of conflagration. They delayed, until these sparks should be quenched, the attack on the barricades Maubuée, de la Chanvrerie, and Saint Merry, that they might have them only to deal with, and might be able to finish all at one blow. Columns were thrown into the streets in fermentation, sweeping the large ones, probing the small on the right, on the left, sometimes slowly and with precaution, sometimes at a double quick step. The troops beat in the doors of the houses from which there had been firing; at the same time manœuvres of cavalry dispersed the groups on the boulevards. This repression was not accomplished without noise, nor without that tumultuous uproar peculiar to shocks between the army and the people. This was what Enjolras caught, in the intervals of the cannonade and the musketry. Besides, he had seen some wounded passing at the end of the street upon litters, and said to Courfeyrac: "Those wounded do not come from our fire."

The hope did not last long; the gleam was soon eclipsed. In less than half an hour that which was in the air vanished; it was like heat lightning, and the insurgents felt that kind of leaden pall fall upon them which the indifference of the people casts over the wilful when abandoned.

The general movement, which seemed to have been vaguely projected, had miscarried; and the attention of the Minister of War and the strategy of the generals could now be concentrated upon the three or four barricades remaining standing.

The sun rose above the horizon.

An insurgent called to Enjolras:

"We are hungry here. Are we really going to die like this without eating?"

Enjolras, still leaning upon his battlement, without taking his eyes off the extremity of the street, nodded his head.

XIV

IN WHICH WILL BE FOUND THE NAME OF ENJOLRAS' MISTRESS

COURFEYRAC, seated on a paving stone beside Enjolras, continued his insults to the cannon, and every time that that gloomy cloud of projectiles which is known by the name of grape passed by, with its monstrous sound, he received it with an outburst of irony.

"You are tiring your lungs, my poor old brute, you trouble me, you are wasting your racket. That is not thunder; no, it is a cough."

And those about him laughed.

Courfeyrac and Bossuet, whose valiant good-humour increased with the danger, like Madame Scarron, replaced food by pleasantry, and, as they had no wine, poured out cheerfulness for all.

"I admire Enjolras," said Bossuet. "His impassive boldness astonishes me. He lives alone, which renders him perhaps a little sad. Enjolras suffers for his greatness, which binds him to widowhood. The rest of us have all, more or less, mistresses who make fools of us, that is to say braves. When we are as amorous as a tiger the least we can do is to fight like a lion. It is a way of avenging ourselves for the tricks which Mesdames our grisettes play us. Roland gets himself killed to spite Angelica; all our heroisms come from our women. A man without a woman, is a pistol without a hammer; it is the woman who makes the man go off. Now, Enjolras has no woman. He is not in love, and he finds a way to be intrepid. It is a marvellous thing that a man can be as cold as ice and as bold as fire."

Enjolras did not appear to listen, but had anybody been near him he would have heard him murmur in an undertone, "*Patria.*"

Bossuet was laughing still when Courfeyrac exclaimed:

"Something new!"

And, assuming the manner of an usher announcing an arrival, he added:

"My name is Eight-Pounder."

In fact, a new personage had just entered upon the scene. It was a second piece of ordnance.

The artillery-men quickly executed the manœuvres, and placed this second piece in battery near the first.

This suggested the conclusion.

A few moments afterwards, the two pieces, rapidly served, opened directly upon the redoubt; the platoon firing of the line and the banlieue supported the artillery.

Another cannonade was heard at some distance. At the same time that two cannon were raging against the redoubt in the Rue de la Chanvrerie, two other pieces of ordnance, pointed, one on the Rue Saint Denis, the other on the Rue Aubry le

Boucher, were riddling the barricade St. Merry. The four cannon made dreary echo to one another.

The bayings of the dismal dogs of war answered each other.

Of the two pieces which were now battering the barricade in the Rue de la Chanvrerie, one fired grape, the other ball.

The gun which threw balls was elevated a little, and the range was calculated so that the ball struck the extreme edge of the upper ridge of the barricade, dismantled it, and crumbled the paving stones over the insurgents in showers.

This peculiar aim was intended to drive the combatants from the summit of the redoubt, and to force them to crowd together in the interior, that is, it announced the assault.

The combatants once driven from the top of the barricade by the balls and from the windows of the wine-shop by the grape, the attacking columns could venture into the street without being watched, perhaps even without being under fire, suddenly scale the redoubt, as on the evening before, and, who knows? take it by surprise.

"We must at all events diminish the inconvenience of those pieces," said Enjolras, and he cried: "fire upon the cannoneers!"

All were ready. The barricade, which had been silent for a long time, opened fire desperately; seven or eight discharges succeeded each other with a sort of rage and joy; the street was filled with a blinding smoke, and after a few minutes, through this haze pierced by flame, they could confusedly make out two thirds of the cannoneers lying under the wheels of the guns. Those who remained standing continued to serve the pieces with rigid composure, but the fire was slackened.

"This goes well," said Bossuet to Enjolras. "Success."

Enjolras shook his head and answered:

"A quarter of an hour more of this success, and there will not be ten cartridges in the barricade."

It would seem that Gavroche heard this remark.

XV
GAVROCHE OUTSIDE

COURFEYRAC suddenly perceived somebody at the foot of the barricade, outside in the street, under the balls.

Gavroche had taken a basket from the wine-shop, had gone out by the opening, and was quietly occupied in emptying into his basket the full cartridge-boxes of the National Guards who had been killed on the slope of the redoubt.

"What are you doing there?" said Courfeyrac.

Gavroche cocked up his nose.

"Citizen, I am filling my basket."

"Why, don't you see the grape?"

Gavroche answered:

"Well, it rains. What then?"

Courfeyrac cried:

"Come back!"

"Directly," said Gavroche.

And with a bound, he sprang into the street.

It will be remembered that the Fannicot company, on retiring, had left behind them a trail of corpses.

Some twenty dead lay scattered along the whole length of the street on the pavement. Twenty cartridge-boxes for Gavroche, a supply of cartridges for the barricade.

The smoke in the street was like a fog. Whoever has seen a cloud fall into a mountain gorge between two steep slopes can imagine this smoke crowded and as if thickened by two gloomy lines of tall houses. It rose slowly and was constantly renewed; hence a gradual darkening which even rendered broad day pallid. The combatants could hardly perceive each other from end to end of the street, although it was very short.

This obscurity, probably desired and calculated upon by the leaders who were to direct the assault upon the barricade, was of use to Gavroche.

Under the folds of this veil of smoke, and thanks to his small size, he could advance far into the street without being seen. He emptied the first seven or eight cartridge-boxes without much danger.

He crawled on his belly, ran on his hands and feet, took his basket in his teeth, twisted, glided, writhed, wormed his way from one body to another, and emptied a cartridge-box as a monkey opens a nut.

From the barricade, of which he was still within hearing, they dared not call to him to return, for fear of attracting attention to him.

On one corpse, that of a corporal, he found a powder-flask.

"In case of thirst," said he as he put it into his pocket.

By successive advances, he reached a point where the fog from the firing became transparent.

So that the sharp-shooters of the line drawn up and on the alert behind their wall of paving stones, and the sharp-shooters of the banlieue massed at the corner of the street, suddenly discovered something moving in the smoke.

Just as Gavroche was relieving a sergeant who lay near a stone-block of his cartridges, a ball struck the body.

"The deuce!" said Gavroche. "So they are killing my dead for me."

A second ball splintered the pavement beside him. A third upset his basket.

Gavroche looked and saw that it came from the banlieue.

He rose up straight, on his feet, his hair in the wind, his hands upon his hips, his eye fixed upon the National Guards who were firing, and he sang:

> On est laid à Nanterre
> C'est la faute à Voltaire,
> Et bête à Palaiseau,
> C'est la faute à Rousseau.

Then he picked up his basket, put into it the cartridges which had fallen out, without losing a single one, and, advancing towards the fusillade, began to empty another cartridge-box. There a fourth ball just missed him again. Gavroche sang:

> Je ne suis pas notaire,
> C'est la faute à Voltaire;
> Je suis petit oiseau,
> C'est la faute à Rousseau.

A fifth ball succeeded only in drawing a third couplet from him.

> Joie est mon caractère,
> C'est la faute à Voltaire;
> Misère est mon trousseau,
> C'est la faute à Rousseau.

This continued thus for some time.

The sight was appalling and fascinating. Gavroche, fired at, mocked the firing. He appeared to be very much amused. It was the sparrow pecking at the hunters. He replied to each discharge by a couplet. They aimed at him incessantly, they always missed him. The National Guards and the soldiers laughed as they aimed at him. He lay down, then rose up, hid himself in a doorway, then sprang out, disappeared, reappeared, escaped, returned, retorted upon the volleys by wry faces, and meanwhile pillaged cartridges, emptied cartridge-boxes, and filled his basket. The insurgents, breathless with anxiety, followed him with their eyes. The barricade was trembling; he was singing. It was not a child; it was not a man; it was a strange fairy *gamin*. One would have said the invulnerable dwarf of the mêlée. The bullets ran after him, he was more nimble than they. He was playing an indescribably terrible game of hide-and-seek with death; every time the flat-nosed face of the spectre approached, the *gamin* snapped his fingers.

One bullet, however, better aimed or more treacherous than the others, reached the Will-o'-the-wisp child. They saw Gavroche totter, then he fell. The whole barricade gave a cry; but there was an Antæus in this pigmy; for the *gamin* to touch the pavement is like the giant touching the earth; Gavroche had fallen only to rise again; he sat up, a long stream of blood rolled down his face, he raised both arms in air, looked in the direction whence the shot came, and began to sing:

> Je suis tombé par terre,
> C'est la faute à Voltaire,
> La nez dans le ruisseau,
> C'est la faute à——

He did not finish. A second ball from the same marksman cut him short. This time he fell with his face upon the pavement, and did not stir again. That little great soul had taken flight.

XVI

HOW BROTHER BECOMES FATHER

THERE were at that very moment in the garden of the Luxembourg—for the eye of the drama should be everywhere present—two children holding each other by the hand. One might have been seven years old, the other five. Having been soaked in the rain, they were walking in the paths on the sunny side;

the elder was leading the little one; they were pale and in rags; they looked like wild birds. The smaller said: "I want something to eat."

The elder, already something of a protector, led his brother with his left hand and had a stick in his right hand.

They were alone in the garden. The garden was empty, the gates being closed by order of the police on account of the insurrection. The troops which had bivouacked there had been called away by the necessities of the combat.

How came these children there? Had they haply escaped from some half-open guardhouse; was there perchance in the neighbourhood, at the Barrière d'Enfer, or on the esplanade of the Observatoire, or in the neighbouring square overlooked by the pediment on which we read: *invenerunt parvulum pannis involutum*, some mountebank's tent from which they had fled; had they perchance, the evening before, evaded the eye of the garden-keepers at the hour of closing, and had they passed the night in some one of those boxes in which people read the papers? The fact is, that they were wandering, and that they seemed free. To be wandering and to seem free is to be lost. These poor little ones were lost indeed.

These two children were the very same about whom Gavroche had been in trouble, and whom the reader remembers. Children of the Thénardiers, rented out to Magnon, attributed to M. Gillenormand, and now leaves fallen from all these rootless branches, and whirled over the ground by the wind.

Their clothing, neat in Magnon's time, and which served her as a prospectus in the sight of M. Gillenormand, had become tatters.

These creatures belonged henceforth to the statistics of "abandoned children," whom the police report, collect, scatter, and find again on the streets of Paris.

It required the commotion of such a day for these little outcasts to be in this garden. If the officers had noticed them, they would have driven away these rags. Poor children cannot enter the public gardens; still one would think that, as children, they had a right in the flowers.

These were there, thanks to the closed gates. They were in violation of the rules. They had slipped into the garden, and they had stayed there. Closed gates do not dismiss the keepers, the oversight is supposed to continue, but it is relaxed and at its ease; and the keepers, also excited by the public anxiety and busier with matters without than within, no longer paid attention to the garden and had not seen the two delinquents.

It had rained the night before, and even a little that morning. But in June showers are of no account. It is with difficulty that we can realise, an hour after a storm, that this fine fair day has been rainy. The ground in summer is as soon dry as the cheek of a child.

At this time of the solstice, the light of the full moon is, so to speak, piercing. It seizes upon everything. It applies itself and spreads itself over the earth with a sort of suction. One would say that the sun was thirsty. A shower is a glass of water; a rain is swallowed immediately. In the morning all is streaming, in the afternoon all is dusty.

Nothing is so admirable as a verdure washed by the rain and wiped by the sunbeam; it is warm freshness. The gardens and the meadows, having water at their roots and sunshine in their flowers, become vases of incense, and exhale all their perfumes at once. All these laugh, sing, and proffer themselves. We feel sweet intoxication. Spring is a provisional paradise; sunshine helps to make man patient.

There are people who ask nothing more; living beings who, having the blue sky, say: "it is enough!" dreamers absorbed in marvel, drawing from idolatry of nature an indifference to good and evil, contemplators of the cosmos radiantly diverted from man, who do not understand how anybody can busy himself with the hunger of these, with the thirst of those, with the nakedness of the poor in winter, with the lymphatic curvature of a little backbone, with the pallet, with the garret, with the dungeon, and with the rags of shivering little girls, when he might dream under the trees; peaceful and terrible souls, pitilessly content. A strange thing, the infinite is enough for them. This great need of man, the finite, which admits of embrace, they ignore. The finite, which admits of progress, sublime toil, they do not think of. The indefinite, which is born of the combination human and divine, of the infinite and the finite, escapes them. Provided they are face to face with immensity, they smile. Never joy, always ecstasy. To lose themselves is their life. The history of humanity to them is only a fragmentary plan; All is not there, the true All is still beyond; what is the use of busying ourselves with this incident, man? Man suffers, it is possible; but look at Aldebaran rising yonder! The mother has no milk, the newborn dies, I know nothing about that, but look at this marvellous rosette formed by a transverse section of the sapwood of the fir tree when examined by the microscope! compare me that with the most beautiful Mechlin lace! These thinkers forget to love. The zodiac has such success with them that it prevents them from seeing the weeping child. God eclipses the soul. There is a family of such minds, at once little and great. Horace belonged to it, Goethe belonged to it, La Fontaine perhaps; magnificent egotists of the infinite, tranquil spectators of grief, who do not see Nero if the weather is fine, from whom the sunshine hides the stake, who would behold the guillotine at work, watching for an effect of light, who hear neither the cry, nor the sob, nor the death-rattle, nor the tocsin, to whom all is well, since there is a month of May, who, so long as there are clouds of purple and gold above their heads, declare themselves content, and who are determined to be happy until the light of the stars and the song of the birds are exhausted.

They are of a dark radiance. They do not suspect that they are to be pitied. Certainly they are. He who does not weep does not see. We should admire and pity them, as we would pity and admire a being at once light and darkness, with no eyes under his brows and a star in the middle of his forehead.

In the indifference of these thinkers, according to some, lies a superior philosophy. So be it; but in this superiority there is some infirmity. One may be immortal and a cripple; Vulcan for instance. One may be more than man and less than man. The immense incomplete exists in nature. Who knows that the sun is not blind?

But then, what! in whom trust? *Solem quis dicere falsum audeat?* Thus certain geniuses themselves, certain Most High mortals, star men, may have been deceived! That which is on high, at the top, at the summit, in the zenith, that which sends over the earth so much light, may see little, may see badly, may see nothing! Is not that disheartening? No. But what is there, then, above the sun? The God.

On the 6th June, 1832, towards eleven o'clock in the morning, the Luxembourg, solitary and unpeopled, was delightful. The quincunxes and the parterres projected themselves into the light in balms and dazzlings. The branches, wild with the noonday brilliance, seemed seeking to embrace each other. There was in the sycamores a chattering of linnets, the sparrows were jubilant, the woodpeckers climbed up the horse-chestnuts, tapping with their beaks the wrinkles in the bark. The flower beds accepted the legitimate royalty of the lilies; the most august of perfumes is that which comes from whiteness. You inhaled the spicy odour of the pinks. The old rooks of Marie de' Medici were amorous in the great trees. The sun gilded, empurpled, and kindled the tulips, which are nothing more nor less than all varieties of flame made flowers. All about the tulip beds whirled the bees, sparks from these flame-flowers. All was grace and gaiety, even the coming rain; that old offender, by whom the honeysuckles and the lilies of the valley would profit, produced no disquiet; the swallows flew low, charming menace. He who was there breathed happiness; life was sweet; all this nature exhaled candour, help, assistance, paternity, caress, dawn. The thoughts which fell from the sky were as soft as the child's little hand which you kiss.

The statues under the trees, bare and white, had robes of shade torn by light; these goddesses were all tattered by the sunshine; it hung from them in shreds on all sides. Around the great basin, the earth was already so dry as to be almost baked. There was wind enough to raise here and there little émeutes of sand. A few yellow leaves, relics of the last autumn, chased one another joyously, and seemed to be playing the *gamin*.

The abundance of light was inexpressibly comforting. Life, sap, warmth, odour, overflowed; you felt beneath creation the enormity of its source; in all these breezes saturated with love, in this coming and going of reflections and reverberations, in this prodigious expenditure of rays, in this indefinite outlay of fluid gold, you felt the prodigality of the inexhaustible; and behind this splendour, as behind a curtain of flame, you caught a glimpse of God, the millionaire of stars.

Thanks to the sand, there was not a trace of mud; thanks to the rain, there was not a speck of dust. The bouquets had just been washed; all the velvets, all the satins, all the enamels, all the golds, which spring from the earth in the form of flowers, were irreproachable. This magnificence was tidy. The great silence of happy nature filled the garden. A celestial silence compatible with a thousand melodies, cooings of nests, hummings of swarms, palpitations of the wind. All the harmony of the season was accomplished in a graceful whole; the entrances and exits

of spring took place in the desired order; the lilacs ended, the
jessamines began; some flowers were belated, some insects in
advance; the vanguard of the red butterflies of June fraternised
with the rearguard of the white butterflies of May. The plane-
trees were getting a new skin. The breeze scooped out waves in
the magnificent vastness of the horse-chestnuts. It was resplendent. A veteran of the adjoining barracks, looking through the
grating, said: "There is spring under arms and in full dress."

All nature was breakfasting; creation was at table; it was the
hour; the great blue cloth was spread in the sky, and the great
green cloth over the earth; the sun shone *à giorno*. God was
serving up the universal repast. Every creature had its food or
its fodder. The ringdove found hempseed, the chaffinch found
millet, the goldfinch found chickweed, the redbreast found
worms, the bee found flowers, the fly found infusoria, the
grossbeak found flies. They ate one another a little, to be sure,
which is the mystery of evil mingled with good; but not an
animal had an empty stomach.

The two little abandoned creatures were near the great basin,
and slightly disturbed by all this light, they endeavoured to hide,
an instinct of the poor and feeble before magnificence, even
impersonal, and they kept behind the shelter for the swans.

Here and there, at intervals, when the wind fell, they confusedly heard cries, a hum, a kind of tumultuous rattle, which was
the musketry, and sullen jars, which were reports of cannon.
There was smoke above the roofs in the direction of the markets.
A bell, which appeared to be calling, sounded in the distance.

These children did not seem to notice these sounds. The
smaller one repeated from time to time in an under tone: "I
want something to eat."

Almost at the same time with the two children, another
couple approached the great basin. This was a goodman of fifty,
who was leading by the hand a goodman of six. Doubtless a
father with his son. The goodman of six had a big bun in his hand.

At that period, certain adjoining houses, in the Rue Madame
and the Rue d'Enfer, had keys to the Luxembourg which the
occupants used when the gates were closed, a favour since suppressed. This father and this son probably came from one of
those houses.

The two poor little fellows saw "this Monsieur" coming, and
hid themselves a little more closely.

He was a bourgeois. The same, perhaps, whom one day Marius, in spite of his love fever, had heard, near this same great basin, counselling his son "to beware of extremes." He had an affable and lofty manner, and a mouth which, never closing, was always smiling. This mechanical smile, produced by too much jaw and too little skin, shows the teeth rather than the soul. The child, with his bitten bun, which he did not finish, seemed stuffed. The boy was dressed as a National Guard, on account of the émeute, and the father remained in citizen's clothes for the sake of prudence.

The father and son stopped near the basin in which the two swans were sporting. This bourgeois appeared to have a special admiration for the swans. He resembled them in this respect, that he walked like them.

For the moment, the swans were swimming, which is their principal talent, and they were superb.

If the two poor little fellows had listened, and had been of an age to understand, they might have gathered up the words of a grave man. The father said to the son:

"The sage lives content with little. Behold me, my son. I do not love pomp. Never am I seen with coats bedizened with gold and gems; I leave this false splendour to badly organised minds."

Here the deep sounds, which came from the direction of the markets, broke out with a redoubling of bell and of uproar.

"What is that?" inquired the child.

The father answered:

"They are saturnalia."

Just then he noticed the two little ragged fellows standing motionless behind the green cottage of the swans.

"There is the beginning," said he.

And after a moment, he added:

"Anarchy is entering this garden."

Meanwhile the son bit the bun, spit it out, and suddenly began to cry.

"What are you crying for?" asked the father.

"I am not hungry any more," said the child.

The father's smile grew broad.

"You don't need to be hungry, to eat a cake."

"I am sick of my cake. It is stale."

"You don't want any more of it?"

"No."

The father showed him the swans.

"Throw it to those palmipeds."

The child hesitated. Not to want any more of one's cake, is no reason for giving it away.

The father continued:

"Be humane. We must take pity on the animals."

And, taking the cake from his son, he threw it into the basin. The cake fell near the edge.

The swans were at a distance, in the centre of the basin, and busy with some prey. They saw neither the bourgeois nor the bun.

The bourgeois, feeling that the cake was in danger of being lost, and aroused by this useless shipwreck, devoted himself to a telegraphic agitation which finally attracted the attention of the swans.

They perceived something floating, veered about like the ships they are, and directed themselves slowly towards the bun with that serene majesty which is fitting to white animals.

"*Cygnes* [swans] understand *signes* [signs]," said the bourgeois, delighted at his wit.

Just then the distant tumult in the city suddenly increased again. This time it was ominous. There are some gusts of wind that speak more distinctly than others. That which blew at that moment brought clearly the rolls of drums, shouts, platoon firing, and the dismal replies of the tocsin and the cannon. This was coincident with a black cloud which abruptly shut out the sun.

The swans had not yet reached the bun.

"Come home," said the father, "they are attacking the Tuileries."

He seized his son's hand again. Then he continued:

"From the Tuileries to the Luxembourg, there is only the distance which separates royalty from the peerage; it is not far. It is going to rain musket-balls."

He looked at the cloud.

"And perhaps also the rain itself is going to rain; the heavens are joining in; the younger branch is condemned. Come home, quick."

"I should like to see the swans eat the bun," said the child.

The father answered:

"That would be an imprudence."

And he led away his little bourgeois.

The son, regretting the swans, turned his head towards the basin, until a turn in the rows of trees hid it from him.

Meanwhile, at the same time with the swans, the two little wanderers had approached the bun. It was floating on the water. The smaller was looking at the cake, the larger was looking at the bourgeois who was going away.

The father and the son entered the labyrinth of walks which leads to the grand stairway of the cluster of trees on the side towards the Rue Madame.

As soon as they were out of sight, the elder quickly lay down with his face over the rounded edge of the basin, and, holding by it with his left hand, hanging over the water, almost falling in, with his right hand reached his stick towards the cake. The swans, seeing the enemy, made haste, and in making haste produced an effect with their breasts which was useful to the little fisher; the water flowed back before the swans, and one of those smooth concentric waves pushed the bun gently towards the child's stick. As the swans came up, the stick touched the cake. The child made a quick movement, drew in the bun, frightened the swans, seized the cake, and got up. The cake was soaked; but they were hungry and thirsty. The eldest broke the bun into two pieces, one large and one small, took the small one for himself, gave the large one to his little brother, and said to him:

"*Stick that in your gun.*"

XVII
MORTUUS PATER FILIUM MORITURUM EXPECTAT

MARIUS had sprung out of the barricade. Combeferre had followed him. But it was too late. Gavroche was dead. Combeferre brought back the basket of cartridges; Marius brought back the child.

"Alas!" thought he, "what the father had done for his father he was returning to the son; only Thénardier had brought back his father living, while he brought back the child dead."

When Marius re-entered the redoubt with Gavroche in his arms, his face, like the child's, was covered with blood.

Just as he had stooped down to pick up Gavroche, a ball grazed his skull; he did not perceive it.

Courfeyrac took off his cravat and bound up Marius' forehead.

They laid Gavroche on the same table with Mabeuf, and they stretched the black shawl over the two bodies. It was large enough for the old man and the child.

Combeferre distributed the cartridges from the basket which he had brought back.

This gave each man fifteen shots.

Jean Valjean was still at the same place, motionless upon his block. When Combeferre presented him his fifteen cartridges, he shook his head.

"There is a rare eccentric," said Combeferre in a low tone to Enjolras. "He finds means not to fight in this barricade."

"Which does not prevent him from defending it," answered Enjolras.

"Heroism has its originals," replied Combeferre.

And Courfeyrac, who had overheard, added:

"He is a different kind from Father Mabeuf."

A notable fact, the fire which was battering the barricade hardly disturbed the interior. Those who have never passed through the whirlwind of this kind of war can have no idea of the singular moments of tranquillity which are mingled with these convulsions. Men come and go, they chat, they joke, they lounge. An acquaintance of ours heard a combatant say to him in the midst of the grape: *This is like a bachelor's breakfast.* The redoubt in the Rue de la Chanvrerie, we repeat, seemed very calm within. Every turn and every phase of fortune had been or would soon be exhausted. The position from critical had become threatening, and from threatening was probably becoming desperate. In proportion as the condition of affairs grew gloomy the heroic gleam empurpled the barricade more and more. Enjolras, grave, commanded it, in the attitude of a young Spartan devoting his drawn sword to the sombre genius Epidotas.

Combeferre, with apron at his waist, was dressing the wounded; Bossuet and Feuilly were making cartridges with the flask of powder taken by Gavroche from the dead corporal, and Bossuet said to Feuilly: *We shall soon take the diligence for another planet*; Courfeyrac, upon the few paving stones which he had reserved for himself near Enjolras, was disposing and arranging a whole arsenal, his sword-cane, his musket, two horse-pistols, and a pocket pistol, with the care of a girl who is putting a little work-box in order. Jean Valjean was looking in silence at the opposite wall. A working-man was fastening on his head with a string a large straw hat belonging to Mother Hucheloup, *for fear of sun-stroke*, said he. The young men of the Cougourde d'Aix were chatting gaily with one another, as if they were in a hurry to talk patois for the last time. Joly, who had taken down the widow Hucheloup's mirror, was examining his tongue in it. A few combatants, having discovered some crusts of bread, almost mouldy, in a drawer, were eating them greedily. Marius was anxious about what his father would say to him.

XVIII
THE VULTURE BECOMES PREY

WE *must* dwell upon a psychological fact, peculiar to barricades. Nothing which characterises this surprising war of the streets should be omitted.

Whatever be that strange interior tranquillity of which we have just spoken, the barricade, for those who are within, is none the less a vision.

There is an apocalypse in civil war, all the mists of the unknown are mingled with these savage flames, revolutions are sphinxes, and he who has passed through a barricade, believes he has passed through a dream.

What is felt in those places, as we have indicated in reference to Marius, and as we shall see in what follows, is more and is less than life. Once out of the barricade, a man no longer knows what he has seen in it. He was terrible, he does not know it. He was surrounded by combating ideas which had human faces; he had his head in the light of the future. There were corpses lying and phantoms standing. The hours were colossal, and seemed hours of eternity. He lived in death. Shadows passed by. What were they? He saw hands on which there was blood; it was an appalling uproar, it was also a hideous silence; there were open mouths which shouted, and other open mouths which held their peace; he was in the smoke, in the night, perhaps. He thinks he has touched the ominous ooze of the unknown depths; he sees something red in his nails. He remembers nothing more.

Let us return to the Rue de la Chanvrerie.

Suddenly between two discharges they heard the distant sound of a clock striking.

"It is noon," said Combeferre.

The twelve strokes had not sounded when Enjolras sprang to his feet, and flung down from the top of the barricade this thundering shout:

"Carry some paving stones into the house. Fortify the windows with them. Half the men to the muskets, the other half to the stones. Not a minute to lose."

A platoon of sappers, their axes on their shoulders, had just appeared in order of battle at the end of the street.

This could only be the head of a column; and of what column? The column of attack, evidently. The sappers, whose duty it is to demolish the barricade, must always precede the soldiers whose duty it is to scale it.

They were evidently close upon the moment which Monsieur de Clermont Tonnerre, in 1822, called "the twist of the necklace."

Enjolras' order was executed with the correct haste peculiar to ships and barricades, the only places of combat whence escape is impossible. In less than a minute, two-thirds of the paving stones which Enjolras had had piled up at the door of Corinth were carried up to the first story and to the garret; and before a second minute had elapsed, these stones, artistically laid one upon another, walled up half the height of the window on the first story and the dormer windows of the attic. A few openings, carefully arranged by Feuilly, chief builder, allowed musket barrels to pass through. This armament of the windows could be performed the more easily since the grape had ceased. The two pieces were now firing balls upon the centre of the wall, in order to make a hole, and if it were possible, a breach for the assault.

When the paving stones, destined for the last defence, were in position, Enjolras had them carry up to the first story the bottles which he had placed under the table where Mabeuf was.

"Who will drink that?" Bossuet asked him.

"They," answered Enjolras.

Then they barricaded the basement window, and they held in readiness the iron cross-pieces which served to bar the door of the wine-shop on the inside at night.

The fortress was complete. The barricade was the rampart, the wine-shop was the donjon.

With the paving stones which remained, they closed up the opening beside the barricade.

As the defenders of a barricade are always obliged to husband their ammunition, and as the besiegers know it, the besiegers perfect their arrangements with a sort of provoking leisure, expose themselves to fire before the time, but in appearance more than in reality, and take their ease. The preparations for attack are always made with a certain methodical slowness, after which, the thunderbolt.

This slowness allowed Enjolras to look over the whole, and to perfect the whole. He felt that since such men were to die, their death should be a masterpiece.

He said to Marius: "We are the two chiefs; I will give the last orders within. You stay outside and watch."

Marius posted himself for observation upon the crest of the barricade.

Enjolras had the door of the kitchen, which, we remember, was the hospital, nailed up.

"No spattering on the wounded," said he.

He gave his last instructions in the basement-room in a quick, but deep and calm voice; Feuilly listened, and answered in the name of all.

"First story, hold your axes ready to cut the staircase. Have you them?"

"Yes," said Feuilly.

"How many?"

"Two axes and a pole-axe."

"Very well. There are twenty-six effective men left."

"How many muskets are there?"

"Thirty-four."

"Eight too many. Keep these eight muskets loaded like the rest, and at hand. Swords and pistols in your belts. Twenty men to the barricade. Six in ambush at the dormer windows and at the window on the first story to fire upon the assailants through the loopholes in the paving stones. Let there be no useless labourer here. Immediately, when the drum beats the charge, let the twenty from below rush to the barricade. The first there will get the best places."

These dispositions made, he turned towards Javert, and said to him:

"I won't forget you."

And, laying a pistol on the table, he added:

"The last man to leave this room will blow out the spy's brains!" "Here?" inquired a voice.

"No, do not leave this corpse with ours. You can climb over the little barricade on the Rue Mondétour. It is only four feet high. The man is well tied. You will take him there, and execute him there."

There was one man, at that moment, who was more impassible than Enjolras; it was Javert.

Here Jean Valjean appeared.

He was in the throng of insurgents. He stepped forward, and said to Enjolras:

"You are the commander?"

"Yes."

"You thanked me just now."

"In the name of the republic. The barricade has two saviours, Marius Pontmercy and you."

"Do you think that I deserve a reward?"

"Certainly."

"Well, I ask one.'

"What?"

"To blow out that man's brains myself."

Javert raised his head, saw Jean Valjean, made an imperceptible movement, and said:

"That is appropriate."

As for Enjolras, he had begun to reload his carbine; he cast his eyes about him:

"No objection."

And turning towards Jean Valjean: "Take the spy."

Jean Valjean, in fact, took possession of Javert by sitting down on the end of the table. He caught up the pistol, and a slight click announced that he had cocked it.

Almost at the same moment, they heard a flourish of trumpets.

"Come on!" cried Marius, from the top of the barricade.

Javert began to laugh with that noiseless laugh which was peculiar to him, and, looking fixedly upon the insurgents, said to them:

"Your health is hardly better than mine."

"All outside?" cried Enjolras.

The insurgents sprang forward in a tumult, and, as they went out, they received in the back, allow us the expression, this speech from Javert:

"Farewell till immediately!"

XIX
JEAN VALJEAN TAKES HIS REVENGE

WHEN Jean Valjean was alone with Javert, he untied the rope that held the prisoner by the middle of the body, the knot of which was under the table. Then he motioned to him to get up.

Javert obeyed, with that undefinable smile into which the supremacy of enchained authority is condensed.

Jean Valjean took Javert by the martingale as you would take a beast of burden by a strap, and, drawing him after him, went out of the wine-shop slowly, for Javert, with his legs fettered, could take only very short steps.

Jean Valjean had the pistol in his hand.

They crossed thus the interior trapezium of the barricade. The insurgents, intent upon the imminent attack, were looking the other way.

Marius, alone, placed towards the left extremity of the wall, saw them pass. This group of the victim and the executioner borrowed a light from the sepulchral gleam which he had in his soul.

Jean Valjean, with some difficulty, bound as Javert was, but without letting go of him for a single instant, made him scale the little intrenchment on the Rue Mondétour.

When they had climbed over this wall, they found themselves alone in the little street. Nobody saw them now. The corner of the house hid them from insurgents. The corpses carried out from the barricades made a terrible mound a few steps off.

They distinguished in a heap of dead, a livid face, a flowing head of hair, a wounded hand, and a woman's breast half naked. It was Eponine.

Javert looked aside at this dead body, and, perfectly calm, said in an under tone:

"It seems to me that I know that girl."

Then he turned towards Jean Valjean.

Jean Valjean put the pistol under his arm, and fixed upon Javert a look which had no need of words to say: "Javert, it is I."

Javert answered.

"Take your revenge."

Jean Valjean took a knife out of his pocket, and opened it

"A *surin!*" exclaimed Javert. "You are right. That suits you better."

Jean Valjean cut the martingale which Javert had about his neck, then he cut the ropes which he had on his wrists, then, stooping down, he cut the cord which he had on his feet; and, rising, he said to him:

"You are free."

Javert was not easily astonished. Still, complete master as he was of himself, he could not escape an emotion. He stood aghast and motionless.

Jean Valjean continued:

"I don't expect to leave this place. Still, if by chance I should, I live, under the name of Fauchelevent, in the Rue de l'Homme Armé, Number Seven."

Javert had the scowl of a tiger half opening the corner of his mouth, and he muttered between his teeth:

"Take care."

"Go," said Jean Valjean.

Javert resumed:

"You said Fauchelevent, Rue de l'Homme Armé?"

"Number Seven."

Javert repeated in an undertone: "Number seven." He buttoned his coat, restored the military stiffness between his shoulders, turned half round, folded his arms, supporting his chin with one hand, and walked off in the direction of the markets. Jean Valjean followed him with his eyes. After a few steps, Javert turned back, and cried to Jean Valjean:

"You annoy me. Kill me rather."

Javert did not notice that his tone was more respectful towards Jean Valjean.

"Go away," said Jean Valjean.

Javert receded with slow steps. A moment afterwards, he turned the corner of the Rue des Prêcheurs.

When Javert was gone, Jean Valjean fired the pistol in the air.

Then he re-entered the barricade and said: "It is done."

Meanwhile what had taken place is this:

Marius, busy rather with the street than the wine-shop, had not until then looked attentively at the spy who was bound in the dusky rear of the basement-room.

When he saw him in broad day clambering over the barricade on his way to die, he recognised him. A sudden reminiscence came into his mind. He remembered the inspector of the Rue de Pontoise, and the two pistols which he had handed him and which he had used, he, Marius, in this very barricade; and not only did he recollect the face, but he recalled the name.

This reminiscence, however, was misty and indistinct, like all his ideas. It was not an affirmation which he made to himself, it was a question which he put: "Is not this that inspector of police who told me his name was Javert?"

Perhaps there was still time to interfere for this man? But he must first know if it were indeed that Javert.

Marius called to Enjolras, who had just taken his place at the other end of the barricade.

"Enjolras!"

"What?"

"What is that man's name?"

"Who?"

"The police officer. Do you know his name?"

"Of course. He told us."

"What is his name?"

"Javert."

Marius sprang up.

At that moment they heard the pistol-shot.

Jean Valjean reappeared and cried: "It is done."

A dreary chill passed through the heart of Marius.

XX

THE DEAD ARE RIGHT AND THE LIVING
ARE NOT WRONG

THE death-agony of the barricade was approaching.

All things concurred in the tragic majesty of this supreme moment; a thousand mysterious disturbances in the air, the breath of armed masses set in motion in streets which they could not see, the intermittent gallop of cavalry, the heavy concussion of artillery on the march, the platoon firing and the cannonades crossing each other in the labyrinth of Paris, the smoke of the battle rising all golden above the roofs, mysterious cries, distant, vaguely terrible flashes of menace everywhere, the tocsin of Saint Merry which now had the sound of a sob, the softness of the season, the splendour of the sky full of sunshine and of clouds, the beauty of the day, and the appalling silence of the houses.

For, since evening, the two rows of houses in the Rue de la Chanvrerie had become two walls; savage walls. Doors closed, windows closed, shutters closed.

In those days, so different from these in which we live, when the hour had come in which the people wished to make an end of a state of affairs which had lasted too long, of a granted charter or of a constitutional country, when the universal anger was diffused in the atmosphere, when the city consented to the upheaval of its pavements, when insurrection made the bourgeoisie smile by whispering its watchword in its ear, then the inhabitant filled with émeute, so to speak, was the auxiliary of the combatant, and the house fraternised with the impromptu fortress which leaned upon it. When the condition of affairs was not ripe, when the insurrection was not decidedly acceptable, when the mass disavowed the movement, it was all over with the combatants, the city changed into a desert about the revolt, souls were chilled, asylums were walled up, and the street became a defile to aid the army in taking the barricade.

A people cannot be surprised into a more rapid progress than it wills. Woe to him who attempts to force its hand! A people does not allow itself to be used. Then it abandons the insurrection to itself. The insurgents become pestiferous. A house is an escarpment, a door is a refusal, a façade is a wall. This wall sees, hears, and will not. It might open and save you. No. This wall is a judge. It looks upon you and condemns you. How gloomy are these closed houses! They seem dead, they are living. Life, which is as it were suspended in them, still exists. Nobody has come out of them for twenty-four hours, but nobody is missing. In the interior of this rock, people go and come, they lie down, they get up; they are at home there; they drink and eat; they are afraid there, a fearful thing! Fear excuses this terrible inhospitality; it tempers it with timidity, a mitigating circumstance. Sometimes even, and this has been seen, fear becomes passion; fright may change into fury, as prudence into rage; hence this saying so profound: *The madmen of moderation.* There are flamings of supreme dismay from which rage springs like a dismal smoke. "What do these people want? They are never contented. They compromise peaceable men as if we had not had revolution enough like this! What do they come here for? Let them get out of it themselves. So much the worse for them. It is their own fault. They have only got what they deserve. It doesn't concern us. Here is our poor street riddled with balls. They are a parcel of scamps. Above all, don't open the door." And the house puts on the semblance of a tomb. The insurgent before that door is in his last agony; he sees the grape and the drawn sabres coming; if he calls, he knows that they hear him, but that they will not come; there are walls which might protect him, there are men who might save him; and those walls have ears of flesh, and those men have bowels of stone.

Whom shall he accuse?

Nobody, and everybody.

The imperfect age in which we live.

It is always at her own risk and peril that Utopia transforms herself into insurrection, and from a philosophic protest becomes an armed protest, from Minerva, Pallas. The Utopia which grows impatient and becomes émeute knows what awaits her; almost always she is too soon. Then she resigns herself, and stoically accepts, instead of triumph, catastrophe. She serves, without complaining, and exonerating them even, those who deny her, and it is her magnanimity to consent to abandonment. She is indomitable against hindrance and gentle towards ingratitude.

But is it ingratitude?

Yes, from the point of view of the race.

No, from the point of view of the individual.

Progress is the mode of man. The general life of the human race is called Progress; the collective advance of the human race is called Progress. Progress marches; it makes the great human and terrestrial journey towards the celestial and the divine; it has its halts where it rallies the belated flock; it has its stations where it meditates, in sight of some splendid Canaan suddenly unveiling its horizon; it has its nights when it sleeps; and it is one of the bitter anxieties of the thinker to see the shadow upon the human soul, and to feel in the darkness progress asleep, without being able to waken it.

"*God is dead perhaps,*" said Gérard de Nerval one day, to him who writes these lines, confounding progress with God, and mistaking the interruption of the movement for the death of the Being.

He who despairs is wrong. Progress infallibly awakens, and, in short, we might say that it advances even in sleep, for it has grown. When we see it standing again, we find it taller. To be always peaceful belongs to progress no more than to the river; raise no obstruction, cast in no rock; the obstacle makes water foam and humanity seethe. Hence troubles; but after these troubles, we recognise that there has been some ground gained. Until order, which is nothing more nor less than universal peace, be established, until harmony and unity reign, progress will have revolutions for stations.

What then is Progress? We have just said. The permanent life of the peoples.

Now, it sometimes happens that the momentary life of individuals offers resistance to the eternal life of the human race.

Let us acknowledge it without bitterness, the individual has his distinct interest, and may without offence set up that interest and defend it: the present has its excusable quantum of selfishness; the life of the moment has its rights, and is not bound to sacrifice itself continually to the future. The generation which has now its turn of passing over the earth is not compelled to abridge it for the generations, its equals, after all, which are to have their turn afterwards. "I exist," murmurs that somebody whose name is All. "I am young and I am in love, I am old and I want to rest, I am the father of a family, I am working, I am prospering, I am doing a good business, I have houses to rent, I have money in the government, I am happy. I have a wife and children, I love all this, I desire to live, let me alone." Hence, at certain periods, a deep chill upon the magnanimous vanguard of the human race.

Utopia, moreover, we must admit, departs from its radiant sphere in making war. The truth of to-morrow, she borrows her process, battle, from the lie of yesterday. She, the future, acts like the past. She, the pure idea, becomes an act of force. She compromises her heroism by a violence for which it is just that she should answer; a violence of opportunity and of expediency, contrary to principles, and for which she is fatally punished. Utopia insurrection fights, the old military code in her hand; she shoots spies, she executes traitors, she suppresses living beings and casts them into the unknown dark. She uses death, a solemn thing. It seems as though Utopia had lost faith in the radiation of light, her irresistible and incorruptible strength. She strikes with the sword. Now, no sword is simple. Every blade has two edges; he who wounds with one wounds himself with the other.

This reservation made, and made in all severity, it is impossible for us not to admire, whether they succeed or not, the glorious combatants of the future, the professors of Utopia. Even when they fail, they are venerable, and it is perhaps in failure that they have the greater majesty. Victory, when it is according to progress, deserves the applause of the peoples; but a heroic defeat deserves their compassion. One is magnificent, the other is sublime. For ourselves, who prefer martyrdom to success, John Brown is greater than Washington, and Pisacane is greater than Garibaldi.

Surely some must be on the side of the vanquished.

Men are unjust towards these great essayists of the future when they fail.

The revolutionists are accused of striking terror. Every barricade seems an outrage. Their theories are incriminated, their aim is suspected, their afterthought is dreaded, their conscience is denounced. They are reproached with raising, building, and heaping up against the reigning social state a mound of miseries, of sorrows, of iniquities, of griefs, of despairs, and with tearing up blocks of darkness from the lower depths with which to entrench themselves and to fight. Men cry to them: "You are unpaving hell!" They might answer: "That is why our barricade is made of good intentions."

The best, certainly, is the peaceable solution. On the whole, let us admit, when we see the pavement, we think of the bear, and his is a willingness about which society is not at ease. But the salvation of society depends upon itself, to its own willingness we appeal. No violent remedy is necessary. Study evil lovingly, determine it, then cure it. To that we urge.

However this may be, even when fallen, especially when fallen, august are they who, upon all points of the world, with eyes fixed on France, struggle for the great work with the inflexible logic of the ideal; they give their life a pure gift for progress; they accomplish the will of Providence; they perform a religious act. At the appointed hour, with as much disinterestedness as an actor who reaches his cue, obedient to the divine scenario, they enter into the tomb. And this hopeless combat, and this stoical disappearance, they accept to lead to its splendid and supreme universal consequences the magnificent movement of man, irresistibly commenced on the 14th of July, 1789; these soldiers are priests. The French Revolution is an act of God.

Still, there are, and it is proper to add this distinction to the distinctions already indicated in another chapter, there are accepted insurrections which are called revolutions; there are rejected revolutions which are called émeutes. An insurrection breaking out is an idea passing its examination before the people. If the people drops its black ball, the idea is withered fruit; the insurrection is an affray.

To go to war upon every summons and whenever Utopia desires it, is not the part of the peoples. The nations have not always and at every hour the temperament of heroes and of martyrs.

They are positive. A priori, insurrection repels them; first, because it often results in disaster, secondly, because it always has an abstraction for its point of departure.

For, and this is beautiful, it is always for the ideal, and for the ideal alone, that those devote themselves who do devote themselves. An insurrection is an enthusiasm. Enthusiasm may work itself into anger; hence the resort to arms. But every insurrection which is directed against a government or a régime aims still higher. Thus, for instance, let us repeat what the chiefs of the insurrection of 1832, and in particular the young enthusiasts of the Rue de la Chanvrerie, fought against, was not exactly Louis Philippe. Most of them, speaking frankly, rendered justice to the qualities of this king, midway between the monarchy and the revolution; none hated him. But they attacked the younger branch of divine right in Louis Philippe as they had attacked the elder branch in Charles X.; and what they desired to overthrow in overthrowing royalty in France as we have explained, was the usurpation of man over man, and of privilege over right, in the whole world. Paris without a king has, as a consequence, the world without despots. They reasoned in this way. Their aim was distant doubtless, vague perhaps, and receding before effort, but great.

Thus it is. And men sacrifice themselves for these visions, which, to the sacrificed, are illusions almost always, but illusions with which, upon the whole, all human certainty is mingled. The insurgent poetises and gilds the insurrection. He throws himself into these tragic things, intoxicated with what he is going to do. Who knows? they will succeed perhaps. They are but few; they have against them a whole army; but they defend right, natural law, that sovereignty of each over himself, of which there is no abdication possible, justice, truth, and in case of need they die like the three hundred Spartans. They think not of Don Quixote, but of Leonidas. And they go forward, and, once engaged, they do not recoil, and they hurl themselves headlong, hoping for unparalleled victory, revolution completed, progress set at liberty, the aggrandisement of the human race, universal deliverance; and seeing at the worst a Thermopylæ.

These passages at arms for progress often fail; why, we have just told. The throng is restive under the sway of the paladins. The heavy masses, the multitudes, fragile on account of their very weight, dread uncertainties; and there is uncertainty in the ideal.

Moreover, let it not be forgotten, interests are there, little friendly to the ideal and the emotional. Sometimes the stomach paralyses the heart.

The grandeur and the beauty of France are that she cares less for the belly than other peoples; she knots the rope about her loins more easily. She is first awake, last asleep. She goes in advance. She is a pioneer.

That is because she is an artist.

The ideal is nothing more nor less than the culminating point of logic, even as the beautiful is nothing more nor less than the summit of the true. The artist people is thus the consistent people. To love beauty is to see light. This is why the torch of Europe, that is to say, civilisation, was first borne by Greece, who passed it to Italy, who passed it to France. Divine pioneer peoples! *Vitai lampada tradunt!*

An admirable thing, the poetry of a people is the element of its progress. The amount of civilisation is measured by the amount of imagination. Only a civilising people must remain a manly people. Corinth, yes; Sybaris, no. He who becomes effeminate becomes corrupt. We must be neither dilettanti nor virtuosi; but we must be artists. In the matter of civilisation, we must not refine, but we must sublime. On this condition, we give the human race the pattern of the ideal.

The modern ideal has its type in art, and its means in science. It is through science that we shall realise that august vision of the poets: social beauty. We shall reproduce Eden by A + B. At the point which civilisation has reached, the exact is a necessary element of the splendid, and the artistic sentiment is not merely served, but completed by the scientific organ; dream must calculate. Art, which is the conqueror, must have its fulcrum in science, which is the mover. The solidity of the mounting is important. The modern spirit is the genius of Greece with the genius of India for its vehicle; Alexander upon the elephant.

Races petrified in dogma or demoralised by lucre are unfit to lead civilisation. Genuflexion before the idol or the dollar atrophies the muscle which walks and the will which goes. Hieratic or mercantile absorption diminishes the radiance of a people, lowers its horizon by lowering its level, and deprives it of that intelligence of the universal aim, at the same time human and divine, which makes the missionary nations. Babylon has no ideal. Carthage has no ideal. Athens and Rome have and preserve, even through all the thick night of centuries, haloes of civilisation.

France is of the same quality of people as Greece and Italy. She is Athenian by the beautiful, and Roman by the great. In addition she is good. She gives herself. She is oftener than other peoples in the spirit of devotion and sacrifice. Only this spirit takes her and leaves her. And here lies the great peril for those who run when she wishes to walk, or who walk when she wishes to stop. France has her relapses of materialism, and, at certain moments, the ideas which obstruct that sublime brain lose all that recalls French greatness, and are of the dimensions of a Missouri or of a South Carolina. What is to be done? The giantess is playing the dwarf; immense France has her childish whims. That is all.

To this nothing can be said. A people, like a star, has the right of eclipse. And all is well, provided the light return and the eclipse do not degenerate into night. Dawn and resurrection are synonyms. The reappearance of the light is identical with the persistence of the Me.

Let us lay down these things with calmness. Death on the barricade, or a grave in exile, is an acceptable alternative for devotion. The true name of devotion is disinterestedness. Let the abandoned submit to abandonment, let the exile submit to exile, and let us content ourselves with imploring the great peoples not to recede too far, when they do recede. They must not, under pretext of a return to reason, go too far in the descent.

Matter is, the moment is, interest is, the belly is; but the belly must not be the only wisdom. The momentary life has its rights, we admit, but the permanent life has its also. Alas! to have risen does not prevent falling. We see this in history oftener than we would wish. A nation is illustrious; it tastes the ideal; then it bites the filth, and finds it good; and if we ask why it abandons Socrates for Falstaff, it answers: "Because I love statesmen."

A word more before returning to the conflict.

A battle like this which we are now describing is nothing but a convulsive movement towards the ideal. Enfettered progress is sickly, and it has these tragic epilepsies. This disease of progress, civil war, we have had to encounter upon our passage. It is one of the fatal phases, at once act and interlude, of this drama, the pivot of which is a social outcast, and the true title of which is: *Progress.*

Progress!

This cry which we often raise, is our whole thought; and, at the present point of this drama, the idea that it contains having still more than one ordeal to undergo, it is permitted us perhaps, if not to lift the veil from it, at least to let the light shine clearly through.

The book which the reader has now before his eyes is, from one end to the other, in its whole and in its details, whatever may be the intermissions, the exceptions, or the defaults, the march from evil to good, from injustice to justice, from the false to the true, from night to day, from appetite to conscience, from rottenness to life, from brutality to duty, from Hell to Heaven, from nothingness to God. Starting point: matter; goal: the soul; hydra at the begining, angel at the end.

XXI
THE HEROES

SUDDENLY the drum beat the charge.

The attack was a hurricane. In the evening, in the obscurity, the barricade had been approached silently as if by a boa. Now, in broad day, in this open street, surprise was entirely impossible; the strong hand, moreover, was unmasked, the cannon had commenced the roar, the army rushed upon the barricade. Fury was now skill. A powerful column of infantry of the line, intersected at equal intervals by National Guards and Municipal Guards on foot, and supported by deep masses heard but unseen, turned into the street at a quick step, drums beating, trumpets sounding, bayonets fixed, sappers at their head, and, unswerving under the projectiles, came straight upon the barricade with the weight of a bronze column upon a wall.

The wall held well.

The insurgents fired impetuously. The barricade scaled was like a mane of flashes. The assault was so sudden that for a moment it was overflowed by assailants; but it shook off the soldiers as the lion does the dogs, and it was covered with besiegers only as a cliff is with foam, to reappear, a moment afterwards, steep, black, and formidable.

The column, compelled to fall back, remained massed in the street, unsheltered, but terrible, and replied to the redoubt by a fearful fusillade. Whoever has seen fireworks remembers that sheaf made by a crossing of flashes which is called the bouquet. Imagine the bouquet, not now vertical, but horizontal, bearing a ball, a buckshot, or a bullet, at the point of each of its jets of fire, and scattering death in its clusters of thunder. The barricade was beneath it.

On both sides equal resolution. Bravery there was almost barbaric, and was mingled with a sort of heroic ferocity which began with the sacrifice of itself. Those were the days when a National Guard fought like a Zouave. The troops desired to make an end of it; the insurrection desired to struggle. The acceptance of death in full youth and in full health makes a frenzy of intrepidity. Every man in this mêlée felt the aggrandisement given by the supreme hour. The street was covered with dead.

Enjolras was at one end of the barricade, and Marius at the other. Enjolras, who carried the whole barricade in his head, reserved and sheltered himself; three soldiers fell one after the other under his battlement, without even having perceived him; Marius fought without shelter. He took no aim. He stood with more than half his body above the summit of the redoubt. There is no wilder prodigal than a miser who takes the bit in his teeth; there is no man more fearful in action than a dreamer. Marius was terrible and pensive. He was in the battle as in a dream. One would have said a phantom firing a musket.

The cartridges of the besieged were becoming exhausted, not so their sarcasms. In this whirlwind of the sepulchre in which they were, they laughed.

Courfeyrac was bareheaded.

"What have you done with your hat?" inquired Bossuet.

Courfeyrac answered:

"They have knocked it off at last by their cannonade."

Or indeed they said haughty things.

"Does anybody understand these men," exclaimed Feuilly bitterly (and he cited the names, well-known names, famous even, some of the old army), "who promised to join us, and took an oath to help us, and who were bound to it in honour, and who are our generals and who abandon us!"

And Combeferre simply answered with a grave smile:

"There are people who observe the rules of honour as we observe the stars, from afar off."

The interior of the barricade was so strewn with torn cartridges that one would have said it had been snowing.

The assailants had the numbers; the insurgents the position. They were on the top of a wall, and they shot down the soldiers at the muzzles of their muskets, as they stumbled over the dead and wounded and became entangled in the escarpment. This barricade, built as it was, and admirably supported, was really one of those positions in which a handful of men hold a legion in check. Still, constantly reinforced and increasing under the shower of balls, the attacking column inexorably approached, and now, little by little, step by step, but with certainty, the army hugged the barricade as the screw hugs the wine press.

There was assault after assault. The horror continued to increase.

Then resounded over this pile of paving stones, in this Rue de la Chanvrerie, a struggle worthy of the walls of Troy. These men, wan, tattered, and exhausted, who had not eaten for twenty-four hours, who had not slept, who had but a few more shots to fire, who felt their pockets empty of cartridges, nearly all wounded, their heads or arms bound with a smutty and blackened cloth, with holes in their coats whence the blood was flowing, scarcely armed with worthless muskets and with old hacked swords, became Titans. The barricade was ten times approached, assaulted, scaled, and never taken.

To form an idea of this struggle, imagine fire applied to a

mass of terrible valour, and that you are witnessing the conflagration. It was not a combat, it was the interior of a furnace;
there mouths breathed flame; there faces were wonderful. There
the human form seemed impossible, the combatants flashed
flames, and it was terrible to see going and coming in that lurid
smoke these salamanders of the fray. The successive and simultaneous scenes of this grand slaughter, we decline to paint. The
epic alone has a right to fill twelve thousand lines with one
battle.

One would have said it was that hell of Brahminism, the most
formidable of the seventeen abysses, which the Veda calls the
Forest of Swords.

They fought breast to breast, foot to foot, with pistols, with
sabres, with fists, at a distance, close at hand, from above, from
below, from everywhere, from the roofs of the house, from the
windows of the wine-shop, from the gratings of the cellars into
which some had slipped. They were one against sixty. The
façade of Corinth, half demolished, was hideous. The window,
riddled with grape, had lost glass and sash, and was now nothing
but a shapeless hole, confusedly blocked with paving stones.
Bossuet was killed; Feuilly was killed; Courfeyrac was killed;
Joly was killed; Combeferre, pierced by three bayonet-thrusts in
the breast, just as he was lifting a wounded soldier, had only
time to look to heaven, and expired.

Marius, still fighting, was so hacked with wounds, particularly about his head, that the countenance was lost in blood, and
you would have said that he had his face covered with a red
handkerchief.

Enjolras alone was untouched. When his weapon failed, he
reached his hand to right or left, and an insurgent put whatever
weapon he could in his grasp. Of four swords, one more than
Francis I. at Marignan, he now had but one stump remaining.

Homer says: "Diomed slays Axylus, son of Teuthras, who
dwelt, in happy Arisbe; Euryalus, son of Mecisteus, extermin-
ates Dresos and Opheltios, Aesepus, and that Pedasus whom
the Naiad Abarbarea conceived by the irreproachable Bucolion;
Ulysses overthrows Pidutes of Percote; Antilochus, Ablerus;
Polypætes, Astyalus; Polydamas, Otus of Cyllene; and Teucer,
Aretaon. Meganthis dies beneath the spear of Euripylus. Aga-
memnon, king of heroes, prostrates Elatus born in the lofty city
which the sounding Satnio laves." In our old poems of exploits,

Esplandian attacks the giant Marquis Swantibore with a two-edged flame, while he defends himself by stoning the knight with the towers which he tears up. Our ancient mural frescoes show us the two dukes of Brittany and of Bourbon, armed, mailed, and crested for war, on horseback, and meeting each other, battle-axe in hand, masked with iron, booted with iron, gloved with iron, one caparisoned with ermine, the other draped with azure; Brittany with his lion between the two horns of his crown, Bourbon with a monstrous *fleur de lys* on the vizor of his casque. But to be superb, it is not necessary to bear, like Yvon, the ducal morion, to handle, like Esplandian, a living flame, or like Phyles, father of Polydamas, to have brought from Ephyræ a fine armour, a present from the king of men, Euphetes; it is enough to give life for a conviction or for a loyalty. That little artless soldier, yesterday a peasant of Beauce or Limousin, who prowls, cabbage-knife at his side, about the children's nurses in the Luxembourg, that pale young student bending over a piece of anatomy or a book, a fair-haired youth who trims his beard with scissors, take them both, breathe upon them a breath of duty, place them opposite each other in the Boucherat square or in the Cul-de-sac Blanche Mibray, and let the one fight for his flag, and the other for his ideal, and let them both imagine that they are fighting for the country; the strife will be colossal; and the shadow which will be thrown upon that great epic field where humanity is struggling, by his blue-coat and this saw-bones in quarrel, will equal the shadow which is cast by Megaryon, King of Lycia, full of tigers, wrestling body to body with the immense Ajax, equal of the gods.

XXII
FOOT TO FOOT

WHEN there were none of the chiefs alive save Enjolras and Marius, who were at the extremities of the barricade, the centre, which Courfeyrac, Joly, Bossuet, Feuilly, and Combeferre had so long sustained, gave way. The artillery, without making a practicable breach, had deeply indented the centre of the redoubt; there, the summit of the wall had disappeared under the balls, and had tumbled down; and the rubbish which had fallen, sometimes on the interior, sometimes on the exterior, had finally made, as it was heaped up, on either side of the wall, a kind of talus, both on the inside, and on the outside. The exterior talus offered an inclined plane for attack.

A final assault was now attempted, and this assault succeeded. The mass bristling with bayonets and hurled at a double-quick step, came on irresistible, and the dense battle-front of the attacking column appeared in the smoke at the top of the escarpment. This time, it was finished. The group of insurgents who defended the centre fell back pell-mell.

Then grim love of life was roused in some. Covered by the aim of that forest of muskets, several were now unwilling to die. This is a moment when the instinct of self-preservation raises a howl, and the animal reappears in the man. They were pushed back to the high six-story house which formed the rear of the redoubt. This house might be safety. This house was barricaded, and, as it were, walled in from top to bottom. Before the troops of the line would be in the interior of the redoubt, there was time for a door to open and shut, a flash was enough for that, and the door of this house, suddenly half opened and closed again immediately, to these despairing men was life. In the rear of this house, there were streets, possible flight, space. They began to strike this door with the butts of their muskets, and with kicks, calling, shouting, begging, wringing their hands. Nobody opened. From the window on the third story, the death's head looked at them.

But Enjolras and Marius, with seven or eight who had been rallied about them, sprang forward and protected them. Enjolras cried to the soldiers: "Keep back!" and an officer not obeying, Enjolras killed the officer. He was now in the little interior court of the redoubt, with his back to the house of Corinth, his sword in one hand, his carbine in the other, keeping the door of the wine-shop open while he barred it against the assailants. He cried to the despairing: "There is but one door open. This one." And, covering them with his body, alone facing a battalion, he made them pass in behind him. All rushed in, Enjolras executing with his carbine, which he now used as a cane, what cudgel-players call *la rose couverte*, beat down the bayonets about him and before him, and entered last of all; and for an instant it was horrible, the soldiers struggling to get in, the insurgents to close the door. The door was closed with such violence that, in shutting into its frame, it exposed, cut off, and adhering to the casement, the thumb and fingers of a soldier who had caught hold of it.

Marius remained without. A ball had broken his shoulder-blade; he felt that he was fainting, and that he was falling. At that moment his eyes already closed, he experienced the shock of a vigorous hand seizing him, and his fainting fit, in which he lost consciousness, left him hardly time for this thought, mingled with the last memory of Cosette: "I am taken prisoner. I shall be shot."

Enjolras, not seeing Marius among those who had taken refuge in the wine-shop, had the same idea. But they had reached that moment when each has only time to think of his own death. Enjolras fixed the bar of the door and bolted it, and fastened it with a double turn of lock and padlock, while they were beating furiously on the outside, the soldiers with the butts of their muskets, the sappers with their axes. The assailants were massed upon this door. The siege of the wine-shop was now beginning.

The soldiers, we must say, were greatly irritated.

The death of the sergeant of artillery had angered them; and then, a more deadly thing, during the few hours which preceded the attack, it had been told among them that the insurgents mutilated prisoners, and that there was in the wine-shop the body of a soldier headless. This sort of unfortunate rumour is the ordinary accompaniment of civil wars, and it was a false report of this kind which, at a later day, caused the catastrophe of the Rue Transnonain.

When the door was barricaded, Enjolras said to the rest:

"Let us sell ourselves dearly."

Then he approached the table upon which Mabeuf and Gavroche were extended. Two straight and rigid forms could be seen under the black cloth, one large, the other small, and the two faces were vaguely outlined beneath the stiff folds of the shroud. A hand projected from below the pall, and hung towards the floor. It was the old man's.

Enjolras bent down and kissed that venerable hand, as in the evening he had kissed the forehead.

They were the only kisses which he had given in his life.

We must be brief. The barricade had struggled like a gate of Thebes; the wine-shop struggled like a house of Saragossa. Such resistances are dogged. No quarter. No parley possible. They are willing to die provided they kill. When Suchet says: "Capitulate," Palafox answers: "After the war with cannon, war with the knife." Nothing was wanting to the storming of the Hucheloup wine-shop: neither the paving stones raining from the window and the roof upon the besiegers, and exasperating the soldiers by their horrible mangling, nor the shots from the cellars and the garret windows, nor fury of attack, nor rage of defence; nor, finally, when the door yielded, the frenzied madness of the extermination. The assailants, on rushing into the wine-shop, their feet entangled in the panels of the door, which were beaten in and scattered over the floor, found no combatant there. The spiral stairway, which had been cut down with the axe, lay in the middle of the basement-room, a few wounded had just expired, all who were not killed were in the first story, and there, through the hole in the ceiling, which had been the entrance for the stairway, a terrific firing broke out. It was the last of the cartridges. When they were gone, when these terrible men in their death-agony had no longer either powder or ball, each took two of those bottles reserved by Enjolras, of which we have spoken, and they defended the ascent with these frightfully fragile clubs. They were bottles of aquafortis. We describe these gloomy facts of the carnage as they are. The besieged, alas, make a weapon of everything. Greek fire did not dishonour Archimedes, boiling pitch did not dishonour Bayard. All war is appalling, and there is nothing to choose in it. The fire of the besiegers, although difficult and from below upwards, was murderous. The edge of the hole in the ceiling was very soon surrounded with the heads of the dead, from which flowed long red and reeking lines. The uproar was inexpressible; a stifled and burning smoke made night almost over this combat. Words fail to express horror when it reaches this degree. There were men no longer in this now infernal conflict. They were no longer giants against colossi. It resembled Milton and Dante rather than Homer. Demons attacked, spectres resisted.

It was the heroism of monsters.

XXIII
ORESTES FASTING AND PYLADES DRUNK

At last, mounting on each other's shoulders, helping themselves by the skeleton of the staircase, climbing up the walls, hanging to the ceiling, cutting to pieces, at the very edge of the hatchway, the last to resist, some twenty of the besiegers, soldiers, National Guards, Municipal Guards, pell-mell, most disfigured by wounds in the face of this terrible ascent, blinded with blood, furious, become savages, made an irruption into the room of the first story. There was now but a single man there on his feet, Enjolras. Without cartridges, without a sword, he had now in his hand only the barrel of his carbine, the stock of which he had broken over the heads of those who were entering. He had put the billiard-table between the assailants and himself, he had retreated to the corner of the room, and there, with proud eye, haughty head, and that stump of a weapon in his grasp, he was still so formidable that a large space was left about him. A cry arose:

"This is the chief. It is he who killed the artillery-man. As he has put himself there, it is a good place. Let him stay. Let us shoot him on the spot."

"Shoot me," said Enjolras.

And, throwing away the stump of his carbine, and folding his arms, he presented his breast.

The boldness that dies well always moves men. As soon as Enjolras had folded his arms, accepting the end, the uproar of the conflict ceased in the room, and that chaos suddenly hushed into a sort of sepulchral solemnity. It seemed as if the menacing majesty of Enjolras, disarmed and motionless, weighed upon that tumult, and as if, merely by the authority of his tranquil eye, this young man, who alone had no wound, superb, bloody, fascinating, indifferent as if he were invulnerable, compelled that sinister mob to kill him respectfully. His beauty, at that moment, augmented by his dignity, was a resplendence, and, as if he could no more be fatigued than wounded, after the terrible twenty-four hours which had just elapsed, he was fresh and rosy. It was of him perhaps that the witness spoke who said afterwards before the court-martial: "There was one insurgent whom I heard called Apollo." A National Guard who was aiming at Enjolras, dropped his weapon, saying: "It seems to me that I am shooting a flower."

Twelve men formed in platoon in the corner opposite Enjolras and made their muskets ready in silence.

Then a sergeant cried: "Take aim!"

An officer intervened.

"Wait."

And addressing Enjolras:

"Do you wish your eyes bandaged?"

"No."

"Was it really you who killed the sergeant of artillery?"

"Yes."

Within a few seconds Grantaire had awakened.

Grantaire, it will be remembered, had been asleep since the day previous in the upper room of the wine-shop, sitting in a chair, leaning heavily forward on a table.

He realised, in all its energy, strength, the old metaphor: dead drunk. The hideous potion, the absinthe-stout-alcohol, had thrown him into a lethargy. His table being small, and of no use in the barricade, they had left it to him. He had continued in the same posture, his breast doubled over the table, his head lying flat upon his arms, surrounded by glasses, jugs, and bottles. He slept with that crushing sleep of the torpid bear and the overfed leech. Nothing had affected him, neither the musketry, nor the balls, nor the grape which penetrated through the casement into the room in which he was. Nor the prodigious uproar of the assault. Only, he responded sometimes to the cannon with a snore. He seemed waiting there for a ball to come and save him the trouble of awaking. Several corpses lay about him; and, at the first glance, nothing distinguished him from those deep sleepers of death.

Noise does not waken a drunkard; silence wakens him. This peculiarity has been observed more than once. The fall of everything about him augmented Grantaire's oblivion; destruction was a lullaby to him. The kind of halt in the tumult before Enjolras was a shock to his heavy sleep. It was the effect of a wagon at a gallop stopping short. The sleepers are roused by it. Grantaire rose up with a start, stretched his arms, rubbed his eyes, looked, gaped, and understood.

Drunkenness ending is like a curtain torn away. We see altogether, and at a single glance, all that is concealed. Everything is suddenly presented to the memory; and the drunkard who knows nothing of what has taken place for twenty-four hours, has no sooner opened his eyes than he is aware of all that has passed. His ideas come back to him with an abrupt lucidity; the effacement of drunkenness, a sort of lye-wash which blinds the brain, dissipates, and give place to clear and precise impressions of the reality.

Retired as he was in a corner and as it were sheltered behind the billiard-table, the soldiers, their eyes fixed upon Enjolras, had not even noticed Grantaire, and the sergeant was preparing to repeat the order: "Take aim!" when suddenly they heard a powerful voice cry out beside them:

"*Vive la République!* I belong to it."

Grantaire had arisen.

The immense glare of the whole combat which he had missed and in which he had not been, appeared in the flashing eye of the transfigured drunkard.

He repeated: "*Vive la République!*" crossed the room with a firm step, and took his place before the muskets beside Enjolras.

"Two at one shot," said he.

And, turning towards Enjolras gently, he said to him:

"Will you permit it?"

Enjolras grasped his hand with a smile.

The smile was not finished when the report was heard.

Enjolras, pierced by eight balls, remained backed against the wall as if the balls had nailed him there. Only he bowed his head.

Grantaire, stricken down, fell at his feet.

A few moments afterwards, the soldiers dislodged the last insurgents who had taken refuge in the top of the house. They fired through a wooden lattice into the garret. They fought in the attics. They threw the bodies out of the windows, some living. Two voltigeurs, who were trying to raise the shattered omnibus, were killed by two shots from a carbine fired from the dormer-windows. A man in a blouse was pitched out headlong, with a bayonet thrust in his belly, and his death-rattle was finished upon the ground. A soldier and an insurgent slipped together on the slope of the tiled roof, and would not let go of each other, and fell, clasped in a wild embrace. Similar struggle in the cellar. Cries, shots, savage stamping. Then silence. The barricade was taken.

The soldiers commenced the search of the houses round about and the pursuit of the fugitives.

XXIV
PRISONER

MARIUS was in fact a prisoner. Prisoner of Jean Valjean.

The hand which had seized him from behind at the moment

he was falling, and the grasp of which he had felt in losing consciousness, was the hand of Jean Valjean.

Jean Valjean had taken no other part in the combat than to expose himself. Save for him, in that supreme phase of the death-struggle, nobody would have thought of the wounded. Thanks to him, everywhere present in the carnage like a providence, those who fell were taken up, carried into the basement-room, and their wounds dressed. In the intervals, he repaired the barricade. But nothing which could resemble a blow, an attack, or even a personal defence came from his hands. He was silent, and gave aid. Moreover, he had only a few scratches. The balls refused him. If suicide were a part of what had occurred to him in coming to this sepulchre, in that respect he had not succeeded. But we doubt whether he had thought of suicide, an irreligious act.

Jean Valjean, in the thick cloud of the combat, did not appear to see Marius; the fact is, that he did not take his eyes from him. When a shot struck down Marius, Jean Valjean bounded with the agility of a tiger, dropped upon him as upon a prey, and carried him away.

The whirlwind of the attack at that instant concentrated so fiercely upon Enjolras and the door of the wine-shop, that nobody saw Jean Valjean cross the unpaved field of the barricade, holding the senseless Marius in his arms, and disappear behind the corner of the house of Corinth.

It will be remembered that this corner was a sort of cape on the street; it sheltered from balls and grape, and from sight also, a few square feet of ground. Thus, there is sometimes in conflagrations a room which does not burn; and in the most furious seas, beyond a promontory or at the end of a cul-de-sac of shoals, a placid little haven. It was in this recess of the interior trapezium of the barricade that Eponine had died.

There Jean Valjean stopped; he let Marius slide to the ground, set his back to the wall, and cast his eyes about him.

The situation was appalling.

For the moment, for two or three minutes, perhaps, this skirt of wall was a shelter; but how escape from this massacre? He remembered the anguish in which he was in the Rue Polonceau, eight years before, and how he had succeeded in escaping; that was difficult then, to-day it was impossible. Before him he had that deaf and implacable house of six stories, which seemed inhabited only by the dead man, leaning over his window; on his right he had the low barricade, which closed the Petite Truanderie; to clamber over this obstacle appeared easy, but above the crest of the wall a range of bayonet-points could be seen. A company of the line was posted beyond this barricade, on the watch. It was evident that to cross the barricade was to meet the fire of a platoon, and that every head which should venture to rise above the top of the wall of paving stones would serve as a target for sixty muskets. At his left he had the field of combat. Death was behind the corner of the wall.

What should he do?

A bird alone could have extricated himself from that place.

And he must decide upon the spot, find an expedient, adopt his course. They were fighting a few steps from him; by good luck all were fiercely intent upon a single point, the door of the wine-shop; but let one soldier, a single one, conceive the idea of turning the house, of attacking it in flank, and all was over.

Jean Valjean looked at the house in front of him, he looked at the barricade by the side of him, then he looked upon the ground, with the violence of the last extremity, in desperation, and as if he would have made a hole in it with his eyes.

Beneath his persistent look, something vaguely tangible in such an agony outlined itself and took form at his feet, as if there were a power in the eye to develop the thing desired. He perceived a few steps from him, at the foot of the little wall so pitilessly watched and guarded on the outside, under some fallen paving stones which partly hid it, an iron grating laid flat and level with the ground. This grating, made of strong transverse bars, was about two feet square. The stone frame which held it had been torn up, and it was as it were unset. Through the bars a glimpse could be caught of an obscure opening, something like the flue of a chimney or the main of a cistern. Jean Valjean sprang forward. His old science of escape mounted to his brain like a flash. To remove the stones, to lift the grating, to load Marius, who was as inert as a dead body, upon his shoulders, to descend, with that burden upon his back, by the aid of his elbows and knees, into this kind of well, fortunately not very deep, to let fall over his head the heavy iron trap-door upon which the stones were shaken back again, to find a foothold upon a flagged surface ten feet below the ground, this was executed like what is done in delirium, with the strength of a giant and the rapidity of an eagle; it required but very few moments.

Jean Valjean found himself, with Marius still senseless, in a sort of long underground passage.

There, deep peace, absolute silence, night.

The impression which he had formerly felt in falling from the street into the convent came back to him. Only, what he was now carrying away was not Cosette; it was Marius.

He could now hardly hear above him, like a vague murmur, the fearful tumult of the wine-shop taken by assault.

BOOK SECOND –
THE INTESTINE OF LEVIATHAN

I
THE EARTH IMPOVERISHED BY THE SEA

PARIS throws five millions a year into the sea. And this without metaphor. How, and in what manner? day and night. With what object? without any object. With what thought? without thinking of it. For what return? for nothing. By means of what organ? by means of its intestine. What is its intestine? its sewer.

Five millions is the most moderate of the approximate figures which the estimates of special science give.

Science, after long experiment, now knows that the most fertilising and the most effective of manures is that of man. The Chinese we must say to our shame, knew it before us. No Chinese peasant, Eckeberg tells us, goes to the city without carrying back, at the two ends of his bamboo, two buckets full of what we call filth. Thanks to human fertilisation, the earth in China is still as young as in the days of Abraham. Chinese wheat yields a hundred and twenty fold. There is no guano comparable in fertility to the detritus of capital. A great city is the most powerful of stercoraries. To employ the city to enrich the plain would be a sure success. If our gold is filth, on the other hand, our filth is gold.

What is done with this filth, gold? It is swept into the abyss.

We fit out convoys of ships, at great expense, to gather up at the south pole the droppings of petrels and penguins, and the incalculable element of wealth which we have under our own hand, we send to the sea. All the human and animal manure which the world loses, restored to the land instead of being thrown into the water, would suffice to nourish the world.

These heaps of garbage at the corners of the stone blocks, these tumbrils of mire jolting through the streets at night, these horrid scavengers' carts, these fetid streams of subterranean slime which the pavement hides from you, do you know what all this is? It is the flowering meadow, it is the green grass, it is marjoram and thyme and sage, it is game, it is cattle, it is the satisfied low of huge oxen at evening, it is perfumed hay, it is golden corn, it is bread on your table, it is warm blood in your veins, it is health, it is joy, it is life. Thus wills that mysterious creation which is transformation upon earth and transfiguration in heaven.

Put that into the great crucible; your abundance shall spring from it. The nutrition of the plains makes the nourishment of men.

You have the power to throw away this wealth, and to think me ridiculous into the bargain. That will cap the climax of your ignorance.

Statistics show that France, alone, makes a liquidation of a hundred millions every year into the Atlantic from the mouths of her rivers. Mark this: with that hundred millions you might pay a quarter of the expenses of the government. The cleverness of man is such that he prefers to throw this hundred millions into the gutter. It is the very substance of the people which is carried away, here drop by drop, there in floods, by the wretched vomiting of our sewers into the rivers, and the gigantic collection of our rivers into the ocean. Each hiccough of our cloaca costs us a thousand francs. From this two results: the land impoverished and the water infected. Hunger rising from the furrow and disease rising from the river.

It is notorious, for instance, that at this hour the Thames is poisoning London.

As for Paris, it has been necessary within a few years past, to carry most of the mouths of the sewers down the stream below the last bridge.

A double tubular arrangement, provided with valves and sluiceways, sucking up and flowing back, a system of elementary drainage, as simple as the lungs of man, and which is already in full operation in several villages in England, would suffice to bring into our cities the pure water of the fields and send back into our fields the rich water of the cities; and this easy seesaw, the simplest in the world, would retain in our possession the hundred millions thrown away. We are thinking of something else.

The present system does harm in endeavouring to do good. The intention is good, the result is sad. Men think they are purging the city, they are emaciating the population. A sewer is a mistake. When drainage everywhere, with its double function, restoring what it takes away, shall have replaced the sewer, that simple impoverishing washing, then, this being combined with the data of a new social economy, the products of the earth will be increased tenfold, and the problem of misery will be wonderfully diminished. Add the suppression of parasitism, it will be solved.

In the meantime, the public wealth runs off into the river, and the leakage continues. Leakage is the word. Europe is ruining herself in this way by exhaustion.

As for France, we have just named her figure. Now, Paris containing a twenty-fifth of the total French population, and the Parisian guano being the richest of all, we are within the truth in estimating at five millions the portion of Paris in the loss of the hundred millions which France annually throws away. These five millions, employed in aid and in enjoyment, would double the splendour of Paris. The city expends them in cloacæ. So that we may say that the great prodigality of Paris, her marvellous fête, her Beaujon folly, her orgy, her full-handed outpouring of gold, her pageant, her luxury, her magnificence, is her sewer.

It is in this way that, in the blindness of a vicious political economy, we drown and let float down stream and be lost in the depths, the welfare of all. There should be Saint Cloud nettings for the public fortune.

Economically, the fact may be summed up thus: Paris a leaky basket.

Paris, that model city, that pattern of well-formed capitals of which every people endeavours to have a copy, that metropolis of the ideal, that august country of the initiative, of impulse and enterprise, that centre and that abode of mind, that nation city, that hive of the future, that marvellous compound of Babylon and Corinth, from the point of view which we have just indicated, would make a peasant of Fok-ian shrug his shoulders.

Imitate Paris, you will ruin yourself.

Moreover, particularly in this immemorial and senseless waste, Paris herself imitates.

These surprising absurdities are not new; there is no young folly in this. The ancients acted like the moderns. "The cloacæ of Rome," says Liebig, "absorbed all the well-being of the Roman peasant." When the Campagna of Rome was ruined by the Roman sewer, Rome exhausted Italy, and when she had put Italy into her cloaca, she poured Sicily in, then Sardinia, then Africa. The sewer of Rome engulfed the world. This cloaca offered its maw to the city and to the globe. *Urbi et orbi.* Eternal city, unfathomable sewer.

In these things, as well as in others, Rome sets the example.

This example, Paris follows, with all the stupidity peculiar to cities of genius.

For the necessities of the operation which we have just explained, Paris has another Paris under herself, a Paris of sewers; which has its streets, its crossings, its squares, its blind alleys, its arteries, and its circulation, which is slime, minus the human form.

For we must flatter nothing, not even a great people; where there is everything, there is ignominy by the side of sublimity; and, if Paris contains Athens, the city of light, Tyre, the city of power, Sparta, the city of manhood, Nineveh, the city of prodigy, it contains also Lutetia, the city of mire.

Besides, the seal of her power is there also, and the titanic sink of Paris realises, among monuments, that strange ideal realised in humanity by some men, such as Machiavelli, Bacon, and Mirabeau: the sublimity of abjectness.

The subsoil of Paris, if the eye could penetrate the surface, would present the aspect of a colossal madrepore. A sponge has hardly more defiles and passages than the tuft of earth of fifteen miles' circuit upon which rests the ancient great city. Without speaking of the catacombs, which are a cave apart, without speaking of the inextricable trellis of the gas-pipes, without counting the vast tubular system for the distribution of living water which ends in the hydrants, the sewers of themselves alone form a prodigious dark network under both banks; a labyrinth the descent of which is its clue.

There is seen, in the humid haze, the rat, which seems the product of the accouchement of Paris.

II

THE ANCIENT HISTORY OF THE SEWER

IMAGINE Paris taken off like a cover, a bird's-eye view of the subterranean network of the sewers will represent upon either bank a sort of huge branch engrafted upon the river. Upon the right bank the belt-sewer will be the trunk of this branch, the secondary conduits will be the limbs, and the primary drains will be the twigs.

This figure is only general and half exact, the right angle,

which is the ordinary angle of this kind of underground ramification, being very rare in vegetation.

We shall form an image more closely resembling this strange
geometric plan by supposing that we see spread upon a background of darkness some grotesque alphabet of the East jumbled
as in a medley, the shapeless letters of which are joined to each
other, apparently pell-mell and as if by chance, sometimes by
their corners, sometimes by their extremities.

The sinks and the sewers played an important part in the
Middle Ages, in the Lower Empire, and in the ancient East. In
them pestilence was born, in them despots died. The multitudes
regarded almost with a religious awe these beds of corruption,
monstrous cradles of death. The pit of vermin of Benares is not
less bewildering than the Pit of Lions of Babylon. Tiglath
Pilezer, according to the Rabbinical books, swore by the sink of
Nineveh. It was from the sewer of Münster that John of Leyden
made his false moon rise, and it was from the cloaca pit of
Kekhschab that his eastern Menæchmus, Mokannah, the veiled
prophet of Khorassan, made his false sunrise.

The history of men is reflected in the history of cloacæ. The
Gemoniæ describe Rome. The sewer of Paris has been a terrible
thing in time past. It has been a sepulchre, it has been an asylum.
Crime, intelligence, social protest, liberty of conscience, thought,
theft, all that human laws pursue or have pursued, have hidden in
this hole; the Maillotins in the fourteenth century, the Tirelaines
in the fifteenth, the Huguenots in the sixteenth, the Illuminati of
Morin in the seventeenth, the Chauffeurs in the eighteenth. A
hundred years ago, the blow of the dagger by night came thence,
the pickpocket in danger glided thither; the forest had its cave;
Paris had its sewer. Vagabondage, that Gallic *picareria*, accepted
the sewer as an affiliation of the Cour des Miracles, and at night,
crafty and ferocious, returned into the Maubué vomitoria as into
an alcove.

It was quite natural that those whose field of daily labour
was the Cul-de-sac Vide-Gousset, or the Rue Coupe-Gorge,
should have for their nightly abode the culvert of the Chemin
Vert or the Hurepoix kennel. Hence a swarm of traditions. All
manner of phantoms haunt these long solitary corridors, putrid-
ity and miasma everywhere; here and there a breathing-hole
through which Villon within chats with Rabelais without.

The sewer, in old Paris, is the rendezvous of all drainages

and all assays. Political economy sees in it a detritus, social philosophy sees in it a residuum.

The sewer is the conscience of the city. All things converge into it and are confronted with one another. In this lurid place there is darkness, but there are no secrets. Everything has its real form, or at least its definitive form. This can be said for the garbage-heap, that it is no liar. Frankness has taken refuge in it. Basil's mask is found there, but we see the pasteboard, and the strings, and the inside as well as the outside, and it is emphasised with honest mud. Scapin's false nose is close by. All the uncleannesses of civilisation when once out of service, fall into this pit of truth, where the immense social slipping is brought to an end. They are swallowed up, but they are displayed in it. This pell-mell is a confession. Here, no more false appearances, no possible plastering, the filth takes off its shirt, absolute nakedness, rout of illusions and of mirages, nothing more but what is, wearing the sinister face of what is ending. Reality and disappearance. Here, the stump of a bottle confesses drunkenness, the handle of a basket tells of domestic life; here, the apple core which has had literary opinions becomes again an apple core; the face on the big sou freely covers itself with verdigris, the spittle of Caïaphas encounters Falstaff's vomit, the louis d'or which comes from the gaming-house jostles the nail from which hangs the suicide's bit of rope, a livid fœtus rolls by wrapped in the spangles which danced at the opera last Mardi Gras, a cap which has judged men wallows near a rottenness which was one of Peggy's petticoats; it is more than brotherhood, it is the closest intimacy. All that paints besmears. The last veil is rent. A sewer is a cynic. It tells all.

This sincerity of uncleanness pleases us, and is a relief to the soul. When a man has passed his time on the earth in enduring the spectacle of the grand airs which are assumed by reasons of state, oaths, political wisdom, human justice, professional honesty, the necessities of position, incorruptible robes, it is a consolation to enter a sewer and see the slime which befits it.

It is a lesson at the same time. As we have just said, history passes through the sewer. The Saint Bartholomews filter drop by drop through the pavements. The great public assassinations, the political and religious butcheries, traverse this vault of civilisation, and push their dead into it. To the reflecting eye, all the historic murderers are there, in the hideous gloom, on their

knees, with a little of their shroud for an apron, dolefully spong-
ing their work. Louis XI. is there with Tristan, Francis I. is there
with Duprat, Charles IX. is there with his mother, Richelieu is
there with Louis XIII., Louvois is there, Letellier is there, Hébert and Maillard are there, scraping the stones, and endeavouring
to efface all trace of their deeds. Beneath these vaults we hear
the broom of these spectres. We breathe the enormous fetidness
of social catastrophes. We see reddish reflections in the corners.
There flows a terrible water, in which bloody hands have been
washed.

The social observer should enter these shades. They are part
of his laboratory. Philosophy is the microscope of thought.
Everything desires to flee from it, but nothing escapes it. Tergiversation is useless. What phase of your character do you show
in tergiversation? the shameful phase. Philosophy pursues evil
with its rigid search, and does not permit it to glide away into
nothingness. In the effacement of things which disappear, in
the lessening of those which vanish, it recognises everything. It
reconstructs the purple from the rag and the woman from the
tatter. With the cloaca it reproduces the city; with the mire it
reproduces its customs. From a fragment it infers the amphora,
or the pitcher. It recognises by the print of a finger nail upon a
parchment the difference between the Jewry of the Judengasse
and the Jewry of the Ghetto. It finds in what remains what has
been, the good, the ill, the false, the true, the stain of blood in
the palace, the blot of ink in the cavern, the drop of grease
in the brothel, trials undergone, temptations welcomed, orgies
spewed out, the wrinkles which characters have received in
abasing themselves, the trace of prostitution in souls which their
own grossness has made capable of it, and, on the vest of the
porters of Rome, the mark of Messalina's elbow.

III
BRUNESEAU

THE sewer of Paris, in the Middle Ages, was legendary. In the
sixteenth century, Henry II. attempted an examination, which
failed. Less than a hundred years ago, the cloaca, Mercier bears
witness, was abandoned to itself, and became what it might.

Such was that ancient Paris, given up to quarrels, to indeci-
sions, and to gropings. It was for a long time stupid enough.

Afterwards, '89 showed how cities come to their wits. But, in the good old times, the capital had little head; she could not manage her affairs either morally or materially, nor better sweep away her filth than her abuses. Everything was an obstacle, everything raised a question. The sewer, for instance, was refractory to all itinerary. Men could no more succeed in guiding themselves through its channels than in understanding themselves in the city; above, the unintelligible, below, the inextricable; beneath the confusion of tongues there was the confusion of caves; Labyrinth lined Babel.

Sometimes, the sewer of Paris took it into its head to overflow, as if that unappreciated Nile were suddenly seized with wrath. There were, infamous to relate, inundations from the sewer. At intervals, this stomach of civilisation digested badly, the cloaca flowed back into the city's throat, and Paris had the aftertaste of its slime. These resemblances of the sewer to remorse had some good in them; they were warnings; very badly received, however; the city was indignant that its mire should have so much audacity, and did not countenance the return of the ordure. Drive it away better.

The inundation of 1802 is a present reminiscence with Parisians of eighty. The mire spread out in a cross in the Place des Victoires, where the statue of Louis XIV. is; it entered the Rue Saint Honoré by the two mouths of the sewer of the Champs-Elysées, the Rue Saint Florentin by the Saint Florentin sewer, the Rue Pierre à Poisson by the sewer of the Sonnerie, the Rue Popincourt by the sewer of the Chemin Vert, the Rue de la Roquette by the sewer of the Rue de Sappe; it covered the curbstones of the Rue des Champs-Elysées to the depth of some fourteen inches; and, on the south, by the vomitoria of the Seine performing its function in the inverse way, it penetrated the Rue Mazarine, the Rue de l'Echaudé, and the Rue des Marais, where it stopped, having reached the length of a hundred and twenty yards, just a few steps from the house which Racine had lived in, respecting, in the seventeenth century, the poet more than the king. It attained its maximum depth in the Rue Saint Pierre, where it rose three feet above the flagging of the water-spouts, and its maximum extent in the Rue Saint Sabin, where it spread out over a length of two hundred and sixty-one yards.

At the commencement of this century, the sewer of Paris was

still a mysterious place. Mire can never be in good repute; but here ill-fame reached even fright. Paris dimly realised that she had a terrible cave beneath her. People talked of it as of that monstrous bog of Thebes which swarmed with scolopendras fifteen feet long, and which might have served as a bathing-tub for Behemoth. The big boots of the sewer-men never ventured beyond certain known points. They were still very near the time when the scavengers' tumbrils, from the top of which Sainte Foix fraternised with the Marquis of Créqui, were simply emptied into the sewer. As for cleansing, that operation was confided to the showers, which obstructed more than they swept out. Rome still left some poetry to her cloaca, and called it Gemoniæ; Paris insulted hers and called it the Stink-Hole. Science and superstitions were at one in regard to the horror. The Stink-Hole was not less revolting to hygiene than to legend. The Goblin Monk had appeared under the fetid arch of the Mouffetard sewer; the corpses of the Marmousets had been thrown into the sewer of the Barillerie; Fagon had attributed the fearful malignant fever of 1685 to the great gap in the sewer of the Marais which remained yawning until 1833, in the Rue Saint Louis, almost in front of the sign of the Gallant Messenger. The mouth of the sewer of the Rue de la Mortellerie was famous for the pestilence which came from it; with its pointed iron grating which looked like a row of teeth, it lay in that fatal street like the jaws of a dragon blowing hell upon men. The popular imagination seasoned the gloomy Parisian sink with an indefinably hideous mixture of the infinite. The sewer was bottomless. The sewer was the barathrum. The idea of exploring these leprous regions did not occur even to the police. To tempt that unknown, to throw the lead into that darkness, to go on a voyage of discovery in that abyss, who would have dared? It was frightful. Somebody came forward, however. The cloaca had its Columbus.

One day in 1805, on one of those rare visits which the emperor made to Paris, the Minister of the Interior came to the master's private audience. In the carousel was heard the clatter of the swords of all those marvellous soldiers of the Grand Republic and the Grand Empire; there was a multitude of heroes at the door of Napoleon; men of the Rhine, of the Scheldt, of the Adige, and of the Nile; companions of Joubert, of Desaix, of Marceau, of Hoche, of Kléber; balloonists of

Fleurus; grenadiers of Mayence, pontooniers of Genoa, hussars whom the Pyramids had beheld, artillery-men whom Junot's ball had bespattered, cuirassiers who had taken by assault the fleet at anchor in the Zuyder Zee; these had followed Bonaparte over the bridge of Lodi, those had been with Murat in the trenches of Mantua, others had preceded Lannes in the sunken road of Montebello. The whole army of that time was there, in the Court of the Tuileries, represented by a squad or a platoon, guarding Napoleon in repose; and it was the splendid epoch when the grand army had behind it Marengo and before it Austerlitz. "Sire," said the Minister of the Interior to Napoleon, "I saw yesterday the boldest man in your empire." "Who is the man," said the emperor quickly, "and what has he done?" "He wishes to do something, sire." "What?" "To visit the sewers of Paris."

That man existed, and his name was Bruneseau.

IV
DETAILS IGNORED

THE visit was made. It was a formidable campaign; a night battle against pestilence and asphyxia. It was at the same time a voyage of discoveries. One of the survivors of this exploration, an intelligent working-man, then very young, still related a few years ago the curious details which Bruneseau thought it his duty to omit in his report to the prefect of police, as unworthy of the administrative style. Disinfecting processes were very rudimentary at that period. Hardly had Bruneseau passed the first branchings of the subterranean network, when eight out of the twenty labourers refused to go further. The operation was complicated; the visit involved the cleaning; it was necessary therefore to clean, and at the same time to measure; to note the entrance of water, to count the gratings and the mouths, to detail the branchings, to indicate the currents at the points of separation, to examine the respective borders of the various basins, to fathom the little sewers engrafted upon the principal sewer, to measure the height of each passage under the keystone, and the width, as well at the spring of the arch as at the level of the floor, finally to determine the ordinates of the levellings at a right angle with each entrance of water, either from the floor of the sewer, or from the surface of the street. They advanced with difficulty. It was not uncommon for the step ladders to plunge into three feet of mire. The lanterns flickered in the miasmas. From time to time, they brought out a sewerman who had fainted. At certain places, a precipice. The soil had sunken, the pavement had crumbled, the sewer had changed into a blind well; they found no solid ground; one man suddenly disappeared; they had great difficulty in recovering him. By the advice of Fourcroy, they lighted from point to point, in the places sufficiently purified, great cages full of oakum and saturated with resin. The wall, in places, was covered with shapeless fungi, and one would have said with tumours; the stone itself seemed diseased in this irrespirable medium.

Bruneseau, in his exploration, proceeded from the head towards the mouth. At the point of separation of the two water pipes from the Grand Hurleur, he deciphered upon a projecting stone the date 1550; this stone indicated the limit reached by Philibert Delorme, who was charged by Henry II. with visiting the subterranean canals of Paris. This stone was the mark of the sixteenth century upon the sewer; Bruneseau also found the handiwork of the seventeenth century, in the conduit of the Ponceau and the conduit of the Rue Vieille du Temple, built between 1600 and 1650, and the handiwork of the eighteenth century in the western section of the collecting canal, banked up and arched in 1740. These two arches, especially the later one, that of 1740, were more cracked and more dilapidated than the masonry of the belt sewer, which dated from 1412, the epoch when the fresh-water brook of Ménilmontant was raised to the dignity of Grand Sewer of Paris, an advancement analogous to that of a peasant who should become first valet de chambre to the king; something like Gros Jean transformed into Lebel.

They thought they recognised here and there, chiefly under the Palais de Justice, some cells of ancient dungeons built in the sewer itself. Hideous *in pace*. An iron collar hung in one of these cells. They walled them all up. Some odd things were found; among other things the skeleton of an ourang-outang which disappeared from the Jardin des Plantes in 1800, a disappearance probably connected with the famous and incontestable appearance of the devil in the Rue des Bernardins in the last year of the eighteenth century. The poor devil finally drowned himself in the sewer.

Under the long arched passage which terminates at the Arche Marion, a ragpicker's basket, in perfect preservation, was the admiration of connoisseurs. Everywhere, the mud, which the workmen had come to handle boldly, abounded in precious objects, gold and silver trinkets, precious stones, coins. A giant who should have filtered this cloaca would have had the riches of centuries in his sieve. At the point of separation of the two branches of the Rue du Temple and the Rue Sainte Avoye, they picked up a singular Huguenot medal in copper, bearing on one side a hog wearing a cardinal's hat, and on the other a wolf with the tiara on his head.

The most surprising discovery was at the entrance of the Grand Sewer. This entrance had been formerly closed by a grating, of which the hinges only remained. Hanging to one of these hinges was a sort of shapeless and filthy rag, which, doubtless, caught there on its passage, had fluttered in the darkness, and was finally worn to tatters. Bruneseau approached his lantern to this strip and examined it. It was of very fine cambric, and they made out at the least worn of the corners a heraldic crown embroidered above these seven letters: LAVBESP. The crown was a marquis's crown, and the seven letters signified *Laubespine*. They recognised that what they had before their eyes was a piece of Marat's winding-sheet. Marat, in his youth, had had his amours. It was when he made a portion of the household of the Count d'Artois in the capacity of physician of the stables. From these amours, a matter of history, with a great lady, there remained to him this sheet. Waif or souvenir. At his death, as it was the only fine linen he had in the house, he was shrouded in it. Old women dressed out for the tomb, in this cloth in which there had been pleasure, the tragic Friend of the People. Bruneseau passed on. They left this scrap where it was; they did not make an end of it. Was this contempt or respect? Marat deserved both. And then, destiny was so imprinted upon it that they might hesitate to touch it. Besides, we should leave the things of the grave in the place which they choose. In short, the relic was strange. A marchioness had slept upon it; Marat had rotted in it; it had passed through the Pantheon to come at last to the rats of the sewer. This rag of the alcove, every fold of which Watteau would once have gladly sketched, had at last become worthy of Dante's fixed regard.

The complete visitation of the subterranean sewer system of

Paris occupied seven years, from 1805 to 1812. While yet he was performing it, Bruneseau laid out, directed, and brought to an end some considerable works; in 1808 he lowered the floor of the Ponceau, and creating new lines everywhere, he extended the sewer, in 1809, under the Rue St. Denis as far as the Fontaine des Innocents; in 1810, under the Rue Froidmanteau and under La Salpêtrière; in 1811, under the Rue Neuve des Petits Pères, the Rue du Mail, the Rue de l'Echarpe, and the Place Royale; in 1812, under the Rue de la Paix and the Chaussée d'Antin. At the same time, he disinfected and purified the whole network. After the second year, Bruneseau was assisted by his son-in-law Nargaud.

Thus, at the beginning of this century, the old society cleansed its double bottom and made the toilette of its sewer. It was always so much cleaned.

Tortuous, fissured, unpaved, crackling, interrupted by quagmires, broken by fantastic elbows, rising and falling out of all rule, fetid, savage, wild, submerged, in obscurity, with scars on its pavements and gashes on its walls, appalling, such was, seen retrospectively, the ancient sewer of Paris. Ramifications in every direction, crossings of trenches, branchings, goose-tracks, stars as if in mines, cœcums, cul-de-sacs, arches covered with saltpetre, infectious cesspools, a herpetic ooze upon the walls, drops falling from the ceiling, darkness; nothing equalled the horror of this old voiding crypt, the digestive apparatus of Babylon, cavern, grave, gulf pierced with streets, titanic molehill, in which the mind seems to see prowling through the shadow, in the ordure which has been splendour, that enormous blind mole, the past.

This, we repeat, was the sewer of former times.

V
PRESENT PROGRESS

At present the sewer is neat, cold, straight, correct. It almost realises the ideal of what is understood in England by the word "respectable." It is comely and sober; drawn by the line; we might almost say fresh from the band-box. It is like a contractor become a councillor of state. We almost see clearly in it. The filth comports itself decently. At the first glance, we should readily take it for one of those underground passages formerly so common and so useful for the flight of monarchs and princes, in that good old time "when the people loved their kings." The present sewer is a beautiful sewer; the pure style reigns in it; the classic rectilinear alexandrine which, driven from poetry, appears to have taken refuge in architecture, seems mingled with every stone of that long darkling and whitish arch; each discharging mouth is an arcade; the Rue de Rivoli rules the school even in the cloaca. However, if the geometric line is in place anywhere, it surely is in the stercorary trenches of a great city. There, all should be subordinated to the shortest road. The sewer has now assumed a certain official aspect. The very police reports of which it is sometimes the object are no longer wanting in respect for it. The words which characterise it in the administrative language are elevated and dignified. What was called a gut is called a gallery; what was called a hole is called a vista. Villon would no longer recognise his old dwelling in case of need. This network of caves has still indeed its immemorial population of rodents, swarming more than ever; from time to time, a rat, an old moustache, risks his head at the window of the sewer and examines the Parisians; but these vermin themselves have grown tame, content as they are with their subterranean palace. The cloaca has now nothing of its primitive ferocity. The rain, which befouled the sewer of former times, washes the sewer of the present day. Do not trust in it too much, however. Miasmas still inhabit it. It is rather hypocritical than irreproachable. The prefecture of police and the health commission have laboured in vain. In spite of all the processes of purification, it exhales a vague odour, suspicious as Tartuffe, after confession.

Let us admit, as, all things considered, street-cleaning is a homage which the sewer pays to civilisation, and as, from this point of view, Tartuffe's conscience is an advance upon Augeas' stable, it is certain that the sewer of Paris has been ameliorated.

It is more than an advance; it is a transmutation. Between the ancient sewer and the present sewer, there is a revolution. Who has wrought this revolution?

The man whom everybody forgets, and whom we have named. Bruneseau.

VI
FUTURE PROGRESS

THE excavation of the sewer of Paris has been no small work. The last ten centuries have laboured upon it, without being able to complete it any more than to finish Paris. The sewer, indeed, receives all the impulsions of the growth of Paris. It is, in the earth, a species of dark polyp with a thousand antennæ which grows beneath at the same time that the city grows above. Whenever the city opens a street, the sewer puts out an arm. The old monarchy had constructed only twenty-five thousand four hundred and eighty yards of sewers; Paris was at that point on the 1st of January, 1806. From that epoch, of which we shall speak again directly, the work was profitably and energetically resumed and continued; Napoleon built, the figures are interesting, five thousand two hundred and fifty-four yards; Louis XVIII., six thousand two hundred and forty-four; Charles X., eleven thousand eight hundred and fifty-one, Louis Philippe, ninety-seven thousand three hundred and fifty-five; the Republic of 1848, twenty-five thousand five hundred and seventy; the existing régime, seventy-seven thousand one hundred; in all, at the present hour, two hundred and forty-seven thousand eight hundred and twenty-eight yards; a hundred and forty miles of sewers; the enormous entrails of Paris. Obscure ramification always at work; unnoticed and immense construction.

As we see, the subterranean labyrinth of Paris is to-day more than tenfold what it was at the commencement of the century. It is hard to realise all the perseverance and effort which were necessary to bring this cloaca to the point of relative perfection where it now is. It was with great difficulty that the old monarchical provostship and, in the last ten years of the eighteenth century, the revolutionary mayoralty, had succeeded in piercing the thirteen miles of sewers which existed before 1806. All manner of obstacles hindered this operation, some peculiar to the nature of the soil, others inherent in the very prejudices of the labouring population of Paris. Paris is built upon a deposit singularly rebellious to the spade, the hoe, the drill, to human control. Nothing more difficult to pierce and to penetrate than that geological formation upon which is superposed the wonderful historical formation called Paris; as soon as, under whatever form, labour commences and ventures into that street of alluvium, subterraneous resistance abounds. There are liquid clays, living springs, hard rocks, those soft and deep mires which technical science calls Moutardes. The pick advances laboriously into these calcareous strata alternating with seams of very fine clay and laminar schistose beds, incrusted with oyster shells contemporary with the pre-adamite oceans. Sometimes a brook suddenly throws down an arch which has been commenced, and inundates the labourers; or a slide of marl loosens and rushes down with the fury of a cataract, crushing the largest of the sustaining timbers like glass. Quite recently at Villette, when it was necessary, without interrupting navigation and without emptying the canal, to lead the collecting sewer under the Saint Martin canal, a fissure opened in the bed of the canal; the water suddenly rose in the works underground, beyond all the power of the pumps; they were obliged to seek the fissure, which was in the neck of the great basin, by means of a diver, and it was not without difficulty that it was stopped. Elsewhere, near the Seine, and even at some distance from the river, as, for instance, at Belleville, Grande Rue, and the Lunière arcade, we find quicksands in which we sink, and a man may be buried out of sight. Add asphyxia from the miasma, burial by the earth falling in, sudden settlings of the bottom. Add typhus, with which the labourers are slowly impregnated. In our day, after having excavated the gallery of Clichy, with a causeway to receive a principal water-pipe from the Ourcq, a work executed in a trench, over ten yards in depth: after having, in spite of slides, by means of excavations, often putrid, and by props, arched the Bièvre from the Boulevard de l'Hôpital to the Seine; after having, to deliver Paris from the swelling waters of Montmartre and to furnish an outlet for that fluvial sea of twenty-two acres which stagnated near the Barrière des Martyrs, after having, we say, constructed the line of sewers from the Barrière Blanche to the Aubervilliers road, in four months, working day and night, at a depth of twelve yards; after having, a thing which had not been seen before, executed entirely underground a sewer in the Rue Barre du Bec, without a trench, twenty feet below the surface, Superintendent Monnot died. After having arched three thousand yards of sewers in all parts of the city, from the Rue Traversière Saint Antoine to the Rue de l'Ourcine; after having, by the branching of the Arbalète, relieved the Censier Mouffetard Square from inundation by the rain; after having built the Saint Georges sewer upon stone-work and concrete in the quicksand; after having directed the dangerous lowering of the floor of the Notre Dame de Nazareth branch, Engineer Duleau died. There are no bulletins for these acts of bravery, more profitable, however, than the stupid slaughter of the battle-field.

The sewers of Paris, in 1832, were far from being what they are today. Bruneseau had made a beginning, but it required the cholera to determine the vast reconstruction which has since taken place. It is surprising to say, for instance, that, in 1821, a portion of the belt sewer, called the Grand Canal, as at Venice, was still stagnating in the open sky, in the Rue des Gourdes. It was only in 1823 that the city of Paris found in its pocket the forty-nine thousand eight hundred and ninety dollars and one cent necessary for the covering of this shame. The three absorbing wells of the Combat, the Cunette, and Saint Mandé, with their discharging mouths, their apparatus, their pits, and their depuratory branches, date only from 1836. The intestinal canal of Paris has been rebuilt anew, and, as we have said, increased more than tenfold within a quarter of a century.

Thirty years ago, at the period of the insurrection of the 5th and 6th of June, it was still, in many places, almost the ancient sewer. A very large number of streets, now vaulted, were then hollow causeways. You very often saw, at the low point in which the gutters of a street or a square terminated, large rectangular gratings with great bars, the iron of which shone, polished by the feet of the multitude, dangerous and slippery for wagons, and making the horses stumble. The official language of roads and bridges gave to these low points and gratings the expressive name of *Cassis*. In 1832, in many streets, the Rue de l'Etoile, the Rue Saint Louis, the Rue du Temple, the Rue Vieille du Temple, the Rue Notre Dame de Nazareth, the Rue Folie Méricourt, the Quai aux Fleurs, the Rue du Petit Musc, the Rue de Normandie, the Rue Pont aux Biches, the Rue des Marais, Faubourg Saint Martin, the Rue Notre Dame des Victoires, Faubourg Montmartre, the Rue Grange Batelière in the Champs-Elysées, the Rue Jacob, the Rue de Tournon, the old Gothic cloaca still cynically showed its jaws. They were enormous, sluggish gaps of stone, sometimes surrounded by stone blocks, with monumental effrontery.

Paris, in 1806, was still almost at the same figure of sewers established in May, 1663: five thousand three hundred and twenty-eight fathoms. According to Bruneseau, on the 1st of January, 1832, there were forty-four thousand and seventy-three yards. From 1806 to 1831, there were built annually, on an average, eight hundred and twenty yards; since then there have been constructed every year eight, and even ten thousand yards of galleries, in masonry of small materials laid in hydraulic cement on a foundation of concrete.

At thirty-five dollars a yard, the hundred and forty miles of sewers of the present Paris represent nine millions.

Besides the economical progress which we pointed out in commencing, grave problems of public hygiene are connected with this immense question: the sewer of Paris.

Paris is between two sheets, a sheet of water and a sheet of air. The sheet of water lying at a considerable depth under ground, but already reached by two borings, is furnished by the bed of green sand lying between the chalk and the jurassic limestone; this bed may be represented by a disk with a radius of seventy miles; a multitude of rivers and brooks filter into it; we drink the Seine, the Marne, the Yonne, the Oise, the Aisne, the Cher, the Vienne, and the Loire, in a glass of water from the well of Grenelle. The sheet of water is salubrious; it comes, first from heaven, then from the earth; the sheet of air is unwholesome, it comes from the sewer. All the miasmas of the cloaca are mingled with the respiration of the city; hence that foul breath. The air taken from above a dunghill, this has been scientifically determined, is purer than the air taken from above Paris. In a given time, progress aiding, mechanisms being perfected, and light increasing, the sheet of water will be employed to purify the sheet of air. That is to say, to wash the sewer. By washing the sewer, of course, we understand: restitution of the mire to the land; return of the muck to the soil, and the manure to the fields. There will result, from this simple act, to the whole social community, a diminution of misery and an augmentation of health. At the present hour, the radiation of the diseases of Paris extends a hundred and fifty miles about the Louvre, taken as the hub of this pestilential wheel.

We might say that, for ten centuries, the cloaca has been the disease of Paris. The sewer is the taint which the city has in her blood. The popular instinct is never mistaken. The trade of sewerman was formerly almost as perilous, and almost as repulsive to the people, as the trade of knacker so long stricken with horror, and abandoned to the executioner. It required high wages to persuade a mason to disappear in that fetid ooze; the well-digger's ladder hesitated to plunge into it; it was said proverbially: *to descend into the sewer is to enter the grave*; and all manner of hideous legends, as we have said, covered this colossal drain with dismay; awful sink, which bears the traces of the revolutions of the globe as well as of the revolutions of men, and in which we find vestiges of all the cataclysms from the shellfish of the deluge down to the rag of Marat.

BOOK THIRD – MIRE, BUT SOUL

I
THE CLOACA AND ITS SURPRISES

IT was in the sewer of Paris that Jean Valjean found himself.

Further resemblance of Paris with the sea. As in the ocean, the diver can disappear.

The transition was marvellous. From the very centre of the city, Jean Valjean had gone out of the city, and, in the twinkling of an eye, the time of lifting a cover and closing it again, he had passed from broad day to complete obscurity, from noon to midnight, from uproar to silence, from the whirl of the thunder to the stagnation of the tomb, and, by a mutation much more prodigious still than that of the Rue Polonceau, from the most extreme peril to the most absolute security.

Sudden fall into a cave; disappearance in the dungeon of Paris; to leave that street in which death was everywhere for this kind of sepulchre in which there was life was an astounding crisis. He remained for some seconds as if stunned; listening, stupefied. The spring trap of safety had suddenly opened beneath him. Celestial goodness had in some sort taken him by treachery. Adorable ambuscades of Providence!

Only, the wounded man did not stir, and Jean Valjean did not know whether what he was carrying away in this grave were alive or dead.

His first sensation was blindness. Suddenly he saw nothing more. It seemed to him also that in one minute he had become deaf. He heard nothing more. The frenzied storm of murder which was raging a few feet above him only reached him, as we have said, thanks to the thickness of the earth which separated him from it, stifled and indistinct, and like a rumbling at a great depth. He felt that it was solid under his feet; that was all; but that was enough. He reached out one hand, then the other, and touched the wall on both sides, and realised that the passage was narrow; he slipped, and realised that the pavement was wet. He advanced one foot with precaution, fearing a hole, a pit, some gulf; he made sure that the flagging continued. A whiff of fetidness informed him where he was.

After a few moments, he ceased to be blind. A little light fell from the air-hole through which he had slipped in, and his eye became accustomed to this cave. He began to distinguish something. The passage in which he was earthed, no other word better expresses the condition, was walled up behind him. It was one of those cul-de-sacs technically called branchments. Before him, there was another wall, a wall of night. The light from the air-hole died out ten or twelve paces from the point at which Jean Valjean stood, and scarcely produced a pallid whiteness over a few yards of the damp wall of the sewer. Beyond, the opaqueness was massive; to penetrate it appeared horrible, and to enter it seemed like being engulfed. He could, however, force his way into that wall of mist, and he must do it. He must even hasten. Jean Valjean thought that that grating, noticed by him under the paving stones, might also be noticed by the soldiers, and that all depended upon that chance. They also could descend into the well and explore it. There was not a minute to be lost. He had laid Marius upon the ground, he gathered him up, this is again the right word, replaced him upon his shoulders, and began his journey. He resolutely entered that obscurity.

The truth is, that they were not so safe as Jean Valjean supposed. Perils of another kind, and not less great, awaited them perhaps. After the flashing whirl of the combat, the cavern of miasmas and pitfalls; after chaos, the cloaca. Jean Valjean had fallen from one circle of Hell to another.

At the end of fifty paces he was obliged to stop. A question presented itself. The passage terminated in another which it met transversely. These two roads were offered. Which should he take? should he turn to the left or to the right? How guide himself in this black labyrinth? This labyrinth, as we have remarked, has a clue: its descent. To follow the descent is to go to the river.

Jean Valjean understood this at once.

He said to himself that he was probably in the sewer of the markets; that, if he should choose the left and follow the descent, he would come in less than a quarter of an hour to some mouth upon the Seine between the Pont au Change and the Pont Neuf, that is to say, he would reappear in broad day in the most populous portion of Paris. He might come out in some gathering of corner idlers. Amazement of the passers-by at seeing two bloody men come out of the ground under their feet. Arrival of sergent de ville, call to arms in the next guardhouse. He would be seized before getting out. It was better to plunge into the labyrinth, to trust to this darkness, and to rely on Providence for the issue.

He chose the right, and went up the ascent.

When he had turned the corner of the gallery, the distant gleam of the air-hole disappeared, the curtain of obscurity fell back over him, and he again became blind. He went forward none the less, and as rapidly as he could. Marius' arms were passed about his neck, and his feet hung behind him. He held both arms with one hand, and groped for the wall with the other. Marius' cheek touched his and stuck to it, being bloody. He felt a warm stream, which came from Marius, flow over him and penetrate his clothing. Still, a moist warmth at his ear, which touched the wounded man's mouth, indicated respiration, and consequently life. The passage through which Jean Valjean was now moving was not so small as the first. Jean Valjean walked in it with difficulty. The rains of the previous day had not yet run off, and made a little stream in the centre of the floor, and he was compelled to hug the wall, to keep his feet out of the water. Thus he went on in midnight. He resembled the creatures of night groping in the invisible, and lost underground in the veins of the darkness.

However, little by little, whether that some distant air-holes sent a little floating light into this opaque mist, or that his eyes became accustomed to the obscurity, some dim vision came back to him, and he again began to receive a confused perception, now of the wall which he was touching, and now of the arch under which he was passing. The pupil dilates in the night, and at last finds day in it, even as the soul dilates in misfortune, and at last finds God in it.

To find his way was difficult.

The track of the sewers echoes, so to speak, the track of the streets which overlie them. There were in the Paris of that day two thousand two hundred streets. Picture to yourselves below them that forest of dark branches which is called the sewer. The sewers existing at that epoch, placed end to end, would have given a length of thirty miles. We have already said that the present network, thanks to the extraordinary activity of the last thirty years, is not less than a hundred and forty miles.

Jean Valjean began with a mistake. He thought that he was under the Rue Saint Denis, and it was unfortunate that he was not there. There is beneath the Rue Saint Denis an old stone sewer, which dates from Louis XIII., and which goes straight to the collecting sewer, called the Grand Sewer, with a single elbow, on the right, at the height of the ancient Cour des Miracles, and a single branch, the Saint Martin sewer, the four arms of which cut each other in a cross. But the gallery of the Petite Truanderie, the entrance to which was near the wine-shop of Corinth, never communicated with the underground passage in the Rue Saint Denis; it runs into the Montmartre sewer, and it was in that that Jean Valjean was entangled. There, opportunities of losing one's self abound. The Montmartre sewer is one of the most labyrinthian of the ancient network. Luckily Jean Valjean had left behind him the sewer of the markets, the geometrical plan of which represents a multitude of interlocked top-gallant-masts; but he had before him more than one embarrassing encounter and more than one street-corner—for these are streets—presenting itself in the obscurity like a point of interrogation; first, at his left, the vast Plâtrière sewer, a kind of Chinese puzzle pushing and jumbling its chaos of T's and Z's beneath the Hôtel des Postes and the rotunda of the grain-market to the Seine, where it terminates in a Y; secondly, at his right, the crooked corridor of the Rue du Cadran, with its three teeth, which are so many blind ditches; thirdly, at his left, the branch of the Mail, complicated, almost at its entrance, by a kind of fork, and, after zigzag upon zigzag, terminating in the great voiding crypt of the Louvre, truncated and ramified in all directions; finally, at the right, the cul-de-sac passage of the Rue des Jeûneurs, with countless little reducts here and there, before arriving at the central sewer, which alone could lead him to some outlet distant enough to be secure.

If Jean Valjean had had any notion of what we have here pointed out, he would have quickly perceived, merely from feeling the wall, that he was not in the underground gallery of the Rue Saint Denis. Instead of the old hewn stone, instead of the ancient architecture haughty and royal even in the sewer, with floor and running courses of granite, and mortar of thick lime, which cost seventy-five dollars a yard, he would have felt beneath his hand the contemporary cheapness, the economical expedient, the millstone grit laid in hydraulic cement upon a bed of concrete, which cost thirty-five dollars a yard, the bourgeois masonry known as *small materials*; but he knew nothing of all this.

He went forward, with anxiety, but with calmness, seeing nothing, knowing nothing, plunged into chance, that is to say, swallowed up in Providence.

By degrees, we must say, some horror penetrated him. The shadow which enveloped him entered his mind. He was walking in an enigma. This aqueduct of the cloaca is formidable; it is dizzily intertangled. It is a dreary thing to be caught in this Paris of darkness. Jean Valjean was obliged to find and almost to invent his route without seeing it. In that unknown region, each step which he ventured might be the last. How should he get out? Should he find an outlet? Should he find it in time? Would this colossal subterranean sponge with cells of stone admit of being penetrated and pierced? Would he meet with some unlooked-for knot of obscurity? Would he encounter the inextricable and the insurmountable? Would Marius die of hæmorrhage, and he of hunger? Would they both perish there at last, and make two skeletons in some niche of that night? He did not know. He asked himself all this, and he could not answer. The intestine of Paris is an abyss. Like the prophet, he was in the belly of the monster.

Suddenly he was surprised. At the most unexpected moment, and without having diverged from a straight line, he discovered that he was no longer rising; the water of the brook struck coming against his heels instead of upon the top of his feet. The sewer now descended. What? would he then soon reach the Seine? This danger was great, but the peril of retreat was still greater. He continued to advance.

It was not towards the Seine that he was going. The saddleback which the topography of Paris forms upon the right bank, empties one of its slopes into the Seine and the other into the Grand Sewer. The crest of this saddleback which determines the division of the waters follows a very capricious line. The culminating point, which is the point of separation of the flow, is in the Saint Avoye sewer beyond the Rue Michel de Comte, in the sewer of the Louvre, near the boulevards, and in the Montmartre sewer, near the markets. It was at this culminating point that Jean Valjean had arrived. He was making his way towards the belt sewer; he was on the right road. But he knew nothing of it.

Whenever he came to a branch, he felt its angles, and if he found the opening not as wide as the corridor in which he was, he did not enter, and continued his route, deeming rightly that every narrower way must terminate in a cul-de-sac, and could only lead him away from his object, the outlet. He thus evaded the quadruple snare which was spread for him in the obscurity, by the four labyrinths which we have just enumerated.

At a certain moment he felt that he was getting away from under the Paris which was petrified by the émeute, in which the barricades had suppressed the circulation, and that he was coming beneath the Paris which was alive and normal. He heard suddenly above his head a sound like thunder, distant, but continuous. It was the rumbling of the vehicles.

He had been walking for about half an hour, at least by his own calculation, and had not yet thought of resting; only he had changed the hand which supported Marius. The darkness was deeper than ever, but this depth reassured him.

All at once he saw his shadow before him. It was marked out on a feeble ruddiness almost indistinct, which vaguely empurpled the floor at his feet, and the arch over his head, and which glided along at his right and his left on the two slimy walls of the corridor. In amazement he turned round.

Behind him, in the portion of the passage through which he had passed, at a distance which appeared to him immense, flamed, throwing its rays into the dense obscurity, a sort of horrible star which appeared to be looking at him.

It was the gloomy star of the police which was rising in the sewer.

Behind this star were moving without order eight or ten black forms, straight, indistinct, terrible.

II

EXPLANATION

DURING the day of the 6th of June, a battue of the sewers had been ordered. It was feared that they would be taken as a refuge by the vanquished, and prefect Gisquet was to ransack the occult Paris, while General Bugeaud was sweeping the public Paris; a connected double operation which demanded a double strategy of the public power, represented above by the army and below by the police. Three platoons of officers and sewermen explored the subterranean streets of Paris, the first, the right bank, the second, the left bank, the third, in the City.

The officers were armed with carbines, clubs, swords, and daggers.

That which was at this moment directed upon Jean Valjean, was the lantern of the patrol of the right bank.

This patrol had just visited the crooked gallery and the three blind alleys which are beneath the Rue du Cadran. While they were taking their candle to the bottom of these blind alleys, Jean Valjean had come to the entrance of the gallery upon his way, had found it narrower than the principal passage, and had not entered it. He had passed beyond. The policemen, on coming out from the Cadran gallery, had thought they heard the sound of steps in the direction of the belt sewer. It was in fact Jean Valjean's steps. The sergeant in command of the patrol lifted his lantern, and the squad began to look into the mist in the direction whence the sound came.

This was to Jean Valjean an indescribable moment.

Luckily, if he saw the lantern well, the lantern saw him badly. It was light and he was shadow. He was far off, and merged in the blackness of the place. He drew close to the side of the wall, and stopped.

Still, he formed no idea of what was moving there behind him. Lack of sleep, want of food, emotions, had thrown him also into the visionary state. He saw a flaring flame, and about that flame, goblins. What was it? He did not understand.

Jean Valjean having stopped, the noise ceased.

The men of the patrol listened and heard nothing, they looked and saw nothing. They consulted.

There was at that period a sort of square at this point of the Montmartre sewer, called *de service*, which has since been suppressed on account of the little interior lake which formed in it, by the damming up in heavy storms of the torrents of rain water. The patrol could gather in a group in this square.

Jean Valjean saw these goblins form a kind of circle. These mastiffs' heads drew near each other and whispered.

The result of this council held by the watch-dogs was that they had been mistaken, that there had been no noise, that there was nobody there, that it was needless to trouble themselves with the belt sewer, that that would be time lost, but that they must hasten towards Saint Merry, that if there were anything to do and any "bousingot" to track out, it was in that quarter.

From time to time parties put new soles to their old terms of insult. In 1832, the word *bousingot* filled the interim between the word *jacobin*, which was worn out, and the word *demagogue*, then almost unused, but which has since done such excellent service.

The sergeant gave the order to file left towards the descent to the Seine. If they had conceived the idea of dividing into two squads and going in both directions, Jean Valjean would have been caught. That hung by this thread. It is probable that the instructions from the prefecture, foreseeing the possibility of a combat and that the insurgents might be numerous, forbade the patrol to separate. The patrol resumed its march, leaving Jean Valjean behind. Of all these movements, Jean Valjean perceived nothing except the eclipse of the lantern, which suddenly turned back.

Before going away, the sergeant, to ease the police conscience, discharged his carbine in the direction they were abandoning, towards Jean Valjean. The detonation rolled from echo to echo in the vault like the rumbling of this titanic bowel. Some plastering which fell into the stream and spattered the water a few steps from Jean Valjean made him aware that the ball had struck the arch above his head.

Slow and measured steps resounded upon the floor for some time, more and more deadened by the progressive increase of the distance, the group of black forms sank away, a glimmer oscillated and floated, making a ruddy circle in the vault, which decreased, then disappeared, the silence became deep again, the obscurity became again complete, blindness and deafness resumed possession of the darkness; and Jean Valjean, not yet daring to stir, stood for a long time with his back to the wall, his ear intent and eye dilated, watching the vanishing of that phantom patrol.

III
THE MAN SPUN

WE must do the police of that period this justice that, even in the gravest public conjunctures, it imperturbably performed its duties watchful and sanitary. An *émeute* was not in its eyes a pretext for giving malefactors a loose rein, and for neglecting society because the government was in peril. The ordinary duty was performed correctly in addition to the extraordinary duty, and was not disturbed by it. In the midst of the beginning of an incalculable political event, under the pressure of a possible revolution, without allowing himself to be diverted by the insurrection and the barricade, an officer would "spin" a thief.

Something precisely like this occurred in the afternoon of the 6th of June at the brink of the Seine, on the beach of the right bank, a little beyond the Pont des Invalides.

There is no beach there now. The appearance of the place has changed. On this beach, two men some distance apart, seemed to be observing each other, one avoiding the other. The one who was going before was endeavouring to increase the distance, the one who came behind to lessen it.

It was like a game of chess played from a distance and silently. Neither seemed to hurry, and both walked slowly, as if either feared that by too much haste he would double the pace of his partner.

One would have said it was an appetite following a prey, without appearing to do it on purpose. The prey was crafty, and kept on its guard.

The requisite proportions between the tracked marten and the tracking hound were observed. He who was trying to escape had a feeble frame and a sorry mien; he who was trying to seize, a fellow of tall stature, was rough in aspect, and promised to be rough in encounter.

The first, feeling himself the weaker, was avoiding the second; he avoided him in a very furious way; he who could have observed him would have seen in his eyes the gloomy hostility of flight, and all the menace which there is in fear.

The beach was solitary; there were no passers; not even a boatman nor a lighterman on the barges moored here and there.

These two men could not have been easily seen, except from the quai in front, and to him who might have examined them from that distance, the man who was going forward would have appeared like a bristly creature, tattered and skulking, restless and shivering under a ragged blouse, and the other, like a classic and official person, wearing the overcoat of authority buttoned to the chin.

The reader would perhaps recognise these two men, if he saw them nearer.

What was the object of the last?

Probably to put the first in a warmer dress.

When a man clad by the state pursues a man in rags, it is in order to make of him also a man clad by the state. Only the colour is the whole question. To be clad in blue is glorious; to be clad in red is disagreeable.

There is a purple of the depths.

It was probably some inconvenience and some purple of this kind that the first desired to escape.

If the other was allowing him to go on and did not yet seize him, it was, according to all appearance, in the hope of seeing him bring up at some significant rendezvous, some group of good prizes. This delicate operation is called "spinning."

What renders this conjecture the more probable is, that the closely buttoned man, perceiving from the shore a fiacre which was passing on the quai empty, beckoned to the driver; the driver understood, evidently recognised with whom he had to do, turned his horse, and began to follow the two men on the upper part of the quai at a walk. This was not noticed by the equivocal and ragged personage who was in front.

The fiacre rolled along the trees of the Champs-Elysées. There could be seen moving above the parapet, the bust of the driver, whip in hand.

One of the secret instructions of the police to officers contains this article: "Always have a vehicle within call, in case of need."

While manœuvring, each on his side, with an irreproachable strategy, these two men approached a slope of the quai descending to the beach, which, at that time, allowed the coach-drivers coming from Passy to go to the river to water their horses. This slope has since been removed, for the sake of symmetry; the horses perish with thirst, but the eye is satisfied.

It seemed probable that the man in the blouse would go up by this slope in order to attempt escape into the Champs-Elysées, a place ornamented with trees, but on the other hand thickly dotted with officers, and where his pursuer would have easily seized him with a strong hand.

This point of the quai is very near the house brought from Moret to Paris in 1824, by Colonel Brack, and called the house of Francis I. A guardhouse is quite near by.

To the great surprise of his observer, the man pursued did not take the slope of the watering-place. He continued to advance on the beach along the quai.

His position was visibly becoming critical.

If not to throw himself into the Seine, what was he going to do?

No means henceforth of getting up to the quai; no other slope, and no staircase; and they were very near the spot, marked by the turn of the Seine towards the Pont d'Iéna, where the beach, narrowing more and more, terminates in a slender tongue, and is lost under the water. There he would inevitably find himself blockaded between the steep wall on his right, the river on the left and in front, and authority upon his heels.

It is true that this end of the beach was masked from sight by a mound of rubbish from six to seven feet high, the product of some demolition. But did this man hope to hide with any effect behind this heap of fragments, which the other had only to turn? The expedient would have been puerile. He certainly did not dream of it. The innocence of robbers does not reach this extent.

The heap of rubbish made a sort of eminence at the edge of the water, which prolonged like a promontory, as far as the wall of the quai.

The man pursued reached this little hill and doubled it, so that he ceased to be seen by the other.

The latter, not seeing, was not seen; he took advantage of this to abandon all dissimulation, and to walk very rapidly. In a few seconds he came to the mound of rubbish, and turned it. There, he stopped in amazement. The man whom he was hunting was gone.

Total eclipse of the man in the blouse.

The beach beyond the mound of rubbish had scarcely a length of thirty yards, then it plunged beneath the water which beat against the wall of the quai.

The fugitive could not have thrown himself into the Seine nor scaled the quai without being seen by him who was following him. What had become of him?

The man in the closely buttoned coat walked to the end of the beach, and stopped there a moment thoughtful, his fists convulsive, his eyes ferreting. Suddenly he slapped his forehead. He had noticed, at the point where the land and the water began, an iron grating broad and low, arched, with a heavy lock and three massive hinges. This grating, a sort of door cut into the bottom of the quai, opened upon the river as much as upon the beach. A blackish stream flowed from beneath it. This stream emptied into the Seine.

Beyond its heavy rusty bars could be distinguished a sort of corridor arched and obscure.

The man folded his arms and looked at the grating reproachfully.

This look not sufficing, he tried to push it; he shook it, it resisted firmly. It was probable that it had just been opened, although no sound had been heard, a singular circumstance with a grating so rusty; but it was certain that it had been closed again. That indicated that he before whom this door had just turned, had not a hook but a key.

This evident fact burst immediately upon the mind of the man who was exerting himself to shake the grating, and forced from him this indignant epiphonema:

"This is fine! a government key!"

Then, calming himself immediately, he expressed a whole world of interior ideas by this whiff of monosyllables accented almost ironically:

"Well! well! well! well!"

This said, hoping nobody knows what, either to see the man come out, or to see others go in, he posted himself on the watch behind the heap of rubbish, with the patient rage of a pointer.

For its part, the fiacre, which followed all his movements, had halted above him near the parapet. The driver, foreseeing a long stay, fitted the muzzles of his horses into the bag of wet oats, so well known to Parisians, to whom the governments, be it said in parenthesis, sometimes apply it. The few passers over the Pont d'Iéna, before going away, turned their heads to look for a moment at these two motionless features of the landscape, the man on the beach, the fiacre on the quai.

IV

HE ALSO BEARS HIS CROSS

JEAN VALJEAN had resumed his advance, and had not stopped again.

This advance became more and more laborious. The level of these arches varies; the medium height is about five feet six inches, and was calculated for the stature of a man; Jean Valjean was compelled to bend so as not to hit Marius against the arch;

he had to stoop every second, then rise up, to grope incessantly for the wall. The moisture of the stones and the sliminess of the floor made them bad points of support, whether for the hand or the foot. He was wading in the hideous muck of the city. The occasional gleams from the air-holes appeared only at long intervals, and so ghastly were they that the noonday seemed but moonlight; all the rest was mist, miasma, opacity, blackness. Jean Valjean was hungry and thirsty; thirsty especially; and this place, like the sea, is one full of water where you cannot drink. His strength, which was prodigious, and very little diminished by age, thanks to his chaste and sober life, began to give way notwithstanding. Fatigue grew upon him, and as his strength diminished the weight of his load increased. Marius, dead perhaps, weighed heavily upon him as inert bodies do. Jean Valjean supported him in such a way that his breast was not compressed and his breathing could always be as free as possible. He felt the rapid gliding of the rats between his legs. One of them was so frightened as to bite him. There came to him from time to time through the aprons of the mouths of the sewer a breath of fresh air which revived him.

It might have been three o'clock in the afternoon when he arrived at the belt sewer.

He was first astonished at this sudden enlargement. He abruptly found himself in the gallery where his outstretched hands did not reach the two walls, and under an arch which his head did not touch. The Grand Sewer indeed is eight feet wide and seven high.

At the point where the Montmartre sewer joins the Grand Sewer, two other subterranean galleries, that of the Rue de Provence and that of the Abattoir, coming in, make a square. Between these four ways a less sagacious man would have been undecided. Jean Valjean took the widest, that is to say, the belt sewer. But there the question returned: to descend, or to ascend? He thought that the condition of affairs was urgent, and that he must, at whatever risk, now reach the Seine. In other words, descend. He turned to the left.

Well for him that he did so. For it would be an error to suppose that the belt sewer has two outlets, the one towards Bercy, the other towards Passy, and that it is, as its name indicates, the subterranean belt of the Paris of the right bank. The Grand Sewer, which is, it must be remembered, nothing more nor less than the ancient brook of Ménilmontant, terminates, if we ascend it, in a cul-de-sac, that is to say, its ancient starting point, which was its spring, at the foot of the hill of Ménilmont-ant. It has no direct communication with the branch which gathers up the waters of Paris below the Popincourt quartier, and which empties into the Seine by the Amelot sewer above the ancient Ile Louviers. This branch, which completes the collecting sewer, is separated from it, under the Rue Ménil-montant even, by a solid wall which marks the point of separa-tion of the waters up and down. Had Jean Valjean gone up the gallery, he would have come, after manifold efforts, exhausted by fatigue, expiring, in the darkness, to a wall. He would have been lost.

Strictly speaking, by going back a little, entering the passage of the Filles du Calvaire, if he did not hesitate at the subterra-nean goose-track of the Boucherat crossing, by taking the Saint Louis corridor, then, on the left, the Saint Gilles passage, then by turning to the right and avoiding the Saint Sébastien gallery, he might have come to the Amelot sewer, and thence, provided he had not gone astray in the sort of F which is beneath the Bastille, reached the outlet on the Seine near the Arsenal. But, for that, he must have been perfectly familiar in all its ramifica-tions and in all its tubes with the huge madrepore of the sewer. Now, we must repeat, he knew nothing of this frightful system of paths along which he was making his way; and, had any-body asked him where he was, he would have answered: In the night.

His instinct served him well. To descend was, in fact, possible safety.

He left on his right the two passages which ramify in the form of a claw under the Rue Lafitte and the Rue Saint Georges, and the long forked corridor of the Chaussée d'Antin.

A little beyond an affluent which was probably the branching of the Madeleine, he stopped. He was very tired. A large air-hole, probably the vista on the Rue d'Anjou, produced an almost vivid light. Jean Valjean, with the gentleness of move-ment of a brother for his wounded brother, laid Marius upon the side bank of the sewer. Marius' bloody face appeared, under the white gleam from the air-hole, as if at the bottom of a tomb. His eyes were closed, his hair adhered to his temples like brushes dried in red paint, his hands dropped down lifeless, his limbs were cold, there was coagulated blood at the corners of his mouth. A clot of blood had gathered in the tie of his cravat; his shirt was bedded in the wounds, the cloth of his coat chafed the gaping gashes in the living flesh. Jean Valjean, removing the garments with the ends of his fingers, laid his hand upon his breast; the heart still beat. Jean Valjean tore up his shirt, bandaged the wounds as well as he could, and staunched the flowing blood; then, bending in the twilight over Marius, who was still unconscious and almost lifeless, he looked at him with an inexpressible hatred.

In opening Marius' clothes, he had found two things in his pockets, the bread which had been forgotten there since the day previous, and Marius' pocket-book. He ate the bread and opened the pocket-book. On the first page he found the four lines written by Marius. They will be remembered.

"My name is Marius Pontmercy. Carry my corpse to my grandfather's, M. Gillenormand, Rue des Filles du Calvaire, No. 6, in the Marais."

By the light of the air-hole, Jean Valjean read these four lines, and stopped a moment as if absorbed in himself, repeating in an undertone: "Rue des Filles du Calvaire, Number Six, Monsieur Gillenormand." He replaced the pocket-book in Marius' pocket. He had eaten, strength had returned to him: he took Marius on his back again, laid his head carefully upon his right shoulder, and began to descend the sewer.

The Grand Sewer, following the course of the valley of Ménilmontant, is almost two leagues in length. It is paved for a considerable part of its course.

This torch of the name of the streets of Paris with which we are illuminating Jean Valjean's subterranean advance for the reader, Jean Valjean did not have. Nothing told him what zone of the city he was passing through, nor what route he had followed. Only the growing pallor of the gleams of light which he saw from time to time, indicated that the sun was withdrawing from the pavement and that the day would soon be gone; and the rumblings of the wagons above his head, from continuous having become intermittent, then having almost ceased, he concluded that he was under central Paris no longer, and that he was approaching some solitary region, in the vicinity of the outer boulevards or the furthest quais. Where there are fewer houses and fewer streets, the sewer has fewer air-holes. The darkness thickened about Jean Valjean. He none the less continued to advance, groping in the obscurity.

This obscurity suddenly became terrible.

V

FOR SAND AS WELL AS WOMAN THERE IS A FINESSE WHICH IS PERFIDY

HE felt that he was entering the water, and that he had under his feet, pavement no longer, but mud.

It sometimes happens, on certain coasts of Brittany or Scotland, that a man, traveller or fisherman, walking on the beach at low tide far from the bank, suddenly notices that for several minutes he has been walking with some difficulty. The strand beneath his feet is like pitch; his soles stick to it; it is sand no longer, it is glue. The beach is perfectly dry, but at every step he takes, as soon as he lifts his foot, the print which it leaves fills with water. The eye, however, has noticed no change; the immense strand is smooth and tranquil, all the sand has the same appearance, nothing distinguishes the surface which is solid from the surface which is no longer so; the joyous little cloud of sand-fleas continues to leap tumultuously over the wayfarer's feet. The man pursues his way, goes forward, inclines towards the land, endeavours to get nearer the upland. He is not anxious. Anxious about what? Only, he feels somehow as if the weight of his feet increased with every step which he takes. Suddenly he sinks in. He sinks in two or three inches. Decidedly he is not on the right road; he stops to take his bearings. All at once, he looks at his feet. His feet have disappeared. The sand covers them. He draws his feet out of the sand, he will retrace his steps, he turns back, he sinks in deeper. The sand comes up to his ankles, he pulls himself out and throws himself to the left, the sand is half leg deep, he throws himself to the right, the sand comes up to his shins. Then he recognises with unspeakable terror that he is caught in the quicksand, and that he has beneath him the fearful medium in which man can no more walk than the fish can swim. He throws off his load if he has one, he lightens himself like a ship in distress; it is already too late, the sand is above his knees.

He calls, he waves his hat or his handkerchief, the sand gains on him more and more; if the beach is deserted, if the land is too far off, if the sandbank is of too ill-repute, if there is no hero in sight, it is all over, he is condemned to enlizement. He is condemned to that appalling interment, long, infallible, implacable, impossible to slacken or to hasten, which endures for hours, which will not end, which seizes you erect, free and in full health, which draws you by the feet, which, at every effort that you attempt, at every shout that you utter, drags you a little deeper, which appears to punish you for your resistance by a redoubling of its grasp, which sinks the man slowly into the earth while it leaves him all the time to look at the horizon, the trees, the green fields, the smoke of the villages in the plain, the sails of the ships upon the sea, the birds flying and singing, the sunshine, the sky. Enlizement is the grave become a tide and rising from the depths of the earth towards a living man. Each minute is an inexorable enshroudress. The victim attempts to sit down, to lie down, to creep; every movement he makes, inters him; he straightens up, he sinks in; he feels that he is being swallowed up; he howls, implores, cries to the clouds, wrings his hands, despairs. Behold him waist deep in the sand; the sand reaches his breast, he is now only a bust. He raises his arms, utters furious groans, clutches the beach with his nails, would hold by that straw, leans upon his elbows to pull himself out of this soft sheath, sobs frenziedly; the sand rises. The sand reaches his shoulders, the sand reaches his neck; the face alone is visible now. The mouth cries, the sand fills it; silence. The eyes still gaze, the sand shuts them; night. Then the forehead decreases, a little hair flutters above the sand; a hand protrudes, comes through the surface of the beach, moves and shakes, and disappears. Sinister effacement of a man.

Sometimes the horseman is enlized with his horse; sometimes the cartman is enlized with his cart; all horrible beneath the beach. It is a shipwreck elsewhere than in the water. It is the earth drowning man. The earth, filled with the ocean, becomes a trap. It presents itself as a plain and opens like a wave. Such treacheries has the abyss.

This fatal mishap, always possible upon one or another coast of the sea, was also possible, thirty years ago, in the sewer of Paris.

Before the important works commenced in 1833, the subterranean system of Paris was subject to sudden sinkings of the bottom.

The water filtered into certain underlying, particularly friable soils; the floor, which was of paving stones, as in the old sewers, or of hydraulic cement upon concrete, as in the new galleries, having lost its support, bent. A bend in a floor of that kind is a crack, is a crumbling. The floor gave way over a certain space. This crevasse, a hiatus in a gulf of mud, was called technically *fontis*. What is a fontis? It is the quicksand of the sea-shore suddenly encountered under ground; it is the beach of Mont Saint Michel in a sewer. The diluted soil is as it were in fusion; all its molecules are in suspension in a soft medium; it is not land, and it is not water. Depth sometimes very great. Nothing more fearful than such a mischance. If the water predominates, death is prompt, there is swallowing up; if the earth predominates, death is slow, there is enlizement.

Can you picture to yourself such a death? If enlizement is terrible on the shore of the sea, what is it in the cloaca? Instead of the open air, the full light, the broad day, that clear horizon, those vast sounds, those free clouds whence rains life, those barks seen in the distance, that hope under every form, probable passers, succour possible until the last moment; instead of all that, deafness, blindness, a black arch, an interior of a tomb already prepared, death in the mire under a cover! the slow stifling by the filth, a stone box in which asphyxia opens its claw in the slime and takes you by the throat; fetidness mingled with the death-rattle; mire instead of sand, sulphuretted hydrogen instead of the hurricane, ordure instead of the ocean? and to call, and to gnash your teeth, and writhe, and struggle, and agonise, with that huge city above your head knowing nothing of it all.

Inexpressible horror of dying thus! Death sometimes redeems its atrocity by a certain terrible dignity. At the stake, in the shipwreck, man may be great in the flame as in the foam, a superb attitude is possible, you are transfigured while falling into that abyss. But not here. Death is unclean. It is humiliating to expire. The last flitting visions are abject. Mire is synonymous with shame. It is mean, ugly, infamous. To die in a butt of Malmsey, like Clarence, so be it; in the scavenger's pit, like d'Escoubleau, that is horrible. To struggle within it is hideous; at the very time that you are agonising, you are splashing. There is darkness enough for it to be Hell, and slime enough for it to be only a slough, and the dying man knows not whether he will become a spectre or a toad.

Everywhere else the grave is gloomy; here it is misshapen.

The depth of the fontis varied, as well as its length, and its density by reason of the more or less yielding character of the subsoil. Sometimes a fontis was three or four feet deep, sometimes eight or ten; sometimes no bottom could be found. The mire was here almost solid, there almost liquid. In the Lunière fontis, it would have taken a man a day to disappear, while he would have been devoured in five minutes by the Phélippeaux slough. The mire bears more or less according to its greater or lesser density. A child escapes where a man is lost. The first law of safety is to divest yourself of every kind of burden. To throw away his bag of tools, or his basket, or his hod, is the first thing that every sewerman does when he feels the soil giving way beneath him.

The fontis had various causes: friability of the soil; some crevasse at a depth beyond the reach of man; the violent showers of summer; the incessant storms of winter; the long misty rains. Sometimes the weight of the neighbouring houses upon a marly or sandy soil pressed out the arches of the subterranean galleries and made them yield, or it would happen that the floor gave way and cracked under this crushing pressure. The settling of the Pantheon obliterated in this manner, a century ago, a part of the excavations on Mount Saint Geneviève. When a sewer sank beneath the pressure of the houses, the difficulty, on certain occasions, disclosed itself above in the street by a kind of sawtooth separation in the pavement; this rent was developed in a serpentine line for the whole length of the cracked arch, and then, the evil being visible, the remedy could be prompt. It often happened also that the interior damage was not revealed by any exterior scar. And, in that case, woe to the sewermen. Entering without precaution into the sunken sewer, they might perish. The old registers make mention of some working-men who were buried in this way in the fontis. They give several names; among others that of the sewerman who was engulfed in a sunken slough under the kennel on the Rue Carême Prenant, whose name was Blaise Poutrain; this Blaise Poutrain was brother of Nicholas Poutrain, who was the last gravedigger of the cemetery called Charnier des Innocents in 1785, the date at which that cemetery died.

There was also that young and charming Vicomte d'Escoubleau of whom we have spoken, one of the heroes of the siege of

Lerida, where they gave the assault in silk stockings, headed by violins. D'Escoubleau, surprised one night with his cousin, the Duchess de Sourdis, was drowned in a quagmire of the Beau-treillis sewer, in which he had taken refuge to escape from the duke. Madame de Sourdis, when this death was described to her, called for her smelling-bottle, and forgot to weep through much inhalation of salts. In such a case, there is no love which persists; the cloaca extinguishes it. Hero refuses to wash Lean-der's corpse. Thisbe stops her nose at sight of Pyramus, and says: "Peugh!"

VI
THE FONTIS

JEAN VALJEAN found himself in presence of a fontis.

This kind of settling was then frequent in the subsoil of the Champs-Elysées, very unfavourable for hydraulic works, and giving poor support to underground constructions, from its excessive fluidity. This fluidity surpasses even that of the sands of the Saint Georges quartier, which could only be overcome by stonework upon concrete, and the clayey beds infected with gas in the quartier of the Martyrs, so liquid that the passage could be effected under the gallery of the martyrs only by means of a metallic tube. When, in 1836, they demolished, for the purpose of rebuilding, the old stone sewer under the Faubourg Saint Honoré, in which we find Jean Valjean now entangled, the quicksand, which is the subsoil from the Champs-Elysées to the Seine, was such an obstacle that the work lasted nearly six months, to the great outcry of the bordering proprietors, espe-cially the proprietors of hotels and coaches. The work was more than difficult; it was dangerous. It is true that there were four months and a half of rain, and three risings of the Seine.

The fontis which Jean Valjean fell upon was caused by the showers of the previous day. A yielding of the pavement, imper-fectly upheld by the underlying sand, had occasioned a dam-ming of the rain water. Infiltration having taken place, sinking had followed. The floor, broken up, had disappeared in the mire. For what distance? Impossible to say. The obscurity was deeper than anywhere else. It was a mudhole in the cavern of night.

Jean Valjean felt the pavement slipping away under him. He

entered into this slime. It was water on the surface, mire at the bottom. He must surely pass through. To retrace his steps was impossible. Marius was expiring, and Jean Valjean exhausted. Where else could he go? Jean Valjean advanced. Moreover, the quagmire appeared not very deep for a few steps. But in proportion as he advanced, his feet sank in. He very soon had the mire half-knee deep and water above his knees. He walked on, holding Marius with both arms as high above the water as he could. The mud now came up to his knees, and the water to his waist. He could no longer turn back. He sank in deeper and deeper. This mire, dense enough for one man's weight, evidently could not bear two. Marius and Jean Valjean would have had a chance of escape separately. Jean Valjean continued to advance, supporting this dying man, who was perhaps a corpse.

The water came up to his armpits; he felt that he was foundering; it was with difficulty that he could move in the depth of mire in which he was. The density, which was the support, was also the obstacle. He still held Marius up, and, with an unparalleled outlay of strength, he advanced; but he sank deeper. He now had only his head out of the water, and his arms supporting Marius. There is in the old pictures of the deluge, a mother doing thus with her child.

He sank still deeper, he threw his face back to escape the water, and to be able to breathe; he who should have seen him in this obscurity would have thought he saw a mask floating upon the darkness; he dimly perceived Marius' drooping head and livid face above him; he made a desperate effort, and thrust his foot forward; his foot struck something solid; a support. It was time.

He rose and writhed and rooted himself upon this support with a sort of fury. It produced the effect upon him of the first step of a staircase reascending towards life.

This support, discovered in the mire at the last moment, was the beginning of the other slope of the floor, which had bent without breaking, and had curved beneath the water like a board, and in a single piece. A well constructed paving forms an arch, and has this firmness. This fragment of the floor, partly submerged, but solid, was a real slope, and, once upon this slope, they were saved. Jean Valjean ascended this inclined plane, and reached the other side of the quagmire.

On coming out of the water, he struck against a stone, and fell upon his knees. This seemed to him fitting, and he remained thus for some time, his soul lost in unspoken prayer to God.

He rose, shivering, chilled, infected, bending beneath this dying man, whom he was dragging on, all dripping with slime, his soul filled with a strange light.

VII

SOMETIMES WE GET AGROUND WHEN WE EXPECT TO GET ASHORE

He resumed his route once more.

However, if he had not left his life in the fontis, he seemed to have left his strength. This supreme effort had exhausted him. His exhaustion was so great, that every three or four steps he was obliged to take breath, and leaned against the wall. Once he had to sit down upon the curb to change Marius' position and he thought he should stay there. But if his vigour were dead his energy was not. He rose again. He walked with desperation, almost with rapidity, for a hundred paces, without raising his head, almost without breathing, and suddenly struck against the wall. He had reached an angle of the sewer, and, arriving at the turn with his head down, he had encountered the wall. He raised his eyes, and at the extremity of the passage, down there before him, far, very far away, he perceived a light. This time, it was not the terrible light; it was the good and white light. It was the light of day.

Jean Valjean saw the outlet.

A condemned soul who, from the midst of the furnace, should suddenly perceive an exit from Gehenna, would feel what Jean Valjean felt. It would fly frantically with the stumps of its burned wings towards the radiant door. Jean Valjean felt exhaustion no more, he felt Marius' weight no longer, he found again his knees of steel, he ran rather than walked. As he approached, the outlet assumed more and more distinct outline. It was a circular arch, not so high as the vault which sank down by degrees, and not so wide as the gallery which narrowed as the top grew lower. The tunnel ended on the inside in the form of a funnel; a vicious contraction, copied from the wickets of houses of detention, logical in a prison, illogical in a sewer, and which has since been corrected.

Jean Valjean reached the outlet.

There he stopped.

It was indeed the outlet, but it did not let him out.

The arch was closed by a strong grating, and the grating which, according to all appearance, rarely turned upon its rusty hinges, was held in its stone frame by a stout lock which, red with rust, seemed an enormous brick. He could see the keyhole, and the strong bolt deeply plunged into the iron staple. The lock was plainly a double-lock. It was one of those Bastille locks of which the old Paris was so lavish.

Beyond the grating, the open air, the river, the daylight, the beach, very narrow, but sufficient to get away. The distant quais, Paris, that gulf in which one is so easily lost, the wide horizon, liberty. He distinguished at his right, below him, the Pont d'Iéna, and at his left, above, the Pont des Invalides; the spot would have been propitious for awaiting night and escaping. It was one of the most solitary points in Paris; the beach which fronts on the Gros Caillou. The flies came in and went out through the bars of the grating.

It might have been half-past eight o'clock in the evening. The day was declining.

Jean Valjean laid Marius along the wall on the dry part of the floor, then walked to the grating and clenched the bars with both hands; the shaking was frenzied, the shock nothing. The grating did not stir. Jean Valjean seized the bars one after another, hoping to be able to tear out the least solid one, and to make a lever of it to lift the door or break the lock. Not a bar yielded. A tiger's teeth are not more solid in their sockets. No lever; no possible purchase. The obstacle was invincible. No means of opening the door.

Must he then perish there? What should he do? what would become of them? go back; recommence the terrible road which he had already traversed; he had not the strength. Besides, how cross that quagmire again, from which he had escaped only by a miracle? And after the quagmire, was there not that police patrol from which, certainly, one would not escape twice? And then where should he go? what direction take? to follow the descent was not to reach the goal. Should he come to another outlet, he would find it obstructed by a door or a grating. All the outlets were undoubtedly closed in this way. Chance had unsealed the grating by which they had entered, but evidently all the other mouths of the sewer were fastened. He had only succeeded in escaping into a prison.

It was over. All that Jean Valjean had done was useless. Exhaustion ended in abortion.

They were both caught in the gloomy and immense web of death, and Jean Valjean felt running over those black threads trembling in the darkness, the appalling spider.

He turned his back to the grating, and dropped upon the pavement, rather prostrate than sitting, beside the yet motionless Marius, and his head sank between his knees. No exit. This was the last drop of anguish.

Of whom did he think in this overwhelming dejection? Neither of himself nor of Marius. He thought of Cosette.

VIII
THE TORN COAT-TAIL

IN the midst of this annihilation, a hand was laid upon his shoulder, and a voice which spoke low, said to him:

"Go halves."

Somebody in that darkness? Nothing is so like a dream as despair, Jean Valjean thought he was dreaming. He had heard no steps. Was it possible? he raised his eyes.

A man was before him.

This man was dressed in a blouse; he was barefooted; he held his shoes in his left hand; he had evidently taken them off to be able to reach Jean Valjean without being heard.

Jean Valjean had not a moment's hesitation. Unforeseen as was the encounter, this man was known to him. This man was Thénardier.

Although wakened, so to speak, with a start, Jean Valjean, accustomed to be on the alert and on the watch for unexpected blows which he must quickly parry, instantly regained possession of all his presence of mind. Besides, the condition of affairs could not be worse, a certain degree of distress is no longer capable of crescendo, and Thénardier himself could not add to the blackness of this night.

There was a moment of delay.

Thénardier, lifting his right hand to the height of his forehead, shaded his eyes with it, then brought his brows together while he winked his eyes, which, with a slight pursing of the mouth, characterises the sagacious attention of a man who is seeking to recognise another. He did not succeed. Jean Valjean, we have just said, turned his back to the light, and was moreover so disfigured, so muddy and so blood-stained, that in full noon he would have been unrecognisable. On the other hand, with the light from the grating in his face, a cellar light, it is true, livid, but precise in its lividness, Thénardier, as the energetic, trite metaphor expresses it, struck Jean Valjean at once. This inequality of conditions was enough to ensure Jean Valjean some advantage in this mysterious duel which was about to open between the two conditions and the two men. The encounter took place between Jean Valjean veiled and Thénardier unmasked.

Jean Valjean perceived immediately that Thénardier did not recognise him.

They gazed at each other for a moment in this penumbra, as if they were taking each other's measure. Thénardier was first to break the silence.

"How are you going to manage to get out?"

Jean Valjean did not answer.

Thénardier continued:

"Impossible to pick the lock. Still you must get away from here."

"That is true," said Jean Valjean.

"Well, go halves."

"What do you mean?"

"You have killed the man; very well. For my part, I have the key."

Thénardier pointed to Marius. He went on:

"I don't know you, but I would like to help you. You must be a friend."

Jean Valjean began to understand. Thénardier took him for an assassin.

Thénardier resumed:

"Listen, comrade. You haven't killed that man without looking to what he had in his pockets. Give me my half. I will open the door for you."

And, drawing a big key half out from under his blouse, which was full of holes, he added:

"Would you like to see how the key of the fields is made? There it is."

Jean Valjean "remained stupid," the expression is the elder Corneille's, so far as to doubt whether what he saw was real. It was Providence appearing in a guise of horror, and the good angel springing out of the ground under the form of Thénardier.

Thénardier plunged his fist into a huge pocket hidden under his blouse, pulled out a rope, and handed it to Jean Valjean.

"Here," said he, "I'll give you the rope to boot."

"A rope, what for?"

"You want a stone too, but you'll find one outside. There is a heap of rubbish there."

"A stone, what for?"

"Fool, as you are going to throw the *pantre* into the river, you want a stone and a rope; without them it would float on the water."

Jean Valjean took the rope. Everybody has accepted things thus mechanically.

Thénardier snapped his fingers as over the arrival of a sudden idea:

"Ah now, comrade, how did you manage to get out of the quagmire yonder? I haven't dared to risk myself there. Peugh! you don't smell good."

After a pause, he added:

"I ask you questions, but you are right in not answering them. That is an apprenticeship for the examining judge's cursed quarter of an hour. And then by not speaking at all, you run no risk of speaking too loud. It is all the same, because I don't see your face, and because I don't know your name, you would do wrong to suppose that I don't know who you are and what you want. Understood. You have smashed this gentleman a little; now you want to squeeze him somewhere. You need the river, the great hide-folly. I am going to get you out of the scrape. To help a good fellow in trouble that puts my boots on."

While approving Jean Valjean for keeping silence, he was evidently seeking to make him speak. He pushed his shoulders, so as to endeavour to see his side-face, and exclaimed, without however rising above the moderate tone in which he kept his voice:

"Speaking of the quagmire, you are a proud animal. Why didn't you throw the man in there?"

Jean Valjean preserved silence.

Thénardier resumed, raising the rag which served him as a cravat up to his Adam's apple, a gesture which completes the air of sagacity of a serious man:

"Indeed, perhaps you have acted prudently. The workmen when they come to-morrow to stop the hole, would certainly have found the *pantinois* forgotten there, and they would have been able, thread by thread, straw by straw, to *pincer* the trace, and to reach you. Something has passed through the sewer? Who? Where did he come out? Did anybody see him come out? The police has plenty of brains. The sewer is treacherous and informs against you. Such a discovery is a rarity, it attracts attention, few people use the sewer in their business while the river is at everybody's service. The river is the true grave. At the month's end, they fish you up the man at the nets of Saint Cloud. Well, what does that amount to? It is a carcass, indeed! Who killed this man? Paris. And justice don't even inquire into it. You have done right."

The more loquacious Thénardier was, the more dumb was Jean Valjean. Thénardier pushed his shoulder anew.

"Now, let us finish the business. Let us divide. You have seen my key, show me your money."

Thénardier was haggard, tawny, equivocal, a little threatening, nevertheless friendly.

There was one strange circumstance; Thénardier's manner was not natural; he did not appear entirely at his ease; while he did not affect an air of mystery, he talked low; from time to time he laid his finger on his mouth and muttered: "Hush!" It was difficult to guess why. There was nobody there but them. Jean Valjean thought that perhaps some other bandits were hidden in some recess not far off, and that Thénardier did not care to share with them.

Thénardier resumed:

"Let us finish. How much did the *pantre* have in his deeps?"

Jean Valjean felt in his pockets.

It was, as will be remembered, his custom always to have money about him. The gloomy life of expedients to which he was condemned, made this a law to him. This time, however, he was caught unprovided. On putting on his National Guard's uniform, the evening before, he had forgotten, gloomily absorbed as he was, to take his pocket-book with him. He had only some coins in his waistcoat pocket. He turned out his pocket, all soaked with filth, and displayed upon the curb of the sewer a louis d'or, two five-franc pieces, and five or six big sous.

Thénardier thrust out his under lip with a significant twist of the neck.

"You didn't kill him very dear," said he.

He began to handle, in all familiarity, the pockets of Jean Valjean and Marius. Jean Valjean, principally concerned in keeping his back to the light, did not interfere with him. While he was feeling of Marius's coat, Thénardier, with the dexterity of a juggler, found means, without attracting Jean Valjean's attention, to tear off a strip, which he hid under his blouse, probably thinking that this scrap of cloth might assist him afterwards to identify the assassinated man and the assassin. He found, however, nothing more than the thirty francs.

"It is true," said he, "both together, you have no more than that."

And, forgetting his words, *go halves*, he took the whole.

He hesitated a little before the big sous. Upon reflection, he took them also, mumbling:

"No matter! this is to *suriner* people too cheap."

This said, he took the key from under his blouse anew.

"Now, friend, you must go out. This is like the fair, you pay on going out. You have paid, go out."

And he began to laugh.

That he had, in extending to an unknown man the help of this key, and in causing another man than himself to go out by this door, the pure and disinterested intention of saving an assassin, is something which it is permissible to doubt.

Thénardier helped Jean Valjean to replace Marius upon his shoulders; then he went towards the grating upon the points of his bare feet, beckoning to Jean Valjean to follow him, he looked outside, laid his finger on his mouth, and stood a few seconds as if in suspense; the inspection over, he put the key into the lock. The bolt slid and the door turned. There was neither snapping nor grinding. It was done very quietly. It was plain that this grating and its hinges, oiled with care, were opened oftener than would have been guessed. This quiet was ominous; you felt in it the furtive goings and comings, the silent entrances and exits of the men of the night, and the wolf-like tread of crime. The sewer was evidently in complicity with some mysterious band. This taciturn grating was a receiver.

Thénardier half opened the door, left just a passage for Jean Valjean, closed the grating again, turned the key twice in the lock, and plunged back into the obscurity, without making more noise than a breath. He seemed to walk with the velvet paws of a tiger. A moment afterwards, this hideous providence had entered again into the invisible.

Jean Valjean found himself outside.

IX

MARIUS SEEMS TO BE DEAD TO ONE WHO IS A GOOD JUDGE

HE let Marius slide down upon the beach.

They were outside!

The miasmas, the obscurity, the horror, were behind him. The balmy air, pure, living, joyful, freely respirable, flowed around him. Everywhere about him silence, but the charming silence of a sunset in a clear sky. Twilight had fallen; night was coming, the great liberatress, the friend of all those who need a mantle of darkness to escape from an anguish. The sky extended on every side like an enormous calm. The river came to his feet with the sound of a kiss. He heard the airy dialogues of the nests bidding each other good-night in the elms of the Champs-Elysées. A few stars, faintly piercing the pale blue of the zenith, and visible to reverie alone, produced their imperceptible little resplendencies in the immensity. Evening was unfolding over Jean Valjean's head all the caresses of the infinite.

It was the undecided and exquisite hour which says neither yes nor no. There was already night enough for one to be lost in it at a little distance, and still day enough for one to be recognised near at hand.

Jean Valjean was for a few seconds irresistibly overcome by all this august and caressing serenity; there are such moments of forgetfulness; suffering refuses to harass the wretched; all is eclipsed in thought; peace covers the dreamer like a night; and, under the twilight which is flinging forth its rays, and in imitation of the sky which is illuminating, the soul becomes starry. Jean Valjean could not but gaze at that vast clear shadow which was above him; pensive, he took in the majestic silence of the eternal heavens, a bath of ecstasy and prayer. Then, hastily, as if a feeling of duty came back to him, he bent over Marius, and, dipping up some water in the hollow of his hand, he threw a few drops gently into his face. Marius' eyelids did not part; but his half-open mouth breathed.

Jean Valjean was plunging his hand into the river again, when suddenly he felt an indescribable uneasiness, such as we feel when we have somebody behind us, without seeing him.

We have already referred elsewhere to this impression, with which everybody is acquainted.

He turned round.

As just before, somebody was indeed behind him.

A man of tall stature, wrapped in a long overcoat, with folded arms, and holding in his right hand a club, the leaden knob of which could be seen, stood erect a few steps in the rear of Jean Valjean, who was stooping over Marius.

It was, with the aid of the shadow, a sort of apparition. A simple man would have been afraid on account of the twilight, and a reflective man on account of the club.

Jean Valjean recognised Javert.

The reader has doubtless guessed that Thénardier's pursuer was none other than Javert. Javert, after his unhoped-for departure from the barricade, had gone to the prefecture of police, had given an account verbally to the prefect in person in a short audience, had then immediately returned to his duty, which implied—the note found upon him will be remembered—a certain surveillance of the shore on the right bank of the Champs-Elysées, which for some time had excited the attention of the police. There he had seen Thénardier, and had followed him. The rest is known.

It is understood also that the opening of that grating so obligingly before Jean Valjean was a piece of shrewdness on the part of Thénardier. Thénardier felt that Javert was still there; the man who is watched has a scent which does not deceive him; a bone must be thrown to this hound. An assassin, what a godsend! It was the scapegoat, which must never be refused. Thénardier, by putting Jean Valjean out in his place, gave a victim to the police, threw them off his own track, caused himself to be forgotten in a larger matter, rewarded Javert for his delay, which always flatters a spy, gained thirty francs, and counted surely, as for himself, upon escaping by the aid of this diversion.

Jean Valjean had passed from one shoal to another.

These two encounters, blow on blow, to fall from Thénardier upon Javert, it was hard.

Javert did not recognise Jean Valjean, who, as we have said, no longer resembled himself. He did not unfold his arms, he secured his club in his grasp by an imperceptible movement, and said in a quick and calm voice:

"Who are you?"

"I."

"What you?"

"Jean Valjean."

Javert put the club between his teeth, bent his knees, inclined his body, laid his two powerful hands upon Jean Valjean's shoulders, which they clamped like two vices, examined him, and recognised him. Their faces almost touched. Javert's look was terrible.

Jean Valjean stood inert under the grasp of Javert like a lion who should submit to the claw of a lynx.

"Inspector Javert," said he, "you have got me. Besides, since this morning, I have considered myself your prisoner. I did not give you my address to try to escape you. Take me. Only grant me one thing."

Javert seemed not to hear. He rested his fixed eye upon Jean Valjean. His rising chin pushed his lips towards his nose, a sign of savage reverie. At last, he let go of Jean Valjean, rose up as straight as a stick, took his club firmly in his grasp, and, as if in a dream, murmured rather than pronounced this question:

"What are you doing here? and who is this man?"

Jean Valjean answered, and the sound of his voice appeared to awaken Javert:

"It is precisely of him that I wished to speak. Dispose of me as you please; but help me first to carry him home. I only ask that of you."

Javert's face contracted, as it happened to him whenever anybody seemed to consider him capable of a concession. Still he did not say no.

He stooped down again, took a handkerchief from his pocket, which he dipped in the water, and wiped Marius' blood-stained forehead.

"This man was in the barricade," said he in an undertone, and as if speaking to himself. "This is he whom they called Marius."

A spy of the first quality, who had observed everything, listened to everything, heard everything, and recollected everything, believing he was about to die; who spied even in his death-agony, and who, leaning upon the first step of the grave, had taken notes.

He seized Marius' hand, seeking for his pulse.

"He is wounded," said Jean Valjean.

"He is dead," said Javert.

Jean Valjean answered:

"No. Not yet."

"You have brought him, then, from the barricade here?" observed Javert.

His preoccupation must have been deep, as he did not dwell longer upon this perplexing escape through the sewer, and did not even notice Jean Valjean's silence after his question.

Jean Valjean, for his part, eseemed to have but one idea. He resumed:

"He lives in the Marais, Rue des Filles du Calvaire, at his grandfather's—I forget the name."

Jean Valjean felt in Marius' coat, took out the pocket-book, opened it at the page pencilled by Marius, and handed it to Javert.

There was still enough light floating in the air to enable one to read. Javert, moreover, had in his eye the feline phosphorescence of the birds of the night. He deciphered the few lines written by Marius, and muttered: "Gillenormand, Rue des Filles du Calvaire, No. 6."

Then he cried: "Driver?"

The reader will remember the fiacre which was waiting, in case of need.

Javert kept Marius' pocket-book.

A moment later, the carriage, descending by the slope of the watering-place, was on the beach. Marius was laid upon the back seat, and Javert sat down by the side of Jean Valjean on the front seat.

When the door was shut, the fiacre moved rapidly off, going up the quais in the direction of the Bastille.

They left the quais and entered the streets. The driver, a black silhouette upon his box, whipped up his bony horses. Icy silence in the coach. Marius, motionless, his body braced in the corner of the carriage, his head dropping down upon his breast, his arms hanging, his legs rigid, appeared to await nothing now but a coffin; Jean Valjean seemed made of shadow, and Javert of stone; and in that carriage full of night, the interior of which, whenever it passed before a lamp, appeared to turn lividly pale, as if from an intermittent flash, chance grouped together, and seemed dismally to confront the three tragic immobilities, the corpse, the spectre, and the statue.

X
RETURN OF THE PRODIGAL SON—OF HIS LIFE

At every jolt over the pavement, a drop of blood fell from Marius' hair.

It was after nightfall when the fiacre arrived at No. 6, in the Rue des Filles du Calvaire.

Javert first set foot on the ground, verified by a glance the number above the porte-cochère, and, lifting the heavy wrought-iron knocker, embellished in the old fashion, with a goat and a satyr defying each other, struck a violent blow. The fold of the door partly opened, and Javert pushed it. The porter showed himself, gaping and half-awake, a candle in his hand.

Everybody in the house was asleep. People go to bed early in the Marais, especially on days of émeute. That good old quartier, startled by the Revolution, takes refuge in slumber, as children, when they hear Bugaboo coming, hide their heads very quickly under their coverlets.

Meanwhile Jean Valjean and the driver lifted Marius out of the coach, Jean Valjean supporting him by the armpits, and the coachman by the knees.

While he was carrying Marius in this way, Jean Valjean slipped his hand under his clothes, which were much torn, felt his breast, and assured himself that the heart still beat. It beat even a little less feebly, as if the motion of the carriage had determined a certain renewal of life.

Javert called out to the porter in the tone which befits the government, in presence of the porter of a factious man.

"Somebody whose name is Gillenormand?"

"It is here. What do you want with him?"

"His son is brought home."

"His son?" said the porter with amazement.

"He is dead."

Jean Valjean, who came ragged and dirty, behind Javert, and whom the porter beheld with some horror, motioned to him with his head that he was not.

The porter did not appear to understand either Javert's words, or Jean Valjean's signs.

Javert continued:

"He has been to the barricade, and here he is."

"To the barricade!" exclaimed the porter.

"He has got himself killed. Go and wake his father."

The porter did not stir.

"Why don't you go?" resumed Javert.

And he added:

"There will be a funeral here to-morrow."

With Javert the common incidents of the highways were classed categorically, which is the foundation of prudence and vigilance, and each contingency had its compartment; the possible facts were in some sort in the drawers, whence they came out, on occasion, in variable quantities; there were, in the street, riot, émeute, carnival, funeral.

The porter merely woke Basque. Basque woke Nicolette; Nicolette woke Aunt Gillenormand. As to the grandfather, they let him sleep, thinking that he would know it soon enough at all events.

They carried Marius up to the first story, without anybody, moreover, perceiving it in the other portions of the house, and they laid him on an old couch in M. Gillenormand's antechamber; and, while Basque went for a doctor and Nicolette was opening the linen closets, Jean Valjean felt Javert touch him on the shoulder. He understood, and went down stairs, having behind him Javert's following steps.

The porter saw them depart as he had seen them arrive, with drowsy dismay.

They got into the fiacre again, and the driver mounted upon his box.

"Inspector Javert," said Jean Valjean, "grant me one thing more."

"What?" asked Javert roughly.

"Let me go home a moment. Then you shall do with me what you will."

Javert remained silent for a few seconds, his chin drawn back into the collar of his overcoat, then he let down the window in front.

"Driver," said he, "Rue de l'Homme Armé, No. 7."

XI

COMMOTION IN THE ABSOLUTE

THEY did not open their mouths again for the whole distance.

What did Jean Valjean desire? To finish what he had begun; to inform Cosette, to tell her where Marius was, to give her perhaps some other useful information, to make, if he could, certain final dispositions. As to himself, as to what concerned him personally, it was all over; he had been seized by Javert and did not resist; another than he, in such a condition, would perhaps have thought vaguely of that rope which Thénardier had given him and of the bars of the first cell which he should enter; but, since the bishop, there had been in Jean Valjean, in view of any violent attempt, were it even upon his own life, let us repeat, a deep religious hesitation.

Suicide, that mysterious assault upon the unknown, which may contain, in a certain measure, the death of the soul, was impossible to Jean Valjean.

At the entrance of the Rue de l'Homme Armé, the fiacre stopped, this street being too narrow for carriages to enter. Javert and Jean Valjean got out.

The driver humbly represented to monsieur the inspector that the Utrecht velvet of his carriage was all stained with the blood of the assassinated man and with the mud of the assassin. That was what he had understood. He added that an indemnity was due him. At the same time, taking his little book from his pocket, he begged monsieur the inspector to have the goodness to write him "a little scrap of certificate as to what."

Javert pushed back the little book which the driver handed him, and said:

"How much must you have, including your stop and your trip?"

"It is seven hours and a quarter," answered the driver, "and my velvet was brand new. Eighty francs, monsieur the inspector."

Javert took four napoleons from his pocket and dismissed the fiacre.

Jean Valjean thought that Javert's intention was to take him on foot to the post of the Blancs-Manteaux or to the post of the Archives which are quite near by.

They entered the street. It was, as usual, empty. Javert followed Jean Valjean. They reached No. 7. Jean Valjean rapped. The door opened.

"Very well," said Javert. "Go up."

He added with a strange expression and as if he were making an effort in speaking in such a way:

"I will wait here for you."

Jean Valjean looked at Javert. This manner of proceeding was little in accordance with Javert's habits. Still, that Javert should now have a sort of haughty confidence in him, the confidence of the cat which grants the mouse the liberty of the length of her claw, resolved as Jean Valjean was to deliver himself up and make an end of it, could not surprise him very much. He opened the door, went into the house, cried to the porter who was in bed and who had drawn the cord without getting up: "It is I!" and mounted the stairs.

On reaching the first story, he paused. All painful paths have their halting-places. The window on the landing, which was a sliding window, was open. As in many old houses, the stairway admitted the light, and had a view upon the street. The street lamp, which stood exactly opposite, threw some rays upon the stairs, which produced an economy in light.

Jean Valjean, either to take breath or mechanically, looked out of this window. He leaned over the street. It is short, and the lamp lighted it from one end to the other. Jean Valjean was bewildered with amazement; there was nobody there.

Javert was gone.

XII
THE GRANDFATHER

BASQUE and the porter had carried Marius into the parlour, still stretched motionless upon the couch on which he had been first laid. The doctor, who had been sent for, had arrived. Aunt Gillenormand had got up.

Aunt Gillenormand went to and fro, in terror, clasping her hands, and incapable of doing anything but to say: "My God, is it possible?" She added at intervals: "Everything will be covered with blood!" When the first horror was over, a certain philosophy of the situation dawned upon her mind, and expressed itself by this exclamation: "it must have turned out this way!" She did not attain to: "*I always said just so!*" which is customary on occasions of this kind.

On the doctor's order, a cot-bed had been set up near the couch. The doctor examined Marius, and, after having determined that the pulse still beat, that the sufferer had no wound penetrating his breast, and that the blood at the corners of his mouth came from the nasal cavities, he had him laid flat upon the bed, without a pillow, his head on a level with his body, and even a little lower with his chest bare, in order to facilitate respiration. Mademoiselle Gillenormand, seeing that they were taking off Marius' clothes, withdrew. She began to tell her beads in her room.

The body had not received any interior lesion; a ball, deadened by the pocket-book, had turned aside, and made the tour of the ribs with a hideous gash, but not deep, and consequently not dangerous. The long walk underground had completed the dislocation of the broken shoulder-blade, and there were serious difficulties there. There were sword cuts on the arms. No scar disfigured his face; the head, however, was as it were covered with hacks; what would be the result of these wounds on the head? did they stop at the scalp? did they affect the skull? That could not yet be told. A serious symptom was, that they had caused the fainting, and men do not always wake from such faintings. The hæmorrhage, moreover, had exhausted the wounded man. From the waist, the lower part of the body had been protected by the barricade.

Basque and Nicolette tore up linen and made bandages; Nicolette sewed them, Basque folded them. There being no lint, the doctor stopped the flow of blood from the wounds temporarily with rolls of wadding. By the side of the bed, three candles were burning on a table upon which the surgical instruments were spread out. The doctor washed Marius' face and hair with cold water. A bucketful was red in a moment. The porter, candle in hand, stood by.

The physician seemed reflecting sadly. From time to time he shook his head, as if he were answering some question which he had put to himself internally. A bad sign for the patient, these mysterious dialogues of the physician with himself.

At the moment the doctor was wiping the face and touching the still closed eyelids lightly with his finger, a door opened at the rear end of the parlour, and a long, pale figure approached.

It was the grandfather.

The émeute, for two days, had very much agitated, exasperated, and absorbed M. Gillenormand. He had not slept during the preceding night, and he had had a fever all day. At night, he had gone to bed very early, recommending that everything in the house be bolted; and, from fatigue, he had fallen asleep.

The slumbers of old men are easily broken; M. Gillenormand's room was next the parlour, and, in spite of the precautions they had taken, the noise had awakened him. Surprised by the light which he saw at the crack of his door, he had got out of bed, and groped his way along.

He was on the threshold, one hand on the knob of the half-opened door, his head bent a little forward and shaking, his body wrapped in a white nightgown, straight and without folds like a shroud; he was astounded; and he had the appearance of a phantom who is looking into a tomb.

He perceived the bed, and on the mattress that bleeding young man, white with a waxy whiteness, his eyes closed, his mouth open, his lips pallid, naked to the waist, gashed everywhere with red wounds, motionless, brightly lighted.

The grandfather had, from head to foot, as much of a shiver as ossified limbs can have; his eyes, the cornea of which had become yellow from his great age, were veiled with a sort of glassy haze; his whole face assumed in an instant the cadaverous angles of a skeleton head, his arms fell pendent as if a spring were broken in them, and his stupefied astonishment was expressed by the separation of the fingers of his aged, tremulous hands; his knees bent forward, showing through the opening of his nightgown his poor naked legs bristling with white hairs, and he murmured:

"Marius!"

"Monsieur," said Basque, "monsieur has just been brought home. He has been to the barricade, and——"

"He is dead!" cried the old man in a terrible voice. "Oh! the brigand."

Then a sort of sepulchral transfiguration made this centenarian as straight as a young man.

"Monsieur," said he, "you are the doctor. Come, tell me one thing. He is dead, isn't he?"

The physician, in the height of anxiety, kept silence.

M. Gillenormand wrung his hands with a terrific burst of laughter.

"He is dead! he is dead! He has got killed at the barricade! in hatred of me! It is against me that he did this! Ah, the blood-drinker! This is the way he comes back to me! Misery of my life, he is dead!"

He went to a window, opened it wide as if he were stifling, and, standing before the shadow, he began to talk into the street to the night:

"Pierced, sabred, slaughtered, exterminated, slashed, cut in pieces! do you see that, the vagabond! He knew very well that I was waiting for him and that I had had his room arranged for him, and that I had had his portrait of the time when he was a little boy hung at the head of my bed! He knew very well that he had only to come back, and that for years I had been calling him, and that I sat at night in my chimney-corner, with my hands on my knees, not knowing what to do, and that I was a fool for his sake! You knew it very well, that you had only to come in and say: 'It is I,' and that you would be the master of the house, and that I would obey you, and that you would do whatever you liked with your old booby of a grandfather. You knew it very well, and you said: 'No, he is a royalist; I won't go!' And you went to the barricades, and you got yourself killed, out of spite! to revenge yourself for what I said to you about Monsieur the Duke de Berry! That is infamous! Go to bed, then, and sleep quietly! He is dead! That is my waking."

The physician, who began to be anxious on two accounts, left Marius a moment, and went to M. Gillenormand and took his arm. The grandfather turned round, looked at him with eyes which seemed swollen and bloody, and said quietly:

"Monsieur, I thank you. I am calm, I am a man, I saw the death of Louis XVI., I know how to bear up under events. There is one thing which is terrible, to think that it is your newspapers that do all the harm. You will have scribblers, talkers, lawyers, orators, tribunes, discussions, progress, lights, rights of man, freedom of the press, and this is the way they bring home your children for you. Oh! Marius! it is abominable! Killed! dead before me! A barricade! Oh! the bandit! Doctor, you live in the quartier, I believe? Oh! I know you well. I see your carriage pass from my window. I am going to tell you. You would be wrong to think I am angry. We don't get angry with a dead man; that would be stupid. That is a child I brought up. I was an old man when he was yet quite small. He played at the Tuileries with his little spade and his little chair, and, so that the keeper should not scold, with my cane I filled up the holes in the ground that he made with his spade. One day he cried: 'Down with Louis XVIII.!' and went away. It is not my fault. He was all rosy and fair. His mother is dead. Have you noticed that all little children are fair? What is the reason of it? He is the son of one of those brigands of the Loire; but children are innocent of the crimes of their fathers. I remember when he was as high as this. He could not pronounce the *d*'s. His talk was so soft and so obscure that you would have thought it was a bird. I recollect that once, before the Farnese Hercules, they made a circle to admire and wonder at him, that child was so beautiful! It was such a head as you see in pictures. I spoke to him in my gruff voice, I frightened him with my cane, but he knew very well it was for fun. In the morning, when he came into my room, I scolded, but it seemed like sunshine to me. You can't defend yourself against these brats. They take you, they hold on to you, they never let go of you. The truth is, that there was never any amour like that child. Now, what do you say of your Lafayette, your Benjamin Constant, and of your Tirecuir de Corcelles, who kill him for me! It can't go on like this."

He approached Marius, who was still livid and motionless, and to whom the physician had returned, and he began to wring his hands. The old man's white lips moved as if mechanically, and made way for almost indistinct words, like whispers in a death-rattle, which could scarcely be heard: "Oh! heartless! Oh! clubbist! Oh! scoundrel! Oh! Septembrist!" Reproaches whispered by a dying man to a corpse.

Little by little, as internal eruptions must always make their way out, the connection of his words returned, but the grandfather appeared to have lost the strength to utter them, his voice was so dull and faint that it seemed to come from the other side of an abyss:

"It is all the same to me, I am going to die too, myself. And to say that there is no little creature in Paris who would have been glad to make the wretch happy! A rascal who, instead of amusing himself and enjoying life, went to fight and got himself riddled like a brute! And for whom? for what? For the republic! Instead of going to dance at the Chaumière, as young people should! It is well worth being twenty years old. The republic, a deuced fine folly. Poor mothers, raise your pretty boys then. Come, he is dead. That will make two funerals under the porte-cochère. Then you fixed yourself out like that for the fine eyes of General Lamarque! What had he done for you, this General Lamarque? A sabrer! a babbler! To get killed for a dead man! If it isn't enough to make a man crazy! Think of it! At twenty! And without turning his head to see if he was not leaving some-body behind him! Here now are the poor old goodmen who must die alone. Perish in your corner, owl! Well, indeed, so much the better, it is what I was hoping, it is going to kill me dead. I am too old, I am a hundred, I am a hundred thousand; it is a long time since I have had a right to be dead. With this blow, it is done. It is all over then, how lucky! What is the use of making him breathe hartshorn and all this heap of drugs? You are losing your pains, dolt of a doctor! Go along, he is dead, stone dead. I understand it, I, who am dead also. He hasn't done the thing half way. Yes, these times are infamous, infamous, infamous, and that is what I think of you, of your ideas, of your systems, of your masters, of your oracles. of your doctors, of your scamps of writers, of your beggars of philosophers, and of all the revolutions which for sixty years have frightened the flocks of crows in the Tuileries! And as you had no pity in getting yourself killed like that, I shall not have even any grief for your death, do you understand, assassin?"

At this moment, Marius slowly raised his lids, and his gaze, still veiled in the astonishment of lethargy, rested upon M. Gillenormand.

"Marius!" cried the old man. "Marius! my darling Marius! my child! my dear son! You are opening your eyes, you are looking at me, you are alive, thanks!"

And he fell fainting.

BOOK FOURTH – JAVERT OFF THE TRACK

I
JAVERT OFF THE TRACK

JAVERT made his way with slow steps from the Rue de l'Homme Armé.

He walked with his head down, for the first time in his life, and, for the first time in his life as well, with his hands behind his back.

Until that day, Javert had taken, of the two attitudes of Napoleon, only that which expresses resolution, the arms folded upon the breast; that which expresses uncertainty, the hands behind the back, was unknown to him. Now, a change had taken place; his whole person, slow and gloomy, bore the impress of anxiety.

He plunged into the silent streets.

Still he followed one direction.

He took the shortest route towards the Seine, reached the Quai des Ormes, went along the quai, passed the Grève, and stopped, at a little distance from the post of the Place du Châtelet, at the corner of the Pont Notre Dame. The Seine there forms between the Pont Notre Dame and the Pont au Change in one direction, and in the other between the Quai de la Mégisserie and the Quai aux Fleurs, a sort of square lake crossed by a rapid.

This point of the Seine is dreaded by mariners. Nothing is more dangerous than this rapid, narrowed at that period and vexed by the piles of the mill of the bridge, since removed. The two bridges, so near each other, increase the danger, the water hurrying fearfully under the arches. It rolls on with broad, terrible folds; it gathers and heaps up; the flood strains at the piles of the bridge as if to tear them out with huge liquid ropes. Men who fall in there, one never sees again; the best swimmers are drowned.

Javert leaned both elbows on the parapet, with his chin in his hands, and while his fingers were clenched mechanically in the thickest of his whiskers, he reflected.

There had been a new thing, a revolution, a catastrophe in the depths of his being; and there was matter for self-examination.

Javert was suffering frightfully.

For some hours Javert had ceased to be natural. He was

1294

troubled; this brain, so limpid in its blindness, had lost its transparency; there was a cloud in this crystal. Javert felt that duty was growing weaker in his conscience, and he could not hide it from himself. When he had so unexpectedly met Jean Valjean upon the beach of the Seine, there had been in him something of the wolf, which seizes his prey again, and of the dog, which again finds his master.

He saw before him two roads, both equally straight; but he saw two; and that terrified him—him, who had never in his life known but one straight line. And, bitter anguish, these two roads were contradictory. One of these two straight lines excluded the other. Which of the two was the true one?

His condition was inexpressible.

To owe life to a malefactor, to accept that debt and to pay it, to be, in spite of himself, on a level with a fugitive from justice, and to pay him for one service with another service; to allow him to say: "Go away," and to say to him in turn: "Be free;" to sacrifice duty, that general obligation, to personal motives, and to feel in these personal motives something general also, and perhaps superior; to betray society in order to be true to his own conscience; that all these absurdities should be realised and that they should be accumulated upon himself, this it was by which he was prostrated.

One thing had astonished him, that Jean Valjean had spared him, and one thing had petrified him, that he, Javert, had spared Jean Valjean.

Where was he? He sought himself and found himself no longer.

What should he do now? Give up Jean Valjean, that was wrong; leave Jean Valjean free, that was wrong. In the first case, the man of authority would fall lower than the man of the galley; in the second, a convict rose higher than the law and set his foot upon it. In both cases, dishonour to him, Javert. In every course which was open to him, there was a fall. Destiny has certain extremities precipitous upon the impossible, and beyond which life is no more than an abyss. Javert was at one of these extremities.

One of his causes of anxiety was, that he was compelled to think. The very violence of all these contradictory emotions forced him to it. Thought, an unaccustomed thing to him, and singularly painful.

There is always a certain amount of internal rebellion in thought; and he was irritated at having it within him.

Thought, upon any subject, no matter what, outside of the narrow circle of his functions, had been to him, in all cases, a folly and a fatigue; but thought upon the day which had just gone by, was torture. He must absolutely, however, look into his conscience after such shocks, and render an account of himself to himself.

What he had just done made him shudder. He had, he, Javert, thought good to decide, against all the regulations of the police, against the whole social and judicial organisation, against the entire code, in favour of a release; that had pleased him; he had substituted his own affairs for the public affairs; could this be characterised? Every time that he set himself face to face with this nameless act which he had committed, he trembled from head to foot. Upon what should he resolve? A single resource remained: to return immediately to the Rue de l'Homme Armé, and have Jean Valjean arrested. It was clear that that was what he must do. He could not.

Something barred the way to him on that side.

Something? What? Is there anything else in the world besides tribunals, sentences, police, and authority? Javert's ideas were overturned.

A galley slave sacred! a convict not to be taken by justice! and that by the act of Javert!

That Javert and Jean Valjean, the man made to be severe, the man made to be submissive, that these two men, who were each the thing of the law, should have come to this point of setting themselves both above the law, was not this terrible?

What then! such enormities should happen and nobody should be punished? Jean Valjean, stronger than the entire social order, should be free and he, Javert, continue to eat the bread of the government!

His reflections gradually became terrible.

He might also through these reflections have reproached himself a little in regard to the insurgent carried to the Rue des Filles du Calvaire, but he did not think of it. The lesser fault was lost in the greater. Besides, that insurgent was clearly a dead man, and legally, death extinguishes pursuit.

Jean Valjean then was the weight he had on his mind.

Jean Valjean confounded him. All the axioms which had

been the supports of his whole life crumbled away before this man. Jean Valjean's generosity towards him, Javert, over-whelmed him. Other acts, which he remembered and which he had hitherto treated as lies and follies, returned to him now as realities. M. Madeleine reappeared behind Jean Valjean, and the two figures overlaid each other so as to make but one, which was venerable. Javert felt that something horrible was penetrating his soul, admiration for a convict. Respect for a galley slave, can that be possible? He shuddered at it, yet could not shake it off. It was useless to struggle, he was reduced to confess before his own inner tribunal the sublimity of this wretch. That was hateful.

A beneficent malefactor, a compassionate convict, kind, helpful, clement, returning good for evil, returning pardon for hatred, loving pity rather than vengeance, preferring to destroy himself rather than to destroy his enemy, saving him who had stricken him, kneeling upon the height of virtue, nearer the angels than men. Javert was compelled to acknowledge that this monster existed.

This could not last.

Certainly, and we repeat it, he had not given himself up without resistance to this monster, this infamous angel, this hideous hero, at whom he was almost as indignant as he was astounded. Twenty times, while he was in that carriage face to face with Jean Valjean, the legal tiger had roared within him. Twenty times he had been tempted to throw himself upon Jean Valjean, to seize him and to devour him, that is to say, to arrest him. What more simple, indeed? To cry at the first post in front of which they passed: "Here is a fugitive from justice in breach of his ban!" to call the gendarmes and say to them: "This man is yours!" then to go away, to leave this condemned man there, to ignore the rest, and to have nothing more to do with it. This man is for ever the prisoner of the law, the law will do what it will with him. What more just? Javert had said all this to himself, he had desired to go further, to act, to apprehend the man, and, then as now, he had not been able; and every time that his hand had been raised convulsively towards Jean Valjean's collar, his hand, as if under an enormous weight, had fallen back, and in the depths of his mind he had heard a voice, a strange voice crying to him: "Very well. Give up your saviour. Then have Pontius Pilate's basin brought, and wash your claws."

Then his reflections fell back upon himself, and by the side of Jean Valjean, exalted, he beheld himself, him, Javert, degraded.

A convict was his benefactor!

But also why had he permitted this man to let him live? He had, in that barricade, the right to be killed. He should have availed himself of that right. To have called the other insurgents to his aid against Jean Valjean, to have secured a shot by force, that would have been better.

His supreme anguish was the loss of all certainty. He felt that he was uprooted. The code was now but a stump in his hand. He had to do with scruples of an unknown species. There was in him a revelation of feeling entirely distinct from the declarations of the law, his only standard hitherto. To retain his old virtue, that no longer sufficed. An entire order of unexpected facts arose and subjugated him. An entire new world appeared to his soul; favour accepted and returned, devotion, compassion, indulgence, acts of violence committed by pity upon austerity, respect of persons, no more final condemnation, no more damnation, the possibility of a tear in the eye of the law, a mysterious justice according to God going counter to justice according to men. He perceived in the darkness the fearful rising of an unknown moral sun; he was horrified and blinded by it. An owl compelled to an eagle's gaze.

He said to himself that it was true then, that there were exceptions, that authority might be put out of countenance, that rule might stop short before a fact, that everything was not framed in the text of the code, that the unforeseen would be obeyed, that the virtue of a convict might spread a snare for the virtue of a functionary, that the monstrous might be divine, that destiny had such ambuscades as these, and he thought with despair that even he had not been proof against a surprise.

He was compelled to recognise the existence of kindness. This convict had been kind. And he himself, wonderful to tell, he had just been kind. Therefore he had become depraved.

He thought himself base. He was a horror to himself.

Javert's ideal was not to be humane, not to be great, not to be sublime; it was to be irreproachable. Now he had just failed.

How had he reached that point? How had all this happened? He could not have told himself. He took his head in his hands, but it was in vain; he could not explain it to himself.

He had certainly always had the intention of returning Jean

Valjean to the law, of which Jean Valjean was the captive, and of which he, Javert, was the slave. He had not confessed to himself for a single moment while he held him, that he had a thought of letting him go. It was in some sort without his knowledge that his hand had opened and released him.

All manner of interrogation points flashed before his eyes. He put questions to himself, and he made answers, and his answers frightened him. He asked himself: "This convict, this desperate man, whom I have pursued even to persecution, and who has had me beneath his feet, and could have avenged himself, and who ought to have done so as well for his revenge as for his security, in granting me life, in sparing me, what has he done? His duty? No. Something more. And I, in sparing him in my turn, what have I done? My duty? No. Something more. There is then something more than duty." Here he was startled; his balances were disturbed; one of the scales fell into the abyss, the other flew into the sky, and Javert felt no less dismay from the one which was above than from the one which was below. Without being the least in the world what is called a Voltairian, or a philosopher, or a sceptic, respectful on the contrary, by instinct, towards the established church, he knew it only as an august fragment of the social whole; order was his dogma and was enough for him; since he had been of the age of a man, and an official, he had put almost all his religion in the police. Being, and we employ the words here without the slightest irony and in their most serious acceptation, being, we have said, a spy as men are priests. He had a superior, M. Gisquet; he had scarcely thought, until today, of that other superior, God.

This new chief, God, he felt unawares, and was perplexed thereat.

He had lost his bearings in this unexpected presence; he did not know what to do with this superior; he who was not ignorant that the subordinate is bound always to yield, that he ought neither to disobey, nor to blame, nor to discuss, and that, in presence of a superior who astonishes him too much, the inferior has no resource but resignation.

But how manage to send in his resignation to God?

However this might be, and it was always to this that he returned, one thing overruled all else for him, that was, that he had just committed an appalling infraction. He had closed his eyes upon a convicted second offender in breach of his ban. He had set a galley slave at large. He had robbed the laws of a man who belonged to them. He had done that. He could not understand himself. He was not sure of being himself. The very reasons of his action escaped him; he caught only the whirl of them. He had lived up to this moment by that blind faith which a dark probity engenders. This faith was leaving him, this probity was failing him. All that he had believed was dissipated. Truths which he had no wish for inexorably besieged him. He must henceforth be another man. He suffered the strange pangs of a conscience suddenly operated upon for the cataract. He saw what he revolted at seeing. He felt that he was emptied, useless, broken off from his past life, destitute, dissolved. Authority was dead in him. He had no further reason for existence.

Terrible situation! to be moved.

To be granite, and to doubt! to be the statue of penalty cast in a single piece in the mould of the law, and to suddenly perceive that you have under your breast of bronze something preposterous and disobedient which almost resembles a heart! To be led by it to render good for good, although you may have said until to-day that this good was evil! to be the watch-dog, and to fawn! to be ice, and to melt! to be a vice, and to become a hand! to feel your fingers suddenly open! to lose your hold, appalling thing!

The projectile man no longer knowing his road, and recoiling!

To be obliged to acknowledge this: infallibility is not infallible, there may be an error in the dogma, all is not said when a code has spoken, society is not perfect, authority is complicate with vacillation, a cracking is possible in the immutable, judges are men, the law may be deceived, the tribunals may be mistaken! to see a flaw in the immense blue crystal of the firmament!

What was passing in Javert was the Fampoux of a rectilinear conscience, the throwing of a soul out of its path, the crushing of a probity irresistibly hurled in a straight line and breaking itself against God. Certainly, it was strange, that the fireman of order, the engineer of authority, mounted upon the blind iron-horse of the rigid path, could be thrown off by a ray of light! that the incommutable, the direct, the correct, the geometrical, the passive, the perfect, could bend! that there should be a road to Damascus for the locomotive!

God, always interior to man, and unyielding, he the true conscience, to the false; a prohibition to the spark to extinguish itself; an order to the ray to remember the sun; an injunction to the soul to recognise the real absolute when it is confronted with the fictitious absolute; humanity imperishable; the human heart inadmissible; that splendid phenomenon, the most beautiful perhaps of our interior wonders, did Javert comprehend it? did Javert penetrate it? did Javert form any idea of it? Evidently not. But under the pressure of this incontestable incomprehensible, he felt that his head was bursting.

He was less the transfigured than the victim of this miracle. He bore it, exasperated. He saw in it only an immense difficulty of existence. It seemed to him that henceforth his breathing would be oppressed for ever.

To have the unknown over his head, he was not accustomed to that.

Until now all that he had above him had been in his sight a smooth, simple, limpid surface; nothing there unknown, nothing obscure; nothing which was not definite, co-ordinated, concatenated, precise, exact, circumscribed, limited, shut in, all foreseen; authority was a plane; no fall in it, no dizziness before it. Javert had never seen the unknown except below. The irregular, the unexpected, the disorderly opening of chaos, the possible slipping into an abyss; that belonged to inferior regions, to the rebellious, the wicked, the miserable. Now Javert was thrown over backwards, and he was abruptly startled by this monstrous apparition: a gulf on high.

What then! he was dismantled completely! he was disconcerted, absolutely! In what should he trust? That of which he had been convinced gave way!

What! the flaw in the cuirass of society could be found by a magnanimous wretch! what! an honest servant of the law could find himself suddenly caught between two crimes, the crime of letting a man escape, and the crime of arresting him! all was not certain in the order given by the state to the official! There might be blind alleys in duty! What then! was all that real! was it true that an old bandit, weighed down by condemnations, could rise up and be right at last? was this credible? were there cases then when the law ought, before a transfigured crime, to retire, stammering excuses?

Yes, there were! and Javert saw it! and Javert touched it! and not only could he not deny it, but he took part in it. They were realities. It was abominable that real facts could reach such deformity.

If facts did their duty, they would be contented with being the proofs of the law; facts, it is God who sends them. Was anarchy then about to descend from on high?

So,—and beneath the magnifying power of anguish, and in the optical illusion of consternation, all that might have restrained and corrected his impression vanished, and society, and the human race, and the universe, were summed up henceforth in his eyes in one simple and terrible feature—so punishment, the thing judged, the force due to legislation, the decrees of the sovereign courts, the magistracy, the government, prevention and repression, official wisdom, legal infallibility, the principle of authority, all the dogmas upon which repose political and civil security, sovereignty, justice, the logic flowing from the code, the social absolute, the public truth, all that, confusion, jumble, chaos; himself, Javert, the spy of order, incorruptibility in the service of the police, the mastiff-providence of society vanquished and prostrated; and upon all this ruin a man standing, with a green cap on his head and a halo about his brow; such was the overturn to which he had come; such was the frightful vision which he had in his soul.

Could that be endurable? No.

Unnatural state, if ever there was one. There were only two ways to get out of it. One, to go resolutely to Jean Valjean, and to return the man of the galleys to the dungeon. The other——

Javert left the parapet, and, his head erect this time, made his way with a firm step towards the post indicated by a lamp at one of the corners of the Place du Châtelet.

On reaching it, he saw a sergent de ville through the window, and he entered. Merely from the manner in which they push open the door of a guardhouse, policemen recognise each other. Javert gave his name, showed his card to the sergent, and sat down at the table of the post, on which a candle was burning. There was a pen on the table, a leaden inkstand, and some paper in readiness for chance reports and the orders of the night patrol.

This table, always accompanied by its straw chair, is an institution; it exists in all the police posts; it is invariably adorned with a boxwood saucer, full of saw-dust, and a pasteboard box full of red wafers, and it is the lower stage of the official style. On it the literature of the state begins.

Javert took the pen and a sheet of paper, and began to write. This is what he wrote:

SOME OBSERVATIONS FOR THE BENEFIT OF THE SERVICE

"First: I beg monsieur the prefect to glance at this.

"Secondly: the prisoners, on their return from examination, take off their shoes and remain barefooted upon the pavement while they are searched. Many cough on returning to the prison. This involves hospital expenses.

"Thirdly: spinning is good, with relays of officers at intervals; but there should be, on important occasions, two officers at least who do not lose sight of each other, so that, if, for any cause whatever, one officer becomes weak in the service, the other is watching him, and supplies his place.

"Fourthly: it is difficult to explain why the special regulation of the prison of the Madelonnettes forbids a prisoner having a chair, even on paying for it;

"Fifthly: at the Madelonnettes, there are only two bars to the sutler's window, which enables the sutler to let the prisoners touch her hand.

"Sixthly: the prisoners, called barkers, who call the other prisoners to the parlour, make the prisoner pay them two sous for calling his name distinctly. This is a theft.

"Seventhly: for a dropped thread, they retain ten sous from the prisoner in the weaving shop; this is an abuse on the part of the contractor, since the cloth is just as good.

"Eighthly: it is annoying that the visitors of La Force have to cross the Cour des Mômes to reach the parlour of Sainte Marie l'Egyptienne.

"Ninthly: it is certain that gendarmes are every day heard relating, in the yard of the prefecture, the examinations of those brought before the magistrates. For a gendarme, who should hold such things sacred, to repeat what he has heard in the examining chamber, is a serious disorder.

"Tenthly: Mme. Henry is an honest woman; her sutler's window is very neat; but it is wrong for a woman to keep the wicket of the trap-door of the secret cells. It is not worthy the Conciergerie of a great civilisation."

Javert wrote these lines in his calmest and most correct handwriting, not omitting a dot, and making the paper squeak resolutely under his pen. Beneath the last line he signed:

"JAVERT,
"Inspector of the 1st class.
"At the Post of the Place du Châtelet.
"June 7, 1832, about one o'clock in the morning."

Javert dried the fresh ink of the paper, folded it like a letter, sealed it, wrote on the back: *Note for the administration*, left it on the table, and went out of the post. The glazed and grated door closed behind him.

He again crossed the Place du Châtelet diagonally, regained the quai, and returned with automatic precision to the very point which he had left a quarter of an hour before, he leaned over there, and found himself again in the same attitude, on the same stone of the parapet. It seemed as if he had not stirred.

The darkness was complete. It was the sepulchral moment which follows midnight. A ceiling of clouds concealed the stars. The sky was only an ominous depth. The houses in the city no longer showed a single light; nobody was passing; all that he could see of the streets and the quais was deserted; Notre Dame and the towers of the Palais de Justice seemed like features of the night. A lamp reddened the curb of the quai. The silhouettes of the bridges were distorted in the mist, one behind the other. The rains had swelled the river.

The place where Javert was leaning was, it will be remembered, situated exactly over the rapids of the Seine, perpendicularly over that formidable whirlpool which knots and unknots itself like an endless screw.

Javert bent his head and looked. All was black. He could distinguish nothing. He heard a frothing sound; but he did not see the river. At intervals, in that giddy depth, a gleam appeared in dim serpentine contortions, the water having this power, in the most complete night, of taking light, nobody knows whence, and changing it into an adder. The gleam vanished, and all became again indistinct. Immensity seemed open there. What was beneath was not water, it was chasm. The wall of the quai, abrupt, confused, mingled with vapour, suddenly lost to sight, seemed like an escarpment of the infinite.

He saw nothing, but he perceived the hostile chill of the water, and the insipid odour of the moist stones. A fierce breath rose from that abyss. The swollen river guessed at rather than perceived, the tragical whispering of the flood, the dismal vastness of the arches of the bridge, the imaginable fall into that gloomy void, all that shadow was full of horror.

Javert remained for some minutes motionless, gazing into that opening of darkness; he contemplated the invisible with a fixedness which resembled attention. The water gurgled. Suddenly he took off his hat and laid it on the edge of the quai. A moment afterwards, a tall and black form, which from the distance some belated passer might have taken for a phantom, appeared standing on the parapet, bent towards the Seine, then sprang up, and fell straight into the darkness; there was a dull splash; and the shadow alone was in the secret of the convulsions of that obscure form which had disappeared under the water.

BOOK FIFTH –
THE GRANDSON AND THE GRANDFATHER

I

IN WHICH WE SEE THE TREE WITH THE
PLATE OF ZINC ONCE MORE

SOME time after the events which we have just related, the Sieur Boulatruelle had a vivid emotion.

The Sieur Boulatruelle is that road-labourer of Montfermeil of whom we have already had a glimpse in the dark portions of this book.

Boulatruelle, it will perhaps be remembered, was a man occupied with troublous and various things. He broke stones and damaged travellers on the highway. Digger and robber, he had a dream; he believed in treasures buried in the forest of Montfermeil. He hoped one day to find money in the ground at the foot of a tree; in the meantime, he was willing to search for it in the pockets of the passers-by.

Nevertheless, for the moment, he was prudent. He had just had a narrow escape. He had been, as we know, picked up in the Jondrette garret with the other bandits. Utility of a vice: his drunkenness had saved him. It could never be clearly made out whether he was there as a robber or as robbed. An order of *nol. pros.*, founded upon his clearly proved state of drunkenness on the evening of the ambuscade, had set him at liberty. He regained the freedom of the woods. He returned to his road from Gagny to Lagny to break stones for the use of the state, under administrative surveillance, with downcast mien, very thoughtful, a little cooled towards robbery, which had nearly ruined him, but only turning with the more affection towards wine, which had just saved him.

As to the vivid emotion which he had a little while after his return beneath the thatched roof of his road-labourer's hut, it was this:

One morning a little before the break of day, Boulatruelle, while on the way to his work according to his habit, and upon the watch, perhaps, perceived a man among the branches, whose back only he could see, but whose form, as it seemed to him, through the distance and the twilight, was not altogether unknown to him. Boulatruelle, although a drunkard, had a correct and lucid memory, an indispensable defensive arm to him who is slightly in conflict with legal order.

"Where the devil have I seen something like that man?" inquired he of himself.

But he could make himself no answer, save that it resembled somebody of whom he had a confused remembrance.

Boulatruelle, however, aside from the identity which he did not succeed in getting hold of, made some comparisons and calculations. This man was not of the country. He had come there. On foot, evidently. No public carriage passes Montfermeil at that hour. He had walked all night. Where did he come from? not far off. For he had neither bag nor bundle. From Paris, doubtless. Why was he in the wood? why was he there at such an hour? what had he come there to do?

Boulatruelle thought of the treasure. By dint of digging into his memory he dimly recollected having already had, several years before, a similar surprise in relation to a man who, it struck him, was very possibly the same man.

While he was meditating, he had, under the very weight of his meditation, bowed his head, which was natural, but not very cunning. When he raised it again there was no longer anything there. The man had vanished in the forest and the twilight.

"The deuce," said Boulatruelle, "I will find him again. I will discover the parish of that parishioner. This Patron-Minette prowler upon has a why, I will find it out. Nobody has a secret in my woods without I have a finger in it."

He took his pickaxe, which was very sharp.

"Here is something," he muttered, "to pry into the ground or a man with."

And, as one attaches one thread to another thread, limping along at his best in the path which the man must have followed, he took his way through the thicket.

When he had gone a hundred yards, daylight, which began to break, aided him. Footsteps printed on the sand here and there, grass matted down, heath broken off, young branches bent into the bushes and rising again with a graceful slowness, like the arms of a pretty woman who stretches herself on awaking, indicated to him a sort of track. He followed it, then he lost it. Time was passing. He pushed further forward into the wood and reached a kind of eminence. A morning hunter who passed along a path in the distance, whistling the air of Guillery, inspired him with the idea of climbing a tree. Although old, he was agile. There was near by a beech tree of great height, worthy of Tityrus and Boulatruelle. Boulatruelle climbed the beech as high as he could.

The idea was good. In exploring the solitude on the side where the wood was entirely wild and tangled, Boulatruelle suddenly perceived the man.

Hardly had he perceived him when he lost sight of him.

The man entered, or rather glided, into a distant glade, masked by tall trees, but which Boulatruelle knew very well from having noticed there, near a great heap of burrstone, a wounded chestnut tree bandaged with a plate of zinc nailed upon the bark. This glade is the one which was formerly called the Blaru ground. The heap of stones, intended for nobody knows what use, which could be seen there thirty years ago, is doubtless there still. Nothing equals the longevity of a heap of stones, unless it be that of a palisade fence. It is there provisionally. What a reason for enduring!

Boulatruelle, with the rapidity of joy, let himself fall from the tree rather than descended. The lair was found, the problem was to catch the game. That famous treasure of his dreams was probably there.

It was no easy matter to reach that glade. By the beaten paths, which make a thousand provoking zigzags, it required a good quarter of an hour. In a straight line, through the underbrush, which is there singularly thick, very thorny, and very aggressive, it required a long half-hour. There was Boulatruelle's mistake. He believed in the straight line; an optical illusion which is respectable, but which ruins many men. The underbrush, bristling as it was, appeared to him the best road.

"Let us take the wolves' Rue de Rivoli," said he.

Boulatruelle, accustomed to going astray, this time made the blunder of going straight.

He threw himself resolutely into the thickest of the bushes.

He had to deal with hollies, with nettles, with hawthorns, with sweet-briers, with thistles, with exceedingly irascible brambles. He was very much scratched.

At the bottom of a ravine he found a stream which must be crossed.

He finally reached the Blaru glade, at the end of forty minutes, sweating, soaked, breathless, torn, ferocious.

Nobody in the glade.

Boulatruelle ran to the heap of stones. It was in its place. Nobody had carried it away.

As for the man, he had vanished into the forest. He had escaped. Where? on which side? in what thicket? Impossible to guess.

And, a bitter thing, there was behind the heap of stones, before the tree with the plate of zinc, some fresh earth, a pick, forgotten or abandoned, and a hole.

This hole was empty.

"Robber!" cried Boulatruelle, showing both fists to the horizon.

II

MARIUS, ESCAPING FROM CIVIL WAR, PREPARES FOR DOMESTIC WAR

MARIUS was for a long time neither dead nor alive. He had for several weeks a fever accompanied with delirium, and serious cerebral symptoms resulting rather from the concussion produced by the wounds in the head than from the wounds themselves.

He repeated the name of Cosette during entire nights in the dismal loquacity of fever and with the gloomy obstinacy of agony. The size of certain gashes was a serious danger, the suppuration of large wounds always being liable to reabsorption, and consequently to kill the patient, under certain atmospheric influences; at every change in the weather, at the slightest storm, the physician was anxious. "Above all, let the wounded man have no excitement," he repeated. The dressings were complicated and difficult, the fastening of cloths and bandages with sparadrap not being invented at that period. Nicolette used for lint a sheet "as big as a ceiling," said she. It was not without difficulty that the chloruretted lotions and the nitrate of silver brought the gangrene to an end. As long as there was danger, M. Gillenormand, in despair at the bedside of his grandson was, like Marius, neither dead nor alive.

Every day, and sometimes twice a day, a very well-dressed gentleman with white hair, such was the description given by the porter, came to inquire after the wounded man, and left a large package of lint for the dressings.

At last, on the 7th of September, four months, to a day, after the sorrowful night when they had brought him home dying to his grandfather, the physician declared him out of danger. Convalescence began. Marius was, however, obliged still to remain for more than two months stretched on a long chair, on account of the accidents resulting from the fracture of the shoulder-blade. There is always a last wound like this which will not close, and which prolongs the dressings, to the great disgust of the patient.

However, this long sickness and this long convalescence saved him from pursuit. In France, there is no anger, even governmental, which six months does not extinguish. Emeutes, in the present state of society, are so much the fault of everybody that they are followed by a certain necessity of closing the eyes.

Let us add that the infamous Gisquet order, which enjoined physicians to inform against the wounded, having outraged public opinion, and not only public opinion, but the king first of all, the wounded were shielded and protected by this indignation; and, with the exception of those who had been taken prisoners in actual combat, the courts-martial dared not disturb any. Marius was therefore left in peace.

M. Gillenormand passed first through every anguish, and then every ecstasy. They had great difficulty in preventing him from passing every night with the wounded man; he had his large arm-chair brought to the side of Marius' bed; he insisted that his daughter should take the finest linen in the house for compresses and bandages. Mademoiselle Gillenormand, like a prudent and elder person, found means to spare the fine linen, while she left the grandfather to suppose that he was obeyed. M. Gillenormand did not permit anybody to explain to him that for making lint cambric is not so good as coarse linen, nor new linen so good as old. He superintended all the dressings, from which Mademoiselle Gillenormand modestly absented herself. When the dead flesh was cut with scissors, he would say: "*aïe! aïe!*" Nothing was so touching as to see him hand a cup of gruel to the wounded man with his gentle senile trembling. He overwhelmed the doctor with questions. He did not perceive that he always asked the same.

On the day the physician announced to him that Marius was out of danger, the goodman was in delirium. He gave his porter three louis as a gratuity. In the evening, on going to his room, he danced a gavot, making castanets of his thumb and forefinger, and he sang a song which follows:

> Jeanne est née à Fougère,
> Vrai nid d'une bergère;
> J'adore son jupon,
>   Fripon.
>
> Amour, tu vis en elle;
> Car c'est dans sa prunelle
> Que tu mets ton carquois,
>   Narquois!
>
> Moi, je la chante, et j'aime,
> Plus que Diane même,
> Jeanne et ses durs tétons
>   Bretons.

Then he knelt upon a chair, and Basque, who watched him through the half-open door, was certain that he was praying.

Hitherto, he had hardly believed in God.

At each new phase of improvement, which continued to grow more and more visible, the grandfather raved. He did a thousand mirthful things mechanically; he ran up and down stairs without knowing why. A neighbour, a pretty woman withal, was amazed at receiving a large bouquet one morning; it was M. Gillenormand who sent it to her. The husband made a scene. M. Gillenormand attempted to take Nicolette upon his knees. He called Marius Monsieur the Baron.

He cried, "*Vive la République!*"

At every moment, he asked the physician: "There is no more danger, is there!" He looked at Marius with a grandmother's eyes. He brooded him when he ate. He no longer knew himself, he no longer counted on himself. Marius was the master of the house, there was abdication in his joy, he was the grandson of his grandson.

In this lightness of heart which possessed him, he was the most venerable of children. For fear of fatiguing or of annoying the convalescent, he got behind him to smile upon him. He was contented, joyous, enraptured, delightful, young. His white hairs added a sweet majesty to the cheerful light upon his face. When grace is joined with wrinkles, it is adorable. There is an unspeakable dawn in happy old age.

As for Marius, while he let them dress his wounds and care for him, he had one fixed idea: Cosette.

Since the fever and the delirium had left him, he had not uttered that name, and they might have supposed that he no longer thought of it. He held his peace, precisely because his soul was in it.

He did not know what had become of Cosette; the whole affair of the Rue de la Chanvrerie was like a cloud in his memory; shadows, almost indistinct, were floating in his mind, Eponine, Gavroche, Mabeuf, the Thénardiers, all his friends mingled drearily with the smoke of the barricade; the strange passage of M. Fauchelevent in that bloody drama produced upon him the effect of an enigma in a tempest; he understood nothing in regard to his own life; he neither knew how, nor by whom, he had been saved, and nobody about him knew; all that they could tell him was that he had been brought to the Rue des Filles du Calvaire in a fiacre by night; past, present, future, all was now to him but the mist of a vague idea; but there was within this mist an immovable point, one clear and precise feature, something which was granite, a resolution, a will: to find Cosette again. To him the idea of life was not distinct from the idea of Cosette; he had decreed in his heart that he would not accept the one without the other, and he was unalterably determined to demand from anybody, no matter whom, who should wish to compel him to live, from his grandfather, from Fate, from Hell, the restitution of his vanished Eden.

He did not hide the obstacles from himself.

Let us emphasise one point here: he was not won over, and was little softened by all the solicitude and all the tenderness of his grandfather. In the first place, he was not in the secret of it all; then, in his sick man's reveries, still feverish perhaps, he distrusted this gentleness as a new and strange thing, the object of which was to subdue him. He remained cold. The grandfather expended his poor old smile for nothing. Marius said to himself it was well so long as he, Marius, did not speak and offered no resistance but that, when the question of Cosette was raised, he would find another face, and his grandfather's real attitude would be unmasked. Then it would be harsh recrudescence of family questions, every sarcasm and every objection at once: Fauchelevent, Coupelevent, fortune, poverty, misery, the stone at the neck, the future. Violent opposition; conclusion, refusal. Marius was bracing himself in advance.

And then, in proportion as he took new hold of life, his former griefs reappeared, the old ulcers of his memory reopened, he thought once more of the past. Colonel Pontmercy appeared again between M. Gillenormand and him, Marius; he said to himself that there was no real goodness to be hoped for from him who had been so unjust and so hard to his father. And with health, there returned to him a sort of harshness towards his grandfather. The old man bore it with gentleness.

M. Gillenormand, without manifesting it in any way, noticed that Marius, since he had been brought home and restored to consciousness, had not once said to him "father." He did not say monsieur, it is true; but he found means to say neither the one nor the other, by a certain manner of turning his sentences.

A crisis was evidently approaching.

As it almost always happens in similar cases, Marius, in order to try himself, skirmished before offering battle. This is called feeling the ground. One morning it happened that M. Gillenormand, over a newspaper which had fallen into his hands, spoke lightly of the Convention and discharged a royalist epiphonema upon Danton, Saint Just, and Robespierre. "The men of '93 were giants," said Marius, sternly. The old man was silent, and did not whisper for the rest of the day.

Marius, who had always present to his mind the inflexible grandfather of his early years, saw in this silence an intense concentration of anger, augured from it a sharp conflict, and increased his preparations for combat in the inner recesses of his thought.

He determined that in case of refusal he would tear off his bandages, dislocate his shoulder, lay bare and open his remaining wounds, and refuse all nourishment. His wounds were his ammunition. To have Cosette or to die.

He waited for the favourable moment with the crafty patience of the sick.

That moment came.

III
MARIUS ATTACKS

ONE day M. Gillenormand, while his daughter was putting in order the vials and the cups upon the marble top of the bureau, bent over Marius and said to him in his most tender tone:

"Do you see, my darling Marius, in your place I would eat meat now rather than fish. A fried sole is excellent to begin a convalescence, but, to put the sick man on his legs, it takes a good cutlet."

Marius, nearly all whose strength had returned, gathered it together, sat up in bed, rested his clenched hands on the sheets, looked his grandfather in the face, assumed a terrible air, and said:

"This leads me to say something to you."

"What is it?"

"It is that I wish to marry."

"Foreseen," said the grandfather. And he burst out laughing.

"How foreseen?"

"Yes, foreseen. You shall have her, your lassie."

Marius, astounded, and overwhelmed by the dazzling burst of happiness, trembled in every limb.

M. Gillenormand continued:

"Yes, you shall have her, your handsome, pretty little girl. She comes every day in the shape of an old gentleman to inquire after you. Since you were wounded, she has passed her time in weeping and making lint. I have made inquiry. She lives in the Rue de l'Homme Armé, Number Seven. Ah, we are ready! Ah! you want her! Well, you shall have her. That catches you. You had arranged your little plot; you said to yourself: I am going to make it known bluntly to that grandfather, to that mummy of the Regency and of the Directory, to that old beau, to that Dorante become a Géronte; he has had his levities too, himself, and his amours, and his grisettes, and his Cosettes; he has made his display, he has had his wings, he has eaten his spring bread; he must remember it well. We shall see. Battle. Ah! you take the bull by the horns. That is good. I propose a cutlet, and you answer: 'A propos, I wish to marry.' That is what I call a transition. Ah! you had reckoned upon some bickering. You didn't know that I was an old coward. What do you say to that? You are spited. To find your grandfather still more stupid than yourself, you didn't expect that, you lose the argument which you were to have made to me, monsieur advocate; it is provoking. Well, it is all the same, rage. I do what you wish, that cuts you out of it, idiot. Listen. I have made inquiries, I am sly too; she is charming, she is modest, the lancer is not true, she has made heaps of lint, she is a jewel, she worships you; if you had died, there would have been three of us; her bier would have accompanied mine. I had a strong notion, as soon as you were better, to plant her square at your bedside, but it is only in romances that they introduce young girls unceremoniously to the side of the couch of the pretty wounded men who interest them. That does not do. What would your aunt have said? You have been quite naked three-quarters of the time, my goodman. Ask Nicolette, who has not left you a minute, if it was possible for a woman to be here. And then what would the doctor have said? That doesn't cure a fever, a pretty girl. Finally, it is all right; don't let us talk any more about it, it is said, it is done, it is fixed; take her. Such is my ferocity. Do you see, I saw that you did not love me; I said: What is there that I can do, then, to make this animal love me? I said: Hold on! I have my little Cosette under my hand; I will give her to him, he must surely love a little then, or let him tell why. Ah! you thought that the old fellow was going to storm, to make a gruff voice, to cry No, and to lift his cane upon all this dawn. Not at all. Cosette, so be it; Love, so be it; I ask nothing better. Monsieur, take the trouble to marry. Be happy, my dear child."

This said, the old man burst into sobs.

And he took Marius' head, and he hugged it in both arms against his old breast, and they both began to weep. That is one of the forms of supreme happiness.

"Father!" exclaimed Marius

"Ah! you love me then!" said the old man.

There was an ineffable moment. They choked and could not speak.

At last the old man stammered:

"Come! the ice is broken. He has called me 'Father.'"

Marius released his head from his grandfather's arms, and said softly:

"But, father, now that I am well, it seems to me that I could see her."

"Foreseen again, you shall see her to-morrow."

"Father!"

"What?"

"Why not to-day?"

"Well, to-day. Here goes for to-day. You have called me

'Father,' three times, it is well worth that. I will see to it. She shall be brought to you. Foreseen, I tell you. This has already been put into verse. It is the conclusion of André Chénier's elegy of the *Jeune malade*, André Chénier who was murdered by the scound——, by the giants of '93."

M. Gillenormand thought he perceived a slight frown on Marius' brow, although, in truth, we should say, he was no longer listening to him, flown off as he had into ecstasy, and thinking far more of Cosette than of 1793. The grandfather, trembling at having introduced André Chénier so inopportunely, resumed precipitately:

"Murdered is not the word. The fact is that the great revolutionary geniuses, who were not evil disposed, that is incontestable, who were heroes, egad! found that André Chénier embarrassed them a little, and they had him guillot——. That is to say that those great men, on the seventh of Thermidor, in the interest of the public safety, begged André Chénier to have the kindness to go—"

M. Gillenormand, choked by his own sentence, could not continue; being able neither to finish it nor to retract it, while his daughter was arranging the pillow behind Marius, the old man, overwhelmed by so many emotions, threw himself, as quickly as his age permitted, out of the bedroom, pushed the door to behind him, and purple, strangling, foaming, his eyes starting from his head, found himself face to face with honest Basque who was polishing boots in the ante-chamber. He seized Basque by the collar and cried full in his face with fury: "By the hundred thousand Javottes of the devil, those brigands assassinated him!"

"Who, monsieur?"

"André Chénier!"

"Yes, monsieur," said Basque in dismay.

IV

MADEMOISELLE GILLENORMAND AT LAST THINKS IT NOT IMPROPER THAT MONSIEUR FAUCHELEVENT SHOULD COME IN WITH SOMETHING UNDER HIS ARM

COSETTE and Marius saw each other again.

What the interview was, we will not attempt to tell. There

are things which we should not undertake to paint; the sun is of the number.

The whole family, including Basque and Nicolette, were assembled in Marius' room when Cosette entered.

She appeared on the threshold; it seemed as if she were in a cloud.

Just at that instant the grandfather was about to blow his nose; he stopped short, holding his nose in his handkerchief, and looking at Cosette above it:

"Adorable!" he exclaimed.

Then he blew his nose with a loud noise.

Cosette was intoxicated, enraptured, startled, in Heaven. She was as frightened as one can be by happiness. She stammered, quite pale, quite red, wishing to throw herself into Marius' arms, and not daring to. Ashamed to show her love before all those people. We are pitiless towards happy lovers; we stay there when they have the strongest desire to be alone. They, however, have no need at all of society.

With Cosette and behind her had entered a man with white hair, grave, smiling nevertheless, but with a vague and poignant smile. This was "Monsieur Fauchelevent;" this was Jean Valjean.

He was *very well dressed*, as the porter had said, in a new black suit, with a white cravat.

The porter was a thousand miles from recognising in this correct bourgeois, in this probable notary, the frightful corpse-bearer who had landed at his door on the night of the 7th of June, ragged, muddy, hideous, haggard, his face masked by blood and dirt, supporting the fainting Marius in his arms; still his porter's scent was awakened. When M. Fauchelevent had arrived with Cosette, the porter could not help confiding this remark to his wife: "I don't know why I always imagine that I have seen that face somewhere."

Monsieur Fauchelevent, in Marius' room, stayed near the door, as if apart. He had under his arm a package similar in appearance to an octavo volume wrapped in paper. The paper of the envelope was greenish, and seemed mouldy.

"Does this gentleman always have books under his arm like that?" asked Mademoiselle Gillenormand, who did not like books, in a low voice of Nicolette.

"Well," answered M. Gillenormand, who had heard her, in the same tone, "he is a scholar. What then? is it his fault?

Monsieur Boulard, whom I knew, never went out without a book, he neither, and always had an old volume against his heart, like that."

And bowing, he said, in a loud voice:

"Monsieur Tranchelevent——"

Father Gillenormand did not do this on purpose, but inattention to proper names was an aristocratic way he had.

"Monsieur Tranchelevent, I have the honour of asking of you for my grandson, Monsieur the Baron Marius Pontmercy, the hand of mademoiselle."

Monsieur Tranchelevent bowed.

"It is done," said the grandfather.

And, turning towards Marius and Cosette, with arms extended in blessing, he cried:

"Permission to adore each other."

They did not make him say it twice. It was all the same! The cooing began. They talked low, Marius leaning on his long chair, Cosette standing near him. "Oh, my God!" murmured Cosette, "I see you again! It is you! it is you! To have gone to fight like that! But why? It is horrible. For four months I have been dead. Oh, how naughty it is to have been in that battle! What had I done to you? I pardon you, but you won't do it again. Just now, when they came to tell us to come, I thought again I should die, but it was of joy. I was so sad! I did not take time to dress myself, I must look like a fright. What will your relatives say of me, to see me with a collar ragged? But speak now! You let me do all the talking. We are still in the Rue de l'Homme Armé. Your shoulder, that was terrible. They told me they could put their fist into it. And then they have cut your flesh with scissors. That is frightful. I have cried; I have no eyes left. It is strange that anybody can suffer like that. Your grandfather has a very kind appearance. Don't disturb yourself, don't rest on your elbow; take care, you will hurt yourself. Oh, how happy I am! So our trouble is all over! I am very silly. I wanted to say something to you that I have forgotten completely. Do you love me still? We live in the Rue de l'Homme Armé. There is no garden. I have been making lint all the time. Here, monsieur, look, it is your fault, my fingers are callous."

"Angel!" said Marius.

Angel is the only word in the language which cannot be worn out. No other word would resist the pitiless use which lovers make of it.

Then, as there were spectators, they stopped, and did not say another word, contenting themselves with touching each other's hands very gently.

M. Gillenormand turned towards all those who were in the room and cried:

"Why don't you talk loud, the rest of you? Make a noise, behind the scenes. Come, a little uproar, the devil! so that these children can chatter at their ease."

And, approaching Marius and Cosette, he said to them very low:

"Make love. Don't be disturbed."

Aunt Gillenormand witnessed with amazement this irruption of light into her aged interior. This amazement was not at all aggressive; it was not the least in the world the scandalised and envious look of an owl upon two ringdoves; it was the dull eye of a poor innocent girl of fifty-seven; it was incomplete life beholding that triumph, love.

"Mademoiselle Gillenormand the elder," said her father to her, "I told you plainly that this would happen."

He remained silent a moment and added:

"Behold the happiness of others."

Then he turned towards Cosette:

"How pretty she is! how pretty she is! She is a Greuze. You are going to have her all alone to yourself then, rascal! Ah! my rogue, you have a narrow escape from me, you are lucky, if I were not fifteen years too old, we would cross swords for who should have her. Stop! I am in love with you, mademoiselle. That is very natural. It is your right. Ah! the sweet pretty charming little wedding that this is going to make! Saint Denis du Saint Sacrement is our parish, but I will have a dispensation so that you may be married at Saint Paul's. The church is better. It was built by the Jesuits. It is more coquettish. It is opposite the fountain of Cardinal de Birague. The masterpiece of Jesuit architecture is at Namur. It is called Saint Loup. You must go there when you are married. It is worth the journey. Mademoiselle, I am altogether of your opinion, I want girls to marry, they are made for that. There is a certain St. Catherine whom I would always like to see with her hair down. To be an old maid, that is fine, but it is cold. The Bible says: Multiply. To save the people, we need Jeanne d'Arc; but to make the people, we used Mother Gigogne. So, marry, beauties. I really don't see the good of being an old maid. I know very well that they have a chapel apart in the church, and that they talk a good deal about the sisterhood of the Virgin; but, zounds, a handsome husband, a fine fellow, and, at the end of the year, a big flaxen-haired boy who sucks you merrily, and who has good folds of fat on his legs, and who squeezes your breast by handfuls in his little rosy paws, while he laughs like the dawn, that is better after all than holding a taper at vespers and singing *Turris eburnea*!"

The grandfather executed a pirouette upon his ninety-year-old heels, and began to talk again, like a spring which flies back:

> Ainsi, bornant le cours de tes rêvasseries.
> Alcippe, il est donc vrai, dans peu tu te maries.

"By the way!"

"What, father?"

"Didn't you have an intimate friend?"

"Yes, Courfeyrac."

"What has become of him?"

"He is dead."

"Very well."

He sat down near them, made Cosette sit down, and took their four hands in his old wrinkled hands:

"She is exquisite, this darling. She is a masterpiece, this Cosette. She is a very little girl and a very great lady. She will be only a baroness, that is stooping; she was born a marchioness. Hasn't she lashes for you? My children, fix it well in your noddles that you are in the right of it. Love one another. Be foolish about it. Love is the foolishness of men, and the wisdom of God. Adore each other. Only," added he, suddenly darkening, "what a misfortune! This is what I am thinking of! More than half of what I have is in annuity; as long as I live, it's all well enough, but after my death, twenty years from now, ah! my poor children, you will not have a sou. Your beautiful white hands, Madame the Baroness, will do the devil the honour to pull him by the tail."

"Mademoiselle Euphrasie Fauchelevent has six hundred thousand francs."

It was Jean Valjean's voice.

He had not yet uttered a word, nobody seemed even to

remember that he was there, and he stood erect and motionless behind all these happy people.

"How is Mademoiselle Euphrasie in question?" asked the grandfather, startled.

"That is me," answered Cosette.

"Six hundred thousand francs!" resumed M. Gillenormand.

"Less fourteen or fifteen thousand francs, perhaps," said Jean Valjean.

And he laid on the table the package which Aunt Gillenormand had taken for a book.

Jean Valjean opened the package himself; it was a bundle of bank-notes. They ran through them, and they counted them. There were five hundred bills of a thousand francs, and a hundred and sixty-eight of five hundred. In all, five hundred and eighty-four thousand francs.

"That is a good book," said M. Gillenormand.

"Five hundred and eighty-four thousand francs!" murmured the aunt.

"This arranges things very well, does it not, Mademoiselle Gillenormand the elder?" resumed the grandfather. "This devil of a Marius, he has found you a grisette millionaire on the tree of dreams! Then trust in the love-making of young folks nowadays! Students find studentesses with six hundred thousand francs. Chérubin works better than Rothschild."

"Five hundred and eighty-four thousand francs!" repeated Mademoiselle Gillenormand in an under tone. "Five hundred and eighty-four! you might call it six hundred thousand, indeed!"

As for Marius and Cosette, they were looking at each other during this time; they paid little attention to this incident.

V

DEPOSIT YOUR MONEY RATHER IN SOME FOREST
THAN WITH SOME NOTARY

THE reader has doubtless understood, without it being necessary to explain at length, that Jean Valjean, after the Champmathieu affair, had been able, thanks to his first escape for a few days to come to Paris, and to withdraw the sum made by him, under the name of Monsieur Madeleine, at M—— sur M——, from Laffitte's in time; and that, in the fear of being retaken, which happened to him, in fact, a short time after, he had concealed and buried that sum in the forest of Montfermeil, in the place called the Blaru grounds. The sum, six hundred and thirty thousand francs, all in bank-notes, was of small bulk, and was contained in a box; but to preserve the box from moisture he had placed it in an oaken chest, full of chestnut shavings. In the same chest, he had put his other treasure, the bishop's candlesticks. It will be remembered that he carried away these candlesticks when he escaped from M—— sur M——. The man perceived one evening, for the first time, by Boulatruelle, was Jean Valjean.——Afterwards, whenever Jean Valjean was in need of money, he went to the Blaru glade for it. Hence the absences of which we have spoken. He had a pickaxe somewhere in the bushes, in a hiding-place known only to himself. When he saw Marius convalescent, feeling that the hour was approaching when this money might be useful, he had gone after it; and it was he again whom Boulatruelle saw in the wood, but this time in the morning, and not at night. Boulatruelle inherited the pickaxe.

The real sum was five hundred and eighty-four thousand five hundred francs. Jean Valjean took out five hundred francs for himself. "We will see afterwards," thought he.

The difference between this sum and the six hundred and thirty thousand francs withdrawn from Laffitte's represented the expenses of ten years, from 1823 to 1833. The five years spent in the convent had cost only five thousand francs.

Jean Valjean put the two silver candlesticks upon the mantel, where they shone, to Toussaint's great admiration.

Moreover, Jean Valjean knew that he was delivered from Javert. It had been mentioned in his presence, and he had verified the fact in the *Moniteur*, which published it, that an inspector of police, named Javert, had been found drowned under a washerwoman's boat between the Pont au Change and Pont Neuf, and that a paper left by this man, otherwise irreproachable and highly esteemed by his chiefs, led to a belief that he had committed suicide during a fit of mental aberration. "In fact," thought Jean Valjean, "since having me in his power, he let me go, he must already have been crazy."

VI

THE TWO OLD MEN DO EVERYTHING, EACH IN HIS OWN WAY, THAT COSETTE MAY BE HAPPY

ALL the preparations were made for the marriage. The physician being consulted said that it might take place in February. This was in December. Some ravishing weeks of perfect happiness rolled away.

The least happy, was not the grandfather. He would remain for a quarter of an hour at a time gazing at Cosette.

"The wonderful pretty girl!" he exclaimed. "And her manners are so sweet and so good. It is of no use to say my love my heart, she is the most charming girl that I have ever seen in my life. Besides, she will have virtues for you sweet as violets. She is a grace, indeed! You can but live nobly with such a creature. Marius, my boy, you are a baron, you are rich, don't pettifog, I beg of you."

Cosette and Marius had passed abruptly from the grave to paradise. There had been but little caution in the transition, and they would have been stunned if they had not been dazzled.

"Do you understand anything about it?" said Marius to Cosette.

"No," answered Cosette, "but it seems to me that the good God is caring for us."

Jean Valjean did all, smoothed all, conciliated all, made all easy. He hastened towards Cosette's happiness with as much eagerness, and apparently as much joy, as Cosette herself.

As he had been a mayor, he knew how to solve a delicate problem, in the secret of which he was alone: Cosette's civil state. To bluntly give her origin, who knows? that might prevent the marriage. He drew Cosette out of all difficulty. He arranged a family of dead people for her, a sure means of incurring no objection. Cosette was what remained of an extinct family; Cosette was not his daughter, but the daughter of another Fauchelevent. Two brothers Fauchelevent had been gardeners at the convent of the Petit Picpus. They went to this convent, the best recommendations and the most respectable testimonials abounded; the good nuns, little apt and little inclined to fathom questions of paternity, and understanding no malice, had never known very exactly of which of the two Fauchelevents little Cosette was the daughter. They said what was wanted of them, and said it with zeal. A notary's act was drawn up. Cosette became before the law Mademoiselle Euphrasie Fauchelevent. She was declared an orphan. Jean Valjean arranged matters in such a way as to be designated, under the name of Fauchelevent, as Cosette's guardian, with M. Gillenormand as overseeing guardian.

As for the five hundred and eighty-four thousand francs, that was a legacy left to Cosette by a dead person who desired to remain unknown. The original legacy had been five hundred and ninety-four thousand francs; but ten thousand francs had been expended for Mademoiselle Euphrasie's education, of which five thousand francs were paid to the convent itself. This legacy, deposited in the hands of a third party, was to be given up to Cosette at her majority or at the time of her marriage. Altogether this was very acceptable, as we see, especially with a basis of more than half a million. There were indeed a few singularities here and there, but nobody saw them; one of those interested had his eyes bandaged by love, the other by the six hundred thousand francs.

Cosette learned that she was not the daughter of that old man whom she had so long called father. He was only a relative; another Fauchelevent was her real father. At any other time, this would have broken her heart. But at this ineffable hour, it was only a little shadow, a darkening, and she had so much joy that this cloud was of short duration. She had Marius. The young man came, the goodman faded away, such is life.

And then, Cosette had been accustomed for long years to see enigmas about her: everybody who has had a mysterious childhood is always ready for certain renunciations.

She continued, however, to say "Father" to Jean Valjean.

Cosette, in raptures, was enthusiastic about Grandfather Gillenormand. It is true that he loaded her with madrigals and with presents. While Jean Valjean was building a normal condition in society for Cosette, and a possession of an unimpeachable state, M. Gillenormand was watching over the wedding corbeille. Nothing amused him so much as being magnificent. He had given Cosette a dress of Binche guipure which descended to him from his own grandmother. "These fashions have come round again," said he, "old things are the rage, and the young women of my old age dress like the old women of my childhood."

He rifled his respectable round-bellied bureaus of Coromandel lac which had not been opened for years. "Let us put
these dowagers to the confession," said he; "let us see what they
have in them." He noisily stripped the deep drawers full of
toilets of all his wives, of all his mistresses, and of all his ances-
tresses. Pekins, damasks, lampas, painted moires, dresses of gros
de Tours, Indian handkerchiefs embroidered with a gold which
could be washed, dauphines in the piece finished on both sides,
Genoa and Alençon point, antique jewellery, comfit-boxes of
ivory ornamented with microscopic battles, clothes, ribbons, he
lavished all upon Cosette. Cosette, astonished, desperately in
love with Marius and wild with gratitude towards M. Gillenormand, dreamed of a boundless happiness clad in satin and
velvet. Her wedding corbeille appeared to her upborne by seraphim. Her soul soared into the azure on wings of Mechlin lace.

The intoxication of the lovers was only equalled, as we have
said, by the ecstasy of the grandfather. It was like a flourish of
trumpets in the Rue des Filles du Calvaire.

Every morning, a new offering of finery from the grandfather to Cosette. Every possible furbelow blossomed out splendidly about her.

One day Marius, who was fond of talking gravely in the
midst of his happiness, said in reference to I know not what
incident:

"The men of the revolution are so great that they already
have the prestige of centuries, like Cato and like Phocion, and
each of them seems a *mémoire antique* (antique memory)."

"Moire antique!" exclaimed the old man. "Thank you,
Marius. That is precisely the idea that I was in search of."

And the next day a magnificent dress of tea-coloured moire
antique was added to Cosette's corbeille.

The grandfather extracted a wisdom from these rags:

"Love, all very well; but it needs that with it. The useless is
needed in happiness. Happiness is only the essential. Season it
for me enormously with the superfluous. A palace and her heart.
Her heart and the Louvre. Her heart and the grand fountains of
Versailles. Give me my shepherdess, and have her a duchess if
possible. Bring me Phillis crowned with bluebells, and add to
her a hundred thousand francs a year. Open me a bucolic out of
sight under a marble colonnade. I consent to the bucolic, and
also to the fairy work in marble and gold. Dry happiness is like

dry bread. We eat, but we do not dine. I wish for the superfluous, for the useless, for the extravagant, for the too much, for
that which is not good for anything. I remember having seen in
the cathedral of Strasbourg, a clock as high as a three-story
house, which marked the hour, which had the goodness to mark
the hour, but which did not look as if it were made for that; and
which, after having struck noon or midnight, noon, the hour of
the sun, midnight, the hour of love, or any other hour that you
please, gave you the moon and the stars, the earth and the sea,
the birds and the fish, Phœbus and Phœbe, and a host of things
which came out of a niche, and the twelve apostles, and the
Emperor Charles V., and Eponine and Sabinus, and a crowd of
little gilded goodmen who played on the trumpet, to boot. Not
counting the ravishing chimes which it flung out into the air on
all occasions without anybody knowing why. Is a paltry naked
dial which only tells the hours, as good as that? For my part I
agree with the great clock of Strasbourg, and I prefer it to the
cuckoo clock of the Black Forest."

M. Gillenormand raved especially concerning the wedding,
and all the pier-glasses of the eighteenth century passed pell-
mell through his dithyrambs.

"You know nothing about the art of fêtes. You do not know
how to get up a happy day in these times," he exclaimed. "Your
nineteenth century is soft. It lacks excess. It ignores the rich, it
ignores the noble. In everything, it is shaven close. Your third
estate is tasteless, colourless, odourless, and shapeless. Dreams of
your bourgeoises who set up an establishment, as they say: a
pretty boudoir freshly decorated in palissandre and chintz.
Room! room! the sieur Hunks espouses the lady Catchpenny.
Sumptuosity and splendour. They have stuck a louis d'or to a
taper. There you have the age. I beg to flee away beyond the
Sarmatians. Ah! in 1787, I predicted that all was lost, the day I
saw the Duke de Rohan, Prince de Léon, Duke de Chabot,
Duke de Montbazon, Marquis de Soubise, Viscount de Thouars,
peer of France, go to Longchamps in a chaise-cart. That has
borne its fruits. In this century, people do business, they gamble
at the Bourse, they make money, and they are disagreeable. They
care for and varnish their surface; they are spruced up, washed,
soaped, scraped, shaved, combed, waxed, smoothed, rubbed,
brushed, cleaned, on the outside irreproachable, polished like a
pebble, prudent, nice, and at the same time, by the virtue of my

mistress, they have at the bottom of their conscience dung-heaps and cloacas enough to disgust a cow-girl who blows her nose with her fingers. I grant to these times this device: Nasty neatness. Marius, don't get angry; let me speak; I speak no evil of the people, you see; I have my mouth full of your people; but take it not amiss that I have my little fling at the bourgeoisie. I am one of them. Who loves well, lashes well. Upon that, I say it boldly, people marry nowadays, but they don't know how to marry. Ah! it is true, I regret the pretty ways of the old times. I regret the whole of them. That elegance, that chivalry, those courtly and dainty ways, that joyous luxury which everybody had, music making part of the wedding, symphony above, drumming below, dances, joyful faces at table, far-fetched madrigals, songs, squibs, free laughter, the devil and his train, big knots of ribbon. I regret the bride's garter. The bride's garter is cousin to the cestus of Venus. Upon what turns the war of Troy? By heavens, upon Helen's garter. Why do they fight, why does Diomede the divine shatter that great bronze helmet with ten points on Meriones' head, why do Achilles and Hector pick each other with great, pike thrusts? Because Helen let Paris take her garter. With Cosette's garter, Homer would make the *Iliad*. He would put into his poem an old babbler like me, and he would call him Nestor. My friends, formerly, in that lovely formerly, people married scientifically; they made a good contract, then a good jollification. As soon as Cujas went out, Gamache came in. But, forsooth! the stomach is an agreeable animal which demands its due, and which wants its wedding also. They supped well, and they had a beautiful neighbour at table, without a stomacher, who hid her neck but moderately! Oh! the wide laughing mouths, and how gay they were in those times! Youth was a bouquet; every young man terminated in a branch of lilac or a bunch of roses; was one a warrior, he was a shepherd; and if, by chance, he was a captain of dragoons, he found some way to be called Florian. They thought everything of being pretty, they embroidered themselves, they empurpled themselves. A bourgeois had the appearance of a flower, a marquis had the appearance of a precious stone. They did not wear straps, they did not wear boots. They were flaunting, glossy, moire, gorgeous, fluttering, dainty, coquettish, which did not prevent them from having a sword at their side. The humming bird has beak and claws. That was the time of the *Indes galantes*. One of the sides of the century was the delicate, the other was the magnificent; and, zookers! they amused themselves. Nowadays, they are serious. The bourgeois is miserly, the bourgeois is prudish; your century is unfortunate. People would drive away the Graces for wearing such low necks. Alas! they hide beauty as a deformity. Since the revolution, everything has trousers, even the ballet girls; a danseuse must be grave; your rigadoons are doctrinaire. We must be majestic. We should be very much shocked without our chin in our cravat. The ideal of a scapegrace of twenty who gets married, is to be like Monsieur Royer Collard. And do you know to what we are coming with this majesty? to being small. Learn this: joy is not merely joyful; it is great. So be lovers gaily then, the devil! and marry, when you do marry, with the fever and the dizziness and the uproar and the tohubohu of happiness. Gravity at the church, all right. But, as soon as mass is over, odzooks! we must make a dream whirl about the bride. A marriage ought to be royal and chimerical; it ought to walk in procession from the cathedral of Rheims to the pagoda of Chanteloup. I have a horror of a mean wedding. 'Zblews! be in Olympus, at least for that day. Be gods. Ah! you might be sylphs, Games and Laughters, Argyraspides; you are elfs! My friends, every new husband ought to be the Prince Aldobrandini. Profit by this unique moment of your life to fly away into the empyrean with the swans and the eagles, free to fall back on the morrow into the bourgeoisie of the frogs. Don't economise upon Hymen, don't strip him of his splendours; don't stint the day on which you shine. Wedding is not housekeeping. Oh! if I had my fancy, it should be gallant, you should hear violins in the trees. This is my programme: sky-blue and silver. I would join the rural divinities in the fête, I would convoke the dryads and the nereids. Nuptials of Amphitrite, a rosy cloud, nymphs with well-dressed heads and all naked, an academician offering quatrains to the goddess, a car drawn by marine monsters.

> Tritton trottait devant, et tirait de sa conque
> Des sons si ravissants qu'il ravissait quiconque!

There is a programme for a fête that is one, or I don't know anything about it, udsbuddikins!"

While the grandfather, in full lyric effusion, was listening to himself, Cosette and Marius were intoxicated with seeing each other freely.

Aunt Gillenormand beheld it all with her imperturbable placidity. She had had within five or six months a certain number of emotions; Marius returned, Marius brought back bleeding, Marius brought back from a barricade, Marius dead, then alive, Marius reconciled, Marius bethrothed, Marius marrying a pauper, Marius marrying a millionaire. The six hundred thousand francs had been her last surprise. Then her first communicant indifference returned to her. She went regularly to the offices, picked over her rosary, read her prayer-book, whispered *Aves* in one part of the house, while they were whispering *I Love Yous* in the other, and, vaguely, saw Marius and Cosette as two shadows. The shadow was herself.

There is a certain condition of inert asceticism in which the soul, neutralised by torpor, a stranger to what might be called the business of living, perceives, with the exception of earthquakes and catastrophes, no human impressions, neither pleasant impressions, nor painful impressions. "This devotion," said Grandfather Gillenormand to his daughter, "corresponds to a cold in the head. You smell nothing of life. No bad odour, but no good one."

Still, the six hundred thousand francs had determined the hesitation of the old maid. Her father had acquired the habit of counting her for so little that he had not consulted her in regard to the consent to Marius' marriage. He had acted with impetuosity, according to his wont, having, a despot become a slave, but one thought, to satisfy Marius. As for the aunt, that the aunt existed, and that she might have an opinion, he had not even thought; and, perfect sheep as she was, this had ruffled her. A little rebellious inwardly, but outwardly impassible, she said to herself: "My father settles the question of the marriage without me, I will settle the question of the inheritance without him." She was rich, in fact, and her father was not. She had therefore reserved her decision thereupon. It is probable that, if the marriage had been poor, she would have left it poor. So much the worse for monsieur, my nephew! He marries a beggar, let him be a beggar. But Cosette's half-million pleased the aunt, and changed her feelings in regard to this pair of lovers. Some consideration is due to six hundred thousand francs, and it was clear that she could not do otherwise than leave her fortune to these young people, since they no longer needed it.

It was arranged that the couple should live with the grandfather. M. Gillenormand absolutely insisted upon giving them his room, the finest in the house. "*It will rejuvenate me*," he declared. "*It is an old project. I always had the idea of making a wedding in my room.*" He filled this room with a profusion of gay old furniture. He hung the walls and the ceiling with an extraordinary stuff which he had in the piece, and which he believed to be from Utrecht, a satin background with golden immortelles, and velvet auriculas. "With this stuff," said he, "the Duchess d'Anville's bed was draped at La Roche Guyon." He put a little Saxony figure on the mantel, holding a muff over her naked belly.

M. Gillenormand's library became the attorney's office which Marius required; an office, it will be remembered, being rendered necessary by the rules of the order.

VII
THE EFFECTS OF DREAM MINGLED WITH HAPPINESS

THE lovers saw each other every day. Cosette came with M. Fauchelevent. "It is reversing the order of things," said Mademoiselle Gillenormand, "that the intended should come to the house to be courted like this." But Marius' convalescence had led to the habit; and the arm-chairs in the Rue des Filles du Calvaire, better for long talks than the straw chairs of the Rue de l'Homme Armé, had rooted it. Marius and M. Fauchelevent saw one another, but did not speak to each other. That seemed to be understood. Every girl needs a chaperon. Cosette could not have come without M. Fauchelevent. To Marius, M. Fauchelevent was the condition of Cosette. He accepted it. In bringing upon the carpet, vaguely and generally, matters of policy, from the point of view of the general amelioration of the lot of all, they succeeded in saying a little more than yes and no to each other. Once, on the subject of education, which Marius wished gratuitous and obligatory, multiplied under all forms, lavished upon all like the air and the sunshine, in one word, respirable by the entire people, they fell into unison and almost into a conversation. Marius remarked on this occasion that M. Fauchelevent talked well, and even with a certain elevation of language. There was, however, something wanting. M. Fauchelevent had something less than a man of the world, and something more.

Marius, inwardly and in the depth of his thought, surrounded this M. Fauchelevent, who was to him simply benevolent and cold, with all sorts of silent questions. There came to him at intervals doubts about his own recollections. In his memory there was a hole, a black place, an abyss scooped out by four months of agony. Many things were lost in it. He was led to ask himself if it were really true that he had seen M. Fauchelevent, such a man, so serious and so calm, in the barricade.

This was not, however, the only stupor which the appearances and the disappearances of the past had left in his mind. We must not suppose that he was delivered from all those obsessions of the memory which force us, even when happy, even when satisfied, to look back with melancholy. The head which does not turn towards the horizons of the past, contains neither thought nor love. At moments, Marius covered his face with his hands, and the vague past tumultuously traversed the twilight which filled his brain. He saw Mabeuf fall again, he heard Gavroche singing beneath the grape, he felt upon his lip the chill of Eponine's forehead; Enjolras, Courfeyrac, Jean Prouvaire, Combeferre, Bossuet, Grantaire, all his friends, rose up before him, then dissipated. All these beings, dear, sorrowful, valiant, charming or tragical, were they dreams? had they really existed? The émeute had wrapped everything in its smoke. These great fevers have great dreams. He interrogated himself, he groped within himself; he was dizzy with all these vanished realities. Where were they all then? Was it indeed true that all were dead? A fall into the darkness had carried off all, except himself. It all seemed to him to have disappeared as if behind a curtain at a theatre. There are such curtains which drop down in life. God is passing to the next act.

And himself, was he really the same man? He, the poor, he was rich; he, the abandoned, he had a family; he, the despairing, he was marrying Cosette. It seemed to him that he had passed through a tomb, and that he had gone in black, and that he had come out white. And in this tomb, the others had remained. At certain moments, all these beings of the past, returned and present, formed a circle about him and rendered him gloomy; then he thought of Cosette, and again became serene; but it required nothing less than this felicity to efface this catastrophe.

M. Fauchelevent almost had a place among these vanished beings. Marius hesitated to believe that the Fauchelevent of the barricade was the same as this Fauchelevent in flesh and blood, so gravely seated near Cosette. The first was probably one of those nightmares coming and going with his hours of delirium. Moreover, their two natures showing a steep front to each other, no question was possible from Marius to M. Fauchelevent. The idea of it did not even occur to him. We have already indicated this characteristic circumstance.

Two men who have a common secret, and who, by a sort of tacit agreement, do not exchange a word upon the subject, such a thing is less rare than one would think.

Once only, Marius made an attempt. He brought the Rue de la Chanvrerie into the conversation, and, turning towards M. Fauchelevent, he said to him:

"You are well acquainted with that street?"

"What street?"

"The Rue de la Chanvrerie."

"I have no idea of the name of that street," answered M. Fauchelevent in the most natural tone in the world.

The answer, which bore upon the name of the street, and not upon the street itself, appeared to Marius more conclusive than it was.

"Decidedly," thought he, "I have been dreaming. I have had a hallucination. It was somebody who resembled him. M. Fauchelevent was not there."

VIII
TWO MEN IMPOSSIBLE TO FIND

THE enchantment, great as it was, did not efface other pre-occupations from Marius' mind.

During the preparations for the marriage, and while waiting for the time fixed upon, he had some difficult and careful retrospective researches made.

He owed gratitude on several sides, he owed some on his father's account, he owed some on his own.

There was Thénardier; there was the unknown man who had brought him, Marius, to M. Gillenormand's.

Marius persisted in trying to find these two men, not intending to marry, to be happy, and to forget them, and fearing lest these debts of duty unpaid might cast a shadow over his life, so luminous henceforth. It was impossible for him to leave all these arrears unsettled behind him; and he wished, before entering joyously into the future, to have a quittance from the past.

That Thénardier was a scoundrel, took away nothing from this fact that he had saved Colonel Pontmercy. Thénardier was a bandit to everybody except Marius.

And Marius, ignorant of the real scene of the battle-field of Waterloo, did not know this peculiarity, that his father was, with reference to Thénardier, in this singular situation, that he owed his life to him without owing him any thanks.

None of the various agents whom Marius employed succeeded in finding Thénardier's track. Effacement seemed complete on that side. The Thénardiess had died in prison pending the examination on the charge. Thénardier and his daughter Azelma, the two who alone remained of that woeful group, had plunged back into the shadow. The gulf of the social Unknown had silently closed over these beings. There could no longer even be seen on the surface that quivering, that trembling, those obscure concentric circles which announce that something has fallen there, and that we may cast in the lead.

The Thénardiess being dead, Boulatruelle being put out of the case, Claquesous having disappeared, the principal accused having escaped from prison, the prosecution for the ambuscade at the Gorbeau house was almost abortive. The affair was left in deep obscurity. The Court of Assizes was obliged to content itself with two subalterns, Panchaud, alias Printanier, alias Bigrenaille, and Demi-Liard, alias Deux Milliards, who were tried and condemned to ten years at the galleys. Hard labour for life was pronounced against their accomplices who had escaped and did not appear. Thénardier, chief and ringleader, was, also for non-appearance, condemned to death. This condemnation was the only thing which remained in regard to Thénardier, throwing over that buried name its ominous glare, like a candle beside a bier.

Moreover, by crowding Thénardier back into the lowest depths, for fear of being retaken, this condemnation added to the thick darkness which covered this man.

As for the other, as for the unknown man who had saved Marius, the researches at first had some result, then stopped short. They succeeded in finding the fiacre which had brought Marius to the Rue des Filles du Calvaire on the evening of the

6th of June. The driver declared that on the 6th of June, by order of a police officer, he had been "stationed," from three o'clock in the afternoon until night, on the quai of the Champs-Elysées, above the outlet of the Grand Sewer; that, about nine o'clock in the evening, the grating of the sewer, which over-looks the river beach, was opened; that a man came out, carry-ing another man on his shoulders, who seemed to be dead; that the officer, who was watching at that point, arrested the living man, and seized the dead man; that, on the order of the officer, he, the driver, received "all those people" into the fiacre; that they went first to the Rue des Filles du Calvaire; that they left the dead man there; that the dead man was Monsieur Marius, and that he, the driver, recognised him plainly, although he was alive "this time;" that they then got into his carriage again; that he whipped up his horses; that, within a few steps of the door of the Archives, he had been called to stop; that there, in the street, he had been paid and left, and that the officer took away the other man; that he knew nothing more, that the night was very dark.

Marius, we have said, recollected nothing. He merely remembered having been seized from behind by a vigorous hand at the moment he fell backwards into the barricades, then all became a blank to him. He had recovered consciousness only at M. Gillenormand's.

He was lost in conjectures.

He could not doubt his own identity. How did it come about, however, that, falling in the Rue de la Chanvrerie, he had been picked up by the police officer on the banks of the Seine, near the Pont des Invalides? Somebody had carried him from the quartier of the markets to the Champs-Elysées. And how? By the sewer. Unparalleled devotion!

Somebody? who?

It was this man whom Marius sought.

Of this man, who was his saviour, nothing; no trace; not the least indication.

Marius, although compelled to great reserve in this respect, pushed his researches as far as the prefecture of police. There, no more than elsewhere, did the information obtained lead to any eclaircissement. The prefecture knew less than the driver of the fiacre. They had no knowledge of any arrest made on the 6th of June at the grating of the Grand Sewer; they had received no officer's report upon that fact, which, at the prefecture, was regarded as a fable. They attributed the invention of this fable to the driver. A driver who wants drink-money is capable of anything, even of imagination. The thing was certain, for all that, and Marius could not doubt it, unless by doubting his own identity, as we have just said.

Everything, in this strange enigma, was inexplicable.

This man, this mysterious man, whom the driver had seen come out of the grating of the Grand Sewer bearing Marius senseless upon his back, and whom the police officer on the watch had arrested in the very act of saving an insurgent, what had become of him? what had become of the officer himself? Why had this officer kept silence? had the man succeeded in escaping? had he bribed the officer? Why did this man give no sign of life to Marius, who owed everything to him? His disinterestedness was not less wonderful than his devotion. Why did not this man reappear? Perhaps he was above recompense, but nobody is above gratitude. Was he dead? what kind of a man was this? how did he look? Nobody could tell. The driver answered: "The night was very dark." Basque and Nicolette, in their amazement, had only looked at their young master covered with blood. The porter, whose candle had lighted the tragic arrival of Marius, alone had noticed the man in question, and this is the description which he gave of him: "This man was horrible."

In the hope of deriving aid in his researches from them, Marius had had preserved the bloody clothes which he wore when he was brought back to his grandfather's. On examining the coat, it was noticed that one skirt was oddly torn. A piece was missing.

One evening, Marius spoke, before Cosette and Jean Valjean, of all this singular adventure, of the numberless inquiries which he had made, and of the uselessness of his efforts. The cold countenance of "Monsieur Fauchelevent" made him impatient. He exclaimed with a vivacity which had almost the vibration of anger:

"Yes, that man, whoever he may be, was sublime. Do you know what he did, monsieur? He intervened like the archangel. He must have thrown himself into the midst of the combat, have snatched me out of it, have opened the sewer, have drawn me into it, have borne me through it! He must have made his way for more than four miles through hideous subterranean galleries, bent, stooping, in the darkness, in the cloaca, more than four miles, monsieur, with a corpse upon his back! And with what object? With the single object of saving that corpse. And that corpse was I. He said to himself: 'There is perhaps a glimmer of life still there; I will risk my own life for that miserable spark!' And his life, he did not risk it once, but twenty times! And each step was a danger. The proof is, that on coming out of the sewer he was arrested. Do you know, monsieur, that that man did all that? And he could expect no recompense. What was I? An insurgent. What was I? A vanquished man. Oh! if Cosette's six hundred thousand francs were mine——"

"They are yours," interrupted Jean Valjean.

"Well," resumed Marius, "I would give them to find that man!"

Jean Valjean kept silence.

BOOK SIXTH – THE WHITE NIGHT

I

THE 16TH OF FEBRUARY, 1833

THE night of the 16th of February, 1833, was a blessed night. Above its shade the heavens were opened. It was the wedding night of Marius and Cosette.

The day had been adorable.

It had not been the sky-blue festival dreamed by the grand-father, a fairy scene with a confusion of cherubs and cupids above the heads of the married pair, a marriage worthy of a frieze panel; but it had been sweet and mirthful.

The fashion of marriage was not in 1833 what it is to-day. France had not yet borrowed from England that supreme delicacy of eloping with one's wife, of making one's escape on leaving the church, of hiding one's self ashamed of one's happiness, and of combining the behaviour of a bankrupt with the transports of Solomon's Song. They had not yet learned all that there is chaste, exquisite, and decent, in jolting one's paradise in a post-chaise, in intersecting one's mystery with click-clacks, in taking a tavern bed for a nuptial bed, and in leaving behind, in the common alcove at so much a night, the most sacred of life's memories pell-mell with the interviews between the diligence conductor and the servant girl of the tavern.

In this second half of the nineteenth century in which we live, the mayor and his scarf, the priest and his chasuble, the law and God, are not enough; we must complete them with the Longjumeau postillion; blue waistcoat with red facings and bell-buttons, a plate for a vambrace, breeches of green leather, oaths at Norman horses with knotted tails, imitation galloon, tarpaulin hat, coarse powdered hair, enormous whip, and heavy boots. France does not yet push elegance so far as to have, like the English nobility, a hailstorm of slippers down at the heel and old shoes, beating upon the bridal post-chaise, in memory of Churchill, afterwards Marlborough, or Malbrouck, who was assailed on the day of his marriage by the anger of an aunt who brought him good luck. The old shoes and the slippers do not yet form a part of our nuptial celebrations; but patience, good taste continuing to spread, we shall come to it.

In 1833, a hundred years ago, marriage was not performed at full trot.

It was still imagined at that day, strange to tell, that a marriage is an intimate and social festival, that a patriarchal banquet does not spoil a domestic solemnity, that gaiety, even excessive, provided it be seemly, does no harm to happiness, and finally that it is venerable and good that the fusion of these two destinies whence a family is to arise, should commence in the house, and that the household should have the nuptial chamber for a witness henceforth.

And they have the shamelessness to be married at home.

The marriage took place, therefore, according to that now obsolete fashion, at M. Gillenormand's.

Natural and ordinary as this matter of marriage may be, the banns to be published, the deeds to be drawn up, the mairie, the church, always render it somewhat complex. They could not be ready before the 16th of February.

Now, we mention this circumstance for the pure satisfaction of being exact, it happened that the 16th was Mardi Gras. Hesitations, scruples, particularly from Aunt Gillenormand.

"Mardi Gras!" exclaimed the grandfather. "So much the better. There is a proverb:

> Mariage un Mardi Gras,
> N'aura point d'enfants ingrats.

Let us go on. Here goes for the 16th! Do you want to put it off, you, Marius?"

"Certainly not!" answered the lover.

"Let us get married," said the grandfather.

So the marriage took place on the 16th, notwithstanding the public gaiety. It rained that day, but there is always a little patch of blue in the sky at the service of happiness, which lovers see, even though the rest of creation be under an umbrella.

On the previous evening, Jean Valjean had handed to Marius, in presence of M. Gillenormand, the five hundred and eighty-four thousand francs.

The marriage being performed under the law of community, the deeds were simple.

Toussaint was henceforth useless to Jean Valjean; Cosette had inherited her and had promoted her to the rank of waiting-maid.

As for Jean Valjean, there was a beautiful room in the Gillenormand house furnished expressly for him, and Cosette had said to him so irresistibly: "Father, I pray you," that she had made him almost promise that he would come and occupy it.

A few days before the day fixed for the marriage, an accident happened to Jean Valjean; he slightly bruised the thumb of his right hand. It was not serious; and he had allowed nobody to take any trouble about it, nor to dress it, nor even to see his hurt, not even Cosette. It compelled him, however, to muffle his hand in a bandage, and to carry his arm in a sling, and prevented his signing anything. M. Gillenormand, as Cosette's overseeing guardian, took his place.

We shall take the reader neither to the mairie nor to the church. We hardly follow two lovers as far as that, and we generally turn our backs upon the drama as soon as it puts its bridegroom's bouquet into his buttonhole. We shall merely mention an incident which, although unnoticed by the wedding party, marked its progress from the Rue des Filles du Calvaire to Saint Paul's.

They were repaving, at that time, the northern extremity of the Rue Saint Louis. It was fenced off where it leaves the Rue du Parc Royal. It was impossible for the wedding carriages to go directly to Saint Paul's. It was necessary to change the route, and the shortest way was to turn off by the boulevard. One of the guests observed that it was Mardi Gras, and that the boulevard would be encumbered with carriages. "Why?" asked M. Gillenormand. "On account of the masks." "Capital!" said the grandfather; "let us go that way. These young folks are marrying; they are going to enter upon the serious things of life. It will prepare them for it to see a bit of masquerade."

They went by the boulevard. The first of the wedding carriages contained Cosette and Aunt Gillenormand, M. Gillenormand, and Jean Valjean. Marius, still separated from his betrothed, according to the custom, did not come till the second. The nuptial cortège, on leaving the Rue des Filles du Calvaire, was involved in the long procession of carriages which made an endless chain from the Madeleine to the Bastille and from the Bastille to the Madeleine.

Masks abounded on the boulevard. It was of no avail that it rained at intervals; Pantaloon and Harlequin were obstinate. In the good-humour of that winter of 1833, Paris had disguised herself as Venice. We see no such Mardi Gras nowadays. Everything being an expanded carnival, there is no longer any carnival.

The cross-alleys were choked with passengers, and the windows with the curious. The terraces which crown the peristyles of the theatres were lined with spectators. Besides the masks, they beheld that row, peculiar to Mardi Gras as well as to Longchamps, of vehicles of all sorts, hackney coaches, spring carts, carrioles, cabriolets, moving in order, rigorously riveted to one another by the regulations of the police, and, as it were, running in grooves. Whoever is in one of these vehicles is, at the same time, spectator and spectacle. Sergents de ville kept those two interminable parallel files on the lower sides of the boulevard moving with a contrary motion, and watched, so that nothing should hinder their double current, over those two streams of carriages flowing, the one down, the other up, the one towards the Chaussée d'Antin, the other towards the Faubourg Saint Antoine. The emblazoned carriages of the peers of France, and the ambassadors, kept the middle of the roadway, going and coming freely. Certain magnificent and joyous cortèges, especially the Fat Ox, had the same privilege. In this gaiety of Paris, England cracked her whip; the postchaise of Lord Seymour, teased with a nickname by the populace, passed along with a great noise.

In the double file, along which galloped some Municipal Guards like shepherds' dogs, honest family carry-alls, loaded down with great-aunts and grandmothers, exhibited at their doors fresh groups of disguised children, clowns of seven, clownesses of six, charming little creatures, feeling that they were officially a portion of the public mirth, penetrated with the dignity of their harlequinade, and displaying the gravity of functionaries.

From time to time, there was a bloc somewhere in the procession of vehicles; one or the other of the two lateral files stopped until the knot was disentangled; one carriage obstructed was enough to paralyse the whole line. Then they resumed their course.

The wedding carriages were in the file going towards the Bastille, and moving along the right side of the boulevard. At the Rue du Pont aux Choux, there was a stop for a time. Almost at the same instant, on the other side, the other file, which was going towards the Madeleine, also stopped. There was at this point of that file, a carriage-load of masks.

These carriages, or, to speak more correctly, these cart-loads of masks, are well known to the Parisians. If they failed on a *Mardi Gras*, or a Mid-Lent, people suspected something, and they would say: "*there is something at the bottom of that. Probably the ministry is going to change.*" A heaping up of Cassandras, Harlequins and Columbines, jolted above the passers-by, every possible grotesqueness from the Turk to the savage, Hercules supporting marchionesses, jades who would make Rabelais stop his ears even as the Bacchantes made Aristophanes cast down his eyes; flax wigs, rosy swaddling-bands, coxcombs' hats, cross-eyed spectacles, Janot cocked hats, teased by a butterfly, shouts thrown to the foot-passengers, arms akimbo, bold postures, naked shoulders, masked faces, unmuzzled shamelessness; a chaos of effrontery marshalled by a driver crowned with flowers; such is this institution.

Greece required the chariot of Thespis, France requires the fiacre of Vadé.

Everything may be parodied, even parody. The saturnalia, that grimace of the ancient beauty, has gradually grown to Mardi Gras, and the bacchanal, formerly crowned with vine branches, inundated with sunlight, showing bosoms of marble in a divine half-nudity, to-day grown flabby under the soaking rags of the north, has ended by calling herself the *chie-en-lit.*

The tradition of the carriages of masks goes back to the oldest times of the monarchy. The accounts of Louis XI. allow to the bailiff of the palace "twenty sous tournois for three masquerade coaches at the street-corners." In our days, these noisy crowds of creatures are commonly carted by some ancient van, the top of which they load down, or overwhelm with their tumultuous group an excise cart whose cover is broken in. There are twenty of them in a carriage for six. They are on the seat, on the stool, on the bows of the cover, on the pole. They even got astride of the carriage lanterns. They are standing, lying, sitting, feet curled up, legs hanging. The women occupy the knees of the men. Their mad pyramid can be seen from a distance above the swarming heads. These carriage-loads make mountains of mirth in the midst of the mob. Collé, Panard, and Piron, flow from them, enriched with argot. They spit the Billingsgate catechism down upon the people. This fiacre, become measureless by its load, has an air of conquest. Uproar is in front, tohubohu is in the rear. They vociferate, they vocalise, they howl, they burst, they writhe with happiness; gaiety bellows, sarcasm flames, joviality spreads itself as if it were purple; two harridans lead on the farce which expands into apotheosis; it is the triumphal car of Laughter.

Laughter too cynical to be free. And, in fact, this laughter is suspicious. This laughter has a mission. Its business is to prove the carnival to the Parisians.

These Billingsgate wagons, in which we feel an indefinable darkness, make the philosopher think. There is something of government therein. In them we lay our finger upon a mysterious affinity between public men and public women.

That turpitudes heaped up should give a total of gaiety, that by piling ignominy upon opprobrium, a people is decoyed; that espionage serving as a caryatid to prostitution, amuses the crowds while insulting them; that the mob loves to see pass along on the four wheels of a fiacre, this monstrous living heap, rag-tinsel, half ordure and half light, barking and singing; that people should clap their hands at this glory made up of every shame; that there should be no festival for the multitudes unless the police exhibit among them this sort of twenty-headed hydra of joy, certainly it is sad! But what is to be done? These tumbrils of beribboned and beflowered slime are insulted and forgiven by the public laughter. The laughter of all is the accomplice of the universal degradation. Certain unwholesome festivals disintegrate the people, and make it a populace. And for populaces as well as for tyrants, buffoons are needed. The king has Roquelaure, the people has Harlequin. Paris is the great foolish town, whenever she is not the great sublime city. The carnival is a part of her politics. Paris, we must admit, willingly supplies herself with comedy through infamy. She demands of her masters— when she has masters—but one thing: "Varnish me the mud!" Rome was of the same humour. She loved Nero. Nero was a titanic lighter-man.

Chance determined, as we have just said, that one of these shapeless bunches of masked women and men, drawn along in a huge calash, stopped on the left of the boulevard while the wedding cortège was stopping on the right. From one side of the boulevard to the other, the carriage in which the masks were, looked into the carriage opposite, in which was the bride.

"Hullo!" said a mask, "a wedding."

"A sham wedding," replied another. "We are the genuine."

And, too far off to be able to accost the wedding party, fearing moreover the call of the sergents de ville, the two masks looked elsewhere.

The whole carriage-load of masks had enough to do a moment afterwards, the multitude began to hoot at it, which is the caress of the populace to the maskers, and the two masks which had just spoken were obliged to make front to the street with their comrades and had none too many of all the weapons from the storehouse of the markets, to answer the enormous jaw of the people. A frightful exchange of metaphors was carried on between the masks and the crowd.

Meanwhile, two other masks in the same carriage, a huge-nosed Spaniard with an oldish air and enormous black moustaches, and a puny jade, a very young girl, with a black velvet mask, had also noticed the wedding party, and, while their companions and the passers-by were lampooning one another, carried on a dialogue in a low tone.

Their aside was covered by the tumult and lost in it. The gusts of rain had soaked the carriage, which was thrown wide open; the February wind is not warm; even while answering the Spaniard, the girl, with her low-necked dress, shivered, laughed, and coughed.

This was the dialogue:

"Say, now."

"What, *daron?*"*

"Do you see that old fellow?"

"What old fellow?"

"There, in the first *roulotte*† of the wedding party by our side."

"Who has his arm hooked into a black cravat?"

"Yes."

"Well?"

"I am sure I know him."

"Ah!"

"I wish that somebody may *faucher* my *colabre* and have never in my *vioc* said *vousaille*, *tonorgue*, nor *mézig*, if I don't know that *pantinois.*"‡

---

* Father.   † Carriage.

‡ I wish that somebody may cut my throat and have never in my life said you, thee, nor me, if I don't know that Parisian.

"To-day Paris is Pantin."

"Can you see the bride by stooping over?"

"No."

"And the groom?"

"There is no groom in that *roulotte*."

"Pshaw!"

"Unless it may be the other old fellow."

"Bend forward well and try to see the bride."

"I can't."

"It's all the same, that old fellow who has something the matter with his paw, I am sure I know him."

"And what good does it do you to know him?"

"Nobody knows. Sometimes!"

"I don't get much amusement out of old men, for my part."

"I know him."

"Know him to your heart's content."

"How the devil is he at the wedding?"

"We are at it, too, ourselves."

"Where does this wedding party come from?"

"How do I know?"

"Listen."

"What?"

"You must do something."

"What?"

"Get out of our *roulotte* and *filer** that wedding party."

"What for?"

"To know where it goes and what it is. Make haste to get out, run, my *fée*, you are young."

"I can't leave the carriage."

"Why not?"

"I am rented."

"Ah, the deuce!"

"I owe my day to the prefecture."

"That is true."

"If I leave the carriage, the first officer who sees me arrests me. You know very well."

"Yes, I know."

---

* Follow.

"To-day I am bought by *Pharos*." *

"It is all the same. That old fellow worries me."

"Old men worry you. You are not a young girl, however."

"He is in the first carriage."

"Well?"

"In the bride's *roulotte*."

"What then?"

"Then he is the father."

"What is that to me?"

"I tell you that he is the father."

"There isn't any other father."

"Listen."

"What?"

"For my part, I can hardly go out unless I am masked. Here, I am hidden, nobody knows that I am here. But to-morrow, there are no more masks. It is Ash Wednesday. I risk failing.† I must get back to my hole. You are free."

"Not too much so."

"More than I, still."

"Well, what then?"

"You must try to find out where this wedding party have gone."

"Where it is going?"

"Yes."

"I know that."

"Where is it going, then?"

"To the Cadran Bleu."

"In the first place, it is not in that direction."

"Well! to the Râpée."

"Or somewhere else."

"It is free. Weddings are free."

"That isn't all. I tell you that you must try to let me know what that wedding party is, that this old fellow belongs to, and where that wedding party lives."

"Not often! that will be funny. It is convenient to find, a week afterwards, a wedding party which passed by in Paris on Mardi Gras. A *tiquante*‡ in a haystack! Is it possible!"

* The government.
† Being arrested.
‡ Pin.

"No matter, you must try. Do you understand, Azelma?"

The two files resumed their movement in opposite directions on the two sides of the boulevard, and the carriage of the masks lost sight of the bride's "roulotte."

II

JEAN VALJEAN STILL HAS HIS ARM IN A SLING

To realise his dream. To whom is that given? There must be elections for that in heaven; we are all unconscious candidates; the angels vote. Cosette and Marius had been elected.

Cosette, at the mairie and in the church, was brilliant and touching. Toussaint, aided by Nicolette, had dressed her.

Cosette wore her dress of Binche guipure over a skirt of white taffetas, a veil of English point, a necklace of fine pearls, a crown of orange flowers; all this was white, and, in this whiteness, she was radiant. It was an exquisite candour, dilating and transfiguring itself into luminousness. One would have said she was a virgin in process of becoming a goddess.

Marius' beautiful hair was perfumed and lustrous; here and there might be discerned, under the thickness of the locks, pallid lines, which were the scars of the barricade.

The grandfather, superb, his head held high, uniting more than ever in his toilet and manners all the elegances of the time of Barras, conducted Cosette. He took the place of Jean Valjean, who, as his arm was in a sling, could not give his hand to the bride.

Jean Valjean, in black, followed and smiled.

"Monsieur Fauchelevent," said the grandfather to him, "this is a happy day. I vote for the end of afflictions and sorrows. There must no longer be any sadness anywhere henceforth. By Jove! I decree joy! Evil has no right to be. That there should be unfortunate men—in truth, it is a shame to the blue sky. Evil does not come from man, who, in reality, is good. All human miseries have for their chief seat and central government Hell, otherwise called the Tuileries of the devil. Good, here am I saying demagogical words now! As for me, I no longer have any political opinions; that all men may be rich, that is to say, happy, that is all I ask for."

When, at the completion of all the ceremonies, after having pronounced before the mayor and the priest every possible yes, after having signed the registers at the municipality and at the sacristy, after having exchanged their rings, after having been on their knees elbow to elbow under the canopy of white moire in the smoke of the censer, hand in hand, admired and envied by all, Marius in black, she in white, preceded by the usher in colonel's epaulettetes, striking the pavement with his halberd, between two hedges of marvelling spectators, they arrived under the portal of the church where the folding-doors were both open, ready to get into the carriage again, and all was over, Cosette could not yet believe it. She looked at Marius, she looked at the throng, she looked at the sky; it seemed as if she were afraid of awaking. Her astonished and bewildered air rendered her unspeakably bewitching. To return, they got into the same carriage, Marius by Cosette's side; M. Gillenormand and Jean Valjean sat opposite. Aunt Gillenormand had drawn back one degree, and was in the second carriage. "My children," said the grandfather, "here you are Monsieur the Baron and Madame the Baroness, with thirty thousand francs a year." And Cosette, leaning close up to Marius, caressed his ear with this angelic whisper: "It is true, then. My name is Marius. I am Madame You."

These two beings were resplendent. They were at the irrevocable and undiscoverable hour, at the dazzling point of intersection of all youth and of all joy. They realised Jean Prouvaire's rhymes; together they could not count forty years. It was marriage sublimated; these two children were two lilies. They did not see each other, they contemplated each other. Cosette beheld Marius in a glory; Marius beheld Cosette upon an altar. And upon that altar and in that glory, the two apotheoses mingling, in the background, mysteriously, behind a cloud to Cosette, in flashing flame to Marius, there was the ideal, the real, the rendezvous of the kiss and the dream, the nuptial pillow.

Every torment which they had experienced was returned by them in intoxication. It seemed to them that the griefs, the sleeplessness, the tears, the anguish, the dismay, the despair, become caresses and radiance, rendered still more enchanting the enchanting hour which was approaching; and that their sorrows were so many servants making the toilet of their joy. To have suffered, how good it is! Their grief made a halo about their happiness. The long agony of their love terminated in an ascension.

There was in these two souls the same enchantment, shaded with anticipation in Marius and with modesty in Cosette. They said to each other in a whisper: "We will go and see our little garden in the Rue Plumet again." The folds of Cosette's dress were over Marius.

Such a day is an ineffable mixture of dream and of certainty. You possess and you suppose. You still have some time before you for imagination. It is an unspeakable emotion on that day to be at noon and to think of midnight. The delight of these two hearts overflowed upon the throng and gave joy to the passers-by.

People stopped in the Rue Saint Antoine in front of Saint Paul's to see, through the carriage window, the orange flowers trembling upon Cosette's head.

Then they returned to the Rue des Filles du Calvaire, to their home. Marius, side by side with Cosette, ascended, triumphant and radiant, that staircase up which he had been carried dying. The poor gathered before the door, and, sharing their purses, they blessed them. There were flowers everywhere. The house was not less perfumed than the church; after incense, roses. They thought they heard voices singing in the infinite; they had God in their hearts; destiny appeared to them like a ceiling of stars; they saw above their heads a gleam of sunrise. Suddenly the clock struck. Marius looked at Cosette's bewitching bare arm and the rosy things which he dimly perceived through the lace of her corsage, and Cosette, seeing Marius look, began to blush even to the tips of her ears.

A good number of the old friends of the Gillenormand family had been invited; they pressed eagerly about Cosette. They vied with each other in calling her Madame the Baroness.

The officer Théodule Gillenormand, now a captain, had come from Chartres, where he was now in garrison, to attend the wedding of his cousin Pontmercy. Cosette did not recognise him.

He, for his part, accustomed to being thought handsome by the women, remembered Cosette no more than any other.

"I was right in not believing that lancer's story!" said Grandfather Gillenormand to himself.

Cosette had never been more tender towards Jean Valjean. She was in unison with Grandfather Gillenormand; while he embodied joy in aphorisms and in maxims, she exhaled love and kindness like a perfume. Happiness wishes everybody happy.

She went back, in speaking to Jean Valjean, to the tones of voice of the time when she was a little girl. She caressed him with smiles.

A banquet had been prepared in the dining-room.

An illumination à giorno is the necessary attendant of a great joy. Dusk and obscurity are not accepted by the happy. They do not consent to be dark. Night, yes; darkness, no. If there is no sun, one must be made.

The dining-room was a furnace of cheerful things. In the centre above the white and glittering table, a Venetian lustre with flat drops, with all sorts of coloured birds, blue, violet, red, green, perched in the midst of the candles; about the lustre girandoles, upon the wall reflectors with triple and quintuple branches; glasses, crystals, glassware, vessels, porcelains, Faënza-ware, pottery, gold and silver ware, all sparkled and rejoiced. The spaces between the candelabra were filled with bouquets, so that, wherever there was not a light, there was a flower.

In the antechamber three violins and a flute played some of Haydn's quartettes in softened strains.

Jean Valjean sat in a chair in the parlour, behind the door, which shut back upon him in such a way as almost to hide him. A few moments before they took their seats at the table, Cosette came, as if from a sudden impulse, and made him a low curtsey, spreading out her bridal dress with both hands, and, with a tenderly frolicsome look, she asked him:

"Father, are you pleased?"

"Yes," said Jean Valjean, "I am pleased."

"Well, then, laugh."

Jean Valjean began to laugh.

A few moments afterwards, Basque announced dinner.

The guests, preceded by M. Gillenormand giving his arm to Cosette, entered the dining-room, and took their places, according to the appointed order, about the table.

Two large arm-chairs were placed, on the right and on the left of the bride, the first for M. Gillenormand, the second for Jean Valjean. M. Gillenormand took his seat. The other arm-chair remained empty.

All eyes sought "Monsieur Fauchelevent."

He was not there.

M. Gillenormand called Basque.

"Do you know where Monsieur Fauchelevent is?"

"Monsieur," answered Basque. "Exactly. Monsieur Fauchelevent told me to say to monsieur that he was suffering a little from his sore hand, and could not dine with Monsieur the Baron and Madame the Baroness. That he begged they would excuse him, that he would come to-morrow morning. He has just gone away."

This empty arm-chair chilled for a moment the effusion of the nuptial repast. But, M. Fauchelevent absent, M. Gillenormand was there, and the grandfather was brilliant enough for two. He declared that M. Fauchelevent did well to go to bed early, if he was suffering, but that it was only a "scratch." This declaration was enough. Besides, what is one dark corner in such a deluge of joy? Cosette and Marius were in one of those selfish and blessed moments when we have no faculty save for the perception of happiness. And then, M. Gillenormand had an idea. "By jove, this arm-chair is empty. Come here, Marius. Your aunt, although she has a right to you, will allow it. This arm-chair is for you. It is legal, and it is proper. 'Fortunatus beside Fortunata.'" Applause from the whole table. Marius took Jean Valjean's place at Cosette's side; and things arranged themselves in such a way that Cosette, at first saddened by Jean Valjean's absence, was finally satisfied with it. From the moment that Marius was the substitute, Cosette would not have regretted God. She put her soft little foot encased in white satin upon Marius' foot.

The arm-chair occupied, M. Fauchelevent was effaced; and nothing was missed. And, five minutes later, the whole table was laughing from one end to the other with all the spirit of forgetfulness.

At the dessert, M. Gillenormand standing, a glass of champagne in his hand, filled half full so that the trembling of his ninety-two years should not spill it, gave the health of the married pair.

"You shall not escape two sermons," exclaimed he. "This morning you had the curé's, to-night you shall have the grandfather's. Listen to me; I am going to give you a piece of advice: Adore one another. I don't make a heap of flourishes. I go to the end, be happy. The only sages in creation are the turtle-doves. The philosophers say: Moderate your joys. I say: Give them the rein. Be enamoured like devils. Be rabid. The philo-

sophers dote. I would like to cram their philosophy back into
their throats. Can there be too many perfumes, too many open
rosebuds, too many nightingales singing, too many green leaves,
too much aurora in life? can you love each other too much? can
you please each other too much? Take care, Estelle, you are too
pretty! Take care, Némorin, you are too handsome! The rare
absurdity! Can you enchant each other too much, pet each
other too much, charm each other too much? can you be too
much alive? can you be too happy? Moderate your joys. Ah,
pshaw! Down with the philosophers! Wisdom is jubilation.
Jubilate, jubilate. Are we happy because we are good: or are we
good because we are happy? Is the Sancy called the Sancy
because it belonged to Harlay de Sancy, or because it weighs
cent-six [a hundred and six] carats? I know nothing about it; life
is full of such problems; the important thing is to have the Sancy,
and happiness. Be happy without quibbling. Obey the sun
blindly. What is the sun? It is love. Who says love, says woman.
Ah, ha! There is an omnipotence; it is woman. Ask this demagogue of a Marius if he be not the slave of this little tyrant of a
Cosette, and with his full consent, the coward. Woman! There
is no Robespierre who holds out, woman reigns. I am no longer
a royalist except for that royalty. What is Adam? He is the realm
of Eve. No '89 for Eve. There was the royal sceptre surmounted
by a fleur de lys; there was the imperial sceptre surmounted by
a globe; there was the sceptre of Charlemagne, which was of
iron; there was the sceptre of Louis XIV., which was of gold,
the revolution twisted them between his thumb and finger like
half-penny wisps of straw; they are finished, they are broken,
they are on the ground, there is no longer a sceptre; but get me
up some revolutions now against this little embroidered handkerchief which smells of patchouly! I would like to see you at it.
Try. Why is it immovable? Because it is a rag. Ah! you are the
nineteenth century! Well, what then? We were the eighteenth!
and we were as stupid as you. Don't imagine that you have
changed any great thing in the universe because your stoop-
galant is called the cholera morbus, and because your boree is
called the cachucha. At heart you must always love women. I
defy you to get away from that. These devilesses are our angels.
Yes, love, woman, the kiss, that is a circle which I defy you to
get out of, and, as for myself, I would like very well to get back
into it. Which of you has seen rising into the infinite, calming

all beneath her, gazing upon the waves like a woman, the star Venus, the great coquette of the abyss, the Célimène of the ocean? The ocean is a rude Alceste. Well, he scolds in vain; Venus appears, he is obliged to smile. That brute beast submits. We are all so. Wrath, tempest, thunderbolts, foam to the sky. A woman enters on the scene, a star rises; flat on your face! Marius was fighting six months ago; he is marrying to-day. Well done. Yes, Marius, yes, Cosette, you are right. Live boldly for one another, my-love one another, make us die with rage that we cannot do as much, idolatrise each other. Take in your two beaks all the little straws of felicity on earth, and build yourselves a nest for life. By Jove, to love, to be loved, the admirable miracle when one is young! Don't imagine that you have invented it. I, too, I have had my dream, my vision, my sighs; I, too, have had a moonlight soul. Love is a child six thousand years old. Love has a right to a long white beard. Methuselah is a *gamin* beside Cupid. For sixty centuries, man and woman have got out of the scrape by loving. The devil, who is malicious, took to hating man; man, who is more malicious, took to loving woman. In this way he has done himself more good than the devil has done him harm. This trick was discovered at the time of the earthly paradise. My friends, the invention is old, but it is quite new. Profit by it. Be Daphnis and Chloë, while you are waiting to be Philemon and Baucis. So act that, when you are with each other, there shall be nothing wanting, and that Cosette may be the sun to Marius, and that Marius may be the universe to Cosette. Cosette, let your fine weather be the smile of your husband: Marius! let your rain be the tears of your wife. And may it never rain in your household. You have filched the good number in the lottery, a love-match; you have the highest prize, take good care of it, put it under lock and key, don't squander it, worship each other, and snap your fingers at the rest. Believe what I tell you. It is good sense. Good sense cannot lie. Be a religion to each other. Every one has his own way of worshipping God. Zounds! the best way to worship God is to love your wife. I love you! that is my catechism. Whoever loves is orthodox. Henry IV.'s oath puts sanctity between gluttony and drunkenness. *Ventre-saint-gris!* I am not of the religion of that oath. Woman is forgotten in it. That astonishes me on the part of Henry IV.'s oath. My friends, long live woman! I am old, they say; it is astonishing how I feel myself growing young again. I would like to go and listen to the bagpipes in the woods. These children who are so fortunate as to be beautiful and happy, that fuddles me. I would get married myself if anybody wished. It is impossible to imagine that God has made us for anything but this: to idolise, to coo, to plume, to be pigeons, to be cocks, to bill with our loves from morning to night, to take pride in our little wives, to be vain, to be triumphant, to put on airs; that is the aim of life. That is, without offence to you, what we thought, we old fellows, in our times when we were the young folks. Ah! odswinkers! what charming women there were in those days, and pretty faces, and lasses! There's where I made my ravages. Then love each other. If people did not love one another, I really don't see what use there would be in having any spring; and, for my part, I should pray the good God to pack up all the pretty things which he shows us, and take them away from us, and to put the flowers, the birds, and the pretty girls, back into his box. My children, receive the benediction of the old goodman."

The evening was lively, gay, delightful. The sovereign good-humour of the grandfather gave the key-note to the whole festival, and everybody regulated himself by this almost centenarian cordiality. They danced a little, they laughed much; it was a good childlike wedding. They might have invited the goodman formerly. Indeed, he was there in the person of Grandfather Gillenormand.

There was tumult, then silence.

The bride and groom disappeared.

A little after midnight the Gillenormand house became a temple.

Here we stop. Upon the threshold of wedding-nights stands an angel smiling, his finger on his lip.

The soul enters into contemplation before this sanctuary, in which is held the celebration of love.

There must be gleams of light above those houses. The joy which they contain must escape in light through the stones of the walls, and shine dimly into the darkness. It is impossible that this sacred festival of destiny should not send a celestial radiation to the infinite. Love is the sublime crucible in which is consummated the fusion of man and woman; the one being, the triple being, the final being, the human trinity springs from it. This birth of two souls into one must be an emotion for space. The lover is priest; the rapt maiden is affrighted. Something of this joy goes to God. Where there is really marriage, that is where there is love, the ideal is mingled with it. A nuptial bed makes a halo in the darkness. Were it given to the eye of flesh to perceive the fearful and enchanting sights of the superior life, it is probable that we should see the forms of night, the winged strangers, the blue travellers of the invisible, bending, a throng of shadowy heads, over the luminous house, pleased, blessing, showing to one another the sweetly startled maiden bride, and wearing the reflection of the human felicity upon their divine countenances. If, at that supreme hour, the wedded pair, bewildered with pleasure, and believing themselves alone, were to listen, they would hear in their chamber a rustling of confused wings. Perfect happiness implies the solidarity of the angels. That little obscure alcove has for its ceiling the whole heavens. When two mouths, made sacred by love, draw near each other to create, it is impossible that above that ineffable kiss there should not be a thrill in the immense mystery of the stars.

These are the true felicities. No joy beyond these joys. Love is the only ecstasy, everything else weeps.

To love or to have loved, that is enough. Ask nothing further. There is no other pearl to be found in the dark folds of life. To love is a consummation.

III
THE INSEPARABLE

WHAT had become of Jean Valjean?

Immediately after having laughed, upon Cosette's playful injunction, nobody observing him, Jean Valjean had left his seat, got up, and, unperceived, had reached the antechamber. It was that same room which eight months before he had entered, black with mire, blood, and powder, bringing the grandson home to the grandfather. The old woodwork was garlanded with leaves and flowers; the musicians were seated on the couch upon which they had placed Marius. Basque, in a black coat, short breeches, white stockings, and white gloves, was arranging crowns of roses about each of the dishes which was to be served up. Jean Valjean had shown him his arm in a sling, charged him to explain his absence, and gone away.

The windows of the dining-room looked upon the street.

Jean Valjean stood for some minutes motionless in the obscurity under those radiant windows. He listened. The confused sounds of the banquet reached him. He heard the loud and authoritative words of the grandfather, the violins, the clatter of the plates and glasses, the bursts of laughter, and through all that gay uproar he distinguished Cosette's sweet joyous voice.

He left the Rue des Filles du Calvaire and returned to the Rue de l'Homme Armé.

To return, he went by the Rue Saint Louis, the Rue Culture Sainte Catherine, and the Blancs Manteaux; it was a little longer, but it was the way by which, for three months, to avoid the obstructions and the mud of the Rue Vieille du Temple, he had been accustomed to come every day, from the Rue de l'Homme Armé to the Rue des Filles du Calvaire, with Cosette.

This way over which Cosette had passed excluded for him every other road.

Jean Valjean returned home. He lighted his candle and went upstairs. The apartment was empty. Toussaint herself was no longer there. Jean Valjean's step made more noise than usual in the rooms. All the closets were open. He went into Cosette's room. There were no sheets on the bed. The pillow, without a pillow-case and without laces, was laid upon the coverlets folded at the foot of the mattress of which the ticking was to be seen and on which nobody should sleep henceforth. All the little feminine objects to which Cosette clung had been carried away; there remained only the heavy furniture and the four walls. Toussaint's bed was also stripped. A single bed was made and seemed waiting for somebody, that was Jean Valjean's.

Jean Valjean looked at the walls, shut some closet doors, went and came from one room to the other.

Then he found himself again in his own room, and he put his candle on the table.

He had released his arm from the sling, and he helped himself with his right hand as if he did not suffer from it.

He approached his bed, and his eye fell, was it by chance? was it with intention? upon the *inseparable*, of which Cosette had been jealous, upon the little trunk which never left him. On the 4th of June, on arriving in the Rue de l'Homme Armé, he had placed it upon a candle-stand at the head of his bed. He went to this stand with a sort of vivacity, took a key from his pocket, and opened the valise.

He took out slowly the garments in which, ten years before, Cosette had left Montfermeil, first the little dress, then the black scarf, then the great heavy child's shoes which Cosette could have almost put on still, so small a foot she had, then the bodice of very thick fustian, then the knit-skirt, then the apron with pockets, then the woollen stockings. Those stockings, on which the shape of a little leg was still gracefully marked, were hardly longer than Jean Valjean's hand. These were all black. He had carried these garments for her to Montfermeil. As he took them out of the valise, he laid them on the bed. He was thinking. He remembered. It was in winter, a very cold December, she shivered half-naked in rags, her poor little feet all red in her wooden shoes. He, Jean Valjean, he had taken her away from those rags to clothe her in this mourning garb. The mother must have been pleased in her tomb to see her daughter wear mourning for her, and especially to see that she was clad, and that she was warm. He thought of that forest of Montfermeil; they had crossed it together, Cosette and he; he thought of the weather, of the trees without leaves, of the forest without birds, of the sky without sun; it is all the same, it was charming. He arranged the little things upon the bed, the scarf next the skirt, the stockings beside the shoes, the bodice beside the dress, and he looked at them one after another. She was no higher than that, she had her great doll in her arms, she had put her louis d'or in the pocket of this apron, she laughed, they walked holding each other by the hand, she had nobody but him in the world.

Then his venerable white head fell upon the bed, this old stoical heart broke, his face was swallowed up, so to speak, in Cosette's garments, and anybody who had passed along the staircase at that moment, would have heard fearful sobs.

IV

IMMORTALE JECUR

THE formidable old struggle, several phases of which we have already seen, recommenced.

Jacob wrestled with the angel but one night. Alas! how many times have we seen Jean Valjean clenched, body to body, in the darkness with his conscience, and wrestling desperately against it.

Unparalleled struggle! At certain moments, the foot slips; at others, the ground gives way. How many times had that conscience furious for the right, grasped and overwhelmed him! How many times had truth, inexorable, planted her knee upon his breast! How many times, thrown to the ground by the light, had he cried to it for mercy! How many times had that implacable light, kindled in him and over him by the bishop, irresistibly dazzled him when he desired to be blinded! How many times had he risen up in the combat, bound to the rock, supported by sophism, dragged in the dust, sometimes bearing down his conscience beneath him, sometimes borne down by it! How many times, after an equivocation, after a treacherous and specious reasoning of selfishness, had he heard his outraged conscience cry in his ear: "A trip! wretch!" How many times had his refractory thought writhed convulsively under the evidence of duty. Resistance to God. Agonising sweats. How many secret wounds, which he alone felt bleed! How many chafings of his miserable existence! How many times had he risen up bleeding, bruised, lacerated, illuminated, despair in his heart, serenity in his soul! and, conquered, felt himself conqueror. And, after having racked, torn, and broken him, his conscience, standing above him, formidable, luminous, tranquil, said to him: "Now, go in peace!"

But, on coming out of so gloomy a struggle, what dreary peace, alas!

That night, however, Jean Valjean felt that he was giving his last battle.

A poignant question presented itself.

Predestinations are not all straight; they do not develop themselves in a rectilinear avenue before the predestinated; they are blind alleys, cœcums, obscure windings, embarrassing cross-roads offering several paths. Jean Valjean was halting at this moment at the most perilous of these cross-roads.

He had reached the last crossing of good and evil. He had that dark intersection before his eyes. This time again, as it had already happened to him in other sorrowful crises, two roads opened before him; the one tempting, the other terrible. Which should he take?

The one which terrified him was advised by the mysterious indicating finger which we all perceive whenever we fix our eyes upon the shadow.

Jean Valjean had, once again, the choice between the terrible haven and the smiling ambush.

It is true, then? the soul may be cured, but not the lot. Fearful thing! an incurable destiny!

The question which presented itself was this:

In what manner should Jean Valjean comport himself in regard to the happiness of Cosette and Marius? This happiness, it was he who had willed it, it was he who had made it; he had thrust it into his own heart, and at this hour, looking upon it, he might have the same satisfaction that an armourer would have, who should recognise his own mark upon a blade, on withdrawing it all reeking from his breast.

Cosette had Marius, Marius possessed Cosette. They had everything, even riches. And it was his work.

But this happiness, now that it existed, now that it was here, what was he to do with it, he, Jean Valjean? Should he impose himself upon this happiness? Should he treat it as belonging to him? Unquestionably, Cosette was another's; but should he, Jean Valjean, retain all of Cosette that he could retain? Should he remain the kind of father, scarcely seen, but respected, which he had been hitherto? Should he introduce himself quietly into Cosette's house? Should he bring, without saying a word, his past to this future? Should he present himself there as having a right, and should he come and take his seat, veiled, at that luminous hearth? Should he take, smiling upon them, the hands of those innocent beings into his two tragical hands? Should he place upon the peaceful andirons of the Gillenormand parlour, his feet which dragged after them the infamous shadow of the law? Should he enter upon a participation of chances with Cosette and Marius? Should he thicken the obscurity upon his head and the cloud upon theirs? Should he put in his catastrophe as a companion for their two felicities? Should he continue to keep silence? In a word, should he be, by the side of these two happy beings, the ominous mute of destiny?

We must be accustomed to fatality and its encounter, to dare to raise our eyes when certain questions appear to us in their horrible nakedness. Good or evil are behind this severe interrogation point. "What are you going to do?" demands the sphynx.

This familiarity with trial Jean Valjean had. He looked fixedly upon the sphynx.

He examined the pitiless problem under all its phases.

Cosette, that charming existence, was the raft of this ship-wreck. What was he to do? Cling on, or let go his hold?

If he clung to it, he escaped disaster, he rose again into the sunshine, he let the bitter water drip from his garments and his hair, he was saved, he lived.

If he loosed his hold?

Then, the abyss.

Thus bitterly he held counsel with his thoughts, or, to speak more truthfully, he struggled; he rushed, furious, within himself, sometimes against his will, sometimes against his conviction.

It was a good thing for Jean Valjean that he had been able to weep. It gave him light, perhaps. For all that, the beginning was wild. A tempest, more furious than that which had formerly driven him towards Arras, broke loose within him. The past came back to him face to face with the present; he compared and he sobbed. The sluice of tears once opened, the despairing man writhed.

He felt that he was stopped.

Alas! in this unrelenting pugilism between our selfishness and our duty, when we thus recoil step by step before our immutable ideal, bewildered, enraged, exasperated at yielding, disputing the ground, hoping for possible flight, seeking some outlet, how abrupt and ominous is the resistance of the wall behind us!

To feel the sacred shadow which bars the way.

The inexorable invisible, what an obsession!

We are never done with conscience. Choose your course by it, Brutus; choose your course by it, Cato. It is bottomless, being God. We cast into this pit the labour of our whole life, we cast in our fortune, we cast in our riches, we cast in our success, we cast in our liberty or our country, we cast in our well-being, we cast in our repose, we cast in our happiness. More! more! more! Empty the vase! turn out the urn! We must at last cast in our heart.

There is somewhere in the mist of the old hells a vessel like that.

Is it not pardonable to refuse at last? Can the inexhaustible have a claim? Are not endless chains above human strength? Who then would blame Sisyphus and Jean Valjean for saying: "it is enough!"

The obedience of matter is limited by friction; is there no limit to the obedience of the soul? If perpetual motion is impossible, is perpetual devotion demandable?

The first step is nothing; it is the last which is difficult. What was the Champmathieu affair compared with Cosette's marriage and all that it involved? What is this: to return to the galleys, compared with this: to enter into nothingness?

Oh, first step of descent, how gloomy thou art! Oh, second step, how black thou art!

How should he not turn away his head this time?

Martyrdom is a sublimation, a corrosive sublimation. It is a torture of consecration. You consent to it the first hour; you sit upon the throne of red-hot iron, you put upon your brow the crown of red-hot iron, you receive the globe of red-hot iron, you take the sceptre of red-hot iron, but you have yet to put on the mantle of flame, and is there no moment when the wretched flesh revolts, and when you abdicate the torture?

At last Jean Valjean entered the calmness of despair.

He weighed, he thought, he considered the alternatives of the mysterious balance of light and shade.

To impose his galleys upon these two dazzling children, or to consummate by himself his irremediable engulfment. On the one side the sacrifice of Cosette, on the other of himself.

At what solution did he stop?

What determination did he take? What was, within himself, his final answer to the incorruptible demand of fatality? What door did he decide to open? Which side of his life did he resolve to close and to condemn? Between all these unfathomable precipices which surrounded him, what was his choice? What extremity did he accept? To which of these gulfs did he bow his head?

His giddy reverie lasted all night.

He remained there until dawn, in the same attitude, doubled over on the bed, prostrated under the enormity of fate, crushed perhaps, alas! his fists clenched, his arms extended at a right angle, like one taken from the cross and thrown down with his face to the ground. He remained twelve hours, the twelve hours of a long winter night, chilled, without lifting his head, and without uttering a word. He was as motionless as a corpse, while his thought writhed upon the ground and flew away, now like the hydra, now like the eagle. To see him thus without motion, one would have said he was dead; suddenly he thrilled convulsively, and his mouth, fixed upon Cosette's garments, kissed them; then one saw that he was alive.

What one? since Jean Valjean was alone, and there was nobody there?

The One who is in the darkness.

BOOK SEVENTH –
THE LAST DROP IN THE CHALICE

I
THE SEVENTH CIRCLE AND THE EIGHTH HEAVEN

THE day after a wedding is solitary. The privacy of the happy is respected. And thus their slumber is a little belated. The tumult of visits and felicitations does not commence until later. On the morning of the 17th of February, it was a little after noon, when Basque, his napkin and duster under his arm, busy "doing his antechamber," heard a light rap at the door. There was no ring, which is considerate on such a day. Basque opened and saw M. Fauchelevent. He introduced him into the parlour, still cumbered and topsy-turvy, and which had the appearance of the battle-field of the evening's festivities.

"Faith, monsieur," observed Basque, "we are waking up late."

"Has your master risen?" inquired Jean Valjean.

"How is monsieur's arm?" answered Basque.

"Better. Has your master risen?"

"Which? the old or the new one?"

"Monsieur Pontmercy."

"Monsieur the Baron?" said Basque, drawing himself up.

One is baron to his domestics above all. Something of it is reflected upon them; they have what a philosopher would call the spattering of the title, and it flatters them. Marius, to speak of it in passing, a republican militant, and he had proved it, was now a baron in spite of himself. A slight revolution had taken place in the family in regard to this title. At present it was M. Gillenormand who clung to it and Marius who made light of it. But Colonel Pontmercy had written: *My son will bear my title.* Marius obeyed. And then Cosette, in whom the woman was beginning to dawn, was in raptures at being a baroness.

"Monsieur the Baron?" repeated Basque. "I will go and see. I will tell him that Monsieur Fauchelevent is here."

"No. Do not tell him that it is I. Tell him that somebody asks to speak with him in private, and do not give him any name."

"Ah!" said Basque.

"I wish to give him a surprise."

"Ah!" resumed Basque, giving himself his second ah! as an explanation of the first.

And he went out.

Jean Valjean remained alone.

The parlour, as we have just said, was all in disorder. It seemed that by lending the ear the vague rumour of the wedding might still have been heard. There were all sorts of flowers, which had fallen from garlands and head-dresses, upon the floor. The candles, burned to the socket, added stalactites of wax to the pendants of the lustres. Not a piece of furniture was in its place. In the corners, three or four arm-chairs drawn up and forming a circle, had the appearance of continuing a conversation. Altogether it was joyous. There is still a certain grace in a dead festival. It has been happy. Upon those chairs in disarray, among those flowers which are withering, under those extinguished lights, there have been thoughts of joy. The sun succeeded to the chandelier, and entered cheerfully into the parlour.

A few minutes elapsed. Jean Valjean was motionless in the spot where Basque had left him. He was very pale. His eyes were hollow, and so sunken in their sockets from want of sleep that they could hardly be seen. His black coat had the weary folds of a garment which has passed the night. The elbows were whitened with that down which is left upon cloth by the chafing of linen. Jean Valjean was looking at the window marked out by the sun upon the floor at his feet.

There was a noise at the door, he raised his eyes.

Marius entered, his head erect, his mouth smiling, an indescribable light upon his face, his forehead radiant, his eye triumphant. He also had not slept.

"It is you, father!" exclaimed he on perceiving Jean Valjean, "that idiot of a Basque with his mysterious air! But you come too early. It is only half an hour after noon yet. Cosette is asleep."

That word: Father, said to M. Fauchelevent by Marius, signified: Supreme felicity. There had always been, as we know, barrier, coldness, and constraint between them; ice to break or to melt. Marius had reached that degree of intoxication where the barrier was falling, the ice was dissolving, and M. Fauchelevent was to him, as to Cosette, a father.

He continued; words overflowed from him, which is characteristic of these divine paroxysms of joy:

"How glad I am to see you! If you knew how we missed you

yesterday! Good morning, father. How is your hand? Better, is it not?"

And, satisfied with the good answer which he made to himself, he went on:

"We have both of us talked much about you. Cosette loves you so much! You will not forget that your room is here. We will have no more of the Rue de l'Homme Armé. We will have no more of it at all. How could you go to live in a street like that, which is sickly, which is scowling, which is ugly, which has a barrier at one end, where you are cold, and where you cannot get in? you will come and install yourself here. And that to-day. Or you will have a bone to pick with Cosette. She intends to lead us all by the nose, I warn you. You have seen your room, it is close by ours, it looks upon the gardens; the lock has been fixed, the bed is made, it is all ready; you have nothing to do but to come. Cosette has put a great old easy chair of Utrecht velvet beside your bed, to which she said: stretch out your arms for him. Every spring, in the clump of acacias which is in front of your windows, there comes a nightingale, you will have her in two months. You will have her nest at your left and ours at your right. By night she will sing, and by day Cosette will talk. Your room is full in the south. Cosette will arrange your books there for you, your voyage of Captain Cook, and the other, Vancouver's, all your things. There is, I believe, a little valise which you treasure, I have selected a place of honour for it. You have conquered my grandfather, you suit him. We will live together. Do you know whist? you will overjoy my grandfather, if you know whist. You will take Cosette to walk on my court-days, you will give her your arm, you know, as at the Luxembourg, formerly. We have absolutely decided to be very happy. And you are part of our happiness, do you understand, father? Come now, you breakfast with us to-day?"

"Monsieur," said Jean Valjean, "I have one thing to tell you. I am an old convict."

The limit of perceptible acute sounds may be passed quite as easily for the mind as for the ear. Those words: *I am an old convict*, coming from M. Fauchelevent's mouth and entering Marius' ear, went beyond the possible. Marius did not hear. It seemed to him that something had just been said to him; but he knew not what. He stood aghast.

He then perceived that the man who was talking to him was

terrible. Excited as he was, he had not until this moment noticed that frightful pallor.

Jean Valjean untied the black cravat which sustained his right arm, took off the cloth wound about his head, laid his thumb bare, and showed it to Marius.

"There is nothing the matter with my hand," said he.

Marius looked at the thumb.

"There has never been anything the matter with it," continued Jean Valjean.

There was, in fact, no trace of a wound.

Jean Valjean pursued:

"It was best that I should be absent from your marriage. I absented myself as much as I could. I feigned this wound so as not to commit a forgery, not to introduce a nullity into the marriage acts, to be excused from signing."

Marius stammered out:

"What does this mean?"

"It means," answered Jean Valjean, "that I have been in the galleys."

"You drive me mad!" exclaimed Marius in dismay.

"Monsieur Pontmercy," said Jean Valjean, "I was nineteen years in the galleys. For robbery. Then I was sentenced for life. For robbery. For a second offence. At this hour I am in breach of ban."

It was useless for Marius to recoil before the reality, to refuse the fact, to resist the evidence; he was compelled to yield. He began to comprehend, and as always happens in such a case, he comprehended beyond the truth. He felt the shiver of a horrible interior flash; an idea which made him shudder, crossed his mind. He caught a glimpse in the future of a hideous destiny for himself.

"Tell all, tell all!" cried he. "You are Cosette's father!"

And he took two steps backwards with an expression of unspeakable horror.

Jean Valjean raised his head with such a majesty of attitude that he seemed to rise to the ceiling.

"It is necessary that you believe me in this, monsieur; although the oath of such as I be not received."

Here he made a pause; then, with a sort of sovereign and sepulchral authority, he added, articulating slowly and emphasising his syllables:

"——You will believe me. I, the father of Cosette! before God, no. Monsieur Baron Pontmercy, I am a peasant of Faverolles. I earned my living by pruning trees. My name is not Fauchelevent, my name is Jean Valjean. I am nothing to Cosette. Compose yourself."

Marius faltered:

"Who proves it to me——"

"I. Since I say so."

Marius looked at this man. He was mournful, yet self-possessed. No lie could come out of such a calmness. That which is frozen is sincere. We feel the truth in that sepulchral coldness.

"I believe you," said Marius.

Jean Valjean inclined his head as if making oath, and continued:

"What am I to Cosette? a passer. Ten years ago, I did not know that she existed. I love her, it is true. A child whom one has seen when little, being himself already old, he loves. When a man is old, he feels like a grandfather towards all little children. You can, it seems to me, suppose that I have something which resembles a heart. She was an orphan. Without father or mother. She had need of me. That is why I began to love her. Children are so weak, that anybody, even a man like me, may be their protector. I performed that duty with regard to Cosette. I do not think that one could truly call so little a thing a good deed; but if it is a good deed; well, set it down that I have done it. Record that mitigating circumstance. Today Cosette leaves my life; our two roads separate. Henceforth I can do nothing more for her. She is Madame Pontmercy. Her protector is changed. And Cosette gains by the change. All is well. As for the six hundred thousand francs, you have not spoken of them to me, but I anticipate your thought; that is a trust. How did this trust come into my hands? What matters it? I make over the trust. Nothing more can be asked of me. I complete the restitution by telling my real name. This again concerns me. I desire, myself, that you should know who I am."

And Jean Valjean looked Marius in the face.

All that Marius felt was tumultuous and incoherent. Certain blasts of destiny make such waves in our soul.

We have all had such moments of trouble, in which everything within us is dispersed; we say the first things that come to mind, which are not always precisely those that we should say. There are sudden revelations which we cannot bear, and which intoxicate like a noxious wine. Marius was so stupefied at the new condition of affairs which opened before him that he spoke to this man almost as though he were angry with him for his avowal.

"But after all," exclaimed he, "why do you tell me all this? What compels you to do so? You could have kept the secret to yourself. You are neither denounced, nor pursued, nor hunted. You have some reason for making, from mere wantonness, such a revelation. Finish it. There is something else. In connection with what do you make this avowal? From what motive?"

"From what motive?" answered Jean Valjean, in a voice so low and so hollow that one would have said it was to himself he was speaking rather than to Marius. "From what motive, indeed, does this convict come and say: I am a convict? Well, yes! the motive is strange. It is from honour. Yes, my misfortune is a cord which I have here in my heart and which holds me fast. When one is old these cords are strong. The whole life wastes away about them; they hold fast. If I had been able to tear out this cord, to break it, to untie the knot, or to cut it, to go far away, I had been saved, I had only to depart; there are diligences in the Rue du Bouloy; you are happy, I go away. I have tried to break this cord, I have pulled upon it, it held firmly, it did not snap, I was tearing my heart out with it. Then I said I cannot live away from here. I must stay. Well, yes; but you are right, I am a fool, why not just simply stay? You offer me a room in the house, Madame Pontmercy loves me well, she says to that armchair: Stretch out your arms for him, your grandfather asks nothing better than to have me, I suit him, we shall all live together, eat in common, I will give my arm to Cosette—to Madame Pontmercy, pardon me, it is from habit—we will have but one roof, but one table, but one fire, the same chimney-corner in winter, the same promenade in summer, that is joy, that is happiness, that, it is everything. We will live as one family, one family!"

At this word Jean Valjean grew wild. He folded his arms, gazed at the floor at his feet as if he wished to hollow out an abyss in it, and his voice suddenly became piercing.

"One family! no. I am of no family. I am not of yours. I am not of the family of men. In houses where people are at home I am an incumbrance. There are families, but they are not for me. I am the unfortunate; I am outside. Had I a father and a mother? I almost doubt it. The day that I married that child it was all over, I saw that she was happy, and that she was with the man whom she loved, and that there was a good old man here, a household of two angels, all joys in this house, and that it was well, I said to myself: Enter thou not. I could have lied, it is true, have deceived you all, have remained Monsieur Fauchelevent. As long as it was for her, I could lie; but now it would be for myself, I must not do it. It was enough to remain silent, it is true, and everything would continue. You ask me what forces me to speak? a strange thing; my conscience. To remain silent was, however, very easy. I have passed the night in trying to persuade myself to do so; you are confessing me, and what I come to tell you is so strange that you have a right to do so; well, yes, I have passed the night in giving myself reasons, I have given myself very good reasons, I have done what I could, it was of no use. But there are two things in which I did not succeed; neither in breaking the cord which holds me by the heart fixed, riveted, and sealed here, nor in silencing some one who speaks low to me when I am alone. That is why I have come to confess all to you this morning. All, or almost all. It is useless to tell what concerns only myself, I keep it for myself. The essential you know. So I have taken my mystery, and brought it to you. And I have ripped open my secret under your eyes. It was not an easy resolution to form. All night I have struggled with myself. Ah! you think I have not said to myself that this is not the Champmathieu affair, that in concealing my name I do no harm to anybody, that the name of Fauchelevent was given to me by Fauchelevent himself in gratitude for a service rendered, and I could very well keep it, and that I should be happy in this room which you offer me, that I should interfere with nothing, that I should be in my little corner, and that, while you would have Cosette, I should have the idea of being in the same house with her. Each one would have had his due share of happiness. To continue to be Monsieur Fauchelevent, smoothed the way for everything. Yes, except for my soul. There was joy every-where about me, the depths of my soul were still black. It is not enough to be happy, we must be satisfied with ourselves. Thus I should have remained Monsieur Fauchelevent, thus I should have concealed my real face, thus, in presence of your cheerfulness, I should have borne an enigma, thus, in the midst of your broad day, I should have been darkness, thus, without openly crying beware, I should have introduced the galleys at your hearth, I should have sat down at your table with the thought that, if you knew who I was, you would drive me away, I should have let myself be served by domestics who, if they had known, would have said: How horrible! I should have touched you with my elbow which you have a right to shrink from, I should have filched the grasp of your hand! There would have been in your house a division of respect between venerable white hairs and dishonoured white hairs; at your most intimate hours, when all hearts would have thought themselves open to each other to the bottom, when we should have been all four together, your grandfather, you two, and myself, there would have been a stranger there! I should have been side by side with you in your existence, having but one care, never to displace the covering of my terrible pit. Thus I, a dead man, should have imposed myself upon you, who are alive. Her I should have condemned to myself for ever. You, Cosette, and I, we should have been three heads in the green cap! Do you not shudder? I am only the most depressed of men, I should have been the most monstrous. And this crime I should have committed every day! And this lie I should have acted every day! And this face of night I should have worn every day! And of my disgrace, I should have given to you your part every day! every day! to You, my loved ones, you, my children, you, my innocents! To be quiet is nothing? to keep silence is simple? No, it is not simple. There is a silence which lies. And my lie, and my fraud, and my unworthiness, and my cowardice, and my treachery, and my crime, I should have drunk drop by drop, I should have spit it out, then drunk again, I should have finished at midnight and recommenced at noon, and my good-morning would have lied, and my good-night would have lied, and I should have slept upon it, and I should have eaten it with my bread, and I should have looked Cosette in the face, and I should have answered the smile of the angel with the smile of the damned, and I should have been a detestable impostor! What for? to be happy. To be happy, I! Have I the right to be happy? I am outside of life, monsieur."

Jean Valjean stopped. Marius listened. Such a chain of ideas and of pangs cannot be interrupted. Jean Valjean lowered his voice anew, but it was no longer a hollow voice, it was an ominous voice.

"You ask why I speak? I am neither informed against, nor pursued, nor hunted, say you. Yes! I am informed against! yes! I am pursued! yes! I am hunted? By whom? by myself. It is I myself who bar the way before myself, and I drag myself, and I urge myself, and I check myself, and I exert myself, and when one holds himself he is well held."

And seizing his own coat in his clenched hand and drawing it towards Marius:

"Look at this hand, now," continued he. "Don't you think that it holds this collar in such a way as not to let go? Well! conscience has quite another grasp! If we wish to be happy, monsieur, we must never comprehend duty; for, as soon as we comprehend it, it is implacable. One would say that it punishes you for comprehending it; but no, it rewards you for it; for it puts you into a hell where you feel God at your side. Your heart is not so soon lacerated when you are at peace with yourself."

And, with a bitter emphasis, he added:

"Monsieur Pontmercy, this is not common sense, but I am an honest man. It is by degrading myself in your eyes that I elevate myself in my own. This has already happened to me once, but it was less grievous then; it was nothing. Yes, an honest man. I should not be one if you had, by my fault, continued to esteem me; now that you despise me, I am one. I have this fatality upon me that, being forever unable to have any but stolen consideration, that consideration humiliates me and depresses me inwardly, and in order that I may respect myself, I must be despised. Then I hold myself erect. I am a galley slave who obeys his conscience. I know well that is improbable. But what would you have me do? it is so. I have assumed engagements towards myself; I keep them. There are accidents which bind us, there are chances which drag us into duties. You see, Monsieur Pontmercy, some things have happened to me in my life?"

Jean Valjean paused again, swallowing his saliva with effort, as if his words had a bitter after-taste, and resumed:

"When one has such a horror over him, he has no right to make others share it without their knowledge, he has no right to communicate his pestilence to them, he has no right to make them slip down his precipice without warning of it, he has no right to let his red cap be drawn upon them, he has no right craftily to encumber the happiness of others with his own misery. To approach those who are well, and to touch them in the shadow with his invisible ulcer, that is horrible. Fauchelevent lent me his name in vain. I had no right to make use of it; he could give it to me, I could not take it. A name is a Me. You see, monsieur, I have thought a little, I have read a little, although I am a peasant; and you see that I express myself tolerably. I form my own idea of things. I have given myself an education of my own. Well, yes, to purloin a name, and to put yourself under it, is dishonest. The letters of the alphabet may be stolen as well as a purse or a watch. To be a false signature in flesh and blood, to be a living false key, to enter the houses of honest people by picking their locks, never to look again, always to squint, to be infamous within myself, no! no! no! no! It is better to suffer, to bleed, to weep, to tear the skin from the flesh with the nails, to pass the nights in writhing, in anguish, to gnaw away body and soul. That is why I come to tell you all this. In mere wantonness, as you say."

He breathed with difficulty, and forced out these final words:

"To live, once I stole a loaf of bread; to-day, to live, I will not steal a name."

"To live!" interrupted Marius. "You have no need of that name to live!"

"Ah! I understand," answered Jean Valjean, raising and lowering his head several times in succession.

There was a pause. Both were silent, each sunk in an abyss of thought. Marius had seated himself beside a table, and was resting the corner of his mouth on one of his bent fingers. Jean Valjean was walking back and forth. He stopped before a glass and stood motionless. Then, as if answering some inward reasoning, he said, looking at that glass in which he did not see himself:

"While at present, I am relieved!"

He resumed his walk and went to the other end of the parlour. Just as he began to turn, he perceived that Marius was noticing his walk. He said to him with an inexpressible accent:

"I drag one leg a little. You understand why now."

Then he turned quite round towards Marius:

"And now, monsieur, picture this to yourself: I have said nothing, I have remained Monsieur Fauchelevent, I have taken my place in your house, I am one of you, I am in my room, I come to breakfast in the morning in slippers, at night we all three go to the theatre, I accompany Madame Pontmercy to the Tuileries and to the Place Royale, we are together, you suppose me your equal; some fine day I am there, you are there, we are chatting, we are laughing, suddenly you hear a voice shout this name: Jean Valjean! and you see that appalling hand, the police, spring out of the shadow and abruptly tear off my mask!"

He ceased again; Marius had risen with a shudder. Jean Valjean resumed:

"What say you?"

Marius' silence answered.

Jean Valjean continued:

"You see very well that I am right in not keeping quiet. Go on, be happy, be in heaven, be an angel of an angel, be in the sunshine, and be contented with it, and do not trouble yourself about the way which a poor condemned man takes to open his heart and do his duty; you have a wretched man before you, monsieur."

Marius crossed the parlour slowly, and, when he was near Jean Valjean, extended him his hand.

But Marius had to take that hand which did not offer itself, Jean Valjean was passive, and it seemed to Marius that he was grasping a hand of marble.

"My grandfather has friends," said Marius. "I will procure your pardon."

"It is useless," answered Jean Valjean. "They think me dead, that is enough. The dead are not subjected to surveillance. They are supposed to moulder tranquilly. Death is the same thing as pardon."

And, disengaging his hand, which Marius held, he added with a sort of inexorable dignity:

"Besides, to do my duty, that is the friend to which I have recourse; and I need pardon of but one, that is my conscience."

Just then, at the other end of the parlour, the door was softly opened a little way, and Cosette's head made its appearance. They saw only her sweet face, her hair was in charming disorder, her eyelids were still swollen with sleep. She made the movement of a bird passing its head out of its nest, looked first at her husband, then at Jean Valjean, and called to them with a laugh, you would have thought you saw a smile at the bottom of a rose:

"I'll wager that you're talking politics. How stupid that is, instead of being with me!"

Jean Valjean shuddered.

"Cosette," faltered Marius—and he stopped. One would have said that they were two culprits.

Cosette, radiant, continued to look at them both. The frolic of paradise was in her eyes.

"I catch you in the very act," said Cosette. "I just heard my father Fauchelevent say, through the door: 'Conscience—Do his duty.'—It is politics, that is. I will not have it. You ought not to talk politics the very next day. It is not right."

"You are mistaken, Cosette," answered Marius. "We were talking business. We are talking of the best investment for your six hundred thousand francs——"

"It is not all that," interrupted Cosette. "I am coming. Do you want me here?"

And, passing resolutely through the door, she came into the parlour. She was dressed in a full white morning gown, with a thousand folds and with wide sleeves which, starting from the neck, fell to her feet. There are in the golden skies of old Gothic pictures such charming robes for angels to wear.

She viewed herself from head to foot in a large glass, then exclaimed with an explosion of ineffable ecstasy:

"Once there was a king and a queen. Oh! how happy I am!"

So saying, she made a reverence to Marius and to Jean Valjean.

"There," said she, "I am going to install myself by you in an arm-chair; we breakfast in half an hour, you shall say all you wish to; I know very well that men must talk, I shall be very good."

Marius took her arm, and said to her lovingly:

"We are talking business."

"By the way," answered Cosette, "I have opened my window, a flock of *pierrots* [sparrows or masks] have just arrived in the garden. Birds, not masks. It is Ash Wednesday to-day; but not for the birds."

"I tell you that we are talking business; go, my darling Cosette, leave us a moment. We are talking figures. It will tire you."

"You have put on a charming cravat this morning, Marius. You are very coquettish, monsieur. It will not tire me."

"I assure you that it will tire you."

"No. Because it is you. I shall not understand you, but I will listen to you. When we hear voices that we love, we need not understand the words they say. To be here together is all that I want. I shall stay with you; pshaw!"

"You are my darling Cosette! Impossible."

"Impossible!"

"Yes."

"Very well," replied Cosette. "I would have told you the news. I would have told you that grandfather is still asleep, that your aunt is at mass, that the chimney in my father Fauche-levent's room smokes, that Nicolette has sent for the sweep, that Toussaint and Nicolette have had a quarrel already, that Nicolette makes fun of Toussaint's stuttering. Well, you shall know nothing. Ah! it is impossible! I too, in my turn, you shall see, monsieur, I will say: it is impossible. Then who will be caught? I pray you, my darling Marius, let me stay here with you two."

"I swear to you that we must be alone."

"Well, am I anybody?"

Jean Valjean did not utter a word. Cosette turned towards him. "In the first place, father, I want you to come and kiss me. What are you doing there, saying nothing, instead of taking my part? who gave me such a father as that? You see plainly that I am very unfortunate in my domestic affairs. My husband beats me. Come, kiss me this instant."

Jean Valjean approached.

Cosette turned towards Marius.

"You, sir, I make faces at you."

Then she offered her forehead to Jean Valjean.

Jean Valjean took a step towards her.

Cosette drew back.

"Father, you are pale. Does your arm hurt you?"

"It is well," said Jean Valjean.

"Have you slept badly?"

"No."

"Are you sad?"

"No."

"Kiss me. If you are well, if you sleep well, if you are happy, I will not scold you."

And again she offered him her forehead.

Jean Valjean kissed that forehead, upon which there was a celestial reflection.

"Smile."

Jean Valjean obeyed. It was the smile of a spectre.

"Now defend me against my husband."

"Cosette!—" said Marius.

"Get angry, father. Tell him that I must stay. You can surely talk before me. So you think me very silly. It is very astonishing then what you are saying! business, putting money in a bank, that is a great affair. Men play the mysterious for nothing. I want to stay. I am very pretty this morning. Look at me, Marius."

And with an adorable shrug of the shoulders and an inexpressibly exquisite pout, she looked at Marius. It was like a flash between these two beings. That somebody was there mattered little.

"I love you!" said Marius.

"I adore you!" said Cosette.

And they fell irresistibly into each other's arms.

"Now," resumed Cosette, readjusting a fold of her gown with a little triumphant pout, "I shall stay."

"What, no," answered Marius, in a tone of entreaty, "we have something to finish."

"No, still?"

Marius assumed a grave tone of voice:

"I assure you, Cosette, that it is impossible."

"Ah! you put on your man's voice, monsieur. Very well, I'll go. You, father, you have not sustained me. Monsieur my husband, monsieur my papa, you are tyrants. I am going to tell grandfather of you. If you think that I shall come back and talk nonsense to you, you are mistaken. I am proud. I wait for you now, you will see that it is you who will get tired without me. I am going away, very well."

And she went out.

Two seconds later, the door opened again, her fresh rosy face passed once more between the two folding-doors, and she cried to them:

"I am very angry."

The door closed again and the darkness returned.

It was like a stray sunbeam which, without suspecting it, should have suddenly traversed the night.

Marius made sure that the door was well closed.

"Poor Cosette!" murmured he, "when she knows——"

At these words, Jean Valjean trembled in every limb. He fixed upon Marius a bewildered eye.

"Cosette! Oh, yes, it is true, you will tell this to Cosette. That is right. Stop, I had not thought of that. People have the strength for some things, but not for others. Monsieur, I beseech you, I entreat you, monsieur, give me your most sacred word, do not tell her. Is it not enough that you know it yourself? I could have told it of myself without being forced to it, I would have told it to the universe, to all the world, that would be nothing to me. But she, she doesn't know what it is, it would appall her. A convict, why! you would have to explain it to her, to tell her: It is a man who has been in the galleys. She saw the chain pass by one day. Oh, my God!"

He sank into an arm-chair and hid his face in both hands. He could not be heard, but by the shaking of his shoulders it could be seen that he was weeping. Silent tears, terrible tears.

There is a stifling in the sob. A sort of convulsion seized him, he bent over upon the back of the arm-chair as if to breathe, letting his arms hang down and allowing Marius to see his face bathed in tears, and Marius heard him murmur so low that his voice seemed to come from a bottomless depth: "Oh! would that I could die!"

"Be calm," said Marius, "I will keep your secret for myself alone."

And, less softened perhaps than he should have been, but obliged for an hour past to familiarise himself with a fearful surprise, seeing by degrees a convict superimposed before his eyes upon M. Fauchelevent, possessed little by little of this dismal reality, and led by the natural tendency of the position to determine the distance which had just been put between this man and himself, Marius added:

"It is impossible that I should not say a word to you of the trust which you have so faithfully and so honestly restored. That is an act of probity. It is just that a recompense should be given you. Fix the sum yourself, it shall be counted out to you. Do not be afraid to fix it very high."

"I thank you, monsieur," answered Jean Valjean gently.

He remained thoughtful a moment, passing the end of his forefinger over his thumb nail mechanically, then he raised his voice:

"It is all nearly finished. There is one thing left———"

"What?"

Jean Valjean had as it were a supreme hesitation, and, voiceless, almost breathless, he faltered out rather than said:

"Now that you know, do you think, monsieur, you who are the master, that I ought not to see Cosette again?"

"I think that would be best," answered Marius coldly.

"I shall not see her again," murmured Jean Valjean.

And he walked towards the door.

He placed his hand upon the knob, the latch yielded, the door started, Jean Valjean opened it wide enough to enable him to pass out, stopped a second motionless, then shut the door, and turned towards Marius.

He was no longer pale, he was livid. There were no longer tears in his eyes, but a sort of tragical flame. His voice had again become strangely calm.

"But, monsieur," said he, "if you are willing, I will come and see her. I assure you that I desire it very much. If I had not clung to seeing Cosette, I should not have made the avowal which I have made, I should have gone away; but wishing to stay in the place where Cosette is and to continue to see her, I was compelled in honour to tell you all. You follow my reasoning, do you not? that is a thing which explains itself. You see, for nine years past, I have had her near me. We lived first in that ruin on the boulevard, then in the convent, then near the Luxembourg. It was there that you saw her for the first time. You remember her blue plush hat. We were afterwards in the quartier of the Invalides where there was a grating and a garden. Rue Plumet. I lived in a little back-yard where I heard her piano. That was my life. We never left each other. That lasted nine years and some months. I was like her father, and she was my child. I don't know whether you understand me, Monsieur Pontmercy, but from the present time, to see her no more, to speak to her no more, to have nothing more, that would be hard. If you do not think it wrong, I will come from time to time to see Cosette. I should not come often. I would not stay long. You might say I should be received in the little low room. On the ground floor. I would willingly come in by the back door, which is for the servants, but that would excite wonder, perhaps. It is better, I suppose, that I should enter by the usual door. Monsieur, indeed, I would really like to see Cosette a little still. As rarely as you please. Put yourself in my place, it is all that I have. And then, we must take care. If I should not come at all, it would have a bad effect, it would be thought singular. For instance, what I can do, is to come in the evening, at nightfall."

"You will come every evening," said Marius, "and Cosette will expect you."

"You are kind, monsieur," said Jean Valjean.

Marius bowed to Jean Valjean, happiness conducted despair to the door, and these two men separated.

II

THE OBSCURITIES WHICH A REVELATION
MAY CONTAIN

MARIUS was completely unhinged.

The kind of repulsion which he had always felt for the man with whom he saw Cosette was now explained. There was something strangely enigmatic in this person, of which his instinct had warned him. This enigma was the most hideous of disgraces, the galleys. This M. Fauchelevent was the convict Jean Valjean.

To suddenly find such a secret in the midst of one's happiness is like the discovery of a scorpion in a nest of turtle-doves.

Was the happiness of Marius and Cosette condemned henceforth to this fellowship? Was that a foregone conclusion? Did the acceptance of this man form a part of the marriage which had been consummated? Was there nothing more to be done?

Had Marius espoused the convict also?

It is of no avail to be crowned with light and with joy; it is of no avail to be revelling in the royal purple hour of life, happy love; such shocks would compel even the archangel in his ecstasy, even the demi-god in his glory, to shudder.

As always happens in changes of view of this kind, Marius questioned himself whether he had not some fault to find with himself? Had he been wanting in perception? Had he been wanting in prudence? Had he been involuntarily stupefied? A little, perhaps. Had he entered, without enough precaution in clearing up its surroundings, upon this love adventure which had ended in his marriage with Cosette? He determined—it is thus, by a succession of determinations by ourselves in regard to

ourselves, that life improves us little by little—he determined
the chimerical and visionary side of his nature, a sort of interior
cloud peculiar to many organisations, and which, in paroxysms
of passion and grief, dilates, the temperature of the soul changing, and pervades the entire man, to such an extent as to make
him nothing more than a consciousness steeped in a fog. We
have more than once indicated this characteristic element of
Marius' individuality. He recollected that, in the infatuation of
his love, in the Rue Plumet, during those six or seven ecstatic
weeks, he had not even spoken to Cosette of that drama of the
Gorbeau den in which the victim had taken the very strange
course of silence during the struggle, and of escape after it. How
had he managed not to speak of it to Cosette? Yet it was so near
and so frightful. How had he managed not even to name the
Thénardiers to her, and, particularly, the day that he met Eponine? He had great difficulty now in explaining to himself his
former silence. He did account for it, however. He recalled his
stupor, his intoxication for Cosette, love absorbing everything,
that uplifting of one by the other into the ideal, and perhaps
also, as the imperceptible quantity of reason mingled with this
violent and charming state of the soul, a vague and dull instinct
to hide and to abolish in his memory that terrible affair with
which he dreaded contact, in which he wished to play no part,
which he shunned, and in regard to which he could be neither
narrator nor witness without being accuser. Besides, those few
weeks had been but a flash; they had had time for nothing,
except to love. Finally, everything being weighed, turned over,
and examined, if he had told the story of the Gorbeau ambuscade to Cosette, if he had named the Thénardiers to her, what
would have been the consequences, if he had even discovered
Jean Valjean was a convict, would that have changed him,
Marius? Would that have changed her, Cosette? Would he have
shrunk back? Would he have adored her less? Would he the less
have married her? No. Would it have changed anything in what
had taken place? No. Nothing then to regret, nothing to
reproach himself with. All was well. There is a God for these
drunkards who are called lovers. Blind, Marius had followed the
route which he would have chosen had he seen clearly. Love
had bandaged his eyes, to lead him where? To Paradise.

But this paradise was henceforth complicated with an
infernal accompaniment.

The former repulsion of Marius towards this man, towards this Fauchelevent become Jean Valjean, was now mingled with horror.

In this horror, we must say, there was some pity, and also a certain astonishment.

This robber, this twice-convicted robber, had restored a trust. And what a trust? Six hundred thousand francs. He was alone in the secret of the trust. He might have kept all, he had given up all.

Moreover, he had revealed his condition of his own accord. Nothing obliged him to do so. If it were known who he was, it was through himself. There was more in that avowal than the acceptance of humiliation, there was the acceptance of peril. To a condemned man a mask is not a mask, but a shelter. He had renounced that shelter. A false name is security; he had thrown away this false name. He could, he, a galley slave, have hidden himself for ever in an honourable family; he had resisted this temptation. And from what motive? from conscientious scruples. He had explained it himself with the irresistible accent of reality. In short, whatever this Jean Valjean might be, he had incontestably an awakened conscience. There was in him some mysterious regeneration begun; and, according to all appearance, for a long time already the scruple had been master of the man. Such paroxysms of justice and goodness do not belong to vulgar natures. An awakening of conscience is greatness of soul.

Jean Valjean was sincere. This sincerity, visible, palpable, unquestionable, evident even by the grief which it caused him, rendered investigation useless and gave authority to all that this man said. Here, for Marius, a strange inversion of situations. What came from M. Fauchelevent? distrust. What flowed from Jean Valjean? confidence.

In the mysterious account which Marius thoughtfully drew up concerning this Jean Valjean, he verified the credit, he verified the debit, he attempted to arrive at a balance. But it was all as it were in a storm. Marius, endeavouring to get a clear idea of this man, and pursuing, so to speak, Jean Valjean in the depths of his thought, lost him and found him again in a fatal mist.

The trust honestly surrendered, the probity of the avowal, that was good. It was like a break in the cloud, but the cloud again became black.

Confused as Marius' recollections were, some shadow of them returned to him.

What was the exact nature of that affair in the Jondrette garret? Why, on the arrival of the police, did this man, instead of making his complaint, make his escape? Here Marius found the answer. Because this man was a fugitive from justice in breach of ban.

Another question: Why had this man come into the barricade? For now Marius saw that reminiscence again distinctly, reappearing in these emotions like sympathetic ink before the fire. This man was in the barricade. He did not fight there. What did he come there for? Before this question a spectre arose, and made response. Javert. Marius recalled perfectly to mind at this hour the fatal sight of Jean Valjean dragging Javert bound outside the barricade, and he again heard the frightful pistol-shot behind the corner of the little Rue Mondétour. There was, probably, hatred between the spy and this galley slave. The one cramped the other. Jean Valjean had gone to the barricade to avenge himself. He had arrived late. He knew probably that Javert was a prisoner there. The Corsican vendetta has penetrated into certain lower depths and is their law; it is so natural that it does not astonish souls half turned back towards the good; and these hearts are so constituted that a criminal, in the path of repentance, may be scrupulous in regard to robbery and not be so in regard to vengeance. Jean Valjean had killed Javert. At least, that seemed evident.

Finally, a last question: but to this no answer. This question Marius felt like a sting. How did it happen that Jean Valjean's existence had touched Cosette's so long? What was this gloomy game of providence which had placed this child in contact with this man? Are coupling chains then forged on high also and does it please God to pair the angel with the demon? Can then a crime and an innocence be room-mates in the mysterious galleys of misery? In this strait of the condemned, which is called human destiny, can two foreheads pass close to one another, the one child-like the other terrible, the one all bathed in the divine whiteness of the dawn, the other for ever pallid with the glare of an eternal lightning? Who could have determined this inexplicable fellowship? In what manner, through what prodigy, could community of life have been established between this celestial child and this old wretch? Who had been able to bind the lamb to the wolf, and, a thing still more incomprehensible, attach the wolf to the lamb? For the wolf loved the lamb, for the savage being adored the frail being, for, during nine years, the angel had had the monster for a support. Cosette's childhood and youth, her coming to the day, her maidenly growth towards life and light, had been protected by this monstrous devotion. Here, the questions exfoliated, so to speak, into innumerable enigmas, abyss opened at the bottom of abysm, and Marius could no longer bend over Jean Valjean without dizziness. What then was this man precipice?

The old Genesiac symbols are eternal; in human society, such as it is and will be, until the day when a greater light shall change it, there are always two men, one superior, the other subterranean; he who follows good is Abel; he who follows evil is Cain. What was this remorseful Cain? What was this bandit religiously absorbed in the adoration of a virgin, watching over her, bringing her up, guarding her, dignifying her, and enveloping her, himself impure, with purity? What was this cloaca which had venerated this innocence to such an extent as to leave it immaculate? What was this Jean Valjean watching over the education of Cosette? What was this figure of darkness, whose only care was to preserve from all shadow and from all cloud the rising of a star?

In this was the secret of Jean Valjean; in this was also the secret of God.

Before this double secret, Marius recoiled. The one in some sort reassured him in regard to the other. God was as visible in this as Jean Valjean. God has his instruments. He uses what tool He pleases. He is not responsible to man. Do we know the ways of God? Jean Valjean had laboured upon Cosette. He had, to some extent, formed that soul. That was incontestable. Well, what then? The workman was horrible; but the work admirable. God performs His miracles as seems good to Himself. He had constructed this enchanting Cosette, and he had employed Jean Valjean on the work. It had pleased Him to choose this strange co-worker. What reckoning have we to ask of Him? Is it the first time that the dunghill has aided the spring to make the rose?

Marius made these answers to himself, and declared that they were good. On all the points which we have just indicated, he had not dared to press Jean Valjean, without avowing to himself that he dared not. He adored Cosette, he possessed Cosette. Cosette was resplendently pure. That was enough for him. What explanation did he need? Cosette was a light. Does light need to be explained? He had all; what could he desire? All, is not that enough? The personal affairs of Jean Valjean did not concern him. In bending over the fatal shade of this man, he clung to this solemn declaration of the miserable being: "*I am nothing to Cosette. Ten years ago, I did not know of her existence.*"

Jean Valjean was a passer. He had said so, himself. Well, he was passing away. Whatever he might be, his part was finished. Henceforth Marius was to perform the functions of Providence for Cosette. Cosette had come forth to find in the azure her mate, her lover, her husband, her celestial male. In taking flight, Cosette winged and transfigured, left behind her on the ground, empty and hideous, her chrysalis, Jean Valjean.

In whatever circle of ideas Marius turned, he always came back from it to a certain horror of Jean Valjean. A sacred horror, perhaps, for, as we have just indicated, he felt a *quid divinum* in this man. But, whatever he did, and whatever mitigation he sought, he was always obliged to fall back upon this: he was a convict; that is, the creature who, on the social ladder, has no place, being below the lowest round. After the lowest of men, comes the convict. The convict is no longer, so to speak, the fellow of the living. The law has deprived him of all the humanity which it can take from a man. Marius, upon penal questions, although a democrat, still adhered to the inexorable system, and he had, in regard to those whom the law smites, all the ideas of the law. He had not yet, let us say, adopted all the ideas of progress. He had not yet come to distinguish between what is written by man and what is written by God, between law and right. He had not examined and weighed the right which man assumes to dispose of the irrevocable and the irreparable. He had not revolted from the word *vengeance*. He thought it natural that certain infractions of the written law should be followed by eternal penalties, and he accepted social damnation as growing out of civilisation. He was still at that point, infallibly to advance in time, his nature being good, and in reality entirely composed of latent progress.

Through the medium of these ideas, Jean Valjean appeared to him deformed and repulsive. He was the outcast. He was the convict. This word was for him like a sound of the last trumpet;

and after having considered Jean Valjean long his final action was to turn away his head. *Vade retro.*

Marius, we must remember, and even insist upon it, though he had questioned Jean Valjean to such an extent, that Jean Valjean had said to him: *You are confessing me,* had not, however, put to him two or three decisive questions. Not that they had not presented themselves to his mind, but he was afraid of them. The Jondrette garret? The barricade? Javert? Who knows where the revelations would have stopped? Jean Valjean did not seem the man to shrink, and who knows whether Marius, after having urged him on, would not have desired to restrain him? In certain supreme conjunctures, has it not happened to all of us, after having put a question, to stop our ears that we might not hear the response? We have this cowardice especially when we love. It is not prudent to question untoward situations to the last degree, especially when the indissoluble portion of our own life is fatally interwoven with them. From Jean Valjean's despairing explanations, some appalling light might have sprung, and who knows but that hideous brilliancy might have been thrown even upon Cosette? Who knows but a sort of infernal glare would have remained upon the brow of this angel? The spatterings of a flash are still lightning. Fatality has such solidarities, whereby innocence itself is impressed with crime by the gloomy law of colouring reflections. The purest faces may preserve for ever the reverberations of a horrible surrounding. Wrongly or rightly Marius had been afraid. He knew too much already. He sought rather to blind than to enlighten himself. In desperation, he carried off Cosette in his arms, closing his eyes upon Jean Valjean.

This man was of the night, of the living and terrible night. How should he dare to probe it to the bottom? It is appalling to question the shadow. Who knows what answer it will make? The dawn might be blackened by it for ever.

In this frame of mind it was a bitter perplexity to Marius to think that this man should have henceforth any contact whatever with Cosette. These fearful questions, before which he had shrunk, and from which an implacable and definitive decision might have sprung, he now reproached himself almost, for not having put. He thought himself too good, too mild, let us say the word, too weak. This weakness had led him to an imprudent concession. He had allowed himself to be moved. He had done wrong. He should have merely and simply cast off Jean Valjean. Jean Valjean was the Jonah, he should have done it, and relieved his house of this man. He was vexed with himself, he was vexed with the abruptness of that whirl of emotions which had deafened, blinded, and drawn him on. He was displeased with himself.

What should be done now? Jean Valjean's visits were very repugnant to him. Of what use was this man in his house? What should he do? Here he shook off his thoughts; he was unwilling to probe, he was unwilling to go deeper; he was unwilling to fathom himself. He had promised, he had allowed himself to be led into a promise; Jean Valjean had his promise; even to a convict, especially to a convict, a man should keep his word. Still, his first duty was towards Cosette. In short, a repulsion, which predominated over all else, possessed him.

Marius turned all this assemblage of ideas over in his mind confusedly, passing from one to another, and excited by all. Hence a deep commotion. It was not easy for him to hide this commotion from Cosette, but love is a talent, and Marius succeeded.

Besides, he put without apparent object, some questions to Cosette, who, as candid as a dove is white, suspected nothing, he talked with her of her childhood and her youth, and he convinced himself more and more that all a man can be that is good, paternal, and venerable, this convict had been to Cosette. All that Marius had dimly seen and conjectured was real. This darkly mysterious nettle had loved and protected this lily.

BOOK EIGHTH – THE TWILIGHT WANE

I

THE BASEMENT-ROOM

THE next day, at nightfall, Jean Valjean knocked at the M. Gille-normand porte-cochère. Basque received him. Basque happened to be in the courtyard very conveniently, and as if he had had orders. It sometimes happens that one says to a servant: "You will be on the watch for Monsieur So-and-so, when he comes."

Basque, without waiting for Jean Valjean to come up to him, addressed him as follows:

"Monsieur the Baron told me to ask monsieur whether he desires to go upstairs or to remain below?"

"To remain below," answered Jean Valjean.

Basque, who was moreover absolutely respectful, opened the door of the basement-room and said: "I will inform madame."

The room which Jean Valjean entered was an arched and damp basement, used as a cellar when necessary, looking upon the street paved with red tiles, and dimly lighted by a window with an iron grating.

The room was not of those which are harassed by the brush, the duster, and the broom. In it the dust was tranquil. There the persecution of the spiders had not been organised. A fine web, broadly spread out, very black, adorned with dead flies, ornamented one of the window-panes. The room, small and low, was furnished with a pile of empty bottles heaped up in one corner. The wall had been washed with a wash of yellow ochre, which was scaling off in large flakes. At the end was a wooden mantel, painted black, with a narrow shelf. A fire was kindled, which indicated that somebody had anticipated Jean Valjean's answer: *To remain below.*

Two arm-chairs were placed at the corners of the fire-place. Between the chairs was spread, in guise of a carpet, an old bed-side rug, showing more warp than wool.

The room was lighted by the fire in the fire-place and the twilight from the window.

Jean Valjean was fatigued. For some days he had neither eaten nor slept. He let himself fall into one of the arm-chairs.

Basque returned, set a lighted candle upon the mantel, and

retired. Jean Valjean, his head bent down and his chin upon his breast, noticed neither Basque nor the candle.

Suddenly he started up. Cosette was behind him.

He had not seen her come in, but he had felt that she was coming.

He turned. He gazed at her. She was adorably beautiful. But what he looked upon with that deep look, was not her beauty but her soul.

"Ah, well!" exclaimed Cosette, "father, I knew that you were singular, but I should never have thought this. What an idea! Marius tells me that it is you who wish me to receive you here."

"Yes, it is I."

"I expected the answer. Well, I warn you that I am going to make a scene. Let us begin at the beginning. Father, kiss me."

And she offered her cheek.

Jean Valjean remained motionless.

"You do not stir. I see it. You act guilty. But it is all the same, I forgive you. Jesus Christ said: 'Offer the other cheek.' Here it is."

And she offered the other cheek.

Jean Valjean did not move. It seemed as if his feet were nailed to the floor.

"This is getting serious," said Cosette. "What have I done to you? I declare I am confounded. You owe me amends. You will dine with us."

"I have dined."

"That is not true. I will have Monsieur Gillenormand scold you. Grandfathers are made to scold fathers. Come. Go up to the parlour with me. Immediately."

"Impossible."

Cosette here lost ground a little. She ceased to order and passed to questions.

"But why not? and you choose the ugliest room in the house to see me in. It is horrible here."

"You know, madame, I am peculiar, I have my whims."

Cosette clapped her little hands together.

"Madame! Still again! What does this mean?"

Jean Valjean fixed upon her that distressing smile to which he sometimes had recourse:

"You have wished to be madame. You are so."

"Not to you, father."

"Don't call me father any more."

"What?"

"Call me Monsieur Jean. Jean, if you will."

"You are no longer father? I am no longer Cosette? Monsieur Jean? What does this mean? but these are revolutions, these are! what then has happened? look me in the face now. And you will not live with us! And you will not have my room! What have I done to you? what have I done to you? Is there anything the matter?"

"Nothing."

"Well then?"

"All is as usual."

"Why do you change your name?"

"You have certainly changed yours."

He smiled again with that same smile and added:

"Since you are Madame Pontmercy I can surely be Monsieur Jean."

"I don't understand anything about it. It is all nonsense; I shall ask my husband's permission for you to be Monsieur Jean. I hope that he will not consent to it. You make me a great deal of trouble. You may have whims, but you must not grieve your darling Cosette. It is wrong. You have no right to be naughty, you are too good."

He made no answer.

She seized both his hands hastily and, with an irresistible impulse, raising them towards her face, she pressed them against her neck under her chin, which is a deep token of affection.

"Oh!" said she to him, "be good!"

And she continued:

"This is what I call being good: being nice, coming to stay here, there are birds here as well as in the Rue Plumet, living with us, leaving that hole in the Rue de l'Homme Armé, not giving us riddles to guess, being like other people, dining with us, breakfasting with us, being my father."

He disengaged his hands.

"You have no more need of a father, you have a husband."

Cosette could not contain herself.

"I no more need of a father! To things like that which have no common sense, one really doesn't know what to say!"

"If Toussaint was here," replied Jean Valjean, like one who is in search of authorities and who catches at every straw, "she would be the first to acknowledge that it is true that I always had my peculiar ways. There is nothing new in this. I have always liked my dark corner."

"But it is cold here. We can't see clearly. It is horrid, too, to want to be Monsieur Jean. I don't want you to talk so to me."

"Just now, on my way here," answered Jean Valjean, "I saw a piece of furniture in the Rue Saint Louis. At a cabinet maker's. If I were a pretty woman, I should make myself a present of that piece of furniture. A very fine toilet table; in the present style. What you call rosewood, I think. It is inlaid. A pretty large glass. There are drawers in it. It is handsome."

"Oh! the ugly bear!" replied Cosette.

And with a bewitching sauciness, pressing her teeth together and separating her lips, she blew upon Jean Valjean. It was a Grace copying a kitten.

"I am furious," she said. "Since yesterday, you all make me rage. Everybody spites me. I don't understand. You don't defend me against Marius. Marius doesn't uphold me against you, I am all alone. I arrange a room handsomely. If I could have put the good God into it, I would have done it. You leave me my room upon my hands. My tenant bankrupts me. I order Nicolette to have a nice little dinner. Nobody wants your dinner, madame. And my father Fauchelevent wishes me to call him Monsieur Jean, and to receive him in a hideous, old, ugly, mouldy cellar, where the walls have a beard, and where there are empty bottles for vases, and spiders' webs for curtains. You are singular, I admit, that is your way, but a truce is granted to people who get married. You should not have gone back to being singular immediately. So you are going to be well satisfied with your horrid Rue de l'Homme Armé. I was very forlorn there, myself! What have you against me? You give me a great deal of trouble. Fie!"

And, growing suddenly serious, she looked fixedly at Jean Valjean, and added:

"So you don't like it that I am happy?"

Artlessness, unconsciously, sometimes penetrates very deep. This question, simple to Cosette, was severe to Jean Valjean. Cosette wished to scratch; she tore.

Jean Valjean grew pale. For a moment he did not answer, then, with an indescribable accent and talking to himself, he murmured:

"Her happiness was the aim of my life. Now, God may beckon me away. Cosette, you are happy; my time is full."

"Ah, you have called me Cosette!" exclaimed she.

And she sprang upon his neck.

Jean Valjean, in desperation, clasped her to his breast wildly. It seemed to him almost as if he were taking her back.

"Thank you, father!" said Cosette to him.

The transport was becoming poignant to Jean Valjean. He gently put away Cosette's arms, and took his hat.

"Well?" said Cosette.

Jean Valjean answered:

"I will leave you, madame; they are waiting for you."

And, from the door, he added:

"I called you Cosette. Tell your husband that that shall not happen again. Pardon me."

Jean Valjean went out, leaving Cosette astounded at that enigmatic farewell.

II
OTHER STEPS BACKWARD

THE following day, at the same hour, Jean Valjean came.

Cosette put no questions to him, was no longer astonished, no longer exclaimed that she was cold, no longer talked of the parlour, she avoided saying either father or Monsieur Jean. She let him speak as he would. She allowed herself to be called madame. Only she betrayed a certain diminution of joy. She would have been sad, if sadness had been possible for her.

It is probable that she had had one of those conversations with Marius, in which the beloved man says what he pleases, explains nothing, and satisfies the beloved woman. The curiosity of lovers does not go very far beyond their love.

The basement-room had made its toilet a little. Basque had suppressed the bottles, and Nicolette the spiders.

Every succeeding morrow brought Jean Valjean at the same hour. He came every day, not having the strength to take Marius' words otherwise than to the letter. Marius made his arrangements, so as to be absent at the hours when Jean Valjean came. The house became accustomed to M. Fauchelevent's new mode of life. Toussaint aided: "*Monsieur always was just so*," she repeated. The grandfather issued this decree: "He is an

original!" and all was said. Besides, at ninety no further tie is
possible; all is juxtaposition; a new-comer is an annoyance.
There is no more room; all the habits are formed. M. Fauchelevent, M. Tranchelevent, Grandfather Gillenormand asked
nothing better than to be relieved of "that gentleman." He
added: "Nothing is more common than these originals. They
do all sorts of odd things. No motive. The Marquis de Canaples
was worse. He bought a palace to live in the barn. They are
fantastic appearances which people put on."

Nobody caught a glimpse of the nether gloom. Who could
have guessed such a thing, moreover? There are such marshes in
India; the water seems strange, inexplicable, quivering when
there is no wind; agitated where it should be calm. You see
upon the surface this causeless boiling; you do not perceive the
Hydra crawling at the bottom.

Many men have thus a secret monster, a disease which they
feed, a dragon which gnaws them, a despair which inhabits their
night. Such a man resembles other people, goes, comes.
Nobody knows that he has within him a fearful parasitic pain,
with a thousand teeth, which lives in the miserable man, who is
dying of it. Nobody knows that this man is a gulf. It is stagnant,
but deep. From time to time a troubling, of which we understand nothing, shows itself on its surface. A mysterious wrinkle
comes along, then vanishes, then reappears; a bubble of air rises
and bursts. It is a little thing, it is terrible. It is the breathing of
the unknown monster.

Certain strange habits, coming at the time when others are
gone, shrinking away while others make a display, wearing on
all occasions what might be called the wall-coloured mantle,
seeking the solitary path, preferring the deserted street, not
mingling in conversations, avoiding gatherings and festivals,
seeming at one's ease and living poorly, having, though rich,
one's key in his pocket and his candle at the porter's, coming in
by the side door, going up the back stairs, all these insignificant
peculiarities, wrinkles, air bubbles, fugitive folds on the surface,
often come from a formidable deep.

Several weeks passed thus. A new life gradually took possession of Cosette; the relations which marriage creates, the visits,
the care of the house, the pleasures, those grand affairs. Cosette's
pleasures were not costly; they consisted in a single one: being
with Marius. Going out with him, staying at home with him,

this was the great occupation of her life. It was a joy to them for ever new, to go out arm in arm, in the face of the sun, in the open street, without hiding, in sight of everybody, all alone with each other. Cosette had one vexation. Toussaint could not agree with Nicolette, the wedding of two old maids being impossible, and went away. The grandfather was in good health; Marius argued a few cases now and then; Aunt Gillenormand peacefully led by the side of the new household, that lateral life which was enough for her. Jean Valjean came every day.

The disappearance of familiarity, the madame, the Monsieur Jean, all this made him different to Cosette. The care which he had taken to detach her from him, succeeded with her. She became more and more cheerful, and less and less affectionate. However, she still loved him very much, and he felt it. One day she suddenly said to him, "You were my father, you are no longer my father, you were my uncle, you are no longer my uncle, you were Monsieur Fauchelevent, you are Jean. Who are you then? I don't like all that. If I did not know you were so good, I should be afraid of you."

He still lived in the Rue de l'Homme Armé, unable to resolve to move further from the quartier in which Cosette dwelt.

At first he stayed with Cosette only a few minutes, then went away.

Little by little he got into the habit of making his visits longer. One would have said that he took advantage of the example of the days which were growing longer: he came earlier and went away later.

One day Cosette inadvertently said to him: "Father." A flash of joy illuminated Jean Valjean's gloomy old face. He replied to her: "Say Jean." "Ah! true," she answered with a burst of laughter, "Monsieur Jean." "That is right," said he, and he turned away that she might not see him wipe his eyes.

III

THEY REMEMBER THE GARDEN IN THE RUE PLUMET

THAT was the last time. From that last gleam onward, there was complete extinction. No more familiarity, no more good-day with a kiss, never again that word so intensely sweet: Father! he was, upon his own demand and through his own complicity, driven in succession from every happiness; and he had this misery, that after having lost Cosette wholly in one day, he had been obliged afterwards to lose her again little by little.

The eye at last becomes accustomed to the light of a cellar. In short, to have a vision of Cosette every day sufficed him. His whole life was concentrated in that hour. He sat by her side, he looked at her in silence, or rather he talked to her of the years long gone, of her childhood, of the convent, of her friends of those days.

One afternoon—it was one of the early days of April, already warm, still fresh, the season of the great cheerfulness of the sunshine, the gardens which lay about Marius' and Cosette's windows felt the emotion of awakening, the hawthorn was beginning to peep, a jewelled array of gilliflowers displayed themselves upon the old walls, the rosy wolf-mouths gaped in the cracks of the stones, there was a charming beginning of daisies and buttercups in the grass, the white butterflies of the year made their first appearance, the wind, that minstrel of the eternal wedding, essayed in the trees the first notes of that grand auroral symphony which the old poets called the *renouveau*—Marius said to Cosette: "We have said that we would go to see our garden in the Rue Plumet again. Let us go. We must not be ungrateful." And they flew away like two swallows towards the spring. This garden in the Rue Plumet had the effect of the dawn upon them. They had behind them in life already something which was like the spring time of their love. The house in the Rue Plumet being taken on a lease, still belonged to Cosette. They went to this garden and this house. In it they found themselves again; they forgot themselves. At night, at the usual hour, Jean Valjean came to the Rue des Filles du Calvaire. "Madame has gone out with monsieur, and has not returned yet," said Basque to him. He sat down in silence, and waited an hour. Cosette did not return. He bowed his head and went away.

Cosette was so intoxicated with her walk to "the garden," and so happy over having "lived a whole day in her past," that she did not speak of anything else the next day. It did not occur to her that she had not seen Jean Valjean.

"How did you go there?" Jean Valjean asked her.

"We walked."

"And how did you return?"

"In a fiacre."

For some time Jean Valjean had noticed the frugal life which the young couple led. He was annoyed at it. Marius' economy was severe, and the word to Jean Valjean had its absolute sense. He ventured a question:

"Why have you no carriage of your own? A pretty brougham would cost you only five hundred francs a month. You are rich."

"I don't know," answered Cosette.

"So with Toussaint," continued Jean Valjean. "She has gone away. You have not replaced her. Why not?"

"Nicolette is enough."

"But you must have a waiting maid."

"Have not I Marius?"

"You ought to have a house of your own, servants of your own, a carriage, a box at the theatre. There is nothing too good for you. Why not have the advantages of being rich? Riches add to happiness."

Cosette made no answer.

Jean Valjean's visits did not grow shorter. Far from it. When the heart is slipping we do not stop on the descent.

When Jean Valjean desired to prolong his visit, and to make the hours pass unnoticed, he eulogised Marius; he thought him beautiful, noble, courageous, intellectual, eloquent, good. Cosette surpassed him. Jean Valjean began again. They were never silent. Marius, this word was inexhaustible; there were volumes in these six letters. In this way Jean Valjean succeeded in staying a long time. To see Cosette, to forget at her side, it was so sweet to him. It was the staunching of his wound. It happened several times that Basque came down twice to say: "Monsieur Gillenormand sends me to remind Madame the Baroness that dinner is served."

On those days, Jean Valjean returned home very thoughtful.

Was there, then, some truth in that comparison of the chrysalis which had presented itself to Marius' mind? Was Jean Valjean indeed a chrysalis who was obstinate, and who came to make visits to his butterfly?

One day he stayed longer than usual. The next day, he noticed that there was no fire in the fire-place. "What!" thought he. "No fire." And he made the explanation to himself: "It is a matter of course. We are in April. The cold weather is over."

"Goodness! how cold it is here!" exclaimed Cosette as she came in.

"Why no," said Jean Valjean.

"So it is you who told Basque not to make a fire?"

"Yes. We are close upon May."

"But we have fire until the month of June. In this cellar, it is needed the year round."

"I thought that the fire was unnecessary."

"That is just one of your ideas!" replied Cosette.

The next day there was a fire. But the two arm-chairs were placed at the other end of the room, near the door. "What does that mean?" thought Jean Valjean.

He went for the arm-chairs, and put them back in their usual place near the chimney.

This fire being kindled again encouraged him, however. He continued the conversation still longer than usual. As he was getting up to go away, Cosette said to him:

"My husband said a funny thing to me yesterday."

"What was it?"

"He said: 'Cosette, we have an income of thirty thousand francs. Twenty-seven that you have, three that my grandfather allows me.' I answered: 'That makes thirty.' 'Would you have the courage to live on three thousand?' I answered: 'Yes, on nothing. Provided it be with you.' And then I asked: 'Why do you say this?' He answered: 'To know.'"

Jean Valjean did not say a word. Cosette probably expected some explanation from him; he listened to her in a mournful silence. He went back to the Rue de l'Homme Armé; he was so deeply absorbed that he mistook the door, and instead of entering his own house, he entered the next one. Not until he had gone up almost to the second story did he perceive his mistake, and go down again.

His mind was racked with conjectures. It was evident that Marius had doubts in regard to the origin of these six hundred thousand francs, that he feared some impure source, who knows? that he had perhaps discovered that this money came from him, Jean Valjean, that he hesitated before this suspicious fortune, and disliked to take it as his own, preferring to remain poor, himself and Cosette, than to be rich with a doubtful wealth.

Besides, vaguely, Jean Valjean began to feel that the door was shown him.

The next day, he received, on entering the basement-room,

something like a shock. The arm-chairs had disappeared. There was not even a chair of any kind.

"Ah now," exclaimed Cosette as she came in, "no chairs! Where are the arm-chairs, then?"

"They are gone," answered Jean Valjean.

"That is a pretty business!"

Jean Valjean stammered:

"I told Basque to take them away."

"And what for?"

"I shall stay only a few minutes to-day."

"Staying a little while is no reason for standing while you do stay."

"I believe that Basque needed some arm-chairs for the parlour."

"What for?"

"You doubtless have company this evening."

"We have nobody."

Jean Valjean could not say a word more.

Cosette shrugged her shoulders.

"To have the chairs carried away! The other day you had the fire put out. How singular you are!"

"Good-bye," murmured Jean Valjean.

He did not say: "Good-bye, Cosette." But he had not the strength to say: "Good-bye, madame."

He went away overwhelmed.

This time he had understood.

The next day he did not come. Cosette did not notice it until night.

"Why," said she, "Monsieur Jean has not come to-day."

She felt something like a slight oppression of the heart, but she hardly perceived it, being immediately diverted by a kiss from Marius.

The next day he did not come.

Cosette paid no attention to it, passed the evening and slept as usual, and thought of it only on awaking. She was so happy! She sent Nicolette very quickly to Monsieur Jean's to know if he were sick, and why he had not come the day before. Nicolette brought back Monsieur Jean's answer. He was not sick. He was busy. He would come very soon. As soon as he could. However, he was going to make a little journey. Madame must remember that he was in the habit of making journeys from time to time. Let there be no anxiety. Let them not be troubled about him.

Nicolette, on entering Monsieur Jean's house, had repeated to him the very words of her mistress. That madame sent to know "why Monsieur Jean had not come the day before." "It is two days that I have not been there," said Jean Valjean mildly.

But the remark escaped the notice of Nicolette, who reported nothing of it to Cosette.

IV
ATTRACTION AND EXTINCTION

DURING the last months of the spring and the first months of the summer of 1833, the scattered wayfarers in the Marais, the storekeepers, the idlers upon the doorsteps, noticed an old man neatly dressed in black, every day, about the same hour, at nightfall, come out of the Rue de l'Homme Armé, in the direction of the Rue Sainte Croix de la Bretonnerie, pass by the Blancs Manteaux, to the Rue Culture Sainte Catherine, and, reaching the Rue de l'Echarpe, turn to the left, and enter the Rue Saint Louis.

There he walked with slow steps, his head bent forward, seeing nothing, hearing nothing, his eye immovably fixed upon one point, always the same, which seemed studded with stars to him, and which was nothing more nor less than the corner of the Rue des Filles du Calvaire. As he approached the corner of that street, his face lighted up; a kind of joy illuminated his eye like an interior halo, he had a fascinated and softened expression, his lips moved vaguely, as if he were speaking to some one whom he did not see, he smiled faintly, and he advanced as slowly as he could. You would have said that even while wishing to reach some destination, he dreaded the moment when he should be near it. When there were but a few houses left between him and that street which appeared to attract him, his pace became so slow, that at times you might have supposed he had ceased to move. The vacillation of his head and the fixedness of his eye reminded you of the needle seeking the pole. However long he succeeded in deferring it, he must arrive at last; he reached the Rue des Filles du Calvaire; then he stopped, he trembled, he put his head with a kind of gloomy timidity beyond the corner of the last house, and he looked into that street, and there was in that tragical look something which resembled the bewilderment of the impossible, and the reflection of a forbidden paradise. Then a tear, which had gradually gathered in the corner of his eye, grown large enough to fall, glided over his cheek, and sometimes stopped at his mouth. The old man tasted its bitterness. He remained thus a few minutes, as if he had been stone; then he returned by the same route and at the same pace; and, in proportion as he receded, that look was extinguished.

Little by little, this old man ceased to go as far as the corner of the Rue des Filles du Calvaire; he stopped half way down the Rue Saint Louis; sometimes a little further, sometimes a little nearer. One day, he stopped at the corner of the Rue Culture Sainte Catherine, and looked at the Rue des Filles du Calvaire from the distance. Then he silently moved his head from right to left as if he were refusing himself something, and retraced his steps.

Very soon he no longer came even as far as the Rue Saint Louis. He reached the Rue Pavée, shook his head, and went back; then he no longer went beyond the Rue des Trois Pavillons; then he no longer passed the Blancs Manteaux. You would have said a pendulum which has not been wound up, and the oscillations of which are growing shorter ere they stop.

Every day, he came out of his house at the same hour, he commenced the same walk, but he did not finish it, and, perhaps unconsciously, he continually shortened it. His whole countenance expressed this single idea; What is the use? The eye was dull; no more radiance. The tear also was gone; it no longer gathered at the corner of the lids, that thoughtful eye was dry. The old man's head was still bent forward; his chin quivered at times; the wrinkles of his thin neck were painful to behold. Sometimes, when the weather was bad, he carried an umbrella under his arm, which he never opened. The good women of the quartier said: "He is a natural." The children followed him laughing.

BOOK NINTH –
SUPREME SHADOW, SUPREME DAWN

I

PITY FOR THE UNHAPPY, BUT INDULGENCE
FOR THE HAPPY

IT is a terrible thing to be happy! How pleased we are with it! How all-sufficient we think it! How, being in possession of the false aim of life, happiness, we forget the true aim, duty!

We must say, however, that it would be unjust to blame Marius.

Marius as we have explained, before his marriage, had put no questions to M. Fauchelevent, and, since, he had feared to put any to Jean Valjean. He had regretted the promise into which he had allowed himself to be led. He had reiterated to himself many times that he had done wrong in making that concession to despair. He did nothing more than gradually to banish Jean Valjean from his house, and to obliterate him as much as possible from Cosette's mind. He had in some sort constantly placed himself between Cosette and Jean Valjean, sure that in that way she would not notice him, and would never think of him. It was more than obliteration, it was eclipse.

Marius did what he deemed necessary and just. He supposed he had, for discarding Jean Valjean, without harshness, but without weakness, serious reasons, which we have already seen, and still others which we shall see further on. Having chanced to meet, in a cause in which he was engaged, an old clerk of the house of Laffitte, he had obtained, without seeking it, some mysterious information which he could not, in truth, probe to the bottom, from respect for the secret which he had promised to keep, and from care for Jean Valjean's perilous situation. He believed, at that very time, that he had a solemn duty to perform, the restitution of the six hundred thousand francs to somebody whom he was seeking as cautiously as possible. In the meantime, he abstained from using that money.

As for Cosette, she was in none of these secrets; but it would be hard to condemn her also.

There was an all-powerful magnetism flowing from Marius to her, which compelled her to do, instinctively and almost mechanically, what Marius wished. She felt, in regard to

"Monsieur Jean," a will from Marius; she conformed to it. Her husband had had nothing to say to her; she experienced the vague, but clear pressure of his unspoken wishes, and obeyed blindly. Her obedience in this consisted in not remembering what Marius forgot. She had to make no effort for that. Without knowing why herself, and without affording any grounds for censure, her soul had so thoroughly become her husband's soul, that whatever was covered with shadow in Marius' thought, was obscured in hers.

We must not go too far, however; in what concerns Jean Valjean, this forgetfulness and this obliteration were only superficial. She was rather thoughtless than forgetful. At heart, she really loved him whom she had so long called father. But she loved her husband still more. It was that which had somewhat swayed the balance of this heart, inclined in a single direction.

It sometimes happened that Cosette spoke of Jean Valjean, and wondered. Then Marius calmed her: "He is absent, I think. Didn't he say that he was going away on a journey?" "That is true," thought Cosette. "He was in the habit of disappearing in this way. But not for so long." Two or three times she sent Nicolette to inquire in the Rue de l'Homme Armé if Monsieur Jean had returned from his journey. Jean Valjean had the answer returned that he had not.

Cosette did not inquire further, having but one need on earth, Marius.

We must also say that, on their part, Marius and Cosette had been absent. They had been to Vernon. Marius had taken Cosette to his father's grave.

Marius had little by little withdrawn Cosette from Jean Valjean. Cosette was passive.

Moreover, what is called much too harshly, in certain cases, the ingratitude of children, is not always as blameworthy a thing as is supposed. It is the ingratitude of nature. Nature, as we have said elsewhere, "looks forward." Nature divides living beings into the coming and the going. The going are turned towards the shadow, the coming towards the light. Hence a separation, which, on the part of the old, is a fatality, and, on the part of the young, involuntary. This separation, at first insensible, gradually increases, like every separation of branches. The limbs, without parting from the trunk, recede from it. It is not their fault. Youth goes where joy is, to festivals, to brilliant lights, to loves. Old age goes to its end. They do not lose sight of each other, but the ties are loosened. The affection of the young is chilled by life; that of the old by the grave. We must not blame these poor children.

II
THE LAST FLICKERINGS OF THE EXHAUSTED LAMP

ONE day Jean Valjean went down stairs, took three steps into the street, sat down upon a stone block, upon that same block where Gavroche, on the night of the 5th of June, had found him musing; he remained there a few minutes, then went upstairs again. This was the last oscillation of the pendulum. The next day, he did not leave his room. The day after he did not leave his bed.

His portress, who prepared his frugal meal, some cabbage, a few potatoes with a little pork, looked into the brown earthen plate, and exclaimed:

"Why, you didn't eat anything yesterday, poor dear man!"

"Yes, I did," answered Jean Valjean.

"The plate is all full."

"Look at the water-pitcher. That is empty."

"That shows that you have drunk; it don't show that you have eaten."

"Well," said Jean Valjean, "suppose I have only been hungry for water?"

"That is called thirst, and, when people don't eat at the same time, it is called fever."

"I will eat to-morrow."

"Or at Christmas. Why not eat to-day? Do people say: I will eat to-morrow! To leave me my whole plateful without touching it! My cole slaw, which was so good!"

Jean Valjean took the old woman's hand:

"I promise to eat it," said he to her in his benevolent voice.

"I am not satisfied with you," answered the portress.

Jean Valjean scarcely ever saw any other human being than this good woman. There are streets in Paris in which nobody walks, and houses into which nobody comes. He was in one of those streets, and in one of those houses.

While he still went out, he had bought of a brazier for a few sous a little copper crucifix, which he had hung upon a nail before his bed. The cross is always good to look upon.

A week elapsed, and Jean Valjean had not taken a step in his room. He was still in bed. The portress said to her husband: "The goodman upstairs does not get up any more, he does not eat any more, he won't last long. He has trouble, he has. Nobody can get it out of my head that his daughter has made a bad match."

The porter replied, with the accent of the marital sovereignty:

"If he is rich, let him have a doctor. If he is not rich, let him not have any. If he doesn't have a doctor, he will die."

"And if he does have one?"

"He will die," said the porter.

The portress began to dig up with an old knife some grass which was sprouting in what she called her pavement, and, while she was pulling up the grass, she muttered:

"It is a pity. An old man who is so nice! He is white as a chicken."

She saw a physician of the quartier passing at the end of the street; she took it upon herself to beg him to go up.

"It is on the second floor," said she to him. "You will have nothing to do but go in. As the goodman does not stir from his bed now, the key is in the door all the time."

The physician saw Jean Valjean, and spoke with him.

When he came down, the portress questioned him:

"Well, doctor?"

"Your sick man is very sick."

"What is the matter with him?"

"Everything and nothing. He is a man who, to all appearance, has lost some dear friend. People die of that."

"What did he tell you?"

"He told me that he was well."

"Will you come again, doctor?"

"Yes," answered the physician. "But another than I must come again."

III

A PEN IS HEAVY TO HIM WHO LIFTED
FAUCHELEVENT'S CART

ONE evening Jean Valjean had difficulty in raising himself upon his elbow; he felt his wrist and found no pulse; his breathing was short, and stopped at intervals; he realised that he was weaker than he had been before. Then, undoubtedly under the pressure of some supreme desire, he made an effort, sat up in bed, and dressed himself. He put on his old working-man's garb. As he went out no longer, he had returned to it, and he preferred it. He was obliged to stop several times while dressing; the mere effort of putting on his waistcoat, made the sweat roll down his forehead.

Since he had been alone, he had made his bed in the ante-room, so as to occupy this desolate tenement as little as possible.

He opened the valise and took out Cosette's suit.

He spread it out upon his bed.

The bishop's candlesticks were in their place, on the mantel. He took two wax tapers from a drawer, and put them into the candlesticks. Then, although it was still broad daylight, it was in summer, he lighted them. We sometimes see torches lighted thus in broad day, in rooms where the dead lie.

Each step that he took in going from one piece of furniture to another, exhausted him, and he was obliged to sit down. It was not ordinary fatigue which spends the strength that it may be renewed; it was the remnant of possible motion; it was exhausted life pressed out drop by drop in overwhelming efforts, never to be made again.

One of the chairs upon which he sank, was standing before that mirror, so fatal for him, so providential for Marius, in which he had read Cosette's note, reversed on the blotter. He saw himself in this mirror, and did not recognise himself. He was eighty years old; before Marius' marriage, one would hardly have thought him fifty; this year had counted thirty. What was now upon his forehead was not the wrinkle of age, it was the mysterious mark of death. You perceived on it the impress of the relentless talon. His cheeks were sunken; the skin of his face was of that colour which suggests the idea of earth already above it; the corners of his mouth were depressed as in that mask which the ancients sculptured upon tombs, he looked at the hollowness with a look of reproach; you would have said it was one of those grand tragic beings who rise in judgment.

He was in that condition, the last phase of dejection, in which sorrow no longer flows; it is, so to speak, coagulated; the soul is covered as if with a clot of despair.

Night had come. With much labour he drew a table and an old arm-chair near the fire-place, and put upon the table pen, ink, and paper.

Then he fainted. When he regained consciousness he was thirsty. Being unable to lift the water-pitcher, with great effort he tipped it towards his mouth, and drank a swallow.

Then he turned to the bed, and, still sitting, for he could stand but a moment, he looked at the little black dress, and all those dear objects.

Such contemplations last for hours which seem minutes. Suddenly he shivered, he felt that the chill was coming, he leaned upon the table which was lighted by the bishop's candle-sticks, and took the pen.

As neither the pen nor the ink had been used for a long time, the tip of the pen was bent back, the ink was dried, he was obliged to get up and put a few drops of water into the ink, which he could not do without stopping and sitting down two or three times, and he was compelled to write with the back of the pen. He wiped his forehead from time to time.

His hand trembled. He slowly wrote the few lines which follow:

"Cosette, I bless you. I am going to make an explanation to you. Your husband was quite right in giving me to understand that I ought to leave; still there is some mistake in what he believed, but he was right. He is very good. Always love him well when I am dead. Monsieur Pontmercy, always love my darling child. Cosette, this paper will be found, this is what I want to tell you, you shall see the figures, if I have the strength to recall them, listen well, this money is really your own. This is the whole story: The white jet comes from Norway, the black jet comes from England, the black glass-imitation comes from Germany. The jet is lighter, more precious, more costly. We can make imitations in France as well as in Germany. It requires a little anvil two inches square, and a spirit-lamp to soften the wax. The wax was formerly made with resin and lamp-black, and cost four francs a pound. I hit upon making it with gum lac and turpentine. This costs only thirty sous, and it is much better. The buckles are made of violet glass, which is fastened by means of this wax to a narrow rim of black iron. The glass should be violet for iron trinkets, and the black for gold trinkets. Spain purchases many of them. That is the country of jet——"

Here he stopped, the pen fell from his fingers, he gave way to one of those despairing sobs which rose at times from the depths of his being, the poor man clasped his head with both hands, and reflected.

"Oh!" exclaimed he within himself (pitiful cries, heard by God alone), "it is all over. I shall never see her more. She is a smile which has passed over me. I am going to enter into the night without even seeing her again. Oh! a minute, an instant, to hear her voice, to touch her dress, to look at her, the angel! and then to die! It is nothing to die, but it is dreadful to die without seeing her. She would smile upon me, she would say a word to me. Would that harm anybody? No, it is over, forever. Here I am, all alone. My God! my God! I shall never see her again."

At this moment there was a rap at his door.

IV

A BOTTLE OF INK WHICH SERVES ONLY TO WHITEN

THAT very day, or rather that very evening, just as Marius had left the table and retired into his office, having a bundle of papers to study over, Basque had handed him a letter, saying: "the person who wrote the letter is in the antechamber."

Cosette had taken grandfather's arm, and was walking in the garden.

A letter, as well as a man, may have a forbidding appearance. Coarse paper, clumsy fold, the mere sight of certain missives displeases. The letter which Basque brought was of this kind.

Marius took it. It smelt of tobacco. Nothing awakens a reminiscence like an odour. Marius recognised this tobacco. He looked at the address: *To Monsieur, Monsieur the Baron Pommerci. In his hôtel*. The recognition of the tobacco made him recognise the handwriting. We might say that astonishment has its flashes. Marius was, as it were, illuminated by one of those flashes.

The scent, the mysterious aid-memory, revived a whole world within him. Here was the very paper, the manner of folding, the paleness of the ink; here was, indeed, the well-known handwriting; above all, here was the tobacco. The Jondrette garret appeared before him.

Thus, strange freak of chance! one of the two traces which he had sought so long, the one which he had again recently made so many efforts to gain, and which he believed forever lost, came of itself to him.

He broke the seal eagerly, and read:———

"Monsieur Baron,—If the Supreme Being had given me the talents for it, I could have been Baron Thénard, member of the Institute (Academy of Ciences), but I am not so. I merely bear the same name that he does, happy if this remembrance commends me to the excellence of your bounties. The benefit with which you honour me will be reciprocal. I am in possession of a secret conserning an individual. This individual conserns you. I hold the secret at your disposition, desiring to have the honour of being yuseful to you. I will give you the simple means of drivving from your honourable family this individual who has no right in it, Madame the Baroness being of high birth. The sanctuary of virtue could not coabit longer with crime without abdicating.

"I attend in the entichamber the orders of Monsieur the Baron. With respect."

The letter was signed "THÉNARD."

This signature was not a false one. It was only a little abridged.

Besides the rigmarole and the orthography completed the revelation. The certificate of origin was perfect. There was no doubt possible.

The emotion of Marius was deep. After the feeling of surprise, he had a feeling of happiness. Let him now find the other man whom he sought, the man who had saved him, Marius, and he would have nothing more to wish.

He opened one of his secretary drawers, took out some bank-notes, put them in his pockets, closed the secretary, and rang. Basque appeared.

"Show him in," said Marius.

Basque announced:

"Monsieur Thénard."

A man entered.

A new surprise for Marius. The man who came in was perfectly unknown to him.

This man, old withal, had a large nose, his chin in his cravat, green spectacles, with double shade of green silk over his eyes, his hair polished and smoothed down, his forehead close to the eyebrows, like the wigs of English coachmen in high life. His hair was grey. He was dressed in black from head to foot, in a well worn but tidy black; a bunch of trinkets, hanging from his fob, suggested a watch. He held an old hat in his hand. He walked with a stoop, and the crook of his back increased the lowliness of his bow.

What was striking at first sight was, that this person's coat, too full, although carefully buttoned, did not seem to have been made for him. Here a short digression is necessary.

There was in Paris, at that period, in an old shanty, in the Rue Beautreillis, near the Arsenal, an ingenious Jew, whose business it was to change a rascal into an honest man. Not for too long a time, which might have been uncomfortable for the rascal. The change was made at sight, for a day or two, at the rate of thirty sous a day, by means of a costume, resembling, as closely as possible, that of honest people generally. This renter of costumes was called *the Changer*; the Parisian thieves had given him this name, and knew him by no other. He had a tolerably complete wardrobe. The rags with which he tricked out his people were almost respectable. He had specialities and categories; upon each nail in his shop, hung, worn and rumpled, a social condition; here the magistrate's dress, there the curé's dress, there the banker's dress, in one corner the retired soldier's dress, in another the literary man's dress, further on the statesman's dress. This man was the costumer of the immense drama which knavery plays in Paris. His hut was the greenroom whence robbery came forth, and whither swindling returned. A ragged rogue came to this wardrobe, laid down thirty sous, and chose, according to the part which he wished to play that day, the dress which suited him, and, when he returned to the street, the rogue was somebody. The next day the clothes were faithfully brought back, and the Changer, who trusted everything to the robbers, was never robbed. These garments had one inconvenience, they "were not a fit;" not having been made for those who wore them, they were tight for this man, baggy for that, and fitted nobody. Every thief who exceeded the human average in smallness or in bigness, was ill at ease in the costumes of the Changer. He must be neither too fat nor too lean. The Changer had provided only for ordinary men. He had taken the measure of the species in the person of the first chance vagabond, who was neither thick nor thin, neither tall nor short. Hence adaptations, sometimes difficult, with which the Changer's customers got along as well as they could. So much the worse for the exceptions! The Statesman's dress, for instance, black from top to toe, and consequently suitable, would have been too large for Pitt and too small for Castelcicala. The Statesman's suit was described as follows in the Changer's catalogue; we copy: "A black cloth coat, pantaloons of black doublemilled cassimere, a silk waistcoat, boots, and linen." There was in the margin: "*Ancient ambassador*," and a note which we also transcribe; "In a separate box, a wig neatly frizzled, green spectacles, trinkets, and two little quill tubes an inch in length wrapped in cotton." This all went with the Statesman, ancient ambassador. This entire costume was, if we may use the word, emaciated; the seams were turning white, an undefined buttonhole was appearing at one of the elbows; moreover a button was missing on the breast of the coat; but this was a slight matter; as the Statesman's hand ought always to be within the coat and upon the heart, its function was to conceal the absent button.

If Marius had been familiar with the occult institutions of Paris, he would have recognised immediately, on the back of the visitor whom Basque had just introduced, the Statesman's coat borrowed from the Unhook-me-that of the Changer.

Marius' disappointment, on seeing another man enter than the one he was expecting, turned into dislike towards the newcomer. He examined him from head to foot, while the personage bowed without measure, and asked him in a sharp tone:

"What do you want?"

The man answered with an amiable grin of which the caressing smile of a crocodile would give some idea:

"It seems to me impossible that I have not already had the honour of seeing Monsieur the Baron in society. I really think that I met him privately some years ago, at Madame the Princess Bagration's and in the salons of his lordship the Viscount Dambray, peer of France."

It is always good tactics in rascality to pretend to recognise one whom you do not know.

Marius listened attentively to the voice of this man. He watched for the tone and gesture eagerly, but his disappointment increased; it was a whining pronunciation, entirely different from the sharp and dry sound of the voice which he expected. He was completely bewildered.

"I don't know," said he, "either Madame Bagration or M. Dambray. I have never in my life set foot in the house of either the one or the other."

The answer was testy. The person, gracious notwithstanding, persisted:

"Then it must be at Chateaubriand's that I have seen monsieur? I know Chateaubriand well. He is very affable. He says to me sometimes: 'Thénard, my friend, won't you drink a glass of wine with me?'"

Marius' brow grew more and more severe:

"I have never had the honour of being received at Monsieur de Chateaubriand's. Come to the point. What is it you wish?"

The man, in view of the harsher voice, made a lower bow.

"Monsieur Baron, deign to listen to me. There is in America, in a region which is near Panama, a village called La Joya. This village is composed of a single house. A large, square, three-story adobe house, each side of the square five hundred feet long, each story set back twelve feet from the story below, so as to leave in front a terrace which runs round the building, in the centre an interior court in which are provisions and ammunition, no windows, loopholes, no door, ladders, ladders to mount from the ground to the first terrace, and from the first to the second, and from the second to the third, ladders to descend into the interior court, no doors to the rooms, hatchways, no stairs to the rooms, ladders; at night the hatchways are closed, the ladders drawn in: swivels and carbines are aimed through the port-holes; no means of entering; a house by day, a citadel by night, eight hundred inhabitants, such is this village. Why so much precaution? because the country is dangerous; it is full of anthropophagi. Then why do people go there? because that country is wonderful; gold is found there."

"What are you coming to?" Marius interrupted, who from disappointment was passing to impatience.

"To this, Monsieur Baron. I am an old weary diplomatist. The old civilisation has used me up. I wish to try the savages."

"What then?"

"Monsieur Baron, selfishness is the law of the world. The proletarian country-woman who works by the day, turns round when the diligence passes, the proprietary country-woman who works in her own field, does not turn round. The poor man's dog barks at the rich man, the rich man's dog barks at the poor man. Every one for himself. Interest is the motive of men. Gold is the loadstone."

"What then? Conclude."

"I would like to go and establish myself at La Joya. There are three of us. I have my spouse and my young lady; a girl who is very beautiful. The voyage is long and dear. I must have a little money."

"How does that concern me?" inquired Marius.

The stranger stretched his neck out of his cravat, a movement characteristic of the vulture, and replied, with redoubled smiles:

"Then Monsieur the Baron has not read my letter?"

That was not far from true. The fact is, that the contents of the epistle had glanced off from Marius. He had seen the handwriting rather than read the letter. He scarcely remembered it. Within a moment a new clue had been given him. He had noticed this remark: My spouse and my young lady. He fixed a searching eye upon the stranger. An examining judge could not have done better. He seemed to be lying in ambush for him. He answered:

"Explain."

The stranger thrust his hands into his fobs, raised his head without straightening his backbone, but scrutinising Marius in his turn with the green gaze of his spectacles.

"Certainly, Monsieur the Baron. I will explain. I have a secret to sell you."

"A secret?"

"A secret."

"Which concerns me?"

"Somewhat."

"What is this secret?"

Marius examined the man more and more closely, while listening to him.

"I commence gratis," said the stranger. "You will see that I am interesting."

"Go on."

"Monsieur Baron, you have in your house a robber and an assassin."

Marius shuddered.

"In my house? no," said he.

The stranger, imperturbable, brushed his hat with his sleeve, and continued:

"Assassin and robber. Observe, Monsieur Baron, that I do not speak here of acts, old, by-gone, and withered, which may be cancelled by prescription in the eye of the law, and by repentance in the eye of God. I speak of recent acts, present acts, acts yet unknown to justice at this hour. I will proceed. This man has glided into your confidence, and almost into your family, under a false name. I am going to tell you his true name. And to tell it to you for nothing."

"I am listening."

"His name is Jean Valjean."

"I know it."

"I am going to tell you, also for nothing, who he is."

"Say on."

"He is an old convict."

"I know it."

"You know it since I have had the honour of telling you."

"No. I knew it before."

Marius' cool tone, that double reply, *I know it*, his laconic method of speech, embarrassing to conversation, excited some suppressed anger in the stranger. He shot furtively at Marius a furious look, which was immediately extinguished. Quick as it was, this look was one of those which are recognised after they have once been seen; it did not escape Marius. Certain flames can only come from certain souls; the eye, that window of the thought, blazes with it; spectacles hide nothing; you might as well put a glass over hell.

The stranger resumed with a smile:

"I do not permit myself to contradict Monsieur the Baron. At all events, you must see that I am informed. Now, what I have to acquaint you with, is known to myself alone. It concerns the fortune of Madame the Baroness. It is an extraordinary secret. It is for sale. I offer it to you first. Cheap. Twenty thousand francs."

"I know that secret as well as the others," said Marius.

The person felt the necessity of lowering his price a little.

"Monsieur Baron, say ten thousand francs, and I will go on."

"I repeat, that you have nothing to acquaint me with. I know what you wish to tell me."

There was a new flash in the man's eye. He exclaimed:

"Still I must dine to-day. It is an extraordinary secret, I tell you. Monsieur the Baron, I am going to speak. I will speak. Give me twenty francs."

Marius looked at him steadily:

"I know your extraordinary secret; just as I knew Jean Valjean's name: just as I know your name."

"My name?"

"Yes."

"That is not difficult, Monsieur Baron. I have had the honour of writing it to you and telling it to you. Thénard."

"Dier."

"Eh?"

"Thénardier."

"Who is that?"

In danger the porcupine bristles, the beetle feigns death, the Old Guard forms a square; this man began to laugh.

Then, with a fillip, he brushed a speck of dust from his coat-sleeve.

Marius continued:

"You are also the working-man Jondrette, the comedian Fabantou, the poet Genflot, the Spaniard Don Alvarès, and the woman Balizard."

"The woman what?"

"And you have kept a chop-house at Montfermeil."

"A chop-house! never."

"And I tell you that you are Thénardier."

"I deny it."

"And that you are a scoundrel. Here."

And Marius, taking a bank-note from his pocket, threw it in his face.

"Thanks! pardon! five hundred francs! Monsieur Baron!"

And the man, bewildered, bowing, catching the note, examined it.

"Five hundred francs!" he repeated in astonishment. And he stammered out in an under tone: "A serious *fafiot*!"

Then bluntly:

"Well, so be it," exclaimed he. "Let us make ourselves comfortable."

And, with the agility of a monkey, throwing his hair off backwards, pulling off his spectacles, taking out of his nose and pocketing the two quill tubes of which we have just spoken, and which we have already seen elsewhere on another page of this book, he took off his countenance as one takes off his hat.

His eye kindled; his forehead, uneven, ravined, humped in spots, hideously wrinkled at the top, emerged; his nose became as sharp as a beak; the fierce and cunning profile of the man of prey appeared again.

"Monsieur the Baron is infallible," said he in a clear voice from which all nasality has disappeared, "I am Thénardier."

And he straightened his bent back.

Thénardier, for it was indeed he, was strangely surprised; he would have been disconcerted if he could have been. He had come to bring astonishment, and he himself received it. This humiliation had been compensated by five hundred francs, and, all things considered, he accepted it; but he was none the less astounded.

He saw this Baron Pontmercy for the first time, and in spite of his disguise, this Baron Pontmercy recognised him and recognised him thoroughly. And not only was this baron fully informed, in regard to Thénardier, but he seemed fully informed in regard to Jean Valjean. Who was this almost beardless young man, so icy and so generous, who knew people's names, who knew all their names, and who opened his purse to them, who abused rogues like a judge and who paid them like a dupe?

Thénardier, it will be remembered, although he had been a neighbour of Marius, had never seen him, which is frequent in Paris; he had once heard some talk of his daughters about a very poor young man named Marius who lived in the house. He had written to him, without knowing him, the letter which we have seen. No connection was possible in his mind between that Marius and M. the Baron Pontmercy.

Through his daughter Azelma, however, whom he had put upon the track of the couple married on the 16th of February, and through his own researches, he had succeeded in finding out many things and, from the depth of his darkness, he had been able to seize more than one mysterious clue. He had, by dint of industry, discovered, or, at least, by dint of induction, guessed who the man was whom he had met on a certain day in the Grand Sewer. From the man, he had easily arrived at the name. He knew that Madame the Baroness Pontmercy was Cosette. But, in that respect, he intended to be prudent. Who was Cosette? He did not know exactly himself. He suspected indeed some illegitimacy. Fantine's story had always seemed to him ambiguous; but why speak of it? to get paid for his silence? He had, or thought he had, something better to sell than that. And to all appearances, to come and make, without any proof, this revelation to Baron Pontmercy: *Your wife is a bastard*, would only have attracted the husband's boot towards the revelator's back.

In Thénardier's opinion, the conversation with Marius had not yet commenced. He had been obliged to retreat, to modify his strategy, to abandon a position, to change his base; but nothing essential was yet lost, and he had five hundred francs in his pocket. Moreover, he had something decisive to say, and even against this Baron Pontmercy, so well informed and so well armed, he felt himself strong. To men of Thénardier's nature every dialogue is a battle. In that which was about to be commenced what was his situation? He did not know to whom he was speaking, but he knew about what he was speaking. He rapidly made this interior review of his forces, and after saying: "*I am Thénardier*," he waited.

Marius remained absorbed in thought. At last, then, he had caught Thénardier; this man, whom he had so much desired to find again, was before him: so he would be able to do honour to Colonel Pontmercy's injunction. He was humiliated that that hero should owe anything to this bandit, and that the bill of exchange drawn by his father from the depth of the grave upon him, Marius, should have been protested until this day. It appeared to him, also, in the complex position of his mind with regard to Thénardier, that here was an opportunity to avenge the colonel for the misfortune of having been saved by such a rascal. However that might be, he was pleased. He was about to deliver the colonel's shade at last from his unworthy creditor, and it seemed to him that he was about to release his father's memory from imprisonment for debt.

Besides this duty, he had another, to clear up, if he could, the source of Cosette's fortune. The opportunity seemed to present itself. Thénardier knew something, perhaps. It might be useful to probe this man to the bottom. He began with that.

Thénardier had slipped the "serious *fafiot*" into his fob, and was looking at Marius with an almost affectionate humility.

Marius interrupted the silence.

"Thénardier, I have told you your name. Now your secret, what you came to make known to me, do you want me to tell you that? I too have my means of information. You shall see that I know more about it than you do. Jean Valjean, as you have said, is an assassin and a robber. A robber, because he robbed a rich manufacturer, M. Madeleine, whose ruin he caused. An assassin, because he assassinated the police-officer, Javert."

"I don't understand, Monsieur Baron," said Thénardier.

"I will make myself understood. Listen. There was, in an arrondissement of the Pas-de-Calais, about 1822, a man who had had some old difficulty with justice, and who, under the name of M. Madeleine, had reformed and re-established himself. He had become in the full force of the term an upright man. By means of a manufacture, that of black glass trinkets, he had made the fortune of an entire city. As for his own personal fortune, he had made it also, but secondarily, and, in some sort, incidentally. He was the foster-father of the poor. He founded hospitals, opened schools, visited the sick, endowed daughters, supported widows, adopted orphans; he was, as it were, the guardian of the country. He had refused the Cross, he had been appointed mayor. A liberated convict knew the secret of a penalty once incurred by this man; he informed against him and had him arrested, and took advantage of the arrest to come to Paris and draw from the banker, Laffitte—I have the fact from the cashier himself—by means of a false signature, a sum of more than half a million which belonged to M. Madeleine. This convict who robbed M. Madeleine is Jean Valjean. As to the other act, you have just as little to tell me. Jean Valjean killed the officer Javert; he killed him with a pistol. I, who am now speaking to you, I was present."

Thénardier cast upon Marius the sovereign glance of a beaten man, who lays hold on victory again, and who has just recovered in one minute all the ground which he had lost. But the smile returned immediately; the inferior before the superior can only have a skulking triumph, and Thénardier merely said to Marius:

"Monsieur Baron, we are on the wrong track."

And he emphasised this phrase by giving his bunch of trinkets an expressive twirl.

"What!" replied Marius, "do you deny that? These are facts."

"They are chimeras. The confidence with which Monsieur the Baron honours me makes it my duty to tell him so. Before all things, truth and justice. I do not like to see people accused unjustly. Monsieur Baron, Jean Valjean never robbed Monsieur Madeleine, and Jean Valjean never killed Javert."

"You speak strongly! how is that?"

"For two reasons."

"What are they? tell me."

"The first is this: he did not rob Monsieur Madeleine, since it is Jean Valjean himself who was Monsieur Madeleine."

"What is that you are telling me?"

"And the second is this: he did not assassinate Javert, since Javert himself killed Javert."

"What do you mean?"

"That Javert committed suicide."

"Prove it! prove it!" cried Marius, beside himself.

Thénardier resumed, scanning his phrase in the fashion of an ancient Alexandrine:

"The — police — of — ficer — Ja—vert — was — found — drowned—under—a—boat—by—the—Pont—au—Change."

"But prove it now!"

Thénardier took from his pocket a large envelope of grey paper, which seemed to contain folded sheets of different sizes.

"I have my documents," said he, with calmness.

And he added:

"Monsieur Baron, in your interest, I wished to find out Jean Valjean to the bottom. I say that Jean Valjean and Madeleine are the same man; and I say that Javert had no other assassin than Javert; and when I speak I have the proofs. Not manuscript proofs; writing is suspicious; writing is complaisant, but proofs in print."

While speaking, Thénardier took out of the envelope two newspapers, yellow, faded, and strongly saturated with tobacco. One of these two newspapers, broken at all the folds, and falling in square pieces, seemed much older than the other.

"Two facts, two proofs," said Thénardier. And unfolding the two papers, he handed them to Marius.

With these two newspapers the reader is acquainted. One, the oldest, a copy of the *Drapeau Blanc*, of the 25th of July, 1823, the text of which can be found on page 360 of this book, established the identity of M. Madeleine and Jean Valjean. The other, a *Moniteur* of the 15th of June, 1832, verified the suicide of Javert, adding that it appeared from a verbal report made by Javert to the prefect that, taken prisoner in the barricade of the Rue de la Chanvrerie, he had owed his life to the magnanimity of an insurgent who, though he had him at the muzzle of his pistol, instead of blowing out his brains, had fired into the air.

Marius read. There was evidence, certain date, unquestionable proof, these two newspapers had not been printed expressly to support Thénardier's words. The note published in the *Moniteur* was an official communication from the prefecture of police. Marius could not doubt. The information derived from the cashier was false, and he himself was mistaken. Jean Valjean, suddenly growing grand, arose from the cloud. Marius could not restrain a cry of joy:

"Well, then, this unhappy man is a wonderful man! all that fortune was really his own! he is Madeleine, the providence of a whole region! he is Jean Valjean, the saviour of Javert! he is a hero! he is a saint!"

"He is not a saint, and he is not a hero," said Thénardier. "He is an assassin and a robber."

And he added with the tone of a man who begins to feel some authority in himself: "Let us be calm."

Robber, assassin; these words, which Marius supposed were gone, yet which came back, fell upon him like a shower of ice.

"Again," said he.

"Still," said Thénardier. "Jean Valjean did not rob Madeleine, but he is a robber. He did not kill Javert, but he is a murderer."

"Will you speak," resumed Marius, "of that petty theft of forty years ago, expiated, as appears from your newspapers themselves, by a whole life of repentance, abnegation, and virtue?"

"I said assassination and robbery, Monsieur Baron. And I repeat that I speak of recent facts. What I have to reveal to you is absolutely unknown. It belongs to the unpublished. And perhaps you will find in it the source of the fortune adroitly presented by Jean Valjean to Madame the Baroness. I say adroitly, for, by a donation of this kind, to glide into an honour-able house, the comforts of which he will share, and, by the same stroke, to conceal his crime, to enjoy his robbery, to bury his name, and to create himself a family, that would not be very unskilful."

"I might interrupt you here," observed Marius; "but continue."

"Monsieur Baron, I will tell you all, leaving the recompense to your generosity. This secret is worth a pile of gold. You will say to me: why have you not gone to Jean Valjean? For a very simple reason: I know that he has dispossessed himself, and dis-possessed in your favour, and I think the contrivance ingenious; but he has not a sou left, he would show me his empty hands, and, since I need some money for my voyage to La Joya, I prefer you, who have all, to him who has nothing. I am somewhat fatigued; allow me to take a chair."

Marius sat down, and made sign to him to sit down.

Thénardier installed himself in a cappadine chair, took up the two newspapers, thrust them back into the envelope, and muttered, striking the *Drapeau Blanc* with his nail: "It cost me some hard work to get this one." This done, he crossed his legs and lay back in his chair, an attitude characteristic of people who are sure of what they are saying, then entered into the subject seriously, and emphasising his words:

"Monsieur Baron, on the 6th of June, 1832, about a year ago, the day of the émeute, a man was in the Grand Sewer of Paris, near where the sewer empties into the Seine, between the Pont des Invalides and the Pont d'Iéna."

Marius suddenly drew his chair near Thénardier's. Thénard-ier noticed this movement, and continued with the deliberation of a speaker who holds his interlocutor fast, and who feels the palpitation of his adversary beneath his words:

"This man, compelled to conceal himself, for reasons foreign to politics, however, had taken the sewer for his dwelling, and had a key to it. It was, I repeat it, the 6th of June; it might have been eight o'clock in the evening. The man heard a noise in the sewer. Very much surprised, he hid himself, and watched. It was a sound of steps, somebody was walking in the darkness; some-body was coming in his direction. Strange to say, there was another man in the sewer beside him. The grating of the outlet of the sewer was not far off. A little light which came from it enabled him to recognise the new-comer, and to see that this man was carrying something on his back. He walked bent over. The man who was walking bent over was an old convict, and what he was carrying upon his shoulders was a corpse. Assassination *in flagrante delicto*, if ever there was such a thing. As for the robbery, it follows of course; nobody kills a man for nothing. This convict was going to throw his corpse into the river. It is a noteworthy fact, that before reaching the grating of the outlet, this convict, who came from a distance in the sewer, had been compelled to pass through a horrible quagmire in which it would seem that he might have left the corpse; but, the sewer-men working upon the quagmire might, the very next day, have found the assassinated man, and that was not the assassin's game. He preferred to go through the quagmire with his load, and his efforts must have been terrible; it is impossible to put one's life in greater peril; I do not understand how he came out of it alive."

Marius' chair drew still nearer. Thénardier took advantage of it to draw a long breath. He continued:

"Monsieur Baron, a sewer is not the Champ de Mars. One lacks everything there, even room. When two men are in a sewer, they must meet each other. That is what happened. The resident and the traveller were compelled to say good-day to each other, to their mutual regret. The traveller said to the resident: *'You see what I have on my back, I must get out, you have the key, give it to me.'* This convict was a man of terrible strength. There was no refusing him. Still he who had the key parleyed, merely to gain time. He examined the dead man, but he could see nothing, except that he was young, well dressed, apparently a rich man, and all disfigured with blood. While he was talking, he found means to cut and tear off from behind, without the assassin perceiving it, a piece of the assassinated man's coat. A piece of evidence, you understand; means of getting trace of the affair, and proving the crime upon the criminal. He put this piece of evidence in his pocket. After which he opened the grating, let the man out with his incumbrance on his back, shut the grating again and escaped, little caring to be mixed up with the remainder of the adventure, and especially desiring not to be present when the assassin should throw the assassinated man into the river. You understand now. He who was carrying the corpse was Jean Valjean; he who had the key is now speaking to you, and the piece of the coat———"

Thénardier finished the phrase by drawing from his pocket and holding up, on a level with his eyes, between his thumbs and his forefingers, a strip of ragged black cloth, covered with dark stains.

Marius had risen, pale, hardly breathing, his eye fixed upon the scrap of black cloth, and, without uttering a word, without losing sight of this rag, he retreated to the wall, and, with his right hand stretched behind him, groped about for a key which was in the lock of a closet near the chimney. He found this key, opened the closet, and thrust his arm into it without looking, and without removing his startled eyes from the fragment that Thénardier held up.

Meanwhile Thénardier continued:

"Monsieur Baron, I have the strongest reasons to believe that the assassinated young man was an opulent stranger drawn into a snare by Jean Valjean, and the bearer of an enormous sum."

"The young man was myself, and there is the coat!" cried Marius, and he threw an old black coat covered with blood upon the carpet.

Then, snatching the fragment from Thénardier's hands, he bent down over the coat, and applied the piece to the cut skirt. The edges fitted exactly, and the strip completed the coat.

Thénardier was petrified. He thought this: "I am floored."

Marius rose up, quivering, desperate, flashing.

He felt in his pocket, and walked, furious, towards Thénardier, offering him and almost pushing into his face his fist full of five hundred and a thousand franc notes.

"You are a wretch! you are a liar, a slanderer, a scoundrel. You came to accuse this man, you have justified him; you wanted to destroy him, you have succeeded only in glorifying him. And it is you who are a robber! and it is you who are an assassin. I saw you, Thénardier, Jondrette, in that den on the Boulevard de l'Hôpital. I know enough about you to send you to the galleys, and further even, if I wished. Here, there are a thousand francs, braggart that you are!"

And he threw a bill for a thousand francs to Thénardier.

"Ah! Jondrette, Thénardier, vile knave! let this be a lesson to you, pedlar of secrets, trader in mysteries, fumbler in the dark, wretch! Take these five hundred francs, and leave this place! Waterloo protects you."

"Waterloo!" muttered Thénardier, pocketing the five hundred francs with the thousand francs.

"Yes, assassin! you saved the life of a colonel there——"

"Of a general," said Thénardier, raising his head.

"Of a colonel!" replied Marius with a burst of passion. "I would not give a farthing for a general. And you came here to act out your infamy! I tell you that you have committed every crime. Go! out of my sight! Be happy only, that is all that I desire. Ah! monster! there are three thousand francs more. Take them. You will start to-morrow for America, with your daughter, for your wife is dead, abominable liar. I will see to your departure, bandit, and I will count out to you then twenty thousand francs. Go and get hanged elsewhere!"

"Monsieur Baron," answered Thénardier, bowing to the ground, "eternal gratitude."

And Thénardier went out, comprehending nothing, astounded and transported with this sweet crushing under sacks of gold and with this thunderbolt bursting upon his head in banknotes.

Thunderstruck he was, but happy also; and he would have been very sorry to have had a lightning rod against that thunderbolt.

Let us finish with this man at once. Two days after the events which we are now relating, he left, through Marius' care, for America, under a false name, with his daughter Azelma, provided with a draft upon New York for twenty thousand francs. Thénardier, the moral misery of Thénardier, the broken-down bourgeois, was irremediable; he was in America what he had been in Europe. The touch of a wicked man is often enough to corrupt a good deed and to make an evil result spring from it. With Marius' money, Thénardier became a slaver.

As soon as Thénardier was out of doors, Marius ran to the garden where Cosette was still walking:

"Cosette! Cosette!" cried he. "Come! come quick! Let us go. Basque, a fiacre! Cosette, come. Oh! my God! It was he who saved my life! Let us not lose a minute! Put on your shawl."

Cosette thought him mad, and obeyed.

He did not breathe, he put his hand upon his heart to repress its beating. He walked to and fro with rapid strides, he embraced Cosette: "Oh! Cosette! I am an unhappy man!" said he.

Marius was in amaze. He began to see in this Jean Valjean a

strangely lofty and saddened form. An unparalleled virtue appeared before him, supreme and mild, humble in its immensity. The convict was transfigured into Christ. Marius was bewildered by this marvel. He did not know exactly what he saw, but it was grand.

In a moment, a fiacre was at the door.

Marius helped Cosette in and sprang in himself.

"Driver," said he, "Rue de l'Homme Armé, Number 7."

The fiacre started.

"Oh! what happiness!" said Cosette. "Rue de l'Homme Armé! I dared not speak to you of it again. We are going to see Monsieur Jean."

"Your father! Cosette, your father more than ever. Cosette, I see it. You told me that you never received the letter which I sent you by Gavroche. It must have fallen into his hands. Cosette, he went to the barricade to save me. As it is a necessity for him to be an angel, on the way, he saved others; he saved Javert. He snatched me out of that gulf to give me to you. He carried me on his back in that frightful sewer. Oh! I am an unnatural ingrate. Cosette, after having been your providence, he was mine. Only think that there was a horrible quagmire, enough to drown him a hundred times, to drown him in the mire, Cosette! he carried me through that. I had fainted; I saw nothing, I heard nothing, I could know nothing of my own fate. We are going to bring him back, take him with us, whether he will or no, he shall never leave us again. If he is only at home! If we only find him! I will pass the rest of my life in venerating him. Yes, that must be it, do you see, Cosette? Gavroche must have handed my letter to him. It is all explained. You understand."

Cosette did not understand a word.

"You are right," said she to him.

Meanwhile the fiacre rolled on.

V

NIGHT BEHIND WHICH IS DAWN

AT the knock which he heard at his door, Jean Valjean turned his head.

"Come in," said he feebly.

The door opened. Cosette and Marius appeared.

Cosette rushed into the room.

Marius remained upon the threshold, leaning against the casing of the door.

"Cosette!" said Jean Valjean, and he rose in his chair, his arms stretched out and trembling, haggard, livid, terrible, with immense joy in his eyes.

Cosette, stifled with emotion, fell upon Jean Valjean's breast.

"Father!" said she.

Jean Valjean, beside himself, stammered:

"Cosette! she? you, madame? it is you, Cosette? Oh, my God!" And, clasped in Cosette's arms, he exclaimed:

"It is you, Cosette? you are here? You forgive me then!"

Marius, dropping his eyelids that the tears might not fall, stepped forward and murmured between his lips which were contracted convulsively to check the sobs:

"Father!"

"And you too, you forgive me!" said Jean Valjean.

Marius could not utter a word, and Jean Valjean added: "Thanks."

Cosette took off her shawl and threw her hat upon the bed.

"They are in my way," said she.

And, seating herself upon the old man's knees, she stroked away his white hair with an adorable grace, and kissed his forehead.

Jean Valjean, bewildered, offered no resistance.

Cosette, who had but a very confused understanding of all this, redoubled her caresses, as if she would pay Marius' debt.

Jean Valjean faltered:

"How foolish we are! I thought I should never see her again. Only think, Monsieur Pontmercy, that at the moment you came in, I was saying to myself: It is over. There is her little dress, I am a miserable man, I shall never see Cosette again, I was saying that at the very moment you were coming up the stairs. Was I not silly? I was as silly as that! But we reckon without God. God said: You think that you are going to be abandoned, dolt? No. No, it shall not come to pass like that. Come, here is a poor goodman who has need of an angel. And the angel comes; and I see my Cosette again! and I see my darling Cosette again! Oh! I was very miserable!"

For a moment he could not speak, then he continued:

"I really needed to see Cosette a little while from time to

time. A heart does want a bone to gnaw. Still I felt plainly that I was in the way. I gave myself reasons: they have no need of you, stay in your corner, you have no right to continue for ever. Oh! bless God, I see her again! Do you know, Cosette, that your husband is very handsome? Ah, you have a pretty embroidered collar, yes, yes. I like that pattern. Your husband chose it, did not he? And then, Cosette, you must have cashmeres. Monsieur Pontmercy, let me call her Cosette. It will not be very long."

And Cosette continued again:

"How naughty to have left us in this way! Where have you been? why were you away so long? Your journeys did not used to last more than three or four days. I sent Nicolette, the answer always was: He is absent. How long since you returned? Why did not you let us know? Do you know that you are very much changed. Oh! the naughty father! he has been sick, and we did not know it! Here, Marius, feel his hand, how cold it is!"

"So you are here, Monsieur Pontmercy, you forgive me!" repeated Jean Valjean.

At these words, which Jean Valjean now said for the second time, all that was swelling in Marius' heart found an outlet, he broke forth:

"Cosette, do you hear? that is the way with him! he begs my pardon,.and do you know what he has done for me, Cosette? he has saved my life. He has done more. He has given you to me. And, after having saved me, and after having given you to me, Cosette, what did he do with himself? he sacrificed himself. There is the man. And, to me the ungrateful, to me the forgetful, to me the pitiless, to me the guilty, he says: Thanks! Cosette, my whole life passed at the feet of this man would be too little. That barricade, that sewer, that furnace, that cloaca, he went through everything for me, for you, Cosette! He bore me through death in every form which he put aside from me, and which he accepted for himself. All courage, all virtue, all heroism, all sanctity, he has it all, Cosette, that man is an angel!"

"Hush! hush!" said Jean Valjean in a whisper. "Why tell all that?"

"But you!" exclaimed Marius, with a passion in which veneration was mingled, "why have not you told it? It is your fault, too. You save people's lives, and you hide it from them! You do more, under pretence of unmasking yourself, you calumniate yourself. It is frightful."

"I told the truth," answered Jean Valjean.

"No," replied Marius, "the truth is the whole truth; and you did not tell it. You were Monsieur Madeleine, why not have said so? You had saved Javert, why not have said so? I owe my life to you, why not have said so?"

"Because I thought as you did. I felt that you were right. It was necessary that I should go away. If you had known that affair of the sewer, you would have made me stay with you. I should then have had to keep silent. If I had spoken, it would have embarrassed all."

"Embarrassed what? embarrassed whom?" replied Marius. "Do you suppose you are going to stay here? We are going to carry you back. Oh! my God! when I think it was by accident that I learned it all! We are going to carry you back. You are a part of us. You are her father and mine. You shall not spend another day in this horrid house. Do not imagine that you will be here to-morrow."

"To-morrow," said Jean Valjean, "I shall not be here, but I shall not be at your house."

"What do you mean?" replied Marius. "Ah now, we shall allow no more journeys. You shall never leave us again. You belong to us. We will not let you go."

"This time, it is for good," added Cosette. "We have a carriage below. I am going to carry you off. If necessary, I shall use force."

And laughing, she made as if she would lift the old man in her arms.

"Your room is still in our house," she continued. "If you knew how pretty the garden is now. The azalias are growing finely. The paths are sanded with river sand: there are some little violet shells. You shall eat some of my strawberries. I water them myself. And no more madame, and no more Monsieur Jean, we are a republic, are we not, Marius? The programme is changed. If you knew, father, I have had some trouble, there was a red-breast which had made her nest in a hole in the wall, a horrid cat ate her up for me. My poor pretty little red-breast who put her head out at her window and looked at me! I cried over it. I would have killed the cat! But now, nobody cries any more. Everybody laughs, everybody is happy. You are coming with us. How glad grandfather will be! You shall have your bed in the garden, you shall tend it, and we will see if your strawberries are as fine as mine. And then, I will do what ever you wish, and then, you will obey me."

Jean Valjean listened to her without hearing her. He heard the music of her voice rather than the meaning of her words; one of those big tears which are the gloomy pearls of the soul, gathered slowly in his eye. He murmured:

"The proof that God is good is that she is here."

"Father!" cried Cosette.

Jean Valjean continued:

"It is very true that it would be charming to live together. They have their trees full of birds. I would walk with Cosette. To be with people who live, who bid each other good morning, who call each other into the garden, would be sweet. We would see each other as soon as it was morning. We would each cultivate our little corner. She would have me eat her strawberries. I would have her pick my roses. It would be charming. Only——"

He paused and said mildly:

"It is a pity."

The tear did not fall, it went back, and Jean Valjean replaced it with a smile. Cosette took both the old man's hands in her own.

"My God!" said she, "your hands are colder yet. Are you sick? Are you suffering?"

"No," answered Jean Valjean. "I am very well. Only——"

He stopped.

"Only what?"

"I shall die in a few minutes."

Cosette and Marius shuddered.

"Die!" exclaimed Marius.

"Yes, but that is nothing," said Jean Valjean.

He breathed, smiled, and continued.

"Cosette, you are speaking to me, go on, speak again, your little red-breast is dead then, speak, let me hear your voice!"

Marius, petrified, gazed upon the old man.

Cosette uttered a piercing cry:

"Father! my father! you shall live. You are going to live. I will have you live, do you hear!"

Jean Valjean raised his head towards her with adoration.

"Oh yes, forbid me to die. Who knows? I shall obey perhaps. I was just dying when you came. That stopped me, it seemed to me that I was born again."

"You are full of strength and life," exclaimed Marius. "Do you think people die like that? You have had trouble, you shall have no more. I ask your pardon now, and that on my knees! You shall live, and live with us, and live long. We will take you back. Both of us here will have but one thought henceforth, your happiness!"

"You see," added Cosette in tears, "that Marius says you will not die."

Jean Valjean continued to smile.

"If you should take me back, Monsieur Pontmercy, would that make me different from what I am? No; God thought as you and I did, and he has not changed his mind; it is best that I should go away. Death is a good arrangement. God knows better than we do what we need. That you are happy, that Monsieur Pontmercy has Cosette, that youth espouses morning, that there are about you, my children, lilacs and nightingales, that your life is a beautiful lawn in the sunshine, that all the enchantments of heaven fill your souls, and now, that I who am good for nothing, that I die; surely all this is well. Look you, be reasonable, there is nothing else possible now, I am sure that it is all over. An hour ago I had a fainting fit. And then, last night, I drank that pitcher full of water. How good your husband is, Cosette! You are much better off than with me."

There was a noise at the door. It was the physician coming in.

"Good day and good-bye, doctor," said Jean Valjean. "Here are my poor children."

Marius approached the physician. He addressed this single word to him: "Monsieur?" but in the manner of pronouncing it, there was a complete question.

The physician answered the question by an expressive glance.

"Because things are unpleasant," said Jean Valjean, "that is no reason for being unjust towards God."

There was a silence. All hearts were oppressed.

Jean Valjean turned towards Cosette. He began to gaze at her as if he would take a look which should endure through eternity. At the depth of shadow to which he had already descended, ecstasy was still possible to him while beholding Cosette. The reflection of that sweet countenance illumined his pale face. The sepulchre may have its enchantments.

The physician felt his pulse.

"Ah! it was you he needed!" murmured he, looking at Cosette and Marius.

And, bending towards Marius' ear he added very low:

"Too late."

Jean Valjean, almost without ceasing to gaze upon Cosette, turned upon Marius and the physician a look of serenity. They heard these almost inarticulate words come from his lips:

"It is nothing to die; it is frightful not to live."

Suddenly he arose. These returns of strength are sometimes a sign of the death-struggle. He walked with a firm step to the wall, put aside Marius and the physician, who offered to assist him, took down from the wall the little copper crucifix which hung there, came back, and sat down with all the freedom of motion of perfect health, and said in a loud voice, laying the crucifix on the table:

"Behold the great martyr."

Then his breast sank in, his head wavered, as if the dizziness of the tomb seized him, and his hands resting upon his knees, began to clutch at his pantaloons.

Cosette supported his shoulders, and sobbed, and attempted to speak to him, but could not. There could be distinguished, among the words mingled with that mournful saliva which accompanies tears, sentences like this: "Father! do not leave us. Is it possible that we have found you again only to lose you?"

The agony of death may be said to meander. It goes, comes, advances towards the grave, and returns towards life. There is some groping in the act of dying.

Jean Valjean, after this semi-syncope, gathered strength, shook his forehead as if to throw off the darkness, and became almost completely lucid once more. He took a fold of Cosette's sleeve, and kissed it.

"He is reviving! doctor, he is reviving!" cried Marius.

"You are both kind," said Jean Valjean. "I will tell you what has given me pain. What has given me pain, Monsieur Pontmercy, was that you have been unwilling to touch that money. That money really belongs to your wife. I will explain it to you, my children, on that account I am glad to see you. The black jet comes from England, the white jet comes from Norway. All this is in the paper you see there, which you will read. For bracelets, I invented the substitution of clasps made by bending the metal, for clasps made by soldering the metal. They are handsomer, better, and cheaper. You understand how much money can be made. So Cosette's fortune is really her own. I give you these particulars so that your minds may be at rest."

The portress had come up, and was looking through the half-open door. The physician motioned her away, but he could not prevent that good, zealous woman from crying to the dying man before she went:

"Do you want a priest?"

"I have one," answered Jean Valjean.

And, with his finger, he seemed to designate a point above his head, where, you would have said, he saw some one.

It is probable that the Bishop was indeed a witness of this death-agony.

Cosette slipped a pillow under his back gently.

Jean Valjean resumed:

"Monsieur Pontmercy, have no fear, I conjure you. The six hundred thousand francs are really Cosette's. I shall have lost my life if you do not enjoy it! We succeeded very well in making glasswork. We rivalled what is called Berlin jewellery. Indeed, the German black glass cannot be compared with it. A gross, which contains twelve hundred grains very well cut, costs only three francs."

When a being who is dear to us is about to die, we look at him with a look which clings to him, and which would hold him back. Both, dumb with anguish, knowing not what to say to death, despairing and trembling, they stood before him, Marius holding Cosette's hand.

From moment to moment, Jean Valjean grew weaker. He was sinking; he was approaching the dark horizon. His breath had become intermittent; it was interrupted by a slight rattle. He had difficulty in moving his wrist, his feet had lost all motion, and, at the same time that the distress of the limbs and the exhaustion of the body increased, all the majesty of the soul rose and displayed itself upon his forehead. The light of the unknown world was already visible in his eye.

His face grew pale, and at the same time smiled. Life was no longer present, there was something else. His breath died away, his look grew grand. It was a corpse on which you felt wings.

He motioned to Cosette to approach, then to Marius; it was evidently the last minute of the last hour, and he began to speak to them in a voice so faint it seemed to come from afar, and you would have said that there was already a wall between them and him.

"Come closer, come closer, both of you. I love you dearly. Oh! it is good to die so! You too, you love me, my Cosette. I knew very well that you still had some affection for your old goodman. How kind you are to put this cushion under my back! You will weep for me a little, will you not? Not too much. I do not wish you to have any deep grief. You must amuse yourselves a great deal, my children. I forgot to tell you that on buckles without tongues still more is made than on anything else. A gross, twelve dozen, costs ten francs, and sells for sixty. That is really a good business. So you need not be astonished at the six hundred thousand francs, Monsieur Pontmercy. It is honest money. You can be rich without concern. You must have a carriage, from time to time a box at the theatres, beautiful ball dresses, my Cosette, and then give good dinners to your friends, be very happy. I was writing just now to Cosette. She will find my letter. To her I bequeath the two candlesticks which are on the mantel. They are silver; but to me they are gold, they are diamond; they change the candles which are put into them, into consecrated tapers. I do not know whether he who gave them to me is satisfied with me in heaven. I have done what I could. My children, you will not forget that I am a poor man, you will have me buried in the most convenient piece of ground under a stone to mark the spot. That is my wish. No name on the stone. If Cosette will come for a little while sometimes, it will give me a pleasure. You too, Monsieur Pontmercy. I must confess to you that I have not always loved you; I ask your pardon. Now, she and you are but one to me. I am very grateful to you. I feel that you make Cosette happy. If you knew, Monsieur Pontmercy, her beautiful rosy cheeks were my joy; when I saw her a little pale, I was sad. There is a five hundred franc bill in the bureau. I have not touched it. It is for the poor. Cosette, do you see your little dress, there on the bed? do you recognise it? Yet it was only ten years ago. How time passes! We have been very happy. It is over. My children, do not weep, I am not going very far, I shall see you from there. You will only have to look when it is night, you will see me smile. Cosette, do you remember Montfermeil? You were in the wood, you were very much frightened; do you remember when I took the handle of the water-bucket? That was the first time I touched your poor little hand. It was so cold! Ah! you had red hands in those days, mademoiselle, your hands are very white now. And the great doll! do you remember? you called her Catharine. You regretted that you did not carry her to the convent. How you made me laugh sometimes, my sweet angel! When it had rained you launched spears of straw in the gutters, and you watched them. One day, I gave you a willow battledore, and a shuttlecock with yellow, blue, and green feathers. You have forgotten it. You were so cunning when you were little! You played. You put cherries in your ears. Those are things of the past. The forests through which we have passed with our child, the trees under which we have walked, the convents in which we have hidden, the games, the free laughter of childhood, all is in shadow. I imagined that all that belonged to me. There was my folly. Those Thénardiers were wicked. We must forgive them. Cosette, the time has come to tell you the name of your mother. Her name was Fantine. Remember that name: Fantine. Fall on your knees whenever you pronounce it. She suffered much. And loved you much. Her measure of unhappiness was as full as yours of happiness. Such are the distributions of God. He is on high, he sees us all, and he knows what he does in the midst of his great stars. So I am going away, my children. Love each other dearly always. There is scarcely anything else in the world but that: to love one another. You will think sometimes of the poor old man who died here. O my Cosette! it is not my fault, indeed, if I have not seen you all this time, it broke my heart; I went as far as the corner of the street, I must have seemed strange to the people who saw me pass, I looked like a crazy man, once I went out with no hat. My children, I do not see very clearly now, I had some more things to say, but it makes no difference. Think of me a little. You are blessed creatures. I do not know what is the matter with me, I see a light. Come nearer. I die happy. Let me put my hands upon your dear beloved heads."

Cosette and Marius fell on their knees, overwhelmed, choked with tears, each grasping one of Jean Valjean's hands. Those august hands moved no more.

He had fallen backwards, the light from the candlesticks fell upon him; his white face looked up towards heaven, he let Cosette and Marius cover his hands with kisses; he was dead.

The night was starless and very dark. Without doubt, in the

gloom some mighty angel was standing, with outstretched wings, awaiting the soul.

VI
GRASS HIDES AND RAIN BLOTS OUT

THERE is, in the cemetery of Père Lachaise, in the neighbourhood of the Potters' field, far from the elegant quartier of that city of sepulchres, far from all those fantastic tombs which display in presence of eternity the hideous fashions of death, in a deserted corner, beside an old wall, beneath a great yew on which the bindweed climbs, among the dog-grass and the mosses, a stone. This stone is exempt no more than the rest from the leprosy of time, from the mould, the lichen, and the droppings of the birds. The air turns it black, the water green. It is near no path, and people do not like to go in that direction, because the grass is high, and they would wet their feet. When there is a little sunshine, the lizards come out. There is, all about, a rustling of wild oats. In the spring, the linnets sing in the tree.

This stone is entirely blank. The only thought in cutting it was of the essentials of the grave, and there was no other care than to make this stone long enough and narrow enough to cover a man.

No name can be read there.

Only many years ago, a hand wrote upon it in pencil these four lines which have become gradually illegible under the rain and the dust, and which are probably effaced:

> *Il dort. Quoique le sort fût pour lui bien étrange,*
> *Il vivait. Il mourut quand il n'eut plus son ange;*
> *La chose simplement d'elle-même arriva,*
> *Comme la nuit se fait lorsque le jour s'en va.*